THE LAST
HERALD-MAGE
TRILOGY

MERCEDES LACKEY

THE LAST HERALD-MAGE TRILOGY

MAGIC'S PAWN

MAGIC'S PROMISE

MAGIC'S PRICE

DAW BOOKS, INC.
DONALD A. WOLLHEIM, FOUNDER
375 Hudson Street, New York, NY 10014

ELIZABETH R. WOLLHEIM
SHEILA E. GILBERT
PUBLISHERS
www.dawbooks.com

INTRODUCTION

I'VE BEEN WRITING for thirty years, professionally.

I began writing a lot earlier than that, as so many of us did; I wrote Andre Norton fanfiction, long before I knew there actually was such a thing as fanfiction. I published short stories in my high school "literary magazine," which were all, of course, fantasy or science fiction. I continued writing through college, and after college, and somewhere in the back of my mind there was always this dream to write for a living.

I made my first professional sale in 1985, to Marion Zimmer Bradley for one of her Darkover anthologies. But my first *published* story was a Tarma and Kethry story for *Fantasy Book* magazine that was published in the same year (the anthology wasn't published until 1986, I believe). By that time, besides working on short fiction, I had started my first book. I scrapped that, after only about ten thousand words, realizing that I didn't (yet) have the skills to pull what I wanted to do off. Later (much later!) that became another trilogy for another company. I then started what would become the first of the *Arrows of the Queen* trilogy.

I sold short stories while working as a computer programmer by day and writing in every bit of my free time. With the help of C. J. Cherryh, I got the manuscript of my first books whipped into shape fit to be seen by a publisher at the same time. C. J. was the one who told me to "commit trilogy" when I presented her with my result. I rewrote them many times under her tutelage, and eventually the books were bought. Several further revisions later, the first two books came out in 1987 and the last in 1988. Elizabeth (Betsy) Wollheim was just starting in her new role as editor-in-chief at DAW, and I think I was one of the first authors who she got to work with from the very beginning.

Once the last of the *Arrows* books were done, Betsy came to me for more material—but the *Herald-Mage* books were not what got done at that point. Instead, I put together some of the Tarma and Kethry stories that I had been doing for magazines and the *Sword and Sorceress* anthologies, and presented Betsy with *Oathbound* and *Oathbreakers*. That was where I tied those stories into the same world as Valdemar. So for my next trick—

Somehow I had to explain how these lands outside of Valdemar *did* have real magic, and Valdemar did not. In the *Arrows* books I had established that Valdemar only had what I referred to as "Mind Magic" (psionics), but no "real" magic. I figured establishing a whole world, the Kingdom of Valdemar, and the Heralds was going to be hard enough without having to come up with a logical system of magic on top of that. (Word to the wise: know your limitations!) But during the course of manuscript revisions, Betsy had said, "This is a fantasy; there has to be some real magic in it." After a lot of thought, I decided to put in the token "real magic" by having my protagonist, Talia, reading about "The Last Herald-Mage," Vanyel, who obviously *did* have "real magic."

And I promptly forgot about that until Betsy wanted another trilogy.

That was when it occurred to me that I had a built-in protagonist (Vanyel), I already knew—thanks to the Tarma and Kethry stories—how I wanted magic to work, and I had a built-in conflict: just how *did* Vanyel become the *last* Herald-Mage? So to me at least, the logical conclusion was that I should write about Vanyel.

However, there was one small potential problem. I had established in those few paragraphs at the beginning of *Arrows of the Queen* that Vanyel was gay . . . and this was back in the late 1980s. While there were any number of established SF/F writers who had portrayed openly gay characters (Marion Zimmer Bradley, Samuel R. Delaney, and Jessica Salmonson, just to name a few), it was still possible that creating a trilogy about a gay protagonist was going to get me, and DAW into a lot of hot water—especially since my target audience was teens and young adults as well as adults. I pointed this out to Betsy.

Betsy said, "Go for it."

So I did. And none of us looked back.

I was very honored to receive the Lambda Award for the last book of the trilogy, although the presenters of the award made it clear that they were actually giving the award for the entire trilogy and not just the third book.

And I've gotten many letters over the years, and many people personally thanking me for writing the trilogy, either because it allowed them to understand a sibling or friend who had just come out, or because it let them know that there were other people out there who were just like them.

It's the latter group I want to say a final thing to.

I'm thrilled that I was the source of material that helped you get through a dreadful and trying time in your life. I could not be happier for you. But *you* were the ones doing the heavy lifting. *You* were the ones who knew that you were not going to let the world put you in a corner. *You* were the ones who were actively looking for something to validate what you knew, deep inside, was perfectly normal. If you hadn't found *The Last Herald-Mage,* you would have found some other writer's work. Maybe Marion's Darkover. Maybe one of Samuel Delaney's books. Maybe one of Charles de Lint's. You would have found *someone* and *something,* because you were looking, and determined not to give up, and that would have given you that boost to keep you going.

You are the real heroes. I am proud and thrilled to have been part of your journey, but you began the journey, and you kept up with it until you came out on top. It was all you. I'm just glad to have been a part of it.

—Mercedes Lackey
Claremore, Oklahoma

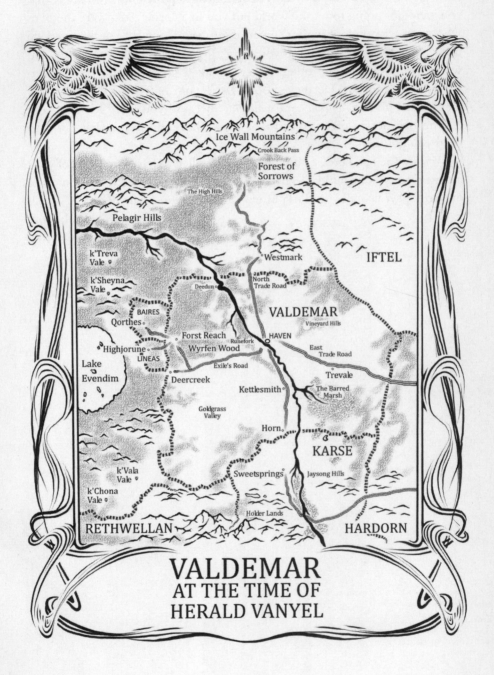

Ice Wall Mountains
Crook Back Pass
Forest of
Sorrows
The High Hills
Pelagir Hills
k'Treva
Vale
k'Sheyna
Vale
Deedun
Westmark
North
Trade Road
BAIRES
Qorthes
Highjorune
LINEAS
Forst Reach
Wyrfen Wood
Runefork
HAVEN
IFTEL
VALDEMAR
Vineyard Hills
East
Trade Road
Exile's Road
Lake
Evendim
Deercreek
Goldgrass
Valley
Kettlesmith
Trevale
The Barred
Marsh
Horn
k'Vala
Vale
k'Chona
Vale
Sweetsprings
Jaysong Hills
KARSE
Holder Lands
RETHWELLAN
HARDORN

VALDEMAR
AT THE TIME OF
HERALD VANYEL

Magic's Pawn

Dedicated to:
Melanie Mar—just because
and
Mark, Carl, and Dominic
for letting me bounce things off them

CHAPTER 1

"**Y**OUR GRANDFATHER," said Vanyel's brawny, fifteen-year-old cousin Radevel, "was crazy."

He has a point, Vanyel thought, hoping they weren't about to take an uncontrolled dive down the last of the stairs.

Radevel's remark had probably been prompted by this very back staircase, one that started at one end of the third-floor servants' hall and emerged at the rear of a linen closet on the ground floor. The stair treads were so narrow and so slick that not even the servants used it.

The manor-keep of Lord Withen Ashkevron of Forst Reach was a strange and patchworked structure. In Vanyel's great-great-grandfather's day it had been a more conventional defensive keep, but by the time Vanyel's grandfather had held the lands, the border had been pushed far past Forst Reach. The old reprobate had decided when he'd reached late middle age that defense was going to be secondary to *comfort*. His comfort, primarily.

Not that Vanyel entirely disagreed with Grandfather; he would have been one of the first to vote to fill in the moat and for fireplaces in all the rooms. But the old man had gotten some pretty peculiar notions about what he wanted where—along with a tendency to change his mind in mid-alteration.

There were good points—windows everywhere, and all of them glazed and shuttered. Skylights lighting all the upper rooms and the staircases. Fireplaces in nearly every room. *Heated* privies, part and parcel of the bathhouse. Every inside wall lathed and plastered against cold and damp. The stables, mews, kennel, and chickenyard banished to new outbuildings.

But there were bad points—if you didn't know your way, you could *really* get lost; and there were an awful lot of places you couldn't get into unless you knew exactly how to get there. Some of those places were important—like the bathhouse and privies. The old goat hadn't much considered the next generation in his alterations, either; he'd cut up the nursery into servant's quarters, which meant that until Lord Withen's boys went into bachelor's hall and the girls to the bower, they were cramped two and three to a series of very tiny attic-level rooms.

"He was *your* grandfather, too," Vanyel felt impelled to point out. The Ashkevron cousins had a tendency to act as if they had no common ancestors with Vanyel and his sibs whenever the subject of Grandfather Joserlin and his alterations came up.

"Huh." Radevel considered for a moment, then shrugged. "He was still crazy." He hefted his own load of armor and padding a little higher on his shoulder.

Vanyel held his peace and trotted down the last couple of stone stairs to hold the door open for his cousin. Radevel was doing him a favor, even though Vanyel was certain that cousin Radevel shared everyone else's low opinion of him. Radevel was far and away the best-natured of the cousins, and the easiest to talk round—and the bribe of Vanyel's new hawking gauntlet had proved too much for him to resist. Still, it wouldn't do to get him angry by arguing with him; he *might* decide he had better things to do than help Vanyel out, gauntlet or no gauntlet.

Oh, gods—let this work, Vanyel thought as they emerged into the gloomy back hall. *Did I practice enough with Lissa? Is this going to have a chance against a standard attack? Or am I crazy for even trying?*

The hallway was as cold as the staircase had been, and dark to boot. Radevel took the lead, feet slapping on the stone floor as he whistled contentedly—and tunelessly. Vanyel tried not to wince at the mutilation of one of his favorite melodies and drifted silently in his wake, his thoughts as dark as the hallway.

In three days Lissa will be gone—and if I can't manage to get sent along, I'll be all alone. Without Lissa . . .

If I can just prove that I need her *kind of training, then* maybe *Father will let me go with her—*

That had been the half-formed notion that prompted him to work out the moves of a different style of fighting than what he was *supposed* to be learning, practicing them in secret with his older sister Lissa: that was what had ultimately led to this little expedition.

That, and the urgent need to show Lord Withen that his eldest son wasn't the coward the armsmaster claimed he was—and that he *could* succeed on martial ground of his own choosing.

Vanyel wondered why he was the only boy to realize that there were other styles of fighting than armsmaster Jervis taught; he'd read of them, and knew that they had to be just as valid, else why send Lissa off to foster and study with Trevor Corey and his seven would-be sword-ladies? The way Vanyel had it figured, there was no way short of a miracle that he would ever succeed at the brute hack-and-bash system Jervis used—and no way Lord Withen would ever believe that another style was just as good while Jervis had his ear.

Unless Vanyel could *show* him. Then Father would *have* to believe his own eyes.

And if I can't prove it to him—

—oh, gods. I can't take much more of this.

With Lissa gone to Brenden Keep, his last real ally in the household would be gone, too; his only friend, and the only person who *cared* for him.

This was the final trial of the plot he'd worked out with Liss; Radevel would try to take him using Jervis' teachings. Vanyel would try to hold his own, wearing nothing but the padded jerkin and helm, carrying the lightest of target-shields, and trusting to speed and agility to keep him out of trouble.

Radevel kicked open the unlatched door to the practice ground, leaving Vanyel to get it closed before somebody yelled about the draft. The early spring sunlight was painful after the darkness of the hallway; Vanyel squinted as he hurried to catch up with his cousin.

"All right, peacock," Radevel said good-naturedly, dumping his gear at the edge of the practice ground, and snagging his own gambeson from the pile. "Get yourself ready, and we'll see if this nonsense of yours has any merit."

It took Vanyel a lot less time than his cousin to shrug into *his* "armor"; he offered tentatively to help Radevel with his, but the older boy just snorted.

"Botch mine the way you botch yours? No thanks," he said, and went on methodically buckling and adjusting.

Vanyel flushed, and stood uncertainly at the side of the sunken practice ground, contemplating the thick, dead grass at his feet.

I never botch anything except when Jervis is watching, he thought bleakly, shivering a little as a bit of cold breeze cut through the gambeson. *And then I can't do anything right.*

He could almost feel the windows in the keep wall behind him like eyes staring at his back. Waiting for him to fail—again.

What's wrong with me, anyway? Why can't I ever please Father? Why is everything I do wrong?

He sighed, scuffed the ground with his toe, and wished he could be out riding instead of trying something doomed to failure. He was the best rider in Forst Reach—he and Star had no equals on the most breakneck of hunts, and he *could*, if he chose, master anything else in the stables.

And just because I won't bother with those iron-mouthed brutes Father prefers, he won't even grant me the accolade there—

Gods. This time I have to win.

"Wake up, dreamer," Radevel rumbled, his voice muffled inside the helm. "You wanted to have at—let's get to it."

Vanyel walked to the center of the practice field with nervous deliberation, waiting until the last minute to get his helm on. He hated the thing; he hated the feeling of being closed in, and most of all hated having his vision narrowed to a little slit. He waited for Radevel to come up to him, feeling the sweat already starting under his arms and down the line of his back.

Radevel swung—but instead of meeting the blow with his shield as Jervis would have done, Vanyel just moved out of the way of the blow, and on his way past Radevel, made a stab of his own. Jervis never cared much for point-work, but Vanyel had discovered it could be really effective if you timed things right. Radevel made a startled sound and got up his own shield, but only just in time, and left himself open to a cut.

Vanyel felt his spirits rising as he saw this second opening in as many breaths, and chanced another attack of his own. This one actually managed to connect, though it was too light to call a disabling hit.

"Light!" Vanyel shouted as he danced away, before his cousin had a chance to disqualify the blow.

"Almost enough, peacock," Radevel replied, reluctant admiration in his voice. "You land another like that with your weight behind it and I'll be out. Try *this* for size—"

He charged, his practice blade a blur beside his shield.

Vanyel just stepped aside at the last moment, while Radevel staggered halfway to the boundary under his own momentum.

It was working! Radevel couldn't get *near* him—and Vanyel was pecking away at him whenever he got an opportunity. He wasn't hitting even close to killing strength—but that was mostly from lack of practice. If—

"Hold, damn your eyes!"

Long habit froze them both in position, and the armsmaster of Forst Reach stalked onto the field, fire in his bloodshot glare.

Jervis looked the two of them up and down while Vanyel sweated from more than exertion. The blond, crag-faced mercenary frowned, and Vanyel's mouth went dry. Jervis looked angry—and when Jervis was angry, it was generally Vanyel who suffered.

"Well—" the man croaked after long enough for Vanyel's dread of him to build up to full force. "—learning a new discipline, are we? *And whose idea was this?*"

"Mine, sir," Vanyel whispered.

"Might have guessed sneak-and-run would be more suited to *you* than an honest fight," the armsmaster sneered. "Well, and how did you do, my bright young lord?"

"He did all right, Jervis." To Vanyel's complete amazement Radevel spoke up for him. "I couldn't get a blow on 'im. An' if he'd put his weight behind it, he'd have laid me out a time or two."

"So you're a real hero against a half-grown boy. I'll just bet you feel like another Veth Krethen, don't you?" Jervis spat. Vanyel held his temper, counting to ten, and did *not* protest that Radevel was nearly double his size and certainly no "half-grown boy." Jervis glared at him, waiting for a retort that never came—and strangely, that seemed to anger Jervis even more.

"All right, *hero*," he snarled, taking Radevel's blade away and jamming the boy's helm down over his own head. "Let's see just how good you really are—"

Jervis charged without any warning, and Vanyel had to scramble to get out of the way of the whirling blade. He realized then that Jervis was coming for him all-out—as if Vanyel was wearing full armor.

Which he wasn't.

He pivoted desperately as Jervis came at him again; ducked, wove, and spun—and saw an opening. This time desperation gave him the strength he hadn't used against Radevel—and he scored a chest-stab that actually rocked Jervis back for a moment, and followed it with a good solid blow to the head.

He waited, heart in mouth, while the armsmaster staggered backward two or three steps, then shook his head to clear it. There was an awful silence—

Then Jervis yanked off the helm, and there was nothing but rage on his face.

"Radevel, get the boys, then bring me Lordling Vanyel's arms and armor," the armsmaster said, in a voice that was deadly calm.

Radevel backed off the field, then turned and ran for the keep. Jervis paced slowly to within a few feet of Vanyel, and Vanyel nearly died of fear on the spot.

"So you like striking from behind, hmm?" he said in that same, deadly quiet voice. "I think maybe I've been a bit lax in teaching you about honor, young milord." A thin smile briefly sliced across his face. "But I think we can remedy that quickly enough."

Radevel approached with feet dragging, his arms loaded with the rest of Vanyel's equipment.

"Arm up," Jervis ordered, and Vanyel did not dare to disobey.

Exactly what Jervis said, then—other than dressing Vanyel down in front of the whole lot of them, calling him a coward and a cheat, an assassin who wouldn't stand still to face his opponent's blade with honor—Vanyel could never afterward remember. Only a haze of mingled fear and anger that made the words meaningless.

But then Jervis took Vanyel on. His way, his style.

It was a hopeless fight from the beginning, even if Vanyel had been *good* at this particular mode of combat. In moments Vanyel found himself flat on his back, trying to see around spots in front of his eyes, with his ears still ringing from a blow he hadn't even seen coming.

"Get up," Jervis said—

Five more times Vanyel got up, each time more slowly. Each time, he tried to yield. By the fourth time he was wit-wandering, dazed and groveling. And Jervis refused to accept his surrender even when he could barely gasp out the words.

Radevel had gotten a really bad feeling in his stomach from the moment he saw Jervis' face when Van scored on him. He'd never seen the old bastard that angry in all the time he'd been fostered here.

But he'd figured that Vanyel was just going to get a bit of a thrashing. He'd *never* figured on being an unwilling witness to a deliberate—

—massacre. That was all he could think to call it. Van was no match for Jervis, and Jervis was coming at him all out—like he was a trained, adult fighter. Even Radevel could see that.

He heaved a sigh of relief when Vanyel was knocked flat on his back, and mumbled out his surrender as soon as he could speak. The worst the poor little snot had gotten was a few bruises.

But when Jervis had refused to accept that surrender—when he beat at

Van with the flat of his blade until the boy *had* to pick up sword and shield just to get the beating to stop—Radevel got that bad feeling again.

And it got worse. Five times more Jervis knocked him flat, and each time with what looked like an even more vicious strike.

But the sixth time Vanyel was laid out, he *couldn't* get up.

Jervis let fly with a blow that broke the wood and copper shield right in the middle—and to Radevel's horror, he saw when the boy fell back that Vanyel's shield arm had been broken in half; the lower arm was bent in the middle, and that could only mean that both bones had snapped. It was pure miracle that they hadn't gone through muscle and skin—

And Jervis' eyes were *still* not what Radevel would call sane.

Radevel added up all the factors and came up with one answer: get Lissa. She was adult-rank, she was Van's protector, and no matter what the arms-master said in justification for beating the crud out of Van, if Jervis laid one finger in anger on Lissa, he'd get thrown out of the Keep with both *his* arms broken. If Withen didn't do it, there were others who liked Liss a lot who would.

Radevel backed off the field and took to his heels as soon as he was out of sight.

Vanyel lay flat on his back again, breath knocked out of him, in a kind of shock in which he couldn't feel much of anything except—except that something was wrong, somewhere. Then he tried to get up—and pain shooting along his left arm sent him screaming into darkness.

When he came to, Lissa was bending over him, her horsey face tight with worry. She was pale, and the nostrils of that prominent Ashkevron nose flared like a frightened filly's.

"Don't move—Van, no—both the bones of your arm are broken." She was *kneeling* next to him, he realized, with one knee gently but firmly holding his left arm down so that he couldn't move it.

"Lady, get away from him—" Jervis' voice dripped boredom and disgust. "It's just his shield arm, nothing important. We'll just strap it to a board and put some liniment on it and he'll be fine—"

She didn't move her knees, but swung around to face Jervis so fast that her braid came loose and whipped past Vanyel's nose like a lash. "*You* have done quite enough for one day, Master Jervis," she snarled. "I think you forget your place."

Vanyel wished vacantly that he could see Jervis' face at that moment. It must surely be a sight.

But his arm began to *hurt*—and that was more than enough to keep his attention.

There wasn't usually a Healer at Forst Reach, but Vanyel's Aunt Serina was staying here with her sister during her pregnancy. She'd had three miscarriages already, and was taking no chances; she was attended by her very own Healer. And Lissa had seen to it that the *Healer*, not Jervis, was the one that dealt with Vanyel's arm.

"Oh, Van—" Lissa folded herself inelegantly on the edge of Vanyel's bed and sighed. *"How* did you manage to get into this mess?"

That beaky Ashkevron nose and her determined chin combined with her anxiety to make her look like a stubborn, mulish mare. Most people were put off by her appearance, but Vanyel knew her well enough to read the heartsick worry in her eyes. After all, she'd all but raised him.

Vanyel wasn't certain how clear he'd be, but he tried to explain. Lissa tucked up her legs, and rested her chin on her knees, an unladylike pose that would have evoked considerable distress from Lady Treesa. When he finished, she sighed again.

"I think you attract bad luck, that's all I can say. You don't do anything *wrong*, but somehow things seem to happen to you."

Vanyel licked his dry lips and blinked at her. "Liss—Jervis was really *angry* this time, and what you told him didn't help. He's going to go right to Father, if he isn't there already."

She shook her head. "I shouldn't have said that, should I? Van, all I was thinking about was getting him away from you."

"I—I know Liss, I'm not blaming you, but—"

"But I made him mad. Well, I'll see if I can get to Father before Jervis does, but even if I do he probably won't listen to me. I'm just a female, after all."

"I know." He closed his eyes as the room began to swing. "Just—try, Liss—please."

"I will." She slipped off the bed, then bent over and kissed his forehead. "Try and sleep, like the Healer told you, all right?"

He nodded.

Tough-minded and independent, like the grandmother who had raised *her*, Lissa was about the only one in the keep willing to stand up to Lord

Withen now that Grandmother Ashkevron had passed on. Not surprising, that, given Grandmother. The Ashkevrons seemed to produce about one strong-willed female in every generation, much to the bemusement of the Ashkevron males, and the more compliant Ashkevron females.

Lady Treesa (anything but independent) had been far too busy with pregnancy and all the vapors she indulged in when pregnant to have anything to do with the resulting offspring. They went to the hands of others until they were old enough to be usefully added to *her* entourage. Lissa went to Grandmother.

But Vanyel went to Liss. And they loved each other from the moment she'd taken him out of the nursery. She'd stand up to a raging lion for his sake.

So Lissa went in search of their father. Unfortunately that left him alone. And unfortunately Lissa didn't return when she couldn't immediately find Lord Withen. And that, of course, left him vulnerable when his father chose to descend on him like the god of thunders.

Vanyel was dizzy with pain as well as with the medicines the Healer had made him drink when Lord Withen stormed into his tiny, white-plastered room. He was lying flat on his back in his bed, trying not to move, and still the room seemed to be reeling around him. The pain was making him nauseous, and all he wanted was to be left in peace. The very last thing he wanted to see was his lord father.

And Withen barely gave him enough time to register that his father was *there* before laying into him.

"What's all this about your cheating?" Withen roared, making Vanyel wince and wish he dared to cover his ears. "By the gods, you whelp, I ought to break your other arm for you!"

"I *wasn't* cheating!" Vanyel protested, stung, his voice breaking at just the wrong moment. He tried to sit upright—which only made the room spin the more. He fell back, supporting himself on his good elbow, grinding his teeth against the pain of his throbbing arm.

"I was," he gasped through clenched teeth, "I was just doing what Seldasen said to do!"

"And just who might this 'Seldasen' be?" his father growled savagely, his dark brows knitting together. "What manner of coward says to run about and strike behind a man's back, eh?"

Oh, gods—now what have I done? Though his head was spinning, Vanyel tried to remember if Herald Seldasen's treatise on warfare and tactics had been one of the books he'd "borrowed" without leave, or one of the ones he was *supposed* to be studying.

"*Well?*" When Lord Withen scowled, his dark hair and beard made him look positively demonic. The drugs seemed to be giving him an aura of angry red light, too.

Father, why can't you ever *believe I might be in the right?*

The book *was* on the "approved" list, Vanyel remembered with relief, as he recalled his tutor Istal assigning certain chapters to be memorized. "It's *Herald* Seldasen, Father," he said defiantly, finding strength in rebellion. "It's from a book Istal assigned me, about tactics." The words he remembered strengthened him still more, and he threw them into his father's face. "He said: 'Let every man that must go to battle fight within his talents, and not be forced to any one school. Let the agile man use his speed, let his armoring be light, and let him skirmish, but not close with the enemy. Let the heavy man stand shoulder to shoulder with his comrades in the shield wall, that the enemy may not break through. Let the small man of good eye make good use of the bow, aye, and let the Herald fight with his mind and not his body, let the Herald-Mage combat with magic and not the sword. *And let no man be called coward for refusing the place for which he is not fit.*' And I didn't *once* hit anybody from behind! If Jervis says I did—well—I *didn't!*"

Lord Withen stared at his eldest son, his mouth slack with surprise. For one moment Vanyel actually thought he'd gotten through to his father, who was more accustomed to hearing him quote poetry than military history.

"Parrot some damned book at me, will you?" Lord Withen snarled, dashing Vanyel's hopes. "And what does some damned lowborn Herald know about fighting? You *listen* to me, boy—you are my heir, my firstborn, and you *damned* well better learn what Jervis has to teach you if you want to sit in my place when I'm gone! If he says you were cheating, then by *damn* you were cheating!"

"But I *wasn't* cheating and I don't *want* your place—" Vanyel protested, the drugs destroying his self-control and making him say things he'd sooner have kept behind his teeth.

That stopped Lord Withen cold. His father stared at him as if he'd gone mad, grown a second head, or spoken in Karsite.

"Great good *gods*, boy," he managed to splutter after several icy eternities during which Vanyel waited for the roof to cave in. "What *do* you want?"

"I—" Vanyel began. And stopped. If he told Withen that what he wanted was to be a Bard—

"You ungrateful whelp—you will learn what I *tell* you to learn, and do what I *order* you to do! You're my heir and you'll do your duty to me and to this holding if I have to see you half dead to get you to do it!"

And with that, he stormed out, leaving Vanyel limp with pain and anger and utter dejection, his eyes clamped tight against the tears he could feel behind them.

Oh, gods, what does he expect *of me? Why can't I ever please him? What do I have to do to convince him that I can't be what he wants me to be? Die?*

And now—now my hand, oh, gods, it hurts—how much damage did they do to it? Am I ever going to be able to play anything right again?

"Heyla, Van—"

He opened his eyes, startled by the sound of a voice.

His door was cracked partway open; Radevel peered around the edge of it, and Vanyel could hear scuffling and whispers behind him.

"You all right?"

"No," Vanyel replied, suspiciously.

What the hell does he want?

Radevel's bushy eyebrows jumped like a pair of excited caterpillars. "Guess not. Bet it hurts."

"It hurts," Vanyel said, feeling a sick and sullen anger burning in the pit of his stomach.

You watched it happen. And you didn't do anything to stop it, cousin. And you didn't bother to defend me to Father, either. None of you did.

Radevel, instead of being put off, inched a little farther into the room. "Hey," he said, brightening, "you should have seen it! I mean, *whack*, an' that whole shield just split—an' you fell down an' that arm—"

"Will you go to hell?" Vanyel snarled, just about ready to kill him. "And you can take all those ghouls lurking out there with you!"

Radevel jumped, looked shocked, then looked faintly offended.

Vanyel didn't care. All that mattered was that Radevel—and whoever else was out there—took themselves away.

Left finally alone, Vanyel drifted into an uneasy slumber, filled with fragmented bits of unhappy dreams. When he woke again, his mother was supervising the removal of his younger brother Mekeal and all Mekeal's belongings from the room.

Well, that was a change. Lady Treesa usually didn't interest herself in any of her offspring unless she had something to gain from it. On the other hand, Vanyel had been a part of her little court since the day he'd evidenced real talent at music about five years ago. She wouldn't want to lose her own private minstrel—which meant she'd best make certain he healed up all right.

"I won't have you racketing about," she was whispering to Mekeal with unconcealed annoyance on her plump, pretty face. "I won't have you keeping him awake when he should be sleeping, and I won't have you getting in the Healer's way."

Thirteen-year-old Mekeal, a slightly shrunken copy of his father, shrugged indifferently. "'Bout time we went to bachelor's hall anyway, milady," he replied, as Lady Treesa turned to keep an eye on him. "Can't say as *I'll* miss the caterwauling an' the plunking."

Although Vanyel could only see his mother's back, he couldn't miss the frown in her voice. "It wouldn't hurt you to acquire a bit of Vanyel's polish, Mekeal," Lady Treesa replied.

Mekeal shrugged again, quite cheerfully. "Can't make silk out o' wool, Lady Mother." He peered through dancing candlelight at Vanyel's side of the room. "Seems m'brother's awake. Heyla, peacock, they're movin' me down t' quarters; seems you get up here to yourself."

"Out!" Treesa ordered; and Mekeal took himself off with a heartless chuckle.

Vanyel spent the next candlemark with Treesa fussing and weeping over him; indulging herself in the histrionics she seemed to adore. In a way it was as hard to deal with as Withen's rage. He'd never been on the receiving end of her vapors before.

Oh, gods, he kept thinking confusedly, *please make her go away. Anywhere, I don't care.*

He had to keep assuring her that he was going to be all right when he was not at all certain of that himself, and Treesa's shrill, borderline hysteria set his nerves completely on edge. It was a decided relief when the Healer arrived again and gently chased her out to give him some peace.

The next few weeks were nothing but a blur of pain and potions—a blur endured with one or another of his mother's ladies constantly at his side. And they all flustered at him until he was ready to scream, including his mother's maid, Melenna, who should have known better. It was like being nursemaided by a covey of agitated doves. When they weren't worrying at him, they were preening at him. *Especially* Melenna.

"Would you like me to get you a pillow?" Melenna cooed.

"No," Vanyel replied, counting to ten. Twice.

"Can I get you something to drink?" She edged a little closer, and leaned forward, batting her eyelashes at him.

"No," he said, closing *his* eyes. "Thank you."

"Shall I—"

"*No!*" he growled, not sure which was worse at this moment, the pounding of his head, or Melenna's questions. At least the pounding didn't have to be accompanied by Melenna's questions.

Sniff.

He cracked an eyelid open, just enough to see her. She sniffed again, and a fat tear rolled down one cheek.

She was a rather pretty little thing, and the only one of his mother's ladies *or* maidservants who had managed to pick up Treesa's knack of crying without going red and blotchy. Vanyel knew that both Mekeal and Radevel had tried to get into her bed more than once. He also knew that she had her heart set on him.

And the thought of bedding her left him completely cold.

She sniffed a little harder. A week ago he would have sighed, and apologized to her, and allowed her to do something for him. Anything, just to keep her happy.

That was a week ago. Now— *It's just a game for her, a game she learned from Mother. I'm tired of playing it. I'm sick to death of all their games.*

He ignored her, shutting his eyes and praying for the potions to work. And finally they did, which at least gave him a rest from her company for a little while.

"Van?"

That voice would bring him out of a sound sleep, let alone the restless drug-daze he was in now. He struggled up out of the grip of fever-dreams to force his eyes open.

Lissa was sitting on the edge of his bed, dressed in riding leathers.

"Liss—?" he began, then realized what *riding leathers* meant. "—oh, gods—"

"Van, I'm sorry, I didn't want to leave you, but Father said it was now or never." She was crying; not prettily like Lady Treesa, but with blotched cheeks and bloodshot eyes. "Van, please say you don't mind too much!"

"It's . . . all right, Liss," he managed, fighting the words out around the cold lump in his throat and the colder one in his gut. "I . . . know. You've got to do this. Gods, Liss, *one* of us has to get away!"

"Van—I—I'll find some way to help you, I promise. I'm almost eighteen; I'm almost free. Father *knows* the Guard is the only place for me; he hasn't had a marriage offer for me for two years. He doesn't dare ruin my chances for a post, or he'll be stuck with me. The gods know you're safe enough *now*—if anybody dared do anything before the Healer says you're fit, he'd make a protest to Haven. Maybe by the time you get the splints off, I'll be able to find a way to have you with me. . . ."

She looked so hopeful that Vanyel didn't have the heart to say anything to contradict her. "Do that, Liss. I—I'll be all right."

She hugged him, and kissed him, and then left him.

And *then* he turned to the wall and cried. Lissa was the only support he had had. The only person who loved him without reservations. And now she was gone.

After that, he stopped even pretending to care about anything. They didn't care enough about him to let Liss stay until he was well—so why should he care about anything or anyone, even enough to be polite?

"Armor does more than protect; it conceals. Helms hide faces—and your opponent becomes a mystery, an enigma."

Seldasen had that right. Just like those two down there.

The cruel, blank stares of the helm-slits gave no clues to the minds within. The two opponents drew their blades, flashed identical salutes, and retreated exactly twenty paces each to end at the opposite corners of the field. The sun was straight overhead, their shadows little more than pools at their feet. Twelve restive armored figures fidgeted together on one side of the square. The harsh sunshine bleached the short, dead grass to the color of light straw, and lit everything about the pair in pitiless detail.

Hmm. Not such enigmas once they move.

One fighter was tall, dangerously graceful, and obviously well-muscled beneath the protection of his worn padding and shabby armor. Every motion he made was precise, perilous—and professional.

The other was a head shorter. His equipment was new, the padding unfrayed, the metal lovingly burnished. But his movements were awkward, uncertain, perhaps fearful.

Still, if he feared, he didn't lack for courage. Without waiting for his man to make a move, he shouted a tremulous, defiant battle cry and charged across the sun-burnt grass toward the tall fighter. As his boots thudded on the hard, dry ground, he brought his sword around in a low-line attack.

The taller fighter didn't even bother to move out of his way; he simply swung his scarred shield to the side. The sword crunched into the shield, then slid off, metal screeching on metal. The tall fighter swept his shield back into guard position, and answered the blow with a return that rang true on the shield of his opponent, then rebounded, while he turned the momentum of the rebound into a cut at the smaller fighter's head.

The pale stone of the keep echoed the sound of the exchange, a racket like a madman loose in a smithy. The smaller fighter was driven back with every blow, giving ground steadily under the hammerlike onslaught—until he finally lost his footing and fell over backward, his sword flying out of his hand.

There was a dull *thud* as he hit his head on the flinty, unforgiving ground.

He lay flat on his back for a moment, probably seeing stars, and scarcely moving, arms flung out on either side of him as if he meant to embrace the sun. Then he shook his head dazedly and tried to get up—

Only to find the point of his opponent's sword at his throat.

"Yield, Boy," rumbled a harsh voice from the shadowed mouth-slit of the helmet. "Yield, or I run you through."

The smaller fighter pulled off his own helm to reveal that he was Vanyel's cousin Radevel. "If you run me through, Jervis, who's going to polish your mail?"

The point of the sword did not waver.

"Oh, all right," the boy said, with a rueful grin. "I yield."

The sword, a pot-metal practice blade, went back into its plain leather sheath. Jervis pulled off his own battered helm with his shield hand, as easily as if the weight of wood and bronze wasn't there. He shook out his sweat-dampened, blond hair and offered the boy his right, pulling him to his feet with the same studied, precise movements as he'd used when fighting.

"Next time, you yield immediately, Boy," the armsmaster rumbled, frowning. "If your opponent's in a hurry, he'll take banter for refusal, and you'll be a cold corpse."

Jervis did not even wait to hear Radevel's abashed assent. "You—on the end—Mekeal." He waved to Vanyel's brother at the side of the practice field. "Helm up."

Vanyel snorted as Jervis jammed his own helm back on his head, and stalked back to his former position, dead center of the practice ground. "The rest of you laggards," he growled, "let's see some life there. Pair up and have at."

Jervis doesn't have pupils, he has living targets, thought Vanyel, as he watched from the window. *There isn't anyone except Father who could even give him a workout, yet he goes straight for the throat every damned time; he gets nastier every day. About all he does give them is that he only hits half force. Which is still enough to set Radev on his rump. Bullying bastard.*

Vanyel leaned back on his dusty cushions, and forced his aching hand to run through the fingering exercise yet again. Half the lute strings plunked dully instead of ringing; both strength and agility had been lost in that hand.

I am never going to get this right again. How can I, when half the time I can't feel what I'm doing?

He bit his lip, and looked down again, blinking at the sunlight winking off Mekeal's helm four stories below. *Every one of them will be moaning and plastering horse liniment on his bruises tonight, and boasting in the next breath about how long he lasted against Jervis this time. Thank you, no. Not I. One broken arm was enough. I prefer to see my sixteenth birthday with the rest of my bones intact.*

This tiny tower room where Vanyel always hid himself when summoned to weapons practice was another legacy of Grandfather Joserlin's crazy building spree. It was Vanyel's favorite hiding place, and thus far, the most secure; a storage room just off the library. The only conventional access was through a tiny half-height door at the back of the library—but the room had a window—a window on the same side of the keep as the window of Vanyel's own attic-level room. Any time he wanted, Vanyel could climb easily out of his bedroom, edge along the slanting roof, and climb into that narrow window, even in the worst weather or the blackest night. The hard part was doing it unseen.

An odd wedge-shaped nook, this room was all that was left of the last landing of the staircase to the top floor—an obvious change in design, since the rest of the staircase had been turned into a chimney and the hole where the roof trapdoor had been now led to the chimney pot. But that meant that although there was no fireplace in the storeroom itself, the room stayed comfortably warm in the worst weather because of the chimney wall.

Not once in all the time Vanyel had taken to hiding here had anything new been added to the clutter or anything been sought for. Like many of the old lord's eccentricities, its inaccessibility made it easy to ignore.

Which was fine, so far as Vanyel was concerned. He had his instruments up here—two of which he wasn't even supposed to own, the harp and the gittern—and any time he liked he could slip into the library to purloin a book. At the point of the room he had an old chair to sprawl in, a collection of candle ends on a chest beside it so that he could read when the light was bad. His instruments were all safe from the rough hands and pranks of his brothers, and he could practice without anyone disturbing him.

He had arranged a set of old cushions by the window so that he could watch his brothers and cousins getting trounced all over the moat while he played—or tried to play. It afforded a ghost of amusement, sometimes. The gods knew he had little enough to smile about.

It was lonely—but Vanyel was always lonely, since Lissa had gone. It was bloody awkward to get to—but he couldn't hide in his room.

Though he hadn't found out until he'd healed up, the rest of his siblings and cousins had gone down to bachelor's hall with Mekeal while he'd been recovering from that broken arm. He hadn't, even when the Healer had taken the splints off. His brothers slandered his lute playing when they'd gone, telling his father they were just as happy for Vanyel to have his own room if he wanted to stay up there. Probably Withen, recalling how near the hall was to his own quarters, had felt the same. Vanyel didn't care; it meant that the room was his, and his alone—one scant bit of comfort.

His other place of refuge, his mother's solar, was no longer the retreat it had been. It was too easy for him to be found there, and there were other disadvantages lately; his mother's ladies and fosterlings had taken to flirting with him. He enjoyed that, too, up to a point—but they kept wanting to take it beyond the range of the game of courtly love to the romantic, for which he *still* wasn't ready. And Lady Treesa kept encouraging them at it.

Jervis drove Mekeal back, step by step. *Fools*, Vanyel thought scornfully, forcing his fingers through the exercise in time with Jervis' blows. *They must be mad, to let that sour old man make idiots out of them, day after day—maybe break their skulls, just like he broke my arm!* Anger tightened his mouth, and the memory of the shuttered satisfaction he'd seen in Jervis' eyes the first time Vanyel had encountered him after the "accident" roiled in his stomach. *Damn that bastard, he* meant *to break my arm, I* know *he did; he's good enough to judge any blow he deals to within a hair.*

At least he had a secure hiding place; secure because getting into it took nerve, and neither Jervis, nor his father, nor any of the rest of them would ever have put him and a climb across the roof together in the same thought—even if they remembered the room existed.

The ill-assorted lot below didn't look to be relatives; the Ashkevron cousins had all gone meaty when they hit adolescence; big-boned, muscled like plow horses—

—and about as dense—

—but Withen's sons were growing straight up as well as putting on bulk. Vanyel was the only one of the lot taking after his mother.

Withen seemed to hold *that* to be his fault, too.

Vanyel snorted as Mekeal took a blow to the helm that sent him reeling backward. *That one should shake up his brains! Serves him right, too, carrying on about what a great warrior he's going to be. Clod-headed beanpole. All he can think about is hacking people to bits for the sake of "honor."*

Glorious war, hah. Fool can't see beyond the end of his nose. For all that prating, if he ever saw *a battlefield he'd wet himself.*

Not that *Vanyel* had ever seen a real battlefield, but he was the possessor of a far more vivid imagination than anyone else in his family. He had no trouble in visualizing what those practice blades *would* be doing if they were real. And he had no difficulty at all in imagining the "deadlie woundes" of the ballads being inflicted on *his* body.

Vanyel paid close attention to his lessons, if not to weapons work. He knew *all* of the history ballads and unlike the rest of his peers, he knew the parts about what happened *after* the great battles as well—the lists of the dead, the dying, the maimed. It hadn't escaped his notice that when you added up those lists, the totals were a lot higher than the number of heroes who survived.

Vanyel knew damned well which list *he'd* be on if it ever came to armed conflict. He'd learned his lesson only too well: why even try?

Except that every time he turned around Lord Withen was delivering another lecture on his duty to the hold.

Gods. I'm just as much a brute beast of burden as any donkey in the stables! Duty. That's bloody all I hear, he thought, staring out the window, but no longer seeing what lay beyond the glass. *Why* me? *Mekeal would be a thousand times better Lord Holder than me, and he'd just* love *it! Why couldn't I have gone with Lissa?*

He sighed and put the lute aside, reaching inside his tunic for the scrap of parchment that Trevor Corey's page had delivered to *him* after he'd given Lissa's "official" letters into Treesa's hands.

He broke the seal on it, and smoothed out the palimpsest carefully; clever Lissa to have filched the scraped and stained piece that no one would notice was gone! She'd used a good, strong ink though; even though the letters were a bit blurred, he had no trouble reading them.

Dearest Vanyel; if only you were here! I can't tell you how much I miss you. The

*Corey girls are quite sweet, but not terribly bright. A lot like the cousins, really. I know I should have written you before this, but I didn't have much of a chance. Your arm should be better now. If only Father wasn't so blind! What I'm learning is ex-*actly *what we were working out together.*

Vanyel took a deep breath against the surge of anger at Withen's unreasonable attitude.

But we both know how he is, so don't argue with him, love. Just do what you're told. It won't be forever, really it won't. Just—hold on. I'll do what I can from this end. Lord Corey is a lot more reasonable than Father ever was and maybe I can get him talked into asking for you. Maybe that will work. Just be really *good, and maybe Father will be happy enough with you to do that. Love, Liss.*

He folded the letter and tucked it away. *Oh, Liss. Not a chance. Father would* never *let me go there, not after the way I've been avoiding my practices. "It won't be forever," hmm? I suppose* that's *right. I probably won't live past the next time Jervis manages to catch up with me. Gods. Why is it that nobody ever asks me what I* want—*or when they do ask, why can't they* mean *it and listen to me?*

He blinked, and looked again at the little figures below, still pounding away at one another, like so many tent pegs determined to drive each other into the ground.

He turned restlessly away from the window, stood up, and replaced the lute in the makeshift stand he'd contrived for it beside his other two instruments.

And everywhere I turn I get the same advice. From Liss—"don't fight, do what Father asks." From Mother—crying, vapors, and essentially the same thing. She's not exactly stupid; if she really cared *about me, she could manage Father somehow. But she doesn't care—not when backing me against Father is likely to cost her something. And when I tried to tell Father Leren about what Jervis was* really *like—*

He shuddered. *The lecture about filial duty was bad enough—but the one about "proper masculine behavior"—you'd have thought I'd been caught fornicating with sheep! And all because I objected to having my bones broken. It's like I'm doing something wrong somewhere, but no one will tell me what it is and why it's wrong! I thought* maybe *Father Leren would understand since he's a priest, but gods, there's no* help coming from that direction.

For a moment he felt trapped up here; the secure retreat turned prison. He didn't dare go out, or he'd be caught and forced into that despised armor—and Jervis would lay into him with a vengeful glee to make up for all the practices he'd managed to avoid. He looked wistfully beyond the practice field to the wooded land and meadows beyond. It was such a beautiful day; summer was just beginning, and the breeze blowing in his open window was heady with the aroma of the hayfields in the sun. He longed to be out walking or riding beneath those trees; he was as trapped by the things he didn't dare do as by the ones he had to.

Tomorrow I'll have to go riding out with Father on his rounds, he gloomed. *And no getting out of* that. *He'll have me as soon as I come down for breakfast.*

That was a new torment, added since he'd recovered. It was nearly as bad as being under Jervis' thumb. He shuddered, thinking of all those farmers, staring, staring—like they were trying to stare into his soul. This was not going to be a pleasure jaunt, for all that he loved to ride. No, he would spend the entire day listening to his father lecture him on the duties of the Lord Holder to the tenants who farmed for him and the peasant-farmers who held their lands under his protection and governance. But that was not the worst aspect of the ordeal.

It was the people themselves; the way they measured him with their eyes, opaque eyes full of murky thoughts that he could not read. Eyes that expected everything of him; that *demanded* things of him that he did not want to give, and didn't know how to give even if he had wanted to.

I don't want them looking to me like that! I don't want to be responsible for their lives! He shuddered again. *I wouldn't know what to do in a drought or an invasion, and what's more, I don't care! Gods, they make my skin crawl, all those—people, eating me alive with their eyes—*

He turned away from the window, and knelt beside his instruments; stretched out his hand, and touched the smooth wood, the taut strings. *Oh, gods—if I weren't me—if I could just have a* chance *to be a Bard—*

In the days before his arm had been hurt he had often imagined himself a Court Bard, not in some out-of-the-way corner like Forst Reach, but one of the Great Courts; Gyrefalcon's Marches or Southron Keep. Or even the High Court of Valdemar at Haven. Imagined himself the center of a circle of admirers, languid ladies and jewel-bedecked lords, all of them hanging enraptured on every word of his song. He could let his imagination transport him to a different life, the life of his dreams. He could actually see himself surrounded, not by the girls of Treesa's bower, but by the entire High Court of Valdemar, from Queen Elspeth down, until the visualization was more real than his true surroundings. He could see, hear, feel, all of them waiting in impatient anticipation for him to sing—the bright candles, the perfume, the pregnant silence—

Now even that was lost to him. Now practices were solitary, for there was no Lissa to listen to new tunes. Lissa had been a wonderful audience; she had a good ear, and knew enough about music to be trusted to tell him the truth. She had been the only person in the keep besides Treesa who didn't seem to think there was something faintly shameful about his obsession with music. And she was the only one who knew of his dream of becoming a Bard.

There were no performances before his mother's ladies, either, because he refused to let them hear him fumble.

And all because of the lying, bullying bastard his father had made armsmaster—

"Withen—"

He froze; startled completely out of his brooding by the sound of his mother's breathless, slightly shrill voice just beyond the tiny door to the library. He knelt slowly and carefully, avoiding the slightest noise. The *last* thing he wanted was to have his safe hiding place discovered!

"Withen, what *is* it you've dragged me up here to tell me that you couldn't have said in my solar?" she asked. Vanyel could tell by the edge in her voice that she was ruffled and not at all pleased.

Vanyel held his breath, and heard the sound of the library door being closed, then his father's heavy footsteps crossing the library floor.

A long, ponderous silence. Then, "I'm sending Vanyel away." Withen said, brusquely.

"*What?*" Treesa shrilled. "You—how—where—*why?* In the gods' names, Withen, *why?*"

Vanyel felt as if someone had turned his heart into stone, and his body into clay.

"I can't do anything with the boy, Treesa, and neither can Jervis." Withen growled. "I'm sending him to someone who can make something of him."

"You can't do anything because the two of you seem to think to 'make something of him' you have to force him to be something he can never be!" Treesa's voice was muffled by the intervening wall, but the note of hysteria was plain all the same. "You put him out there with a man twice his weight and expect him to—"

"To behave like a man! He's a sniveler, a whiner, Treesa. He's more worried about damage to his pretty face and delicate little hands than damage to his honor, and you don't help matters by making him the pet of the bower. Treesa, the boy's become nothing more than a popinjay, a vain little peacock—and worse than that, he's a total coward."

"A *coward!* Gods, Withen—only *you* would say that!" Lady Treesa's voice was thick with scorn. "Just because he's too clever to let that precious *arms-master* of yours beat him insensible once a day!"

"So what does he do instead? Run off and hide because once—just *once*—he got his poor little arm broken! Great good gods, I'd broken every bone in my body at least once by the time I was his age!"

"Is that supposed to signify virtue?" she scoffed. "Or stupidity?"

Vanyel's mouth sagged open. *She's—my gods! She's standing up to him! I don't believe this!*

"It signifies the willingness to endure a little discomfort in order to *learn*," Withen replied angrily. "Thanks to you and your fosterlings, all Vanyel's ever learned was how to select a tunic that matches his eyes, and how to warble a love song! He's too damned handsome for his own good— and you've spoiled him, Treesa; you've let him trade on that pretty face, get away with nonsense and arrogance you'd never have permitted in Mekeal. And now he has no sense of responsibility whatsoever, he avoids even a hint of obligation."

"You'd prefer him to be like Mekeal, I suppose," she replied acidly. "You'd like him to hang on your every word and never question you, never challenge you—"

"Damned right!" Withen roared in frustration. "The boy doesn't know his damned place! Filling his head with book-learned nonsense—"

"He doesn't know his *place?* Because he can think for himself? Just because he can read and write more than his bare name? *Unlike* certain grown men I could name—gods, Withen, that priest of yours has you parroting every little nuance, doesn't he? And you're sending Van away because he doesn't measure up to *his* standards of propriety, aren't you? Because Vanyel has the intelligence to question what he's told, and Leren doesn't like questions!" Her voice reached new heights of shrillness. "That *priest* has you so neatly tied around his ankle that you wouldn't *breathe* unless he declared breathing was orthodox enough!"

—ah, Vanyel thought, a part of his mind still working, while the rest sat in stunned contemplation of the idea of being "sent away." Now Treesa's support had a rational explanation. Lady Treesa did not care for Father Leren. Vanyel was just a convenient reason to try to drive a wedge between Withen and his crony.

Although Vanyel could have told her that this was *exactly* the wrong way to go about doing so.

"I expected you'd say something like that," Withen rumbled. "You have no choice, Treesa, the boy is going, whether you like it or not. I'm sending him to Savil at the High Court. *She'll* brook no nonsense, and once he's in surroundings where he's not the only pretty face in the place he *might* learn to do something besides lisp a ballad and moon at himself in the mirror."

"*Savil?* That old harridan?" His mother's voice rose with each word until she was shrieking. Vanyel wanted to shriek, too.

He remembered his first—and last—encounter with his Aunt Savil only too well.

Vanyel had bowed low to the silver-haired stranger, a woman clad in impeccable Heraldic Whites, contriving his best imitation of courtly manner. Herald Savil—who had packed herself up at the age of fourteen and hied herself off to Haven without word to anyone, and then been Chosen the moment she passed the city gates—was Lissa's idol. Lissa had pestered Grandmother Ashkevron for every tale about Savil that the old woman knew. Vanyel couldn't understand *why*—but if Lissa admired this woman so much, surely there must be more to her than appeared on the surface.

It was a pity that Liss was visiting cousins the one week her idol chose to make an appearance at the familial holding.

But then again—maybe that was exactly as Withen had planned.

"So this is Vanyel," the woman had said, dryly. "A pretty boy, Treesa. I trust he's something more than ornamental."

Vanyel went rigid at her words, then rose from his bow and fixed her with what he hoped was a cool, appraising stare. Gods, she *looked* like his father in the right light; like Lissa, she had that Ashkevron nose, a nose that both she and Withen thrust forward like a sharp blade to cleave all before them.

"Oh, don't glare at me, child," the woman said with amusement. "I've had better men than you try to freeze me with a look and fail."

He flushed. She turned away from him as if he was of no interest, turning back to Vanyel's mother, who was clutching a handkerchief at her throat. "So, Treesa, has the boy shown any sign of Gift or Talent?"

"He sings beautifully," Treesa fluttered. "Really, he's as good as any minstrel we've ever had."

The woman turned and stared at him—stared through him. "Potential, but nothing active," Savil said slowly. "A pity; I'd hoped at least one of your offspring would share my Gifts. You can certainly afford to spare one to the

Queen's service. But the girls don't even have potential Gifts, your four other boys are worse than this one, and this one doesn't appear to be much more than a clotheshorse for all his potential."

She waved a dismissing hand at him, and Vanyel's face had burned.

"I've seen what I came to see, Treesa," she said, leading Vanyel's mother off by the elbow. "I won't stress your hospitality anymore."

From all Vanyel had heard, Savil was, in many ways, not terribly unlike her brother; hard, cold, and unforgiving, preoccupied with what she perceived as her duty. She had never wedded; Vanyel was hardly surprised. He couldn't imagine *anyone* wanting to bed Savil's chill arrogance. He couldn't imagine why warm, loving Lissa wanted to be like her.

Now his mother was weeping hysterically; his father was making no effort to calm her. By that, Vanyel knew there was no escaping the disastrous plan. Incoherent hysterics were his mother's court of last resort; if *they* were failing, there was no hope for him.

"Give it up, Treesa," Withen said, unmoved, his voice rock-steady. "The boy goes. Tomorrow."

"You—unfeeling *monster*—" That was all that was understandable through Treesa's weeping. Vanyel heard the staccato beat of her slippers on the floor as she ran out the library door, then the slower, heavier sound of his father's boots. Then the sound of the door closing—

—as leaden and final as the door on a tomb.

CHAPTER 2

VANYEL STUMBLED OVER to his old chair and collapsed into its comfortable embrace.

He couldn't think. Everything had gone numb. He stared blankly at the tiny rectangle of blue sky framed by the window; just sat, and stared. He wasn't even aware of the passing of time until the sun began shining directly into his eyes.

He winced away from the light; that broke his bewildered trance, and he realized dully that the afternoon was gone—that someone would start looking for him to call him for supper soon, and he'd better be back in his room.

He slouched dispiritedly over to the window, and peered out of it, making the automatic check to see if there was anyone below who could spot him. But even as he did so it occurred to him that it hardly mattered if they found his hideaway, considering what he'd just overheard.

There was no one on the practice field now; just the empty square of turf, a chicken on the loose pecking at something in the grass. From this vantage the keep might well have been deserted.

Vanyel turned around and reached over his head, grabbing the rough stone edging the window all around the exterior, and levered himself up and out onto the sill. Once balanced there in a half crouch, he stepped down onto the ledge that ran around the edge of the roof, then reached around the gable and got a good handhold on the slates of the roof itself, and began inching over to his bedroom window.

Halfway between the two windows, he paused for a moment to look down.

It isn't all that far—if I fell just right, the worst I'd do is break a leg—then they couldn't send me off, could they? It might be worth it. It just might be worth it.

He thought about that—and thought about the way his broken arm had hurt—

Not a good idea; with my luck, Father would send me off as soon as I was patched up; just load me up in a wagon like a sack of grain. "Deliver to Herald Savil, no special handling." Or worse, I'd break my arm again, or both arms. I've got a chance to make that hand work again—maybe—but if I break it this time there isn't a Healer around to make sure it's set right.

Vanyel swung his legs into the room, balanced for a moment on the sill, then dropped onto his bed. Once there, he lacked the spirit to even move. He slumped against the wall and stared at the sloping, whitewashed ceiling.

He tried to think if there was anything he could do to get himself out of this mess. He couldn't come up with a single idea that seemed at all viable. It was too late to "mend his ways" even if he wanted to.

No—no. I can't, absolutely can't face that sadistic bastard Jervis. Though I'm truly not sure which is the worst peril at this point in the long run, Aunt Ice-and-Iron or Jervis. I know what he'll do to me. I haven't a clue to her.

He sagged, and bit his lip, trying to stay in control, trying to think logically. *All* he knew was that Savil would have the worst possible report on him; and at Haven—the irony of the name!—he would have no allies, no hiding places. That was the worst of it; going off into completely foreign territory *knowing* that everybody there had been told how awful he was. That they would just be waiting for him to make a slip. All the time. But there was no getting out of it. For all that Treesa petted and cosseted him, Vanyel knew better than to rely on her for anything, or expect her to ever *defy* Withen. That brief flair during their argument had been the exception; Treesa's real efforts always lay in keeping her own life comfortable and amusing. She'd cry for Vanyel, but she'd never defend him. Not like Lissa might well have—

If Lissa had been here.

When the page came around to call everyone to dinner, he managed to stir up enough energy to dust himself off and obey the summons, but he had no appetite at all.

The highborn of Forst Reach ate late, a candlemark after the servants, hirelings and the armsmen had eaten, since the Great Hall was far too small to hold everyone at once. The torches and lanterns had already been lit along the worn stone-floored corridors; they did nothing to dispel the darkness of Vanyel's heart. He trudged along the dim corridors and down the stone stairs, ignoring the servants trotting by him on errands of their own. Since his room was at the servants' end of the keep, he had a long way to go to get to the Great Hall.

Once there, he waited in the sheltering darkness of the doorway to assess the situation in the room beyond.

As usual he was nearly the last one to table; as far as he could tell, only his Aunt Serina was missing, and she might well have eaten earlier, with the children. Carefully watching for the best opportunity to do so undetected, he slipped into his seat beside his brother Mekeal at the low table during a moment when Lord Withen was laughing at some joke of Father Leren's. The usually austere cleric seemed in a very good mood tonight, and Vanyel's heart sank. If Leren was pleased, it probably didn't bode *Vanyel* any good.

"Where were *you* this afternoon?" Mekeal asked, as he wiggled over to give Vanyel a place on the bench, interrupting his noisy inhalation of soup.

Vanyel shrugged. "Does it matter?" he asked, trying to sound indifferent. "It's no secret how I feel about that nonsense, and it's no secret how Jervis feels about me. So does it really matter where I was?"

Mekeal chuckled into his bowl. "Probably not. You know Jervis'll just be harder on you when you do get caught. And you're going to get caught one of these days. You're looking for another broken arm, if you're lucky. If that's the way you want it, on your head be it."

So Father hasn't said anything yet—Vanyel thought with surprise, his spoon poised above the soup. He glanced over at the head table. Lady Treesa *was* in her accustomed place beside her lord. And she didn't look any more upset than she usually did; she certainly showed no signs of the hysterics Vanyel had overheard this afternoon.

Could she actually have stood up for me, just this once? Could she have gotten him to back down? Oh, gods, if only!

The renewal of hope did not bring a corresponding renewal of appetite; the tension only made his stomach knot up all the more. The room seemed far too hot; he loosened the laces of his tunic, but that didn't help. The flames of the lamps on the wall behind him made the shadows dance on the table, until he had to close his eyes and take several deep breaths to get his equilibrium back. He felt flushed and feverish, and after only a few mouthfuls of the thick, swiftly cooling soup that seemed utterly tasteless, he signaled to a servant to take it away.

He squirmed uncomfortably on the wooden bench, and pushed the rest of his meal around on his plate with one eye always on the high table and his father. The high table *was* high; raised on a dais a good hand above the rest of the room, and set at the head of the low table like the upper bar of a "T." That meant that it overlooked and overshadowed the low table. Vanyel could feel the presence of those sitting there looming over him even at those few times when he *wasn't* watching them. With each course his stomach seemed to acquire another lump, a colder and harder one, until he finally gave up all pretense of eating.

Then, just at the dessert course, when he thought he might be saved, his father rose to his feet.

Lord Withen towered over the table as he towered over Vanyel and everything belonging to Forst Reach. He prided himself on being a "plain man," close enough in outlook to any of his men that they could feel easy with him. His sturdy brown leather tunic and linen shirt were hardly distinguishable from the garb of any of the hireling armsmen; the tunic was decorated with polished silver studs instead of copper, but that was the only token of his rank. The tunic strained across his broad shoulders—and across the barest hint of a paunch. His long, dark hair was confined in a tail at the nape of his neck by a silver band, his beard trimmed close to his square jawline.

Vanyel's changeling appearance, especially when contrasted with Mekeal's, may have been one reason why Withen seemed to be irritated whenever he looked at his eldest son. Vanyel was lean, and not particularly tall; Mekeal was tall and muscular, already taller than Vanyel although he was two years younger. Vanyel's hair was so black it had blue highlights, and his eyes were a startling silver-gray, exactly like his mother's—and he had no facial hair to speak of. Mekeal's eyes were a chestnut brown, he already had to shave, and his hair matched his father's so closely that it would not have been possible to tell which of them a particular plucked hair came from.

Mekeal made friends as easily as breathing—

I never had anyone but Lissa.

Mekeal was tone-deaf; Vanyel lived for music. Mekeal suffered through his scholastic lessons; Vanyel so far exceeded his brother that there was no comparison.

In short, Mekeal was completely his father's son; Vanyel was utterly Withen's opposite.

Perhaps that was all in Withen's mind as he rose and spared a glance for his first-and-second-born sons, before fixing his gaze on nothing in particular. The lanterns behind Withen danced, and his shadow reached halfway down the low table. As that stark shadow darkened the table, it blackened Vanyel's rising hope.

"After due consideration," Withen rumbled, "I have decided that it is time for Vanyel to acquire education of a kind—more involved than we can give him here. So tonight will be the last night he is among us. Tomorrow he will begin a journey to my sister, Herald-Mage Savil at the High Court of Valdemar, who will take official guardianship of him until he is of age."

Withen sat down heavily.

Treesa burst into a tearful wail, and shoved herself away from the table; as she stood, her chair went over with a clatter that sounded, in the unnatural silence that now filled the Great Hall, as loud as if the entire table were collapsing. She ran from the room, sobbing into her sleeve, as Withen maintained a stony silence. Her fosterlings and ladies followed her, and only Melenna cast an unreadable glance over her shoulder at Vanyel before trailing off in the wake of the others.

Everyone in the silent room seemed to have been frozen by an evil spell.

Finally Withen reached forward and took a walnut from the bowl before him; he nestled it in his palm and cracked it in his bare hands. Vanyel jumped at the sound, and he wasn't the only one.

"Very good nuts last year, don't you think?" Withen said to Father Leren.

That seemed to be the signal for the entire room to break out in frantic babbling. On Vanyel's right, three of his cousins began laying noisy bets on the outcome of a race between Radevel and Kerle on the morrow. On his right, Radevel whispered to Mekeal, while across the table from him his youngest brother Heforth exchanged punches and pokes with cousin Larence.

Vanyel was pointedly ignored. He might just as well have been invisible, except for the sly, sidelong looks he was getting. And not just from the youngsters, either. When he looked up at the high table once, he caught Father Leren staring at him and smiling slyly. When their eyes met, the priest nodded very slightly, gave Vanyel a look brimming with self-satisfaction, and only then turned his attention back toward Withen. During that silent exchange—which nobody else seemed to have noticed—Vanyel had felt himself grow pale and cold.

As the dessert course was cleared away, the elders left the hall on affairs of their own, and a few of the girls—more of Vanyel's cousins—returned; a sign that Lady Treesa had retired for the night.

The boys and young men remaining now rose from their seats; the young usually reigned over the hall undisturbed after dinner. With the girls that had returned they formed three whispering, giggling groups; two sets of four and one of eleven—all three groups blatantly closing Vanyel out. Even the girls seemed to have joined in the conspiracy to leave him utterly alone.

Vanyel pretended not to notice the muttering, the jealous glances. He rose from the bench a few moments after the rest had abandoned him, making it a point of honor to saunter over to stare into the fire in the great fireplace. He walked with head high, features schooled into a careful mask of bored indifference.

He could feel their eyes on the back of his neck, but he refused to turn, refused to show any emotion at all, much less how queasy their behavior was making him feel.

Finally, when he judged that he had made his point, he stretched, yawned, and turned. He surveyed the entire room through half-closed eyelids for a long moment, his own gaze barely brushing each of them, then paced lazily across the endless length of the Great Hall, pausing only to nod a cool good night to the group nearest the door before—finally!—achieving the sanctuary of the dark hallway beyond it.

"Ye gods, you'd think he was the Heir to the Throne!" Sandar exclaimed, rolling his eyes and throwing up his hands. "Queen Elspeth herself wouldn't put on such airs!"

Eighteen-year-old Joserlin Corveau stared after the lad for a long moment, putting his thoughts together. He was the oldest of the fosterlings, and the latest-come. Really, he wasn't properly a fosterling at all, nor a close cousin. A true cousin, childless after many years, had decided on Joserlin as his Heir and (as he himself was not in the best of health) requested he be fostered to Lord Withen to learn the ways of governance of one's Holdings. He was broad and tall as any of the doors to the keep, and even Jervis respected the power of his young muscles. After a single practice session with young Jos, Jervis had decreed that he was old enough to train with Withen's armsmen. After seeing the way Jervis "trained" the boys, Jos had been quite content to have it so.

Some of the younger boys had made the mistake of thinking that his slow speech and large build meant that he was stupid. They had quickly discovered their mistake when he'd gotten them with well-timed jokes.

He liked to say of himself that while he didn't think quickly, he *did* think things through all the way. And there were aspects of this vaguely disturbing evening that were not adding together properly in his mind.

Meanwhile the rest of his group continued dissecting Withen's least-beloved offspring.

"He thinks he *is* the Heir to the Throne," giggled Jyllian, swishing her skirts coquettishly. "Or at least, that the rest of us are that far below him. You should *see* him, lording it over us in the bower!" She stuck her nose in the air and mimed looking down it while playing a make-believe lute. "But just *try* and get anything out of him besides a song! Brrr! Watch the snow fall! You'd think we were poison-vellis, the way he pulls away and goes cold!"

Mekeal snorted, tossing his head. "Thinks he's too good for you, I s'ppose! Nothing high enough for *him* but a lady of the blood-royal, no doubt! Thinks girls like you aren't lofty enough."

"Or not pretty enough," snickered Merthin. "Havens, give it a thought—none of you little lovelies are even a close match for His Majesty's sweet face. Can't have his lady less beautiful than *he* is, after all."

"I don't doubt." Larence put in his bit, coming up behind Merthin. "Well, he'll find he's not the only pretty face when he gets to the High Court. He *just* might find himself standing in somebody's shadow for a change! Take my word for it, dear little Vanyel is going to get a rude awakening when he gets to Haven."

"Dammit, it's not *fair*," Mekeal grumbled, face clouding at this reminder of Vanyel's destination. "I'd give my arm to go to Haven! I mean, think of it; the best fighters in the country are there—it's the center of everything!" He flung his hands wide, nearly hitting Merthin, in a gesture of total frustration. "How'm I ever going to get a—an officer's commission or any kind of position when nobody with any say at Court is ever going to see me? That's why they sent m'sister off to be fostered right near there! You have a chance to get *noticed* at Court! She's going to be an officer, you can bet on it, an' best I'll ever get is *maybe* a Sector command, which means not one damn thing! I *need* to be at Court; I ain't going to inherit! *I'm* the one that should be going, not Vanyel! It's not *fair!*"

"Huh. You've got that right," Larence echoed, shifting his feet restlessly. "Dammit, we're all seconds, thirds—we *all* need a chance like that, or we'll be stuck doing nothing at the end of nowhere for the rest of our lives! We're never going to get anywhere, stuck off here in the back of beyond."

"And think of the ladies," added Kerle, rolling his eyes up and kissing his hand at the ceiling. "All the loveliest darlings in the kingdom."

He ducked, laughing, as Jyllian feinted a blow at his head, then shook her fist at him in mock-anger.

"Dammit, think a bit," Mekeal persisted. "What in Haven's name has he *done* to deserve getting rewarded like that? All he does around here is play he's a minstrel, look down that long nose of his at the rest of us, and shirk every duty he can!" Mekeal glowered and pounded his fist into the palm of his other hand to emphasize his words. "He's *Mother's* little darling, but— there's no way she'd have talked Father into sending him off, you all saw how she acted! So *why?* Why him, when the rest of us would *die* to get a chance to go to the capital?"

Joserlin continued to stare off into the dark; he was still putting together what he'd been observing. Everyone looked expectantly at him when Mekeal subsided and he cleared his throat. They all knew at this point that he was not the bright intellectual light among his brothers and cousins that Vanyel was, but he had a knack of seeing to the heart of things, and they wanted to hear if *he* had an answer for them. He usually did, and as they had half expected, this time was no exception.

"What makes you all think it's a reward?" he asked quietly.

The astonishment in the faces turned to his, followed by the light of dawning understanding, made him nod as he saw them come to the same conclusion he had made.

"You see?" he said, just as quietly as before. "It isn't a reward for Vanyel— it's an exile."

Vanyel didn't have to control his trembling when he reached the safe, concealing shelter of the hallway, but he didn't dare pause there. Someone might take it into his or her head to follow him.

But what he *could* do—now that he was out of the range of prying, curious eyes and ears—was run.

So he did, though he ran as noiselessly as he could, fleeing silently behind his shadow through the dim, uncertain light of the hallways. His flight took him past the dark, closed doorways leading to the bower, to bachelor's hall, to the chapel. His shadow sprang up before him every time he passed a lantern or torch, splaying out thin and spidery on the floor. He kept his head down so that if anyone should happen to come out of one of those doorways, they wouldn't see how close he was to tears.

But no one appeared; he reached the safe shelter of the servants' wing without encountering a single soul. Once there he dashed heedlessly up the stone staircase. Someone had extinguished the lanterns on the staircase itself; Vanyel didn't care. He'd run up these stairs often enough when half blind from trying not to cry, and his feet knew the way themselves.

He hit the top landing at a dead run, and made the last few feet to his own door in a few heartbeats. He was sobbing for breath as he fumbled out his key in the dark and unlocked it—and the tears were threatening to spill.

Spill they did as soon as he got the door open. He shut and locked it behind him, leaning his back against it, head thrown back and resting against the rough wood. He swallowed his sobs out of sheer, prideful refusal to let *anyone* know of his unhappiness, even a servant, but hot tears poured down his cheeks and soaked into the neck of his tunic, and he couldn't make them stop.

They hate me. They all hate me. I knew they didn't much like me, but I never knew how much they hated me.

Never had he felt so utterly alone and nakedly vulnerable. At that moment if he could have *ensured* his death he'd have thrown himself out of his window. But as he'd noted earlier, it wasn't *that* far to the ground, and pain was a worse prospect than loneliness.

Finally he stumbled to his bed, pulled his clothing off, and crawled under the blankets, shivering with the need to keep from crying out loud.

But despite his best efforts, the tears started again, and he muffled his sobs in his pillow.

Oh, Liss—oh, Liss—I don't know what to do! Nobody cares, nobody gives a damn about me, nobody would ever risk a hangnail for me but you—and they've taken you out of reach. I'm afraid, and I'm alone, and Father's trying to break me, I know he is.

He turned over, and stared into the darkness above him, feeling his eyes burn. *I wish I could die. Now.*

He tried to will his heart to stop, but it obstinately ignored him.

Why can't they just leave me alone? He closed his burning eyes, and bit his lip. *Why?*

He lay in his bed, feeling every lump in the mattress, every prickle in the sheets; every muscle was tensed until it ached, his head was throbbing, and his eyes still burned.

He lay there for at least an eternity, but the oblivion he hoped for didn't come. Finally he gave up on trying to sleep, fumbled for the candle at his bedside, and slid out into the stuffy darkness of the room. He grabbed up his robe from the foot of the bed and pulled it on over his trembling, naked body, and began crossing the floor to the door.

Though the room itself was warm—too warm—the tiled floor was shockingly cold under his feet. He felt his way to the door, and pressed his ear against the crack at the side, listening with all his might for any sounds from the corridor and stairs beyond.

Nothing.

He cautiously slipped the inside bolt; listened again. Still nothing. He cracked the door and peered around the edge into the corridor.

It was thankfully empty. But the nearest lantern was all the way down at the dead end.

He took a deep breath and drew himself up; standing as tall and resolutely erect as if he were Lord of the Keep himself. He walked calmly, surely, down the empty corridor, with just as much arrogance as if all his cousins' eyes were on him. Because there was no telling when one of the upper servants who had their rooms along this hall might take it into their heads to emerge—and servants talked. Frequently.

And they would *talk* if one of them got a glimpse of Vanyel in tears. It would be all over the keep in a candlemark.

He lit his candle at the lantern, and made another stately progress back to his room. Only when he had securely bolted the door behind him did he let go of the harpstring-taut control he'd maintained outside. He began shaking so hard that the candle flame danced madly, and spilled drops of hot wax on his hands.

He lit the others in their sconces by the door and over the bed as quickly as he could, and placed the one he was clutching in the holder on his table before he could burn himself with it.

He sat down heavily on the rucked-up blankets, sucking the side of his thumb where hot wax had scorched him, and staring at his belongings, trying to decide what his father was likely to let him take with him.

He didn't even bother to consider his instruments. They were far safer where they were. Maybe someday—if he survived this—he could come back and get them. But there was *no* chance, none at all, that he could sneak them out in his belongings. And if his father found them packed up—

He'd smash them. He'd smash them, and laugh, and wait for me to say or do something about it.

He finally got up and knelt on the chill stone beside the chest that held his clothing. He raised the heavy, carved lid, and stared down at the top layer for a long moment before lifting it out.

Tunics, shirts, breeches, hose—all in the deep, jewel-tones of sapphire and aquamarine and emerald that he knew looked so good on him, or his favorite black, silvery or smoky gray. All clothing he wore because it was one tiny way to defy his father—because his father could wear the same three outfits all year, all of them identical, and never notice, never care. Because his father didn't give a damn about what he or anyone else wore—and it angered him that Vanyel did.

Vanyel pondered the clothing, stroking the soft raime of a shirt without much thinking about what he was doing. *He won't dare keep me from taking the clothes, though I bet he'd like to. I'll have to look presentable when I get there, or I'll shame him—and the stuff Mekeal and the rest scruff around in is not presentable.*

He began rolling the clothing carefully, and stowing it into the traveling packs kept in the bottom of the chest. Though he didn't dare take an instrument, he managed to secrete some folded music, some of his favorite pieces, between the pages of the books he packed. *Bards are thick as birds in a cherry grove at Haven*, he thought with a lump in his throat. *Maybe I can get one to trade an old gittern for a cloak-brooch or something. It won't be the same as my lovely Woodlark, but it'll be better than nothing. Provided I can keep Aunt Unsavory from taking it away from me.*

It was all too quickly done. He found himself on the floor beside the filled packs with nothing more to do. He looked around his room; there was nothing left to pack that he would miss—except for those few things that he wanted to take but didn't dare.

Pretty fine life I've led, when all of it fits in four packs.

He got slowly to his feet, feeling utterly exhausted, yet almost too weary to sleep. He blew out all the candles except the one at his bedside, slipped out of his robe, tucked it into the top of the last pack, and climbed back into bed.

Somehow he couldn't bring himself to blow out the last candle. While there was light in the room he could keep the tears back. But darkness would set them free.

He lay rigid, staring silently at the candlelight wavering on the slanted ceiling, until his eyes burned.

All the brothers and fosterlings shared rooms; Mekeal had shared his with Vanyel until his older brother's broken arm had sent Mekeal down here a year early. And when Vanyel hadn't made the move down—Mekeal hadn't been particularly unhappy.

So for a while he had this one to himself, at which point he found that he really hadn't liked being alone after all. He liked company. Now, though—at least since late spring—he'd shared with Joserlin.

That had been *fine* with him. Jos was the next thing to an adult; Mekeal had been excited to have him move in, pleased with his company, and proud that Jos had treated him like an equal. And Jos talked to him; he didn't talk much, but when he did it was worth listening to. But he'd already said his say earlier tonight—so Mekeal had thought.

So he was kind of surprised when Jos' deep voice broke the silence right after they'd blown the candles out.

"Mekeal, why are you younglings so hard on your brother?"

Mekeal didn't have to ask *which* brother, it was pretty plain who Jos meant. But—"hard on him?" How could you be hard on somebody who didn't give a damn about anything but himself?

" 'Cause he's a—*toad*," Mekeal said indignantly. "He's got no more backbone than a mushroom! He's a baby, a coward—an' the only thing he cares about's hisself! He's just like Mama—she's gone and made him into a mama-pet, a shirker."

"Hmm? Really? What makes you so sure of that last?"

"Father says, and Jervis—"

"Because he won't let Jervis pound him like a set of pells." Joserlin snorted with absolute contempt. "Can't say as *I* much blame him, myself. If I was built like him, with Jervis on my back, reckon I'd find a hiding-hole, too. I sure's Haven wouldn't go givin' Jervis more chances t' hit on me."

Mekeal's mouth fell open in shock, and he squirmed around in his bed to face where Joserlin was, a dark bulk to his right. "But—but—Jervis—he's *armsmaster!*"

"He's a ham-handed lackwit," came the flat reply. "You forget, Meke, I was fostered with Lord Kendrick; I learned under a *real* armsmaster; Master Orser, and he's a good one. Jervis wouldn't be anything but another arms-man if he hadn't been an old friend of your father's. He *don't* deserve to be armsmaster. Havens, Meke, he goes after the greenest of you like you was his age, his weight, and his experience! He don't pull his blows half the time; and he don't bother to show you how to take 'em, just lets you fumble it out for yourselves. An' he don't know but *one* bare style, an' that one's Holy Writ!"

"But—"

"But nothin'. He's no great master, let me tell you; by *my* way of thinkin' he's no master at all. If I was Vanyel, I'd'a poisoned myself before I let the old goat take his spleen out on me again! I *heard* what happened this spring— about how he took after Van an' beat him down a half dozen times, an' then broke his arm."

"But—he was cheating!" Mekeal protested.

"No such thing; Radevel told me what really happened. *Before* that bastard managed to convince you lot that you *didn't* see Van getting beaten up 'cause he bested the old peabrain. That weren't nothing but plain old bullying, an' if *my* old armsmaster had treated one of *his* pupils that way, he'd have been kicked off the top of the tower by Lord Kendrick hisself!"

Mekeal could hardly believe what he was hearing. "But—" he protested again. "But Father—"

"Your father's a damn fool," Joserlin replied shortly. "An' I won't beg your pardon for sayin' so. He's a damn fool for keepin' Jervis as Master, an' he's a damn fool for treatin' young Vanyel the way he does. He's beggin' for trouble ev'ry time he pushes that boy. Half of what Vanyel does he *made* him do—to spite him. You mark my words; I seen this before, only the opposite. Place next to where I was fostered at your age, old Lady Cedrys at Briary Holding. Old Cedrys, she was big on scholarly stuff; nothin' would do but for *her* oldest t' be at the books night and day. 'Cept her oldest was like you, mad for the Guard. And the more Cedrys pushed books, the more Liaven ran for the armsmaster at our place, till one day he kept right on running and didn't stop till he'd signed up with a common mercenary-company, an' she never saw him again."

"But—Jos—you've *seen* him, the way he lords it over us like he was King of the Gods or something—keeping his nose in the air every time he looks at us."

"Uh-huh," Joserlin replied out of the dark, "And some of it's 'cause he's spoiled flat rotten by Lady Treesa. I won't deny that; he's one right arrogant little wart an' he sure knows he's the prettiest thing on the holding. Makes sure everybody else knows it, too. But I can't help but wonder how much he sticks that nose in the air around you lot 'cause you seem so bent on rubbin' it in the dirt. Hmm?"

Mekeal could find nothing to say in reply.

*   *   *

I could run away, Vanyel thought, almost dizzy with weariness, but still finding sleep eluding him. *I could run away—I think—*

He chewed his lip until it bled. *If I did, what could I do? Go for sanctuary? Gods, no—there is no way I was meant to be a priest! I don't write well enough to be a scribe, and besides, there isn't a lord would hire me once they found out who I was. Father would see to that, I know he would. Oh, gods, why didn't you make me a Bard?*

He licked the corner of his mouth, struck with a kindred thought. *I could try my hand at minstrelsy, couldn't I? I couldn't, I daren't show my face at any large courts, but there's a bit of coin to be had singing almost anywhere else.*

For a moment it seemed the way out. He need only slip across to the storeroom and get his instruments, then run off before dawn. He could be far away before anyone realized he was gone, and not just hiding again.

But—no.

My hand—my hand. Until it's working right, I can't do anything but the barest simple music. If I can't play right, there's no way I could look for a place in a household. And without the kind of noble patronage I can't look for, I won't be able to do much more than keep myself fed. I can't live like that, I just can't! I can't sing for farmers in the taverns and the folks in the fairs, I can't go begging like that, not to peasants. Not unless it looks like Savil is going to poison me, and I don't bloody think that's likely. She's a Herald; Heralds don't do that sort of thing even to please their brothers. He sighed, and the candle went out. *No, it won't work. There's no way to escape.*

He waited, feeling the lump growing in his throat, threatening to undermine him again. The tears were going to come—going to weaken him still further, push him down into helplessness.

The darkness closed around him like a fist, and he fought against crying with such single-mindedness that he never quite knew when he passed from a half-daze into troubled, dream-haunted sleep.

He was alone, completely alone. For once in his life there was no one pushing him, no one mocking him. Above him was only dull gray sky; around him a plain of ice and snow stretched glittering to the horizon.

Everywhere he looked there was nothing but that barren, white plain. Completely empty, completely featureless. It was so cold he felt numb.

Numb. Not aching inside. Not ready to weep at a single word. Just—cold.

No pain. Just—nothing. He just stood, for several long moments, savoring the unfeeling, the lack of pain.

Safe. He was safe here. No one could touch him. As long as he stayed in this isolation, this wilderness, no one could touch him.

He opened his eyes wide in the dream, and breathed the words out. "If no one touches me—no one can hurt me. All I have to do is never care."

It was like a revelation, a gift from the hitherto-uncaring gods. This place, this wilderness of ice—if he could hold it inside him—if he could not-care enough—he could be safe. No matter what happened, who hated him, no one could ever hurt him again.

Not ever again.

CHAPTER 3

IN THE MORNING all he had to do was think of his dream, and he was cold inside, ice filling the place within him where the hurt and loneliness had been. He could be as remote and isolated as a hermit on a frozen mountaintop, any time he chose.

It was like taking a drug against pain. An antidote to loneliness.

Indifference was a defense now, and not just a pose.

Could this armor of indifference serve as an offensive weapon too? It was worth a try.

After all, he had nothing to lose; the worst had already occurred.

He dressed quickly; riding leathers that had originally been brown that he had ordered redyed to black—without his father's knowledge. He was very glad that he'd done so, now. Black always made him look taller, older—and just a little bit sinister. It was a good choice for a confrontation. It was also the color of death; he wanted to remind his father of just how often the man had Vanyel—elsewhere.

He had second thoughts about his instruments, at least the lute, which he *had* been permitted. He wouldn't pack it, but it should *be* here, else Lord Withen might wonder where it was.

Besides, if he could confront Withen *with* it, then force the issue by packing it in front of his eyes—

It might gain him something. So he slipped quickly across to his hiding place and back before the sun actually rose, and when Withen came pounding on his door, he was ensconced below the window with the instrument in his hands, picking out a slow, but intricate little melody. One where his right hand was doing most of the work. He had staged the entire scene with the deliberate intent to make it seem as if he had been there for hours.

Lord Withen had, no doubt, expected to find his oldest son still in his bed—had expected to rouse out a confused and profoundly unhappy boy into the thin, gray light of post-dawn. Had undoubtedly counted on finding Vanyel as vulnerable as he had been last night.

That would have pleased you, wouldn't it, Father—it would have given you such confirmation of my worthlessness. . . .

Instead, he flung the door open after a single knock—to find Vanyel awake, packed, and already dressed for travel, lute suddenly stilled by his entrance.

Vanyel looked up, and regarded his father with what he hoped was a cool and distant arrogance, exactly the kind of expression one would turn upon a complete stranger who had suddenly intruded himself without invitation.

His surprise and the faint touch of unease in his eyes gave Vanyel the first feelings of gratification he'd had in a long time.

He placed his lute on the bed beside him, and stood up slowly, drawing himself up as pridefully erect as he could. "As you see, sir"—he lifted a single finger and nodded his head very slightly in the direction of his four packs—"I am prepared already."

Lord Withen was obviously taken further aback by his tone and abstracted manner. He coughed, and Vanyel realized with a sudden surge of vindictive joy that *he*, for once, had the advantage in a confrontation.

Then Withen flushed as Vanyel stooped quickly and caught up the neck of his lute, detuning it with swift and practiced fingers and stuffing it quickly into its traveling bag.

That was a challenge even Withen recognized. He glowered, and made as if to take the instrument from his son—

And Vanyel drew himself up to his full height. He said nothing. He only gave back Withen a stare that told him—

Push me. Do it. See what happens when you do. I have absolutely nothing to lose and I don't care what happens to me.

Withen actually backed up a pace at the look in his son's eyes.

"You may take your toy, but don't think this means you can spend all your time lazing about with those worthless Bards," Withen blustered, trying to regain the high ground he'd lost the moment he thrust the door open. "You're going to Savil to learn something other than—"

"I never imagined I would be able to for a moment—sir," Vanyel interrupted, and produced a bitter not-smile. "I'm quite certain," he continued with carefully measured venom, "that you have given my aunt very explicit instructions on the subject. And on my education. Sir."

Withen flushed again. Vanyel felt another rush of poisonous pleasure. *You know and I know what this is really about, don't we, Father? But you want me to pretend it's something else, at least in public. Too bad. I don't intend to make this at all easy on you, and I don't intend to be graceful in public. I have the high ground, Father. I don't give a damn anymore, and that gives me a weapon you don't have.*

Withen made an abrupt gesture, and a pair of servants entered Vanyel's room from the corridor beyond, each picking up two packs and scurrying out of the door as quickly as they could. Vanyel pulled the shoulder strap of the lute over his own head, arranging the instrument on his back, as a clear sign that he did not intend anyone else to be handling it.

"You needn't see me off, sir," he said, when Withen made no move to follow the servants with their burdens. "I'm sure you have—more important things to attend to."

Withen winced, visibly. Vanyel strolled silently past him, then turned to deliver a parting shot, carefully calculated to hurt as much as only a truth that should not be spoken could.

"After all, sir," he cast calmly over his shoulder, "it isn't as if I mattered. You have four other potential—and far worthier—heirs. I *am* sorry you saw fit not to inform my mother of my hour of departure; it would have been pleasant to say farewell to someone who will miss my presence."

Withen actually flinched.

Vanyel raised one eyebrow. "Don't bother to wish me well, sir. I know what Father Leren preaches about the importance of truth, and I would not want you to perjure yourself."

The stricken look on Withen's face made a cold flame of embittered satisfaction spring up in Vanyel's ice-shrouded soul. He turned on his heel and strode firmly down the corridor after the scuttling servants, not giving his father the chance to reply, nor to issue orders to the servants.

He passed the two servants with his packs in the dim, gray-lit hallway, and gestured peremptorily that they should follow him. Again, he felt that blackly bitter satisfaction; obviously Lord Withen had intended that his son should have scampered along in the servants' wake. But the sudden reversal of roles had confused Withen and left the servants without clear instructions. Vanyel seized the unlooked-for opportunity and held to it with all his might. For once, just this once, Vanyel had gotten the upper hand in a situation, and he did not intend to relinquish it until he was forced to.

He led them down the ill-lit staircase, hearing them stumbling blindly behind him in the darkness and thankful that *he* was the one carrying his lute and that there was nothing breakable in the packs. They emerged at the end of the hall nearest the kitchen; Vanyel decided to continue to force the issue by going out the *servants'* door to the stables. It was closer—but that wasn't why he chose it; he chose it to make the point that he *knew* his father's thoughts about him.

The two servitors, laden as they were with the heavy packs, had to stretch to keep up with him; already they were panting with effort. As Vanyel's boots crunched in the gravel spread across the yard between the keep and the stables, he could hear them puffing along far behind him.

The sun was barely over the horizon, and mist was rising from the meadows where the horses were turned loose during the day. It would likely be hot today, one of the first days of true high summer. Vanyel could see, as he came around the side of the stable, that the doors were standing wide open, and that there were several people moving about inside.

Couldn't wait to be rid of me, could you, Father dear? Meant to hustle me off as fast as you could throw me into my clothes and my belongings into packs. I think in this I will oblige you. It should keep you sufficiently confused.

Now that he had this set of barriers, for the first time in more than a year he was able to think clearly and calmly. He was able to make plans without being locked in an emotional morass, and carry them out without losing his head to frustration. Gods, it was so simple—just don't give a damn. Don't care what they do to you, and they do nothing.

If I were staying, I'd never have dared to say those things. But I'm not, and by the time Father figures out how to react, I'll be far beyond his ability to punish me. Even if he reports all this to Aunt Unsavory, it's going to sound really stupid—and what's more, it'll make him look a fool.

He paused in the open doors, feet slightly apart, hands on his hips. After a few moments, those inside noticed him and the buzz of conversation ceased altogether as they turned to gape at him in dumbfounded surprise.

"Why isn't my mare saddled?" he asked quietly, coldly. The only two *horses* bearing riding saddles were two rough cobs obviously meant for the two armsmen beside them, men who had been examining their girths and who had suddenly straightened to attention at the sound of his voice. There was another beast with a riding saddle on it, but it wasn't a horse—it was an aging, fat pony, one every boy on the holding had long since outgrown, and a mount that was now given to Treesa's most elderly women to ride.

"Beggin' yer pardon, m'lord Vanyel," said one of the grooms, hesitantly, "but yer father—"

"I really could not care less what my father ordered," Vanyel interrupted, rudely and angrily. "*He* isn't going to have to ride halfway to the end of the world on that hobbyhorse. *I* am the one being sent on this little exile, and I am not going to ride *that*. I refuse to enter the capital on a beast that is going to make me look like a clown. Besides, Star is *mine*, not his. The Lady Treesa gave her to *me*, and I intend to take her with me. Saddle her."

The groom continued to hesitate.

"If you won't," Vanyel said, his eyes narrowing, his voice edged with the coldest steel, "I will. Either way you'll have trouble. And if *I* have to do it, and my lady mother finds out, you'll have trouble from her as well as my father."

The groom shrugged, and went after Star and her tack, leaving his fellow to strip the pony and turn it into the pasture.

Lovely. Put me on a mount only a tyro would have to ride, and make it look as if I was too much a coward to handle a real horse. Make me look a fool, riding into Haven on a pony. *And deprive me of something I treasured. Not this time, Father.*

In fact, Vanyel was already firmly in Star's saddle by the time Lord Withen made a somewhat belated appearance in the stableyard. The grooms were fastening the last of the packs on the backs of three mules, and the armsmen were waiting, also mounted, out in the yard.

Vanyel patted the proudly arched neck of his Star, a delicately-boned black palfrey with a perfect white star on her forehead, a star that had one long point that trailed down her nose. He ignored his father for a long moment, giving him a chance to absorb the sight of his son on his spirited little blood-mare instead of the homely old pony. Then he nudged Star toward the edge of the yard where Lord Withen stood—by his stunned expression, once again taken by surprise. She picked her way daintily across the gravel, making very little sound, like a remnant of night-shadow in the early morning light. Vanyel had had all her tack dyed the same black as his riding leathers, and was quite well aware of how striking they looked together.

So was she; she curved her neck and carried her tail like a banner as he directed her toward his father.

Lord Withen's expression changed as they approached; first discomfited, then resigned. Vanyel kept his the same as it had been all this morning; nonexistent. He kept his gaze fixed on a point slightly above his father's head.

Behind him, Vanyel could hear the mules being led out to have the lead rein of the first fastened to the cantle of one of the armsmen's saddles. He halted Star about then, a few paces from the edge of the yard. He looked down at his father, keeping his face completely still, completely closed.

They stared at each other for a long moment; Vanyel could see Withen groping for something appropriate to say. And each time he began to speak, the words died unspoken beneath Vanyel's cold and dispassionate gaze.

I'm not going to make this easy for you, Father. Not after what you've done to me; not after what you tried to do to me just now. I'm going to follow my sire's example. I'm going to be just as nasty as you are—but I'm going to do it with more style.

The silence lengthened almost unbearably; even the armsmen began picking up the tension, and shifted uneasily in their saddles. Their cobs fidgeted and snorted restlessly.

Vanyel and Star could have been a statue of onyx and silver.

Finally Vanyel decided he had prolonged the agony enough. He nodded, once, almost imperceptibly. Then, without a word, he wheeled Star and nudged her lightly with his heels. She tossed her head and shot down the road to the village at a fast trot, leaving the armsmen cursing and kicking at their beasts behind him, trying to catch up.

He reined Star in once they were past the Forst Reach village, not wanting her to tire herself so early in the journey, and not wanting to give the armsmen an excuse to order him to ride between them.

Father's probably told them that they're to watch for me trying to bolt, he thought cynically, as Star fought the rein for a moment, then settled into a more-or-less sedate walk. And indeed, that surmise was confirmed when he saw them exchange surreptitious glances and not-too-well concealed sighs of relief. *Huh. Little do they know.*

For once they got beyond the Forst Reach lands that lay under the plow, they entered the completely untamed woodlands that lay between Forst Reach and the nearest eastward holding of Prytheree Ford. This forest land had been left purposely wild; there weren't enough people to farm it at either Holding, and it supplied all of the wood products and a good half of the meat eaten in a year to the people of both Holdings.

It took skilled foresters to make their way about in a wood like this. And Vanyel knew very well that he had no more idea of how to survive in wilderland than he did of how to sprout fins and breathe water.

The road itself was hardly more than a rutted track of hard-packed dirt meandering through a tunnel of tree branches. The branches themselves were so thick overhead that they rode in a kind of green twilight. Although the sun was dispersing the mist outside the wood, there were still tendrils of it wisping between the trees and lying across the road. And only an occasional sunbeam was able to make its way down through the canopy of leaves to strike the roadway. To either side, the track was edged with thick bushes; a hint here and there of red among the green leaves told Vanyel that those bushes were blackberry hedges, probably planted to keep bears and other predators off the road itself. Even if he'd been thinking of escape, he was not fool enough to dare their brambly embrace. Even less did he wish to damage Star's tender hide with the unkind touch of their thorns.

Beyond the bushes, so far as he could see, the forest floor was a tangle of vegetation in which *he* would be lost in heartbeats.

No, he was not in the least tempted to bolt and run, but there were other reasons not to run besides the logical ones.

There were—or seemed to be—things tracking them under the shelter of the underbrush. Shadow-shapes that made no sound.

He didn't much like those shadows behind the bushes or ghosting along with the fog. He didn't at all care for the way they moved, sometimes following the riders on the track for furlongs before giving up and melting into deeper forest. Those shadows called to mind far too many stories and tales—and the Border, with all its uncanny creatures, wasn't all *that* far from here.

The forest itself was too quiet for Vanyel's taste, even had those shadows *not* been slinking beneath the trees. Only occasionally could he hear a bird call above the dull clopping of the horses' hooves, and that was faint and far off. No breeze stirred the leaves above them; no squirrels ran along the branches to scold them. Of course it *was* entirely possible that they were frightening all the nearby wildlife into silence simply with their presence; these woods *were* hunted regularly. That was the obvious explanation of the silence beneath the trees.

But Vanyel's too-active imagination kept painting other, grimmer pictures of what might be lurking unseen out there.

Even though it became very warm and a halt would have been welcome, he really found himself hoping they wouldn't make one. The armor that had so far been proof against pressure from without cracked just a little from the pressure within of his own vivid imagination. He was uneasy when they paused to feed and water the horses and themselves at noon, and was not truly comfortable until they saddled up and moved off again. The only way he could keep his nerves in line was to concentrate on how well he had handled Lord Withen. Recalling that stupefied look he'd last seen on Withen's face gave him no end of satisfaction. Withen hadn't seen Vanyel the boy—he'd seen a man, in some sort of control over his situation. And he plainly hadn't enjoyed the experience.

It was with very real relief that Vanyel saw the trees break up, then open out into a huge clearing ahead of them just as the woods began to darken with the dying of the day. He was more than pleased when he saw there was an inn there, and realized that his guardians had been undoubtedly intending to stay there overnight.

They rode up the flinty dirt road to the facade of the inn, then through the entryway into the inn yard. That was where his two guardians halted, looking about for a stableboy. Vanyel dismounted, feeling very stiff, and a lot sorer than he had thought he'd be.

When a groom came to take Star's reins, he gave them over without a murmur, then paced up and down the length of the dusty stableyard, trying to walk some feeling back into his legs. While he walked, one of the armsmen vanished into the inn itself and the other removed the packs from the mules before turning them and their cobs over to more grooms.

It was at that point that Vanyel realized that he didn't even know his captors' names.

That bothered him; he was going to be spending a lot of time in their company, yet they hadn't even introduced themselves during the long ride. He was confused, and uncomfortable. Yet—

The less I feel, the better off I'll be.

He closed his eyes and summoned his snow-field; could almost *feel* it chilling him, numbing him.

He began looking over the inn, ignoring the other guard, and saw with mild surprise that it was huge; much bigger than it had looked from the road. Only the front face of it was really visible when he'd ridden up to it; now he could see the entire complex. It was easily five times the size of the little village inn at Forst Reach, and two-storied as well. Its outer walls were of stone up to the second floor, then timber; the roof was thickly thatched, and the birds Vanyel had missed in the forest all seemed to have made a happy home here, nestling into the thatch with a riot of calls and whistles as they settled in for the night. With the stables it formed two sides of a square around the stable yard, the fourth side being open on a grassy field, probably for the use of traders and their wagons. The stables were extensive, too; easily as large as Lord Withen's, and he was a notable horsebreeder.

Blue shadows were creeping from the forest into the stableyard, although the sky above had not quite begun to darken very much. And it was getting quite chilly; something Vanyel hadn't expected, given the heat of the day. He was just as glad when the second armsman finally put in an appearance, trailed by a couple of inn servants.

Vanyel pretended to continue to study the sky to the west, but strained his ears as hard as he could to hear what his guardians had to say to each other.

"Any problems, Garth?" asked the one who'd remained with Vanyel, as the first bent to retrieve a pack and motioned to the servants to take the ones Vanyel recognized as being his own.

"Nay," the first chuckled. "This early in th' summer they be right glad of custom wi' good coin in hand, none o' yer shifty peddlers, neither. Just like m'lord said, got us rooms on second story wi' his Highness there on t' inside. No way he gets out wi'out us noticin'. Besides we bein' second floor, 'f's needful we just move t' bed across t' door, an' he won't be goin' nowhere."

Vanyel froze, and the little corner of him that had been wondering if he could—perhaps—make allies of these two withdrew.

So that's why they're keeping their distance. He straightened his back, and let that cool, expressionless mask that had served so well with his father this morning drop over his features again. *I might have guessed as much. I was a fool to think otherwise.*

He turned to face his watchers. "I trust all is in order?" he asked, letting nothing show except, perhaps, boredom. "Then—shall we?" He nodded slightly toward the inn door, where a welcoming, golden light was shining.

Without waiting for a reply, he moved deliberately toward it himself, leaving them to follow.

Vanyel stared moodily at the candle at his bedside. There wasn't anything much else to look at; *his* room had no windows. Other than that, it wasn't that much unlike his old room back at Forst Reach; quite plain, a bit stuffy—not too bad, really. Except that it had no windows. Except for being a prison.

Inventory: one bed, one chair, one table. No fireplace, but that wasn't a consideration given the general warmth of the building and the fact that it was summer. All four of his packs were piled over in the corner, the lute still in its case leaning up against them.

He'd asked for a bath, and they'd brought him a tub and bathwater rather than letting him go down to the bathhouse. The water was tepid, and the tub none too big—but he'd acted as if the notion had been his idea. At least his guardians hadn't insisted on being in the same room watching him when he used it.

One of them *had* escorted him to the privy and back, though; he'd headed in that direction, and the one called Garth had immediately dropped whatever it was he'd been working on and attached himself to Vanyel's invisible wake, following about a half dozen paces behind. That had been so humiliating that he hadn't spoken a single word to the man, simply ignored his presence entirely.

And they hadn't consulted him on dinner either; they'd had it brought up on a tray while he was bathing.

Not that he'd been particularly hungry. He managed the bread and butter and cheese—the bread was better than he got at home—and a bit of fresh fruit. But the rest, boiled chicken, a thick gravy, and dumplings, and all of it swiftly cooling into a greasy, congealed mess on the plate, had stuck in his throat and he gave up trying to eat the tasteless stuff entirely.

But he really didn't want to sit here staring at it, either.

So he picked up the tray, opened his door, and took it to the outer room, setting it down on a table already cluttered with oddments of traveling gear and the wherewithal to clean it.

Both men looked up at his entrance, eyes wide and startled in the candlelight. The only sound was the steady flapping of the curtains in the light breeze coming in the window, and the buzzing of a fly over one of the candles.

Vanyel straightened, licked his lips, and looked off at a point on the farther wall, between them and above their heads. "Every corridor in this building leads to the common room, so I can hardly escape you that way," he said, in as bored and detached a tone as he could muster. "And besides, there's grooms sleeping in the stables, and I'm certain you've already spoken with *them*. I'm scarcely going to climb out the window and run off on foot. You might as well go enjoy yourselves in the common room. You may be my jailors, but that doesn't mean you have to endure the jail yourselves."

With that, he turned abruptly and closed the door of his room behind him.

But he held his breath and waited right beside the door, his ear against it, the better to overhear what they were saying in the room beyond.

"Huh!" the one called Garth said, after an interval of startled silence. "Whatcha think of *that?*"

"That he ain't half so scatterbrained as m'lord thinks," the other replied thoughtfully. "*He* knows damn well what's goin' on. Not that he ain't about as nose-in-th'-air as I've ever seen, but he ain't addlepated, not a bit of it."

"Never saw m'lord set so on his rump before," Garth agreed, speaking slowly. "Ain't never seen him taken down like that by a *lord*, much less a grass-green youngling. An' never saw *that* boy do anythin' like it before, neither. Boy's got sharp a'sudden; give 'im that. Too sharp?"

"Hmm. No—" the other said. "No, I reckon in this case, he be right." Silence for a moment, then a laugh. "Y'know, I 'spect his Majesty just don't want to have t' lissen t' us gabbin' away at each other. Mebbe we bore 'im, eh? What th' hell, I could stand a beer. You?"

"Eh, if you're buyin', Erek—"

Their voices faded as the door to the hall beyond scraped open, then closed again.

Vanyel sighed out the breath he'd been holding in, and took the two steps he needed to reach the table, sagging down into the hard, wooden chair beside it.

Tired. Gods, I am so tired. This farce is taking more out of me than I thought it would.

He stared numbly at the candle flame, and then transferred his gaze to the bright, flickering reflections on the brown earthenware bottle beside it.

It's awful wine—but it is wine. I suppose I could get good and drunk. There certainly isn't anything else to do. At least nothing they'll let me do. Gods, they think I'm some kind of prig. "His Majesty" indeed.

He shook his head. *What's wrong with me? Why should it matter what a couple of armsmen think about me? Why should I even want them on my side? Who are they, anyway? What consequence are they? They're just a bare step up from dirt-grubbing farmers! Why should I care what they think? Besides, they can't affect what happens to me.*

He sighed again, and tried to summon a bit more of the numbing disinterest he'd sustained himself with this whole, filthy day.

It wouldn't come, at first. There was something in the way—

Nothing matters, he told himself sternly. *Least of all what they think about you.*

He closed his eyes again, and managed this time to summon a breath of the chill of his dream-sanctuary. It helped.

After a while he shifted, making the chair creak, and tried to think of something to do—maybe to put the thoughts running round his head into a set of lyrics. Instead, he found he could hear, muffled, and indistinct, the distracting sounds of the common room somewhere a floor below and several hundred feet away.

The laughter, in particular, came across clearly. Vanyel bit his lip as he tried to think of the last time he'd really laughed, and found he couldn't remember it.

Dammit, I am better *than they are, I don't* need *them, I don't* need *their stupid approval!* He reached hastily for the bottle, poured an earthenware mug full of the thin, slightly vinegary stuff, and gulped it down. He poured a second, but left it on the table, rising instead and taking his lute from the corner. He stripped the padded bag off of it, and began retuning it before the wine had a chance to muddle him.

At least there was music. There was always music. And the attempt to get what he'd lost back again.

Before long the instrument was nicely in tune. That was one thing that minstrel—*What was his name? Shanse, that was it*—had praised unstintingly. Vanyel, he'd said, had a natural ear. Shanse had even put Vanyel in charge of tuning *his* instruments while he stayed at Forst Reach.

He took the lute back to the bed, and laid it carefully on the spread while he shoved the table up against the bedstead. He curled up with his back against the headboard, the bottle and mug in easy reach, and began practicing those damned finger exercises.

It might have been the wine, but his hand didn't seem to be hurting *quite* as much this time.

The bottle was half empty and his head buzzing a bit when there was a soft tap on his door.

He stopped in mid-phrase, frowning, certain he'd somehow overheard something from the next room. But the tapping came a second time, soft, but insistent, and definitely coming from his door.

He shook his head a little, hoping to clear it, and put the lute in the corner of the bed. He took a deep breath to steady his thoughts, uncurled his legs, rose, and paced (weaving only a little) to the door.

He cracked it open, more than half expecting it to be one of his captors come to tell him to shut the hell up so that they could get some sleep.

"Oh!" said the young girl who stood there, her eyes huge with surprise; she was wearing the livery of one of the inn's servants. He had caught her with her hand raised, about to tap on the door a third time. Beyond her the armsmen's room was mostly dark and quite empty.

"Yes?" he said, blinking his eyes, which were not focusing properly. When he'd gotten up, the wine had gone to his head with a vengeance.

"Uh—I just—" The girl was not as young as he'd thought, but fairly pretty; soft brown eyes, curly dark hair. Rather like a shabby copy of Melenna. "Just—ye wasn't down wi' th' others, m'lord, an' I wunnered if ye needed aught?"

"No, thank you," he replied, still trying to fathom why she was out there, trying to think through a mist of wine-fog. Unless—that armsman Garth might well have sent her, to make certain he was still where he was supposed to be.

The ties of the soft yellow blouse she was wearing had come loose, and it was slipping off one shoulder, exposing the round shoulder and a goodly expanse of the mound of one breast. She wet her lips, and edged closer until she was practically nose-to-nose with him.

"Are ye sure, m'lord?" she breathed. "Are ye sure ye cain't think of nothin'?"

Good gods, he realized with a start, *she's trying to seduce me!*

He used the ploy that had been so successful with his mother's ladies. He let his expression chill down to where it would leave a skin of ice on a goblet of water. "Quite certain, thank you, mistress."

She was either made of sterner stuff than they had been, or else the subtler nuances of expression went right over her head.

Or, third possibility, she found either Vanyel or his presumably fat purse too attractive to let go without a fight.

"I c'd turn yer bed down fer ye, m'lord," she persisted, snaking an arm around the door to glide her hand along Vanyel's buttock and leg. He was only wearing a shirt and hose, and felt the unsubtle caress with a startlement akin to panic.

"No, please!" he yelped in shock; the high-pitched, strangled shout startled her enough that she pulled back her arm. He slammed the door in her face and locked it.

He waited with his ear pressed up against the crack in the door; waited for an explosion of some kind. Nothing happened; he heard her muttering to herself for a moment, sounding very puzzled, then finally heard her retreating footsteps and the sound of the outer door opening and closing again.

He staggered back to the bed, and sat down on it, heavily. Finally he reached for the lute, detuned it, and put it back in its traveling case.

Then he reached for the bottle and gulped the wine as fast as he could pour it down his throat.

Oh, lord—oh, gods. A fool. After everything this morning, after I start to feel like I'm getting a grip on things, and I go and act like a fool. Like a kid. Like a baby who'd never seen a whore before.

He burned with humiliation as he imagined the girl telling his guards what had just passed between them. And drank faster.

He *did* remember to unlock his door and blow out the candle before he passed out. If Sun and Shadow out there decided to take it into their heads to check on him, he didn't want them breaking the door down. That would be even more humiliating than having them follow him to the privy, or laughing at him with the girl.

I've never been this drunk before, he thought muzzily, as he sank back onto the bed. *I bet I'll have a head in the morning. . . .*

He snorted then, a sound with no amusement in it. *At least if I'm hung over, it'll make Trusty and Faithful happy. If they can't report to Father that I tried to escape, at least they can tell him I made a drunken sot of myself at the first opportunity. Maybe I should have let the girl in after all. It wouldn't be the first time I've bedded something I didn't much care for. And it would have given them one more story to tell. Oh, gods, what's wrong with me? Mekeal would have had her tumbled before she blinked twice! What is wrong with me?*

He rolled over, and it felt a lot like his head kept on rolling after he'd stopped moving.

Then again—I don't think so. Not even for that. The wine's bad enough here. I hate to think where the girls come from . . . or where they've been.

But why can't I react the way everyone else seems to? Why am I so different?

His head hurt, but not unbearably. His stomach was not particularly happy with him, but he wasn't ready to retch his guts up. In short, he was hung over—though less than he'd expected. In an odd sort of way, he was feeling even more detached than before. Perhaps his intoxication had purged something out of him last night; some forlorn hope, some last grasping at a life no one would ever let him have.

He pulled on his riding leathers and groomed himself as impeccably as he could manage without a mirror, leaving only the tunic off, since he intended to soak his aching head in cold water before he mounted Star—in the horse trough if he had to. He walked out into the morning light pouring in through the outer room, surveying the pathetic wrecks that had been his alert and vigilant guardians only the night before with what he hoped was cool, distant impassiveness.

And he spared a half a moment to hope that the girl *hadn't* told them—

His guards were in far worse case than he was, having evidently made a spectacular night of it. *Quite* a night, judging by their bleary eyes, surly, yet satiated expressions, and the rumpled condition of the bedding. And Vanyel was not such an innocent as to be unable to recognize certain—aromas— when he detected them in the air before Garth opened the window. He was just as pleased to have been so drunk as to be insensible when they had been entertaining their temporary feminine acquaintances. Could be the chambermaid had found what she'd sought in the company of Garth and Erek after being rebuffed by Vanyel.

They weren't giving him the kind of sly looks he'd have expected if the girl *had* revealed his panicked reaction.

Well—maybe she was too busy. Thank you, gods.

He managed to deal with his hangover in a fairly successful fashion. Willowbark tea came for his asking, hot from the kitchen; on the way to the privy, with the faithful Garth in queasy attendance, he managed to divert long enough to soak his head under the stable pump until his temples stopped pounding. The water was very cold, and he saw Garth wincing when he first stuck his head beneath it.

That dealt with the head; the stomach was easier. He drank nothing but the tea and ate nothing but bread, very mild cheese, and fruit.

He was perfectly ready to ride out at that point. His guards were not so fortunate. Or, perhaps, so wise, since *their* remedies seemed to consist of vile concoctions of raw eggs and the heavy imbibing of the ale that had *caused* their problem the night before.

As a result, their departure was delayed until midmorning—not that this disturbed Vanyel a great deal. They'd be outside the bounds of the forest before dark; at least according to what the innkeeper told Garth. That was all *Vanyel* cared about.

Garth and Erek were still looking a bit greenish as they mounted their cobs. And neither seemed much inclined toward talk. That suited Vanyel quite well; it would enable him to concentrate on putting just a bit more distance between himself and the world. And it would allow him to do some undisturbed thinking.

The forest did not seem quite so unfriendly on the eastern side of the inn—perhaps because it was hunted more frequently on this side. The underbrush certainly wasn't as thick. The boughs of the trees overhead weren't, either, and Vanyel got a bit of nasty satisfaction at seeing Garth and Erek wincing out of the way of sunbeams that were *much* more frequent on this side of the woods.

But it was hotter than yesterday, and Vanyel finally stripped off his leather tunic and bundled it behind him.

Seeing no lurking shadows beneath the trees, he felt a bit easier about turning his attention inward to think about just what, exactly, he was heading toward.

I can guess at what Father's told the old bat. That's easy enough. The question is what she's likely to do about it.

He tried to dig everything he could remember out of the dim recesses of memory—not just about his aunt in particular, but about Heralds in general.

He'll tell her I'm to be weapons-schooled, that's for certain. But how—that's up to her. And now that I think of it—damn if it wasn't a Herald that wrote that book that got me in such trouble! I may, I just might *actually be better off in that area! Huh—now that I think about it, I can't see any way I'd be worse off.*

A bird called overhead, and Vanyel almost felt a bit hopeful. *No matter who I get schooled under, he can't possibly be worse than Jervis—because whoever he is, he* won't *have a grudge against me. The absolute worst I can get is a Jervis-type without a grudge. That might just be survivable, if I keep myself in the background, if I manage to convince him that I'm deadly stupid and clumsy. Stupid and clumsy are* not *possible to train away, and even Jervis knew that.*

Another bird answered, reminding him that there was, however, the matter of music.

He's bound to have issued orders that I'm not to be allowed anywhere near the Bards except right under Savil's eye—and if she's like Father, she has no ear at all. Which means she'll never go to entertainments unless she has no choice. He sighed. *Oh, well, there's worse. I won't be any worse off than I was at home, where I saw a real, trained Bard once in my entire lifetime. At least they'll be* around. *Maybe if I can get my fingering back and play where one is likely to overhear me—*

He sternly squelched that last. *Best not think about it. I can't afford hope anymore.*

Star fidgeted; she wanted her usual early-morning run. He reined her in, calmed her down, and went back to his own thoughts. *One thing for sure, Father is likely to have told Savil all kinds of things about how rotten I am. So she'll be likely looking for wrong moves on my part—and I'll bet she'll have her proteges and friends watching me, too. It's going to be hell. Hell, with no sanctuary, and no Liss.*

He studied Star's ears as he thought, watching her flick them back with alert interest when she heard him sigh.

Well, everyone else is going to hate me, but you *still love me.* He patted Star's neck, and she pranced a little.

To the lowest hells with all of them. I do not need them, I don't need anybody, not even Liss. I'll do all right on my own.

But there was one puzzle, one he was reminded of later, when they passed one of the remote farms, and Vanyel saw the farmer out in the field, talking with someone on horseback who was likely his overlord. *Huh*—he thought, *I can't figure how in Havens Father expects Savil to train me in governance. . . .*

Then he felt a cold chill.

Unless he doesn't really expect me to ever come home again. Gods—he could *try to work something out in the way of sending me off to a temple. He could do that*— *and it bloody wouldn't matter if Father Leren could find him a priest he could bribe into accepting an unwilling acolyte. It would work*—*it would* work. *Especially if it was a cloistered order. And with me out of the way in Savil's hands, he has all the time he needs to find a compliant priest. He doesn't even have to tell Savil; just issue the order to send me back home again when it's all arranged. Then spirit me off and announce to anyone who asks that I discovered I had a vocation. And I would spend the rest of my life in a little stone cave somewhere*—

He swallowed hard, and tried to find reasons to dismiss the notion as a paranoid fantasy, but all he could discover were more reasons why it was a logical move on Lord Withen's part.

He tried to banish the fear, telling himself that it was no good worrying about what might only be a fantasy until it actually happened. But the thought wouldn't go away. It kept coming back, not only that day, but every day thereafter. It wasn't quite an obsession—but it wasn't far off.

It was quite enough to keep him wrapped in silent, apprehensive thought for every day of the remainder of the journey, and to keep him sleepless for long hours every night. And not even dreams of his isolated snow-plain helped to keep it from his thoughts.

CHAPTER 4

"ALL RIGHT, TYLENDEL, that was passable, but it wasn't particularly smooth," Herald-Mage Savil admonished her protege, tucking her feet under the bottom rung of her wooden stool, and absently smoothing down the front of her white tunic. "Remember, the power is supposed to *flow*; from you to the shield and back again. Smoothly, not in spurts. You tell me why."

Tylendel, a tall, strikingly attractive, dark blond Herald-trainee of about sixteen, frowned with concentration as he considered Savil's question. She watched the power-barrier he had built about himself with her Mage-Sight, and Saw the pale violet half-dome waver as he turned his attention to her question and lost a bit of control over the shield. She could feel the room pulsing as he allowed the shield to pulse in time with his heartbeat. If he let this go on, it would collapse.

"Tylendel, you're losing it," she warned. He nodded, looked up and grimaced, but did not reply; his actions were reply enough. The energy comprising the half-dome covering him stopped rippling, firmed, and the color deepened.

"Have you an answer to my question yet?"

"I think so," he answered. "If it doesn't flow smoothly, I'll have times when it's weak, and whatever I'm doing with it will be open to interruption when it weakens?"

"Right," Savil replied with a brisk nod. "Only don't think in terms of 'interruption,' lad. Think in terms of 'attack.' Like *now*."

She flung a levinbolt at his barrier without giving him any more warning than that, and had the satisfaction, not only of Seeing it deflected harmlessly upward to be absorbed by the Work Room shields, but Seeing that he shifted his defenses to meet it with no chance to prepare at all.

"Now *that* was good, my lad," she approved, and Tylendel's brown eyes warmed in response to the compliment. "So—"

Someone knocked on the door of the Work Room, and Savil bit off what she was going to tell him with a muffled curse of annoyance. "*Now what?*" she muttered, shoving back her tall stool and edging around Tylendel's mage-barrier to answer the door.

The Work Room was a permanently shielded, circular chamber within the Palace complex that the Herald-Mages used when training their proteges in the Mage-aspects of their Gifts. The shielding on this room was incredibly ancient and powerful. It was *so* powerful that the shielding actually muffled physical sound; you couldn't even hear the Death Bell toll inside this room. One of the duties of every Herald-Mage in the Circle was to augment the protections here whenever they had the time and energy to spare. This shielding had to be strong; strong enough to contain magical "accidents" that would reduce the sparse furniture within the room to splinters. Those "accidents" were the reason why the walls were stone, the furniture limited to a couple of cheap stools and an equally cheap table, and why *every* Herald-Mage put full personal shields on himself and his pupil immediately on entering the door of this room.

Those accidents were also the reason why anyone who disturbed the practice sessions going on in the Work Room had better have a damned good reason for doing so.

Savil yanked the door open, and glared at the fair-haired, blue-uniformed Palace Guard who stood there, at rigid and proper attention. "Well?" she said, letting a bit of ice creep into her voice.

"Your pardon, Herald-Mage," he replied, his expression as stiff as his spine, "but you left orders to be notified as soon as your nephew arrived." He handed her a folded and sealed letter. "His escort wished you to have this."

She took it and stuffed it in a pocket of her breeches without looking at it. "Oh, bloody hell," she muttered. "So I did."

She sighed, and became a bit more civil. "Thank you, Guard. Send him and whatever damned escort he brought with him to my quarters; I'll get with them as soon as I can."

The Guard saluted and turned sharply on his heel; Savil shut the door before he finished his pivot, and turned back to her pupil.

"All right, lad, how long have we been at this?"

Tylendel draped an arm over his curly head and grinned. "Long enough for my stomach to start growling. I'm sorry, Savil, but I'm hungry. That's probably why my concentration's going."

She shook her finger at him. "Tchah, younglings and their stomachs!

And just what do you plan to do if you get hungry in the middle of an arcane duel? Hmm?"

"Eat," he replied impishly. She threw up her hands in mock despair.

"All right, off with you—ah, ah," she warned, wagging her finger at him as he made ready to dispel the barrier the quick and dirty way; by pulling the energies into the ground. "*Properly*, my lad—"

He bowed to her in the finest courtly manner. She snorted. "Get on with it, lad, if you're in such a hurry to stuff your face."

She Watched him carefully as he took down the barrier—properly— with quite a meticulous attention to little details, like releasing the barrier-energy back into the same flow he'd taken it from. She nodded approvingly when he stepped across the place where the border had been and presented himself to have the shields she'd put on him taken off.

"You're getting better, Tylendel," she said, touching the middle of his forehead with her index finger, and absorbing the shield back into herself. Her skin tingled for a moment as she neutralized the overflow. "You're coming along much faster than I guessed you would. Another year—no, less, I think—and you'll be ready to try your hand at a Border stint with me. And not much longer than that, and I'll shove you into Whites."

"It's my teacher," he replied impishly, seizing her hand and kissing it, his long hair falling over her wrist and tickling it. "How can I help but succeed in such attractive surroundings?"

She snatched her hand back, and cuffed his ear lightly. "Get on with you! Even if I *wasn't* old enough to be your grandmother, we *both* know I'm the wrong sex for you to find me attractive!"

He ducked the blow, grinning, and pulled the door open for her. "Oh, Savil, don't you know that the real truth is that I'd lost my heart to my teacher, knew I had no hope, and couldn't accept a lesser woman than—"

"*Out!*" she sputtered, laughing so hard she nearly choked. "Liar! Before I do you damage!"

He ran off down the wood-paneled hallway, his own laughter echoing behind him.

She closed the Work Room door behind her and leaned against the wall, still laughing, holding her aching side. *The imp. More charm than any five younglings, and all the mischief of a young cat! I haven't laughed like this in years— not the way I have since I acquired Tylendel as a protege. That boy is such a treasure—if I can just wean him out of that stupid feud his family is involved in, he'll make a fine Herald-Mage. If I don't kill him first!*

She gulped down several long breaths of air, and composed herself. *I'm going to have to deal with that spoiled brat of a nephew in a few minutes*, she told herself sternly, using the thought to sober herself. *And I haven't the foggiest notion of what to do with him. Other than have him strangled—no, that's not such a good notion, it would please Withen too much. Great good gods, the man has turned into such a pompous ass in the last few years! I hardly recognized him. That ridiculous letter a week ago could have come from our father.*

She smoothed her hair with her hands (checking to see that the knot of it at the base of her neck had not come undone), tugged on the hem of her tunic, and made sure that the door of the Work Room was closed and mage-locked before heading up the hall toward her personal quarters. The heels of her boots clicked briskly against the stone of the hallway, and she nodded at courtiers and other Heralds as they passed her.

If only Treesa hadn't spoiled the lad so outrageously, there might be something there worth salvaging. Now, I don't know. I certainly don't have the time to find out for myself. Huh. I wonder—if I put the boy into lessons with the other Herald-trainees, then leave him to his own devices the rest of the time, that just might tell me something. If he doesn't turn to gambling and hunting and wild parties—if he becomes bored with the flitter-heads in the Court—

She pushed open one half of the double doors to the new Heralds' quarters, and strode through. Her own suite was just at the far end and on the left side of the hall.

Changes, changes. Five years ago we were crammed in four to a room, and not enough space to throw a tantrum in. Now we rattle around in this shiny-new barracks like a handful of peas in a bucket. And me with a suite and not getting forlorn looks from Jays or Tantras because one of the rooms is vacant. I can't see how we'll ever get enough bodies to fill this place . . .

The door stood slightly ajar; she shoved it out of the way, and paused a few steps into her outer room, crossing her arms and surveying the trio on the couch beneath her collection of Hawkbrother featherwork masks at the end of the room.

Only one of them was actually *on* the couch; Vanyel. Beside him, only too obviously playing his jailers, stood a pair of Withen's armsmen. On Vanyel's right, a short, stocky man—axeman, if Savil was any judge. On his left, one about a head taller and very swarthy; a common swordsman. And Vanyel, sitting very stiffly on the edge of the couch.

Savil heaved a strictly internal sigh. *Lad, a year obviously hasn't improved you except in looks—and that's no advantage. You're too damned handsome, and you know it.*

Since she'd last seen him, Vanyel's face and body had refined. It was a face that could (and probably did) break hearts—broad brow, high cheekbones, pointed chin, sensuous lips—fine-arched black brows, and incredible silver eyes; all of it crowned with thick, straight, blue-black hair most women would kill to possess. The body of an acrobat; nicely muscled, if not over-tall.

And the posture was arrogant, the mouth set in sullen silence; the eyes sulky, and at the same time, challenging her.

Lord and Lady. Do I believe my fool brother, or do I take the chance that a good portion of what's wrong with the boy is due to Withen trying to mold him into his own image?

While she tried to make up her mind, she nodded at the two armsmen. "Thank you, good sirs," she said, crisply. "You have performed your duty admirably. You may go."

The taller one coughed uneasily, and gave her an uncomfortable look.

"Well?" she asked, sensing something coming—something she wasn't going to like. Something petty and small-minded—

"The boy's horse—"

"Stays, of course," she interrupted, seeing the flash of hurt in Vanyel's eyes before he masked it, and reacting to it without needing to think about which way she was going to jump.

"But, Herald, it's a valuable animal!" the armsman protested, his mouth thinning unhappily. "Lord Withen—my lord—surely you've beasts enough here—"

"What do you think this is?" she snapped, turning on him with unconcealed anger. Gods, if this was symptomatic of the boy's trip here, no wonder he was sullen.

Take the boy's horse, will you? You bloody little— She took control of herself, and gave them irrefutable reasons to take back to their master. They were, after all, only following orders.

"You think we run a damned breeding farm here? We haven't horses to spare. The boy will be taking equitation lessons, of course, and he's hardly going to be able to go over the jumping course on foot!"

"But—" the armsman sputtered, not prepared to give up. "Surely the Companions—"

"Bear their *Chosen* and *no other*." She took a deep breath and forced her temper to cool. The man was making her more than annoyed with his obstinacy, he was making her quite thoroughly enraged, and if this was a measure of what Vanyel had been subjected to over the past few years, well, perhaps the boy wasn't entirely to blame for his current behavior.

"I said," she told the men, glaring, "you may go."

"But—I have certain orders—certain things I am to tell you—"

"I am countermanding those orders," she answered swiftly, invoking all of her authority, not just as a Herald, but as one of the most powerful Herald-Mages in the Heraldic Circle, second only to Queen's Own, Seneschal's, and Lord-Marshal's Herald. "This is *my* place, and *my* jurisdiction. And you may tell my brother Withen that I will make up my own mind what is to be done with the boy. If he wants to deposit young Vanyel in my care, then he'll have to put up with my judgments. And you can tell him I said so. Good day, gentlemen." She smiled with honeyed venom. "Or need I call a Guard to escort you?"

They had no choice but to take themselves off, though they did so with extreme reluctance. Savil waited until they had gone, and were presumably out of hearing range, before taking the letter she'd been given out of her pocket. She held it up so that Vanyel could see that it had not been opened, then slowly, deliberately tore it in four pieces and dropped the pieces on the floor.

Margret is going to have my hide, she thought wryly. *If she's told me once not to throw things on the floor, she's told me a hundred times—*

"I don't know what Withen had to say in that letter," she told the strange and silent boy. Was that sullenness in the set of his mouth, or fear? Was that suspicion in the back of his eyes, or arrogance? "Frankly, I don't care. This much I can tell you—young man, you are going to stand or fall with me by your own actions. I tell you now that I very much resent what Withen has done; I have three proteges to train, and no time to waste on cosseting a daydreamer." *Might as well let him know the truth about how I feel right out and right now; he'll find out from the gossip sooner or later. I can't afford to have him pulling something stupid in the hopes I'll pull him out of it and give him some attention.* "I have no intention of trying to make you into something you aren't. But I also have no intention of allowing you to make a fool out of me, or inconvenience me."

There was a whisper of sound at the door.

Without turning around, Savil knew from the brush of embarrassed

Mindspeech behind her that Tylendel and her other two proteges, Mardic and Donni, had come in behind her, not expecting to find anyone except Savil here. They had stopped in the doorway—startled at finding their mentor dressing down a strange boy, and more than a bit embarrassed to have walked in at such a touchy moment.

And of course, now it would be even more embarrassing for them to walk back out and try to pretend it hadn't happened.

"You'll be taking lessons with some of the Herald-trainees and with some of the young courtiers as soon as I get a chance to make the arrangements," Savil continued serenely, gesturing slightly with her right hand for her three "children" to come up beside her. "Now—Vanyel, this is Donni, this Mardic, and this Tylendel. As Herald-trainees, they outrank you; let's get that straight right now."

"Yes, Aunt," Vanyel said without changing his expression a hair.

"Now what that actually *means* is not one damned thing, except I expect you to be polite."

"Yes, Aunt."

"My servant Margret tends to us; breakfast and lunch are cold and left over on that table over there. Supper will be with the Court for you once I get you introduced. If you miss it, you can take your chances with us. Lessons, hmm. For now—oh—Donni, I want you to take him with you in the morning and turn him over to Kayla; Withen was rather insistent on his getting weapons work, and for once I agree with him."

"Yes, Savil," the short, tousle-haired trainee said calmly. Savil blessed the girl's soothing presence, and also blessed the fact that she was lifebound to Mardic. Nothing shook a lifebond except the death of one of the pair. Vanyel's handsome face wasn't going to turn *her* head.

She rather dreaded the effect of that face on the rest of the younglings at the Court, though.

"Mardic?"

The imperturbable farmer's son nodded his round head without speaking.

"Take him to Bardic Collegium in the afternoon for me, and get them to put him into History, Literature, and—" She wrinkled her brow in thought as her three proteges arranged themselves around her.

"How about Religions?" Tylendel suggested. He raised one dark-gold eyebrow and Mindspoke his teacher in Private-mode, his lips thinning a little. :*He's lovely, Savil. And he Feels like he's either an arrogant little bastard, or somebody's been hurting him inside for an awfully long time. Frankly, I couldn't tell you which. Is he going to be as much trouble as I think?:*

　:Don't know, lad,: Savil Mindspoke soberly. *:But don't get wrapped up with him, not until we know. And don't fall in love with him. I have no idea where his preferences lie, but even Withen didn't hint he was* shay'a'chern. *I don't want to have to patch your broken heart up. Again.:*

　:Not a chance, Teacher,: Tylendel mind-grinned. *:I've learned better.:*

　:Huh. I should hope. Oh, Lord of Light—I did give all of you grabs at Dominick's old room, didn't I? I don't want to start this off with hurt feelings—:

　:Yes, you did, and none of us wanted to move,: Tylendel mind-chuckled. *:The garden door may be nice but it's drafty as the Cave of the Winds. If I had someone to keep me warm—:*

　:I could get you a dog,: she suggested, and watched his lips twitch as he tried not to smile. *:Well, that's one worry out of the way.:* Then said aloud, "All right, Vanyel, History, Literature and Religions it is, and weapons work with Kayla in the morning. She teaches the young highborns, and she's very good—and if I find out you've been avoiding her lessons, I'll take a strap to you."

Vanyel flushed at that, but said nothing.

"Donni, Mardic, Tylendel, give Vanyel a hand with his things; we'll put him in the garden chamber. I had Margret get it ready for him this morning."

As the three trainees scooped up a pack apiece, and Vanyel bent slowly to take the fourth, Savil added a last admonition.

"Vanyel, what you do with your free time is your own business," she said, perhaps a bit more harshly than she intended. "But if you get yourself into trouble, and there's plenty of it to get into around here, don't expect me to pull you out. I can't, and I won't. You're an imposition. It's your job to see that you become less of one."

Vanyel thanked the trainees for their help as they dropped his packs to one side of the door, speaking in a voice that sounded dull and exhausted even in his own ears.

The blond one hesitated for a moment—just long enough to give him what *looked* like a genuine smile, before slipping out the door.

But despite that smile, Vanyel was mortally glad when they didn't linger. He closed the door behind them, then leaned up against it with his eyes shut. The entire day had been confusing and wearying, an emotional obstacle course that he was just happy to have survived.

The worst of it had been the past couple of hours; first, being shuttled off to Savil's quarters with Erek and Garth suddenly deciding to act like the jailers that they were, then the interminable wait—then the Interview.

Her words had hurt; he willed them not to. He willed himself not to care.

Then he moved to the middle of his new room and looked around himself, and blinked in surprise.

It was—amazing. Warm, and welcoming, paneled and furnished in goldenoak, and as well-appointed as his mother's private chamber. Certainly *nothing* like his room back at Forst Reach. A huge bed stood against one wall, a bed almost wide enough for *three* and covered with a thick, soft red comforter. In the corner, a wardrobe, not a simple chest, to hold his clothing. Beside it a desk and *padded* chair—Havens, an *instrument* rack on the wall next to the weapons-rack! Next to the window a second, more heavily padded chair, both chairs upholstered in red that matched the comforter. His own fireplace. A small table next to the bed, and a bookcase. But that wasn't the most amazing thing—

His room had its own private entrance, something that was either a small, glazed door or an enormous window that opened up on a garden.

I don't believe this, he thought, staring stupidly through the glass at the sculptured bushes and the glint of setting sun on the river beyond. *I just do not believe this. I expected to be in another prison. Instead—*

He tried the door/window. It was unlocked, and swung open at a touch.

—instead, I'm given total freedom. I do not believe this! His knees went weak, and he had to sit down on the edge of the bed before he collapsed. The breeze that had been allowed to enter when he opened the window made the light material used as curtains flap lazily.

Gods—he thought, dazedly. *I don't know what to think. She saves Star—then she humiliates me in front of the trainees. She gives me this room—then she tells me I'm the next thing to worthless and she threatens to beat me herself. What am I supposed to believe?*

He could hear the murmuring of voices beyond the other door, the one the tall blond had closed after himself. *They sound so comfortable out there, so easy with each other*, he thought wistfully. They were terribly unalike, the three of them. The one called Donni could have been Erek's twin sister; they looked to have been cast from the same mold—dark, curly-haired, phlegmatic. The shorter boy, Mardic, had the look of one of Withen's small-holders; earthy, square, and brown. But the third—

Vanyel was experiencing a strange, unsteady feeling when he thought about the tall, graceful blond called Tylendel. He didn't know why.

Not even the minstrel Shanse had evoked this depth of—disturbance—in him.

There was a burst of laughter beyond the door. *They sound so happy,* he thought a bit sadly, before his thoughts darkened. *They're probably laughing at me.*

He clenched his teeth. *Damn it, I don't care, I won't care. I don't need their approval.*

He closed his walls a little tighter about himself, and began the mundane task of settling himself into his new home. And tried not to feel himself left on the outside, telling himself over and over again that nothing mattered.

The slender girl Vanyel's aunt had called "Donni" looked askance at all the padding and armor Vanyel picked off his armor-stand and weapons-rack. "Are you really taking all that?" she asked, hazel eyes rather wide with surprise.

He nodded shortly.

She shook her head in disbelief, her tight, sable curls scarcely moving. "I can't see why you want all *that* stuff, but I guess it's your back. Come on."

There'd been no one in the suite when Vanyel woke, but there *had* been cider, bread and butter, cheese, and fruit waiting on a sideboard in the central room. He had figured that was supposed to be breakfast, seeing that *someone*—or several someones, more like—had already made hearty inroads on the food. He had helped himself, then found a servant to show him the way to the bathing-room and the privies, and cleaned himself up.

He'd pulled on some of his oldest and shabbiest clothing in anticipation of getting them well-grimed at the coming weaponry-lesson. He was back in his own room and in a very somber mood, sitting on the floor while putting some new leather lacings on his practice armor, when Donni came hunting him.

He gathered up his things and followed one step behind her out through his garden door and into the sunlit, fragrant garden, trying not to let any apprehension seep into his cool shell. She took him on a circuitous path that led from his own garden door, past several ornamental grottoes and fish ponds, down to a graveled pathway that followed the course of the river.

They trudged past what looked like a stable, except that the stalls had no doors on them, and past a smaller building beside it. Then the path took an abrupt turn to the right, ending at a gate in a high wooden fence. By now

Vanyel's arms were getting more than a little tired; he was hot, and sweating, and he hoped that this was at least close to their goal.

But no; the seemingly placid trainee flashed him what *might* have been a sympathetic grin, and opened the gate, motioning for Vanyel to go through.

"There," she said, pointing across what seemed to be an expanse of carefully manicured lawn as wide as the legendary Dhorisha Plains. At the other end of the lawn was a plain, rawly new wooden building with high clerestory windows. "That's the salle," she told him. "That's where we're going. They just built it last year so that we could practice year-round." She giggled. "I think they got tired of the trainees having bouts in the hallways when it rained or snowed!"

Vanyel just nodded, determined to show no symptoms of his weariness. She set off across the grass with a stride so brisk he had to really push himself to keep up with her. It was all he could do to keep from panting with effort by the time they actually reached the building, and his side was in agony when she slowed down enough to open the door for him.

Once inside he could see that the structure was one single large room, with a mirrored wall and a carefully sanded wooden floor. There were several young people out on the floor already, ranging in apparent age from as young as eleven or twelve to as old as their early twenties. Most of them were sparring—

Vanyel was too exhausted to take much notice of what they were up to, although the pair nearest him (he saw with a sinking heart) were working out in almost *exactly* the weapons style Jervis used.

"This him?"

A woman with a soft, musical contralto spoke from behind them, and Vanyel turned abruptly, dropping a vambrace.

"Yes, ma'am," Donni said, picking the bracer up before Vanyel had a chance even to flush. "Vanyel, this is Weaponsmaster Kayla. Kayla, this stuff is all his; I guess he brought it from home. I've got to get going, or I'll miss my session in the Work Room."

"Havens forfend," Kayla said dryly. "Savil would eat me for lunch if you were late. Don't forget you have dagger this afternoon, girl."

Donni nodded and slipped out the door, leaving Vanyel alone with the redoubtable Weaponsmaster.

For redoubtable she was. From the crown of her head to the soles of her feet she was nothing but sinew and muscle. Her black hair, tightly braided to her head, showed not a strand of gray, despite the age revealed by the fine net of wrinkles around her eyes and mouth. Those gray-green eyes didn't look as if they missed much.

For the rest, Kayla's shoulders were nearly a handspan wider than his, and her wrists as thick as his ankles. Vanyel had no doubt that she could readily wield *any* of the blades in the racks along the wall, even the ones as tall or taller than she. He did *not* particularly want to face this woman in *any* sort of combat situation. She looked like she could quite handily take on Jervis *and* mop the floor with his ugly face.

Vanyel remained outwardly impassive, but was inwardly quaking as she in turn studied him.

"Well, young man," she said quietly, after a moment that was far too long for his liking. "You might as well throw that stuff over in the corner over there"—she nodded toward the far end of the salle, and a pile of discarded equipment—"we'll see what we can salvage of it. *You* certainly won't be needing it."

Vanyel blinked at her, wondering if he'd missed something. "Why not?" he asked, just as quietly.

"Good gods, lad, that stuff's about as suited to you as boots on a cat!" she replied, with a certain amusement. "Whoever your last master was, he was a fool to put you in *that* gear. No, young man—you see Redel and Oden over there?"

She pointed with her chin at a pair of slender, androgynous figures involved in an intricate, and possibly deadly dance with very light, slender swords.

"I'll make Duke Oden your instructor; he'll be pleased to have a pupil besides young Lord Redel. That's the kind of style suited to you, so *that's* what you'll be doing, young Vanyel," she told him.

His heart rose to its proper place from its former position—somewhere in the vicinity of his boots.

Kayla graced him with a momentary smile. "Mind you, lad, Oden's no light taskmaster. You'll find you work up as healthy a sweat and collect just as many bruises as any of the hack-and-bashers. So let's get you suited for it, eh?"

If the morning was an unexpected pleasure—and it was; for the first time in his life he received *praise* for weapons work, and preened under it—the afternoon was an unalloyed disaster.

It started when he returned with equipment that weighed a third of what he'd carried over. He racked it with care he usually didn't grant to weaponry, and sought the central room of the suite.

Someone—probably the hitherto invisible Margret—had taken away the food left on the sideboard this morning and replaced it with meat rolls, more fruit and cheese, and a bottle of light wine.

Tylendel was sprawled on the couch, a meat roll in one hand, a book in the other, a crease of concentration between his brows. He didn't even look up as Vanyel moved hesitantly just into the common room itself.

Once again he got that strange, half-fearful, fluttery feeling in the pit of his stomach. He cleared his throat, and Tylendel jumped, dropping his book, looking up with his eyes widened and his hair over one eye.

"Good gods, Vanyel, make some *noise*, next time!" he said, bending to retrieve his book from the floor. "I didn't know there was anyone here but me! That's lunch over there—"

He pointed with the half-eaten roll.

"Savil says to eat and get yourself cleaned up; she's going to present you to the Queen before the noon recess. Then you'll be able to have dinner with the Court; the rest of us get it on the fly as our schedules permit. Savil will be back in a few minutes so you'd better move." He tilted his head to one side, just a little, and offered, "If you need any help . . ."

Vanyel stiffened; the offer hadn't sounded at all unfriendly, but—it could be Tylendel was looking for a way to spy on him. Savil hadn't necessarily told the truth.

—if only—

"No," he replied curtly, "I don't need any help." He paused, then added for politeness' sake, "Thank you."

Tylendel gave him a dubious look, then shrugged and dove back into his book.

Savil *was* back in moments; Vanyel had barely time to make himself presentable before she scooped him up and herded him off to the Throne Room.

The Throne Room was a great deal smaller than he had pictured; long and narrow, and rather dark. And stuffy; there were more people crammed into this room than it had ever been intended to hold. Somewhere down at the farther end of it was the Throne itself, beneath a huge blue and silver tapestry of a rampant winged horse with broken chains on its throat and legs that took up the entire wall over the Throne. Vanyel could see the tapestry, but nothing else; everyone else in the room seemed to be at least a hand taller than he was, and all he could see were heads.

The presentation itself was a severe disappointment. Vanyel waited with Savil at his side for nearly an hour while some wrangle or other involving a pair of courtiers was ironed out. Then Savil's name was called; the two of them (Vanyel trailing in Savil's formidable wake) were announced by a middle-aged Herald in full Court Whites. Vanyel was escorted to the foot of the Throne by that same Herald, where Queen Elspeth (a thin, dark-haired woman who was looking very tired and somewhat preoccupied) nodded to him in a friendly manner, and said about five words in greeting. He bowed and was escorted back to Savil's side, and that was all there was to it.

Then Savil hustled him back to change *out* of Court garb and into ordinary day-garb for his afternoon classes. Mardic practically flew in the door from the hallway and took him in tow. They traversed a long, dark corridor leading from Savil's quarters, out through a double door, to a much older section of the Palace. From there they exited a side door and out into more gardens—herb gardens this time, and kitchen gardens.

Mardic didn't seem to be the talkative type, but he could certainly move. His fast walk took them past an L-shaped granite building before Vanyel had a chance to ask what it was, and up to a square fieldstone structure. "Bardic Collegium," Mardic said shortly, pausing just long enough for a couple of youngsters who were running to get past him, then opening the black wooden door for him.

He didn't say another word, just left him at the door of his first class before vanishing elsewhere into the building.

He was finding it hard to believe that Savil was going so far in ignoring his father's orders as to put him in *lessoning* with the Bardic students. Nevertheless, here he was.

Inside Bardic Collegium. Actually inside the building, seated in a row of chairs with three other youngsters in a small, sunny room on the first floor.

More than that, pacing back and forth as he lectured or questioned them was a real, live Bard in full Scarlets; a tall, powerful man who was probably as much at home wielding a broadsword as a lute.

At home Vanyel had always been a full step ahead of his brothers and cousins when it came to scholastics, so he began the hour with a feeling of boredom. History was the proverbial open book to him—or so he had always thought. He began the session with the rather smug feeling that he was going to dazzle his new classmates.

The other three boys looked at him curiously when he came in and sat down with them, but they didn't say anything. One was mouse-blond, one chestnut, and one dark; all three were dressed nearly the same as Vanyel, in ordinary day-clothing of white raime shirt and tunic and breeches of soft brown or gray fabric. He couldn't tell if they were Heraldic trainees or Bardic; they wore no uniforms the way their elders did. Not that it mattered, really, except that he would have liked to impress them with his scholarship if they *were* Bardic students.

The room was hardly bigger than his bedroom in Savil's suite; but unlike the Heralds' quarters, this building was old, worn, and a bit shabby. Vanyel had a moment to register disappointment at the scuffed floor, dusty furnishings, and faded paint before the leonine Bard at the window-end of the room began the class.

After that, all he had a chance to feel was shock.

"Yesterday we discussed the Arvale annexation; today we're going to cover the negotiations with Rethwellan that followed the annexation." With those words, Bard Chadran launched into his lecture; a dissertation on the important Arvale–Zalmon negotiations in the time of King Tavist. It was fascinating. There was only one problem.

Vanyel had never even heard of the Arvale–Zalmon negotiations, and all he knew of King Tavist was that he was the son of Queen Terilee and the father of Queen Leshia; Tavist's reign had been a quiet one, a reign devoted more to studied diplomacy than the kind of deeds that made for ballads. So when the Bard opened the floor to discussion, Vanyel had to sit there and try to look as if he understood it all, without having the faintest idea of what was going on.

He took reams of notes, of course, but without knowing why the negotiations had been so important, much less what they were about, they didn't make a great deal of sense.

He escaped that class with the feeling that he'd only just escaped being skinned and eaten alive.

Religions was a *bit* better, though not much. He'd thought it was Religion, singular. He found out how wrong he was—again. It was, indeed, Religions in the plural sense. Since the population of Valdemar was a patchwork quilt of a dozen different peoples escaping from various unbearable situations, it was hardly surprising that each one of those peoples had their own religion. As Vanyel heard, over and over again that hour, the law of Valdemar on the subject of worship was "there is no 'one, true way.'" But with a dozen or more "ways" in practice, it would have been terribly easy for a Bard—or Herald—to misstep among people strange to him. Hence this class, which was currently covering the "People of the One" who had settled about Crescent Lake.

It was something of a shock, hearing that what *his* priest would have called rankest heresy was presented as just another aspect of the truth. Vanyel spent half his time feeling utterly foolish, and the other half trying to hide his reactions of surprise and disquiet.

But it was Literature—or rather, an event just before the Literature class—which truly deflated and defeated him.

He had been toying with the idea of petitioning one of the Bards to enroll him in their Collegium before he began the afternoon's classes, but now he was doubtful of being able to survive the lessons.

Gods, I—I'm as pig-ignorant compared to these trainees as my cousins are compared to me, he thought glumly, slumping in the chair nearest the door as he and the other two with him waited for the teacher of Literature to put in her appearance. *But—maybe this time. Lord of Light knows I've memorized every ballad I could ever get my hands on.*

Then he overheard Bard Chadran talking out in the hallway with another Bard; presumably the teacher of this class. But when he heard his own name, and realized that they were talking about *him*, he stretched his ears without shame or hesitation to catch all that he could.

"—so Savil wants us to take him if he's got the makings," Chadran was saying.

"Well, has he?" asked the second, a dark, sensuously female voice.

"Shanse's heard him sing; says he's got the voice and the hands for it, and I trust him on that," said Chadran, hesitantly.

"But not the Gift?" the second persisted.

Chadran coughed. "I—didn't hear any sign of it in class. And it's pretty obvious he doesn't compose, or we'd have heard about it. Shanse would have said something, or put it in his report, and he didn't."

"He has to have two out of three; Gift, Talent, and Creativity—you *know* that, Chadran," said the woman. "Shanse didn't see any signs of Gift either, did he?"

Chadran sighed. "No. Breda, when Savil asked me about this boy, I looked up Shanse's report on the area. He *did* mention the boy, and he *was* flattering enough about the boy's musicality that we could get him training as a minstrel if—"

"If—"

"If he weren't his father's heir. But the truth is, he said the boy has a magnificent ear, and aptitude for mimicry, and the talent. But no creativity, and no Gift. And that's not enough to enroll someone's heir as a mere minstrel. Still—Breda, love, *you* look for Gift. You're better at seeing it than any of us. I'd really like to do Savil a favor on this one. She says the boy is set enough on music to defy a fairly formidable father—and we owe her a few."

"I'll try him," said the woman, "but don't get your hopes up. Shanse may not have the Gift himself, but he knows it when he hears it."

Vanyel had something less than an instant to wonder what they meant by "Gift" before the woman he'd overheard entered the room. As tall as a man, thin, plain—she still had a *presence* that forced Vanyel to pay the utmost attention to every word she spoke, every gesture she made.

"Today we're going to begin the 'Windrider' cycle," she said, pulling a gittern around from where it hung across her back. "I'm going to begin with the very first 'Windrider' ballad known, and I'm going to present it the way it should be dealt with. Heard, not read. This ballad was *never* designed to be read, and I'll tell you the truth, the flaws present in it mostly vanish when it's sung."

She strummed a few chords, then launched into the opening to the "Windrider Unchained"—and he no longer wondered what the "Gift" could be.

Because she didn't just *sing*—not like Vanyel would have sung, or even the minstrel (or, as he realized now, the *Bard*) Shanse would have. No—she made her listeners *experience* every word of the passage; to feel every emotion, to see the scene, to live the event as the originals must have lived it. When she finished, Vanyel knew he would never forget those words again.

And he knew to the depths of his soul that he would never be able to do what she had just done.

Oh, he tried; when she prompted him to sing the next Windrider ballad while she played, he gave it his best. But he could tell from the look in his fellow classmates' eyes—interest, but *not* rapt fascination—that he hadn't even managed a pale imitation.

As he sat down and she gestured to the next to take a ballad, he saw the pity in her eyes and the slight shake of her head—and knew then that *she* knew he'd overheard the conversation in the hallway. That this was her way of telling him, gently, and indirectly, that his dream could not be realized.

It was the pity that hurt the most, after the realization that he did not have the proper material to be a Bard. It cut—as cruelly as any blade. All that work—all that fighting to get his hand back the way it had been—and all for nothing. He'd never even had a hope.

Vanyel threw himself onto his bed, his chest aching, his head throbbing—

I thought nothing would ever be worse than home—but at least I still had dreams. Now I don't even have that.

The capper on the miserable day was his aunt, his competent, clever, selfless, damn-her-to-nine-hells aunt.

He flopped over onto his stomach, and fought back the sting in his eyes. She'd pulled him aside right after dinner; "I asked the Bards to see if they could take you," she'd said. "I'm sorry, Vanyel, but they told me you're a very talented musician, but that's all you'll ever be. That's not enough to get you into Bardic when you're the heir to a holding."

"But—" he'd started to say, then clamped his mouth shut.

She gave him a sharp look. "I know how you probably feel, Vanyel, but your duty as Withen's heir is going to have to come first. So you'd better resign yourself to the situation instead of fighting it."

She watched him broodingly as he struggled to maintain his veneer of calm. "The gods know," she said finally, "*I* stood in your shoes, once. I wanted the Holding—but I wasn't firstborn son. And as things turned out, I'm glad I didn't get the Holding. If you make the best of your situation, you may find one day that you wouldn't have had a better life if you'd chosen it yourself."

How could she know? he fumed. *I hate her. So help me, I hate her. Everything she does is so damned perfect! She never says anything, but she doesn't have to; all she has to do is give me that look. If I hear one more word about how I'm supposed to like this trap that's closed on me, I may go mad!*

He turned over on his back, and brooded. It wasn't even sunset—and he was stuck here with his lute staring down at him from the wall with all the broken dreams it implied.

And nothing to distract him. Or was there?

Dinner was over, but there were going to be people gathered in the Great Hall all night. And there were plenty of people his age there; young people who *weren't* Bard trainees, nor Herald proteges. Ordinary young people, more like normal human beings.

He forgot all his apprehensions about being thought a country bumpkin; all he could think of now was the admiration his wit and looks used to draw at the infrequent celebrations that brought the offspring of several Keeps and Holdings together. He needed a dose of that admiration, and needed its sweetness as an antidote to the bitterness of failure.

He flung himself off the bed and rummaged in his wardrobe for an appropriately impressive outfit; he settled on a smoky gray velvet as suiting his mood and his flair for the dramatic.

He planned his entrance to the Great Hall with care; waiting until one of those moments that occur at any gathering of people where everyone seems to choose the same moment to stop talking. When that moment came, he seized it; pacing gracefully into the silence as if it had been created expressly to display *him*.

It worked to perfection; within moments he had a little circle of courtiers of his own flocking about him, eager to impress the newcomer with their friendliness. He basked in their attentions for nearly an hour before it began to pall.

A lanky youngster named Liers was waxing eloquent on the subject of his elder brother dealing with a set of brigands. Vanyel stifled a yawn; this was sounding *exactly* like similar evenings at Forst Reach!

"So he charged straight at them—"

"Which was a damn fool thing to do if you ask me," Vanyel said, his brows creasing.

"But—it takes a *brave* man—" the young man protested weakly.

"I repeat, it was a damn fool thing to do," Vanyel persisted. "Totally outnumbered, no notion if the party behind him was coming in time— great good gods, the *right* thing to do would have been to turn tail and run! If he'd done it convincingly, he could have led them straight into the arms of his own troops! Charging off like that could have gotten him killed!"

"It worked," Liers sulked.

"Oh, it worked all right, because nobody in his right mind would have done what he did!"

"It was the *valiant* thing to have done," Liers replied, lifting his chin.

Vanyel gave up; he didn't dare alienate these younglings. They were all he had—

"You're right, Liers," he said, hating the lie. "It was a valiant thing to have done."

Liers smiled in foolish satisfaction as Vanyel made more stupid remarks; eventually Vanyel extricated himself from *that* little knot of idlers and went looking for something more interesting.

The fools were as bad as his brother; he could *not*, would *never* get it through their heads that there was nothing "romantic" about getting themselves hacked to bits in the name of Valdemar or a lady. That there was nothing uplifting about losing an arm or a leg or an eye. That there was nothing, *nothing* "glorious" about warfare.

As soon as he turned away from the male contingent, the female descended upon him in a chattering flock; flirting, coquetting, each doing her best to get Vanyel's attention settled on *her*. It was exactly the same playette that had been enacted over and over in his mother's bower; there were more players, and the faces were both different and often prettier, but it was an identical script.

Vanyel was bored.

But it was marginally better than being lectured by Savil, or longing after the Bards and the Gift he never would have.

"—Tylendel," said the pert little brunette at his elbow, with a sigh of disappointment.

"What about Tylendel?" Vanyel asked, his interest, for once, caught.

"Oh, Tashi is in love with Tylendel's big brown eyes," laughed another girl, a tall, pale-complected redhead.

"Not a chance, Tashi," said Reva, who was flushed from a little too much wine. She giggled. "You haven't a chance. He's—what's that word Savil uses?"

"*Shay'a'chern*," supplied Cress. "It's some outland tongue."

"What's it mean?" Vanyel asked.

Reva giggled, and whispered, "That he doesn't like girls. He likes boys. Lucky boys!"

"For Tylendel I'd turn into a boy!" Tashi sighed, then giggled back at her friend. "Oh, what a waste! Are you sure?"

"Sure as stars," Reva assured her. "Only just last year he broke his heart over that bastard Nevis."

Vanyel suppressed his natural reaction of astonishment. Didn't—like girls. He knew at least that the youngling courtiers used "like" synonymously with "bedding." But—didn't "like" girls? "Liked" boys?

He'd known he'd been sheltered from some things, but he'd never even guessed about this one.

Was this why Withen—

"Nevis—wasn't he the one who couldn't make up his mind *which* he liked and claimed he'd been seduced every time he crawled into somebody's bed?" Tashi asked in rapt fascination.

"The very same," Reva told her. "I am *so* glad his parents called him home!"

They were off into a dissection of the perfidious Nevis then, and Vanyel lost interest. He drifted around the Great Hall, but was unable to find anything or anyone he cared to spend any time with. He drank a little more wine than he intended, but it didn't help make the evening any livelier, and at length he gave up and went to bed.

He lay awake for a long time, skirting the edges of the thoughts he'd had earlier. From the way the girls had giggled about it, it was pretty obvious that Tylendel's preferences were something short of "respectable." And Withen—

Oh, he knew now what Withen would have to say about it if he knew that his son was even sharing the same quarters as Tylendel.

All those times he went after me when I was tiny, for hugging and kissing Meke. That business with Father Leren and the lecture on "proper masculine behavior." The fit he had when Liss dressed me up in her old dresses like an overgrown doll. Oh, gods.

Suddenly the reasons behind a great many otherwise inexplicable actions on Withen's part were coming clear.

Why he kept shoving girls at me, why he bought me that—professional. Why he kept arranging for friends of Mother's with compliant daughters to visit. Why he hated seeing me in fancy clothing. Why some of the armsmen would go quiet when I came by—why some of the jokes would just stop. Father didn't even want a hint of this to get to me.

He ached inside; just ached.

I've lost music—no; even if Tylendel is to be trusted, I can't take the chance. Not even on—being his friend. If he didn't turn on me, which he probably would.

All that was left was the other dream—the ice-dream. The only dream that couldn't hurt him.

The chasm wasn't too wide to jump, but it was deep. And there was something— terrible—at the bottom of it. He didn't know how he knew that, but he knew it was true. Behind him was nothing but the empty, wintry ice-plain. On the other side of the chasm it was springtime. He wanted to cross over, to the warmth, to listen to bird- song beneath the trees—but he was afraid to jump. It seemed to widen even as he looked at it.

"Vanyel?"

He looked up, startled.

Tylendel stood on the other side, wind ruffling his hair, his smile wide and as warm and open as spring sunshine.

"Do you want to come over?" the trainee asked softly. He held out one hand. "I'll help you, if you like."

Vanyel backed up a step, clasping his arms tightly to his chest to keep from inadvertently answering that extended hand.

"Vanyel?" The older boy's eyes were gentle, coaxing. "Vanyel, I'd like to be your friend." He lowered his voice still more, until it was little more than a whisper, and gestured invitingly. "I'd like," he continued, "to be more than your friend."

"No!" Vanyel cried, turning away violently, and running as fast as he could into the empty whiteness.

When he finally stopped, he was alone on the empty plain, alone, and chilled to the marrow. He ached all over at first, but then the cold really set in, and he couldn't feel much of anything. There was no sign of the chasm, or of Tylendel. And for one brief moment, loneliness made him ache worse than the cold.

Then the chill seemed to reach the place where the loneliness was, and that began to numb as well.

He began walking, choosing a direction at random. The snow-field wasn't as featureless as he'd thought, it seemed. The flat, smooth snow-plain that creaked beneath his feet began to grow uneven. Soon he was having to avoid huge teeth of ice that thrust up through the crust of the snow—then he could no longer avoid them; he was having to climb over and around them.

They were sharp-edged; sharp as glass shards. He cut himself once, and stared in surprise at the blood on the snow. And, strangely enough, it didn't seem to hurt—

There was only the cold.

CHAPTER 5

TYLENDEL WAS SPRAWLED carelessly across the grass in the garden, reading. Vanyel watched him from behind the safety of his window curtains, half sick with conflicting emotions. The breeze was playing with the trainee's tousled hair almost the same way it had in his dream.

He shivered, and closed his eyes. *Gods. Oh, gods. Why me? Why now? And why, oh why,* him? *Savil's favorite protege—*

He clutched the fabric of the curtain as if it were some kind of lifeline, and opened his eyes again. Tylendel had changed his pose a little, leaning his head on his hand, frowning in concentration. Vanyel shivered and bit his lip, feeling his heart pounding so hard he might as well have been running footraces. No girl had ever been able to make his heart race like this. . . .

The thought made him flush, his stomach twisting. *Gods, what am I? Like him? I must be. Father will—oh, gods. Father will kill me, lock me up, tell everyone I've gone mad. Maybe I have gone mad.*

Tylendel smiled suddenly at something he was reading; Vanyel's heart nearly stopped, and he wanted to cry. *If only he'd smile at me that way—oh, gods, I can't, I can't, I daren't trust him, he'll only turn on me like all the others.*

Like all the others.

He turned away from the window, invoking his shield of indifference with a sick and heavy heart.

If only I dared. If only I dared.

Savil locked the brassbound door of her own private version of the Work Room with fingers that trembled a little, and turned to face her favorite protege, Tylendel, with more than a little trepidation.

Gods. This is not going to be easy. She braced herself for what was bound to be a dangerous confrontation; both for herself and for Tylendel. She didn't *think* he was going to go for her throat—but—well, this time she was going to push him just a little further than she had dared before. And there was always the chance that it would be *too* far, this time.

He stood in the approximate center of the room, arms folded over the front of his plain brown tunic, expression unwontedly sober. It was fairly evident that he had already gathered this was not going to be a lesson or an ordinary discussion.

There was nothing else in this room, nothing at all. Unlike the public Work Room, this one was square, not circular; but the walls here were stone, too, and for some of the same reasons. In addition there was an inlaid pattern of lighter-colored wood delineating a perfect circle in the center of the hardwood floor. And there was an oddness about the walls, a sense of presence, as if they were nearly alive. In a way, they were; Savil had put no small amount of her own personal energies into the protections on this room. They were, in some senses, a part of her. And because of that, she should be safer here than anywhere else, if something went wrong.

"You didn't bring me in here to practice," Tylendel stated flatly.

Savil swallowed and shook her head. "No, I didn't. You're right. I wanted to talk with you; I have two subjects, really, and I don't want anyone to have a chance at overhearing us."

"The first subject?" Tylendel asked. "Or—I think I know. My family again." His expression didn't change visibly, but Savil could sense his sudden anger in the stubborn setting of his jaw.

"Your family again," Savil agreed. "Tylendel, you're a Herald, or nearly. Heralds *do not* take sides in anyone's fight, not even when their own blood is involved. Your people have been putting pressure on you to do something. Now *I* know you haven't interfered—but I also know you want to. And I'm afraid that you might give in to that temptation."

His mouth tightened and he looked away from her. "So Evan Leshara can pour his poison into the ear of anyone at Court who cares to listen—and I'm not allowed to do or say anything about it, is that it? I'm not even allowed to call him a damned liar for some of the things he's said about Staven?" He pulled his gaze back to her, and glared at her as angrily as if she were the one responsible for his enemy's behavior. "It's more than just my blood, Savil, it's my *twin*. By all he believes, by all he holds true, we've got blood-debt to pay here—and *Staven*, for all that he's young, is the Lord Holder now. It's his decision; the rest of us Frelennye must and *will* support him. And besides all that, he's in the *right*, dammit!"

"Lord Holder or not, *young* or not, *right* or not, he's a damned hotheaded fool," Savil burst out, flinging up both her hands before her in a gesture of complete frustration. "Blood-debt be hanged, it's that kind of fool thinking that got your people and the Leshara into this *stupid* feud in the first damned place! *You can't bring back the dead with more blood!*"

"It's honor, dammit!" He clenched his hands into fists. "Can't you even *try* to understand that?"

"It has nothing to do with *real* honor," she said scornfully. "It has everything to do with plain, obstinate pride. 'Lendel, you *cannot* be involved."

She froze with her heart in her mouth as he made one angry step toward her. He saw her reaction, and halted.

She plowed onward, trusting in the advice she'd gotten. *Please, Jaysen, be right this time, too.*

"This whole feud is *insanity*! 'Lendel, listen to me—it has got to be stopped, and if it goes on much longer it's the Heralds who'll have to stop it and you *cannot* take sides!"

All right so far; she hadn't said anything new. Now for the fresh goad. And hope it wasn't too much of a goad, too soon.

"'Lendel, I know you've never been able to figure out why both you *and* Staven weren't taken by Companions—well, dammit, it's *exactly* this insanity that's the reason your beloved twin *didn't* get Chosen and *you* did. You at least can *see* the futility of this when you aren't busy defending him—he's too full of vainglory and too damned stubborn to *ever* see any solution to this but crushing the Leshara, branch and root! Your twin is an *idiot*, 'Lendel! He's just as much an idiot as Wester Leshara, but that doesn't change the fact that he's going to get people killed out of plain stupidity! And I will not permit this to go on for very much longer. If I have to denounce Staven to end your involvement with this, I will. *Never* doubt it. You have more important things to do with your life than waste it defending a fool."

Tylendel's fists clenched again; he was nearly rigid with anger, as his eyes went nearly black and his face completely white with the force of his emotions—and for one moment Savil wondered if he'd strike her this time. Or strike *at* her, that is; if he came for her, she didn't intend to be where his fist landed. Or his levinbolt, if it came to that.

Please, Lord and Lady, don't let him lose it this time, let him stay in control— I've never pushed him this far before. And don't let him try magic. If he hits out, I may not be able to save him from what my protections will do.

She prayed, and looked steadfastly (and, she hoped, compassionately) into those angry eyes.

She could Feel him vibrating inside, caught between his need to strike

out at the one who had attacked his very beloved twin and his own conscience and good sense.

Savil continued to hold her ground, refusing to back down. The tension
in the room was so acute that the power-charged walls picked it up, reverberating with his rage. And that fed back into Savil, will-she, nill-she. It was
all *she* could do to hold fast, and maintain at least the appearance of calm.

Then he whirled and headed blindly into a corner. He rested his forehead against the cool stone of the wall with one arm draped over his head,
pounding the fist of his free hand against the gray stones, cursing softly
under his breath.

Now Savil let him alone, saying absolutely nothing.

*Once you get him worked into a rage, let him deal with his anger and his internal
turmoil in his own way*, had been Jaysen's advice. *Leave him alone until he's
calmed* himself *down*.

Finally he turned back to the room and her, bracing himself in the corner, eyes nearly closed, breathing as hard as if he'd been running a mile.

"You'll never get me to agree to stop supporting Staven, you know," he
said in a perfectly conversational tone. "I won't interfere with the Heralds,
I won't help with the feud, and I won't call Evan Leshara a damned liar—but
I *will* defend Staven and what he thinks is right, if only to you. I love him,
and I will not give that up."

There was no sign that a moment before he'd been in—literally—a killing rage.

"I know," Savil replied, just as calmly, giving no indication that *she* was
still shaking inside. "I'm not asking you to give up loving Staven. All I want
is for you to *think* about this mess, not just react to it. If it was only your two
families, it would be bad enough, but you're involving the whole region in
your feuding. We know very well that you've both been looking for mages
to escalate this thing—and 'Lendel, I do not want to hear a single word
about which side started *that*. The important thing is that you've done it.
The *important* thing is that if either side involves magic in this, the Heralds
must and *will* take a hand. We can't afford to have wild magic loose and
hurting innocent people. You are a Herald, or nearly. You have to remember that you *cannot* take a side. You *have* to be impartial. No matter what
Evan Leshara does or says."

Tylendel shrugged, but it was *not* an indifferent shrug. His pain was very
real, and only too plain to his mentor; she hurt *for* him. But this was one of
the most important lessons any Herald had to learn—that he *had* to be

impartial, no matter what the cost of impartiality was. And no matter whether the cost was to himself, or to those he cared for.

"All right," he said, tonelessly. "I'll keep out of it. So. Now that you've turned my guts inside out, what else did you want to discuss?"

"Vanyel," Savil said, relaxing enough that her voice became a little dulled with weariness. "He's been here for more than a month. I want you to tell me what you think."

"Gods." He sagged back against the wall, and opened his eyes completely. They had returned to their normal warm brown. "You would bring up His Loveliness."

"What's the matter?" Savil asked sharply, and took a closer look at him; he was wearing a most peculiar half-smile, and she smelled a rat—or at least a mouse. "'Lendel, *don't* tell me you've gone and fallen in love with the boy!"

He snorted. "No, but the lad is putting a lot of stress on my self-control, let me tell you that! When I don't want to smack that superior grin off his face, I want to cuddle and reassure him, and I don't know which is worse."

"I don't doubt," Savil replied dryly, walking over to where he leaned, and draped herself against the wall opposite him. "All right, obviously you've had your eye on him; tell me what you've figured out so far. Even speculation will do."

"Half the time I think you ought to drown him," her trainee replied, shaking his golden head in disgust. "That miniature Court he's collected around himself is sickening. The posing, the preening—"

Savil made a little grimace of distaste. "You don't have to tell *me*. But what about the other half?"

"In my more compassionate moments, I'm more certain than ever that he's hurting, and all that posing is just that—a pose, a defense; that the little Court of his is to convince *himself* that he's worth something. But I've made overtures, and he just—goes to ice on me. He doesn't hit at me, he just goes unreachable."

"Well—" Savil eyed her protege with speculation. "That particular scenario hadn't occurred to me. I thought that now he'd been given his head, he was just showing his true colors. I was about ready to wash my hands of him. Foster him with—oh—Oden or somebody—somebody with more patience, spare time, and Court connections than me."

"Don't," Tylendel said shortly, a new and calculating look on his face. "I just thought of something. Didn't you tell me one of the things his father was absolutely livid about was his messing about with music?"

"Yes," she said, slowly, pretending to examine the knuckles of her right hand as if they were of intense interest, but in reality concentrating on Tylendel's every word. The boy was a marginal Empath when he wasn't thinking about it. She didn't want to remind him of that Gift just now, not when she needed the information she could get from it. "Yes," she repeated. "Point of fact, he told me flat I was to keep the boy away from the Bards."

"And you told me Breda let him down gently, or as gently as she could, about his ambitions. *How often has he played since then?*"

Now Savil gave him a measuring look of her own. "Not at all," she said slowly. "Not a note since then. Margret says there's dust collecting on that lute of his."

"Lord and Lady!" Tylendel bit his lip, and looked away, all his attention turned inward. "I didn't know it was that bad. I thought he might at least be playing for those social butterflies he's collected."

"Not a note," Savil repeated positively. "*Is* that bad?"

"For a lad who's certainly good enough to get a lot of praise from his sycophants? For one whose *only* ambitions lay with music? It's bad. It's worse than bad; we broke his dream for him. Savil, I take back the first half of what I said." Tylendel rubbed his neck, betraying a growing unease. He looked up at the ceiling, then back down at her, his eyes now frank and worried. "We have a problem. A serious problem. That boy is bleeding inside. If we can't get him to open up, he may bleed himself to death."

"How do we get at him?" Savil asked, taking him at his word. Her weakness—and what made her a *bad* Field Herald, although it was occasionally an asset in training proteges—was in dealing with people. She didn't read them well, and she didn't really know how to handle them in a crisis situation. This business with Tylendel and his twin and the feud, for instance—

I would never have thought of this solution—desensitizing him, weaning him into thinking about it logically by bringing him to the edge over and over but never letting him slip past that edge. Bless Jaysen. And damn him. Gods, every time we play this game it wreaks as much damage on me as it does on poor 'Lendel. I'm still vibrating like a harpstring.

Tylendel pondered her question a long time before answering, his handsome face utterly quiet, his eyes again turned inward. "I just don't know, Savil. Not while he's still rebuffing every overture he gets. We need some time for this to build, I think, and then some event that will break his barricades for a minute. Until that happens, we won't get in, and he'll stay an arrogant bastard until he explodes."

She felt herself grow cold inside. "Suicidal?"

To her relief, Tylendel shook his head. "I don't think so; he's not the type. It wouldn't occur to him. Now *me*—never mind. No, what he'll do is go out of control in one way or another. He'll either do it fast and have some kind of breakdown, or slowly, and debauch himself into a state where he's got about the same amount of mind left as a shrub."

"Wonderful." She placed her right hand over her forehead, rubbing her eyebrows with thumb and forefinger. "Just what I wanted to hear."

Tylendel made one of his expressive shrugs. "You asked."

"I did," she said reluctantly. "Gods, why me?"

"If it's any comfort, it's not going to happen tomorrow."

"It better not. I have an emergency Council session tonight." She sighed, and rubbed her hands together. "I'll probably be up half the night, so don't wait up."

"Does that mean the interview is over?" he asked quirking one corner of his mouth.

"It does. You can have the suite all to yourself tonight—just don't leave crumbs on the floor or grease on the cushions. *I* wouldn't care, but Margret will take your hide off in one piece. And don't look for the lovebirds, either—they're out on a fortnight Field trial with Shallan and her brood. So you'll be all alone for the evening."

"Oh, gods, all alone with the beautiful Vanyel—you *really* want to test my self-control, don't you!" He laughed, then sobered, shoving away from the wall and straightening. "On the other hand, this might give me the chance I was talking about. If I get him alone, maybe I can get him to open up a bit."

Savil shrugged and pushed away from the wall herself. "You're better than I with people, lad, that's why I asked your advice. If you think you have an opportunity, then take it. Meanwhile, *I* have to go consult with the Queen's Own."

"And from there, straight to the meeting? No time for a break?" Tylendel asked, sympathetically. She nodded.

He reached for her shoulders and embraced her closely. "See that you eat, teacher," he murmured into her hair. "I want you to stay around for a while, not wear yourself into another bout of pneumonia, and maybe kill yourself this time. Even when I hate you, you old bitch, you know I love you."

She swallowed down another lump in her throat, and returned the embrace with a definite stinging in her eyes.

"I know, love. Don't think I don't count on it." She swallowed again, closed her eyes, and held him as tightly, a brief point of stability in a world that too often was anything but stable. "I love you, too. And don't you ever forget it."

The *emptiness* of the suite almost oppressed Tylendel. With the "lovebirds" gone, Savil due (so the dinnertime rumor in the kitchens had it) for a till-dawn Council session in her capacity as speaker for those Heralds teaching proteges, and Vanyel presumably entertaining his little coterie of followers, there was nothing and no one to break the stifling silence. It closed around him like a shroud, until the very beating of his heart was audible. Outside the windows it was as dark as the heart of sin, and so overcast not even a hint of moon came through. His scalp was damp, hot, and prickly. Sweat trickled down the back of his neck and soaked into his collar. It felt a whole lot later than it actually was; time was crawling tonight, not flying.

Tylendel gave up trying to read the treatise on weather-magic Savil had assigned him and switched to a history instead. A handwritten pamphlet on weatherworking was *not* what he needed to be reading right now, anyway; not with a storm threatening. His energy control often wasn't as good as he'd like, and he didn't want to inadvertently augment what was coming in. He was a lot better at controlling his subconscious than he *had* been, but there was no point in taking chances with Savil out of reach.

That storm was at least part of what was making the suite seem stuffy; Tylendel Sensed the thunderheads building up in the west even though he couldn't see them from where he was sprawled on the couch of the common room. That *was* the Gift that made him a Herald-Mage trainee and not just a Herald-trainee; the ability to See (or otherwise Sense) and manipulate energy fields, both natural and supernatural. His Gifts had come on him early and a long time before he was Chosen; they'd given him trouble for nearly half of his short life, and only his twin's support had kept him sane in the interval between their onset and when his Companion Gala finally appeared—

:*Are you tucked safe away, dearling?*: he Mindspoke to her. :*When this blow comes, it's going to be a good one.*:

The drowsy affirmative he got told him that she was half-asleep; heat did that to her.

Heat mostly made *him* irritable. He had propped every window and door wide open (and to hell with bugs), but there wasn't even a whisper of breeze to move the air around. The candle flames didn't even waver, and the honey-beeswax smell of the candles placed all around the common room was almost choking him with its sweetness.

He shook back his damp hair, rubbed his eyes, and tried to concentrate on his book, but part of him kept hoping for a flash of lightning in the dark beyond the windows, or the first *hint* of cooling rain. And part of him kept insisting that all he had to do was *nudge* it a little. He told *that* part of himself to take a long walk, and waited impatiently for the rain to come of itself.

Nothing happened. Just an itchy sort of tension building.

He gave up trying to concentrate, got up and went to the sideboard for a glass of wine; he needed to get centered and calmed, and a little less sensitive, and he wasn't going to be able to do it on his own. The only wine left was a white, and it was a bit dry for his taste, but it did accomplish what he wanted it to. With just that hint of alcohol inside him, he finally managed to relax and get *into* the blasted book.

He got so far into it, in fact, that when the first simultaneous blast of wind and thunder came, he nearly jumped off of the couch.

Half the candles—the ones not sheltered in glass chimney-lamps—blew out. Wind whipped through the suite, sending curtains flying and carrying with it a welcome chill and the scent of rain. The shutters in Mardic's and Donni's room banged monotonously against the walls; not hard enough to shatter the glass yet, but it was only a matter of time. He dropped the book and got up to head for their door just as Vanyel stumbled in through the corridor door and into the brightness of the common room.

The boy stood as frozen as a statue, blinking owlishly at the light. Tylendel's stomach gave a little lurch; Vanyel looked like death.

It was bad enough that the boy was light-complected; bad enough that he was wearing stark black tonight, which only accentuated his fair skin. But his face had *no* color at the moment; it was so white it was almost transparent. His eyes looked sunken, and his expression was of someone who has seen, but been denied, the Havens.

"Vanyel—" Tylendel said—whispered, really—his voice barely audible above the banging shutter and the sound of the storm. He cleared his throat and tried again. "Vanyel, I didn't expect you back so—uh—soon. Is something wrong?"

For one moment—for one precious moment—Tylendel thought he had him; he was sure that the boy was going to open up to him. His eyes begged for pity; his expression, so hungry and haunted, nearly cracked Tylendel's own calm. The trainee made a tentative step toward him—

It was the wrong move; he knew that immediately. Vanyel's face shut-tered and assumed his habitual expression of flippant arrogance. "Wrong?" he said, with false gaiety. "Bright Lady, no, of course there's nothing wrong! Some of the Bards just came over from their Collegium and started an im-promptu contest; it got so damned hot in the Great Hall with all those people crowded in that I gave up—"

Just then the shutters in both the lifebonded's room *and* Savil's crashed against the walls with such force that it was a wonder that the windows *didn't* shatter.

"Havens!" Vanyel yelped. "She'll kill us!" and dove for Savil's room. Tylendel dashed into the other, mentally cursing his own clumsiness, and cursing himself for letting *his* reaction to the boy cloud his reading of him.

By the time he got everything secured and returned to the common room, Vanyel had retreated into his *own* room and the door was firmly and irrevocably shut.

"Vanyel," the trainee said, softly, his eyes dark with compassion and understanding, "Is something wrong?"

"I—" Vanyel began, then closed his eyes as a fit of trembling hit him. "I—the music—I—"

Suddenly Tylendel was beside him, holding him, quieting his shivering. "It's all right," he murmured into Vanyel's ear, his breath warm and like a caress in his hair. "It's all right, I understand."

Vanyel stood as unmoving as a dead stick, hardly daring to breathe, afraid to open his eyes. Tylendel stroked his hair, the back of his neck, his hands warm and light— and Vanyel thought his heart was going to pound itself to pieces. "I understand," he repeated. "I know what it's like to want something, and know you'll never have it."

"You—do?" Vanyel faltered.

Tylendel chuckled. It was a warm, rich sound.

And his fingers traced the line of Vanyel's spine, slowly, sensuously. Vanyel started to relax in Tylendel's arms—and his eyes popped open in startlement when his own hands at Tylendel's chest encountered, not cloth, but skin.

The trainee was starkly, gloriously nude.

"Then again," Tylendel whispered, looking deeply into Vanyel's eyes. "Maybe I will get it."

Vanyel made a strangling noise, wrenched himself away, and fled into darkness, into cold—

Into the middle of his old dream.

First there had been the snow-plain, then as he walked across it, the teeth of ice had begun poking their way up through the granular snow. They'd grown higher as he walked, but what he hadn't known was that they were growing behind him as well. Now he was trapped inside a ring of them. Trapped inside walls of ice, smoother than the smoothest glass, colder than the coldest winter. He couldn't break out; he pounded on them until his arms were leaden, to no effect. Everywhere he looked—ice, snow, nothing alive, nothing but white and pale blue and silver. Even the sky was white. And he was so alone—so terribly alone.

Nothing soft, nothing comforting. Nothing welcoming. Only the ice, only the unyielding, unmoving ice and the white, grainy snow.

He was cold. So appallingly cold—so frozen that he ached all over.

He had to get out.

Hoping to climb over the barrier, he reached for the top of one of the ice-walls, and pulled back his hands as pain stabbed through them. He stared at them stupidly. His palms were slashed nearly to the bone, and blood oozed sluggishly from the cuts to pool at his feet.

There was blood on the snow; red blood—but as he stared at it in numb fascination, it turned blue.

Then his hands began to burn with the cold, yet fiery pain of the wounds. He gasped, and tears blurred his vision; he wanted to scream, but could only moan. Gods, it hurt, *he'd give anything to make it stop hurting!*

Suddenly, the pain did *stop; his hands went numb. His eyes cleared and he looked down at his injured hands again—and saw to his horror that the slashes had frozen over and his hands were turning to ice; blue, and shiny, and utterly without feeling. Even as he gazed at them, the ice crept farther up; over his wrists, crawling up his forearms—and he cried out—*

Then he wasn't there anymore, he was somewhere else. It was dark, but he could see; by the lightning, by a strange blue glow about him. Lightning flickered overhead, and seemed to be controlled by what he did or thought; he was standing on a mound of snow in the center of a very narrow valley. To either side of him were walls of ice that towered over his head, reaching to the night sky in sheer, crystalline perfection. Behind him—there was nothing—somehow he knew this. But before him—

"Vanyel!"

Before him an army; an army of mindless monsters—creatures with only one goal. To get past him. Already he was wounded; he twisted to direct the lightning to lash into their ranks, and felt pain lancing down his right side, felt the hot blood trickling down his leg into his boot and freezing there. There were too many of them. He was doomed. He gasped and wept at the horrible pain in his side, and knew that he was dying. Dying alone. So appallingly alone—

"Vanyel!"

He struggled up out of the canyon of ice, out of the depth of sleep; shaken out of the nightmare by hot, almost scorching hands on his shoulders and a commanding voice in his ears.

He blinked; feeling things, and not connecting them. His eyes hurt; he'd been crying. His hair, his pillow were soggy with tears, and he was still so cold—too cold even to shiver. That was why Tylendel's hands on his bare shoulders felt so hot.

"Vanyel—" Tylendel's eyes were a soft sable in the light of the tiny bedside candle; like dark windows on the night, windows that somehow reflected concern. His hands felt like branding irons on Vanyel's skin. "Gods, Vanyel, you're like ice!"

As he tried to sit up, Vanyel realized that he was still leaking tears.

As soon as he started moving he began shivering so hard he couldn't speak. "I—" he said, and could get nothing more out.

Tylendel snagged his robe from the foot of the bed without even looking around, and wrapped it about his naked shoulders. It wasn't enough. Vanyel shook with tremors he could not stop, and the robe wasn't doing anything to warm him.

"Vanyel," Tylendel began, then simply wrapped his arms around Vanyel and held him.

Vanyel resisted—tried to pull away.

He blinked.

The snow-plain stretched all around him, empty—but not asking anything of him. Cold, but not a threat. But lonely, lonely—oh, gods, how empty—

But not asking, not hurting—

He blinked again, and Tylendel was still there, still staring into his eyes with an openness and a concern he could not doubt.

"Go away!" he gasped, waiting for pain, waiting to be laughed at.

"Why?" Tylendel asked, quietly. "I want to help you."

He was turning to ice; soon there would be no feeling and nothing to feel—and he would be trapped.

Tylendel took advantage of his distraction to get his arms around him. "Van, I wouldn't hurt you. I *couldn't* hurt you."

He closed his eyes and gasped for breath, his chest tight and hurting.
—*oh, gods—I want this—*

"I'm just trying to get you warm again," Tylendel said with a hint of
impatience. "That's *all*. Relax, will you?"

He *did* relax; he couldn't maintain his indifference—and to his shame,
began crying again—and he couldn't stop the tears any more than he could
the shivering.

But not only did Tylendel not seem to mind—

"Come on, Vanyel," he soothed, pulling him into a comfortable position
on his shoulder, supporting him like a little child. "It's all right, I told you
I won't hurt you. I wouldn't *ever* hurt you. Cry yourself out, it's just you and
me, and I'll never tell anyone. On my honor. Absolutely on my honor."

It was already too late to save his battered dignity anyway—

Vanyel surrendered appearance, self-respect, everything. He sagged
against Tylendel's shoulder, burying his face in Tylendel's soft, worn, blue
robe. He let the last of his pride dissolve, releasing all the tears he'd been
keeping behind his walls of indifference and arrogance. Soon he was crying
so hard he couldn't even think, just cling to Tylendel's shoulders and sob.
He didn't really hear what Tylendel was saying, only the tone of his voice
registered in his sleep-mazed grief; comforting, compassionate, caring.

He cried his eyes sore and dry; he cried until his nose felt swollen to the
size of an apple. All the time he shivered with the terrible cold that seemed
to have become one with his very bones; shivered until the bed shook.

Finally there just weren't any tears left—and he wasn't shivering anymore, he was warm—and more than warm; protected. And completely
exhausted. Tylendel held him as carefully as if he was made of spun glass and
would shatter at a breath; just held him. That was all.

It was enough. It was more than he ever remembered having. He wished
it could last forever.

—*may the gods help me. I've always wanted this—*

"Done?" Tylendel asked, very quietly, a good while after the last of the
sobs and the tremors had finished shaking his body.

He nodded, reluctantly, and felt the arms holding him relax. He sat up
again, and Tylendel cupped both his hands around his face, turning him
into the light. He winced away from it, knowing what he must look like;
the trainee chuckled, but it had a kindly, not a mocking, sound.

"You're a mess, peacock," he said, somehow making the words a joke to be shared between them. Vanyel smiled, tentatively, and Tylendel dabbed at his eyes with the corner of the sheet.

"Do you have so common a thing as a handkerchief around here?" he asked, quite casually. Vanyel nodded, and fumbled at the drawer of the bed-side table until Tylendel patted his hand away and got the square of linen out of it himself.

"Here," he gave it to Vanyel, then settled back a little. "I couldn't sleep; got up to get some wine and heard you. Do this often?"

Vanyel blew his nose, and looked up at the older boy through half-swollen eyes. "Often enough," he confessed.

"Nightmare?"

He nodded, and looked down at his hands.

"Know why?"

"No," he whispered. But he did. He did. It was hearing the Bards—hearing what he'd never, ever have—and then encountering Tylendel and knowing—

Gods.

"Want to tell me about it?"

He dared another glance at the trainee; the quiet face of the older boy was not easy to read, but there were no signs of deception there that Vanyel could see.

But—

"You'll laugh at me," he said, ready to pull away again.

"No. On my honor. Van, *I don't lie*. I won't laugh at you, and nothing you tell me will go outside this room unless you want it to."

Vanyel shivered again, and without any warning at all, the words came spilling out.

"It's—ice," he said, sniffing, studying his hands and the handkerchief he had twisted up in them. "It's all around me; I'm trapped, I can't get out, and I'm so cold—so cold. Then I cut myself, and *I* start to turn into ice. Then—sometimes, like tonight—I'm somewhere else, and I'm fighting these things, and I know I'm going to die. And the worst of it isn't the pain, or the dying—it's that—that—" He faltered. "—I'm—all alone. So totally alone—"

It sounded so banal, so incredibly foolish, just put into words like that. Especially when he didn't, *couldn't*, tell Tylendel the rest, the part about *him*. He looked up, expecting to see mockery in the older boy's face—and froze, seeing nothing of the kind.

"Van, I think I know what you mean," Tylendel said slowly. "There are times when—when being alone is a hurt that's worse than dying. When it's easier to die than to be alone. Aren't there?"

Vanyel blinked, caught without words.

Tylendel's voice was so soft he might well have been speaking to himself. "Sometimes, maybe it's better to have had someone and lost them than to have never had anyone—"

Then Tylendel's eyes focused for a moment on Vanyel. And Vanyel's heart spasmed at the flash of emotion he saw. A longing he'd not *ever* dreamed to see there. Directed at him.

—oh—gods. I never—I thought—he can't—

He does. He is. Father will—

I don't care!

He snatched at what was proffered before it could be taken away.

"Vanyel—" the blond began.

"'Lendel—" Vanyel interrupted, urgently, daring the nickname he'd heard his aunt use. "Stay with me—please. Please." His words tumbled over one another as he hurried to get them out before Tylendel could interrupt; he caught hold of the older boy's wrist. "The ice is still there, I *know* it is, it's inside me and it's freezing me from the inside out—it's killing my—feelings. I think it's killing me. Please, please, don't leave me alone with it—"

"You *don't* know what you're asking," Tylendel said, almost angrily, pulling his hand out of Vanyel's, his eyes no longer readable. "You can't know. You don't know what *I* am."

"But I *do*," Vanyel protested desperately. "I do, the girls tell me things to get my attention—they told me you're—uh—*shay'a'chern*, they said. That you don't sleep with girls; that you—" He felt himself blush, the rush of blood almost painful, his cheeks were so sore from crying.

"Then *dammit*, Vanyel, what do you think I'm made of?" Tylendel cried harshly, his face twisted and his eyes reflecting internal pain. "What do you think I am? Marble? You're *beautiful*, you're bright, you're everything I'd ever ask for—you think I can stay here and not want you? Good gods, I *won't* take advantage of an innocent, but what you're asking of me would try the control of a saint!"

"You don't understand. I *know* what I'm asking," Vanyel replied, catching his wrist again before he could get up and stalk off into the dark. "I *do* know."

Tylendel shook his head violently and looked away.

"'Lendel—look at me," Vanyel pleaded, pouring his heart out in a confession he'd never have dared to make before this. "Listen—I don't like girls either. I'm *not* an innocent, I know what I want, 'Lendel, please, listen—I've been—I've *bedded* enough of them to know that they don't do anything for me. It's—about as mechanical as dancing, or eating. They just don't *mean* anything to me."

Tylendel stopped trying to pull away, and turned a face to Vanyel that was so full of dumbfounded surprise that the younger boy had to fight hysterical laughter.

"And I do? You—" Tylendel began, then his face hardened. "Don't play with me, Vanyel. Don't toy with me. I've had that game played on me once already—and I don't want to hear you crying to Savil in the morning that I seduced you."

Vanyel bit his lip, and looked directly into Tylendel's eyes, pleadingly. "I'm not playing, 'Lendel. Please." He felt his eyes sting, and this time didn't try to hide the two tears that spilled down his raw cheeks. "I—I've been thinking about this for a long while. Almost since I got here, and they—told me about you. And you never laughed at me. You—were—kind to me. You kept being kind to me even when I was pretty rude. It meant a lot to me. And I didn't know how to thank you. I—started feeling—things around you. I was scared. I didn't dare let you guess. I didn't want to admit what I wanted; now I do."

The older boy looked at him sideways. "Which is?"

Vanyel gulped. "I want to be with you, 'Lendel. And if you go—I won't have any choice but the ice—"

Once again Tylendel cupped his face between his strong hands, and gently brushed the tears away with hesitant fingers. He stared deeply into Vanyel's eyes for so long, and so searchingly, that Vanyel thought he surely must be reading right down to the depths of his soul. Vanyel held his gaze, and tried to make his own eyes say that he meant every word he'd said. Tylendel finally nodded, once, slowly.

Then he reached out, quite deliberately, and snuffed the candle before taking Vanyel back into his arms.

It was very dark; no light outside, no sound but the rain falling. After a moment, Tylendel chuckled with what sounded like surprise, and said softly into Vanyel's ear, "I'm beginning to wonder just who's taking advantage of who, here."

Then, a bit later, another chuckle to tell Vanyel that he was teasing. "Move over, you selfish little peacock, I'm about to freeze to death."

Then no words at all.

Then again, they didn't need words.

The halls were totally deserted, chill, and lit by lamps that were slowly flickering out as they used up the last of the night's oil. Savil's slow, weary footsteps echoed before and behind her without disturbing so much as a spider. At one point on the long walk back to her quarters from the Council Chamber, Savil wasn't entirely certain she was going to make it. She was so damned tired she was about ready to give up and lie down in the middle of the cold hall.

I'm getting too old for this, she told herself. *No more younglings after this lot. I can't take the emotional ups and downs. And I truly cannot take these all-night sessions with a lot of stubborn old goats.*

She grinned a little ironically at herself.

Of which I am one of the most stubborn. But gods—hours like this are for the young. I hurt. And I think I'm going to beg off 'Lendel's weather working lesson today, else my bones are going to ache more. Gods bless—the door at last.

She pushed open the door to the suite; Tylendel had left a night-candle burning, but it, too, was guttering. No matter, there was the pearly gray light of an overcast dawn creeping in through the windows of her room, the lifebonded's, and Tylendel's—

She froze. Tylendel's bed was unoccupied; she could see it through the door.

Don't panic, old woman— she cautioned herself. *Just do a bit of a trace, first—you've shared magic; you've got the line to his mind. See where it leads.*

She found the little energy-link that said *Tylendel* and followed it back to where Tylendel himself was. It wasn't very far. Still in the suite, in fact. In Vanyel's room.

Vanyel's room?

Her first reaction was to fling the door open and demand to know what was going on. Her second was to chuckle; with aura overtones like *that* she bloody well *knew* what was going on!

But—*Vanyel?* Gods have mercy. No sign he was *shay'a'chern*—

Then again, given Withen's prejudices, he *might* have feared for a long time that the boy was fey. And Withen's answer to that fear would have been—

Exactly what he'd been doing. Keeping the boy sheltered at home rather than fostering him out and trying to shove him in the direction Withen wanted. Trying to force the boy into a mold he was totally unsuited for. And he also might well have protected the boy from even the *idea* that same-sex pairings were possible. So the boy himself wouldn't have known what he was—until he first found out about 'Lendel.

Which answered a great many questions indeed. The question now was—what had led to this, and what was it going to mean for the future?

She took a deep breath of the chilly, damp air, and groped her way back to her own room. No use rushing things; questioning could be done just as easily with herself lying in her own warm bed. Easier, actually, given how she felt.

She stripped herself down to the skin, promised her weary bones a bath *later*, and dragged on a bedgown before crawling into the blankets. The *warm* blankets, and she blessed Tylendel's thoughtfulness for putting the warming spell on her bed before he'd taken to his own. Or—whatever.

She settled herself comfortably, and reached out a thin tendril of Mind-speech in Private-mode. If the imp was awake—

He was.

:*Savil?*: came the sleep-blurred thought, dense with a feeling of content-ment. :*Thought I heard you come in. Found me, hmm?*:

:*Aye. And I have a pile of questions.*: She shifted herself until her left shoul-der stopped aching quite so much. :*The only important one is, how did you talk him into it?*:

:*I didn't. It was all Van's idea.*:

She almost lost the Mindspeech thread with her start of surprise, and had to grope after it. :*Sounds like I really missed something! What in the name of the Havens* happened *last night?*:

:*Too much to talk about now.*: There were overtones of mental and physical weariness to his Mind-voice. :*But he's going to be all right, Savil. We did more than—just the physical. I think we must have talked for hours, before and after. He handed me the key to himself, and he wanted* me *to have it.*:

She raised a sardonic mental eyebrow. :*'Lendel—I don't want to drench you with cold water, but may I remind you of what happened the* last *time morning arrived with you in someone else's bed?*:

:*It's all right, Savil, it really is this time.*: A feeling of faint surprise. :*You know, you're always teasing me about falling in love—but—I don't know, this feels different.*:

Savil snorted. :*Right; it always does. No, don't let an old cynic disturb you.*:

:*Teacher—I think this is going to be something more than just a one-time; I think he needs me.*:

:Oh, Havens. All right, if that's the way you think it's going—just let me know in the morning if you plan to move in with him. Or him with you, though his is the better chamber. We could use a spare for guests.:

Flavor of laughter like crisp apples. :You just want my room back.:

:If you aren't using it—seriously, 'Lendel, this is important. I want to have a long talk with him when I get up, and I want you there. He really should know what he's letting himself in for as shay'a'chern. I don't think we should let that get out, and I'll Mindspeak with you on that before we talk with him. Hmm—cancel your classes this morning; I'm too tired, and I have the feeling you weren't exactly early to sleep.:

Another apple-feeling of laughter, and the mind-link faded. And she let exhaustion pull her down into a slumber that she really didn't want, not anymore.

One last thought before sleep came.

Great good gods, what am I going to tell Withen?

Tylendel raised himself up on his elbow and looked down at the slumbering boy beside him. Rest had repaired the damages that several hours of soul-wrenching weeping had done to Vanyel's face; relaxed, and with all his barriers down, he looked as innocent as an unawakened child—

—which he was, as Tylendel now knew quite intimately, not. Not in any way; except, perhaps, his vulnerability.

"Van," he whispered, touching his shoulder, and feeling just a faint chill of apprehension despite his words to his mentor, "can you wake up a little?"

Vanyel stirred, wrinkled his nose, and half-opened his eyes. And when he saw who was beside him, he smiled with heart-stopping sweetness. With all his masks gone, he was as charming as he was beautiful.

"Hmm?" he said, blinking, as Tylendel felt a surge of relief and gratitude that this was not going to be a repeat of the infamous Nevis affair.

"Want a roommate?"

"You—why?"

He grinned; he knew now that you had to show Van that something was a joke, or often he'd taken it seriously. "Savil seems to want my room back—for guests, she says. Besides, I like your company."

Vanyel's reply, though not verbal, was a definite and unmistakable affirmative.

*　　*　　*

"We have," Savil said dryly, "several problems, here."

She'd had that Mindspeech conference with Tylendel as she'd gotten herself put together for the day. Nice thing, Mindspeech; let you cover more than one thing at once. And after giving it thorough consideration while she bathed, she decided to have her "little talk" with Vanyel in *his* room. With any luck, he'd feel less threatened there.

She did usurp the most comfortable chair in the room, though. *The privilege of age*, she told herself, waiting for the two young men to settle themselves. Without seeming to consult about it, Tylendel sat on the edge of the bed, and Vanyel arranged himself cross-legged on the floor at his feet.

And the flexibility of youth. Would that I could still do that! The body language gave her spirits a lift, though; the way Vanyel had positioned himself was interesting. At Tylendel's feet, below both her head and his lover's. That could well show he'd given up that pose of arrogant superiority. Very interesting.

I wonder if having a steady lover at his side might well give 'Lendel something to think about besides his twin and that damned feud. On the other hand—this lad's been so affection-starved—this could be another sort of trouble.

"Yes, indeed, we have quite a few little problems here," she repeated.

Tylendel nodded at her words; Vanyel looked puzzled, at first, then thoughtful.

"The first problem and the one that's going to tie in to all the others, Vanyel, is your father." She paused, and Vanyel bit his lip. "I'm sure that you realize that if he finds out about this, he is going to react badly."

Vanyel coughed, and bowed his head, hiding his face for a moment. When he looked back up, he was wearing a weary, ironic half-smile, a smile that had as much pain in it as humor. It was, far and away, the most open expression Savil had ever seen him wear.

" 'Badly' is something of an understatement, Aunt," he replied, rubbing his temple with one finger. "He'll—gods, I can't predict what he'll do, but he'll be in a rage, that's for certain."

"He'll pull you home, Van," Tylendel said in a completely flat voice. "And he can do it; you're not of age, you aren't Chosen, and you aren't in Bardic."

"And *I* can't protect you," Savil sighed, wishing that she could. "I can stall him off for a while, seeing as he officially turned guardianship of you over to me, but it won't last more than a couple of months. Then—well, I'll give you my educated guess as to what Withen will do. I *think* he'll put you under house arrest long enough for everybody to forget about you, then find himself a compliant priest and ship you off to a temple. Probably one *far* away, with very strict rules about outside contact. There are, I'm sorry to say, several sects who hold that *shay'a'chern* are tainted. They'd be only too happy to 'purify' you for Withen and Withen's gold. And under the laws of this kingdom, none of us could save you from them."

Vanyel nodded; by the startled agreement in his eyes, Savil reckoned that this was a speculation he'd entertained before this, although for different causes. "So is there *anything* I can do?" he asked quietly.

"Obviously," she said, "Or I wouldn't be talking to you now. But you aren't going to like the solution to your problem. It's pretty heartbreakingly simple. Outside of this room, Vanyel, *nothing is to change.*"

"But—" He twisted his head around to see what Tylendel thought about this, only to find that his lover was nodding, in complete agreement with her.

"Savil's right, Van," Tylendel said sadly.

"But—" Vanyel protested, holding out one hand toward him in entreaty, then turning the same pleading eyes on Savil when Tylendel shook his head.

"Mardic and Donni are discreet, and I'd trust Margret to keep what she knows behind her teeth even under torture, but if you want to *stay* here, Vanyel, you won't say or do anything to betray your relationship to 'Lendel. The moment people start to talk, it'll get back to your father."

"The quickest way to make them talk, love," Tylendel said in what was almost a whisper, "is to change. Is to even be *friendlier* to me than you have been. You told me the girls told you I was a pervert." Vanyel's eyes widened at Tylendel's directness. "It can't have escaped your notice how they sniggered and giggled about it, and they were being *polite.* My preferences are not generally socially acceptable. There are only two reasons why I have as little trouble as I do. The first is that I'm a Herald-trainee, and Heralds are allowed a bit more license than ordinary mortals. And my patron is Savil. She just happens to outrank everybody in the Circle except the Queen's Own."

"And the other reason?" Vanyel said in a very subdued voice.

What stretched Tylendel's mouth was something less than a smile. "The fact that I took a couple of the worst offenders on and kept knocking them down until they didn't get up."

"Oh."

Tylendel caught up one of his hands in both of his own. "I *know* you want everyone to know about us. I can't tell you how much that means to me. But it will mean a lot more to me to know you were going to be able to *stay* with me."

"And to do that, young Vanyel," Savil said, intruding into the intense interaction between them, "you are going to have to begin a performance a Master Player couldn't equal. 'Lendel and I have been talking about you this afternoon."

From the complete astonishment on his face, Savil could tell that he *hadn't* guessed they'd been in conference via Mindspeech. For that matter, it might be that he didn't know they both had that Gift.

"We share the Mindspeech Gift, lad, and it's damned useful at times like this. He's told me some of what you told him, and it rather changed my mind about you. But I will not lie to you; I'm going to help you because *he* wants it, because he wants you here. So now I'm going to *order* you; outside of this suite you are to be the same arrogant little bastard that arrived here. And if you can manage to be *slightly* rude to 'Lendel, that's even better. And in return, I'll make this suite a little sanctuary for the two of you. Is it a bargain?"

Vanyel, who had gone rather pale, gulped, and nodded.

Savil smiled for the first time since she'd begun this conference.

"That's a good lad. If you're half of what 'Lendel claims for you, I'm going to come to like you a great deal, and I'm sorry for the treatment you've had from your father. I'll tell you that he *isn't* the same person I knew when I was Chosen. He's gone stiff and stubborn, and altogether hidebound. Maybe it's age; maybe it's that a lot of his old friends have taken the Long Walk and he's seeing Death looking for him, too. Maybe it's that priest he's gotten tied up with—I just don't know." She coughed. "Well, that's not to the point; what *is* to the point is that you'll only have to keep up this charade until you're eighteen; you'll be your own man then, and can do what you please. And I'll see to it that 'Lendel begins having trouble with his Mage-lessons." She winked, and Tylendel chortled. "I think we can keep him out of Whites until you're of age. After that," *if this love affair lasts that long,* "you'll have to make your decisions on your own. Fair enough?"

"More than fair, Aunt Savil." Vanyel looked very subdued, and quite unlike the boy that had faced her something like a month ago. She couldn't quite pinpoint why.

:'Lendel, what is it about him?: she Mindspoke, letting her puzzlement drift over.

:No masks,: came the immediate answer. *:This is the real Vanyel, dearheart. The one nobody but me—and maybe his sister—has seen. Now see why I love him?:*

The last thought stopped her cold. *:Are you that sure, ke'chara? Are you really that sure?:*

His eyes caught hers over Vanyel's head; caught and held them. *:I'm that sure.:*

:And him?:

:I don't know; but he was willing to defy his father for me, and I think that says something.:

She closed her own eyes against that burning, intense gaze. *:Then may the gods help and guard you.:*

She turned her attention back to Vanyel, and quickly. He was still looking toward Tylendel, and the very same look was in his eyes—and a vulnerability and apprehension that cut at her heart.

"I'll help you all I can, son," she said quietly. "I'll help you all I can."

CHAPTER 6

"**D**ON'T GO YET," Tylendel said abruptly, as Vanyel picked himself up off the floor. Vanyel gave him a look of uncertainty. He was still too new to this—being open. He was still waiting for blows that never came.

But Tylendel seemed to know that.

"It's all right, Van," he said softly. "It's really all right. I have a good reason."

"I've got a lesson," he protested. "History, and I'm still behind the other three."

Tylendel made a wry face. "You're a law unto yourself, remember? At least that's what you're supposed to be acting like. You skipped your lessons this morning, skip the rest of them today; tell 'em you were sick. Tell 'em the storm last night gave you a headache."

"But—"

"It's important," Tylendel coaxed. "Really, it is. More important than that history lesson. If you're behind, I'll coach you. Please?"

It didn't take much encouragement from Tylendel to get him to do what he already *wanted* to do; lessons were hardly as attractive as more of Tylendel's company. *Here* he wasn't going to be hurt. Here—someone cared for him. It was as heady as a little too much wine, only without the hangover.

Vanyel closed the door to his room, then turned an expectant face toward his lover, poised with one hand still on the latch.

Tylendel stretched lazily, reaching for the ceiling with his head tilted back. Then he dropped his arms, rose from his seat on the bed, and walked over to put his hand behind Vanyel's shoulder.

"There's somebody I want you to meet," he said, gently pushing Vanyel in the direction of the room's outside door.

"But—" Vanyel protested weakly. "I thought—"

"You're awfully fond of that word 'but,' love," Tylendel chuckled. "What does it take to get you to say something else?"

He opened the door, still without enlightening Vanyel as to the reason why he was going to introduce Vanyel to someone after Savil had just got done telling them both that they were to keep the relationship a secret—

—and Tylendel had agreed with her.

Vanyel started to protest again, realized that the only thing he could think of to say was "but," and subsided, as Tylendel guided him out the door to the gardens beyond.

"You see that bridge?" Tylendel pointed northward to the first of the two bridges crossing the Terilee River on the Palace grounds. "And that stand of pines on the other side?"

Vanyel nodded; it was quite a healthy grove, in fact, and the trees extended a good distance back into the Field. They were tall, very thick, and a deep green that was almost black, with huge branches that drooped beneath their own weight until they touched the ground.

"You count to fifty after you see me go in there, then you follow," Tylendel ordered. "In case anybody happens to come by, though, or looks out a window, you'd better try your hand at acting the arrogant little prig."

Vanyel nodded again; completely mystified, but willing to go along with about anything that Tylendel wanted. He posed himself carefully, leaning against the doorframe with his arms crossed over his chest, attempting to look as if he were simply idling about in the gardens, while Tylendel sauntered off.

This is going to be harder than it was before, he thought somberly, trying to look anywhere except after Tylendel. *I didn't have anything to lose, before. Now I have everything to lose if I slip.* He closed his eyes, and turned his face up to the sun, as if he were savoring the warmth. *But if I don't slip—oh, gods, whichever one of you is responsible for this—it's worth anything. I swear, it's worth anything you ask of me!*

He chanced a sideways glance across the river; Tylendel was only just reaching the pine grove. He looked away, strolled over to a stand of daylilies, admired them for a moment, then glanced across the river again. Tylendel's blond hair gleamed against the dark boughs like a tangled skein of spun sunlight, then vanished as the branches closed behind him.

Vanyel transferred his admiration to a bed of rose vines, languidly bending to inhale their perfume, all the while counting to the requisite fifty. He had no sooner reached the required number, though, when a giggling flock of his admirers rounded a hedge, saw him, and altered their course to intersect with his.

Oh, no! he thought, dismayed, and looked surreptitiously about for an escape route, but saw no way to avoid them. Sighing, he resigned himself to the inevitable, and waited for their arrival.

"*Vanyel*, what are you doing out here?" asked slim, barely-adolescent Jillian, batting her sandy lashes at him. "Aren't you supposed to be at lessons?"

Vanyel covered a wince. *It would* have *to be Jillian. No common sense, and the moral fiber of a hound in heat. And after me with all the dedication you'd see in a hawk stooping on a pigeon. Lord. I hope her father marries her* off *quick, or she'll be sleeping her way around the Court before long.*

But he smiled at her, a smile with a calculated amount of pain in it. "A rotten headache, pretty one. It took me last night when the storm came in, and I *cannot* be rid of it. I tried sleeping in, but—" He shrugged. "My aunt *suggested* I take a long walk."

The entire covey giggled in near-unison. "Suggested with a stick, I'll bet," dark Kertire said sardonically, squinting into the sunlight. "Sour Savil. Well, we'll walk with *you* then, and keep you from being bored."

Vanyel bit his lip in vexation and thought quickly. "She *suggested* my course, as well," he told them, grimacing. "To the end of Companion's Field and back. And I have no doubt she's watching from her window."

He pouted at them. "Much as I would adore your company, my pretties, I rather doubt those slippers you're wearing are equal to a hike across a field full of—er—"

"Horseturds," said Jesalis inelegantly, wrinkling her nose and tossing her blond curls over her shoulder. "Bother. No, you're right," she continued, sticking her foot out a little, and surveying the embroidered rose-satin slipper on it with regret. "I *just* finished the embroidery on these and got them back from the cobbler; I don't want them spoiled, and they would be before we'd gotten half across." The others murmured similar sentiments as their faces fell. "We're *never* going to forgive you for deserting us, Vanyel."

"Now *that's* unfair," he exclaimed, assuming a crushed expression. "Blaming me for the orders of my crotchety old aunt!" He rolled his eyes mournfully at them.

Jesalis giggled. "We'll only forgive you if you promise to make it up to us tonight after dinner."

"Tonight?" he asked, pained by the idea of spending the evening with them instead of with Tylendel as they'd planned this morning.

They mistook his expression for headache. "Well, not if you still aren't feeling well," Jesalis amended.

"After a tramp across a perilous obstacle course like *that*," he gestured flamboyantly at the Field across the river, "I much doubt I'm going to be feeling *better.*"

"Well—"

"A bargain; if you'll forgive me, I'll come and play for you while you're doing finework tomorrow morning," he said, quite desperately, willing to promise them almost anything to avoid losing his evening, and recalling that they'd all been pestering him to play for them. Before it hadn't been possible; it would have hurt too much. Now, though—well, becoming—or not becoming—a Bard didn't seem all that important anymore. And consequently the thought of music didn't hurt anymore. Or not as much. Certainly it was a small price to pay for having his evening free.

"You will?" squealed Wendi, whose older sister was fostered with Vanyel's mother. "Really? Ratha told me you were as good as a Bard!"

"Well," he shrugged, then smirked. "I won't say I'm a bad hand at the lute. And I know a ballad and a dance or two."

"Done," said Jesalis. "A bargain."

"Bless you, my dear," he replied, with honest thankfulness. "I wouldn't be able to live without your forgiveness. Now, if you'll all excuse me—the sooner I get this nonsense over, the sooner I'll be able to go back to my bed."

They giggled and turned back, retracing their footsteps. While he watched them, they disappeared behind the hedge again, heading in the direction of the maze.

When they were safely out of sight, he trudged—to all appearances, *most unwillingly*—across the bridge and up a little rise, heading a little indirectly for the pine grove.

He went past it, walking through soft grasses that ranged from knee-high to closely cropped. And despite what he had told the girls, there were no "traps" lurking beneath the grass for the unwary. That *did* surprise him, a bit; he was no stranger to long walks across pastureland and the hazards thereof.

What on earth do the Companions do—drop it all in one corner? I suppose—the stories say they're as intelligent as a human. I suppose it's possible. Likely, really. They still eat grass, like horses, and who'd want to eat in the privy?

After first making certain that there was no one about to see him, Vanyel doubled back to the pine grove, and pushed aside the heavy, scratchy boughs. He almost had to force his way past them; the needles caught in his hair and clothing and the branches closed over his head almost immediately, shutting off most of the sunlight. A few feet inside the grove there was no direct light; he walked through a pine-scented twilight gloom, with boughs lacing together just barely above his head, and a thick carpet of dry needles at his feet. The needles crunched a little, releasing more piny scent, but otherwise his own footsteps were almost noiseless. Somewhere in the distance he could hear birds calling, but their songs seemed to be furlongs away. This place looked enormous now that he was inside it, much larger than it had appeared from outside; magical, almost mystical, and far removed from the bright green-and-gold Field just a few feet away.

This wasn't *the* Grove; that was a good deal farther into the Field—but this stand of ancient pines was giving Vanyel a pleasant, shivery sort of feeling, making him feel somehow more aware and alive.

"'Lendel?" he called softly into the blue-green quiet under the pine boughs, his voice muffled by the rows of straight, columnar trunks of shaggy ebony all about him. He turned, slowly, trying to see past the shadows, peering beneath the feathery branches.

"Right here," came the reply from slightly behind him, and a white shape ghosted up on his right, resolving itself into—

A Companion. The first that Vanyel had ever seen at close range. And Tylendel beside her, one hand on her snowy, arched neck.

"This is who I wanted you to meet. Van—this is Gala. She already knows about you, Van, she knew last night. We're mind-linked; I told her everything, and she wanted to see you right away."

Vanyel felt strange and awkward. Those sapphire eyes held an intelligence that was rather frightening, but the *form* was a horse. How in the *Havens* did you introduce yourself to a horse?

The silence grew; he stared into Gala's eyes, swallowed, and finally made the attempt.

"Hullo," he said, shyly, looking straight into those eyes and hoping to speak directly to the intelligence there, trying to ignore the fact that he was feeling more than a bit intimidated and foolish. "I—I hope you don't mind—"

Gala snorted, and Tylendel chuckled. "She says to tell you that she's been hoping I'd 'find a nice mate and give her a chance for a little peace' for a long time. She says it's altogether disconcerting to be sidling up to a hand-some stallion and find *me* in her head asking for bedtime stories!"

That was the *last* response he'd expected. Vanyel choked down a laugh. "'Lendel, you didn't!"

He nodded, as Gala tossed her own head. "I most certainly did, but *only* once. It was after Nevis, and I was," he faltered, and looked to the side, "rather lonely."

Vanyel touched the hand still resting on Gala's neck. "Not anymore, I hope."

Tylendel glanced from the hand resting lightly on his own to Vanyel's face, and half-smiled into his eyes. "No," he replied quietly. "Not anymore."

The quiet, the peace of the shadowed grove let them ignore everything except each other. Caught in the spell of that place and that pose, neither paid any attention to the passing of time—

Until Vanyel stumbled forward, propelled by a hard shove in the small of his back. Tylendel grabbed him to keep him from falling, both of them too startled to do more than emit rather undignified squeaks of surprise.

Gala danced backward a few steps, making sounds Vanyel would have been willing to stake his life were *laughter*. It was pretty obvious that she'd shoved him into Tylendel's arms with her nose.

Tylendel burst into gales of laughter; he clutched his stomach, nearly incoherent, and gasped for breath. Gala snorted and bobbed her head, and he doubled over again.

They're talking, Vanyel finally realized, as Tylendel wheezed. *Or—well, I guess she's teasing him. Gods above and below, all the stories are true! I wish I could hear them.*

His stomach fluttered uncertainly, and he tasted the sour bite of what could only be jealousy. Tylendel and Gala were sharing something he never could—something they'd had for years before he had come along. In this, he was, he would always be, the outsider. That realization condensed into a hard, cold lump in his throat, and besides the bitter taste of jealousy, he shivered in a sudden chill of loneliness. And just a touch of doubt.

He could really have about anyone he wanted, couldn't he? So why should he bother with me? How can I know if he means what he told me?

But before he could throw himself into a mire of depression he found he had his hands full, keeping the trainee from falling over while Tylendel struggled to breathe around his laughter and gasped like a stranded fish.

"You wouldn't!" Tylendel choked, as tears ran down his cheeks, and he pulled away from Vanyel to advance on his Companion in mock threat—the effect somewhat spoiled by the fact that he had to catch hold of a tree trunk as something she "said" made him bend over again with laughter. "Don't you dare! Gala, I'll do *no* such thing! You *rude* little bitch!"

Gala danced in place, her hooves making no sound at all in the thick carpet of needles. Her eyes sparkled with mischief, and Vanyel had, for one moment, a disconcerting double-vision image of the prancing Companion and an equally mischievous young woman of about Tylendel's age, laughing soundlessly at her Chosen.

This was worse than before. Vanyel felt *completely* alone—and left altogether on the outside.

Tylendel, not noticing his distress in the least, managed to get himself back under control, and wiped his eyes with the back of his hand as he straightened up.

He assumed a stern expression. "Now see here, you wicked young lady," he began, when she turned the tables on him by whickering and reaching out to nuzzle his cheek.

Vanyel saw his eyes soften as he folded immediately. "Oh, all right, I forgive you," he sighed in defeat, putting his arms around her neck and resting his cheek against hers. "But you had damn well *better* not—"

What it was Gala had "better not" do, Tylendel did not verbalize, nor was Vanyel entirely certain he wanted to know. He had the sneaking suspicion that it would be more than a little embarrassing.

Finally Gala shook herself free and shoved her Chosen in Vanyel's direction—a good bit more gently than she'd shoved the latter. And as if in apology, she paced forward and gave Vanyel a brief caress with her nose, rather like a soft kiss, before trotting off into the blue twilight under the pine boughs and out of sight among the trunks.

Silence followed her going.

"Well," Tylendel said, at last. "That was Gala."

Vanyel replied with the first thing that came into his head. "You really love her, don't you?"

"More than anything or anybody except you and Staven," Tylendel replied, almost apologetically. "I'm not sure I can explain it—" He bit off what he was saying, as if something in Vanyel's expression told him how depressed this meeting had made him.

"Van." He reached out hesitantly toward Vanyel's shoulder, then pulled his hand back, as if unsure whether to touch him. "I didn't bring you here to hurt you."

His very real distress forced Vanyel to pull himself together and try to *analyze* his feelings, instead of just wallow in them.

They were, to say the least, mixed. "I think I'm jealous," he said, after an uncomfortable pause. "I know it's stupid, she can't ever have you the way I do—but I can't ever share your thoughts the way she does."

"Huh. You wouldn't *want* to—" Tylendel began.

"But that's not the point," Vanyel interrupted, backing a few steps away. "I can't *know* that. You can tell me, but I can't ever *know* that, can I?" He wasn't sure what to do or what else to say, and so fell silent, turning away slightly and looking out past Tylendel into the shadows that had swallowed the Companion.

"Van." He felt Tylendel's hand fall lightly on his shoulder, and turned to look into his eyes. "Do you want to talk about this? Do you want to hear about what it's like for us, how it started? Do you think that will help you understand?"

Not trusting his voice, Vanyel nodded.

"This will take a while; pick a spot to sit. Unless you'd rather go back to the room?" Tylendel raised one eyebrow inquiringly.

"No, I like it here; it somehow seems more private." Vanyel faltered, and covered his hesitation by looking around for a good place. He finally chose a spot at the base of one of the bigger trees beside them, between two roots that were each as thick as his leg. He put his back against the trunk and slid down it to be cradled where the roots joined the tree.

Tylendel pondered his choice for a moment. "Well, I can only see two ways I can talk and look at you at the same time, and since I don't fancy shouting across the clearing—"

Before Vanyel had time to react, he'd stretched himself out along the ground and put his head in Vanyel's lap. "—*much* better," he sighed.

Vanyel froze.

"Van," Tylendel said quietly, closing his eyes. "*I won't hurt you.* Not for any reason. I like being near you, with you. I need to touch people; and I won't *ever* hurt you."

Vanyel relaxed a little.

"I like this grove, too, though hardly anyone else seems to. It feels like there's no time in here." He kept his eyes closed, and Vanyel saw a little pain-crease between his eyebrows.

He gets those headaches; he told me last night—I wonder—if he'd mind—if it would help—

Vanyel hesitated for a moment, then began massaging Tylendel's temples with gentle fingertips.

The trainee chuckled and Vanyel felt his shoulders relax. "You have about a hundred years to stop doing that," he said.

"You were going to tell me about you and Gala and being Chosen," Vanyel prompted, though the thought made him a little uncomfortable still. "I mean, you practically got my whole life story last night, and I still don't know that much about you."

"To begin at the beginning—I have a twin, Staven. He's the elder by about an hour. Nothing like me, by the way; he's taller, thinner, darker, and *much* handsomer. He's the leader, I'm the follower. We've had a primitive sort of mind-link ever since we were born. Things happened between us all the time. Things like—oh, I blacked out when he fell down the well; he acted like he'd broken his leg when I broke *mine*. We always knew what the other one was up to." He took a deep breath. "People knew all about *that*, but I had other Gifts, too, that I could use. Besides that mind-link, from the time I was about nine I had a touch of Thought-sensing for people besides Stav, and I had an ability to—make accidents happen to people I didn't like."

"Did that cause you problems?" Vanyel asked. "With other people, I mean. I should think they wouldn't much appreciate that last."

Tylendel shook his head slightly. "It didn't crop up often enough for people to really notice—or if they did, they were too afraid of my father to say anything about it. I didn't do it often, the accident-causing, I mean; it made me sick, after. Staven sometimes tried to egg me on, but it wasn't something I'd give in to him about." Tylendel paused, and bit his lip; his expression flickered briefly into one both dark and brooding before it lightened again. "It was the link between me and Staven that was the strongest and most predictable of the Gifts; it was pretty much limited to physical sensations, but once we figured out how to use it—"

Vanyel chuckled. "I bet you were unholy terrors."

Tylendel echoed the chuckle, and winked at him. "I wouldn't mind having a link like that with you."

Vanyel blushed, but answered with exactly what he was thinking. "I wouldn't mind either."

Tylendel's expression sobered. "Now comes the part where things got odd. Staven matured pretty early; by twelve he was as tall as most at fifteen, and all the girls were starting to flirt with him. And not just the girls, but grown women as well. I think he got all his share of female-attraction *and* mine, if you want to know the truth. That summer we were hosting a tournament and everything from goosegirls to visiting highborn were after him and he was acting like a young and randy rooster in a henyard. It all climaxed—if you'll forgive the expression—when one of the ladies who'd come to visit Mother dropped him a note that said in no uncertain terms that she'd be quite pleased to find him in her bed that night. Well—"

He closed his eyes for a moment, then looked up into Vanyel's face, his own expression ironic. "Understand. I was just as curious as any twelve-year-old about what Doing It was like. *I* said I'd cover for him if *he* let me—uh—eavesdrop."

"Something tells me it didn't go according to plan," Vanyel guessed.

"Dead in the black," Tylendel said soberly. "I was 'with' him for about as long as it took for things to get interesting. I had been feeling odd from the start, but I tried to ignore it, and concentrated on the link. Then things got—I don't know how to describe it, except that I started losing my grip on *me* and started merging with *him*. And the more I concentrated, the stranger it all got. It was a bit like those times I'd made accidents happen; the room faded in and out, I was in a kind of sickish fever, my heart was racing—and I couldn't tell what was 'me' and what was Stav. Under any other circumstances I think I would have quit and shut everything down, but I was stubborn and I was a little afraid of Stav making fun of me for diving out, after this was over. I kept holding to that link, figuring that if I could just weather it out, things would get fun again. Then—" He shook his head a bit, and his mouth twitched. "Just as things were about to come to the cusp for Staven, something—broke loose in me. I just barely remember the start of it, like I'd suddenly been dropped into a fire. I was in unbelievable pain. It felt like being in the middle of a lightning storm, and from the wreck I made of our room, that's exactly what I may have created. Something about what was going on, something about the link I had with Staven, triggered *all* my potential Gifts—explosively. I was unconscious for about a day, and when I woke up—"

He shuddered. "—nothing would ever be the same."

He closed his eyes, and Vanyel stroked his forehead. His mouth was tight, with lines of unhappiness at the corners. Far off in the distance, Vanyel could hear meadowswifts crying like the lost souls of ghost-children.

"So there I was," Tylendel continued, his voice thin and strained. "I had the Mage-Gift, Thought-sensing, Fetching, a bit of Empathy—none of it predictable, none of it controlled, and all of it likely to burst out at any moment." He took a look at Vanyel's face and read the puzzlement there. "Gods, I keep forgetting you aren't a trainee. Fetching—that means I can move things without touching them; Empathy means I can feel what someone else is feeling, which is why I knew when you had that nightmare last night. Thought-sensing—if someone isn't shielding, I can tell what they're thinking. The Mage-Gift is harder to explain, but it's what makes it possible for a Herald-Mage to do magic."

"You can tell what I'm thinking?" Vanyel said dubiously. He would have liked being able to share Tylendel's thoughts the way Gala did, but wasn't entirely sure he wanted the relationship to hold that kind of one-sided intimacy.

"I can, but I *won't*," Tylendel said, with such firmness that Vanyel couldn't find it in his heart to doubt him. "Even if it wasn't so unfair to you, it's counter to all the ethics that go with being a Herald. Basically I just use it to talk with Gala and Savil."

Vanyel nodded, comforted. "So you had all these—Gifts—sort of thrown at you, and no way to control them."

"Exactly," Tylendel said soberly. "And all this at twelve. It was *two years* before Gala came for me. If it hadn't been for Staven, I'd have gone mad."

"Why?" Vanyel whispered. "What was happening?"

"What *wasn't*? I'd drop into a fit—when I'd wake up again, I'd be in the middle of a fifty-foot circle of wreckage. That was the Mage-Gift and Fetching working together in a way Savil and I haven't been able to duplicate under control. Seems I have to go berserk."

He frowned, and reached up to rub his forehead between his eyebrows. "Staven was the only one who could get near me—who was *willing* to stay near me, in or out of a fit. They said I'd been taken by a demon. They said that because of what Staven and I had tried to share, I had been possessed. When I—started to show signs of being *shay'a'chern*, they said I was cursed, too."

"That's—that's stupid!" Vanyel cried indignantly.

"They still said it; if they'd dared, they'd have outcast me. But they didn't; Staven swore if they did he'd go with me, and *he* was the heir, the only possible heir with me acting the way I was. Mother wasn't capable of having any more children, Father wouldn't remarry, and he'd been completely faithful to her, so there weren't any bastards around. They didn't have a choice. They had to allow me to stay, but they didn't have to make it comfortable for me."

Vanyel thought with wonder that Tylendel's situation was actually worse than his own.

"They kept me pretty well isolated; even when I was fine they avoided me. But when everyone else abandoned me in one of my fits, *he* stayed, *he* took care of me, absolute and unshakable in the belief that I would never hurt him. Positive that, despite what was whispered, what had happened was *not* that I'd been possessed, but was something that would somehow be worked out."

Tylendel shuddered again, his eyes haunted, and plainly seeing another time and place. Vanyel, feeling *his* pain, put both his hands on his shoulders, trying to just be a comforting presence without disturbing him; Tylendel looked up at him, patted his hand, and half-smiled.

"You see? I think maybe that's why we understand each other. Well, finally Gala came—gods. I cannot ever tell you what it was like, looking into her eyes for the first time. It was—like souls touching. And the relief— knowing that I *wasn't* mad, that I *wasn't* demon-possessed—I went from hell to the Havens in the space of a heartbeat."

He sighed and seemed to sink into his own thoughts for a long while.

"What did she do?" Vanyel asked.

"For one thing, she put me under her shielding; got me controlled until we arrived here and Savil took me under her wing. That's more than enough reason to love her, even without the bond to her. She's my very best friend and the sister of my soul."

He reached up, and touched Vanyel's cheek. His hand was cool, almost cold. "But she'll never be what you are. Can you understand what I'm saying, love? I owe her my sanity, but in a lot of ways she's *more* than I am; I love her the way I love Savil or my mother—inferior to superior. *Not* brother to sister, or lover to lover; not *ever* as equals."

Vanyel put his own hand over the one touching his cheek, and held it, warming it in his own. "What am I, then?"

"You're my partner, my equal, my friend—and my love. Vanyel, I didn't say this in so many words last night—but I *do* love you."

Those words were *not* expected; certainly the implied level of commitment was not what Vanyel had expected. "But—" he stuttered, not sure whether what he was feeling was joy or fear.

"Van, I know we haven't known each other long, but I do *love* you,"

Tylendel said, ignoring the "but," holding Vanyel's gaze with his own. "And I love you because I love you, not because I owe you anything, or because some god somewhere decided I was going to be a Herald, or because you're a beloved teacher. I love you because you're Vanyel, and we belong together, and together we can stand back-to-back against anything."

Much to his confusion, Vanyel felt his eyes start burning. "I don't know—really know what to say," he replied awkwardly, blinking hard. "Except—'Lendel, I think after last night—I can't ever remember being this *happy*. I've never loved anyone, I don't know what it's like, but if—" He tried to say what he felt. "—if wanting to die for you is love—"

His eyes burned; he rubbed at them with his free hand, and tried to put his feelings into coherent words. He groped after his thoughts, totally awkward and altogether out of his depth, but he *needed* to articulate his bewildering emotions. He'd never felt so vulnerable and exposed in his life. "I'd do anything for you; I'd take the sneers, the pointed fingers—I wouldn't care, so long as they didn't take me away from you. If I could, I'd give you anything. I'd do anything I could to make *you* happy. And—I'll gladly share you with Gala."

"Havens, don't say that," Tylendel chuckled, though his voice sounded suspiciously thick and *his* eyes glistened in the shadows. "*She* wanted to 'eavesdrop,' you know. She'd take you up on that, the randy little bitch."

Vanyel's face flamed hotly, and he laughed, using his own embarrassment to get past that moment of complete vulnerability. "I *knew* she was saying something that would make me blush, I just *knew* it!"

"Well, she is *not* going to have her prurience satisfied, I promise you," Tylendel said firmly. "*I* am not going to share *you*, and that's that."

Vanyel entered their room through the garden door, blinking until his eyes adjusted to the semidarkness after the noontide sunlight of the gardens. He was carrying his lute by the neck in his right hand, and holding his left, wrapped in a handkerchief, curled against his chest.

Ye gods, I should have known better, he thought ruefully, as his left hand throbbed. *I am such a damned fool.*

"'Lendel?" he called into the outer room, racking the lute with care, still using only his right hand. "Are you out there?"

"Of course I am." Tylendel strolled in, a half-eaten slice of bread and cheese in one hand. "It's lunchtime, you know I'm always here when the food is!"

Vanyel began unwrapping his hand—slowly—

Tylendel stopped chewing, then tossed his lunch, forgotten, onto the table. "Gods, Van—what did you do to yourself? Sit!"

The ends of Vanyel's fingers were blistered, and the blisters had broken and were bleeding. The muscles of the hand were cramped so hard he couldn't have gotten his fingers uncurled to save his soul. He looked at the wreckage he'd made of his hand with a kind of pained disbelief.

Tylendel pushed him down onto the bed, and took the injured hand in both his own.

"I made a fool of myself, is what I did," Vanyel told him, regretfully. "I told the girls yesterday that if they'd leave me alone I'd play for them this morning. I forgot how long it's been since I played—and, well, I'll tell you the truth, I forgot I lost some feeling in those fingers when the arm got broken. I didn't even realize what I'd done to my finger-ends until *after* the muscles in my hand started to cramp."

"Stay right there." Tylendel went to the little chest at the foot of the bed that he'd moved into Vanyel's room with the rest of his things, bent over it for a moment, and came back with bandages and a little pot of salve. "I'm no Healer," he said, sitting down and taking Vanyel's hand back into his, "but I've banged myself up a time or two, and this is good stuff."

He took some of it on the ends of his fingers and massaged it into the palm of Vanyel's hand. A pleasant, sharp odor came from it, both green and spicy, and his fingers began to relax from their cramped position, both from the warming effect of the salve and the massage.

"What is that?" Vanyel asked, sniffing. "I'm going to smell sort of like a pastry."

Tylendel laughed. "Don't tempt me this early in the day, Vanyel-*ashke*. It's cinnamon and marigold. Good for the cramped muscles *and* the poor, battered fingers."

He had worked all the way out to the ends of Vanyel's fingers; the cramps were mostly gone, and the salve, rather than burning as Vanyel had half feared it would, was numbing the areas where Tylendel was spreading it.

"Now just let me get you bandaged up."

"What was that you just called me?"

"*Ashke?* It's *Tayledras*. Hawkbrother-tongue. All those feathered faces and masks Savil has on the wall out in the common room are from the *Tayledras;* she studied with one of their Adepts, Starwind k'Treva, and they made her a Wingsister. That's like a blood brother for them."

Tylendel was wrapping each finger carefully and taking his time about it. Vanyel didn't mind in the least. Now that he wasn't in much pain, there was something a bit sensual about Tylendel's ministrations.

"She uses a lot of their expressions when there isn't a good word for the thing in our tongue. Like *shay'a'chern*—it translates as—oh—'one whose lover is like self,' with a sexual connotation to the word 'self' that makes it clear that they aren't talking about incest *or* similar interests. It's a very complicated language." He looked up from his bandaging, and Vanyel could see laughter-glints lurking in the depths of his eyes. "You smell delicious; are you *sure* you have lessons this afternoon?"

"We promised Savil we'd be virtuous today," Vanyel reminded him, feeling greatly tempted anyway.

Tylendel heaved an exaggerated sigh. "Too true. Well, *ashke* translates simply to 'beloved.' And it's part of your name already—*ashke*, Ashkevron. See?"

He tied off the last bit of bandage with a flourish.

"*Ashke*," Vanyel mused. "I—like it."

"It suits you, *ashke;* Savil says the Hawkbrothers seldom go by their born-names, they take use-names when they become mages. Maybe that's the name you always should have had. Now let's go eat lunch and be virtuous—before I decide to break my sworn word to Savil!"

Savil looked up from her book and rubbed her tired, blurring eyes. Tylendel and Vanyel had taken over the couch across from her to study. Candlelight from the lantern beside them made a halo of Tylendel's dark gold curls and highlighted the golden brown of his tunic; beside him, in deep blue, Vanyel seemed to be an extension of his shadow. They shared Vanyel's history text; it rested on their knees with each holding a corner. Tylendel's arm was around Vanyel's shoulder, their heads nestled closely together. From time to time Savil could catch the murmur of a question from her nephew and Tylendel's slightly higher reply.

Strange that it's the older who has the tenor voice and the younger who's the deeper, she mused, blinking sleepily at them. *Though the pairing is strange all around. I would never have reckoned Vanyel for shay'a'chern. Not with Withen for a father.*

She yawned silently, and half-closed her eyes. The two young ones across the room from her blurred into a haze of gold and darkest blue. *He's got 'Lendel thinking about something other than that damned feud, at least; for that I'd warm to* him. *Even if I want to knock him into the wall occasionally for being a little prig. 'Lendel does seems to be getting some notion of responsible behavior into his head. And a bit more politeness. Though it's a damn good thing Mardic and Donni are inclined to take everything he says generously, or they might have knocked him into the wall for me! Bless them. He can be so damned rude sometimes—and not mean it.*

She worried a hangnail with the end of her thumb. *He's been so isolated I suppose I shouldn't be surprised. Gods be thanked, 'Lendel seems to be civilizing him. There's more patience there than there was before—and I think maybe, a little more kindness. Less arrogance, for certain. Withen should be pleased enough with the reports he's getting to let him stay.* She noted Vanyel's intense concentration on his book, and restrained the corners of her mouth from quirking up. *Looks like he's enjoying himself. Can't say that I'd mind studying with my 'Lendel coaching! Poor little lad; when he gives his heart to a thing, he certainly doesn't do it halfway. Still, I'm not certain I like the way he's becoming so dependent on 'Lendel. That isn't healthy, not for either of them. It could make for trouble later on.*

A thin tendril of contact reached for her from across the room, although Tylendel's eyes remained on the book. :*A silver for your thoughts, teacher-mine.*:

:*How pretty you look together, young demon,*: she replied the same way. :*And how grateful I am that you've managed to stay discreet.*:

:*Discipline, discipline,*: came the laughter-tinged answer. :*Seriously, you've heard no gossip?*:

:*Only that I'm likely to find you two at knife-point one day.*:

The aura of amusement deepened. :*Well, well, so it worked. I owe Van a forfeit.*:

Savil raised her eyebrows in surprise, and opened her eyes again to catch Tylendel looking at her with a smile lurking in the corners of his mouth. :*How so, demon-child?*:

:*He's been insulting me behind my back. Popinjay pecking. Mostly on my proclivities. So if anything gets back to Withen . . . We decided I should "find out about it" and go for him if the insults got noticed.*:

:*Great good gods!*: She bit her lip to keep from laughing :*Pot calling kettle, oh my hope of the Havens! What were you planning on doing? Are you going to call him out? I'd rather you didn't have at each other with anything sharp.*:

:*Oh, probably I'll make a major confrontation, with as many witnesses as possible. But not with blades, teacher-love; he's too good for me, and we figured he should lose so he gets the sympathy of his flock of doves. Barehanded, we think. Wrestling; we'll try to keep fists out of it as much as possible too. We had some vague notion of trying it the next time it rains, in the mud. It should be lots of fun.*:

Savil had to drop the mind-link for a moment until she got herself back under control. *Lots of fun indeed—great good gods, both of them tussling in the open in front of everyone and no one guessing how much they're enjoying it.*

:Demon-child, I think I'll put you in for envoy when I grant you your Whites; you have altogether too twisted a mind!:

:Well, doing it that way we can avoid the chance of hurting each other, and I've already established that I go after people very directly. Poor Van is going to have to decide which outfit of his I'm going to ruin, though. I intend to rip it to rags for verisimilitude.:

Savil nearly choked to death, trying not to laugh at the mind-pictures and overtones that came across with that last sending. *:Verisimilitude, my behind! You just want—:*

:Why, Savil!: The eyes across from her were wide with assumed innocence. *:How could you think such a thing?:*

:Easy enough,: she replied, her own mental tone so dry that it had a metallic taste. *:Given who I've got for a protege.:*

:Well—:

Well, indeed. 'Lendel—just a word of caution, and I may be being reactionary— but I don't like the way Van is coming to lean on you for everything. It isn't healthy; he needs to learn how to depend on himself a little.:

:Oh, Savil.:

:I'm serious.:

:It's just a phase. He's young, and he needs so badly. Great good gods, nobody's ever bothered to love him except his sister. After he's had me around for a bit and knows I won't vanish on him, he'll grow out of it.:

:'Lendel, I'm not the expert on people that Lancir is, but in my experience people don't grow out of a habit of dependence.: She glanced at the time-candle. *:Ah, we'll just leave it at that, all right? Keep it in mind. And that's enough study for one night. Both of you to bed.:*

Again the mental laughter. *:Why, Savil—:*

:To sleep, dammit!:

Tylendel nudged the other boy, and closed the book, then looked across the room at his mentor with that ironic half-smile she knew so well. "Let's pack it up for the night, Van," he said quietly—

—and *:Of course, teacher. To sleep,:* she Mindheard.

Then, as they disappeared into their room—

:Eventually.:

*   *   *

Savil had forgotten all about the planned "fight" by the time a good, soaking rain actually put in an appearance, nearly a fortnight later. She had reserved the Work Room for Mardic and Donni that afternoon; for all that they were lifebonded they were having a tremendous difficulty in working together, magically speaking. Donni had a tendency to rush into something at full tilt; Mardic was entirely the opposite, holding reserves back until the very last moment and dithering about full commitment. That meant that when they worked together their auras pulsed and had some serious weak spots, and their shields never quite meshed. Savil was putting them through an exercise designed to force them to synchronize their energy-levels and work as a unit rather than as an uneven team, when someone pounded urgently on the door.

The union of energy fields disintegrated at the first knock; dissipating with a "pop" into a shower of visible sparks and separating into the auras—green for Donni, yellow for Mardic—surrounding each of her crestfallen students. Savil swore an oath sufficiently heated to blister paint. She looked the couple over with Othersight and swore another nearly as strong.

Dammit, their concentration's gone completely. Look at those auras pulse! Oh, hellfires! If this isn't important, I'll kill whoever's out there!

She banished the violet shield she had placed about the pair with an abrupt gesture, and stalked to the door, yanking it open and glaring at the agitated Guard standing just outside.

"*Yes?*" she said, with an edge to her voice that was sharp enough to shave with.

"Herald Savil, your nephew and your protege Tylendel—they're fighting—" The man gulped, stepping back involuntarily at the sight of her angry face. "Tylendel's put up a barrier and we can't get at them to break it up; he's got your nephew down and we're afraid he may do him true harm—"

"*Damn!*" The word exploded from her, as for one moment she thought that something had *really* happened between the pair and the fight was *serious*.

Then she recalled the plan, and almost ruined it for them all by laughing in the man's face.

She schooled her expression to the one she would have been wearing if this had been a *genuine* fight; mouth tight and eyes narrowed in feigned anger. "Show me," she barked. "I'll deal with this nonsense right now."

The Guard scurried ahead of her down the hallway; she followed at a

near-trot, wincing a little at the aches the rain had called up in the depths
of her joints.

*I'll bet 'Lendel put up the mage-barrier to keep people from seeing that he and
Van aren't* really *hitting each other,* she decided, hastening her pace a bit as the
Guard pulled ahead. *And to keep folks from breaking up the fight too soon. I'd
better make a major scene over this or he'll never forgive me.*

There was no doubt of where the fight was taking place—Herald-proteges,
young courtiers, Bard-trainees, and other assorted young people were clustered tightly around the door to the gardens on the southeast side of the
Palace, all of them babbling like a pack of fools. The Guard pushed his way
through them with no regard for rank or ceremony whatsoever; Savil followed behind him and peered out the door into the pouring rain.

The combatants were about fifty paces beyond the door, in a spot beside
the paved path where all the grass had been worn away. There was, indeed,
a mage-barrier over the area where they were struggling, a place that looked
more like a pig-wallow at this point. The barrier and the rain were blurring
the combatants badly enough that it was hard to see exactly what was going
on. Vanyel was down, on his back; at least Savil assumed it was Vanyel, since
the current loser was slightly smaller and his hair was mostly dark under the
mud. Tylendel was sitting on his chest, and if Savil hadn't known better,
she'd have sworn he was strangling the younger boy.

"You take that back, you little bastard!" Tylendel roared. "You take that
back, unless you want another pound of mud shoved down your throat!"

Savil steeled herself and barked—in her best stop-a-mob-in-full-cry
voice—a single word.

"ENOUGH!"

Instantly the fighters froze.

Savil strode out into the deluge, her dignity somewhat diminished when
her feet squelched instead of coming down firmly, and the rain immediately
plastered her hair to her skull, sending tendrils of it straggling into her eyes
and mouth.

Nevertheless, she reckoned she looked imposing enough, since all the
babbling behind her ceased as she reached the edge of Tylendel's mage-
barrier and stopped.

"Take it down, trainee," she said, her tone so cold it could have turned
the rain into snow.

Tylendel scrambled to his feet and dismissed the barrier. Now that he
could be seen clearly, he truly looked as if he'd been through the wars. His

hair was full of mud and straggling around his face in dirty coils. One eye
was turning black and starting to swell; his lower lip was split and bleeding.
His tunic was torn and muddy and so were his breeches; one of his boots
had come unlaced and sagged around his ankle. He wore a very un-Tylendel-
like expression; sullen and full of barely-smothered anger.

Vanyel remained prone for several moments longer with his chest heaving as he gulped for air, long enough that Savil began to think he might
really be hurt. She breathed a little easier when he levered himself up out of
the mud and got slowly to his feet.

He was in worse case than Tylendel; his tunic had been all but stripped
from his body. There wasn't much left of it, and what there was hung in
strips from his belt and his wrists. He had several angry-looking scratches
on his arms and chest, and a split lip to match Tylendel's; but more seriously,
he was favoring his right foot, wincing in real pain when he had to put any
weight on it.

He didn't move once he'd gotten to his feet, just stood with his hands
clasped before him, wearing an expression so like Tylendel's that Savil began
to be alarmed.

:'Lendel?: she Mindspoke, layering the name with her anxiety and
distress.

Tylendel's expression didn't change by so much as a twitch of an eyelid,
but the Mindvoice was as cheerful and amused as his face was angry and
sullen. :No fear, teacher-mine. It's still going mostly as planned.:

She sighed mentally with relief. :Mostly?:

:Well, we couldn't practice this much, so we made some miscalculations. Van got
me in the eye with his elbow, we both managed to sock each other in the mouth somehow, and I think I made him sprain his ankle when I tackled him. Hurry up and
lecture us, I can't keep a straight face much longer!:

She straightened, and looked down her long nose at both of them, ignoring the water dripping off the end of it. "A fine thing," she said acidly,
"when I can't trust my protege and ward to conduct themselves like civilized adults in my absence! What am I to do with you? Find you
keepers?"

Tylendel made as if to say something, but shrank under her icy glare, the
rain slowly washing the mud out of his hair.

"Trainee Tylendel, *you* should have known better! You are a Herald-in-
training; I expect you to act in accordance with the dignity and honor of
our office. I do *not* expect to find you thrashing about in the mud like a

six-year-old brat with no manners and no sense! No matter how much Vanyel provoked you, you should have come to *me* first, not taken the matter into your own hands!"

Tylendel hung his head and mumbled something in the direction of the puddle around his feet.

"Louder, trainee," she snapped. "I can't hear you."

"Yes, Herald Savil," he repeated, his voice harsh, and full of suppressed emotion. "I was wrong."

"Go—back to your quarters. Now. Make yourself presentable. I'll deal with you when I'm done with Vanyel."

Tylendel bowed slightly, and without another word, walked past her and through the crowd at the doorway. Savil didn't turn around to watch his progress, but even above the steady beat of the rain she could hear the sound of the crowd parting behind her to let him through. One or two in the group snickered a little, but that was all.

She turned her dagger-gaze on Vanyel, who was glaring at her from under a wet comma of black hair that was obscuring one eye.

"And *you*. Fine state of affairs *this* is." She walked forward a bit and folded her arms, trying not to shiver in the cold rain. "I've heard about those snide little comments of yours, the backbiting, and all the rest of it. You've been picking at 'Lendel ever since you arrived here, young man, and I won't have it!"

Vanyel raised his head, glaring back at her with every bit of the arrogance he'd ever shown. "He's nothing but a—"

"He outranks *you*, young man, and you'd do well to remember that!" she snapped. "Consider yourself confined to your quarters for the duration! If I learn you've set one foot out of the suite when you aren't at lessons, I'll ship you back to your father so fast the wind of your passing will tear the thatch from the roofs! Now *march*!"

Vanyel set his jaw, and pivoted where he stood, setting off toward Savil's suite through the rain—taking the opposite course that Tylendel had followed. He was more than half staggering, and it made Savil's ankle ache in sympathy to see him struggling through the mud, but she made no move to help him. Instead, she stalked along behind him, as if making certain that he reached his goal.

But once they had rounded the corner and were out of sight of the doorway, she dropped her pose and her dignity and scrambled through the slippery grass to reach his side.

"Lean on me, lad," she said, coming up beside him, and pulling his arm over her shoulder. "I've been called an old stick before this, I might as well act like one."

"Aunt—thank the gods—" he gasped. "I thought we'd never get out of sight." He stumbled and nearly fell, all of his weight suddenly landing on Savil, making her stagger. "Please, I've got to rest a minute. Gods above, this *hurts*."

"How bad is it?" she asked, as he shivered beside her in the cold rain.

"Don't know." He managed a wan grin. "Hurts more than a thorn in the toe, less than when I broke my arm. That tell you anything?"

"Hardly," she snorted. "Come on, the sooner I get you inside, the happier I'll be. And I hope my protege has the sense to *think* and not come running out to help."

The lights of Savil's windows were in sight—and her heart sank for a moment when she *did* see someone running toward them through the rain. Then she saw a second silhouette beside the first, and realized that it was not Tylendel who was coming to help them in, but Mardic and Donni.

The youngsters took over the task of supporting Vanyel. That left Savil free to go on ahead of them, for which she was truly grateful. She was chilled right down to the bone, and those bones were starting to ache rather persistently.

She stepped in through Vanyel's outer door; almost as soon as she'd stepped across the threshold she found herself enveloped in a warm blanket and practically carried into the common room. It was Tylendel, of course; he stayed with her just long enough to settle her in her favorite chair and put a mug of mulled wine in her hand, then he was gone.

He was back again in a moment, Vanyel's arm around his shoulder, the latter hopping awkwardly beside him.

There was already a blanket waiting on the couch; Tylendel got Vanyel bundled into it and pressed another mug of the wine into his hands.

Mardic and Donni piled in right behind them; giggling, shaking the rain out of their hair, and heading straight for the kettle of wine on the hearth. Vanyel was more interested in his lover's black eye and swollen lip than the wine.

"Gods—'Lendel, I did *not* mean that—" he mourned, reaching out hesitantly to touch the edge of the bruise. "Oh Lord and Lady, *why* do I have to be so clumsy?"

"Oh, you just fight like a girl," Tylendel teased. "All flying knees and elbows. It was *my* own stupid fault for getting my face in the way. It's your ankle I'm worried about." He started unlacing Vanyel's boot, fighting the wet laces and swearing under his breath when they wouldn't cooperate.

"I'm all—*ouch!*"

Tylendel froze. "Did I—"

"*No,*" Vanyel said around clenched teeth. "Just get that damned boot off before you have to cut it off."

But Tylendel dithered over the task until Mardic pushed him out of the way and took over, getting the boot off with an abrupt yank that blanched Vanyel to the color of pure beeswax. He clutched Tylendel's hand while Mardic examined the ankle, pronounced it "probably not broken," and bound it up.

"Havens, teacher," Mardic laughed, rescuing his cup from Donni and returning to sit at her feet across from Savil. "Were *we* as moonstruck as that? Gods, I feel like I'm being smothered in syrup!"

He nodded at the two on the couch, each assuring the other that his own hurts were less than nothing and fussing over the other's injuries.

"For at least the first five or six months," Savil replied dryly, after sipping her wine. "Just as moonstruck, and just as cloying. And even more sentimental." She raised her voice a bit. "You two *might* thank me."

"Certainly, Savil," Tylendel replied, craning his head around. "If you'd tell us what we're thanking you for."

"Gods. Vanyel, don't you ever listen?"

"I'm sorry, Aunt," he said, looking confused, his hair still trailing over one eye. "My foot hurt so much I wasn't paying any attention; it wasn't a *real* lecture, after all."

She cast her eyes up to the ceiling. "Give me strength. I just confined you completely to the suite for as long as I care to enforce my decision, you little ninny. I just got you *away* from the girl-gaggle and gave you *orders* to stay here indefinitely. Except for lessons, you'll be here waking and sleeping. That includes taking meals here."

"You did?" he said, dazed. "I am? You mean I can stay here?"

"With 'Lendel, and not arouse any suspicions," she interrupted. "That's exactly what I mean. Fact of the matter is, your damnfool father will probably be pleased to hear that you were—"

She broke off, seeing that she no longer had the attention of either of them. Across from her she heard Mardic snicker.

She favored the lifebonded with a sardonic glance. "Don't feel too smug," she told them. "Or I'll start trotting out tales about *you* two."

"Yes, Savil," Mardic replied, not in the least repentant. "Whatever you say. Would you care for honey in that wine?"

Savil spared a glance back toward the couch. Tylendel was rebandaging Vanyel's ankle, treating it as if it were as fragile as an insect's wing. She made a face.

"I think not," she replied. "We've got enough sweetness around here for one night."

Tylendel looked up, and stuck his tongue out at her, while Vanyel blushed.

Savil chuckled and sat back in her chair, well content with her world. *At least for the moment*, she thought, taking another sip of spiced wine, *which is all any Herald can reasonably hope for. I'll worry about tomorrow when tomorrow gets here.*

CHAPTER 7

TYLENDEL SPRAWLED IN his favorite chair, and watched Vanyel restringing his lute, sitting cross-legged on the bed. Candlelight reflected in a honey-colored curve along the round belly of the instrument.

Is it time? he wondered. *He plays for the girls, but they don't matter. He doesn't care if he plays well or badly for them. Will he play for someone he loves, someone who does matter? Can he? Has he recovered enough?*

Only one way to find out, though.

"*Ashke*," he said quietly, extending his little Gift of Empathy as far as it would go. Van lifted his head from his work; he looked rather comical with the old strings dangling from his mouth like the feelers on a catfish.

"Mph?" he replied.

"When you get Woodlark in tune, would you play for me?"

Vanyel froze. Tylendel *Felt* the startlement—and the ache. And reacted to them.

"Please? I'd like it."

Vanyel took the strings out of his mouth, and Tylendel could sense his withdrawal. "Why?" he asked, bitterly, his eyes shining wetly. "There's dozens better than I am right here at Bardic. Why listen to a half-crippled amateur?"

Tylendel restrained his natural reaction—which was to go to him, hold him, ease his hurt that way. That would ease it all right, but it wouldn't cure it. "Because you *aren't* half-crippled anymore," he replied. "Because you aren't an amateur. You're good; the Bards all say so."

"But not good enough to be one of them." Vanyel turned away, but not before Tylendel saw tears in his eyes. And Felt the anguish.

"That's not true," he insisted gently. "Look, Van, it's *not* that you aren't good enough. It's that you just don't have the Gift. Can a blind man paint?"

Vanyel just shook his head, and Tylendel could sense his further withdrawal. "It's not the same thing," he said, tightly. "The blind man can't see a painting. But there's nothing wrong with my ears."

Tylendel searched for something that might reach this wounded corner of his beloved, and finally found it.

"*Ashke*, why do you think there are minstrels trained at Bardic? Why do you think that people welcome minstrels when there are Bards about?" He'd asked that same question of Breda, who had all three Bardic Talents: the Gift, the Skill, and the Creativity. Her answer had been enlightening.

Vanyel shook his head, still tightly bound up inside himself. "Because there aren't enough Bards to go around, just like there aren't enough Heralds or Healers."

"Wrong," Tylendel said firmly, "and I have this from Breda. *There are times when the Gift gets in the way of the music.*"

"What?" Vanyel's head whipped around in startlement, and Tylendel saw the shine of tears on his cheek. "What do you mean by that?"

"Just what I said." *Now* was the time to rise and go to Vanyel's side, and Tylendel did just that. "Listen to me; just what is the Bardic Gift, hmm? It's the ability to make others *feel* the things you want them to through music. But when a Bard does that, you can't keep your mind on the music, can you? You never really hear how beautiful it is; you're too busy with what the Bard is doing. You never really hear it for itself, and when you remember it, you don't remember the music, you remember the emotions. There's another reason; when the Bard performs, you put nothing of yourself into the listening. But when a minstrel performs, or a Bard without the Gift, you get out of the music exactly what you put into the listening." He chuckled, and reached for Vanyel's limp hands. "Breda said that in some ways it's a little like making love with a paid courtesan or with your lover. Your lover may not be as expert, but the experience is a lot more genuine."

"Breda said that?" Vanyel faltered.

"In her cups, yes." He didn't add it had been here, in Savil's quarters, the evening she'd tested and failed Vanyel. Breda had a very soft heart beneath that bony chest; she'd not enjoyed destroying Vanyel's hopes, even indirectly. "They do say that there's truth in the bottom of every wine bottle." He paused, and raised one eyebrow at his lover. "She also said that if you *weren't* your father's heir, they'd snap you up so fast you'd leave your boots behind."

"She did?" He could Feel Vanyel uncoiling from around that lump of hurt.

"She did." He picked up the lute and put it back in Vanyel's hands. "And since my personal preference is *not* for courtesans, however expert—will you play for me?"

"Just—" Vanyel swallowed, and finally met his eyes. The hurt was still there, but already fading. "—just let me get her in tune."

To Vanyel Ashkevron from Lord Withen Ashkevron: greetings. I have received good reports of you from Herald Savil, except for the instance of your quarrel with her protege. While I cannot condone your actions, I can understand that it may be irritating to share the same roof with the young man. You must keep your temper and not provoke him further, as it is obvious that he cannot be relied upon to keep his. I am also given to understand that you have abandoned your pretensions as a musician and relegated such nonsense to its proper place; an amusing hobby, no more. I am pleased with this development; it seems to me this is evidence of maturity and acceptance of your proper place in life, and I have sent a small token of my approval. Inscribed by Father Leren Benevy, By my hand and seal, Lord Withen Ashkevron.

To Lord Withen Ashkevron from Vanyel Ashkevron: greetings. I have received your letter and your token, for which my thanks. I am endeavoring to follow all of Herald Savil's instructions to the best of my ability. I have found her to be a wise and knowledgeable mentor, and hope to better please her in the future. By my hand, Vanyel Ashkevron.

Dearest Son: I Pray with all my Heart that this finds you Well, and that you were not Hurt by that Brutal Boy. I Feared that something of this Nature would Occur from the Instant your Father Told me of this Foolish Scheme and have had Dark and Fell Dreams from the moment you Departed. Savil is plainly Not To Be Relied Upon to keep her Creatures in Order. I pray you, do not Provoke the Barbarian further; I am endeavoring to Persuade your Father to fetch you Home again, but thus far it is All In Vain. I am Prostrate with Worry—and if your Absence were not enough, I have been visited with a Further Grief. My maid Melenna has been rendered With Child—and by your Brother Mekeal! So she Claims, and so Mekeal Admits. Your Father is No Help; he seems to Think it is All Very Amusing. Indeed, I am at my Wit's End and I know not What To Do! But even in my Extremity, I have not forgotten my Beloved Child, nor that your Birthday is this very day. I enclose a Small Token—All that I could Manage, and not Nearly your Desert. I Beg you that if you are in Need that you will Tell Me at Once. I shall Manage something More from your Father, Hard-Hearted as he is. Your Loving Mother, Lady Treesa Ileana Brendywhin-Ashkevron.

*   *   *

"Purple ink?" Tylendel said incredulously, looking over Vanyel's shoulder. "Am I really seeing purple ink? And *pink* paper?"

"Costs a fortune, and it's all she'll use," Vanyel answered absently, pondering how to reply without setting his mother off again. The pink page lay on the blotter of the desk, its very existence a maternal accusation that he hadn't written since he arrived here. Beside it were two piles of silver coins—absolutely equal in value.

One reward for beating up a pervert, one consolation for getting beaten up by a pervert. He sighed. *Gods, there are times I wish I was an orphan.*

"May I?" Tylendel asked.

Vanyel shrugged. "Go ahead. You'll encounter her eventually, I'm sure. You ought to know what she's like."

Tylendel worked his way through the ornamented and scrolled calligraphy, and gave it back to Vanyel with a grimace that said more than words could have.

"You think this is bad—you should see the letters she writes to friends, or worse, people she thinks have slighted her. Three, four, and five pages, purple ink and tear-blotches, and everything capitalized." He sighed again. "And *appalling* grammar. When she gets really hysterical, she goes into formal mode and she *cannot* seem to keep her 'thees' and 'thous' straight."

He contemplated the letter for a moment. "What's really awful, she *talks* like that, too."

Tylendel laughed, threw himself down on the bed, and got back to the book he'd been reading.

Dear Mother: I really am all right. Please don't worry about me—worry about yourself. If you don't take care of yourself, if you let your fine sensibilities get the better of you, you'll make yourself ill. Savil is quite kind, and the problems I had with Tylendel have been taken care of. Every rumor that comes out of this Court is an exaggeration at best and an outright lie at worst, so pay no attention to what your friends are telling you. I am sorry to hear about Melenna; this must be a terrible burden for you. Your present was very kind, and very much appreciated, and far in excess of my needs. I love you, and I think about you often. Be well, Vanyel.

Dear Vanyel; what in Havens is going on? Are you all right? If it's unbearable, for the gods' sake let me know and I'll lead the Seven Corey Swordmaids to your rescue—they're dying to play avenging angels, although given their figures, it's more like avenging angles. All my love, Lissa.

Vanyel laughed aloud, and passed the note to Tylendel.

Tylendel grinned broadly and handed it back to him. "Now *this* one I like. What're my chances of meeting her?"

"Pretty good," Vanyel replied, stretching. "Once the secret's out about us, Father will disinherit me, Mother will have vapors, and Lissa will show up, sword in hand, to defend me from Father's wrath. She's gotten a lot spunkier since she went over to the Coreys to foster. Lord Trevor has just about promised her a commission in the Guard."

"Which he can give her, since he's in charge of recruitment for the Guard," Tylendel said thoughtfully. "Is that your last letter?"

"One more after this—"

Dearest Lissa; Don't worry, it's all right. I'm fine, and I'm happier than I've been in my life here. Savil is on my side against Father, and some of what you've been hearing is to keep him happy. Trust me, it really is all right. I love you, and I miss you, Van.

To Vanyel Ashkevron from Evan Leshara; greetings. I believe we have mutual interests and I would be honored and pleased if we could meet to discuss them. I am at your disposal any evening. By my hand and seal, Evan Leshara.

"'Lendel—" Vanyel said slowly, sorely puzzled by this last note, which had been delivered to the suite by a page that very afternoon. "Who is Evan Leshara?"

Tylendel paced the confines of the bedroom, as restless as a caged wolf. Savil thought both of them were in here; he hadn't told her that Vanyel had slipped his leash to go see what Evan Leshara wanted. He glanced over at the time-candle; it hadn't burned down any since the last time he'd looked at it.

I shouldn't have let him go. If Leshara figures out the fight was all a ruse—

Up and back, up and back. It was damned hot for an autumn night, or was it being on edge that was making him sweat? His scalp prickled, and he felt a headache beginning just under his right eye. Shadows cast by the light of the time-candle danced and flickered, shrank and grew.

—if he figures out the game we're playing, he'll be able to use blackmail on Van against me, and me against Staven. Oh, gods, I shouldn't have let him go. I should have told him to ignore Leshara's invitation. I should have. I—

The creak of the garden door broke into his worries, and his tensions evaporated when Vanyel slipped in from the darkness and latched the door behind himself.

"*Ashke?*" Tylendel began, then hesitated, seeing the troubled expression in Vanyel's eyes.

"He's a damned persuasive man, this Leshara," Vanyel said softly, sitting himself in the chair in front of the cold fireplace.

"That's why he's here," Tylendel replied grimly. "It's the Leshara countermove to my being here. Since they can't buy into the Heralds, they've sent the one of their kin with the sweetest tongue to get the ear of the Queen, if he can."

"He says he's got it. He said a lot of things. 'Lendel, there was an awful lot of what he said that made sense."

"Of course there was!" Tylendel interrupted. "I'll be willing to bet that half of what he told you was the absolute truth even by *my* standards. It's the *way* he said it, the context, and what he was prompting you to infer from what he told you that counts! You ought to know yourself from what you've been writing home that the best possible lie is to tell only the truth—just not all of it!"

"But 'Lendel." Vanyel still looked uncertain. "'Lendel, he says his people have been willing to settle for months now, a settlement the Queen approves, and yours refuse to go along with it—"

"He didn't tell you what that 'plan' was, did he?"

Vanyel shook his head.

"To marry my thirty-year-old maiden-cousin who's never been outside of a cloister to a fifty-year-old lecher, take Staven out of being Lord Holder and put *her* in," he said savagely, "which effectively means putting *him* in, since there's no way she'd ever be able to stand up to him. She'd dry up and blow away the first time he spoke harshly to her. *That's* the Leshara notion of an equitable settlement." He glared at Vanyel, angry and a little hurt that Vanyel would even *consider* taking Evan Leshara's word as the whole truth. "He's using the fact that Staven's only seventeen as a way to imply that he's incompetent, too young to make any kind of rational decision. And a lot of the powers at Court, being old goats themselves, are buying into the idea. After all, seventeen's only old enough to be told you have to go fight and die for something—it's *not* old enough to have any say in the matter!"

Vanyel's eyes had gotten very distressed, and he had shrunk back into the chair as far as he could. "'Lendel," he faltered. "I didn't mean—I wasn't doubting you—"

Tylendel gave himself a mental kick in the posterior for upsetting him. "*Ashke*, I didn't mean to shout at you," he said, kneeling beside the chair and putting one hand on Vanyel's knee. "I'm sorry—I'm just so damned frustrated. He can say any damned thing he wants, and because I'm a Herald-trainee, I can't even refute him. It makes me a little crazy, sometimes."

Vanyel brightened, and put his hand over Tylendel's. "That's all right. I know how you feel. Like me and Father and Jervis."

"Something like it."

"'Lendel, would you . . ." Vanyel hesitated. "Would you tell me your side?"

Tylendel took a deep breath. "If I do, I'll be breaking a promise I made to Savil, not to get you involved."

"I'm already involved. I—why? That's what I really want to know. What's keeping this thing going?"

"Something Wester Leshara did," Tylendel replied, fighting down the urge to get up, grab a horse, and ride out to strangle Wester with his bare hands. The white-hot rage that always filled him whenever he called that particular memory up was very hard to control. "Savil says I have to be absolutely fair—so to be absolutely fair, I'll tell you that this was in retaliation for a raid that accidentally killed his youngest son. We—our people—went in to stampede his cattle. The boy fell off his horse and wound up under their hooves. But I don't think that excuses what Wester did."

"Which was?"

"My father had just died; he hired some kind of two-copper conjuror to convince Mother that Father's ghost wanted to speak with her. She wasn't very stable—which Wester was damned well aware of, and this pushed her over the edge. We got rid of the charlatan, but not before he'd gotten her convinced that if she found just the right formula, she'd be able to communicate with Father's spirit. She started taking all manner of potions, trying to see him. Finally she *did* see him—she ate Black Angel mushrooms."

He did not add that he and Staven had been the ones to find her. Vanyel looked sick enough. Tylendel got a lid on his anger, and changed the subject. "What did the bastard want, anyway?"

"He wanted me to let him know any time I heard anything about you or your family, and he wanted me to talk my father 'round to his side."

"What did you tell him?"

Vanyel grimaced. "I guess I was playing the same game of telling not all of the truth. I told him that I heard more about your people directly from you than I heard casually, and let him draw his own conclusions."

Tylendel relaxed, and chuckled. Vanyel brightened a little more. "What about your father?"

"I told him the truth; that I had been sent here as punishment, because I wouldn't toe the line at home, and that father would take advice from a halfwit before he'd take it from me. He was rather disappointed."

Now Tylendel laughed, and hugged him. "*Ashke, ashke*, you couldn't have done better if I'd given you a script!"

"So I did all right?" Now Vanyel was fairly glowing.

"You did better than all right."

Gods, he thought, seeing Vanyel so elated, *he fades like an unwatered flower when he thinks I'm angry at him—and now this—you'd have thought I'd offered him a Bard's laurel. Does my opinion mean so much to him? Do I mean so much to him?*

The thought was a sobering one. And it was followed inevitably by another. *Maybe Savil's right. . . .*

"He said he wants to stay in touch with me anyway, just in case I hear something. I told him that was all right with me. In fact, I acted pretty eager about it." He turned his head a little to one side, and offered, tentatively, "I thought we could sort of tell him what we wanted him to hear."

Ha. "We," not "you." No, Savil's not right. He depends on me, but I depend on him, and if he's leaning on me a little, well, that isn't going to hurt anyone. He's just not used to making decisions on his own, that's all.

"That's perfect," he said, leaning on the arm of the chair. "Absolutely perfect. Now, after facing off the dragon for me, oh noble warrior, in what way can I *ever* reward you?" He batted his eyelashes at Vanyel, who laughed, and drew himself up as if he sat in a throne. "I'll do *anything*—"

"Oh?" Vanyel replied archly. "*Anything?*"

"Savil told me something funny today," Tylendel murmured quietly into Vanyel's ear. His voice roused Vanyel out of the sleepy half-dream he'd been in ever since he and Tylendel had settled into their favorite spot in all of the Field.

It was the first time either of them had broken the silence since they'd entered the pine copse.

The suite had seemed far too stuffy for the warm autumnal evening, even with all the windows open. And Vanyel had scarcely left it since they'd staged their "fight"—except for lessons and the obligatory evenings with Evan Leshara to feed him misinformation. And the appearances he *had* to make at Court to keep his circle of admirers happy and deceived.

It was moon-dark, and the chance of anyone seeing them heading out into Companion's Field together was practically nonexistent. So when Vanyel had looked up from his Religions text and tentatively suggested a walk, Tylendel had shut his own book and flung the garden door open with a mocking bow and a real grin.

It was inevitable that Gala should join them when they crossed the river; Vanyel had come to take her presence for granted on the precious few joint excursions they'd judged safe from detection. It was equally inevitable that they should seek "their" pine grove; it drew them as no other place within walking distance could.

It was blacker than Sunsinger's despair beneath the branches on this moonless night, but Tylendel had made a tiny mage-light once they'd gotten past the first line of trees and were safely out of sight. They'd just rambled for a long time, from one end of the peaceful grove to the other and back again; not speaking, but not needing to. Not touching, either—but again, not needing to.

It wasn't until they'd walked out the last of their end-of-the-day tensions that they'd finally decided to settle next to the oldest tree in the grove and just relax in silence. Gala provided a willing backrest, and the two of them leaned up against her soft warmth, with Vanyel resting his head on Tylendel's shoulder. Tylendel had put out the mage-light, leaving them in near-total darkness. There were still a few crickets that hadn't been killed by the first frost, calling from a dozen different directions, and once Vanyel had heard geese crying by high overhead. But other than that, and the sigh of Gala's breathing, they might have been the only two living creatures in an endlessly empty, pine-fragrant universe.

Which was exactly the way Vanyel wanted it. This continual charade of theirs was proving to be both harder and easier than he'd thought it would. Easier, because he was no longer trying to block out his feelings, no longer trying to convince himself that he didn't need anyone. Easier, because the arrogant pose, the flirtation games, were no longer anything more than an elaborate set of games. But harder, because one single slip, one hint getting back to Withen of what was really going on, and he'd lose everything that was making his life something more than a burden to be endured. And harder, because of the double-game he was playing with Leshara. One slip *there* and Leshara would know what was really going on—and it would be child's play for him to use that knowledge as a double-weapon against Vanyel *and* Tylendel.

And there was no way of knowing how much—or how little—Evan Leshara believed out of all the things Vanyel was telling him. All he could do was trust that 'Lendel knew enough to seed the falsehoods with exactly the right amount of truth—because *he* certainly didn't know enough.

The pretense was a constant drain on his emotional energy, and it wasn't often that he felt safe enough to forget and enjoy the moment. The insecurity of the situation was the first thing on his mind when waking and the last when going to sleep.

That wasn't the only strain. Since the fight, he'd been virtually ostracized by the Bards, Heralds, and all their trainees. Tylendel was (somewhat to his own surprise) highly regarded among the "working" members of Queen Elspeth's High Court. But that meant that Vanyel was bearing the burden of *their* scorn for provoking the fight. And while his teachers remained within the bounds of polite civility, they were making no secret of their disdain. Lessons had become ordeals, and only Tylendel's insistence that he was going to *have* to continue if the charade was going to work had kept Vanyel persisting in the face of the hostility he was facing. The only one of his teachers that seemed oblivious to the whole mess was Lord Oden—possibly because the Lord-Marshall's second-in-command was pretty well indifferent to anything not involving the martial arts. Vanyel had ample occasion to reflect on the irony that his situation was now precisely the opposite of what he had endured at Forst Reach. There he'd been the pet of his tutors, except for the armsmaster, and despised by everyone his own age. Here—discounting the trainees— his peers were fawning on him, but his teachers were doing their icily gracious best to get him to give up and drop out of their lessons—except for his armsmaster. It was *not* his imagination that they were being harder on him than the others being lessoned; Mardic was in his Religions group now, and had confirmed his suspicions.

"So what did Savil say?" he replied, closing his weary eyes, and shifting a bit so that he wasn't resting so much of his weight on Tylendel's arm. Tylendel responded by holding him a little closer.

"That she can't understand why we haven't had at least one fight," Tylendel said, laughing a little. "She says we're sickening."

"She has a point," Vanyel conceded, with a ghost of a chuckle. "We are, a bit."

"She told me she can't understand how we stay so dotingly devoted to each other. She says we act like a couple of spaniels—you know, kick 'em, and they just come back begging to be kicked again—only worse, because we aren't kicking each other."

"She just doesn't realize," Vanyel said, sobered by a moment of introspection. "'Lendel, there is no way I'd fight with you, when any moment my father might find out about us and pull me home. I couldn't bear the idea of our last words being angry ones. I have to make every moment we have together a good memory."

"Don't let it eat at you," Tylendel interrupted. "You're sixteen now; I'm seventeen. It's only two years before you're of age. We'll be all right so long as you can keep your end of things going with Lord Evan."

Vanyel sighed. "Gods, gods, two years—it seems like forever. It seems like it's been years already. I just can't imagine coming to the end of this."

Tylendel stroked his hair, his hand as light as a breath of wind. "You'll manage, *ashke*. You're stronger than you think. I sometimes think you're stronger than I am. I doubt I could be dealing successfully with the plate you've been handed. And whether or not you believe this, I think I depend as much on you as you do on me. Gala says so."

"She does?" Vanyel's voice rose with his surprise. "Really?"

"Frequently." He sighed, and Vanyel wondered why. There were times when it seemed that there were some serious points of disagreement between Gala and her Chosen, usually involving Tylendel's tacit and unshakable support of his twin. Vanyel personally couldn't see what all the fuss was about. Even if 'Lendel *hadn't* had the close bond he did with Staven, even if Wester Leshara *hadn't* connived the painful suicide of 'Lendel's mother, it would still have been his duty to support Staven. Even though Vanyel himself had a rather bitter and uncomfortable relationship with his own brother Mekeal, if it came to an interHouse confrontation there was no doubt in his mind where *he* would stand, and he knew Mekeal was likely to feel the same. And given how much Tylendel owed to his brother for supporting *him* in the face of all opposition—well, Vanyel couldn't see what else he *could* do, in all decency and honor.

But then, there was a great deal about all this "Herald" business he didn't understand. For instance—

"'Lendel, if we make it that far—all the way to when you get your Whites—"

"'If?' Don't think in terms of 'if,' love," Tylendel chided, softly. "It may not be easy, but we'll make it. Havens, I should talk about not being easy, when it's you that is having to take the worse share on your shoulders. But I'll help you, I'll help you all I can, and we *will* see this through to the other side."

"Well, what's going to happen with us? When you get your Whites and I'm of age—what then?"

There was a long pause, and Tylendel's hand stopped moving, resting on the back of his neck. "That's the easy part, really. First thing, you make up your mind about exactly what you want to do about Lord Withen. I mean, you could flat tell him about us, or you could just—let him find out. Whichever way you want. At that point the worst he could do is disown you, and you *know* everything I have is yours for the asking. The Circle won't stint me; I'll have more than enough to support two."

"He probably will disown me," Vanyel said bitterly. "Which will mean I'll *have* to ask, 'Lendel."

"So? We're partners, aren't we? It won't be charity, *ashke;* it'll be sharing."

Vanyel squelched the automatic retort that it would still *feel* like charity. "All right, assume I've told my father and I'm free to do what I want. Then what?"

"After that, Savil will turn the lovebirds over to another Herald and take me—us—out on a Field assignment. Us, because obviously I won't go without you; Savil knows that, so it's a given. That's a year, or thereabouts. But then—I don't know. I'm a Herald-Mage trainee; they usually give us permanent positions rather than having us ride circuit like the straight Heralds do. They'll probably put me either here at Haven, or out along the Border at the places where magic is needed. Down by White Foal Pass, around the edge of the Pelagirs—"

"Why? That's something that has me baffled. Why?" Vanyel asked. "I mean, why are you going to do what somebody else wants? Why do you have to go where *they* say? Who *are* 'they,' anyway?"

"'They'—that's the Heraldic Circle. Queen's Own, Seneschal's Herald,

Lord-Marshal's Herald, the speaker for the Heralds with trainees—that's Savil—the speaker for the Herald-Mages, and the speaker for the Heralds on circuit. And the Queen, of course, and the Heir. They're the ones who decide where Heralds and Herald-Mages will serve and what they'll do. That's—that's just the way it is. Van, I don't understand *you* now." There was hurt in Tylendel's voice. "Don't you *want* to go with me?"

"Oh, gods—" Vanyel groped for Tylendel's free hand, and held it tightly. "'Lendel, I didn't mean that. I'd rather lose my arms and legs than lose you. I'll go wherever you go, and glad to. I'm just trying to get all this to make sense. *Why* are you doing this, going where they tell you, doing what they tell you to do? Why is this—Herald stuff—so important to you?"

Vanyel could almost feel Tylendel fumbling after the right words. "It's, I don't know, it's a kind of hunger. I can't help it. I've got these abilities, these Gifts, and I can't *not* use them. I couldn't sit here, knowing that there were people out there who need *exactly* the kind of help I can give them and not make the effort to find them and take care of them. It's like backing Staven—it's just something I could not even see myself *not* doing. I can't explain it, Van, I can't. I have to, or—or I'm not me anymore."

Vanyel just shook his head a little. "All right, I'll accept that. But I still can't really grasp it," he confessed. "Giving up everything to play nursemaid to a pack of people you don't even know. Won't you have any life of your own? Who are these hypothetical people that need you, that you're sacrificing your whole life for them?"

"Huh," Tylendel said. "You sound just like Stav—"

Suddenly he went rigid; "Staven?" he whispered. "Stav—"

Then his entire body convulsed as he screamed Staven's name. And the night erupted into chaos around them.

The scream went on and on, filling the entire universe with pain and loss. An unbearable pressure rose around them, and shattered, all in the moment, the eternity of that scream. The still air churned, and began pummeling them with fists of heat and turbulence.

Gala scrambled to her feet; Vanyel caught and held his lover, trying to support him as he thrashed in uncontrolled spasms. Tylendel's forehead cracked against the bridge of his nose; he saw stars and tasted blood, but gritted his teeth against the pain and held on.

A gale-force wind sprang up out of the confusion and chaos. It went howling about them, moving outward in a spiral, nearly tearing the clothes from Vanyel's body as it passed. Tylendel was—glowing; angry red light pulsed around him. In it, Vanyel could see his face set in a mask of madness. His teeth were clenched in a grimace of pain, and there was no sense in his eyes, no sign of intelligence.

The trees closest to them literally exploded in a shower of splinters; those farther away spasmed in convulsions much like Tylendel's before they began tearing themselves apart.

The wind picked up in strength; trees farther away began thrashing and the wind spiraled outward a little farther than it had a moment before. The light surrounding Tylendel—and now Vanyel—throbbed, ebbing and strengthening with each paroxysm of his body. And something frighteningly like lightning was crackling off the edges of that glow, striking at random all about them. Where it hit, the effect was exactly like natural lightning; trees split, and the ground was scorched and pitted.

The wind was scouring the earth bare, making projectiles of dead needles and bits of wood. Even the ground was shuddering, heaving like a horse trying to throw a rider.

Vanyel held Tylendel as tightly as he could, looking wildly about for Gala. Finally he saw her, off on the edge of the circle of chaos. She, too, was glowing, bluely; the edge of her glow seemed to be deflecting the debris and the lightning, but it looked as if she was unable to *do* anything. Not that she wasn't trying—she stretched her neck out toward her Chosen, her eyes bright and terrible with distress—but all she seemed able to do was shield herself. She couldn't even get *near* them.

"Gala!" Vanyel shouted, over the screaming of the wind, restraining Tylendel as his lover spasmed in another convulsion. "Get help! Get Savil!" He couldn't think. If Gala were helpless to do anything. Savil was the only possible source of aid.

She shook her head, tried to force her way through the gale toward them, but was actually pushed back by whatever force was controlling the raging wind. She tried twice more; twice more was shoved farther back, as the circle of destruction grew. Finally she reared, screamed like a terrified human, pivoted on her hind feet, then sprang off into the darkness.

Vanyel closed his eyes and clasped Tylendel against his chest, trying to protect him from the wind, trying to keep him from hurting himself as he continued to convulse. He was well beyond fear, his mind numb, his mouth dry, his heart pounding—praying for an end to this, praying for help. He couldn't think, couldn't move—all he could do was *stay*.

'Lendel, I'm here—he thought, as hard as he could, hoping somehow that Tylendel would "hear" him. *'Lendel, come back to me*—

The trainee spasmed once more, his back arcing—and suddenly, it was over. The light vanished, and with it, the wind. The ground settled—and there was nothing but a deadly silence, hollow darkness, and the weight of his lover's unmoving body in Vanyel's arms.

"'Lendel?" He shook Tylendel's shoulders, and bit back a moan when he got no response. "Oh, gods—" Tylendel was still breathing, but it was strange, shallow breathing—and the trainee's skin was clammy and almost cold.

A moment later Savil and two other Heralds came pounding up on their Companions, mage-lights glowing over their heads. By their light, Vanyel could see that Tylendel was limp and completely unconscious, his head lolling back, his eyes rolled up under half-open lids. He swallowed down fear, as Savil slid off Kellan's back without waiting for her to come to a full stop, landing heavily and stumbling to them. As the light of the pulsing balls strengthened, Vanyel saw with shock that there was not so much as a single pine seedling left standing in what had been a healthy grove of trees.

"I—I-I d-d-don't know what h-h-happened," he stuttered, as Savil went to her knees beside them, pulled open Tylendel's eyelids and checked his pulse, her face gray and grim in the blue light of her globe. The other two Heralds dismounted slowly, looking about them at the destruction with expressionless faces. "He was a-a-all right one minute, and then—Aunt Savil, please, *I* d-d-didn't do this t-t-t-to him—did I?"

"No, lad," she said absently. "Jaysen, come over here and confirm, will you?"

The taller of the two Heralds knelt beside Savil and made the same examination she had. "Backlash shock," he said succinctly. "Bad. Best thing we can do for him is get him in a bed and put someone he trusts with him."

"What I thought," she replied, getting to her feet and motioning to the older Herald to come help Jaysen take up the unconscious trainee. "No, Vanyel, it had nothing to do with you." She finally *looked* at him. "Did you know your nose is broken?"

"It is?" he replied, mind still fogged with fear for Tylendel.

"It is. Hold still; Jaysen's got just about enough of the Healing Gift to do something—"

The tall, bleached-looking Herald freed a hand from his task just long enough to touch his face. There was an odd tugging sensation, and a flash of pain that sent him blind for a moment, then numbness.

Savil looked him over briefly. "Good enough; it'll hurt like hell for the next few days, but it'll heal up straight. We'll wash the blood off your face later. Jaysen, Rolf, get 'Lendel back to my quarters; this isn't anything a Healer's going to be able to treat. We'll take care of him ourselves."

"Aunt, please, what happened?" He staggered to his feet, holding Tylendel's hand tightly as the other two picked him up, still limp as a broken doll and showing no signs of consciousness. He was not willing to let go until he *knew* what was wrong.

Savil gently loosed his fingers from their grip. "If what we got from Gala is right—the moment he went mad is the moment someone assassinated his twin," she said angrily. "You know the bond he had with Staven."

Vanyel nodded, and his whole face throbbed.

"He felt it; felt the death, knew what had happened. Lost all control, lost his mind for a while, like the fits he used to have—only, I think, worse this time. Now he's depleted himself down to next to nothing, his whole body's in collapse from the energies he put through it, his mind's in trauma from Staven's death. That's backlash shock."

Vanyel wasn't sure he understood, but nodded anyway.

Savil's face darkened to pure rage. "May all the gods damn those fools and their feuding! Death after death, and *still* they aren't satisfied! Van, our job is to see we don't lose Tylendel as well."

"Lose him?" Vanyel's voice broke, and he looked wildly after the Heralds and their unconscious burden. "Oh no—oh gods—Aunt, tell me what to *do*, I can't let him—"

"I don't intend to let him die," she interrupted him, pushing him after the other Heralds. "The masquerade has been canceled, and to hell with what your father finds out; I'll deal with Withen myself, and I'll keep you here if I have to get the Queen's order to do it. You go with them, and don't you leave him, no matter what happens." Savil bit her lip, and gave Vanyel another push when he looked at her with a fear that held him nearly paralyzed. "Go—go on. He needs you, lad—like he's never needed anyone before. You're my only hope of getting him through this sane."

The two Heralds that Savil had called Jaysen and Rolf got Tylendel stripped and into bed without the trainee giving any sign of returning consciousness.

Vanyel hovered at the edge of the room, his hands clenched, his face throbbing and feeling as if it were nearly as white as Tylendel's. When they left—after giving him more than one dubious and curious glance—he installed himself in a chair at Tylendel's side, took his lover's limp, cold hand in his own, and refused to be moved.

He stayed there for the rest of the night, unable to sleep, unable to even think very clearly. Tylendel looked ghastly; his skin had gone transparent and waxy, there was no muscle tone in the hand Vanyel held, and the only thing showing he was alive was the shallow movement of his chest as he breathed.

Savil looked in once or twice during the night, but said nothing. Mardic came in at dawn to try to persuade him to get some rest, but Vanyel only shook his head stubbornly. He would not, he *could* not, rest, until he knew that Tylendel would be all right.

Savil left for a Council session—probably dealing with the feud—right after sunrise; with some reluctance, Mardic and Donni departed for their lessons a couple of candlemarks later. When Mardic failed to convince Vanyel to rest, Donni had tried to talk him into some food. He'd refused that as well, suspecting that—with all the best intentions in the world—she might have slipped something into it to make him sleep.

"'Lendel, they've gone," he said, when he heard the door open and close, just to have some other sound in the room besides Tylendel's breathing. "It's just you and me. 'Lendel, you have to come back—please. I *need* you, 'Lendel." He laughed, right on the edge of hysteria. "Look, you know yourself that I'm too far behind on my History for Mardic to help me."

He thought—maybe—he saw a flicker of response. His heart leapt, and he continued talking, coaxing, reciting bits of Tylendel's favorite poems—anything to bring him out of that unnatural sleep. He talked until his mouth and throat were dry, talked his voice into a harsh croak, left just long enough to get water, and returned to begin the monologue again. He lost track of what he was saying, somewhere around mid-afternoon; he was vaguely aware of someone checking on them, but ignored the other presences to keep up the flow of words. For by afternoon, there was no doubt; there *was* some change going on in Tylendel's condition, and for the better. He didn't know if it was the talking that was doing it, but he couldn't take any chances. He just kept holding to Tylendel's hand, saying anything that came into his head, however foolish-sounding.

Sunset arrived, turning the river beyond the windows briefly to a sword of flame; the light faded, the room darkened, and still he refused to move. Savil came in long enough to light the candles and whisper something—that he was doing the right thing, he thought; he wasn't sure. He didn't care; his whole world had narrowed to the white face resting on the pillow, and the slowly warming hand in his.

His eyes grew heavy, and his whole body ached, and his voice had thinned down to a whisper not even he could make out. He finally put his head down on his arms, intending to just rest for a moment—

And woke, feeling a hand tentatively caressing his hair. He started, jerking his head up off the coverlet, making his face pulse with pain.

Tylendel regarded him out of blue-ringed, weary eyes; eyes so full of anguish and loss that Vanyel nearly started weeping. "I heard you," he whispered. "I heard you, I just didn't have the strength to answer. Van—Staven—"

His face crumpled, and Vanyel slid off the chair and onto the side of the bed, taking him into his arms and holding him as tightly as he could; supporting him against his shoulder, giving him what little comfort his presence would give. Tylendel's body shook with sobs and he clung to Vanyel as to the only source of consolation left to him in the entire world, and Vanyel wept with him.

They finally fell asleep like that; true sleep, not the state of shock Tylendel had been in—Vanyel still fully clothed and sprawled between his chair and the side of the bed, Tylendel clinging to him like a heartbroken child.

"Eat," Vanyel ordered, setting the tray down in Tylendel's blanket-covered lap.

Tylendel looked nauseated and shook his head. "Can't," he whispered hoarsely.

"You mean 'won't,'" Vanyel retorted almost as hoarsely, trying to ignore the fact that talking made the whole of his face ache. "You've gone all day without food. Savil says if you don't get something down, you'll go into backlash shock again. I didn't spend all that time talking you out to have you drop back in again. Now *eat*, dammit!" He crossed his arms over his chest and glared down at Tylendel. The trainee eased a little higher up on the pillows supporting him in a sitting position and tried to shove the tray away. Unfortunately he was so weak he couldn't even lift it; he just moved it a palm-length away. Vanyel put it back precisely where he had placed it the first time.

Tylendel gave the perfectly good soup on the tray a look that would have been better bestowed on a bowl of pig swill, but picked up the spoon any-way. He swallowed the first spoonful with the air of someone who expects what he's just eaten to make a precipitate reappearance, but when nothing happened, gingerly ventured a second mouthful, and a third.

Vanyel sat warily on the edge of the bed, careful not to overset the tray between them. There was something very different about Tylendel since he'd reawakened—something secretive, but at the same time, impassioned. He could sense it in every word they'd exchanged. He thought he knew what it was, but he wanted to be sure.

"They're afraid I'm going to go mad, you know," Tylendel whispered in a matter-of-fact tone when he was about halfway through the bowl.

"I know," Vanyel replied, just as matter-of-factly, sensing that the secret was about to be revealed. "That's why they have me here. Are you?"

Tylendel looked up from his meal, and there was that strange, burning *something* Vanyel had felt searing sullenly at the back of his eyes. "They might think so. Van, you've got to help me."

"You didn't have to ask," Vanyel replied soberly. "Tell me what you want, and I'll get it for you."

"Vengeance." The thing at the back of his eyes flared for a moment, before subsiding into half-hidden, secretive smoldering again.

Vanyel nodded. This was rather what he had expected. If Tylendel wanted revenge— "Tell me. If I can do it, I will."

Tylendel slumped back on the pillows piled behind him, his head tilted back a little, his eyes closed, his features gone slack with relief. "Oh, gods— Van—I thought—"

"Eat," Vanyel growled. "I've told you before this that *I* understand, even if Savil doesn't. The only question *I've* got is how you think two half-grown, half-trained younglings are going to get revenge on people who live a good fortnight away by fast horse. I assume you've got an answer for that problem."

Tylendel opened his eyes and nodded soberly, but the spoon was still lying in the bowl of soup where he'd left it—and Vanyel was concentrating on the more immediate goal of getting him back on his feet. He'd worry about this plan when Tylendel was in shape to execute it, and not before.

"Dammit, 'Lendel, if you *don't* eat, I *won't* help you!"

Tylendel started guiltily, and leaned forward again to finish his meal.

Vanyel stole his mug long enough to get a sip of wine. His face hurt as badly as it looked, and when he'd taken one glance in the mirror, he'd had to look away again. His circle of admirers would have little to sigh over at the moment. He looked like he was wearing a black-and-blue domino mask and a putty nose. And he hurt. Gods, he hurt. The only reason he'd slept at all, once he'd comforted Tylendel last night, was because he'd been utterly, utterly exhausted.

"Did I do that?" Tylendel asked softly, finally *looking* at his face, as he scraped the last spoonful of soup from the bottom of the bowl.

Vanyel nodded, seeing no reason to deny it. "You weren't exactly yourself," he said, taking the tray away and stretching across Tylendel to put it on the table beside the bed.

"Oh, gods—Van, I'm sorry—" The smothered fury faded from Tylendel's eyes for a moment, and was replaced by concern as he reached in the direction of Vanyel's nose. The concern was replaced by hurt as Vanyel winced away.

"Touch me anywhere but *there;* it hurts bloody awful and it wasn't your fault, all right?" To counteract that flash of hurt in Tylendel's eyes, he moved closer, close enough to give 'Lendel a quick hug before taking his hand in both his own. "Now—you want to talk? I think maybe it's my turn to listen."

The deeply-buried fire returned, warring with anguish in his expression. "That link between Staven and me—it was different from what they think. Most of the time distance matters in a link like that, distance makes it weaker. It never did, for us. But Savil thought it did, and I let her go on thinking that. She would have been on me to break it, otherwise." He tensed, and closed his eyes; Vanyel held his hand a little more tightly. "All I ever had to do was think about him for him to be *with* me; it was the same for him. They—the Leshara—they ambushed him; killed his escort. Killed him. And it wasn't just an assassination, Van. *They used magic.*"

Vanyel felt his mouth drop open. "They what? How? How could a Herald—"

"It wasn't a Herald. They've hired a mage from outKingdom. They turned some—*things*—loose on the Holding. Magic monsters, maybe from the Pelagirs. Staven went after them with an escort, but when he got there, they were gone. He must have spent all day trying to track them down, and just exhausting himself, the fighters, and their horses. That's when the mage brought them back and ambushed Staven with them." Tylendel's eyes were horrible, like he was looking into hell. "These things, they *hurt* him before they killed him, hurt him awfully. On purpose; on their master's orders. I think on Leshara's orders. I can't tell you—"

He shuddered. "Stav reached for me—he reached for me through the link—Van, I was *with* him, I *felt* him die!"

He gripped Vanyel's hand so tightly that *both* their hands went white, and his voice quavered.

"He knew I was there with him; he knew it the moment I linked. Thank the gods—he knew he wasn't alone. But the last thing, the very last thing he did was to beg me, plead with me, to *pay them back*." His eyes opened, and they no longer smoldered; they flamed with fury and pain. "I promised him, Van. I *promised* him. Those bastards killed Staven—but they *won't* get away with it."

Vanyel met that fury, and bowed before it. "I told you, 'Lendel," he replied quietly. "Just ask."

"Oh, love—" The voice broke on a sob, and Vanyel looked up to see tears trickling down Tylendel's cheek. "I shouldn't get you into this—gods, I shouldn't. It isn't fair, it isn't right. You've got no stake in this."

"You told me yourself that we're partners, that whatever you had I'd share," Vanyel replied, as forcefully as he could. "That means the bad as well as the good, by *my* way of thinking." Now it was his turn to fumble in the drawer of the bedside table for a handkerchief. "Here," he said, pressing it into Tylendel's hand. "Now, tell me what you want me to do."

Tylendel scrubbed the tears away, his hand shaking. "We can't let Gala know what we're doing; she'd try to stop me. I can block her from knowing; I've already blocked her from knowing about the link to Staven. I'll—play sick—"

"You *are* sick; look at your hand shake."

Tylendel looked at the trembling of his hands with a certain amount of surprise. "Sicker, then. Too sick to do anything but lie here. What I need you to do is to sneak into Savil's room and get me two books. They're proscribed; nobody except very high-level Herald-Mages are even supposed to know they exist, and Savil is one of only three here at Haven who have copies."

Vanyel felt stirrings of misgiving. "In that case, won't they be locked up?"

The corner of Tylendel's mouth twitched. "Oh, they are. She's got them under protections. *But the protections don't work against someone with no Mage-Gift*."

"What?" Vanyel's jaw dropped again.

"Margret has to get in there and clean, so Savil only put up a protection against someone with a Mage-Gift touching them. That way Margret can handle them and put them away if she leaves them out by accident. She figured nobody without the Gift would ever know what to look for. So *you* can get them, even though I can't."

"Now?" Vanyel asked dubiously.

Tylendel shook his head. "No, I can't—can't handle much of anything right now. Later—" He choked, and whispered, "Oh, gods—Staven—"

His breath caught again, and this time he couldn't control himself. He dissolved into hopeless sobbing, and Vanyel turned his attention instantly from plans of revenge to comfort.

"You'll have to turn the pages," Tylendel told him, looking down at the plain, black-bound book lying on the coverlet between them. "I don't dare touch them."

Vanyel shrugged, and obliged, opening the ordinary-looking book to the first page.

The ruse had worked admirably well; Tylendel had feigned a far greater weakness than he actually felt, and all Savil had shown was simple concern that he rest as much as possible. She hadn't evidenced any signs that she thought his recovery was taking overlong; she hadn't even brought in a Healer when Vanyel had tentatively suggested (as a test) that Tylendel didn't seem to be improving that much.

"Backlash is a nasty thing, lad," she'd said with a sigh. "Takes weeks to bounce back from it; months, sometimes. I didn't expect him to come out of this as well as he did, and I think perhaps I've got *you* to thank for it."

Vanyel had blushed, and mumbled something deprecating. Savil had ruffled his hair and told him to get back to his charge, and not be an idiot. In a way, he'd felt a bit guilty at that moment, knowing what he knew, knowing that they were plotting something she wouldn't have permitted.

But she couldn't possibly understand, he told himself for the hundredth time. *She couldn't possibly. She cut her family ties long ago, and they were never that strong to begin with.* From time to time the strength of Tylendel's desire for revenge frightened him a little, but he told himself that it was *Tylendel* who was within his rights in this.

And when the thought occurred that his lover had grown to be obsessed with his revenge, he dismissed the thought as unworthy. Unworthy of 'Lendel, of Staven. This wasn't revenge—it was justice. Certainly the Heralds hadn't made any move toward dealing with the Leshara.

This afternoon Savil had scheduled Donni and Mardic for the Work

Room, and threatened murder on anyone who interrupted her *this* time. With the coast thus completely cleared, Vanyel had slipped into her room.

The books, so Tylendel had told him, would be in a small bookcase built into the wall beside the door that led to her own work room. He'd felt a chill of apprehension when he'd found the two volumes Tylendel wanted on the top shelf. He'd reached for them, expecting any moment to be flung across the room or fried by a lightning bolt.

But nothing had happened.

He'd returned to the bedroom where Tylendel waited, tucked up in bed with pen and paper. He slipped in furtively, clutching the books to his chest and shutting the door behind him.

Tylendel's fierce look of joy as he placed the books on the coverlet sent a shiver down his spine that he told himself was a thrill of accomplishment.

"What are you looking for?" he asked curiously, turning the pages slowly, Tylendel nodding to signal when he should.

"Two spells. We don't use spells a lot, but that doesn't mean they don't work," Tylendel said absently. "They do, and they work really well for somebody with a Mage-Gift as strong as the one I've got. Savil says I can pull energy out of rocks—well, most of us can't, so that's why we don't use spells much. The first one I want is something called a 'Gate'; it'll let us cover that distance from here to the Leshara lands in under an hour."

"You have *got* to be joking," Vanyel replied in disbelief. "I've never heard of anything like that."

"Herald-Mages would rather that people didn't know they could do that—really, only the best of them can; Savil can, and she said once that I should be able to, and Mardic and Donni if they ever learn how to work together. Most of the ones that can, *won't*, if they're on their own. That's because to do it, you need a lot of energy; it takes everything a mage has, and then what's he going to do when he gets where he wants to go?"

"Good point; what *are* you going to do?"

"I'm going to borrow *your* energy—if—you'll let me—" Tylendel faltered, and looked up from the book in entreaty.

Vanyel firmed his chin. "What do you mean, 'if'? *Of course* you can borrow it, what other good am I going to do?"

"Gods—*ashke, ashke,* I don't deserve you," Tylendel said softly, half-smiling, his voice shaking in a way that told Vanyel he was on the verge of tears again.

"It's the other way around, love," Vanyel replied, cutting him off. "Who was it kept me from—killing myself by inches? Who showed me what happiness was about? Who loves me when nobody else does? Hmm?"

"Who blacked your eyes, broke your nose, and nearly fractured your ankle?"

"Well, that proves it, doesn't it?" Vanyel retorted, trying to make a feeble joke. "They say if you don't hurt, you don't love."

Tylendel shook his head. "I—gods, don't let me go all to pieces again. Vanyel-*ashke*, I could *never* hope to do this without you. There's no one else that I would trust in this that could help me with a Gate-spell—and Van, I should warn you, you're going to feel damn seedy afterward, like you've had a case of backlash to match mine."

"*Can* you borrow this stuff?" Vanyel interrupted dubiously. "I mean, I don't have any Mage-Gifts or anything."

"Not active; you've got something, you've got the potential, but it's locked. I wouldn't have known, but I think we're linking a little, on a deeper level than Savil and I have—or even Gala and I. It's more like what I had with my twin; it isn't conscious, but—I know you know when I'm—"

"—unhappy," Vanyel finished for him, thoughtfully. "And other things. Uh-huh, I think you're right. I thought it might just be because I'm worried about you, but it seems to be going further than that. Like last night, when I woke you up before you'd barely started to have a nightmare."

Tylendel nodded. "So I think we're linking. I think it happened sometime between when I started the fit and when I came out of the backlash coma. I can feel—something—in you. Something very deep, but very strong. That's when I thought about the Gate-spell, and I used Othersight on you. I sort of felt the link, and then I saw you had Mage-energies I could tap into using that link."

"Gods—'Lendel, *don't* tell me I'm going to turn into a Herald-Mage," he said, alarmed by the very idea.

"If you haven't by now, it isn't too bloody likely," Tylendel replied, to Vanyel's profound relief. "Savil says a lot of people have the potential, but nothing ever triggers it. You've just got the potential."

"So *don't* trigger it," Vanyel replied, shivering with an unexplained chill. "I don't *want* to be a Herald or a Herald-Mage, or anything like them."

Tylendel gave him an odd look, but only said, "I doubt I could, even if you wanted it. There's stories that there's a couple of Mage-schools that know how to trigger potential, but nobody I know has ever seen it done, so even if it's possible, the people that can do it are keeping the means a deep secret."

"Good," Vanyel replied, still fighting down his chill of apprehension. "That's exactly the way I want it. So—you make this Gate thing. Then what?"

"When we get to the other side of the Gate, we'll be on Leshara land; right on top of the keep, if I can manage it. I'll use the other spell I'm looking for—and that will be the end of it."

Vanyel suddenly *knew*, without knowing how he knew, that he did not *want* to know what this "other spell" was.

"Fine," he replied shortly, turning another page. "You keep looking. Just tell me when to stop."

CHAPTER 8

$\diamond$

VANYEL STARED NERVOUSLY at his own reflection in the window—a specter, pale and indistinct; ghostlike, with dark hollows for eyes. Beyond the glass, night blanketed the gardens; a moonless night, a night of wind and cloud and no light at all, not even starlight.

Sovvan-night; the night of celebration of the harvest, but also the night set apart for remembering the dead of the year past. The night when—so most traditions held—the Otherworld was closer than on any other night. A night of profound darkness, like the one a moon ago when Staven had been slain.

Savil was with the rest of the Heralds, mourning *their* dead of the year. Donni and Mardic, having no one in need of remembrance, were with some of the other trainees at a Palace fete, indulging in a certain amount of the superstitious foolery associated with Harvestfest that was also a part of Sovvan-night, at least for the young.

Lord Evan Leshara had gone home to Westrel Keep. Presumably well satisfied with himself. There was no doubt in Vanyel's mind that Lord Evan had somehow extracted enough good information from what had been fed to him to deduce exactly what bait would serve best to lure Staven to his death. They had tried to use him—and had ended up being used by him.

And that was a blackly bitter thought.

Tylendel and Vanyel had been left alone in the suite—

Tylendel and Vanyel would not be mewed up in the suite much longer.

"Are you ready?" Tylendel asked from the door behind him.

Vanyel nodded, and pulled the hood of his dark blue cloak up over his head, trying not to shiver at his own reflection. With the hood shrouding his face, he looked like an image of Death itself. Then Tylendel moved silently to his side, and there were *two* of the hooded figures reflected in the clouded glass: Death, and Death's Shadow.

He shook his head to free it of such ominous thoughts, as Tylendel opened the door and they stepped out into the cold, blustering night.

This morning he had slipped out into Haven and bought a pair of nondescript horses from a down-at-the-heels beast-trader, using most of the coin he and Tylendel had managed to scrape together over the past three weeks. He'd taken them off into the west end of the city and stabled them at an inn just outside the city wall.

Tylendel had told Vanyel that before he worked the spell to take them within striking distance of the Leshara holding, he wanted to be out of the easy sensing range of the Herald-Mages. They needed transportation, but it didn't matter how broken-down the beasts were; their horses only needed to last long enough to get them an hour's ride out of the city. After that it wouldn't matter what became of them.

Obviously, riding Gala was totally out of the question. They weren't taking Star or "borrowing" any of the true horses from the Palace stables, because if their absence were noticed, Tylendel didn't want any suspicions aroused until it was too late to stop them. Vanyel had concurred without an argument; if they couldn't force their mounts through Tylendel's Gate—and the trainee had indicated that they might not be able to or might not want to—they were going to have to turn them loose to fend for themselves. He didn't want to lose Star, and he didn't want to be responsible for the loss of anyone else's prized mount, either.

The ice-edged wind caught at their cloaks, finding all the openings and cutting right through the heavy wool itself. Vanyel was shivering long before they slipped past the Gate Guard at the Palace gates and on out into the streets of the city. The Guard was preoccupied with warming himself at the charcoal brazier beside the gate; he didn't seem to notice them as they hugged the shadows of the side of the gate farthest from him and took to the cobblestoned street beyond.

Now they were out in the wealthiest district of the city. The high buildings on either side of them served only to funnel the wind right at them, or so it seemed. Tylendel, who was still not entirely steady on his feet, grabbed Vanyel's arm and hung on. Vanyel could feel him shivering, partly with cold, but from the way his eyes were gleaming in the shadows of his hood, partly also with excitement.

These mansions of the wealthy and highborn were mostly dark tonight; the inhabitants were either at Temple services or attending the Harvestfest gathering at the Palace. Vanyel had *not* received an invitation—and although he was anything but displeased, he wasn't entirely certain why he had not. His apparent about-face with regard to Tylendel had confused not only his own little circle, but the trainees and Heralds as well. And no one had enlightened them; Savil had reckoned that keeping the rumormongers confused would keep the real story from reaching Withen for a while and buy them additional time.

Assuming Lord Evan hadn't told him, just for the pure spite of making things difficult for Tylendel and Tylendel's lover. It would suit the man's character.

Vanyel thought briefly of the Sovvan-fete he was missing. It was possible that those in charge of the festivities had assumed he would be staying at Tylendel's side, especially tonight. It was also possible that they blamed him for Tylendel's condition (Mardic had reported several stories to that effect) and were "punishing" him for his conduct.

Whatever the reason, this had proved to be too good an opportunity to slip out undetected to let pass by.

They turned a corner, and the buildings changed; now they were smaller, crowded closer together, and no longer hidden behind walls. Each had candles in the otherwise darkened windows—another Sovvan-custom. It was by the light of these candles that the two were finding their way; the torches that usually illuminated the street by night had long since blown out.

Tylendel had been growing increasingly strange and withdrawn in the past several days since Vanyel had purloined Savil's magic books for him. Vanyel would wake up in the middle of the night to find him huddled in the chair, studying his handwritten copies of the two spells with fanatic and feverish concentration. During waking hours he would often stare for hours at nothing, or at a candleflame, and his conversation had become monosyllabic. The only time he seemed anything like his old self was when he'd begin a nightmare and Vanyel would wake him from it; then he would cry for a while on Vanyel's shoulder, and afterward talk until they both fell asleep again. *Then* he sounded like the old Tylendel—not afraid to share his grief or his fears with the one he loved. But when day arrived, he would be back inside his shell, and nothing Vanyel could do or say seemed to crack that barrier.

Vanyel had long since begun to think that he would *never* be his old self again until his revenge had been accomplished, and he had begun to long for that moment with a fervor that nearly equaled his lover's.

They reached the sector of shops and inns long before they saw another human out on the streets, and that was only the Nightwatch. The patrol of two men gave them hardly more than a passing glance; they were obviously unarmed except for knives, were too well-dressed to be street-toughs, and not flashy enough to be young highborns out to find some trouble. The two men of the Watch gave them nearly simultaneous nods, curt and preoccupied, nods which they returned as the light from the Watchlantern in the hands of the rightmost one fell on them. Satisfied by what they saw, the Watch passed on, and so did they, boot-heels clattering on the cobbles.

Here the buildings were only one or two stories tall, and the wind howled and ramped about them unimpeded. The quality and state of repair of these buildings—mostly shops, inns, lodging-houses, and workshops—declined steadily and rapidly as they neared the west city-wall of Haven.

The Guards on the great gates of Haven were not in evidence tonight, although there was a viewport in the wall, and Vanyel could almost feel eyes on him as they passed below it. Obviously the Guards found as little to alarm them in the two younglings as the Watch had; they passed out under the wall with no challenge whatsoever.

Once outside the west wall, they were in the lowest district in the city. Vanyel led the way to the ramshackle inn where he'd left their sorry nags; fighting the wind every inch of the way, as it nearly tore the edges of his cloak out of his half-frozen hands.

The Red Nose Inn was brightly lit and full to bursting with roisterers; Vanyel heard their out-of-tune singing and hoarse laughter even over the moaning of the wind as they passed by the open door. Smoke and light alike spilled out that door, and the wind carried a random puff of the smoke into their eyes as they passed, a noisome smudge that made them cough and their eyes water for a moment before cleaner air whipped it out of their faces again. They ignored that open door and passed around the side of the inn to the dirty courtyard and the stabling area.

There was a single, half-drunk groom on duty, slumped on a stack of hay bales by the stable door, illuminated by a feebly burning lantern. His head lolled on his chest as he snored, smelling, even in this wind, as if he'd fallen into a vat of cheap beer. Tylendel waited in the shadows beyond reach of the light from the smoking lantern that had been hung in the lee of the stable door, while Vanyel shook the man's shoulder until he roused.

"Eh?" the man grunted, peering into the shadows under Vanyel's hood in an unsuccessful attempt to make out his features. His breath was as foul as his clothing; his face was filthy and unshaven, and his hair hung around his ears in lank, greasy ringlets. "What ye want, then? Where be yer nags?"

"Already here," Vanyel replied, in a tone as adult, brusque, and gruff as he could manage. "Here—" He shoved the claim-chits at the groom, together with two silver pieces. The man stared stupidly at them for a moment, blinking in surprise, as if he were having trouble telling the chits from the coins. Then he grinned in sudden comprehension, displaying a mouthful of half-rotten teeth, and nodded.

"'Nuff celebratin', eh, master? Just ye wait, just ye wait right here." He shoved the coins and chits together into the pocket in the front of his stained, oily leather apron, heaved himself up off his couch of hay bales, and staggered inside the stable door. He emerged a great deal sooner than Vanyel would have thought possible, leading a pair of scruffy-looking, nondescript brown geldings that were already saddled and bridled with patched and worn tack. Vanyel squinted at them in the smoky light, trying to make out if they were the same ones he'd bought this morning, then realized that it didn't matter if they were or not. It wasn't as if the horses he'd purchased were any kind of prize specimens—in fact, if these *weren't* "his" horses, they were likely as not to be an improvement over the ones he'd bought!

He took the reins away from the groom without another word, turned, and led them across the dirt court to where Tylendel was waiting, huddled against the inn wall in a futile attempt to avoid the biting wind. When he looked back over his shoulder, he could see that the groom had already flopped down on the straw bales and resumed his interrupted nap.

He handed Tylendel the reins of the better of the two mounts, and scrambled into his own saddle. His flea-bitten beast skittered sideways in an attempt to avoid being mounted, and gave a half-hearted buck as Vanyel settled into his seat. Vanyel made a fist and gave it a good rap between the ears; the nag stopped trying to rid itself of its rider and settled down.

The spine of his saddle was broken; the horse itself was swaybacked, and its gait was as rough as he'd ever had the misfortune to encounter. He hoped, as Tylendel took the lead and they headed down Exile's Road into the west, that they wouldn't be riding for too very long.

The wind had died down—at least momentarily—when Tylendel finally stopped. It was so dark that the only way he really knew that Tylendel had pulled up was because the sound of hooves on the hard surface of the road ahead of him stopped. They'd trusted to the fact that Exile's Road was lined on either side with hedges to keep their sorry beasts on the roadway. He kicked at his own mount and forced it forward until he could feel the presence of Tylendel and his horse bulking beside him.

There was a flare of light; Vanyel winced away from it—it was quite painful after the near-total darkness of the last candlemark or so. When he could bear to look again, he saw that Tylendel had dismounted and was leading his horse, a red ball of mage-light bobbing along above his head.

He scrambled off of his own mount, glad enough to be out of that excruciatingly uncomfortable saddle, snatched the reins of the beast over its head, and hastened to catch up.

"Are we far enough away yet?" he asked, longing for even a single word from the trainee to break the silence and tension. Tylendel's face was drawn and fey, strained; Tylendel's attention was plainly somewhere else, his whole aspect wrapped up in the kind of terrifying concentration that had been all too common to him of late.

"Almost," he replied, after a long and unnerving silence. His voice had a strange quality to it, as if Tylendel was having to work to get even a single word out past whatever it was he was concentrating on. "I'm—looking for something. . . ."

Vanyel shivered, and not from the cold. "What?"

"A place to put the Gate." They came to a break in the hedge. No—not a break. When Tylendel stopped and led his horse over to it, Vanyel could see that it was the remains of a gated opening in the hedge, long since overgrown. Beyond the gap something bulked darkly in the dim illumination provided by the mage-light. Tylendel nodded slightly. "I thought I remembered this place," he muttered. He didn't seem to expect a response, so Vanyel didn't make one.

It was obvious that the horses were not going to be able to force themselves through so narrow a passage; Tylendel stripped the bridle from his, hung it on the saddlebow, and gave the gelding a tremendous slap on the hip that made it snort with surprise and sent it cantering off into the darkness. Vanyel did the same with his, *not* sorry to see it go, and turned away from the road to see that Tylendel had already forced his way past the gap in the hedge and was now out of sight. Only the reddish glow of the mage-light through the leafless branches of the hedgerow showed where he had gone.

Vanyel shoved his way past the branches, cursing as they caught on his cloak and scratched at his face. When he emerged, staggering, from the prickly embrace of stubborn bushes, he found that he was standing knee-deep in weeds, in what had been the yard of a small building. It could have been anything from a shop to a cottage, but was now going to pieces; the yard was as overgrown as the gate had been. The building seemed to be entirely roof-less and the door and windows were mere holes in the walls. Tylendel was examining the remains of the door with care.

The gap where the door had been was a large one, easily large enough for a horse and rider to pass through. Tylendel nodded again, and this time there was an expression of dour satisfaction on his face. "This will do," he said softly. "Van, think you're ready?"

Vanyel took a deep breath, and tried to relax a little. "As ready as I'm ever likely to get," he replied.

Tylendel turned and took both Vanyel's hands in his; he looked search-ingly into Vanyel's eyes for a long moment. "Van, I'm going to have to force that link between us wide open for this to work. I may hurt you. I'll try not to, but I can't promise. Are you still willing to help me?"

Vanyel nodded, thinking, *I've come this far; it would be stupid to back out at this point. Besides—he needs this. How can I not give it to him?*

Tylendel closed his eyes; his face froze into as impassive a mask as Vanyel had ever worn. Vanyel waited, trembling a little, for something to happen.

For a long while, nothing did. Then—

Rage flamed up in him, a consuming, obsessive anger that left very little room for anything else. One thing mattered: Staven was dead. One goal drove him: deal the same painful death to Staven's murderers. There was still a tiny corner of his mind that could think for itself and wonder at the overwhelming power of Tylendel's fury, but that corner had been locked out of any position of control.

The truism ran "Pain shared is pain halved"—but this pain was doubled on being shared.

He turned to face the ancient doorway without any conscious decision to do so, Tylendel turning even as he did. He saw Tylendel raise his arms and cast a double handful of something powderlike on the ground before the door, heard him begin a chant in some strange tongue and hold his now-empty hands, palm outward, to face that similarly empty gap.

He felt something draining out of him, like blood draining from a wound, and felt that it was taking his strength with it.

The edges of the ruined doorway were beginning to glow, the same sullen red as the mage-light over Tylendel's head, like the muted red of em-bers, as if the edge of the doorway smoldered. As more and more of Vanyel's energy and strength drained from him, the ragged border brightened, and tiny threads of angry scarlet wavered from them into the space where the door had stood. More and more of these threads spun out, waving like water-weeds in a current, until two of the ends connected across the gap.

There was a surge of force out of him, a surge that nearly caused his knees to collapse, as the entire gap filled with a flare of blood-red light—

Then the light vanished, and the gap framed, not a shadowed blackness, but a garden—a formal garden decorated for a festival, and filled with people, light, and movement.

He had hardly a chance to see this before Tylendel grabbed his arm and pulled him, stumbling, across the threshold. There was a moment of total disorientation, as though the world had dropped from beneath his feet, then—

Sound: laughter, music, shouting. He stood, with Tylendel, facing that garden he had seen through the ruined doorway, and beyond the garden, a strange keep. Lanterns bobbed gaily in the branches of a row of trees that stood between them and the gathered people, and trestle tables, spread with food and lanterns, were visible on the farther side. Near the trees was a lighted platform on which a band of motley musicians stood, playing with a vigor that partially made up for their lack of skill. Before the platform a crowd of people was dancing in a ring, laughing and singing along with the music.

Vanyel's knees would not hold him; as soon as Tylendel let go of his arm, his legs gave way, and he found himself half-kneeling on the ground, dizzy, weak, and nauseated. Tylendel didn't notice; his attention was on the people dancing.

"They're *celebrating*," Tylendel whispered, and the anger Vanyel was inadvertently sharing surged along the link between them. "Staven's *dead*, and they're *celebrating*!"

That small, rational corner still left to Vanyel whispered that this was *only* a Harvestfest like any other, that the Leshara weren't particularly gloating over an enemy's death. But that logical voice was too faint to be heard over the thunder of Tylendel's outrage. A wave of dizziness clouded his sight with a red mist, and he could hear his heart pounding in his ears.

When he could see again, Tylendel had stepped away from him, and was standing between him and the line of trees with his hands high over his head. From Tylendel's upraised hands came twin bolts of the same vermilion lightning that had lashed the pine grove a moon ago. Only *this* lightning was controlled and directed, and it cracked across the garden and destroyed the trees standing between him and the gathered Leshara-kin in less time than it took to blink.

In the wake of the thunderbolt came startled screams; the music ended in a jangle of snapped strings and the squawk of horns. The dancers froze, and clutched at each other in clumps of two to five. Tylendel's mage-light was blazing like a tiny, scarlet sun above his head; his face was hate-filled and twisted with frenzy. Tears streaked his face; his voice cracked as he screamed at them.

"He's *dead*, you bastards! He's *dead*, and you're *laughing*, you're *singing*! Damn you all, I'll teach you to sing a different song! You want magic? Well, *here's* magic for you—"

Vanyel couldn't move; he seemed tethered to the still-glowing Gate behind him. He could only watch, numbly, as Tylendel raised his hands again—and this time it was not lightning that crackled from his upraised hands. A glowing sphere appeared with a sound of thunder, suspended high above him. About the size of a melon, it hung in the air, rotating slowly, a smoky, sickly yellow. It grew as it turned, and drifted silently away from Tylendel and toward the huddled Leshara-folk, descending as it neared them, until it came to earth in the center of the blasted, blackened place where the trees had been a moment before.

There it rested; still turning, still growing, until it had swelled to twice the height of a man.

Then, between one heartbeat and the next, it burst.

Another wave of disorientation washed over him; Vanyel blinked eyes that didn't seem to be focusing properly. Where the globe had rested there seemed to be a twisting, twining mass of shadow-shapes, shapes as fluid as ink, as sinuous as snakes, shapes that were *there* and *not there* at one and the same time.

Then they slid apart, those shapes, separating into five writhing mist-forms. They solidified—

If some mad god had mated a viper and a coursing-hound, and grown the resulting offspring to the size of a calf, the result *might* have looked something like the five creatures snarling and flowing lithely around one another in the gleaming of Tylendel's mage-light. In color they were a smoky black, with skin that gave an impression of smooth scales rather than hair. They had long, long necks, too long by far, and arrowhead-shaped heads that were an uncanny mingling of snake and greyhound, with yellow, pupil-less eyes that glowed in the same way and with the same shifting color that the globe that had birthed them had glowed. The teeth in those narrow muzzles were needle-sharp, and as long as a man's thumb. They had bodies like greyhounds as well, but the legs and tails seemed unhealthily stretched and unnaturally boneless.

They regarded Tylendel with unwavering, saffron eyes; they seemed to be waiting for something.

He quavered out a single word, his voice breaking on the final, high-pitched syllable—and they turned as one entity to face the cowering folk of Leshara, mouths gaping in unholy parodies of a dog's foolish grin.

But before they had flowed a single step toward their victims, a shrill scream of equine defiance rang out from behind Vanyel.

And Gala thundered through the Gate at his back, pounding past him, then past Tylendel, ignoring the trainee completely.

She screamed again, more anger and courage in her cry than Vanyel had ever thought possible to hear in a horse's voice, and skidded to a halt halfway between Tylendel and the things he had called up. *She* was glowing, just like she had during 'Lendel's fit; a pure, blue-white radiance that attracted the eye in the same way that the yellow glow of the beasts' eyes repelled. She continued to ignore Tylendel's presence entirely, turning her back to him; rearing up to her full height and pawing the air with her forehooves, trumpeting a challenge to the five creatures before her.

They reversed their positions in an instant as her hooves touched the ground again, facing her with silent snarls of anger. She pawed the earth, and bared her teeth at them, daring them to try to fight her.

"Gala!" Tylendel cried in anguish, his voice breaking yet again. "*Gala! Don't—*"

She turned her head just enough to look him fully in the eyes—and Vanyel heard her mental reply as it rang through Tylendel's mind and heart and splintered his soul.

:*I do not know you,*: she said coldly, remotely. :*You are not my Chosen.*:

And with those words, the bond that had been between them vanished. Vanyel could feel the emptiness where it had been—for he was still sharing everything Tylendel felt.

Tylendel's rage shattered on the cold of those words.

And when the bond was broken, what took its place was utter desolation.

Vanyel moaned in anguish, sharing Tylendel's agony, and the torment and bereavement as he called after Gala with his mind and received not even the echo of a reply. Where there had been warmth and love and support there was now—nothing; not even a ghost of what had been.

The link between them surged with loss, and Vanyel's vision darkened.

He heard Tylendel cry out Gala's name in utter despair, and willed his eyes to clear.

And to his horror he watched her fling herself at the five fiends, heedless of her own safety.

They swarmed over and about her, their darkness extinguishing her light. He heard her shriek, but this time in pain, and saw the red splash of blood bloom vividly on her white coat.

He tried to stagger to his feet, but had no strength; his ears roared, and he blacked out.

He barely felt himself falling again, and only Tylendel's scream of anguish and loss penetrated enough to make him fight his way back to consciousness.

He found himself half-sprawled on the cold ground. He shoved himself partially erect despite his spinning head, and looked for Gala—

But there was no Companion, no fight. Only a mutilated corpse, sprawling torn and ravaged, throat slashed to ribbons, the light gone from the sapphire eyes. Tylendel was on his knees beside her, stroking the ruined head, weeping hoarsely.

Beside her lifeless body lay one of the five monstrosities, head a shapeless pulp. The others flowed around the Companion's body, as if waiting for the corpse to rise again so that they could attack it. Two of the others limped on three legs—but two were still unharmed, and given what they had done to Gala in a few heartbeats, two would be more than enough to slaughter every man, woman, and child of the Leshara.

Finally they left off their mindless, sharklike circling, and turned to face the terrified celebrants. They took no more notice of Tylendel than of the dead Companion.

A man bolted from the crowd. With a start, Vanyel recognized him for Lord Evan. Whether he meant to attack the beasts, or simply to flee, Vanyel couldn't tell. It really didn't matter much; one of the beasts that was still unhurt flashed across the intervening space and caught him. He did not even have time to cry out as it disemboweled him.

A woman screamed—and that seemed to signal the beasts to move again. They began to ooze in a body toward their victims—

And a bolt of brilliantly white lightning cracked from behind Vanyel to scorch the earth before the leader.

There was a pounding of hooves from the Gate. Vanyel was momentarily blinded by the light and by another surge of weakness that sent him sagging back to the ground.

When his eyes cleared again, there were three white-clad Heralds and their three Companions closing on the fiends, lightnings crackling from their upraised hands. They were using the lightnings to herd the beasts into a tight little knot and barring their path to their prey.

He barely had time to recognize two of the three as Savil and Jaysen before battle was joined.

Once again he started to black out, feeling as if something was trying to pull his soul out of his body. He fought against unconsciousness, though he felt as if he had nothing left to fight *with*; both the rage and the despair were gone now, leaving only an empty place, a void that ached unbearably.

He felt a tiny *inflowing* of strength; it wasn't much, but it was enough to give him the means to fight the blackness away from his eyes, to fight off the vertigo, and to finally get a precarious hold on the world again.

The first thing he saw was Tylendel; still on his knees, but no longer weeping. He was vacant-eyed, white as bleached linen, and staring at his own blood-smeared hands. Where the five creatures had been there was now nothing; only the mangled body of Gala and the burned and churned-up earth.

Taking her hand away from his shoulder was Savil—her face an unreadable mask.

Savil pulled her attention away from Tylendel, who was slumped in a kind of trance of despair beside her, and back to what Vanyel was telling the other two Heralds.

". . . then she said, 'I don't know you, you aren't my Chosen,'" the boy whispered, eyes dull and mirroring his exhaustion, voice colorless. "And she turned her back on him, just turned away, and charged those things."

"Buying time for us to get here," Jaysen murmured, his voice betraying the pain he would not show. "Oh, gods, the poor, brave thing—if she hadn't bought us those moments, we'd have come in on a bloodbath."

"She *repudiated* him," said Lancir, the Queen's Own, as if he did not believe it. "She repudiated him, and then—"

"Suicided," Savil supplied flatly, her own heart in turmoil; aching for

Tylendel, for the loss of Gala, for all the things she should have seen and hadn't. "Gods, she *suicided*. She knew, she *had* to know that no single Companion could face a pack of *wyrsa* and survive."

Tylendel sat where they had left him, unseeing, unspeaking—all of hell in his eyes. Mage-lights of their own creation bobbed overhead, pitilessly illuminating everything.

Jaysen contemplated Savil's trainee for a long moment, but said nothing, only shook his head slightly. Then he spared a glance for Vanyel, and frowned; Savil heard his thought. *:The boy is still tied to the Gate, sister. He grows weaker by the moment. If you want him undamaged—:*

Unspoken, but not unfelt, was the vague thought that perhaps it would be no bad thing if Vanyel were to be "forgotten" until it was too late to save him from the aftereffects of the Gate-magic. That undercurrent of thought told Savil that Jaysen placed all of the blame for this squarely on Vanyel's shoulders.

:It wasn't his fault, Jaysen,: she answered, heartsick and near to weeping, but unable to be anything other than honest. *:He didn't do anything worse than go along with what 'Lendel wanted without telling me. What happened was as much due to my negligence as anything he did.:*

Jaysen gave a curt nod, but a skeptical one. *:In that case, we need to get that Gate closed down as soon as possible, or the boy will sicken—or worse.:*

No need to ask what that "worse" was; Vanyel was already looking drawn, almost transparent, as the Gate pulled more and more of his lifeforce from him. How Tylendel, half-trained, and Vanyel, unGifted, had managed that, Savil had no notion—but they dared not break the link until they didn't need the Gate anymore.

:Fine, but what are we going to do about all that mess?: Savil asked, nodding her head at the milling crowd, the mangled corpse of the single victim the *wyrsa* had killed, and the pathetic body of the Companion. *:Somebody had better take them in hand, or no telling what they'll get up to. Go in for a wholesale slaughtering-party on Tylendel's people, make up some kind of tale about Heralds being in on this—:* Even a hair away from breaking down into tears, she was still *thinking*; she couldn't help it.

:I'll stay here,: Lancir volunteered. *:Elspeth can do without me for a moon or so. I'll take care of the Leshara and see to—:* his thought faltered. *:—Gala.:*

:And you'll get home how?: Jaysen asked, concerned. *:We're going to shut the Gate from the other side as soon as we're through, and you aren't up to Gating by yourself these days.:*

:Like ordinary mortals,: he replied, with a deathly seriousness. *:On our feet.:*

:What—what are we going to do about—: Savil's eyes flicked to Tylendel and back; the boy was still staring vacantly into space, his face pale and blank, his eyes so full of inward-turned torment that she could scarcely bear to look into them for fear she *would* break down and cry.

:I don't know,: Lancir replied bleakly. *:I just don't know. There's no precedent. Get the boy home; worry about it when you've got time to think about it. Ask your Companions; it was one of their number that died. That's all I can think of. But you'd better get on with it if you expect to leave the other boy with a mind.:*

"Jays, take Tylendel, will you?" Savil said aloud, reaching for Vanyel's arm and pulling him to his feet. "Lance—"

"Gods with you, heart-sibs," said the Queen's Own, pity and compassion momentarily transforming his homely face into something close to saintly, like that of a beautiful carved statue. "You'll need their help. Taver?"

His Companion sidled up to him and held rock-still for Jaysen to help him to mount; like the Queen, like Savil, Lancir was feeling his age these autumn days, and needed the boost into place that Jaysen gave him. But once in the saddle, he resumed the strength and dignity of a much younger Queen's Own—the man he had been twenty years ago. Taver tossed his head, and walked with calm and quiet steps toward the shocked, confused mob of Leshara at the other end of the garden.

Jaysen tugged on Tylendel's arm; the boy rose, but with the automatic movements of someone spellbound, his attention still turned within himself. The Seneschal's Herald led the way to the Gate, followed closely by his Companion, and guided the boy with a hand at his shoulder.

He cast a look back at Savil. "I don't fancy the notion of the ride we have ahead of us—too many things to go wrong on the way. You know more about this spell than I do—do you think you can reset this Gate to bring us out at the Palace?"

She wrenched her attention away from the unanswerable problem of what to do about the boys, and contemplated the structure of the Gate. The portal at *this* end was an ornamental gazebo in the center of the blasted garden. Through the arch of the entrance lay the dark of the ruinous cottage yard.

"I don't see any problem," she replied, after study. "I can bring us out in the Grove Temple, if that's all right."

"That should do," Jaysen said, eyeing the sky on the other side of the portal, which was flickering with lightnings. "Good gods—why did *that* blow in? There wasn't a storm due."

"Don't look so surprised, Jays," she growled, needed to lash out at *something* and using his absentmindedness to make him the target. "I've told you a dozen times that Gating plays merry cob with the weather. That's why I don't like to use Gates. It's going to get worse when I reset it, and all hell will break out when I collapse it."

He pursed his lips and frowned, but didn't reply, just waved at her with his free hand. She let go of Vanyel, who sagged back to his knees, too weakened to stay standing without her support. She raised both her hands high above her head, and made an intricately weaving little gesture. Filaments of dull red light floated from the Gate toward her, and were caught up on her fingers by that complex weaving. When she had them fast, she clenched her hands on them and sent her will coursing down them in a surge of pure, commanding power, the filaments turning from red to white as *her* will flowed back along them.

When the wave of white reached the Gate, the portal misted over, then flared incandescently. When the light died, the scene framed in the gazebo arch was that of Companion's Field, seen by the fitful flashes of lightning, as viewed from the porch of the Grove Temple.

Savil reached down and caught the fabric of Vanyel's tunic, pulling him to his feet again. She dragged him with her as she followed closely on Jaysen's heels. He hurried across the Gate threshold, pushing Tylendel before him; she half-ran a step behind him, dragging Vanyel with her by main force.

The Gate-crossing hit her with its all-too-familiar, sickening sensation of falling. Then—hard, smooth marble was beneath her feet, and they were home.

Lighting struck a nearby tree, and thunder deafened her for a moment. She cleared out of the path of the Gate and Kellan and Felar darted across, ears laid back, as soon as she and Vanyel were out of the way.

She let go of Vanyel, who stumbled the two steps to one of the pillars and clung to it. She turned to face the Gate even as another bolt struck nearby. The Gate was going unstable, wavering from red to white and back again, the instability in the energy fields mirrored in the increasing fury of the lightning storm overhead. She raised her hands and began the dismissal—and encountered unexpected resistance.

She tried again, wincing at the crack of thunder directly above her. There was something wrong, something very wrong. The Gate was fighting her.

"Jays"—she shouted over the growl of thunder and the whine of the wind—"I need a hand, here."

Jaysen let go of Tylendel to add his strength to hers—their united wills worked at the spell-knot, forcing it to unravel faster than it could knit itself back up again.

With a surge of wild power that brought a half-dozen lightning strikes down on the Belltower of the Temple itself, the Gate collapsed—

Then again the unexpected; the Gate-energy, instead of dissipating back into the air and ground, flared up, and surged back down the one conduit left to it. The force-line that had tied it into Vanyel. Savil Saw it—but not in time to stop it.

Vanyel screamed in agony, convulsing, clutching the pillar as the released power arced back into him—and from him, a second, weaker arc leapt to Tylendel.

Tylendel jerked into sudden alertness—and uttered the most painful cry of despair Savil had ever heard; it was a cry that would haunt her nightmares for the rest of her life.

She pivoted and grabbed for him as quickly as she could as Vanyel collapsed in a moaning heap at the foot of the pillar.

But it was too late. No longer held in deceptive docility by his shock, he dodged her outstretched hand. She saw his face in another of the lightning flashes; his eyes were all pupil, his face a twisted mask of nothing but pain. He looked frantically about him with those terrible eyes that held no sanity at all, dodged her again, and then dashed past her into the tangled trees of the Grove.

Jaysen gave chase; Savil limped after both of them. Lightning was striking so often overhead now that the sky was almost as bright as day. She tried to use the line of their shared magic to get at Tylendel's mind as she ran, hoping to bring him back to her, but stumbled in shock and fell when she touched his thoughts. There was nothing to get a hold on—the boy was a chaotic, aching void of grief and loneliness. It was so empty, so unhuman, that for a moment she could only crouch in the cold, dry grass and listen to her overworked heart beat in panic. It took every ounce of discipline she had to get her own mind back under control after touching that terrible, all-consuming sorrow.

Belatedly she thought of Vanyel. If anyone could reach Tylendel, surely *he* could.

She lurched painfully to her feet and stumbled back toward the Temple. In the lightning flashes she could make out the younger boy staggering blindly out of the Temple, clutching himself as if he were freezing—saw him stumble and fall on his shoulder, without trying to save himself.

Then she saw Tylendel dart out of the tree-shadows to her right and race past her, past his fallen lover, and back into the Temple itself.

And her heart went cold with a sudden premonition of disaster.

She forced her exhausted legs into a stumbling parody of a run, but she wasn't fast enough.

Just as she reached the place where Vanyel lay, panting and moaning in pain, she saw his head snap up as if in response to a call only he could hear. He seemed to be looking up at the Tower that held the Death Bell. She heard him cry out something unintelligible, and followed his horror-stricken glance—

—and saw Tylendel poised against the lighting-filled sky, arms spread as if to fly—

—and saw him leap—

He seemed to hang in the air for a moment, as if he *had* somehow mastered flight.

But only a moment; in the next heartbeat he was falling, falling—she couldn't tell if the scream she heard was hers, or Vanyel's, or both. It wasn't Tylendel's; his eyes were closed, and his mouth twisted and jaw clenched in a rictus of pure grief.

She felt the impact of his body with the unforgiving ground as if it had been her own body that had fallen—

—and the scream ended.

Jaysen stopped dead beside her, frozen in mid-step.

She whimpered in the back of her throat, and Jaysen walked slowly to the crumpled thing lying on the ground, not twenty paces from where she now stood. He went to his knees beside it, then looked up, and she saw him shake his head slowly, confirming what she already knew.

And at that moment, the Death Bell began solemnly tolling.

She stumbled to Jaysen's side, each step costing her more in pain than she had felt in a lifetime of sacrifice to Queen and Circle. She went heavily to her knees, and gathered up the limp, pitiable body to her breast.

She held him, cradling him against her shoulder, gently rocking a little as if she held a small child. Tears coursed silently down her face to mingle with the rain that was pouring from the sky; it seemed that the whole world echoed her grief. Jaysen knelt beside her, his head bowed, his shoulders shaking with sobs, as the Companions gathered about them and the Death Bell tolled above them.

It was only when the rest of the Heralds arrived to take their burden from them that they thought of Vanyel, and sent someone to look for him.

But the boy was gone.

CHAPTER 9

V ANYEL STUMBLED THROUGH the pouring, frigid rain. He was
  half-blinded with grief, with no hope of finding comfort anywhere in
this world. There was nothing left for him—nothing.

He's dead—oh, gods, he's dead, and it's all my fault—

His whole body seemed to be on fire, a slow, smoldering pain that was
burning away at him from the inside the way the ice of his dream had
chilled him.

There was no reason to fight ice *or* fire anymore. Let either or both eat
him; he couldn't care.

Rain pounded him, hail struck like slung stones. His head reeled and
pounded with his pulse. He hurt, but he welcomed the pain.

It's all I deserve. It was all my fault—

He couldn't see where he was going, and he didn't give a damn. He
tripped and fell any number of times, but bruises and cuts didn't matter; he
just picked himself back up and kept running in whatever direction he happened to be facing.

His whole universe had collapsed the moment Tylendel had thrown
himself off that tower. Somewhere down in the depths of his soul was the
dim thought that if he ran far enough, ran fast enough, he might run off the
edge of the world and into an oblivion where there would be no more feeling, and no more pain.

He didn't run off the edge of the world, quite. He ran off the bank into
the river.

The ground just disappeared under his feet, and he flailed his arms
wildly as he half-fell, half-tumbled down the bank and somersaulted at the
bottom into the icy water. It closed over his head, and the cold shocked him
into an instant of forgetfulness; he lost the desire for oblivion as instinct took
over, and he fought back to the surface.

He gulped air, shook water out of his eyes, and in a flash of lightning
saw an oncoming tree limb too late to dodge it. He managed to turn away

from it, but it hit him across the back of the head and knocked him under again. The second time his head broke the surface, he was dazed and unthinking; in another glare of lighting he saw the branches of a bush beside him and grabbed at them—

They were too far away, far out of his frantic reach—

Then the bush shook violently, and seemed to stretch toward *him*. He snatched at the ends of the branches—

He caught them, somehow; they cut into his hand, but he managed to pull himself into the shallows.

He had just enough strength left to crawl halfway up into the rain-slick bank, and just enough mind left to wonder why he'd bothered to save himself.

He lay facedown in the sodden, dead grass on the bank; chilled and numb, and growing colder, and wracked with anguished guilt and mourning.

'Lendel, 'Lendel, it was all my fault—oh, gods, it was all my fault—I should have told Savil. I should have tried to stop you.

He sobbed into the rough grass, the damp-smelling earth, longing inarticulately for the power of a god to reverse time, to unmake all that had happened.

I'm sorry—oh, please, someone, take it all back! If you have to have someone, take me instead! Make it a dream, oh, gods—please—

But it wasn't a dream; no more than the rain that was diluting his tears, or the icy water that tugged at his legs. And no god intervened to unmake the past. The wintry cold was closing in on him, chilling the fire along his veins; he was too weak to move, and too tired, and far too grief stricken to care. It occurred to him then that he might die here, as alone as Tylendel had died.

It was no less than his deserts, and he changed his prayers. *Please—* he asked, desperately, of powers that were not answering. *Please—let me die.*

He thought of every mistake he had made, every wrong turning, and moaned. *I deserve to die*, he thought in anguish, closing his eyes. *I want to die.*

:No.: The mind-voice was bright, bright as a flame, and sharp as steel, piercing his dark hope for death. *:No, you must not. You must live, Chosen.:*

He raised his head a little, but couldn't get his eyes open, and really didn't want to. *:You don't know,:* he thought bleakly back at the intruder. *:Let me alone. No one wants me, nobody should want me; I kill everything I care for.:*

But someone grabbed him by the back of the collar and half-dragged him up the bank. He tried to twist away, but his body wouldn't work right anymore, and all he did was thrash feebly. Heartbeats later the rain was no longer pounding his back, and the green-smelling, soft moss under his weakly moving hands was dry; he'd been pulled into some kind of shelter. Whatever had him let go of his collar, after lowering him gently down onto the moss; he managed to get his eyes open, but with the lightning fading off in the distance, he could see nothing but darkness.

Something warm and large lay down beside him with a sigh. A soft nose nuzzled his cheek—

—like Gala had—

The sensation brought up memories that cut him into little shreds. He brought his knees up under his chest and curled up on himself, sobbing uncontrollably, driven to the edge of sanity by grief and loneliness.

:—but I am here—:

He brought his head up a little, and looked for the speaker with vision blurred by tears—and in a last glare of the lightning met a pair of glowing sapphire eyes—eyes so full of compassion and love that he knew their owner would forgive him anything. That love reached out for him, and flowed over into him. It couldn't erase his loss, but it could share the pain—and it didn't blame him for what had happened.

He uncurled, and groped for the smooth white neck and shoulder the way he had seized on the branches of the bush to keep from drowning.

He sobbed himself into exhaustion on that shoulder, wept until he hadn't the strength to shed another tear, and into a kind of fevered half-sleep. And all the while, that bright voice murmured, like a litany, over and over, into his mind—

:I am here, my Chosen. I love you. I will never leave you.:

"Savil, we found him." Mardic burst into the room that had been Vanyel's and Tylendel's, dripping from head to toe, and shivering in the draft from the door behind him.

As he turned to close the door, Savil dredged up energy she hadn't dreamed she still possessed, and started to rise. Jaysen and Healer Andrel simultaneously seized her shoulders and pushed her back down into her chair.

"Where?" she demanded, in a voice hoarsened by weeping. "Who found him? Is he all right?"

"I dunno, the Companions found him; Yfandes did, anyway," Mardic replied vaguely, swaying with weariness, looking colorless with exhaustion in the yellow candlelight. "She found him on the garden side of the river and dragged him into a grotto. Tantras thinks he's sick, something like backlash, but he can't tell for sure. He's trying to persuade her to let him bring Van back here so Andrel can take care of him."

Savil shook her head, trying to make sense of his words. "Mardic, what are you trying to tell me? What has Yfandes got to do with anything?"

"She won't let anyone lay a finger on him, Savil," Mardic replied, blinking, and still shivering despite the warmth of the room. "She's adamant about it; damned near took Tantras' hand off when he tried to get at Van. She told my Fortin that she doesn't trust us to protect him and keep him under shield properly—that we won't understand what we've got—that he's hurt, all torn up inside his mind, and we can't begin to help him—"

"Mardic," Jaysen said, slowly, "are you saying that Yfandes *Chose* Vanyel? The only full-grown Companion in the Field that hasn't Chosen—the Companion that hasn't Chosen for over ten years—and *now* she's Chosen *Vanyel*?"

"She didn't come out and say so, but I guess she did," Mardic said, fatigue slurring his words as he slumped against the doorframe. "I dunno why in hell she'd be curled up around him like he was her foal otherwise, and not letting us near him. We think he's unconscious; he isn't moving, and he isn't responding when we talk to him, but Yfandes won't let anyone close enough to get a good look at him."

Savil exchanged startled looks with the Seneschal's Herald, but it was Healer Andrel who put their thoughts into words.

"By the Lady Bright," he murmured, green eyes gone round with consternation. "What in the Havens is *this* going to mean?"

Vanyel swam up out of a feverish, fitful nightmare, prodded by an insistent voice in his head. He moaned, and opened dry, hot eyes that ached and burned. His head still pounded, and moving it even a little made his vision blur. He felt as if his whole body was a hot, tight, painfully constrictive garment; it felt like it didn't belong to him.

Sunlight gleamed weakly in through a rocky opening; he could see the river gurgling by just a few paces beyond it. It looked as if he were in a cave, but there were pink marble benches beside the entrance. Caves didn't have pink marble benches. They didn't have cultivated, moss-covered floors, either.

Then he recognized the place for what it was—one of the garden grottoes set into the riverbank. They were popular with courting couples or people seeking a moment of solitude from the Court. Tylendel had often wistfully expressed the wish that they dared to use one—

Tylendel. Grief closed around his throat and stopped his breath.

:*No, Vanyel, Chosen. Not now. Mourn later; now get up.*:

Without knowing quite how he had gotten there, Vanyel found himself on his feet, leaning heavily on the silky shoulder of a Companion.

His Companion. Yfandes.

He tried to make sense of that, but his head spun too much and he couldn't get a good grip on any of the thoughts that half-formed and then blew away.

:*You are ill,*: said the worried voice inside his mind. :*I cannot care for you. I did not wish to let you away from my protection, but I cannot help you. You have fever, you need a Healer. Move your foot. One step. Another—*:

He discovered that he was shaking, and clung a little tighter to the Companion's back. Obedient to that voice in his head, he put one hesitant foot in front of the other, learning quickly that he had to rest most of his weight on the arm clinging to Yfandes' shoulder. He had to close his eyes after the first couple of steps and trust her to guide him; he was so dizzy and nauseated he couldn't make any sense out of what he was seeing.

They emerged into sunlight that was far too much for his eyes; he opened them once, and shut them again, quickly. The Companion suddenly stepped away from him, and he literally fell into the arms of a strange Herald; and once out of contact with Yfandes there were *dozens* of voices in his head, all of them clamorous, all of them confusing. He whimpered, tried to pull away, and hid his head in his arms. They hurt, they *hurt*, and he couldn't make out which were his own thoughts and which belonged to someone else.

:*Tell your fool Chosen to shield him, Delian!*:

That voice he recognized, although Yfandes had never spoken that sharply to him. The stranger bit off a curse and touched Vanyel's forehead, and the voices cut off. Vanyel opened his eyes again, and wished he hadn't; the world was spinning around with him as the center of the chaos. He shut them immediately, vowing not to reopen them.

"Let me, Tantras." The soft voice was that of yet another stranger.

Two cool hands rested lightly on his head, and brought with them the promise of comfort and the peace of sleep. He took what they offered, falling into oblivion gratefully.

With any luck, he'd never wake up.

*   *   *

The bed looked far too big for the boy; never tall, he seemed to have collapsed in on himself. He was as pale as the sheets and—it might have been his dark hair and naturally fair complexion, but it seemed to her that he looked worse than Tylendel had after his fit. That was something Savil had not thought possible until now.

Tylendel. Oh, my 'Lendel, my poor, poor 'Lendel.

Unshed tears made a hard knot in her throat and misted her eyes. So she missed the moment that Andrel took his hand away from the boy's forehead and sagged back into his chair with a sigh of weariness, his graying red hair damp with sweat, his freckles twice as evident with his skin so washed out and pale.

It was that sigh that brought her back to the urgent present.

"Andrel?" she said softly. "Can you tell me anything?"

"I did what I could for him—and more, I've got a line established," the Green-robed Healer to the Heralds replied, without looking up. "I want you to follow it—or if you feel you can't, find me a Herald-Mage your equal. I don't believe what I Saw, to be frank, and I want a confirmation."

Savil tightened her jaw, and told herself again that none of this had been Vanyel's fault. Besides, she was the only Herald-Mage at the Palace who was likely to have *any* feelings of charity toward the boy.

"I'll follow it. Have you got more to say, or—"

"I want you in there first. What I have to say is going to depend on whether you think I've gone over the edge or not."

Savil raised one eyebrow in surprise, but moved in to stand beside the Healer. She reached out for Andrel's soothing Presence as easily as she could have reached for his hand; they'd been lovers, once, and had worked together often, both before and since.

They meshed auras exactly as hand would close on hand, and Savil followed the "line" the Healer had established down past the churning chaos of Vanyel's sleeping surface mind to the dark, grief-stricken core of him. The measure of that grief would have reconciled her to him even had she felt him blameworthy; she'd known the depth of Tylendel's feelings, but it seemed as if Vanyel's had run at least as deep. Certainly his grief and loss were as profound as her own. More—

Oh, gods—it's just what I warned 'Lendel against. He's lost, he's utterly lost without 'Lendel—

But that was not what rocked her back onto her heels with real shock.

Savil had spent most of the past twenty years of her life as the one Herald-Mage most intimately involved in training young Herald-Mages, and the one most often set to identify youngsters with active Gifts and the potential of being Chosen. She had seen children with one, two, or (most commonly) no Gifts. Tylendel had been unusual in having Mindspeech, Fetching, Empathy, and the Mage-Gift, all at near-equal strength. Most Heralds or Herald-Mages had one or two strong Gifts—and few had as many as three.

Vanyel had them all. Each channel she tested—with the sole exception of Healing—was open; most of them had been forced open to their widest extent. The boy had Mindspeech, Fetching, Farsight, Foresight, as much Empathy as Tylendel had shown, even enough Fire-starting to ensure he'd never need to use a tinderbox again, and the all-important Mage-Gift. His Mindspeech was even of both types, Thought-sensing and Projecting.

And—irony of ironies—as if the gods were taking with one hand and offering a pittance as compensation—the Bardic Gift.

This boy had more Gifts than any five full Heralds—and all of them had come into full activity in less than a day.

To her horror she could See that all the channels were as raw and sensitive as so many open wounds. The channels had not been "opened," they'd been *blasted* open. It was a wonder the boy wasn't mad with the pain alone.

Savil came up out of Vanyel's mind with a rush like a startled fish jumping out of a stream, and looked from the boy to the Healer and back in a state of surprise that closely resembled shock.

"Great good *gods*," she said. "What the hell happened to do *that*?"

Andrel shook his head. "Your guess would be better than mine. I never cared much where our powers came from, I was just concerned with learning to use them effectively. But do you see what I'm up against with this boy?"

"I think so," Savil replied, groping for the bedpost and sitting down carefully on the foot of the bed. "Let me add this up. You've got backlash trauma from when the Gate-energy got pulled from him, and more trauma from when we sent it back *into* him; you've got the problems inherent when you wake Gifts late or early. You've got the problems with them being at full power from the moment they woke. Worst of all, you've got channels that were *burned* open or *torn* open instead of opening of themselves."

"That, and more mundane emotional trauma and physical shock. I hope to the Havens that he doesn't come down with pneumonia on top of it all. I already fought off one fever, one his own body produced when it couldn't handle the energy-overload." Andrel touched the back of his hand to the boy's waxen cheek, checking his temperature. "So far, so good, but it's a real possibility. And I'm fighting off the effects of exposure, too. Savil, the child is a mess."

"Lover, you have a talent for understatement." Savil contemplated Vanyel's pinched, grief-twisted face.

Even in sleep he doesn't lose his pain.

"Now I see why Yfandes was so reluctant to let him out of her care. Until she gets him firmly bonded to her, he's going to have to be in physical contact with her for her to protect him. But what can we do? I can't fit her in here, I can't put him in the stables, not with the weather being what it is."

"Try, and I'll call you up on charges," Andrel replied, and Savil could tell that he was not joking. "Do that in this chill, and you'll kill him. It's going to be touchy enough with him tucked up in a warm bed."

"Well, how in hell do I protect him from his own powers?"

"Put your own shields on him, and hope nothing gets through."

"I can't keep them up forever," Savil reminded him acidly. "I'm fairly well fagged out myself. A couple of hours is about all I can manage at this point."

"*Then go order two graves, dammit!*" the Healer snarled in sudden frustration. "Because you're going to lose *this* one, too, if you don't do *everything* right with him!"

Savil pulled back, taken very much aback by the sudden explosion of temper. "I," she faltered, then as his words penetrated, and she thought of what was lying in the Grove Temple at this moment, lost her own precarious hold on calm.

She got up, stumbling a little; turned away from him and leaned against the doorframe, her shoulders shaking with her silent weeping.

"Savil—"

Strong but trembling hands on her shoulders turned her back to face the room, and pulled her into an embrace against a bony chest covered in soft, green wool. "Savil, I'm sorry," Andrel murmured into her hair. "I shouldn't have said that. You're exhausted, I'm exhausted, and neither of us are up to facing the problem this boy represents. Is there *anyone* you can turn him over to, for a day, at least? Long enough for you to get some rest and a chance to think?"

A white square of linen appeared just when she needed it. She mopped at her eyes with the handkerchief he offered, and blew her nose. "Under any other circumstances I'd just let *any* of the others spell me—but I don't know, Andy. A lot of them still think he's responsible for all this. Even if they shield—with Gifts like his, what's he going to pick up? *You* of all people should know how leaky we all are to a new, raw Gift, even when we aren't stressed."

Andrel sighed. "Dearheart, I don't think you have a real choice. You'll just have to hope that if surface thoughts leak past, he won't be able to understand them yet. If you don't get some rest, *you're* going to collapse, and even a novice Healer would be able to tell you that."

She bowed her head, feeling the weight of all her years and all her sorrows falling on her back. "All right," she said, acting against her better judgment, but unable to see any other option open to her. "See if you can round up Tantras for me, will you? At least he didn't know poor 'Lendel all that well."

Vanyel woke from a dream in which Tylendel was alive again, and had teased him gently about how much he had been grieving. For a confused moment after waking, he wasn't certain which had been the dream, and which the reality.

Then he opened his eyes, and found that he was in his own bed, and his own room, now illuminated by carefully shaded candle-lanterns. And there was something odd about the room.

After a long moment, he finally figured out what it was. The feeling of "Tylendel," the sense of his being there even when he wasn't physically present, was missing.

That told him. He swallowed a moan of despair, and closed his eyes against the resurgence of tears—and just in time, for the door opened softly and closed again, and he felt a new presence in the room with him.

He froze for a moment, then sighed, as if in sleep, and turned onto his side, hiding his face away from the light.

He was hearing things—like someone talking to himself, only—only, *inside* his head, the way Yfandes' voice had been inside his head. It hurt to listen, but he couldn't stop the words from coming in. And from the feel of that mind-voice, he knew who it was that was sitting by his bedside, too; it was one of the Heralds that had been with Savil, the one called Jaysen.

And Jaysen did not in the least care for Vanyel.

:—gods—: Vanyel heard, a little garbled by the pain that came with the words. :—trade this arrogant little toad for Tylendel. Damn poor bargain.:

Vanyel could feel brooding eyes on him, and the words in his head came clearer, more focused. :*No matter what Savil said, I'll never believe he didn't have something to do with the boy's death. If they'd been all that close, Tylendel would have listened to him, and even if 'Lendel was crazed on revenge, this one wasn't. 'Lendel may have loved him, but he could never have cared for the lad in the same way, or he'd have stopped him. 'Lendel was just one more little addition to his stable of admirers. If he'd left 'Lendel alone, if he hadn't played on his—weaknesses—:*

Vanyel cringed beneath the pitiless words, and the vision of himself that came with them: arrogant, self-centered, self-serving. Using Tylendel, not caring for him. And worse, worse than that, feeding him what he craved, like feeding a perpetual drunk the liquor he shouldn't have.

Without thinking about it, he reached beyond his room; it was a little like straining his ears to hear a conversation in the distance, and the pain that came with the effort felt like muscles pulling against a broken bone, but he found he could catch other snatches of—it must be thoughts—that touched on him.

They could have been echoes of Jaysen's thoughts.

He pulled his awareness back, as a child pulls its singed hand from the fire that has burned it. There were only two creatures in all the world that he could be certain cared for him despite what he was; Tylendel and Yfandes. Neither were to be trusted to know the truth about him. The second was besotted by whatever magic had made her Choose him; the first was—

The first was dead. And it was his fault. Jaysen was right; if he'd really *cared* for 'Lendel, he'd have stopped him. It wouldn't even have been hard; if he hadn't agreed to get those books, if he hadn't agreed to help with that spell, Tylendel would be alive at this moment. And if he hadn't seduced 'Lendel with his own needs, none of this ever would have happened.

Bad on top of worst; now he was a burden on the Heralds, who hated him, but felt honor-bound to take him in Tylendel's place. And he could *never* replace Tylendel, not ever; even *he* knew that. He had none of Tylendel's virtues, and *all* of his vices and more.

He *listened* to the mind-voice of the one beside him with all his strength, ignoring the pain it cost, hoping beyond hope that the Herald would somehow give him the chance to get away—get away and do something to make this right. If the Herald would just—go away for a moment, or—or better yet, fall asleep—

Jaysen *was* tired; though he'd done less magic than Savil, and had more time to rest, he was still very weary. He'd set himself up in the room's really comfortable chair, the one Tylendel had sometimes fallen asleep in. Vanyel could feel Jaysen's mind drifting over into slumber, and held his breath, hoping he'd drift all the way.

Because he'd gleaned something else from those minds out there—

Because the Death Bell had rung for him, despite what he'd done, Tylendel was being accounted a full Herald and tomorrow would be buried with all the honors.

Tomorrow. But tonight—he was in the Temple in the Grove. And if he could get that far, Vanyel was going to try to right the wrongs he had done to all of them, atoning with the only thing he had left to give.

Jaysen's thoughts slipped into the vague mumbles of sleep, and in the next moment a gentle snore from the chair beside the bed told Vanyel that he was completely gone.

Vanyel turned over, deliberately making noise.

Jaysen continued to snore, undisturbed.

Vanyel sat up, slowly, taking stock of himself and his surroundings.

About a candlemark later, he was dressed; even if he had *not* needed to move slowly for fear of waking the Herald, he would have had to for weakness. He had even needed to hold onto the furniture at first, because his legs were so unsteady. Even now his legs trembled with every step he took, but at least he was moving a bit more surely.

He stole soundlessly across the floor and unlatched the door, opened it just enough to squeeze himself through, and shut it again. It was dark out here, a still, cloudless night. He wouldn't be seen, but it was a long way to the Grove.

He steeled himself and stepped shakily onto the graveled path that ran from his door through the moonlit garden.

But someone had been waiting for him.

Yfandes glided out of the darkness to his side almost before he had made five steps along that path.

:No—: she said, sternly, barring his way. :You are ill; you should be in bed.:

For a moment he was ready to collapse right where he stood.

—gods, she's going to stop me—

Then he saw a way to get Yfandes to help him—without her knowing she was doing so.

:Please—: He directed everything he could on part of the truth. He couldn't lie mind-to-mind, he knew that, but he *didn't* have to reveal everything unless Yfandes should ask a direct question about it. And besides that, the link to her was fading in and out (and it hurt, like everything else) and he would bet she wouldn't want to force anything. *:Please, Yfandes, I have to—:* he faltered *:—to say—good-bye.:*

She bowed her head almost to the earth as he let his grief pour out over her. *:Very well,:* he heard, the mind-voice heavy with reluctance. *:I will help you. But you must rest, after.:*

:I will,: he promised, meaning it, though not in the way she had intended.

She went to her knees so that he could mount; he, once the best rider at Forst Reach, could not drag himself onto her back without that help. His arms and legs trembled with weakness as he clung to her back, and if it had not been that she could have balanced a toddler there and not let it fall, he would have lost his seat within the first few moments.

He concentrated on his weariness, on how physically miserable he was feeling, and spent not so much as an eyeblink on his real intentions. He closed his eyes, both to concentrate, and because seeing the ground move by so fast in the moonlight *was* making him nauseated and disoriented again.

He had had no notion of how fast the Companions could travel at a so-called walk. She was stepping carefully up to the porch of the Grove Temple long before he had expected her to get there; the clear ringing of her hooves on the marble surprised him into opening his eyes.

:We are here,: she said, and knelt for him to dismount.

The marble of the Temple porch glistened wetly in the moonlight, and he could see candlelight shining under the door. He slid from Yfandes' back, and "listened" with this new, mental ear for other minds within the Temple.

None.

He shivered in the cold wind; he'd dressed carefully, in the black silk tunic and breeches Tylendel had thought he looked best in, and once off Yfandes' warm, broad back, the wind cut right through his clothing.

:Not for long,: she admonished, as he clung to the doorframe and negotiated unlatching the door into the Temple itself.

:No, Yfandes,: he said, sincerely. *:Not for long.:*

He got the door open and closed again—then, as quietly as he could, locked it.

There was no clamor from the opposite side, so he assumed she had not heard the bolt shoot home. He turned, bracing himself for what he was about to do, and faced the altar.

The Temple itself was tiny; hardly bigger than the common room of their suite. It had been built all of white marble, within and without. The walls took up the candlelight, and reflected it until they fairly glowed. There were only two benches in it, and the altar. Behind the altar were stands thick with candles; behind the candles, the wall had been carved into a delicate bas-relief; swirling clouds, the moon, stars, and the sun—and in the clouds, suggestions of male and female faces, whose expressions changed with the flickering of the candles.

Before the altar stood the bier.

Vanyel's legs trembled with every step; he made his way unsteadily to that white-draped platform, and looked down on the occupant.

They'd dressed Tylendel in full Whites; his eyes were closed, and there was no trace of his grief or his madness in that handsome, peaceful face. His hands were folded across his waist, those graceful, strong hands that had held so much of comfort for his beloved. He looked almost exactly as he had so many mornings when Vanyel had awakened first. His long, golden curls were spread against the white of the pallet, a few of them tumbled a little untidily over his right temple; long, dark-gold lashes lay against his cheeks. Only the pose was wrong. Tylendel had never, in all the time Vanyel had known him, slept in anything other than a sprawl.

Vanyel reached out, hesitantly, to touch that smooth cheek—almost believing, even now, that he had only to touch him to awaken him.

But the cheek was cold, as cold as the marble of the altar, and the eyes did not flutter open at his touch. This was no child's tale, where the sleeping one would wake again at the magic touch of the one who loved him.

"Please, 'Lendel, forgive me," he whispered to the quiet face, and took the knife from the white sheath on Tylendel's belt. "I—I'm going to try to—pay for all of what I did to you."

His hands shook, but his determination remained firm.

Quickly, before he could lose his courage, he bent and kissed the cold lips—hoping that this, too, would be forgiven, and caught in a grief too deep for tears. Then he knelt on the icy white marble of the floor beside the bier, and braced the hilt of the dagger between his knees, clasping his hands with the dagger between his wrists, resting them on either side of the blade-edge.

"'Lendel, there's nothing without you. Forgive me—if you can," he whispered again, both to Tylendel and the brooding Faces behind the altar.

And before he could begin to be afraid, he pulled both wrists up along the knife-edges, slashing them simultaneously.

The dagger was as sharp as he had hoped—sharper than he had expected. He cut both wrists almost to the bone; gasped as pain shot up his arms, and the knife fell clattering to the marble, released when his legs jerked involuntarily.

He sagged with sudden dizziness, and fell forward over his bent knees; his head bowed over his hands, his arms lying limp on the marble floor. Blood began to spread on the white marble, pooling before him under his slashed wrists. He stared at it in morbid fascination.

Red on white. Like blood on the snow—

It was only at that moment that Yfandes seemed to realize what it was he was doing.

She screamed, and began kicking at the door.

But it was far too late; his eyes were no longer focusing properly anymore, and his wrists didn't even hurt.

But he was feeling so cold, so very cold.

:I'm sorry,: he thought muzzily at the frantic Companion, beginning to black out, and feeling himself falling over sideways. *:Yfandes, I'm sorry . . . you'll find someone . . . better than me. Worthy of you.:*

"Gone?" Savil's voice broke. "What the hell do you mean, *gone?*"

"Savil, I swear to you, the boy was asleep. I dozed off for a breath or two, and when I woke up he was gone," Jaysen answered, one hand clutched at the side of his head on a fistful of hair, his expression frantic and guilt-ridden. "I thought maybe he'd gone to the privy or something, but I can't find him anywhere."

Savil swung her legs out of the bed and rubbed her eyes, trying to think. Where would Vanyel have gone, and in the name of the gods, *why?*

But in a heartbeat she had her answer—the frightened, frantic scream of a Companion rang across the river, and her Kellan's voice shrilled into her head.

:Savil—the boy—: and an image of where he was and what he had done.

From the stricken look on Jaysen's face, his own Felar had given him the same information.

"*Gods!*" Savil snatched her cloak from the chair beside her bed and ran out in her bare feet, through the common room, and headed for the door of Vanyel's room, Jaysen breathing down her neck.

She hit the garden door at a dead run, and it was a damned good thing that it wasn't locked, because if it had been, she'd have broken it off the hinges. The cold of the night slapped her in the face like an impious hand; *that* stopped her for a moment, but *only* a moment. In the next instant Felar and Kellan pounded up at a gallop. Felar skidded around in a tight pivot, presenting his hind-quarters to his Chosen, who leapfrogged up into his seat with an acrobatic skill that would have had Savil muttering about "show-offs" had the situation been less precarious. Instead, she waited for Kellan to come to a dead halt, and clambered onto her back anyhow, her bedgown rucked up around her legs. Kellan launched herself into a full, frantic gallop as Savil clung on as best she could.

Now Savil was a breath behind Jaysen, as the young Seneschal's Herald led the way across the nearest bridge and up the Field to the Temple of the Grove. Nor were they the only two summoned by the frantic screaming, mind and voice, of Yfandes. Heralds and trainees were boiling out of the Palace like aroused fire ants, rendezvousing with their Companions, and heading across the river at breakneck speed.

But Jaysen and Savil were the first two on the scene; it was their dubious privilege to see Yfandes trying to batter down the solid bronze door of the Temple single-handedly, and not budging it by so much as a thumb's-breadth. Her hooves were screeching across the metal, leaving showers of sparks in their wake, and her anguished screams were far too like a human's for comfort.

Jaysen vaulted off Felar's back and hit the ground at a run, ducking fearlessly under Yfandes' flying hooves to make a trial of the door himself.

"It's locked from the inside," he shouted unnecessarily, as Savil slid from Kellan's back to limp to his side. He put his shoulder against the door, and rammed it, with no more luck than Yfandes had had.

"Vanyel!" Savil put her mouth up against the crack between door and frame, and shouted through it. "Van, lad, let us in!"

She put her ear to the crack and listened, but heard nothing.

:Kellan—:

:Yfandes says he's still alive, but unconscious and weakening,: came the grim reply, as Yfandes danced in place, her sapphire eyes gone nearly black with anguish.

"Somebody get me a mage-light on that damned tower!"

It was Mardic; he had his hands on Donni's shoulders and was staring up at the tower. Donni was holding a crossbow with a bulky missile cocked and ready.

Savil responded first, running far enough back from the door that she could see the top of the Belltower. It was glowing faintly, but obviously too faintly for Donni to make out a target. Savil raised her hands, and sent up such a burst of power that the entire top of the tower flowered with light.

While Mardic closed his eyes and scowled in concentration, Donni raised the crossbow, squinted carefully along it, and fired.

The oddly-shaped arrow flew strangely, and slowly, trailing something light colored behind it—and in a moment, Savil realized why and what it was. Donni had been a bright little apprentice-thief when she'd been Chosen; this was a grapnel-arrow, meant to carry a light, but strong line through an open window and catch on the sill. Mardic had a very weak, but usable Fetching-Gift; he had invoked it to help the arrow carry something heavier than a light line. A climbing-rope.

It lobbed through the loop of the Bell-house, clanging ominously off the Death Bell itself. Savil felt a chill, and made a warding-gesture, nor was she the only one. She could see most of the others shivering at the least, and Yfandes moaned like a dying thing at the sound of the Bell.

Donni, her normally mobile face gone blank, was paying no attention to anything other than her arrow and line; all her concentration was on the task in her hand. She drew the rope to her with agonizing slowness; Savil fought down the urge to shout at her to hurry. Finally Donni's careful pulling met resistance; she tugged, then pulled harder, then yanked on the rope with all her might.

Then, before Savil had time to blink, she was swarming up it like a squirrel.

One or two of the trainees gave a ragged cheer; Donni ignored them. She reached the opening and squeezed through, and Savil saw to her surprise that Mardic was following her. She'd been so intent on Donni's progress that she'd missed seeing him altogether until he got into the glow of the mage-light.

Savil sprinted back for the door—the crowd there parted to let her through—and waited, trembling with impatience, with the rest.

:Hang on, Savil,: she heard Mardic's mind-voice, in Broadsend-mode. *:He's alive; thank the gods he didn't know the right way to slit his wrists. Donni's got the blood stopped, but we'll need a Healer, fast. 'Fandes warped the door pounding on it; it's going to take a bit of work to get it open.:*

A tall figure in Healer's Greens pushed through to Savil's side as Mardic began pounding on the door, forcing the bolt back thumblength by thumblength; Andrel opened his arms and wrapped Savil inside the warmth of his fur-lined cloak with him.

Finally the door creaked open; Andrel deserted her, leaving her suddenly in sole possession of the heavy cloak. She followed inside, hard on his heels.

Donni knelt in front of the bier; there was a frighteningly wide scarlet stain on the marble of the floor, and her hands looked as if she had dipped them in vermilion dye. She was holding Vanyel's wrists; the boy was sprawled on the floor beside her at the foot of the bier, his face as transparently white as the marble under his head, and slackly unconscious. Andrel was just beginning to kneel in the pool of blood on the other side of the boy, heedless of his robes, and as Savil limped across the floor toward them, followed by the rest of the would-be rescuers, he reached out and set his hands firmly over Donni's bloodstained ones.

His face was fixed in a mask of absolute concentration, and Savil could feel the power beginning to flow from him. But he'd been hard-pressed today, and had little time to rest. And she knew that his few reserves were not going to be enough—

She ran the last few steps and placed her hands on his shoulders as he began to falter, sending energy coursing down into his center. And in a moment, she felt herself joined by Jaysen—then Mardic—then Donni. The four of them meshed in a union that was as nearly perfect as any magic she'd ever witnessed, and sent Andrel all he needed and more, in a steady, steadfast, stream.

Finally the Healer sighed, and lifted his hands away from Donni's; the other three disengaged with something that was a little like reluctance. It wasn't often that even Heralds experienced the peace that came with a perfect Healing-meld; it was nearly a mystical experience, and as close to the peace of the Havens as Savil ever wanted to get until she was Called.

Donni lifted her hands away from Vanyel's wrists, and Savil could see that the skin, veins, and tendons beneath were whole again. For a moment the wrists were marred by angry red scars, then gradually those scars faded to thin white lines.

Jaysen moved swiftly to gather the unconscious boy in his arms; blood from the boy's sleeves stained the front of his Whites, but Jaysen didn't seem to notice.

Vanyel's head sagged against the Herald's chest. Despite being moved, he showed no signs of reviving.

Savil helped Andrel to rise and go to him. The Healer reached out a hand that shook uncontrollably and checked the pulse at the hinge of Vanyel's jaw, lifted an eyelid, then shook his head.

"Nearer than I like, and he lost too much blood, given what he's been through," Andrel said, grimacing. "Jays, can you and Felar get him back into his bed as of a candlemark ago?"

"No," Savil interrupted. "No, you leave that to me and Yfandes. Jays, give him to me as soon as I get mounted."

She pushed her way through the silent, shocked crowd and found Yfandes waiting as close to the open door as she could get. The Companion looked deeply into Savil's eyes, her own eyes back to a quiet, depthless sapphire, then went to her knees for the Herald to mount.

Savil mounted, and Yfandes rose gracefully to her feet, not in the least unsteady on the smooth marble. Savil held out her arms, amazed by her own calm, and Jaysen lifted the limp form of Vanyel up into place before her. She cradled the boy against her shoulder, wrapping Andrel's cloak about both of them; he was no burden at all, really—almost *too* light a weight for the ease of her heart and conscience.

Oh, lad, lad— She sighed, nudging Yfandes lightly with her heels to tell her to go on. *Poor little lad—we've made a right mess of your life, haven't we? And all for lack of listening to you. I don't know who is guiltier, me or Withen.*

She held him a bit tighter as Yfandes headed at a gentle walk toward the beckoning beacon of the open door of her suite. He was all the legacy Tylendel had left to her, and she pledged the silent sleeper in the Temple behind her that she would take better care of him from this moment on.

And the first task is to put you back together, my poor, bewildered, heart-broken lostling. If ever I can.

CHAPTER 10

Y EARS LATER—or so it seemed—Savil finally crawled into some clothing. She wanted, needed, to collapse somewhere, wanted rest as a starving man wants bread, but dared not leave Vanyel alone. She finally dragged the chair Jaysen had been using close to the bedside and wrapped herself in the first warm thing that came to hand (which turned out to be Andrel's fur-lined cloak), intending, despite her exhaustion, to stay awake as long as possible.

But she dozed off, sometime around dawn, and woke at the sound of a strangled sob.

She fought her way out of the tangled embrace of the cloak; when she got her head free of the folds of the hood, the first things she saw were Vanyel's silver eyes looking at her with a kind of accusative sorrow.

"Why?" he whispered mournfully. "Why did you stop me?"

Savil finally untangled the rest of her, sat up in her chair, and took a quick look around. As she'd ordered, Mardic was still standing weary guard over the door to the rest of the suite, and Donni was drowsing, slumped against the door to the garden. Vanyel was not going to give them the slip a second time, however unlikely the prospect seemed. It hadn't seemed possible the *last* time.

She gave Mardic a jerk of her head and a Mindsent order; .*Out, love, this needs privacy,*: and woke Donni with a quick Mindtouch. Donni came completely awake as soon as Savil touched her, a talent the Herald-Mage envied. She pulled herself to her feet with the help of the doorframe at her back. Then both of them left for their own quarters, closing the door into the common room of the suite behind them.

Savil got up stiffly, every joint aching, and sat on the side of the bed, taking both of Vanyel's hands in her own. They were like ice, and bloodless-looking. "I stopped you because I had to," she replied. "Because—Vanyel, self-destruction is no answer. Because we've already lost one we loved—and I couldn't lose you, too, now—"

"But I deserve to die—" His voice was weak, and broke on the last word. And he wouldn't look her in the eyes.

Oh, gods—what was going through that head of his? What had he convinced himself of? "For what?" she asked, her voice sounding rough-edged even to her. "Because you made some mistakes? Gods, if *that* was worthy of a death sentence, I should have been sharing that knife!"

His hands were chilling hers; she tried to warm them, chafing them as gently as she could. "Listen to me, Vanyel—this whole wretched mess was one mistake piled on top of another. *I* made mistakes; I should have watched 'Lendel more carefully. I should have insisted he talk to Lancir when his brother was killed. That's one of Lancir's jobs; to keep our heads clear and our minds able to think straight. Dammit, *I* knew what 'Lendel was capable of where Staven was concerned! And he would *not* have been able to hide that obsession from a Mindhealer! 'Lendel made mistakes—the gods themselves know that. He should have thought before he acted; I'd been trying to get him to do that. We—the Heralds—accept mental evidence! All he had to do was ask for a hearing, and we'd have had the material we needed from his own mind to put the Leshara down. You made mistakes, yes, but you made them out of love. He needed help, asked you for it, and you tried to help him the only way anyone had ever taught you was right. And, gods, even *Gala* made mistakes!"

Her voice was harsh with tears, and with her own guilt, and she was not ashamed to let him hear it. "Van, Van, we're only simple, fallible mortals— we aren't saints, we aren't angels—we fall on our faces and make errors and sometimes people die of them—sometimes people we love dearly—"

She choked on a sob, and bowed her head.

He freed a hand and touched her cheek hesitantly; his fingers were still snow-cold. She caught and held it, and looked back up into his eyes, seeing worse than grief there before he dropped them.

"You thought the world would be better with you out of it, is that it?"

He nodded, dumbly, and his hands trembled in hers.

"Did you stop to think how *I* would feel? You were 'Lendel's love. Didn't you think I'd come to care for you at least a bit, if only for his sake?"

How was she to reach him—when she'd *never* been good with words? "I've buried him today. Did you think I'd be indifferent about burying you as well? What about Jaysen? I'd left him to watch you. How do you think *he* feels right now about his carelessness? What do you think he'd have felt if you'd died? And—gods help us—what did you think Yfandes would do?"

"I thought—I thought she'd find somebody better," he faltered, his voice quavering a bit.

"She'd *die*, lad; Companions very seldom outlive their Chosen. And she Chose *you*. If you die, she dies; she'd probably pine herself to death, and she does *not* deserve that."

He shrank into himself, pulling even further away from her, and she cursed her clumsy words, her inability to tell him what she really meant without hurting him further. "Van—oh, *hell*—I'm not saying any of this the way I wanted to. Listen to me; you're sick, you need to rest and get well. We'll deal with this later, all right? Just—don't take yourself out of this world right now, there are folks who'll have holes in their lives if you go. And I'm one of them."

He nodded; he didn't look convinced, but now she had exhausted what little eloquence she possessed, and didn't know what else to say to him.

So she tried one last tactic. *Let me just keep him alive—if I can do that, maybe we can help him.*

"Will you promise me, on your word of honor, that you won't try to do yourself in again? If you will, I'll trust you, and I won't leave guards on your doors."

He swallowed, pulled his hands out of hers, and whispered, haltingly, "I—promise. Word of honor." He still wouldn't look her in the face, but she trusted that sworn word.

She nodded. "Accepted. Now is there anything, anything at all, that I can do for you?" *Maybe—* "Need to talk?"

He shook his head, and she sensed his complete withdrawal, and cursed again. *Dammit, just when I need Lance the most, he's not here.*

"Sure?" She persisted, even in the face of defeat; that was her nature. "Vanyel—Vanyel, you're the only person I've got who knew 'Lendel from the inside the way I did. If—if you need somebody to mourn with . . ."

He shook his head again, avoiding her eyes altogether, and she sighed, giving up. "If you change your mind—well, rest, lad. Get better. Call, if you need anything—mind or voice, either, I'll hear you."

He nodded slightly, and closed his eyes again, leaning back and turning his face to the wall. That face was as white as the pillows beneath it, and it made her hurt all over again to see that lost look of his. She waited for another response or a request of some kind, but he slipped right back into an uneasy, shallow slumber. Finally she eased off the bed, gathered up Andrel's cloak from the chair, and left him alone.

*   *   *

Andrel arrived at sunset in response to her invitation to fetch his cloak and share food and thoughts. They'd had more than one intimate little supper in their lives, many of them in this very room, but none so gloom-ridden. Mardic and Donni had gone off to cautiously interview some of Vanyel's circle of admirers, to see if there was someone else they could contact that might help to bring him out of this mental abyss.

Savil's Hawkbrother masks on the wall behind Andrel's left shoulder gazed at her from dispassionate and empty eyeholes. Candles flickered on the table between them.

Neither of them had much interest in food at the moment; both their minds were on the boy sleeping behind the closed door behind Savil's chair. "What we need," she told Andrel glumly, eating a dinner she did not taste, "is Lancir. We need his Mindhealing; the boy's pulling further away from *touching* with every moment he's awake, and I cannot get him to let me inside. He's barricading himself again; a different kind of barricade than that old arrogance, but it's there all the same. And Lance bloody *would* be out of touch right now."

He sighed, his breath making the candleflame flutter, and pushed his own food around on his plate with his fork. "I have to agree with you. Is there no chance you can get Lance back via Gate?"

She shook her head, shoving her frustration back down out of her way. She'd already been over this with Jaysen. "Not without knowing where he is, and he's not a strong enough Thoughtsenser to read a Broadcast-sending. And we don't know what route he's taking home; could be one of half a dozen. If something were wrong with Elspeth we could afford to send out half-a-dozen Heralds to look for him, but—Vanyel just is not that important." Her tone turned acid. "Or so I've been told."

Andrel frowned, and his eyebrows met. "He may become that important; I'm shielding him as much as I can, but his trauma is still leaking through. Half the trainees are depressed to the point of tears right now, Gifted Bardic, Healer, *and* Herald, and it's all due to Vanyel's leakage."

"Well, what do you expect?" she countered, letting him see her very real anger. "*You* saw the strength and depth of his Gifts. Even with raw channels he's Broad-sending without knowing it, and he has no more notion of how to shield than how to fly! And it's not every day you've got one half of a lifebonded pair left after the other half suicides. If he were *trained*, he'd be leaking. But nobody else believes how strong he is; they all think I'm letting my affection for Tylendel magnify everything that was connected with him out of all proportion to reality."

"Gods!" he looked up from his plate with the expression of a stunned sheep. "Vanyel and Tylendel—*lifebonded*?"

She nodded unhappily. "I'm pretty damned sure of it; what's more, so are Mardic and Donni, and if anyone would recognize a bonding, it would be another bonded pair. I expected grief, mourning, the natural responses for a youngster who's lost his first love under rotten bad circumstances—I did *not* expect to find the kind of gaping emotional wounds I saw before he started shutting me out today. I've never seen that depth of feeling before in *anyone*, Herald or no, *except* Mardic and Donni. So tell me; what the hell do I do about a broken lifebond?"

He shook his head, obviously at a loss. "I can't tell you; I don't know. I don't Heal minds, I Heal bodies. And I don't know of anyone who Heals hearts."

She sighed, and looked down at her congealing dinner. "That's what I was afraid you'd tell me. I have more bad news; the relationship between them was one where 'Lendel was the leader and Van the follower. Van had gotten totally dependent on 'Lendel for all his emotional needs. I tried to warn 'Lendel, but—" She shrugged. "And to put the snow on the mountain, Van's got some guilt he's hiding from me, and all I can think is that he's convinced he cursed 'Lendel because he seduced him. Mind you, he didn't; from all I know I'm positive the seduction, if seduction it was, was mutual, but—there it is."

"Jaysen," Andrel said positively.

She nodded. "Good bet, my friend. Jays has got all those Kleimar prejudices about same-sex pairings. He accepted 'Lendel, but mostly after I rammed his prejudices right up in his face. But Vanyel? Vanyel wasn't even a Herald-candidate when he and 'Lendel paired. Jays hasn't *said* a word, but you can bet on what he was thinking when he was keeping watch on him. Resentment that Van is alive and 'Lendel dead would be the least of it."

"And Vanyel picked it up," Andrel said sadly.

"Probably." She took a bite, found it catch in her throat, and gave up trying to eat, shoving the plate away. "From what I can tell, he's sensitive enough to pick up things *you've* forgotten for years and do it right through your shielding. Ah, gods."

She rested both elbows on the table, and covered her sore eyes with her hands. A moment later she felt one of Andrel's hands stroking her hair, and dropped her own back on the table, giving him a good long look across the candleflames. His deeply green eyes were fixed on her face, reflecting a profound concern.

"And what about you?" he asked, barely above a whisper.

"I am *trying* to reach out to him," she said, feeling old and tired and about ready to give up. "I think I've convinced myself that none of this was any more his fault than it was anyone else's. I bloody well hope so, or he's going to be getting knives in the gut from me, too. And he doesn't deserve that. The rest—gods, I don't know what to do."

"That isn't what I meant," he replied, taking his hand away from her hair and reaching for her wrist. "I want to know how *you're* weathering this. Need a shoulder?"

"Want the truth?" She tensed all over, trying to keep from bawling like a little child. "Yes, I need a shoulder, and no, I am *not* taking this well. I want 'Lendel back, Andy—he was my soul-son, and I loved him, and I want him back with me."

Her voice cracked; she lost her veneer of calm, and just dissolved into tears. Andrel got up, gracefully, and without letting go of her wrist. He moved around the table, and pulled her to her feet, then led her over to the couch and gave her that shoulder she needed so badly.

The peaceful night rocked; Vanyel convulsed, wailing—

His cry sounded like something in its death agonies, and made Savil's hair stand on end.

The room trembled, literally. The walls shook as Vanyel's muscles spasmed.

His eyes were wide open, but saw nothing, and his pupils dilated with fear. He convulsed again, and the very foundation of the Palace rocked. The bed shook as if it were alive. His lute fell from the wall, landing with a sickening crack that surely meant it was broken past all repair; his armor-stand crashed over and scattered his equipment across the floor, and Savil was tossed from his bedside to the floor before she realized it.

She picked herself up off the floor beside his bed without thinking about safety or bruises, and flung herself at him again.

He thrashed beneath her, fighting her with a paranormal strength; he couldn't know where he was or who she was. All she could read from him was terrible agony—and beneath the pain, confusion, panic, entrapment. She caught his wrists and tried to pinion them against the pillows, then tried to pin him down with the blankets. His chest arched against hers. He screamed, and the walls shook again.

Mardic lay in the corner behind her, quite unconscious; Donni had his head in her lap and she was trying to protect him from falling objects with her own body. Vanyel had thrown him against the wall when this nightmare—or whatever it was—had started, and Mardic had made the mistake of trying to touch his mind to wake him.

:Donni—: Savil used a moment of lull to Mindtouch her pupil, taking a tiny fragment of her attention from the attempt—*attempt*, for it wasn't succeeding—to shield Vanyel, to get him under some kind of control. :— *Donni, how's Mardic?*:

:*He's all right, just stunned,*: came the reassuring reply. :—*I can spare you something. Catch this, quick*—:

The girl "threw" her a mental line, and began sending additional, sorely-needed energy down it as soon as Savil "caught" it.

It helped to keep Savil from blacking out as Vanyel lashed out with *his* mind, but that was about all.

Jaysen was coming on the run; Savil could Feel him reaching out to find out what the hell was going on, and Felt the panic in *his* mind when he realized they had a powerful Gifted trapped in a pain-loop and hallucination. He all but broke down the door, trying to get in, and flung himself into the affray without a second thought.

"*Shield* him, dammit," he shouted, throwing himself across Vanyel's legs, as the walls (but, thank the gods, not the foundations again) shook.

"I'm *trying*," she snapped back, giving up on the uneven struggle to pin Vanyel down, and settling for securing his arms. "He breaks them as fast as I get them up!"

Jaysen succeeded in getting Vanyel physically restrained where she, being lighter, had failed. He added his strength to Savil's and Donni's on the crumbling shields they were trying to get on the boy. But it wasn't even stalemate; they were losing him to his own nightmares.

Andrel appeared. Savil didn't even see or Sense him run in; he was just *there* all in an instant. But instead of flinging himself into the melee, he grabbed their arms and pulled both of them *off* the boy.

Then he reached down for something at his feet, and came up with a bucket of icy water. He doused the boy, bed and all, without a heartbeat of hesitation.

The convulsions stopped as Vanyel came abruptly awake.

He sat up—stared—then he suddenly went limp.

The room stopped shaking.

"Savil, get me a blanket," Andrel ordered quietly. "Jays, help me get him out of that wet bed before he goes into shock, then get the bedding stripped before the mattress gets soaked."

By the time Savil returned with the goosedown comforter from her bed, the two men had pulled the half-stunned boy from the tangled mess of water-soaked bedcoverings, and the bedding was piled on the floor. Andrel was carefully shaking the boy's shoulders while Jaysen supported him.

Behind them, Mardic was groggily climbing to his knees, Donni steadying him, but the two of them waved Savil off when she made a half-step in their direction.

:We're all right,: Donni Mindspoke. :I'll get Mardic into bed myself, and then I'll come make up the bed in here again.:

Savil turned her attention back to the boy, knowing she could trust Donni to deal with the situation if she had said she could.

"Come on, Vanyel," Andrel was saying, coaxingly. "Come on, lad, come back to us. Wake up, come out of it."

Vanyel blinked, blinked again, and sense came back into his eyes. He looked about him, momentarily confused, then the destruction about him seemed to register on him. He closed his eyes, a soft, hardly audible moan coming from the back of his throat.

And for one instant, Savil was nearly flattened beneath an overwhelming load of blackest despair, terrible guilt, and a grief so heavy she felt her knees start to give way beneath the weight of it.

Then it was gone, absolutely cut off, and so completely that for a moment even she doubted that she had felt it.

But one look at Andrel and Jaysen convinced her otherwise; the former was deeply shaken, and the latter white-lipped.

She expected tenderness and concern from Andrel—but strangely enough, it was Jaysen who carefully got the boy into a chair, wrapped in the comforter, and from the chair back into the bed when Donni had stripped it of the wet coverings and remade it. It was Jaysen who stayed beside him, leaving Savil free to see to it that Mardic was truly all right. Savil wasn't in a mood to ask questions about his apparent change of heart.

Mardic was fine, and relatively cheerful. "I'll have a godsawful headache," he told her. "Poor Van thought I was going to kill him, took me for an enemy in his dream. When he realized it *was* a dream, he pulled most of it—"

"*Most* of it?" Savil choked. "He flattened you, and he pulled *most* of it?"

"Near as I can tell." Mardic put both hands to his temples and massaged a little. "Well, when he pulled the blow, the energy overflowed into those raw channels and hurt him, and he went over the edge; couldn't control *anything*. Then—I *think*—he lost his center and got lost in his own pain. Andrel had the right notion; physical shock is what gave him something to home in on."

"But you *are* going to be all right?"

He gave her half a grin. "If you'll let me get some sleep."

Savil took the statement as an unsubtle request and made a hasty exit.

She got back just in time to see Andrel give Vanyel some kind of sedative to drink. But it was Jaysen who sat with the boy until Andrel's sedative took effect. And it was Jaysen who righted the armor-stand, and picked up the broken-backed lute from the floor with a wince at seeing the fine instrument so ruined.

"I'll see to getting this fixed, if it can be," he said, when he saw Savil watching him before she knelt to put out the fire. They daren't have a fire here while Vanyel slept, nor candles burning, either—not unless Andrel could do something to keep him from going into another fit.

"Jays, what am I going to do with him?" she asked, quietly, standing up with a wince as a pulled muscle in her back told her what a fool she'd been. He motioned that she should precede him out the door, and she half turned to see his face as she walked past him. "He's sick with backlash, and he's getting sicker, not better. His channels are all raw; you can't Mindtouch him without doing *that* to him, throwing him into convulsions. That was what set all this off, Mardic trying to soothe him out of a bad dream. What am I going to do the *next* time he has a nightmare?"

Jaysen shrugged helplessly, and shut the door behind her. She made a circuit of the common room, setting candles erect and lighting them. "If you don't know, be damned if I do. Andy, can we keep him sedated long enough to heal?"

Andrel grimaced, looking as if he'd swallowed something sour. "With any other patient I'd tell you where to put that question—what I just gave the boy was argonel."

Jaysen and Savil both started with surprise, and in Savil's case the surprise was not unmixed with shock. "Great good gods, Andy!"

"Ease up; he's safe enough," Andrel interrupted her, throwing himself down on the couch with his usual lack of concern for the furniture. He groaned, stretched, and then raised an eyebrow at the Seneschal's Herald. "Jaysen, may I mention that you have lovely legs?"

Jaysen, who was attired only in shirt and hose and only just now really realized this, blushed a furious scarlet, but refused to be distracted. "Argonel, Andy—" he began, taking a chair and crossing his legs primly.

"He's burning it off at a respectable rate, or I wouldn't have given it to him," Andrel replied. "The benefit of it is that it's a muscle relaxant *and* a sedative; he won't be able to go into convulsions again even if you Mindtouch him. I *won't* speak for him tossing the Palace around, but he won't go into *physical* convulsions. As for him healing, well that depends entirely on what you mean."

Savil took another chair, flopping down into it with a tired *thud* as loud as the one Andrel had made connecting with the couch cushions.

"Physically," she said, flatly. "Pure physical healing. Backlash symptoms, exhaustion, blood loss. I'll worry about raw channels later."

"Yes, I can keep him sedated long enough for the effects of backlash to wear off, for his physical energy to recover and for him to replace the blood he lost. I can combine the argonel with jervain, and dull out all the Gift-senses enough so that they aren't so sensitive. That *might* let the channels heal. I don't know for sure; I've never seen nor read of anything like this, Gifts being blasted open like his were."

"Mentally?" Jaysen prodded, frowning. "Emotionally?"

"At this point I don't think even Lance can help him," Andrel replied sadly. "You both felt—"

Jaysen nodded, ruefully. "That's—I think perhaps I picked up something more than either of you," he said, a shadow of guilt crossing his face. "He—he thinks that everything he touches is doomed, cursed. Because of—what he and 'Lendel were. And I know *exactly* where he got that particularly poisonous little thought. Only it isn't a 'little thought' anymore. It's as much an obsession as Tylendel's was."

He hung his head, and wouldn't look at her. "I never thought—" he faltered. "I never guessed—I thought he was just a user—"

Savil was not feeling charitable just now. "Damn right, you never thought," she snapped. "You never thought at all! You and your damned provincial—"

"Savil," Andrel said, warningly, his head turned slightly to the side, nodding at the door to Vanyel's room.

She subsided. If she got angry, Van might pick it up; it might set him off again. "Sorry, Jays," she finally said grudgingly, not feeling sorry at all.

"At least you didn't send somebody out to cut their wrists," he answered unhappily.

She winced. "No—I just—hell, this isn't getting us anywhere. Andy, you think you can get him *physically* recovered, right?"

Candlelight reflected in his eyes, which had gone inward-looking. "I would say yes, cautiously."

"Let's worry about that, then, for a couple of days. I have a germ of an idea, but whether or not I can pull it off is going to depend very strongly on whether or not *you* can get Vanyel fit to ride."

"If I can't get him to that point in the next couple of weeks or so, it's never going to happen," Andrel replied.

"What's the chance we can do something about the way he's barricading himself—or even help him get some of his power under his own control?"

He pondered her question while the fire crackled beside him. "Why don't you ask your Companions? He may be able to barricade against you, but I doubt he can do much against Yfandes."

She pressed her hand to her eyes and shook her head. "Gods, why in hell didn't I think of that?" And at the same time, Mindsent :*Kellan?*: knowing that Jaysen was doing the same with Felar.

:*Here,*: came the reply, immediately.

She sent their dilemma in a complicated thought-burst, and waited while Kellan digested the information, and possibly conferred with Felar and Yfandes.

:*Yfandes says that the bonding is weak,*: came the reply, flavored with the acid tang of concern. :*It fades in and out—and it hurts the boy, sometimes, to speak with her.*:

:*Can we do anything about that?*: Jaysen fell into the rapport, and if there was anything other than genuine distress there on Vanyel's behalf, Savil couldn't feel it. Through him, she could Hear Felar.

:*Physical contact,*: Felar said shortly.

Kellan agreed. :*As much as possible. That is what strengthens the bonding; now she cannot help him to get control of what he does.*:

:*And if the bond is strengthened?*: Jaysen asked.

:*Perhaps,*: said Felar.

:*A hope,*: added Kellan.

Jaysen looked into Savil's eyes from across the room, and nodded, a little grimly. At this point they would accept even a hope, however tenuous.

Nothing hurt much, now, not since he'd drunk that fiery stuff the red-haired Healer had given him. Those places inside him, the mind-things, that had burned so—they still burned, but remotely, as if the hurting belonged to somebody else. He couldn't concentrate on much of anything for very long, and none of it really seemed to matter.

Only the empty place in him was pretty much the same; only that continued to ache in a way the Healer's potions couldn't seem to touch. The place where Tylendel had been—and now—

But the potions let him sleep, a sleep without dreams. And he'd had the snow-dreams again—that was what had thrown him into that fit.

Oh, gods—he'd thought—he'd thought they'd never come again. He'd thought 'Lendel had driven them away.

But they weren't the dreams about being walled in by ice, so maybe 'Lendel had—

Maybe not. He couldn't tell. It was the other dream, anyway. Clear, vivid as no other dream he'd dreamed had ever been, and much more detailed than the last time he'd had it.

He'd been in a canyon, a narrow mountain pass with walls that were peculiarly smooth. He'd known, in the dream, that this was no real pass—that this passage had been *created*, cut armlength by armlength, by magic.

He'd known, too, that the magic had been wrong, skewed. It had an aura of pain and death about it, as if every thumblength of that canyon had been paid for in spilled blood.

It had been night, cloudy, with a smell of snow on the wind. Where he stood the canyon had narrowed momentarily, choked by avalanches on either side. He'd been very cold, despite the heavy weight of a fur cloak on his shoulders; his feet had been like blocks of the ice that edged the canyon walls.

He had felt a feeling of grim satisfaction, when he'd seen that at this one point the passage was wide enough for two men, but no more. And he knew that *he* had somehow caused those blockages, to create a place where one man could, conceivably, hold off an army.

Because an army was what was coming down that canyon.

He'd sent for help, sent Yfandes and Tylendel—

Tylendel? But Tylendel was dead—

—but he'd also known that help was unlikely to arrive in time.

He had waited until they were almost on him, suspecting nothing, and knowing that they could not see him yet because he willed it so. Then he had raised his right hand high over his head, and a mage-light had flared on it, so bright that the front ranks of that terrible army winced back, and their shadows fell black as the heart of night on the snow behind them. He had said nothing; nothing needed to be said. He barred the way; that was all the challenge required.

They were heavily armored, those fighters: armor of some dull, black stuff, and helms of the same. They carried the weight of that armor as easily as Vanyel wore his own white fur cloak. They bore unornamented round shields, again of the same dull, black material, and carried long broadswords. For the rest, what could be seen of their clothing under the armor and their cloaks over it, they were a motley lot. But they *moved* with a kind of sensitivity to the presence of the next-in-line that had told Vanyel in the dream that they had been drilled together by a hand more merciless than ever Jervis had been.

They stared at him, and none of them moved for a very long time—

Until the front ranks parted, and the wizard stepped through.

Wizard he was, and no doubt; Vanyel could feel the Power heavy within him. But it was Power of the same kind as that which had cut this canyon; paid for in agony. And when it was gone, there would be no more until the wizard could torture and kill again. Vanyel had all the power of life itself behind him; the power of the sleeping earth, of the living forest—

He spread his arms, and the life-energy flowed from him, creating a barricade across the valley—

—like the barricade across his heart—

—and a shield behind which he could shelter. He faced the wizard, head held high, defiance in the slightest movement, daring him to try and pass.

But the ranks of the fighters parted again, and the first wizard was joined by a second, and a third. And Vanyel felt his heart sinking, seeing his own death sentence written in those three-to-one odds.

Still, he had stood his ground—

Until Mardic touched his mind.

It had *hurt*, that touch, salt on raw flesh. He'd interpreted it as an attack of the wizards, and had struck back, struck to kill, and only as he'd made his strike had realized that—

—a dream, oh, gods—it's a dream, it isn't real, and that's Mardic—

And had tried to pull the blow; *had* pulled the blow, but that sent the aborted power coursing back down places that burned in agony when it touched them. And he'd tried to stop the flow, but that had only twisted things up inside him, until he was a thrashing knot of anguish and he didn't know where he was or what he was doing. It all hurt, everything hurt, everything burned, and he was trapped in the pain, in the torment, crying out and knowing no one could hear him, and lost—he couldn't feel his body anymore, couldn't hear or see; he was foundering in a sea of agony—

Then a shock—like being struck—

He found himself gasping for breath, frozen to his teeth, but back in a normal body that hurt in a normal way.

Then he had blacked out for a moment; he came to with the Healer shaking him, talking to him.

He was soaking wet, and shivering.

Mardic? What about Mardic?

The Herald Jaysen was holding him upright, more than half supporting him—

Tylendel, dead, crumpled at Jaysen's feet. My fault, oh, gods, my fault—

The grieving came down on him full force, but somewhere at the back of his mind he *knew* that *they* were feeling what *he* was feeling and he clamped down on it—closed that line off—

In the stunned, mental silence he heard Jaysen's anguished thoughts, as clearly and intimately as if he was speaking them into Vanyel's ear.

:Gods—oh, gods, I didn't know, I didn't guess—I thought he was playing with the boy, I thought he was—oh, gods, what have I done?:

He shuddered away from the unwanted sympathy, from the mind-words that were like acid in his wounds, and blocked *that* line just as ruthlessly.

Then had come the potions—and the numbness. The blessed *unfeeling*. He drifted, nothing to hold him, not even his worry for Mardic. It was pitchy dark; they hadn't left a single flame in the room, which under the circumstances was probably wise. Scraps of what he now knew were thoughts drifted over to him; now Savil's mind-voice, now Jaysen's (dark with guilt, and Vanyel wondered why), now Mardic's.

If he had been on his feet, he would have staggered with relief at hearing that last. *I didn't kill him—thank the gods, I didn't kill him.*

He drifted further, until he couldn't hear anything anymore. Until he lost even his own thoughts. Until there was nothing left but sleep, and the sorrow that never, ever left him.

* * *

Savil stood beside the garden door with one hand on the frame, and prayed. She didn't pray often; most Heralds didn't. Praying usually meant asking for something—and the kind of person that became a Herald tended to be the kind that didn't look outside of himself for help until the last hope had been exhausted.

For Savil, at least, it had gotten to that point.

Just beyond the window, bundled in quilts and blankets and half-lying against Yfandes' side, Vanyel dozed in the sun, still kept in a sleepy half-daze by Andrel's potions. Jaysen had carried him out there, with his own mind so tightly shielded against leaking his thoughts that Savil fair Saw him quivering under the strain. Jaysen would be back for the boy in another two candlemarks, which was all Andrel would allow in this cold. This was the third day of the routine; there had been no real repetition of the crisis that had precipitated it, but Savil more than half expected one every night.

Vanyel sighed in sleep, and one arm stole out of the blankets to circle around Yfandes' neck. The Companion nuzzled his ear, and instead of pulling away, he cuddled *closer* to her.

But before Savil had a chance to really take in this first, positive sign that the Herald–Companion bond was taking root in the boy, someone *pounded* on her outer door. She half-turned, and heard Donni pattering across the common room to answer it. There was a murmur too indistinct to make out.

The voice from outside the door strengthened. "Please, I'm Van's sister—let me at least talk to my aunt—"

Savil started, and strode quickly across Vanyel's room, pulling open the door. There could only be one of Vanyel's sisters likely to show up on her doorstep at this point, the one that had fostered out in hopes of a career in the Guard.

"Let her in, Donni," Savil said—and blinked in surprise. The girl in the doorway could have been herself at seventeen or eighteen.

God help her—no wonder she went for the Guard, Savil thought irrelevantly. *She's got that damned Ashkevron nose.*

Evidently the same thought was running through the girl's mind. "You must be my Aunt Savil," she said forthrightly, standing at what was almost "attention" in the doorway. "You have the nose. I'm Lissa. Can I help?"

Savil decided that she liked this blunt girl. "Perhaps, I don't know yet," she replied. "First, Lissa, come in and tell me what you've heard."

*   *   *

Lissa turned away from the garden door with a shudder. "He looks like he's been dragged through the nine hells facedown," she said.

"And at that he looks better than he did three days ago," Savil replied. She would have said more, but there was another pounding on the suite door and a voice she knew only too well rumbled angrily when Donni answered it.

"Like bloody hell she's too busy," Lord Withen Ashkevron snarled. "I didn't bloody ride my best horse to foundering to be put off with a 'too damned busy!' Now where in hell is she?"

Savil, with Lissa at her side, strode across to the door, flung it open, and stood facing Withen with her back poker-straight, feet slightly apart, arms crossed over her chest.

"What do you want, Withen?" she asked flatly, narrowing her eyes in mingled annoyance and apprehension.

"What the hell do you think I want?" he growled, ignoring Lissa and Donni as if they weren't there, placing his fists on his hips, and taking an aggressive, wide-legged stance. "I want to know what the hell you've been doing with the boy I sent you! I sent him down here for you to make a *man* out of him, not turn him into a perverted little catamite!" His face darkened and his voice rose with every word. "I—"

"*I* think that's more than enough, Withen," she snapped, cutting him off before he could build up to whatever climax he had in mind. "I, I, I— dammit, you blustering peabrain, is *that* all you ever think of? Yourself? Vanyel almost *died* four days ago, he almost died *again* three days ago, and he could die *or* go mad in the next candlemark, and all *you* can think of is that he did something your back-country prejudices don't approve of! Gods above and below, you can't even call him by his bloody name, just 'the boy'!"

She advanced on him with such anger in her face that he actually fell back a pace, alarm and surprise chasing themselves across his eyes. Lissa moved with her, and stood beside her with every muscle tensed, and her fists clenched into hard knots.

"You come storming in here when we've maybe—*maybe*—got him stable, without so much as a 'please' or a 'may I,' you don't even ask if he's in any shape to put two words together in a sensible fashion! Oh, no, all *you* can do is scream that *I've* made him into a catamite when you sent him to be made into a man. A *man*!" She laughed, a harsh cawing sound that clawed its way up out of her throat. "My *gods*—what the hell did you think he was? Tell me, Withen, what kind of a *man* would send his son into strange hands just because the poor thing didn't happen to fit his image of masculinity?"

Savil ran out of things to say—but Lissa hadn't.

"What kind of a *man* would let a brutal bully break his son's arm for *no damned reason?*" the girl snarled. "What kind of a *man* would drive his son into becoming an emotional eunuch because every damned time the boy looked for a little bit of paternal love he got slapped in the face? What kind of a *man* would take *anyone's* word over his son's with *no cause* to *ever* think the boy was a liar?" Lissa faced down her father as if he had become her enemy. "You tell *me*, Father! What right do you have to demand *anything* of him? What did you ever give him but scorn? When did you *ever* give him a single thing he really needed or wanted? When did you ever tell him he'd done well? When did you *ever* say you loved him?"

Withen backed up another two paces, his back against the wall beside the door, his expression that of someone who has just been poleaxed.

Savil found her tongue again. "A *man*—may all the gods give you what you deserve, you fathead! *What kind of a man would care more for his own reputation than his son's life?*" She was backing him into the corner now, unleashing on Withen all the pain and frustration and anger she'd been keeping bottled up inside her over the past week. He had gone pale—and started to try to say something, but she cut him off.

"Let me tell you this, Withen," she hissed. "Everything that Vanyel's become, *you* had a hand in making—and mostly because *you* didn't want a son, you just wanted a little toy copy of yourself to parade around so that people could congratulate you on your bedroom prowess. You helped make him what he is—gave him a set of values so distorted it's a wonder he even recognized love when he saw it, and taught him that he had to keep everything he felt secret because adults couldn't be trusted. And *now* I have one boy dead, and one a hair from dying, and all you care about is that somebody *might* think you weren't *manly* enough to father *manly* sons! Oh, get out of here, get out of my sight—"

She turned away from him before he could see the tears in her eyes. Lissa put a steadying hand on her shoulder and glared at her father as if she would be perfectly happy to take a piece out of him if he said one wrong word.

"S-S-Savil—I—I—" he stammered. "They said—but I didn't believe—is Vanyel—"

"One wrong word, one wrong move, and he will die, Withen," she said flatly, her eyes shut tightly as she reestablished control over herself. "One wrong *thought* almost killed him. He slit his wrists because he discovered that someone he trusted believed that his *love* was the reason Tylendel died. Are you pleased with what you made? It was certainly the *honorable* thing for him to do, wasn't it?"

"I—I—"

"I am very gratified to be able to tell you that he *isn't* yours anymore, Withen, he's mine. He's been Chosen—*if* he lives that long, he'll be a Herald-trainee, and as such, he is *my* charge. You've forfeited any claim on him. So you can have what you've always wanted—little Mekeal can be your heir-designate, and you can wash your hands of Vanyel with a clear conscience."

Withen flinched at her pitilessly accurate words, and seemed to almost shrink in size.

"Savil—I didn't mean—I didn't want—"

"You didn't?" She raised an ironic eyebrow.

He winced. "Savil, can I—see him? I won't hurt him, I—dammit, he's still my son!"

"Lissa, do you think we should?"

Lissa looked at her father as one looks at a not-particularly-trustworthy stranger. "I don't know that he can behave himself."

Withen's face darkened. "You ungrateful little—"

Lissa shrugged, and said to Savil, "See what I mean?"

Savil nodded. "I see—but he has a point. Maybe he ought to see his handiwork." She nodded toward the door to Vanyel's room. "Follow me, Withen. And keep a rein on that mouth of yours, or I'll have you thrown out."

He stopped dead at the garden door, and pressed his hands and face against the glass in stunned disbelief. "My *gods*—" he gasped. "They said—but I didn't believe them. Savil, I've seen men dead a week that looked better than that!"

Lissa snorted. Savil pushed him away from the door impatiently, and opened it, flinching a bit as the cold air hit her. She looked back at him; he'd made no move to follow. "Are you coming, or not?" she asked, keeping her voice low so as not to startle Vanyel.

He swallowed, his own face set and very white, and followed her with slow, hesitant steps. She walked quickly to the patch of sheltered, sun-gilded brown grass where the boy was lying with Yfandes; he hadn't moved since she'd left. He didn't seem to notice she was there as she knelt in the harsh, dry grass that prickled her knees through the cloth of her breeches and hose.

"Van—Van, wake up a little, can you?" she said softly, not touching him at all, either with hand or mind. "Van?"

He moved his head a little, and blinked in a kind of half-dazed parody of sleepiness. "A-aunt?" he murmured.

"Your father's here—Withen—he wants to see you. Vanyel, he can't take you home, he has no power over you now that you're Chosen. You don't have to see him if you don't want to."

Vanyel blinked again, showing a little more alertness. "N-no. S'all right. 'Fandes says s'all right; says I should."

Savil rose quickly and returned to where Withen waited uncertainly on the worn path, halfway between the door and where the boy lay. "Go ahead," she said roughly. "Don't raise your voice, and speak slowly. We've got him pretty heavily drugged, so keep that in mind. You might trigger more than you want to hear if you aren't careful."

She followed a few steps behind him, with Lissa behind her, and remained within earshot as he knelt heavily in the dry grass and started to reach out to touch Vanyel's shoulder. She very nearly snapped at him, but Vanyel roused a bit more, and waved the blunt fingers away.

"Vanyel—" the man said, seeming at a complete loss for words. "Vanyel, I—I heard you were sick—"

Vanyel gave a pitiful little croak of a laugh. "You h-heard I was playin' ewe t' 'Lendel's ram, y'mean. Don' lie t' me, Father. You lied t' me all m'life an' I couldn' prove it, but I *know* when people lie t'me now."

Withen flushed, but Vanyel wasn't through yet.

"Y're thinkin' now that—I—I'm perv'rt'd, unclean or somethin', an' that I—I'm just bad an' ungrateful an' I n-never p-p-pleased you an'—*dammit*, all I ev' wanted was f'r you t' tell me I did *somethin'* right! Just *once*, Father, j-j-just one time! An' all *you* ever d-d-did was let J-J-Jervis knock me flat, an' then kick me y'rself! 'Lendel *loved* me, an' I loved *him* an' you can *stop* thinkin' those—god—damned—*rotten*—*things*—"

Withen pulled back and started to his feet—opened his mouth like he was about to roar at his son—

But that was as far as he got. Vanyel's eyes blazed; his face went masklike with rage. And before Withen could utter a single syllable, Vanyel surged up out of his cocoon of blankets and knocked Withen head over heels into the bushes with the untrained, half-drugged power of his mind alone.

Withen struggled up. Vanyel knocked him flat. Lissa made as if to go to one or the other of them, but Savil caught her arm.

"Look at Yfandes," she said. "She's calm, she hasn't even moved. Let them have this out. Between us I think Yfandes and I could keep the lad from killing his father, but that isn't what he wants to do."

Twice more Withen tried to get his feet, and twice more Vanyel flung him back. He was crying now, silent, unnoticed tears streaking his white cheeks. "How's it *feel*, Father? Am I *strong* enough now? How's it *feel* t' get knocked down an' stepped on by somethin' you can't reason with an' can't fight? You *happy*? I'm as big a bully as J-J-Jervis now—*does that make you bloody happy?*"

Withen's mouth worked, but no sound came out of it.

Vanyel stared at him, then the angry light faded from his eyes and was replaced by a disgusted bitterness. "It doesn't make *me* happy, Father," he said, quietly, and clearly; the last of the drug-haze gone from his speech. "Knowing I can do this to you just makes me sick. *Nothing* makes me happy anymore. Nothing ever will again."

He sank back down to the ground, pulled his blankets around himself, and turned his face into Yfandes' shoulder. "Go away, Father," he said, voice muffled. "Just go away."

Withen got slowly and awkwardly to his feet. He stood, shaken and pale, looking down at his son for a long time.

"Would it make any difference if I said I was sorry?" he asked, finally, from the bewildered expression on his face, acutely troubled—and more than that, vaguely aware that he had just had his entire world knocked head-over-heels, and was entirely uncertain of what to do or say or even *be* next.

"Maybe—someday," came the voice, thickened with tears. "Not now. Go *away*, Father. Please—leave me alone."

Dear Withen: I think you are right for once in your life. The boy is not a boy any-more. He never was the boy you thought he was. If you can adapt yourself to treating him as an adult and an acquaintance rather than your offspring, I think you can come to some kind of a reconciliation with him eventually.

"Savil?"

Savil looked up. Mardic peeked around Savil's half-open door, uncertainty in his very posture.

Huh. I'm getting better at reading people.

She gave a quick glance out her window. Vanyel was sitting on the bench just outside it, talking with Lissa, Yfandes hovering over both of them.

Bless the child; I don't know what I'd do without her.

For a moment she forgot Mardic; a terrible weariness bowed down her shoulders like a too-heavy cloak.

Gods. What am I going to do? He's not getting better, just a little stronger. He keeps trying to make me or Liss into a substitute for 'Lendel, into someone else to follow. I can't let him do that. It'll just make things ultimately worse. But when we try and push him into standing on his own feet, he goes into a sulk. She sighed. *It makes me so angry at him that I want to slap him into next week. And he's had too much of that already. He doesn't really deserve it, either. Hellfires, those sulks are the closest he's ever gotten to normal behavior! Oh, gods—*

Mardic cleared his throat, and she jumped. "I'm sorry, lad, I'm wool-gathering. Must be getting old. Come on in."

He edged into the room, crabwise. "Savil, Donni and I want to ask you something," he faltered, hands behind his back, rubbing his left foot against his right ankle. "We—Savil, you're the best there is, but—Vanyel needs you more than we do."

"Gods," she sighed, rubbing her right temple. "I have been shorting you two—I am sorry—"

"No, really, we don't mind," Donni interrupted, poking her curly head past the edge of the door just behind Mardic's shoulder.

"I was wondering when you'd put in your silver-worth," Savil replied.

"We *do* come as a set," she pointed out. "No, Savil, you haven't been shorting us. It's more that we're afraid you're going to split yourself in half, trying to do too many things. *Vanyel* needs you; we've finally *got* what we needed from you—there wasn't anybody else likely to be able to teach us to work in concert, but look—"

Mardic moved farther into the room; Donni stayed by the door. They reached out to one another, arms extended, hands not *quite* touching, and—

Where there had been two auras there was now one; a golden-green flow over and around them that was seamless—and considerably *more* than either aura had been alone. Savil blinked in surprise. "Just when did you two start to do that?" she asked.

"The night—when we had to get the Temple open," Mardic supplied. "When we had to get the arrow up, and then even more when we meshed in the Healing-meld. That's when what you'd been showing us sort of fell into place. So, well, now any Herald-Mage could teach us, and really, given what we do together, it probably ought to be Jaysen, or Lancir. But Jaysen hasn't got anyone right now."

"Piffle. You'd make a three-hour tale of a limerick," Donni sniffed. "Savil, we asked Jaysen; he said he'd take us if you allow it."

Savil put down her pen, and closed her gaping mouth. "I think I may kiss you both," she replied, as Donni gave Mardic an "I told you so" grin. "I was trying to think of a way to get you another mentor and coming up blank because I'm the only one who knows how to teach concert work. Bless you, loves."

She rose and took both of them in her arms; they returned the embrace, their support as much mental as physical.

"Savil," Donni said quietly, as she released them with real reluctance. "What are you going to do with Vanyel? He's—he's still so broken—and everything here has just *got* to keep reminding him of 'Lendel. It's too bad you can't take him somewhere really different."

"Gods, that's only too true," she replied.

—really different—gods—oh, gods, thank you for bright little proteges!

"Donni," she said slowly, "I think you may just have found my answer for me. Now I'm even more grateful to you for finding yourselves a new teacher."

"You've got an idea?"

Savil nodded. "And kill two birds with one stone. Those things the Leshara had brought in—they *had* to be from the Pelagirs, just like what 'Lendel conjured in retribution. I'd have had to go out there anyway, to find out who's been tampering. So—what I'm going to do is take Vanyel there to some friends of mine, the Hawkbrothers. They're self-appointed guardians of the Pelagirs, so they should be told if there's been a mage tampering with their creatures. And they follow a different discipline; maybe they can help Van. And if they can't, I know they can at least contain him."

"But you really think they can help him?" Donni asked hopefully.

"Well, *I* can't; I know for a fact that Starwind is better than I am. Besides, if we keep Van drugged much longer, Andrel is afraid he'll become addicted, but if we take him off—"

"He could wreck the Palace." Mardic nodded solemnly. "When are you taking him?"

"When—within the next few days, I think. The sooner the better." She looked over his head, to the Wingsister talisman on her wall. "The only problem is that to find Starwind k'Treva and Moondance k'Treva I'll have to go to *them*—because they don't *ever* come out of the Pelagirs. That means two things. I'll have to build a Gate, and I'll have to hope that I still know *how* to find them."

CHAPTER 11

"GODS, I *HATE* GATING," Savil muttered to Andrel, squinting against the glare of sun on snow as she scanned the sky for even a hint of cloud.

"Why? Other than the recent rotten associations—"

"It's damned dangerous at the best of times. It plays fast and loose with local weather systems, for one thing; it's a spell that sets up a local energy field, a kind that disrupts any kind of high-energy weather pattern that's around it. Usually for the worse." She closed her eyes, centered and grounded, and extended her Mage-Gift sense up and out, looking farther afield for anything that *might* move in while she had the Gate up. To her vast relief there didn't seem to be anything of consequence anywhere nearby; the only energy-patterns she could read were a few rising air currents over warm spots, too small to be any hazard.

She sighed. "Well, the weather's not going to cause any problems. How was the lad?"

"Drugged to his teeth, and I would stake my arm that he won't be able to count to one before some time tonight. And I am damned glad you told me that you were planning on Gating out of here." Andrel tucked his long, sensitive hands inside his cloak, and peered across the open Field through the sunlight. "Since it was Gate-energy that blew his channels open—"

"Probably," Savil interrupted.

"All right, *probably* blew his channels open—he's going to be doubly sensitive to it for the rest of his life. He'll likely know when someone's opening a Gate within a league of him. And actually going through one *may* touch off another fit. Which is why—"

"—you drugged him to the teeth. I have no objection; it's a little awkward, but that's why we have the kind of saddles for our Companions that we do."

They crunched their way across Companion's Field, now covered with the first snowfall of the season. Savil repeated a quieting exercise for every step she made, for she knew she needed to establish absolute calm within herself; she would be Gating to her absolute physical limits (in terms of the distance she planned to cover) and that would take every reserve she had.

In light of that, she had turned everything (other than establishing the Gate itself) over to the hands of others. Mardic and Donni had done all her packing, Lissa had taken care of Vanyel's, and Lissa had taken charge of the boy once Andrel was finished with him. They were all waiting at the Grove Temple at this very moment.

"So why else don't you like Gating?" Andrel asked, while the Field around them glowed under the sun.

"Because when I get there, I'm going to be pretty damned worthless," she replied dryly, "and I'd better hope the Talisman performs the way Starwind claimed it was supposed to, or we'll be a pretty pathetically helpless pair, Vanyel and I."

"Why don't you do what Tylendel did, use someone else's energy?"

"Because I don't really know what he did," she said, after a long pause that was punctuated only by the sound of their footsteps breaking through the light crust of snow. "None of us do. That may be why we ended up feeding the energy back through poor Van instead of grounding and dissipating it. I personally do not care to take the chance of doing that to another living soul and neither do any of the others. Vanyel lived through it; someone else might not. And it may well be that you have to have a lifebound pair to carry it off at all. So," she shrugged, "we do this the hard way, and I fall on my nose on the other side."

They entered the Grove, the leafless trees making a lacework of dark branches against the bright blue sky. The peace of the Grove never left it, no matter what the season was. That was one reason why Savil had chosen to set up the Gate here. The other was that it was the safest place on the Palace grounds that she could put a Gate; no one but Heralds ever came here without invitation. There should be no accidents caused by a stranger wandering by at the wrong moment.

The group waiting by the Temple, which looked today as if it had been newly-made of the same pure snow that covered the ground around it, was a small one. Jaysen, Donni and Mardic, and Lissa. There were only two Companions there; Kellan and Yfandes. Companions tended to avoid the Grove except when a Herald died. Vanyel was slumped over in Yfandes' saddle, wrapped in the warmest cloak Savil could find and strapped down securely enough that his Companion could fight or flee without losing him.

Avert— Savil thought, a little superstitiously. *Let there be no reason for her to have to fight. We've had enough bad fortune without that.*

She went first to his side; his hands had been loosely tied together at the wrist and the bindings were hooked over the pommel of the saddle. The stirrup-irons were gone, probably stored in one of the packs bundled behind his saddle; the stirrup-leathers had been turned into straps binding his calves to the saddle itself. He was belted twice at the waist; once to the pommel, once to the high cantle, using rings on the saddle meant for exactly that purpose. He was *not* going to come off.

Andrel reached her side; he reached up and pried open one of Vanyel's eyelids. The boy didn't react at all, and his pupils were mere pinpoints. The Healer's eye unfocused for a moment as he "read" the boy; then he nodded with satisfaction.

"He should be all right, Savil. No more drugs, though, after this. Not even if those friends of yours—"

Savil shook her head. "They don't like this kind of drug. Not for any reason. Drugs like you've been giving him are too easy to abuse."

"I don't like them either, but there are times you've got no other choice, and this was one of them." Andrel touched the boy's hand; his green eyes darkened as he brooded for a moment. "Gods. I hope you're right about these people. His channels haven't healed at all, not really."

"If they can't help us, no one can." Savil turned her back on her semiconscious charge and faced the door of the Temple, and put herself into the right mindset to invoke her spell.

To build a Gate—

It was the most personal of spells. Only one person could build a Gate, because only one mind could direct the energy needed to build it. The spell-wielder had to have a very exact notion of *where* the Gate was to exit, and no two people ever had precisely the same mental image of a place. In any event, only Savil had ever been in the k'Treva territory of the Pelagirs. She couldn't be "fed" by another Herald-Mage, since she would need every bit of her attention for the Gate itself and would have none to spare to channel incoming energy. Lastly, because the energy had to be so intimately directed, it could come from only one place—

From *within* the builder of the Gate. Or—perhaps—one soul-bound to the builder of the Gate? A lifebond was at such a deep level that it wasn't conscious, so perhaps that was why Tylendel had succeeded in using Vanyel as his source of energy.

The kind of power needed to build a Gate was the kind that *could* be stored, could be planned for. But like a vessel that could only hold so much liquid, a mage could only hold so much energy within himself. Savil had prepared for this; she could replenish herself within a day when the spell was completed and the Gate dismissed. But for that critical period of twenty-four candlemarks she would be exhausted—physically, mentally, and magically.

No time to think of that. Get to it, woman. First, the Portal, then the Weaving.

The Temple door had been used so many times before as one end of a Gate that it needed no special preparation. She needed only to—reach—

She raised her hands, closed her eyes, and centered herself so exactly that everything about her vanished from her attention. There was only the power within her, and the place where the Gate would begin.

I call upon the Portal—

She molded the power into a frame upon the physical frame of the doorway; building it layer upon layer until it was strong enough to act as an anchor to hold *this* place when she warped space back upon itself.

Then she began spinning out threads of energy from the framework; they drifted outward, seeking.

This is the place, she told them, silently willing them to find the real-world counterpart of the image in her mind. *Where the rocks are* so *and the trees grow* thus *and the feel of the earth is in this manner—*

They spun out, longer, finer, more attenuated. When they weakened, she fed them from within herself, spinning her own substance out and feeling it drawn out of her.

Now she was losing strength; it felt exactly as if she were bleeding from an open wound. And the power was not merely draining from her anymore, it was being *pulled* from her by the Gate itself. This was the point of greatest danger for a Herald-Mage; she was having to fight the Gate to keep from being drained right down to unconsciousness.

Then one of those questing power-threads caught on something, out beyond the farthest range of her sensing; another followed—

There was a silent explosion of light that she could see even through her closed lids, and the Gate Wove itself in an instant into a temporary, but stable, whole.

She dropped her hands, opened her eyes, and swayed with uttermost exhaustion; Kellan was there beside her in time for her to catch the pommel of her saddle to keep from falling.

The door of the Temple has no longer within the doorframe. Instead, the white marble—glowing now, even in the bright sunlight—framed a strange and twisted bit of landscape.

"*That's* where you're going?" Jaysen said doubtfully, looking at the weird shapes of rock, snow, and sand that lay beyond the portal. It was snowing there, from black, lowering clouds; fat flakes drifting down through still, dark air. Savil nodded.

"That's it; that's the edge of the Pelagirs near Starwind's territory. The other end is a cave entrance, so we'll have some shelter on the other side until Starwind and Moondance get there."

"And if they don't?" Jaysen asked. "Savil, I don't like to think of you two alone out in a place like that. The boy is next to useless, and you're exhausted."

"Jays, it's quite possible that they'd take one look at you and kill you if they didn't see me right there with you," she said, clinging to the saddle and trying to muster enough strength to climb into it. "They're unbelievably territorial and secretive, and for good reasons—think for a minute, will you? They *have* to have known someone was tampering, stealing creatures they thought safely locked up. If they see a stranger and Sense he's Mage-Gifted, they're likely to strike first and ask questions of the corpse. And I mean that literally. I'm taking enough risk bringing the boy in, and he's plainly in need of help, and branded as *mine*."

She gave up trying to be self-sufficient. "Boost me up, will you?" she asked humbly.

Jaysen went her one better; with the help of Andrel he lifted her into place. "Have you got everything you need?"

"I think so." In actual fact, she was too tired to think; it was all she could do to keep her mind on the next step of the journey. "Toss the firewood through."

Four heavy bundles of dry, seasoned wood went through the Gate to land in the snow on the other side.

Vanyel whimpered beside her; she could see his face was creased with lines of pain. *He's feeling it, like Andy thought he might. Better hurry.*

"Mardic—" she said quietly. "Donni—"

Savil's proteges came solemnly to her stirrup; she held out her hands to them, and shared a moment of mind-melded intimacy with them that was more than "farewell"; it was a sharing of gifts. Her pride in them and love and blessing—and their love and well-wishing for her.

"Lissa—"

The girl came to stand beside her students.

"I can't begin to thank you," Savil began, awkward, as ever, with words.

"Thank me by bringing Van home well," Lissa replied earnestly. "That's all I want." She reached up and squeezed Savil's hand once, then backed away.

The youngsters moved out of the way, and Jaysen and Andrel came to take their place without any prompting. She gave a hand to each, closing her eyes again, and opening herself to them in a melding even more intimate than she had shared with her students, for there were no secrets among the three of them, and nothing held back. What she had not told Mardic and Donni was that there might be no returning from this journey. If she failed with Vanyel, he might well destroy both of them; his Gifts were that powerful. Even now he moaned again in his drug-induced slumber, feeling the Gate energies despite a dose of narcotic that would have rendered a less sensitive Gifted unconscious for a week.

For a moment, she was angry. *He could kill us, and do it without knowing what he was doing. Oh, gods. Gods, you owe him, dammit! You've taken his love— at the least give him something in return.*

But she was too tired, too depleted to sustain even her anger at Fate or the gods or—whatever. Especially when this might *really* be farewell.

So this was a moment when she asked forgiveness of her friends for anything she might have done in the past—and they asked for and received the same from her.

When she raised her heavy, weary head, the two pairs of eyes, green and gray, that met hers were bright with tears that would not be shed—at least not now. She squeezed their hands, and let go; they stepped away from her as she straightened in her saddle, took a deep breath, and faced the Gate and the gray landscape beyond it. It looked no more welcoming now than it had before, and dallying wasn't going to make the leaving easier.

:*All right, Kellan,*: she Mindspoke. :*Let's go.*:

And they rode into the stomach-churning vertigo she had come to hate.

Savil huddled beside the fire with her legs curled under her, forcing herself to stay awake. There was, thank the gods, no wind; the cave was warming fairly quickly. It smelled of damp, though, and of the musty taint of the half-rotten leaves that had blown in here with the autumn winds. That damp meant that if she let the fire die, it would chill down very quickly, a chill that would penetrate even their thick wool cloaks.

Once she'd taken the Gate down, she'd had just enough strength to lay the fire, and start it with the coal she'd brought in a fire-safe. After that she'd sunk to the sand next to it, pulling Vanyel close in beside her. He was curled up against her now, bundled with her inside her cloak, his head in her lap; he shook like a reed in the wind. From time to time he moaned and his hand groped for something that seemed to elude him; she soothed him back into sleep, stroking his hair until he finally recognized that she was still with him and calmed a little.

The Gate-crossing had been hard on him, as hard as she'd feared. When she'd gone to take him from Yfandes' back, he'd been half-roused out of his drugged daze; his eyes had been wide open, his jaws clenched. He had been held paralyzed, not by the drugs, but by unfocused and overwhelming ter-ror and pain. It had taken a candlemark to get him soothed down again.

Somewhere just outside were Kellan and Yfandes, standing a watchful guard in the falling snow. Still in their tack, poor things—she'd barely been able to get Vanyel unstrapped from the saddle before collapsing beside him. She had nearly forgotten to activate the Wingsister Talisman. It had taken Kellan's sharp reminder to shake her out of her fog of exhaustion long enough to stab her finger and let the prescribed three drops of her blood fall on it.

Memory came, then, as sharply defined as if she had bid farewell to the Hawkbrothers scant days ago instead of years.

"Blood calls to blood, and heart to heart," Starwind told her gravely, his ice-blue eyes focused inward. He held his slashed palm above the Wingsister Talisman of silver wire and crystals, and his blood dripped onto the heart-stone of the piece, dyeing the clear crystal a vivid ruby.

Savil watched, silently, feeling the power flowing and weaving itself into the intricate design of rainbow crystal and silver wire.

This was nothing like the kind of magic she was used to using; it really wasn't much like that the Hawkbrothers had taught her, either. This was older magic, much older, dating, perhaps, from the times of the Mage Wars, the wars that had wrecked the world and left the Pelagirs a twisted, magic-riddled ruin. She shivered a little, and Starwind looked up, one of his brief and infrequent smiles lighting his face for a moment.

He closed his hand; Moondance touched the back of it, and he opened it again. The slash in his palm had been Healed with the speed of a thought. At eighteen the young outlander now calling himself "Moondance" was well on his way to becoming that rarest of mages, a Healer-Adept.

Starwind fixed the Talisman in its place on the mask of feathers and crystal beads; it resembled a palm-sized diadem perched on the brow of the mask above the eye-slits. He handed the whole mask to her, and nodded at the Talisman. "When you need us again, come to us, and let three drops of your own blood fall upon the heart-stone. I shall know, and come to you."

In all those years since, the heart-stone's bright scarlet had not faded. She only hoped that the set-spell had not faded either. It did seem to her that the heart-stone began pulsing with a dim, inner light from the moment that her blood touched it. But that could have been the flickering of the fire, or the wavering of her own vision; she was too spent to tell, and too drained to begin to sense power even if it was moving under her own nose.

Vanyel stirred at her side, curling his knees tighter against his chest. She shifted a bit, glad that the floor of the cave was covered in several inches of dry, soft sand.

Poor child, she thought, her mind dark with despair. *I'm at a loss for what to do with you. You keep reaching out to me for support, and I want to give it to you, and I can't, I mustn't. If I do, you'll just fall right back into the pattern you danced with poor 'Lendel.* She stroked the fine, silky hair beneath her hand, and her heart ached for him. *You don't know what to think anymore, do you? You're afraid to touch again, afraid to open yourself, you're full of such fear and such pain—gods, when you told Withen that nothing would ever make you happy again—*

She swallowed the lump in her throat that threatened to choke her, and blinked at the dancing flames, then closed her stinging eyes and felt tears bead up on her lashes. *Starwind, old friend*, she thought desperately, *where are you? I'm out of my depth; I don't know what to do. I need your help—*

:And you have it, sister-of-my-heart.:

She started. There was a swirl of snow at the cave entrance, white-gold and shadow in the dancing firelight. There had been no alert from either Companion—

But when the snow settled and cleared, he was there.

He hadn't changed, not at all.

The sword of ice, she had called him when she'd first seen him. Flowing silver hair still reached past his waist when he put back the hood of his white cloak and let the silky mass of it tumble free. There still were no wrinkles in his face, not even around the obliquely-slanting, ice-blue eyes; he was still tall and unbent, still slender as a boy. Only the cool deeps of his eyes showed his age, and the aura of power that pulsed about him. No mage would ever have any doubts that this was an Adept, and a powerful one.

He smiled at her, and held out his hands. "Welcome, heart-sister, Wingsister Savil," he said in the liquid *Tayledras* tongue, gliding to her to take the hands she held up to him in his own. "Always welcome, and well come thou art."

"Starwind, *shaydra*," her sight darkened for a moment, and when it cleared, the *Tayledras* Adept was kneeling at her side, holding her upright.

"Savil, you stubborn, headstrong woman," he chided, as she felt an inrushing of energy from his center to hers. She swayed a little, and he held her upright. "What need could possibly have been so great that you drain yourself to a wraith to Gate yourself here?"

"This need—" She pulled back her cloak to show him the boy curled against her side, his face taut with pain.

"God of my fathers—" He reached out with his free hand and barely touched Vanyel's brow. He pulled back his hand as if it had been burned. "Goddess of my mothers! What have you brought me, sister?"

"I don't know," she said, slumping wearily against him. "He's been blasted open, and he can't heal—more than that—I'm too tired to tell you right now. So much has happened, and to both of us—I just can't think what to do anymore. All I know is that he's hurting, and I can't help him, and if I'd left him where he was he'd have destroyed himself at the best, and half the capital at the worst."

"There is nothing wrong with your judgment, I pledge you that," Starwind replied, sitting back on his heels and regarding the boy dubiously. "There is such potential there—he frightens me. And such darkness of the soul—no, Wingsister, not *evil*; there is nothing evil in him. Just—darkness. Despair is a part of it, but—denial of what he is and must become is another. Self-willed darkness; he wills himself not to see, I think."

"You see more than I do," she told him, rubbing her aching forehead. "I haven't the right to ask it of you, but—will you help me with him? *Can* you help me?"

The firelight turned the ice of his eyes to blue-gold flame. "You have the right, sister to brother, to ask what you will of me. Did you not gift me with the greatest of all gifts, in the person of my *shay'kreth'ashke*?"

She had to smile a little at that. Bringing Starwind another boy long ago had been one of the few unalloyed good things she'd ever done. "Where is Moondance, anyway?"

:*Moondance stands in the snow, defending his head and his lifeblood. Telling the stranger-*lasha'Kaladra *not to eat me*,: came the laughter-flavored reply. :*I frightened her. She does not trust me, I think.*:

:Kellan—: Savil Mindspoke tiredly.

:He popped up right under Yfandes' nose and scared the liver out of her, Chosen,: Kellan replied apologetically. *:She went for him before we knew who it was. It's all right now, he's just making amends.:*

:Bright Havens, Kell, you *know him, at least!:* she snapped, her tiredness making her impatient.

:Not anymore—:

"I fear I have greatly changed, Wingsister," Moondance said contritely from the entrance. "And I also fear I had forgotten the fact."

Savil looked over Starwind's shoulder and felt her mouth gaping. Starwind put one finger beneath her chin, and shut it for her with a chuckle.

"Great good gods!" she said after a moment of stunned silence. "You *have* changed!"

The Moondance she had known—he hadn't had the name "Moondance" for long at that point—had been brown-haired and brown-eyed and as ordinary as a peasant hut. Not surprising for one of peasant stock. But now—now the hair was as long and as silver and the eyes as ice-blue as Starwind's. The lines of his face were still the same; square to Starwind's triangle, but the cheekbones were far more prominent than Savil remembered, and the body had grown out of adolescent gawkiness and into a slender grace so like Starwind's that they could have been brothers by birth instead of by blood.

:He even smells *different,:* Kellan complained.

"How did you *do* that?" Savil demanded.

Moondance made a fluid shrug, and tossed the sides of his white cape over his shoulders, showing that he wore only thin gray breeches and a sleeveless gray leather jerkin with matching boots. Savil shivered at this reminder that the *Tayledras* never seemed to notice the cold. "It's the magic we use," he said. "It makes us into what it wants us to be. I think."

"As always, an oversimplification," Starwind corrected him fondly. "*Ka'sheeleth.* Savil has brought us a problem. Come look at this boy—"

Moondance drifted over to Savil's other side, sat on his heels beside her, and studied Vanyel's face for several breaths.

"*Hai'yasha,*" he breathed. "*Shay'a'chern,* hmm? And Lovelost? No, it goes deeper than that." He reached out as Starwind had, and touched Vanyel's forehead, but unlike Starwind, did not pull away. "*Ai'she'va*—Holiest Mothers! The *pain!*" His jaw tightened and the pupils of his eyes contracted to pinpoints. "Reft and bereft of *shay'kreth'ashke.*" His face took on the tranquility of a statue. "Pawn he is now—pawn he has been—" he said, his tone flat, his voice dropping half an octave. "Pawn to what he is and what he wills not to be. But will or no, the pawn is in play—and the play is a trial—"

"And what of the game?" Starwind asked in a whisper.

Moondance hesitated, then life came back to his face as he shrugged again, and his pupils went back to normal. "No way of knowing," he replied, slowly taking his hand from Vanyel's forehead. "That depends entirely upon whether he is willing to become more than a pawn. But yours to be the Teaching, I think," he said, looking up sharply at the Adept. "It is like your powers that he holds. As for Healing, I think that half of it will be his doing—if he Heals at all—"

"And the other half yours," the Adept stated with an ironic smile.

Moondance turned Vanyel's wrist up, showing the scar across it—then turned over his own hand, and the firelight picked out the scar that ran from the gold-skinned hand halfway to the elbow, a scar that followed the course of the blue vein pulsing beneath the skin. "Who better?" he asked. "We have something in common, I think."

Savil swayed again, caught in a sudden dizziness, and Starwind took hold of her shoulders to steady her. "You need rest," he said in concern. "Will you have it here, or can you ride?"

Savil thought longingly of just lying down where she was, and then reflected on being able to do so in a bed.

And also on the Companions, out there in the snow and cold, and still in their harnesses.

"The Companions can and will carry double," she sighed, feeling just about ready to fade away. "If you're willing to ride them. Or strap us in, I don't much care which. But I'd like *them* in the warm."

"Then we ride," Starwind said, as Moondance scooped Vanyel up in his arms as if he weighed next to nothing. The older Adept rose to his feet and offered her his hand, and it took every scrap of will she had left to her to stumble erect. "It is not far, Wingsister."

"I hope not," she told him earnestly, staggering out into the snow, while Moondance put the fire out with a single backward glance. "Because if it isn't, you're going to be carrying me as well as the boy."

First there was darkness, and the peace that came with being so drugged that there was no thought at all. It was the only time he felt anything like peace, these days, and he welcomed the drugs and the red-haired Healer who brought them. There were times without counting when he hoped that *this* time the Healer had miscalculated—that *this* time he wouldn't wake.

Then there was pain, unfocused, but somewhere near at hand. Like the touch of sun on skin already reddened and burned. It got past the drugs, somehow; he tried to push it away, but it continued to throb in those half-healed places in his mind, promising him more pain to come.

Then—nothing *but* pain, fire in his veins and under his skin, flames dancing along his nerves and scorching his mind. Gate-fire, Gate-energy—it was unmistakable, and unbearable, and yet it continued long past the moment he thought his sanity would shatter or his heart stop. He screamed, or thought he did. He was lost in it, and there was no way out—not even death, for the pain would not let him die.

Then it was gone. But it left him aching, all the channels burned raw again, and worse, all the memories replaying themselves over and over—Gala dying, Tylendel throwing himself from the Tower, Tylendel lying in state in the Temple—

Then, without warning, the Dream.

He stood blocking the way, a one-mage barricade across Crook-Back Pass. Mage-light from his upraised hand reflected from the impassive faces and hollow, empty eyes of the three wizards who opposed him.

This was *not* like the old dream—the dream of being alone in the ice. This was—something else. He could sense things, shards of meaning, just under the surface of it, but couldn't seem to bring them out to where he could read them.

But it felt—real. Fearfully real.

"Why do you bother with this nonsense?"

The voice from behind the wizards was sweet, lilting. One more figure paced forward as the ranks of the army backing the wizards parted to let him pass.

"You are quite alone, Herald-Mage Vanyel." One of the wizards stepped two paces to the side to allow the newcomer through to the center, to face Vanyel.

He was beautiful; there was no other word for him. A perfectly sculptured face and body, hair and eyes of twilight shadow, a confidence, poise, and power so complete they were works of art.

Except for the dark eyes, he could have been Vanyel's brother; except that he was too perfect, he could almost have been a younger Vanyel.

He was clad in dull black armor, like his soldiers, but carried no weapon. He didn't need one; he was a weapon. He was a weapon with no other purpose than the destruction and death he molded into his power. Unlike the knife which could cut to heal or harm, this weapon would never serve any other purpose than pain. Vanyel knew that as well as he knew himself.

"You are," the beautiful young man repeated, smiling, choosing his words to hurt, "quite alone."

Vanyel nodded. "You tell me nothing I was not already aware of. I know you. You are Leareth." The word meant—

"Darkness." Leareth laughed. "I am. Darkness. And these are my servants. A quaint conceit, don't you think?"

Vanyel said nothing. Every moment he kept Leareth here was one more moment speeding Yfandes down the road with Tylendel—

—but Tylendel was dead—

"You need not remain alone," Leareth continued, moistening his lips with his tongue, sensuously. "You have only to stretch out your hand to me, Vanyel, and take my Darkness to you—and you would never be alone again. We could accomplish much together, we two. Or if you wish—I could even—" He stepped forward a pace; two. "I could even bring back your long-lost love to you. Think of him, Vanyel. Think of Tylendel—alive, and once more at your side."

"NO!"

He struck at the terrible, beautiful face, struck with all the power at his command— and wept as he struck.

:Dreams, young Vanyel.: A blue-green voice froze him in mid-strike. *:Nothing but dreams. They vanish into mist if you will it.:*

The army, the pass, Leareth, all whirled away from him into another kind of darkness; this was a darkness that soothed, and he embraced it as eagerly as he had repudiated the other.

Cool, green-gold music threaded into the darkness, not dispelling it, but complementing it. It wound its way into his mind, and wherever it went, it left healing behind it; in all the raw, bleeding places, in all the burning channels. It flowed through him and he sank into it, drifting, drifting, and content to drift. It surrounded him, bathed him in balm, until there was nothing left of hurt in him—

—except the place Tylendel had left behind—the place that still ached so emptily—

The green-gold music was joined by another, a blue-green harmony like the voice that had spoken to dispel the dream. And this music was no longer letting him drift aimlessly. It was leading him; it had wound around his soul and he had no choice but to follow where it wanted him to go.

The blue-green music took the melody, the green-gold faded to a descant, and the voice spoke in his dreams again. *:Look; you wish control*—here *is your center*—so *to center and* so *to ground*—:

The music led him in a dance wherein he found a balance he hadn't known he craved until he found it. The music spun him around; he spun with it, and he knew that having found this point of equilibrium he would not lose it again.

:So, so, so, exactly *so,:* the music chuckled. *:Now, you would protect yourself*—thus *the barrier, see? Dense, and it keeps all out, flexible to your will. Always your will, young Vanyel, it is will and nothing less*—

It spun him walls to keep others out of his mind; he saw the way of it and spun them thicker, harder—then raveled them again down to the thinnest of barricades, knowing he could build them up again when he wanted to.

Then the blue-green music faded, leaving the green-gold to carry the melody alone. It sang to him then, sang of rest, sang of peace, and he dreamed. Dreamed of waking, moving to another's will, to drink and care for himself and sleep again. But no more dreams that hurt, only dreams full of the verdant music.

Then he woke—truly woke, not dreams of waking—to the sound of it; breathy, haunting notes that wandered into and out of melodies that he half recognized, but couldn't identify. There was a scent of ferns, a smell of growing things, a whiff of freshly-turned earth, and a hint of something metallic. Behind the music, he heard the sound of gently falling water.

He was no longer drugged. And the mind-channels within him no longer burned and tormented him.

He opened his eyes, slowly.

He thought for one mad moment that he was somehow suspended in a tree. He was surrounded on all sides by greenery, and luxuriantly-leaved branches hung over his head. Then he saw that while the branches were real, and the leaves, they were not the same organism. The branches supported huge ferns whose fronds draped down like a living canopy over his bed, and the greenery about him was a curtaining of multi-layered, multi-shaded green fabric hung from a framework of more branches, each layer as light and transparent as a spiderweb, and cut to resemble a cascade of leaf shapes. He had never in his life imagined that there could be so many colors of green.

Weak beams of sunlight threaded past the fern fronds. The blankets—if that was what they were—were a darker green, like moss, and felt as soft as velvet, but were thick and heavy.

He tried to sit up, and discovered that he couldn't. He was absolutely spent, with no strength left at all.

The music beyond the curtains finished with a breathless, upward-spiraling run, and a few moments later, the curtains parted.

Vanyel blinked in surprise at the young man who stood there, framed by the green of the curtain material; he knew he was staring, and rudely, but he couldn't help himself. He'd never seen anyone who looked like this—

A young man—silver-haired as any oldster, with hair longer than most women had, and with eyes of light blue that measured and weighed him, full of secrets and thoughts that Vanyel couldn't begin to read. He wore a sleeveless green jerkin, and breeches of a darker green, and in the hand that held back the curtains there was a white flute that looked as if it had been carved from luminescent, opaque crystal.

Vanyel suddenly realized that, indeed, he *couldn't* read the young man's thoughts; there was *presence* there, but nothing spilling over into his own mind.

He stammered out the first things in his mind—not terribly clever, and certainly not original but—"W-w-where am I? W-w-who are you?"

The young man tilted his head to one side a little, and Vanyel saw a faint hint of smile as he replied, very slowly and with a strange accent, "Well. 'Where am I?' you ask me—better than I had feared. I had half dreaded hearing 'who am I?' young Vanyel." He tilted his head the other way, and this time the smile was definite. "You are in k'Treva territory in the Pelagir Hills, and before you ask, your aunt, our Wingsister Savil, brought you here. We are her friends; she asked us to help her with your troubles. I am Moondance k'Treva; I am *Tayledras*, and I have been your Healer. That is my bed you are lying in. Do you like it? Starwind says it is a foolish piece of conceit, but *I* think that this is only because he did not think of it first."

Vanyel could only blink at him in bewilderment.

Moondance shook his head, ruefully. "I go too fast for you. Simple things first. Are you hungry? Thirsty? Would you like to bathe?"

All at once he *was* hungry—and thirsty—and disgustingly aware that his skin was crawling with the need for a bath.

"All three," he said, a little hesitantly.

"Then we remedy all three." Moondance pulled the curtains back to the foot and the head of the bed, and—

—and reached to pull off the blankets. At which point Vanyel realized that he was quite nude beneath the bedcoverings. He flushed, and clutched at the blanket.

Moondance gave him an amused look. "Who do you think it was that undressed you and put you where you are?" he asked. "I pledge you, it was not the Eastern Wind."

Vanyel flushed again, but did not release the blanket.

"So, so—here, my modest one—" Moondance reached up to one side among the hangings, and detached something which he tossed onto the blankets. Vanyel reached for it—a wrap-robe of something green and silken that was, thankfully, much more substantial than the hangings. As Moondance pointedly turned his back, he eased out of the bed and wrapped it around himself.

And reached for one of the bed-supports as dizziness made the room spin around him.

"That will *never* do." There was a cool touch between his eyes, and the room steadied.

"Come," Moondance was just in front of him, holding out his hands encouragingly. "Keep your eyes on me—yes. A step. Another. You have been long abed, young Vanyel, you must almost learn to walk again."

The *Tayledras* Healer walked backward, slowly, as Vanyel followed, looking only at his eyes. But he did not move to give the boy support in any way, except the one time Vanyel stumbled and nearly fell. Then Moondance caught him, held him until he could find his balance again, and only when Vanyel was standing firmly again did he draw away.

Vanyel was vaguely aware that they had crossed a threshold into another room, but just *walking* was costing him so much sweating, concentrated effort he didn't dare look around any. It seemed to take years before Moondance stopped, caught his elbow, and guided him to a seat on a smooth rock ledge that rimmed a raised pool of water so hot that it steamed.

"Now, look about you." Moondance waved at the pool and the rest of the room. "This is the pool for washing. Here is soap. When you are clean, go *there*, the pool for resting."

Though the pool Vanyel was sitting beside was deep, it was quite small. Next to the "pool for washing" was another, much larger, much deeper, and slightly above it, with an opening in the side that spilled hot water down into this pool. Both pools looked natural, rock-sided and sandy-bottomed.

"I think even weak as you are, you shall be able to find your way there. I shall return with food and drink." The young man hesitated a moment— then with the swiftness of a stooping hawk, leaned over and kissed Vanyel full on the lips. "You are very welcome, young Vanyel," he said, before

Vanyel had a chance to get over his surprise. "We are pleased to have you, Starwind and I, and not just for the sake of Wingsister Savil."

He vanished before Vanyel had a chance to react.

Vanyel found that if he moved slowly and carefully he didn't exhaust himself. He shed the robe and eased himself into the water with a sigh, and soaped and rinsed until he *finally* felt clean again. His pool emptied itself over the side and down a channel in the floor—and where the water went from there he couldn't say. He had figured by now that this was some kind of hot spring, which accounted for the metallic tang in the air.

With Moondance gone, he had a chance to get a good look around while trying to sort himself out. There didn't appear to be any "doors" as such in this dwelling, just doorways. This bathing room was multileveled; the highest level was the "pool for resting" which cascaded to the next level and the "pool for washing," which in turn was above the "floor" and the channel carrying the water away that was cut into it. There were no windows in the walls of natural rock; the whole was lit by a skylight taking up the entire ceiling, and there were green and flowering plants and ferns standing and hanging everywhere. There was only one entrance into this room—that led back to the bedroom, also rock-walled and roofed with a skylight, from what Vanyel could see of it.

The ledge between the pools was *not* that high, though it took far more of Vanyel's strength to get over it than he would have believed. Once in the larger pool he discovered that his surmise was right; crystalline hot water bubbled up from the sand in the center of the pool; someone had improved on nature by forming the rock of the pool sides below the waterline into smooth benches.

It was wonderful; the water was about as hot as was comfortable, and was forcing him to relax whether or not he wanted to. He closed his eyes and sat back, deliberately thinking of absolutely nothing, and only opened them again when he heard light footsteps crossing the stone floor below him.

It was, as he expected, Moondance, who had brought with him an earthenware beaker of what proved to be cider and a plate of sliced bread and cheeses and fruit.

"Eat lightly," the young man warned, climbing to Vanyel's level and setting his burdens down on the rim of the pool at Vanyel's right hand. "You have been three weeks without true food, and spent more than one of those days drugged."

"Three weeks?"

Moondance shrugged. "You needed Healing, of a kind your good

Healer Andrel could not give you. I think perhaps no Healer among your folk could have given you such Healing; they know nothing of the Healing of hurts caused by magic, only of illness and wounding. *That* is a study only a few have made, and most of those few *Tayledras.* Eat, young Vanyel. There are herbs in the bread and the drink to strengthen you."

"Where—where is Savil?" he asked, suddenly a little worried at being alone with a stranger.

"With Starwind. She was very weary, both in body and in soul. This—thing that has happened. It has been a deep grief to her, as well to you. Her heart is as sore, I think. They are old friends, my *shay'kreth'ashke* and Savil, and there are no secrets between them, and much love. She has need of such love. Perhaps more than you, for *she* has had no one to lend her support."

Vanyel had looked up at him sharply at that—with the word *ashke* striking him with the force of a cold slap in the face, making his heart pound painfully.

Moondance looked down at him, something speculative in his glance. He weighed Vanyel for a moment, then cleared his throat and looked away, deliberately. "I have a thing to say to you, a thing I wish you to think upon."

Vanyel put down his cider, and waited, apprehensively, to hear the rest.

"I have shared your thoughts; I know more of you than anyone, except, perhaps, your *shay'kreth'ashke.*"

Moondance changed his position so that he was sitting with his back to the pool, leaning his weight against his hands and staring up at the clouds visible through the skylight. He was being very careful *not* to look at Vanyel.

"As you have guessed from my words," he said, "I am *shay'a'chern.* As is Starwind. As you." Now he gave Vanyel a very brief, sidelong glance. "I am a Healer-Adept and I Heal more than people—I Heal *places.* I know the natural world as only one who wishes to restore it to its rightful balances can. This is the thing I wish to tell you; in all the world, there are more creatures than just man that make lifetime matings. Among them, some of the noblest—wolves, swans, geese, the great raptors—all creatures man could do worse than emulate, in many, many ways. And with all of them, *all,* there are those pairings, from time to time, within the same gender. Not often, but not unheard of either."

Vanyel found himself unable to move, and unable to anticipate the direction this was taking.

Now Moondance dropped his eyes to catch and hold Vanyel's in a joining of glances and wills that was unbreakable.

"There is in you a fear, a shame, placed there by your own doubts and the thoughts of one who knew no better. I tell you to think on this: the *shay'a'chern* pairing occurs *in nature*. How then, 'unnatural'? *Usual*, no, and not desirable for the species, else it would die out for lack of offspring. But not *unnatural*. The beasts of the fields are innocent as man can never be, who has the knowledge of good and evil and the choice between, and they do not cast out of their ranks the *shay'a'chern*. There was between you and your *shay'kreth'ashke* much love—only love. There is no shame in loving."

Vanyel couldn't breathe; he could only see those ice-blue eyes.

"This I think I have learned: where there is love, the form does not matter, and the gods are pleased. This I have observed: what occurs in nature, comes by the hand of nature, and if the gods did not approve, it would not be there. I give you these things as food for your heart and mind."

Once again, before Vanyel could move, he bent deliberately and kissed him, but this time on the forehead.

"I leave you for a moment with both kinds of nourishment." He smiled, and gave Vanyel a slow wink. "Since you are not to stay in the pool forever, I must needs find you clothing. *I* would not mind, but your aunt grows anxious and wishes to see you awake and aware, and we would not wish to put her to the blush, hmm?"

And with that, he jumped down from the pool ledge to the floor, and vanished again.

CHAPTER 12

"**HERE.**" MOONDANCE, a crease of worry between his brows, was back in a few moments with a towel and what looked like folded clothing: green, like his own. "You shall have to care for yourself, I fear. There is trouble, and I have been called to deal with it. Starwind and Savil will be with you shortly." He hesitated a moment, visibly torn. "Forgive me, I *must* go."

He put his burdens down on the pool edge and ran back out the doorway before Vanyel could do more than blink.

Gods—I feel like somebody in a tale, going to sleep and waking up a hundred years later. It seems so hard to think—like I'm still half asleep.

He dressed slowly, trying to collect his thoughts, and making heavy work of it. He *did* remember—vaguely—Savil telling him that he was too ill for Andrel to help, and he definitely remembered—despite the fog of drugs about the words—being told that she was going to take him to some friends of hers. He hadn't much cared what was happening at that point. He'd either been too drugged to care, or been hurting too much.

Presumably Moondance, and the absent Starwind, were the friends she meant. They were fully as strange as those weird masks of beads and feathers that Savil had on her wall. As was this place. Wherever it was.

He pulled the deep green tunic over his head, and suddenly realized something. He wasn't drugged—and he wasn't hurting, either. Those places in his mind that had burned—he could still feel them, but they weren't giving him pain.

Moondance said he Healed me. Is that why it feels like I halfway know him? Tayledras. *Didn't Aunt Savil tell us stories about them? I thought that was all those were—stories. Not real.* He looked around at the strange room, half-structure, half-natural, each half fitting into the other so well he could scarcely tell where the hand of nature left off and the hand of man began. *Real. Gods, if I were to describe this place, nobody would ever believe me. This—it's all so different. I even feel different.*

He could sense some kind of barrier around him, around his thoughts. At first it made him wary, but he tested it, tentatively, and found that it was a barrier that *he* could control. When he thinned it, he became aware of presences, what must be minds, out beyond the limits of this room. Animals, surely, and birds, for their thoughts were dim and *here*-centered. Then two close together—very bright, but opaque and unreadable. One "felt" like Savil and the other must be the mysterious Starwind. Then two more; just as bright, just as opaque—but one he recognized by the "feel" as being Yfandes. Then a scattering of others . . .

Yfandes. A Companion. My Companion.

So—it was no hallucination, then. He *had* somehow gotten Herald-Gifts and a Companion.

Gifts I never wanted, at a cost I never thought I'd pay. I'd trade them and half my life to have—him—back again.

That hit like a blow to the gut. He descended from the level of the uppermost pool to the floor and sat heavily on one of the stone benches around the edge of the room, too tired and depressed to move.

Oh, 'Lendel . . . gods, he thought, bleak despair overcoming him. *What am I doing here? Why didn't they just let me die?*

:Do you hate me, Chosen?: said a bright, reproachful voice in his mind, *:Do you hate me for wishing you to live?:*

:Yfandes?: He remembered what Savil had said, about how his Companion would pine herself to death if he died, and sagged with guilt. *:Oh, gods, Yfandes, no—no, I'm sorry—I just—:*

He'd been able to not-think about it when he'd been drugged. He'd been able to concentrate on nothing more complicated than the next moment. Now—now his mind was only too clear. He couldn't ignore the reality of Tylendel being gone, and there were no drugs to keep him in a vague fog of forgetting.

:You miss him,: she replied, gently. *:You need him, and you miss him.:*

:Like my arm. Like my heart. I just can't imagine going on without him. I don't know what to do with myself, where to go, what to do next.:

If Yfandes had a reply, he never heard it; just at that moment Savil and a second *Tayledras,* this one in white breeches, soft, low boots and jerkin, entered the room. Vanyel started to stand; Savil motioned for him to stay where he was. She and the stranger walked slowly across the stone floor and took places on the bench beside him.

Vanyel was shocked at her appearance. Although her hair had always been a pure silvery white, she'd never looked *old* before. Now she did; she looked every year of her age and more. He recalled what Moondance had said about Tylendel's death being as hard on her as it was on Vanyel. Now he believed it.

"Aunt Savil," he said, hesitantly, as she and the stranger arranged themselves comfortably beside him. "Are you all right? I mean—"

"Looking particularly haglike, am I?" she asked dryly. "No, don't bother to apologize; I've got a mirror. I don't bounce back from strain the way I used to."

He flushed, embarrassed, and feeling guilty.

"Van, this is Starwind k'Treva," she continued. "He and Moondance are the *Tayledras* Adepts I told you younglings about a time or two. This," she waved her hand around her, "is his, mostly, being as he's k'Treva Speaker."

"In so much as any *Tayledras* can own the land," Starwind noted with one raised eyebrow, his voice calling up images of ancient rocks and deep, still water. "It would be as correct, Wingsister, to say that this place owns me."

"Point taken. This is k'Treva's *voorthayshen*—that's—how would you translate that, *shayana*?"

The *Tayledras* at her side had a triangular face, and his long hair was arranged with two plaits at each temple, instead of one, like Moondance—and he *felt* older, somehow. At least, that was how he felt to Vanyel.

"Clan Keep, I think would be closest," Starwind said, "Although k'Treva is not a clan as your people know the meaning of the word. It is closer to the *Shin'a'in* notion of 'Clan.'"

His voice was a little deeper in pitch than Moondance's and after a moment Vanyel recognized the "feel" of him as being the same as the "blue-green music" in his dreams.

"My lord," Vanyel began hesitantly.

"There are no 'lords,' here, young Vanyel," the Adept replied. "I speak for k'Treva, but each k'Treva rises or falls on his own."

Vanyel nodded awkwardly. "Why am I here, sir?" he asked—then added, apprehensively, "What did you do to me? I—forgive me for being rude, but I *know* you did something. I feel—different."

"You are here because you have very powerful Mage-Gifts, awakened painfully, awakened late, and out of control," the Adept replied. His expression was calm, but grave, and held just a hint of worry. "Your aunt decided, and rightly, that there was no way in which you could be taught by the Heralds that would not pose a danger to you and those about you.

Moondance and I are used to containing dangerous magics; we do this constantly, it is part of *what* we do. We can keep you contained, and Savil believes we can teach you effectively. And if we cannot teach you control, then she knows that we can and *will* contain you in such a way that you will pose no danger to others."

Moondance had not looked like this—so impersonal, so implacable. Vanyel shivered at the detached calm in Starwind's eyes; he wasn't certain what the Adept meant by "containing" him, but he wasn't eager to find out.

"As to what we have done with you—Moondance Healed your channels, which are the conduits through which you direct energy. And I have taught you, a little, while you were in Healing trance. I could not teach you a great deal in trance, but what I have given you is very important, and will go a great way toward making you safe around others. I have taught you where your center is, how to ground yourself, and how to shield. So that now, at least, you are no longer out of balance, and you may guard yourself against outside thoughts and keep your own inside your mind where they belong. And there will be no more shaking of the earth because of dreams."

So *that* was what had happened—with the music, the colors—and this new barricade around his mind.

Starwind leaned forward a little, and his expression became far more human: concerned, and earnest. "Young Vanyel, we. Moondance and I, we are perfectly pleased to have you with us, to help you. But that is *all* we can do—help you. *You* must learn control; we cannot force it upon you. *You* must learn the use of your Gifts, or most assuredly they will use you. Magic is that kind of force; I beg you to believe me, for I know this to be true. If you do not use it, it will use you. And if it begins to use you"—his eyes grew very cold—"it must be dealt with."

Vanyel shrank back from that chill.

"But this is neither the place nor the time to speak of such things," Starwind concluded, rising. "We have you under shield, and you are too drained to cause any problems for the nonce. Youngling, can you walk? If you can, you would do well with exercise and air, and I would take you to a vantage to show you our home, and tell you a little of what we do here."

Vanyel nodded, not eager to be left to his aching memories again; he found on rising that he was feeling considerably stronger than he had thought. He couldn't move very fast, but as long as Starwind and Savil stayed at a slow walk, he could keep up with them.

They went from the bathing room back through the bedroom; it looked even more like a natural grotto than the bathing room had. Vanyel almost couldn't distinguish the real foliage from the fabric around the bed, and the "furniture," irregularly shaped chairs, benches, and tables with thick green cushions and frames of bent branches, fitted in with the plants so well as to frequently seem part of them. There was a curtained alcove (with more of those leaf-mimicking curtains) that seemed to be a wardrobe, for the curtains had been drawn back at one side enough to display a bit of clothing.

From there they passed into a third, most peculiar room. There was no furniture, and in the center of it, growing up from the stone floor, was the living trunk of a tree, one a dozen people could not have encircled with their arms. Attached to the trunk was a kind of spiral staircase. They climbed this—Vanyel feeling weak at the knees and clinging to the railing for most of the climb—to a kind of covered balcony that gave them a vantage point to see all of Starwind's little kingdom.

This was a valley—no, a *canyon*; the walls were nearly perpendicular—of hot springs; Vanyel saw steam rising from the lush growth in more places than he could count. Although there was snow rimming the lip of the canyon high above, vegetation within the bowl ran riot.

"K'Treva," Starwind said, indicating the entire valley with a wave of his hand. "Though mostly only Moondance and I dwell here-below. Beneath, the living-spaces for the *hertasi* and those who do not wish the trees."

Vanyel looked over the edge of the balcony; below him was a collection of rooms, mostly windowless, but with skylights, the whole too random to be called a "house."

"There are other living places above—which is where most of us dwell," Starwind continued, with an ironic smile. "Moondance is not *Tayledras* enough to be comfortable above the ground. The *hertasi* you may or may not see; they serve us, we protect them and allow them to dwell here. They are shy of strangers—even of *Tayledras*; really, only Moondance is a friend to all of them. They are something like a large lizard, but they are full human in wit. If you should see one, I pray you strive not to frighten it. And although you may go where you will here-below, pray do not come here-above without invitation."

Vanyel looked up, but couldn't see any sign of these "living places"—only the staircase spiraling farther up the trunk and vanishing into the branches. The very thought of being up·that high was dizzying, and he thought it was likely to take a great deal more than an invitation to get him to climb above.

"Tchah—I stand on Moondance's side," Savil replied. "I remember the first time I was here, and you made me try to sleep up in one of your perches. Never again, my friend."

"You have no sense of adventure," Starwind countered, putting his palms down on the rail and leaning forward a little. "The last thing, one that you may sense, so that you know it is indeed there—the barrier about the vale. It protects us from that which we would not have pass within and it keeps the vale always warm and sheltered. So—this is k'Treva. What we do here—two things. Firstly, we make places where the magic creatures of the Pelagirs may live in peace. Secondly, we take the magic out of those places where they do not live, making the land safe for man. We use the magic we take to make boundaries about the places of refuge, so that none may pass who do not belong. That is what the k'Varda, the Mage-Clans of the *Tayledras*, do. We guard the Pelagirs from despoilers as our cousins, the *Shin'a'in*, guard the Dhorisha Plains."

"As I keep saying, you're like we are. You guard the Pelagirs as the Heralds guard Valdemar," Savil said.

Starwind nodded, his braids swaying. "Aye, save that your Heralds concern themselves with the people, and the *Tayledras* with the land."

"Valdemar *is* the people; we could pack up and flee again, as we did at the founding, and still be Valdemar. I suspect the same would be true of you, if you'd only admit it."

"Na, the *Tayledras* are bound to the land, cannot live outside the Pelagirs; we must—" Starwind was interrupted by the scream of a hawk somewhere above his head. He threw up his forearm, and a large, white raptor plunged down out of the canopy of leaves to land on Starwind's arm. Vanyel winced, then saw that the *Tayledras* wore white leather forearm guards, which served to keep the wicked talons from his flesh.

It was a gyrefalcon; its wings beat the air for a moment before it settled, its golden eyes fixed on Starwind's face. The *Tayledras* smoothed its head with one finger, then stared into the hawk's eyes for a long, long time, seeming to be reading something there.

Then, without warning, he flung up his arm, launching it back into the air from his wrist. The falcon's wings beat against the thick, damp air, then it gained height and vanished back up into the tree branches.

"Bad news?" Savil asked.

"Nay—good. The situation is not so evil as we feared. Moondance is wearied, but he shall return by sunrise."

"I'm glad to hear something is going right for someone," Savil replied, sighing.

"Indeed," the Adept replied, turning those strange, unreadable eyes on Vanyel. "Indeed. Young Vanyel, I would advise you to walk about, regain your health, eat and rest. When Moondance returns and is at full strength, your schooling will begin."

So he did as he was told to do, exploring what Starwind called "the vale" from one end to the other. It was shaped like a teardrop, and smaller than it seemed; there were so many pools and springs, waterfalls and geysers, and all cloaked in incredible greenery that effectively hid paths that came within whispering distance of each other, that it gave the illusion of being an endless wilderland.

It kept him occupied, at least. The vale was so exotic, so strange, that he could lose himself in it for hours—and forget, in watching the brightly colored birds and fish, how very much alone he was.

Half of him longed for the time—before Tylendel. The isolation of that dream-scape. The other half shrank from it. He no longer knew what he wanted, anymore, or what he was.

He certainly didn't know what to do about Yfandes; he needed her, he loved her, but that very affection was a point of vulnerability, another place waiting to be hurt. She seemed to sense his confusion, and kept herself nearby, but not at hand, Mindspeaking only when he initiated the contact.

Savil was staying clear of him, which helped. When Moondance finally made an appearance, he made some friendly overtures, but didn't go beyond them; Vanyel was perfectly content to leave things that way.

When he asked, the younger *Tayledras* acted as a kind of guide around the vale, pointing out things Vanyel had missed, explaining how the mage-barrier kept the cold—and other things—out of the vale.

The elusive *hertasi* never appeared, although their handiwork was everywhere. Clothing vanished and returned cleaned and mended, food appeared at regular intervals, rooms seemed to sweep themselves.

When the vale became too familiar, Vanyel tried to catch a glimpse of them. Anything to keep from thinking.

Then he was given something else to think about.

:You fail,: Starwind said in clear Mindspeech. He was seated cross-legged on the rock of the floor beyond the glowing blue-green barrier, imperturbable as a glacier. *:Again, youngling.:*

:*But*—: Vanyel protested from the midst of the barrier-circle the Adept had cast around him, :*I*—: He was having a hard time shaping his thoughts into Mindspeech.

:*You,*: Starwind nodded. :*Exactly so. Only you. Until you match your barrier and merge it with mine, mine will remain. And while mine remains, you cannot pass it, and I will not take you from this room.*:

Vanyel drooped with weariness; it seemed that the *Tayledras* mage had been schooling him, without pause or pity, for days, not mere hours. This was the seventh—or was it eighth?—such test the Adept had put him to. Starwind would go *into* his head, somehow, show him what was to be done. Once. Then Vanyel fumbled his way through whatever it was. As quickly as Vanyel mastered something, the Adept sprang a trial of it on him.

There was no sign of exit or entrance in this barren, rock-walled room where he'd been taken, and no clue as to where in the complex of ground-level rooms it was. There was only Starwind, his pointed face as expressionless as the rock walls.

Vanyel didn't know what to think anymore. These new senses of his—they told him things he wasn't sure he wanted to know. For instance—there was something in this valley. A power—a living power. It throbbed in his mind, in time with his own pulse. He had told Savil, thinking he must be ill and imagining it. She had just nodded and told him not to worry about it.

He hadn't asked her much, or gone to her often. *If I don't touch, I can't be hurt again.* The half-unconscious litany was the same, but the meaning was different. *If I don't open myself, I won't be open to loss either.*

The *Tayledras*, Starwind and Moondance, alternately frightened and fascinated him. They were like no one he'd ever known before, and he couldn't read them. Starwind in particular was an enigma. Moondance seemed easier to reach.

But there was always that danger. *Don't reach; don't touch,* whispered the part of him that still hurt. *Don't try.*

There had been a point back at Haven when he'd tried to reach out, first to Savil, then to Lissa. He'd wanted someone to depend on, to tell him what to do, but the moment he'd tried to get them to make his decisions for him, they'd pushed him gently away.

Now—no more; all he wanted was to be left alone.

It seemed, however, that the *Tayledras* had other plans.

Savil had come to get him in the morning, after several days of wandering about on his own, reminding him of what Starwind had said about being schooled in controlling these unwanted powers of his. He'd followed her through three or four rooms he hadn't seen before into—

—something—

He wasn't sure what it was; it had felt a little like a Gate, but there was no portal, just a spot marked on the floor. He'd stumbled across it, whatever it was, and found himself on the floor of this room, a room with no doorways.

Savil had appeared behind him, but before he could say anything, she'd just given him a troubled look, said to Starwind, "Don't hurt him, *shayana*," and left. Stepped into thin air and was gone. Left him alone with this—this madman. This unpredictable creature who'd been forcing him all morning to do things he didn't understand, using the powers he hadn't even come to terms with possessing, much less comprehending.

"Why are you doing this to me?" he cried, ready to weep with weariness. Starwind ignored the words as if they had never been spoken.

:*Mindspeech, Chosen,*: came Yfandes' calm thought, :*That is part of his testing. Use Mindspeech.*:

He braced himself, sharpened his thoughts into a kind of dagger, and *flung* them at Starwind's mind.

:*Why are you DOING this to me?*:

:*Gently,*: came the unruffled reply. :*Gently, or I shall not answer you.*:

Well, that was more than he'd gotten out of the Adept in hours. :*Why?*: he pleaded.

:*You are a heap of dry tinder,*: Starwind replied serenely. :*You are a danger to yourself and those around you. It requires only a spark to send you into an uncontrolled blaze. I teach you control, so that the fires in you come when you will and where you will.*: He stared at Vanyel across the shimmering mage-barrier. :*Would you have this again?*:

He flung into Vanyel's face memories that could only have come from Savil—a clutch of Herald-trainees weeping hysterically, infected with *his* grief; Mardic flying through the air, hitting the wall, and sliding down it to land in an unconscious heap; the very foundations of the Palace shaking—

:*No—*: he shuddered.

:*There could be worse—*: Starwind showed him what he meant by "worse." A vivid picture of Withen dead—crushed like a beetle beneath a boot—by the powers Vanyel did not yet comprehend and could not direct.

:*NO!*: He tried to deny the very possibility that he could do anything of the kind, rejecting the image with a violence that—

—that made the floor beneath him tremble.

:You see?: Starwind said, still unperturbed. *:You see? Without control, without understanding, you can—and will—kill, without ever meaning to. Now—:*

Vanyel hung his head, and wearily tried to match the barrier one more time.

Savil ran for the pass-through, in response to Starwind's urgent summons, Moondance a bare pace behind her. She hit the permanent set-spell, a kind of low-power Gate, at a run; there was the usual eyeblink of vertigo, and she stumbled onto the slate floor of Starwind's Work Room and right into the middle of a royal mess.

Starwind was only now picking himself up off the floor behind her; there was a smell of scorched rock and the acrid taint of ozone in the air. And small wonder; the area around all around Vanyel in the center of the Work Room was burned black.

Lying sprawled at one side of the burned area was the boy himself, scorched and unconscious.

Moondance popped through the pass-through, glanced from one fallen body to the other, and made for the boy as needing him the most. That left Starwind to Savil.

She gave him her hands and helped him to his feet; he shook his head to clear it, then pulled his hair back over his shoulders. "God of my fathers," he said, passing his hand over his brow. "I feel as if I have been kicked across a river."

Savil ran a quick check over him, noted a channel-pulse and cleared it for him. "What happened?" she asked urgently, keeping one hand on his elbow to steady him. "It looks like a mage-war in here."

"I believe I badly frightened the boy," Starwind said, unhappily, checking his hands for damage. "I intended to frighten him a little, but not so badly as I did. He was supposed to be calling lightning and he was balking. He plainly refused to use the power he had called. I grew impatient with him—and I cast the image of *wyrsa* at him. He panicked, and not only threw his own power, he pulled power from the valley-node. Then he realized what he had done and aborted it the only way he could at that point, pulling it back on himself." Starwind gave her a reproachful glance. "You told me he could sense the node, but you did not tell me he could pull from it."

"I didn't know he could, myself. Great good gods—*shayana*, it was *wyrsa* that his *shay'kreth'ashke* called down on his enemies, didn't I tell you?" Savil's gut went cold; she bit her lip, and looked over her shoulder at Moondance and his patient. The Healer-Adept was kneeling beside the boy with both hands held just above his brow. "Lord and Lady, no wonder he nearly blew the place apart!"

Starwind looked stricken to the heart, as Moondance took his hands away from the boy's forehead and put his arm under Vanyel's shoulder to pick him up and support him in a half-sitting position. "You told me—but I had forgotten. Goddess of my mothers, what did I do to the poor child?"

"*Ashke*, what did you do?" Moondance called worriedly, one hand now on Vanyel's forehead, the other arm holding him. "The child's mind is in shock."

"Only the worst possible," Starwind groaned. "I threw at him an image of the things his love called for vengeance."

"*Shethka*. Well, no help for it; what is done cannot be unmade. *Ashke*, I will put him to bed, and call his Companion, and we will deal with him. We will see what comes of this." He picked the boy up, and strode through the pass-through without a backward glance.

"Ah, gods—this was going well, until this moment," Starwind mourned. "He was gaining true control. Gods, how could I have been so *stupid*?"

"It happens," Savil sighed. "And with Van more so than with anyone else, it seems. He almost seems to attract ill luck. *Shayana*, why did you throw anything at him, much less *wyrsa*?"

"He finally is willing enough to learn the controls, the defensive exercises, but *not* the offensive." Starwind put his palms to his temples and massaged for a moment, a pain-crease between his eyebrows. "And if he does not master the offensive—"

"The offensive magics will *remain* without control," Savil said grimly, the smell of scorched rock still strong about her. "Like Tylendel. I couldn't get past his trauma to get those magics fully under conscious lock. I should have brought *him* to you."

"Wingsister, hindsight is ever perfect," Starwind spared a moment to send a thread of wordless compassion her way, and she smiled wanly. "The thing with this boy—I told you, he *had* the lightnings in his hand, I could see him holding them, but he would not cast them. I thought to frighten him into taking the offense." He lowered his hands and looked helplessly at Savil. "He is a puzzle to me; I cannot fathom why he will not fully utilize his powers."

"Because he still doesn't understand why he should, I suppose," Savil brooded, rocking back and forth on her heels. "He can't see any reason to use those powers. He doesn't want to help anyone, all he wants now is to be left alone."

Starwind looked aghast. "But—so *strong*—how can he *not*—"

"He hasn't got the hunger yet, *shayana*, or if he's got it, everything else he's feeling has so overwhelmed him that all he can register is his own pain." Savil shook her head. "That, mostly, would be my guess. Maybe it's that he hasn't ever seen a reason to care for anyone he doesn't personally know. Maybe it's that right now he has no energy to care for anyone but himself. Kellan tells me Yfandes would go through fire and flood for him, so there has to be *something* there. Maybe Moondance can get through to him."

"Only if he survives what we do to him," Starwind replied, motioning her to precede him into the pass-through, and sunk in gloom.

Vanyel woke with an ache in his heart and tears on his face; the image of the *wyrsa* had called up everything he wanted most to forget.

He could tell that he was lying on his bed, still clothed, but his hands and forearms felt like they'd been bandaged and the skin of his face hurt and felt hot and tight.

The full moon sent silver light down through the skylight above his head. He saw the white rondel of it clearly through the fronds of the ferns. His head hurt, and his burned hands, but not so much as the empty place inside him, or the guilt—the terrible guilt.

'Lendel, 'Lendel—my fault.

He heard someone breathing beside him; a Mindtouch confirmed that it was Moondance. He did not want to talk with anyone right now; he just wanted to be left alone. He started to turn his face to the wall, when the soft, oddly young-sounding voice froze him in place.

"I would tell you of a thing—"

Vanyel wet his lips, and turned his head on the pillow to look at the argent-and-black figure seated beside him on one of the strange "chairs" he favored.

Moondance might have been a statue, a silvered god sitting with one leg curled beneath him, resting his crossed arms on his upraised knee, face tilted up to the moon. Moonlight flowed over him in a flood of liquid silver.

"There was a boy," Moondance said, quietly. "His name was Tallo. His parents were farmers, simple people, good people in their way, really. Very tied to their ways, to their land, to the cycle of the seasons. This Tallo . . .

was not. He felt things inside him that were at odds with the life they had. They did not understand their son, who wanted more than just the fields and the harvests. They did love him, though. They tried to understand. They got him learning, as best they could; they tried to interest the priest in him. They didn't know that what the boy felt inside himself was something other than a vocation. It was power, but power of another sort than the priest's. The boy learned at last from the books that the priest found for him that what he had was what was commonly called magic, and from those few books and the tales he heard, he tried to learn what to do with it. This made him—very different from his former friends, and he began to walk alone. His parents did not understand this need for solitude, they did not understand the strange paths he had begun to walk, and they tried to force him back to the ways of his fathers. There were—arguments. Anger, a great deal of it, on both sides. And there was another thing. They wished him to wed and begin a family. But the boy Tallo had no yearning toward young women—but young *men*—that was another tale."

Moondance sighed, and in the moonlight Vanyel saw something glittering wetly on his eyelashes. "Then, the summer of the worst of the arguments, there came a troupe of gleemen to the village. And there was a young man among them, a very handsome young man, and the boy Tallo found that he was not the only young man in the world who had yearnings for his own sex. They quickly became lovers—Tallo thought he had never been so happy. He planned to leave with the gleemen, to run away and join them when they left his village, and his lover encouraged this. But it happened that they were found together. The parents, the priest, the entire village was most wroth, for such a thing as *shay'a'chern* was forbidden even to speak of, much less to be. They—beat Tallo, very badly; they beat the young gleeman, then they cast Tallo and his lover out of the village. Then it was that the young gleeman spurned Tallo, said in anger and in pain what he did not truly mean, that he wanted nothing of him. And Tallo became wild with rage. He, too, was in pain; he had suffered for this lover, been cast out of home and family for his sake, and now he had been rejected—and he called the lightning down with his half-learned magic. He did not mean to do anything more than frighten the young man—but that was not what happened. He killed him; struck him dead with the power that he could not control."

Moonlight sparkled silver on the tears that slowly crept down Moondance's face.

"Tallo had heard his lover's thoughts, and knew that the young man had not meant in truth the hurtful things he had said. Tallo had wanted only for the boy to say with words what he had heard in the other's mind. So he called the lightning to frighten him, but he learned that the lightning would not obey him when called by anger, and not by skill. And he heard the boy crying out his name as he died. Crying out in fear and terrible pain, and Tallo unable to save him. Tallo could not live with what he had done. With the dagger from his lover's belt, he slashed his own wrist and waited to die, for he felt that only with his own death could he atone for murdering his love."

Moondance raised his left arm to push some of his heavy hair back from his face, and the moon picked out the white scar that ran from his wrist halfway to his elbow.

"There was, however, a stranger on the road, an outlander who had sensed the surge of power and read the signs and knew that it was uncontrolled. She came as quickly as she could—though not quickly enough to save both. She found the young men, one dead, one nearly—she saved the one she could, and brought him to a friend who she thought might understand."

Moondance was so silent and for so long, that Vanyel thought he was through speaking. He stared up at the moon, eyes and cheeks shining wetly, like a marble statue in the rain.

Then he spoke again, and every syllable carried with it a sense of terrible pain. "So here is the paradox. If the boy Tallo had not misused his fledgling powers and struck down his lover, they would have gone off together, and, in time, parted. Tallo would likely have been found by a Mage and taught, or—who knows?—gotten as far as Valdemar and been taken by a Companion. Those with the power are not left long to themselves. It might even have been that the Mage that found him was a dark one, and Tallo might have turned for a time or for all time to evil. But that is not what happened. The boy killed—murdered in ignorance—and was brought to k'Treva. And in k'Treva he found forgiveness, and the learning he needed as the seed needs the spring rain—and one thing more. He found his *shay'kreth'ashke.* In your tongue, that means 'lifebonded.' "

Vanyel started. Moondance nodded without turning to look at him. "You see? Paradox. Had things not fallen as they did, Tallo would never have met with Starwind. The *Tayledras* are very secretive and Wingsister Savil is one of the first to see one of us, much less to see k'Treva, in years beyond counting. The two meant to be lifebonded would never have found each other. There would be no Healer-Adept in k'Treva, and much *Tayledras* work would have gone undone because of that. So—much good has come of this, and much love—but it has its roots in murder. Murder unintentional, but murder all the same."

Moondance sighed again. "So what is the boy Tallo to think? Starwind's solution was to declare the boy Tallo dead by his own hand, a fitting expiation for his guilt, and to bring to life a new person altogether, one Moondance k'Treva. So there is no more Tallo, and there is one that magic has changed into a man so like *Tayledras* that he might have been born to the blood. But sometimes the boy Tallo stirs in the heart of Moondance—and he wonders—and he weeps—and he mourns for the wrongs he has done."

He turned his head, then, and held out his hand to Vanyel. "*Ke'chara*, would you share grief with Tallo? Weeping alone brings no comfort, and your heart is as sore as mine."

Vanyel started to reach for that hand, then hesitated.

If I don't touch—

"If you do not touch," said Moondance, as if he read Vanyel's thought, "you do not *live*. If you seal yourself away inside your barriers, you seal out the love with the pain. And though love sometimes brings pain, you have no way of knowing if the pain you feel now might not bring you to love again."

"Tylendel's dead." There; he'd said it, said it out loud. It was real—and couldn't be changed. The tight, burned skin on his face hurt as he held back tears. "*Nothing* is going to bring him back. I'll *never* be anything but alone."

Moondance nodded, slowly, and left his hand resting on the edge of the bed; Vanyel couldn't see his face, shadowed as it was by the white wing of his hair.

"The great love is gone. There are still little loves—friend to friend, brother to sister, student to teacher. Will you deny yourself comfort at the hearthfire of a cottage because you may no longer sit by the fireplace of a palace? Will you deny yourself to those who reach out to *you* in hopes of warming themselves at your hearthfire? That is cruel, and I had not thought you to be cruel, Vanyel. And what of Yfandes? She loves you with all her being. Would you lock her out of your regard as well? That is something more than cruel."

"Why are you telling me, asking me this?" The words were torn out of him, unwilling.

"Because I nearly followed the road you are walking." The *Tayledras* shifted slightly in his chair and Vanyel heard the wood creak a little. "Better, I thought, not to touch at all than to touch and bring hurt upon myself and others. Better to do nothing than to make a move and have it be the wrong one. But even deciding to not touch or to be nothing is a decision, Vanyel, and by deciding not to touch, so as to avoid hurt, I then hurt those who tried to touch me." He waited, but Vanyel could not bring himself to answer him.

Moondance's expression grew alien, unreadable, and he shrugged again. "It is your decision; it is your life. A Healer cannot live so; it may be that you can."

He uncoiled himself from his chair and in a kind of seamless motion was standing on his feet, shaking back his hair. The tears were gone from his eyes, and his expression was as serene as if they had never been there as he looked down on Vanyel. "If you are in pain, Mindcall, and I shall come."

Before Vanyel could blink, he was gone.

Morning came—but the expected summons to Starwind's Work Room did not. The sun rose, and he wandered from room to empty room, in the small area that he knew, without finding anyone. He began to wonder if his rejection of Moondance last night had led them all to abandon him here.

Finally he found a way out into the valley itself, and stood by the rock-arch of the doorway, blinking a little at the bright sunlight, unfiltered by the tinted skylight. There were ferns the size of a small room, bushes and small trees with leaves he could have used as a rain shelter, and the larger trees, while not matching the one growing up through the middle of the "house" in girth, were still large enough that it would take five people to encircle their trunks with their arms.

:*Yfandes?*: he Mindcalled tentatively. He wasn't at all sure he'd get a reply.

But he did. :*Here,*: she said—and a few moments later, she came frisking through the undergrowth, tail and spirits held banner-high. She nuzzled his cheek. :*Are your hands better?*:

He had unwrapped them this morning from their bandages, and aside from a little soreness, they seemed fine—certainly nothing near as painful as they had been last night.

:*I think so.*: He rested his forehead against her neck. It was incredibly comforting just to be in her presence, and hard to remember to barricade himself around her. :*Where is everybody?*:

:Savil is up above, in Starwind's place.: She gave him a mental picture of a kind of many-windowed room perched in the limbs of what could only be the tree growing up through the center of the "house." *:She doesn't much care for it, and having her up there makes Kellan nervy, but he was upset over the accident yesterday and he feels happier up in the boughs. They're talking.:*

:With the other k'Treva?:

:I think perhaps.:

:Where's Moondance?:

:By himself. Thinking,: Yfandes said.

:'Fandes—did I—: He swallowed. *:Did I do something wrong last night?:*

She looked at him reproachfully. *:Yes. I think you ought to talk to him. You hurt him more deeply last night than he showed. He's never told that story to anyone; Savil and Starwind know it, but he never told them. And he's never even told Starwind how badly he still feels. It cost him a great deal to tell it to you.:*

His first reaction was guilt. His second was anger.

By his own admission, Moondance's tragic affair had been nothing more than that—an affair doomed to be brief. How could he even *begin* to compare his hurt with Vanyel's? Moondance wasn't alone—

Moondance hadn't murdered Starwind—just some stupid gleeman, who would have passed out of his life in a few weeks. A common player, and no great love.

Moondance still had Starwind. Would always have Starwind. Vanyel would be alone forever. So how *could* Moondance compare the two of them?

Yfandes seemed to sense something of what was going on in his mind; she pulled away from him, a little, and looked—or was it *felt?*—offended.

That only made him angrier.

Without another word, spoken or thought, he turned on his heel and ran—away from her, away from the *Tayledras*—away from all of them. Ran to a little corner at the end of the vale, a sullen grove of dark, fleshy-leaved trees and ferns, where very little light ever came. He pushed his way in among them, and curled up around his misery and his anger, his stomach churning, his eyes stinging.

They don't give a damn about me—just about what I can do. They don't care how much I hurt, all they want is for me to do what I'm told. Savil just wants to see me tricked into being a Herald, that's all. They don't any of them understand! They don't any of them know how much—I—

He began crying silently. *'Lendel, 'Lendel, they don't know how much of me died with you. All I want is to be left* alone. *Why can't they leave me* alone? *Why can't they stop trying to make me do what they want? They're all alike, dammit, they're just like Father, the only thing different is what they want out of me! Oh 'Lendel—I need you so much—*

He stayed there, crying off and on, until full dark—then crept as silently as he could back to the building—part of him hoping to find them waiting for him.

Only to find it as vacant as when he'd left it. In fact, only the night-lamps were burning and those were only left for the benefit of any of the *Tayledras* who might care to come down to the ground during the night. It didn't even look as if he'd been missed.

They don't care, he thought forlornly, surveying the empty, ill-lit rooms. *They really* don't *care. Oh, gods—*

His stomach knotted up into a hard, squirming ball.

No one cares. No one ever did except 'Lendel. And no one ever will again.

His shoulders slumped, and a second hard lump clogged his throat. He made another circuit of the rooms, but they stayed achingly, echoingly empty. No sign of anyone. No sign anyone would ever come back.

After pacing through the place until the echoes of his own footsteps were about to drive him into tears, he finally crawled into bed.

And cried himself to sleep.

CHAPTER 13

LEARETH LAUGHED; his icy laughter echoed off the cliffs as he held up one hand and made the simplest of gestures. A rage-storm swirled into being precisely at the edge of Vanyel's defenses. Vanyel poured power into his shielding; this was the last, the very last of his protections. He was drained, the energy-sources were drained, and he himself had taken far more damage in the duel than he would allow Leareth to know.

He was no match for the scouring blast that peeled his shields away faster than he could replace them. Leareth smiled behind his mage-storm, as if he knew that Vanyel was weakening by the moment. Sweat ran into his eyes and started to freeze there; he went to his knees, still fighting, and knowing he was going to lose. Leareth seemed not even wearied.

A final blast struck down the last of his protections. Vanyel screamed as agony such as he'd never known before arced through his body—

Vanyel woke up; the bed was soaking with sweat, and he was shaking so hard the ferns over his head quivered. He was afraid that he had screamed out loud.

But when no one came running into the room, he knew that he hadn't; that everything had been in the dream. At least this time he hadn't awakened anyone, and hadn't been trapped in the dream.

Dream. Oh, gods, it isn't just a dream. He shivered, despite the warmth of the room, and stared up through the fern fronds at the descending moon. The nightmare had him in a grasp of iron claws and would not let him go. *This is going to be real, it feels real. It's Foresight. It has to be. Leareth calls me "Herald-Mage Vanyel," and I'm in Whites. I'm dreaming my own death. This is what is going to happen to me, how I'm going to die, if I become a Herald. Alone. In terrible pain, and all alone, fighting a doomed battle.*

He shivered harder, chilled by the cold of the dream, chilled even more with fear. He finally threw the covers back, grabbed his robe, and padded into the room with the hot pools, finding his way by moonlight and habit.

For this was not the first time he'd awakened in the middle of the night, dream-chilled and needing warmth. This was just the first time since he'd arrived here that the dream had been clear enough to remember.

He climbed into the uppermost pool, easing himself down into the hot water with a sigh and a shiver. *Oh, gods. I don't want to die like that. They can't want me to have to face that, can they? If they knew about this dream, would they still want me to be a Herald? Gods, I know the answer to that—*

He eased a little farther down into the hot water, until it lapped at his chin. He was fighting blind, unreasoning panic, and losing. *What am I going to do? Oh, gods—I can't think—*

I have to get away. I can't stay here. If I do, they'll try and talk me around. Where can I go? I don't even know where "home" is from here. But I can't stay—I'll just go, I'll just pack up and go, and hope something turns up, it's all I can do. It means leaving Yfandes—

For a moment that thought was more than he could bear. But—fear was stronger. *It's lose her, or lose my life. No. I can't. I can't face an end like that. Besides,* he choked on a sob, *she just wants me to be a Herald, too—*

He looked up, judging the hour by the moon. *I've got a few hours until dawn. I can be out of the valley and well away before they even start looking for me. And they might not—Starwind still isn't ready to deal with me again; they might just think I've gone off somewhere to be alone, especially if I block Yfandes out now and keep her out.*

He climbed out of the pool and dried himself with his robe; he knew exactly where the clothing he'd arrived in was hung—the far end of Moondance's closet. He pulled it on as quickly as he could, taking the heavy cloak and draping it over one arm. One of the packs was in there, too, the one with the rest of his winter clothes. They were too warm to wear in the valley, so he'd never unpacked them, wearing instead Moondance's outgrown things. There was always food out in the room beside the one with the staircase; *Tayledras* sometimes kept odd hours. He filched enough bread and cheese to last several days and stuffed it into the pack with his clothing.

It took him most of a candlemark to reach the entrance to the valley. If it hadn't been snowing, he might have turned back at that moment—but it was, lightly, enough to cover his tracks. He swung the heavy cloak over his shoulders, braced himself for the shock of the temperature change, and stepped out into the dark and cold, remembering just in time to put up a shield so that he could not be tracked by his own aura.

*   *   *

"Two steps forward, one step back," Moondance's voice drifted up the ladder—Savil refused to call anything that steep a "staircase"—to Starwind's *ekele*; it was a good three breaths before Moondance himself appeared. His head poked through the hatchway in the gleaming wooden floor just as a gust of wind made the whole tree sway and creak.

Savil gulped, and gripped the arms of her low chair, looking resolutely away from the windows and their view of the birds flying by *below* them. Starwind never would tell her what it was they used in those windows instead of glass—which wouldn't have lasted ten breaths in a high wind. It was the same thing they used for the skylights, only thinner. Some kind of tough, flexible, transparent membrane—and Savil could not bring herself to believe that it would hold if you fell against it. The *ekele* creaked again, and she shuddered as she saw the window-stuff ripple a little with the warping of the window frames.

"Would you mind explaining that cryptic remark?" she asked, as the rest of Moondance emerged from the "entrance."

"Oh, thy pupil, Wingsister," he said, at his most formal, closing the hatchway against another gust of chill air. The ladder was sheltered, but not entirely enclosed—that would have been impractical—and Starwind couldn't see wasting a mage-barrier on the entrance to his "nest" when the hatchway served perfectly well most of the time. "Bright the day, Master-*ashke*."

"Wind to thy wings," Starwind replied automatically, turning away from the window, his gloom brightening a little. "*Shay'kreth'ashke*, there is no 'Master' here for thee."

"Nay, till the day thy wings bear thee upwards, thou'rt my Master." Moondance glided across the unsteady floor to Starwind's side, as surefooted as a sailor on a moving deck.

"Enough, I'm drowning," Savil groaned. "Gods, lifebonded—it's enough to make me celibate. What about my pupil? And will you *please* come away from that window? I keep thinking the next gust is going to pitch you out."

"The window would hold. Besides, no *Tayledras* has fallen from his *ekele* in years beyond counting, Wingsister," Starwind said, turning his back to the window and leaning on the ledge.

"So the time is long past for it to happen, and I don't want it to be you, all right?" Another gust made the whole tree groan, and she clutched at the arms of the chair, her knuckles going white.

"Very well," Starwind was actually smiling as he stepped away from the window and folded himself bonelessly into one of the chairs bolted to the floor of his *ekele*. He got a certain amount of pleasure out of teasing Savil about her acrophobia.

Each *ekele* was something like an elaborate treehouse; there was one for each major branch of the King Tree, some twenty in all. Not all were tenanted, and they were mostly used for meditation, sleeping, teaching, and recreation. For everything else, the "place below" served far better. But when a *Tayledras* needed to think, he frequently retreated to his *ekele*, sometimes for weeks, touching foot to ground only when he needed to.

An *ekele* consisted of a single windowed room, varying in size, made of polished wood so light in color that it was almost white, and furnished at most with a few chairs bolted to the floor, a table likewise bolted, and rolled pads stored in one corner for sleeping. Starwind's was one of the highest, hence, one of the smallest. The view was majestic. It was wasted on Savil.

Moondance took a third chair, and sat in it sideways, legs draped over the arms. "Well?" Savil demanded. "Are you going to explain yourself?"

"Your pupil. First, we strive to bring him to not depend upon others. So—then he pulls in upon himself, confiding not even in his Companion, hiding his pain within. Then I try to bring him to confess the pain, to share it, to reach out—"

"So?"

Moondance shrugged, and Savil sensed he hadn't told everything.

"What did you tell him?"

Moondance's moods could be read from his eyes; they were a murky gray-blue. "I—told him of myself. I thought if he could see that he is not the only soul in the world that feels pain, he might be brought to share it."

Savil's eyes narrowed; Moondance was unhappy. "*Shayana*, did he hurt you? If he did—"

"Na, the only one who hurt me was myself." His eyes cleared, and he gave her a wry smile. "He only pushed me away, is all. So, he hides all day, and this morning he is hiding again. His bed is empty, the *hertasi* say he went to the end of the vale, and his Companion says he has blocked her out entirely. To put it rudely, Wingsister, he is sulking."

Savil sighed, forgetting to clutch the arms of the chair. "Gods, what are we to do with him?"

Starwind's expression sobered again, and he began to answer—but was interrupted. Both *Tayledras* snapped to attention; their heads swung to face the window as if a single string had pulled them in that direction.

Two birds shot up from below and hovered there, just outside that window; the white gyrefalcon, and a second, of normal plumage. Starwind leaped out of his chair and flung the window open; the birds swirled in on the blast of wind that entered, and he slammed the window shut again.

Moondance had jumped to his feet, holding both arms out, ready for the birds, the moment Starwind went for the window. The falcons homed for him unerringly and were settling on the leather guards on his forearms before Starwind had finished latching the window closed.

The elder *Tayledras* held out his arm, and the buff falcon lofted to his forearm with a flutter of pinions, settling immediately.

Both *Tayledras* stared into their birds' eyes in silent communion. Savil kept as still as she could; while the bond between Hawkbrother and his birds was a strong one, and the magic-bred birds *were* considerably more than their wild brethren, their minds were something less than that of a very young child, perhaps a trifle superior to a cat, and it didn't take much to distract them.

The white falcon mantled; the buff cried. The *Tayledras'* eyes refocused, and Savil read "trouble" in the grim lines of their mouths.

"What?" she asked.

"First—tampering, as you had reported it to us, but this time on *our* ground and not on k'Vala," Starwind said, soothing his bird by stroking its breast-feathers. "A clutch of colddrakes, from the look of it. Something has *made* them move, so when we deal with the drakes, we shall have to look farther afield; there are folk settled in that direction under k'Treva protection. This is the first time we have caught the culprit in the act, and I do not intend to take this lightly."

"I hope you're counting me in that 'we'; a clutch of drakes needs every mage you can muster," she said, getting carefully to her feet and bracing herself against the sway of the *ekele*.

"If you would—you would be welcome." Starwind looked relieved. "But Vanyel—"

"If he's hiding, he'll only come out when he's ready. He's not going to come to any harm while he's in the vale. How far are these monsters, anyway?"

"Half a day's footpace; perhaps less," Moondance replied. "The which I do not like. It speaks for them being harried, or even Gated. In which case, why and who?"

"Good questions, both of them," Savil agreed. "Who can we count on?"

"Nothing under an Adept, not with drakes; not even Journeymen should handle drake-swarms, at least not to my mind. *Shethka.*"

"Don't tell me, we're the only three in any shape to take them on, right?"

"Sunsong is still recovering from moving the firebirds to sanctuary, Brightwind is too old to travel, Stormwing is pregnant."

"Lord and Lady—*lock* her up!" Savil exclaimed.

"No fear, she's steadied since she reached Adept. No more headlong races into danger just for the thrill. So—Rainstar is out already, with another call from the *kyree*, as is Fireflight. And that is the total of k'Treva Adepts." Starwind grimaced. "If this were summer . . ."

"If this were summer, it wouldn't be colddrakes, *ashke*," Moondance reminded him. "We work with what we have, and grateful that Wingsister Savil is with us."

"Let's get on with it," Savil said, steadying herself for the long climb down, as the *Tayledras* transferred their birds from forearm to shoulder for the descent. "So far as *I'm* concerned, I'll take a colddrake over your bedamned ladder any time!"

The snow cleared just before dawn, and the sun rose, pale and glorious, shining through the bare branches of the trees. The forest was filled with light; with the light came a resurgence of Vanyel's good sense.

He sat down on a stump, tired and winded, and suddenly seemed to wake out of the hold of his nightmare. *What am I doing out here?* he thought, panting. *I don't know where I'm going, I don't know what I'm going to do when I get there, I have no idea where I am! I just—hared off into nowhere, like a complete idiot!*

He put his pack down at his feet and scooped up some of the new snow in his mitten and ate it; it numbed his tongue, but it didn't do much for his thirst. *I can't believe I did anything this stupid.*

He wrapped his cloak tighter, and tucked his knees up under his chin, staring at the delicate tracery of white branches against the painfully blue sky. He began to think things through, slowly, one small, painful step at a time.

He flushed with shame. *I can't believe I did this. Dammit, I know how much Savil loves me, I've felt it—and Yfandes, and—damn, I am a rotten fool. Moondance was just trying to say that it's—easier to have other people around who hurt when* you *hurt, not that he thought he hurt worse than me. I hurt* him *by pushing him away.*

His blush deepened. *Worst of it is, he'll likely forgive me without my asking. They didn't abandon me yesterday; they were busy—probably over my welfare. They gave me exactly what I wanted; to be left alone. I should have been knocked up against a wall.*

He brooded, watching the birch branches swaying in the breeze. He was alone, completely alone, as he had not been since he left Forst Reach. The only thing breaking the silence was the whisper of the breeze and the occasional call of a winter bird. It was the kind of solitude he had sought—and not found—in the ice-dream. And now that he had it, he didn't want it.

Not that this place wasn't peaceful—but a sanctuary, as he had discovered with his little hideaway at the keep, could all too easily become a prison.

When you lock things out, he thought slowly, *you lock yourself in. I think maybe that was what Moondance was trying to tell me.*

He stared at the white branches, not seeing them, and not really thinking, just letting things turn over in the back of his mind. There was a half-formed thought back there, an important one. But it wasn't quite ready to come out yet.

Finally he sighed, and turned his thoughts back to his own stupidity. *Even if that dream is Foresight, there's probably ways around it. Nobody's going to force me into being a Herald. I could probably stay here if I asked to. There was no reason to go running off into the wilderness with nothing but what I could carry and no weapons. Gods, what a fool I am!*

He swiveled around to look down his backtrail. Even as he watched, the brisk breeze was filling in the last of his tracks with the light, powdery snow.

He groaned aloud. *Oh, fine. Just fine. I probably won't be able to find my way back now! I don't need teachers, I need nursemaids!*

Then he blinked, caught in sudden astonishment at the tone of his own thoughts. He sat up a little straighter and took stock of himself, and found that he was—feeling *alive* again. Feeling ready to *be* alive.

It's like I've been sick, fevered, and the fever just broke. Like I've been broken inside, somehow, and I'm finally starting to feel healed. I haven't felt this—good— since Tylendel—died—

He closed his eyes, expecting pain at that thought. There *was* pain, but not the debilitating agony of loss it had been.

'Lendel, he thought with a tinge of wonder, *I still miss you. It still hurts,*

you not being here. But I guess Moondance was right. I have to get on with my life, even though you aren't here to share it.

He opened his eyes on the snow-sparkling forest, and actually managed a weak smile at his own folly. "I really *am* an idiot, a right royal moon calf. And you'd have been the first to laugh at me, wouldn't you, 'Lendel?" He shook his head at himself. "All right, I guess I'd better figure out how to find my way back without a trail to follow."

Then the answer came to him, and he laughed at his own stupidity. "Lord and Lady, it's a good thing you take care of fools. All I have to do is look for *mages*. It's not like there's too many enclaves of mages out here, after all! The power should be there for even a dunderhead like *me* to see."

He closed his eyes again. and took a deep breath of the cold, crisp air. *Center—ground—and open—well, just like I figured, there they are—*

The surge of Gate-energy hit him with a shock, knocking him senseless.

When Vanyel came to again. the sun was high overhead, shining down on his cheek; it was noon, or nearly. He was lying where he'd fallen, on his side, braced between his pack and the stump. He'd curled up around the pack, and the roots from the stump were digging into his side and leg. His ears were ringing—or was it his head? Whatever; it felt as if he'd been graced with one of Jervis' better efforts.

Gods. He glanced up at the sun, and winced. *That was a Gate. Nothing else feels like that. Oh, I hurt. It's a good thing I was wrapped up in this cloak when I fell over, or I'd have frozen.*

He pushed the pack away, and rolled over onto his stomach. That at least got the sun out of his eyes. He got his knees under him, and pushed himself up off the snow with his arms; he was stiff and cold, but otherwise intact. Only his head hurt, and that in the peculiar "inside" way that meant he'd "bruised" those new senses of his. He knelt where he was for a moment, then pushed his hood back and looked around. It looked as if he'd fallen right over sideways when the shock hit him.

Guess I'd better get moving. Before I turn into a snow-statue. He pulled himself to his feet with the help of the stump, then stamped around the snow for several moments, trying to get his blood moving again.

I hope nobody noticed I'm gone. I hope that Gate wasn't somebody out looking for me. I feel enough of a fool as it is.

He hitched his pack over his shoulder, and took his bearings. *All right, let's try again. Center—and ground—and open—and If I find out that Moondance had anything to do with this I'll—*

His head rang again, and he swayed and almost fell, but this time the shock was a clear, urgent, and unmistakable wordless cry for help. It sobered him as quickly as Andrel's bucket of cold water.

There was no "presence" to the cry, not like any of the Gifted or the *Tayledras* had; it was just simple and desperate. This was no trained mage or Herald. It could only be an ordinary person in mortal fear.

Gods! His head swiveled toward the source of the cry as a needle to a lodestone. And without any clear notion of *why* he was doing so, except that it was a cry for help, and he *had* to answer it, Vanyel began stumbling toward the source at a clumsy run.

He had been following a game-trail; now he was right off any path. He ran into a tangle of bushes, and could find no way around it. Driven nearly frantic by the call in his head, he finally shoved his way through it. Then he was in a beech grove; there was little or no growth between the straight, white columns of the trunks, and he picked up his pace until he was at an all-out run.

But the clear, growth-free area was too soon passed; his breath was burning in his lungs as the forest floor became rougher, liberally strewn with tangles of briar and rocks, and hillier as well. His cloak kept hanging up on things, no matter how hard he tried to keep it close to his body. He tripped, stumbled wildly into the trunk of a tree, and picked himself up only to trip a second time and fall flat in the snow. The breath was knocked out of him for a moment, but that panicked, pleading voice in his "ear within" would not let him give up. He scrambled to his feet, pulled his cloak loose from a bramble, and started running again.

He must have tripped and fallen a good dozen times over obstacles hidden in the snow, and he surely made enough noise to have warned anything that wasn't deaf of his coming.

Anything that wasn't deaf—or very busy.

Winded, floundering blindly, and unable to focus on anything more than a few feet ahead of him, he fell over a root just as he reached the crest of a low hill, and dropped into a thicket of bushes that crowned it.

He saw the danger before he got up and broke through their protective cover. He froze where he was. The "danger" was too intent on its victims to have paid any attention to the racket he'd been making. Likely an entire cavalry troupe could have come on it unawares.

This was the very edge of the cleared lands of some smallholder; a fertile river-valley, well-watered, sheltered from the worst of the winter weather and summer storms. Arable land like this could well tempt an enterprising farmer out into the possible perils of the Pelagirs. There had been a stockade around the house and barns to guard against those hazards that could be foreseen.

But the stockade, of whole tree trunks planted in a ring around the buildings, was flattened and uprooted. It could not have held more than a few moments against what had come at the settlers out of the bright winter morning.

Vanyel had never seen a colddrake, but he knew what it was from descriptions in far too many songs and tales to count.

Less like a lizard, and more like a snake with short, stubby legs, it was the largest living creature Vanyel had ever seen. From nose to tail it was easily as long as six carts placed end-to-end. Its equine head was the size of a wine barrel; it had row upon row of silvery needle-sharp spines along its crest and down its back, and more spines formed a frill around its neck. It snarled silently, baring teeth as long as Vanyel's hand, and white and sharp as icicles. Its wickedly curved claws had torn the earth around it. Vanyel knew what *those* looked like; Moondance had a dagger made from one. Those claws were *longer* than his hand, and as sharp as the teeth. Huge, deep-purple eyes, like perfect cabochon amethysts, were fixed unwaveringly upon its prey, a young woman and her two children. It was a pure silver-white, like the cleanest of snow, and its scales sparkled in the sunlight; it was at least as beautiful as it was deadly.

As one mangled body beneath its forefeet testified, the creature knew very well how to use its wickedly sharp claws and teeth.

But neither tail nor fangs and claws was what held the terrified woman and her two children paralyzed almost within reach. It was the colddrake's *primary* weapon—the hypnotic power of its eyes.

It stared at them in complete silence, a silence so absolute that Vanyel could hear the woman panting in fear where he lay. The drake was not moving; it was going to bring its prey to within easy reaching distance of it.

Vanyel hadn't reshielded since he'd first been impaled upon that dreadful dagger of the woman's fear. He could still sense her thoughts—incoherent, hysteric, and hopeless. Her mind wailed and scratched at the walls that the colddrake's violet gaze had set up around it. She was trapped, *they* were trapped, their wills gone, their bodies no longer obeying them.

That was how her husband, the children's father, had died; walking right into the creature's grasp, his body obedient to *its* will, not his own. The beast was *slow*, that was the true horror of it—if they could just distract it for a crucial moment, break its gaze, they could escape it.

Vanyel could "hear" other minds, too—out there on the opposite side of the clearing. The *rest* of the extended family—there must have been dozens of them—had made it past the slow-moving drake to the safety and shelter of the woods. Only these four had not: the woman, burdened with her toddlers, and the man, staying to protect them. He could "hear" bits of their anguish, like a chorus wailing beneath the woman's keening fear.

Vanyel stared at the trapped three, just as paralyzed as they were. His mouth was dry, and his heart hammered with fear. He couldn't seem to think; it was as if those violet eyes were holding *him* captive, too.

There was movement at the edge of his field of vision.

No—not all had fled to the woods. From around the corner of the barn came a man, limping, painfully, slowly, but moving so quietly that the snow didn't even creak beneath his boots. He was stalking the drake. A new set of thoughts invaded Vanyel's mind, fragmentary, but enough to tell him what the man was about.

:—*get close enough to stick 'im*—:

It was an *old* man, a tired, old man; it was the woman's grandfather. He'd been caught in the barn when the thing attacked and knocked the stockade flat, and he'd seen his granddaughter's husband walk into the thing's jaws. He'd recognized the drake for what it was, and he'd armed himself with the only weapon he could find. A pitchfork. Ridiculous against a colddrake.

:—*get them eyes off 'er an' she kin run fer it*—:

The colddrake was paying no attention to anything except the prey right before it. The old man crept up behind it without it ever noticing he was there.

The old man knew, with calm certainty, that he was going to die. He knew that his attack was never going to do anything more than anger the creature. But it *would* break the thing's concentration; it *would* make it turn its head away for one crucial moment.

His attack was suicidal, but it would give his grand-daughter and her children a chance to live.

He came within an arm's length of the colddrake—he poised the pitchfork as casually as if he were about to stab a haybale—and he struck, burying the pitchfork tines in the colddrake's side with a sound like a knife burying itself to the hilt in a block of wood.

The drake screamed; its whistling shriek shattered the dreadful silence, and nearly shattered Vanyel's eardrums. It whipped its head around on its long, snaky neck, and it seized the old man before he even let go of the pitchfork. With a snap of its jaws that echoed even above its shrill screeching, it bit the old man's head neatly off his shoulders.

Vanyel screamed as he felt the old man die—and the oldster's desperate courage proved to be too much of a goad for him to resist.

Anger, fear, other emotions he couldn't even name, all caught him up, raised him to his feet, drove him out into the open and exploded out of him with a force that dwarfed the explosion he'd caused when Starwind had tried to make him call lightning.

He was thinking just enough to throw up a shield around the woman and her children with one shouted word. Then he hit the drake with everything he had in him. The blast of raw power caught the drake in the side and sent it hurtling up over the roof of the house—high into the sky—and held it suspended there for one agonizing moment while Vanyel's insides felt as if they were tearing loose.

Then the power ran out, and it fell to the earth, bleeding in a hundred places, every bone in its body shattered.

And Vanyel dropped to his knees, then his hands, then collapsed completely, to lie spent in the open field under the pale winter sun, gasping for breath and wondering what he had done.

Savil surveyed the last of the colddrake carcasses, and turned to Starwind, biting her lip in anxiety. "Where's the queen-drake?"

"No sign of her," he replied, shortly, holding to his feet with pure will. He'd taken the brunt of the attack, and he was dizzy and weak from the effort of holding the center while Savil and Moondance closed the jaws of the trap about the colddrake swarm.

"I have not seen her, either," Moondance called up the hill. He was checking each carcass in case one should prove to be an immature queen. It was unlikely to see a swarm with a juvenile queen, but it wasn't unheard of, either.

Yfandes had consented to carry the *Tayledras* double—the need to get to the place where the drake swarm was before the swarm reached inhabited areas was too great for any other consideration. Starwind had then served as the "bait" afoot, while Moondance on Yfandes and Savil on Kellan had been the arms of the trap.

"No queens," he said, flatly, having checked the sixth and final body.

The fight had stripped the snow from the hilltop, exposing the blackened slope. The six drakes lay upon the scorched turf in twisted silver heaps, like the baroque silver ornaments of a careless giantess strewn across black velvet.

"*Ashke*, are you well?" Moondance asked anxiously, leaving the last of the bodies and climbing the hill with a certain amount of haste. Starwind looked as if his legs were going to give out on him at any moment, and Yfandes had moved up to lend him her shoulder as support. He leaned on it with a murmur of gratitude as the Healer-Adept reached his side.

"I will do well enough, once I have a chance to breathe," the elder *Tayledras* replied, as Moondance added his support to Yfandes'. "I am more worried that we did not find the queen."

"Do you suppose," Savil began—

Then all three of them felt an incredible surge of raw, wild power—and it had Vanyel's "presence" laced through it.

"M'lord?"

Someone was tugging at his shoulder. Vanyel lifted his head from his arms; that was just about the limit of his capabilities right now.

"Gods," he said, dazedly, as the stocky young cloak-shrouded woman at his side tried to get him to sit up. "Oh, please—just—don't do that right now."

"M'lord? Ye be hurt?" she asked, thick brows knitting with concern. "Ye bain't hurt, best ye get inside fore 'nother them things comes."

"Aren't . . . anymore," he replied heavily, giving in to her urging and hauling himself into a sitting position. The sun seemed very bright and just on the verge of being painful to his watering eyes.

Gods, it's one of the holders. She's going to lay into me for not coming sooner, he thought, squinting at her, and already wincing in anticipation of harsh words. *She's going to want to know why I didn't save the old man, or come in time to save the young one. What can I tell her? How can I tell her it was because I was too scared to move until the old man threw himself at the thing?*

"Ye saved us, m'lord," she said, brown eyes wide, the awe in her voice plain even to Vanyel's exhausted ears. "Ye came t' save us, I dunno how ye knew, but, m'lord, I bain't got no way t' thank ye."

He stared at her in amazement. "But—"

"Be ye with the bird-lords, m'lord? Ye bain't their look, but they be the only mages abaht that give a bent nail fer folks' good."

"Bird-lords?" he repeated stupidly.

"Tchah, Menfree, 'tis only a boy an' he's flat paid out!" The newcomer was an older woman, a bit wrinkled and weathered, but with a kindly, if careworn, face. She bunched her cloak around her arms and bent over him. "Na, lad, ye come in, ye get warm an' less a'mudded, an' then ye tell yer tale, hmm?"

She took Vanyel's elbow, and he perforce had to get up, or else pull her down beside him. The next thing he knew, he was being guided across the ruts of the plowed field, past the carcass of the colddrake (he shuddered as he saw the *size* of it up close) up to the battered porch of the house and into the shadowed doorway.

He was not only confused with exhaustion, but was feeling more than a little awkward and out of place. These were the kind of people he had most tried to avoid at home—those mysterious, inscrutable peasant-farmers, whose needs and ways he did not understand.

Surely they would turn on him in a moment for not being there when they needed help.

But they didn't.

The older woman pushed him down onto a stool beside the enormous fireplace at the heart of the kitchen, the younger took his cloak and pack, and a boy brought him hot, sweetened tea. When one of the bearded, dark-clad men started to question him, the older woman shooed him away, pulling off her own dun cloak and throwing it over a bench.

"Ye leave th' boy be fer a bit, Magnus; I seen this b'fore with one a' them bird-laddies. They does the magickin', then they's a-maundered a whiles." She patted Vanyel on the head, in a rather proprietary sort of fashion. "He said there bain't no more critters, so ye git on with takin' care a' poor old Kern an' Tansy's man an' let this lad get hisself sorted."

Vanyel huddled on the stool and watched them, blinking in the half-dark of the kitchen, as they got their lives put back together with a minimum of fuss. Someone went to deal with the bodies, someone saw to the hysterical young mother, someone else planned the rites. Yes, they were mourning the deaths; simply and sincerely, without any of the kind of hysterics he'd half feared. But they were not allowing their grief to get in the way of getting on with their lives, nor were they allowing it to cripple their efforts at getting their protections back in place.

Their simple courage made him somehow feel very ashamed of himself.

It was in that introspective mood that the others found him.

*   *   *

"—I know it was a stupid thing to do, to run off like that, but—" Vanyel shrugged. "I won't make any excuses. I've been doing a lot of stupid things lately. I wasn't thinking."

"Well, don't be too hard on yourself. Foresight dreams have a way of doing that to people," Savil said, crossing her legs and settling back on her stool beside the hearth. "They tend to get you on the boil and then lock up your ability to think. You wouldn't be the first to go charging off in some wild-hare direction after waking up with one, and you probably won't be the last. No, thank you, Megan," she said to the wide-eyed child who offered her tea. "We're fine."

If the settlers had been awed by Vanyel, they'd been struck near speechless by the sight of the *Tayledras*. They didn't know a Herald from a birch tree, but they knew who and what the Hawkbrothers were, and had accorded them the deference due a crowned head.

All three of the adults were weary, and relief at finding both that Vanyel was intact and that the queen-drake was indisputably deceased had them just about ready to collapse. So they'd taken the settlers' hospitality with gratitude, settling in beside the hearth and accepting tea and shelter without demur.

Vanyel had waited just long enough for them to get settled before launching into a full confession.

"So when I finally managed to acquire some sense," he continued, "I figured the best way to find my way *back* would be to look for where all the mage-energy was. I did everything like you told me, Master Starwind, and I opened up—and the next thing I knew it was nearly noon. Somebody'd opened up a Gate—I think somewhere nearby—and it knocked me out cold."

"Ha—I *told* you those things were Gated in!" Savil exclaimed. "Sorry, lad, I didn't mean to interrupt you. Then what?"

"Well, I didn't think there was anyone around here but *Tayledras*, so I thought one of them had done it. I started to open up again to find the vale, and I heard a call for help. I got here, and when I saw that colddrake—kill the old man—I just—I just couldn't stand by and not do anything. I didn't even think about it. I wish I had, I think I overdid it."

"With a colddrake, particularly a queen, better overkill," Savil replied, exchanging a look of veiled satisfaction with Starwind. "You may have acted a fool, but it put you in the right place at the right time, and I am not going to berate you for it."

"Aunt Savil, I—" He flushed, and hunched himself up a little. "I got here before the old man came out. I didn't *do* anything until he—I mean—I was just hiding in the bushes. I guess," he said, in a very small voice, "I guess Father's right. I *am* a coward. I could have saved him, and I didn't."

"Did you *know* you could have saved him?" Moondance asked, quietly, his square face still. "Did you *know* that your mage-powers would work against the drake?"

"Well—no."

"You ran *toward* the danger when you Mindheard the call for help, right?" Savil asked. "Not *away?*"

"Well—yes."

"And you simply froze when you saw the strange monster. You did not flee?" Starwind raised one long eyebrow.

"I guess that's what happened."

"I think perhaps you have mistaken inexperience for cowardice, young Vanyel," Starwind said with conviction. "A coward would have run away from a plea for help. A coward would have fled at the first glimpse of the drake. You were *indecisive*—but you remained. It is experience that makes one decisive, and you have precious little of that."

"M'lord Starwind?" One of the homespun-clad men of the settlement was standing diffidently at the *Tayledras'* elbow.

"Phellip, I *wish* you would not call me 'lord,' " Starwind sighed, shaking his head. "You hold your lands under our protection, yes, but it is a simple matter of barter, foodstuffs for guardianship, and no more than that."

"Aye, m'—Master Starwind. Master, this drake—she just be chance-come, or be there anythin' more to it?"

Starwind turned to look at him more closely, and with some interest. "Why do you ask that?"

Phellip coughed, and flushed. "Well, m'lord, I was born 'n bred west a' here. M'people held land a' Magelord Grenvis—*he* were all right, but—well, when 'is neighbors had a notion t' play war, they useta bring in drakes an' th' like aforehand."

"And you think something of the sort might be in the offing? Phellip, I congratulate you on your foresight. The thought had only just occurred to me—"

"Da?" One of the boys couldn't contain himself any longer, and bounced up beside his father. "Da, there gonna be a war? With fightin' an' magic an'—"

Phillip grabbed the loose cloth of the boy's tunic and pulled him close. "Jo—I want ye t' *lissen* t' what m'lord Starwind is gonna tell ye—m'lord, *you* tell 'im; 'e don' believe 'is ol' man that fightin' ain't good fer nothin' but fillin' up graveyards."

"Young man," Starwind fixed the boy with an earnest stare. "There is *nothing* 'fine' about warfare. There is nothing 'glorious' about battle. All that a war means to such as you and I is that people we know and love will die, probably senselessly; others will be crippled for life—and the fools who began it all will sit back in their high castles and plot a way to get back what *they* lost. If there *were* to be a war—which, trust me, Phillip, I shall try most earnestly to prevent—the very *best* you could hope for, young man, would be to see these lovely fields around you put to the torch so that you would face a very hungry winter. *That* is what warfare is all about. The only justifiable fight is a defensive one, and in *any* fight it is the innocents who ultimately suffer the most."

The boy didn't look convinced.

Vanyel cleared his throat, and the boy shot a look at him. "Pretty exciting, the way that drake just nipped off that fool old man's head, wasn't it, Starwind?" he drawled, in exaggerated imitation of some of the young courtiers of his own circle.

The boy paled, then reddened—but before he could burst into either tears or angry words, Vanyel looked him straight in the eyes so fiercely that he could not look away.

"*That's* what you'll see in a war, Jo," he said, harshly. "Not people in tales getting killed—*your* people getting killed. Younglings, oldsters—everybody. And some fool at the rear crowing about how *exciting* it all is. *That's* what it's about."

Now Jo looked stricken—and, perhaps, convinced. Out of the corner of his eye Vanyel saw the farmer nodding in approval.

Out of nowhere, Vanyel felt a sudden rush of kindred feeling for these people. Suddenly they weren't faceless, inscrutable monoliths anymore—suddenly they were *people*. People who were in some ways a great deal more like him than his own relatives were. They had lives—and loves and cares.

Their outlook on warfare was certainly closer to his than that of any of his blood relations.

They aren't that much different than me. Except—except that I can do something they can't. I can—I can protect them when they can't protect themselves. And they can do things I can't. But I could learn to grow a carrot if I had to. It probably wouldn't be a very good carrot, but I could grow one. They won't ever be able to blast a colddrake.

What does that mean, *really? What does that say about* my *life? Why can* I *do these things, and not someone else—and what about the people out there who—who send drake-swarms out to eat helpless farmers? If I can protect people like this from people like them—doesn't that mean—that I really* have *to?*

He looked up and saw his aunt's eyes; she was watching the children at their chores, cleaning and chopping vegetables for a stew. Her expression was at once protective and worried.

It's the way Savil feels—it's got to be. That's why she's a Herald.

And suddenly Tylendel's words came back to him; so clearly that it seemed for a moment as if Tylendel were sitting beside him again, murmuring into his ear.

". . . it's a kind of hunger. I can't help it. I've got these abilities, these Gifts, and I can't not *use them. I couldn't sit here, knowing that there were people out there who* need *exactly the kind of help I can give them and not make the effort to find them and take care of them."*

Now he understood those words. Oh, the irony of it, this part of Tylendel that he had never been able to comprehend—*now* it was clear. Now that Tylendel was gone—*now* he understood.

Oh, gods—

He closed his eyes against the sting of tears.

Oh, yes—*now* he understood. Because now he felt that way, too.

Too late to share it.

CHAPTER 14

⟶ ◇ ⟵

:*W*ELL?*: To all appearances, Savil was asleep beside the settlers' stone hearth as she Mindspoke Starwind in Private-mode. In actuality, despite her weariness she was anything but sleepy, and was watching the fire through half-slitted eyes as she waited for the opportunity to confer with him. Her single word contained a world of overtones that she was fairly certain he'd pick up.

:*Interesting, on several levels,*: he replied. He was lying on his back, arms beneath his head, his eyes also closed.

The settlers—Savil had learned before the evening was over that they were calling their lands "Garthhold," and that there were seven loosely-related families in the group—had offered the *Tayledras* and their friends unlimited hospitality. All four of them were bone-tired even after rest and tea, and it was agreed among the three adults that it would be no bad thing to take them up on it. They refused, however, to put anyone out of his bed. So after a dinner of bread and stew, they made it plain that they intended to sleep by the fireside. The four of them were currently rolled up in their cloaks, on sacks of straw to keep them off the stone of the floor, beside the glowing coals of the kitchen hearth.

Vanyel was genuinely asleep. Savil wasn't certain of Moondance; he was curled on his side, his face to the fire, as peaceful and serene as a child's.

By all rights, he should really be asleep. There'd been several injuries related to the colddrake's attack and the hasty escapes, and Moondance had had his hands full Healing them. Then he had delegated himself magical assistant to getting the stockade back up. It had saved the Garthholders no end of effort to have the logs spell-raised back into place. He *should* have been exhausted.

So Savil thought, until he Mindspoke both of them. :*May I enter the conversation? I assume there is one.*:

So much for Moondance being weary.

:*Be welcome, but keep it in private,*: she replied. :*Among other things, we're discussing the boy. Starwind, go on please.*:

:From the small things to the great—I think perhaps *you may cease to fear for the boy. I think he now feels the hunger you spoke of, and understanding has been attained. Herein the question is if the boy can conquer his fears.:*

:I wondered about that. He's been wearing a very odd look on his face this evening, and I've never *known him to be as friendly with common folk as he was tonight.:* She opened her eyes wide and stared at the glowing embers of the hearth without really seeing them. *:Poor Van. If that dream of his is Foresight— that's a hell of a burden to carry around.:*

:It still may never come to be,: Moondance reminded them, and the straw of his bedding crackled as he shifted. *:We still See only the thing most likely* at this moment. *And the moment is always changing. I would change the subject. We have a more urgent consideration. Those colddrakes were Gated here. That speaks of—:*

:—great trouble to come,: Starwind replied, his mind-voice dark and grim. *:There is no doubt in my mind at this moment that the drakes were sent to harry this area in advance of a fighting force.:* The fire popped once. *:This has gone beyond tampering. There was a village to the west of here under tacit k'Treva protection. I can no longer sense it; it is under foreign shield.:*

:Someone moved in and took it over, hmm?: Savil brooded on that a moment. *:What would you say to us organizing a little surprise for whoever sent those drakes? I doubt anyone is expecting k'Treva response this soon. By rights, dividing the swarm should have kept us busy for a week.:*

Starwind's mind-voice was troubled. *:I would say that you are not k'Treva—:*

:And I would reply that I am Wingsister, which makes me just as much k'Treva as Moondance. I would say also that two mages tampering in this area is a very unlikely coincidence. It is far more likely that this is the same mage who was hired by the Leshara of Valdemar. Which makes it the more my fight.:

More straw rustled, and Savil moved her head slightly, just enough to see Starwind's ironic gaze bent on her for a long moment.

:And I,: Moondance put in, *:would say that my shay'kreth'ashke is unlikely to win a battle of wills with such a stubborn one as I know the Wingsister to be. I would also say that three Adepts are better in this than two.:*

Starwind sighed. *:I fear I am defeated ere I begin. What do we do with the boy, then? We cannot leave him here, and I mislike taking the time to take him back to the vale. That* will *lose us the element of surprise.:*

:He may prove useful,: Moondance said unexpectedly. *:He did defeat the queen-drake.:*

:We bring him, I suppose,: Savil agreed, though with some misgiving. *:Surely Yfandes can be counted on to keep him out of serious trouble.:*

:I cannot like it, but I must agree,: Starwind replied reluctantly. *:This is a great deal of danger to be taking one so untested and so newly-healed into.:*

:I know,: Savil said, wishing the coals burning in the fireplace didn't look so much like a burning town. *:Believe me, I know.:*

It had been snowing all day, not heavily, but steadily. The air felt almost warm. The Companions moved like white spirits through the drifts of flurries, each carrying double. White horses, white riders—all but one; the one riding pillion behind the second Companion was in smoky black and dark gray, a shadow to a ghost.

"You all look like Heralds," Vanyel said, from the pillion-pad behind Moondance. "Everyone does except me."

"How so?" Moondance asked, somewhat surprised.

"It's your white outfits," Savil supplied, as Kellan lagged a little so that she could reply without having to turn her head. "Heralds always wear white uniforms when they're on duty."

"Ah—youngling, *Tayledras* always wear the colors best suited to blend into the treetops. In winter—white. In summer, obviously, green." Moondance was carefully plaiting a new bowstring using both hands. He wasn't even bothering with the reins; he had those looped up on the pommel of the saddle. Vanyel didn't much care for riding pillion, but it wasn't bad behind Moondance; the younger *Tayledras* didn't mind talking to him. As Vanyel had suspected, he had forgiven Vanyel even before he made his apology to the *Tayledras*. Which he had done as soon as he could get Moondance alone; it only seemed right. Now it was as if the incident had never occurred; Moondance even seemed to welcome his questions and encouraged him to ask them.

They'd talked about Vanyel's Gifts, mostly. Vanyel hadn't actually *talked* about them to anyone; Savil hadn't had much opportunity to do so, and Starwind had just gone directly into his head, showed him what to do, and then expected him to do it.

"So, what were we up to?" Moondance asked.

"Foresight." Vanyel shivered. "Moondance, I don't like it. I don't *want* to know what's going to happen. Is there any way I can block it?"

"Now that it is active? Not to my knowledge. But you must not let it cripple you, *ke'chara*. You are not seeing the *irrevocable* future, you see the future as it may be if nothing changes. The most likely at this moment. These things may change; *you* can change them."

"I can?" Vanyel perked up at this.

"Assuredly. But it may be that the cost of such a change is to dissolve a friendship or a love you would not willingly forgo. You may feel such a bond is worth the price." He smiled crookedly back over his shoulder. "If I were to have the certain knowledge that my lifebond to Starwind would send me to my death tomorrow, I would go willingly to that fate. But I would not tell Starwind of my foreknowledge. Think on that, if you will."

Vanyel did brood on that for several furlongs.

It was Moondance in Yfandes' saddle and not Vanyel, because if they were surprised by an attack, Vanyel had been ordered to drop off the pillion pad and stay out of the fight.

It was humiliating—but sensible. Vanyel was rather more acutely interested in "sensible" than in "humiliating" at the moment. If an attack came, he'd obey those orders. He'd learned his lesson with the colddrake.

"Well, are there no more questions, *ke'chara*?"

Vanyel shook his head.

"Then I have one for you. Starwind has said that when you were frightened in practice you pulled power from the valley-node. Is this true?"

"What's the valley-node?"

"Savil did not tell you?" Moondance made a face. "No patience, that one. You surely have felt that all things have energy about them, yes?"

"Even rocks—"

"*Ge'teva*, if you sense that, then your Mage-Gift is a most strong one! Even I have some difficulty with seeing that. So; have you seen that this energy flows along lines, as rainwater to streams?"

Vanyel hadn't, but when he closed his eyes and *extended* he could see that Moondance was right.

"I do now."

"Then follow a stream to the place where it meets another."

He did. There was a kind of—knot. A concentration of power. He told Moondance so.

"That is a node." Moondance nodded. "*Tayledras* can direct the course of these streams on occasion, which is how we take the magic from places where the wars left it and move it to a place where it is useful. We build our strongholds over places where two or more powerful streams meet: nodes. The energy of the node is such that all of us can use it, but we have found that many outland mages not only cannot sense the streams, they cannot sense nor use the nodes. This may be something only those outsiders at the level of our Adepts do well; I think it is perhaps unique to the *Tayledras* that all of us, from the time we start to feel our Gifts awaken, manipulate this energy as easily as a child plays with building bricks. There was a time—*very* long ago—when the *Tayledras* adopted outlanders very commonly, and it is said that these outlanders changed even as I have. I think that the key to change is using this magic under the direction of *Tayledras* born. So; of outland Adepts we have known, only Wingsister Savil can link into the nodes as well as *Tayledras;* her Gift is very strong. So, it seems, is yours."

Vanyel was confused as to where all this was leading. "But what does that mean, Moondance?"

"For now—you exhausted yourself when you killed the colddrake. That is something you need not do *quite* so quickly, if you remember that you can pull from the life-energy nodes within your sensing range. When *they* are drained—*then* you use your own strength."

:*That's what I've been trying to tell you,*: Yfandes said unexpectedly in his mind.

That gave him food for thought for several more candlemarks.

They'd journeyed westward from Garthhold with the rising of the sun, stopping three times on the way to question folk Starwind knew. The first had been a fur trapper, who'd told them of rumors of a renegade wizard, who was half-human, half-Pelagir changeling and had sorcerous skills and a taste for worldly power. The second was a *kyree*, a wolflike creature with a mind fully the equal of any human. *He* stopped *them*, Mindspeaking to warn them of the same wizard, but his stories were more than mere rumors. To his certain knowledge the changeling was planning to carve himself a realm of his own as quickly as he could, and had already begun that task.

The third *had been* one of k'Treva's border-guards—not *Tayledras* herself, but another of the Pelagir changelings, a *tervardi*, a kind of flightless bird-woman.

She was no longer among the living.

When Starwind had been unable to Mindcall her, they had detoured to the grove of trees that held her *ekele*. There was no sign of a struggle, but they found the fragile, white-plumaged wraith in her *ekele*, dead, without a mark upon her, but with her bow in her hand, bowstring snapped, and her empty, glazed eyes wide with what Vanyel assumed was fear.

Starwind spent some moments beside the body, working some kind of subtle magic. Vanyel could feel things stirring, even if he couldn't yet read them. What it was Starwind found, he would not tell Vanyel, but the three adults grew very grim—and Moondance took the bow and its arrows when they left.

They had been riding all day, cutting cross-country at the ground-eating pace only a Companion could maintain; it was nearing sunset when they slowed, on coming to what looked to be a fairly well-traveled road.

Savil and Kellan halted while they were still within the cover of the forest, and Yfandes came up beside them as silently as it was possible for something the size and weight of a Companion to do. The snow-laden branches of an enormous evergreen shielded them from the view of anyone on that road, although the road itself looked deserted. There didn't seem to be any new tracks on it, and all the old ones had been softened with a layer of new, undisturbed snow. The road was lined on both sides by a row of these evergreens, though, and anything could lie in wait undetected behind them.

"The village of Covia lies a few furlongs up that road," Starwind whispered, as the sun sank in sullen glory ahead of them. "There is still a shield upon it, and I do not like the feel of the power behind that shield. I do not, however, sense that the power is presently in the village."

"Nor I," replied Savil, after a moment.

:Nothing,: Yfandes said to Vanyel.

"'Fandes says she doesn't feel anything either," he reported, feeling rather in the way.

"My thought is to enter the village and see how much is amiss—and what the people know. Then—Vanyel, it is in my mind to leave you with the villagers. You have enough mage-training to be some protection to them, and they may be of some physical protection to you."

"I—yes, Master Starwind," he replied, not much liking the idea, but not seeing any other choice. "What about 'Fandes?"

:I don't like it, but I'll go with them,. Yfandes said reluctantly. :If you need me, I'll know, and they need a second mount.:

Vanyel reported Yfandes' words with a sinking heart. Starwind nodded. "I think she has the right of it; we can cover more ground mounted. Well." He peered up the road through the gathering evening gloom. "I think it is time to see the handiwork of our enemy."

*   *   *

Vanyel was doing his best not to be sick. Again. He'd already lost control over his stomach once, just outside of Covia, when they'd found the wizard's—warn-off.

It was well after sundown, and pitchy dark outside of the village square. The entire population of the village, upwards of seventy people, was jammed into the tiny square. Many of them had brought lanterns and torches. They were crowding about the four strangers and two Companions, like baby chicks seeking the shelter of the hen's wings—although they were paying scant attention to Savil and less than that to Vanyel and the Companions. The Herald was a dubious and unknown quantity, and the boy and the "horses" were being dismissed out of hand.

The party had made a kind of impromptu dais out of the low porch of the Temple, which was barely large enough to hold the four humans; the Companions were serving as living barricades on either side, to keep them from being totally overwhelmed. As it was it was getting a little cramped, behind the two *Tayledras*. But Vanyel was beginning to be rather glad he was being ignored. Between the tales the villagers were telling Starwind—and the physical evidences they were displaying in the flickering of the torch-light to substantiate those stories—it wasn't easy for Vanyel to control his nausea.

This *had* been a pleasant little village, as safe as any place inside the Pelagirs. People could feel comfortable about raising children; had time for celebrations now and again.

It was no longer pleasant, nor safe. It was now a place under siege, with no way out.

Two weeks ago a stranger had come to the village, mounted on some-thing that was *not* a horse, and accompanied by a retinue of some of the Pelagirs' least attractive denizens. He had announced that the town and its inhabitants were now *his*, and had helped himself to whatever he wanted. After one demonstration of his power had left a heap of ash where the vil-lage inn had once stood, these folk had more sense than to resist—but they *had* attempted to send for help. The remains of their messenger were found the next morning, impaled on a stake in the middle of the outbound road. The frozen corpse was still there; the Companions had passed it on the way in. From the look of the man, simple impalement had come as a relief.

He had come back about every other night, each time taking both goods and victims. The villagers told Starwind that they had been praying for help;

they assumed he was the answer to those prayers. He seemed, to Vanyel at least, to be agreeing with that assumption.

Vanyel was just grateful that the fitful torchlight wasn't bright enough for him to see much of the details of what had been done to some of the wizard's victims. He was equally grateful that he was in the dark at the back of the porch, behind Savil.

"—this's the last, Master Starwind," the swarthy, unshaven headman said, wearily, his red-rimmed eyes those of one who had seen far too much of horror in the past few days. "This girl."

He pushed a mousy blond female right up onto the porch, where Vanyel couldn't avoid looking at her. The young woman would still have been attractive—if she hadn't been vacant-eyed and drooling. She was filthy, her hair matted and hanging in lank snarls. Starwind flinched at the sight of her, but Moondance fearlessly took her face in both his slender hands and gazed into her blank brown eyes for a long time.

When he finally released her, his face and voice were tight with anger. "I think that Brightwind may be able to bring her mind back," he said, slowly and carefully, as if he was trying to keep from saying something he had rather not speak aloud. "It will require many months—and she will never be able to bear the touch of a man; she has been too far hurt within. Even so, all those channels meant for pleasure have been warped, and now can only carry pain. I do not know if even I can Heal that. I do not think that anything will be able to Heal her heart and soul of what was done to her, not entirely. It may be it is better not to try; it may be that it is better to wipe all away and begin with her as with a small child."

The balding headman nodded as if that was what he had expected to hear. "She was one of the first he took," he said heavily. "Her and her mother. Her father was the messenger we sent—we never found anything of her mother."

"And he grows stronger, this Krebain, with every person he takes?" Starwind asked.

The torches wavered in the wind, casting weird shadows across the man's hollow-cheeked face as he nodded. Vanyel could scent the coming of more snow in that wind. "He seems to. Seems to me he's doing blood-magic, wouldn't you say, Master Starwind?"

Starwind nodded, and narrowed his eyes in thought. "Aye, Gallen; you know your lore well, I think. So. This Krebain has retreated to whatever place he has made for a fastness, and it is bound to be somewhere near; I think we shall continue with my original plan. Gallen, I shall leave young Vanyel here with you. He knows something of material strategy and warfare; he is also Mage-Gifted."

Vanyel shivered at the thought of being left alone here. The headman cast one doubtful look at him and ventured a protest; Vanyel didn't much blame him. "Master Starwind—I beg you—this is only a boy—"

"He destroyed a queen colddrake, alone and unaided," Moondance said quietly, pushing Vanyel forward and putting one hand on Vanyel's shoulder. "It is in my mind that he could deal with more than you would reckon."

"He did?" This time the look Headman Gallen gave him was a little less doubtful, but it was still not overly confident.

"Gallen, I do not expect Vanyel to have to defend you from this Krebain," Starwind said patiently. "He could never be a match for a bloodbound Adept, and I would not expect it of him. I expect him to have to deal with some of this renegade's creatures at worst. My thought is that the three of us shall find Krebain and deal with him—and that when his control over his slaves is gone, some of them may think to attack here. I see no reason why, among you, you folk and Vanyel could not defend yourselves against such lesser dangers. Does that content you?"

It didn't—that was obvious. But it was all that Headman Gallen was going to get, and he well knew it. Vanyel attempted to put himself into the mindset of a warleader. He didn't feel particularly successful at it.

"Van, see what you can do about organizing these folk," Savil said quietly. "You know most of those old ballads by heart, and there's lots of good advice in them; that's why we make you learn them. I don't want you to try anything more than a token defense if something does come at you that you can't handle. Just call Yfandes for help and delay things as long as you can. For the rest—the creatures they've described are strong, but not particularly bright. Barricades across the road and fire should keep most of them at bay. You took that queen colddrake; remember that. You can take just about anything else except this Krebain himself so long as it isn't a small army."

Vanyel gulped, and tried to look competent and brave. *This is what it all comes down to, doesn't it? This is what I have to do; I have to, like 'Lendel said. Because these people need me.* "Yes, Aunt," he said carefully. "Barricades and fire."

Savil looked worried and preoccupied. "Do your best, lad. Remember that 'voice' I used to stop you and 'Lendel fighting? It makes people listen;

goes right to their guts. Imitate that if you can." She mounted Kellan from the porch; Starwind took Yfandes' saddle, but Moondance hesitated a moment before taking the pillion behind him.

"Vanyel, *ke'chara*, remember what I told you about the nodes. *Use* them. There are—" He paused, and his eyes unfocused for a moment. "There are three that I can sense that you should be able to use. I wish you could reach the valley-node as we can, but I think it is beyond your strength for now. None of the three nearby are as strong as the valley-node, but taken together they should serve." He took Vanyel's face between his hands and kissed him on the forehead. "Gods be with you, youngling. With fortune, this will be no more than an interesting exercise for you."

He mounted behind Starwind, and the crowd of villagers parted to let them through. Vanyel watched them vanish into the darkness with a heavy heart.

If he hadn't been so frightened himself, he'd have lost his temper a dozen times over. He had to keep explaining to these people, time and time again, exactly *what* he wanted of them and *why* he wanted it—and would turn his back on one group, thinking that he had *finally* gotten through to them, only to return to find they'd abandoned the project and were staring apprehensively off into the darkness.

It wasn't that they were stupid; it was that they were so completely without hope. They couldn't see any *chance* of holding off anything, and so they had abandoned any thought of being able to do so. After all, *their* best efforts hadn't done anything but get folks killed. Vanyel, who was counting on *them* to be as much protection for him as he would be for them, was nearly frantic. It took hours before he was finally able to get them going under their own power.

Then there was the matter of defense.

When dawn came and he asked for their weaponry, he got as ill-used and motley an assortment of near-junk as he'd ever seen, and there wasn't a one of them who knew how to use any of it. These were farmers born and farmers bred; most of them off lands held of lords or mage-lords who were bound to protect *them*. The k'Treva had bartered protection for made-stuffs and foodstuffs, and they had never thought they'd need to raise a blade in their own defense.

So Vanyel was faced with the task of showing rank amateurs the way of the sword. *Forget* teaching them point-work; *forget* the finer points of defense. In the end he padded them to the eyebrows and set them to bashing at each other. Teach them to hold something long and poke with it, or hold something heavy and smash with it—and if it was something with an edge, hope that the edge, rather than the flat, connected.

By the second day of this he was tired to the bone, half-mad with frustration, and frantic with the fear he dared not show. So when Veth, Gallen's half-grown son, came at him wide open for the hundredth time, he lost his temper completely and hit him with a full force blow he had not consciously intended to deliver. And tried to pull it too late to do any good.

He knocked the boy halfway across the square.

Veth landed sprawled on his back—and didn't move—

And Vanyel's heart stopped—

And in his mind he saw—Jervis—standing over *him*—

Oh, gods!

Vanyel's sword went flying; his helm followed it as he ran to kneel at Veth's side in the cold dust of the square.

Oh, gods—oh, gods—I've done to him what Jervis did to me. Oh, please, gods, please don't let me have hurt him—

He unlaced the boy's helm and pulled it off; about then Veth blinked up at him and started to sit up of himself, and Vanyel nearly cried with relief.

"Veth—please, Veth, I'm sorry, I—I lost my temper—I didn't mean it—"

The boy looked at him with bewilderment. "Eh, Master Van, I be all right. I been kicked by our old mule worse nor this—just let me get a bit of a drink, eh?"

Vanyel sagged back on his heels, shutting his eyes against the harsh sunlight, limp with relief. The boy got gingerly to his feet.

Oh, gods. I—I'm as bad as Jervis. I'm worse than Jervis; I know better. Oh, gods—

"Vanyel, young sir—"

He looked up; it was Reva, Veth's mother, her tired face anxious. He winced, and waited for her to give him the tongue-lashing he deserved.

It didn't come. "If you'll forgive me for being an interfering old hen," she said, with a little quirk of her mouth, "I think you've about worn yourself into uselessness, young sir. I know you haven't eaten since last night. Now here—"

She offered him her hand; astounded, he took it, and to his utter befuddlement she hauled him to his feet. "Now," she put one arm around his shoulders, the other about Veth's. "I think it's time you both got a bit of food in you. The time it takes to eat won't make Veth a better fighter, nor you a better teacher." She hugged them both, as if they were both her sons, then released them.

The words he had thrown into Withen's face—was it only a year ago?—came back to shame him further.

"Let every man that must go to battle fight within his talents, and not be forced to any one school."

I've been treating them exactly the way Jervis treated me. Forcing them to use things they don't know, to go outside of their talents. I am a complete and incompetent fool.

Vanyel blushed. And stammered. "I—I'm no kind of a teacher, Mistress Reva, or I'd not have chosen what I did to teach." He raised his voice so the rest of those practicing in the square could hear him. "This is getting us nowhere. It's like you trying to teach me to—to plow and spin, for a Midsummer contest a week away. We haven't the time, and I'm a fool. Now, please, what are your *real* weapons? Any of you know the use of bow? Or sling? Boar-spear, maybe?"

It was not his imagination; there were looks of real relief all across the square—and the beginnings of smiles.

But in the end, all his preparations were in vain.

The villagers willing to fight were on the barricades; there were really only two blockades—there was only one road going through the village, and it led directly through the pounded-dirt square. The square itself was fairly defensible now; not even a colddrake would have been able to get past the buildings. The folk too frightened or unable to defend themselves had faded away into the shadows as they did every night to scatter and hide in the cellars and attics of the buildings around the square. Headman Gallen had by now come to the conclusion that Vanyel knew something of what he was about; he and two or three of the other folk not too cowed to take a stand (including the old herb-witch, who took a dim view of this young upstart wizard taking over *her* village) were having a hasty conference with Vanyel on supplies—when a surge of Gate-energy invoked practically under Vanyel's nose knocked him to his knees and very nearly knocked him out.

The only thing that saved him from unconsciousness this time was that he was completely under shield. He found himself gasping for breath, and completely disoriented for a moment. His eyes had flashing lights in front of them, and he shook his head to try and clear it. *That* was a mistake; his head reacted poorly to the abrupt movement.

He could hardly think, much less see. *Gods—what in—*

"What do we have here?"

The clear, musical tenor voice sounded amused—and Vanyel froze. The voice carried clearly; the petrified silence in the square was as deep as the Nine Pits.

He looked up when his eyes cleared, and found that all he could see were the backs of people. The members of his erstwhile war-council were standing huddled together as if to keep him hidden in the shadows behind them. Vanyel got hold of the splintery side of the storehouse and pulled himself cautiously to his feet, ducking his head behind Gallen's and standing on tiptoe to peek over the shoulders of the men in front of him. His gut went cold when he saw the flamboyantly dressed stranger in the middle of the cleared square.

This could *only* be the wizard Krebain.

The torches falling from the hands of the stunned villagers were unneeded; the wizard had brought his own mage-light with him. It hung over his head, a tiny green-yellow sun. People were slowly backing away until they ran into the walls and the barricades, leaving the stranger standing in arrogant isolation in the exact center of the dusty square.

The wizard was a gaudy sight. He wore scarlet and gold; skin-tight breeches, close-cut gold-embroidered velvet tunic, scarlet cloak with cloth-of-gold lining. Even his boots and velvet gloves were scarlet. He had a scarlet helm that was more than half mask, ornamented with a preposterous crest of a rampant dragon in gold. With one hand on his hip, he tapped at his chin with a gloved finger as he turned to survey the people surrounding the square.

"A rebellion—I do believe this is a rebellion! How *droll!*" He laughed; it had a nasty sound to it.

He was graceful, slim, and very tall. White-blond hair tumbled from beneath the helm in wavy, shining cascades. What could be seen of his face was like elegantly sculptured marble. Vanyel found himself caught by the wizard's sheer charismatic beauty. None of the villagers had said anything about *that.*

Vanyel felt almost sick. Evil such as had been described to him *shouldn't* be—beautiful!

But then he thought, *Artificial—that really is what he is. He's changed himself, I'm sure of it, like—painting his face, only more so. If I had a lot of power and didn't care how I used it, I suppose I'd make myself beautiful, too.*

"I wonder what could have roused you worms to think to stand against me?" Krebain mused aloud. "None of you had half an ounce of courage before this. But then—none of you smelled of the mage-born before this, either, other than that foolish old witch of yours over there." He smiled slyly. "I think I detect a stranger among you—hmm? Now where have you hidden him?"

Ice crawled up Vanyel's spine. *All they have to do is point a finger at me—and even if they don't, if I call Yfandes for help, he'll know where I am. Oh, gods, can I hide? I can't challenge him! They can't expect it of me—I'm no match for him!*

But to his surprise, not a single one of those remaining in the square answered the wizard's question. In fact, the men standing in front of Vanyel moved closer together, as if to shield him from the wizard's chance sight.

The wizard's voice sharpened with impatience. "I grow weary, curs. Where is the stranger I sensed?"

Silence.

Except for the herb-witch, who whispered back at Vanyel, with the merest breath—"Stay quiet, boy. You're no fit opponent for him, and we know it. Won't do any of us any good for you to get caught, and he just may take us apart for spite even if he gets you. Maybe if he gets bored, he'll go away."

"I *said*, I want to know where the stranger is." The wizard looked about him, both hands on his hips now, and anger in his pose. "Very well. I see it's time you learned another lesson." He turned slightly, so that he was staring right at the group clustered in front of Vanyel, and raised his left hand. "You—Gallen." He made a little summoning motion. "Come here. . . ."

Gallen made a staggering step, then another. He was fighting the wizard with his will, but losing. Sweat popped out all over his brow, and he made a whimpering noise in the back of his throat.

Behind him, the group closed ranks, still shielding Vanyel from view. Before him, the wizard grinned sadistically. "You really haven't a hope of fighting me, you know," he said pleasantly. "It's like a babe challenging an armed warrior. Come along, there's a good dog."

Gallen ran the last few steps, coming to a trembling halt at the wizard's side. Krebain strolled around him, looking him over carefully. The mage-light followed in faithful attendance above his head. "Let's see—I believe you have a wife." He swept his gaze over the rest of the villagers. "Yes, indeed—and there she is. Reva—my goodness. A would-be sword-lady, are you? Come here, my dear."

He crooked his finger, and dusky Reva stumbled out of the group at the barricade on the west road, still clutching her improvised pike of a knife strapped to the end of a staff. Her face was strained, white—and a mask of despair.

Krebain shook his head. "Really, my dear, you have no use for a weapon like that. Take it from her, Gallen."

Gallen did not move; sweat poured down his face, glistening in the mage-light.

"I said, *take it*." Krebain's voice sharpened with command, and Gallen's gnarled hands slowly reached forward to take the pike from his wife.

"Now—just rest the point of that wicked little knife on her stomach, why don't you." Gallen his face reflecting his agony, lowered the pike until the point of the blade touched his wife's stomach. He whimpered again as Krebain's will made him brace it. Krebain's smile grew broader. "Of course, Reva, it would be very painful if you were to walk forward just now—"

Vanyel couldn't bear it. He gathered what little there was of his courage, and shouted, his voice breaking.

"*Stop it!*"

He pushed his protectors aside and walked out from behind them to stand in the open, a pace or two in front of them.

And in the moment when Krebain turned to face him, licking his lips, he Mindcalled with all his strength—

:*Yfandes! The mage—he's here! 'Fandes—*:

"That's enough, child."

Vanyel felt a barrier close down around the village, a barrier that allowed no thought to escape, and no further call for help.

He raised his chin with the same bleak defiance that had served him against his father.

"Let them alone, wizard," he said, his voice trembling despite his efforts to keep it steady. He could feel sweat trickling coldly down the back of his neck, and his mouth was dry and sour with fear. "I'm the one you wanted."

Krebain made a dismissing gesture, and Reva and Gallen staggered as his hold over them was released. Gallen threw down the pike and seized her shoulders, and together they melted into the crowd at Krebain's back.

"Come where I can see you," the wizard said, mildly.

Vanyel walked, with slow and hesitant steps, into the area where the mage-light was striking.

"What a *pleasant* surprise—"

Unless Krebain was feigning it—which was possible—he *was* surprised. And—pleased.

If Vanyel could keep him in that mood, maybe he could keep them all safe a little longer. He began to feel a tiny stirring of hope.

"What a truly pleasant surprise. My would-be enemy is a *beautiful* young man. What is your name, lovely one?"

Vanyel saw no reason not to answer him. If nothing else—if Yfandes had heard him, he'd be buying time for help to arrive. He allowed himself a moment to hope a little more, then replied, "Vanyel Ashkevron."

"Vanyel—I do *not* believe this—Vanyel Ashkevron?" The wizard laughed, throwing back his head. "What a joke! What a magnificent *jest!* I come a-hunting you, and *you* walk unarmed into my very hand!"

Vanyel shook his head, bewildered.

The wizard grinned. "Dear, lovely boy. You have enemies, you know, enemies with no appreciation of beauty and a great deal of coin to spend. Wester Leshara holds you to blame for the death of his cousin Evan, didn't you know that? He sent me an additional commission to deal with you as I had with young Staven Frelennye. *I* had thought to attend to my own pursuits a while here, then deal with you at my leisure, allowing matters to cool first. But—now I don't know that I am going to oblige him by killing you. Not when you turn out to be so very beautiful. Come closer, would you?"

Vanyel felt no magical coercion, which rather surprised *him.* "If you don't mind," he said carefully, "I'd really rather not."

This time Krebain's smile held a hint of real humor. "Then I shall have to come to you, beautiful Vanyel."

He paced gracefully across the pounded dirt of the village square, taking each step as though he walked on a carpet of petals strewn especially for his benefit. The mage-light continued to follow him faithfully. He strolled around Vanyel as he had walked around Gallen, but his expression this time was less cruelly cheerful and more acquisitive. His path was an inward-turning spiral, with Vanyel as the center, so that he completed his circuit facing Vanyel and less than a handspan away. He reached out with one crimson-gloved hand, ignoring the presence of everyone in the square as if he and Vanyel were alone together, and laid it along Vanyel's cheek. Vanyel looked steadily into his blue-black eyes within the shadowed eyeholes of the helm-mask and did not flinch away. Those eyes were the first indication he had seen that the wizard was something other than human. Those dark and frightening eyes were slitted like a cat's—and under the velvet of the glove, Vanyel could feel something very sharp and talonlike resting on his cheek.

"My goodness," Krebain breathed, "Silver eyes. Rare and beautiful, Vanyel Ashkevron. How wonderful, and how strange, that you should be here, at this moment. And I wonder, now—given what I know of Tylendel Frelennye—were you only the *friend* of Tylendel, or were you something more than friend?"

Still ignoring everyone else, he leaned forward and kissed Vanyel passionately and deeply.

Vanyel trembled with an unexpected reaction comprised of both revulsion and desire.

Half of him wanted to pull away and strike at this creature who could casually force a man to stab his own wife, who could regard the villagers about them so lightly as to totally ignore them at this moment.

The other half of him wanted to melt into the wizard's arms.

He fought the temptation to yield. *This—dammit, it's nothing but sex, that's all it is. I* know *what real love feels like—and this—isn't—close.*

He closed his eyes, as his knees went to water.

A dream-flash—

"Surrender to me, Herald-Mage Vanyel," Leareth said. "Take my darkness to you."

Had that dream been, not Foresight, but a warning?

He fought to think clearly, battling silently, but daring to give no outward sign of his struggle. It was at that moment that he realized that whatever other powers this wizard had, he did *not* share Vanyel's Mind-Gifts. Like— Thought-sensing, for instance. The shield over the village was spellcast, not mindcast. Which meant that Vanyel should be able to read the wizard, without Krebain knowing he was being read.

Krebain finally brought an end to the kiss, pulling away slowly and reluctantly, taking his hand from Vanyel's cheek with a tender caress of his velvet-clad fingers.

"Oh," he whispered, his eyes half-shut, the slits in them narrowed to near-invisibility. "Oh, beautiful and rare, *lovely* Vanyel. Come with me. Come with me, be my love. I can teach you more than you have ever dreamed. I could carve you a kingdom, give you power, pleasure—anything you desired. Name it, and it would be yours."

The temptation was incredible. And the thought—*I could guide him. I could bring him to compassion. He doesn't have to be this way. I could make him into something better. Couldn't I? Even if I don't love him—wouldn't that be worthwhile?*

Wouldn't that be a worthy goal? And I don't love him—but I could care for him, I think. There's a mutual need—isn't that enough?

His heart raced. *I have to know—what is Krebain truly made of? If there's something there to work with—something I can influence—*

Krebain smiled. "I could even," he whispered, "grant you the finest revenge upon Wester Leshara the world has ever witnessed. A revenge so complete that it would even satisfy Tylendel's lover."

The wizard's mind was open to Vanyel's at that crucial instant; completely open and unguarded.

Vanyel saw *how* Krebain had gotten his power; how—and from what— he had learned it. And the uses he had put it to. And how he had *enjoyed* what he had done. There was nothing there that was human or humane.

Gods! Never—never would I give myself to that!

Utter revulsion killed all trace of desire—and *now* Vanyel flinched away, his nausea plain for anyone to read.

Krebain stepped back an involuntary pace, his face flushed. He frowned with anger, and his expression hardened. "I will have you, Vanyel Ashkevron—with or *without* a mind."

Vanyel had that much warning to get a shield up; had that much warning to scream "*Run—*" at the villagers.

At least, he *thought* he screamed that warning at them. They certainly scattered as quickly as if he had, scrambling up and over the barricades that they had built to keep the menace out, leaving him alone with the wizard.

Who called the lightnings down on him.

Vanyel's body screamed with pain, despite the shielding; his hair stood on end, and fire ran along his nerves. He went to his knees beneath the onslaught, reinforced his shielding and felt it weakening—and then remembered what Moondance had said about the power-nodes.

He reached, desperately; found them, tapped into them, and felt their power flowing into him, giving him a heady surge of strength, driving out the pain and renewing the will to *fight* this monster in human guise.

He staggered to his feet, backed up a pace, and deflected Krebain's own lightnings back into his face.

The fires arced across the square and the wizard retreated, getting his own shields up just in time. Vanyel did not give him a chance to recover from his surprise, but launched an attack of his own: not lightnings this time, but a vise of power, a glowing shroud that he closed around the wizard and began tightening.

But Krebain broke it after a moment's struggle, and countered with a circle of flame that roared up about him and began eating its way inward. Vanyel could smell his boot-soles scorching, and his skin tightened and hurt.

Vanyel in his turn, sweating with the heat, and his fear and effort, called upon the dust of the square to rise and snuff the flames.

This time Krebain gave him no chance to invoke a counterattack, but summoned a mage-storm like the one in Vanyel's dream. It howled down out of the night sky and surrounded him in a cloud of wind and energy, crackling with it, screaming with it.

And like the one in Vanyel's dream, this one ate away at his shields as fast as he could bring them up.

The whirlwind howled and raged, obscuring sight—he couldn't see— couldn't see anything anymore, just the flickering storm of power shrieking around him, coming closer by the moment.

One by one the nodes went drained and dead; now there was only his own strength left.

He went to his knees, holding the last of his shields up with little more than desperation left to sustain him—

—and a final hammer-blow blew the storm away and *smashed* him to the earth.

Vanyel lay stunned in the sudden silence of the square, broken and bleeding.

He was sprawled half on his back, and the silence howled in his ears as the storm had. The square was deserted now, but for the silent scarlet figure of the wizard.

Vanyel was utterly spent, and everything hurt so much he could hardly think. He coughed, and tasted blood, and when he tried to breathe, he felt stabbing pains in his chest and back.

He was oddly conscious of little things, of a pebble digging into his cheek, of his ankle bending the wrong way, of a strand of hair tickling his nose, of blood running into his eyes—of a single flake of snow spiraling down into the mage-light.

His vision began to darken as Krebain strode toward him from across the square; he seemed to be seeing things through a shadowy mist.

The wizard stood over him.

And strangely, he felt like laughing. *Gods. All that being afraid of that dream, for nothing.* He saw the wizard's expression, and sobered. *So. This is what it comes to. This is how it ends. At least—he looks a little tired. At least I put up some kind of a fight.*

He thought he heard someone, something, whimper. *Please, gods—let those people have gotten away. Don't let this have been for nothing. Let the others come in time to save them.*

"I told you, Vanyel Ashkevron, that I would have you with or without a mind," Krebain said softly. "But I would rather you were mine wholly, and of your own will. You see? I can be merciful. I can be kind to those I love. I give you another chance, beautiful Vanyel. Surrender to me, and I will heal your hurts, and give you all that I promised you. Will you come with me now?"

No. Not ever. Not at the cost of my life. He looked up at those inhuman, chillingly cold eyes. *And it will be at the cost of my life. But—gods—I can't let it cost more lives than my own!*

He reached, as far as he could, hoping for a tiny bit of energy left in the power-nodes—hoping to find another node, undrained—

—and touched the valley-node instead.

Gods—it isn't possible!

For a moment he thought he saw a way out, not only for the villagers, but for himself. But when he assessed his own capabilities, he saw that to use the raw, elemental force of the vale *would* surely kill him. He no longer had the strength to control it. The effect would be like what he had done to himself in practice with Starwind—only a hundred times worse.

He could die painlessly, letting the wizard destroy his mind and soul— or he could die in agony, saving the people of Covia.

I was willing to die before, for 'Lendel—why would I be afraid of pain and dying now? he thought, with a catch in his throat. *I surely owe a price for not stopping 'Lendel. All right. Gods, let this be my expiation. Give me this last strength to stop him.*

"No," he breathed. "Never."

The wizard's face twisted with anger, and he stepped back to deliver the final blow. Vanyel closed his eyes and *reached—*

In this last moment, peace came to him. A strange and heart-tight inner stillness, born of total acceptance that what he was about to do would kill him without Moondance near to heal what he would do to himself. With a feeling oddly like the lifting of his heart, he opened himself to the valley-node—and focused—

And the raw power poured through him and blasted from his eyes.

He screamed in agony, but his own cry was lost in the shriek Krebain made as the bolt of power caught him unshielded, in the face.

Then Vanyel fell, into true peace, and darkness.

Oh, 'Lendel, wherever you are, I'm coming. Please, please be there—

Dear Withen; I think you would be very proud of your son today—

A faint sound from the fern-canopied bed beside her made Savil set down her pen and paper beside her chair, unwrap herself from her cloak, rise, and draw the silky hangings aside.

Vanyel—bandaged, splinted, and bruised, and looking very pale against the dark green of Moondance's bedding—moved his head again on the pillow, and opened dazed eyes.

Savil swallowed hard; he looked so battered, so bewildered.

Oh, my little love, we so nearly lost you this time—so close, so close. I half expect you to ask me to let you stay here, sheltered and safe. And the gods know, you've earned it.

He blinked, as if he didn't quite believe what he saw.

"Aunt—Savil?" he said faintly. "Are you—real?"

She sat carefully on the edge of the bed, and touched his cheek, giving him a faint smile. "That real enough for you?"

He nodded, and blinked again. "The people—the villagers—Gallen and Reva—are they all right?"

"They're fine, *ke'chara*," she replied, her heart filling with pride and love at the question. *His first thought—for others. There's no doubt; Starwind was right. There is no doubt of him.* "We got there just in time for Moondance to keep you from getting away from us. Gods—it's a good thing that bastard wasn't still alive. I don't think I've ever seen him so angry in my life, and Yfandes was white-hot with rage. There wasn't much left for us to do. Basically all *I* did was make a Gate to get us all back to k'Treva so Moondance could put you back together again."

"Then everyone's all right?" he asked insistently, as if he didn't quite dare to believe her. "Are they protected now? Are you and Starwind and Moondance all right, too? That wizard—he was the one *Leshara* hired—he told me so. He told me—"

"Later," she soothed. "Tell me all that later. We're all fine. K'Treva sent out some of the Journeyman *Tayledras* to help get Covia back on its collective feet and give the region a little more in the way of protections. *You're* the only one who sustained any damage, love." She glanced up at the skylight to gauge the time. "I expect Moondance will be along any moment to give you another Healing."

He sighed, and made a tiny choking sound. She looked down, and saw to her confusion that he was crying.

"Vanyel," she asked, bewildered by the tears, and the strange, lost look in his eyes, "Van, what's wrong?"

"I—" he choked hopelessly. "I—after 'Lendel—they won't want me. The Heralds—they won't want me—"

"Oh, Van—" She closed her eyes against a surge of tears of her own, but these were born of joy. *Child—oh, child, you rise above my expectations. That was the very last thing I ever thought I'd hear from your lips right now.* "Van—*ke'chara*—the Heralds *will* want you. How can they not want you? You *are* a Herald already."

"I—am? I am?" He stared at her, bewildered, clearly unable to believe her.

She reached over to the chair and pulled her white cloak from it, draping it carefully over him. He clutched it, his eyes wide, his face reflecting all of his changing emotions, as he moved from hopelessness through surprise, to a joy that equaled her own.

"—there. There's your Whites to prove it. You have a bit more to learn; we'll be staying here for a few moons yet while Starwind teaches you—but Vanyel, what makes a Herald is the *heart*. A caring heart, that cares for others before itself. And *you are* a Herald."

He smiled then, a smile so sweet and so *happy* that it stopped her breath, and closed his eyes in absolute contentment, falling asleep with one hand still clutching the cloak to him.

—yes, Withen. You would be very proud. I know I am.

MAGIC'S
PROMISE

Dedicated to:
Elizabeth (Betsy) Wollheim
Who said—"Go for it"

CHAPTER 1

T HE BLUE LEATHER SADDLEBAGS and a canvas pack, all bulging
with filthy clothing and miscellaneous gear, landed in the corner of
Vanyel's room with three dull *thuds*. The lute, still in its padded leather case,
slithered over the back of one of the two overstuffed chairs and landed with
a softer *pumph*, to rest in the cradle of the worn red seat cushion. Once safely
there it sagged, leaning over sideways like a fat, drunken child. The dark
leather lute case glowed dully in the mid-morning sun still coming in the
single eastward-facing window. Two years of mistreatment had not marred
the finish *too* much, although the case was scuffed here and there, and had
been torn and re-mended with tiny, careful stitches along the belly.

Vanyel grimaced at the all-too-visible tear. *Torn? No; no tear would be that
even. Say* cut, *or* slashed *and it would be nearer the truth. Pray nobody else notices that.*

*Better the lute case than me . . . that came closer than I really want to think
about. I hope Savil never gets a good look at it. She'd know what that meant, and
she'd have a cat.*

Herald-Mage Vanyel took the other chair gracelessly, dropping all his
weight at once into the embrace of comfortable upholstered arms.

Home at last. Havens, I sound like the pack hitting the corner.

"O-o-oh." Vanyel leaned back, feeling every muscle in his body crying
out with long-ignored aches and strains. His thoughts fumbled their way
into his conscious mind through a fog of utter exhaustion. He wanted, more
than anything, to close his gritty eyes. But he didn't dare, because the moment he did, he'd fall asleep.

*Someday I'm going to remember I'm not sixteen anymore, and keep in mind that
I can't stay up till all hours, then rise with the dawn, and not pay for it.*

A few moments ago his Companion Yfandes had fallen asleep, standing
up in the stable, while he was grooming her. They'd started out on this last
leg of their journey long *before* dawn this morning, and had pushed their
limits, eating up the last dregs of their strength just to get to the sanctuary
of "home" the sooner.

Gods. If only I would never *have to see the Karsite Border again.*

No chance of that. Lord and Lady, if you love me, just give me enough time to get my wind back. That's all I ask. Time enough to feel like a human again, and not a killing machine.

The room smelled strongly of soap and the beeswax used to polish the furniture and wall paneling. He stretched, listening to his joints crack, then blinked at his surroundings.

Peculiar. Why doesn't this feel like home? He pondered for a moment, for it seemed to him that his modest, goldenoak-paneled quarters had the anonymous, overly-neat look of a room without a current occupant. *I suppose that's only logical,* he thought reluctantly. *They haven't been occupied, much. I've been living out of my packs for the last year, and before that I was only here for a couple of weeks at a time at most. Gods.*

It was a comfortable, warm—and quite average—room. Like any one of a dozen he'd tenanted lately, when he'd had the luxury of a guest room in some keep or other. Sparsely furnished with two chairs, a table, a desk and stool, a wardrobe, and a curtained, canopied bed in the corner. That bed was enormous—his one real indulgence: he tended to toss restlessly when—and if—he slept.

He smiled wryly, thinking how more than one person had assumed he'd wanted that particular bed for another reason entirely. *They'd never believe it if I told them Savil gets more erotic exercise than I do. Oh, well. Maybe it's a good thing I don't have a lover; he'd wake up black and blue. Always assuming I didn't strangle him by accident during a nightmare.*

But other than that bed, the room was rather plain. Only one window, and that one without much of a view. It certainly wasn't the suite he could have commanded—

But what good is a suite when I hardly see Haven, much less my own room?

He put his feet up on the low, scarred table between the chairs, in defiance of etiquette. He could have requisitioned a footstool—

But somehow I never think of it until I'm five leagues down the road headed out. There's never enough time for—for anything. Not since Elspeth died, anyway. And gods—please let me be wrong about Randale.

His eyes blurred; he shook his head to clear them. Only then did he see the pile of letters lying beside his feet, and groaned at the all-too-familiar seal on the uppermost one. The seal of Withen, Lord of Forst Reach and Vanyel's father.

Twenty-eight years old, and he still makes me feel fifteen, and in disgrace. Why me? he asked the gods, who did not choose to answer. He sighed again, and eyed the letter sourly. It was dauntingly thick.

Hellfire. It—and every other problem—can damned well wait until after I've had a bath. A bath, and something to eat that doesn't have mold on it, and something to drink besides boiled mud. Now, did I leave anything behind the last time I was here that was fit to wear?

He struggled to his feet and rummaged in the wardrobe beside his bed, finally emerging with a shirt and breeches of an old and faded blue that had once been deep sapphire. *Thank the gods.* Not *Whites, and I* won't *be wearing Whites when I get home. It's going to be so nice to wear something that doesn't stain when you look at it.* (Unfair, nagged his conscience—properly treated, the uniform of Heraldic Whites was so resistant to dirt and stains that the non-Heralds suspected magic. He ignored the insistent little mental voice.) *Although I don't know what I'm going to do for uniforms. Dear Father would hardly have known his son, covered in mud, stubbled, ashes in his hair.*

He emptied the canvas pack on the floor and rang for a page to come and take the mishandled uniforms away to be properly dealt with. They were in exceedingly sad shape; stained with grass and mud, and blood—some of it his own—some were cut and torn, and most were nearly worn-out.

He'd have taken one look and figured I'd been possessed. Not that the Karsites didn't try that, too. At least near-possession doesn't leave stains . . . not on uniforms, anyway. What am I going to do for uniforms? Oh, well—worry about that after my bath.

The bathing room was at the other end of the long, wood-paneled, stone-floored hallway; at mid-morning there was no one in the hall, much less competing for the tubs and hot water. Vanyel made the long trudge in a half-daze, thinking only how good the hot water would feel. The last bath he'd had—except for the quick one at the inn last night—had been in a cold stream. A *very* cold stream. And with sand, not soap.

Once there, he shed his clothing and left it in a heap on the floor, filled the largest of the three wooden tubs from the copper boiler, and slid into the hot water with a sigh—

—and woke up with his arms draped over the edges and going numb, his head sagging down on his chest, and the water lukewarm and growing colder.

A hand gently touched his shoulder.

He knew without looking that it had to be a fellow Herald—if it hadn't been, if it had even been someone as innocuous as a *strange* page, Vanyel's tightly-strung nerves and battle-sharpened reflexes would have done the unforgivable. He'd have sent the intruder through the wall before he himself had even crawled out of the depths of sleep. *Probably* by nonmagical means, but—magical or nonmagical, he suddenly realized that he could easily hurt someone if he wasn't careful.

He shivered a little. *I'm hair triggered. And that's not good.*

"Unless you plan on turning into a fish-man," Herald Tantras said, craning his head around the partition screening the tub from the rest of the bathing room and into Vanyel's view with cautious care, "you'd better get out of that tub. I'm surprised you didn't drown yourself."

"So am I." Vanyel blinked, tried to clear his head of cobwebs, and peered over his shoulder. "Where did *you* pop out of?"

"Heard you got back a couple of candlemarks ago, and I figured you'd head here first." Tantras chuckled. "I know you and your baths. But I must admit I didn't expect to find you turning yourself into a raisin."

The dark-haired, dusky Herald came around the side of the wooden partition with an armload of towels. Vanyel watched him with a half-smile of not-too-purely artistic appreciation; Tantras was as graceful and as handsome as a king stag in his prime. Not *shay'a'chern*, but a good friend, and that was all too rare.

And getting rarer, Vanyel thought soberly. *Though, Havens, I haven't exactly had my fill of romantic companionship either, lately . . . well, celibacy isn't going to kill me. Not by any stretch of the imagination. Gods, I should apply for the priesthood.*

There was concern in the older Herald's deep, soft eyes. "You don't look good, Van. I figured you'd be tired—but from the way you passed out here—it must have been worse out there than I thought."

"It was bad," Vanyel said shortly, reluctant to discuss the past year. Even for the most powerful Herald-Mage in the Circle, holding down the positions of *five* other Herald-Mages while they recovered from magical attack, drainage, and shock was *not* a mission he wanted to think about for a long while, much less repeat. He soaped his hair, then ducked his head under the water to rinse it.

"So I heard. When I saw you playing dead in the tub, I sent a page up to your room with food and wine and sent another one off for some of my spare uniforms, since we're about the same size."

"Name the price, it's yours," Vanyel said gratefully, levering himself out of the tub with a groan and accepting the towel Tantras held out to him. "I have *nothing* worth wearing right now in the way of uniforms."

"Lord and Lady—" the other Herald swore, looking at him with shock. "*What* have you been doing to yourself?"

Vanyel paused in his vigorous toweling, looked down, and was a little surprised *himself* at the evidence of damage. He'd always been lean—but now he was whipcord and bone and nothing else. Then there were the scars—knife and sword scars, a scoring of parallel claw marks on his chest where that demon had tried to remove his heart. Burn marks, too—he was striped from neck to knee with three thin, white lines where mage-lightning had gotten through his shields. And there were a few other scars that were souvenirs of his bout with a master of mage-fire.

"My job. Living on the edge. Trying to convince the Karsites that I was five Herald-Mages. Playing target." He shrugged dismissively. "That's all. Nothing any of you wouldn't have done if you could have."

"Gods, Van," Tantras replied, with a hint of guilt. "You make me feel like a shirker. I hope to hell it was worth what you went through."

Vanyel compressed his lips into a tight line. "I got the bastard that got Mardic and Donni. And you can spread that as official."

Tantras closed his eyes for a moment, and bowed his head. "It *was* worth it," he said faintly.

Vanyel nodded. "Worth every scar. I may have accomplished something else; that particular necromancer had a flock of pet demons and I turned them back on Karse when I killed him." He smiled, or rather, stretched his mouth a little. "I hope it taught the Karsites a lesson. I hope they end up proscribing magic altogether on their side of the Border. If you can believe anything out of Karse, there's rumor that they're doing just that."

Tantras looked up again. "Hard on the Gifted—" he ventured.

Vanyel didn't answer. He was finding it very hard to feel sorry for *anyone* on the Karsite side of the Border at the moment. It was uncharitable, un-Heraldic, but until certain wounds healed—and *not* the physical ones—he was inclined to be uncharitable.

"There's more silver in your hair, too," Tantras observed, head to one side.

Vanyel made a face, just as glad of the change in subject. "Node-magic. Every time I tap into it, more of my roots go white. Moondance k'Treva was pure silver by the time he was my age; I guess I'm more resistant." He smiled, it was faint, but a *real* smile this time. "One nice thing; all those white hairs give me respect I might not otherwise get!"

He finished drying himself and wrapped the towel around his waist.

Tantras grimaced again—probably noting the knife wound on his back—and handed him another towel for his hair.

"You already paid that forfeit, by the way," he said, plainly trying to lighten the conversation.

Vanyel stopped toweling off his hair and raised an eyebrow.

"You stood duty for me last Sovvan."

Vanyel clamped down on the sudden ache of loss and shrugged again. *You know you get depressed when you're tired, fool. Don't let it sink you.* "Oh, that. Any time, Tran. You know I don't like Sovvan-night celebrations, I can't handle the memorial services, and I don't like to be alone, either. Standing relay duty was as good as anything else to keep my mind off things."

He was grateful when Tantras didn't press the subject. "Think you can make it to your room all right?" the other asked. "I said you don't look good; I mean it. Falling asleep in the tub like that—it makes me wonder if you're going to pass out in the hall."

Vanyel produced something more like a dry cough than a laugh. "It's nothing about a week's worth of sleep won't cure," he replied. "And I'm sorry I won't be able to stand relay for you this year, but I have the Obligatory Familial Visit to discharge. I haven't been home in—gods, four years. And even then I didn't stay for more than a day or two. They're going to want me to make the long stay I've been promising. There's a letter from my father waiting for me that's probably reminding me of just that fact."

"Parents surely know how to load on the guilt, don't they? Well, if you're out of reach, Randale won't find something for you to do—but is that going to be *rest*?" Tantras looked half-amused and half-worried. "I mean, Van, that family of yours—"

"They *won't* come after me when I'm sleeping—which I fully intend to do a lot of." He pulled on his old, clean clothing, reveling in the feel of clean, soft cloth against his skin, and started to gather up his things. "And the way I feel right now, I'd just as soon play hermit in my rooms when I get there—"

"Leave that stuff," Tantras interrupted. "I'll deal with it. You go wrap yourself around a decent meal. You don't look like you've had one in months."

"I haven't. They don't believe in worldly pleasures down there. Great proponents of mortification of the flesh for the good of the spirit." Vanyel looked up in time to catch Tantras' raised eyebrow. He made a tragic face. "I know what you're thinking. That, too. *Especially* that. Gods. Do you have *any* idea what it was like, being surrounded by all those *devastatingly* hand-some young men and not daring to so much as *flirt* with one?"

"Were the young ladies just as devastatingly attractive?" Tantras asked, grinning.

"I would say so—given that the subject's fairly abstract for me."

"Then I think I can imagine it. Remind me to avoid the Karsite Border at all costs."

Vanyel found himself grinning back—another real smile, and from the heart. "Tran, gods—I'm glad to see you. Do you know how long it's been since I've been able to talk freely to someone? To *joke,* for Lady's sake? Since I was around people who don't wince away when I'm minus a few clothes?"

"Are you *on* about that again?" Tantras asked, incredulously. "Do you *really* think that people are nervous around you because you're shaych?"

"I'm *what?*" Van asked, startled by the unfamiliar term.

"Shaych. Short for that Hawkbrother word you and Savil use. Don't know where it came from, just seems like one day everybody was using it." Tantras leaned back against the white-tiled wall of the bathing room, folding his arms across his chest in a deceptively lazy pose. "Maybe because you're as prominent as you are. Can't go around calling the most powerful Herald-Mage in the Circle a 'pervert,' after all." He grinned. "He might turn you into a frog."

Vanyel shook his head again. "Gods, I *have* been out of touch to miss *that* little bit of slang. Yes, of course because I'm *shay'a'chern,* why else would people look at me sideways?"

"Because you scare the hell out of them," Tantras replied, his smile fading. "Because you *are* as powerful as you are; because you're so quiet and so solitary, and they never know what you're thinking. Havens, these days half the *Heralds* don't even know you're shaych; it's the Mage-Gift that makes them look at you sideways. Not that anybody around *here* cares about your bedmates a quarter as much as you seem to think. They're a lot more worried that—oh—a bird will crap on you and you'll level the Palace."

"Me?" Vanyel stared at him in disbelief.

"You. You've spent most of the last four or five years in combat zones. *We* know your reflexes are hypersensitive. Hellfire, that's why *I* came in here to wake you up instead of sending a page. We know what you can do. Van, nobody I've *ever* heard of was able to take the place of *five* Herald-Mages by himself! And the very idea of *one* person having that much power at his beck and call scares most people witless!"

Vanyel was caught without a reply; he stared at Tantras with the towel hanging limply from his hands.

"I'm telling you the plain truth, Van. I wish you'd stop wincing away from people with no cause. It's *not* your sexual preferences that scare them, it's *you*. Level the Palace, hell—they know you could level Haven if you wanted to—"

Vanyel came out of his trance of astonishment. "What do they think I am?" he scoffed, picking up his filthy shirt.

"They don't know; they haven't the Mage-Gift and most of them weren't trained around Herald-Mages. They hear stories, and they think of the Mage Wars—and they remember that once, before there *was* a Valdemar, there was a thriving land to the far south of us. Now the Dhorisha Plains are there—a *very* large, circular crater. No cities, no sign there ever *was* anything, not even two stones left standing. Nothing but grass and nomads. Van, *leave* that stuff; I'll pick up after you."

"But—" Vanyel began to object.

"Look, if *you* can spend most of a year substituting for five of *us,* then *one* of us can pick up after you once in a while." Tantras took the wet towels away from him, cutting off his objections before he could make them. "Honestly, Van."

"If you insist." He wanted to touch Tantras' mind to see if he really *meant* what he said. It seemed a fantastical notion.

But Tran had not invited, and a Herald did not intrude uninvited into another's mind, not unless there was an overriding need to do so.

"Is . . . that how *you* feel?" he asked in a whisper.

"I'm not afraid of you, but let me tell you, I wouldn't have your powers for *any* reward. I'm *glad* I'm just a Herald and not a Herald-Mage, and I don't know how you survive it. So just let me spoil you a little, all right?"

Vanyel managed a weak smile, troubled by several things—including that "just a Herald" business. That implied a division between Heralds and Herald-Mages that made him very uneasy. "All right, old friend. Spoil me. I'm just tired enough to let you."

The fog of weariness came between him and the corridor, and he was finding it all he could do to put one foot in front of the other. *Lady, bless you for Tantras. There aren't many even among the Heralds I trained with that will accept what I am as easily as he does. Whether it's that I'm a Mage or that I'm fey— although I can't see why Mage-powers would frighten someone. We've had Herald-Mages since there was a Valdemar.*

I wish he was as right about that as he thinks he is; I still think it's the other thing.

The stone was so cool and soothing to his feet; it eased the ache in them that was the legacy of too many hours—days—weeks—when he had slept fully clothed, ready to defend the Border in the blackest, bleakest hours of the night.

That reminder brought bleaker thoughts. Every time he came back to Haven it was with the knowledge that there would be fewer familiar faces to greet him. *So many friends gone—not that I ever had many to begin with. Lancir, Mardic and Donni, Regen, Dorilyn. Wulgra, Kat, Fretor. All gone. Not many left besides Tran. There's—Jays. Savil. Andy, and he's a Healer. Erdane, Breda, a couple of the other Bards. How can I be anything but solitary? Every year I'm more alone.*

True to Tantras' promise, Vanyel found an overflowing plate waiting for him beside the pile of letters. It held a pair of meat pies, soft white cheese, and apples, and beside the generous plate of food was an equally generous pitcher of wine.

I'd better be careful with that stuff. I'm not used to it anymore, and I bet it'll go straight to my head.

He stifled a groan as he sagged down into the empty chair, poured a goblet of wine, then picked up the topmost letter. He broke the seal on it, gritted his teeth, and started in.

To Herald-Mage Vanyel from Lord Withen Ashkevron of Forst Reach: My dear Son—

Vanyel nearly dropped the letter in surprise, and reread the salutation to be certain that his eyes hadn't played tricks on him.

Great good gods. "My dear Son?" I haven't been "dear," much less "Son" for—years! I wonder what happened—

He took a long breath and continued.

Though you might find it difficult to believe, I am pleased and grateful that you are going to be able to find the time for an extended visit home. Despite our differences, and some hard words between us, I am very proud of my Herald-Mage son. I may not care for some aspects of your life, but I respect your intelligence and good sense. I confess, Vanyel, that your old father has need of some of that good sense. I need your help in dealing with your brother Mekeal.

Vanyel nodded to himself with cynicism. *Now we come to it.*

He has made some excessively poor judgments since I turned over the management of some of the lands to him, but this spring he has outdone himself. He's taken the cattle—good, solid income-producing stock—off Long Meadow and installed sheep down there instead!

Vanyel chuckled. Whoever Withen had roped into being his scribe on this letter had reproduced his father's tones perfectly. He could *feel* the indignation rising from the page.

And as for that so-called "Shin'a'in warsteed" *he bought—and a more ill-tempered, ill-favored beast I never saw—the less said, the better! All these years I spent in building up the Forst Reach line—and he'll undo it all with one unmanageable stud! I feel sure he'll listen to you; you're a Herald—the King himself trusts your judgment. The boy has me ready to throw him down the blamed well!*

Vanyel shifted a little and reached for a wedge of cheese. This letter was proving to be a lot more enlightening than he'd had any reason to expect.

This is no time for Meke to be mucking about; not when there may be trouble across the Border. Maybe you remember that alliance marriage between Deveran Remoerdis of Lineas and Ylyna Mavelan of Baires? The one that brought a halt to the Linean-Baires war, and that brought that minstrel through here that you were so taken with as a boy? It doesn't seem to be working out. There've been rumors for years that the oldest child was a bastard—now Deveran seems to have given substance to those rumors; he's disinherited the boy in favor of the next in line. In some ways I can't blame him too much; even if the lad didn't look so much like his uncle—I've seen both the boy and the man, and the resemblance is uncanny—the rumors alone would have been enough to make his inheritance shaky. I wouldn't trust that entire Mavelan family, frankly. A pack of wizardly snakes, the lot of them, the only time they stop striking at each other is when they take on an outsider. I only thank the gods that they've stayed at each other's throats all this time. But there've been some nasty noises out of them about Tashir's disinheritance and if it gets to be more than noises, we may have trouble across the Border. Your brother is all fired up for a war, by the way. Gods, that is the last thing we need. I just thank the Lady that Randale had the good sense to send a plain Herald into Lineas as envoy, and not a Herald-Mage. A good solid Herald might be able to keep this from growing into another feud like the one the marriage was supposed to stop in the first place. The Lineans will certainly be far more inclined to listen to a plain Herald; they don't trust anything that smacks of wizardry, and given what the Mavelans did to them, who can blame them?

Vanyel bit his lip, the half-eaten scrap of cheese dangling forgotten from his fingers. Withen was showing a great deal more political astuteness than he'd ever given his father credit for. But this business in Lineas—

Please, he sent up a silent prayer. *Not now—*

It's evidently worrisome enough that Randale sent your sister Lissa and her Guard Company to keep a cross-Border eye on the Mavelans. You'd know what that would mean better than your old father, I think. If we're lucky and things stay calm, perhaps she can slip off for a few days' visit herself. I know you'd both like that. By the way—I hope you aren't planning on bringing any of your—friends—home with you, are you? You know it would upset your mother. You wouldn't want to upset your mother. By the hand of Radevel Ashkevron and my seal, Lord Withen Ashkevron.

Vanyel grimaced, dropped the letter back down on the table, and reached for the wine to take the bitter taste of those last words out of his mouth. He held the cool metal of the goblet to his forehead for a moment, an automatic reaction to a pain more emotional than physical.

:He doesn't mean to hurt, Chosen.: Yfandes' mind-voice touched the bitterness, but could not soothe it.

:Awake again, dearling? You should sleep—:

:Too much noise,: she objected. *:Equitation lessons, and I'm too tired to find a quiet corner of the Field. I'll just stand here by the stable and let the sun bake my sore muscles and wait for the babies to go away. Your father truly does not mean to hurt you.:*

Vanyel sighed, and picked up a meat pie, nibbling the flaky crust listlessly. *:I know that. It doesn't stop it from hurting. If I weren't so tired, it probably wouldn't hurt as much. If I weren't so tired, it might even be funny.:* He swallowed another gulp of wine, painfully aware that even the simple act of chewing was becoming an effort. He put the pie down.

:You have nothing left,: she stated. *:No reserves at all.:*

:That's ridiculous, love. It's just that last push we made. And if I haven't anything left, then neither have you—:

:Not true. I may be spent physically, but you are spent emotionally, magically, mentally. Chosen, beloved, you have not spared yourself since Elspeth Peacemaker died.:

:That's because nobody had a choice,: he reminded her, reaching for a piece of cheese, but holding it up and staring at it, not eating it, seeing other times and places. *:Everybody else has been pushed just as hard. The moment poor Randale took the throne that fragile peace she had made for us fell to pieces. We had no warning it was going to come to that. Mardic and Donni—:*

The cold hand of grief choked his throat. The lifebonded couple who had been such steadfast friends and supporters to him had been two of the first victims of the Karsite attacks. He could feel the echo of his grief in the mourning of Yfandes' mind-voice.

:Poor children. Goddess hold them—:

:'Fandes—at least they died together. I—could wish—: he cut off the thought before he could distress her. He contemplated the white wedge of cheese in his hand as if he had never seen anything like it, and then blinked, and began nibbling at it, trying to force the food around the knot of sorrow blocking his throat. He had to eat. He'd been surviving on handfuls of parched corn, dried fruit, and dried beef for too long. He *had* to get his strength back. It wouldn't be long before Randale would need him again. Well, all he really needed was a couple of weeks of steady meals and sleep. . . .

:You ask too much of yourself.:

:Who, me? Strange thoughts from a Companion. Who was it who used to keep nagging me about duty?: He tried to put a measure of humorous teasing into his own mind-voice, but it felt flat.

:But you cannot be twenty places at once, Chosen. You are no longer thinking clearly.:

The cheese had finally migrated inside him, and most of the lump in his throat was gone. He sighed and reached for the meat pie again. With enough wine to help, he *might* be able to get that down, too.

The trouble was, 'Fandes was right. For the past few months he'd been reduced to a level where he really wasn't thinking much at all—just concentrating on each step as it came, and trying to survive it. It had been like climbing a mountain at the end of a long and grueling race; just worrying about one handhold at a time. Not thinking about the possibility of falling, and not able to think about what he'd do when he got to the top. If he got to the top. If there was a top.

Stupid, Herald. Looking at the bark and never noticing the tree was about to fall on you.

The sun coming in his window had crept down off the chair and onto the floor, making a bright square on the brown braided rug. He chewed and swallowed methodically, not really tasting what he was eating, and stared at the glowing square, his mind going blank and numb.

:Randale uses you beyond your strength, because of the nodes,: Yfandes said accusingly, breaking into his near-trance. *:You should say something. He'd stop if he realized what he was doing to you. If you were like other Heralds, unable to tap them—:*

:If I were like other Heralds, the Karsites would be halfway to Haven now, instead of only holding the disputed lands,: he replied mildly. *:Dearest, there is no choice. I lost my chance at choices a long time ago. Besides, I'm not as badly off as you think. All I need is a bit of rest and I'll be fine. We're damned lucky I can use the nodes—and that I don't need to rest to recharge.:*

:Except that you must use your power to focus and control—:

He shook his head. *:Beloved, I appreciate what you're telling me, but this isn't getting us anywhere. I have to do what I'm doing; I'm a Herald. It's what any of the others would do in my place. It's what 'Lendel—:*

Grief—he fought it, clenching his hand hard on the arm of his chair as he willed his emotions into control. *Control yourself, Herald. This is just because you're tired, it's maudlin, and it doesn't do you or anyone else any good.*

:I could wish you were less alone.:

:Don't encourage me in self-pity, love. It's funny, isn't it?: he replied, his lips twitching involuntarily, though not with amusement. *:Dear Father seems to think I've been seducing every susceptible young man from here to the Border, and I've been damned near celibate. The last was—when?:* The weeks, the months, they all seemed to blur together into one long endurance trial. A brief moment of companionship, then a parting; inevitable, given his duties and Jonne's.

:Three years ago,: Yfandes supplied, immediately. *:That rather sweet Guardsman.:*

Vanyel remembered the person, though not the time.

"Hello. You're The Herald-Mage, aren't you?"

Vanyel looked up from the map he was studying, and smiled. He couldn't help it—the diffident, shy smile the Guardsman wore begged to be answered.

"Yes—are you—"

"Guardsman Jonne. Your guide. I was born not half a league from here." The guileless expression, the tanned face and thatch of hair, the tiny net of humor lines about the thoughtful hazel eyes, all conspired to make Vanyel like this man immediately.

"Then you, friend Jonne, are the direct answer to my prayers," he said.

Only later, when they were alone, did he learn what other prayers the Guardsman had an answer for—

:Jonne. Odd for such a tough fighter to be so diffident, even gentle. Though why he should have been shy, when he was five years older and had twice my—uh—experience—:

:Your reputation, beloved. A living legend came down off his pedestal and looked to him for company.: Yfandes sent him an image of a marble saint-statue hopping out of its niche and wriggling its eyebrows in a come-hither look. There was enough of a tired giggle in her mind-voice to get an equally tired chuckle out of him. But he sobered again almost immediately. *:And that lasted how long? Two months? Three? Certainly not more.:*

:You were busy—you had duties—both of you. It was your duties that parted you.:

:I was,: he replied bitterly, *:a fool. More than duties would have parted us in*

time. I know exactly what I'm trying to do—when I admit it to myself. I'm trying to replace 'Lendel. I can't, I can't ever, so why do I even bother to try? A love like that happens once in a lifetime, and I'm not doing myself or my would-be partners any favor by trying to recreate it. I know it, and once the first glow wears off, they know it. And it isn't fair to them.:

Silence from Yfandes. There really wasn't much she *could* say. He was left to contemplate the inside of his own thoughts, as faint sounds of distant people and a bit of birdsong drifted in his window.

Damn it, I'm feeling sorry for myself again. Heralds are all lonely; it isn't just me. We're different, made different by our Gifts, made even more so by the Companions, then driven even further away from ordinary people by this fanatic devotion to duty of ours. Herald-Mages are one step lonelier than that. He couldn't help himself; the next thought came automatically, despite his resolution not to fall into a morass of self-pity. *Then there's me. Between the level of my Gift and my sexual preferences—*

He buried his face in his free hand. *Gods. I am a fool. I have 'Fandes. She loves me in a way no one else ever will or ever did, except 'Lendel. That ought to be enough. It really ought—if I wasn't so damned selfish.*

She interrupted his thoughts. *:Van, you almost need a friend more than a lover. A different kind of friend than me; one that can touch you. You need to be touched, you humans—:* Her mind-voice trailed off, grew dim, in the way that meant she was losing her battle to fatigue and had fallen asleep again.

"You humans." That phrase said it all. *That* was the telling difference, he realized suddenly. The telling lack. Yfandes was not human—and she never *felt* exactly the way a human would. There was always the touch of the "other" about her, and the strange feeling he got, sometimes, that she was hiding something, some secret that she could only share with another Companion. It was not a comfortable feeling. He was just as glad she wasn't awake to pick it up from him.

He dragged himself up out of the depths of his chair to rummage paper and a pen and inkpot out of his desk. He slouched back down into the cushions and chewed thoughtfully on the end of the pen, trying to compose something that wouldn't set Withen off.

To Lord Withen Ashkevron of Forst Reach from Herald-Mage Vanyel Ashkevron. So far, so good.

Dear Father: I'm sorry I've had to put off spending any length of time at home— but duty must always come before anything else, and my duty as a Herald is to the orders of my King.

He licked his lips, wondering if that was a bit excessively priggish. *Probably not. And I don't think I'll say anything about how visits of less than a day keep Mother from having vapors at me.* He reached for the goblet again, and another swallow of wine, before continuing.

As for Meke, I'll do my best with him, Father. You must remember though, that although I am a Herald I am also his brother—he may be no more inclined to listen to me than he does to you. With regard to your news about Baires and Lineas—may the gods help us—I have seen far too much of conflict of late. I was praying for some peace, and now you tell me we may have a Situation on our very doorstep. Unless Randale asks me to intervene, there isn't much I can do. Let us hope it doesn't come to that. I promise I will try to put some sense into Meke's head about that as well; perhaps when he has heard some of what I have seen, a war will no longer seem quite so attractive. Perhaps when he sees some of what war has done to me—no, Father, I was not badly hurt, but I picked up an injury or two that left scars. It may be that will impress him.

He closed his eyes and carefully picked out the least loaded words he could think of for the next sentence. When he thought he had it, he concentrated on setting it carefully down on the paper so that there could be no mistake.

With regard to my—friends; I promised you ten years ago that I would never indulge in anything that you did not approve of or that made you uncomfortable under your roof. Do you still find it so difficult to believe that I would keep my word?

He nobly refrained from adding—"Odd, no one else seems to have that problem." That would *not* serve any purpose, and would only make his father guilty, and then angry.

I do have a request to make of you, and a reminder of a promise you made to me at the same time. You pledged to keep Mother from flinging young women at me—under other conditions I would not feel that I needed to remind you of this promise, but I truly cannot handle that particular situation this time, Father. I'm exhausted; you can't know how exhausted. All I really want is some peace, some quiet time to rest and catch up with the family matters. Please do me this one small favor; I don't think it's too much to ask. Yours, Vanyel.

He folded the letter and sealed it quickly, before he had a chance to add a postscript to that temptingly empty space at the bottom. *All I want from you and Mother is to be left alone. I need that rest. Before I fall on my face.*

He picked up the second letter, and heaved a sigh of relief. *Liss. Oh, bless you, big sister. My antidote to Father.*

To Herald-Mage Vanyel Ashkevron from Guard-Captain Lissa Ashkevron:

Dearest Van—if half of what I've been hearing about you is true, I'm tempted to abandon my command and kidnap you and hide you someplace until you've had some rest! Thank the gods somebody saw enough reason to give you a leave! And before you bleat to me about "duty," just you remember that if you kill yourself with over-work you won't be around to do that duty!

Vanyel smiled, biting his lip to keep from chuckling. Good old Liss!

I should tell you what's going on out here, since you may be riding right into another hotbed of trouble. Deveran of Lineas has disinherited his eldest. The boy supposedly has mage-power, which, since his mother does not, is being read that he is probably a bastard. The Lineans in any case are not likely to allow anyone with Mage-Gifts to rule over them—but this Tashir is altogether too like his Uncle Vedric for comfort. And Vedric is protesting the tacit slur on his "good name"—not that he has one—and is being backed by the entire Mavelan Clan. I suppose it is a bit much to imply that your brother-in-law was fornicating with his own sister before your marriage to her. Havens bless—talk about soiled goods!

At any rate, I suspect there's far more to it than that; what, I don't know, but the Mavelans seldom unite for anything and they're uniting on this one. I much doubt it's over concern for Vedric's reputation or tender feelings for Tashir. My guess is there's another attempt at acquiring Lineas in the offing—but since they're both clients-by-alliance to Valdemar, the Mavelans can't just begin flinging mage-fire over there. Randale would definitely take exception to that.

So here we are, camped on the Border, and watching for one false note. What really worries me is that it's Vedric who's fronting this; they're all snakes, but he's a viper. The only reason he's not Lord Mavelan is because his brother's been very lucky—or smart enough to buy some really good spies and bodyguards. Vedric is definitely the most ambitious of the lot; my guess is he's been promised Lineas if he can get it quietly. Through Tashir, perhaps.

Vanyel found his eyebrows rising with every sentence. Lissa had come a long way from the naive swordswoman who had accepted that commission in the Guard. She was a *lot* more politically astute than Van would have dreamed—which gave him the second surprise of the day. First Father, then Liss—no bad thing, either. No one living in the days of King Randale could afford to be politically naive.

I hope to steal away long enough to spend at least a little time with you, love, but don't count on it. There's nothing going on overtly, but the whole thing feels very touchy to me, like the moments before the storm hits. If I feel the situation has calmed down enough, I'll come. Be well. Love, Liss.

That was by far and away the easiest letter to answer he'd had in a long time. He scrawled a quick reply of affection, including the fact that he missed her badly, sealed the note, and laid it with the other.

There were two or three other letters, all nothing more than invitations to various entertainments; hunting parties, mostly, at noble estates, parties meant to last a week or more. Despite the fact that he *never* attended these things—wouldn't have even if he'd had the *time*—the invitations never stopped coming. He wrote brief, polite notes, and sat back again, staring at the packs in the corner. He knew he had to sort things out of his traveling kit for his trip home—and he just couldn't muster the energy. It was so much easier just to sit and let all the kinks in his muscles respond to the soft—motionless!—chair.

A rap at the door interrupted his lethargy; it was the page sent by Tantras, with the promised uniforms. And one more thing; a note—and Vanyel recognized Randale's handwriting on the outside.

Oh, gods—no, no! For a moment he tensed, fearing another call to duty on the eve of his promised chance to rest. Then he saw that it wasn't sealed, not even by Randale's personal seal.

He relaxed. No seal meant it wasn't official. He took it from the wide-eyed page and motioned to the youngster to stay for a reply.

Vanyel; come by after Court and say good-bye—don't come before then; if I'm not being official, I don't have to find something for you to do. Or rather, I don't have to assign you to one of the hundred messes that needs dealing with. I'm sorry you aren't staying, but I understand, and if you weren't planning on leaving, I'd probably tie you to Yfandes and drive you off before I work you to death. But do come by; Jisa wants to see her "Uncle Van" before he vanishes again. Randale.

:*If you don't make the time to see her, I'll bite you when you try to saddle me.*:

Vanyel had to smother a laugh. :*Woke up again, did you? Why is it anything about Jisa snags your attention like nothing else does?*:

:*Because she's adorable—as most six-year-old humans are not. Besides, she's your daughter.*:

:*I'm just grateful she doesn't look anything like me,*: he replied, sobering. :*If she'd gotten these silver eyes of mine, for instance—or black hair when both Randale and Shavri are light brown. Don't you dare let that slip to anyone!*:

:*Not even another Companion,*: she reassured him. :*I'm not sure I understand what the problem could be, though. Shavri won't let Randale marry her, so should it matter who Jisa's father is?*:

:*It would disturb some folk, because they're lifebonded. Besides, we don't want anyone to know that Randale's sterile. If he has to make an alliance marriage—that* could ruin it. And there are damn few people even inside the Heralds who would understand someone wanting a child badly enough to go to bed with someone other than her lifebonded.:

Yfandes' mind-voice was hesitant. :Truth, Chosen—it seems to bother you.:

Vanyel leaned farther back into the chair, scrawling replies to the invitations with half his attention. It did bother him, and in a way that made him reluctant to even think about Shavri, sometimes. :It's not that,: he temporized. :It's just that I'm worried about them.:

But the uneasy feeling continued, an uncomfortable unhappiness that he couldn't define. So he continued hastily, :Poor Shavri; you can't know how much she wanted that child. That was the only reason we did it.:

:You like her.:

:Of course I like her!: he answered—again, just a shade too quickly. :She and Randale—they're friends; how could I have told them no?: He shied away from examining his feelings too closely. :Besides, it was never anything more than a—physical exercise for either of us. No more involved for me, certainly, than dancing. Shavri being a Healer, she could make sure she "caught" the first time. Neither of us were emotionally involved, or ever likely to be.:

:I suppose that could have been a problem,: she replied.

:Exactly. That's why Shavri and Randale asked me to help in the first place: I was perfect; a Herald, already a friend, physically able, and not going to get romantically entangled.:

:Don't you . . . want the child, sometimes?: Yfandes sounded wistful. Vanyel was a bit surprised.

:Frankly, no. I'm not very paternal. It takes more than seed to make a father, love. Great good gods, can you see me as a parent? I'd be awful. Randale has what I lack in that department.: His thoughts darkened, as he recalled what had been bothering him since he scanned the palace when they rode in. :'Fandes, I'm worried about them. When Lancir died—truth, I almost expected Taver to Choose me King's Own. Instead—instead he chose Shavri, and I'm desperately afraid it wasn't because she was Randale's lifebonded. I'm afraid it was because she's a Healer.:

There was a long silence on Yfandes' part. Then, :Why haven't you said something before this?:

:Because—I wasn't sure. I've been wrong about things so many times—and I didn't really want to think about it. Shavri told me once that she was afraid that Randale's sterility was a symptom of something worse. I didn't know what to say, so I told her not to worry about it. But now—you know how sensitive I am; follow my line to Randale—:

Vanyel could "feel" every Herald and Herald-Mage in Haven, all tied to him by a kind of tenuous network of lines of life-energy, with every identity as plain to him as if he could see the faces. Most Herald-Mages could follow the line to anyone who had shared magic with them; Vanyel could follow the line of anyone who had "shared magic" just by virtue of being a Herald. He had the line that led to Randale without even thinking about it, and "felt" Yfandes follow it down with him, Seeing what he Saw.

:There's—something not right.: she said, after a moment's study. :Something out of balance. Physically, not mentally or emotionally. But I can't tell what it is.:

:Exactly,: he agreed. :I felt it as soon as we came in; he wasn't like that when we left. I wish I was a Healer-Adept like Moondance k'Treva or even little Brightstar. They're much better at understanding imbalances than I am.: He rubbed his forehead, his headache starting again.

:I don't think I will ever forget the look on Shavri's face when you told her this wasn't the first time you'd done someone the favor of—uh—stud service.: Yfandes' mind-voice colored yellow with laughter, and he was just as pleased to change the subject.

:Moondance and Starwind wanted a child to raise, and neither of them can function with a female,: he reminded her, :and Snowlight was willing to have twins, one for her, one for them.:

:You certainly produce lovely children.:

:Brightstar is a good lad,: he said, shyly. :They're rightly proud of him—and that's their doing, not mine. But I'm beginning to think I ought to rent myself out. Do you think I could command the same fees as a Shin'a'in stud?:

:Oh, at least,: she giggled, as he reached for pen and paper. :Double if your Gift and beautiful silver eyes breed true!:

He smothered a chuckle, and turned all his attention to the reply the page was waiting for. Dearest friends; of course I'm coming by. Don't you realize that you're my last taste of sanity before I spend the fall with my lunatic family?

He sealed this last note and handed them all to the page to take away. He stood and hauled the packs over to his bed, resisting the temptation to throw himself there instead of his belongings, and began sorting out the items he'd need for his visit home.

There was an awful lot of money in there—money he didn't remember getting, but it all seemed to be in those silly little sealed "stipend" bags, most of them still unopened. At least a half-dozen. Then again—he hadn't had much to spend it on, going from post to post like a madman, never getting regular meals, seldom sleeping in a real bed. He combined all the bags into one, and tossed the empties onto the table for the servants to collect. Then had second thoughts, and added some coins to the pile of empty bags. No harm in leaving a little something for the ones who kept things picked up for him; they did a good job. They *could* have just sealed the room up until he returned, but they kept it open and aired, even though that meant extra work. He'd acquired a much greater appreciation for good servants since he'd become a Herald.

He returned to his packs; there were a lot of small, valuable trinkets he just barely remembered being gifted with in there.

:Why do people insist on giving me all this stuff?: he asked Yfandes, a little irritably. *:It isn't bribery; I'd have sensed that and given it back.:*

:I told you,: she replied. *:They wanted something of the excitement of your life to rub off on them, so they give you things. That's what it means to be Herald Vanyel, second only to King's Own.:*

He made a sound of contempt, as he sorted through the things; jewelry mostly. *:I bet they think I have everything I could want. I suppose on a lot of levels, I do. I'm ungrateful, I guess. I don't know why I'm not happier.:*

:Vanyel Ashkevron, you are being an idiot,: she replied acidly. *:Stop feeling guilty about feeling like you're overworked and unhappy! You're only human!:*

:Beloved, I think you know me better than I know myself.: He laughed to keep from wincing; she was cutting a bit too close to the truth. His hand fell on more jewelry, and he changed the subject. *:Ah, now these I remember; I bought them honestly.:* He selected the three trinkets that he had thought would please Randale, Shavri, and Jisa when he'd seen them; a cloak-clasp for Randale in the form of a vine of Heal-All twining around a beryl the green of a Healer's robes—a pendant that matched for Shavri—and a wonderful little articulated carving of a Companion complete with formal panoply for Jisa. The rest went back into the pack; he would need presents for the mob at Forst Reach, and there was surely enough there to make a start. He paused with the last piece, a crystal mage-focus stone (rose-quartz, sadly, and not a stone he cared to work with) still in his hand.

:Think Savil would like this?:

:You know she would. Rose-quartz is her Prime Focus, and you don't often see a crystal that big or that clear.:

:Good.: He put it with the little gifts on his bedside table.

The bed looked better than ever.

:Courtesy calls,: Yfandes reminded him. *:Then you can take a nap. Lazy.:*

He groaned. *:Too true. Oh, well.:* He picked up the crystal and slipped it into his pocket. *:Savil first. She'll put me in a good mood for the others.:*

There was a touch of smile in Yfandes' mind-voice as he slipped out his door and down the hall—still barefoot. *:You don't really need to be put in a good mood for Jisa do you?:*

He grinned; although she couldn't see it, she would feel the rise in his spirits. *:No—but if Randi ends up giving me an assignment anyway, I won't feel so bad about it!:*

CHAPTER 2

◆

VANYEL'S ROOM WAS in the "old Palace," the original building dating back to King Valdemar, in the oldest section still used for Heralds' quarters. Savil's suite was in the new wing added some fourteen years ago. She no longer occupied the suite he'd had when he first was put in her custody by Lord Withen—she didn't teach more than one pupil at a time these days, so having no use whatsoever for a suite with four bedrooms, she'd moved instead to another suite, still on the ground floor, though without an outside door to the gardens. Moving had been something of a relief to both of them; her former quarters held too many sad memories, memories of the painful weeks following Tylendel's suicide.

Vanyel had helped with that move, since it had coincided with their return—him in full Whites—from the Pelagir Hills and the Vale of the *Tayledras* k'Treva. The touchiest part had been moving the magic Work Room: a transfer of energies rather than physical furniture. Savil had left that to *him*; since they'd shared magic so intimately and so often he knew her "resonances," and more importantly, her protections "recognized" him.

The magical transfer had been a kind of graduation exercise for him—not to prove to Savil that he could do it, but to prove his ability—and his training—to the rest of the Herald-Mages. He could still remember Jaysen Kondre's face, when he'd stood in the middle of the new Work Room and "called" the shields and protections—and they'd swarmed up and followed him like bees with a migrating queen, settling into place as solidly as if they'd been cast on the new room from the beginning. Jays had looked as if he'd just swallowed a live fish.

Savil's suite now was of four rooms only; her protege's bedroom, and her bedroom, sitting room, and Work Room.

:Van—: Yfandes said sleepily into his mind. *:Ask Jays to get you a Work Room this time. You need a Work Room.:*

:I thought you were asleep. How many times do I have to tell you that I don't need one before you'll believe me?: he replied.

:*But*—: Even after all these years, Yfandes *still* wasn't used to the idea that Vanyel's methods weren't *quite* the same as the other Herald-Mages'.

:*I can use Savil's if I'm working formal magic. When I'm in the field, I don't have time to muck about with formalities.*.:

:*But*—:

He shook his head, glad that the only other people about were used to Heralds and the way they seemed to mutter at themselves. When he'd been in the field, he'd frequently gotten knowing looks and averted eyes. :*Go back to sleep, 'Fandes.*:

She gave up. *You ought to know by now that you can't out-stubborn me, sweetling.*

Savil was still his master when it came to magic that required long, painstaking setups. Vanyel's talents lay elsewhere. He had neither master nor even peer when a crisis called for instant decision and instant action. It was that ability to use his powers on a moment's notice that made him second-rank to no one in power, and second only to Shavri in the Heraldic Circle; that, and the ability to use the lines and currents of power, and the nodes where they met, as the Ancients had done and the *Tayledras* could still do, though none of the other Herald-Mages except Savil could.

He squinted against the light as he entered the new wing. The paneling of the new section had not had time to darken with age: the halls here seemed very bright, though they no longer smelled "new."

This section feels even emptier than the old quarters; I don't think more than half the ground-floor rooms have claimants, there's less than that on the second floor, and none at all on the third. I can't see how we'll ever fill it.

The hall was so quiet he could hear the murmur of voices from one of the farther suites without straining his ears at all. A quick Look gave him identities; Savil and Jays. He paused for a moment and sent the tentative little mind-probe on ahead of him that was the Thought-sensing equivalent of a knock on the door, and got a wave of welcome from both minds before he had taken two steps.

Now sure of his reception—and that he wasn't interrupting anything—he crossed the remaining distance to Savil's door and pushed it open.

Savil, her silver hair braided like a coronet on the top of her head, was enthroned in her favorite chair, a huge, blue monstrosity as comfortable as it was ugly. Tall Jaysen (who always looked bleached, somehow) was half-sprawled on her couch, but he rose at Vanyel's entrance—then did a double take, and staggered back a step hand theatrically clutched to his chest.

"My heart!" he choked. "Savil, *look* at your nephew! Barefoot, shaggy-headed, and *shabby*! Where in Havens has our peacock gone?"

"He got lost somewhere south of Horn," Vanyel replied. "I last saw him in a tavern singing trios with my mind and my wits. I haven't seen either of *them* in a while, either."

"Well, you surely couldn't tell it from the reports we got back," Jaysen answered, coming quickly forward and clasping his forearms with no sign of the uneasiness he'd once had around the younger Herald. "There's three new songs about you out of your year down south, in case you didn't know. Very accurate, too, amazingly enough."

Vanyel sighed. "Gods. Bards."

Jaysen cocked his graying head to the side. "You should be used to it by now. You keep doing things that make *wonderful* songs, so how can they resist?" He grinned. "Maybe you should stop. Become a bricklayer, for instance."

Vanyel shook his head and groaned. "It's not my fault!"

Jaysen laughed. "I'd best be off before that trio wrecks my workroom. Did Savil tell you? I've been given the proteges *you'd* have gotten if you hadn't been in a combat zone. Count your blessings—one's a farmgirl who had *much* rather be a fighter than a Herald-Mage, thank you; one's a very bewildered young man who can't for a moment imagine why *he* was Chosen and as a result has no confidence whatsoever; and the third is an *overly* confident sharpster who's actually a convicted lawbreaker!"

"Convicted of what?" Vanyel asked, amused at the woebegone expression on Jaysen's face.

"Chicanery and fraud. The old shell-and-pea game at Midsummer Fair; he was actually Chosen on the way to his sentencing, if you can believe it."

"I can believe it. It's keeping you busy, anyway."

"It is that. It's good to see you, Van." Jaysen hesitated a moment, and then put one hand on his shoulder. "Vanyel—" He locked his pale, near-colorless blue eyes with Vanyel's, and Van saw disturbance there that made *him* uneasy. "Take care of yourself, would you? We *need* you. I don't think you realize how much."

He slipped out the door before Vanyel could respond. Van stared after him with his mouth starting to fall open.

"What in the name of sanity was *that* about?" he asked, perplexed, turning back to his aunt, who had not left the comfortable confines of her chair. She looked up at him measuringly.

"Have you any notion how many Herald-Mages we've lost in the last four years?" she asked, her high-cheekboned face without any readable expression.

"Two dozen?" he hazarded.

Now she looked uneasy. Not much, but enough that he could tell. "Slightly more than half the total we had when you and I came back from k'Treva. We can't replace them fast enough. The Mage-Gift was never that common in the first place, and with a rate of attrition like that—" She grimaced. "I haven't told you about this before, because there was nothing you could do about it, but after the deaths of the last year, you should know the facts. You become more important with each loss, Van. You were the *only* one available to send to replace those five casualties on the Karsite Border. You were the only one who *could* replace all five of them, all by yourself. That's why we couldn't relieve you, lad, or even send you one other Herald-Mage to give you a breather. We simply didn't have anyone to send. Speaking of which—" She raised one eyebrow as she gave him such a penetrating look that Vanyel felt as if she was seeing past his clothes to count his ribs and mark each of his scars. "—*you* look like hell."

"Can't *anyone* greet me without saying that?" he complained. "You, Tran, Jays—Can't you tell me I'm looking seasoned? Or poetic? Or something?"

"Horseturds; you don't look 'seasoned,' you look like hell. You're too damned thin, your eyes are sunken, and if my Othersenses aren't fooling me, you've got no reserves—you're on your last dregs of energy."

Vanyel sighed, and folded himself up at her feet, resting his back against the front of her chair and his head against her knee. *That* was "home," and always would be—as Savil was more his mother than his birth-mother ever could be. "It's nothing," he replied. "At least nothing a little sleep won't cure. Come on, you know how you feel at the end of a tour of duty. You're still *your* old tactful self, Savil."

"Tact never was one of my strong traits, lad," she replied, and he felt her hand touch, and then begin stroking his hair. He closed his eyes and relaxed; muscles began to unknot that must have been tensed up for the past year. For the first time in months there was no one depending on him, looking to him for safety. It was nice to feel sheltered and protected, instead of *being* the shelter and protection. *There are times when I'd give anything to be a child again, and this is perilous close to one of them.*

"I am mortally tired, Savil," he admitted, finally. "I need this leave. It won't take long to rest up—but I do need the rest. You know, I didn't *ask* for this. I didn't *want* to be a Herald-Mage, I wanted to be a Bard. I sure as Havens didn't *ask* to be 'Vanyel Dragonsbreath,' or whatever it is they're calling me."

"Demonsbane."

The increasingly shrill tone of his own voice finally penetrated his fog. "Savil, I—am I whining?"

She chuckled throatily. "You're whining, son."

"Hellfire," he said. "I swear, every time I lose a little sleep, I turn fifteen. A *bratty* fifteen, at that. I'm amazed you put up with me."

"Darling boy," she said, her hand somehow stroking his headache away, "you've earned a little whine. You're thinned out in more ways than one." She sighed. "That's the one thing I regret most about the past few years— you never do or say anything anymore without thinking about it. That's good for Herald-Mage Vanyel, but I'm not entirely certain about Vanyel Ashkevron." There was a long silence behind him, then—"There's no joy in you anymore, *ke'chara*. No joy at all. And that bothers me more than the circled eyes and thin cheeks."

"We've all endured too much the last five years to be able to afford to do things without thinking. As for joy—is there joy anywhere, anymore? We've all lost so much—so many friends gone—"

Another long silence. "I don't know."

He cleared his throat, and changed the subject. "I didn't feel a third here. You aren't teaching?"

"Can't; don't have the stamina anymore. Not and be Guardian, too."

He'd half expected that. And he half expected what quarter. "So they made you Guardian? In whose place?"

"Lancir's. Shavri can't; she tried, and she can't. The four Guardians *have* to be Herald-Mages. We'd hoped Healing-Gift was close enough, but she didn't pass the last trial. I think she's relieved. It's a pity; the Guardian of the East has always been King's Own, but—"

"In that case, the present I brought you may be handy." He shifted so that he could get at his pocket, and pulled out the crystal. He closed his hand around it, feeling all the smooth planes and angles pressing into his palm. "Don't you need a Prime Focus stone of your own to set in the Web? I thought you didn't have a good Prime to use for anything but personal stuff."

"You do, and I put a stone there, but it was a Secondary Focus, an am- ethyst, and not what I'd have—"

He raised the hand holding the crystal above his head, parting his fingers so she could see it, but not opening his eyes or moving his head.

"Sunsinger's Glory!" she breathed. "Where did you find that?"

"Gifted me," he said, as the weight left his hand. "People keep *giving* me things, Savil. An opal or amber I could have used—still—*you* can use it, so do."

"I shall." Her hand began to stroke his hair again, and he heard the little *click* as she set the stone down on the table beside her. "That will make my job a bit easier." She chuckled richly. "I thought I was so lucky when it turned out my resonances worked best with rosequartz—not like Deedre who was stuck with topaz, or Justen, with ruby. Nice, cheap stone, I thought. Won't have to go bankrupt trying to get a good one. Little did I know how hard it was to find a good, unflawed, *large* crystal!"

"Little did you know you were going to turn out a Guardian," he replied drowsily.

"Hmm, true." Her mind touched softly on his. :*Vanyel, ke'chara, you are not well. There's more silver in this lovely black hair.*:

He couldn't lie mind-to-mind, not to her, so he temporized. :*The silver's from working with the nodes; you should know that. As for the rest—I'm just weary, teacher-love. Just weary. Too many hours fighting too many battles, and all of it too much alone.*:

:*Heart-wounded?*: Her Mind-voice was etched and frosted with concern.

:*No, heart-whole. Just lonely. Only that. You know. I haven't time these days to go courting a friend. Not on battle-lines. And I won't ask for more than friendship—gods, how could I ask anyone to make an emotional commitment to somebody who's out trying daily to get himself killed? I'm better off alone.*:

The hand on his hair trembled a little, and rested.

:*I know,*: she replied, finally. :*There are times when I wish with all my heart I could take some of that from you.*:

:*Now, now, don't encourage me in my self-pity. Honestly, you and 'Fandes—*: "If wishes were fishes, we'd walk on the sea, teacher-love," he said aloud. "I'd rather you could keep Father and Mother off when I'm home."

"So you're finally making that major visit they've been plaguing you for?" She took the unspoken cue and switched to less-intimate vocal speech.

"Randale sent me word just as I was leaving the Border. Several weeks leave of absence at least. And I must say, that while I'm looking forward to the rest, I'm not at all sanguine about this little sojourn in the bosom of my loving family."

"Out of experience I'm forced to tell you: even if they behave themselves, you're all too likely to find yourself the court of appeal for every family feud that's been brewing for the last ten years," she said, and laughed. "And no one will like your judgments and everyone will accuse you of favoritism."

He opened his eyes and moved his head around, propping his chin against the seat cushion. "And Mother will haul every eligible female for *leagues* about in on 'visits,' and Father will go cross-eyed trying to see if I'm attempting to seduce *any* of the young men on the estate. And dear Father Leren will thunder sermons about fornication and perversity every holy day, and glare. Jervis will snipe at me, try to get me angry, and glare. And Mother's maid Melenna will chase me all over the property. And on and on." He made mournful eyes at her. "If I hadn't promised, I'd be greatly tempted to take my chances with Randale finding another emergency and stay here."

"I thought Lissa was stationed right near Forst Reach. She always *used* to be able to protect you." Savil gave him a half smile. "She was a very *good* little protector when you were a child."

"I don't think she's going to feel she can leave her assigned post," he said. "It seems *that* Border is heating up."

"Just what we need. Another Situation."

"Exactly."

"You could have dealt with this earlier, I suppose."

He snorted. "Not likely. That whole monstrous mess of tangled emotions and misconception is why I never have spent more than a day at home if I can help it. If it isn't Mother flinging women at me, it's Father watching me out of the corner of his eye." He throttled down savagely on the wave of bitterness that crawled up his throat, but some of it emerged despite his good intentions. "Gods, Savil, I am *so damned tired* of the whole dance. I really need to take a couple of weeks to rest, and where else can I go? *You* know I daren't stay here; if I do, Randale will recruit me. He won't want to, he won't mean to, but something will come up, and he'll have to—and *I* won't be able to say no. If I went to Liss—assuming she *has* someplace to put me!—she'd end up doing the same thing. I'm a tool, and neither of them dares let a tool stand idle, even when it might break."

"Easy, lad," Savil cautioned, her face clouded and troubled.

He grimaced. "Did it again. Sorry. I won't break. I'm not sure I *can* break. The fact is, I still look all right, and I really *don't* want Randi to guess how drained out I am. If he knows, he'll feel guilty, and there's nothing he can do. He *has* to do what he does to me. So—" Vanyel shrugged. "The strain doesn't show; it won't take long to put right. I'm as much to blame for the overload as Randi. I *could* say 'no'—but I never have the heart to."

"Maybe you should choose somewhere to go besides Forst Reach. Or only stay there for a day or two, then go off visiting friends, or by yourself."

"I don't want to go off somewhere alone, I'll just brood. And I haven't anyone to go *to;* k'Treva is too far away. You, at least, have had Andy for longer than I've known you." He sighed. "I'm sorry, I'm whining again. I can't seem to help it, which might be a symptom of how on edge I am. *That* is the only thing that really worries me; I'm hair-triggered and dangerous, and I need some peace to get balanced again. All I can hope is that Mother and Father decide that I look as bad as you and Jays think, and leave me alone for a bit. Long enough to get some reserves back, anyway."

It was the closest he'd come to admitting that he wasn't really certain how much—or how little—reserves he still had, and he quelled the rest of what he almost said.

"You don't look good; even *they* should see that, *ke'chara.*" She toyed with a bit of his hair, and worried at her lower lip with her teeth. "You know, *I* haven't been back in—ye gods, not since I checked you all for Mage-Gift! *My* Familial Visitation is more than overdue."

"But—you're a Guardian—" Hope rose in him. If only Savil would be there, he'd have *one* kindred soul in the lions' den! He had no doubt she was more than up to the trip; he could feel *her* strength even as he leaned on it.

"Won't take me but a day to set my focus in the Web and then I can Guard from Forst Reach as easily as from here. It's only a matter of Sensing threat and sending the alert, you know. It's not as if I actually had to *fight* anything. And it's only because I need to keep that little corner of my mind tuned to the Web waking and sleeping that I don't have a protege—ten years ago I could have done what Jays is doing; Guard *and* teach three." She nodded. "This is *no* bad notion. Provided you don't mind having me there—"

"Mind?" He seized her hand and kissed it.

"Then expect me in about—oh, two weeks after you arrive. It'll take Kellan a little longer to make the trip than you youngsters."

"Savil, if you only knew how grateful I am—"

"Pish. I'm selfish, is what I am." A smile started to twitch at the corners of her mouth. "We can guard *each other's* backs this way. I'm counting on you to save me from Withen as much as you are counting on me to save you."

He rose and kissed her forehead. "I don't care what you say, it's the most generous, *unselfish* thing anyone's done for me in a year. And you just may save this visit from becoming the legend of how Herald Vanyel went berserk and left his entire family tied to trees with rags stuffed in their mouths! About what time is it? I'm all turned round about from being so far south."

She checked the angle of the sun coming in her window. "I'd guess just after Court."

"Good; I have to catch Randale and Shavri and say good-bye. *He* promised if I didn't come when he was being 'official' he wouldn't find something for me to do."

"Then off with you, *ke'chara*, and I'll see you at Forst Reach—and thank you for thinking of me," she finished, touching the stone on the table beside her.

"Because you think of me, love." He kissed her cheek, then her forehead again, and left her suite.

He stopped first at his room to change back into a set of Tran's Whites and put on the soft, low boots Heralds wore indoors; not as comfortable as going barefoot, but they beat the riding boots hands down. And if he didn't change, he *might* not be let into the King's quarters—every time he came back, it seemed fewer folk knew his face.

That accomplished, and now every inch his usual neat self, he headed down to the oldest part of the Palace, the extensive set of rooms shared by King Randale; his lifebonded and King's Own, Shavri; and their daughter.

He had scarcely crossed the threshold of the sparsely furnished audience chamber—his unfamiliar face giving a moment's apprehension to the two Guards posted at the door—when a six-year-old, curly-headed, miniature whirlwind burst through the farther door and flung herself across the audience chamber at him, evidently blithely certain he would catch her before she fell.

Which he did, and swung her around, up and over his head while she squealed with excitement and delight. "Uncle Van!" she crowed at the top of her lungs. "UncleVanUncleVanUncleVan!"

He started to put her down, but she demanded a hug and a kiss with the same infectious charm her "father" Randale could display whenever he chose. Vanyel hoisted her into a comfortable carrying position and complied without an argument, thinking as he did so that it was a good thing that she was still so tiny.

"Now how did you know I was coming?" he asked her, as her bright brown eyes looked solemnly down into his.

"Felt you," she said, giving him another hug. "Felt you in my head, all blue-glowy and swirly."

He nearly dropped her in shock. That was surely the most vivid—and accurate—description of his aura he'd ever heard out of anyone but another high-ranking Herald-Mage.

"Or a Healer," said Shavri, coming up beside him as he gaped at the child, and Jisa giggled at the face he was making. "Healers see you that way, too, Van. And no, I wasn't eavesdropping on your thoughts—they were plain enough from that poleaxed look on your face." There was strain and fear under Shavri's light tone, as if she walked a narrow bridge above a bottomless chasm. "Besides, you aren't the only one she's 'felt in her head' during the last three months. Let's start this greeting over; hello, Van, have you a hug for me?"

"Always." He was already bracing himself for trouble; with *that* look on her face there was something seriously wrong. And that meant *he'd* have to be the strong one.

He included Shavri in his arms, while Jisa flung her arms around both their necks and cuddled. "Jisa sweet, can I put you down long enough for presents?"

"Presents?" Jisa was no different from any other six-year-old when *that* word came up. She squirmed a little, and he set her down, then extracted the little Companion-figure from his pouch and handed it to her. She shrieked with delight, and ran outside to show it to the two Guards. Shavri watched her go, her gypsy-dark eyes darker with unconcealed love—and something else. Something secret and profoundly unhappy. His first reaction was to want to hold her, protect her, make that unhappiness go away.

Randi's lifebonded—

"That's quite a little impling you're raising, Shavri," he said, instead. "Incredibly unspoiled, given that I'd lay odds she's the pet of the Circle."

"You say that every time you see her, beast," she replied, flashing an uncertain smile, startlingly bright in her sober, dark face.

"Well, it's true." Vanyel Looked quickly around, ascertained that they were going to be alone for a few moments, and asked quickly, "How is he?"

The smile vanished, and the fear and unhappiness were plain for anyone who knew her to read. :*Oh, gods—Van, he's sick, I can't make it go away, and I think he's dying. And I don't know why.*:

:What?: He gathered his scant resources to support her—and to hide the fact that *her* fear was making *him* tremble inside.

"He's well enough," she said lightly, but Mindspoke him with a vastly different tone. *:There's something wrong; it isn't affecting him much at the moment other than steady weakness and a dizzy spell now and again—but—it keeps getting worse with each spell. And—oh, Van—I'm so afraid—:*

He tightened his arm around her shoulders. *:Easy, flowerlet—:* "Then it sounds like there's no problem with my taking this leave." *:How long has this been going on?:*

Her unshed tears knotted both their throats. *:Eight months. It's something I can't Heal; the gods know I've tried!:*

He felt chill creep over him. *:Forgive me, Shavri, but I have to ask this. Given worst case—if it is something life-threatening, and it keeps getting worse, how long do you think he has?:*

:If he keeps weakening at the same rate? Fifteen years—maybe less, certainly not more. Gods, Van, he won't even see fifty—he won't even see his grandchildren! Elspeth was seventy-six when she was Called!:

There was another thought, unspoken—but Vanyel felt it, since it touched so nearly on his own private loneliness.

I'll have to go on alone—

He held her close to his chest, with her face pressed into his shoulder as she struggled not to cry, and clamped down a tight shield to prevent any stray thought from reaching her and frightening her. *Savil supported you. You support Shavri the same way,* he told himself, below the threshold of her ability to Mindhear. *Let her know she won't be alone. Gods, gods, they're both so young, not even twenty-five . . . and so sheltered all their lives. Oh, Shavri—your pain hurts me—*

"Easy, love," he murmured into her hair. *:Does he know?:*

:No. Not yet. Healer's Collegium does; they're working on it. We don't want him to know until it's certain. Now you know why I won't marry him. Van, I couldn't, I'm not strong enough, I can't rule! Not alone! And when he dies—and I won't have Jisa forced onto the throne too young, either.: Her mind-voice strengthened with stubbornness. *:So long as we're unwedded, it can't be forced on me nor on Jisa until all the collateral lines are exhausted. I—:*

He felt the surge of terror and grief, and tried to project strength to her, not allowing her to see how fragile that strength was at the moment. With grim certainty he knew that she would not be able to cope if the worst came—unless someone she trusted was there to help. And the only one she trusted to that extent—the only one Randi trusted—was him. *Gods. They really think I can do anything—and I'm no more ready for this than she is.*

He pushed the thought away, concentrated on trying to ease some of that fear. *:Gently, sweet. Don't borrow trouble. Don't assume anything. You may cure him yet; this may turn out to be something ridiculous—and you both may get run over by a beer-wagon tomorrow!:*

That startled a weak chuckle out of her, and she blinked up at him through tears she was doing her best not to release.

:Worry about tomorrow when it comes; enjoy now. Now, what's all this with Jisa "feeling people in her head?":

Footsteps made both of them look up. "Are you seducing my lady, Herald Vanyel?" asked Randale, King of Valdemar, holding out his arms to embrace both of them.

"I'd *rather* seduce you, you charmer," Vanyel replied coyly, batting his eyelashes at the King. But there was an edge of bitterness there in his banter, and despite his best intentions it must have crept into his voice. He saw a hint of startlement, then of worry, creep into both their expressions.

Lighten up, dammit, he told himself angrily. *They've got their own problems—they don't need yours.*

He grinned and winked, and both of them relaxed again.

Randale laughed heartily, and hugged him hard, taking Shavri away from Vanyel as he did so. And Vanyel felt a strange twinge, another flash of uneasiness.

Gods, what's wrong with me?

He didn't stop to think about it. The hug wasn't as hard as it had been a year ago—and there was a transparency about Randale that made Vanyel's heart lurch. Randale had grown a neat brown beard—was it to hide the fact that his cheeks were a little hollower? Was that tidy-to-a-fault brown hair a little lackluster? There *were* shadows under his dark eyes; were they there from lack of sleep, or some more sinister reason? Within a few breaths Vanyel had noted a dozen small signs of "something wrong"—all of them little things, things that someone who saw him day-in, day-out might not have noticed. But *Vanyel* had been away for a year, and the things he saw shook him. *Gods, gods—my King, my friend—Shavri is right. You're ill, at the very least—*

Randale was *not* a Herald-Mage; his Gift was Farsight, and his Mindspeech was not as sure a thing as Vanyel's and Shavri's. For once Vanyel was grateful for that lack. He changed the subject before Randale could note his unease.

"It seems your little shadow is developing precocious Gifts," he said. "At least she said she 'felt me coming in her mind.'" Jisa ran back in, and attached herself to Vanyel's leg. "Didn't you, imp?" He looked down at her, surprised by the surge of love he felt for the child.

She nodded, very well pleased with herself.

"We thought about taking her to Savil, but she's been so busy," Randale replied, shrugging. "I don't suppose *you'd* test her, would you? That's a major spell for anyone else but you and Savil."

"*Now* I see the reason for all the concern that I stop by!" Vanyel teased. "*Not* that you've missed me!"

"*Van*—" Shavri said indignantly. "I never—"

Randale chortled, and she hit his shoulder. "You can just *stop* that, you beast."

Jisa giggled, and Vanyel looked down at her. "Hold still for a minute, impling," he said. "I'm about to make your head feel funny, like Mama did when you had the measles."

"All right," Jisa said calmly, and Vanyel had the sudden unsettling feeling that she would permit her totally-trusted "Uncle Van" to chop off her hand if he wanted to.

He rested his palm on the top of her brown curls, and focused *out* and *down*—

—and came out again, blinking. "Well."

"Well, *what*?" Shavri and Randale demanded in the same breath.

"She won't be a Herald-Mage, not unless she gets blasted open the way I did—which I do *not* recommend," he added lightly, trying to catch his breath. Even that little magic had been more of a strain than he had thought it would. "But she's carrying the potential in a double dose; she'll certainly pass it to her children. She *will be* a Mindhealer; she *is* an active Empath, and her Mindspeech center is opening early, too. With that combination, Randale, she'll very likely be King's Own after Shavri."

Gods, she is so like me. Right down to the Mage-potential. Jisa, sweetling, I swear I will do anything to keep you safe—

Shavri trembled, and Randale's arm tightened around her shoulder. "Is she likely to be Chosen anytime soon?"

Vanyel did not answer immediately. :*'Fandes?*: he called, softly. :*Are you awake?*:

:*And following the conversation. Yes, provided it's needful for her to get the training and she stays as sweet as she is. I'd say by age ten. Maybe sooner, two years from now.*:

"Yfandes guesses that if she needs the training, between age eight and ten. Remember, for the presumptive King's Own, that won't be a bonded Choosing—she won't bond until—until she gets the office. Then she'll bond with Taver." Vanyel ignored both Shavri's frightened face and Randale's elation. "So, given that—there's a little something she and I ought to do."

He focused himself *down* again, pulling on Yfandes' strength to assist his own, and thanking the gods he could do so, because Jisa should not remain as open as she was now. This time he did not close his eyes, but locked them with the child's, and showed her without words—for she did not yet have sufficient Mindspeech to use words—how to shield herself from unwanted thoughts and emotions, and unshield again at will. He was, he feared, the only person who *could* have taught her at this stage, Empathy not being a normal Heraldic Gift, and most Healers not using it in the way a Herald-Mage could.

He showed her how to find her center—she knew with an instant of studying *him* how to ground. The fundamentals it had taken him so long and so painfully to learn came to her with the ease of breathing, perhaps because learning *was* as easy as breathing at her age, and perhaps because *his* learning had come at the cost of so much loss and pain that had nothing to do with his Gifts.

"—there. That should hold her until she's got enough to be taught formally. Teach her yourself, Shavri. You won't find anyone in the Heralds with Empathy as strong as hers. When she's got it at full power, she'll be able to control a mob in full cry."

Shavri had herself back under control again, and the smile she gave Vanyel was genuine. "Thank you, love."

He shrugged. "No thanks needed. Before I forget it—I brought you two some 'pretties' also."

Shavri took the pendant with an exclamation of genuine delight as he handed the matching cloak-brooch to Randale. "Van, you shouldn't have—" she began.

"Of course I should have," he said. "Who else have I got to bring things to?" It came out bleaker than he intended.

"Oh, Van—" Her eyes softened, and Randale cleared his throat and blinked. They reached out in the same moment and each took one of his hands. He closed his eyes, and for an instant allowed himself to feel a part of their closeness.

But it was *their* closeness, not his.

And I have no right.

"Mama, I have lessons," said a small voice, still at Vanyel's knee.

"Bright Havens, so you do!" Shavri exclaimed. "Van—"

"Go," he said, wrinkling his nose at her. "I'll be back in a few weeks, and maybe this tyrant of a King will let me stick around for a while this time."

She shooed Jisa out and followed her with the light step of a young girl. Randale's gaze followed both of them.

"You sire wonderful children, Van," he said softly.

"*You* raise better ones," Vanyel replied, uneasily. "*You* are Jisa's papa, don't you ever forget it. I was nothing more than the convenient means to a rather attractive little end."

The King relaxed visibly. "I keep thinking you're going to want her back—especially now that she's showing Gifts. She's more like you than you know."

Vanyel laughed. "Whatever would I *do* with her? Great good gods, what kind of a parent would *I* make? I can't even train the palace cats to stay off my pillow! No, Randi, she's all yours, in everything that counts. *I* would rather be Uncle Van, who gets to spoil her."

Randale reached out without looking and snagged a chair with one hand. He swung it around and put it in front of Vanyel. "She'd make a good Queen."

"She'd make a very bad Queen," Vanyel replied, draping himself over it as Randale took another. "The things that make a *good* Monarch's Own are weakness in the Monarch."

"Like?"

"Empathy. She'd be vulnerable to everyone with a petition and the passion to back it. She'd be tempted to use projective Empathy on her Council to make them vote *her* way. Mindhealers are *drawn* to the unbalanced; but a Monarch can't waste time dealing with every Herald in trauma she encounters." Vanyel shook his head. "No. Absolutely not. Jisa is going to be a lovely young woman and a good Monarch's Own; be satisfied with that."

Randale gave him a wry look. "You sound very sure of yourself."

"Shouldn't I be?" Vanyel folded his arms over the back of the chair and rested his chin on them. "Forgive me if I sound arrogant, but other than Savil, I *am* the expert in these things. Ask my aunt when I'm not around and I'll bet money she'll tell you the same thing."

Randale shrugged, and scratched the back of his head. "I guess you're right. I was hoping you'd back me, though—"

"Why?" Vanyel interrupted. "So you can have something else to pressure Shavri into marrying you?"

Randale winced at his bluntness, and protested weakly, "But that's—I mean—dammit, Van, I *need* her!"

Gods, so young . . . so uncertain of himself, of her. So afraid that without bonds *he won't hold her.* "You think she doesn't need you? Randi, she's your *life-bonded,* do you really *need* any further hold on her than that? She'd rather die than lose you!"

Randale studied the back of his hand. "It's just . . . I want something a little more—"

"Ordinary?" Vanyel finished wryly. "Randi, Heralds are *never* ordinary. If you wanted 'ordinary,' you should have become a blacksmith."

Randale shook his head.

Vanyel gritted his teeth and prepared to say to Randale what no one else could—or *would.* "Now you *listen* to me. You're making her miserable with the pressure you've been putting on her. She's doing exactly what she should; she's putting Valdemar and Valdemar's King ahead of her own wishes."

Mostly.

"She knows the situation we have just as well as you do, but *she's* willing to face it. Things went to pieces when your grandmother Elspeth died, and they've been getting worse since—steadily."

"I'm not *blind,* Van," Randale interrupted. "I—"

"Quiet, Randi. I'm making a speech, and I don't, often. I want you to *think.* There's a very real probability that you'll have to buy us peace on one of our Borders with an alliance marriage—*exactly* how your grandmother bought us peace with Iftel. And why do you think she never married Bard Kyran after your grandfather died, hmm? She knew her duty, and so should you. You *have* to stay free for that."

Randale was flushing; Vanyel didn't need Empathy to know he was getting angry. "So what business is it of yours?" he burst out. "I thought you were a friend—"

"I am. But I'm a Herald first. And my first duty is to Valdemar, not to you." Vanyel sat straight up and let his face grow very cold; knowing what he was doing and hating himself for it. Randi *wanted* his friend, and at some levels, *needed* his friend. He was going to get Herald-Mage Vanyel Ashkevron. "You, Herald-King Randale, cannot permit your personal feelings to interfere with the well-being of this kingdom. You are as much Herald as I. If you cannot reconcile yourself to that—give up the Crown."

Randale slumped, defeated. No one knew better than he that there was no Heir or even Heir-presumptive yet. The Crown was his, like it or not. "I . . . I wish I . . . there's no one else, Van. No one old enough."

"Then you can't resign your Crown, can you." Vanyel made it a statement rather than a question.

"No. *Damn*. Van—you know I never wanted this—"

Memory.

Balmy spring breezes played over the lawn. Randi laughing at something, some joke he had just made—Shavri playing with the baby in a patch of sun. Bucolic, pastoral scene—

Shattered by the arrival on a lathered horse of a Queen's Messenger. In black.

Randi jumped to his feet, his face going white. The man handed Randale a sealed package wrapped in silk, but Randi didn't open it.

"Herald Randale—your grandmother the Queen sends me to tell you that your father—"

The package fell from Randale's fingers. The blue silk wrappings unwound from the contents.

The silver coronet of the Heir.

An accident. A stupid accident—a misstep on a slippery staircase in full view of everyone—and the Heir, Herald-Mage Darvi, was dead of a broken neck. And Randale was Heir.

Vanyel's heart ached for him. And he dared not show it. Pity would be wrong at this moment, but he softened his voice and his expression.

"I *told* you Jisa would make a bad Queen. I meant every word. Shavri knows all this, too, you can bet on it. And I'm telling you you're tearing her in pieces, putting her between love for you, and what she knows is her duty." Randale looked at him as if he wanted to interrupt. "No, hear me out—you've sympathized often enough with me and my matchmaking mother. How in Havens do you think Shavri feels with you putting that same kind of pressure on her?"

"Not good," Randale admitted, after a long moment.

"Then stop it, before you put her under more pressure than she can take. Leave her alone. Let it lie for another ten years; if things haven't come to a conclusion one way or another, *then* bring it up. All right?"

"No," Randale said slowly. "It's not all right. But you're absolutely correct about there being no choice. Not for any of us."

Vanyel rose, and swung the chair he'd been slouched over out of the way. Randale did the same.

"Don't spoil what you have with what you only *think* you want, Randale," he said softly, taking his friend and King's arm. "This is experience talking; the one thing about the brief time *I* shared with my love that I have *never* regretted is that I never consciously did anything to make him unhappy. Had our time been longer, maybe I would have; I can't ever know. But at least I have no memories of quarrels or hard words to shadow the good memories."

Randale took his hand. "You're right; I'm wrong. I'll stop plaguing her."

"Good man."

Randi—oh, Randi— Close; Randale was coming too close. It was beginning to hurt—

Then Randale's servant entered behind him, the King's formal uniform draped over one arm, the royal circlet in the other hand, and a harried expression on his face. Vanyel forced a laugh, and took the welcome opportunity to escape. "Now unless I haul myself out of here, I'm going to make your man there very unhappy."

"What?" Randale turned, startled. "Oh. Oh, hellfire. I *have* got that damned formal audience before dinner, don't I?"

"Yes, sire," the servant replied, as expressionless as a stone.

"Then I'd better get changed. Vanyel—"

Vanyel put his arm around the younger man's shoulders and gave him an affectionate embrace. "Just go do *your* duty, and make her happy. That's what counts. I'm off; I'll see you by Midwinter, certainly."

"Right. Van, be well." Randale looked at him—really *looked* at him, for the first time. He started to reach for Vanyel's arm with an expression of concern; Vanyel ducked his head to conceal the signs of weariness.

"I'm never ill. Go, go, go—before your man kills me with a look!"

Randale managed a grin, and followed the servant back into the private rooms of the suite. Vanyel spent a moment with his eyes closed in unvoiced prayer for him, then took himself back to his own room and his longed-for reunion with his bed.

CHAPTER 3

⟶ ◇ ⟵

MORNING. VANYEL WOKE slowly, surrounded by unfamiliar warmth and softness, and put bits of memory together as they drifted within reach.

He vaguely remembered getting to his room, surrounded by fatigue that increasingly fogged everything; recalled noting a brief message from Tran, and getting partially undressed. He did not remember lying down at all; he didn't even remember sitting on the bed.

By the amount of light leaking around the bedcurtains it was probably midmorning, and what had wakened him was hunger.

His soft bed—*clean* sheets, a *real* featherbed, and those wonderful dark curtains to block out the light—felt so *good*. Good enough to ignore the demands of his stomach and give preference to the demands of his weary body. He'd had a fair amount of practice in shutting off inconvenient things like hunger and thirst; there'd been plenty of times lately when he'd had no other choice.

He almost did just exactly that, almost went back to sleep, but his conscience told him that if he didn't get up, he'd probably sleep for another day. And he couldn't afford that.

Clothing, clothing, good gods, what am I going to do about clothing?

There was no way his uniforms would be cleaned and mended, and he was going to need to *take* a few with him even if he didn't plan to wear them. And he had to have uniforms to travel in, anyway; technically a Herald traveling was on duty.

Wait a moment; wasn't there something in that note from Tran about uniforms?

He pushed off the blankets with a pang of regret, pulled the bed curtains aside, winced away from the daylight flooding his room, and sat on the edge of the bed, waiting for leftovers from half-recollected dreams to clear out of his brain. His shoulders hurt.

Have to do something about that muscle strain before I start favoring that arm . . . remember to put liniment on it, and do some of those exercises.

Birds chirped news at one another right outside his window. It had been a very long time since he'd paid any attention to birdcalls—except as signals of the presence or absence of danger.

The musical chatter was quite wonderful, precisely because it was so sanely ordinary. *Ordinary. Peaceful. Gods, I am so tempted just to fall back onto the mattress and to hell with starting for Forst Reach today.*

But a promise was a promise. And if he delayed going one day, it would be easy to rationalize another delay, and another, all of which would only lead to Randale's recruiting him. Which was what the trip was supposed to *prevent.*

He pulled himself up out of bed with the aid of the bedpost and reached for one of Tantras' uniforms. *Clean, Lord and Lady, clean and smelling of nothing worse than soap and fresh air.* Once he managed to get himself started, habit took over.

He reached with one hand for one of yesterday's leftover apples in their bowl on the table, and Tantras' note with the other.

Go ahead and take my stuff with you. I don't need these; they're spares that were made before I put on all that muscle across the shoulders. A bit tight on me, they should be just a little big on you. Tell me what you want done and get out of here; I don't mind taking care of some of your paperwork for you. I'll see that your new uniforms are ready by the time you get back; Supply told me there's no chance of salvaging your old ones. Tran.

More than a little big, Vanyel thought wryly, standing up and surveying himself in the rather expensive glass mirror (a present from Savil) on the back of the door. He'd had to tie the breeches with an improvised drawstring just so they'd stay up, and the tunic bagged untidily over his belt. He looked— except for the silver in his hair—rather like an adolescent given clothing "to grow into." *They'd have been all right a year ago, but—oh, well. Nobody's going to see me except the family. I certainly don't have anyone to impress!*

But Tran's volunteering gave him a notion about some other things he needed. He rummaged out the pen and paper he'd used yesterday; by now he reckoned those notes were well on the way to the Border and Forst Reach.

Another reason to hail out of here. If I don't arrive soon after the letter, they'll worry. His letters should beat him to the holding by a few days, at least.

He wrote swiftly, but neatly; "neat as a clerk," Tran was wont to tease. *Order me new cloaks, would you? And new boots. I need them badly; I'd be ashamed to stand duty the way they are now.*

And since you're being so kind as to keep track of this, ask Supply to work me up a set of spare uniforms to leave here, and have them keep a set here at all times. Next time there might not be anyone my size with extras for me to borrow! Thanks, Van.

He packed quickly, without having to think about what he was doing, now that he'd finally gotten his momentum. After the last four years, he could pack fatigue-drunk, pain-fogged, drugged to his eyebrows, or asleep—and he *had*, at one time or another.

He swung his cloak—it was more gray than white, and a little shabby, but there was nothing to be done about *that*—over his shoulder, picked up his packs, plucked his lute off the chair, and headed out. In the dark and echoing hall on his way to Companion's Field and the stable, he intercepted a page, gave the child the note for Tantras, and asked for some kind of breakfast to be brought to him while he saddled Yfandes.

She was already waiting calmly for him at the entrance to the tackshed. *:They've cleaned all my tack,:* she told him, *:but the saddle needs mending and the rest isn't what it should be. I wouldn't trust the chestband to take any strain at all, frankly.:*

:Swordcuts and burns aren't fixed with saddlesoap,: he reminded her. *:We'll just have to—wait a moment—what about your formal gear? That's next thing to brand new. Gods know we've used it what—once? Twice?:*

Her ears went up—her sapphire eyes fixed on him—

And he had that curious and disorienting doubled image of her that he'd gotten sometimes in the past, the image of a dark, wise-eyed woman, weary, but smiling with newly-kindled anticipation, flickering in and out with the graceful white horse.

Gods, if I needed a sign of how dragged-out I am, that's it. Hallucinating again. Dreaming awake. Got to be because I never really think of her as a "horse" even when I'm riding her.

He blinked his eyes and forced himself to focus properly as she replied, as excited as a girl being told she could wear her holiday best—*:Chosen, could we use it? Please?:*

He chuckled. *:You like being dressed up and belled like a gypsy, don't you?:*

She tossed her head, and arched her neck. *:Don't you? I've heard you preening at yourself in the mirror of a morning, especially when there was someone to impress!:*

"You fight dirty," he said aloud, and went in search of her formal tack, grinning.

* * *

One of the kitchen wenches, a bright-eyed little brunette, barely adolescent, brought him hot bread and butter, cider, and more apples about the time he managed to find where Yfandes' formal panoply had been stored. The saddle was considerably lighter than the field saddle, and fancier; it was tooled and worked with silver and dyed a deep blue. The chest and rump bands had silver bells on them, as did the reins of what was essentially an elaborate hackamore. The reins were there more for *his* benefit than his Companion's, and more for show than either. There was light barding that went along with the outfit, but after regarding it wistfully for a moment, Yfandes agreed that the barding would be far more trouble than it was worth and Vanyel bundled it away.

He paused a moment and bit into the bread; it was dripping with melted butter, and he closed his eyes at the unexpected pleasure the flavor gave him.

Oh, gods—fresh bread!

The taste was better than the manna that the priests said gods ate. "Bread" for the past year had meant rock-hard journey-bread at best, moldy crusts at worst, and anything in between—and it was *never* fresh, much less hot from the oven. There *had* been butter—sometimes—rancid in summer, as rock-hard as the journey-bread in winter.

It's the little things we miss the most—I swear it is! Ordinary things, things that spell "peace" and "prosperity." He thought briefly of the sword-comrades he'd left on the Border, and sent up a brief prayer. *Brightest gods, grant both, but especially peace. Soon, before more blood is shed.*

After that he alternated between bites of food and adjusting of harness. The kitchen wench lingered to watch him saddle Yfandes, draped over the open half-door of the stable, squinting into the sunlight. There was something between hero-worship and starry-eyed romance in her gaze; finally Vanyel couldn't stand it any longer and gently shooed her back to her duties.

He noted out of the corner of his eye—with more than a little alarm—that she was clutching the mug he'd drunk from to her budding bosom as though it had been transformed into a holy chalice.

:Looks like you've got another one, Chosen,: Yfandes commented sardonically as he fastened his packs behind her saddle.

:Thank you for that startling information. That's just what I needed to hear.:

:It's not my fault you have a face that breaks hearts.:

:But why—oh, never mind.: He gave the girth a last tug and swung up into the saddle. *:Let's get out of here before someone else decides she's fallen in love with me.:*

*   *   *

They got through the city as quickly as they could, and out onto the open road where it was possible to breathe without choking on the thick cloud of dust and other odors of the crowded city. It was a little strange to ride with the soft chime of the bells marking every pace Yfandes took; it made him nervous for the first few leagues, until he managed to convince his gut that they were in *friendly* territory, and in no danger of alerting enemy scouts with the sound. After that, the sound began to soothe him. Like muted, rhythmic windchimes—

I've always adored windchimes. And I never get to meditate to them anymore.

He slowly began to relax. Yfandes was in no great hurry, although her "traveling" pace would have run a real horse into the ground after half a day. This had been a gentle summer, turning into a warm and even gentler fall, with just enough frost to ensure that the harvests ripened, not enough yet to turn the leaves. Once out of Haven, Exile's Road wound lazily through rustling, golden grainfields, and fields of sweetly ripening hay. The morning air was slightly cool, but the sun was warm enough that Vanyel soon rolled his cloak and bundled it behind his saddle.

It was very hard to stay awake, in fact. His muscles relaxed into the familiar configurations of riding.

Memory flicker—the k'Treva Vale. Savil, schooling him on Yfandes. *"You think you're a rider now, lad. When I'm done with you, you'll be able to do* anything *ahorse that you can do on the ground."*

Himself, slyly. "Anything?"

She threw a saddlebag at him.

From here to the Border the land was the next thing to flat; long, rolling hills covered with cultivated fields, interrupted by fragrant oak groves that occasionally amounted to small forests.

:You really could *sleep, you know,:* Yfandes chided him. *:I'm not going to let you fall off. It won't be the first time you've taken a nap that way.:*

"I'm hardly going to be company for you like that."

She shook her head, and the bells on her halter laughed for her. *:Your presence is company enough, Chosen. I ran lone for ten years before you bonded to me. Just having you with me, whole and healthy, is pleasure; you needn't think I need entertaining when we aren't working.:*

With a brief flash of pain and pleasure he remembered how *he* had never needed anything but Tylendel's presence either. . . .

:Yes,: she agreed, following the thought. *:Exactly.:*

So he hooked his leg around the saddle pommel, crossed his arms and tucked the ends of his fingers into his belt, then sagged into a comfortable slouch, chin on chest. It didn't take long.

He came awake all at once, his hand reaching automatically for the sword he wasn't wearing. There was an instant of panic before he remembered where he was going, and why he was going there.

"Why did you stop?" he asked Yfandes, who had come to an unmoving halt—which was what had waked him—in the middle of the completely deserted road. There was nothing but open meadow on either side of him, dotted with sheep, though there was no sign of the shepherd. Crows cawed overhead, and the sheep bleated in their pastures; otherwise silence prevailed. The sun was low enough ahead of them to force him to squint. *It must be late afternoon, early evening.*

:There's an inn just beyond the next curve, sleepy one,: Yfandes said, a hint of amusement tingeing her thought. *:It's later than lunch and earlier than dinner, but I'm tired and I'd really like to stop before I go any farther.:*

"Havens, love, you should have—"

:No, I shouldn't have. This is the first time you've really relaxed in I don't know how long. Have you thought about the way we resonate?:

He saw instantly what she meant. "So—you were relaxing with me."

:In very deed, and reveling in it. First journey I've been able to enjoy in a while. But I would like to stop now.:

"Then so would I." He unwrapped his leg from the pommel and stretched it; she waited until his foot was back in the stirrup, then resumed her easy amble, not quite a walk, not quite a canter. "Is this a temporary halt, or are we stopping for the night?"

:The night?: she asked, wistfully. There was a hint of something more there than she was sending.

"You're not telling me everything," he accused. "Why *this* inn?"

:Well—you won't be the only Herald there. Herald-Courier Sofya is there—:

"Chosen by?" He had a shrewd hunch where this was leading.

She curved her neck coquettishly, and looked up and sideways at him out of one huge blue eye. *:Gavis.:*

He shook his head at her. "Ah, yes—the one that has been setting all the courier-records lately. Why this penchant for over-muscled courier-types, all legs and no brains—"

:He is not over-muscled,: she replied indignantly, breaking into a teeth-rattling trot to punish him.

"But brainless?" he taunted, feeling unusually mischievous.

:He just doesn't speak up unless he has something to say. Unlike certain Herald-Mages I know.: She kicked once, jarring every vertebra in his spine, before settling, all four feet braced in the dust of the road, and plainly going nowhere.

He reached forward before she could stop him, and tweaked her ear. "Well, since you want to arrange a little assignation, don't you think you'd better get the cooperation of *your* Chosen?"

:I can't imagine why,: she replied.

"We *could* move out of the center of the road, and I *could* groom you so that you looked your usual lovely self when we rode into that inn yard, instead of being all covered with road dust. I *could* even braid your tail up with some of the blue and silver cord that was with the barding. *If* I felt like it."

:I—Vanyel—I—: she floundered.

"And I *do* feel like it, you ridiculously vain creature," he said, leaning down and putting both arms around her neck, resting his cheek on her crest. "And to think that they call *me* a peacock! Has it been so long since I teased you that you've forgotten what it sounds like?"

:Oh, Vanyel—it has been a long time.:

"Then we'll have to remedy that." He dismounted, still a bit stiff from his long doze, and opened the pack with the currycomb in it. Something else occurred to him as he wormed his hand down inside the pack. "Just— do me a very big favor, sweetling—"

:Hmm?: She turned her head and blinked back at him.

He fished out the comb and the cords. "Please, *please* remember to shield me out of your trysting, all right? You forgot to, the last time. Here, let's get out of the road." He stifled a sigh, as they moved under the shade of tree beside the roadway. "I don't grudge you any pleasure at all, but it's been a very long time since I did any number of things—and teasing you is only one of them."

Yfandes twitched, the closest to blushing a Companion could come.

Vanyel allowed no hand to tend Yfandes but his own, no more than he would have permitted a stranger to see to the comfort of his sister, the cloistered priestess. 'Fandes frequently protested this wasn't necessary, but this afternoon she wasn't complaining. Especially not when young Gavis pranced up to the fence of the inn's open wagon-field with a proud curve to his neck and a certain light of anticipation in his eye. Vanyel kept his amused thoughts to himself as Yfandes flirted coyly with the handsome Companion, and wished her nothing more risque than a "pleasant evening" when he opened the gate into the meadow for her.

She gave him a long look over her shoulder. :*Vanyel, you aren't made of stone. I wish you would find a—comrade. You would be much happier.*:

He winced away from the idea. :*I've been over this with Savil. And you. Until I can stop trying to replace 'Lendel, I'm not going to cheat myself and my would-be partner.*:

:*I don't see that. If you're friends, it wouldn't be cheating . . . never mind.*:

:*Go, and enjoy yourself.*:

:*Oh, I think I can manage that,*: she said with deliberate innocence, gave him a slow wink, then frisked off with Gavis in close attendance.

The tack he *did* entrust to the stableboy, though the lad's wide-eyed awe in his presence left him feeling just a bit uneasy. "Awe" was not something he wanted aimed in his direction. It felt too close to "fear."

He stepped into the open door of the inn's common room with his packs over one shoulder, and stood blinking in the sawdust-scented gloom, waiting for his eyes to adjust. The lean and nervous innkeeper was at his elbow in a breath, long before Vanyel could see anything other than shadows, more shadows, and a dim white form in one corner that was probably Herald Sofya. It seemed as if he and the other Herald were the only guests this early in the afternoon, but this *was* harvest-season. The locals were undoubtedly making the maximum use of every moment of daylight.

"Milord Herald, an honor, a pleasure. How may this humble inn serve you, milord?"

"Please—" Vanyel flushed at his effusiveness. "Just dinner, a room if you've one to spare, use of your bathhouse, food for my Companion—I took the liberty of turning her loose with Companion Gavis." Now his eyes had adjusted enough that he could see what he was doing; he fumbled in his belt-pouch and pressed coins into the innkeeper's hand. "Here; I'm on leave, not on duty. This should cover everything." Actually it was too much, and he knew it—but what else did he have to spend it on? The man gaped at the money, and began babbling about the room: "Royalty slept there, indeed they did, King Randale himself before his coronation—" Vanyel bore with it as patiently as he could, and when the man finally wound down, thanked him in a diffident voice and entrusted everything but the lute to the hands of one of the servants to be carried away to the rented room.

Now he could make out Herald Sofya in the corner; a dark, pretty woman, quite young, *quite* lean, and not anyone he recognized. She was paying studious, courteous attention to her jack of ale; Vanyel drifted over to her table when the innkeeper finally fled to the kitchen vowing to bring forth a dinner instantly, which—from the description—would have satisfied both the worst gourmand and the fussiest gourmet in the Kingdom.

"Herald Sofya?" he said quietly, and she looked at him in startlement. He surmised the cause, and smiled. In all probability her Companion had been so taken up with Yfandes that he'd neglected to tell *his* Chosen Vanyel's identity. Or else she wasn't much of a Mindspeaker, which meant Gavis wouldn't be able to give her more than images. She had probably assumed the same was true for him. "Your Gavis Mindspoke my Yfandes on the road, and she told me both your names before we arrived. Might I join you?"

"Certainly," she replied, after swallowing quickly.

He sat on the side of the table opposite her, and saw the very faint frown as she took in the state of his Whites. "I apologize for my appearance." He smiled, feeling a little shy. "I know it won't do much for the Heraldic reputation. But I only *just* got leave, and I didn't want to wait for replacement uniforms. I was afraid that if I did, they'd find some reason to cancel my leave!"

Sofya laughed heartily, showing a fine set of strong, white teeth. "I know what you mean!" she replied. "It seems like all we've done is wear out saddle-leather for the past three months. There're four of us on this route, and the farmers are beginning to count on us like a calendar; one every three days, out to the Border and back."

"To Captain Lissa Ashkevron?"

"The same. And let us hope the Linean Border doesn't heat up the way the Karsite Border did."

Vanyel closed his eyes, as a chill crawled up his backbone and shivered itself along all of his limbs. "Gods spare us *that*," he said, finally.

When he opened his eyes again, she was staring at him very oddly, but he was saved from having to say anything by the appearance of the innkeeper with his dinner.

Vanyel started in on the smoked-pork pie with an appetite he didn't realize he'd had until the savory aroma of the gravy hit him. Sofya leaned back against the wall and continued to nurse her drink, giving him an odd and unreadable glance from time to time.

He'd been too numb from the long, grueling ride to appreciate his meal yesterday. He'd stowed it away without tasting it, as if it had been the iron rations or make-do of the combat zone. But this morning—and now—the home fare seemed finer than anything likely to be set before Randale.

"I hope you don't mind my staring," Sofya said at last, as he literally cleaned the plate of the last drop of gravy, "but you're going after that pie as if you hadn't seen food in a week, and you're rather starved-looking, and that seems very odd in a Herald—unless you've been standing duty somewhere extraordinary."

He noticed then the "blank" spot in the back of his mind that meant 'Fandes was keeping her promise and shielding him out. He grinned a little to himself; that probably meant that Gavis was doing the same, so Sofya's curiosity about him must be eating her alive.

"I've seen nearly no food for a week," he replied quietly, and paused for a moment when the serving girl took the plate away and replenished his mug of cider. "I don't know if you'd call my duty extraordinary, but it was harder than I expected. I've been on the Karsite Border for the last year. Meals weren't exactly regular, and the food was pretty awful. There were times I shared 'Fandes' oats because I couldn't even attempt eating what they gave me; half-rotten meat and moldy bread aren't precisely to my taste. All too often there wasn't much to go around. And, to tell you the truth, sometimes I just forgot to eat. You know how it is, things start happening, and the next thing you know, it's two days later. That's why—" He gestured at his too-large uniform, and grinned wryly. "The situation was harder on clothing than on stomachs."

Her sable eyes widened, and softened. "You were on the Karsite duty? I don't blame you for running off," she replied, with a hint of a chuckle. "I think I would, too, Herald—you never did give me your name."

"Vanyel," he said. "Vanyel Ashkevron. Lissa's brother. I know, we don't look at all alike—"

But her reaction was not at all what he had expected. Her eyes widened even further, and she sat straight up. "Herald-Mage *Vanyel*?" she exclaimed, loud enough that the farmers and traders who'd begun trickling in while Vanyel was eating stopped talking and turned to look with their mouths dropping open. "You're *Vanyel*?" Her voice carried embarrassingly well, and rose with every word. "Vanyel Demonsbane? The Shadow Stalker? The Hero of—"

"Please—" Vanyel cut her off, pleadingly. "Please, it—yes, I'm Vanyel. But—honestly, it wasn't like you think." He groped for the words that would make the near-worship he saw on her face go back to ordinary friendliness. "It wasn't like that, it really wasn't—just—things had to get done, and I was the only one to do them, so I did. I'm not a hero, or—I'm just—I'm just—another Herald," he finished lamely.

He looked around the common room, and to his dismay saw the same worship in the expressions of the farmfolk around him. And something more.

Fear.

An echo of that fear was in Sofya's eyes as well, before she looked down at her ale.

He closed his eyes, settling his face into a calm and expressionless mask, that belied the ache that their fear called up in him. He'd wanted—acceptance, only that.

Tran, Tran, you were right, I was wrong. "Be careful what you ask for, you may get it." Gods, I asked for signs that Tran was right. And now I have them. Don't I?

He opened his eyes again, but the reverence and adulation hadn't vanished. There was a palpably clear space around him where the "common folk" had moved a little away, as if afraid to intrude too closely on him.

Even Sofya.

And the room had taken on the silence of a chapel.

I'm about to ruin their evening as well as mine. Unfair, unfair—there must be something I can do to salvage this situation, at least for them.

"You know," he said, with forced lightness, "if there was one thing I missed more than anything, it was a chance for a little music—"

He reached blindly down beside him for the lute he'd left leaning against the wall, stripped the case off it and tuned it with frantic speed. "—and I hate to sing alone. I'll bet you all know 'The Crafty Maid,' don't you?"

Without waiting for an answer, he launched into the song. He sang alone on the first verse—but gradually other voices joined his on the chorus; Sofya first, with a kind of too-hearty determination, then a burly peddler, then three stout farmers. The local folk sang timidly to begin with, but the song was an old and lively one, and the chorus was infectious. By his third song the whole room was echoing, and they were no longer paying much more attention to him than they would have to a common minstrel.

Except between songs.

And except for Sofya, who worshiped him with eyes that sent a lump of cold to live in the bottom of his throat. She waited on him herself, as if he was some kind of angel, to be adored, but not touched.

He slipped out of the room early, when she was getting something;

another musician had joined the crowd, a local, and he used the lad's talent as a screen to get out during a particularly rowdy song. He thought he'd gotten away without anyone noticing, but the innkeeper intercepted him in the hallway.

"Milord—Vanyel—" The tallow candles lighting the hall smoked and flickered and made the shadows move like the Shadows he'd once hunted. The memory knotted his stomach. He concentrated on the innkeeper, but the man gulped and would not meet his eyes. A breath of cooked onions drifted up the hall from the common room. "Milord, if I'd known who it was I was serving, I'd have made you special fare, and I'd not have accepted your coin."

"*Please,*" Vanyel interrupted, trying to conceal his hurt. The innkeeper jumped back a pace. "Please," he said, softly this time. "I told you, I'm not on duty, I'm on leave. I'm just another traveler. You fed me the best meal I've had in months, truly you did. You've earned every copper I paid you, and honestly."

"But milord Vanyel, it was nothing, it was common plowman's pie— surely you'd have preferred wine to cider; venison or a stuffed pheasant— and you paid me far too much—"

Vanyel felt a headache coming on. "Actually, no, innkeeper. The truth is I've been on iron-rations for so long anything rich would likely have made me ill. And venison—if I *never* have to see another half-raw deer—Your good, solid fare was feast enough for me. I'll tell you what—" He decided on the lie quickly. "I've been too long within walls. I have a fancy for trees and sky tomorrow; if you'll have your *excellent* cook make me up a packet for breakfast and lunch, I'll consider us more than even. Will that serve your honor, good sir?"

The innkeeper stared, chewing his mustache ends nervously, as if he thought Vanyel might be testing him for some reason, and then nodded agreement.

"Now I—I'm just a little more tired than I thought. If I could use the bathhouse, and get some sleep, do you think?"

To the man's credit, he supplied Vanyel with soap and towels and left him alone. In the steamy quiet of the bathhouse Vanyel managed to relax again. But the cheer of this morning was gone.

He sought release in sleep, finally, in what must have been the finest room in the inn—a huge bed wide enough for an entire family, two feather-beds and a down comforter, and sheets so fresh they almost crackled, all of it scented with orris and lavender. Far below he could still hear the laughter and singing as he climbed into the enormous bed. He blew out the candle then, feeling as lonely as he had ever been in his life, and prayed that sleep would come quickly.

For once his prayers were answered.

"I wish I dared Gate," he mused aloud, carefully examining, then peeling a hard-boiled egg. Yfandes had not said anything about his early-morning departure from the inn, or the fact that he had not waited for breakfast. It was chilly enough that he needed his cloak, and there was a delicate furring of frost on some of the tall weeds beside the roadway. "Gating would shorten this trip considerably."

:*You try and I'll kick you from here to Haven*,: Yfandes replied sharply, the first time she'd spoken to him this morning. :*That is absolutely the stupidest thing you've said in months!*:

He bit into the egg and looked at her backward-pointing ears with interest. "Havens, ladylove—didn't your tryst go well?"

:*My "tryst" went just fine, thank you*,: she replied, her mind-voice softening. :*I just get sick every time I think about what happened the last time.*:

"Oh, 'Fandes, it wasn't that bad."

:*Not that bad? When you were unconscious before you crossed the threshold? And hurting so badly I nearly screamed?*:

"All right, it was bad," he admitted, popping the rest of the egg into his mouth and reaching into the "breakfast packet." "And I'm not stupid enough to Gate without *urgent* need." He studied a roll, weighing it in his hand. It seemed *awfully* heavy. As good as the food had been so far, it didn't seem likely that it was underbaked, but he was *not* in the mood to choke down raw dough. He nibbled it dubiously, then bit into it with a great deal more enthusiasm when it proved to have sausage baked into the middle of it. "It would just be very convenient to not have to stop at inns."

:*Don't tell them your real name*,: she interrupted.

"What?"

:*If reactions like last night bother you, you don't have to tell them your real name. Tell them you're Tantras. Tran won't mind.*:

"'Fandes, that's not the point—never mind." He finished the last of his breakfast and dusted his hands off. A skein of geese flew overhead, honking. The farmers already out in the fields beside the road, scything down the grain and making it into sheaves, paused a moment and pointed at the "v" of birds. "Tran was right, and I'm going to have to get used to it, I guess. And I can't do that hiding behind someone else's name." He managed a wan smile. "It could be worse. They could be treating me like a leper because I'm *shay'a'chern*, instead of treating me like a godlet because I'm Herald-Mage Vanyel Demonsbane." He grimaced. "Gods, that sounds pretentious."

She slowed her pace a trifle. :*It isn't that important—is it?:*

"It's that important. I'm a very fallible mortal, not an Avatar. Magic is a force—a force I control, no more wonderful than a Mindspeaker's ability, or a Healer's. But *they* don't see it that way. To them it's something beyond anything they understand, and they're not sure it *can* be controlled." He sighed. "Or worse, they think magic can solve every problem."

:*You thought that, once.:*

"I know I did. When I was younger. Magic seemed to offer solutions to everything when I was nineteen." He shook his head, and stared out at the horizon. "For a while—for a little while—I thought I held the world. Even Jays respected me, came to be a friend. But magic couldn't force my father to tell me I'd done well in his eyes—or rather, it *could* force him, when I *wanted* the words to come freely from him. It couldn't make being *shay'a'chern* any easier. It couldn't bring back my Tylendel. It was just power. It's dividing me from ordinary people. Worse than that—it seems to be doing the same between me and other Heralds—and 'Fandes, *that* scares the hell out of me."

:*You won't be getting any of the godlet treatment from your kin, I can promise you that.:*

"I suppose not."

It was getting warmer by the moment. He bundled his cloak, and wondered if he should get out his hat. *Gods! Change the subject—before you brood yourself into depression again.* "Do *you* think Father will be able to keep Mother off my back?"

:*Not to put too fine a point upon it, no.:*

"I didn't think so." His shoulders were beginning to hurt again. He clasped his arms behind him and arched his back, looking up at the blue, cloudless sky. "Which means she'll keep trying to cure me by throwing every female above the age of consent within *leagues* at me. I could almost feel sorrier for the girls than I do for myself."

:*You ought to, Van.:*

He looked down at Yfandes' ears in surprise.

:*Did it ever occur to you that you could well have broken a fair number of susceptible young hearts?:*

He raised an eyebrow, skeptically. "Aren't you exaggerating?"

:*Think! What about the way you charmed that poor little kitchen girl back at the Palace?*:

He winced a little, recalling the romance in her eyes, but then irritation set in. "'Fandes, I've never done anything other than be polite to any of them."

She snorted. :*Exactly. Think about it. You're polite to them. Gallant. Occasionally even attentive. Think about the difference in your station and that kitchen maid's. What in Havens do you* think *she was expecting when you were polite to her? What does any young man of rank want when he notices a servant or a farmer's daughter?*:

Now he was something more than irritated. "I don't *suppose* it's occurred to you that it *might* just be the simple fact that I'm a Herald, a safe sort of romance object? Great good gods, 'Fandes, I doubt she had any notion of my rank!"

:*Well, what about all those young women your mother parades before you—telling them they're prospective brides? What do they think that gallantry is?*:

"I would imagine that *Mother* tells them plenty," he replied with heat, beginning to flush, and *very* glad there was no one about to overhear this conversation.

:*Well, you imagine wrong. Talking to servants is beneath her. As for the others, all* she *ever tells them is that you—and I quote—"lost your first love tragically." Now what in the Lady's name do you think that makes them want to do?*:

"Gods, 'Fandes, is that somehow *my* fault? Was I supposed to interrogate them while they were chasing me?"

:*You*,: she said, ice dripping from every word, :*never asked. Or bothered to ask. Or wanted to ask. It never occurred to you that Withen might not want it spread about the neighborhood that his first-born son prefers men?*:

"'Fandes," he replied, after a long, bitter moment of silence. "I don't see where it's any of your business. It has nothing to do with my duties as a Herald."

Silence on her part. Then, :*You're right. I'm sorry. I . . . overstepped myself. I—I just wanted you to think about what was going on.*:

"Is that what I've been doing?" he asked quietly.

:*Well—yes.*:

"Then I *should* apologize. I can't afford to react automatically to things—not even in my personal life. And—gods. Not when I'm *hurting* people."

A wash of relief. Then a tinge of sarcasm. :*You're thinking. And about time, too. Now are you going to enjoy a long wallow in self-accusation?*:

Something about the tone of her mind-voice—and the exact wording she'd used—made him pause for a moment. "Wait a minute—let me look at this from another angle." He made a mental checklist of all the young women Lady Treesa had pushed off on him, and what they'd done when he'd failed to succumb to their various charms. And the more he thought about it—

"You *are* exaggerating, aren't you?" he accused.

:*Well—yes. But the situation exists. What are you going to do about it?*:

"Be careful, I suppose. But I'll have to watch what I say."

:*Good. You're still thinking.*:

"The ones Mother keeps flinging at me are the hardest. If I tell them the truth, I'll hurt Father. I'll shame him, at the least. Even if I pledge them to silence, it'll get out."

:*So?*:

"I don't know. But I'll think about it."

:*Now* that *is the Vanyel I Chose.*: Her mind-voice was warm with approval. :*You're not "just" reacting anymore.*:

"Havens, I've been going numb between the ears for the past year, haven't I?"

:*Well—yes. You had reason but—.*:

He nodded, slowly. "This last year—I've gotten into a lot of habits."

:*Exactly. You can't let your heart or your habits control you. Not when you're who you are, and wield the power you do. Think about reacting emotionally in a battle situation. Think about even reacting reflexively, instead of tactically.*:

He did, and shuddered.

He always stopped at Halfway Inn—the name, he'd learned since, was a conscious pun—the hostelry that sat in the middle of the forest that cut Forst Reach off from the rest of the Kingdom.

In a way, what he had become had started here. The Inn had certainly marked his passage into a different world, though young Vanyel Ashkevron, more than half a prisoner of his escort, had not gotten the attention that Herald-Mage Vanyel got now.

It was an enormous place, and in the normal run of things very few travelers even saw the Innkeeper. A Herald was an exception. The Innkeeper himself saw to Vanyel's every whim—not that there were very many of those. The Inn was quite comfortable even for those who were less noteworthy than Vanyel.

There was less of the hero-worship here than there had been in other inns along the road. Vanyel was "local"; everyone attached to the inn and most of those staying there knew his family, his holding. They seemed to regard him with proprietary pride rather than awe, as if the things he had done were somehow reflections on *them*; as if his fame brought *them* fame. And as if *they* had something to do with what he had become.

In a way, perhaps they had. If events that occurred here had not made him feel so utterly alienated from the rest of the world, he might not have responded as strongly as he had to Tylendel.

He left Halfway Inn just after dawn, hoping to reach Forst Reach by early afternoon at the very latest. He had always made excellent time on this last leg of his journey every other time he'd made his trips home—though he always *left* much faster than he arrived. . . .

But he stopped Yfandes before they had traveled more than a candle-mark, while fog still wreathed the undergrowth and it was dark beneath the silent trees. The air was damp-smelling, with the tang of rotting leaves, and a hint of muskiness. No birds sang, and nothing rustled the fallen leaves underfoot or the branches overhead. This forest was *always* quiet, but this morning it was *too* quiet.

"Something's wrong," he said, straightening in his saddle, and pulling his cloak a little tighter around his shoulders.

:I can feel it, too,: Yfandes agreed, *:but it's very subtle.:*

This forest—unnamed, so far as he knew—had frightened him to the point of near-hysteria the first time he'd traveled this road. *Now* he knew why; there was magic here, old magic of the kind that the *Tayledras* used, that they frequently drained off in order to weaken it, and open the lands to more "normal" human settlements. The kind of magic that made the Pelagir Hills the changeling-haunted places they were. Anyone with so much as the potential for the Mage-Gift could feel enough to make them unhappy and uncomfortable.

But this magic had been dormant for a very long time.

"I'm going to probe," he said, and closed his eyes, going *in,* then opening *out*—

The magic was still there, but it lay even deeper below the fabric of the forest than it had the last time he had passed this way. Now that his Gift was fully trained, he could even see the traces that told him it *had* been drained by the *Tayledras* at least twice, which meant it should be "safe." The Hawk-brothers never left wild magic behind when they abandoned an area.

But that draining and abandonment had been long ago—very long ago.

Yes, the magic still slept, deeper than the taproots of the trees and harder to reach—but it slept uneasily. All magic was akin, and all magic touched all other magic—an affinity that made the Gate-spell possible. But close proximity meant stronger ties to magics that neighbored one another; disturbance to one site frequently disturbed another.

Vanyel could feel that disturbance in the magics here. A resonance with another pole of power at a distance—probably across the Border, and *most* probably in Baires, given that the ruling family was composed of mages. Something somewhere was powerfully warping kindred magic fields, and this field housed in the forest was resonating to that disturbance, like a lute string resonating to a touch on the one beside it.

But it was too far away, and the resonances too tenuous, for Vanyel to determine *who* was causing it, or *where* it originated, or even *what* was being done. Although—

Vanyel brought himself up out of his scanning-trance, and bit his lip in thought.

"'Fandes, did you get anything?"

:*No more than you,*: she replied uneasily, resuming her pace without his prompting. :*Except—the root of all this is evil.*:

"And I know better than to ask you to probe anything I can't reach. But I don't like it either. I like it even less now, with the Border uneasy. It makes me wonder if someone is forcing an issue—and if so, what, and to what end?"

:*Tell Lissa. That's all you can do for now.*:

He glanced uneasily to either side of him. "I'm afraid you're right, lady-love," he agreed. "I am afraid you're only too right."

CHAPTER 4

◆

DESPITE EVERYTHING HE'D told himself, despite being adult and with experiences behind him Withen could not even imagine, Vanyel felt his shoulders beginning to knot with anxiety the moment he crossed the gate marking the edge of the Forst Reach lands. By the time he rode through the gate in the wall that surrounded the Great House of the estate, he was fighting to keep himself from hunching down in the saddle like a sullen, frightened child.

It never changes. Outside these walls I may be a Herald-Mage who can admonish the King himself; inside—I'm Vanyel, prodigal son, with habits we don't talk about, and tastes best politely ignored. Gods, when are they ever going to accept me for who I am?

:Perhaps never. Perhaps when you accept yourself, Chosen.:

The unsolicited reply nettled him a little.

:Perhaps,: she continued, *:when you know who you are, and know it well enough that you can't be reduced to an adolescent just by riding through the gates.:*

He glanced down at Yfandes' ears, and then ahead, down the road to the destination that was causing him such discomfort. *:Are you saying I don't know who I am?:*

She didn't reply, but picked her pace up to a trot—the easy kind—and rounded the final curve and hill that brought them within sight of Forst Reach itself, bulking heavy and gray against the brilliant autumn sky.

The building had once been a defensive keep, and still had something of that blocky, no-nonsense look about it. It had long since been renovated and converted into a dwelling far more comfortable, though even at this distance Vanyel could see the faint outline of the moat under the lush grass surrounding it. Surrounded as it was by newer, smaller outbuildings of whitewashed stucco, it resembled a vast and rather ill-natured gray granite hen squatting among a flock of paler chicks.

Someone had been watching for him. Vanyel saw a small, fairly androgynous figure leave a position on a little rise beside the road and run toward the main building. It vanished somewhere in the vicinity of one of the old postern gates, which were now doors, and Vanyel assumed he (or she, though it was probably a page) had gone to tell the rest of the household that he had arrived. Heralds were distinctive enough to be spotted at any distance, and few enough that it would be safe to assume that any Herald coming to Forst Reach was going to be Vanyel.

Sure enough, people began emerging from doors all over the building, and by the time Vanyel and Yfandes reached the main doors—impressive black oaken monstrosities that had been set into a frame in what had once been the gateway to the center court—there was a sizable group waiting for him.

There was the usual babble of greetings—Treesa wept all over him, Withen gingerly clapped him on the shoulder, his brothers all followed Withen's example. There was the usual little dance when Withen told a page to "take Vanyel's horse" and Van—*again*—had to explain that Yfandes *wasn't* a horse, she was a Companion and his partner and that *he* would see to her. And as usual, Withen looked puzzled and skeptical, as if he was wondering if his son wasn't a bit daft.

But Vanyel was firm—as usual—and got his way. Because if he hadn't insisted (and the first visit home, he hadn't) Yfandes would be stripped of tack and given a good rubdown, then locked into a stall like the "valuable animal" she seemed to Withen to be. Van hadn't known what had happened that time until she wistfully Mindspoke him at dinner, asking if he'd come let her out, since she couldn't reach the lock on the door of the stall.

That night he had gone immediately down to the stable leaving his dinner half-eaten, and with profligate use of magic, created a new split door to the outside in one of the big loose boxes Withen used for mares in foal. Whenever he came home now, *that* stall was Yfandes', no matter if he had to move a mare out and scour it down to the wooden floor with his own two hands first. And no matter what sort of contrivance Withen had installed on the new door to keep it locked, Vanyel magicked it so that Yfandes could come and go as she pleased. Maybe Withen wondered why the box never had to be cleaned; certainly the stablehands did But Withen never seemed to grasp that Yfandes was *exactly* what his son said she was; a brilliant, thinking, creative lady, with all of a great lady's manners and daintiness, who just happened to be living in a horse's body.

Yfandes was still moderately amused. But Vanyel frequently thought that it was a good thing he'd never mentioned Withen's proposition on that first visit to breed her to the best of his palfrey-studs, or he'd have been using his magic to repair the gaping holes in the stable, instead of adding a door.

This time, at least, Withen had learned enough through repetition that the loose box had been vacated, scoured and bleached, and then filled with straw. But he *still* had left the outer door latched and double-locked.

Vanyel just sighed, magicked the locks in the *open* position, and pulled the top half of the door wide. He moved the latchstring for the lower half back through the hole to where Yfandes could get at it, then rummaged through his own packs for a longer bit of string so that she could pull it closed if she chose. Needless to say, the strap he'd attached there last time was gone.

"How hungry are you?" he asked her, stripping her tack and hanging it over the edge of the stall for the stablehands to clean, then beginning to rub her down. Straw dust tickled his nose and made him want to sneeze.

:Very,: she replied, testing the depth of the straw with a forehoof and nodding approval. :Just take the sweat off and get the knots out of my tail; I'm going to roll when I get out, and maybe swim in the pond.:

He heard Withen's footsteps on the path to the stable, and switched to Mindspeech. :Fine, love, just have your swim when nobody's watching or they'll send half the stablehands to pull you out. Now watch; I will bet you money that Father says, "Are you sure you should leave her that much food so soon after a long ride? She might founder.": He finished currying her, took the bucket off its hook, and went after grain for her.

"Are you sure you should leave her that much food so soon after a long ride?" Withen said dubiously from the stable-door proper, his square bulk blocking nearly all the light. "She might founder."

"Father, she isn't a horse; she knows better than to stuff herself silly. She told me she's very hungry. It's been a hard tour of duty for both of us, and both of us need to get back a little weight." Vanyel hung the bucket of mixed grains where Yfandes could get at it easily. :Now he'll say, "I suppose you know best, son, but—":

"I suppose you know best, son, but—" Withen moved cautiously up to the loose box as Vanyel forked in hay.

"Father, would *you* stuff yourself sick after a long day at the harvest?" At harvest-time Withen made it a point of spending one day with each of his tenants and several days with his own fieldhands, working beside them. It was one of the many things he did that endeared him to his people.

"Well—" Withen's heavy brows creased, and for once he looked uncertain. "—no."

"So, neither will she." He rinsed her water-bucket until it squeaked, filled it with absolutely clear, cold water, and hung it beside the grain bucket. Withen stepped forward as if he couldn't help himself.

"Son, she'll foul the water."

"Would Mother drop food into the wine in her goblet?" Vanyel sighed.

"Well—no."

"So, Yfandes wouldn't." *Since she has better manners than Mother.*

He Mindtouched Yfandes gently. *:All set, ladylove?:*

:Quite, beloved.: Yfandes' mind-voice was yellow and effervescent with amusement. *:Does he do that to you every time we come?:*

Vanyel rubbed her forehead between her eyes and she closed them with pleasure. *:Just about. Normally he doesn't follow me into the stable, but I get it when he hears from the stablehands what I did with you. Watch out for that so-called "Shin'a'in stallion"; I think he's sometimes allowed to run loose in this field. He might try and bully you; he might decide you're one of his mares and give you a little excitement.:*

She bared her front teeth delicately. *:I'd rather like to see him try anything on me. I could use a good fight.:*

He nearly choked. *:Now, love, you'll scare him impotent, and how will I explain that to Meke?:*

:Cleverly, of course. Go on with you; I'm fine and your father is fretting.:

"All right, Father, she says she's comfortable," he said aloud, forcing himself *not* to grin. "Let's go."

"Are you sure she should be left like that? What if she gets out?"

"Father," Vanyel sighed, sending the gods a silent plea for patience. "I *want* her to be able to come and go as she pleases."

"But—"

Vanyel wondered if his father ever really heard anything he said. "She's *not*," he repeated for the hundredth time, "a *horse*."

Vanyel was in time for dinner, a pleasure he would just as soon have done without. But once bathed, settled into the best guest room, and dressed in clean clothing—*not* a uniform, he wasn't on duty now, not even technically—his good sense prevailed over his reluctance. When the summons for dinner came, he followed the page and took his place at the high table. Withen *tried* to put him at his right, between himself and Vanyel's mother. Vanyel managed to convince him to let him take the usual seat guests took, on the end, displacing Radevel, who didn't look at all unhappy to be sitting down at the low table.

Sitting at the end he was spared having to make conversation with two people at once. His seat-mate proved to be Mekeal's thin, little red-haired wife Roshya, who took *all* the burden of conversation from him. She chattered nonstop, sparrowlike, without ever seeming to pause for breath. All *he* had to do was nod and make vague noises of agreement or disagreement from time to time, and he actually didn't mind; Roshya's gossip was cheerful and never malicious—if she had a fault it was that she seemed to assume he *must* know every highborn and family member for leagues around. After all, *she* did.

The dark, high-ceilinged hall seemed far more cramped than Vanyel remembered—until he counted heads, and realized that there were twice the number of folk dining than there had been when he was fifteen. He blinked, but the number didn't change. The low table had been lengthened, and a second table set at right angles to it at the other end, making an "H" shape with the high table.

And the high table had been lengthened, too; when Van had been sent to Haven and his aunt Savil, only Withen, Treesa, Jervis, Father Leren, and any guests they might have had been seated there—which had then included Vanyel's Aunt Serina and her Healer. Now, besides the original four, the table included the unmarried children, all three married sons, and their wives.

Great good gods, this isn't a family, it's a tribe!

The only one missing since his last visit seemed to be his youngest sister Charis; it looked like the only ones still home were the boys. After a moment of thought it seemed to him that he recalled getting word of Charis' wedding to somebody-or-other just after Elspeth's death. *Did I send a present? I must've, or I'd have heard about it five breaths after being greeted. That's right—I remember now—I sent that hideously pious tapestry of the Lady of Fertility. Aunt Savil took care of Meke and Roshya for me, and I sent Deleran those awful silver-and-crystal candlesticks. . . .*

But gods, did I do anything about Kaster and whatever-her-name-is? That was just seven or eight months ago, I was so tangled up in the Border-fight—I don't remember—

He continued to fret about that until Roshya's dropped comment about the "delightful bedcurtains, Kaster and Ria were *so* pleased," told him that if *he* hadn't, *Savil* must have sent something in his name. At that point he relaxed a little. From Roshya's chatter, Vanyel learned that she and Mekeal had *six* children thus far; Deleran and *his* wife had two, and Kaster's rather plump new bride—

Looks ready to spawn at any moment. Lord and Lady, they certainly didn't waste any time.

It made his head swim to think about it. Forst Reach was hardly a small holding, but it must be near to bursting at the seams.

He must have looked as if he were marginally interested in the new bride. Roshya waved her beringed hands in an artful imitation of Treesa, and launched into a dissertation on Lady Ria that was partly fact and mostly fancy—Vanyel was in a position to know. She'd been one of the young women his mother had thrown into his path the last time he'd been home. She looked content enough now with Kaster, which was something of a relief to his conscience.

He looked back down at the low table in one of Roshya's infrequent pauses for breath.

No wonder she's thin. She never stops talking to eat.

Radevel was the only face he recognized down there, although a good half the youngsters had the Ashkevron build and look. Radevel was stolidly munching his way through a heaping plateful of bread and roast when he caught Vanyel looking at him, and gave the Herald a shrug of the shoulders aimed at the mob of children, then a slow and quite deliberate wink.

Vanyel stifled a laugh. *So Father is still fostering dozens of cousins, and Radevel is still stuck here. Poor Rad; what is he, fifth son? Nowhere else to go, I guess. I bet Father's put him in charge of the younglings. Good choice. He'll keep them moderately in line. Better him than Jervis.*

He looked back up in time to catch crag-faced Jervis, the Forst Reach armsmaster, giving him an ugly glare. He met the glare impassively, but with an inward feeling of foreboding. *He's going to try something, I feel it in my bones. Great, that means I'll get to play cat-and-mouse with him through the whole visit.* He looked away when the armsmaster's eyes fell, only to find that saturnine Father Leren was giving him a look of ice and calculation, too, from beneath hooded lids. *Delightful, so I have both of them to deal with. Just what I needed. What a wonderful friendly visit this is going to be.*

He continued to make the appropriate noises at Roshya, and ignored the further stares of Jervis and Leren.

Mekeal had become so like Withen that Vanyel had to blink, seeing them together. Broad shoulders, brown beards trimmed identically, brown hair held back in identical tails with identical silver rings, dark brown eyes as open and readable as a dog's—dissimilar clothing was about all that differentiated them. That, and a few wrinkles in Withen's face, a few gray streaks in his hair and beard. Meke was perhaps a touch less muscular; not surprising since Withen's muscles had been built up in actual fighting during his career as a guard officer, and Meke had never seen any fighting outside of an occasional skirmish with bandits. But otherwise—Withen did *not* look his age; with all the silver in *his* hair and the stress-lines around his eyes, *Vanyel* could be taken for older than his father.

Treesa, on the other hand, had not aged gracefully. She was still affecting the light, diaphanous gowns and pale colors appropriate to a young girl. Even if he had not been aware of the various cosmetic artifices employed by the ladies of Randale's Court, Vanyel would have known the coloring of her hair and cheeks to be false.

She's holding onto youth with teeth and nails, and it's still getting away from her, he thought sadly. *Poor Mother. All she ever had to make her feel like she had some worth was being pretty and me, and she's losing both. Every year I become more of a stranger to her; every year her looks fade a little more.* He glanced over at Roshya, who seemed to be doing her best to imitate Lady Treesa, and was relieved to see a gleam of lively good humor in her green eyes, and to hear a little of that sense of humor reflected in what she was saying. Treesa would likely become a bitter, unpleasant old woman on her own—but not with Roshya around.

The rest of Vanyel's brothers had become thinner, more reckless copies of Meke. They ate heavily and drank copiously and roared jokes at each other across the length of table, emphasizing points with a brandished fork. *They're probably terrors on the hunt—and I bet they hunt every other day. And probably fighting when they aren't hunting. They need something to keep them occupied, can't Father see that?*

The more Vanyel saw, the uneasier he became. There was a restlessness in Withen's offspring that demanded an outlet, but there wasn't any. *No wonder Meke is hoping for a Border-war,* he realized as the meal drew to a close. *This place is like a geyser just about to blow. And when it does, if there isn't any place for that energy to go, someone is going to get hurt. Or worse.*

Servants began clearing the tables, and the adults rose and began to drift out on errands of their own. By Forst Reach tradition, the Great Hall belonged to the youngsters after dinner. Vanyel lingered until most of the others had gone out the double doors to the hallway; he was not in the mood to argue with anyone right now, or truly, even in the mood to make polite conversation. What he wanted was a quiet room, a little time to read, and more sleep.

It didn't seem as if the gods were paying much attention to *his* wants, lately.

Withen was waiting for him just beyond the doors.

"Son, about that horse—"

"Father, I keep telling you, Yfandes is *not*—"

Withen shook his head, an expression of marked impatience on his square face. "Not your Companion—*Mekeal's* horse. That damned stud he bought."

"Oh." Vanyel smiled sheepishly. "Sorry. Lately my mind stays in the same path unless you jerk its leash sideways. Tired, I guess."

For the first time Withen actually *looked* at him, and his thick eyebrows rose in alarm. "Son, you look like *hell*."

"I know," Vanyel replied. "I've been told."

"Bad?" Withen gave him the same kind of sober attention he gave to his own contemporaries. Vanyel was obscurely flattered.

"Take all the horror stories coming north from the Karsite Border and double them. *That's* what it's been like."

For once Withen's martial background was a blessing. He *knew* what Border-fighting was like, and his expression darkened for a moment. "Gods, son—that is *not* good to hear. So you'll be *needing* your rest. Well, I won't keep you too long, then—listen, let's take this out to the walk."

The "walk" Withen referred to was a stone porch, rather like a low balcony and equipped with a balustrade, that ran the length of the north side of the building. Why Grandfather Joserlin had put it there, no one knew. It overlooked the gardens, but not usefully, most of the view being screened off by the row of cypresses he'd had planted just beneath the railing. It could be accessed by one door, through the linen storeroom. Not many people used it, unless they wanted to be alone.

Which actually made it a fine choice for a private discussion.

Blue, hazy dusk, scented with woodsmoke, was all that met them there. Vanyel went over to the balustrade and sat on the top of it, and Withen began again.

"About that horse—have you seen it?"

"I'm afraid so," Vanyel replied. His window overlooked the meadows where the horses were turned loose to graze, and he'd seen the "*Shin'a'in* stud" kicking up his heels and attempting to impress Yfandes who was in the next field over. *She* had been ignoring him. "I hate to say this, Father, but Meke was robbed. I've *seen* a *Shin'a'in* warsteed; they're ugly, but not like that beast. They're smaller than that stud; they're not made to carry men in armor, they're bred to carry nomad horse-archers. They have *very* strong hindquarters, but their forequarters are just as strong, and they're a little short in the spine. 'Bunchy,' I guess you'd say. And their heads are large all out of proportion to the rest of them. The only thing a *Shin'a'in* warsteed has in common with Meke's nag is color. And besides, the only way an outsider could get a warsteed would be to steal a *young*, untrained one—and then kill the entire Clan he stole it from—and then kill the other Clans that came after him. No chance. Maybe somewhere there's *Shin'a'in* blood in that one, but it's cull blood if so."

Withen nodded. "I thought it might be something like that. *I've* seen their riding-beasts, the ones they *will* sell us. Beautiful creatures—so I knew that stud wasn't one of those, either: the animal is stupid, even for a horse, and that's going some. It's vicious, too—even with other horses; cut up the one mare Meke put it to before they could stop it. It's never been broken to ride, and I'm not sure it can be—and you know how I feel about that."

Vanyel half-smiled; one thing that Withen knew was his horses, and it was an iron-clad rule with him that *all* studs had to be broken for riding, the same as his geldings, and exercised regularly under saddle. No stud in *his* stable was allowed to laze about; when they weren't standing, they were working. It made them that much easier to handle at breeding-time. Most of Withen's own favorite mounts were his studs.

A mocker-bird shrilled in one of the cypresses, and Vanyel jumped at the unexpected sound. As he willed his heart to stop racing, Withen continued. "It hasn't taken a piece out of any of the stablehands yet, but I wonder if that isn't just lack of opportunity. And *this* is what Meke wants to breed half the hunter-mares to!"

Vanyel shook his head. *Damn! I hope this jumping-at-shadows starts fading out. If I can't calm myself down, I'm going to hurt someone.*

"I don't know what to tell you, Father. *I'd* have that beast gelded and put in front of a plow, frankly; I think that's likely all he's good for. Either that, or use the damned thing to train your more experienced young riders how to handle an unmanageable horse. But I'm a Herald, not a landholder; I have no experience with horsebreeding, and Meke is likely to point that out as soon as I open my mouth."

"But you *have* seen a real *Shin'a'in* warsteed," Withen persisted.

"Once. With a real *Shin'a'in* on its—her—back. The nomad in question told me they don't allow the studs anywhere near the edge of the Dhorisha Plains. Only the mares 'go into the world' as he put it." Even in the near dark and without using any Gift, Vanyel could tell his father was alive with curiosity. Valdemar saw the fabled *Shin'a'in* riding horses once in perhaps a generation and very few citizens of Valdemar had even seen the *Shin'a'in* themselves. Probably no one from Valdemar had ever seen a nomad on his warsteed until *he* had.

"Bodyguard, Father," he said, answering the unspoken question. "The nomad was a bodyguard for one of their shamans, and I met them both in the k'Treva Vale. I doubt the shaman would have needed one, except that he must have been nearly eighty. I tell you, he was the *toughest* eighty-year-old I'd ever seen. He'd come to ask help from the *Tayledras* to get rid of some monster that had decided the Plains looked good and the horses tasty, and moved in."

Withen shivered a little; talk of magic bothered him, and the fact that his son had actually been taught by the ghostly, legendary Hawkbrothers made him almost as uneasy as Vanyel's sexual inclinations.

The mocker-bird shrieked again, but this time Vanyel was able to keep from leaping out of his skin. "At any rate, I don't promise anything more except to try. But I want to warn you, I'm going to go at this the same way I'd handle a delicate negotiation. You won't see results at once, assuming I get any. Meke is as stubborn as that stud of his, and it's going to take some careful handling and a lot of carrots to get him to come around."

Withen nodded. "Well, that's all I can ask. I certainly haven't gotten anywhere with him. And that's *why* I asked you to stick your nose into this. I'm no diplomat."

Vanyel got up off the railing and headed for the door. "The fact is, Father, you and Meke are too damned much alike."

Withen actually chuckled. "The fact is, son, you're too damned right."

Vanyel slept until noon. The guest room was at the front of the building, well away from all the activity of the stables and yards. The bed curtains were as thick and dark as he could have wished. And someone had evidently given the servants orders to stay out of his room until he called for them. Which was just as well, since Van was trusting his reflexes not at all.

So he slept in peace, and rose in peace, and stood at the window overlooking the narrow road to the keep feeling as if he *might* actually succeed in putting himself back together if he could get a few more nights like the last one. A mere breath of breeze came in the window, and mocker-birds were singing—pleasantly, this time—all along the guttering above his head.

He could easily believe it to be still summer. He couldn't recall a gentler, warmer autumn.

He sent out a testing thought-tendril. *:'Fandes?:*

:Bright the day, sleepy one,: she responded, the Hawkbrother greeting.

He laughed silently, and took a deep breath of air that tasted only faintly of falling leaves and leafsmoke. *:And wind to thy wings, sweeting. Would you rather laze about or go somewhere today?:*

:Need you ask? Laze about, frankly. I think I'm going to spend the rest of the day the way I did this morning—napping in the sun, doing slow stretches. That pulled tendon needs favoring yet.:

He nodded, turning away from the window. *:I don't doubt. Makes me glad I was running lighter than normal after you pulled it.:*

She laughed, and moved farther out into her field so that he could see her from the window. *:I won't say it didn't help. Well, go play gallant to your mother and get it over with. With any luck, she hasn't had a chance to bring in one of the local fillies.:*

He grimaced, rang for a servant. One appeared with a promptness that suggested he'd been waiting right outside the door. Vanyel felt a pang of conscience, wondering how long he'd been out there.

"I'd like something to eat," he said, "and wash water, please. And—listen, there is no reason to expect me to wake before midmorning, and noon is likelier. I surely won't want anyone or anything before noon. So pass that on, would you? No use in having one of you cool his heels for hours!"

The swarthy manservant looked surprised, then grinned and nodded before hurrying off after Vanyel's requests. Vanyel hunted up his clothing, deciding on an almost-new dark blue outfit about the time the wash water arrived. It felt rather *strange* not to be wearing Whites, but at the same time he was reveling in the feel of silk and velvet against his skin. The Field uniforms were strictly utilitarian, leather and raime, wool and linen. And he hadn't had many occasions to wear formal, richer Whites. *No wonder they call me a peacock. Sensualist that I am—I like soft clothing. Well, why not?*

The manservant showed up with food as Vanyel finished lacing up his tunic. He considered his reflection in the polished steel mirror, and ended up belting the tunic; it had fit perfectly when he'd last worn it, but now—it looked ridiculously baggy without a belt.

He sighed, and applied himself to his breakfast. It was *always* far easier to gain weight than to lose it, anyway, that was one consolation!

After that he felt ready to face his mother. And whatever lady-traps she had baited and ready.

She always asked him to play whenever he stayed long enough, so he stripped the case from his lute and tuned it, then slung it on his back, and headed for her bower. Maybe he could distract her with music.

"Hello, Mother," Vanyel said, leaning down to kiss Treesa's gracefully extended, perfumed fingertips. "You look younger every time I see you."

The other ladies giggled, pretended to sew, fluttered fans. Treesa colored prettily at the compliment, and her silver eyes sparkled. For that moment the compliment wasn't a polite lie. "Vanyel, you have been away *far* too long!" She let her hand linger in his for a moment, and he gently squeezed it. She fluttered her eyelashes happily. Flirtation was Treesa's favorite game; courtly love her choice of pastime. It didn't matter that the courtier was her son; she had no intention of taking the game past the graceful and empty movements of the dance of words and gesture, and he knew it, and she knew he knew it, so everyone was happy. She was never so alive as when there was someone with her willing to play her game.

He fell in with the pretense, quite pleased that she hadn't immediately introduced anyone to him; that might mean she didn't have any girls she planned to fling at him. And she hadn't pouted at him either, so he was still in her good graces. He had *much* rather play courtier than have her rain tears and reproaches on his head for not spending more time with his family.

In the gauze-bedecked bower, full of fluttering femininity in pale colors and lace, he was quite aware that he looked all the more striking in his midnight blue. He *hoped* it would give him enough distinction—and draw enough attention to the silver in his hair—so that Treesa would remember he wasn't fifteen anymore. "Alas, first lady of my heart," he said with a quirk of one eyebrow, "I fear I had very little choice in the matter. A Herald's duty lies at the King's behest."

She dimpled, and patted the rose-velvet cushion of the stool placed beside her chair. "We've been hearing so many *stories* about you, Vanyel. This spring there was a minstrel here who sang *songs* about you!" She fussed with the folds of her saffron gown as he took his seat at her side. Her maids (those few who weren't at work at the three looms placed against the wall) and her fosterlings all gathered up their sewing and spinning at this unspoken signal and gathered closer. The sun-bright room glowed with the muted rainbow colors of their gowns, and Vanyel had to work to keep himself from smiling, as faces—young, and not-so-young, pretty and plain—turned toward him like so many flowers toward the sun. He'd not gotten *this* kind of attention even when he was the petted favorite of this very bower.

But then, when he'd been the bower pet, he'd only been a handsome fifteen-year-old, with a bit of talent at playing and singing. *Now* he was Herald-Mage Vanyel, the *hero* of songs.

:And all too likely to have his foot stepped on if he comes near me with a swelled head,: said Yfandes.

He bent his head over the lute and pretended to tune it until he could keep his face straight, then turned back to his mother.

"I know better songs than those, and far more suited to a lovely lady than tales of war and darkness."

There was disappointment in some faces, but Treesa's eyes glowed. "*Would* you play a love song, Van?" she asked coquettishly. "Would you play 'My Lady's Eyes' for me?"

Probably the most inane piece of drivel ever written, he thought. *But it has a lovely tune. Why not?*

He bowed his head slightly. "My lady's wish is ever my decree," he replied, and began the intricate introduction at once.

He couldn't help noticing Melenna sitting just behind a knot of three adolescents, her hands still, her eyes as dreamy as theirs. *She* was actually prettier now than she had been as a girl.

Poor Melenna. She never gives up. Almost fourteen years, and she's still yearning after me. Gods. What a mess she's made out of her life. He wondered somewhere at the back of his mind what had become of the bastard child she'd had by Mekeal, when pique at his refusing her had led her to Meke's bed. Was it a boy or girl? Was it one of the girls pressed closely around him now? Or had she lost it? Loose ends like that worried him. Loose ends had a habit of tripping you up when you least expected it, particularly when the loose ends were human.

He got the answer to his question a lot sooner than he'd guessed he would.

"Oh, Van, that was *lovely,*" Treesa sighed, then dimpled again. "You know, we haven't been *entirely* without Art and Music while you've been gone. I've managed to find myself another handsome little minstrel, haven't I, 'Lenna?"

Melenna glowed nearly the same faded-rose as her gown—one of Treesa's, remade; Vanyel definitely recollected it. "He's hardly as good as *Vanyel* was, milady," she replied softly.

"Oh, I don't know," Treesa retorted, with just a hint of maliciousness. "Medren, why don't you come out and let Vanyel judge for himself?"

A tall boy of about twelve with an old, battered lute of his own rose slowly from where he'd been sitting, hidden by Melenna, and came hesitantly to the center of the group. There was no doubt who his father was—he had Meke's lankiness, hair, and square chin, though he was smaller than Mekeal had been at that age, and his shoulders weren't as broad. There was no doubt either who his mother was—Melenna's wide hazel eyes stared at Vanyel from two faces.

The boy bobbed at Treesa. "I can't come close to those fingerings, milord, milady," he said, with an honesty that *felt* painful to Vanyel.

"Some of that's the fact that I've had near twenty years of practice, Medren," Vanyel replied, acutely aware that both Treesa and Melenna were eyeing him peculiarly. He was not entirely certain what was going on. "But there's some of it that's the instrument. This one has a very easy action—why don't you borrow it?"

They exchanged instruments; the boy's hands trembled as he took Vanyel's finely crafted lute. He touched the strings lightly, and swallowed hard. "What—" His voice cracked, and he tried again. "What would you like to hear, milord?"

Vanyel thought quickly; it had to be something that wouldn't be so easy as to be an insult, but *certainly* wouldn't involve the intricate fingerings he'd used on "My Lady's Eyes."

"Do you know 'Windrider Unchained'?" he asked, finally.

The boy nodded, made one false start, then got the instrumental introduction through, and began singing the verse.

And Vanyel nearly dropped the boy's lute as the sheer *power* of Medren's singing washed over him.

His voice wasn't *quite* true on one or two notes; that didn't matter. Time, maturity, and practice would take care of those little faults. His fingerings were sometimes uncertain; that didn't matter either. What mattered was that, while Medren sang, Vanyel *lived* the song.

The boy was Bardic Gifted, with a Gift of unusual power. And he was singing to a bowerful of empty-headed sweetly-scented marriage-bait, wasting a Gift that Vanyel, at fifteen, would willingly have sacrificed a leg to gain. *Both* legs. And counted the cost a small one.

It was several moments after the boy finished before Vanyel could bring himself to speak—and he really only managed to do so because he could see the hope in Medren's eyes slowly fading to disappointment.

In fact, the boy had handed him back his instrument and started to turn away before he got control of himself. "Medren—*Medren!*" he said insistently enough to make the boy turn back. "You are *better* than I was, even at fifteen. In a few years you are going to be *better* than I could ever hope to be if I practiced every hour of my life. You have the Bardic-Gift, lad, and that's something no amount of training will give."

He would have said more—he *wanted* to say more—but Treesa interrupted with a demand that *he* sing again, and by the time he untangled himself from the concentration the song required, the boy was gone.

The boy was on his mind all through dinner. He finally asked Roshya about him, and Roshya, delighted at having actually gotten a question out of him, burbled on until the last course was removed. And the more Vanyel heard, the more he worried.

The boy was being given—at Treesa's insistence—the same education as the legitimate offspring. Which meant, in essence, that he was being educated for exactly *nothing*. Except—perhaps—one day becoming the squire of one of his legitimate cousins. Meanwhile his *real* talent was being neglected.

The problem gnawed at the back of Vanyel's thoughts all through dinner, and accompanied him back to his room. He lit a candle and placed it on the small writing desk, still pondering. It might have kept him sleepless all night, except that soon after he flung himself down in a chair, still feeling somewhat stunned by the boy and his Gift, there came a knock on his door.

"Come—" he said absently, assuming it was a servant.

The door opened. "Milord Herald?" said a tentative voice out of the darkness beyond his candle. "Could—you spare a little time?"

Vanyel sat bolt upright. "Medren? Is that you?"

The boy shuffled into the candlelight, shutting the door behind him. He had the neck of his lute clutched in both hands. "I—" His voice cracked again. "Milord, you said I was good. I taught myself, milord. They—when they opened up the back of the library, they found where you used to hide things. Nobody wanted the music and instruments but me. I'd been watching minstrels, and I figured out how to play them. Then Lady Treesa heard me, she got me this lute. . . ."

The boy shuffled forward a few more steps, then stood uncertainly beside the table. Vanyel was trying to get his mind and mouth to work. That the boy was this good was amazing, but that he was entirely self-taught was miraculous. "Medren," he said at last, "to say that you astonish me would be an understatement. What can *I* do for you? If it's in my power, it's yours."

Medren flushed, but looked directly into Vanyel's eyes. "Milord Herald—"

"Medren," Vanyel interrupted gently, "I am *not* 'Milord Herald,' not to you. You're my nephew; call me by my given name."

Medren colored even more. "I—V-Vanyel, if you could—if you would—teach me? Please? I'll—" He coughed, and lowered his eyes, now turning a red so bright it was painful to look at. "I'll do anything you like. Just teach me."

Vanyel had no doubt whatsoever what the boy thought he was offering in return for music lessons. The painful—and very potently sexual—embarrassment was all too plain to his Empathy. *Gods, the poor child—* Medren wasn't even a temptation. *I may be shaych, but—not children. The thought's revolting.*

"Medren," he said very softly, "they warned you to stay away from me, didn't they? And they told you why."

The boy shrugged. "They said you were shaych. Made all kinds of noises. But hell, you're a Herald, Heralds don't *hurt* people."

"I'm shaych, yes," Vanyel replied steadily. "But you—you aren't."

"No," the boy said. "But hell, like I said, I wasn't worried. What you could teach me—that's worth anything. And I haven't got much else to repay you with." He finally looked back up into Vanyel's eyes. "Besides, there isn't anything you could do to me that'd be worse than Jervis beating on me once a day. And they all seem to think *that's* all right."

Vanyel started. "Jervis? What—what do you mean, Jervis beating on you? Sit, Medren, please."

"What I said," the boy replied, gingerly pulling a straight-backed chair to him and taking a seat. "I get treated just like the rest of them. Same lessons. Only there's this little problem; I'm *not* true-born." His tone became bitter. "With eight *true-born* heirs and more on the way, where does that leave me? Nowhere, that's where. And there's no use in currying favor with *me*, or being a little easy on *me*, 'cause I don't have a thing to offer anybody.

So when time comes for an example, who gets picked? Medren. When we want a live set of pells to prove a point, who gets beat on? Medren. And what the hell do I have to expect at the end of it, when I'm of age? Squire to one of the *true-born* boys if I'm lucky, the door if I'm not. Unless I can somehow get good enough to be a minstrel."

Vanyel's insides hurt as badly as if Medren had punched him there. *Gods*—His thoughts roiled with incoherent emotions. *Gods, he's like I was— he's just like I was—only he doesn't have those thin little protections of rank and birth that I had. He doesn't have a Lissa watching out for him. And he has the Gift, the precious Gift. My gods—*

"'Course, my mother figures there's another way out," Medren continued, cynically. "Lady Treesa, she figures you've turned down so many girls, she figures she's got about one chance left to cure you. So she told my mother you were all hers, she could do whatever it took to get you. And if my mother could get you so far as to marry her, Lady Treesa swore she'd get Lord Withen to allow it. So my mother figures on getting into your breeches, then getting you to marry her—then to adopt me. She says she figures the last part is the easiest, 'cause she watched you watching me, and she knows how you feel about music and Bards and all. So she wanted me to help."

Poor Melenna. She just can't seem to realize what she's laying herself open for. "So why are you telling me this?" Vanyel found his own voice sounding incredibly calm considering the pain of past memories, and the ache for this unchildlike child.

"I don't like traps," Medren said defiantly. "I don't like seeing them being laid, I don't like seeing things in them, and I don't much like being part of the bait. And besides all that, you're—special. I don't want anything out of you that you've been tricked into giving."

Vanyel rose, and held out his hand. Medren looked at it for a moment, and went a little pale despite his brave words. He looked up at Vanyel with his eyes wide. "You—you want to see my side of the bargain?" he asked tremulously.

Vanyel smiled. "No, little nephew," he replied. "I'm going to take you to my father, and we're going to discuss your future."

Withen had a room he called his "study," though it was bare of anything like a book; a small, stone-walled room, windowless, furnished with comfortable, worn-out old chairs Treesa wouldn't allow in the rest of the keep. It was where he brought old cronies to sit beside the fire, drink, and trade tall tales; it was where he went after dinner to stare at the flames and nurse a last mug of ale. That's where Vanyel had expected to find him, and when Vanyel ushered Medren into the stuffy little room, he could tell by his father's stricken expression that Withen was assuming the absolute worst.

"Father," he said, before Withen could even open his mouth, "do you know who this boy is?"

Candlelight flickered in his father's eyes as Withen looked at him as if he'd gone insane, but he answered the question. "That's—uh—Medren. Melenna's boy."

"Melenna *and Mekeal's,* Father," Vanyel said forcibly. "He's Ashkevron blood, and by that blood, we owe him. Now just how are we paying him? What future does he have?" Withen started to answer, but Vanyel cut him off. "I'll tell you, Father. None. There are *how* many wedlock-born heirs here? And *how* much property? Forst Reach is big, but it isn't *that* big! Where does that leave the little tagalong bastard when there may not be enough places for the legitimate offspring? What's he going to do? Eke out the rest of his life as somebody's squire? What if he falls in love and wants to marry? What if he doesn't *want* to be somebody's squire all his life? You've given him the same education and *the same wants* as the rest of the boys, Father. The same expectations, *the same needs.* How do you plan on making him content to take a servant's place after being raised like one of the heirs?"

"I—uh—"

"Now I'll tell you something else," Vanyel continued without giving him a chance to answer. "This young man is Bardic-Gifted. That Gift is as rare—and as valued in Valdemar—as the one that makes me a Herald. And we Ashkevrons are letting that rare and precious Gift rot here. Now what are we going to do about it?"

Withen just stared at him. Vanyel waited for him to assimilate what he'd been told. The fire crackled and popped beside him as Withen blinked with surprise. "*Bardic-Gifted? Rare?* I knew the boy played around with music, but—are you telling me the boy can make a future out of *that?*"

"I'll tell you more than that, Father. Medren *will be* a first-class Bard *if* he gets the training, and gets it *now.* A Full Bard, Father. Royalty will pour treasure at his feet to get him to sing for them. He could earn a noble rank, higher than yours. But only if he gets what he needs now. And I mean *right* now."

"What?" Withen's brow wrinkled in puzzlement.

Vanyel could see that he was having a hard time connecting "music" with "earning a noble rank."

"You mean—send him to Haven? To Bardic Collegium?"

"That's exactly what I mean, Father," Vanyel said, watching Medren out of the corner of his eye. The boy was in serious danger of losing his jaw, or popping his eyes right out of their sockets. "And I think we should send him as soon as we can spare him an escort—when the harvest is over at the very latest. I will be *happy* to write a letter of sponsorship to Bard Chadran; if Forst Reach won't cover it, I'm sure my stipend will stretch enough to take care of his expenses."

That last was a wicked blow, shrewdly designed to awake his father's sense of duty and shame.

"That won't be necessary, son," Withen said hastily. "Great good gods, it's the least we can do! If—if that's what *you* want, Medren."

"What I want?" the boy replied, tears coming to his eyes. "Milord—I— oh, Milord—it's—" He threw himself, kneeling, at Withen's feet.

"Never mind," Withen said hastily, profoundly embarrassed. "I can see it is. Consider it a fact; we'll send you off to Haven with the Harvest-Tax." The boy made as if to grab Withen's hand and kiss it. Withen waved him off. "No, now, go on with you, boy. Get up, get up! Don't grovel like that, dammit, you're Ashkevron! And don't thank me, I'm just the old fool that was too blind to see what was going on under my nose. Save your thanks for Vanyel."

Medren got to his feet, clumsy in his adolescent awkwardness, made clumsier by dazed joy. Before the boy could repeat the gesture, Vanyel took him by the shoulders and steered him toward the door.

"Why don't you go tell your mother about your good news, Medren?" He winked at the boy, and managed to get a tremulous grin out of him. "I'm certain she'll be very surprised."

That sentence made the grin widen, and take on a certain conspiratorial gleam. Medren nodded, and Vanyel pushed him out the door, shutting it tightly behind him.

He turned back to face Withen, and there was *no* humor in his face or his heart now.

"Father—we have to talk."

CHAPTER 5

"WHAT?" WITHEN ASKED, his brow wrinkling in perplexity.
"I said, we have to talk. Now." Vanyel walked slowly and carefully toward his father, exerting every bit of control he possessed to keep his face impassive. "About you. About me. And about some assumptions about me that you keep making."

He stood just out of arm's length of Withen's chair, struggling to maintain his composure. "When I brought Medren in here, I *knew* what you were thinking, just looking at your expression."

The fire flared up, lighting Withen's face perfectly.

And you're still *thinking it—*

Vanyel came as close as he ever had in his life to exploding, and kept his voice down only by dint of much self-control. It took several moments before he could speak.

"Dammit, Father, *I'm not like that!* I don't *do* things like that! I'm a Herald—and dammit, I'm a decent man—I *don't* molest little boys! Gods, the idea makes me want to vomit, and that *you* automatically assumed I had—"

He was trembling, half in anger, half in an anguished frustration that had been held in check for nearly ten years.

Withen squirmed, acutely uncomfortable with this confrontation. "Son, I—"

Vanyel cut him off with an abrupt shake of his head, then held both his hands outstretched toward Withen in entreaty. "Why, Father, *why? Why* can't you believe what I tell you? What have I *ever* done to make you think I have no sense of honor? When have I ever been anything other than honest with you?"

Withen stared at the floor.

"Look," Vanyel said, grasping at anything to get his point across, "let's turn this around. I know damned good and well you've had other bedpartners than Mother, but do I assume *you* would try to—to seduce that little-girl chambermaid of hers? Have I looked sideways at *you* whenever you've been around one of her ladies? So why should *you* constantly accuse me in your mind—*assuming* that I would *obviously* be trying to seduce every susceptible young man and vulnerable little boy in sight?"

Withen coughed, and flushed crimson.

He'd probably be angry, Vanyel thought, in a part of his mind somewhere beyond his anguish, *except that this frontal assault isn't giving him time to be anything other than embarrassed.*

"You—could use your reputation. As a—the kind of person they write those songs about." Withen flushed even redder. "A hero-worshipping lad would find it hard to—deny you. Might even think it your due and his duty."

"Yes, Father, that's only too true. Yes, I *could* use my reputation. Don't think I'm not acutely aware of that. But I *won't*—would *never*! Can't you understand that? I'm a Herald. I have a moral obligation that I've pledged myself to by accepting that position."

By the blankness of Withen's expression, Vanyel guessed he had gone beyond Withen's comprehension of what a "Herald" was. He tried again. "There're more reasons than that; I'm a *Thought-senser,* Father, did you ever think what *that* means? The constraints it puts on me? The things I'm open to? It's a harder school of honor than *ever* Jervis taught. There are no compromises, mind-to-mind. There are no falsehoods; there can't be. A relationship for me has to be one of absolute equals, freely giving, freely sharing—or nothing." Still no flicker of understanding. He used blunter language. "No rape, Father. No unwilling seduction. No lies, no deception. No harm. No one who doesn't already know what he is. No one who hasn't made peace with what he is, and accepted it. No innocents, who haven't learned what they are. *No children.*"

Withen looked away, fidgeting a little in his chair. Vanyel moved swiftly to kneel between him and the fire, where Withen couldn't avoid looking at him. "Father—dammit, Father, I *care* about you. I don't want to make you unhappy, but I can't help what I am."

"Why, Van?" Withen's voice sounded half-strangled. "Why? What in hell did I do wrong?"

"Nothing! Everything! *I* don't know!" Vanyel cried out, his words trembling in the air, a tragic song tortured from the strings of a broken lute. "Why am I Gifted? Why am I *anything*? Maybe it's something I was born with. Maybe the gods willed it. Maybe it's nothing more than the fact that the only person I'll *ever* love happened to be born into the same sex body that I was!" Grief knotted his throat and twisted his voice further. "All I know is that I *am* this way, and nothing is going to change that. And I care for my father, and nothing is going to change *that*. And if you can't believe in me, in *my* sense of honor—oh, *gods*, Father—"

He got to his feet somehow, and held out his open hands toward Withen in a desperate plea for understanding. "Please, Father—I'm not asking for much. I'm not asking you to *do* anything. Only to believe that I am a decent human being. Believe in Herald Vanyel if you won't believe in your son. Only—*believe*; believe that no one will ever come to harm at my hands. And *try* to understand. Please."

But there still was no understanding in Withen's eyes. Only uncertainty, and acute discomfort. Vanyel let his hands fall and turned away, defeated. The last dregs of his energy had been burned out, probably for nothing.

"I—I'm sorry, son—"

"Never mind," Vanyel said dully, bleakly, walking slowly toward the door. "Never mind. I've lived with it this long, I should be used to it. Listen; I'm going to make you a pledge, since you won't believe me without one. Medren is safe from my advances, Father. Your grandsons are safe. *Every damned thing on this holding down to the sheep is safe.* All right? You have my damned oath as a damned Herald on it. Will that be enough for you?"

He didn't wait to hear the answer, but opened the door quickly and shut it behind him.

He leaned against it, feeling bitterness and hurt knotting his gut, making his chest ache and his head throb. And eleven years' experience as a Herald was all that enabled him to cram that hurt back down into a little corner and slap a lid on it, to fiercely tell the lump in his throat that it was *not* tears and it *would* go away. Maybe he would deal with all this later—not now. Not when he was drained dry, and not when he was alone.

"Heyla, Van!" The voice out of the dark corridor beside him startled him, and he whirled in reaction, his hands reaching for weapons automatically.

He forced himself to relax and made out who it was.

Gods—just what I needed.

"Evening, Meke," he replied; tired, and not bothering to hide it. "What brings you out tonight?"

Lady Bright, that sounds feeble even to me.

"Oh," Mekeal replied vaguely, moving into the range of the lantern beside the study door. "Things. Just—things. Where were you off to?"

"Bed." Vanyel knew his reply was brusque, even rude, but it was either that or let Meke watch him fall to pieces. "I'm damned tired, Meke; I've got a lot of rest to catch up on."

Mekeal nodded, his expression softening a little with honest concern. "You look like hell, Van, if you don't mind my saying so."

Gods. Not again.

"The last year hasn't been a good one. Especially not on the Borders."

"That's exactly what I wanted to talk to you about," Mekeal interrupted eagerly, coming so close that Vanyel could see the lantern flames reflected in his eyes. "Listen, can you spare me a little time before you go off to bed? Say a candlemark or so?"

Vanyel stifled a sigh of exasperation. *All right, stupid, you gave him the opening, you have only yourself to blame that he took it.* "I suppose so."

"Great! Come on." Mekeal took Vanyel's elbow and hauled him down the ill-lit corridor, practically running in his eagerness. "You've seen that stud I bought?"

"From a distance," Vanyel replied cautiously.

"Well, I want you to come have a good look at him, and he really doesn't settle down until well after dark."

I can believe that.

They walked rapidly down the hollow-sounding corridor, Mekeal chattering on about his acquisition. Vanyel made a few appropriately conversational sounds, but was far more interested in reestablishing his "professional" calm than in anything Meke was saying. Meke was obviously heading for the corridor that led to one of the doors to the stable yard, so Vanyel pulled his arm free and picked up his own pace a little. *Might as well get this over with now, while I'm still capable of standing.*

Mekeal obviously had this planned, for when they emerged into the cool darkness and a sky full of stars, Vanyel saw the dim glow of a lantern in the stable across the yard. They crossed the yard at something less than a run, but not for lack of Mekeal's trying to hurry his steps.

The famous stud had pride of place, first stall by the entrance, by the lantern. Vanyel stared at it; if anything it was worse up close than at a distance.

Ugly is not the word for this beast.

It glared over its shoulder at him as if it had heard his thought, and bared huge yellow teeth at him.

I've never seen a nastier piece of work in my life. You couldn't pay me enough to try and saddle-break this nag!

"Well?" Meke said, bursting with pride. "What do you think?"

Vanyel debated breaking the bad news easily, then remembered what his little brother was like. He not only did not take hints well, he never even knew there was such a thing as a subtle hint. Vanyel braced himself, and told the truth. "Meke—there's no way to say this tactfully. That monster is no more *Shin'a'in* than I am. You were robbed."

Mekeal's face fell.

"I've *seen* a *Shin'a'in* warsteed," Vanyel said, pressing his advantage. "She was under a *Shin'a'in*. The nomad told me then that they don't ever sell the warbeasts, and that they literally would not permit one to be in the hands of an outsider. And they never, *never* let the studs off the Dhorisha Plains. I'll give you a full description. The mare I saw was three hands shorter than this stud of yours, bred to carry a *small* horse-archer, not anyone in heavy plate; she was short-backed, deep-chested, and her hindquarters were a little higher than her forequarters. She had a *big* head in proportion to the rest of her, and if anything, this stud's head is small. Besides being large, her skull had an incredibly broad forehead. *Lots* of room for brains. Need I say more? About the only things she had in common with your stud are color and muscles." He sighed. "I'm sorry, Meke, but—"

"A half-breed? Couldn't he be a cross?" Mekeal asked desperately.

"*If* a common stud caught the mare in season and *if* she didn't kill him first and *if* the mare's owner decided—against all tradition—to sell the foal instead of destroying it or sending it back to the Plains. Maybe. Not bloody likely, but a very bare possibility. It is also a *very* bare possibility that this stud has *Shin'a'in* cull blood somewhere *very* far back in his line." Vanyel rubbed his nose and sneezed in the dust rising as the stud fidgeted in his stall. The precious stud laid his ears back, squealed, and cow-kicked the door to the box as hard as he could. More dust rose, there was a clatter of hooves all through the stable, and startled whinnies as the rest of the horses reacted to the stud's display of ill-temper. "Meke, *why* did you buy this monster? Forst Reach has the best line of hunters from here to Haven."

"Hunters won't do us a hell of a lot of good when there's an army marching toward us," Mekeal said, turning to look at him soberly. "And even if this lad isn't *Shin'a'in*, crossed into our hunters he'll sire foals with the muscle to carry men in armor. I just hope to hell we have them *before* we need them."

Incredulous at *those* words coming from *this* sibling, Vanyel looked across his shoulder at his younger brother. "*That's* what this is about?"

Meke nodded, the flickering lantern making him look cadaverous—and *much* older. "There's trouble coming up on the West. Even if it *doesn't* come from Baires and Lineas, one or both, it'll come from the changeling lands beyond them. It's been building since Elspeth died. Every year we get more weird things crossing over into Valdemar. Plenty of them here. Check the trophy room some time while you're visiting; you'll get an eyeful. Liss thinks they're either being driven here by something worse, or they're being sent to test our defenses; neither notion makes me real comfortable. Hunters are all very well, but they *can't* carry a fighter in full armor. And the tourney-horses I've been seeing lately don't have the stamina for war. One thing this lad *does* have is staying power."

Gods. Oh, gods. If the problems are so evident even Meke is seeing them— Vanyel's spine went to ice.

"Do you want my advice with this beast?" he asked bluntly.

Mekeal nodded.

"Given what you've told me, he might be useful after all. Breed him to the best-tempered and largest of the hunter-mares. *And* see what comes of breeding him to plowhorse mares. Maybe make a second-generation three-way cross—if you have time."

Meke nodded again, smoothing his close-cropped beard. "I hadn't thought about plowbeasts; that's a good notion. He is vicious. I like the willingness to fight, but I can do without viciousness. So, you agree with me?"

Vanyel turned slowly, a new respect for his brother coloring his thoughts. "Meke, even if this Border stays quiet, there's Karse, there's Hardorn, there's Iftel—Rethwellan *seems* quiet, but *their* king is old and that could change when he dies. There's even the north, if those barbarians ever find a leader to weld them into a single fighting force. May the gods help us—you'll have a ready market all too soon if you can breed the kind of horses you're talking about." Vanyel pondered the worn, scrubbed wooden floor of the stable. "What have *you* heard? About here, I mean."

"The Mavelans want Lineas. Badly enough to chance a war with us, I don't know. The Lineans don't much like either Baires or Valdemar, but they figure Valdemar is marginally better, so they'll put up with us enforcing the peace as third-party. It all comes down to what's going to happen with this mess with Tashir being disinherited."

Lady Bright, more words of political wisdom where I never expected to find them. His view may be shortsighted—he may not see the larger picture—but where his neighbors are concerned, my little brother seems to have them well weighed and measured.

"I heard Lord Vedric is behind the protests," Vanyel ventured. Mekeal looked skeptical.

"One thing I've learned watching them, anything the Mavelans do openly has about fifty motives and is hiding a dozen other moves. The protest might be a covering move for something else. Vedric might have the backing of the family. Vedric might be operating under orders. Vedric might be acting on his own. Vedric might have nothing to do with it. And Vedric might really be Tashir's father—and might actually be trying to do something for the boy. The gods know he hasn't any true-born offspring and it's not that he hasn't tried."

Vanyel nodded and stowed that tidbit away. "I'll tell you what, Meke, I'll do what I can to get Father to see why you want to breed this stud—and persuade him that since you *aren't* breeding hunters, he ought to leave you alone to see what you can come up with. But those sheep—"

Mekeal coughed and blushed. "Those sheep were a damnfool thing to do. There's no market, not with Whitefell just south of us, with furlongs of meadow good for nothing *but* sheep. But dammit, the old man goes *on* and *on* about it until I'm about ready to bash him with a damned candlestick! I am *not* going to give in to him! We aren't *losing* money, we just aren't making as much. And if I give in to him on the sheep, he'll expect me to give in to him on the stud."

Vanyel groaned. "Lady bless! The two of you are stubborn enough to make an angel swear! Look—if I manage to get him to agree on the stud, will you *please* agree to clear out the damned sheep? Bright Havens, can't *one* of you show a little sense in the interests of peace and compromise?"

Mekeal glowered, and Mekeal grumbled, but in the end, on the way back to the keep, Mekeal grudgingly agreed.

The silken voice stopped Vanyel halfway between the keep and the stables, dimming the bright autumn sunlight and casting a pall on the sweetness of the late-morning sky.

"Good—morning. Herald Vanyel." The slight hesitation before the second word called pointed attention to the fact that it lacked little more than a candlemark till noon. The cool tone made it clear that Father Leren did not approve of Vanyel's implied sloth.

Vanyel paused on the graveled path, turned, and inclined his head very slightly in the priest's direction. "Good afternoon, Father Leren," he replied, without so much as an eyebrow twitching.

The priest emerged from the deeply recessed doorway of the keep's miniature temple, a faithful gray-granite replica of the Great Temple at Haven. Leren had persuaded Withen to build it shortly after his arrival as Ashkevron priest, on the grounds that the chapel, deep within the keep it-self, couldn't possibly hold the family and all of the relatives on holy days. It had been a reasonable request, although the old priest had managed by holding services in shifts, the way meals were served in the Great Hall. Vanyel alone had resented it; the little gray temple had always seemed far too confining, stifling, for all that it was five times the size of the chapel. The homely wood-paneled chapel made the gods seem—closer, somehow. Forgiving rather than forbidding. He had hated the temple from the mo-ment he'd first stepped into it at the age of five—and from that moment on, had refused to enter it again. In fact, Vanyel wasn't entirely certain that Leren had ever even set foot in the *old* chapel—which was why, as a boy, he had accomplished his own worship *there*.

"I have seen very little of you, my son," came the cool words. The priest's lean, dusky face beneath his slate-gray cowl was as expressionless as Vanyel's own.

Vanyel shrugged, shifted his weight to one foot, and folded his arms across his chest. *If he wants to play word-games*—"I'm not surprised, sir," he replied with detached civility. "I have spent very little time outside of my room. I've been using this time alone to catch up on a year's worth of lost sleep."

Leren allowed one black eyebrow to rise sardonically. "Indeed? Alone?" His expression was not quite a sneer.

Oh, what the hell. In for a sheep— Vanyel went into a full-scale imitation of the most languid fop at Haven.

The man in question *wasn't* inclined to *shay'a'chern,* as it happened: ru-mor had it he played the effeminate to irritate . . . not Vanyel—but certain of his colleagues—and he *also* happened to be one of the finest swordsmen outside of the Circle or the Guard.

Following that sterling example, Vanyel set out to be *very* irritating.

"*Quite* alone, sad to say," he pouted. "But then again, I *am* here for a *rest.* And company would *hardly* be *restful.*"

The priest retreated a step, surprise flashing across his face before he shuttered his expression. "Indeed. And yet—I am told young Medren spends an inordinate amount of time in your rooms." His tone insinuated what he did not—quite—dare say.

I won't take that from Father, you snake. I'm damned if I'll take that from you. Vanyel transformed the snarl he wanted to sport into an even more petulant pout. "Oh, *Medren.* I'm teaching him music. He is a sweet child, don't you think? But still, a child. *Not* company. I prefer my companions to be—somewhat older." He took a single slow step toward the priest, and twitched his hip *ever* so slightly. "Adult, and able to hold an adult conversation, to have adult—interests." He took another step, and the priest fell back, a vague alarm in his eyes. "More—masterly. Commanding." He tilted his head to one side and regarded the priest thoughtfully for a moment. The alarm was turning to shock and panic. "Now, someone like *you,* dear Leren—"

The priest squawked something inarticulate about vessels needing consecrating, and groped behind him for the handle of the open temple door. Within a heartbeat he was through it, and had the gray-painted door shut—tightly—behind him.

Vanyel grinned, tucked his head down to hide his expression, and continued on toward the stables and Yfandes.

"Meke, is there going to be a Harvest Fair this year?" he asked, brushing Yfandes with vigor, as she leaned into the brush strokes and all but purred.

Mekeal did not look up from wrapping the ankles of one of his personal hunters. "Uh-huh," he grunted. "Should be near twice as big as the ones you knew. Got merchants already down at Fair Field."

"Already?" This was more than he'd dared hope. "Why?"

"Liss an' her company, dolt." Meke finished wrapping the off hind ankle and straightened with another grunt, this time of satisfaction. "Got soldiers out here with pay burnin' their pockets off, and nothin' to spend it on. There're only two ladies down at Forst Reach village that peddle their assets, and three over to Greenbriars, and it's too far to walk except on leave-days anyway. So they sit in camp and drink issue-beer and gripe. Can you see a merchant allowin' a situation like *that* to go unrelieved? There's a *good* girl," he said to the mare, patting her ample rump. "We'll be off in a bit."

:Keep brushing. You can talk and brush at the same time.:

Vanyel resumed the steady strokes of the brush, working his way down Yfandes' flank. "Would there be any instrument makers, do you think?" Forst Reach collected a peddling fee from every merchant setting his wagon up at the two Fairs, Spring and Harvest. Withen found that particular task rather tedious—and Vanyel hoped now he'd entrusted it to Mekeal.

Meke sucked on his lip, his hand still on the mare's shoulder. "Now that I think of it, there's one down there already. Don't think we'll likely get more than one. Why?"

"Something I have in mind," he replied vaguely. And, to Yfandes, :*Lady-my-love, do you think I can interest you in a little trip?*:

She sighed. :*So long as it's a little trip.*:

:*This soft life is spoiling you.*:

:*Mmh,*: she agreed, blinking lazily at him. :*I like being spoiled. I could get used to it very quickly.*:

He chuckled, and went to get her gear.

Before Vanyel even found someone who knew which end of Fair Field the luthier was parked in, he had picked up half a dozen trifles for Shavri and Jisa.

He paused in the act of paying for a jumping jack, struck by the fact that they were so uppermost in his mind.

What has gotten into me? he wondered. *I haven't thought about them for a year, and now—*

Well, I haven't seen them for a year. That's all. And if I can give Shavri a moment of respite from her worry—

He pocketed the toy and headed for the grove of trees at the northern end of the field.

He spotted the faded red wagon at once; there was an old man seated on the back steps of it, bent over something in his hands.

Shavri, bent over a broken doll some child in the House of Healing had brought to her. Looking up at me with a face wet with tears. Me, standing there like an idiot, then finally getting the wits to ask her what was wrong. "I can't bear it, Van, I can't—Van, I want a baby—"

He shoved the memory away, hastily.

"Excuse me," Vanyel said, after waiting for the carver perched on the back steps of his scarlet traveling-wagon (part workshop, part display, and part home) to finish the wild rose he was carving from a bit of goldenoak. He still hesitated to break the old man's concentration in the middle of such a delicate piece of work, but there wasn't much left of the afternoon. If he was going to find the purported luthier—

But the snow-pated craftsman's concentration had evidently weathered worse than Vanyel's gentle interruption. "Aye?" he replied, knobby fingers continuing to shape the delicate, gold-sheened petals.

"I'm looking for Master Dawson."

"You're looking at him, laddybuck." Now the oldster put down his knife, brushed the shavings from his leather apron, and looked up at Vanyel. His expression was friendly in a shortsighted, preoccupied way, his face round, with cloudy gray-green eyes.

"I understand you have musical instruments for sale?"

The carver's interest sharpened, and his eyes grew less vague. "Aye," he said, standing, and pulling his apron over his head. There were a few shavings sticking to the linen of his buff shirt and breeches, and he picked at them absently. "But—in good conscience I can't offer 'em before Fair-time, milord. Not without Ashkevron permission, any rate."

Vanyel smiled, feeling as shy as a child, and tilted his head to one side. "Well, I'm an Ashkevron. Would it be permissible if I made it right with my father?"

The old man looked him over very carefully. "Aye," he said, after so long a time Vanyel felt as if he was being given some kind of test. "Aye, I think 'twould. Come in the wagon, eh?"

Half a candlemark later, with the afternoon sun shining into the crowded wagon and making every varnished surface glow, Vanyel sighed with disappointment. "I'm sorry, Master Dawson, none of these lutes will do." He picked one at random off the rack along the wall of the wagon interior, and plucked a string, gently. It resonated—but not enough. He put it back, and locked the clamp that held it in place in the rack. "Please, don't mistake my meaning, they're beautiful instruments and the carving is fine, but—they're—they're student's lutes. They're all alike, they have no voice of their own. I was hoping for something a little less ordinary." He shrugged, hoping the man wouldn't become angered.

Strangely enough, Dawson didn't. He looked thoughtful instead, his face crossed by a fine net of wrinkles when he knitted his brows. 'Huh. Well, you surprise me, young milord—what did you say your name was?"

Vanyel blushed at his own poor manners. "I didn't, I'm sorry. Vanyel."

"Vanyel—that—Vanyel Ashkevron—my Holy Stars! The *Herald*?" the luthier exclaimed, his eyes going dark and round. "Herald Vanyel? The Shadow—"

"Stalker, Demonsbane, the Hero of Stony Tor, yes," Vanyel said wearily, sagging against the man's bunk that was on the wall opposite the rack of instruments. The instrument maker's reaction started a headache right behind his eyes. He dropped his head, and rubbed his forehead with one hand. "Please. I really—get tired of that."

He felt a hard, callused hand patting his shoulder, and he looked up in surprise into a pair of very sympathetic and kindly eyes. "I 'magine you do, lad," the old man said with gruff understanding. "Sorry to go all goose-girl on you. Just—person don't meet somebody folks sing about every day, an' he sure don't expect to have a hero come strollin' up to him at a Border Harvest Fair. Now—you be Vanyel, I be Rolf. And you'll have a bit of my beer before I send you on your way—hey?"

Vanyel found himself smiling. "Gladly, Rolf." He started to pick his way across the wagon to the door at the rear, but the man stopped him with a wave of his hand.

"Not just yet, laddybuck. As I was startin' to tell you, I got a few pieces I don't put out. Keep 'em for Bards. And I got a few more I don't even show to just any Bard—but bein' as you are who you are—an' since they say you got a right fine hand with an instrument—" He opened up a hatch in the floor of the crowded wagon, and began pulling out instruments packed in beautifully wrought padded leather traveling bags. Two lutes, a harp—and three instruments vaguely gittern-shaped, but—much larger.

Rolf began stripping the cases from his treasures with swift and practiced hands, and Vanyel knew that he had found what he was looking for. The lutes—which were the first cases he opened—bore the same relationship to the instruments on the wall as a printed broadside page bears to an elegant and masterfully calligraphed and ornamented proclamation.

He took the first, of a dark wood that glowed deep red where the light from the open door struck it, tightened a string, and sounded a note, listening to the resonances.

"For you, or for someone else?"

"Someone else," he said, listening to the note gently die away in the heart of the lute.

"High voice or low?"

"High now, but I think he may turn out to be a baritone when his voice changes. He's my nephew; he's Gifted, and he is going to be a *fine* Bard one day."

"Try the other. That one is fine for a voice that don't need any help, it's loud, as lutes go—and all the harmonics are low. The other's better for a young voice, got harmonics up and down, and a nice, easy action. That one he'd have to grow into. The other'll grow with him."

Vanyel looked up in surprise at the old man.

Rolf gave him a half-smile. "A good craftsman knows how his work fits in the world," he said. "I got no voice, but I got the ear. Truth is, the ear is harder to find than the voice. Though I doubt you'd find a Bard who'd agree."

Vanyel nodded, and picked up the second lute, this one of wood the gold of raival leaves in autumn. He tightened a string and sounded it; the note throbbed through the wagon, achingly true. He tried the action on the neck; easy, but not mushy.

"You were right," he said, holding the chosen instrument out to the luthier. "I'll take it. No haggling." He looked wistfully over at the other. "And if I didn't already have a lute I love like an old friend. . . ."

Rolf waggled his bushy eyebrows, and grinned, as he took the golden lute from Vanyel and began carefully replacing it in its bag. "Care to try a friend of a new breed?" He nodded at the gittern-shaped objects.

"Well . . . what *are* those things?"

"Something new. Been trying gitterns with metal strings, 'stead of gut; you tell *me* how it came out." He laid the chosen lute carefully down on his bunk, and stripped the case from the first of the gitterns. "I keep 'em tuned; *this* one is a fair bitch to demonstrate if I don't. Hoping to get to Haven one day, show 'em to the Collegium Bards."

"Great good gods." Vanyel's jaw dropped. "*Twelve* strings? I should say."

"Fingers like a gittern. That one's like it; the other has six. Use metal harpstrings."

Vanyel took it carefully, and struck a chord—

It rang like a bell, sang like an angel in flight, and hung in the air forever, pulsing to the beat of his heart.

He closed his eyes as it died away, lost in the sound, and when he opened them, he saw Rolf grinning at him like a fiend.

"You," he said, sternly, "are a *terrible* man, Rolf Dawson."

"Oh, I know," the old man chortled. "It don't hurt that the inside of this wagon's tuned, too. That's one reason why them student lutes sound as good as they do. But *that* lady'll sound good in a privy."

"Well, I hope you're prepared to work your fingers to the bone," Vanyel replied, snatching up the leather case and carefully encasing *his* gittern. "Because when I take her back to Haven and Bard Breda hears her, *she* will send packs of dogs out to find you and bring you there!"

Rolf chuckled even harder. "Why d'you think I pulled her out and had you try her? You're going to do half my work for me, Herald Vanyel. With you t'speak for me, an' that lady, I won't spend three, four fortnights coolin' my heels with the other luthiers, waitin' my turn to see a Collegium Bard."

Vanyel had to chuckle himself. "You are a *very* terrible man. Now—you might as well tell me the worst."

"Which is?"

He felt a twinge for his once-full purse. Well, what else did he have to spend money on? "How much I owe you."

Vanyel shut the door to his room behind him, and set his back against it, breathing the first easy breath he'd taken since he left his chamber this morning. "Gods!" he gasped. "Sanctuary at last! Hello, Medren. Oh, you brought wine—thank you, I need it badly."

The boy looked up from tuning the new strings on his new lute. Giving it to him had given Vanyel one of the few moments of unsullied joy he'd had lately, a reaction worth ten times what Vanyel had paid.

Medren grinned. "Mother?"

"That was this morning," Vanyel replied, pushing away from the door, heading for the table beside the window seat and the cool flask of wine Medren had brought. "I swear, she chased me all over the keep, with stars in her eyes and the hunt in her blood."

Poor Melenna. Gods. She's driving me insane, but I can't *bring myself to hurt her. I've been the cause of so much hurt, I can't bear any more.*

"And lust in her—"

"Medren!" Vanyel interrupted. "That's your mother you're slandering!"

"—heart," the boy finished smoothly. "What did you do?"

"I took a bath," Vanyel replied puckishly. "I took a very *long* bath. When I finally came out, she'd given up."

"So who was chasing you this time, if it wasn't Mother?"

"Lord Withen. On the Great Sheep Debate. Meke wants to keep the sheep on Long Meadow until spring shearing; Father wants yearling cattle back there *immediately*, if not sooner." Vanyel groaned, and held both hands to his head. "If it wasn't for the fact that once this door is shut they leave me alone—gods, the *Border* was more peaceful!"

Water droplets beaded the side of the flask and ran down the sides as Vanyel picked it up. "Whoever gets you as protege will bless you for your thoughtfulness, lad." He poured himself a goblet of wine, and took it with him to sip while he stood over Medren at the window seat. No breath of air stirred without or within, and even the birds seemed to have gone into sun-warmed naps. "That instrument still as much to your liking?"

Medren nodded emphatically, if with a somewhat preoccupied expression. He was tuning the last string, a frown of concentration making his young face look adult.

Vanyel warmed inside, as he picked up his own lute. *It takes so little to make the child so happy—and gods, the talent.*

"Well, then," he said, laying a hand on the boy's shoulder, "Ready for your les—"

The boy winced away from the light touch on his shoulder. Not in emotional reaction—but in physical pain.

Vanyel snatched his hand away as if it had been a redhot iron he'd inadvertently set on the bare skin of the boy's back. "Medren! What did I—"

"It's all right," the boy said, and shrugged—which called up another grimace of pain. "Just—old Jervis reckoned we all ought to see how you could trick somebody into dropping his shield and then come in overhand. Guess who got to be the victim." His tone was so bitter Vanyel could taste it in the back of his own mouth. "Like always."

The blur of the blade coming for him, always coming for him; the weight of the shield on his arm getting heavier by the moment. The shock of each blow that he couldn't dodge; shock first and then pain. Breath burning in lungs, side aching with bruises, cramps knotting his calves. Stumbling backward, head reeling, vision clouding.

"Van?"

Cold sweat down his back and the taste of blood in his mouth. Bitter, absolute humiliation. Metallic taste of hate and fear.

"Hey, Vanyel—are you all right?"

Vanyel shook his head to clear it, and locked down his own agitation as best he could, but the memories were crowding in on him so vividly he was almost reliving that moment so many years ago when Jervis finally got him in a corner he couldn't escape.

"I'm all right." His left arm began to ache, and he massaged the arm and wrist, reflexively. *It still aches, after all these years. I still have numb fingers. Oh, gods, not Medren.*

"We could skip the lesson," he began, with carefully suppressed emotion.

"No!" Medren exclaimed, clutching the lute to his chest and jumping to his feet. "No, it's nothing! Really! I'm fine!"

"If you're sure," Vanyel said, wondering how much of that was bravado on the boy's part.

"I'm sure. I got some horse-liniment, I'd have rubbed it on right after, but I didn't want to stink up your room." The boy grinned half-heartedly and sat down again, his eyes anxious.

"I've got something better than that—if you aren't afraid I'll seduce you!"

The boy made an impudent face at him. "You *had* your chance, Vanyel. What's this stuff you got? I don't mind telling you my shoulder hurts like blazes."

"Willow and wormwood in ointment, with mint to make it smell reasonable. I *always* have some." He put his lute down and leaned over to rummage in the chest at the foot of his bed. "I'm one of those people who bruise just thinking about it. Get your shirt off, would you?"

When he turned around with the little jar in his hand, the boy had stripped to the waist, revealing a nasty bruise the size of his hand spreading all over the left shoulder. It was an ugly thing; purple the next thing to black in the center, blue-gray and red mottled through it.

Crack like lightning striking as the shield split. Sudden darkness, dizziness. Waking to Lissa's anxious face, and a pain in his left arm that sent the blackness to take him again.

"Good gods!"

Medren shrugged with one shoulder. "I bruise that way. Looks worse than it is, I guess. Young Mekeal took one just as hard and you can't hardly see a mark on him." He looked longingly at the pot of salve. "Vanyel, you going to stand there and stare all day, or use that stuff?"

"I'm sorry, Medren." He shook off his shock, got several fingersful of the ointment, and began to massage it as gently as possible into the bruised area, working his way from the edges inward. The boy hissed with pain at first, then gradually relaxed.

Vanyel, on the other hand, was profoundly disturbed, and growing tenser by the moment, his own shoulder muscles knotting up like snarled harpstrings. *Gods, what can I do? Damned if I'll let Jervis ruin Medren the way he ruined me—but how? If I force a confrontation, he'll only take it out on Medren. If I take him on myself—gods, I do not trust my temper, not with that old bastard. Not with the hairtrigger I've got right now. He'd make one wrong move, or say something at the wrong time—and I'd kill him before I could stop myself. What can I do? What can I do?*

"Lady Bright," the boy sighed. "I feel like I got a shoulder again, instead of a piece of pounded meat."

"Medren, is there *any* way you can avoid practices until you're safely out of here?" Vanyel asked.

Medren considered a moment. "Now and again," he said, slowly. "Not on a regular basis."

"Are you *sure*?" Vanyel pursued, urgently. "Isn't there any place you can hide?"

"Not since they opened up the back of the library. Anyplace I go, they'll find me, eventually. Isn't there anything *you* can do?"

Vanyel shook his head with bitter regret. "I wish there were. I can't think of anything at the moment. I'll work on it; if there's a way out for you, I'll find it. Look, avoid him as much as you can. Try and stay out of his line-of-sight when you can't avoid the practices. If he doesn't actually see you in front of him, sometimes you can manage to keep from becoming his target for the day."

Medren sighed, and shrugged his shirt back on. "All right. If that's all I can do, that's all I can do." He twisted his head around and gave Vanyel a slightly pained grin. "At least you believe me. You even sound like you know what I'm going through."

Vanyel stared at the wall, but what he was seeing was not wood panels, but a thin, undersized boy being used as an object upon which a surly ex-mercenary could vent his spleen. "I do, Medren," he replied slowly, a cold lump settling just under his heart. "Believe me, I do."

Vanyel was more than happy to see his Aunt Savil's serene, beaky face again. And was glad he'd decided to ride out and meet her. It was a lot easier to tell her what had been going on without wondering who was going to overhear.

". . . so that's the state of things," Vanyel concluded, Yfandes matching her pace to Savil's taller Companion. "The only real problems—other than the fact that Lineas and Baires could go for each other's throats any day—is Medren. Melenna I can avoid. The Great Sheep Debate is going to go on until the sheep are gone from Long Meadow. Father seems to have accepted Meke's breeding program, although he's got *his* agent out looking for an alternative to that awful stud Meke bought. But Medren—Savil, I *know* what you're thinking; you're thinking I'm overreacting to seeing another lad in the same position I was in. You didn't see that monster bruise he showed up with. He's not getting love-pats. That bruise was the size of my spread hand, finger-tip to thumb-tip, easily."

"Huh," Savil replied, frowning in thought.

"And to make it worse, Meke told me Jervis wants to—I quote—'go a few rounds with me.' To spar." Vanyel snorted. "'Spar' indeed. It'll be a cold day—"

She nodded. "Probably a damned good idea to avoid him. He'll push you, Van; he'll push you all he can."

"And I've just spent the last year on the Border."

"Exactly. If he pushed you too far—well, you know that better than me. Kellan, can you and 'Fandes kindly wait until you're loose for the chatter and gossip? We're trying to have a serious briefing here."

Vanyel chuckled. :*Trading stories about the muscular, young courier-types?*:

:*Shut up and ride.*:

Vanyel caught Savil's eye, and they exchanged a look full of irony. "I can see," she said aloud, "that this is going to be a very—lively—visit."

CHAPTER 6

THE ARGUMENT HAD been in full flower since Vanyel had arrived at the stable, and from all that he could tell it had evidently begun (well fertilized with invective) long before then. The stable was a good fifty paces from the keep itself, but the voices reached with unmistakable clarity well beyond the stable. The stablehands were doing their best to pretend they weren't listening, but Vanyel could all but see their ears stretching to catch the next interchange.

Havens, Savil has a strong set of lungs!

"Now *listen*, you stubborn old goat—"

"Stubborn!" The indignation in Withen's voice was thick enough to plow. "You're calling *me* stubborn? Savil, that's pot calling kettle if I ever—"

"—and provincial, hidebound, and muddle-headed to boot!"

Vanyel smothered a grin and kept the movement of the brush steady along Yfandes' glossy flank. She sighed with contentment and leaned into each stroke.

:Feel good?:

:Wonderful. All Companions should choose musicians; you have such talented hands. Speaking of which—: She flicked an ear at the open window through which Savil and Withen's argument was coming so very clearly.

:Music to my ears. If he's yelling at Aunt Savil, he can't be yelling at me. You're looking better. Those hollows behind your withers are gone. And your coat is much healthier.: He paused for a moment to admire the shine.

:I'm recovering faster than you are.: She swung her head around to fix him with a critical blue eye. *:Are you getting enough sleep?:*

:If I slept any longer, I'd wake up with headaches.: He turned his mental focus up toward that open window, avoiding any more of Yfandes' questions.

The fact was, he didn't *know* why he was still sleeping so long, and tiring so easily. He always felt hollow, somehow, as if there were an enormous empty place inside him that he couldn't fill. But he *had* recovered enough that all the problems, major and minor, were starting to make him feel restless because he couldn't *do* anything about them.

Other problems were starting to eat at him, too.

Shavri; I like her—too much? Gods. I must think about her and Jisa every night. I loved 'Lendel. I know I loved him. But have I let Shavri get into me deeper than I'd thought? Gods, she's Randi's lifebonded. He must be my best friend in the world next to Savil. She's one of my best friends. How can I even be thinking this? Gods, gods. Am I really even shaych? Or am I something else?

The question ate at him, more than he cared to admit.

Am I avoiding Melenna because I'm shaych, or because I hate to be hunted?

He shied away from the uncomfortable thoughts, and sent out a thin, questing thought-tendril toward Savil.

:*What can I do for you, demon-child?*: came her prompt reply.

:*Just wondering if you needed rescuing.*:

The answer came back laughter-tinged. :*Havens, no! I'm enjoying this one! I'm opening your father's eyes to politics and policies under Randale. Elspeth was always conservative, and got more so as she grew older. Randale is her opposite. This is coming as quite a shock to Withen.*:

Vanyel fought down another grin. :*What's he up in arms about now?*:

:*The mandatory education law Randale and the Council just passed.*:

:*Remind me; I'm behind.*:

:*Every child in Valdemar is to be taught simple reading, writing, and arithmetic in the temples from now on; every child, not just the highborn, or the few the priests single out as having vocations or being exceptional. Morning classes in the winter from harvest-end to first planting. And it's the duty of the Lord Holders to see that they get it.*:

Vanyel blinked. :*Oh, my. I can see where he wouldn't be pleased. I know where Randale's coming from on this one, though; he talked it over with me often enough. I just didn't know he'd managed to get it past the Council intact.*:

:*Enlighten me, I need ammunition.*:

:*He believes that an informed populace is more apt to trust its leaders than an ignorant populace, assuming that they feel the leaders are worthy of trust.*:

:*That isn't much of a problem in Valdemar,*: Savil replied.

:*Thanks be to the gods. Well. The only way to have an informed populace is to educate them, so they don't have to rely on rumors, so they're willing to wait for the official written word. It was the near-panic when Elspeth died that decided him.*:

:*I didn't know that; good points, ke'chara. Young as he is, our Randale can be brilliant at times. As soon as your father pauses for breath—*:

"Now see here, you old boneheaded windbag! Do you *want* those farmers of yours to be the prey of every scoundrel with a likely rumor under his hat?" Savil had the bit in her teeth and she was off again. Vanyel gave up trying to control himself, and leaned all his weight against Yfandes, laughing silently until his eyes teared.

This is ridiculous, Vanyel thought irritably, pausing for a moment on the narrow staircase. *Absolutely ridiculous. Why should I have to act as though I was sneaking through enemy-held territory just to get to my own bed every night?*

He took the last flight of back stairs to the fourth floor, poorly lit as they were, with not so much as the betraying squeak of a stair tread. He flattened himself against the wall at the top, and probed cautiously ahead.

No Melenna.

So far, so good.

His right eye stung and watered, and he rubbed at it with one knuckle; his eyelids were sore and felt puffy. *I should have gotten to bed candlemarks ago, except every time I tried, Melenna was lurking around a corner to waylay me. I hope she's given up by now.*

He peered down the dark corridor one more time before venturing out into it. This was the servants' floor, and if she were still awake and hoping to ambush him, Melenna wouldn't think to look for him up here.

He counted the doors—the fifth on the right opened, not into a room, but into a tiny spiral staircase that only went as far as the third floor. He probed again, delicately. Nothing in the staircase, or at the foot of it.

The stair was of cast iron, and in none too good repair. He clung to the railing, gritted his teeth, and moved a fingerlength at a time to keep it from rattling. The journey through the stuffy darkness seemed to take all night.

Then his foot encountered wood instead of metal, and he slipped off the staircase and groped for the door. He put one hand flat against the wooden panel and concentrated on what lay beyond it. This stair let out only two doors from his own room, and if Melenna were waiting, she'd be in the corridor.

Politeness—and Heraldic constraints—forbade Mindsearching for her, even if he had the energy to spare. Which he didn't, he had been chagrined to discover.

And anyway, the non-Gifted were always harder to locate by Mindsearch than the Gifted.

I'm getting very tired of this. I don't want to set Mother off, and I don't really want to hurt Melenna, but if this cat-and-mouse game keeps on much longer, I may have to do just that. I tell her "no," politely, and she doesn't believe it. I avoid her, and she just gets more persistent. I almost killed her two days ago when she popped out of hiding at me. He leaned his forehead against the door for a moment, and closed his aching eyes. *I'm about at my wits' end with that woman. Damn it all, she's old enough to know better! I don't want to hurt her; I don't even want to embarrass her.*

Well, there was no sign of her in the corridor. He relaxed a little and stepped out onto the highly polished wood of the hall of the guest rooms, where the brighter lighting made his smarting eyes blink and water for a moment.

He opened the door to his own room—

And froze, hand still on the icy metal of the doorhandle.

Candles burned in the sconces built into the headboard. Melenna smiled coyly at him from the middle of his bed. She allowed the sheet to slide from her shoulders as she sat up, proving that she hadn't so much as a single thread to grace her body.

Vanyel counted to ten, then ten again. Melenna's smile faltered and faded. She tossed her hair over one shoulder and began to pout.

Vanyel snatched his cloak from the peg beside the door, turned on his heel without a single word, and left, slamming the door behind him hard enough to send echoes bouncing up and down the corridor.

:'Fandes, beloved,: he Mindsent, so angry he was having trouble staying coherent. *:I hope you don't mind sharing sleeping-space.:*

Straw was not the most comfortable of beds, although he'd had worse. And he'd spent nights with his head pillowed on Yfandes' shoulder before this. But "day" for the occupants of the stable began long before *he'd* been getting up. The stablehands had no reason to be quiet—and neither did the horses. Meke's famous stud was the worst offender; he began cow-kicking the side of his stall monotonously from the moment color touched the east.

:Stupid brute thinks that if he keeps kicking, somebody will come to let him out,: came Yfandes' sleepy thought. *:I usually move out under a tree about now.:*

Vanyel raised his head and yawned. He'd gotten some sleep, but not nearly as much as he would have liked. *:You move. I think I'll go back to my room. If Melenna hasn't taken herself off to her own room by now, I swear I'll throw her out. Maybe a dose of humiliation will convince her to leave me alone.:*

:Sounds as good a plan as any.: Yfandes waited for him to move out of the

way, then got herself to her feet and nudged open the outside door. Vanyel stood up, shoulders aching from the strange position he'd slept in, and brushed bits of straw off his clothing. He ignored the startled glances of the stablehands, picked up his cloak and shook it out as Yfandes ambled out into her meadow.

:*Go get some more sleep, dearheart,*: she Mindsent back toward him.

:*I'll try,*: he replied, smoldering. :*Maybe I'll bring my sleeping roll down here. Maybe when word gets around that I'm sleeping with horses she'll stop this nonsense.*:

:*And if she's stupid enough to try and waylay you down here, I'll chase her around the meadow a few times to teach her better manners,*: Yfandes sent, irritation of her own coloring her thoughts a sullen red. :*This is getting exasperating. I don't care if she thinks she's in love with you, that doesn't excuse imbecilic behavior.*:

Vanyel didn't reply; he was too close to temper that could do the woman serious damage. He folded his cloak tidily over his arm, pretending he didn't notice the whispers of the stablehands as he let himself out of the stall and shut the door behind him.

"There was a problem with my bed last night," he told Tam, the chief stableman and Withen's most trusted trainer.

Tam was no fool, and he'd been quietly on Vanyel's side since Van was old enough to ride. He was one of the few at Forst Reach who hadn't changed his behavior toward Vanyel when the nature of Vanyel's relationship with Tylendel became known at the holding. Since his wife was one of the cooks, he was quite conversant with "house" gossip. He smiled slowly, showing the gap where he'd had three teeth kicked out. "Aye, milord Van. I ken. There's some invites a body wish t' give hisself."

Van winced inwardly a little, knowing that this was going to do Melenna's reputation no good at all once this tale got around the keep.

The stablehands went back to their chores, and he wound his way past them, out into the yard between the outbuildings and the keep. He blinked at the sunlight, seeing just one other person, a vague, unidentifiable shadow in the door of the armory.

"Vanyel," called a raspy, far-too-familiar voice. "A word with you."

Jervis. The armsmaster moved out past the door of the armory to stand directly in his path and Vanyel felt his stomach start to churn. In no way could he successfully avoid a confrontation this time. Jervis was between him and the keep.

"Yes, armsmaster?" he said.

"I left you messages, Meke told me he'd passed them on." Jervis moved closer, a frown making his seamed and craggy face more forbidding than usual.

Vanyel kept his own feelings behind an expressionless mask. "That you wanted to spar, yes I know. He did tell me. I'd rather not, thank you."

"Why not?"

"Frankly, because I don't feel up to it," Vanyel replied with cool neutrality, though his back was clammy with nervous sweat. *Because I know damned well it won't stay polite exercise for long. Because I know you're going to push me just as far as you can, armsmaster. I'm going to have to* hurt *you. And dammit, I don't want to let you do that to me.*

"What's that supposed to mean?" Jervis growled, his face darkening. "You think this old man isn't good enough for you?"

"I'm *worn out,* for one thing. I just spent the night in the stable because there was an unwelcome visitor in my room; that's *not* my bed of choice, and Meke's damned stud makes more noise than a herd of mules. For another—Jervis, I've been on a battle-line for the last year. *You* were a mercenary, what does that tell you?"

I don't want to inflict more pain when I don't have to. And I'm on a hair-trigger; gods, think about this, you old bastard! Remember what it was like, how some things became reflex, no matter how hard you tried to control them.

Jervis narrowed his eyes. "You look in good enough shape to me. There's nothing you can do, young Vanyel, that *I* can't handle. Unless you're really no better than, say, young Medren, no matter what all those songs say about you."

The reminder of the treatment Medren was receiving at Jervis' hands was the spark to the tinder. Vanyel's temper finally snapped. "On your head be it," he growled. "I take *no* responsibility. You want to spar so badly, all right, let's get it over with."

He stalked off toward the armory, a sturdy wooden building between the stables and the keep, with Jervis at his heels. He had a set of practice gear here, made up soon after he returned from k'Treva, gear put together at Withen's insistence and unused until now. It was gear unlike any other set at Forst Reach: light, padded leather gambeson; arm, thigh, and shin guards; main-gauche and heavy rapier; and a very light helm, all suited to his light frame and strike-and-run style.

The armory was not dark; there were clerestory windows glazed with bubbly, thick third-rate glass; stuff that wouldn't admit a view, just light. Vanyel found the storage chest with his name on it. He pulled his gear out and stripped off yesterday's tunic, pulling on the soft, thick linen practice tunic, strapping on the gambeson and guards, and gathering up his helm and weighted wooden practice blades.

This armory was new; built since Vanyel had left home. There was enough room for sparring inside; most of the interior had been set up as a salle. Vanyel was just as pleased to see that. The older building had been so small that all practices had to be held outside. So far as Vanyel was concerned, the fewer eyes there were to witness the confrontation, the better he'd like it.

He was shaking and sick inside; he was going to give Jervis a lesson the old man would never forget, and the very idea made his gut knot. He was *not* proud of what he was going to do.

But the old man asked for it. He wouldn't take "no," and he wouldn't back down. Dammit, it's going to be his fault, not mine!

Van dwelled on that while he armed up; a sullen anger making him feel justified, and burning the knots out of his gut with self-righteousness and a growing elation that he was *finally* going to pay Jervis back for every bruise and broken bone.

Until he realized where *that* train of thought was leading him.

I'm rationalizing the fact that I want to beat him bloody. That I want revenge on him. Oh, gods.

The realization made him sick again.

He went to the center of the practice area, crossing the unvarnished wooden floor with no more noise than a cat. Jervis looked around after donning his own gear—*much* heavier than Vanyel's—as if he had actually expected Van to have slipped out while he was arming. He seemed surprised to see Vanyel standing on the challenger's side, waiting for him.

I'll let him make the first move, Van thought, keeping himself under tight control. *He's probably going to give me a full rush, and I wouldn't be surprised if he tried to hurt me. Damned bully. But I will not lose my temper. I can't stop my reflexes, but I can keep my temper. I will not let him do that to me.*

But Jervis astonished him by simply walking up to his side of the line, giving a curt salute that Vanyel returned, and waiting in a deceptively lazy guard position.

Dust tickled Vanyel's nose, and somewhere in the building a cricket was chirping. *Well, do something, damn you!* he thought in frustration, as the moments continued to pass and Jervis did nothing but stand in the guard position. Finally the waiting was too much for his nerves. *He* rushed Jervis, but he pulled up short at the last second, so that the armsmaster was tricked into overextending. There was a brief flurry of blows, and with a neat twist of his wrists, Vanyel bound Jervis's blade and sent it flying out of his hands to land with a noisy clatter on the floor to Vanyel's left.

Now it comes. Vanyel braced himself for an explosion of temper.

But it didn't. No growl of rage, no snatching off of helm and spitting of curses. Jervis just *stood*, shield balanced easily on left arm, glaring. Vanyel could feel his eyes scorching him from within the dark slit of his helm for several heartbeats, while Vanyel's uneasiness grew and his blood pounded in his ears with the effort of holding himself in check. Finally the armsmaster moved—only to fetch the blade, return to his former position, and wait for Vanyel to make another attack.

Vanyel circled to Jervis' right, bouncing a little on his toes, waiting for a moment when he could get past that shield, or around it. Sweat began running down his back and sides, and only the scarf around his head under his helm kept it out of his eyes. He licked his lips, and tasted salt. His concentration narrowed until all he was aware of was the sound of his own breathing, and the opponent in front of him.

Jervis returned his feints, his blows, sometimes successfully, sometimes not. Vanyel scored on him *far* more often than vice versa. But every time he made a successful pass, Jervis would back out of reach for a moment. It was maddening and inexplicable; he'd just fall completely out of fighting stance, shuffle and glare, and mutter to himself, before returning to the line and mixing in again.

This little series of performances began to wear on Vanyel's nerves. It was far too like the stalking he used to get when Jervis wanted to beat him to a pulp and didn't quite dare—and at the same time, it was totally unlike anything in the old man's usual pattern.

What's he doing? What's he waiting for? Those aren't any love-taps he's been giving me, but it isn't what I know he's capable of, either.

Finally, when he was completely unnerved, Jervis made the move he'd been expecting all along—an all-out rush, at full-strength and full-force, the kind that had bowled him over time after time as a youngster—the kind that had ended with his broken arm.

Blade a blur beside Jervis' shield and the shield itself coming at him with the speed of a charging bull, the horrible crack as his shield split—the pain as the arm beneath it snapped like a green branch.

But he *wasn't* an adolescent; he was a battle-seasoned veteran.

His boot-soles scuffed on the sanded wood as he bounced himself out of range and back in again; he engaged and used the speed of Jervis' second rush to spin himself out of the way, and delivered a good hard stab to Jervis' side with the main-gauche as the man passed him—

—or meant to deliver it. For all his bulk, Jervis could move as quickly as a striking snake. He somehow got his shield around in time to deflect the blow and then continued into a strike with the shield-edge at Vanyel's face.

Vanyel spun out of the way, and let the movement carry him out of sword range. But now his temper was gone, completely shattered.

"*Damn* you, you bullying bastard! Preach about honor and then turn a shield-bash on me, will you!" His voice cracked with nerves. "Come on! Try again! *Try* and take me! I'm not a child, *armsmaster* Jervis. I'm not as *easy* to knock down and beat up anymore! You can't make a fool and a target of me the way you do with Medren! I *know* what I'm doing, damn you, and my style is a match for yours on any damned field!"

Jervis pulled off his battered helm with his shield hand, and sweat-darkened tendrils of gray-blond hair fell into his eyes. "That's enough," he said. "I've seen what I wanted t' see. Seems those songs got a grain of truth in 'em."

Vanyel choked his temper down. "I trust you won't require any more *sparring sessions*, armsmaster?"

Jervis gave him another long, measuring look. "I didn't say that. I'll be wantin' t' practice with you again, master Vanyel."

And he turned on his heel and left Vanyel standing in the middle of the salle, entirely uncertain of who had won what.

Have we got a truce? Have we? Or is this another kind of war?

"*My Shadow-Lover, bear me into light,*" Vanyel sang softly, as the odd, minor chords blended one into another, each leaving a ghost of itself hanging in the air for the next to build from. This new gittern did things to this particular song that carried it beyond the poignant into the unearthly. He paused a moment, brushed the last chording in a slow arpeggio, and finally opened his eyes.

Medren sat on the edge of the bed, his mouth open in a soundless "O."

Vanyel shook off the melancholy of the song with an effort. "How long have you been there?" he asked, racking the gittern on its stand, and uncoiling from his window seat.

"Most of the song," Medren shivered. "That's the *weirdest* love song I ever heard! How come I never heard it before?"

"Because Treesa doesn't like it," Vanyel replied wryly, stretching his fingers carefully. "It reminds her that she's mortal." He saw the incomprehension on Medren's face, and elaborated. "The lover in the song is Death, Medren."

"Death? As—" The boy gulped. "—a lover?"

The stricken look on the boy's face recalled him to the present, and he chuckled. "Oh, don't look that way, lad. I'm in no danger of throwing myself off a cliff. I have too much to do to go courting the Shadow-Lover."

The boy's face aged thirty years for a moment. "But if He came courting you—"

I'd take His kiss of peace only too readily, Vanyel thought. *Sometimes I'm so damned tired.* He *thought* that—but smiled and said, "He courts me every day I'm a Herald, nephew, but He hasn't won me yet. What brings you here?"

"Oh," Medren looked down at his hands. "Jervis. Some of the other kids—they told me he's got something special going today. For me."

Vanyel thought of the "sparring session" and went cold. And a seed of an idea finally sprouted and flowered. He stood, and walked slowly to the bed, to put his hand lightly on Medren's shoulder. "Medren, would you rather deal with Jervis, or be sick?"

"What?" The boy looked up at him with the same incomprehension in his eyes he'd shown when Vanyel had spoken of the Shadow-Lover.

"I have just enough of the Healing-Gift that I can *make* you sick." That wasn't exactly what he would do, but it was close enough. "Then I can *keep* you sick; too sick to go to practice, anyway." There was measles in the nursery; that would keep the boy down for a good long time.

"Will I lose my voice?" The boy looked up at him with the same complete trust Jisa had, and that shook him.

He grinned, to cover it. "No, you'll just come out in spots, like Brendan. In fact, I want you to sneak into the nursery and spend a candlemark with Brendan when I'm done with you." *As much as I'm going to depress his body, if he isn't fevered by nightfall I'll eat my lute.* "Make sure nobody sees you, and go straight to your mother after and tell her you have a headache."

"As long as I won't lose my voice," Medren said, grinning, "I think I can take spots and itching."

"It won't be fun."

"It's better than being beat on."

"All right." Vanyel put his hand on Medren's shoulders, and focused *down* and *out*—

"Funny about Medren," Radevel said, "coming down with spots so sudden-like. I would've sworn he had 'em once already."

Vanyel just shrugged. He was in Radevel's room following another "sparring session"—this time one in which *he* sparred with Rad under Jervis' eye. It had been easier to deal with than the last one, but Jervis was still acting out of character. *We have a truce of sorts. I don't know why, but I won't take the chance that it will extend to cover Medren. I daren't.*

Radevel had invited him here afterward in a burst of hearty comradeship, and Vanyel had decided to take him up on it. Over the past hour he'd come to discover he *liked* this good-natured cousin more than he'd ever dreamed.

" 'Nother funny thing I can't figure," Radevel continued, feet propped up on a battered old table, mug of watered wine in hand. "Old Leren. Saw him watching you an' Jervis an' me at practice this afternoon, an' if looks were arrows, you'd be a damned pincushion. What in hell did you ever do to him?"

Vanyel shrugged, took a long drink of the cool wine, and turned his attention back to repairing his torn leather gambeson with needle and fine, waxed thread in a neat, precise row of carefully placed stitches. The past four years had seen him out more often than not beyond the reach of the Haven-bred comforts and the servants that saw to the needs of Heralds. He'd gotten into the habit of repairing things himself, and around Radevel, that habit (which Radevel shared) made itself evident at the smallest excuse. "Don't know," he said shortly. "Never did. I would almost be willing to pledge to you that he's hated me from the moment he came here. Mother swears it's because I asked too many questions, but I thought priests were supposed to *encourage* questions. Our old priest did. I may have been only four when he died, but I remember *that*."

Radevel nodded agreement. "Aye, I remember that, too. Jervis always said that Osen was a good man. Made you feel like taking things to him, somehow. 'The gods gave you a brain, boy,' he'd say. 'If you want to honor them, *use* it.' Never made you feel like you were beneath him." He brooded over his mug, his plain face quiet with thought. "This Leren, now—huh. I

dunno, Van. You know, I stopped going to holydays *here* a long time ago—
hike down into the village with Jervis when we feel like we need a dose of
priest-talk. Tell you something else—young Father Heward down in the
village don't care much for Leren either. He did his best not to let on, but
he was downright gleeful to see us come marching down to the village
temple, an' I *know* he don't care much for fighters, being a peace-preacher.
Figure *that*."

"I can't," Vanyel replied.

He "felt" Savil's distinct "presence" coming up to the door of Radevel's
room, so he didn't jump when she spoke. "Is this a 'roosters only' discussion,
or can an old hen join?"

Vanyel did not bother to turn around. Radevel grinned past Vanyel's
shoulder at Savil, and reached—without needing to look—into the cupboard over his head for another mug. "I dunno," he mused. "Old hens,
welcome, but old bats—?"

"*Give* me that, you shameless reprobate," she mock-snarled, snatching
the clean mug out of his hand and pouring herself wine from the jug. She
tasted it and made a face. "Gods! What's that made of, old socks?"

"Standard merc ration, milady Herald ma'am, an' watered down, too.
Grows on you, though. Got into liking it 'cause of Jervis."

"Huh. Grows on you like foot-rot."

Vanyel stuck the needle under a line of stitches and moved over to make
room for her. She sat down beside him, careful to avoid unbalancing the
bench. She sipped again. "You're right. Second taste has merit—unless it's
just that the first swallow ate the skin off my tongue. What was all this about
Leren?"

"Radevel said he was watching me and Rad spar with Jervis this afternoon," Vanyel supplied, frowning at his work. The leather was scraped thin
here, and likely to tear again if he wasn't careful where he placed his stitches.

"To be precise, he was watching Herald Van, here. Like he was hoping
me or Jervis would slip-up like and break his neck for him," Radevel said.
"I'll tell you again, I *do* not like that man, priest or no priest. Makes my skin
fair crawl with some of those looks he gives."

"I've noticed," Savil said soberly. "*I* don't like him either, and damned if
I know why."

Radevel held up one hand in a gesture of helplessness. "I spent more
time around him than either of you, and I just can't put a finger on it. Treesa
doesn't like him either; only reason she goes to holyday services is 'cause she

reckons herself right pious, and facing him's better'n not going. But if she had her druthers, he'd be away and gone. It's about the one thing I agree with that featherhead on. Pardon, Van."

"Mother *is* a featherhead; I won't argue there. But—Savil, did you realize that she's very slightly sensitive? Not Thought-sensing, not Empathy, but like to it—something else, some kind of sensitivity we haven't identified yet. The gods only know what it is; *I* haven't got it nor have you. But it's a sensitivity she shares with Yfandes."

"Treesa? Sensitive like a *Companion*?" Savil gave him a look of complete incredulity. "Be damned! I never thought to test *her*."

He nodded. "The channel's in 'Fandes, wide open. The same channel Treesa has, only hers is to 'Fandes the way a melting icicle is to a waterfall. *I* don't know what it is, but I'd say we shouldn't discount feelings of unease just because Treesa shares them. She could *very* truly be feeling something."

"Huh," Radevel said, after a moment. Then he grinned. "I got a homely plain man's notion. That mare of yours ever dropped a foal?"

"Why, yes, now that you mention it. Two, a colt and a filly—both before she Chose me. Dancer and Megwyn. Why?"

"Just that about every mother *I* ever saw, human to hound, knew damned well when somebody had bad feelings toward her children, no matter how much that somebody tried to make out like it wasn't true. Even Milady Treesa." He grinned as Vanyel's jaw fell, and Savil's expression mirrored his. "Now Savil, you never had children, and it'd take a miracle from the Twain themselves to make Van a momma. So, no—what you call—channel. Make sense?"

"Damned good sense, cousin," Vanyel managed to get out around his astonishment. "For somebody who has no magic of his own, you have an uncanny grasp of principles."

Savil nodded. "You know, this enmity could also be partially that the man was pushed into the priesthood by his family and hates it. A priest with no vocation is worse than no priest at all."

"Could be," Radevel replied. "One thing for sure, it wasn't this bad 'fore Van came home. It's like something about Van brings out the worst in the old crow. Thought I'd say something." He shrugged. "I don't like him, Jervis don't like him. Jervis's got a feel for things like enemies sneakin' up on your back. You might want to keep an eye on Leren."

Oh, yes, cousin, Vanyel thought quietly. *If you are seeing the hint of trouble, stolid as you are, I will surely keep an eye on him.*

*   *   *

:Things in your bed again?: Yfandes asked sweetly.

Vanyel snarled, hung the lantern he was carrying on a hook, climbed up on the railings of the box, and hauled his bedroll down from the rafters above her stall. "This is *not* my idea of a good time," he replied. "I didn't come home with the intention of sleeping in the stable!" The bedroll landed on the floor, and he jumped down off the top rail to land beside it. "Here I thought I'd get past her by getting dinner with the babies and sneaking up to my room at sunset, and there she is waiting for me, bold as a bad penny. Not nude this time, but *in my bed.* 'Fandes, this is the *third* night in a row! Has the woman *no* shame? And I locked the damned door!"

:Why didn't you just put her out the door?:

He glared at her, and heaved the bedding into the stall. "I do not," he said between clenched teeth, "feel like engaging in a wrestling match with the woman. Dammit, there's going to be frost on the ground in the morning. It's getting *chilly* at night."

:Poor abused baby. I know somebody who'll gladly keep you warm.:

He glared at her again, poised halfway over the railings of the box-stall, one foot on either side. "'Fandes, you're pushing my patience."

:Me.:

"Oh, 'Fandes. . . ." His tone cooled a little, and he swung his leg over the top rail of the stall, and hopped down beside her to hug her neck. "I'm sorry. I shouldn't take the fact that I'm ready to kill *her* out on *you.*"

She rubbed her cheek against his, her smooth coat softer than any satin, and nibbled at his hair. Her breath puffed warm against his ear, sweet, and hay-scented. Farther down in the stable, beyond the light of Vanyel's lantern, one of the horses whickered sleepily, and another stamped.

:I'm rather selfishly glad to have you with me,: she said, watching him heap up straw and spread his sleeping roll on it. *:I like having you here with no danger to keep us wakeful, a quiet night, nothing to really disturb us. Remember how you used to spend nights out in the Vale with me, watching the stars?:*

"And waiting for Starwind to take a header out of his treehouse!" Vanyel laughed, with her rich chuckle bubbling in his mind. "You're right; that *was* a good time, even if I *did* spend the first few months of it in various states of hurting. Gods of Light, 'Fandes, I miss them. It's been far too long since I last saw them. Brightstar must be—what—nearly ten? I wish we had time to go back there."

They don't shake me to my shoes the way Shavri and Randi do. Is it only because I don't see them too often, or—

Yfandes' interrupted his thought.

:*You'd have to Gate, or else spend months on the road,:* she replied sadly. :*We daren't take the time, and I won't let you Gate yet, not unless it's an emergency. You're still drained.:*

Her tone cheered him a little. "Yes, little mother," Vanyel chuckled, climbing into his crude bed, good humor fully restored. And to prove that he wasn't *quite* so drained as Yfandes seemed to think, he snuffed the lamp with a thought.

:*Show-off,:* she teased, settling down carefully next to him so that he could curl up beside her, for all the world like a strange sort of gangly foal. He wriggled himself and blankets in against her warm, silken side, and slipped one hand out to rest on her foreleg.

He yawned. With his anger gone, his energy seemed to be gone too. "'Night, dearheart," he mumbled, suddenly unable to keep his eyes open.

She nuzzled his cheek. :*Goodnight, beloved.:*

They howled around him, trying to crawl inside his mind. Horrible, vile, they made him retch to look at them, but he couldn't look away from their distorted faces and maimed bodies. They drove fear before them and raised terror about them, making a whirlwind with himself in the center; they had knives for teeth and scythes for claws, red eyes full of madness and an insatiable hunger he could feel beating at his frail shell of protection in waves of heat. They were shadows, deadly, killing shadows, and they couldn't get at him, but they could and would find other prey. They howled off and away on the wind, and he screamed (or tried to) and hid his head and made himself as small as he could while the killing and dying began. And he wept with terror and shrieked—

Vanyel shook off the grip of the nightmare and came up out of it with a rush, choking against the black bile of fear in his throat. He clawed his way out of his blankets, and lay panting and unthinking against Yfandes' side in the aftermath of all-consuming horror, while his heart pounded in his ears.

The night about him was quiet, peaceful, undisturbed.

On the surface. But—

Beneath the surface?

Automatically he reached *out* with his Othersenses, to touch the energy currents that lay beneath the material night.

No, it hadn't been a nightmare; his Othersenses showed him the new, churning eddies in the currents of power all about him. *Something* had happened tonight. Somewhere out there *something* had used Power, used it freely, and to a terrible end. His nightmare had only been the far-off echo of something much, much worse. There was evil on the Otherwinds—and the world beneath shivered to feel it.

If I'd been in my room, I'd never have felt this, he realized, coming fully awake. *My room is shielded and so is Savil's. But I never shield when I'm with Yfandes. That means Savil hasn't felt this. I'm the only one who knows there's something wrong.*

"'Fandes?" He reached out for her shoulder; the muscles were bunched with tension, and her head was up, sniffing the crisp breeze.

:Hush. Listen.:

Faint, and far off—a Mind-cry for help? Or just a mind crying in despair? It wavered maddeningly in and out of his sensing-range.

:That's because he's bonded. It's a Companion, a young one. He's Chosen, and his Chosen is emperiled. I can hardly hear him.: She stretched her neck out, as if simply trying harder could make what she sensed clearer. *:That's—he's caught in his Chosen's fear, and he's nearly hysterical.:*

"Which, Companion or Chosen?" Vanyel scrambled completely out of his bedroll, and flared the lamp to life with a blink of thought. *We'd better deal with this. We may be the only ones close enough to hear them.*

:Both—the Companion, at least.: She lurched to her feet, her eyes black with distress. Moonlight poured in through the open upper half of the door to the paddock, silvering her. *:Vanyel, please—we* must *go to them!:*

"What's it look like I'm doing?" he demanded, throwing her blanket over her, then pulling down the saddle itself. "I'll have you saddled in half a moment. Where is this?"

:Lineas. Highjorune.:

"The Linean throne-seat." He made a quick check of his mental maps. "That's relatively near our Border. Can we be there by dawn?"

:Before.: All her attention was back on the West.

"Good, because I have the feeling what we're about to do isn't legal, at least by Linean standards, and I'd rather not break laws while people are awake to catch me. Kellan!"

A stamp and a whicker told him that Savil's Companion had heard him.

"Get Savil awake and tell her what we know and where we're going. And why."

Snort of agreement.

"'Fandes, wait a minute, I'd better change." He began stripping his clothing off, cursing the laces that wouldn't come undone, and snapping them when he realized how much time this was taking.

She swung her head around to stare at him frantically. :*We can't afford the time!*:

"We can't afford *not* to take the time," he said reasonably. "Think about it, love. I had damn well *better* be in uniform. Even the Lineans will think twice about stopping a Valdemar Herald, but a man on a white horse won't rate that second thought. I am something less than fond of being a target, even a moving one." He rummaged in the saddlebags, coming up with a slightly crumpled set of Whites. "Thought I left those here. Thank the gods for battle-line habits." He shrugged on the breeches and tunic and belted them tight; pulled on the boots he'd pulled off when he'd wormed into his blankets. "Good thing I've only got the one pair of boots. Damn, I wish I'd thought to leave a sword here."

:*Meke left one in the tack bin by the stud.*:

"Bless you—"

He vaulted the railings to fetch it; it was not a good blade, but it was serviceable. He strapped it and his long dagger on, inserted the short ones into their pockets in his boots.

His cloak—he looked for it quickly; he'd need it out there. There it was, half tangled with the blankets. He pulled it out of the tangle, shook it out, flung it over his shoulders, fastened the throat-latch, and returned to the task of harnessing Yfandes. He swung the saddle onto her back, gave a quick pull of the cinch, got chest- and rump-bands buckled and snugged in—she was ready.

He snatched her hackamore off its peg and tossed it over her head; he mounted while she shook it into place as the bells on it jangled madly. She booted the bottom of the door into the paddock open with her nose while he grabbed for the reins and brought them over her neck, and then with a leap a wild deer would envy she was off into the darkness.

CHAPTER 7

GODS, IT'S LIKE another Border-alert. Though Yfandes was frantic with the call in her mind, Vanyel kept his wits about him and reached out with a finger of power to snuff the lantern as they cleared the stable-door.

Yfandes raced across the black velvet of the paddock, hooves pounding dully on the turf, uncannily surefooted in all the moon-cast, dancing shadows. He'd forgotten for a moment that their path out was going to be blocked. He glanced ahead barely in time to see the fence at the far end coming at them and set himself instinctively when he felt her gather under him. They flew over the bars and landed with a jar that drove his teeth together and threw him against the pommel of the saddle. He fought himself back into balance and felt her begin to hesitate in midstride.

:Van?:

He clenched his teeth and wrenched himself into place. *:Just go—I'm fine.:*

She stretched out flat to the ground and ran with all the heart that was in her. Vanyel pulled himself down as close to the level of her outstretched neck as he could, kept his silhouette low and clean, and balanced his weight just behind her shoulders where she could carry it easiest. And fed her with his power.

No one except another Herald could know how exhausting "just riding" could be, especially on a ride like this. He was constantly moving, altering his balance to help her without thinking about it. It was *work*, and involved tiny muscle adjustments to complement her exertions.

He kept his cloak tucked in all around, but it didn't help much; the wind cut right through it, and chilled him terribly. His hands and face were like ice before a candlemark had passed. The wind whipped his hair into snarls and numbed his ears, and there was *nothing* he could do except endure it all, and keep his Othersenses alert for trouble.

I'll have to do something about the Border Guards when we get there. Something that isn't intrusive.

The Border—friendly in name only, neutral in truth—was guarded by sentries and watchtowers. They reached it at just about midnight, and Vanyel blinked in amazement when the first of those towers loomed up above the trees on the horizon, a black column against moon-whitened clouds. He'd had no way to judge Yfandes' speed in the dark, only the wind in his face and the thin, steady pull of power from him, power that he in turn drew from the nodes and power-streams they passed as they came into sensing range. Her speed wasn't natural, and required magic to sustain over any distance.

:The watchtowers—: That was the first time she'd Mindspoken him since they'd leapt the paddock fence, and her mind-voice, though preoccupied, was dark with apprehension. *:The Border Guards—:*

:I've got it figured,: he told her; got a wash of relief, and then felt her turn her attention back to the race and her footing, secure in the belief that he would handle the rest.

He closed his eyes against distractions, and Looked out ahead. He found and identified each mind that could *possibly* see them passing—those who were awake and those who were not—he left nothing to chance anymore. Not after he'd once been detected on a crawl through the enemy camp by a cook who happened to head for the privy-trench at *just* the wrong time. So, calling on more of that node-energy he'd garnered on the run, he built a *Seeming* that touched all those minds.

There is nothing on the road, his mind whispered to theirs. *Only shadows under the moon, the drumming of a partridge, the hooves of startled deer. You see nothing, you hear only sounds you have heard before. There is nothing on the road.*

There were plenty of circumstances that could break this *Seeming.* It was too delicate to hold against a counterspell and it would certainly break if they had the misfortune to run into someone physically. But anyone touched by the spell would see only shadows, hear only sounds that could easily be explained away.

More importantly, they would feel a subtle aversion to investigating those sounds, a bored lassitude that would keep them in the shelter of their posts.

They passed the Border-Guard station, vaulting the twin gates that barred the road, Valdemar and Lineas sides, as lightly as leaves on the wind. The Linean Guard was actually leaning on the gatepost, lounging beneath a lantern, his face a startlingly pale blur above his dark uniform. He looked directly at them, and Vanyel felt him yawn as they leaped the gate. Then he was lost in the dark behind as they raced on. Vanyel did not look back, but set the spell to break the moment they were out of sight. He would cloak his own passing; he would not leave the Border to spell-mazed guardians.

He spent no more magical energies in such spells; he didn't particularly care if the common folk of Lineas saw them. They were familiar enough with the uniform of the Heralds. If any Lineans saw him, they would assume, reasonably enough, that he'd been properly dealt with at the Border and belonged here.

Yfandes raced on, through pocket-sized villages in tiny, sheltered river-hollows, even through a larger town or two. All were as dark as places long abandoned. Finally, in the dead hours of the night, the time when death and birth lie closest, they came to Highjorune.

Most of the city was as dead and dark as the villages, but not all; no city slept the night through. More and stronger magic would be required to get them to their goal—whatever it was—without being stopped. Vanyel reached, seeking node-energy to use to pass the city gates as they had the Border, and recoiled a little in surprise.

For a place so adamantly against mages and their Gifts, Highjorune was *crawling* with mage-energy. It lay on the intersection of three—five—*seven* lines of force, none of them trivial, all flowing to meet at a node beneath it, liquid rainbows humming the random songs of power, strong enough for even new-made Adepts to use, provided they had the sensitivity to detect them—though the node where they met would be too wild, too strong for any but an experienced Adept.

:*Yfandes, stop a bit.*:

Yfandes obeyed. He raised his hands, preparing to spin out a true spell of illusion and sound-dampening, taking the power directly from the closest stream, bracing himself for the shock as his mind met the flow of energy.

The city gate was too well-guarded and well-lit, and the city itself too crowded with people to chance the kind of spell he'd worked on the Border Guards. He wanted to hurry the spell, but knew he didn't dare. *Careful*—he told himself. *This is Savil's area of expertise, not yours. Rush it, and you could lose it.*

Yfandes fidgeted, her bridle-bells chiming, her hooves making a deeper ringing on the hard paving of the road. :*Hurry,*: she urged, her own Mind-voice dense with fear. :*Please. He'll die, they'll die—there's another Companion, she's nearly gone mad, she can't speak*—:

:'*Fandes, don't interrupt. I'm working as fast as I can, but if I don't pull power now, I won't have anything when we need it.:* The raw power was beginning to fill him, fill all the echoing *emptiness.* Natural, slow recovery had not been able to do *this!* He was going to have to wait until the achingly empty reservoirs of power within him were full again before he could spin a shield this complicated, though at this rate it wasn't going to take long. Besides, he was all too likely to *need* power. If everything went to hell and he had to Gate out of here—

Gods. It's like—eating sunlight, breathing rainbows, drinking wind— Force poured into him, wild and untamed, and for the first time in months he felt complete and revived. There was *nothing* this strong anywhere near Forst Reach.

No mystery now why the Mavelans wanted Lineas, not with this kind of power running through Highjorune going untapped and unused. He could almost pity the magelords. It must be like living next to people who mined up precious gems with their copper, and threw the gems out with the tailings, but wouldn't let *you* in to glean them. *Got to hurry this. We're running out of time.*

Cautiously he *pulled* at the power, until it responded, flowing faster into him. *That's it. Now I make it mine.*

He tapped into the wild power he'd taken, learned it, tamed it to his hand.

He was sweating now, both with effort and impatience. *Gods, this takes too much time, but I can't afford any surprises.*

Slowly, carefully, he began to spin the energy out into threads, visible only to his Othersight, making a cocoon of the threads that would absorb sound within it, and send the eyes that lit upon it to looking elsewhere. Layer on layer, thread on delicate thread, this was a spell that required absolute concentration and attention, for the slightest defect would mean a place where the eye could catch and hold, where sound could leak out. Yfandes stood like a statue of ice in the moonlight, no longer fidgeting.

Finally, with a sigh of relief, he completed the web. He replaced what he had spent, then cut off his connection to the mother-stream.

His arms hurt, but he had the feeling that more was going to hurt than his arms before this was over.

:Go!: he told Yfandes, who leaped off into the dark, heading for the open city gates ahead of them.

He grabbed for the reins and pommel as she shot forward, a white arrow speeding toward a target only she knew.

:'Fandes! Where are we going?:
:The palace!:

The streets wound crazily round about, with no sense and no pattern; some
were illuminated by torches and lanterns, some only by the moon. They
sped from dark to light to dark again, Yfandes' hooves sliding on the slippery cobbles. They splashed through puddles of water and less pleasant liq-
uids. He could hear her hooves, oddly muffled, beneath him, and both
intriguing scents and noisome, foul stenches met his nose only to be snatched
away before he could recognize them. There *were* people about; street clean-
ers, beggars, whores, drunks, others he couldn't identify. The spell held; the
eyes of the townsfolk they passed slid past the two of them with no interest
whatsoever.

:*The first Companion, the young one—I can't even reach him now, he's too
crazed, Van, he's so frightened!*: Yfandes was not particularly coherent herself;
stress was distorting her mind-voice into a wash of emotion through which
it was hard to pick up words. :*The second one—she's—her Chosen—she can't
bear what he's doing, she's shutting everything out.*:

Vanyel clung to the pommel and balanced out sideways a bit as Yfandes
rounded a corner, hindquarters skewing as her hooves slipped a little. This
"second one"—she was probably the Companion with Randale's envoy. But
what could a *Herald* be doing that would stress his Companion to the point
of breakdown?

Vanyel didn't have long to wait to discover the answer; they entered a
zone of wider streets and enormous residences, homes of the noble and rich.
The streets were near daylight-bright with cressets and lanterns of scentless
oils. *The palace can't be far*, he thought, and just as he finished the thought,
they pounded around a corner and into a huge square, then down a broad
avenue. At the end of that processional avenue was a huge structure, half
fortress, half fantasy, looming above the city, a black eagle mantling above
her nest against the setting moon. And at the eagle's feet, an egg of light—
the main courtyard, brightly lit. Vanyel banished the spell of *unsight* as they
thundered in the gilded gates.

The dark-charcoal palace walls cupped the courtyard on three sides, the
wall they'd just passed beneath forming the fourth. There must have been a
hundred lanterns burning.

He only got a glimpse of confusion; to his right, half a dozen armed and armored men, and a Companion down and moaning on the black cobbles. To his left—a younger Companion, blood streaked shockingly red on his white coat, teeth bared and screaming with rage and battlefury; a blond boy clinging dazedly to his back, and—

It was like something out of his worst nightmares. A *Herald*, with a heavy carter's whip, *beating* the stallion until his skin came away in strips and blood striped bright on the snowy hide, trying to separate him from the boy.

Yfandes literally rode the Herald down, swerving at the last moment to shoulder him aside instead of trampling him. Vanyel leaped from her saddle as he had so many times before in Border-fights, hit the cobbles and tumbled to kill his momentum, and sprang to his feet with sword drawn.

He didn't give the other Herald a breath to react. Whatever insanity was going on here had to be *stopped*. Without thinking, Van reversed the grip on the sword in his hand.

And lashed up to catch the stranger squarely on the chin with a handful of metal.

The other Herald went flying backward, and landed in an untidy heap. *Damn, he's still moving.*

Vanyel put himself in fighting stance between the young stallion and his abuser. He touched the young ones' minds just long enough to try and get some sense out of either the boy or the stallion—but from the first picked up only shock, and from the second, fear that drowned everything else out.

Vanyel pulled on the power within him, feeling it leap, wild and undisciplined, as the other Herald staggered to his feet, bleeding from a split lip, and prepared to lash out with the whip again. Flinging out his left hand, Van sent a lash of his own, a lash of lightning from his outstretched finger to the whipstock. The spark arced across the space between them with a crackle and the pungent smell of burning leather, and the dark, sallow-faced Herald dropped the whip with an exclamation of pain. Behind him, Yfandes was holding off the armsmen with squeals, lashing hooves and bared teeth; faced with her anger, they were not inclined to come to the Herald's rescue.

"What in *hell* do you think you're doing?" Vanyel thundered, letting the other feel his outrage, a wave of red anger. The older man backed up an involuntary pace. "What in the name of the gods themselves is going on here?"

Vanyel sheathed his sword then. The other Herald drew himself up, nursing his injured hand against his chest, rubbing the blood off his bruised chin with the other. "Who are *you* to interfere—" he began, his face a caricature of thwarted authority.

Vanyel tried to Mindspeak, but the other's channel was weak, and he was blocking it besides. And the personality was not one for much hope of compromise. Stolid and methodical—and affronted by the stranger's intervention in *his* jurisdiction. The *young* stranger, too young, surely, to have any authority.

Gods bless—I'm going to have to pull rank on this thickheaded idiot. And he's never going to forgive me for that.

And the only reason I didn't put him out is because he's so damn thick-headed!

"Herald-Mage Vanyel Ashkevron," Vanyel cut him off. "Called Demonsbane, called Shadowstalker, First Herald-Mage in Valdemar. I outrank you, Herald, and your damn fool actions tonight called me out of my bed and across the Border. You've exceeded your authority, and I'm ordering you to *let this boy be.* Who in hell are *you?*"

Vanyel could feel the older man's resentment and smoldering anger, heavy and hot, a ponderous weight of molten emotional metal. "Herald Lores," he said sullenly, rubbing his hand. "King Randale's envoy to the court of Lineas."

Over his shoulder, Vanyel watched Yfandes backing away from the armsmen. She cautiously nudged the downed Companion's shoulder—still keeping one eye on them. After a couple of false tries, the other mare managed to get back to her feet, but stood with her head down and her legs splayed and shaking.

:*'Fandes?*:

:*She's Hearing again, and Speaking, a little; when you got her Chosen to stop, it resolved the conflict inside her—but she is not well. She is still in turmoil, and her heart bleeds.*:

:*Take care of her.*: He turned his attention back to Lores. "Tell me—slowly—just *what* you thought you were doing, taking a *whip* to a Companion, trying to drive him away from his Chosen."

Lores snarled. "That *boy* is a bloody-handed murderer, and that *thing* you call a Companion is his demon shape-changed! He called it up and was trying to escape on it."

"What?" Vanyel backed up a step, inadvertently bumping into the young stallion, who snorted in alarm but stood rock-steady, ready to protect his Chosen against *anything,* be it man, beast, or creature of magic. Vanyel reached out, still keeping his eyes on Lores, and laid his hand along the stallion's neck. If *anyone* in the wide world would know what a demon "felt" like, *he* did, after having them close enough to score his chest with their claws, and after turning them back against Karse! He extended his mind toward the young stallion's, and touched again, gently. No demonic aura met his mind, only the pure, bright, blue-white pulsing that was the signature of a Companion, an aura that *only* a Companion, of all the creatures he had ever Mindtouched, possessed.

Anger rose in him, as his hand came away bloody, and the young stallion shivered in fear and pain. He clenched his fist and stared at the older Herald. "You—" He groped for words. "If I didn't *know* Randale, and *know* that neither he nor Shavri would send anyone at all unbalanced out here as an envoy, I'd say you were insane." The man gaped at him, taken completely aback. "As it is, I'm forced to say I've never encountered anyone so incredibly *stupid* in my life!" He relaxed his clenched fist and patted the stallion's neck without looking around, then advanced on Lores with such anger filling him that he was having trouble keeping his voice controlled. "What in *hell* makes you think this youngster is a demon?"

"You could be fooled, spell-touched—"

"Not bloody likely! And a demon could *never* fool my Companion, *nor* yours. Gods, man, if *they* wouldn't know a real Companion, who would? Look, you fool—*look!*" He reached Lores—withstood the desire to strangle the older man—and spun him around so that he could see his *own* Companion, legs bowed and shivering from nose to tail with shock, head nearly touching the cobbles. His right hand left a bloody smudge on Lores' shoulder. "Look what you've *done* to her! Didn't you *feel* it? You came *quite* close to driving her catatonic. She couldn't obey you, and she couldn't stop you! *Look at her!*"

Lores took one step toward her—two—and the third step became a stumbling run that ended with him on his knees beside her, stroking her neck, whispering in her ear. Her trembling stopped; she began to relax. He got to his feet, and urged her a little more upright, until she finally stood naturally, with her head pressed against the front of his tunic.

She was so anguished that Vanyel nearly wept. He finally had to block her out of his mind, or he knew he would lose control of his own small Gift of Empathy.

:*'Fandes,*: he Mindsent softly, :*what about the other? Can you calm him now?*:

:*Yes.*: She picked her way across the cobbles, hooves chiming on the hard black stone, until she was behind him and presumably dealing with the young stallion. Vanyel took a few steps closer to Lores. The armsmen began edging toward the gate and slipping out of the courtyard, and Vanyel was not inclined to stop them.

Lores looked up, his face twisted and tear-streaked. "I—didn't know. I couldn't—I don't feel anything from Jenna, not really, I—my Gift—it's Fetching. I don't Mindspeak even with her, much—I—told her what to do, but she didn't do it, I thought the demon must have—" His eyes fell upon the boy, and his face hardened. "It doesn't matter. That boy is *still* a murderer."

Vanyel lost his hold on his temper. "*Dammit* man, Companions *don't* Choose murderers!"

"Oh, no?" Lores spat back. "*Gala* did!"

Lightning and rain; madness and grief.

Present rage replaced past grief.

"That," he said angrily, "was *after* she Chose. And she repudiated him, cast him off. As *you* should know. *After* she Chose, and after—her Chosen— was pressed past all sanity. It has *no* bearing on what happened here. *You* would not listen to your *own Companion* try to tell you the truth."

He took a step toward the other, bloody finger pointed in accusation. "You blocked her out with *your* anger and *your* fear. You allowed *your* emotions to interfere with your ability to see the truth. You blocked her so you couldn't hear what you didn't *want* to hear."

Lores' resentment smoldered in his eyes, but he could not deny Vanyel's accusations.

:Van—the boy—:

Vanyel spun, just in time to see the young man losing his death grip on his Companion's mane, sliding to the ground. He sprinted to the boy's side, startling the young stallion so that he threw up his head and rolled his eyes, and caught the boy in mid-collapse, draping the boy's arm over his own neck and shoulder, supporting him, and looked around for an open door— *any* door—

:Your left,: Yfandes prompted; one of the double doors into the main entranceway was cracked open. He half-carried, half-dragged the boy there, with Lores following sullenly behind, and kicked the door open enough to squeeze through.

*   *   *

It was pitchy dark in the palace—which was *damned* odd for the throne-seat, even at a few hours till dawn. Even odder, all that commotion in the main courtyard had brought *no one* out to see what the ruckus was about. Van couldn't see a thing past the little light coming in the doorway. The building might just as well have been deserted.

First things first; they needed light. So—*Be damned to local prejudice*, he thought, and set a globe of blue mage-light to spinning above his head. Behind him, he heard a stifled gasp as Lores watched it appear out of nowhere.

They were in a bare entryway; that was all he had time to notice in his brief glance. *Someplace to put this boy*—A seat was what he was looking for, and he spotted one: a highly-polished wooden bench, bare of cushions and bolted to the floor, over against the wall just clear of the door. Presumably it was for the use of low-rank servants waiting for something or someone at the main entrance. Whatever, it was a seat. He supported the boy over to it, and got him seated, shoved his head down between his legs, and worked the little Healing he knew to clear the shock out and get him conscious again.

The boy was aware enough to interpret that as some kind of coercion or confinement; he tried to fight, and raised his head into the light.

And Vanyel saw his face for the first time.

It was Tylendel's face, dazed with shock and vacant-eyed, that looked up at him in confusion beneath the blue mage-light.

Vanyel choked, and the floor seemed to heave beneath him. Only one hand on the wall saved him. For a moment he thought that his heart had stopped, or that his mind had snapped.

His eyes cleared again, and he took a closer look, reached out to tip the boy's face into the light, and *almost* Mindtouched—

But he stopped himself, as he began to see the little differences. The boy couldn't be more than sixteen, and looked it; 'Lendel had always looked *older* than he really was. The boy's nose was snubbed, or more than 'Lendel's had been; the eyes were farther apart and larger, the chin rounded and not squared, the hair wavy, not curly, and darker than the golden-brown of Tylendel's. Subtle differences, but enough to let him shake off his ghosts, enough to tell him that this *was not* Tylendel.

Whatever the boy in turn saw or sensed in *his* eyes, it reassured him enough that he stopped fighting, and obeyed Vanyel's half-audible order to keep his head down.

Not now, he told himself. *Deal with your ghosts later, not now.*

For the first time since entering the gilded door, he looked around to see if there was *finally* anyone coming. He looked past the barren entryway—and froze at the sight of the wreckage in the mage-light.

He'd seen less destruction after the sacking of a keep.

No wonder no one came, he thought, dumbly. *Nobody human could have survived this.*

Vanyel stood at the edge of the staircase and stared. This entry was hardly more than twenty feet long, and made of the same black stone as the exterior, but polished to a reflective shine; it led to a short stone stair that in turn led down into the wood-paneled Great Hall. This Hall had been a reception area—lit by chandeliers and wall sconces, hung with tapestries, lined with dark wood tables and chairs polished to mirror-brightness. It was demolished.

The chandeliers had been torn from the beams, tapestries ripped from the walls. The walls, the floor, the ceiling beams themselves were scored and gouged as though with the marks of terrible claws. The tapestries had been shredded, the furniture reduced to splinters, the wreckage scattered across the floor as though a whirlwind had played here.

Vanyel remembered his dream, and felt his hair rise and a chill creep up his backbone.

"What—" His voice cracked, and he tried again. "What *happened*?"

Lores' lip lifted a little, but he answered civilly enough. "That boy—that's Tashir. You know who he is?"

Vanyel nodded. "Tashir Remoerdis. Deveran of Lineas' oldest child."

"You know Deveran figured him for a bastard, the worst kind, fathered on Ylyna by her own brother, so they say."

"Is that really germane?" Van looked back at the wreckage.

"Damn right it's *germane*." Lores lifted his lip scornfully. "It's why the brat *did* all this."

"Lores, you'd better tell me everything you know," Vanyel requested simply, still trying to take in the implications of the wrecked palace.

Lores snorted and rambled on. "Ylyna was no virgin, though in honesty the Mavelans never claimed she was. Still, fourteen's a bit young to have been as—let's say—*experienced* as she was. Tashir was born eight months after the wedding. That's suspicious enough. Boy looks like his uncle Vedric and *nothing* like Ylyna or Deveran did. That's the second reason; another is that he's known to have Gifts; Fetching, for one—things have been flying around when he got upset ever since he was thirteen. No Gifts manifested in Ylyna, and there's *never* been any in Deveran's line. The locals called it wizardry and pressured Deveran to disinherit Tashir."

"I'd heard about the Gift," Vanyel said, looking back at the boy to see if he'd overheard them. They were only twenty paces away, and Lores was making no effort to keep his voice down. Tashir was still sitting where they'd left him, head and hands dangling between his knees. "How did the boy take being disinherited?"

"The boy?" For a moment Lores seemed puzzled. "That was the odd part; boy seemed relieved. It was Vedric Mavelan that made all the fuss. But tonight—something happened at dinner, and I'm not sure exactly what." Lores wrapped his arms around his chest, and his expression turned introspective, and a little fearful.

"Were you there?" Vanyel asked.

Lores nodded. "Always, as the Valdemar envoy. Tonight . . ." He looked into the distance, frowning. "I remember I was chatting with Deveran's armsmaster and the boy came up to the high table to say something to Deveran. Next thing I knew, they're at it hammer and tongs, screaming at each other, the boy going white and Deveran going red. Then Deveran backhanded the boy, knocked him to the floor."

Vanyel chewed his lip. "Was that unusual?"

Lores shrugged. "Well, it had never happened in public before. Deveran asked us all to leave in the kind of voice that makes an order out of a request. We left—don't look at me like that, what else could we do?"

"I don't know," Vanyel replied soberly. "I wasn't there. But I don't think I would have left a situation that volatile."

"Well, *I* left; it's not Valdemar and it wasn't my business. I went out to the stable and Jenna, was outside with her for a while." He shook his head. "They'd moved the fight up to Deveran's study, toward the back of the palace; I could hear 'em both shouting at each other through the window. Then it got real quiet for a bit—and then all hell broke loose." He gestured at the wreckage in the Great Hall, and his expression became strained. "You can figure what *that* sounded like; enough screaming for a war. Nobody wanted to break in on that, and anyway we found out that the doors were all like they were welded shut."

His voice was casual, but he was trembling and sweating, and his skin was dead white.

"It didn't last long. Then it was quiet again, sudden, like everything had been cut off. Me, the outside servants, and Deveran's armsmen from the palace, and the town guard and a couple of the town council with some courage in them, we all broke the doors open."

"And you found?"

"*That's* what we found. The boy knocked out under that bench, and when we went to look for bodies—gods. Everyone inside these walls . . . was dead. The boy's sibs, the servants, everybody. Torn to pieces, just like . . . that stuff. *Nothing* bigger than palm-sized pieces of everybody else." He was shaking now, his teeth chattering, and his pupils dilated. *"Nothing,"* he repeated.

"You're not saying *Tashir* did all that?" Vanyel said incredulously. "That's impossible—it's insane!" The mage-light flared a little, setting shadows shrinking and growing again, flickering as he whirled to look at the boy, and his attention wavered.

Lores turned away from the wreckage, clutching his arms against his chest, and gradually stopped trembling. His eyes fell on Tashir again; just the sight of the boy seemed to reawaken his anger. "What's insane about it?" he demanded. "Fetching can wreck, or even kill. I should know that better than *you*, it's *my* Gift."

"It's one of my Gifts, too, you damned fool!" Vanyel growled. "And at one point I *almost* got out of control, but my Gift was blasted open and I was in pain enough to drive a strong man mad. Nothing like that happened here! This boy *never* showed a hint of anything on *this* scale! And he was *untrained*? Not bloody likely!"

"How do we know he was untrained?" Lores demanded, his eyes reflecting blue glints from the mage-light over Vanyel's head. "He was the *only* one left alive! He *had* to have done it!"

Vanyel had a dozen retorts on the tip of his tongue, but none of them seemed wise.

So how did you come to be such an expert on Gifts and magic, you idiot? And did you search to find someone who might have hidden himself—or herself—until you'd found and dealt with Tashir? Or did you identify everyone, or at least count all the bodies and come up with the same number as those known to be in the palace?

He kept his teeth shut on all those questions. It was obvious that this had been bungled from the start, and dressing down this fool wasn't going to undo the bungling.

"We couldn't really believe it, not at first," Lores admitted reluctantly.

"We thought it must have been—oh, something out of the Pelagir wilder-lands, or even something cooked up by the Mavelans. We really didn't know what it could have been, especially not the Lineans, but there wasn't anyone or anything else, and when we tried to question Tashir, the boy wouldn't answer. At first he was—dazed-like. Then he just refused to speak except to say he didn't remember." Lores shook his head. "Not *remember*? How could he not remember something that did *that*? Unless he was lying, or he'd done it in anger and had blanked it out of his mind." Lores clasped his folded arms still tighter against his chest, as if he was trying to protect himself. "What could we do? The guards were spooked, nobody wanted something like *that* on their hands. In the end, we just threw him in the guardhouse at the front gate there, since the townsfolk didn't want him in *their* jail and nobody wanted to have to go down to the cells under the palace. We sent off a mes-senger for Vedric, since he was the one making all the fuss about the boy in the first place. He may be a Mavelan, but he's not going to be able to talk the boy out of *this* mess. He'll have to deal with him, and he *is* a mage. We reckoned it was better for one mage to deal with another. *Especially* a murderer."

"That's not proved."

Lores glared at him. Vanyel repeated his words stubbornly. "That's *not* proved. *Nothing* is proved. And furthermore, I'd like to know how the hell a *Herald* could come to attack a Companion."

Lores began pacing, four steps away from Vanyel, four steps back. "We shoved him in there, picked up the bodies—what was left of them. Things quieted down. Then, less than a candlemark ago, that *demon* showed up."

"*Companion.*"

Lores wheeled to glare again, but the look in Vanyel's eyes cowed him. "That *Companion* showed up; he began breaking down the door. The guard got me, I sent for reinforcements—*I* thought it was a demon—more men showed up about the time the de—Companion got the door smashed in and started to run off with the boy. That whip was in the guardhouse and I grabbed it—figuring demon or not, it was horse-shaped." He shrugged. "You know the rest."

"Didn't you even try the boy under Truth Spell?" Vanyel snarled, out of patience with the lack of *thought*, the complete bullheaded stupidity of the man.

Lores looked baffled. "'Truth Spell'? Why? What's that got to do with me?"

"Goddess Incarnate! *Any* Herald can work first-stage Truth Spell! Didn't your mentor ever—" Vanyel paused at the dumbfounded look on Lores' face. "Your mentor never told you?"

Lores shook his head.

"*Gods,*" Vanyel strode over to the adolescent, who was still slumped over his own knees. "Tashir?" he said, gently, kneeling beside him. He braced himself when the young man looked up, it still made his heart lurch to see those eyes, that face—and that dazed, lost, and pleading expression. "Tashir, do you remember anything that happened tonight? Anything at all?"

Tashir's eyes were still not focusing well; he shook his head dumbly.

Vanyel shook him gently. "Think. Dinner. Do you remember your father calling you up at dinner?"

"I . . ." The boy's voice was quite low, almost a match for Vanyel's baritone. "I think so. Yes. He . . . wanted me to go somewhere."

"Where, Tashir?" Vanyel prompted.

"I . . . don't remember."

"Do you remember arguing with him?"

A hesitant nod. There were shadows under Tashir's eyes that had nothing to do with the way the light was falling on him. "I didn't want to go. He wanted to send me somewhere. I don't remember where, I just remember that I didn't want to go. I told him I wouldn't. He hit me."

"Did he hit you very often?"

The eyes cleared for a moment, bright with fear. "Often enough," the boy confessed cautiously. "When I was around too much. I tried not to get in his way. Sometimes he'd get mad about something, and take it out on me. But not in front of people, not before tonight."

"So he hit you. Then he sent everyone else away. What then?"

"He . . . came around the table. He grabbed me before I could get away, twisted my arm up behind my back, and made me go with him to his study. And . . ."

The eyes clouded again.

"And?"

"I don't remember!" Tashir wailed softly. "Please, I *don't remember*!"

Vanyel set in motion the spell that called the *vrondi,* the mindless air elemental that could not abide the emotional emanations associated with falsehood. In *his* hands, because he could give it energy beyond its own, the *vrondi* would be able to settle within the youngster's mind: he would be incapable of lying so long as it was there. Vanyel watched the *vrondi* settle into place, a glowing blue mist like a visible aura about Tashir's head and shoulders. *He* would not see it, but Vanyel and Lores certainly could. He glanced over at Lores, and saw the older man's lips compress, his face grow speculative.

"Are you sure, Tashir?" he urged. "Think. Your father took you up to his study; what happened in the study?"

"I don't remember!" Tashir whimpered. "I *don't!*"

Vanyel sighed, and dismissed the *vrondi* with a word. The mist dissolved, faded away, but slowly, not all at once as it would have if it had met with a lie. There was only one other thing he could try. He reached out tentatively with a Mindtouch.

Tashir should not have been able to detect it. But suddenly he jerked away, his eyes wild and unreasoning, and a shield snapped up so quickly Vanyel barely had time to pull back his Touch.

"Look out!" Lores cried, diving for the floor, as half a vase rose from the wreckage, flung itself across the room and smashed against the door. More fragments followed it, all rising from the wreckage to smash against the door, creating a rain of flying shards that pelted them both like fine hail.

Vanyel didn't move so much as a hair. He clenched his jaw, and reached out with his own power to damp Tashir's Gift with an external shield.

Sudden silence.

"Tashir," he reached out for the youngster, with his hand this time, not his mind. "Tashir, I want to help you. I *believe* you. I *will not* allow anyone to harm you, or to imprison you for something you didn't do."

The adolescent's eyes slowly calmed, grew saner. He stared at Vanyel for a long moment, then buried his face in his hands and began sobbing, trembling on the jagged edge of hysteria.

"I—don't—remember—" he choked. "Oh, *please,* I don't, I really don't."

Before he could do anything to comfort or calm the youngster, Vanyel heard a noise in the distance, muffled by the door, that made his hair stand on end.

The sullen, angry roaring of a mob—

Lores' head snapped up, and a look of grim satisfaction spread over his face. "The armsmen," he said smugly. "They must have spread the word. That's the people of Highjorune out there, *Milord Herald-Mage.* You don't rank *them*, and they aren't likely to listen to you. What's your plan *now*? They're going to want the boy. I think you should let them have him."

Tashir gave a kind of choking gasp, and looked straight into Vanyel's eyes, his whole body pleading for rescue. His eyes were swollen, tears smeared across his face, and hair tumbled into one eye; his expression was tragic and hopeless.

Vanyel could no more have resisted a boy who looked like *that* than he could have given up Yfandes.

"I still outrank *you*, Lores," he said coldly. "You are still under *my* orders. Get out there and do what you can to keep them off."

"*Keep them off?* You're madder than *he* is!"

"*Move!*" Vanyel snapped, rising to his feet, as the flickering of torches lit the gap in the open door.

Lores made no further protest; he snorted, and stalked across the entry-way to the door, his backbone stiff with unspoken resentment.

Vanyel followed him as far as the door, and once he had barely cleared it, slammed it shut practically on his heels. He heard a muffled exclamation, and the muttering of the mob grew louder and nearer. Vanyel threw the bolt into place across the door; it was metal, but it was *not* going to hold up against a concerted attack.

"That . . . isn't going to hold them for long," Tashir said fearfully, brushing the hair out of his eyes with the back of one hand.

"It won't have to," Vanyel answered absently, moving his Othersenses *out* and *down* and hoping that it was no coincidence.

There was that node, the most powerful node he'd ever encountered outside *Tayledras* lands. Given that Highjorune was situated *on top* of the convergence of those energy-streams, given that the node *had* to be around here somewhere. . . .

Had the palace been built where *he'd* have put it?

It was no coincidence. The palace was situated *directly* over the node; a node so strong it roared in Vanyel's mind.

"Now that pompous peabrain is going to find out *why* I outrank him," he growled to himself, and reached—

The current-power had been wild; it was nothing to this. He had compared channels in his mother and Yfandes to a dripping icicle and a waterfall. *This* was to those streams what a raging Firestorm was to a campfire. But Vanyel knew its secrets and how to control it, and it raged to *his* will.

He set his mind in the spell-cycle; he murmured a few words, gathered his will, and cupped his hands, unconsciously mirroring the *shape* he wanted to create.

Then he snapped his hands open, crying out a single word of *command*.

A flash of light made his closed eyelids burn red for a moment. Tashir cried out fearfully.

Absolute and complete silence descended on them like sudden deafness.

He opened his eyes; a steady, yellow glow on the outer walls was just barely visible to his Othersight.

He had erected a mage-barrier about the palace that would keep out anything *he* didn't want in, including such intangibles as thought—or other magic. *He* could pass through: so could anything he brought with him. No one and nothing else.

With effort his thoughts passed it.

:Yfandes? How are you and the stranger?:

:They are ignoring us,: she said. *:You have frightened the Young One, and angered Lores. The mob has not made up its mind.:*

:Even if they do, it won't get them anywhere. Give me a moment to make up my mind.:

Vanyel severed the connection between himself and the node. He could control it, yes, but at a price. He'd just earned himself another scattering of silver hairs. Among other things.

He opened his eyes and saw Tashir huddled up against the wall, shaking so hard his teeth rattled. He walked stiffly to the bench, and touched the young man's shoulder. He got no response. He turned Tashir's face into the light, and saw his eyes glazed over in withdrawal.

"Damn." Vanyel sat down heavily beside him. "Now what?"

He thought hard for a moment; made up his mind quickly, and *reached* for the node again.

The shock as he touched it the second time was a little less. When he could catch his breath again, he used the node-energy to boost his own Mindspeech far beyond what he could have reached alone, sending his mind out questing for a Mindpresence so dear and familiar it could almost have drawn him on its own.

Touch.

Startlement. *:Who?:*

:Savil?:

Recognition and relief. *:Gods! Ke'chara, what has been bloody going on? Where are you?:*

He told her everything that had happened, from the time he'd been awakened by the nightmare. He compressed as much of it as he could, warned her in advance before he Mindsent her an image of Tashir, and even so, the close resemblance to Tylendel came as a shock to her that mirrored his own. He had been Tylendel's lover—but Savil had been mentor, friend, confidant, and near-mother to Tylendel, the role she filled now for Vanyel.

:*So,*: she sent, after she regained her mental balance. :*Plans?*:

:*I'm taking him into protective custody, and getting him out of here.*:

:*How, with a mob—oh, gods.*: Realization and fear. Flatly—:*You're going to Gate.*:

:*Do you see any other choice?*: he asked. :*Even if the mob weren't there—I tried to remember what little I've heard about investigative procedures.* Preserve the evidence. *If I break the shield-spell to get out, anybody can get in, and I don't have the power to set a second spell, not this solid, not from the outside. From the inside I can tap the node, but the interference I'd create with the shield would keep me effectively out of the node. You know that. Shields are permeable to the creator, but they still resist penetration. We have to find out what happened here, and we won't if anyone can get in and muddle things up.*:

Her mind-voice was gritty and gray with grim concern. :*Far too logical to make me happy, love. But you rank me these days, and there's reasons enough for that for me to follow your lead. Where are you coming in?*:

He'd thought about that very carefully. :*The door to the old chapel. It's on sanctified ground, it's one of the few doors inside Forst Reach big enough to use as a Gate-terminus, but it's not under constant use, and I know it as well as I will ever know any place. So be ready for me, because I'm not going to be worth much when I come through.*:

:*As if I didn't know. Be careful—please.*:

:*I'll try.*:

He cut the connection to the node, which dropped him out of the link with Savil, and turned his mind to one nearer at hand.

:*Brightlove—*:

:*Chosen—*:

:*I'm Gating myself and Tashir out of here. You and the Young One make a run for it. If that damned fool calling himself a Herald can't take the hint, it's not my fault; I've got too many balls in the air as it is.*:

She trembled with concern. :*I will warn Jenna; if she can get him to mount, she can carry him off whether he likes it or not. I won't tell you not to use that means of escape, only—take care!*:

He touched her with a mental caress. :*I shall.*:

He opened his eyes, and considered the possibilities, finally deciding on the open archway onto the stairs as his best bet. Putting a Gate-terminus on the outer door where the shield was would be risking more magically than he cared to. At full powers, maybe. Not now.

But first—

He shoved outward a little, chuckling nastily as the expanding shield shoved Lores down the stairs and into the courtyard. *There. That should keep them quiet for a bit.*

He walked to the center of the hallway, raised his hands, and *began.*

He spun bits of himself, his stored powers, into the structure. He could not tap the node for this; the only *possible* way to use external mage-energy for a Gate would be—at least as far as he had learned—if two mages were lifebonded, for at some deep level, two lifebonded were *one.* And, as always, as soon as he had formed the Portal around the edge of the archway, his uniquely sensitized channels began to burn painfully as he resonated to Gate-energy. When the Gate was complete, he'd be in torment.

But that was something he had learned to accept and work around.

The Weaving—

He spun *himself,* his own substance, out into threads that quested for the unique *place* he sought, the place where he would build the other end of the Gate. At some point he was no longer having to *send* those searching filaments; they were *pulling* on him, and it was all he could do to keep them from spinning away from him and taking everything that *was* him with them. Then, finally, one of them *found* the chapel door—another—a third—

There was a flare of light, not so bright as the one when he'd built the shield, and his knees gave.

Oh, hell— he thought dazedly. *I wasn't as ready as I thought I was.*

He crouched on the filthy, shard-covered floor, panting in pain, for a long, long moment before he had the strength to look up. But when he did, he saw, not the wreckage of the Highjorune Great Hall, but the welcoming, familiar corridor that led to the old Forst Reach chapel. And thrice-blessed Savil, tunic on backward, waiting.

The pain—

I . . . think I'm in trouble. I've never . . . been this drained . . . before, he thought, somewhere under the red wash of burning. *Oh, gods—if I'd known it was going to be like this, I'd never have had the courage. . . .*

He got to his feet, somehow; he staggered like a mortally-wounded drunk trying to get to Tashir. He was so dizzy he could hardly see, and only concentrating on each step, one at a time, enabled him to cross the hallway to the young man.

"Ta—shir," he croaked, and prayed for a little intelligence in those eyes. His prayers were answered *this* time; the young man stared at him with a kind of foggy awareness, though he still trembled in every limb. "Go . . . get up . . ." His feeble tugs on Tashir's arm were answered; the young man stumbled to his feet. "Go . . . there . . ." He pushed Tashir toward the Gate, every step bought with black-red waves of pain.

Maddeningly, Tashir *stopped*, right on the edge.

Vanyel screamed in frustration and torment, and *shoved*, sending the young man stumbling through, and unable to keep his balance, fell right through after him.

Fell from torment into agony; strength gone, control gone, sight, sound, all senses. There was only the pain—

And then there was nothing.

CHAPTER 8

"**Y**OU LOOK LIKE HELL," said a rough voice just above his head. *What an amazing coincidence, Savil,* Vanyel thought without opening his eyes. *I feel like hell.*

"I seem," his aunt continued dryly, "to spend an inordinate amount of time at your bedside. And don't try to pretend you're not awake."

"I wouldn't think of it," he whispered, cracking his right eye open. Savil was lounging in the chair she'd pulled up next to his bed, feet *on* his bed. "Mother will have a cat," he observed, prying his left eye open as well. "You *know* how she feels about boots on the bedcovers."

"Your mother isn't here at the moment. How are you feeling?"

He took a quick inventory. "Other than some assorted joint-aches, about the same as when I got back to Haven. Which is to say, as you pointed out, like hell. What's been going on? How long was I out this time?"

"Your outside matches your inside, we're not in a war with Lineas *quite* yet, and three days." She quirked one corner of her mouth as he groaned, and continued. "I took the liberty of deep-scanning you while you were wit-wandering, and I got in touch with a couple of merchant-contacts in Highjorune. Useful birds, pigeons. Particularly when one can *tell* their little heads *exactly* where you want them to go. You want your briefing in sequence, or by specifics?"

He had been inching into a sitting position while she was talking. She poured a goblet of cider from a pitcher next to her, and handed it to him when he was secure.

"In sequence," he said, after a sip to help moisten his throat. "And you'd better start with how Father is taking the new houseguest."

"Your father doesn't know about him, thank the gods." The other corner of her mouth twitched up to make a real smile. "Your old aunt is no fool, *ke'chara;* he was due to make his Harvest-tide inspection round of the freeholders the same morning you Gated back and fell on your nose. I simply installed Tashir in the guest room next to yours and didn't bother to tell anyone until after Withen was gone." She hesitated a moment before continuing. "I have to tell you, having that boy around is unnerving. He acts like a ghost, whisking out of sight when he sees me coming; he's given me chills more than once. He's too like our lost one. . . . Well. He is *not* well-wrapped, even I can tell that, and I'm no Mindhealer."

Vanyel nodded thoughtfully. "I've got too many questions, and nowhere near enough answers. So Tashir is here, and Father doesn't know about it. A not insignificant blessing. Keep going."

"Yfandes and the new Companion got back about noon. By nightfall I'd gotten a pigeon or two back with news. Lores is going back to Haven to protest your actions to Randale, and he's carrying a demand from what's left of Deveran's Council that Tashir be turned over to them. Vedric finally stuck his nose in; he showed up the next day. *He* seems to be on the side of the Lineans, but he wants Tashir turned over to the Mavelans for trial and sentencing." She paused for breath. "That's the bad news. The good news is that since that fathead Lores—yes, dear, I know him, he's a fathead and always has been one—*isn't* a Herald-Mage, he can't Gate back to Haven. It's going to take him a good long while to get there, especially since the Companions are in on our little conspiracy."

"The—how?"

"Jenna is going to be an invalid all the way home. If he makes the same time he'd make on a spavined horse, he'll be lucky."

He coughed on a swallow of cider. Savil patted his back, a gleam of amusement in her eye. "I got that from 'Fandes through Kellan. Jenna is *not* happy with her Chosen, and intends to make him pay for it. So, Lores is going to be delayed. So far as I know, nobody knows where you and the lad are; *Lores* assumed you'd gone to Haven. That's more good news. So you're safe for a bit, maybe long enough to find out what *really* happened."

"Even when people do find out where we are," Vanyel pointed out, "I can't be countermanded by anyone other than Randale. Randi is going to stall, I *know* him. He knows that if there weren't something damned odd going on, I'd have Gated to Haven with Tashir. So—what about our guest?"

"Well, I told you, he's been acting like a ghost. He's been hovering over *you* whenever there wasn't someone in here, but he seems to know when someone is coming, and slips back into his own room just before they get here. Fortunately I scanned you *before* I tried to read his mind. *Someone* or *something* certainly made him sensitive to *that*. I judged we didn't need any broken vases."

"Exactly." Vanyel sat up a little straighter, feeling better by the moment. "I *wish* I dared Mindtouch him long enough to figure out what his Gifts are. Fetching for certain—probably Mindspeech; that would account for knowing when someone was coming. Has anybody been seeing that he's fed?"

"Oh, he comes to meals, but not with the family. He slips down to the kitchen at First Call for the servants and the armsmen, gets himself something portable, and pelts back up here. I *guess* he returns whatever dishes he takes after the kitchen shuts down for the night; nobody's complained to me about missing plates. Your mother is alive with curiosity about him, and he won't get any nearer to her than he will to me."

"*Why* is he so—I don't know what to call it; battleshy, maybe?" Vanyel chewed at a fingernail. "I never heard that Deveran was all that bad a man."

"Rumor and the truth are sometimes fairly different things, *ke'chara*," Savil reminded him. "And Deveran was a man well-beset by problems, saddled with a wife he didn't care for, an enemy on one of his Borders which forced him to make his little kingdom into a client-state of Valdemar, his eldest was a problematical bastard, and he was unsteady enough on his throne that his people could pressure him into disinheriting the boy." She shrugged eloquently. "This doesn't make for happy times in Lineas. Men under pressure have been known to take their unhappiness out on the defenseless."

"Tashir." Vanyel sighed. "So we have a new presumptive Herald with major problems. Not good, Savil. What do we tell Father when he gets back?"

"Good question. No more than that you've retrieved Tashir newly-Chosen and—damaged. The less he knows of this mess, the better. I can't remember if he's ever *seen* Vedric or Tashir; if he hasn't, it might be best not to—"

:*FearfearfearTRAPPED. Away! Get away! DON'T TOUCH ME! FEAR!*:

"What in hell!" Savil exclaimed.

"Tashir," Vanyel croaked, throwing himself out of bed, staggering across the room.

"Van!"

He ignored Savil, and pulled open the door to his room. "He's in the bower. Treesa must have cornered him somehow, and frightened him."

He stumbled down the hall at an unsteady run, bare feet slapping on the wooden floor, weaving a little from side to side, but not slowing. He was halfway down the hallway before Savil caught up with him and threw a robe over him.

"Treesa would *not* appreciate a naked man breaking into her solar," she rasped at him, as he wrestled it on, then outraced his aunt again.

It was a damned good thing that Treesa's bower wasn't far from the guest quarters, because he was winded when he got there, and holding his aching side.

Feminine shrieks met him halfway there. The pain—that was Tashir's and *that* was all emotional. So whatever was happening, it *wasn't* a repetition of the slaughter at Highjorune.

He yanked open the door on chaos. Heavy furniture was dancing all over the room; lighter things like embroidery frames and stools circled the ceiling like demented bats, now and again pausing to throw themselves at the wall before circling again. Piles of shards showed where a few fragile ornaments had performed the same maneuvers to a more fatal end. Tashir was cowering in the corner nearest the doorframe, head buried in his arms; the women were cowering against the far wall, screaming at the tops of their lungs.

Vanyel and Savil acted in concert. *He* clamped down on Tashir; the furniture froze in mid-dance, and the flying pieces began gently lowering themselves to the floor. Savil took the women, collectively paralyzing their throats so they couldn't scream.

It was a fragile solution, at best; Vanyel sensed that the moment he or Savil loosed control, the young man would continue to panic.

The clatter of boots on the staircase heralded the unlikely answer to his prayers; Withen and Jervis stormed into the mess with drawn swords, probably expecting looting and rapine from all the screams. They stopped cold on the threshold. Vanyel would remember the looks on their faces for a long time.

Then Tashir looked up at the intruders; Vanyel got ready to tighten down on the youngster if another surge of fear broke him out of control. But instead, he felt the first flickers of hope and something very like trust when Tashir focused on Jervis.

Jervis? Lady have mercy—but I am not looking sideways at a gift horse!

The women clearly saw Withen and Jervis as deliverers; they relaxed immediately, and Savil let them go, one at a time. "Sorry about this, Withen. We've got a presumptive Herald here with a problem," Savil said, slowly and carefully. "Van rescued him, he's very jumpy—his Gift is Fetching, ladies, and he was just trying to get you to leave him alone. He panicked when you started screaming. It's all right, Withen, nobody's hurt, and it looks like the only damage is a couple of ornaments."

Treesa, white and shaking, actually managed a tremulous smile. "Th-they were those horrible ch-cherubs Thorinna insisted on g-g-giving me," she stammered. "I shan't m-m-miss them."

Vanyel, meanwhile, managed to snag Jervis' elbow and draw him away from Withen. "I've got a *very* frightened lad here, Jervis," he whispered. "I'll tell you everything I can later. For now, he seems to see you as somebody he can depend on. Do you think you can handle him, get him calmed down?"

Jervis didn't waste any time with questions or arguments. He took one look at Tashir's strained, white face, sheathed his sword, and nodded.

Vanyel, with Jervis at his elbow, moved toward Tashir as quietly and unthreateningly as he could. The youngster looked up at them with a measure of both hope and fear. "I'm going to take the shields off you, Tashir," Vanyel said, as if none of this had happened, projecting calm with all his power. Empathy was not one of his strong Gifts, but he *did* have it, and he used it to the limit. "I want you to go back to your room with Jervis. Jervis, this is Tashir. Lad, Jervis is our armsmaster."

Again that flash of hope and trust—stronger this time—in response to the identification of Jervis.

"I want you to get yourself calmed down. I know you can. Once you do, all these strange things will stop happening. What you have is something we call a Gift, and it's no more unnatural than being able to paint well or fight well. And the proof of *that* is that you're going to feel exhausted in a minute, *just* like you'd been fighting. You *have*—only with your mind. We'll help you figure out how to keep it under control so that things like this won't happen again. No one is angry at you—you heard Lady Treesa— and no one is going to punish you for any of this. These things happen to some people, and we understand that here in Valdemar; we *look* for people like you, Tashir, and we train them to *use* what they have. This little mess wasn't your fault, and I won't allow anyone to blame you for it."

"Vanyel's all right," Jervis said gruffly, clapping Vanyel on the shoulder and making him stagger a little. "If he says you're going to be fine, you will be. He won't lie, and he keeps his promises."

Without daring to Mindtouch, Vanyel couldn't tell what the youngster was thinking; he was forced to rely on what Tashir was projecting that *he* was picking up Empathically. There was doubt there—but a trust in Jervis that was increasing by the moment. Clearly, Tashir would trust Jervis where he wouldn't trust anyone else.

There was a glimmering, a hint of something else for a moment, then it was gone, slithering away before Vanyel could read it. *That* was frustrating in the extreme, but he certainly didn't want to set Tashir off again. So he slowly let his control over the youngster fade, little by little, until it was gone. Tashir slumped against the wall in total exhaustion, closing his eyes.

"Here, lad," Jervis stepped forward and took him by the elbow; the boy transferred his weight from the wall to Jervis, a sign Vanyel read with relief. "Come on, let's get you back to your room, hey? If what young Van here says is true, you're probably feeling like you've just gone through a round-robin tourney in weighted armor."

Tashir nodded, and let Jervis lead him out, stumbling a little with fatigue.

With Tashir gone, the tension left the solar, and everyone in it reacted to the relief differently. Treesa and her ladies were twittering in their corner like a flock of flustered sparrows. Vanyel found a chair and sat in it before his knees gave out on him. Withen suddenly seemed to remember the sword in his hand, and sheathed it.

"Fine, we've got Tashir taken care of, now can *any* of you tell us what happened?" Vanyel asked wearily.

The women started, and stared at him—with fear. Even his mother. Everyone except Melenna.

Their fear hit him like a blow to the heart, making him feel sick. That fear—*Gods. They never saw me work magic before. The stories were just—stories. Now I've conjured myself from Highjorune in a night, brought a wizardling with me—dispelled his magic with a look. Now I'm Vanyel Demonsbane. I'm not anyone they know anymore. I'm not anyone they could know. I'm someone with powers they don't understand, someone to fear.*

He could deal with this now—or let the situation worsen. He chose for the Heralds; chose to withdraw *himself*, Vanyel, inside a kind of mental shell and let Herald-Mage Vanyel come to the fore.

"Ladies, please," the Herald-Mage said, gently, and with a winning smile, exerting all the charm he had. "This is important to all of you if I'm to understand what set the lad off. The idea *is* to keep him from doing it again, after all."

One or two tittered nervously, the rest looked at him with wide, frightened eyes. Then after a moment during which his smile remained steady, they relaxed a little.

His heart sank when Melenna worked her way to the front of the group. He wasn't hoping for much coherency out of *her*.

But she was surprisingly calm. "Lady Treesa found the young man with Medren," she said quietly, her eyes downcast. "She's been *terribly* curious about him—well, we *all* were, really—so she ordered him to come with her to the solar and present himself properly right then. He didn't want to—well, that's what Medren said—but she ordered him, so he followed her. He was *very* polite, but even I could see that he was very unhappy, and the more Treesa asked about his family—because he told us who he was right off—the unhappier he got. As soon as Treesa noticed it, that was when she did—like she does with you, milord Van. You know, she gets sort-of flirty, but at the same time she starts getting very *mothering*. She got up and started to go to him, to put him at ease—and he sort of jumped back, and one of the couches jumped right between him and Treesa. It just—jumped, like a trained dog, or something. Lady Treesa nearly had heart failure, and she screamed, she was so surprised—that was when Tashir went absolutely white and everything in the room began flying around."

She paused, then looked up, very shyly, with none of her usual coquettishness. "We were terribly frightened, milord Van. I mean, I know you and milady Savil are magicians, and I'm sure it all seems very tame to you, but—we've never seen magic like that. Furniture—just shouldn't *do* that. I'm going to feel funny sitting on a chair for the next *week*, wondering if it's going to take it into its head to fly."

Vanyel almost felt himself liking her, for the first time in years. "I can't say I blame you; I keep forgetting most of you have never even seen me do—oh, *this*."

He made a tiny mage-light in the center of the palm of his outstretched hand. It was about all he had the energy for, and it impressed the ladies out of all proportion to its size. They *ooh*'d and *ah*'d, but they did not come any nearer.

"Milord Van," Melenna said, recapturing his attention, "there's something you really need to know. *Nothing hit anyone*. Nothing even came close. Even when those horrid cherubs hit the wall and shattered, no one was cut, no one was hurt. And do you know, that almost made the whole thing scarier."

Vanyel nodded; this incident only confirmed his feeling that the youngster *couldn't* have been guilty of that wholesale slaughter in Lineas. If he didn't remember what had happened, it could have been sheer terror that made his mind hide the memory.

But he found himself seeing the other possibilities.

That works both ways. He could have done it, just as Lores pointed out. And because he's basically a good lad, the sheer horror of what he did made his mind hide the memory so deeply there was no sign of it.

He shivered, in a preoccupied way, and drifted out of the bower, ignoring the following gazes of Treesa, her ladies, and Melenna.

He dressed and ate, all in a fog comprised of weariness and preoccupation. It was hours later when he finally faced the obvious—that he'd put a very vulnerable young man in the hands of someone who had abused *him.*

He wouldn't. Would he? Oh, gods.

He went looking for Jervis in a state of increasing alarm, and found him in the salle, working out against the pells. And by the time he found the armsmaster, he was ready to kill the man himself if Jervis had even *thought* of bullying the boy.

Bluff him. He doesn't know how worn out I am. If I go on the offensive right away, he won't have time to think.

Planting both feet firmly on the sanded wooden floor, he took an aggressive stance, arms crossed over his chest. "Jervis," he called, loudly enough to be heard over the racket of practice blade against pells.

The armsmaster pivoted and pulled off his helm. He must have been at the exercise for some time; sweat beaded his brow, and dripped off the ends of his hair. "Aye?"

Vanyel did not move. "One word for you. I don't know what this game you've been playing with me means, and at this point I don't dare take any chances. I'm warning you now; harm Medren—harm Tashir—you'll be dealing with me. *Not* Herald Vanyel—plain Vanyel Ashkevron. And you know now I can take you; any time, any place; with magic, *or* without. And I *won't* hesitate to use any weapon I've got."

Jervis flushed; looked dumbfounded. "*Harm* 'em? *Me?* What d'you take me for?"

"The man who broke my arm, Jervis. The man who's been trying to intimidate me on this very floor for the past week. The man that was too damned inflexible to suit the style to the boy—so he tried to break the boy."

Jervis flung his helm down, going scarlet with anger. The helm dented the floor and rolled off. "*Dammit,* you fool! Don't you see that was what I was tryin' t'do? I was *tryin'* t'learn *your* damned style—and *for* Medren! Hellfire! A fool could see that poor little sprout Medren was no more suited t' my way then puttin' armor on a palfrey!"

Vanyel felt as if someone had just dropped him into a vat of cold water. He blinked, relaxed his stance, and blinked again. *Feeling poleaxed is getting to become a regular occurrence*, he thought, trying to get his jaw hinged again. His knees were trembling so much with reaction that he wasn't certain they'd hold him.

Jervis saved him the trouble. He threw his gear over into his chest at the side of the practice area, stalked over to Vanyel's side, and took his elbow. "Look," he said, gruffly, "I'm tired, and we've got a lot between us that needs talking about. Let's go get a damned drink and settle it."

I shouldn't be drinking unwatered wine this tired, Vanyel thought, regarding the plain clay mug Jervis was filling with unease.

It seemed Jervis had already thought of that. "Here," he said, taking a loaf of coarse bread, a round of cheese, and a knife out of the same cupboard that had held the mugs and wine bottle, and shoving them across the trestle table at Vanyel. "Eat something first, or you'll be sorry. Not a good idea t' be guzzling this stuff if you ain't used t' it, but there's some pain between us, boy, and *I* need the wine t' get it out, even if you don't."

They were still in the armory, in a little back room that was part office, part repair-shop, and part infirmary. Vanyel was sitting on a cot with his back braced against the wall; Jervis was on the room's only chair, with the table between and a little to one side of them, a table he'd cleaned of bits of harness and an arm-brace and tools by the simple expedient of sweeping it all into a box and shoving the box under the table with his foot.

The armsmaster followed his own advice by hacking off a chunk of bread and cheese and bolting it, before taking a long swallow of his wine. Vanyel did the same, a little more slowly. Jervis sat hunched over for a long moment, his elbows on his knees, contemplating the contents of the mug held between his callused hands.

"Do you begin," Van asked awkwardly, "or should I?"

"Me. Your father—" Jervis began, and coughed. "You know I owe him, owe him for takin' me on permanent. Oh, he owed me some, a little matter of watchin' his back once, but not what I figured would put me here as armsmaster. So I figure that put me on the debit side of the ledger, eh? Well, that was all right for a while, though it weren't no easy thing, makin' fighters out of a bunch of plowboys an' second an' third sons what couldn't find the right end of a spear with both hands an' a map. Your granther—he reckoned it best t'hire what he needed. Your father—he figured best t' train his own, an' that was why he kept me. Gods. Plowboys, kids, it was a damn mess. No, it weren't easy. But I did it, I did it—an' then along comes you, first-born, an' Withen calls in the *real* debt."

The former mercenary sighed, and wiped his forehead with the back of his hand. He gave Vanyel a measuring look before taking another drink and continuing. "I 'spect by now it ain't gonna come as a surprise t' hear your old man figured you for—what're they sayin' now, *shaych?*—yeah, figured you for that from the time you came outa the nursery. Times were you looked more girl than boy—gah, that stuck in his craw for sure. Hangin' about with Liss, fightin' shy of th' foster-boys—then you took up with music, an' gods, he was sure of it. Figured he could cure you if he made sure you never knew there was such a thing, and he got somebody t' beat you into shape. That somebody was s'pposed t' be me."

He stabbed a gnarled thumb toward his chest and snorted. "Me! Kernos' Horns! 'Make the boy a man,' he says. 'I don't care what you have to do, just make 'im a man!' An' every day, just about, askin' me how you was shapin' up. I been under pressure before, but *damn*, this was enough t' make an angel sweat. I *owed* that man, an' what the hell was I supposed t' do? Tell him I never saw no beatin's turn no kids from fey if that was how they was bent? Tell him there were no few of the mercs his father'd hired was shield-mates, an' looked about as fey as me an' fought like hell's own demons?"

"You could have *tried*—"

Jervis snarled a little. "*And lose my place?* You think there's jobs for old mercs 'round any corner? I was flat *desperate*, boy! What in hell was I supposed to do?"

Vanyel bit back his resentment. "I didn't know," he said finally. "I didn't guess."

Jervis grimaced. "You weren't supposed to, boy. Well, hell, my style suited you, you poor little scrap, 'bout as well as teats on a bull. 'Bout the same as Medren."

"If you knew that—" Vanyel bit back his protest.

"Yeah, I knew it. I just couldn't face it. Then *you* went all stubborn on me, you damned well wouldn't even *try*, an' I didn't know what the hell t' do! I was 'bout ready t' bust out, you made me so damned mad, an' your old da *on* me every time I turned around—an' if that weren't enough, gods, I useta get nightmares 'bout you."

"Nightmares?" Vanyel asked. He knew he sounded skeptical, mostly because he *was*.

"Yeah, *nightmares*," Jervis said defensively. "Shit, you can't live on the damn Border without seein' fightin' sooner or later. An' you likely t' get shoved out there with no more sense of what t' do t' keep yourself alive than a butterfly. Look, smart boy—you was *firstborn;* you *bet* I figured you for bein' right in th' front line some day, an' I figured you for dead when that happened. An' I *don't* send childer outa my damned hands t' get killed, dammit!"

His face twisted and his shoulders shook for a moment, and he finished off the wine in his mug at a single gulp. Vanyel could sense more pain than he'd ever dreamed the old man could feel behind that carved-granite face. Somewhere, some time, Jervis *had* sent ill-prepared "childer" out of his hands to fight—and die—and the wounds were with him still. His own anger began to fade.

"Well, that's what you were headin' *straight* for, boy, an' I just plain didn't know how t' keep it from happening. *You* made me so damned mad, an' then your old man just gave me too much leash. Told me I had a free hand with you. An' I—lost it. I went an' took the whole mess out of your hide."

He shook his head, staring at the floor, and his hands trembled a little where he was clutching the empty mug. "I lost my damned temper, boy. I'm not proud of that. I'm not proud of myself. Should have known better, but every time you whined, it just made me madder. An' I was *wrong*, dead wrong, in what I was trying t' force into you; I knew it, an' that made me mad too. Then you pulled that last little stunt—that was it. You ever thought about what you did?"

"I never stopped thinking about it," Vanyel replied, after first swallowing nearly half the contents of his own mug. The wine could not numb the memories, recollections that were more acid on the back of his tongue than the cheap red wine.

He looked fiercely into Jervis's eyes. "I hated you," he admitted angrily. "If I'd had a real knife in my hands that day, I think I'd have gone for your throat." All the bitterness he'd felt, then and after, rose in his gullet, tasting of bile. He struggled against his closing throat to ask the question that had never been answered and had plagued him for more than a decade. "Why,

Jervis, *why*?" he got past his clenched jaw. "If you *knew* what I was doing, why did you *lie* and tell Father I was cheating?"

Silence; Jervis stared at him with anger mixed with shame, but it was the shame that won out. "Because I couldn't admit I was wrong," Jervis replied, subdued and flushing a dark red. "Because I couldn't admit it to myself or anybody else. Couldn't believe a kid had come up with the answer I couldn't find. So I told Withen you'd cheated. Half believed it myself; couldn't see how you'd've touched me, otherwise. But I—I've had a lot of time t' think about it. Years, since you left. An' you turnin' out the way you did, a Herald an' all—shit, anybody turned out like that wouldn't cheat. Came to me after a while I never caught you in a lie, neither. Came to me that the only lies bein' told were the ones *I* was tellin'. Then when I started t' tell myself the truth, began t' figure out how close I came t' breakin' more'n your arm."

He hung his head, and he wouldn't look at Vanyel. And Vanyel found his anger and bitterness flowing away from him like water from melting ice.

"Boy, I was wrong, and I am sorry for it," he said quietly. "I told Withen the truth a while back, when they sent you out on the Karsite Border; told him everything I just told you. *He* didn't know what they was sendin' you to, but *I* did. Damn, I—if anythin' had happened, an' I hadn't told him—"

He shuddered. "I told him more things, best I could. Told him that he's got a damned fine son, an' that there've been plenty of shieldmated fighters I'd'a been glad t' have at m'back, an' I'd've trusted with m' last coin and firstborn kid—an' just as many lads whose tastes ran t' wenchin' that I'd've just as soon set up against a tree an' shot. Told him if he let *that* stand between him an' you, he was a bigger fool than me. Did m' best for you, boy. Gonna keep on with it, too. Figure if I tell him enough, he might start believin' me. An' Van—I'm damned sorry it took me so long t' figure out how wrong I was."

There was profound silence then, while Vanyel waited for his thoughts and emotions to settle into coherency. Jervis was as silent as a man of rock, eyes fixed on the floor. The cricket in the salle broke off its singing, and Vanyel could hear the thud of hooves and sharp commands, faint and muffled, as Tam took one of the young stallions around on the lunge just outside.

Finally, everything within him crystallized into a new pattern—

Vanyel took Jervis' mug from limp fingers and refilled it. But instead of giving it back, he offered the armsmaster his own outstretched hand.

The former mercenary looked up at him in surprise, one of the first times Vanyel had ever seen the man register surprise, and began to smile, tentatively at first, then with real feeling.

He took Vanyel's hand in both of his, and swallowed hard. "Thank you, boy," he said hoarsely. "I wasn't sure you'd—you're a better *man* than—oh, hell—"

Vanyel shrugged, and handed him his refilled mug. "Let's call it truce. *I* was a brat. And if you hadn't done what you did, I wouldn't be a Herald." *And I wouldn't have had 'Lendel.*

"Listen," Jervis said, after first clearing his throat. "About Medren—that boy has no future here, a blind man could see that. What with all the right-born boys—an' I couldn't see *that* one bein' happy as anybody's dogsbody squire, you know? Figured the only chance for him was the way I came up; merc armsman. Lord Kernos knows he's got all the brains t' make officer right quick. So that's what I was tryin' to work him to."

"There *was* music."

"Yeah, his other shot was *maybe* music. I'd heard him, boy sounded all right, but what the hell do I know about music? Not a damn thing. But I figured, I figured I could make a damned fine armsman out of him, what with his reactions an' his brains an' speed an' all, if I could just figure out what they'd taught you over to Haven. Been tryin'—*damn* if I haven't been tryin'. *Could* not seem t'get it worked out, an'—shit, Van, hate t' use th' boy like a set of pells, but it seemed like th' only way t' work it out was to work it out usin' *him*. But," Jervis held up a knotted finger, "just on th' chance th' boy *was* good at the plunkin' I been *damned* careful of his hands. *Damned* careful."

Vanyel's arm began to ache, and he put his mug down to rub it. "I never did get all the feeling back," he said, still resentful, still feeling the last burn of the anger he'd nursed all these years. "If things hadn't turned out the way they did—even being *careful* you could have hurt him, and *ruined* his chance at music."

Jervis visibly stifled an angry retort, but in the face of Vanyel's own anger, winced and looked away. "Can't undo what I did, boy," he said, after an uncomfortable silence. "Nobody can. But the least I can do is keep from makin' the same mistake twice. An' I *was* tryin'. I swear it."

Vanyel sat on his anger.

Jervis gulped his wine. "Truth now, between you an' me. Were you any good? Did I—"

"No," Vanyel said honestly. "I didn't have the Gift. And it's taken a while, but I learned how to make up for the lost feeling. You didn't take anything away from me, not really."

Jervis' shoulders sagged a little. "How about the bastard? Medren, I mean."

"I'm sponsoring him into the Bardic Collegium. He's better than I was at fifteen, and he's got the Bardic Gift." Vanyel nodded at Jervis' swift intake of breath. "Exactly; he'll make a full Bard."

The memory suddenly sprang up, unprompted, of Medren and his succession of bruises—just bruises. Nasty ones, some of them, but not broken bones, not even sprains. No worse than Vanyel had seen his brothers and cousins sport, back in the long ago. And Vanyel began to look a little closer at those memories, while Jervis stared at him askance. Finally he began to smile.

"It just occurred to me—Medren. With a full Gift. He has been *manipulating* me, the little demon, using that Gift of his. Doing it just fine, too, and with no Bardic training. Given that, I'd say he's going to be outstanding, and I think I'd better have a little word with him on the subject of ethics!"

Jervis chuckled. "I don't think it's a-purpose; at least, I don't think he knows he shouldn't. He's another one that's good at bottom. An' let me tell you, even *without* havin' a decent style, he's no slouch with a blade!"

Vanyel cut them both more bread and cheese, and reached for the wine to refill both mugs. He leaned back against the wall, with a feeling that something that had been festering for a long time had begun to heal. He didn't *like* Jervis, quite. Not yet, anyway. But he was beginning to see why Jervis had done what he'd done, and beginning to respect the courage that made the armsmaster admit—if belatedly—that he was wrong.

"You know," Vanyel said slowly, "he'll be taught blade right along with music; Bards end up finding themselves in some fairly unpleasant places from time to time. *They're* in Valdemar's service no less than Heralds are, so being handy with a sword surely can't hurt. Hellfire, you should have seen Bard Chadran in his prime; he'd have been a match for *both* of us together!"

Jervis looked up with interest. "Chadran—that the one that was s'pposed t' have got picked up by bandits, got 'em t' trust 'im, then fought himself an' a handful of prisoners loose?"

"That's the one, only he went in on Elspeth's request."

When he finished that story, Jervis managed to coax the Shadow Stalker tale out of him, after half the bottle was gone. Most people never heard the real story. It took half a bottle before he was ready to face those memories.

Before *that* tale was over and the bottle was empty, Vanyel had decided he had an ally he could count on. He was certain of it after Jervis' final words when Vanyel got up to leave.

"Never understood Heralds before," the armsmaster admitted. "Never could figure out what all the fuss and feathers was about. Didn't *really* have any notion of what you people did, until them stories about you started up. Never paid much attention t' who the hero was before, then I started noticin' that in the Valdemar songs most of the heroes turn out t' be Heralds. Somethin' else I started noticin'—most of the Heralds ended up comin' down with a serious case of dead in them stories. *You* come pretty close to it, a time or two, eh?"

Vanyel nodded ruefully, stretching sore muscles. "Stupidity, mostly."

Jervis snorted. "My ass. Wasn't stupidity so much's puttin' yourself in harm's way. Right, so tell me this—a merc like me, he puts himself on the line for money. Knows what he bought himself into, knows what he'll get out of it if he lives. An' he only gives so much; what he was paid for, but not past it. But—you—you Heralds? What's in it for you? I mean, look at you right now—you've about wore yourself down to a thread, somethin' *no* merc would do. And you showed up *here* in th' same state. What for?"

Vanyel shook his head. "It's hard to tell you; it's a feeling, more than anything. Something like a priestly vocation, *I* would guess." He looked inside himself for the answer, an answer he hadn't really looked for since he first realized what it was that had made Tylendel *need* to be a Herald. "I do it because I have to. Because I'm needed. There isn't anybody—I'm not boasting, Jervis, you can ask Savil—there isn't *anybody* else in the whole Kingdom that can do what I can do. I can't give up, I can't just shrug things off and tell myself somebody else will take up the slack, because there *isn't* anybody else. There are too many people out there who need my protection; *because* I'm this powerful I have an obligation to use that power. I'm the lone Guard at the Gate—I daren't give up, because there's nobody behind me to take up what I lay down."

Jervis' face went absolutely still. Vanyel wished he knew what the old man was thinking. "Nobody?" he asked.

Vanyel shook his hair out of his eyes. "Nobody," he echoed, staring into space. "I have no choice; it's that, or know *my* inaction dooms others. Sometimes lots of others. Too many times, others I know and care for."

Jervis's eyes grew deep and thoughtful, and Vanyel could feel them on his back as he left, headed for the bathhouse.

＊　　＊　　＊

There was a light tap at Vanyel's door that woke him from the nap he was trying to take—in part to make up for the sleep he had been losing to Melenna. It hadn't been a very successful attempt. He was still too on edge; his mind was too active. He yawned, and then grinned, identifying Medren by a stray thought-wisp. *So we've recovered from the measles, hmm? And about to have a little moment of truth with Uncle Vanyel. Or rather, though he doesn't know it, Herald Vanyel.*

"Come," he said, sitting up and stretching, then swinging his legs off the bed.

"Vanyel?" Medren plodded into the room and sagged down into the window seat. "Can I hide up here? I just found out from young Meke that old Jervis is gonna have some 'special demonstration' this afternoon, and you *know* what that means." The boy shuddered. "Good old Medren for pells."

"Actually, no, not this time." Vanyel grinned. "It means 'good old Radevel for pells.' I've been teaching Rad my style, and the pells plan on giving Jervis as good as he gets. Then you and Radevel will have at each other while I coach so Jervis can watch. He says he wants to know my style 'because sooner or later he's going to get another puny 'un.' And some time this week, my young friend, you will have another sparring partner; once I recover, you and *I* are going to pair off. And *I'll* run you around the field for a while. And *meanwhile* we'll find out what Tashir is good for."

The boy's mouth dropped open, and Vanyel continued mercilessly.

"This is for your benefit. Bardic Collegium includes bladework for Bards right along with the music lessons, and I wanted you to have as much of a head start as possible. A Bard's duty has been known to carry him into some dangerous places, and the Bardic Circle can't spare Guards to tag along behind you to keep you out of trouble."

The boy's mouth worked, but for a long moment, no sound emerged.

"Oh—" he said weakly. "I—ah—"

"Medren, I have a very serious question to ask you." Vanyel let the smile drop from his mouth and eyes, and moved to stand over the boy. "When you were fishing for my sympathy, what else were you doing? And don't tell me that you weren't doing anything. We both know better than that."

"I . . ." the boy gulped, and dropped his eyes. "I was trying to make you feel sorry for me. That's why I was kind of . . . playing while I was talking to you, singing but not singing, you know? Putting music behind what I was doing. I . . . it feels sort of like when I really get taken up by a song. Like I'm pushing something. Only with the inside of my head."

"Did you ever think about whether that was a good idea?" Vanyel asked, with no inflection in his voice.

"No. Not really." A long pause, then Medren hung his head. "It isn't, is it?" he asked, in a very small, and very subdued voice. "I was doing something I shouldn't have. I . . . I guess it's something like being a bully because you're bigger than somebody, isn't it?"

Vanyel nodded, relief relaxing his shoulders. *Good. He knows, now. He saw it for himself. He'll be all right.* But he spoke sternly. "It is. And if you do it at Bardic, they'll have the Heralds block your Gift, and they'll turn you out. That *is* your Gift; this ability to make people feel what you want them to feel through music. And there are only three times it's permissible for you to use that Gift; when you're performing, when you're helping someone who *needs* help, and at the King's orders."

"Yessir," Medren whispered, head sunk between his shoulders, where he'd pulled it when Vanyel spoke of having his Gift blocked and being turned out of the Collegium. "Nossir. I'll remember."

"You'd better. On this, you get *one* chance. Now, come on, lad," Vanyel said with a renewal of cheerfulness, urging Medren up out of his chair and propelling him out the door with a hand behind his shoulders. "Time for you to show those plowhorse cousins of yours how a *real* fighter does things."

CHAPTER 9

THEY RETURNED TO his room after practice; Vanyel had *thought* to give Medren another music lesson, but even though *he* hadn't done any fighting, he realized as he directed Medren's movements that he was drained—and that was long before the practice was over.

Medren was no fool; he could see how exhausted Vanyel was. *He* suggested that the lesson be put off; he even offered to have servants bring Vanyel's dinner to his room.

Vanyel accepted both offers; he bolted the food as soon as the servant brought it, and threw himself facedown on his bed again with a groan. The bed had somehow been made up in his absence, *despite* all the hurly-burly in Treesa's bower. *Baby Heralds wrecking rooms, adult Heralds making magic Gates and then falling through them half-dead, a possible war on the Border, and* still somehow the beds get made. What a world.

He tried to think of what he would have done if Tashir hadn't run berserk, and realized he hadn't *yet* spoken with Yfandes. She probably knew what was going on, of course; since the moment he had first accepted the notion of becoming a Herald she had made a habit—which he encouraged—of eavesdropping on just about everything as a kind of silent observer in the back of his mind. He didn't in the least mind her using his eyes and ears; it saved a lot of explaining, and if there was something he *didn't* want her "present" for, he'd tell her. But it was very rude of him not to have *said* something, at least in greeting, before this. He rolled over on his back and closed his eyes.

:'Fandes?: he called, tentatively. :*I'm sorry—I got tangled—and then I fell on my nose for a while—and then I had a visit to make—and then I had a visitor myself.:*

She chuckled. :*So I saw. You're forgiven.:*

:*Have you got anything for me? I'm sorry I made you run all the way home instead of taking the shortcut.:*

:*You're forgiven. And oddly enough,:* she replied promptly, :*I have got*

something for you. Brightest gods, let me tell you, it hasn't been the easiest informa-
tion to obtain. And I am not *sorry I was apart from you for a bit; I am very glad you*
were far away by the time you completed the Gate. I felt your pain quite enough as it
was.: The love in her mind-voice softened her words. *:The Young One—I*
have taken to calling him "Ghost," for he has been haunting this place like the veriest
spirit, never coming near enough to touch and only rarely to be seen, and frightening
the farmers no end. He is quite *closely locked into his Chosen's mind. I can speak*
with him, but only distantly; most of his attention and his concentration are with
Tashir. But I can Mindtouch with him as you cannot his Chosen; Mindtouch does
not frighten him. And so, because of the close bond between him and the youngling,
I can sometimes pick up things as if I was in Mindtouch with Tashir.: Overtones of
deep uneasiness. *:The youngling is something less than steady; his mind is fragile*
and unbalanced. There are terrible things which haunt him, and which he fears to tell,
and which he even blocks from his thoughts. Still. Ghost may yet balance him, if he
can regain balance; the stallion is something of a Mindhealer.:

Vanyel sat bolt upright. *:A Mindhealer? A* Companion? *But—:*

:It happens from time to time,: she interrupted, the overtones of her mind-
voice telling him clearly that she was very reluctant to speak of it. *:It happens*
when it is needed. . . . Listen, I was in Mindtouch when the boy was making such
a ruin of Treesa's bower, and I remained in touch. I saw what you only glimpsed.
Here.:

It was a feeling she Sent, as well as an image. A feeling of profound trust,
and the image of an older man, much like Jervis, in practice armor.

:Looks like Jervis may be our key,: Vanyel mused, lying back down again,
and putting his hands behind his head. *:Could that man have been Deveran's*
armsmaster?:

:I cannot tell you; that is all I could obtain,: she replied. *:Tashir is much too*
traumatized for any questioning, I would say. He—: she slipped out of the link
for a moment, then slipped back in again. *:—he is better, steadier, and Jervis is*
with him again. They are taking supper in the Great Hall, though with the ser-
vants, not the family. But I would not disturb him.:

He winced at the thought. *:Even if I wanted to, I'm not up to dealing with*
him, beloved,: he confessed, feeling every joint in his body ache. *:I'm not en-*
tirely certain I could contain him again. I am about down to my last dregs. This is
getting to be a habit I'd rather not have.:

:Then rest. This won't be solved in a day.:

He grimaced silently. *:I know. I told Savil that I have more questions than*
answers. Like—why are Highjorune and that palace built where they are? I can't

*believe that it's accident. Why are the people of Lineas so against magic—and yet
have no laws forbidding its use? Where did Deveran want to send Tashir, and why
did the prospect frighten him enough to defy his father in public? And why is the boy
so afraid of women that a bowerful could send him skirting the edges of hysteria?:* He
made a mental shrug. *:I know some of those questions seem trivial, yet it all ties
together, somehow, but how—:*

:Rest,: Yfandes repeated. Then, mischievously, *:There is at least one thing
you will not need to beware of.:*

:Which is?:

*:Visitors in your bed. I do believe you have frightened Melenna enough that she
is thinking about things you might choose to do with her.:*

:Such as?:

:Flying her out the window in the nude.:

He laughed aloud, and decided to stay in his room. Right now what he
wanted was some quiet and solitude. . . .

Three days of unconsciousness seems to make for insomnia, he thought, after trying
to fall asleep for what seemed like half the night. He gave up, finally, and
moved to the window seat. He lit the candle beside it the ordinary way—
from the coals in the fireplace—and found a book. It was a volume of history
he would have found perfectly fascinating under normal circumstances, but
he found himself rereading pages two and three times and *still* not getting the
sense of them.

He abandoned it in favor of the new gittern, letting his fingers wander
across the strings as he tried to relax. It was earlier than he'd thought. This
evening was very much like the one three nights ago; cool and crisp, with
a light breeze. The moon was waning now into her last quarter, so there was
less light, but the same kind of clouds raced across her face.

Gods, how life can change in one night.

This afternoon had been hard. Hard on emotions. Dealing with Jervis—
purging that old hate. And before that, Tashir. Seeing Tashir in daylight,
looking *so* much like Tylendel, only a younger, more vulnerable Tylendel,
had reawakened all the old hurt and loss. He was trying to deal with the
young man *as himself,* but it was not easy, not with his insides in knots every
time Tashir turned those eloquent eyes on him . . . all he wanted to do was
take the young man in his arms and . . . never mind.

And is that because he looks like 'Lendel? Or is it because of me? He picked
out the refrain of "Shadow-Lover," as he tried to sort himself out. *I don't*

know what I am anymore. Shavri and Randi, they're more to me than friends. And Shavri more than Randi. A lot more. I don't know what that means. I just don't. *Now Tashir—hellfire. But the reason—is it because he's attractive, or because he reminds me of 'Lendel?* He tried to think if he'd ever been the *least* bit attracted to any other women but Shavri, and couldn't think of any. *But how much of that is because they kept throwing themselves at me? Gods, I* hate *being pursued. I especially hate being pursued in public. And the idea of going to bed with somebody I don't care for—* His stomach knotted. *Gods, gods, where does friendship end and love start? How much of my being shaych was being shaych, and how much was just because of 'Lendel?*

His unhappy thoughts were interrupted by a knock on the door, and he started. He'd already dealt with Medren. Melenna was *not* likely to show up, according to Yfandes. He wasn't expecting anyone; not even Savil.

He turned away from the window with the gittern cradled against his chest, and racked the instrument carefully. He walked soundlessly across the room and answered the door just as the would-be visitor made a second, more tentative knock.

It was Tashir; pale as bleached linen, with the eyes of a lost soul. As Vanyel stood there stupidly, the young man slipped inside and closed the door behind him, putting his back to it, and facing Vanyel with a fear-filled and haunted expression, a strange expression Vanyel could not interpret.

And in the dim light the young man looked even more like Tylendel. Vanyel's heart seemed to be squeezed up into an area just below his throat, and his chest hurt. "I heard you playing," the youngster said, hoarsely. "I wouldn't have troubled you if you hadn't been awake. Can I—bother you?"

"Please, sit," Vanyel managed, finding it very hard to get his breath. "Certainly, you're welcome here, and it isn't 'bothering me.' How can I help you?"

The young man walked hesitantly toward the table, and paused, with his hands on the back of one of the chairs. He looked back over his shoulder at Vanyel. His face—thank the gods!—was in shadow. Vanyel succeeded in getting two full breaths in a row.

"Jervis says you're . . . shaych," Tashir whispered. "Are you?"

Vanyel moved over to the other chair and motioned him to sit; he did so, but on the very edge of the chair. Vanyel had a flash of image, a young stag at the edge of a bright meadow in the midst of hunting season. Which was also mating season. Wanting, needing, looking for something, not knowing *what* he needed, and full of fear and less definable emotions. "It's no secret," Vanyel replied cautiously, unable to predict what was coming. "Yes. Yes, I am."

"Would you be my lover?" Tashir blurted desperately.

Vanyel found he *needed* to sit down. He did, just before his legs refused to hold him. He stared at Tashir, quite unable to speak for a moment.

Do you have any idea what you're doing to me, lad? No, you can't. Poor boy. Poor, confused child—

He gathered his emotions and put a tight rein on them. The youngster did *not* have the feel of *shay'a'chern,* not in any way. This was the last question Vanyel would ever have expected from him. And his initial reaction was to tell him "no."

And yet—and yet—he looked so like Tylendel. *And I've enough experience I could be certain he'd enjoy it—* was the unbidden thought. *I could convince him he was. It would be so easy. And I'm so lonely. Oh, gods. Oh, gods. The temptation—*

Instead of answering, he stood slowly and moved to stand before the boy, gently reaching out and placing the fingers of his right hand just beneath the line of Tashir's jaw. Ostensibly, this was to make the youngster look up into his eyes—but Vanyel wanted to *know* something of what was going on in the young man's mind, and if he could not Mindtouch, well, physical contact made his Empathy *much* sharper. As the dark eyes met his silver, he could feel the youngster's pulse racing beneath the tip of his middle finger. And the *feel* he received was of fear and unhappiness, *not* attraction. Not in the slightest. *That* was both relief and disappointment.

"Why?" Vanyel asked, much more calmly than he felt, striving with all his might for impartiality. "Why do you want me as a lover?"

Tashir flushed, and his fear deepened. And there was something new: shame. "It—this afternoon—" he stammered. "Lady Treesa—I was so—I—I—she—Vanyel, she—" His voice dropped to a humiliated whisper. "She scares me, ladies scare me—I—"

"Oh." Vanyel made the one word speak volumes, not of contempt, but understanding and compassion. "*Now* I think I see what the problem is, and why you're here. My mother frightened you, and women in general frighten you, so you think you *must* be *shay'a'chern,* right?"

Tashir nodded a little, and paled again.

Vanyel sternly told his insides to leave him alone. They didn't listen. They ached. He ignored them, grateful that training had made it possible for him to control his voice and his face, if not his emotions. "Well, let's really analyze this before we go making assumptions, shall we? Do you know my aunt, Herald Savil? Have you met her formally yet?"

"The o—the lady who was with you?" Now Vanyel picked up only respect, mixed with the good-natured contempt of the young for the old.

"Does *she* frighten you?" He half-smiled, stiffly. "She should, you know, she's a *terrible* tyrant!"

Tashir shook his head.

"How about Kylla? She's the baby who's always getting out of the nursery, usually without a stitch on. I expect she's done it at least once while I was sleeping. Does *she* bother you?"

Bewilderment. "She's kind of cute. Why should I be afraid of *her*?"

Vanyel worked his way up and down the age scale of all the women at Forst Reach that he thought the youngster might have seen. Only when he neared women between twenty and Treesa's age did he get any negative responses, and when he mentioned a particularly pretty fourteen-year-old niece, there was *definite* interest—and real attraction.

From time to time Vanyel dropped in questions about his feelings toward *men*; not just himself, but Jervis, Medren, some of the servants the youngster had encountered. And at no time, even as he began to relax, did Tashir evidence any attraction to men in general or Vanyel in particular—except, perhaps as a protector. Certainly not as a potential lover. Whenever that topic came up, the fear came back.

Finally Vanyel sighed, and took his hand away. It ached, ached as badly as the injured left did when it rained. He rubbed it, wishing he could massage away the ache in his own heart. "Tashir—let me say that I'm very flattered, but—no. I will *not* oblige you. Because you've come to me for all the wrong reasons. You aren't here because you *know* you're *shay'a'chern*; you aren't even here because you're attracted to me. You're here because women of a certain age frighten you. That's not enough to base a relationship on, not the kind you're asking me for. You don't *know* what you want; you only know what you don't want."

"But—" the youngster said, his eyes all pupil, "but you—when you were *younger* than me—Jervis said—"

Vanyel *had* to look away; he couldn't bear that gaze any more. "When I was younger than you I *knew* what I was, and I *knew* what I wanted, and who I wanted it with. You're looking for—for someone to like you, for someone to be close to. You're just grasping at something that looks like a solution, and you're hoping I'll make up your mind for you. And I *could* do that, you know. Even without using magic, I could probably convince you that you *were shay'a'chern,* at least for a little while. I could . . . do things, say things to you, that would make you very infatuated with me." He paused, and forced a breath into his tight chest, looking back down at Tashir's bewildered eyes. "But that wouldn't solve your problems, it would only let you postpone finding a solution for a while. And I truly don't think that would help you in the least. Any answers you find, Tashir, are going to have to be answers you decide on for yourself. Here—" He offered the youngster his hand. Tashir looked at it in surprise, then tentatively put his own hand in Vanyel's.

He looked even more surprised when Vanyel hauled him to his feet, put his palm between his shoulderblades, and shoved him gently toward and out the door. "Go to bed, Tashir," Vanyel said, trying to make his tones as kindly as he could. "You go have another chat with Jervis. Go riding with Nerya. Try making some friends around the Reach. We'll talk about this later."

And he shut the door on him, softly, but firmly.

He began to shake, then, and clung to the doorframe to keep himself standing erect. He leaned his forehead against the doorpanel for a long time before he stopped trembling. When he thought he could walk without stumbling, he turned and went back to his chair, and sat down in it heavily.

He hurt. Oh, gods, he hurt. He felt so empty—and twice as alone as before. He stared at the candleflame while it burned down at least half an inch, trying to thaw the adamantine lump of frozen misery in his stomach, and having a resounding lack of success.

:You did the right thing, Chosen.: The bright voice in his mind was shaded with sympathy and approval both.

:I know I did,: he replied, around the ache. *:What else could I do? Just—tell me, beloved—why can't I feel happy about it? Why does doing the right thing have to hurt so damned much?:*

She had no answer for him, but then, he hadn't really expected one.

If I were just a little less ethical—and how much of that is because he looks like 'Lendel? Gods. It isn't just my heart that hurts. And I'm so damned lonely.

Eventually he slept.

It took a week before he felt anything like normal. Challenging Jervis when he had been straight out of his bed had been pure bluff. He wouldn't have been able to stand against the armsmaster for more than a few breaths at most. He wondered if Jervis had guessed that.

Arms practice was interesting. He and Jervis circled around each other, equally careful with words *and* blows. There was so much between them that was only half-healed, at best, that it was taking all his skill at diplomacy to keep the wounds from reopening. And no little of that was because it sometimes seemed that Jervis might be regretting his little confession.

But they were civil to each other, and working with each other, which was a *damn* sight more comfortable than being at war with each other.

"That boy's got more'n a few problems, Van," Jervis said, leaning on his sword, and watching Tashir work out with Medren. The young man was being painstakingly careful with the younger boy, and he was wearing the first untroubled expression Vanyel had seen on his face. And for once, there was no fear in him. For once, he was just another young man; a little more considerate of the smaller, younger boy than most, but still just another young man.

"I know," Vanyel replied, shifting his weight from his right foot to his left. "And I know you aren't talking about fighting style." He chewed his lip a little, and decided to ask the one question that would decide whether or not he was going to be able to carry out the plan he'd made in the sleepless hours of the last several nights. "Tell me, do you feel up to handling him by yourself for a bit? You'll have Savil in case he does anything magical again, though I don't think he will, but I don't think he'll open up to Savil the way he will to you."

Jervis gave him a long look out of the corner of his eye. "And just where are *you* going to be?"

Vanyel looked straight ahead, but spoke in a low voice that was just loud enough for Jervis to hear him. The fewer who knew about this, the better. "Across the Border. All the answers to our questions are over *there*, including the biggest question of all—if Tashir didn't rip a castle full of people to palm-sized pieces, who did? And why?"

And away from him, maybe I can get my thinking straight.

Jervis considered his words, as the *clack* and *thwack* of wooden practice blades echoed up and down the salle. "How long do you think you'll be out over there? You're not going as *yourself*, I hope?"

"No." He smiled wanly. A Herald was not going to be a popular person in Highjorune right now. "I've got a disguise that's been very useful in the past; Herald Vanyel is still going to be resting in the bosom of his family.

The gentleman who's going to cross the Border is a rather scruffy minstrel named Valdir. Nobody notices a minstrel asking questions; they're *supposed* to. And since the only person who saw my face *clearly* is now on his way to Haven with a rock in his craw, I should be safe. I expect to take a fortnight at most."

"*Get that guard up, Medren!* Huh. Sounds good to me. Gods know we aren't getting any answers out of the boy at the moment. What's Savil say?"

Vanyel winced as Medren got in a particularly good score on Tashir. "That she never could stand clandestine work, so she's not about to venture an opinion. Father's not to know. Savil is going to tell him I'm visiting with Liss. Yfandes is in favor, since she's going to be with me most of the time, and within reach when she's not actually *with* me."

Jervis' shoulders relaxed a trifle. "That had me worried, a bit. But if you're taking the White Lady, I got no objections. If *she* can't get you out of a mess, nobody can. I got a lot of respect for that pretty little thing."

:Tell him thank you, Chosen.:

Vanyel grinned. Jervis, unlike Withen, had no problem remembering that Yfandes was not a horse. He'd always offered her respect; since he and Vanyel had made their uneasy peace, he'd offered her the same kind of treatment she'd have gotten from another Herald. Yfandes was a *person* to Jervis; a little oddly shaped, but a person. Jervis actually got along with her better than he did with Vanyel. "She says to tell you, 'thank you.' I think she likes you."

"She's a lovely lady, and I like her right back." Jervis grinned at him. "There's been a couple of times I've wished I could talk to her straight out; I kind of wanted her to know I'm real pleased that she's on *my* side these days. *Tashir! The boy won't break! Put some back in that swing! He's* supposed *to learn how to get out of the way, dammit!*" Jervis stalked onto the floor of the salle, and Vanyel took the opportunity to get back to his room and pack up.

There was one other person who needed to know where Vanyel was going to be: Medren. This was in part because Vanyel needed to borrow his old lute. Disreputable minstrel Valdir could never afford Herald Vanyel's lute or the twelve-stringed gittern. And going in clandestine like this, Vanyel knew he'd better have *no* discrepancies in his persona. Vanyel *had* a battered old instrument he'd picked up in a pawn shop that he carried as Valdir, but he'd left it at Haven, not thinking he'd need it.

But there was a further reason; Tashir was relaxed and open with the boy in a way he was not with either Jervis or Vanyel. Vanyel had come to the conclusion that his nephew was older than his years in a great many ways, and Vanyel had confidence in his inherent good sense.

And, last of all, the boy had the Bardic Gift. That could be very useful in dealing with an unbalanced youngster that no one dared to Mindtouch.

In a kind of bizarre coincidence, they'd given Medren Vanyel's old room, up and under the eaves and across from the library. Vanyel stared out the window, and wondered if he was still up to the climb across the face of the keep to get to that little casement that let into the library.

"How long do you reckon you'll be over there?" Medren asked, sitting on his bed and detuning his old instrument carefully.

"Not long; about a fortnight altogether. Anything I can't find out in that time is going to be too deep to learn as a vagabond minstrel, anyway." Vanyel turned away from the window.

"You aren't planning on going into that palace are you?"

"No. Why?"

Medren shook his head. "I dunno. I just got a bad feeling about it. Like, you shouldn't go in there alone. As long as I think of you going in *with* somebody, the bad feeling goes away. That sound dumb?"

"No, that sounds eminently sensible." Vanyel sat down beside him on the bed. Medren picked up the patched and worn canvas lute case and slid the instrument into it. "I want you to keep an eye on Tashir for me; a *Bardic* eye, if you will."

The boy contemplated that statement for a moment, whistling between his teeth a little. "You mean keep him calmed down? He's as jumpy as a deer hearing dogs. I been trying to do a little of that. I—" He blushed. "I remembered what you told me, about misusing the Gift. I thought this might be what you meant about using it right. He likes music well enough, so I just—sort of make it soothing."

Vanyel ruffled his hair approvingly, and Medren gave him an urchinlike grin. "Good lad, that is *exactly* what I meant about using it properly. When you aren't enhancing a performance, *proper* use is to the benefit of your audience, or to the King's orders. And poor Tashir could certainly benefit by a little soothing. So keep him soothed, hmm? There's one other thing, and this is a bit more delicate. He may tell you things, things about himself. I hesitate to ask you to betray confidences, but we just don't know anything about him."

Medren thought that over. "Seems to me that the awfuller the thing he'd tell me, and the less he'd want it known, the more *you'd* want to know it." He chewed his lip. "That's a hard one. That's awful close to telling secrets I've been asked to keep. And if I've been making him feel like he could trust me, it doesn't seem fair."

"I know. But I remind you that he's been accused of murdering fifty or sixty people. What he tells you might be a clue to whether or not he actually did it." Vanyel forestalled Medren's protests with an uplifted hand. "I know what you're going to say, and *if* he did it, I *don't* believe he did it on purpose. But if—say—you found out where it was that his father wanted to send him, and why it frightened him so, we could have mitigating circumstances. I doubt the Lineans would totally accept it, but *we* would, and he could make a very pleasant home here with the Valdemar Heralds, even if he could never return to Lineas. That's not exactly a handicap."

Medren nodded so vigorously that his forelock fell into his eyes. "Makes sense. Fine, then if he tells me stuff, I'll tell it to you."

The boy stuffed a handful of the little coils of spare lute strings into a pocket on the back of the case and handed the whole to Vanyel. Vanyel stood, and pulled the carry strap over his shoulder. "Do I look the proper scruffy minstrel?" he asked, grinning.

Medren snorted. "You're *never* going to look scruffy, Van. You *do* look underfed, which is good. And if you didn't shave for a couple of days, that would be better. Then, again—" He contemplated Vanyel with his head tilted to one side. "If you didn't shave you'd look like a bandit, and people don't tell things to bandits. Better just stick to looking clean, starving, and pathetic. That way women'll feed you and tell you everything while they're feeding you. Hey, don't worry about that lute—if you gotta leave it, leave it. If you feel bad about leaving it, replace it."

Vanyel placed his right hand over his heart and bowed slightly. "I defer to your judgment. Clean and starving it is, and if speed requires I leave the instrument, I shall. And I *shall* replace it. It's a good thing to have one old instrument that you needn't worry about; you never know when you'll want to take one—oh, on a picnic or something. Thank you, Medren. For everything." He glanced out the window. "I want to get to Highjorune by nightfall, so we'd better get on it. Remember, I'm supposed to be on a side trip to see Liss. I sent her a message by one of Savil's birds, so Liss knows to cover for me."

Medren nodded. "Right. And I'll keep a tight eye on Tashir for you, best I can."

"That's all I can ask of anyone."

Sunset was a thing of subdued colors, muted under a pall of gray clouds. Vanyel slipped off Yfandes' back, and uncinched the strap holding the folded blanket he'd used as a makeshift riding pad. Bareback for most of a day would not have been comfortable for either of them, but he had no place to hide her harness. No problem; they'd solved *this* little quandary the first time he became minstrel Valdir. She wore no halter at all, and only the blanket that *he* would use if he had to sleep in stables or on the floor of some inn. Nothing to hide, and nothing to explain. Yfandes would keep herself fed by filching from farms and free-grazing. If she got *too* hungry, he'd buy or steal some grain and toss it out over the wall to her at night.

:*Be careful,*: she said, nuzzling his cheek. :*I love you. I'll be staying with you as much as I can, but this is awfully settled land. I may have to pull off quite a ways to keep from getting caught.*:

:*I have all that current-energy to pull on if I have to call you,*: he reminded her. :*It's not the node, but it wouldn't surprise me to find out I could boost most of the way back to Forst Reach with it. I'm planning on recharging while I'm here, anyway.*:

:*If Vedric is still here, that could be dangerous.*:

:*Only if he detects it.*: He cupped his hand under her chin and gazed into those bottomless blue eyes. :*I'll be careful, I promise. This isn't Karse, but I'm going to behave as if it was. Enemy territory, and full drill.*:

:*Then I'm satisfied.*: She tossed her head, flicking her forelock out of her eyes. :*Call me if you need me.*:

:*I will.*: He watched her fade into the underbrush of the woodlot beside him with a feeling of wonderment. How something that big and that *white* could just—vanish like that—it never ceased to amaze him.

He rolled the cinch-belt, folded the blanket, and stuffed both into the straps of his pack. With a sigh for his poor feet, he hitched the lute strap a little higher on his shoulder, and headed toward the city gates of Highjorune.

The road was dusty, and before he reached the gates he looked as if he'd been afoot all day. He joined the slow, shuffling line of travelers and workers returning from the farms, warehouses, and some of the dirtier manufactories that lay outside the city walls. Farmworkers, mostly; most folk owning farms within easy walking distance of Highjorune lived within the city walls, as did their hirelings, a cautious holdover from the days when Mavelan attacks out of Baires penetrated as far as the throne city. The eyes of the guard at the gate flickered over him; noted the lute, the threadbare, starveling aspect, and the lack of weaponry, and dismissed him, all in a breath. Minstrel Valdir was not worth noting, which made minstrel Valdir very happy indeed.

Well, the first thing a hungry minstrel looks for is work, and Valdir was no exception to that rule. He found himself a sheltered corner out of the traffic, and began to assess his surroundings.

The good corners were all taken, by a couple of beggars, a juggler, and a man with a dancing dog. He shook his head, as if to himself. Nothing for him here, so close to the gates. He was going to need a native guide.

He loitered about the gate, waiting patiently for the guard to change. He put his hat out, got the lute in tune, and played a little, but he really didn't expect much patronage in this out-of-the-way nook. He actually drew a few loiterers, much to his own amazement. To his further amazement, said loiterers had money. By the time the relief-guard arrived with torches to install in the holders on either side of the gate, he'd actually collected enough coppers for a meager supper.

He had something more than a turnip and stale breadcrust on his mind, however. It was getting chilly; his nose was cold, and his patched cloak was doing very little to keep out the bite in the air. He chose one of the guards to follow, a man who looked as if he ate and drank well, and had money in his pocket; he slung the lute back over his shoulder, and sauntered along after him at a discreet distance.

It *was* possible, of course, that the man was married—but he was unranked, and young, and that made it unlikely. There was an old saying to the effect that, while higher-ranked officers *had* to be married, anyone beneath the rank of sergeant was asking for trouble if *he* chose matrimonial bonds. "Privates can't marry, sergeants *may* marry, captains *must* marry." Valdir had noticed that, no matter the place or the structure of the armed force, that old saying tended to hold true.

So, that being the case, an unranked man was likely to find himself a nice little inn or taphouse to haunt. And establishments of the sort he would frequent would tend to cater to his kind. They would have other entertainments as well—and they were frequently run by women. Valdir had traded off his looks to get himself a corner in more than one such establishment.

The man he was following turned a corner ahead of him, and when Valdir turned the same corner, he knew he'd come to the right street. Every third building seemed to be an alehouse of one sort or another; it was brightly lit, and women of problematical age and negotiable virtue had set up shop—as it were—beneath each and every one of the brightly burning torches and lanterns. Valdir grinned, and proceeded to see what he could do about giving those coppers in his purse some company.

The first inn he stuck his nose into was *not* what he was looking for. It was all too clearly a place that catered to appetites other than hunger and thirst. The second was perfect—but it had a musician of its own, an older man who glared at him over the neck of his gittern in such a way as left no doubt in Valdir' mind that he intended to *keep* his cozy little berth. The third had dancers, and plainly had no need of him, not given the abandon with which the young ladies were shedding the scarves that were their principle items of clothing. The fourth and fifth were run by men; Valdir approached them anyway, but the owner of the fourth was a minstrel himself, and the owner of the fifth preferred his customers with cash to spare to spend it in the dice and card games in the back room. The sixth was— regrettable. The smell drove him out faster than he'd gone in. But the seventh—the seventh had possibilities.

The Inn of the Green Man it was called; it was shabby, but relatively clean. The common stew in a pot over the fire smelled edible *and* as if it had more than a passing acquaintance with meat, though it was probably best not to ask what species. It was populated, but not overcrowded, and brightly lit with tallow dips and oil lamps, which would discourage pickpockets and cutpurses. The serving wenches—whose other properties were also, evidently, for sale—were also relatively clean. They weren't fabulous beauties, and most of them weren't in the first bloom of youth, but they *were* clean.

There was a good crowd, though the place wasn't exactly full. And Valdir spotted his guide here as well, which was a good omen.

Valdir stuck a little more than his nose in the door, and managed to get the attention of one of the serving wenches. "Might I have a word with the owner?" he asked, diffidently.

"Kitchen," said the hard-faced girl, and gave him a second look. He contrived to appear starving and helpless, and she softened, just a little. "Back door," she ordered. "Best warn you, Bel don't much like your kind. Last songbird we had, run off with her best girl."

"Thank you, lady," Valdir said humbly. She snorted, and went back to table-tending.

Valdir had to make his way halfway down the block before he could find an accessway to the alley. He caught a couple of young toughs eyeing him with speculation, but his threadbare state evidently convinced them that he didn't have much to steal—

That, and the insidious little voice in their heads that said, *Not worth bothering with. He doesn't have anything worth the scuffle.*

The alley reeked, and not just of garbage, and he was just as glad that he hadn't eaten since morning. He risked a mage-light, so that he could avoid stepping in anything—and when it became evident that there were places he couldn't do that, he risked a little more magic to give him a clean spot or two to use as stepping stones.

Kind of funny, he thought, stretching carefully over a puddle of stale urine. *It was because I couldn't face situations like this that I never ran away to become a minstrel. And now, here I am—enacting one of my own nightmares. Funny.*

He finally found the back door of The Green Man and pushed it open. The kitchen, also, was relatively clean, but he didn't get to see much of it, because a giantess blocked his view almost immediately.

If she was less than six feet tall, Valdir would have been surprised. The sleeves of her sweat-stained linen shirt were rolled up almost to the shoulder, leaving bare arms of corded muscle Jervis would have envied. She wore breeches rather than skirts, which may have been a practical consideration, since enough materials to make *her* a skirt would have made a considerable dent in a lean clothing budget. Her graying brown hair was cut shorter than Valdir's. And no one would ever notice her face—not when confronted with the scar that ran from left temple to right jawbone.

"An' what d'*you* want?" she asked, her voice a dangerous-sounding growl.

"The—the usual," faltered Valdir. "A place, milady . . . a place for a poor songster. . . ."

"A place. Food and drink and a place to sleep in return for some share of whatever paltry coppers ye manage to garner," the woman rumbled disgustedly. "Aye, and a chance t' run off with one o' me girls when me back's turned. *Not* likely, boy. And ye'd better find yerself somewhere else t' caterwaul; there ain't an inn on th' Row that needs a rhymester."

Valdir made his eyes large and sad, and plucked at the woman's sleeve as she turned away. "My lady, please—" he begged shamelessly. "I'm new-come, with scarce encugh coppers to buy a crust. I pledge you, lady, I would treat your other ladies as sisters."

She rounded on him. "Oh, ye would, would you? Gull someone else! If ye're new-come, then get ye new-gone!"

"Lady," he whimpered, ducking her threatened blow. "Lady, I swear—lady—I'm—" He let his voice sink to a low, half-shamed whisper. "—lady, your maids are safe with me! More than safe—I'm—shaych. There are few places open for such as I—"

She stared, she gaped, and then she grinned. "'Struth! Ye could be at that, that pretty face an' all! Shaych! I like that!" She propelled him into the kitchen with a hand like a slab of bacon. "All right, I give ye a chance! Two meals an' a place on th' floor for half yer takin's."

He knew he had to put up at least the appearance of bargaining—but not much, or he'd cast doubt on his disguise. "Three meals," he said, desperately, "and a quarter."

She glared at him. "Ye try me," she said warningly. "Ye try me temper, pretty boy. Three an' half."

"Three and half," he agreed, timidly.

"Done. An' don't think t' cheat me; me girls be checkin' ye right regular. Now—list. I got armsmen here, mostly. I want lively stuff, things as put 'em in mind that me girls serve more'n ale. None of yer long-winded ballads, nor sticky love songs, nor yet nothin' melancholy. Not less'n they asks for it. An' if it be melancholy, ye make 'em cry, ye hear? Make 'em cry so's me girls an' me drink can give 'em a bit 'o comfort. Got that?"

"Aye, lady," he whispered.

"Don't ye go lookin' fer a bedmate 'mongst them lads, neither. They wants that, there's the Page, an' that's where they go. We got us agreements on the Row. I don' sell boys, an' I don' let in streetboys; the Page don' sell girls."

"Aye, lady."

"Ye start yer plunkin' at sundown when I open, an' ye finish when I close. Rest of th' time's yer own. Get yer meals in th' kitchen, sleep in th' common room after closin'."

"Aye, lady."

"Now—stick yer pack over in that corner, so's I know ye ain't gonna run off, an' get out there."

He shed pack and cloak under her critical eye, and tucked both away in the chimney corner. He took with him only his lute and his hat, and hurried off into the common room, with her eyes burning holes in his back.

She was in a slightly better mood when she closed up near dawn. Certainly she was mollified by the nice stack of copper coins she'd earned from his efforts. That it was roughly twice the value of the meals she'd be feeding him probably contributed to that good humor. That no less than three of the prettiest of her "girls" had propositioned him and been turned down probably didn't hurt.

She was pleased enough that she had a thin straw pallet brought down out of the attic so that he wouldn't be sleeping on the floor. He would be sharing the common room with an ancient gaffer who served as the potboy, and the two utterly silent kitchen helpers of indeterminate age and sex. Her order to all four of them to strip and wash at the kitchen pump relieved him a bit; he wasn't looking for comfort, but he had hoped to avoid fleas and lice. When the washing was over, he was fairly certain that the kitchen helpers were girls, but their ages were still a mystery.

When Bel left, she took the light with her, leaving them to arrange themselves in the dark. Valdir curled up on his lumpy pallet, wrapped in his cloak and the blanket that still smelled faintly of Yfandes, and sighed.

:Beloved?: He sent his thought-tendril questing out into the gray light of early dawn after her.

:Here. Are you established?:

:Fairly well. Valdir's seen worse. At least I won't be poisoned by the food. What about you?:

:I have shelter.:

:Good.: He yawned. :This is strictly an after-dark establishment; if I go roaming in the late morning and early afternoon, I should find out a few things.:

:I wish that I could help,: she replied wistfully.

:So do I. Good night, dearheart. I can't keep awake anymore.:

:Sleep well.:

One thing more, though, before he slept. A subtle, and very well camouflaged tap into the nearest current of mage-power. He needed it; the tiny trickle he would take would likely not be noticed by anyone unless they were checking the streams inch by inch. It wouldn't replenish his reserves immediately, but over a few days it would. It was a pity he could only do this while meditating or sleeping. It was an even greater pity that he couldn't just tap straight in as he had the night he'd rescued Tashir; he'd be at full power in moments if he could do that.

But *that* would tell Lord Vedric Mavelan that there was another mage here.

And if it comes to that, I' á rather surprise him.

He'd intended to try and think out some of his other problems, but it had been a full day since he'd last slept, and the walking he'd done had tired him out more than he realized. He started to try and pick over his automatic reactions to Bel's "girls"; had he led them on, without intending to? Had he been *flirting* with them, knowing deep down that he was going to turn them down and enjoying the hold his good looks gave over them? It was getting so that *nothing* was simple anymore.

But before he could do more than worry around the edges of things, his exhaustion caught up with him.

He slept.

CHAPTER 10

—→———◇———←—

"**B**OY?"

The harsh whisper in the dark startled him out of unrestful sleep; it jerked him into full awareness, dry-mouthed, heart pounding.

"Boy, be ye awake?"

"Yes," Valdir replied. *I am now, anyway.*

Hot, onion-laden breath near his elbow. "Lissen, boy, ye needs warnin'. The reason this place don' prosper. Bel drinks up th' profit."

Valdir calmed his heart, nodded to himself. That explained a lot. "I'd wondered," he whispered back.

"She be at the keg in 'er room right now. Come mornin' she'll be up wi' a temper like a spring bear. She won't go hittin' on th' girls, not them as makes her profit—but me an' Tay an' Ri be fair game. An' now you. Ye take my meanin'?"

"I think so."

"Don' doubt me. An' don' go thinkin' ye got anywhere's else. Ev'ry inn on th' Row's got its singster or dancer. Bel's the only one did wi'out. That be 'cause she don't care for ye singsters, an' no dancin' girl'll stay where the profits be so lean. How long ye plan on stayin'?"

Valdir was profoundly grateful that he was not locked into this life. "I hadn't thought I'd be here long. I really sort of thought I'd look for a place at the Great Houses or the Palace," he began timidly. "I—used to be with a House. They mostly keep at least one minstrel, and I figure the Palace must use—"

The old man choked with laughter, and then broke into a fit of terrible coughing. Valdir acted as would be expected. "I'm not that bad!" he sputtered indignantly. "I'm just—out of luck, lately."

The old man convulsed again. "Outa more'n luck. *First* off, there ain't no Great Houses in the city. They all be outside the walls. Second, the Remoerdis Family's dead. Ain't nobody in th' Palace but ghosts."

Valdir gasped, and let the old gaffer tell the tale as he pleased. It was amazingly consistent with what Lores had told him, save only that the Herald who'd carried off Tashir had been seven feet tall, cut down a dozen guards, and rode away on a fanged white demon. "An' third thing," the rheumy voice continued, "they wouldn't have anyone next or nigh the palace as *wasn't* blood kin; even the servants be blood kin on the backside. So even if they'd been alive an' ye'd been t' see, they'd not 'ave took ye."

"Why?" Valdir asked, bewildered. "That doesn't make any sense! What does being blood relation have to do with serving—or talent?"

The old man coughed again. "Damn if I know. Been that way f'rever. Anyway, I'm tellin' ye, if ye wanta keep that purty face purty, save yer coppers an' get outa here soon as ye can; afore the snow flies be best. Otherwise ol' Bel likely to start seein' how far she can push ye. I've warned ye, now I'm goin' t' sleep." And not another word could Valdir get out of him.

He found out how right the warning was the next day, when Bel stumbled down the stairs, red-eyed and touchy, smelling like a brewery. She started in on the two kitchen girls, looking for excuses to punish one of them. She found plenty; the girls sported a black eye each before she was through with them.

Valdir managed to stay out of her way long enough to get his pack and bed stowed safely and his lute placed beside the door. But then—then he got an unexpected and altogether unpleasant shock. Bel tried—him. First flirting, then, when that brought no result, threatening.

She disgusted and frightened him, and he knew he dared not retaliate in *any* way. Instead he had to stand and take her pawing, while his skin crawled and his stomach churned, trying *not* to show anything except his very real and growing fear of her. She finally convinced herself that she wasn't going to get any pleasure out of him in *that* way, so she chose another.

In the end he escaped with no worse than a darkening bruise on his cheekbone where she'd backhanded him into a wall—without his promised breakfast or lunch, and not willing to endure either more of her clumsy caresses *or* her brutality to get it. He flew out the door as soon as she unlocked it, resolving not to return until nightfall and the time appointed for him to perform. He paused long enough in his flight to snatch up his lute; he would not leave the means of his livelihood unguarded, and anyway, there might be the chance of making a few coins on the street as he had last night. Enough, maybe, to feed him.

Herald Vanyel would not have tolerated that treatment, but Herald

Vanyel was far, far away. There was only poor, timid Valdir, fallen indeed on bad luck, scrawny, fearful, and no little desperate.

Gods help her people. If I was what I'm pretending to be, I think I'd go hunting a sharp knife, and I'm not sure if I'd use it on her first, or myself. . . .

"Thought you might end up here," drawled a strange, well-trained voice, as he bolted out the door and into the street. He turned, blinking in the bright sunlight. Lounging against a wall across the street was the grizzled minstrel who'd been playing the gittern in one of the other taverns the night before. He was dressed in dull colors that blended with the wall; he'd taken up a post right opposite The Green Man. He looked bored and lazy; as Valdir watched him suspiciously, he pushed away from the wall and walked slowly toward him across the cobblestones. In the light of day he was clearly much older than Valdir; hair thinning and mostly gray, square face beginning to wrinkle and line. But as he approached Valdir, it was also plain that he had kept his body in relatively good shape; beneath the loose, homespun shirt, leather tunic and breeches, he had only the tiniest sign of a paunch, and the rest of him looked wiry and strong enough to survive just about any tavern brawl.

. To someone like Valdir, this stranger meant danger of another sort. The man could be looking to eliminate a rival, or intending to bully him—or worse.

Talk about luck being out. Have I leaped out of the pan into the fire?

Valdir backed up a pace, letting his uncertainty show on his face.

A tired horse pulled a slops-wagon down the center of the street, and the stranger stepped deliberately toward him once it had passed.

"Ah, ease up, boy, I'm not about to pummel you," the minstrel said, a faint hint of disgust twisting his lips. Valdir continued to step back, until the minstrel had him trapped in a corner where a fence met the inn wall. Valdir froze, his hands pressed against the unsanded wood behind him, and the minstrel reached for his face, grabbing his chin in a hand rough with chording-calluses. He turned Valdir's cheek into the light, and examined the slowly purpling bruise.

"Got you a good one, did she?" He touched the edge of the bruise without hurting his captive. "Huhn. Not as bad as it could be."

The minstrel let him go and backed up a few steps. Valdir huddled where he was, watching him fearfully. The stranger scratched his chin thoughtfully. "Heard you last night when I went on break. You aren't bad."

"Thank you," Valdir replied timidly.

"You're also going to get your hands broken if you stay with Bel for very long," the other continued. "That's what she did to the one before the one that ran off with her girl."

Valdir did not reply.

"Well? Aren't you going to say anything?"

"Why are you telling me all this?" Valdir asked, letting his suspicion show. He stood up a little straighter, and rubbed his sweaty palms on his patched and faded linen tunic in a conscious echoing of an unconscious gesture of nervousness.

"Because the one before the one that ran off with her girl was a good lad," the older man said, impatience getting the better of him. "He was pretty, like you, and he was fey, like I bet you are, and I don't want it happening to another one. All right?" He turned on his heel and started to walk away.

Don't turn away a possible ally!

"Wait!" Valdir cried after him. "Please, I—I didn't mean—"

A bit of breeze blew dry leaves up the street. The minstrel halted, turned slowly. Valdir walked toward him, holding out his hand. "I'm Valdir," he said shyly. "I've been—north. Baires." The other showed his surprise with a hissing intake of breath. "I made a bit of a mistake, and I had to make a run for it." He looked down at his feet, then back up again. "It hasn't been easy; not while I was there, and not getting across the border to here. They got me out of the habit of looking for friends up there, and into the habit of looking for enemies.'

"Renfry," said the older minstrel, clasping his hand, with a slow smile that showed a good set of even, white teeth. "Not many real musicians on the Row. I s'ppose I should be treating you as a rival—but—hell, a man gets tired of hearing and singing the same damn things over and over. Bel had Jonny for a long while before she ruined him, and he trained here."

"What happened to him? After, I mean."

"We clubbed together and sent him off to a Healer the very next day, ended up having to send him across the Border. Uppity palace Healer didn't want to 'waste his time on tavern scum.' Never heard anything after that." He shrugged. "If the poor lad ended up not being able to play again, I don't imagine he'd want anyone to know."

Valdir shuddered, genuinely.

"Ol' Bel don't believe in letting the help sample the goods. She got drunk and thought Jonny had his eye on one of the girls." He snorted in contempt. "Not bloody likely."

"She must have slipped up once—" Valdir ventured. "I mean—the one that romanced her girl, like you said."

Renfry laughed, and started up the dusty, near-empty street with Valdir following. The thin autumn sunlight stretched their shadows out ahead of them. "She did, because she was bedding the fellow herself. She never figured him for having the stamina to be double-dipping! Truth to tell, I hope he was good in bed, because he surely had a voice like a crow in mating season, and maybe four whole chords to his name."

Valdir thought about the way Bel had tried to come on to *him,* and could actually feel a shred of sympathy for the unknown minstrel. "Were you waiting out here for *me?*" Valdir asked, as they approached the closed door of The Pig and Stick, the tavern Renfry had been playing in last night.

Renfry nodded, holding the door to "his" inn open.

"Why?"

"To warn you, like I said. Let you know you'd better make tracks."

Valdir shook his head, and his hair fell over one eye. "I can't. I—I haven't got a choice," he confessed sadly. "I haven't anywhere else to go."

Renfry paused in surprise, half in, half out of the doorway. "*That* lean in the pocket?" he asked. "Lad, you aren't *that* bad. You're a good enough musician, for true. Unless you *really* made more than just a mistake."

Valdir nodded unhappily. "Made a bad enemy. Sang the wrong song at the wrong time. Used to be with a House. Now I've got the clothes on my back, my lute, and that's mostly it."

"Save your coppers and head over the Border into Valdemar," the other advised. "Tell you what, I'll stand you a drink and a little better breakfast than you'd get from old Bel, then I'll steer you over to a decent corner. Not the best, but with the palace a wreck, there's a lot of guards standing about with nothing to do but make sure our High and Mighty Lord Visitor doesn't get himself in the way of a stray knife round about the Town Elder's house. You ought to collect a bit there, hmm?" He grinned. "Besides, I got an underhanded motive. You're about as good as me, and you know some stuff new to our folk. I'm going to bribe you with food to learn it, and then I'm going to get you out of town so you aren't competition anymore."

Valdir smiled back hesitantly, at least as far as his sore cheek permitted. "Now *that* I understand!"

By nightfall Bel was sober, and when Valdir crept in at the open door she waved him to his place on the hearth with nothing more threatening than a scowl. He sat down on the raised brick hearth with his bruised cheek to the fire, and began tuning the lute. There were one or two customers; nothing much. Valdir was just as glad; it gave him a chance to think over what he'd picked up.

It had been a very profitable day. The Town Elder's servants were entertainment-starved and loose-tongued; once Valdir had gotten them started they generally ran on quite informatively and at some length before demanding something in return.

Ylyna had been a child-bride; that made Tashir's arrival eight-and-a-half months after the wedding so much more surprising. Several of the Mavelan girls had been offered as prospective treaty-spouse, but of them all, only Ylyna had lacked mage-powers, so only Ylyna had been acceptable to Deveran Remoerdis *or* his people. It was generally agreed that she was "odd, even for a Mavelan." And strangely enough, it was also generally agreed that up until the night of the massacre Tashir had been a fairly decent, if slightly peculiar, young man. "A bit like you, lad," one of the guards had said. "Jumpin' at shadows, like. Nervy." If it had not been for his mage-powers there likely would have been no objection to his eventual inheritance of the throne of Lineas. But once those powers manifested, it became out of the question. No Linean would stand by and see a mage take the seat of power.

"We seen what comes o' that, yonder," an aged porter had told him a bit angrily, pointing with his chin at the north. "Put a mage in power, next thing ye know, he's usin' magic t' get any damn thing 'e want out 'o ye. No. No mages here."

So as soon as it had become evident that several of Tashir's younger brothers—all of whom markedly resembled Deveran—were going to live into adulthood, the Council demanded that Deveran disinherit the boy. They didn't have to pressure him, according to the Lord Elder's first chambermaid; he gave in at once, so quickly that the ink wasn't even dry on the copies of the proclamation when his heralds cried the news.

And strangely enough, Tashir didn't seem the least unhappy about it. "Didn' 'xactly jump for joy, but didn' seem t' care, neither," a fruitseller had observed.

Lord Vedric—that was who Valdir assumed was the "Lord Visitor," though he was never referred to as anything but "that Mavelan Lord"—had come as something of a surprise to the folk of Highjorune. They'd expected him to attempt to defend Tashir; instead he'd listened to the witnesses with calm and sympathy, and had expressed his horrified opinion that the boy *had* gone rogue. He'd kept displays of magery to a minimum, and had made himself available to the Council as a kind of advisor until someone figured out how to get Tashir back to be punished, and until they determined who the new ruler of Lineas would be.

As for the startling resemblance between Lord Vedric and Tashir—

"'E said th' boy could be 'is, 'e didn't know," one of the chambermaids—a pretty one that Valdir suspected of getting gossip fodder via pillow talk—had whispered, sniggering, to Valdir. "'E said th' girl couldn' keep 'er skirts down, an' that she'd bribed 'er way inta lots o' beds, takin' the place o' th' girls as was s'pposed t' be there. Said 'e'd found 'er in 'is bed more'n once, an' that 'e didn't know it were 'is own 'alf-sister an' not the wench 'e'd called fer till mornin'. That was why 'e were tryin' t' keep th' boy heir, so 'e says; tryin' t' do right by 'im, like, just in case." She sniggered again. "*I* 'eard 'nough fr'm m' cousin 'bout 'Er 'Ighness an' 'er lightskirt ways *I* believe 'im."

And the cousin, it seemed, had been one of Ylyna's personal maids. More importantly, she had been *out* of the palace the night everyone else had been killed. The chambermaid had promised an introduction in a day or two.

"You gonna sit there all night diddlin' that thing, or you gonna play?" Bel growled, breaking into his thoughts. With a start and a cowed look, he began playing.

The young girl scampered back to her duties, leaving Valdir alone with the last surviving member of the palace staff, her cousin. The woman pondered him for a moment, then, a trifle reluctantly, invited him into her tiny parlor. The cousin was old; that surprised Valdir. And the odd look she gave him as he took the seat she indicated surprised him more.

"Why are ye askin', lad?" she queried, as she settled into her own chair. "If it's just morbid curiosity . . ."

He rubbed the bruise Bel had gifted him with this morning—it matched the first—and tried to get her measure. She was a bit younger than Savil, and small, but proudly erect. There was something very dignified about her, and out of keeping with her purported position; she didn't hold herself with the air of a servant. She was plainly clothed, in dark wool dress and white linen undertunic, but the wool was fine lambswool, tightly woven, and costly, and the linen as fine as he had ever seen on his mother. She watched him from under half-closed lids. Her eyes seemed full of secrets.

She had been out of the palace that fatal evening, the girl had told him, because she had been here, in the home of her aged mother, who had fallen and could not be left alone at night. There was a great deal about her that prompted Valdir to trust in her honesty; enough that he decided to tell her a certain measure of the truth.

"I want to find out what really happened," he said, as sincerely as he could manage. "The stories I've heard so far don't make a lot of sense. If there's something that needs to be told, perhaps I'm the one to tell it. A minstrel can tell an unpleasant truth with more success, sometimes, than anyone else. I'm a stranger, with no interests to protect. It might be I'd be believed more readily than a Linean."

She looked away from him, and her face was troubled. "I don't know," she said, finally. "This . . ." She looked down at her hands, and her attention seemed to be caught by a ring she wore.

It was an unusual ring in the fact that it was so very plain; burnished, unornamented silver, centered with a dull white stone. The stone was nothing Valdir recognized; it looked like an ordinary, water-worn quartz pebble.

Then her attention was more than caught—

The stone flared with an internal, white flame for a moment, and it seemed that she could not look away from it.

The woman's face took on a blankness of expression he'd only seen in the spell-bound.

Valdir felt the back of his neck chill. There was a Power moving somewhere, one he didn't recognize. He longed to be able to unshield and probe, and maddeningly knew he dared not. This felt *almost* like someone was working a Truth Spell, only the feel of this was old—old—

"Lady Ylyna—" she said, in a strangely abstracted voice. "At the bottom of this, it all comes down to Lady Ylyna."

"Tashir's mother?" Valdir asked, biting his lip in vexation when it occurred to him that his words might break whatever spell it was that held her. But her expression remained rapt, and he ventured more. "But—how—"

"She was hardly more than a child when she came here," the woman said, still gazing into the stone of her ring, "but I've never seen a more terrified girl in my life. She'd been the ignored one, until Deveran refused to take any girl to wife that had mage-powers. *Then* she was valuable, and you can believe her family *kept* the strings on her. She was terrified of them. She was so happy when she was first pregnant—Deveran made a great deal of her, you see. But then Tashir came early—there was no telling him that it was just accident the boy looked like his uncle. So he only came to her to get her pregnant, and once pregnant, he ignored her until the children were born."

"But—"

She didn't seem to hear him. "He ignored the boy, too. *She* was scarcely old enough to have left off with dolls, she hadn't a clue what to do with a child. Then the letters started coming—letters from Baires, with the royal seal on them, from *The* Mavelan. She never let us see them, but they terrified her. And she took it all out on the boy. The other children, the ones that took after Deveran, *they* had nursemaids, and careful watching, but not Tashir. *He* was left to *her*. Poor child. Half the time she petted and cosseted him like a lapdog—*that* was when her letters seemed to be good. The other half of the time she'd take a riding crop to him till the poor boy was bruised all over. That was when the letters frightened her. Then the boy started showing wizard-power, and it got worse. I watched her watching him one day—I've never seen such jealousy in my life on a human face."

"Why would she be *jealous* of him?" Valdir wondered aloud.

The old woman shook herself, and gave him a sharp look. "I've said more than I intended," she told him, almost accusingly.

He tried to look innocent and trustworthy. "But what you've said is important."

She rose and walked slowly across the tiny sitting room to the door, and opened it. "Come back in two days," she said, in tones that brooked no argument. "I may decide to tell you more then."

Nearly ready to burst with frustration, Valdir left, doing his best to show none of it.

She shut the door behind him, and he wandered back down to the Row, looking for a good place to set out his hat for a few more hours.

He still had to eat, after all.

:*How much of this can you trust?*: Yfandes asked.

:*Well, I'm hardly going to be able to run Truth Spell on her,*: he replied, staring up into the darkness and listening to old Petar snoring loud enough to shake the chimney down. :*Although—gods help me, it seems as if something was doing that for me. And you have to admit, this report of alternate petting and abuse certainly explains some of his reaction toward women. "Mothers" in particular.*:

:*But it doesn't explain what happened that night.*:

One of the two girls murmured in her sleep. Vanyel shivered, and pulled his blanket a little closer. The cold of the dirt floor was seeping through his thin straw pallet. *:There's more. I know there's more. I think she—or whatever it was that made her talk—is testing me, and I don't know why. Gods, and the questions I have—why allow only blood relations to serve the Remoerdis Family? And why does it feel as if the old lady is—Gifted? Or geased, bespelled. Or both, I don't know. And I don't dare test her to find out, with Vedric in the city.:*

:Mm,: she agreed. *:Wise. What's he up to?*

:Being utterly charming,: Valdir replied. *:He's got the locals coming more and more over to his side. And he's agreeing with them on every point. It's hard to believe that this is the same man my sister called a viper.:*

:Interesting. And these Lineans are a hard-headed lot.:

:It would just about take an angel to change their minds about the Mavelans,: Vanyel told her. *:But Vedric seems to be doing just that.:*

Petar snorted, coughed, and turned over. There was silence for a moment, then he snorted again, and the snores did *not* resume.

:Take the chance to get to sleep while you can,: Yfandes advised dryly.

But sleep refused to come.

Tonight had been particularly bad. Not only had Bel made another try, but Valdir had fended off the attentions of someone else as well.

Even if he *hadn't* taken Bel's glare as warning that she meant what she'd said about not taking up with her customers, he'd have avoided this one. *Shaych*, yes—but in a way that made Valdir's skin crawl as much as Bel did. The man hadn't been physically repulsive, but there was something twisted about him, something unhealthy. Like a fine velvet glove over a taloned hand. The man had looked at him with a hunger that made him shiver with reaction even now. He had reminded Vanyel—not Valdir—of the mage that had called himself "Krebain."

I don't know what to think anymore. If I'm not shaych, then why can't I just do what Bel wants and get it over with? If I am, then why did that hunter revolt me? He turned onto his side, curling into a ball against the cold, the ache of his empty stomach, the misery his own uncertainty was causing.

And today—gods. That sick little game I was playing on the serving girls. Leading them on—knowing I was leading them right down a dead end. Yes, I got information—but I was actually enjoying deluding them, having a little power over them. Gods, that was sick. And I would have gone right on *playing little sex-flirtation games if 'Fandes hadn't threatened to kick me into next week. I'm turning into something I don't much like.*

He curled up a little tighter. *I don't even know my own feelings any more.*

He tightened his lips in exasperation. *Look, Van, you're supposed to have been trained in logic. So why don't you try putting things into some kind of category, you goose? Maybe you don't know what you feel, but you certainly know what you don't feel. You've been agonizing over that enough lately! Then figure out what it is that everything you don't care for has in common.*

:*It's about time*,: came Yfandes' sardonic comment.

He was startled—and then angry. He very nearly made some kind of nasty retort back to her, but *she* was blocking, and he wasn't so angry that he'd try to breach her shields just to tell her off. For one thing, he wasn't sure he could—for another, the attempt *might* give him away to Vedric.

But he certainly wanted to. . . .

The next several days were some of the worst Valdir had ever spent. He played his fingers to the bone every night until the last customer left. He dodged Bel, not always successfully, by day. He took her beatings with teeth-gritting meekness, avoided her increasingly heavyhanded attempts to trap him, and did his best to minimize the damage she inflicted. He was cold at night, and starved by day; Bel's idea of "meals" being scarcely enough to keep a mouse alive. And his own unhappy thoughts kept him awake more often than not.

He went back to the former maid Reta's tiny house faithfully every two days, only to be turned away with nothing.

Then, finally, after close to a fortnight—an endless series of attempts to see the old woman and being turned away from her door—Reta finally agreed to speak with him again.

"I wasn't sure you'd be back." Reta held the door open for him, and he slipped past her into the tiny, painfully neat sitting room. She closed the door carefully, and sat down on her settle beside the hearth. Valdir took the only other seat, a stool. The old woman regarded him thoughtfully while he curbed his impatience, and hoped that *this* time some more information would be forthcoming.

"No, I wasn't certain you'd be back," she repeated.

"Why wouldn't I?" he asked, just as quietly, as he ignored the hollow feeling in his stomach. He'd been here long enough that the meager rations and short sleep were beginning to affect him, and while he'd recharged his mage-energies fully, his physical energies were becoming exhausted. He woke up five and six times a night, cramping with cold, and even with the supplementary food he was spending his pittance of earnings on, he was beginning to have spells of light-headedness. Most of his money was going to buy Yfandes grain, anyway. But Reta held the key, he was sure of it. If only he could persuade her to part with the information. Her—or whatever power had controlled her the first time he came to her door.

"This isn't a tale of high adventure," she pointed out dryly. "And it isn't a bedroom farce. It's not terribly interesting, it's not good song-fodder, and it's sad."

"Sad?" He raised an eyebrow. "Why sad?"

She examined the hands she held folded in her lap, as if they were of great interest. "That poor child Ylyna, she never really had a chance to grow up. Oh, she was grown in body, but—*They* kept her a child, a frightened child they could manipulate. I find that sad."

"They" meaning the Mavelans. "Why didn't you say something?" he asked, trying to understand what could have led her to stand by and watch, and not act.

She shrugged. "Who would have listened? I was Her Highness' personal maid, as I was Deveran's mother's. Deveran would have thought me either besotted or bewitched. He wasn't known for thinking much of women in the first place." She shook her head and stared at the ring on her finger. The peculiar, dull white stone seemed to brighten for a moment, and her voice and expression became abstracted, as it had the first time she'd spoken openly.

It's happening again! Valdir held his breath, all his exhaustion, his personal concerns forgotten, hoping against hope. . . .

"No, Deveran had no faith in the good sense *or* the honesty of women. After all, his own mother had betrayed him by dying when he most needed her, or so his own father kept claiming. And Ylyna—*not* a virgin, possibly mad, and surely little better than a trollop—certainly didn't help matters."

Valdir could not stay silent; he protested such inexcusable, willful blindness. "But the way she treated Tashir—"

"Was likely the way *she'd* been treated." The old woman shook her head again, continuing to stare at the stone of her ring. "When you reach my age, you have generally seen a great deal. Adults who have been beaten as children beat their own children. And—other things. I sometimes wonder if *that* isn't what Holy Lerence meant when he said 'the sins of the fathers shall be taken up by the sons.'" Her eyes grew even more thoughtful—or entranced. She didn't seem to be paying any attention to him.

There was something stirring here. Again he felt some Power moving under the powers he could detect easily. *Gods! I don't dare try to probe for it.* The frustration maddened him. He could *feel* it, something deep, and powerful, it vibrated so that he felt it rather than "detected" it, the way he could sometimes "feel" the vibrations of a note too low to actually hear.

But it was *stronger* this time, much stronger, and it seemed to be stirring to *his* good, for the old chambermaid was saying things she hadn't more than hinted at before.

"What other things was she doing?" Valdir prompted in a whisper, hands clenched together so tightly they ached. This was it. This was what he was looking for. The secret no one knew. The key to it all.

She sounded as if she was talking to herself. "When Tashir grew older— and handsomer—she started looking at him differently. The gods know Deveran hadn't come to her bed for four years, and wouldn't allow any male servants near her, only women. She had never had *any* pleasure except in bed, I think. I wonder if that wasn't the only thing she thought she could do well." The old woman was gazing deeply into her stone and not at all at him now, and her voice was very low, so that he had to strain to hear it. She shifted just a little, and he caught the sharp smell of lavender from the folds of her dress. "Tashir began looking more and more like his uncle, and he was *still* terrified of her. Of *her*, who never frightened anyone, and couldn't even command respect from her servants. It must have been too seductive to resist, that combination: fear, and the handsome young face and body. She set out to seduce her own son into her bed."

Valdir froze. *No—that's—my gods—*

She continued on, still speaking in that same, dreamy voice, as if she was speaking only to herself. "That frightened him even more, I think, once he realized what was going on. Poor child. I hardly believed it at first; I just thought the petting was getting a little—overwarm. She'd use any excuse to get her hands on him. Any excuse at all."

Valdir licked his dry lips, but couldn't make his voice work.

Reta sighed. "And Deveran either didn't know or didn't care; I tend to think the latter. He had what he wanted; three sons indisputably his, and likely to reach maturity. What happened to Tashir didn't matter. The *only* person who cared what was happening to him was the old armsmaster, the one Deveran had retired. Karis. *He* had taken to teaching the boy, when he saw no one else would. He protected him as much as he could. Which wasn't much, but it was something. He gave the boy a place to hide—and a person to look up to who was stable, sane, and fond of him."

"A good man?"

And possibly another way to get Tashir to open up—

"A very good man. A pity he was in the palace with the rest of them."

Valdir wanted to curse, and restrained himself only by a strong effort of will.

"Finally it got to the point that Tashir *couldn't* keep her away—and that wizard-power of his intervened. He had a kind of fit; smashed half the bower before it was over. That was when Deveran decided."

"Decided what?" Valdir asked.

At that moment, the power faded abruptly. One breath it was there. Then it was gone. Her eyes finally came back to their normal sharp focus. "What?" she asked him, looking up at him suddenly.

Gods—the spell's broken. Oh, Lady of Light, help me persuade her. Would she finish the sentence? Could he convince her on his own? "You were going to tell me what Deveran had decided to do about Tashir," he prompted. "That night."

"Oh." She shrugged, indifferently. "That. I thought everyone knew about that."

"*I* don't," he pointed out. "And nobody wants to talk about it, much."

"It's simple enough. Since Vedric was making such a big to-do over the boy, Deveran decided to let *him* deal with the problem. Deveran was going to send the boy to his Mavelan relatives—permanently. That was what he told Ylyna after they cleared the boy and the mess out of her bower. That he intended to tell the boy at dinner." She sighed. "And I can only assume, given that Tashir was even more frightened of that den of madmen than he was of his mother, that this was exactly what happened, and what brought—everything—down."

He hadn't realized how much time he'd spent in the little sitting room; when he took his leave of Reta, he was appalled. *One* candlemark to sundown.

Panic stole thought. He could only think of *one* thing.

Home.

He *had* to get home, before it was too late. He didn't *dare* try to Mindtouch Savil from here; that would be as stupid, with Vedric so near, as riding through the gates in full Whites on Yfandes.

He ran across town, dodging through foot and beast traffic, trying to reach the east gate before they closed it for the night. Once closed—he wouldn't get out until morning. He didn't *dare* cast any kind of spell to get him by, no more than he dared Mindtouch Savil. Vedric would detect spell-casting even faster than the use of a Mind-Gift. And every moment he stayed here was another moment the same disaster that wiped out Tashir's family could move to harm *his*.

The sun was dropping inexorably toward the horizon; he had a pain in his side, and he was gasping for breath—and *still* he wasn't more than half-way to his goal. He stumbled against a market-stall; recovered; ran on. He realized with despair that he was *not* going to make it in time.

And candlemarks could count; could be fatal, given what he knew now.

It *was* only too possible that Tashir had done exactly what he'd been accused of; that he had been pushed too far by his father's ultimatum, and he had lost his hold temporarily on his Gift and his sanity. It was only too likely that he had unleashed power gone rogue and had destroyed his own home and everything and everyone in it.

Valdir stopped, unable to run any farther; clung to the corner of a build-ing at a cross street, and watched the sun turn to blood and sink below the horizon.

Taking with it his hope.

Valdir slipped into The Pig and Stick, keeping to the wall and the shadows as much as he could. He managed to get within touching distance of Ren-fry, and froze there, unmoving, in the shadows behind him.

He prayed that Renfry was about to finish a set, and that he had not just *begun* one. The tavern was hot, and he was sweating from his run. His side still hurt, and he wanted to cough so badly his chest ached with the effort of holding it back. Sweat ran down his back, and into his eyes. Odor of bread and stew and spilled ale made his stomach cramp up with hunger, and his eyes watered. The lamps flickered, and he gripped the wall behind him, as the room swam before his eyes.

Too long on too little. Oh, gods, keep me going!

Finally Renfry finished, and waved aside requests for more. "Not now, lads," he said genially. "Not until I wet my throat a bit."

He turned, and saw Valdir behind him. He started to say something—then took a second, closer look at him, and his eyes grew alarmed.

He picked up the gittern by the neck, and grabbed Valdir's elbow with his free hand. Without a single word, he propelled the unresisting Valdir before him through the door leading to the kitchen.

It was light enough in here, though twice as hot as the tavern common room, what with two fires and the brick bake-oven all roaring at once. A huge table dominated the center of the room; an enormously fat man in a floury, stained apron was pulling fresh loaves out of the oven with a long wooden paddle and putting them to cool on the table. There were two boys at each of the fireplaces, one turning a spit, one watching a kettle. A fifth boy was sitting on a stool right by the door, peeling roots.

Renfry pushed the boy peeling roots off his perch and shoved Valdir down onto it.

"What's wrong?" he said. "And don't tell me it's nothing. You look like somebody seeing a death sentence."

Valdir just nodded; he'd already concocted a story for Renfry, and one that fit in with what he'd already told the man. "I've—" He finally coughed, rackingly; swallowed. "I've got to get out of here. Now. Tonight."

Renfry looked at him narrowly. "Wouldn't be that little matter of a song, would it?"

Valdir just looked at him, pleadingly. "If Vedric finds out I'm here," he whispered truthfully, "he'll probably kill me. You didn't tell me it was *Vedric* here."

"*Vedric!*" Renfry exploded. "Great good gods, boy, you sure don't pick your enemies too carefully! Oh, *hell*."

He folded his arms and gazed up at the ceiling, brows knitted together so that they came close to meeting. "Let's see. First off, we got to get your things away from Bel. Huh . . . got it!"

He slipped out into the taproom and returned within a few moments. "I just paid that little sneak brat of the cook's to pinch your things. If *he* can't nip 'em, nobody can. Now—how much coin you got?"

Valdir turned out his purse. There wasn't much. Renfry counted it carefully. "Tel!" he shouted into the chaos of the kitchen. "How much day-old bread and stuff can I get you to part with for twenty coppers? Be generous, the boy has to run for it."

The massive cook blundered over to their side of the big central work-table, peered at Valdir, and then at the tiny heap of coin. "Huh. Apples is cheap right now; got some with bad spots. All right fer the road, no good t' store. Bread, uh—got some I was gonna use fer stuffin'. Let ye have it all. Got some cheese w' mold all through. Mold won' hurt ye, just looks like hell an' tastes mighty sharp; people round about here don't care for sharp cheese. Skinny runt like you, hold ye least a fortnight."

Renfry gave Valdir a look brimming with satisfaction. "That'll get you across the Border, easy, and there's a Harvestfest going on over there right now. Boy with a voice like yours that can't get coin at a Harvestfest don't deserve t' call himself a minstrel."

"Hey, 'Fry!" An insolent urchin slid in under Renfry's elbow, Valdir's pack and blanket in one hand, his lute in the other. "These whatcha lookin' fer?"

Valdir snatched the lute out of the child's hand and held it to his chest, his eyes going moist. "Oh, gods—Renfry, I—"

I never dared hope for this much help from him. Never even prayed for it.

"*Don't* you cry on me!" Renfry growled, cuffing his ear. "Just getting my competition out of town, I told you. Tel, here—pack up the boy's food." He scraped everything but two small silver pieces off the table and poured them into the cook's hand. The handful of copper bits vanished into a pocket of the stained apron, and a hand rivaling Bel's for size and strength took the pack. "Now, listen careful, because I'm only going to tell you this once. You go down to the *west* gate. I know it's the wrong way, just circle around the city walls once you get outside. You ask for Asra. You got that?"

"Asra," Valdir repeated, nodding. "West gate."

"You tell him Renfry sent you, and you give him *one* silver. That's his standard bribe to let folks out after dark, and don't let him tell you different. Then when you get to the Border, you give the other to our lads. That'll get you past them. Valdemar folk don't give a hang about who crosses to their side, so long as you don't look like a fighter or a trader. Fighter they'd question, trader they'd tax. You got that?"

"One silver to Asra at the west gate, one to the Border Guards."

"Good lad." Renfry nodded approvingly. "Now belt that blanket around you under your cloak; you're going to need it, it's cold out there. When you get 'round the walls, you take the east road as far as the *second* farm on the right tonight. You stop there. There's a haybarn right on the road and the old boy that owns it don't give a hang if people sleep there so long as they don't build fires. After that, you're on your own."

Valdir was pulling his threadbare cloak on over the blanket when the cook returned with his pack bursting at the seams. He tucked the two tiny coins into his now-empty purse, slung pack over one shoulder and lute over the other, and turned to Renfry, trying to think of some way to thank him.

Renfry took one look at his eyes, and softened. "Damn. Wish you could have stayed a while," he said gruffly, and suddenly pulled Valdir into a quick, rough embrace. "Now get out of here, before Bel comes looking for you."

* * *

Vanyel made the best meal he'd had in a fortnight of half a loaf, the cheese, and a couple of apples. Yfandes got the rest.

:*Funny, how you seem to be able to find friends in the most unexpected places,*: she mused. :*Sometimes I wonder . . .*:

"Friends? What are you talking about?" he asked her, cinching the blanket pad in place, and pulling himself up on her back. "Gods." He clung there for a moment, as another wave of disorientation washed over him.

:*Never mind. Are you all right?*:

"I'll be fine. Just low on resources, and worn out." Anxiety cramped his stomach a moment. He wouldn't have stopped long enough to eat if he hadn't found his legs giving out as he circled around the city to his meeting place with Yfandes. The shadows under the trees seemed sinister. The wind in the near-naked branches moaned as if in pain. He *had* to get back—

—*but the old man was one of those that died.* The thought kept nagging at him. *He must have loved that old man, given his reaction to Jervis. That wasn't feigned. I can't believe that he would have killed the only person he trusted, even in a fit of uncontrolled rage and fear.*

Never mind. The important thing was to take this knowledge back, *now*—before it was too late. Before the same thing could happen at Forst Reach. It still might not have been Tashir who killed the Remoerdis Family, but he dared not take that chance.

"All right, 'Fandes," he said aloud. "Let's get *out* of here."

And she leaped out onto the moon-flooded road.

CHAPTER 11

$\leftarrow$ $\diamond$ $\leftarrow$

IF VANYEL HAD dared to Gate so close to Vedric Mavelan he *would* have. But he didn't; he didn't dare alert him to the fact that a mage powerful enough to Gate had been within the city. *If* the Mavelans were somehow behind the disaster after all, he would be a fool to alert his quarry. So he and Yfandes pounded into Forst Reach just after dawn—

To find everything as peaceful as when they'd left.

:*I told you*,: Yfandes said, in a maddeningly reasonable tone of mind-voice as she pulled into a tired walk. :*I told you if anything had gone wrong we'd have* felt *it, the way we felt the first surge. Didn't I tell you?*:

Visions of slaughter and mayhem melted, taking with them the fear that had strengthened and supported him. When they got to the stable, Vanyel just slid wearily off her back, vowing not to say a word.

Because if he did, he'd take her head off. He *hated* it when she said, "I told you so."

And he did not want to get into a fight with her, didn't even want to have words with her; she didn't deserve it.

Much.

He hurt; he ached all over, and he was half numb with cold. His legs trembled a little as he walked beside her into the stable, his boots and her hooves echoing hollowly on the wooden floor. He managed to get her stall open, and he spent as much time as he could leaning against something while he groomed her. There was, thank the *gods*, hay and water already waiting.

"Get some rest," he told her, fatigue dulling his mind and slurring his words. "I'm going to do the same."

He didn't remember how he got to his room; all he really remembered was leaving Medren's lute by the door, stripping his filthy rags off and dropping them on the floor as he staggered to his bed, and falling *into* the bed. Literally falling; his legs gave out at that point. He held onto consciousness just long enough to pull off the patched breeches and his boots, drag the blankets over himself and wrap them around his chilled, numb body; as soon as he stopped shivering, he was asleep, and oblivious to the world. At that point, Tashir *could* have replicated the massacre in Highjorune, and he'd have slept right through it.

He woke about mid-afternoon, still tired, but no worse than when he'd first arrived home. The filthy rags he'd worn were gone. Evidently one of the servants had come in and picked up after him, and it was a measure of his exhaustion that he not only hadn't woken, he hadn't even *heard* the intruder. He was not pleased with himself; carelessness like that could get him killed all too easily under other circumstances.

On the other hand, it means I'm obviously nowhere near as jumpy as I was, which is all to the good.

The first order of business was food and a bath, and stopping by the kitchen on the way to the bathhouse solved both at the same time.

But the *next* order of business—and one that made him wolf down the first decent meal he'd had in a fortnight practically untasted, and *while* he bathed—was a long talk with Jervis and Savil.

"The boy's staying so close to Jervis you'd think he'd been grafted there," Savil said. Vanyel followed her out to the salle as the late afternoon sunlight gilded everything with a mellowing glow. "It's been entirely quiet, *ke'chara.* Not so much as a murmur out of the boy, or a single plate gone skyward." She looked at him quizzically, with a touch of worry. "To see you practically *flying* back, and in this state—I wish you'd tell me what's going on."

Vanyel shook his head, and his hair fell annoyingly into his eyes again. He hadn't had a chance to get it cut; it was a lot longer than he was used to wearing it, and he wasn't sure if he ought to find the time to do something about it or not. He raked it back with his fingers and suppressed his flash of annoyance at it. "I will, as soon as I have both you and Jervis together. I don't want to have to repeat myself, and I want to hear *both* of your opinions at the same time. It's—some of what I found out is terrifying, and *none* of it is pretty. And I *don't* know what to make of it."

Savil brooded on that. "I thought you were going to find answers over there."

"I did," he replied, deeply troubled. "But the answers I found only gave me more questions."

Jervis was alone in the workroom of the salle. *Which might be the first piece*

of good luck I've had in a while, Vanyel thought with reluctance. Jervis' eyebrows went up when he saw the expression on Vanyel's face, but he didn't
move from his chair; he only put down the vambrace he'd been repairing,
and waited for them to settle themselves.

"You're back, hmm?" the armsmaster said quietly. "From the look of
you, I don't know as I'm going to like what you're going to tell me."

Vanyel shut the door carefully behind Savil; he would have *preferred* to
stand, but he was just too tired. He compromised by perching on a tall stool,
and then looked from Jervis to his aunt and back again, at a real loss as to
how to broach the whole subject.

"Did you find out who put fear in the boy?" Jervis prompted.

That's about as good a place to start as any. Vanyel took a deep breath. "Yes,"
he said, and began his tale.

Jervis and Savil heard him out in complete silence, hardly even breathing. Savil's face was expressionless; Jervis, though, looked ready to call *somebody* out. Vanyel, for starters.

"That's it," Vanyel finished, starting to slump with weariness, his shoulders aching with tension. "That's what I found out. And you have to admit,
the answers I got certainly fit the symptoms."

"Dammit Van," Jervis said tightly, plainly holding his temper in check,
"I am bloody well tempted to call you a damned liar to your face!"

"Why?" Vanyel asked bluntly, too weary for diplomacy.

Jervis colored, and growled. "Because that's *nothing* like the things
Tashir's been telling *me*! The way *he* tells it—"

"Wait a minute! Do you mean Tashir's been talking about his family
to *you*?"

"He trusts me! Can't the boy trust somebody other than you?"

Vanyel told himself that Jervis was only reacting much the way *he* would
if the boy were in *his* protection, and managed to cool his rising temper.
"Why don't you begin at the beginning, and tell me what *you* heard?"

What emerged was nothing less than a fantasy, if what *Vanyel* had learned
was true. In his long talks with Jervis (and it seemed that there had been
several), Tashir had painted a perfect, idyllic family for himself, one in
which the members were forced by circumstance and enemies to present a
very different face to the outside world than the one they showed each
other. His mother, for instance; Tashir depicted her as the long-suffering
plaything of her Mavelan relatives. According to him, once she discovered
Deveran's kindness, she took a stand firmly by the side of her wedded lord,

but played the part of the discarded, unwanted spouse so as to give the Mavelans no reason to think she could be used against Lineas and its ruler.

And according to Tashir's tale, Deveran was not the bitter, half-impotent dancer on the line between Baires threat and Lineas politics. He was supposedly a stern but kindly patriarch of the Linean throne. Deveran, so Tashir had told Jervis, had only disinherited him under pressure from his people. No, there was never any question in Deveran's mind as to who Tashir's father was. No, there had never been a fight, never been anything other than a small misunderstanding that they had settled that very night.

Fiction, first to last.

"That doesn't even square with what the boy told me!" Vanyel retorted, disgusted with the game the youngster seemed to be playing. "*He* told *me* that his father hated him—that knocking him to the ground that night was only out of the ordinary because Deveran hadn't knocked him about much in public before!"

"Hell!" Jervis replied, his face flushing. "The boy was half-crazed an' scared outa his wits."

"All the more reason that he should have told me the *truth*—he didn't have time to make up some tale!"

Jervis started to protest, and Vanyel raised his voice to interrupt him. "And the part about the fight *wasn't* just from Tashir, it was from Herald Lores!"

"A fathead," Savil put in reluctantly, "but an honest fathead."

Jervis lunged to his feet. "An' how much of this is 'cause you *want* that boy's tail?" he snarled, hands knotting into fists at his sides.

Vanyel went hot, then cold. "If *that's* what you think, I see no point in any further discussion. Think what you like—*do* what you like—but obstruct me, and I'll haul you off to Lissa in manacles."

Jervis froze.

"Before I am anything else, armsmaster, I am *Herald* Vanyel, and my first priority is to my king and land. If I judge this boy is a danger to either, I will give him into Randale's custody. *Not* mine, armsmaster. But I must, and *will* have answers, and I will not permit anyone to even attempt preventing me from finding those answers."

Vanyel rose stiffly from his stool, pivoted, and stalked towards the door.

He hadn't taken more than a few steps, when Jervis' strangled, halfsmothered "wait" stopped him in his tracks.

"Why?" he asked, not turning.

"Because—I—we gotta figger *out* this thing." Jervis cleared his throat. "All of us."

Vanyel turned back, still angry, but suppressing it. "Very well. If we're going to figure this mess out, you'll have to take *my* word as being at least as good as the boy's."

Jervis plainly didn't like that, but only protested, "How in *hell* can we take two stories that're *that* different?"

"Look at the one that fits the symptoms," Vanyel's voice was grim, and his face felt tight. "He's afraid to let women between the ages of eighteen and forty even *touch* him—assume the story he told you is true—Ylyna alternately beating him and loving him, and *then* trying to seduce him—"

He wiped his forehead, and his hand came away wet with nervous sweat.

"Gods. Think about how Treesa treats *every* attractive male, including me. She comes on to every man like a flirt. It's only a *game* to her, but *think* how that must have looked to Tashir—the way he'd react. Given my version is true, you could predict he'd do *just what he did*—panic, and let his Gift act up and frighten her off—*just* as I was told he did with his mother. Think about how he *hides* from Withen! And think about the way he clings to *you,* Jervis! *Everything* makes sense."

Jervis faltered. "Well, yes, but—"

"And everything points straight at Tashir as the unconscious murderer," Vanyel continued, heartsick.

"Now that I *will* not believe!" Jervis shouted, surging to his feet. "That boy is no *kind* of a killer! Hell, he damn near castrated himself in practice yesterday, pulling a cut when Medren lost his helm!"

"Who *else* could it be?" Vanyel shouted back, overriding Jervis' protests by sheer volume. "He had the power, he was at the scene, and he *had the motive*! There's nobody, *nobody*, with any kind of a motive *except* Tashir!"

"*No!*" Jervis insisted, eyes going black with anger. "No, I *won't* accept that! Look how he kept from hurting anybody in Treesa's bower."

"But crazed with fear, wild with anger, can you speak for that?"

"Even crazed—how could he kill that Karis? He *loved* that old man, he must have, to trust me so much just because I look like him!"

Vanyel sat heavily back down onto the stool. "I don't know," he admitted in a low voice. "That's only *one* of the things that's been bothering me. In all of the cases of Gifts gone rogue that I've ever heard of, the rogue never hurts anyone but the ones directly in his way. *Everybody* was killed in this case, and that *doesn't* make sense. It *might* make sense if he panicked completely and thought he was killing witnesses, but he didn't have enough time to reason something like that out, not from all I learned. And from what I know of his personality—no. I can't see him killing in cold blood even to save himself." He rubbed his pounding temples with his fists. Fits of anger always gave him a headache. "The first half of the story fits, but the second doesn't. I just can't reconcile the two."

"There're other questions," Savil pointed out from her seat on the cot. Vanyel looked at her in surprise; he'd forgotten she was there. "Lots of other questions. Some of them may tie in, others may not, but the fact is there's too many of them. Lord Vedric's behavior is certainly peculiar. It doesn't in the least match what I've heard of him. Either the man has reformed, or he's up to something. Then there's the puzzle of the Remoerdises, the Linean Royal Family. Why did Deveran insist that only those related to his family serve in the palace? Why is the place *built* on top of a damned mage-node? Why are the Lineans so completely against mage-craft?"

Vanyel shook his head. "You think those questions are crucial?"

"Don't you?" She stood, and smoothed down the front of her tunic. "You know damned well they are, or you wouldn't have brought them up. I tend to agree with Jervis; Tashir is no killer. I agree with you that *your* tale of how the boy was treated fits his behavior a lot better than the one he told Jervis. And there is *something* we're missing. Something important. *I* think we ought to all think about it."

"What about that tale he's been feeding Jervis?" Vanyel asked.

"I think whoever runs into him next ought to call him on it—no, let me amend that. Whichever of the two of *us*, Van. Jervis, I'm sorry, but if it comes to magic, you're defenseless. I'm pretty certain Van and I could contain the worst of anything he could do."

"The boy wouldn't hurt anybody, and especially not me," he insisted stubbornly. "I *know* it, damn it, I just *know* it!"

"Forgive me, but I'd rather not take the chance," Savil said dryly. "I hate picking up my acquaintances in palm-sized pieces. We've eaten this particular bird down to bones; let's let things simmer for a bit, and let's do something about dinner."

"Gods." Vanyel slid off the stool, held out his hands and watched them shake with a certain bemusement. "I *just ate*, and after this to-do, my stomach should be in knots. Instead, I could eat a cow."

"Don't fill up," Savil cautioned him, as they left Jervis mulling over the unpleasant things he'd heard. "There's Harvestfest tonight."

"What?" He looked at her, bewildered. "Harvest—can't be—oh, gods—"

He counted up the passing days in his mind, and when he arrived at *today*, he could feel the blood draining out of his face. "Oh, gods. It's Sovvan. I lost track of time. . . ." He stopped dead in the path, legs gone leaden, mind gone numb. Sovvan-night. Year's turning.

The night Tylendel had died.

Coming on top of all the rest of it—exhaustion, confusion, the verbal fight with Jervis—

It was too much. What little emotional balance he had left evaporated so quickly that he felt dizzy, as if he was dangling over a precipice.

His internal turmoil must have been mirrored clearly on his face. Savil moved closer to him, brows knitting in concern. "Van—*ke'chara*—let it go. You aren't helping yourself by brooding." She put her arm around his shoulders. "Go down to the barns with the others. I'm going to—"

He scarcely felt it. All he could see was—

—*a crumpled, lifeless shape.*

He clamped an iron control down over his face. "That's not something I can do," he replied stiffly. "I can't forget, *especially* not tonight. I won't ever forget. . . ."

"Then, for the gods' sake, for your *own* sake, find something to distract you—music, dancing—"

"No, Savil." He pulled away from her, and forced himself to walk steadily toward the keep. "You deal with grief your way, and leave me to deal with it in mine."

"But—"

He shook his head stubbornly, unwilling to say more, and not sure that he could. *Forget 'Lendel? How can I forget—how can I ever forget?*

Oh, 'Lendel—

There was only one place where he could escape the sounds of celebration; the stone porch on the north side of the keep. All other interests had vanished when he realized what night it was; now all he wanted was solitude.

The lingering warmth of this fall had fooled him; usually Sovvan-tide was marked by ice-edged rains and bitter winds.

Like the storm that night—

Usually he tried to find something useful to do—like stand guard-duty, or spell someone at courier, or even take the place of one of the Guardians watching the Web. Anything, so long as it was work, and didn't involve interacting with people, only serving them.

He'd completely forgotten that he'd be spending Sovvan here, in presumed idleness; leisure that would only give him the opportunity to remember how utterly alone he was.

It hadn't been this bad the first few years; in the first two, in fact, there had been moments when he thought he'd felt that treasured and familiar presence waiting, watching. But as the years passed—and it became clear that he was and would *always* be alone, Sovvan-night had become an occasion for profound depression unless he was very careful not to give in to it. *This* Sovvan-night bid fair to be an ordeal; he was too exhausted, and too shaken, to put up any kind of fight against himself.

He watched the sun die in glory; watched the stars come out, flowering against the velvet sky. He closed his eyes when the sparks of white began to waver in his vision, and struggled anyway in a losing battle against self-pity and heartache. *I've wept enough; tears won't ease this, they'll only make it worse. I wish I was being Valdir. I wish I was back at Haven.*

He thought briefly of Yfandes, and rejected the notion of going to her. She couldn't help him, much as he loved her. Her presence would only serve as a reminder of how much he had lost to gain her.

I need something to keep me occupied. Savil was right about that. Something that will take concentration.

There was only one task he knew that could possibly fill all his thoughts, take all his attention. *Magic. I'll build some illusions, good, tight ones. I can use the practice. I need the practice.*

He perched on the edge of one of the stone benches, the gritty granite warm from the sun it had absorbed this afternoon, and concentrated on a point just in front of him. *People, they're hardest. Starwind. He's vivid enough.*

He closed his eyes, and *centered*.

It took very little to cast an illusion, just a wisp of power, and he didn't even need to take it from his reserves. The ambient energy around him was enough. He visualized a vibrant column of light growing in the air in front of him, then began forming the shapeless energy into an image, building it carefully from the feet up. Green leather boots, silky green breeches, and sleeveless tunic, all molding to a tall, slender, wiry body. Implicit strength, not blatant. Waist-length silver hair, four braids in the front, the rest falling free down his back, a cascade of ice-threads. Golden skin. Then the face: pointed chin, high cheekbones, silver-blue eyes with a wisdom and humor lurking in them that could not be denied, and a smile just hovering at the edge of the thin lips.

He opened his eyes—and before him stood the *Tayledras* Healer-Adept Starwind k'Treva.

For one moment he had it; perfect in every detail.

Then the hair shortened and darkened to curly blond, the face squared, and the eyes began warming and darkening to a soft and gentle brown.

His heart contracted, and he banished the illusion and began another, quickly: Savil. This one started to go wrong from the very beginning, and with a gasp of pain, he wiped it out and started on a third. Not even a human this time—one of the little lizards that served the *Tayledras*, the *hertasi*.

But the *hertasi* began growing taller, and developed blond hair.

"Oh, *gods*—" He banished the third illusion, and buried his face in his hands, shaking in every limb and battling against grief.

This—this is the worst Sovvan I've ever had, he thought, feeling sorrow tearing at his chest until it hurt to breathe. *It's the worst since you died. Oh, 'Lendel, ashke, I can't bear it, and I have no choice! I'm so tired, so very tired—my balance is gone. And, to know it's going to go on like this, year after year, alone. . . .*

I don't know how to cope anymore. I don't know how anyone can be this lonely and still be sane. . . . I don't even know how sure I am of myself. I thought you were the only person I could ever love, but this business with Shavri has me all turned 'round about. And Tashir—I came so close to giving in to temptation with him. . . .

All I am certain of is that I need you as much as I ever did. And I'd give anything to have you back.

He bit his lip and tasted the sweet-salt of blood; took his hands away from his face, and willed his eyes open. Nightshadows of leafless trees moved ebony against charcoal; the last frost had killed the insects, and the birds had mostly flown south by now. There was no sign of anything alive out there, just barren shadows dark as his soul, as empty as his heart.

A wisp of glow drifted in the air in front of him, and he gave in to his anguish, to the perverse need to probe at his heartache.

To hell with it—how can I hurt any more than I do now? And everything I try turns to 'Lendel. Not Shavri—which ought to have told me who I love more.

Once again he closed his eyes and began to build a new illusion, one formed with passionate care, and at a level of detail only love could have discerned in the original. The way that one lock of gold-brown sunstreaked hair used to fall—just touching the eyebrow. The depth of the clear, brown eyes, sometimes sable, sometimes golden, but so bottomless you could lose yourself in them. The square chin, so—high cheekbones, so—the generous mouth, so ready to smile or laugh, the strong pillar of the neck. Shoulders ready to take the weight of the world's troubles. Body of a fighter or a dancer; gentle hands of a healer—

It didn't take long, now that he was no longer fighting with himself.

Oh, Tylendel—

Vanyel looked up to see his handiwork, and sobbed, once, reaching out involuntarily to touch empty air.

The illusion was nothing less than heartbreakingly perfect. The Tylendel of the joyous days of their one summer together stood before him, so *alive* Vanyel fancied he could see him breathing, that in a moment he would speak.

And I could do that, too; I could make him breathe and talk to me. No, I couldn't bear that. It's hollow enough as it is. Oh, gods, why? 'Lendel—

Someone gasped behind him, and as he started and lost control of it, the illusion shattered, exploded outward into a hundred thousand glittering little bits that rained down and vanished, melting away before they touched the pale stone of the porch. Vanyel whipped around to see a dark and indistinct shape beside the black hole of the door.

"Who's there?" he snapped, hastily wiping his eyes with the back of his hand. "What do you want?"

"I—it's Tashir." The young man came toward him hesitantly. "Medren told me you were back. I wondered where you were. Where you've been."

Depression abruptly became anger at being disturbed, and the desire to hurt fountained in him. He wanted someone, *anyone*, any creature at all, to suffer inside as much as he did at this moment. He *knew* it was base; knew that Tashir would be an easy target, and that he *could* hurt him. He hated the desire even as he felt it, and it sickened him as much as he wanted it. He fought it down, but the anger remained, red and sullen. This young man, for whom Vanyel had been risking his life, had been undermining everything he'd built here. It wasn't just that Tashir had been lying; it was that what he had told Jervis had come close to destroying the fragile beginnings of friendship that had cost both of them so much pain and soul-searching to create, had set them at each other's throats like enemies, and had left them, once again, uneasy and grudging allies at best.

"I've been finding out the truth," he said softly. "While *you* seem to have been busy trying to hide it." The anger blossomed, and he briefly lost control over it, just long enough that he growled a single sentence.

"Why did you lie to Jervis?"

"I didn't!" Tashir's voice cracked as Vanyel rose and walked toward him, one hand flaring with mage-light. The blue light reflected off Tashir's face, revealing the youngster's surprise and growing fear. The young man's eyes widened, his expression froze, and he backed away from the Herald step by forced step. He didn't stop until his thighs hit the stone railing and Vanyel had him backed into a corner with nowhere to go.

"You did," Vanyel whispered. "All those stories you told him about your perfect, loving family—that's all they were, stories. Lies. I've been in High-jorune, Tashir. I spent the last fortnight there, talking to people. One of them was your mother's maid, Reta."

The branches of the bushes nearest Tashir began to thrash as if tossed by a wind, though not a breath of air stirred anywhere else. Vanyel didn't have to see them to know that the young man had unleashed his Gift in panic. He let it go for a moment, waiting to see how violent Tashir would become. Fallen leaves whirled up in a mad dance to engulf both of them, beating at Vanyel ineffectually. But with nothing more at hand to work with than leaves, the attack wasn't even a distraction. Vanyel savagely clamped down on the young man with a shield not even an Adept could have cracked, and the leaves drifted back down to the ground and the porch.

Tashir cowered against the stone railing, averting his eyes as the mage-light on Vanyel's hand flared. Perversely, the display of subservience only made him angrier. He fought down his temper and got himself back under control, managing at last to gaze down upon the youngster with his anger held in check.

"Well, Tashir?" Vanyel whispered tonelessly. "Are we ready to hear a little truth now?"

"A-about wh-what?" Tashir croaked.

Vanyel formed the light into a ball and sent it to hover just over his head with a flick of his wrist. He folded his arms, and compressed his lips, forcing his anger to cool a little more.

I'll invoke Truth Spell on him. Then at least I'll bloody well know when he's lying.

"I think," he said, finally, "that we can start with your father."

He called up the *vrondi,* and when it surrounded him with faint blue light, Tashir's pale face stood out with sharp-edged distinctness against the night-dark shadows behind him. Word by agonized word, he dragged a story out of Tashir that was virtually identical to the one that Reta had told him.

Three times more, whenever Vanyel dealt with the subject of his mother, the boy unconsciously attempted to evoke his Gift; he failed to break the shield Vanyel still held on him each time. Vanyel noted with a smoldering, sullen calm that while Tashir *did* freeze physically when this happened, he was *quite* conscious, if not in conscious control of what he was doing.

Finally Vanyel decided to force the issue—to deliberately evoke the same state of mind the younger man must have been in on that fatal night.

"The night I found you," he said, "your father told you something, and you refused him, and he hit you. Do you remember what that was?"

Tashir shook his head, a breath away from hysterical breakdown. The blue aura of the Truth Spell continued to glow.

"He told you that he was going to send you to your Mavelan relatives to stay; that he was washing his hands of you."

It was hard to tell in the blue glows of mage-light and Truth Spell, but Tashir seemed to become paler. Vanyel shook his head regretfully, and deliberately turned his back on the youngster. "*I* don't know what to do about you," he said expressionlessly. "You've brought me nothing but trouble, and you're about to cause a major diplomatic incident between Valdemar and Lineas. You *could* even start a war. I'm sorry, Tashir, but your uncle Vedric is petitioning that you be put into his custody. King Randale is likely to order just that. Given the circumstances, I think it would be the wisest thing if I admitted where you are and my part in this mess and turned you over to Vedric in the morning."

He waited for an attack; he waited for the shield to break under the stress of Tashir's Gift at the kind of level of manifestation that was indicated by the slaughter at Highjorune.

Instead, he heard a peculiar little whimper, and felt the pressure within the shield go null.

Vanyel pivoted in surprise just in time to catch the youngster as he fell over in a dead faint.

It took him the better part of a candlemark to revive Tashir. It took longer to convince him that although it might be the *wisest* thing to do, it was *not* the course of action Vanyel intended to take. The youngster was totally terrified of being sent into Mavelan hands, yet even under the stress of this absolute terror, his Gift manifested at no higher level than before.

Eventually Tashir believed him when he told the youngster that he would continue to shelter him, to try to find out what had really happened.

And then, when the young man had settled a little, he began the questioning again.

With a cool and calculated assessment of the stress he was putting Tashir under, Vanyel brought him to the breaking point over and over, until he was *certain* that nothing was going to evoke the kill-storm.

Finally the boy was too exhausted to be pressed further. And Vanyel wasn't too far behind him—at least emotionally. "Why, Tashir?" he asked, looking for *any* clue as to the truth of that night. "Why *did* you make up that fantasy for Jervis?"

"Because—because I wanted him to *like* me!" the young man blurted desperately. "How could he like me if my own father hated me? How could he like me if he knew what my mother wanted to—"

Vanyel interrupted, trying not to show the frustration he was feeling. "Tashir, *Karis* tried to protect you. Why did you think Jervis would be any different?"

"But Karis was *there*, he saw what was happening. If I told anybody else they'd think I was *lying*, Mother said so."

Tashir paled again, but Vanyel assumed it was only the stress of having to face that unnatural relationship squarely.

"Karis," he whispered, "was *there*."

"Tashir, from what I've been told, *she* was the one who lied; why would you think she'd have told you the truth about—"

"V-Vanyel," the young man interrupted. "Karis—they never told me *who* besides—was Karis—one of—was he—"

Then Vanyel saw what Tashir had finally realized; saw the plea in Tashir's eyes to be told that Karis was still alive, and couldn't answer it. He looked away—which was answer enough.

The youngster crumpled, holding the stone balustrade for support, his entire body shaking with harsh, racking sobs. Vanyel remembered, as he banished the shield and uncast the Truth Spell, that one of the most telling pieces of evidence *against* the youngster—in the eyes of Herald Lores, at any rate—was Tashir's *lack* of emotion when he'd been told what had happened.

Lores should see him now, he thought grimly, putting his arm around Tashir's shoulders and letting him weep himself out with Vanyel supporting him. His own anger was quite gone, and he was recalling his desire to make Tashir hurt as much as *he* did with a sick, shamed feeling in the pit of his stomach. Then Tashir turned to cry on Vanyel's shoulder, and it was all

Vanyel could do to keep from losing control again, this time for a very different reason.

Finally the youngster pulled away, and Vanyel let him go. He walked back to his former seat on the bench at the farther side of the porch and slumped there, his head in his hands, not really thinking, only aching.

Because Tashir was *so* like Tylendel.

Holding him while he wept had been like reliving the past. The dead past. . . .

Hesitant footsteps behind him, and a shy sniffle.

Vanyel wished with all his heart that the boy would go—find Jervis, go back to his room, or seek solace at the festivities, *anything* but stay here with that far-too-familiar face, providing a ready-made knife to the heart, and not even knowing that he was doing so.

"Vanyel?" came the halting whisper. "Vanyel, who was that man? The one that disappeared when I startled you? I thought it was me, at first, but he was different."

"It was just an illusion," Vanyel replied, rubbing his temples, staring at the dark blot of his own feet against the gray stone. "I was practicing."

The youngster hovered just beside him. "But who is it?" he persisted. "It wasn't me, and it wasn't Uncle Vedric. And why were you casting a seeming of him?"

"Tylendel," Vanyel replied shortly. "His name was Tylendel. He's dead. He—*was*—my lover."

And half of my soul and all of my heart.

Tashir started back at that, out of touching distance, projecting clear revulsion and fear so clearly that Vanyel felt it like a blow.

Vanyel's temper snapped.

"*Dammit,*" he snarled, rounding on the youngster, "will you *not* act like I'm going to pounce on you and rape you? I *don't* make a habit of hitting attractive young men over the head and dragging them off to my bed, no matter *who* they look like!"

Tashir put out a hand as if to keep him away.

Vanyel could no longer control his temper or his words. "*You* came to *me* not all that long ago," he snarled, "and I'll thank you to remember that I didn't take advantage of the situation! So you've changed your mind about being shaych; fine, I have no quarrel with you or with that, that is *your* decision and yours alone to make. I have no intention of making you change your mind. But kindly remember that I'm a human being, and I lost somebody—"

He fought the words past the grief. "—lost somebody I loved more than anyone else on earth. He was my lifebonded, and I will be *without* him for the rest of my life. You're not the *only* one in the world who's alone! You're not the only one who's suffered!"

He turned away abruptly, got up, and stalked stiffly to the stone railing, staring out into the lattice of bare tree branches and trying to keep from breaking down completely. Behind him he could hear Tashir shuffling his feet, the sound betraying uncertainty.

Go away, boy. Leave me alone. Leave me to mourn my dead, my beloved, and go chase my niece. Just leave me.

But the footsteps shuffled nearer, hesitated, then came nearer still, until Tashir stood at his right elbow. Vanyel stared out ahead of him, at the branches, and the stars that seemed to be caught there.

"Was he a Herald?" The voice was timid.

"No. A trainee."

Stop driving knives in me. Go away.

"How long ago?"

"Twelve years, tonight."

Twelve years forsaken. Twelve long, lonely years, knowing I'll never be whole again.

"What happened?" the youngster persisted, sounding very young indeed.

"He killed himself."

There. Are you happy? Now will you go away?

"But—" No condemnation, just bewilderment. "—*why?* How could he—when he had a Companion?"

So you know that already, do you? How if we die, they die? But you don't know everything, laddy-boy.

"She repudiated him. That's why he did it. He—couldn't bear—the—" He couldn't finish.

Silence, a silence marked only by the occasional rustle of leaves. Vanyel hung his head and wrestled with his grief and hoped the youngster would take the hint and finally go away.

Tashir moved a little closer. "I don't understand," he said, humbly. "I can't imagine what could have happened. Please—"

Vanyel took a deep, shuddering breath. Obviously the boy wasn't going to leave until he had his curiosity satisfied.

So tell him, and get it over with.

He looked back up at the remote and uncaring stars. " 'Lendel was Savil's trainee when my father sent me to her because I wasn't the kind of man he thought I should be," he began, trying to recite the words as if they described someone else. "What I didn't know then was that he was afraid I was fey, and he was trying to keep me from being shaych. He kept me amazingly sheltered, really; I had no idea that—well, I suppose—anyway, I knew I was different, but I didn't know why." His chest ached when he took a breath. "I was disliked at home. The fosterlings, my brothers, they all figured me for Mother's darling. And I just couldn't seem to fit in with them. Granted, I didn't make much effort to *be* liked after a while, but—well."

It was all coming back with the impact of something that had happened only yesterday. "So Withen sent me off to Haven, where I was even more a stranger." He tried to laugh; it sounded like a croak. "I was put with Savil and her proteges, and Savil was supposed to 'make a man out of me'—turn me into something like Meke, I suppose. What Father didn't know was that her favorite protege 'Lendel was shaych—openly shaych. Exactly what he'd tried to keep me from. I was lonely and desperately unhappy, and 'Lendel was kind to me even when I was rotten to him. Then I found out certain things about *him* from other sources and suddenly a lot of inexplicable things about myself had answers."

I watched you and wanted more from you than friendship—for days, weeks. And at the same time—I was so afraid. Not like this young fool is afraid; I was afraid that once I broke my isolation, you'd hurt me like everyone else had. But you didn't, 'Lendel. At least not in the way I'd feared. And in the end, it wasn't you who hurt me; it was losing you—

"Things—happened. 'Lendel and I became lovers, then lifebonded. I know that now, I didn't know that then; all I knew then was that I'd have done anything for him, committed any crime to avoid losing him."

"You weren't a Herald?"

"No, not even a trainee." His eyes blurred and burned. Vanyel blinked, and tears splashed down onto the balustrade beside his hand. "Tylendel had a twin; his twin was murdered in a feud. Murdered by magic. No one seemed willing to do anything about it. 'Lendel and Staven had been mindlinked; losing Staven drove him more than a little mad. He decided to take matters into his own hands, and I helped him by stealing the proscribed books of magic. I couldn't believe—I was outraged that no one had done anything about Staven's murder. I didn't know what I should have done, and

I didn't see anything wrong with going out for revenge—especially not when 'Lendel was hurting so much. We slipped away on Sovvan-night—"

Dark and cold it was, and wind blowing fit to tear the clothes from your body. But not so dark and cold as the place inside 'Lendel that only revenge would heal—I thought. I only wanted him satisfied so I could have the Tylendel I knew back again. I never thought further than that.

"—we Gated to where the other family was celebrating. Since we were lifebonded and I had Mage-*potential*, 'Lendel could use my energy to make the Gate and his own to call up his vengeance. Which he did. He called up a pack of *wyrsa* and turned them loose."

He felt the young man beside him shudder, but he was too caught in his memories to pay much attention. He could still see it; the image was burned into his mind for all time.

'Lendel, his face twisted with grief and rage, his eyes no longer gentle, and holding a black gleam of madness. The cowering people, seeing no escape—and Evil made flesh in the form of the four wyrsa, *unholy meldings of snake and ferret, with their dagger-teeth and their burning sulfur eyes and their insatiable hunger that he could feel beating against his mind even now. And then the thunder of hooves behind him and the equine shriek of defiance and loss—*

"Gala came through the Gate when the *wyrsa* had made only one kill. She challenged the whole pack—she repudiated 'Lendel."

Sweet blue eyes gone dead and empty, mind-voice reverberating coldly down the link that bound him and 'Lendel. I do not know you. You are not my Chosen. Then the internal snap of something breaking, and the utter desolation where love had been—

"She attacked the pack. They pulled her down and killed her."

Tylendel's eyes with all of hell in them. Tylendel's heart a churning storm of loss and agony. Tylendel's soul a shattered thing past all repairing. Tylendel's mind holding no sane thoughts at all—

"Savil and two other Heralds came through the Gate and destroyed the *wyrsa*—too late, oh, gods—'Lendel's heart, his mind, his *soul* were broken. He got away from them when we reached Haven. They backlashed the Gate energy through me by accident, and my collapse distracted them just long enough for him to break free of them. He couldn't bear it—the pain of losing Gala, then having her *die* before his eyes—so he threw himself—off the Belltower—"

I wish they'd let me die with you. I wish they hadn't saved me when I tried to kill myself. Oh, 'Lendel, Tylendel, it wasn't supposed to end that way—

He couldn't look at Tashir. Couldn't. Tears fell silently and splashed onto his hands. He gripped the railing until his knuckles ached. There was nothing inside him but the same throbbing emptiness that had been left twelve years ago.

Twelve years, 'Lendel. Twelve years, and it hurts more, not less. Twelve years, and all I really look forward to is the moment it's all over—

Tashir was very quiet; Vanyel couldn't even hear him breathing, and only the sense of *presence* still at his side told him that the young man was still there.

"I'm sorry," Tashir said awkwardly. "That's a stupid thing to say, but it's all I can think of. I wish it had never happened. I wish I could bring him back for you, Herald Vanyel. Karis always told me people *could* feel that way about each other, could really *love* each other and not just pretend to, but I never—I never knew anybody who did. I'm sorry I made you unhappy. I apologize for reacting like I did. If I'd known what you just told me, I'd have realized how stupid I was."

"It's all right," Vanyel answered him huskily, after a pause to get the lump out of his throat. "You couldn't know. Lifebonds don't happen very often. When they do, well, it's like Companion-bond; when one partner dies, the other dies with him, usually. The only thing that kept me alive was that I bonded to Yfandes that night. It doesn't hit me like this very often, it's just—Sovvan-night, and I'm bloody damned tired, and you—gods, Tashir, you could have been him. It hurts every time I see you, because half the time I don't see *you*, I see *him*."

The young man was silent again, but it was a silence that implied he was going to speak. And he did.

"I'm probably saying things I shouldn't, but you said it yourself, Vanyel. It's been *twelve years*. Don't you think that's an awful long time to be holding onto a memory so tightly that it strangles you?"

He stepped away a little, as Vanyel finally turned to look at the dark shape of him in shock and astonishment. "People need you, and you can't help them when you're like this. Jervis told me that you said that's important. And *you* aren't the only one in the world who's suffering, either. You aren't the only one who's ever lost his love."

He backed up a little, then broke and ran for the door, leaving Vanyel standing stiffly beside the railing, trying to collect his wits.

Have I been that selfish? he wondered. *Is it selfish to grieve for someone like this?*

I don't know.

But he's right. I'm not the only one in the world who's lost someone they loved. He lost Karis, and Karis was the only person he ever knew who loved him. I have Savil; I have 'Fandes. I have—

Friends.

Gods.

He blinked, as answers finally put themselves together in his mind. *I said it myself; it wasn't Shavri everything turned into, it was 'Lendel. I do love Shavri, but not like that. It's just that I've been so long without caring for anyone that deeply that I couldn't untangle what it meant. I want to protect her, care for her, but because she's a friend who needs me more than anyone has ever needed me except 'Lendel. And because she cares for me. It was only 'Lendel who gave me love without asking for anything—*

—good gods. That's it, isn't it. That's where the sticking point is. Everybody wants something from me, or seems to. Mother, first of all; Melenna, Randi—they all want me to be something for them. Only 'Lendel wanted me to be myself. Only 'Lendel gave without asking what he was going to get. And now Shavri. And Jisa, who just loves, like only a child can love, without any questions at all.

But that's not wrong, either; I can't blame the ones who need things from me. But that may be something of the difference between friends and lovers. Interesting. But how is it that I can go to bed with a friend—

Ah. I can't go to bed with someone who's not a friend. How could I have lost what I knew when I was fifteen? That was what I knew when Krebain tried to seduce me. Sex and love aren't *the same thing. But love and friendship are so close that you can't have love without having friendship. I could have continued to love 'Lendel even without sex. That's what had me confused. We became friends and lovers and beloved all at the same instant. There was something about him I would always have liked, even if I'd never loved him.*

The stars weren't any brighter for having just found some of his answers, but they seemed that way. *Poor Tashir—he doesn't have anyone. I had* a true love. *Not too many people can say that.*

He contemplated that for a moment. *I've been thinking awfully hard about how I lost him. Maybe it would be better to remember how I had him.*

Once again he set himself to build the illusion that had shattered with Tashir's gasp; just as carefully, just as lovingly.

But this time remembering the good times.

Once again Tylendel stood before him, frozen in a moment of gentle joy. He remembered that moment well.

You gave me a gift I never expected to have; you gave me my music back, beloved. You told me that it was more important to you to hear music played for itself than to hear it enhanced by the strongest of Bardic Gifts. He found himself smiling, a smile with tears on the edge of it, but smiling. *Then I sang you a love song. The first one I ever sang for you. It was the first time I'd ever sung one with my heart in it.*

Tylendel had given himself up completely to the music he'd woven for him. It had been a moment completely free of any shadows because 'Lendel had chased the only one that haunted him.

Beloved, you knew how much I needed that back, and you gave it to me with open hands.

Memory *could* be sweet—even if it held an edge of sorrow.

I won't ever forget you, ashke, *but I can choose how I remember you. And I promise I'll try to remember with love, not tears.*

He allowed the image to fade.

So it's time I started doing something about people who need me, hmm? Just like you told me. And the most urgent of those is Tashir.

He yawned suddenly, then laughed a little at himself. *And I'm not going to do* anyone *any good falling asleep on my feet. So best I seek my virtuously empty bed. Morning is going to come far too soon.*

He looked once more into the sky—or beyond it. Even he wasn't certain which.

Good night, ashke. Wherever you are. Wind to thy wings—

CHAPTER 12

NEWS, SPED BY Herald, Mind- and Mage-Gifts, and Herald-guided messenger birds, moved quickly in Valdemar when the King and Circle chose. But when they didn't—

They had not chosen to speed either edicts *or* news in the matter of Tashir and the mysterious slaughter of the Linean Royal Family. *That* news moved with the same plodding slowness as it did outKingdom. And that gave Vanyel and the youngster a respite.

But it was a short respite only; Vanyel had known that from the beginning. Vanyel wasn't much surprised when a messenger arrived the day after Sovvan from Captain Lissa. He had a fair notion of just what the sealed message-tubes the courier carried contained.

And he wasn't at all surprised to be summoned to Lord Withen's study when the messenger had departed.

The door stood open; Vanyel tapped on the frame, then entered when his father looked up. Withen wore a troubled expression, the look of a man who is uneasy about things over which he had little or no control. He motioned to Vanyel to take a chair, but Van only shook his head, preferring to stand. If Withen meant to take him to task, let him do so with Vanyel in some kind of "formal" stance.

"This—" Withen settled back into his own chair and lifted a corner of one of the papers lying on his desk. "I had the messenger read it for me; I wasn't sure I wanted Radevel to know what was going on until I talked to you. It's a politely worded 'request' from Lissa for permission to move her company of the Guard to the Ashkevron personal estates. And an explanation of why she's been ordered to move."

Vanyel nodded. Given what he had seen on his way home—the way the Linean side of the Border had been fortified in just under a fortnight—he had realized it would be only a matter of time before Liss got orders to move from the Border-section facing Baires to that facing Lineas. And the Ashkevron family land sat squarely on the only road suitable for troop movements.

Withen coughed uncomfortably. "Van, son—the boy you brought here—he's *that* Tashir, isn't he? Tashir Remoerdis. The Linean."

"He is," Vanyel replied levelly. "And the fact that he was Chosen *after* the Remoerdis Family died is reason enough to presume him innocent." He straightened a little. "Father, you *know* I wouldn't have brought anyone dangerous here, but he needed a sanctuary, and this was the only place I could think of where no one would look for him."

Withen interrupted him with a wave of his hand. "That's not what I'm worried about. That boy wouldn't hurt a fly, I'd swear to it myself. It's— what do I do if Liss or somebody else comes looking for *you*?"

"You could give us up." Vanyel sighed, his muscles going to knots. "In fact, you should."

"Like *hell* I will!" Withen rumbled. "You brought him here for sanctuary, and by the gods, he's going to get it!"

Vanyel relaxed and grinned; the expression startled his father. "Father mine," he said warmly, "you have just eased my last worry. I was *not* going to foist this walking diplomatic incident on you unwilling, but if *you* have no qualms about continuing to shelter him—"

Withen snorted. "I'll pick up blade and defend him m'self, if I have to."

"I *hope* you won't have to; I *hope* I'll be able to find out who really did this, and clear Tashir entirely. If you don't mind, I'll take that chair you offered." Withen nodded, and Vanyel lowered himself into its support gratefully. "Randale's playing a very tricky game here; Liss' troop is mostly made up of men from Forst Reach and the holdings in fealty to us. He knows damned well that no matter what the 'official' word is, they'll protect me, with silence, if nothing else, unless *you*—or Liss—indicate differently. Randale trusts my judgment, and he's giving me time to get this sorted out."

Withen nodded, one eyebrow raised in tribute to Randale's cleverness.

"Don't worry, Father, I'll have word and time to get us out of Forst Reach and into hiding in the forest long before anyone dangerous could actually arrive here."

"That was all I was worried about, except"—Withen tugged his short beard unhappily—"*is* there a chance the Lineans would make a Border-war out of this?"

Vanyel weighed all the factors in his mind, including Vedric's apparent unwillingness to force the issue. He ruminated a long time, for the most part ignoring his father's increasingly gloomy countenance, before he was able to make a tentative conclusion. He stood then, hoping he looked more

confident than he felt. "I don't think so, but I pledge you, Father," he said
steadily, holding Withen's eyes with his own, "before it comes to that, I'll
turn both of us over to them myself."

And I hope to Havens I never have to make good on that pledge.

The reaction to the news contained in the missive was mixed. On the
whole, Vanyel's younger brothers seemed to welcome the prospect of "a
little excitement" with cheerful bloodthirstiness. Mekeal alone of all of
them seemed of two minds about the whole thing, first joining in the boasting and enthusiastic weaponry practices, then taking to pacing about the
keep muttering about "line-of-sight" and "defensibility" with a worried
frown creasing his forehead.

Withen made it very plain when the youngster's identity became generally known that he shared Jervis' conviction of Tashir's innocence, and
Tashir reacted to his show of faith with disbelief at first. But when Withen
himself assured him of his sanctuary, Tashir reacted with a pitiful gratitude
that would have softened harder hearts than Withen's.

It was because of *this* that Withen actually got embroiled in a shouting
match with Father Leren over Tashir and the question of his disposition,
guilt, or innocence; the first time Withen had ever disagreed with the cleric
to Vanyel's knowledge.

Tashir's Companion had finally come in to take up nervous residence
with Yfandes. This was something of a relief to Vanyel, since Ghost had
been frightening the whey out of most of the workers on the holding; they'd
see only a flash of something white, usually by night, and then it would be
gone, and the rumors of a "demonhorse" were spreading. Vanyel was trying
to coax both the young man and the Companion into a calmer state of mind
in which deeper bonding and Mindspeech between the two would be possible, but neither of them were at all willing to be calmed. Ghost, in fact,
showed a marked tendency to panic if even the lower half of the outer door
to Yfandes' stall was closed while he was in it. Vanyel was about ready to
give it up as a hopeless task when Jervis came looking for him, a startling
grin transforming his craggy face into a mask of unholy glee.

Relations between the two of them were improving again—slowly.
Vanyel suspected Tashir may have had a hand in that, though whether or
not that was on purpose he had no idea. But although they were speaking
without daggers behind the words, Vanyel had *not* expected to see that kind
of expression on the armsmaster's face—ever.

"Van," Jervis whispered, while Tashir communicated with Ghost in his own way, with brush and murmured words Vanyel couldn't catch. "If you're done here, there's somethin' you *have* to hear."

Vanyel shrugged, and vaulted over the stall railings. "Tashir," he called over his shoulder, "why don't you two work off some of that nerve in a good long ride? You're too edgy to trance and I don't blame you.'

Tashir looked relieved; Ghost lowered his head in a clear gesture of agreement. The young Companion stood steadily for Tashir while his Chosen pulled himself up onto his back, then nosed the stall door open and trotted out into the paddock.

"All right," Vanyel said, turning back to Jervis. "What is all this about?"

"Just come with me," Jervis said gleefully, and led Vanyel out of the stable to stand just under one of the windows in the tiny temple.

"—possessed at the best, a red-handed murderer at the worst!" Father Leren was shouting, his voice muffled by all the intervening stone.

"That boy's no more a murderer than I am!" Withen shouted back. "You were dead wrong about Vanyel, and by the gods, you're even more wrong about this boy! Van asked me for sanctuary for him, *I* pledged it, and I'm *not* taking back my sworn word!"

"You're putting your soul in jeopardy, Lord Withen," the priest thundered. "The gods—"

"The gods, my ass!" Withen roared, in full and magnificent outrage. "There isn't an evil hair on that poor boy's head! Who made *you* the spokesman for the gods? Last *I* was taught, if the gods want something done, they don't bother with a damned mouthpiece, they do it themselves—*or* they choose a vessel and make their power plain! I haven't seen *you* glowing with holy light, old man!"

Leren sputtered, incoherent, obviously taken aback by this revolt of his erstwhile supporter.

"And I'll tell you one thing more, *I* judge who's to be Forst Reach priest. I put you *in*, and I can throw you *out* just as easy! If you want to *stay* Forst Reach priest, you'll keep your mouth off Tashir—aye, and while we're at it, off Vanyel as well! When you've done as much for Valdemar as he has, you can call him pervert and catamite to your heart's content, but till you do, you keep a respectful tongue in that head of yours! He's *Herald* Vanyel, first-rank Herald-Mage of Valdemar and confidant of the King, and furthermore he's *my son* and you'd better *damned* well remember that fact!"

Leren tried to say something else, but Withen's roar drowned him out.

Vanyel signaled that they probably ought to move on; Jervis nodded as he stifled snickers with his hand, biting the edge of it to keep from laughing out loud as they slipped away. Vanyel was too surprised to laugh; it felt as if his eyebrows were about to make a permanent home in his hair.

It was certainly the *last* argument he'd ever expected to overhear.

The falling-out found Leren taking his meals with the hirelings instead of with the family, a circumstance that Vanyel *tried* not to rejoice in, but couldn't help enjoying. It certainly made mealtime easier for *him* to face. The quarrel also gave Jervis ascendancy, and as a result of *that*, Vanyel thought he *might* be detecting a certain softening of Withen's attitude toward his firstborn, although what with everything and everyone stirred up it was impossible to be sure.

That was the state of things when Captain Lissa Ashkevron rode in through the gates of Forst Reach at the head of her company.

"Lord Withen," said the solemn hatchet-faced woman in dress blues, bowing slightly over her horse's neck in the salute of equals. She waited his response with her helm tucked at a precise angle under her left arm, her bay's reins held at an equally precise angle in her right. The blue-dyed rooster feathers mounted in a socket at the top of the light dress helm fluttered across her arm in the light breeze. Her brown hair had been braided and coiled atop her head with the same military precision that characterized the rest of her equipage.

This was the first time Vanyel had seen his sister "on duty," or in any kind of official capacity. She was certainly a far different creature from the careless, untidy hoyden he remembered her being as a child, or even the wild rogue she could become off-duty.

"Captain Ashkevron." Withen returned her salute, visibly torn between worry and pride.

"Permission to bivouac the troops, sir."

"Granted." Pride won out, and Withen beamed. "The South Home Pasture's been vacated; it's all yours, Captain."

"Thank you, my lord," she replied formally. "Sergeant Grayse, front and center!"

A Guardsman with a brown, round face that seemed vaguely familiar to Vanyel marched crisply from the front rank to Lissa's right stirrup, and waited.

"South Home Pasture; lead the troops there and bivouac. I'll join you shortly."

The sergeant saluted and pivoted, heel and toe, and Vanyel realized why he seemed familiar; Grayse was one of the holding families, and this solid young man must be one of the sons. He barked out a series of orders as Lissa moved her horse off the road, turned again, and stepped out with the rest of the troop following as promptly as if they hadn't just spent all day on their feet. Lissa stayed on her horse at semi-attention until the last of her troop was out of sight, then grinned and tossed Vanyel her helm. She dropped her horse's reins as she vaulted out of her saddle, ground-tethering him. As soon as her feet hit the ground she made straight for Withen.

Vanyel caught the tumbling helm as she flung her arms around her father's neck and kissed him soundly, and then he held it out of the way as she made it his turn for an enthusiastic embrace, an embrace which he returned one-handed.

"Well, Father," she said, after kissing Vanyel just as thoroughly. "What do you think of my youngsters?"

"Fine!" Withen glowed. "Damn fine! Gods, I hardly knew my little daughter, up there on her warhorse and in her uniform and all!"

"I've never seen you on duty either, Liss," Vanyel reminded her. "I think you look wonderful."

She hugged him again, then stood beside him with her arm around his waist. "I'm just sorry it has to be under alert-conditions," she said soberly. "I'm sorry, Father. The last thing I ever wanted to do was—"

"Don't worry about it," Withen interrupted. "Now, is there anybody you want to quarter at the keep?"

"My Healer; I want him to have an infirmary set up. I bivouac with the troops."

Withen looked a little disappointed, but Vanyel found himself grinning with approval. "Good!" he said. "I didn't think it was my place to say anything, but it seemed to me down at the Karsite Border that all the best officers stayed with their troopers."

"So I'm told," Lissa replied. "Don't worry, Father, you'll see more of me than you think." She hugged Vanyel hard. "Come on, little brother, help me get this nag in a stall, hmm?"

He let her go and handed back her helm. She caught up the bay's reins and walked beside him to the stable.

"Lord Marshal doesn't like the way things are shaping up," she said in a quiet voice as soon as they got out of earshot. "Vedric has been making himself into the Linean patron saint, what with supporting their protests to Randale and all. I *wish* I knew what he was up to; this doesn't square with any of the intelligence I've had on him up until now. As for you, my impetuous little brother, I've got *official* orders that if I find Tashir I'm to take him in, but I've also got this—"

She reached into her belt-pouch and took out a much-creased note with Randale's private seal on it, and handed it to him. Vanyel noticed that it was addressed only to her, and opened it.

Captain Ashkevron; it read. *Show this to your brother—you know which one I mean. This is an order. It overrides any other orders you may receive until you hear differently under my hand and seal. You haven't seen either Vanyel or the boy Tashir Remoerdis. You won't see them until I tell you that you have. Randale.*

Vanyel handed it back to her with no other comment than a slightly raised eyebrow.

"He's covering for you, Van," she said worriedly, "but he can't do that for much longer. Have you got any idea of what you can do?"

"Not at the moment," he told her. "But I soon will."

His generous room seemed very crowded with both Savil and Jervis sprawled across the window seat and a chair, respectively.

"Ideas?" Vanyel asked, looking from Savil to Jervis and back again. "I've got one, but I want to hear yours first."

Savil wedged herself in the window seat, back flat against one wall, feet braced against the opposite wall, fingers laced together across her knees. "You said you went across the Border to get answers," she said, as if she was thinking out loud.

"And I found them—some of them," he agreed, eyes half-closed, staring at the patterns that firelight and shadows made on her Whites.

"But you also found more questions. I'm wondering if you just weren't there long enough. And I wonder if we *all* really ought to go back there. With two Adept-class mages it ought to be ridiculously simple to come up with illusion-disguises for four of us."

"Hide the boy in plain sight you mean?" Jervis was sitting backwards on one of the straight-back chairs, with his chin resting on his arms. He'd blinked sleepily while Savil spoke. Now he raised his head and looked alert. "I like that! Last place they're going to look for the boy is back where he came from!"

Vanyel nodded. "That was something of the same idea I had. We could further confuse the issue—go across the Border as, say, four Heralds making up a peace envoy to Vedric. Once outside Highjorune, we could switch to magic disguises and come into the city by pairs—Jervis and me, Tashir and Savil. One thing they won't be expecting, and that's Tashir with a woman. We meet up at an inn, say, on the better side of town. I could be a Bard this time, instead of a minstrel; you lot could be my entourage. Nose around, see what we can find out."

"Van, I think you and I need to actually get into the palace," Savil put in, staring up at the ceiling. "I think we ought to try and find out exactly what happened and what that attack was. If it was magic, that alone would rule Tashir out."

"Hmm." Moisture beaded the outside of his goblet. He ran his finger down the side, collecting the droplets, and traced little patterns on the table in front of him with a wet forefinger. "Do you think getting Tashir back into the palace might trigger his memory as well?"

"It might," Savil said, moving her gaze down until she caught his eyes. "It's worth a try."

"Then let's do it."

"I never thought I'd see *this* nag cowed!" Jervis chuckled, the rising sun at his back throwing their shadows far ahead of them on the dark-paved road. Three of the four shadows were as long-limbed and graceful as the Companions that threw them. The fourth crow-hopped from time to time as the raw-boned, ugly stud Jervis sat made his displeasure as obvious as he could.

Savil laughed. "He doesn't look too cowed to *me*!"

"Compared to what he was like before your two ladies chased him up and down the paddock all night, he's an angel!" Jervis chuckled, reaching out and hitting the stud between the ears with his fist when he bucked a little too hard. The gray stud squealed and laid his ears back; an answering squeal from Kellan and a showing of her formidable teeth settled him back down.

"I hate to think what Meke is going to do to me when he finds out what we've done," Vanyel murmured. He was still feeling guilty about "borrowing" the stud without a "by your leave."

"What else were we going to use?" Savil asked in a sweetly reasonable tone of voice, as Yfandes snorted. "That blasted stud of Meke's was the closest thing to white on the holding, besides being the only beast with the endurance to keep up with three Companions!" She chortled. "Come to that, he's a good match for Jervis as a Herald, provided you're seeing the real Jervis and not the glamour you put on him."

Jervis *did* make a very unlikely looking Herald. Tashir fit a set of Vanyel's cast-off Whites, left from when *he* was seventeen, fairly well. Vanyel and Savil *had* their uniforms, of course. But for Jervis it had been a case of hasty make-do. He wore one of his own shirts, and had squeezed himself into a pair of Vanyel's white breeches, but they'd had to sacrifice a sleeveless leather tunic of Savil's, opening the seams on both sides and punching holes, then lacing it onto him. He wore his own boots—brown—but they hoped no one would notice that.

"So long as we aren't dealing with anyone who can see through the glamour we'll be all right."

"Are you sure any spy Vedric might have on the Border won't pick this up?" Savil asked.

"Well, Heralds are *supposed* to feel a little of magic. A *full* illusion would radiate *far* too much, but an enhancement should pass without any trouble."

"But won't Vedric pick up the illusion-disguises once we're in town?" Jervis said suddenly. The stud took advantage of his distraction to try to buck him off.

Yfandes nipped the stud's flank, Kellan kicked him, and Jervis bashed him between the ears, all simultaneously. Vanyel choked down a laugh.

The stud shrilled his indignation, but settled again.

"He would, if the ambient magic in Highjorune wasn't going to mask *my* relatively weak spells. The illusion is *only* going to be on the Companions, to make them something else. Hardly a whisper on the wind."

The stud tried to rid himself of the bit. "You fixed his outside," Jervis said wistfully. "If you could only do something about the *inside* of his ugly head. . . ."

Held to the pace of the stud, it took them three days to reach Highjorune. To pass the gates, Kellan and Ghost became donkeys led by an old peasant woman and her son. Vanyel became a Bard on a showy gold palfrey, and Jervis his man-at-arms and general servant. If attention was to be drawn, Vanyel wanted it drawn to *him*.

And indeed, he drew enough attention coming through the gates to more than distract the guards from the old woman and her offspring behind them. Vanyel and Yfandes pranced and preened, sidled and danced—and in general made a thoroughgoing nuisance of themselves. Jervis grunted, looked long-suffering, and earned the sympathy of the gate guards. The stud tried to take off someone's hand and got a fist in his teeth for his trouble.

No row taverns for Vanyel, not this time. He lodged in the best inn in Highjorune, right across from the residency of the Master of the Weaver's Guild. *Not* so incidentally, that put the palace and all its mage-energies and shield-spells between him and the house where Lord Vedric was staying. Hopefully, any disturbances the illusions were creating would be lost in the greater wash of the shields and the node beneath the shields.

"Somebody's tried to break the shields," Vanyel observed, staring fixedly out the window.

"You can tell that from here?" Jervis asked, surprised, looking up from sharpening his dagger.

"Uhm-hmm." Vanyel probed deeper, and let his eyes unfocus. "I can even tell what spells he used. And that it was a *he* and not a *she*. Nobody I recognize, but I'd bet it was Vedric."

"Couldn't you—I don't know—get a look at Vedric so you'd know for certain?"

Vanyel turned restlessly away from the window and shook his head. "No. Probing him to get his signature would tell him I was here. Having the palace between us wouldn't hide me long if he started looking for another mage. I don't like it, though. I wish I knew for certain. And I wish I knew why whoever it was tried to breach the shields. It can't be pure curiosity, not with spells that powerful being used. Oh, I can *guess* that it's Vedric, and that he wants to get in there to destroy some kind of evidence, but I'd much rather know for certain if my guess is wrong or right."

"Well, *I* wish Savil and the boy would get here," Jervis growled. "I don't like the notion of us bein' split up like this."

"I agree," Vanyel began, when a tap at the door interrupted him.

He whirled, but it was Jervis who answered it and with a grimace of relief let in Savil and Tashir.

"Where in *Havens* have you been?" he demanded. "You were s'pposed to be here long before sundown!"

"Detained," she replied, smugly. "And what I got was worth the delay! What would you two say to a motive for the Mavelans to destroy the entire Remoerdis Royal House?"

"What?" Jervis and Vanyel exclaimed simultaneously.

"We were playing peasants seeing the sights," Tashir said tiredly. "One of the sights is the Great Hall of Justice. They keep important documents in there, under glass, so that anybody who can read can see them. I remembered one of them was the treaty between Baires and Lineas and told Savil, so that's why we went there."

"It took a fair amount of Tashir playing gawker to give me time to read it; by then it was dinnertime, and they shooed us all out." Savil threw herself down in a chair beside the table, picked up the knife Jervis had been sharpening, and examined it critically. "What it all comes down to is this: if one of the two Royal Houses dies out—and there are provisions about it being 'through misadventure, pestilence, or acts of the gods,' in other words, it can't be because of *proven* assassination by the other House—the surviving House gets the thrones of both. And that's all in ink and parchment under the signature and seal of Elspeth. Remember? Valdemar oversaw the treaty in the first place, and Valdemar is responsible for administering the provisions of it."

"If I ever knew that, I'd forgotten it," Tashir confessed into the silence.

"In other words, if Tashir is declared guilty of murder, the Linean throne gets handed over to the Mavelans—and Valdemar has to *enforce* this?" Vanyel said, incredulously.

"In a nutshell," Savil replied.

"Great good gods—"

"That ain't real likely to make Valdemar popular around here," Jervis observed. "Not that they're real popular after Van runnin' off with the boy. And if that ain't a pretty good reason for the Mavelans to kill off the Linean House and slap the blame on Tashir—who's Linean, even if he was disinherited—I don't know what would be."

"Nor I," Savil agreed grimly. "*Very* tidy little plot. Well, Van, you wanted a motive."

"I certainly got one." He returned to the window, and stared out of it. "And I have an *excellent* reason for Vedric making himself so popular with the Lineans." There was still some lingering sunset afterglow to make the sky a pearly light blue—and against it, the palace loomed ominously dark.

"Exactly. When everyone finally gets around to checking that treaty, Vedric will be the *only* Mavelan the Lineans will accept. And they *might* even do it with good grace, if he's done his job right."

"Savil," he said slowly, "I think our very first order of business is going to be—"

"The palace," she supplied.

"These seals were definitely tampered with," Vanyel observed. "A little more power behind the attacks and the shields might well have come down."

Yfandes paced up beside him and extended her nose to the door, closing her eyes. :Blood-magic,: she judged. :Faint, but there. Most of the energy traces are ordinary sorcery, but whoever set the spells is used to using blood-magic, and that will taint everything he does.:

"Which means it's not Heraldic—which we figured. And probably not a local. Working mage-craft around here would get you into trouble with your neighbors quickly, but working blood-magic would get you caught and hung." Vanyel licked his lips, and glanced around at the darkened courtyard. Acting on a hunch from Savil, they'd cleaned out their belongings from the inn and brought everything with them. Now he was glad they had. He raised his voice just a little. "Conference—" he called softly.

Four humans and three Companions made a huddle. Mekeal's stud was tethered as far away as possible. "Whoever tried to break the shields used something tainted with blood-magic," he said. "Yfandes smelled it out. Now I have a problem of defense here. Jervis, Tashir, every time we pass the threshold we're going to weaken those shields further. I think maybe we'd better change our plans because I don't think those shields are going to take much more weakening, and the only way for me to reinforce them will be from inside."

"That won't necessarily work either," Savil observed. "You'll just be patching. The weak spot will still be there."

"Exactly." Vanyel nodded. "It isn't going to be pleasant, but what I'd like to do is to just cross once, to keep the strain to a minimum."

His immediate answer was a silence in which the sound of dead leaves skittering across the cobbles was enough to set his nerves jumping. "Set up in residence, until we figure out what happened, you mean?" Savil asked. He nodded. She pursed her lips, and gave a reluctant assent. "I'm inclined to agree. Blood-magic will break shields the way nothing else can, and I'd rather this place wasn't left open to tampering. But what about the Companions?"

"They leave," Vanyel said unhappily. Yfandes Sent a wordless burst of protest. "I'm sorry, but I can't think of any place that's safe for them inside the city walls. The west gate stays open at night, but it's guarded. If I put a no-see, no-hear spell on them, they'll make it out all right. And if Vedric detects it, it won't matter; the stir I'm going to make by opening the shield ought to keep him thoroughly occupied."

Jervis cleared his throat. "'Nother thing; we run into trouble, that way *they're* free t' run for help."

Vanyel bit his lip thoughtfully. "Good point. 'Fandes, *I* don't like it either, but—"

:I see no other recourse,: she answered, pawing the cobbles and radiating unwillingness.

"And you'll have to look after that damned stud."

:May I kick him if he won't behave?: she asked, raising her head and ears hopefully.

Vanyel grinned to himself. Other than Jervis, Yfandes had suffered the most from the stud's behavior; the beast kept trying to induce her to mate. "As much as you have to. From here to Karse if necessary. Be my guest."

:Then this is not altogether an unpleasant prospect. Kellan, Leshya—: She waited for the humans to remove their packs from the saddles, then trotted to the tethered stud and freed him with her strong white teeth. With heads high and eyes fixed on Vanyel with acute interest, they waited for him to cast the spell.

Since the four of *them* already knew that the four mounts were there, the spell had very little effect on the onlookers. But Vanyel could See them surrounded with a distorting shimmer that meant the cloaking was in effect. Yfandes Mindsent him a wordless wave of love and concern, and with the stud's reins still in her teeth, turned toward the open gate to the courtyard. Then, with squeals and nips, the three Companions drove the stallion out of the gates and into the swiftly darkening streets.

Vanyel focused his inner eye on the place where he meant to set a portal in the fabric of the shields, then moved his hands in a complicated, mirror-imaged gesture. Through closed eyelids, he Saw the energy walls of the shields part just enough to let a tall man through.

"It's open." He looked with outer eyes again, and watched Jervis feel his way along the invisible—but patently tangible—shield-wall, until he came to the spot opposite Vanyel. Vanyel wasn't sure which was funnier, his expression when he couldn't force his way past the shields, or his expression when he found the "hole."

"I can't hold this too long," he warned; the other three snatched up their packs and his, and Medren's poor, battered, secondhand lute, and hurried up the stone stairs as far as the double door. They waited, white against the dark bulk of the door, while Vanyel slipped across the boundary and re-sealed the shields behind himself.

He took the stairs slowly, and regarded the purely physical barrier. "Tashir," he began.

The boy looked at him in startlement.

"Young friend, this is where you see how *useful* that Gift of yours is. *My* strong suit is *not* Fetching, and I've only seen this door once, remember." Vanyel folded his arms and raised an eyebrow at him. "I also distinctly recall that I barred the door behind Lores. *You* surely remember what the door and bar look like, and your Gift *is* Fetching. Let's see you raise that bar."

"But—" Tashir began to protest. Savil looked as if she might object as well, but Vanyel silenced her with a look.

"Do it, Tashir. You're better at this than I am."

The young man took a deep breath, closed his eyes and took a wide-legged stance in what may have been an unconscious imitation of the one Vanyel had taken, and frowned.

Vanyel *had* been giving him what rudimentary instruction he could, when he could. It wasn't much. But as Vanyel had half suspected, away from the disapproval of his family and *into* an environment in which "magic" was actually encouraged, he'd begun practicing, probably in an attempt to get his rogue Gift under some kind of conscious control. All of them could clearly hear the grate of the bar in its sockets on the other side of the closed metal-sheathed door; Jervis clapped Tashir on the back, startling him, as the door creaked open a thumb's-breadth.

Vanyel did the same, a bit more gently. Tashir grinned at both of them, teeth flashing whitely in the first of the moonlight. "Good work, young man," Vanyel congratulated him. "Now let's get ourselves under cover be-fore somebody curious comes by."

Savil was already pushing the door open; the rest of them followed her into the absolute darkness of the entry hall. She waited until Vanyel had closed the door and rebarred it before fashioning a mage-light and sending it upward to dance and flare above her head.

"Gods!" she hissed, shocked at the extent of the wreckage in the next room.

Jervis moved past her to stand at the top of the stairs, shaking his head. "I've seen wars and looters that weren't *this* thorough. What'n hell did that?"

Vanyel glanced over at Tashir, who had lost his expression of triumph and had become very pale. His eyes were shadowed; his expression haunted. Vanyel put his hand lightly on the youngster's shoulder in encouragement, and felt him tremble.

Savil joined Jervis, oblivious to Tashir's distress, walking very slowly. "I can tell you what *didn't*," she said, unexpectedly. "Tashir."

The youngster jerked in startlement.

"You're sure?" Vanyel asked softly, feeling a tense core inside him go limp with relief. He really *hadn't* believed it was the boy, but still. . . .

"Positive. You get under the glare of the node-energy, and this place is dusted all over with magic." She closed her eyes, and reached out her hand as if to touch something. "There's a very old spell tied to the node that's rooted somewhere just ahead of us. But there's a second spell overlaid on the walls themselves, and *that's* what caused this mess. Van, let me handle that one; it's a trap-spell, and I'd rather you didn't trigger it."

"I'll second that. You're much better with set-spells than I am. Tashir, Jervis, did you understand that?"

Jervis nodded.

Tashir looked both frightened and hopeful. "She said that there was a magic spell on the palace that—did all this? But why does that eliminate me?"

"Because you haven't even Mage-*potential*. Your Gift isn't *magic,* as we use the term. Real magic leaves traces of itself behind, like the dust a moth's wings leave on your hands when you catch it. You *couldn't* have done something that would leave those traces; you're not capable of it; for you, manipulating mage-energies would be like trying to carry water in a bucket with no bottom."

"And that's good enough evidence for Valdemar," Jervis put in. "Trouble is, I'd bet it ain't good enough evidence for Lineas."

Tashir's face fell. "That's only too true," he said, crestfallen.

"So our job is to *find* good enough evidence for Lineas." Vanyel took on unconscious authority. "First off, let's clean out one of the smaller chambers and set up living quarters. Then we'll get some sleep; we'll be better off working by daylight."

Savil dropped out of her half-trance and rejoined them. "I agree. I don't want to tackle anything that tricky without a full night's sleep. Tashir, this was your home; what would be the best place for us to set up where we aren't likely to be seen or disturbed?" She shivered in a sudden chilly draft.

"*And* where we can build a fire; I don't fancy freezing to death in my sleep, and there's a winter bite to the air at night."

Tashir looked about; although he had lost some of his apprehension, there was still fear and great unhappiness in him that Vanyel could Sense without effort. *Small wonder. Everyone he ever knew died here.*

"The kitchen, I think," Tashir replied. "And there wouldn't have been anybody back there when—" He shuddered, and not from the cold.

"Another thing to consider," Vanyel said gravely. "We're all likely to come on some very grisly relics, and of us all, Tashir is the least used to such things. Tashir, *don't* go off alone. Stay with one of us; Jervis, by preference. If at any time this gets too much for you, just go straight back to the kitchen until you get yourself settled again. I *do* want you to try and remember what happened that night. I *don't* want a repetition of what you did in Mother's bower. It's not that I think you'll hurt anybody because I know you won't." He managed a little smile of encouragement. "It's that you'll be *noisy*, lad. There's not supposed to be anybody here. I'm sure Vedric has figured it out, but he might not dare act on his knowledge just yet. We want to keep him from having reasons. We don't need someone sending for your Uncle Vedric to lay the ghosts, now, do we?"

Tashir paled, and Vanyel was immediately sorry he'd mentioned either ghosts or Vedric. The youngster shook his head wordlessly.

"All right, then let's get to the first stage." He shouldered his pack; the others did the same. "Tashir, it's up to you. Find us that kitchen."

CHAPTER 13

N ONE OF THEM slept particularly well. The first light of dawn saw three of the four lying open-eyed and tense on their sleeping mats, held prisoner by cold, nebulous fears, each waiting for someone *else* to make a sound that indicated rising. Vanyel was actually the last to claw his way out of uneasy half-dreams, which wasn't surprising, considering how exhausted he was. *He* felt the wakefulness around him after a confused moment or two and made a mage-light without thinking. Three gasps of startlement answered the first flare of the light; three pairs of eyes reflected blue flickers back at him.

"If you were all awake," he said, still sleep-mazed and confused, "why didn't you just get up?"

He told Jervis later that—on reflection—he was surprised no one killed him for that question.

There were still usable supplies in the kitchen; dried, salted, or otherwise preserved, and the kitchen had its own pump and well, which solved the problem of where they were going to get water. Trying to ignore the nagging thought that they were robbing the dead, Vanyel helped Jervis cobble together a tolerable meal of bacon, tea, and biscuits.

They sat on folded blankets beside the hearth to eat it; the windowless kitchen was dark, and it somehow *echoed* more than it should. Even Jervis was affected by the somber atmosphere, casting surreptitious glances over his shoulder at the shadows behind him.

"I think we're going to have to divide our attentions," Vanyel said quietly, as they sipped their tea from an assortment of whatever containers had come to hand. "Does anyone object to my taking charge?" He waited, but no one said anything. "Fine. Savil, I'd like you to look into the trap-spell; find out what it does, or did, if you can. *And* how it was set here in the first place. Jervis, Tashir, I'd like you two to start going over the palace, room by room. Jervis, you've been in and out of highborn homes for a good part of your life; you know what *belongs* and what doesn't. I want you to look for anything that seems odd or out of place. Tashir, you're to try and trigger your memory of that night. While you're both at it, we need candles down here, and a bit more in the way of blankets and bedding would be nice."

"And you'll be—?" Jervis raised a thick, grizzled eyebrow. His tone was not accusatory, just inquiring. Once again he and Vanyel had achieved a delicately balanced friendship. It was beginning to grow into something closer and less tentative, something more like a reliable partnership.

A partnership built on respect, and concern for the boy. That Tashir had confessed his fictions hadn't hurt.

"I'll be doing exactly the same, but from the bottom up; I want you two to work from the top down." Vanyel grimaced. "I don't think things are going to be very pretty in the cellars, and, to be brutal, I'm the one of us most recently off a battle-line. I *don't* want Tashir to have to deal with the kind of things I may find down below. I *did* learn that your father wasn't holding any prisoners, Tashir, but I doubt the searchers spent much time in the cellars looking for victims."

Tashir blanched, and took a large, audible gulp of tea.

"Eventually there's one more thing I'll be doing—I've got a hunch that the magic-node beneath the palace plays a major part in the *why* of all this; I want to find out just what the connection is, if I can. There has to be some kind of a connection; I cannot believe that *Tayledras* Adepts just *left* a powerful node like that undrained and unattended. That kind of carelessness goes counter to everything I know about them. *Even if they were forced out,* they'd have come back to release the mage-lines and drain the node—if not the original clan, then the descendants, or allied clan. I think that old spell Savil mentioned is very likely to have something to do with that."

Tasks assigned, they parted. Vanyel had taken the cellars for another reason; he and Savil were the only ones capable of producing their own light without needing to resort to candles or lanterns. They *had* no such physical lights, and there obviously were no windows in the cellars.

He had cause to be grateful for a strong stomach before the morning was over. He'd been right about searchers not checking below. And Lores had not exaggerated the violence of the massacre in the least. Even this old, the shredded remains were appalling. But he had seen remains as bad, or worse, over the past year. And he began to discover a pattern: where there had been no people present, the damage to *things* was minimal, or nonexistent. The more people, the greater the damage.

He did find candles, and the wine cellar. The former he took up the

stairs and left at the kitchen landing; the latter he sealed. Half the casks had
been split and all the bottles shattered. And as for what remained intact—he
rather doubted anyone would ever want to drink from casks that had been
stained and spattered with—

Well, it was better not to dwell on it.

They could drink what they found in the kitchen, or water.

From the look of things, four of the servants had been drinking and
dicing down there when the disaster had struck. At least, he *thought* it was
four. There were four overturned mugs beside the dice and pile of coins, but
he couldn't find more than six hands before he gave up searching.

And the hands were the only parts still recognizably human.

It was odd though; four of those six hands had worn rings exactly like
the one the maid Reta had worn; dull silver with strange, dead-white stones.
Reta's ring had plainly been something other than ornament, but although
he Mindtouched one of the rings cautiously, Van could find nothing out of
the ordinary about it.

And yet he had seen a ring identical to these acting on his behalf. They
could be just the badge of the household, yet in magic-fearing Highjorune,
why would the ruler's own household wear something spell-touched?

Vanyel wondered; it all tied in, somewhere, somehow. He had to find
the key.

But answers were not forthcoming; not yet.

He lost track of time down there, and certainly under these circumstances his stomach was not likely to remind him. It felt like being on the
Border again; every muscle tensed and waiting for something to leap on him
from behind. And no Yfandes to guard his back. He'd never been so conscious of being completely alone before; he might easily have been the only
living being in the entire palace. And it was far too easy for his overactive
imagination to people the shadows beyond his mage-light with pathetic or
vengeful spirits.

When he finally completed his inspection of the cellars and their occasionally grisly contents, it was with profound relief that he climbed the
kitchen stairs to emerge, blinking, into brilliant light.

That was the first welcome surprise in a long while. Someone had taken
it upon himself to remove the bundles of candles. That same someone had
stuck them on every available surface all over the kitchen, and lit them.
Light transformed the look of the place from that of a gloomy cave to a
normal island of commonplace, a bright and cheerful haven of sanity. It was

a profligate use of candles, but there were hundreds of them. Vanyel stepped into the kitchen with a feeling of having left a little hell behind him.

Tashir and Jervis were by the hearth, sorting through several large bundles.

"Where's Savil?" Vanyel asked. He squinted into the light. "What time is it?"

Tashir jumped, and stared at Vanyel with a momentary expression of panic, as if he did not recognize him immediately. Jervis continued with his sorting, unperturbed. "She's tryin' to track down *where* that trap was set up," the armsmaster replied. "And it's early evening. Give us a hand here, eh? We come up with some likely stuff out of closets and chests; if you get it sorted out an' made up as beds, I'll see to dinner."

Jervis was as good as his word; by the time Savil drifted in, still a little unfocused, he had another fair meal put together.

The blankets, comforters, and sheets that Tashir and Vanyel had made into tolerably comfortable beds smelled strongly of sendle and lavender; proof enough that they'd been laid away in storage. Vanyel judged by Tashir's silence and white lips that the two had probably come across the same appalling signs and stains of slaughter that he had, though probably not the actual remains. The party that had searched the palace had most likely dealt with the actual bodies. Which was all to the good; if Tashir had seen what Vanyel had been dealing with, the boy might well have snapped. Vanyel gave Jervis high marks for unexpected sensitivity; in the state of nerves the young man was in now, one bloodstained sheet come upon in a bundle of bedding he was expected to *use* would likely send him into hysterics. Safer, far, to have searched out the linen closets and taken things sealed away for winter use.

And it was also probable that the pattern below had been continued above; rooms that had been occupied at the time of the massacre might not *have* anything usable in them anymore.

Savil wandered over to the fire and sat down absently on the bed nearest her pack. "Any luck?" he asked her. She shook off her vagueness and finally looked *at* him instead of *through* him.

"Yes and no. I think I've got the site narrowed to the second floor, and I think I know *how* it was set. Someone brought in a catalyst, then using that catalyst, enlarged and strengthened the spell's compass over a long period of time. With no shields on this place, it would have been apprentice work once the initial spell had been set." She accepted a plate from Jervis without looking at it. "It's nasty stuff, *ke'chara*. Makes my skin crawl. Hard to force myself to probe it, now that I know it's there. Like some kind of web with something incredibly evil at the heart—and I'm over on the edge of it, trying to see into the heart without waking what's there. And there's something very, very odd about it. It reeks of blood-magic, as you might well expect, but there's 'blood' involved in it in a *much* subtler way."

"Eat," Vanyel advised, guessing that she hadn't paused for food or drink since this morning. "Jervis, did you and Tashir find anything?"

The armsmaster chewed and swallowed before answering. "Maybe. If you're done below, I'd like your word on it. It's a room, first floor, smack square in the center of this building. Not much bigger than a closet, an' has just one thing in it; a floor-t'-ceiling pillar; same stone as the outside. Might just be a kinda kingpost for the palace, it's bigger around than I can reach, but I never seen anything like it. You said look for odd, well, that's odd."

"Tashir?"

The young man froze in mid-bite, and stared at him like a cornered rabbit.

Vanyel felt an uncomfortable sympathy for him. His own Empathy told him Tashir was dancing on a hair-thin thread of nerve at the moment. There was no doubt in Vanyel's mind that he *was* trying to jar his memories loose. There was also no doubt in his mind that the youngster was, literally, going through hell. But there was no help for it; if the mystery was to be solved and Tashir cleared of guilt, it was likely to take all four of them to do it.

"Tashir, what do you know about this room Jervis found?" he prompted.

Tashir swallowed and licked his lips. "Nothing," he replied faintly. "They wouldn't ever let me in there. Everybody else got taken in at least once, but not Mother, and not me."

"Tashir, that's *something*," Vanyel chided gently. "You said 'everybody'; do you mean that literally? Servants, too?"

The young man nodded so hard he started to tip his plate off his knee. Jervis caught it before it spilled. Tashir hardly noticed, he was so intent on Vanyel. "Servants, too, Vanyel. Everybody."

"That's more than odd; that's smacking of a mystery." He brooded for a moment, staring at the crackling flames in the hearth. He was greatly tempted to seek the place out now, this instant.

But then he thought of the empty rooms filled with wreckage and the long, haunted halls he'd have to traverse to get there. He hesitated, and shivered. Strong stomach, battle-trained or not, there was a limit.

I don't think so. I'm not up to it. Besides, I'd rather not chance a light being seen from outside. It'll be there in the morning.

"D-d-d-do you want to go there tonight?" Tashir stuttered, patently not relishing the thought at all.

"No, Tashir, not tonight," he replied, half-smiling as a rush of relief brought a little more color to the youngster's cheeks. "Not tonight," he repeated, echoing his own thought. "We've all had enough for one day. It's been there all this time; it'll be there in the morning."

Jervis broke the silence that followed. "Van, I was noticin' something. Rooms where there wasn't any folks, hardly anything's smashed. Maybe a curtain torn, chair broken, that kind of thing. Rooms where there was people, they're wrecked. The more people, the worse."

"It's the same down below," Vanyel told him, as Jervis continued demolishing his dinner thoughtfully. "Savil, does that kind of pattern suggest anything to you?"

She scowled with concentration. "Yes, but I can't think what. Damn!"

Vanyel followed a stray thought. "Tashir, when they broke in and found the mess, where were you?"

"Th-the Great Hall," he faltered. "I just sort of woke up and I was there."

"And the worst wreckage was in the Great Hall?" Vanyel turned to Jervis for confirmation.

"Near as I can tell from what I've seen so far."

As he tried to trigger his own memory, he had a momentary flash of that dream he'd had, of being surrounded by a whirlwind of devilish creatures. He realized with a start that made him sit up straight that *that* dream actually had an echo in *his* recent experience. The fire flared on the hearth, and with it, memory.

He'd been playing bait, at the beginning of the Karsite campaign, sitting all alone in an old keep just behind the Border.

The keep was supposed to be held by nothing more formidable than an old man and a handful of retainers. Certainly the Guard was days away at the best forced march pace, though that shouldn't have mattered. Because no one was supposed to know that the keep was held so weakly. And no one was supposed to know that it guarded a very strategic supply route.

But someone did know; someone had been leaking information to the Karsites. Poorly-guarded keeps of strategic importance behind the Valdemar lines were being decimated, the occupants slaughtered, leaving holes the strategists didn't learn about until it was too late. Or worse—when the strategists checked on their supposed hold-ings, they found keeps somehow occupied by hostile forces.

Vanyel read the signs of magic, and had known only magic could counter these attacks. So Vanyel had ridden Yfandes to exhaustion to reach this one, a likely target. He'd cleared out the old man and his following, and waited.

And the attack had come, in the form of a gretshke-Swarm; demi-demonic crea-tures (mostly head, teeth, and appetite) that, taken individually, were inconsequential. An ordinary fighter could deal with one—or two; they certainly were not immune to cold iron. But a Swarm—that was another matter. The Swarm contained hundreds, if not thousands, of the creatures. You could kill them by the dozens, and still they would overwhelm you, like encountering an avalanche of starving rats.

A mage didn't control a Swarm; he just unleashed it. When the food was gone, or when they were sated, they would return to their own plane if they were given an exit. So a mage using them would customarily lure a Swarm to the Portal to their plane that he had opened within his target area and cast a shield about the target to keep the Swarm from escaping. He would wait an appropriate length of time—usually no more than a candlemark; the Swarm was fast—and open the Portal again to pull whatever of the Swarm remained back to their own plane. He would take the shield down then, and an occupying force could move in.

All this required someone on the level of Adept; which made it likely that the mage in question was one of the three Adepts the Karsites had hired when they began this. One of the three had threatened, then launched the brutal incineration of an entire town; the town had been saved, but in stopping him, Mardic and Donni had called the flames on themselves in a desperate attempt to confine them.

It had worked. It had been a brave, unselfish—and ultimately fatal—ploy. The best that could be said was that their pain had been mercifully short.

Vanyel had been determined that before he was pulled off the lines, he would have that particular mage's life. By preference, given the other things they'd done, he would have all three, but he wanted that one.

The only problem was, the mages themselves refused confrontation, striking time and time again where he wasn't.

By the time of this ambush he'd had enough. He had begun hunting them with the patience and stealth that would eventually earn him the name "Shadowstalker" when he tracked down the second Adept.

But that was in the future; at that moment, the first step on his self-appointed road of revenge, he had been waiting in the darkened keep, fueling the delicate illusion that made it appear to that unknown enemy that only the old man and his dozen retainers and fighters were within those walls, and all were asleep.

He felt the shields go up; he felt the Portal open.

The Swarm descended on the Hall of the keep, where he waited for them beside the firepit in the center. And he threw up his own shield, abandoning the illusion, and watched as the Swarm ravened outside it, tearing the scant furnishings of the Hall to shreds in frustration, unable to reach the meat so tantalizingly out of reach.

While he smiled grimly and set up a second shield between the Swarm and the Portal. When the mage opened the Portal again, then established a probe to check on the results of his work, Vanyel would seize on the probe before he could withdraw it, and use it to send him an unexpected surprise.

It was the image of the Swarm shredding cushions, furnishings, and tapestries that interested him now; an image he sent swiftly to Savil, who seized on it with an exclamation. Jervis raised his eyebrow.

"We think we may have an explanation for all the destruction," Vanyel explained absently, as he and Savil conferred in Mindspeech. "It's complicated, and there's a lot of 'ifs' and 'buts.' It may take us a while to unravel them, but the explanation fits the current evidence."

Jervis just shook his head. "If that's magery, then it's too much for me, Van," he said, yawning. "I'll leave that to you. I'll just show you that room and let *you* deal with it, eh?"

"I'll do that," Vanyel replied, then turned his mind to looking for the traces that would tell him *what* kind of things had torn the hall to shreds—because that would tell him a great deal about *how strong* the enemy was—and importantly, might even give a clue as to *who*.

But in the end, he and Savil sought their beds without any answers but one. *How strong* was *very*. Adept at least.

Because the traces that would have distinguished what the trap-spell had unleashed had been skillfully wiped away. All that remained was the heavily camouflaged spell itself (which only an Adept could have detected under the camouflage) and the bare traces of *magic* that had alerted them in the first place.

Jervis and Tashir were already asleep when they gave up.

"Sleep?" he asked Savil, hoping she'd answer in the affirmative.

"We might as well. We aren't going to get anything more tonight." She stretched once, and began burrowing into her blankets, practically radiating exhaustion. Vanyel realized then what kind of strain she was under—all this complicated, involved sorcery, *and* maintaining her position as the Web's Eastern Guardian. He resolved to take more of the burden from her as soon as he could. This was not fair to her, nor was it good for her.

I wonder if there's a way to tie all the Heralds into the Web, as power-source at least. That would take fully half the burden off the Guardians.

"Want me to put out the candles?" he asked, glancing around at the burning tapers still bedecking corners of the kitchen.

She opened one eye thoughtfully. "No. Just leave them, if you would. It isn't as if we need to hoard them, and I don't think I want to go to sleep in darkness for a while."

Vanyel thought it over a moment, and nodded. "You know what, teacher-mine?" he said softly. "Neither do I."

She chuckled wearily, and closed her eyes again. "Absurd, isn't it? Here we are, two of the ranking Herald-Mages in Valdemar—afraid of the dark."

He wrapped himself up in his own blankets. "If you promise not to tell anyone, I won't either."

A light snore was his only answer, and he fell asleep with the comforting glow of the candles all about them.

The tiny room vibrated with power.

It was a round room; stone-walled and wooden-floored-and-ceilinged. The walls were pale sandstone, the rest pale birch. The pillar of stone clearly reached higher than the ceiling and lower than the floor. And the room, with barely enough space to walk around the dark pillar was, very clearly, set up with permanent shields, like those in the communal magic Work Room at the Palace in Haven. Small wonder neither he nor Savil had detected this artifact before. Vanyel set a cautious hand to the pillar of charcoal-gray, highly polished stone, as Tashir and Jervis watched him curiously. It was warm, not cool, and felt curiously alive.

And very familiar.

This was a *Tayledras* heart-stone. The Vale of k'Treva had such a stone, a place where the physical, material valley itself merged and melded with the energy-node and intersection of power-flows "below" it. Such a stone was the physical manifestation of the energies fueling the *Tayledras* magics, and this physical manifestation was peculiarly vulnerable to tampering. So the heart-stones were guarded jealously—and *always* deactivated when *Tayledras* left a place.

This one *should not* be here, except, perhaps, as a dead relic of former inhabitants. It should not be alive, and more, responding to his touch, physical and magical, upon it.

"This—" He faltered, and pulled his hand away with a wrench. "Jervis, you were right. This is *not* something I would expect here. I'm going to have to Mindtouch it."

"Anything we can do to help?" the armsmaster asked quietly.

"To tell you the truth, I'd rather you took Tashir out to the Great Hall to see if you can help him remember," Vanyel said, trying to keep the fascination of the heart-stone from recapturing him. "There isn't much you can help me with, and you two *being* here would be a little distracting. But if you'd poke your nose in here from time to time—"

"Anything I should watch for?"

"Well," Vanyel replied wryly, "if I'm turning blue, that's probably a sign something's wrong. Other than that, trust your own judgment."

Jervis' answering laugh was gruff, and sounded a little like churning gravel, but it proved that of the four of them, he was the one least affected by their macabre surroundings. "All right, let me take the boy out, and we'll see if we can make some progress."

"Thanks." *And thank you, Jervis, that we can trust each other now. I don't think I could be doing this otherwise.* Without waiting to see them go, Vanyel turned back to the stone pillar, and placed both palms and his forehead against it—

And it took him into itself.

For a very long time he was conscious only of the incredible, seething maelstrom of the energy-node itself. It was like plunging into the heart of the sun, and yet remaining curiously unscathed and untouched. It was different from tapping into the node; there he was outside, separate from the energy he sought to control, and he was dealing with a single, thin stream of force. Now he was a part of the force, with no intent—or chance—to control it. But control was not what he wanted; he wanted only observation, and answers.

But to have an answer, one must first ask a question. He framed it in his mind, carefully inserting all the nuances into it he could.

In words, it would have been a simple "Who left this here?" In thought, it was infinitely more complex than that; asking "who" specifically, and "who" as a class.

The heart-stone was not an intelligence, but it *remembered.* And every question that was balanced by an answer would call that answer out of the stone. Vanyel got a very clear picture of *Tayledras* Adepts; several of them, all of them radiating great power, including one with the peculiar blue-green aura of the rare Healer-Adept. That particular Adept was much clearer, and lingered longer in the mind, and the implication was that it was this Healer-Adept that was responsible for having left both stone and node still in their active state.

If Vanyel could have started with surprise, he would have. Although they could, and on occasion *did,* act as ordinary Healers, *Tayledras* Healer-Adepts concerned themselves with Healing, not people, but environments. At restoring the balance nature had intended. At Healing the hurts that either magic or the hand of man had dealt there. That a Healer-Adept would have deemed it necessary to *leave* this potentially disastrously-dangerous energy source in lands soon to be settled by ordinary humans—that seemed to indicate that there was a terrible need that overrode all other considerations.

"Why?" he asked, urgently.

And felt himself being drawn down—deeper—below the bedrock, and into the roots of the earth itself. And he realized with a shock that the pillar was that deeply rooted, too.

There was tension here, a tension that increased as he went deeper, a vast pressure to either side of him that squeezed him until he could scarcely breathe. And still the force that had seized him to answer his question drew him deeper, and deeper still, to a point where the rock began to warm about him.

Then he saw it. Running from north to south, invisible from above, yet carrying implied within it such peril that his blood ran cold, was a crack in the last layer of rock itself. A fault, a place of slippage, following the river bottom.

That was natural enough; what was *not* natural was the hole punched through the fault down to the molten core of the planet, something probably left from the Mage Wars. *That* was what the heart-stone was planted above.

And all of Highjorune was built directly on that fault. More, it extended the width of Lineas and out into the unsettled lands. If it slipped—

And it was only a matter of time before it slipped and caused a catastrophe that would destroy the city in fire and earthquake—and much of the surrounding country beside. Vanyel could not imagine why it hadn't happened *before* this—until he *Saw* where the energy of the node was going.

It was feeding into a complicated spell so convoluted and involved he could *never* have set it himself. It could only be the handiwork of that *Tayledras* Healer-Adept—and it looked to be the masterwork of an entire lifetime as a mage and an Adept. It was holding the wound closed, and keeping the fault from slipping.

More, it would, given time enough, *Heal* the wound and the fault, re-distributing the strain elsewhere, until this was no longer an area of insta-bility. But it would take time, hundreds of years or more, and any great siphoning away of the node-energy would deprive the spell of needed power. And if *that* occurred—depending on the amount of energy stolen from its proper usage, there would come anything from a minor tremor to the major, devastating disaster the Adept had been trying to prevent.

The force that had him let him go, and he drifted back to the "surface" more than a little dazed.

But he still had one more question. What was the connection between Tashir's family and this artifact at the heart of their palace?

That answer came immediately, and almost as words.

They were the Guardians.

And with that came a rush of knowledge that rocked him physically away from the stone. He opened his eyes to find himself pressed back against the wall, staring at the pillar of dark, volcanic basalt, with his mind seething with information.

He staggered out of the tiny room, carefully closing the door behind him, and made his unsteady way into the kitchen, bypassing the Great Hall entirely. He wanted to lie down, very badly. This was not the first time he'd queried a heart-stone, but it was the first time one had responded with such a flood of facts and memories. The heart-stones *he'd* merged with had been slow, old, and so peaceful that the answer you wanted might take *candlemarks* to drift within grasping. By contrast, this one practically flung responses at you before you finished the question.

He made the kitchen easily enough, and spent some time sticking up new candles and lighting them before wobbling back to his bed and falling facedown into the blankets.

He must have slept, because the next thing he knew, the others were clattering about the kitchen, there was a smell of frying bacon, and his stomach was declaring war on his backbone.

He rolled over on his back, stiffly, painfully, and Savil immediately knelt at his side and peered into his eyes. "You were in shock-sleep," she said. "We couldn't wake you. I hope to hell you got something worth it."

He took a deep breath, and discovered that his ribcage was sore, that all his muscles ached. He must have held them tensed for hours. He nodded. "Answers," he said—croaked, rather. "I got answers. I got *answers*. Savil, that's a heart-stone in there. And it's awake!"

Her mouth had dropped open the moment he'd said the words "heart-stone." She shut it again with a snap. "Eat first, and get something to drink. *Then* tell us."

He sat up slowly, more than ever grateful for all the soft comforters to cushion his aching body from the stone floor of the kitchen. There was a fire in the hearth, and the other three seemed warm, but he was cold—cold.

Jervis shoved a plate into his hand, Tashir a cup of tea into the other. Savil and Jervis then pretended to deal with the remnants of their dinners. Tashir made no such pretense, hovering at Vanyel's side and watching every mouthful he took with impatience.

It was a little embarrassing, but Vanyel could not find it in his heart to blame him.

When he put down the empty plate, the other two gave up all pretensions and hovered around him.

"I'll try to make this short," he said, feeling a little awkward with all their attention so fixed on him. "This palace is situated on top of a place where several lines of magical energy meet and collect—we call that a 'node.' Nodes—the very powerful ones, that is—frequently aren't natural. They can be created artificially by a particular group of Adepts called the *Tayledras*—the 'Hawkbrothers.'" At Jervis' and Tashir's look of blank nonrecognition, he added, "They live in the Pelagirs. Most people have never heard of them. Fewer still will ever see them. Savil and I are among the few."

Savil nodded. "They're very secretive, and for a good reason. They do—almost as naturally as breathing—something damned few other mages are even capable of *imagining*. They manipulate the energy fields of the world around us."

Vanyel interrupted her gently. "They do two things, really; they drain magic left from the old wars away from lands that ordinary people are moving into, and they use that magic both to Heal those lands and to create sanctuaries for magical creatures that are displaced by the folk moving in. When they settle in a place, they generally create a node under it to use. When they *leave* that place they *always*—or so *I* always thought—deactivate and drain the node, and reroute the power-lines running to it."

"That's what Starwind always told me," Savil agreed, shifting her position so that she rested her chin on her knees.

"Well, they didn't this time," Vanyel replied. "The node is *still* fully active, and the heart-stone that is the physical link to it is still alive. That's what that pillar is, Tashir, the heart-stone. And that brings me to *why*."

He licked his lips and closed his eyes for just a moment, to center himself. "Some time when people first moved into this area, Tashir, one of the *Tayledras* remained behind, and selected your remote forefather to be the hereditary guardian of the heart-stone. He charged him to keep it safe, and to see that *no one* in Lineas ever dabbled in magic. That charge has been passed down to *everyone* with the blood of the Remoerdis Family—because that blood carries Mage-potential with it, and because that very wise ancestor of yours saw no reason to limit the guardianship to a favored few. The more guardians, he thought, the safer—and I think he was right. After all, this has gone on for generations without *any* inkling of the power here leaking outside of Lineas. That's the meaning of those rings everyone—except you and your mother—wore. They link the wearer to the heart-stone and the guardianship, and the spell that binds wearer to ring and to the guardianship allows the stone to act upon *the wearer* to keep them safe, and to safeguard itself. I actually saw that last in action—your mother's maid Reta was moved by the heart-stone to tell me some of what I needed to know. It was quite uncanny; she acted for all the world as if someone had put a second-stage Truth Spell on her. Back to the subject. *You* didn't get one, and weren't sealed to the stone, because your father didn't believe you were of his blood. To settle *that* question, the stone says otherwise. The stone recognized you as being of the blood the moment you entered the room. You *are* the true-born son of Deveran Remoerdis of Lineas. And if your father had ever conquered his own doubts and suspicions, and allowed you into the room, even as an infant, he would have known that, too."

Tashir hung his head, and Vanyel could see his shoulders shaking. He laid his hand on top of one of the youngster's, and Jervis put his arm around the young man's shoulders for a moment.

"Now—the reason *why* the node was left active; there's an instability underneath Lineas; *right* underneath Highjorune. The node is literally holding it together. If it were to be disturbed, *especially* if it were to be drained, as a careless or ignorant mage might manage, Highjorune would certainly be destroyed by a terrible earthquake, and quite probably all of Lineas, a good section of Baires, and even some of Valdemar. *That* is why the people of Lineas have been trained to shun and discourage mages. *That* is what your people have held in trust for centuries—and I think that the power of the node is also why the Mavelans want Lineas. Unfortunately, I suspect they see only the powerful node, and have made no effort at discovering why it is there."

"I doubt they'd care," Savil said dryly.

"I wish I knew differently." He put down his mug, and rested his forehead on his own knees. "Gods," he said, his voice muffled. "Well, we have part of the puzzle."

He felt a hand on his shoulder; Savil's. "Tired, *ke'chara?*" she asked.

"Not *tired*, precisely," he replied, raising his head and smiling into her eyes. "Just a little—divided. You know what querying a heart-stone is like; you become part of it. It's *hard* being a rock; they have such a strange sense of time—and priorities." He shook off his feeling of disorientation and patted her hand. "No matter, now that I've got that solved, I can help you with that trap-spell. If you can get me safely inside it, I *think* I can unravel the components enough to tell what triggers it and what it acts on."

"We're getting somewhere, too," Jervis put in diffidently. Tashir raised his head and sniffed, once, then scrubbed the tears from his cheeks with the back of his hand and nodded. "You want to tell 'em, Tashir, or you want me?"

"I can," he said, though his voice quavered a little. "I remember *why* those things couldn't get me the way they got the others. I was—pushing them away with my head. I remember doing that; I remember them trying to get at me, and I remember just shoving—like this—"

He screwed up his face with effort, and Vanyel found himself being pushed across the floor, away from the boy, bedding and all. When he reached out his hand, he encountered what was almost a surface, as if the air itself had solidified.

Tashir dropped the effort with a gasp. "It hurts to do that," he said, "but it hurt less when I was scared."

Vanyel nodded. "And the reason that the others held their attackers off for a little while—which was why the rooms with people in them were torn apart—was because of the rings. The stone told me that there's some limited protections spelled into the rings by the ceremony of binding. Unfortunately those protections were mainly meant to be used against someone trying to probe a guardian's mind, not against someone trying to kill him."

"One more day should see us with all the answers," Savil observed.

"Let's just hope they aren't answers we don't want to hear," Jervis replied grimly.

Sensitized by the heart-stone to what magically *should* and *should not* be associated with the palace itself, Vanyel took the lead the next morning, making a check of every room in the palace. Once they found the trap-spell catalyst, they would have a much better chance of unraveling the roots of the spell itself.

There was nothing on the first floor, and nothing in the private quarters, not even Ylyna's. But when they reached the guest rooms—

The taste of evil was in the air of the primary suite so thick that Vanyel could hardly believe that Savil didn't sense it, too. This was a set of five rooms reserved for the most important of visitors, the suite that the Mavelan representatives had undoubtedly occupied during the signing of the treaty and the wedding. The effluvium of *wrong* was strongest in the reception chamber, a room of linen-paneled walls hung with weaponry and the heads of many dead animals, and furnished with a variety of impractical and uncomfortable unpadded wooden chairs, and one large desk. He traced it, growing more and more nauseated by the moment, to, of all things, an ornamental dagger hung in plain sight on the wall above the hearth.

He didn't touch it—he couldn't bear to—but he didn't need to. It had been there for years; perhaps as long as eighteen or twenty. The spell had been given plenty of time to permeate through the physical fabric of the palace like a slow poison in the veins of an unsuspecting victim.

"That's it?" Savil said incredulously. "I must have passed this room a dozen times."

Vanyel shrugged, and found himself a marginally comfortable chair. They were likely to be here a long while, once Savil got started. "Did you test that dagger, or were you looking for something hidden?" he asked.

"Something hidden," she admitted ruefully, walking slowly and reaching for—but *not* touching—the dagger. Her eyes unfocused. "That's it," she replied after a moment.

"All right. I'll link to you, and you slip me inside the spell," Vanyel told her, bracing himself in the chair. "Get out as soon as you can; you've been draining yourself quite enough as it is."

"Not as much as you, *ke'chara*," she retorted, her lips thinning, as she took a seat on the floor at his feet, and laid her hands over his wrists.

"But *I'm* not a Web-Guardian," he pointed out with ruthless logic. "Come on; let's get this over with."

He closed his eyes and evoked a light trance-state, *centered*, then *reached* for a deeper level of Savil than he touched in Mindspeech.

Like hand taking hand, he linked with her, followed her blindly through a twisting, torturous maze of fire and shadow and confusing shapes in which the slightest misstep would mean things he preferred not to think about.

Savil knew what she was doing; if *she* couldn't weave her way through this thing, no one outside of k'Treva could.

:Brace yourself, love. I'm going to toss you in.:

He "made" himself as compact and small a "bundle" as he could—and felt himself hurled—

He crawled on hands and knees into consciousness. He opened burning eyes, his stomach in knots, his head pounding, and wanting a bath more than he'd ever wanted anything in his life. He felt filthy inside as well as out.

Savil was still kneeling beside him, holding both of his cold hands in hers, staring intently into his eyes. "You're back," she said.

"I'm back," he replied, swallowing bile. "You won't like it."

"I don't like it now." She released his hands, and he rubbed his eyes with his knuckles.

"Remember what you said, about 'blood' being involved very subtly in this? It is; and given what I found out about the guardianship of the heart-stone, it's sickeningly logical. When this spell is triggered *on* someone, it not only goes for them—but for *everyone* sharing blood-relationship with that person that is also a mage or carries the potential. *Everyone*, right down to babes in the womb."

Savil's face grayed a little. "So whoever did this—"

"I've got that, too. Last person to trigger it was *dear* Uncle Vedric Mavelan. Last person targeted was Tashir. So much for all his protests about wanting to help the lad."

"Tashir?" Her voice rose at least half an octave. "But then—that means that Vedric *knew* the boy wasn't his!"

Vanyel grimaced, and tried to sit up straighter. "Exactly. He knew it all along, and made *no* attempt to clear either his sister, or the youngster. Now, I have a few guesses as to why there seem to be inconsistencies. The biggest is why the maid Reta I spoke to survived. My *guess* is that Vedric shielded the palace to avoid blood in the streets and the question of why Tashir would murder people he didn't even know existed. If he hadn't, it's pretty likely that people would have looked elsewhere for a perpetrator, rather than to Tashir. And that shield would explain why the Mavelans weren't at-tacked, since they were related to Tashir through Ylyna."

"And why Ylyna was killed with everyone else; she must have been carrying Mage-potential," Savil mused aloud.

"The thing is—this is a trap that resets itself. Until we destroy the maker, anyone that knows how can set it against anyone else."

He sat bolt upright, as the shields on the palace buckled and weakened under a furious attack.

"Did you—" Savil exclaimed, blanching. "—gods, of course you felt that; they're your shields. There's somebody out there trying to get in!"

"*Will* get in," Vanyel corrected grimly, launching himself out of the chair. "It's Vedric. He knows we're in here. He's probably figured out that we know what happened—or soon will. He can't afford to let us escape."

The shields shrieked in his mind as another attack battered at them. Vanyel started down the hall at a run, followed by his Aunt.

:*Yfandes!*: he called, snaking the Mindtouch around Vedric, hoping the mage would be too preoccupied with his attack to sense it

:*Here*—:

Grateful that thought took less time to send than words, he told her all they'd learned. :*Time to run for it, love. Have Kellan stay with the stud, you and Ghost head over the Border at top speed. Vedric's on to us. If we lose this*—:

:*I will see that the Kingdom knows,*: she replied grimly. :*I will see you avenged. Then I will come to you.*:

She cut him off before he could protest, and there was no more time to spare for protests.

"We have," he cast over his shoulder at Savil, "maybe a candlemark or two to figure out what we're going to do."

CHAPTER 14

THEY SKIDDED INTO the Great Hall, feet slipping on the debris, startling Jervis and Tashir considerably as they came to a halt beside them. Savil held her side and panted a little.

"What—" Jervis began.

"Vedric's out there," Vanyel interrupted him. "He's trying to break through the shields. I expect he knows we're in here; I expect he figures we've learned the truth of what happened. *He's* the one that triggered the trap-spell; he used Tashir for the target, and the damned thing's set to take *anyone* of the bloodline of the target with Mage-potential."

Tashir had been sitting on a cleared space on the floor. He stood, slowly, his expression frozen, his face drained. *"I remember,"* he said, his voice tight and strained, *"I remember now."* He turned away from them, and pointed a shaking hand at the door that led to the second-floor stairs. "I was running down those stairs. I was going to run away. I told Father that—I told him that I'd rather dig ditches than go to Baires. He laughed at me, he said he doubted I had the spine—and I hit him. I didn't mean to, but it just happened. I was afraid he'd do something horrible and I ran. I ran through here and out the door, and—and—*I couldn't get out!* It was like hitting a wall! I didn't even think, I just turned around and started running for the stable door, and when I got *here*—" He pointed at his feet. "I—it—happened. Like, I don't know, like a whirlwind, only there were all these teeth and eyes, and pretty soon it was filling the whole room and tearing everybody and everything around into *shreds*—"

His voice spiraled up into hysteria, and Jervis shook his shoulders.

"Tashir, come on, lad, we've got troubles *now*, don't you fall apart on me."

The young man shivered like a trapped rabbit, but he nodded, and there was still some sense in his eyes.

"I repeat; Vedric's out there." Vanyel shuddered as he felt his shields buckle a little more. "He'll be in *here* soon. I sent the Companions out of here; Kellan's minding the stud, she and Ghost and Yfandes are going for home. One way or another, the truth is going to get out, but there's only one way out now for us. Savil, I'll hold him, while you build a Gate and get Jervis and Tashir out of here."

She nodded, face gray and grim. "Where?"

"Haven, by choice; no one is going to extract him from Randale's hands once he hears the whole story." He was only giving half his attention to the conversation; the other half was busy weaving reinforcements to his disintegrating shields.

"But—" she protested.

"Dammit, Savil, just *do* it; *I* can't. Gating that far would probably kill me!"

"Vanyel," she interrupted urgently, "what happens when he triggers the trap on *you*?"

He felt himself pale, felt his spellcasting falter. "Oh, gods—let me think—*you* should be all right if I can just hold him off long enough for you to alert somebody to protect you. Medren is Bard-Gifted with no Mage-potential, he should be safe enough. My sibs—no potential. Father!"

"Is safe," she told him. "How do you think I got half these white hairs? I spent a week in the nodes weaving protections for him when I first met Starwind. When I realized how powerful an Adept I was, I also realized that very few enemies were going to be able to come at me directly, so they *might* choose to come at me through my brother. I made *sure* there was no chance of that while I had the energy and leisure. Is there *anybody* else?"

"No," he said. But his mind was screaming the real truth at her even as his lips formed the lie. *:Savil! Jisa—oh, gods, the children—:*

:What?:

He grabbed her shoulders so tightly it surely must have hurt enough to leave bruises as his fingertips dug into the flesh. *:I have three children. Brightstar and his twin are in k'Treva, under their own shields, Starwind's and Moondance's, so they're safe enough, but Jisa—*

:Jisa? How? Why?:

His thoughts were not particularly ordered or coherent, but he did his best to get the sense across to her. *:Savil, don't ask; she's mine by blood, Randale and Shavri wanted it, that's all you need to know. She's not under shield.:* He wanted to *pound* the fear he felt for them into Savil. *:And Shavri's at risk through Jisa. I don't know if Shavri's got the potential or not. You have to get back there—gods—I never meant anyone else to know, but there's no choice—Jays. Trust Jays. Tell him the truth; I think he'll understand.* No one else. *Gods, if Randale* *was only a mage—go, Savil!:* The battering at his shields grew fiercer. *:Just go! I can't hold him much longer!:*

He released her shoulders, and Savil turned without another word and faced one of the open doorways. She held up her hands, and Vanyel felt the slight disorientation that always accompanied the moment when someone invoked Gate-energy around him. He left the little group of three and sprinted across the wreckage-strewn hall and up the staircase to face the door and try to keep Vedric in check long enough for them to escape.

He fought silently, fighting as he had never fought before, fighting not only for himself, but for his friends—and for his land, for without Shavri, Randale would fall to pieces. The last of his shield reinforcements cracked and fell away just as he felt the wave of dizziness that signaled the opening of the Gate itself. And the outer door exploded open, breaking two of its hinges and shattering every window in that wall, just as he felt a wash of pain—

Pain that signaled the Gate being traversed, and then going down again.

That pain nearly did him in; he was barely able to get his own personal shield up in time to deflect the lightnings Vedric called down on him.

"Hold him, boy!" came an urgent voice behind him. "He *knows* we know—he doesn't dare let us live!"

"Jervis!" Vanyel tapped recklessly into the node, and flung fire into Vedric's face. He didn't dare look around, but he spat a stream of heartfelt curses in four languages at the armsmaster. *"Damn* you," he screamed, deflecting a paralysis-dagger and countering with an ice-storm. "Get under cover! What in the *hell* do you think you're doing?"

"What Savil told me," came the unperturbed voice from behind and to his right, as Vanyel tried to shatter Vedric's shields with hammering blows of pure force. Vedric turned them, though not easily; Vanyel could spare no more attention to the armsmaster. To deal with Vedric would take every scrap of concentration.

They were equals, or so close as made no difference. Vanyel had the node to draw on, but Vedric was being fed from somewhere outside himself, too. The entryway shook; the glass of the windows that had been shattered in the first exchange rose up and flew at him. He pulverized the flying shards of death with a single blow. Now flakes of stone and plaster rained down on them, and the paving beneath their feet cracked.

Then Vedric smiled—and triggered the trap-spell.

Hastily Vanyel extended his shield to cover Jervis. A whirlwind Swarm of creatures—as Tashir had described, seeming mostly teeth and eyes—circled them, screaming their outrage at not being able to reach them. They weren't the *gretshke* beings he'd encountered—they were at once less *hungry* and more evil. The Swarm he knew attacked to feed, these things attacked only to rend and tear, to maim and destroy, for the pleasure of destruction and the pain it caused.

Shrieking in frustration, the Swarm spiraled up and away, passing through the ceiling unhindered—and were gone.

Vedric smiled again. "Well, Herald Vanyel—I presume that is who you are—aren't you going to try to rush off to the rescue of your family, your kindred?"

Vanyel just laughed at him.

That was *not* the response Vedric had expected, and it shook him. But what shook him even more was the backlash a moment later as his Swarm attempted to find victims, and were thwarted again—and again—and again—

Failed spells recoiled on their caster; that was one of the first lessons Starwind had taught him. And a spell this powerful, if backlashed, *should* have knocked Vedric to his knees.

But it didn't.

It seemed as if the Mavelan mage-lord took the backlash, and siphoned it off somewhere.

That was when Vanyel realized exactly where Vedric was getting his unprecedented power. The entire Mavelan family had united (for once) and was feeding this, their chosen representative, with all their combined powers.

Vanyel could hammer at him until dark with no effect.

He deflected another lightning-strike, and thought frantically. Even if he defeated Vedric, that *wouldn't* take care of the rest of the family unless he could somehow get at *them* through the linkage to the mage-lord.

Then he knew *how* to manage that.

Raw node-power.

Only *Tayledras*-trained or an Adept with the dearly bought control he and Savil shared could handle it. He remembered how when he had defeated the changeling-mage Krebain, he had nearly killed himself by flooding it through his system. Only one thing had saved him; the fact that Moondance, a k'Treva Healer-Adept, had gotten to him within heartbeats after he'd blasted himself. If he poured *that* through Vedric and into the meld before they realized what he was doing, there would be no saving of any of them. Without being prepared to handle that kind of power, they would be destroyed.

But to do that, he would have to drain the node to a level where he might trigger a quake. And he would have to *touch* Vedric.

He had been very carefully avoiding looking at the mage-lord. Now he looked across the space intervening between them and saw—

Tylendel. As Tylendel would have looked *now*, had he survived into full manhood.

He froze.

The momentary pause in the parry-riposte of the mage-duel broke Vedric's rhythm and concentration. He looked up and stared at Vanyel as if wondering what the other was up to.

That broke the grip of heartache holding him, for *nothing* could have been less like the Tylendel Vanyel had loved than the creature that looked at him out of the mask of Tylendel's face. There was craft there, and guile— and a terrible cruelty. The kind of cruelty that would see nothing wrong with setting an innocent boy up to be abused and neglected most of his life. A heartlessness that had finally served the helpless boy up as a sacrifice, as the expendable tool that gave Vedric power, and never once felt a twinge of guilt or regret.

A strengthening surge of anger galvanized him, and he re-engaged with every resource he had, fighting his way through lightning, fire, force-walls, everything Vedric could throw into his path. He could see the puzzlement in Vedric's eyes as he won each step across the room, paying for each fingerlength in pain when Vedric's weaponry penetrated his shielding and scored on him, but taking those fingerlength gains despite the pain. He forgot Jervis, forgot Tashir, forgot everything but the fight to win to within arm's-reach of the mage-lord.

Multicolored curtains of power danced in front of him, barring his way. They scorched him as he parted them.

Two steps to go.

One.

He reached out and seized Vedric's arms, and at that moment the mage seemed to figure out what his goal was. Panic spasmed across his face.

But it was a realization that came too late.

Vanyel opened himself up to the node *completely*, and let the power use him as a channel, as he had when he melded with the heart-stone. It poured through him, meeting no resistance—

And into the meld that was the Mavelan family.

Vedric's spine arced; his mouth opened, but no sound emerged. For one moment he glowed like a young sun—

—Vanyel's mind rocked under a multivoiced scream of agony that seemed to go on and on forever—

Then it was gone, and so was Vedric. There was nothing left but a pile of white ash at Vanyel's feet and two handfuls of ash that he dropped onto the pile.

Vanyel stared at the ash, dully—and when the entryway swayed, he thought for a moment that it was his own fatigue that made him stumble and lose his footing.

But as Jervis scrambled toward him to grab his arms and shake him, he understood. The node—he'd drained enough power so that the fault had gone unstable.

The building rocked again, as Jervis continued to shake him. "Come *on*, you damned fool!" he shouted, right into Vanyel's face. "Those damned shields that Vedric set up t' keep us from gettin' away are still there! Gate us outa here before the building comes down on our heads!"

He wrenched himself out of Jervis' hands and faced the ruined outer door, holding up his hands and beginning the Gate-spell, while around him the room bucked and heaved like a boat in a storm.

The pain was incredible.

Letting the node-force use him had left him raw; it was only knowing that Jervis would perish with him that kept him going. He could see the court beyond the door—or rather, what the quake was leaving of it. The palace was disintegrating around them, and nothing living was going to stay that way for long here.

Finally the Gate was complete; the courtyard winked out with a wrench that felt as if someone had torn Vanyel's guts out, and in its place was the corridor just outside the Ashkevron family chapel.

Vanyel's knees gave out and he collapsed. He had just enough energy to wince a little as half the wall collapsed between him and the Gate.

There was nothing but pain now, and he lacked even the strength to weep.

Jervis was shaking him; he tried to push the man's hands away, but it was like a babe trying to push away the hand of an adult. "Go," he panted, too spent even to moan. "Can't—hold it—stable."

There's nothing left. I overestimated again—

He could feel the Gate pulsing with the beating of his own heart. In a moment it would collapse.

"Go—now," he tried to urge the armsmaster. He was so tired; he'd give anything to be able to rest, beyond the pain.

Shadow-Lover—

Death had long since lost any fear for him. He had been courted by the Shadow-Lover for so long that His embrace would be welcome, if only it would bring him peace. There was nothing left—not even his will.

But Jervis had enough will for two.

"I'm not goin' without you!" the old man growled, as the palace walls cried in a hundred agonized voices around them. "You remember what you said about giving up? Dammit, Van, don't do it now! *There's nobody to pick up your load if you give up on me!*"

The words reached through the haze of pain and weakness as nothing else could have. He struggled to his feet, Jervis supporting him, as the palace bucked around them. Jervis started for the open Gate, more than half dragging him over the rubble, and finally draped his arm across his own shoulders and *carried* him through the Gate itself.

He'd thought there could be no worse pain than passing that Gate.

He discovered a heartbeat later that he was wrong.

There was a flash of light on metal as Jervis' boots clattered onto the stone of the corridor floor. It was training, a training that refused to admit to having no strength, that made him squirm sideways in Jervis' grip.

But it wasn't quite enough. There was a rush of dark cloth toward them, and the hard impact of something driving into his stomach and jerking upward—

"*Leren!*" Jervis roared. "What in—"

And pain that blacked out everything else sent him bonelessly to the floor as Jervis let go of him.

Somewhere—in some other world beyond the pain—there was a sound of scuffling. All *he* knew was the pain, the agony that was the center of him, as he lay on his side and clutched his stomach, something hot and wet trickling between his fingers.

Heal—I have to Heal myself— He *had* just enough Healing-Gift to save himself. He *reached*, feebly. *— no strength—*

:Chosen!: Yfandes' mind-voice, faint and far-off—and a brief, unsteady surge of energy from *her* to *him*, all unlooked-for; energy that could Heal him.

But something else brushed his mind, a sense of dark and evil wings.

It was *with* Leren. A dark force that ruled Leren, and it was poised to strike at the armsmaster.

He had a choice; save himself—or save Jervis.

Which was not a choice at all.

No!

Vanyel took that borrowed strength and hurled it at the unprotected, unsuspecting darkness like a spear of light.

It penetrated.

But it did not kill. The darkness fled, wounded, but not conquered, as Vanyel began fading into a darkness of his own.

Gods—Leren—controlled.

Jervis' voice. "Bastard got distracted. Got him with a chair," the man said, from that other world. "He won't be going anywhere for a while. Boy—boy, did he mark you?"

It was becoming very hard to breathe; his frantic gasps after air just made the pain worse, and didn't seem to be bringing anything into his lungs.

Someone rolled him onto his back and he cried out.

"Lady's tits!" Jervis swore. "Bloody bastard!"

Vanyel opened his eyes, but he couldn't see anything but a tiny spot of brightness in a sea of black. The blackness called him—

Jervis slapped his face lightly, and the blackness receded for a moment. "*Don't* leave on me, boy," he said urgently, supporting Vanyel in his lap. "Stay with me!"

Vanyel did his best to obey, as Jervis bellowed somewhere over his head for a Healer, but he was cold, and getting colder, and there didn't seem to be any room for anything but agony.

He tried to open his eyes again, when he heard frantically running feet. There was a strange Herald in Whites on his left, and a swirl of green robes as a Healer dropped down beside him on his right.

"Gods!" he heard the latter swear, in an audible panic. There were hands pulling his away, and a wash of weakening that followed a gush of something, warmth that poured out of him, and over the hands that replaced his. "I—oh, gods, we're losing him!"

"Like hell!"

"I—"

Everything—voices, vision, even the pain—began to fade. Everything except the stranger kneeling at his left side. Though his face remained oddly shadowed, there was a soft, argent glow about him, like starlight, that brightened with each passing moment.

:Take my hand, Herald Vanyel.:

Vanyel blinked, struggled against his fading sight, tried to hold to consciousness.

:My hand.: The strange Herald held his right hand out to Vanyel, and there was entreaty in that mind-voice. *:Will you not take it?:*

The urgency in the request pulled at him; this was important. Important that he fight past the pain to obey the stranger. Moved by some deep conviction that he didn't understand, he found a tiny crumb of strength; just enough to move the fingers of his left hand and place them, sticky and warm with his own blood, into the stranger's outstretched palm. The stranger's hand closed over his, and his lips curved in a smile of triumph.

He was standing. The pain was gone.

So was the wound. The strange Herald still held his hand, but about them was—nothing. Only a kind of peaceful, tranquil gray emptiness.

The stranger's face was still shadowed—except for the eyes, a blazing glory of sapphires and light, a light never seen in Vanyel's world.

Not in the mortal world that Vanyel knew. *Not* the natural world.

Therefore this was not the natural world—and this was no mere Herald.

Vanyel released the stranger's hand and sank slowly to one knee, unable to look away from those incandescent eyes. Then the stranger smiled, and the smile was as brilliant and overpowering as the gaze. That smile was no sight for mortal eyes, and Vanyel managed to drop his gaze before he was lost to it. He bowed his head over his knee in profound obeisance to the Power that had chosen to wear the guise of a human, and a Herald.

"Lord," he whispered, unable to muster enough coherent thought to say anything more.

"Vanyel, no," replied a voice of amber, silk, and steel.

He felt hands, gentle hands on his shoulders, hands that drew him up to his feet. He dared a glance at the Power's face, and was caught again, a moth in sapphirine flame.

"No, Vanyel," He said, shaking His head, denying Vanyel's assumption. "Not 'Lord.' Only a messenger, a servant. You mustn't kneel to me."

The longer he looked into those eyes, the easier it became. "I'm—dead," he said steadily, feeling nothing at the words except a soul-deep relief that it was finally over, that he could rest.

But the Other shook His head again. "No. Not yet Vanyel." He hesitated a moment, and His eyes were shadowed with pity. "Vanyel, because of what you are, what you have become, and that you stand at the crossroads of many possibilities, it is given to you to choose."

"Choose?" he said, honestly bewildered. "Choose how?"

"Life," replied the Power, His eyes dimmed, as if with unshed tears, "Life, or—" He touched His hand to His own heart. "—or myself."

Then he understood what stood with him in this timeless nothingness, what gazed at him with eyes of sorrow; beautiful, perfect, and serene.

The Shadow-Lover.

"Ask me what you will," Death said, eyes radiant, and voice soft with compassion. "You must choose in full knowledge of *what* your choice will mean."

"What do I go to," Vanyel asked, marveling at his own steadiness, as he ached for the peace those eyes promised him, "if I choose to live?"

"Pain," Death replied, bowing His own head so that Vanyel could no longer see those eyes. "Loss. You will see good friends die, one by one, until you are alone. You will find yourself growing apart from others, day by day, until there seems to be nothing but loneliness and your duties. You will receive hurts and will not die of them, though you may long to. And the end—will be only more pain."

"And—the alternative."

"For you—peace. And an end to pain and loneliness and grieving."

Vanyel felt all the burdens of his existence heavy upon him, felt taxed beyond his strength. But he had not missed that subtle phrasing, and he asked a further question, though he knew in his heart that he would hate the answer.

"And what of those I leave behind?"

Death looked up again, and held his gaze with those brilliant, depthless eyes—and was it his imagination, or did a sad, proud smile touch those sculptured lips for a moment?

"They will come to me," Death said quietly. "And sooner, and in greater numbers, than if you choose to live. The Valdemar you knew will be no more; her people will struggle to maintain their freedom in a shrunken land, bereft of allies and hemmed about by enemies. You are not the only hope, Vanyel, but you are Valdemar's best hope."

Vanyel closed his eyes in a spasm of despair, struggling to maintain his composure. He was so tired—so very tired. So tired of pain, of loneliness, of a life that seemed harder to endure each day. But what he had told Jervis was no less than the truth. He could no more leave his duties unfulfilled than he could repudiate Yfandes. Especially not now—not *knowing,* by the word of a Power that would not tell him false, that there was no one else to do what he could do.

But he was so tired.

"What is magic's promise, Vanyel?" asked the vibrant voice. "You thought you knew the answer once. Is it still the answer you would give now?"

He rose out of his own soul-deep weariness, and realized that—no, the promise of magic's power—*to a Herald*—was *not* what he had thought at seventeen. And *that* was the difference between what *he* was, and what those of Vedric and Krebain's ilk were.

"It isn't a promise made to me," he replied, slowly opening his eyes and meeting Death's unblinking, steadfast gaze. "It's a promise made to those who depend on me, on my strength; it's a promise I haven't fulfilled, not yet, not completely." He closed his eyes again, and bowed his head, feeling tears of weariness slipping from beneath his lashes and not wanting the Other to see them and his weakness. "It's a promise that gives me no choice. I—have to go back. No matter how—tired—I am—"

There was a whisper of sound, and a feather-light touch on his jaw. He opened his eyes, and Death's hand lifted his chin so that his gaze again met those beautiful eyes. There were tears in Death's eyes, tears that matched his own, and a tender, sorrowful smile on Death's lips.

"I have never been so grieved—and so glad—to lose," he said, and touched his lips to Vanyel's. Their tears mingled on his lips as Vanyel closed his eyes; he tasted them in the kiss, his own salt, bitter tears—and Death's sweet—Strong arms closed about him, supporting him, holding him against a comforting shoulder, as Death held him with all the sensitivity of the lover that He could be.

Vanyel yielded to the greater strength, and crumpled in his arms, his shoulders shaking with silent sobs. Gentle hands caressed his hair, and gentle words came to his ears.

"Not yet, beloved," Death murmured, breath moving against his ear, lightly stirring his hair. "There is no time here, while I will it so. You need not take up your burden until you feel ready to meet your life again."

So he wept out his weariness, his longing for respite. He wept, and then he rested on Death's shoulder.

"Vanyel, is it only duty that calls you back?"

"No." He found another tiny crumb of strength and slowly straightened in the Power's arms. "No—it's more than that. Moondance said it a long time ago. I lost my own hearth-fire, but that's no reason why I can't warm myself at the hearths of my friends, not when they've offered that warmth." He blinked, and realized that he was smiling. "Not so many friends," he said, half to himself, "but all of them—*good* friends."

"Worth returning for, Vanyel?"

"Yes," he replied simply.

Death actually laughed softly. "So long to learn what Moondance meant?"

"Sometimes I'm a bit dense." He wiped his eyes with the back of his hand. "For some reason I never had any trouble figuring out what death was all about; but life—that's taken me until now."

The Power held him for a moment longer, then let him go. He met the compassionate, luminous blue eyes for one final time, and saw them flare with a strange mixture of pride, grief, and joy. "Vanyel," Death whispered. "One thing more—there is one who would make his farewell to you."

Vanyel *felt* someone behind him, a lesser presence than the Shadow-lover, and turned.

"Hello, Vanyel," said Jaysen, holding out his hand. "Or—I guess it's good-bye."

"Jays?" Vanyel took the hand, momentarily stunned. "Oh, Jays, no—I didn't—"

"No, *you* didn't. Don't go all guilty on me." Jaysen actually smiled, rue-fully. "It was my own stupid fault for being so distracted by the fact that you went and fathered our little pet that I gave those things of Vedric's a chance to get at me."

Tears burned his eyes. "But—"

"*Stop* that. I *knew* you'd take it that way, that's why I asked—Her—Lady Death—to let me see you. *It's not your fault.* Now *listen* to me, neither of us have much more time."

"The Web—you're the Northern Guardian—"

"Exactly. You'll have to take my place. More than that, remember what you were thinking earlier? About making *all* the Heralds the power source? *Do* that, Van. Figure out how." Jaysen squeezed his hand urgently. "It's important. Figure out how to change the Web-spell so that it doesn't *need* Guardians anymore, just the Heralds themselves. You're the only one of us that can do that. I'm *charging* you with that, Van."

He nodded, and met Jaysen's eyes evenly. "I promise."

"I—" Jaysen's eyes softened for a moment. "There's something else She told me I could tell you. Maybe it'll help. She said you won't be alone."

He released Vanyel's hand, and stepped backward, already beginning to fade.

"She promised, Van. And I promise."

Then he was falling, falling—

For a confused moment after he opened his eyes, he thought that the slumped form in Whites in the chair beside his bed was the Messenger—

But his hiss of pain as he tried to move woke the other, and he saw that it was a mortal and a friend, after all.

"Tran?" he whispered. "Tantras? What are you—"

Tantras' face was lined with exhaustion, and his eyes were red with weeping.

"Van, I have to tell you—"

"We lost Jays," he whispered, remembering, feeling the emptiness.

Oh, gods— He was not aware that he was weeping until a sob shook him and made him gasp with pain.

Tantras just handed him a square of linen, and, moving to sit gingerly on the side of the bed, held him until exhaustion left him no more tears to weep.

"We thought you ought to hear it from a friend," Tantras told him, helping him to lie back. "I should have known you already knew."

"How?" Vanyel whispered. "He didn't tell me how."

"He couldn't keep the Swarm off—so he and his Companion—you know better than me how that works."

"Final strike," Vanyel answered numbly. "Take your last target with you. Oh, *gods*—if I'd just been there."

"What good would you have done?" Tantras chided. "No one can be two places at once, Van. Not even you. Lady Bright, we came within a hair of losing *you*, and that's something I'd rather not think about. Lissa's Healer *still* doesn't know how he pulled it off. He swears he had divine help at the last moment."

Vanyel just stared at him, finding it hard to imagine a world without Jaysen in it.

A gentle tap broke the silence between them, and a maid hurried in, face blank—hiding fear.

"Milord Herald-Mage?" she faltered, holding a pitcher.

Not "Vanyel," or even "milord Van," he thought, with a catch in his throat. *Now I terrify even the ones who grew up with me around. I'm a stranger even to my own.*

"Yes, Sondri?" he said, as gently as he could.

"I brought ye summat t' drink."

"Thank you."

She left the pitcher and glass beside the bed, and hurried out.

Fear. Vanyel felt another wrench inside. And there was only one way to deal with the pain of it.

Tantras had enough Empathy to feel something of his withdrawal. "Van—" He touched Vanyel's shoulder. "Van, what are you doing?"

Van looked at him bleakly. "You saw her," he whispered. "It's just like you told me. I frighten people. And now even more than before. I wiped out the *entire* Mavelan family, or at least all of the ones in the meld. I had *divine aid* in being Healed, or at least that's what they're telling each other out there. I frightened them before, now I terrify them. It *hurts*, Tran. It *hurts* to feel that fear."

"So you're withdrawing behind walls again." Tantras shook his head. "Van, that's not the answer."

"What is?"

Tantras only shook his head dumbly.

"At least my walls give me a little peace. And I won't wall my friends out, I promise." He tried to smile, at least a little.

"But you won't look for new friends either. *Or* love. Van, you're making a serious mistake."

"It's mine to make."

"I can't stay," Tantras said, after a long silence. "I have to courier messages back. I only waited to tell you."

Vanyel nodded, grief too profound to be purged with one spate of weeping rising to block his words. "Duty; we all have it. That's what kept me, Tran, that, and finally figuring out what I'm doing here. And that's what Jays died for—duty, and protecting the ones we all love." He stared at a spot on the opposite wall while his eyes burned and blurred. "Thanks for waiting to tell me."

Tantras eased off the bed, and squeezed his hand. "Rest. When there's more to tell, we'll get the word to you."

"Thank you," he murmured, closing his eyes. He heard soft footsteps crossing the floor, heard the door open and close. Then knew nothing more for a very long time.

The Healer had done his best, but the wound Father Leren's knife had left was only half healed, and still very sore. Vanyel had just discovered that getting from his bed to the chair beside his table was a sweating and pain-filled ordeal. The Healer had sternly warned him about the consequences of tearing open half-healed tissues, and Vanyel was inclined to take him very seriously, given the way he was hurting. He didn't want to make a bigger mess of his midsection than it already was. As it was, he'd have an L-shaped scar for the rest of his life. Gut wounds were definitely not on his list of favored ways to earn a little rest.

Getting dressed had been an ordeal, too, but the Healer had said he could have visitors, and he *wasn't* going to see them bundled in bed like an invalid.

He eased himself down into the chair with a hiss as someone knocked on the door to his room. "Come," he called, wiping the sweat from his forehead with the back of his hand.

It was not anyone he had expected. It was Melenna.

A much subdued, sobered Melenna.

"I came to see if you were really all right," she said, shyly, "and to ask Herald Vanyel for a favor, and some advice."

Herald Vanyel. Not Van. And the fear is in her, too.

"Please, Melenna, sit down. I can't imagine why you'd want my advice, but—"

She remained standing. "Vanyel," she said softly. "You—and me. There's no hope, is there?"

He looked up, and the honest longing in her eyes made his heart go out to her, the anger and frustration of the past few weeks evaporating. The gods knew, he knew *exactly* how it felt to long for something you'd never have—or never have again. "I'm sorry, Melenna, but I won't lie to you. It was hopeless from the start. A woman can never be anything more than my friend. I *do* value you as a friend, and the mother of my very young friend Medren, but I can't offer you any more than that."

She bent her head, and quickly wiped her eyes, all coquettishness gone.

"I—you know how I feel. Couldn't you—pretend? It would make Lady Treesa and Lord Withen awfully happy. And I wouldn't mind, really I wouldn't."

He looked away from those sad, sad eyes. The offer was terribly tempting. But ultimately, a lie. "I know it would make them happy, but I'm a Herald, Melenna. I can't *tell* lies—how could I live one? And you *would* care, eventually. It would make you very unhappy. There are other men—*shay'a'chern*—who've talked with me, who tried just what you're suggesting. In the end, instead of two people who were only moderately happy most of the time, there were two people who were desperately unhappy all the time. The wife was jealous of his lovers, and his lovers were jealous of her, and it went downhill from there." He shook his head. "No, my friend, it won't work. I'm sorry."

She wiped another tear away. "I'm sorry, too," she said. "But to tell you the truth, I'm mostly sorry for myself, and a little bit for Treesa." She sighed. "Can I—ask you a favor? And you can say no. It's about Medren."

"If it's about Medren, the answer is probably 'yes,'" he said. "Your son is a delight to any musician, and a charmer all by himself."

"Would you—sort of be his guardian until he's settled? He's never been away from home at all. I know he isn't shy, but that's the problem. He seems a lot older than he really is, and that's my fault, I guess. He could get in with a faster crowd than he can handle."

He stared at her, astounded. "You'd trust *me*—?"

She returned his astonished stare levelly. "I'm not very clever, sometimes," she replied, "but I listen, I listen a lot. You're very honorable, and in all the stories about you and—others, there's only been *men*. Not boys. Besides, Medren told me how he offered to pay for lessons, and how you turned him down. Yes, I trust you. I'll always trust you. I've loved you, Vanyel . . . for a very long time."

Greatly moved, Vanyel took her hand and kissed the back of it gently. "Then I will be very honored to see Medren settled properly," he replied. "And I can only pray that I will always be worthy of your trust."

She got up before he could say another word, and headed for the door—only to be run over by the rush of people crowding in, as the door slammed open.

"Now *look*, you peabrain—" Savil was shouting, as Vanyel's head began to spin.

"Look *yourself*," Withen shouted back, shaking his finger at her. "The damned Lineans won't accept anything *but* the boy!"

"But he's a *Herald*," Lores wailed over the din.

Vanyel's head began to spin, and he clutched the edge of his table. Rescue came from an unexpected source.

"Shut UP!" Jervis roared, in a tone of voice that harkened back to the parade ground.

Silence descended so suddenly that Vanyel's ears rang.

"Would someone mind explaining what all this is about?" he whispered into it.

"Let me see if I have all this straight," he said, after everyone had said his or her piece—except Melenna, who'd found herself trapped by the influx of people and hadn't had the courage to push past them to escape. "Tashir now holds both thrones according to the treaty. Now that he's been acquitted, the Lineans are willing to accept him, and the Bairens are willing to take about anybody so long as it isn't a Mavelan. The problems with this are: first, he's a Herald, which means he has to be trained, and would normally mean he'd abdicate lands and titles; second, he doesn't *want* to be a King; third, he's very young, which would be a temptation to others to come and attack, and would drag Valdemar into defending his kingdom for him."

"Something like that," Withen admitted, as the others nodded.

"Why me?" he demanded. "Why am *I* suddenly the arbitrator?"

Savil flourished a piece of parchment. "Because according to this little piece of paper I have, under Randale's *official* seal, you understand the problems, so you're appointed full and final authority."

:*I'll get you for this, Savil.*:

:*You can try.*:

He massaged his temples, and wished for wine. "All right, let's take this slowly. First of all, we've waived the rules for Heralds before when they were the only heirs. It isn't done often, but I think it's called for in this case. Lores, your Gift is Fetching, right?"

Startled, the Herald nodded.

"Fine, I hereby appoint you Tashir's mentor, to stay with him and teach him until you feel he's ready for Whites. You can serve double duty that way; mentor and envoy. Now—Tashir, would you be willing to take the ruling seat if we arranged for you to make the two lands a vassal-state? That means you are holding the lands of Randale, and it would make them part of Valdemar."

Tashir considered that for a moment, his face sober. "D-does it have to be—do I have to be a King? I don't want to be a King. It's pretty stupid, anyway, to be a King of something you can ride across in a few days."

"Provided you can get your people to agree, I can't see what difference it makes."

"Then I'll be a Baron," Tashir replied, sitting up very straight. "Lord-Baron of the March of Lineas-Baires. If there aren't any straight-line heirs, it all goes back to Valdemar."

Vanyel sighed his relief. If Tashir hadn't been willing to take the damned power seat—civil wars were *not* what Valdemar needed on the Border.

"Now, when there's a ruler as young as you, he usually has a Council of older people to advise him—"

"There isn't one," Tashir interrupted. "Father had one, but they all died."

"True. Have you any objections to my appointing you one?"

Tashir shook his head, and Vanyel plowed on before anyone could stop him. "First Councilor and Chamberlain, Herald Lores. Second Councilor and Seneschal, Kaster Ashkevron. He's Meke's right hand, Father, *and* he's Meke's accountant. Any objections so far?"

Withen snapped his mouth shut on whatever he was going to say, and shook his head.

"Right. Third Councilor, have somebody sent over from your local temple—pick a scholar. Fourth Councilor, the current Chief Elder of High-jorune. Fifth Councilor—huh. You'll need a Marshal, a good military advisor, I would think. Jervis."

"Huh?" Jervis responded, "I what?"

"He'll be very good," Vanyel continued before he could object, "and Radevel is *certainly* capable of taking over here as armsmaster. And since you're a bachelor, you'll need a Castelaine—otherwise you're never going to have cooked meals or clean shirts." He went blank for a moment—until his eyes fell on Melenna.

"'Lenna?"

She jumped.

"Think you'd be able to keep Tashir in roasts, herbs, and clean linen?"

"Me?" she squeaked. "Me? Castelaine?"

"Of course, there's a catch." Vanyel was beginning to enjoy this. "You'll have to be ennobled, but Randi *did* give me full powers." He saw with a hidden smile that Tashir was beginning to look happier. Melenna had stood up for him once already and she was the mother of his good friend Medren—two points already in her favor, at least in his eyes.

"But—but I—but I don't know a thing about—"

"B—beanshucks," Withen rumbled, changing his epithet in midsyllable. "You've been doing Castelaine duty here for years. Treesa'll have vapors, of course."

Savil interrupted him. "Let her have vapors. If she doesn't want to mind Forst Reach, let Meke's lady deal with it. I know young Roshya. She's a bright little thing, and I know she's been properly trained. That's one of your worst problems here, Withen—too many trained hands and not enough jobs for them."

Melenna turned anxious eyes toward Vanyel. "Herald Vanyel? Do you think that I—could—"

"I think you'll do just fine. Now—does that solve all the problems?"

Because I'm about to run out of brilliant ideas, energy, and the ability to hold off pain.

"I think so," Savil replied. "I think we can start off by collecting Kaster and showing Tashir something of what he'll be dealing with."

"You won't need me, will you?" Jervis asked suddenly.

"Probably not—at least not for a while."

"Then I need a word or two with young Van here. Could you send to fetch me when you need me?"

Savil raised one eyebrow, but nodded.

The mob left, and Vanyel sagged as Jervis put a pitcher down on the table before him.

"Gods. That was a *hell* of a way to spend my first day out of bed." He cast a wistful glance at the pitcher. "I don't suppose that's wine, is it?" The Healer, used to fighters, who would use the infirmary as a good place to hold an impromptu party, had forbidden him wine. He was getting *very* tired of cider.

Besides, the drugs the Healer had given him were too strong. He wasn't taking them except to sleep, and the pain-dulling effects of alcohol would have been welcome.

"Well—cider," Jervis said slyly, "and help." He reached inside his jerkin and held up a little bottle of apple brandy. "Couldn't get wine past that snoop, but I could this. Figured you could use it. Little bird told me you probably weren't taking those pills."

He poured a generous dollop of brandy into each mug before adding the cider; Vanyel accepted his gratefully. "What little bird?"

"One name of Lissa. I've been playin' her eyes an' ears over here."

"She could be right," he admitted. "She knows I hate to be muddle-headed these days."

Jervis grimaced. "*Anybody* been on front-lines hates t' be muddle-headed. Wish them Healers'd figure that out."

"Have you heard anything out of Highjorune? Like about the palace, and the heart-stone?"

"Buried, and gonna leave it that way. Seemed safest. Van, you *really* think I should do this?"

"Why? Don't you?"

Jervis chewed his lip. "I dunno," he said after a moment. "Tashir trusts me. I'm getting too old to try and beat sense into more young heads than one at any one time. What do you think of the notion? Too damned foolish to believe?"

"I think you'd make a good Marshal," Vanyel replied honestly. "You've certainly proved that you aren't too old to change."

Jervis snorted. "You say that after I nearly ruined your life for you?"

"But you saved it," Vanyel pointed out. "If you hadn't been there, I would either have let the palace bury me, or I'd have gone down under Leren's knife. I'd have been dead before anyone found me. I think we're even."

"Huh." They drank in silence for a moment. The pain of Vanyel's wound seemed a bit eased.

"About Leren—you heard anything yet?"

Vanyel shook his head. "I was hoping you'd get around to him. I have some information for *you*, since you're relaying to Liss. Leren *was* mage-controlled."

Jervis swore under his breath. "So he *was* tryin' t' take us both out a-purpose. If he hadn't gotten distracted—"

"Exactly—and I'm the one that distracted him for you; there was—I felt something about him, but it got away from me."

Jervis shook his head. "Damn. We found out he was planted on us by the Mavelans. And *now* the priests of Astera are sending 'finders' into every damn temple along the Border here, to see how many more there are like him. Seems the Mavelans *bought* themselves a temple-school. The High Prelate is not what you'd call pleased. But I guess Leren's even twistier than we thought?"

Vanyel nodded. "I told Savil this morning and she relayed it to Haven, but Liss might as well get it from you. He may have been serving the Mavelans, but he was serving somebody else, too. And I don't know who or what. It was no power I recognized."

"And you won't ever find it from him. Liss couldn't get it out of him, and whoever it was killed him before she could turn him over to Heralds."

Vanyel swore creatively and descriptively in *Tayledras*. "Savil didn't tell me *that*."

Jervis grimaced. "She didn't know. Liss' sergeant found him dead in his cell just this mornin', guts torn out, and nobody next or nigh him since they'd brought him dinner. But Savil an' Lores an' Tashir showed up right after that, an' *that* kinda got lost in tryin' t' figger out what to' do 'bout Tashir."

"Magic."

"Seems so."

Vanyel pondered for a moment. "Did you ever find out why he tried to kill me?"

"Oh, aye. That was easy enough. Leren knew what was goin' on here; that Mavelan bastard was keepin' him briefed. That much Liss got outa him afore he got his insides tore out. Vedric figured you were getting too close to the truth about the boy. When he breached the shields, he *didn't* know we'd unraveled everything. *He* had it figured that his spell was too good to unravel. What *he* meant to do was send you Gating home, and the boy with you. Leren was supposed to knife you both. They figured you'd use the same place to Gate into as last time, so Leren was waiting once Vedric contacted him. What they didn't figure on was Savil and me bein' there, nor you and Savil splitting up, and they didn't figure on *me* bein' with you an' not the boy."

"I'm glad you were," Vanyel said, softly. "If it hadn't been for you throwing my own words back in my face—well, I wouldn't be here."

"Is that a thing to thank me for?" Jervis asked unexpectedly. "How much you going to take before you crack?"

"As much," Vanyel replied deliberately, "as I have to."

Jervis pondered that a moment. "Van—are we friends now?"

Vanyel closed his eyes. "We're friends. And I think I know what your next question is going to be. You want to know why I'm sending you away with Tashir."

"Somethin' like."

"I'm trying to scatter my targets. I had a lot of time to think, the past couple of days. I figured out something. Enemies might not be able to get *me*, but they can get at me through the people I care for. Some of them—they're pretty well protected. But ordinary people, like you, Medren—" He shook his head. "So I'm trying to send you all away—*far* away from me. The farther away you are, the safer you are. Either you'll be too distant to get at, or it will look as if I don't care. Either way, *you'll* be all right."

"And you'll be alone."

"That's better than knowing you took a mage-bolt because someone wanted to rock *me*," he retorted, and swallowed the contents of the mug at a gulp.

Silence, then Jervis reached out and refilled his mug. Vanyel found himself getting a little light-headed. "Let me ask about something inconsequential; how's Medren? Is he going to forgive me for wrecking his old lute?"

"Lute?" Jervis chortled. "He'd have forgiven you for wrecking Forst Reach so long as you came back safe. Funny thing; remember you said Medren'd be safe from the Swarm because he was Bardic-Gifted and not Mage? You was almost right. Seems like the instant the Swarm tried t' find a target here, ev'ry one of his lute strings snapped. How's that for strange?"

Vanyel shook his head. *Too close. Too damned close. I was right.*

"Anyway, he's safe at Bardic; word came back from a Bard called Breda that 'if there's any more at home like him, they're staging a raid'."

"So he's doing well?"

"Better than well. I think that's the reason Melenna decided to take that Castelaine position. I think she's startin' to look at being something other than 'Somebody's lady' or 'Somebody's momma.' I think maybe she wants to take a shot at being Somebody, herself."

"Good," Vanyel said, and meant it.

"You know," Jervis raised one eyebrow, "your father still don't half believe but what you were after Tashir's tail the whole time. Aye, and Medren, too."

Vanyel snorted.

"In fact," Jervis continued, "to hear *him* in his cups, you've had half the boys in Valdemar."

Vanyel put his mug down. "If that's a question," he replied acidly, "you can tell him from me that it's been so damned long that both you and those damned sheep in Long Meadow are starting to look good!"

Jervis gave him a long, thoughtful look, and Vanyel wondered if he'd said too much, too freely. He tried to ready an apology—when Jervis gave him a long, slow grin.

"Stick to the sheep," the armsmaster advised impudently. "They don't snore."

MAGIC'S PRICE

To
Russell Galen
Judith Louvis and Sally Paduch
and everyone who dreams of wearing Whites

CHAPTER 1

SWEAT RAN DOWN Herald Vanyel's back, and his ankle hurt a little—he hadn't twisted it, quite, when he'd slipped on the wooden floor of the salle back at the beginning of this bout, but it was still bothering him five exchanges later.

A point of weakness, and one he'd better be aware of, because his opponent was watching for such signs of weakness, sure as the sun rose.

He watched his adversary's eyes within the shadows of his helm. *Watch the eyes*, he remembered Jervis saying, over and over. *The eyes will tell you what the hands won't.* So he studied those half-hidden eyes, and tried to hide his entire body behind the quillons of his blade.

The eyes warned him, narrowing and glancing to the left just before Tantras moved. Vanyel was ready for him.

Experience told him, just before their blades touched, that this would be the last exchange. He lunged toward Tantras instead of retreating as Tran was obviously expecting, engaged and bound the other's blade, and disarmed him, all in the space of a breath.

The practice blade clattered onto the floor as Tantras shook his now-empty hand, swearing.

"Stung, did it?" Vanyel said. He straightened, and pulled at the tie holding his hair out of his eyes, letting it fall loose in damp strands. "Sorry. Didn't mean to get quite so vigorous. But *you are* out of shape, Tran."

"I don't suppose you'd accept getting old as an excuse?" Tantras asked hopefully, as he took off his gloves and examined the abused fingers.

Vanyel snorted. "Not a chance. Bard Breda is old enough to be my mother, and she regularly runs me around the salle. You are woefully out of condition."

The other Herald pulled off his helm, and laughed ruefully. "You're right. Being Seneschal's Herald may be high in status, but it's low in exercise."

"Spar with my nephew Medren," Vanyel replied. "If you think *I'm* fast, you should see him. That'll keep you in shape." He unbuckled his practice gambeson while he spoke, leaving it in a pile of other equipment that needed cleaning up against the wall of the salle.

"I'll do that." Tantras was slower in freeing himself from the heavier armor he wore. "The gods know I may need to face somebody using that cut-and-run style of yours some day, so I might as well get used to fights that are half race and half combat. And *entirely* unorthodox."

"That's me, unorthodox to the core." Vanyel racked his practice sword and headed for the door of the salle. "Thanks for the workout, Tran. After this morning, I needed it."

The cool air hit his sweaty skin as he opened the door; it felt wonderful. So good, in fact, that between his reluctance to return to the Palace and the fresh crispness of the early morning, he decided to take a roundabout way back to his room. One that would take him away from people. One that would, for a moment perhaps, take his mind off things as well as his bout with Tantras had.

He headed for the paths to the Palace gardens.

Full-throated birdsong spiraled up into the empty sky. Vanyel let his thoughts drift away, following the warbling notes, leaving every weighty problem behind him until his mind was as empty as the air above—

:Van, wake up! Your feet are soaked!: Yfandes' mind-voice sounded rather aggrieved. *:And you're chilling yourself. You're going to catch a cold.:*

Herald-Mage Vanyel blinked, and stared down at the dew-laden grass of the neglected garden. He couldn't actually see his feet, hidden as they were by the long, dank, dead grass—but he could feel them, now that 'Fandes had called his attention back to reality. He'd come out here wearing his soft suede indoor boots—they'd been perfect for sparring with Tran, but now—

:They are undoubtedly ruined,: she said acidly.

She sounded so like his aunt, Herald-Mage Savil, that he had to smile. "Won't be the first pair of boots I've ruined, sweetheart," he replied mildly. His feet *were* very wet. And very cold. A week ago it wouldn't have been dew out here; it would have been frost. But Spring was well on the way now; the grass was greening under the dead growth of last year, there were young leaves unfolding on every branch, and a few of the earliest songbirds had begun to invade the garden. Vanyel had been watching and listening to a pair of them, rival male yellowthroats, square off in a duel of melody.

:Probably not the last article of clothing you'll ruin, either,: she said with resignation. *:You've come a long way from the vain little peacock I Chose.:*

"That vain little peacock you Chose would still have been in bed." He yawned. "I think he was the more sensible one. This hour of the day is positively unholy."

The sun was barely above the horizon, and most of the Palace inhabitants were still sleeping the sleep of the exhausted, if not the just. This half-wild garden was the only one within the Palace grounds with its eastern side unblocked by buildings or walls, and the thin, clear sunlight poured across it, making every tender leaf and grass blade glow. Tradition claimed this patch of earth and its maze of hedges and bowers to be the Queen's Garden—which was the reason for its current state of neglect. There was no Queen in Valdemar now, and the King's lifebonded had more urgent cares than tending pleasure gardens.

An old man, a gardener by his earth-stained apron, emerged from one of the nearby doors of the Palace and limped up the path toward Vanyel. The Herald stepped to one side to let him pass and gave him a friendly enough nod of greeting, but the old man completely ignored him, muttering something under his breath as he brushed by.

His goal, evidently, was a rosevine-covered shed a few feet away; he vanished inside it for a moment, emerged with a hoe, and began methodically cultivating the nearest flowerbed with it. Van might as well have been a spirit for all the attention the old man gave him.

Vanyel watched him for a moment more, then turned and walked slowly back toward the Palace. "Did it ever occur to you, love," he said to the empty air, "that you and I and the entire Palace could vanish overnight, and people like that old man would never miss us?"

:Except that we wouldn't be trampling his flowers anymore,: Yfandes replied. :It was a bad morning, wasn't it.: A statement, not a question. Yfandes had been present in the back of Vanyel's mind during the whole Privy Council session.

"One of Randi's worst yet. That's why I was taking my frustration out with Tran." Vanyel kicked at an inoffensive weed growing up through the cobbles of the path. "And Randi's got some important things to take care of this afternoon. Formal audiences, for one—ambassadorial receptions. I won't do, not this time. It has to be the King, they're insisting on it. Sometimes I wish I didn't have to be so politic, and could knock a few diplomatic heads together. Tashir, bless his generous young heart, handled things a bit better with his lot."

Another gardener appeared, and looked at Vanyel oddly as he passed.

Van suppressed the urge to call him back and explain. *He must be new; he'll learn soon enough about Heralds talking to thin air.*

:What did Tashir do with his envoys? I was talking to Ariel's Darvena while you were dealing with them. You know, I still can't believe your brother Mekeal produced a child sensitive enough to be Chosen.:

"Neither can I. But then, illogic runs in the family, I guess. As for Tashir; his envoys have been ordered to accept me as the voice of the King—" Vanyel explained. "The trouble's with the territories he annexed on Lake Evendim. This lot from the Lake District is touchy as hell, and being received by anyone less than Randi is going to be a mortal affront."

:Where did you pick that tidbit up?:

"Last night. After you decided that stallion from up North had a gorgeous—"

:Nose,: Yfandes interrupted primly. *:He had a perfectly lovely nose. And you and Joshe were boring me to tears with your treasury accounts.:*

"Poor Joshe."

He meant that. *Less than a year in the office, and trying to do the work of twenty. And wishing with all his soul he was back as somebody's assistant. And unfortunately, Tran knows less about the position than he does.*

:He's not comfortable as Seneschal.:

"In the black, love. He's young, and he's nervous, and he wanted somebody else to go over his figures before he presents them to the Council." Vanyel sighed. "The gods know Randi can't. He'll be lucky to make it through this afternoon."

:Esten will help. He'll do anything for Randi.:

"I know that, but—'Fandes, the pain-sharing a Companion can do and the strength a Companion can lend just aren't enough anymore. And it's time we all admitted what we know. Randi's too sick for anything we know to cure—" Vanyel took a deep breath to steady his churning insides. "—and the very best we can hope for is to find some way to ease his pain so he can function when he has to. And hope we can get Treven trained soon in case we can't."

:Get Treven trained in time, you mean,: Yfandes replied glumly. *:Because we're running out of it. I hate this, Van. We can't do anything, the Healers can't do anything—Randale is just dying by inches, and none of us can do anything about it!:*

"Except watch," Van replied with bitterness. "He gets a little worse every day, and not only can't we stop it, we don't even know why! I mean, there are some things not even the Healers can cure, but we don't even know what this illness that's killing Randi *is*—is it inheritable? Could Treven have it, too? Randi didn't show signs until his mid-twenties, and Trev is only seventeen. We could be facing the same situation we have now in another ten or fifteen years."

Unbidden thoughts lurked at the back of his mind. *A good thing Jisa isn't in the line of succession, or people would be asking that about her, too. And how could I explain why she's in no danger without opening a much bigger trouble-box than any of us care to deal with? Especially her. She takes on too much. It's bad enough just being fifteen and the King's daughter. To have to deal with the rest of this—thank the gods there are some difficulties I can spare her.*

He stared down at the overgrown path as he walked, so deep in thought that Yfandes tactfully withdrew from contact. There were some things, or so she had told him, that even a Companion felt uncomfortable about eavesdropping on.

He walked slowly through the neglected garden. He took the winding path back to the door from the Palace, setting his feet down with exaggerated care, putting off his return to the confines of the building as long as he could. But his troubles had a tendency to pursue him beyond the walls.

"Uncle Van?" a breathless young female voice called from behind him. He heard the ache in the familiar voice, the unshed tears; he turned and opened his arms, and Jisa ran into them.

She didn't say anything; she didn't have to. He knew what brought her out here; the same problems that had driven him out into the unkempt maze of the deserted garden. She'd been with her mother and father all morning, right beside Van, doing what she could to ease Randale's pain and boost Shavri's strength.

Van stroked her long, unbound hair, and let her sob into his shoulder. He hadn't known she was behind him—

Ordinarily that would have worried him. But not since it was Jisa. She was very good at shielding; so good, in fact, that she could render herself invisible to his Othersense. That was no small protection to her—since if she could hide her presence from *him*, she could certainly hide it from enemies.

Vanyel was tied to every other Herald alive, and was able to sense *them* whenever he chose, but since Jisa wasn't a Herald, he wouldn't "know" where she was unless he was deliberately Looking for her.

Jisa had not yet been Chosen, which Vanyel thought all to the good. To his way of thinking, she didn't need to be. As an Empath she was getting full Healer's training, and Van and his aunt Savil were instructing her exactly as they would have a newly-Chosen Herald. If people wondered why the child of two full Heralds wasn't yet Chosen when every Companion at Haven loved her and treated her as one of their own, let them continue to wonder. Vanyel was one of the few who knew the reason. Jisa hadn't been Chosen because her Companion would be Taver, and Taver was the Companion to the King's Own, Jisa's mother Shavri. So Jisa and Taver would not bond until Shavri was dead.

Not an event anyone cared to rush.

None of them, not Randale, Shavri nor Vanyel, were ready for even the Heraldic Circle to know *why* she hadn't been Chosen. Jisa knew—Vanyel had told her—but she seldom said anything about it, and Van didn't push her. The child had more than enough to cope with as it was.

Being an Empath and living in the household of your dying parent—

It was one thing to know that someone you loved was going to die; to share Randale's pain as Jisa did must be as bad as any torture Van could think of.

Small wonder she came to Vanyel and cried on his shoulder. The greater wonder was that she didn't do so more often.

He insinuated a tiny thread of thought into her mind as he stroked her tangled, sable-brown hair. Not to comfort; there was no comfort in this situation. Just something to let her know she wasn't alone. *:I know, sweetling. I know. I'd give my sight to take this from you.:*

She turned her red-eyed, tear-smudged face toward his. *:Sometimes I think I can't bear it anymore; I'll kill something or go mad. Except that there's nothing to kill, and going mad wouldn't change anything.:*

He smoothed the hair away from her face with both hands, cupped her chin in one hand, and met her hazel eyes with his own. *:You are much too practical for me, sweetling. I doubt that either of those considerations would hold me for a second in your place.:* He pretended to think for a moment. *:I believe, on the whole, I'd choose to go mad. Killing something is so very messy if you want it to be satisfying. And how* would *I get the blood out of my Whites?:*

She giggled a little, diverted. He smiled back at her, and blotted the tears from her eyes and cheeks with a handkerchief he pulled from the cuff of one sleeve. *:You'll manage as you always do, dearest. By taking things one day at a time, and coming to me or Trev when you can't bear it all on your own shoulders.:*

She sniffled, and rubbed her nose with her knuckle. He pulled her hand away with a mock-disapproving frown and handed her his handkerchief.

:*Stop that, little girl. I've told you a hundred times not to go out without a hand-kerchief. What will people think, to see the King's daughter wiping her nose on her sleeve?*:

:*That she's a barbarian, I suppose,*: Jisa replied, taking it with a sigh.

:*I swear, I'll have your women sew scratchy silver braid on all your sleeves to keep you from misusing them.*: He frowned again, and she smiled.

:*Now wouldn't that be a pretty picture? Sewing silver braid on my clothing would be like putting lace on a horseblanket.*: Jisa dressed plainly, as soberly as a priestly novice, except when coerced into something more elaborate by her mother. Take now; she was in an ordinary brown tunic and full homespun breeches that would not have been out-of-place on one of the Holderkin beyond the Karsite Border.

:*Jisa, Jisa,*: he sighed, and shook his head. Her eyes lit, and her pretty, triangular face became prettier with the mischief behind them. There were times he suspected her of dressing so plainly just to annoy him a little. :*Any other girl your age in your position would have a closet full of fine clothing. My mother's maids dress better than you do!*:

Mindspeech with Jisa was easier than talking aloud; she'd been a Mind-speaker since she was six and use of Mindspeech was literally second-nature to her. On the other hand, that made it very difficult to keep things from her. . . .

:*Then no one will ever guess you are my father, will they?*: she replied impu-dently. :*Perhaps you should be grateful to me, Father-Peacock.*:

He tugged a lock of hair. :*Mind your manners, girl. I get more than sufficient back-chat from Yfandes; I don't need it from you. Feeling any better?*:

She rubbed her right eye with the back of her hand, ignoring the hand-kerchief she held in it. :*A bit,*: she admitted.

:*Then why don't you go find Trev? He's probably looking for you.*: Van chuck-led. Everyone who knew them knew that the two had been inseparable from the moment Treven stepped onto the Palace grounds. That pleased most of the Circle and Court—except those young ladies of the Court who cherished an infatuation with the handsome young Herald Treven was a finely-honed, blond copy of his distant cousin Herald Tantras, one with all of Tran's defects—not that there were many—corrected. He had half the girls of the Court trailing languidly after him.

And he was Jisa's, utterly and completely. His loyalty was without question—and no one among the Gifted had any doubts as to his love for her.

Sometimes that worried Van; not that they were so strongly attracted to each other, but because Treven was likely to have to make an alliance-marriage, just the way his grandmother, Queen Elspeth, had.

It would never be a marriage in more than name, Vanyel was certain of that. There were conditions in Treven's case that his grandmother and cousin had not ever needed to consider. Elspeth had not been a Mind-speaker; Randi wasn't much of one. No one but another Herald with that particular Gift could guess how distasteful it would be for a powerful Mind-speaker like Trev to make love to someone who was not only mind-blocked, but a total stranger. Probably a frightened, unhappy stranger.

One wonders how any Mindspeaking Monarch could be anything but chaste. . . .

Yet the Monarchs of Valdemar had done their duty before, and likely would do so again. Probably Trev would have to, as well. Yes, it was heart-rending, but it was a fact of life. Heralds did a lot of things they didn't always like. As far as that went, for the good of Valdemar, *Vanyel* could and would have bedded anyone or anything.

In fact, he had done something of the sort, though it hadn't been exactly disagreeable; Van had fathered Jisa with poor, dear Shavri, when Randale proved to be sterile—even though his *preference* was, then and now, for his own sex. . . .

Shaych, they called it now—from the *Tayledras* word *shay'a'chern*, though only a handful of people in all of Valdemar knew that. Though openly shaych, he'd given Shavri a child because Randale couldn't, and because she'd wanted one so desperately—Randi needed his lifebonded stable and whole, and the need for a child had been tearing her apart.

And her pregnancy had stilled any rumors that Randale might not be capable of fathering a child, which kept the channels open for proposals of alliance-marriages to *him*, at least until his illness became too severe to hide.

But because Randale had needed to keep those lines open—and because Shavri was terrified of even the *idea* of ruling—he'd never married his life-bonded. So when it became evident that Randale was desperately ill, and that the Companions "inexplicably" were not going to Choose Jisa, Ran-dale's collateral lines had been searched for a suitable candidate.

Treven was the only possible choice at that point; he'd been Chosen two years ago, and he was a Mindspeaker as powerful as Vanyel. He understood the principles of governing—at least so far as they applied to his own par-ents' Border-barony, since he'd been acting as his father's right-hand man since he was nine.

Jisa had loved him from the moment he'd crossed the threshold of the

Palace. It wasn't obligatory for the King's Own to be in love with her monarch, but Vanyel was of the opinion that it helped. . . .

Except that it makes things awfully complicated.

:*She's not a child anymore,*: Yfandes reminded him. At that point he really *looked* at her, and saw the body of a young woman defining the shape of what had been shapeless before this year.

:*Let's not borrow trouble before we have to,*: he thought back at his Companion, avoiding the topic.

Jisa looked back at him with those too-old, too-wise eyes. :*Trev's waiting for me; he sent me to you. Sometimes he knows what I need before I do.*:

He released her, and stepped back a pace. :*Think you still need me?*:

She shook her head, and pulled her hair back over her shoulders. :*No, I think I'll be all right, now. I don't know how you do it, Father—how you manage to be so strong for all of us. I'll go back in now, but if you need me for anything—*:

He shook his head, and she smiled weakly, then turned and threaded her way across the overgrown flowerbeds, taking the most direct route back, the route he had avoided.

Soaking *her* shoes. And not caring in the least.

:*Like father, like daughter,*: Yfandes snorted.

:*Shut up, horse,*: Van retorted absently.

His own thoughts followed his daughter. *It's a lifebonding, the thing between her and Trev. I'm positive. The way she's always aware of him, and Trev of her . . . in a way that's not a bad thing. She's going to need all the emotional help she can get when Randi dies, and she surely won't get it from Shavri. Shavri is going to be in too much pain herself to help Jisa—assuming Shavri lives a candlemark beyond Randi. . . .*

But the problems . . . gods above and below! Is she old enough to understand what Trev is going to have *to do—that the good of Valdemar may—will—take precedence over her happiness? How* can *any fifteen-year-old understand that? Especially with her heart and soul so bound up with his?*

But—she was old enough to understand about me. . . .

How well Vanyel remembered. . . .

. . . the provisions of the exclusion to be as follows. . . .

"Uncle Van?"

Vanyel had looked up from the proposed new treaty with Hardorn. He had the odd feeling that there was something hidden in the numerous clauses and subclauses, something that could cause a lot of trouble for

Valdemar. He wasn't the only one—the Seneschal was uneasy, and so were any Heralds with the Gift of Foresight that so much as entered the same room with it.

So he'd been burning candles long into the night, searching for the catch, trying to ferret out the problem and amend it before premonition became reality.

He'd taken the infernal thing back to his own room where he could study it in peace. It was past the hour when even the most pleasure-loving courtier had sought his or her bed; it was long past the hour when Jisa should have been in hers. Yet there she stood, wrapped in a robe three sizes too big for her, half-in, half-out of his doorway.

"Jisa?" he'd said, blinking at her, as he tried to pull his thoughts out of the maze of "whereas"es and "party of the first parts." "Jisa, what are you doing still awake?"

"It's Papa," she'd said simply. She moved out of the doorway and into the light. Her eyes were dark-circled and red-rimmed. "I can't do anything, but I can't sleep, either."

He'd held out his arms to her, and she'd come to him, drooping into his embrace like an exhausted bird into its nest.

:Uncle Van—: She'd Mindtouched him immediately, and he could sense thoughts seething behind the ones she Sent. :Uncle Van, it's not just Papa. I have a question. And I don't know if you're going to like it or not, but I have to ask you, because—because I need to know the answer.:

He'd smoothed her hair back off her forehead. :I've never lied to you, and I've never put you off, sweetling,: he'd replied. :Even when you asked uncomfortable questions. Go ahead.:

She took a deep breath and shook off his hands. :Papa isn't my real father, is he? You are.:

He'd had less of a shock from mage-lightning. And he'd answered without thinking. :I—yes—but—:

She'd thrown her arms around his neck and clung to him, not saying anything, simply radiating relief.

Relief—and an odd, subdued joy.

He blinked again, and touched her mind, tentatively. :Sweetling? Do—:

:I'm glad,: she said. And let him fully into her mind. He saw her fears—that she would become sick, as Randale had. Her puzzlement at some odd things she'd overheard her mother say—and the strange evasions Shavri had given instead of replies. The frustration when she sensed she wasn't being told the truth. The bewilderment as she tried to fathom questions that became mystery. And the love she had for *him*. A love she now felt free to offer him, like a gift.

Perhaps it was that last that surprised him the most. :*You don't mind?*: he asked, incredulously. He could hardly believe it. Like many youngsters in adolescence, she'd been a little touchy around him of late. He'd assumed that it was because she felt uncomfortable around him—and in truth, he'd expected it. Jisa knew what he was, that he was shaych, and what that meant, at least insofar as understanding that he preferred men as close companions. Neither he nor her parents had seen any point in trying to hide that from her; she'd always been a precocious child, as evidenced by *this* little surprise. :*You really don't mind?*: he repeated, dazed.

"Why should I *mind*?" she asked aloud, and hugged him harder. "Just—tell me why? Why isn't Papa my father—and why is it you?"

So he had, as simply and clearly as he could. She might have been barely over twelve, but she'd taken in his words with the understanding of someone much older.

She left him amazed.

She'd finally gone off to her bed—but had sent him back to his treaty both bewildered and flattered, that she admired him so very much. . . .

And loved him so very much.

She still loved him, admired him, and trusted him; sometimes she trusted him more than her "parents." Certainly she confided more in him than in Shavri.

He shook his head a little, and continued down the cobbled path that would lead him eventually to the door out of the garden. *Poor Jisa. Shavri leans on her as if she were an adult—depends on her for so much—it hardly seems fair. Then again, maybe I should envy the little minx. I still can't get my parents to think of me as an adult.*

All too soon he came to the end of the path. Buried in a tangle of hedges and vines was the chipped, green-painted door. He opened it, and stepped into the darkened hallway of the Queen's suite.

The rooms were just as neglected as the garden had been; dark, full of dusty furniture, and with a faint ghost of Elspeth's violet perfume still hanging in the air. Shavri had never felt comfortable here, and Randale had deemed it politic (after much discussion) to leave this suite empty as a sign that he *might* take a Queen.

That "might" had been hard-won from Randi—because although Shavri was both his King's Own and his lifebonded love, his advisors (Vanyel among them) had managed to convince him that he should at least *appear* to be free to make an alliance and seal it with a wedding.

Shavri had seen the need, but Randale had been rebellious, even angry with them. But after hours of argument, even he could not deny the fact that Valdemar's safety would be ill-served if he acted to please only himself. It was a lesson Trev was going to have to learn all too soon.

Fortunately Shavri—lovely, quiet Shavri—had backed them with all the will in her slender body. And that was considerable, for she was a full and powerful Healer as well as being a Herald. Herald-Mages were rare; before Taver Chose Shavri, Valdemar had never seen a Herald-Healer. Van hoped the need would never arise for there to be another.

Vanyel eased through the rooms with a sense, as always, that he was disturbing something. Dust motes hung in the sunbeams that shone through places where the curtains had parted. Despite that hint of perfume, there was no sense of "presence"—it was rather as though what he was disturbing were the rooms themselves rather than something inhabiting them. There were several places in the Palace like that, places where it seemed as if the walls themselves were alive. . . .

Taver had Chosen Shavri when Lancir had died—just before Elspeth herself had passed. The Heralds had been puzzled; they hadn't known why a Healer should be Chosen, though most assumed it was for lack of a more suitable candidate, or simply because Shavri and Randale were lifebonded. Only later, when Shavri couldn't seem to conceive for all her trying, did *she* suspect that the reason for Taver's taking her was that something was wrong with Randi.

And only *much* later did they all learn that her suspicion was correct.

At that point, wild horses couldn't have dragged her to the altar to marry Randale. If there was one thing Shavri *didn't* want, it was the responsibility of rule.

Vanyel eased open one side of the heavy double doors to the main corridor, and shut it behind him. His own responsibilities settled over him like a too-weighty cloak. He straightened his back, squared his shoulders, and set off down the stone-floored hall toward his own quarters in the Heralds' Wing.

Shavri was, if truth were to be told, entirely unsuited to ruling. *I guess we should be just as pleased that she doesn't want Consort status*, Vanyel thought, nodding to an early-rising courtier, one already clad in peacock-bright, elaborately embellished Court garb. *For her own sake, and Jisa's sake, I think she made the right decision. I know she didn't want Jisa forced into the position of Heir, and really, this was the only way to keep that from happening. She can't be sure that Jisa wouldn't be Chosen if the Companions thought it necessary. And if she were Chosen and rightborn—*

But Jisa's legally a bastard and can't inherit, and not being Chosen makes her doubly safe.

The stone floor gave way to wood; the "Old Palace" to the New. Vanyel ran over the plans for the day in his mind; first *his* audience with Tashir's people, then a session with the Privy Council, then with the Heraldic Circle. Then the audiences with Randale and the Lake District envoys. Shavri would be there, of course; Randale needed her Gift and her strength. She spent it all on him, which left her no time or energy for any of the normal duties of the King's Own. No matter; Vanyel took those—and even if she'd had the strength to spare, Shavri had not been very skilled at those tasks. . . .

:*Shavri was abysmal at those tasks,:* Yfandes said tartly. :*The only reason she wasn't a total failure was that she relied on Taver and on you to tell her what to do and say.:*

Vanyel stopped long enough to have a few words with one of Joshe's aides, an older girl-page with a solemn face, his mind only vaguely on what he was saying to the girl. :*'Fandes, that isn't kind.:*

:*Maybe. But it's true. The only thing she showed any real talent in was managing Randi and in knowing where her skills weren't up to the job. If Shavri'd let Randale go through with wedding her,* she'd *be next in line even before Jisa, and that would be a disaster.:*

Vanyel wanted to be able to refute her, but he couldn't. Shavri *wasn't* a ruler; she wasn't even a Herald except in having Taver. Vanyel did most of her work, from playing ambassador with full plenipotentiary powers, to creating and signing minor legal changes into effect. From being First in the Circle to being First in the Council, to being Northern Guardian of the Web; he did it all. He even took Randale's place in the Council in the King's absence.

:*That's most of the time, now,:* Yfandes observed sadly.

Van got the answer he wanted out of the child, despite his distraction. She smoothed her tunic nervously, plainly anxious to be gone, and Vanyel obliged her. He was still analyzing the overtones of his conversation with Jisa. :*We've got a new problem. Did you pick up what I did from Jisa?:* he asked, hurrying his steps toward his room. His feet were beginning to ache with the cold, and the wet leather had begun to chafe his ankles.

:About the real reason why she came to cry on your shoulder? The one she doesn't want to think about? It was too cloudy for me to read.:

Vanyel sensed someone in his room as he neared it, but it was a familiar presence, though one without the "feel" of a Herald, so he didn't bother to identify his visitor. *:Shavri,:* he said grimly. *:It's what she's picking up from her mother. Jisa knows Randi's doomed; she's coming to grips with that. What she can't handle is that Shavri's getting more desperate by the moment, more afraid of being left alone. Jisa's afraid that when Randi leaves us—her mother will follow.:*

He felt Yfandes jerk her head up in surprise. *:She's a Healer!:* the Companion exclaimed. *:She can't—she wouldn't—:*

:Don't count on it, dearheart,: Vanyel answered, one hand on the door latch. *:Even I can't tell you what she'll do. I don't think she'd actively suicide on us—but she is a Healer. She knows enough about the way that the body works to kill herself through lacking the will to live. And that's what Jisa's afraid she'll do; just pine away on us. And the worst of it is, I think she's right.:*

He pushed the door to his spare quarters open; it was full of light and air, but not much else. Just a bed, a low, square table, a few floor-pillows, a wardrobe, and a couch.

On the couch was his visitor—and despite his worries, Vanyel felt his mouth stretching in a real smile.

"Medren!" he exclaimed, as the lanky, brown-haired young Bard-trainee rose and reached across the table to embrace him. "Lord and Lady, nephew, I think you get taller every week! I'm sorry about not being able to get to your recital, but—"

Medren shook long hair out of his warm brown eyes, and smiled. "Tripes, it isn't my first, and it isn't going to be my last. That's not what I came after you for, anyway."

"No?" Vanyel settled himself down in his favorite chair, and raised an inquiring eyebrow. "What brings you, then?"

Medren resumed his seat, leaning forward over the table, his eyes locking with Van's. "Something a hell of a lot more important than a stupid recital. Van, I think I have something that can help the King."

CHAPTER 2

$\Large V$ ANYEL CLOSED THE door behind him, balanced with one hand still on the door handle, and reached down to pull one of his boots off. "What exactly do you mean?" he asked, examining it, and deciding that it was going to survive the soaking after all. "Forgive me if I sound skeptical, Medren, but I've heard that particular phrase dozens of times in the past few years, and in the end nothing anyone tried made any difference. I'm sure you mean well—"

Medren perched in a chair beside the window, with not only his expression but his entire body betraying how tense he was. The curtains fluttered in a sudden gust of breeze, wrapping themselves over his arm. He pushed them away with an impatient grimace. "That's why I waited so long, I really thought about this for a while before I decided to talk to you," Medren told him earnestly. "You've had every Healer, herbalist, and so-called 'physician' in the Kingdom in and out of here—I wasn't going to come to you unless it wasn't just me who was sure we had something."

Vanyel pulled off his other boot, and regarded his nephew dubiously. He'd never known Medren to go overboard—but there had been so many times when a new treatment had sounded promising and had achieved nothing. . . . Medren's judgment was unlikely to be better than anyone else's.

Still—there was always the chance. There was little doubt that in Medren Van was dealing with a rational adult now, not an overly impressionable boy. Medren had grown taller in the years since Vanyel had sent him off to Bardic Collegium, and even though he hadn't put on any bulk at all he was obviously at full growth. He actually looked like a pared-down, thin version of his father, Vanyel's brother Mekeal. Except for one small detail—he had his mother Melenna's sweet, doelike eyes.

He must be just about ready to finish Journeyman's status at least, Vanyel realized with a start. *He might even be due for Full Bard rank. Ye holy stars, he must be nearly twenty!*

The curtains flapped, and Medren pushed them away again "You know

I wouldn't bring you anything trivial or untried. I know better, and anyway, I've got my ranking to think of. I'm one master-work away from Full Bard," he finished, confirming Vanyel's startled assessment. He combed his fingers restlessly through his long hair. "I can't start my career by getting a reputation for chasing wild geese. I've had Breda check this for me, and she's confirmed it. It seems my roommate, Stefen, has a Wild Talent. He can sing pain away."

Van had made his way to the side of the bed by the end of this speech; he sat down on it rather abruptly, and stared at his young cousin. "He can—what?"

"He sings pain away." Medren shrugged, and the cloth of his red-brown tunic strained over his shoulders. "We don't know how, we only know he can. Found it out when I had that foul case of marsh-fever and a head like an overripe pumpkin."

Vanyel grimaced in sympathy; he'd had a dose of that fever himself, and knew the miserable head and bone aches it brought with it.

"Stef didn't know I was in the room; came in and started practicing. I started to open my mouth to chase him out, I figured that was the *last* thing I needed, but after the first two notes *I couldn't feel any headache.* Point of fact, I fell asleep." Medren leaned forward, and his words tumbled out as he tried to tell Vanyel everything at once. "I woke up when he finished, he was putting his gittern away, and the headache was coming back. Managed to gabble something out before he got away from me, and we tried it again. Damned if I didn't fall asleep again."

"That could have been those awful herbal teas the Healers seem to set such store by," Vanyel reminded him. "They put *me* to sleep—"

"Put you to sleep, sure, but they don't do much about the head. Besides, we thought of that. Got at Breda when I cured up, told her, got her to agree to play victim next time she had one of her dazzle-headaches, and it worked for her, too." He took a deep breath, and looked at Vanyel expectantly.

"It did?" Vanyel was impressed despite his skepticism. Breda, as someone with the Bardic Gift, wasn't easily influenced by the illusions a strong Gift could weave. Besides, so far as he knew, nothing short of a dangerous concoction of wheat-smut could ease the pain of one of her dazzle-headaches.

Medren spread his hands. "Damned if I know how he does it, Van. But Stef's had a way of surprising us over at Bardic about once a week. Only eighteen, and *he's* about to make Full Bard. Just may beat me to it. Anyway, you were telling me how Randale hates to take those pain-drugs because they make him muddled—"

"But can't endure more than an hour without them, yes, I remember." Vanyel threw the abused boots in the corner and leaned forward on his bed, crossing his arms. "I take it you think we can use this Stefen instead of the drugs? I'm not sure that would work, Medren—the reason Randi hates the drugs is that his concentration goes to pieces under them. How can he do anything and listen to your friend at the same time?"

Medren swatted the curtains away again, jumped to his feet and began pacing restlessly, keeping his eyes on Vanyel. "That's the whole beauty of it—this Wild Talent of his seems to work whether you're consciously listening or not! Honest, Van, I thought this out—I mean, if it would work when Breda and I were *asleep*, it should work under any circumstances."

Vanyel stood up, slowly. This Wild Talent of Stefen's might not help— but then again, it might. It was worth trying. These days anything was worth trying. . . .

And they had tried anything and everything once the Healers had confessed themselves baffled. Hot springs, mud baths, diets that varied from little more than leaves and raw grains to nothing but raw meat. There had been no signs of a cure, no signs of improvement, just increasing pain and a steadily growing weakness. Nothing had helped Randale in the last year, not even for a candlemark. Nothing but the debilitating, mind-numbing drugs that Randi hated.

"Let's go talk to Breda," Van said abruptly, kneeling and fishing his outdoor boots out from under the bed. He looked up to catch Medren's elated grin. "Don't get excited," he warned. "I know you're convinced, but this may be nothing more than pain-sharing, and Randi's past the point where that's at all effective." He stood up, boots in hand, and pulled them on over his damp stockings. "But as you pointed out, it's worth trying. Astera knows we've tried stranger things."

Medren kept pace with his uncle easily, despite Vanyel's longer legs and ground-devouring strides. After all, *he* had just spent his Journeyman period completely afoot, in the wild northlands, where villages were weeks apart. *Fortunately it was also the shortest Journeyman trial in the history of the Collegium,* he reflected wryly, recalling his aching feet, sore back, and the nights he spent half-frozen in his little tent-shelter. *And it wasn't even winter yet! Three months up there gave me enough material for a hundred songs. Although so far half of them seem to be about poor souls freezing to death—*

Medren watched his uncle out of the corner of his eye, trying to gauge his feelings, but he couldn't tell what Van was thinking. In that, as in any number of things, Vanyel hadn't changed much in the past few years, though he had altered subtly from the uncle Medren had first encountered.

Gotten quieter, more focused inside himself. Doesn't even talk to anybody about himself anymore, not even Savil. Medren frowned a little. *Uncle Van isn't doing himself any favors, isolating himself like that.*

Vanyel had the kind of fine-boned, ascetic face that aged well, with no sign of wrinkling except around the eyes and a permanent worry-line between his brows. His once-black hair was thickly streaked with white, but that wasn't from age, that was from working magic with what he and his aunt, Herald-Mage Savil, called "nodes." Medren had gathered from Vanyel's complicated explanations that these node-things were collecting points for magical energy—and that they were infernally hard to deal with.

For whatever reason, the silver-streaked hair, when combined with the ageless face and a body that would have been the envy of most of Medren's peers, made Vanyel's appearance confusing—even to those who knew him. Young-old, and hard to categorize.

Add eyes the color of burnished silver, eyes that seemed to look right through a person, and you had the single most striking Herald in Whites. . . .

Medren frowned again. *And the least approachable.*

His nephew guessed that Vanyel had been purposefully learning how to control his expressions completely in the same way a Bard could. Probably for some of the same reasons. Not even a flicker of eyelid gave his thoughts away; over the past couple of years control had become complete. Even Medren, who knew him about as well as anyone, never knew what was running through his mind unless Van wanted him to know.

Vanyel was as beautiful as a statue carved from the finest alabaster by the hand of a master. But thanks to that absolute control, he was also about as remote and chill as that same statue.

Which is the way he wants it, Medren sighed. *Or at least, that's what he says. "I can't afford hostages," he says. "I can't let anyone close enough to be used against me." He doesn't even like having people know that he and I are as friendly as we are*—and we're *related. He thinks it makes me a target. . . .*

There actually had been at least one close scrape, toward the end of the Tashir affair. Medren hadn't realized how close that scrape had been until long after, in his third year at Bardic. And in some ways, Van was absolutely right, in that he couldn't afford close emotional relationships. If he'd been the marble statue he resembled, his isolation would likely have been a good thing.

But he wasn't. He was a living human being, and one who would not admit that he was desperately lonely.

To the lowest hells with that. If he doesn't find somebody he can at least talk to besides Savil, he's going to go mad in white linen one of these days. He's keeping everyone else sane, but who can he go to?

Nobody, that's who. Medren gritted his teeth. *Well, we'll see about that, uncle. If you can resist Stef, you're a candidate for the Order of Saint Thiera the Immaculate.*

They left the Palace itself, and followed a graveled path toward the separate building housing the Bardic Collegium; a three-storied, gray stone edifice. The first floor held classrooms, the second, the rooms of such Bards as taught here, and the third, the rooms of the apprentices and Journeymen about to be made Masters. There were only two of the latter, himself and Stefen. Some might have objected to being roomed with Stef, for the younger boy was shaych, and made no bones about it—but not Medren.

Not with Vanyel for an uncle, Medren reflected, with tolerant amusement. *Not that Stef's anything like Van. If uncle's a candidate for the Order of Saint Thiera, Stef's a candidate for the Order of the Brothers of Perpetual Indulgence! No wonder he writes good lovesongs; he's certainly had enough experience!*

One of the brown-tunicked Bardic apprentices passed them, laboring under a burden of four or five instruments. They stepped off the path long enough to let her pass; her eyes widened at the sight of Vanyel, and she swallowed and sketched a kind of salute as they passed by her. Van didn't notice, but Medren did; he winked at her and returned it.

Medren had gotten Stef as a roommate before this, back when he was an apprentice. *That was surely an experience! I'm not sure which was stranger for me; Stef as he arrived, or Stef once he figured out what he was.* Medren mentally shook his head. *What a country-bred innocent I was!*

Stef had arrived at the Collegium in the care of Bard Lynnell; barely ten, and frightened half to death. He had no idea what was going on, or why this strange woman had plucked him off his street corner and carried him off. Lynnell wasn't terribly good with children, and she hadn't bothered to explain much to young Stefen. That had been left to Medren, the only apprentice at the time who had no roommate.

And first I had to explain that this wasn't a bordello. He'd thought Lynn was a procurer.

Lynnell had heard the boy singing on the street corner, attracting good crowds despite being accompanied only by an unskilled hag with a bodhran.

While the Bard had no talent for taking care of children, she *was* both skilled and graced with the Bardic Gift herself. She had recognized Stefen's Gift with the first notes she heard. And she knew what would happen if that child was left unprotected much longer—some accident would befall him, he could be sold to a whoremaster, some illness left untreated could ruin his voice for life—there were a thousand endings to this child's story, and few of them happy.

Until Lynnell had entered it, anyway. *One thing about Lynn; she goes straight for what she wants so fast that most people are left gaping after her as she rides out of sight.*

She'd made enough inquiries to ascertain that the crude old woman playing the drum and collecting the coins was *not* Stef's mother, nor any kind of relative. That was all it took for her to be on the sunny side of legality; once that was established, she had invoked Bardic Immunity and kidnapped him.

Then dumped him on me. Medren smiled. *Glad she did. He may have gotten me into trouble, but it was generally fun trouble.*

There were some who opined that Stefen's preference for his own sex stemmed from some experience with that nasty old harridan that was so appalling he'd totally repressed the memory. Privately Medren thought that was unlikely. So far as he was able to determine, she'd never laid a finger on Stefen except for an occasional hard shaking, or a slap now and then.

From everything Stef said, when she was sober, she knew where her money was coming from. She wasn't cruel, just crude, and not too bright. So long as her little songbird kept singing, she wasn't going to do anything to upset him.

He held the door to the Bardic Collegium open for his uncle, and followed closely on his heels.

All that Stef had suffered from was neglect, physical and emotional. The emotional neglect was quickly remedied by every adult female in the Collegium, who found the half-starved, big-eyed child irresistible.

Stef's spirits certainly revived quickly enough once he discovered the attention was genuine—and also learned he was to share the (relative) luxuries of the Bardic Collegium.

Like a roof over his head every night, a real bed, all he could eat whenever he wanted it, Medren thought, following Vanyel up the narrow staircase to the second floor. *Poor little lad. Whatever his keeper had been spending the money on, it certainly wasn't high living. Drugs, maybe. The gods know Stef's death on anybody he catches playing with them.*

Bard Breda's rooms were right by the staircase; Collegium lore had it that she'd picked that suite just so she could humiliate apprentices she caught sneaking in late at night.

The *fact* was that she had chosen those rooms because she was something of an Empath and something of a chirurgeon; she'd gotten early herbalist training before her Gift was discovered. Bardic apprentices tended to get themselves in trouble with alarming regularity. Sometimes that trouble ended in black eyes—and occasionally in worse. Breda's minor Talents had come to the rescue of more than one wayward apprentice since the day she'd settled in to teach.

Like every other female in the place, she'd taken a liking to Stef, which was just as well. Once Stef had reached the age of thirteen his preferences were well established—and his frail build combined with those preferences got him into more fights than the rest of the apprentices combined. Breda had patched Stefen up so many times she declared that she was considering having the Healers assign him to one of *their* apprentices as a permanent case study.

Vanyel paused outside the worn wooden door, and knocked lightly.

"Come," Breda replied, her deep voice still as smooth as cream despite her age, and steadier than the Palace foundations. Vanyel pushed the door ajar, and let them both into the dim cool of Breda's quarters.

Medren often suspected that Breda was at least half owl. She was never awake before noon, she stayed alert until the unholiest hours of the dawn, and she kept the curtains drawn in her rooms no matter what time of day or night it was. Of course, that could have been at least in part because she was subject to those terrible headaches, during which the least amount of light was painful . . . still, walking into her quarters was like walking into a cave.

Medren peered around, trying to see her in the gloom, blinking as his eyes became accustomed to it. He heard a chuckle, rich and throaty. "By the window. I do read occasionally."

Medren realized then that what he'd taken for an empty chair did in fact have the Bard in it; he'd been fooled by the shadows cast by the high back. "Hullo, Van," the elderly Bard continued serenely. "Come to verify your scapegrace nephew's tale, hmm?"

"Something like that," Vanyel admitted, finding another chair and easing himself down into it. "You must admit that most of the rumors of cures we've chased lately have been mist-maidens."

Medren groped for a chair for himself; winced as the legs scraped discordantly against the floor, and dropped down onto its hard wooden seat.

"Sad, but true," Breda admitted. "I must tell you, though, I was completely skeptical, myself. I'm difficult to deceive at the best of times; when I have one of my spells I really don't have much thought for anything but the pain. And that youngling *dealt* with the pain. I've no idea how, but he did it."

"So I take it you're in favor of this little experiment?" Medren thought Van sounded relieved, but he couldn't be sure.

A faint movement from the shadows in the chair signaled what might have been a shrug. "What have we got to lose? The boy can't hurt anyone with that Wild Talent, so the very worst that could happen is that the King will have one of our better young Journeymen providing appropriately soothing background music for the audiences. He'll have to have *someone* there entertaining in any case—someone with the Gift, to keep those ambassadors in a good mood. No reason why it can't be Stefen. The boy's amazingly good; very deft, so deft that even most Gifted Bards don't notice he's soothing them."

"No reason at all," Vanyel agreed. "Especially if he's that good. Can he do both at once?"

"Can you Mindspeak with 'Fandes and spellcast at the same time?" Breda countered.

"If the spell is familiar enough." Vanyel pondered. "But I don't know, he's not very experienced, is he? Medren told me he's still a Journeyman."

"He may not be experienced, but he's a damned remarkable boy," Breda replied, with an edge to her voice. "You ought to pay a bit more attention to what's going on under your nose, Van; the lad's been the talk of the Collegium for the past couple of years. That's why we kept him *here* for his Journeyman period instead of sending him out. The boy's got all *three* Bardic requirements, Van, not just two. The Gift, the ability to perform, and the creative Talent to compose. Three of his ballads are in the common repertory already, and he's not out of Journeyman status."

Vanyel coughed. "I stand rebuked," he replied, a hint of humor in his voice. "Well, let's give this Stefen a chance. Do you want to tell him, or shall I?"

Breda laughed. "You. I'd just gotten comfortable when you two sailed in. And at my age, one finds stairs more than a little daunting."

Vanyel rose, and Medren scrambled to join him. "You're just lazy, that's all," he mocked gently. "You can outdance, outfight, outdrink, and outlast people half your age when you choose."

"That's as may be," Breda replied as Vanyel turned toward the door, her own voice just as mocking. "But right now I don't choose. Let me know how things work out, youngling."

Medren felt a hand between his shoulderblades propelling him out the door and into the corridor. "Just for that," Vanyel said over his shoulder as he closed the door, "I think I'll see that someone tells you—sometime next week."

A pungent expletive emerged, muffled, through the door. Medren hadn't known Breda knew *that* particular phrase . . . though anatomically impossible, it certainly would have been interesting to watch if she'd decided to put his uncle in that particular position. . . .

Stefen—or rather, Stefen's appearance—came as something of a surprise to Van. Vanyel had been expecting something entirely different—a youngster like Medren, but perhaps a little plainer, a little taller. At some point he'd formed a vague notion that people gifted with extraordinary abilities tended to look perfectly ordinary.

Stefen was far from ordinary—

Van hung back when they'd gotten to the room Medren shared with the boy, prompted by the feeling that Stefen might be uneasy in his presence. Stef had just been leaving, in fact. Medren intercepted him right at the door, and Vanyel had lingered in an alcove while Medren explained to the boy what they wanted of him. That gave Van ample opportunity to study the musician while the youngster remained unaware of the Herald's scrutiny.

Vanyel's first impression was of fragility. Stefen was slight; had he been a girl, he'd have been called "delicate." He was a little shorter than Vanyel, and as slim. That didn't matter, though—Vanyel could tell that Stef's appearance was as deceptive as his own. Stefen was fine-boned, yes, but there was muscle over that bone; tough, wiry muscle.

I wouldn't care to take him on in a street fight, Van observed, eyes half-closed as he studied the boy. *Something tells me he'd win.*

Dark auburn hair crowned a triangular face; one composed, at first impression, of a pair of bottomless hazel eyes, high cheekbones, and the most stubborn chin Van had ever seen.

He looks like a demented angel, like that painting in the High Temple of the Spirit of Truth. The one that convinced me that knowing too much truth will drive you mad. . . . Vanyel watched carefully as Stef listened to Medren's plans. Once or twice, the boy nodded, and some of that wavy hair fell into his eyes. He brushed it out of the way absently, all his attention given to his roommate.

He was tense; that was understandable. Vanyel was very glad that he had chosen to keep himself out of the way now. The boy was under quite enough pressure without the added stress of Herald Vanyel's presence. Van was quite well aware how much he overawed most of the people he came into contact with—that gardener this morning was the exception. Most folk reacted the way that young Bardic apprentice had on the way over here— the kind of mix of fear and worship that made her try to bow to him despite having both arms full, and despite custom that decreed otherwise. Heralds were not supposed to be "special." Rank was not supposed to matter except inside Circle and Council.

Rules, apparently, did not apply to Herald-Mage Vanyel Ashkevron.

Well, that's neither here nor there, he thought, watching the young Journeyman-Bard carefully. *:'Fandes, what do you think of this youngster?:*

He felt her looking out of his eyes, and felt her approval before she voiced it. *:I like him, Van. He'll give you everything he has, without holding back. He has a very powerful Bardic Gift, and he does indeed have a secondary Gift as well that is nearly as powerful. It's something like Mindhealing, but very specific. I can't tell you any more than that until I See it in action.:*

For the first time that day, Vanyel allowed his hope to rise a little. *:Then you think this might work?:*

:I don't know any more than you do,: she replied, *:But the boy has something unusual, and I think you'd be a fool not to give him all he needs to wield it.:*

Van blinked. *:Huh. Well, right now, the only other thing I can give him is to stay out of the way. I don't want to frighten him into freezing by having The Great Herald-Mage Vanyel Demonsbane descend on him.:*

:The Great Herald-Mage indeed,: she snorted. *:Sounds like someone I know may not fit his hats before too long.:*

Medren opened the door to their room and waved Stefen inside. He looked back over his shoulder at Van, who just nodded at him. The boy was doing just fine; so long as Stefen got to the Throne Room in time for the audiences, Vanyel didn't see any reason to interfere in the way things were going. He turned and headed back down the hallway to the stairs.

:I won't fit my hats, hmm?: he replied as he descended the stairs. *:Isn't that interesting. I was just thinking that it's been too long since the last time you and I went over the advanced endurance course together. Who was it I overheard boasting about the times she used to make over the course?:*

If she'd been human, she'd have spluttered. *:Van! That was a long time ago! The trainees are going to be out on the course at this time of the day—I'm going to look like an out-of-shape old bag of bones in front of them!:*

Vanyel chuckled, and pushed open the door to the outside with one hand. *:And who was it who told me she could run those trainees into the ground?:*

He hadn't known Yfandes knew that particular curse. He wondered if she'd learned it from Breda.

Stefen sagged bonelessly into the room's single comfortable chair, and stared at a discolored spot on the plastered wall.

This was what I wanted, right? That's why I let Medren talk me into trying that trick on Breda. I used to "cure" old Berte's hangovers by singing them away—I was sure I could do the same for what ailed Medren and Breda. And that would get me what I needed, since I knew damn well he has connections up into the Court. I knew he'd get me in to see if I could help the King. This is the only way I could think of to get Court favor, and get it honestly. Now, I know I can help King Randale. What I can do is better for him than his taking a lot of drugs. It'll be a fair exchange. So why am I so nervous about this?

He couldn't stand sitting there idle; he reached automatically for the gittern he kept, strung and tuned, beside the chair. It was one of his first student instruments—worn and shabby, a comforting old friend. He ran his fingers over the strings, in the finger exercises every Bard practiced every day of his life, rain or shine, well or ill.

He'd known about this trick of his, this knack of "singing pain away" for a long time—he'd had it forced on him, for all practical purposes, by the old woman who had cared for him for as long as he could remember. It was either sing her pain away, or put up with her uncertain temper and trust he could get out of her reach when she was suffering a "morning after."

Old Berte wasn't his mother—but he couldn't remember anyone who might have been his mother. There had only been Berte. Those memories were vivid, and edged with a constant hunger that was physical and emotional. Berte teaching him to beg before he could even walk. Berte making false sores of flour-paste and cow's blood, so that he looked ill. Berte binding up one of his legs so that he had to hobble with the help of a crutch.

The hours of sitting beside her on a street corner, learning to cry on cue.

Then the day when one of the other beggars brought out a tin whistle, and Stef had begun to sing along, in a thin, clear soprano—and when he'd finished, there was a crowd about the three of them, a crowd that tossed more coppers into Berte's cracked wooden bowl than he'd ever seen in his short life.

I looked up, and I saw the expression on her face, and I knew I'd never have to limp around on a crutch again.

He closed his eyes, and let his fingers walk into the next set of exercises. *Berte bought us both a real supper of cooked food from a food stall at the market. Fresh food, not stale, not crumbs and leavings—and we shared a pallet and a blanket that she bought from a ragman that night. That was the best day of my life.*

It remained the best day of his life for a long while, for once she had a steady source of income, Berte returned to the pleasures that had made her a beggar in the first place. Liquor, and the drug called "dreamerie."

She drank and drugged away every copper we made. At least I didn't have to spend half of every night trying to run the cramps out of my legs, he thought, forcing the muscles in his shoulders to relax while he continued to play. *Things were a little better. I could take care of her hangovers—enough so that we could get out every morning. I was hungry, but I wasn't quite as hungry as when we'd just been begging for a living. The worse she got, the easier it was to hide a coin or two, and once she was gone into her dreams, I could sneak out and buy something to eat. But I kept wondering when she was going to run afoul of whoever it was that sold her the drugs—how long it would be before the craving got too much and she sold me the way she'd sold her own children.* An involuntary shudder made both his hands tremble on the strings. *I was sure that was what had happened when Lynnell grabbed me that night.*

It had been late; Berte had just sunk into snoring oblivion, and Stef had eased out between the loose boards at the back of their tenement room, a couple of coppers clutched in his fist. He had intended to head straight for Inn Row where he knew he could buy a bowl of soup and all the bread he could eat for those two coppers—but someone had been waiting for him. A woman, tall, and sweet-smelling, dressed all in scarlet.

She'd grabbed his arm as he rounded the corner, and there had been two uniformed Guardsmen with her. Terror had branded her words into his memory.

"Come with me, boy. You belong to Valdemar now."

He hadn't the faintest idea what she'd meant. He hadn't known that "Valdemar" was the name of the kingdom where he lived. He hadn't even known he lived in a Kingdom! All he'd ever known was the town; he'd never even been outside its walls. He'd thought this "Valdemar" was a person, and that Berte had either sold him or traded him away.

*I was in terror—too frightened to object, too petrified to even talk. I kept wondering who this "Valdemar" was, and whether it was a he or a she—*He smiled at the next set of memories. *Poor Lynn. When she finally figured out what I thought she'd bought me for, she blushed as red as her tunic.*

She'd done her best to try and convince him otherwise, but he really didn't believe her. He really didn't believe any of it until a week or two after he'd been brought to the Collegium, tested, and confirmed in his Gifts.

It was really Medren that convinced me. Bless him. Bless Breda for putting us together. He was a complete country bumpkin, and I was an ignorant piece of street scum, and together we managed to muddle through. If he was just shaych, he'd have been perfect. He wasn't even jealous when he found out I had all three Gifts, too, and in a greater measure than he did. . . .

It took two of what were commonly called "the Bardic Gifts" to ensure entry into Bardic Collegium as a Bardic apprentice rather than a simple minstrel. The first of those two were the most common: the ability to compose music, often referred to as the "Creative Gift," and the unique combination of skills and aptitudes that comprised the "Gift of Musicianship." The third was more along the lines of the Gift of Healing or one of the Heraldic Gifts—and that was simply called the "Bardic Gift."

It seemed to be related to projective Empathy; a person born with it had the ability to manipulate the moods of his audience through music. Some of the Bards of legend had been reputed to be able to *control* their listeners with their songs.

Stef had all three Gifts, just as Lynnell had suspected. Medren, who until Stefen had arrived had been the star apprentice, also had all three, but not to the extent Stef did.

Take the Creative Gift, for instance. Medren cheerfully admitted that he could no more compose anything more complicated than a simple ballad than he could walk on water. Or Musicianship; there were few even among the Master Bards that were Stef's peers in skill on his chosen instruments. In sober truth, there were few who even played as many instruments as he did. Although his favorite by far was the twelve-stringed gittern, he played virtually every string and percussion instrument known to exist, and even a few wind instruments, like the shepherd's pipes.

But it was Stefen's Bardic Gift that was the most impressive. Even before he had revealed his ability to come between the listener and his pain, the Master Bards had marveled at the strength of his Gift. Untrained, he could easily hold an audience of more than twenty; and when he exerted himself they would be deaf and blind to anything other than himself and his music.

Anybody but Medren would have been jealous. He just felt sorry for me, because I was alone. Stefen smiled, and modulated the last exercise into a lullaby. *There I was, the cygnet among the chicks, and instead of trying to peck me to bits like anyone else would have, he decided I needed a protector. Life would have been a lot harder without him. He kept me from making a lot of enemies. . . .*

He hadn't known until much later that a number of the sharp-tongued boys who initially closed their ranks against the stranger were children of high-ranking nobles, or were nobles in their own right. When he would have gone after them in the straight-forward "fight-or-be-beaten" manner of the streets, Medren had kept him from losing his head.

He helped me to at least get them to accept me. And I may need them. I certainly couldn't afford to have any of them holding grudges. He sighed and racked his instrument. *That's my only hope; court favor. And it's a damned good thing Medren kept me from losing it before I even had a chance at it. Being a Bard is better than being a beggar, but it's still a risky profession to be in, with no real security. A Healer can always rely on the Temple to care for him if something happens to him, and if a Herald ends up hurt or ill—Havens, most of them end up dead—there are always places for them here, at the Palace. But a Bard has only himself to rely on. If he loses his voice, or the use of his hands. . . .*

The harsh reality was that Stefen had come from the streets, and if something happened to him, the streets were likely where he'd end. Unless he built himself some kind of secure future.

Otherwise—

No. He got up, and stared for a moment out his window, at the Palace, the heart of all his hopes. *No. I'll do it. I'll make my own luck. I swear I won't go back to that. I won't end up like Berte.*

He gazed at the Palace for a moment more, then picked up the case holding his good gittern, squared his shoulders, and headed for the door.

So now "Valdemar" needs me, after all. That should work. I serve Valdemar, and we both get what we need. He nodded to himself, and closed the door behind him. *Fair enough.*

CHAPTER 3

◆

"**A**RE YOU GOING to be all right?" Vanyel asked in an undertone. Then he thought savagely in the next instant, *Of course he isn't going to be all right, you fool.* The King was as pale as paper, thin to transparency, with pain-lines permanently etched about his mouth and eyes. Under any other circumstances, Vanyel would have ordered him back to his bed; beads of sweat stood out all over his forehead with the effort of walking as far as the Audience Chamber, and Vanyel didn't have to exert his Empathy to know how much pain his joints were causing him. Vanyel would have traded away years of his life to give the King a few moments' respite from that agony. But he allowed none of this to show as he settled the colorless wraith that was King Randale into the heavily-padded shelter of his throne.

"I'll be fine," Randale replied, managing a strained smile. "Really, Van, you worry too much." But he couldn't restrain a gasp of pain as he slipped a little and hit his arm against the side of the throne.

Vanyel cursed his own clumsiness, and did his best not to clutch at Randale's fragile arms, as he caught Randale before he could fall and lowered the King carefully the rest of the way down into his seat. *Another bruise the size of my hand, and he doesn't need ten more where my fingers were.*

"Really, Van," Randale repeated with patently false cheer, once he'd been settled as comfortably as possible. "You worry too much." Vanyel stepped back a pace, ready to aid in any way he could, but sensing the King's irritability at his own weakness and helplessness. *He also doesn't need to be reminded of how little he can do anymore.*

The slight noise of the chamber's side door opening and shutting caught Randale's attention. He craned his head around a little to see who it was, as young Stefen entered the Audience Chamber, put down a stool, and began setting up near the throne.

"Is that a new Bard?" he asked with more real interest than he'd shown in anything all day. "I don't remember seeing that youngster in Court, and I'd surely remember that head of hair! He looks like a forest fire at sunset."

:*Should I tell him, 'Fandes?*:

:*No,*: came the immediate reply. :*It would be cruel to raise his hopes. Stefen is either going to be able to help him, or not. And if not, better that the King simply enjoy the music, as best he can.*:

Vanyel sighed. Yfandes could be coldly pragmatic at the oddest times. "Breda sent him over," Van temporized. "She says he's very good, and you can probably use him with this particular lot of hardheads."

"Gifted, hmm?" Randale looked genuinely interested.

"Quite remarkably, according to Breda." Vanyel coughed. "I gather she caught something in the wind about the Lake District lot, and sent him over specially. I understand he's to concentrate on something soothing."

Randale actually chuckled. "Breda is a very wise woman. Remind me to thank her."

At that moment, the delegation from the Lake District arrived, a knot of brightly-clad figures beside the door, who waited impatiently for the Seneschal to announce them. Vanyel stepped back to his place behind the throne and to Randale's left, while Shavri stepped forward to her position as King's Own at his right.

Please, he sent up a silent plea, *just let him get through this audience.*

Shavri nodded to the young Journeyman Bard, and Stefen began to play as the delegation formed themselves into a line and approached the throne.

Stefen fought down the urge to stare at the King, and concentrated on his tuning instead. Each brief glance at Randale that he stole appalled him more than the one before it. Only the thin gold band holding his lank hair back, and the deference everyone gave this man, convinced him that the man on—or rather, *in*—the throne was Valdemar's King. There were two other Heralds on the dais, one on either side of the throne; a dusky woman, and a man Stefen couldn't see because the woman was in his line-of-sight. Either one of them was a more kingly figure than Randale.

He'd known that Randale was sick, of course—that was no secret, and hadn't been for as long as Stefen had *been* in Haven. But he hadn't known just how sick Randale was; after all, apprentice and Journeymen Bards hardly were of sufficient rank to join the Court, especially not bastards like Medren and gutter rats like himself. The Bards didn't gossip about the King, at least not where their students could hear them. And Stef had never believed more than a quarter of what the townsfolk and nobly-born students would tell the presumptive Bards. He'd imagined that Randale would look ill; thin and pale, perhaps, since his illness was obviously serious. He'd never thought that the King could actually be dying.

Randale looked like a ghost; from colorless hair to skeletal features to corpse-pale complexion, if Stef had come upon this man in a darkened hallway, he'd have believed all the tales of spirits haunting the Palace. That the King wore Heraldic Whites didn't help matters; they only emphasized his pallor.

Stefen was stunned. He couldn't have imagined that the King was in *that* bad a state. It didn't seem possible; Kings weren't supposed to die in the ways ordinary mortals did. When Kings were ill, the Healers were supposed to take heroic measures, and cure them. Kings weren't supposed to have pain so much a part of their lives that every movement was hesitant, tremulous.

Kings were supposed to be able to command miracles.

Except this one can't. This one can't even command his own body to leave him in peace. . . .

There was something so heroic about this man, this King—sitting there despite the fact that he obviously belonged in bed, doing his job in spite of the fact that he was suffering—Stefen wanted to *do* something for him, to protect him. For the first time in his life, Stefen found himself wanting to help someone for no reason other than that the person needed the help.

And for a moment he was confused.

But I am getting something out of this, he reminded himself. *Notice at Court. Maybe even the King's favor, if I really do well. Come on, Stef, you know what's at stake here; settle down and do your work. If he needs your help, that's all the more reason that he'll be grateful when he gets it.*

There was a stir among the group of people beside the door, and they began to sort themselves out and move toward the throne. Stefen looked back to the three on the dais for instructions, and the dark-haired woman with the sorrowful eyes nodded at him purposefully.

Taking that as a signal, he began to play, dividing his power as he'd been instructed. The greater part went to King Randale. Once that was established, the remainder went toward the approaching delegates, soothing their fears, their suspicions—and they *were* suspicious, he could read that in their attitudes, just as he'd been taught. Bards weren't Thoughtsensers, but the kind of instruction they had in reading movement and expression sometimes made it seem that they were. It was plain to Stef that this lot thought Randale had been playing some kind of political game with them, calculatedly insulting them by making them wait for their audience.

Look, you fools, he thought at them, surprising himself with his anger at their attitude. *See what he's going through? He wasn't putting you off, the man's in agony; every moment he spends with you he's paying for in pain.*

He tried to put some of that behind his music, and it worked. He saw the mistrust in their hard, closed faces fade; watched the expressions turn to shock and bewilderment, then faint shame.

He allowed himself a moment of triumph before turning his attention back to the King.

He hadn't quite known what to expect from Randale in the way of an indication that he was doing some good. He had known he would manage *something* in the way of relief for the King; he had been completely confident of that. But how much—and whether there would be any outward sign—

It was the woman's reaction that surprised him the most. She clutched at the other Herald's arm, her expression astonished and incredulous. Randale simply looked—well, better. He sat up straighter, there was a bit more alertness in the set of his head and shoulders, and he moved with more freedom than he had before.

But then Stefen caught a glimpse of his face.

Breda had been transfigured when his Gift had taken away the pain of her dazzle-headache; Medren had revived when it had eased the misery of the fever—but those reactions compared to the relief Randale showed now—well, there simply was no comparison.

Only at that moment did Stefen realize how the King must have been living with this pain as a constant companion, day and night, with no hope of surcease.

He couldn't bear to bring that relief to an end, not after seeing that. So even when the audience concluded, he played on, allowing himself to drift into a trance-state in which there was nothing but the music and the flowing of the power through him—all of it directed to Randale now. A cynical little voice in the back of his mind wondered at that; wondered why he was so affected by this man and why he was giving so much of himself with no promise of reward.

He ignored that thought; though he might have heeded it an hour ago, now it seemed petty and ugly, not sensible and realistic.

Besides, it really wasn't important anymore. All that was important was the music, and the places it was reaching.

There was only the flow of melody, no real thought at all. This was the world he really lived for once he'd discovered it, the little universe woven entirely of music. This was where he belonged, and nothing could touch him here; not hunger, not pain, not loneliness.

He closed his eyes, and let the music take him deeper into that world than he had ever gone before.

Something brushed against Stefen's wandering thoughts; a presence, where no one had ever intruded until now. *What?* he thought, and his fingers faltered for a moment.

That slight hesitation broke the spell he had woven about himself, and suddenly *he* was in pain, real pain, and not some echo from Randale. His fingers ached with weariness, threatening cramps—the tips burned in a way that told him he'd played for much longer than he should have. . . .

In fact, when he opened his eyes, slowly, then pulled fingers that felt flayed off the strings and looked at his chording hand, the reddened and slightly swollen skin told him of blisters beneath the callus.

Blisters that are really going to hurt in a moment.

But that wasn't what had broken his trance; there was someone standing near enough to him to have intruded on his trance, but not so near as to loom over him.

He felt himself flushing; why, he wasn't quite sure. It wasn't quite embarrassment, it was more confusion than anything else. He glanced up from his mangled hand at whoever it was that was standing beside him.

The Audience Chamber had been nearly empty when he'd lost himself in his music—now it was filled to overflowing. But it wasn't the crowd that had broken his entrancement; it was that single person.

The other Herald, the one he hadn't been able to see clearly because the woman had been in the way. And *now* Stefen knew him, knew exactly who he was. Long, silvered black hair, the face every woman in the Court sighed over, silver eyes that seemed to look straight into the heart—there was no mistaking *this* Herald for any other. This was Herald-Mage Vanyel Ashkevron. *Demonsbane*, they called him sometimes, or *Firelord*, or *Shadowstalker*.

There were a hundred names for him, and twice as many tales about him, ballads about him; he was probably *the* most sung-about Herald alive.

Stefen knew every song, and he knew things about Vanyel that were *not* in the ballads. For one thing, he knew that Vanyel's reputation of being a lone wolf was well-founded; he'd held himself aloof from non-Heralds for years, and even those he called "friend" were scarcely more than casual acquaintances.

He had no lovers—not even the rumor of a lover for as long as Stef had been at the Collegium. *So the ladies set their wits to catch him, each one hoping she'll be the one to capture his fancy, to break through that shell of ice.*

Stef would have felt sorry for them if the situation hadn't been so ridiculous. The ladies were doomed to sigh in vain over Vanyel; their hopes could never bear fruit. He knew what they didn't—thanks to the fact that Vanyel might just as well have taken a vow of celibacy, and that the few older Heralds who knew him from his younger days were not inclined to gossip. Because of Medren, Stef was well aware that Vanyel, like Stef himself, was shaych. And that his current state of solitude was not due to a lack of capability or desire.

It was due to fear, according to Medren. Fear that being close to Vanyel would put prospective partners in danger. Fear that others he cared for could be used against him.

The past seemed to have proved Vanyel right, in some ways. Certainly the Herald had not had a great deal of good luck in his emotional life. . . .

Especially with Tylendel.

Stef knew all about Tylendel, the Herald-trainee no one talked about— at least not willingly. They'd talk about his *Companion*, but they'd avoid mentioning his name, if they could. "Gala repudiated her Chosen," they'd say—

As if by mentioning Tylendel's name, his mistake would rub off on them.

There were no songs and few people were willing to discuss the deceased young trainee, even though that repudiation had led to Vanyel's coming into his powers in the first place.

People knew that Herald Vanyel had been Tylendel's closest friend—and some even remembered that they'd been lovers—but it sometimes seemed to Stefen that despite that, they wanted to forget that Tylendel had ever existed.

That struck him as unfair, somehow. The whole tragic mess had been directly responsible for Vanyel becoming the most respected and powerful Herald-Mage in the Circle—and from what Stefen had learned, Tylendel hadn't been *sane* when he'd pursued revenge at the cost of all else. The Companions knew that; they'd rung the Death Bell for him. That was why he'd been buried with full honors, *despite* the repudiation, which told Stef that *some-one* thought he'd have been worth his Whites if he hadn't gone over the edge.

Someone besides Vanyel. Stefen was one of the few outside of the Heraldic Circle who knew that doomed Tylendel had been Vanyel's very first lover—and according to Medren, his lifebonded, and only love.

And Medren should know, seeing that Vanyel is his uncle, Stefen thought, staring stupidly into those incredible silver eyes. This was the closest by far he'd ever been to the famous Herald-Mage, though he'd secretly worshiped Vanyel and daydreamed about him for—well, years.

Medren had offered an introduction, but Stef just couldn't scrape up the courage. Certainly Medren was Stef's friend, and certainly Medren was Vanyel's favorite nephew—but the Herald himself was as far from Stef's reach as a beggar child from a star.

Still, he could dream.

In all those daydreams, Stefen imagined himself doing something wonderful—writing a ballad that would bring tears to the eyes of everyone who heard it, perhaps, or performing some vague but important service for the Crown. He had pictured himself being presented to the Court, then being formally introduced to Herald Vanyel. He'd invented a hundred witty things to say, something to make the Herald laugh, or simply to entertain him. And from there the daydreams had always led to Vanyel's seeking out his company—and finally courting him. Because, thanks to Medren's gossip, Stefen was very well aware that before the Herald-Mage had gotten so bound up in assuming most of the duties rightfully belonging to the King's Own—and before he'd decided that his attentions could prove dangerous to those around him—Vanyel hadn't been at all celibate.

Now the moment was here; Herald-Mage Vanyel was within arm's reach, and looking at him with both gratitude and concern. Now was the time to say or do something clever—

The music limped to a faltering conclusion as Stefen stared back at his idol, unable to think of a single word, clever, or otherwise.

Vanyel pivoted and strode back over to the dais, while Stefen's ears burned with chagrin.

I had my chance. I had it. I should have said something, anything, dammit! Why couldn't I say anything? Oh, ye mothering gods, how can I be such a gap-faced idiot?

The King was talking with someone in Healer's Greens; this looked like more of an interview than an audience—though judging by the way they were leaning toward each other and the intensity of their concentration, there was no doubt that it was an important exchange. While Stefen sat dumbly, berating himself for being such a dolt, the Herald-Mage interrupted the earnest colloquy with a whispered comment.

Both Randale and the Healer turned their heads in his direction, and

Stefen suddenly found himself the focus of every eye in the Audience Chamber.

He felt his face growing hot, a sure sign that he was blushing. He wanted to look away, to hide his embarrassment, but he didn't dare. He knew that if he did, he'd look like a child, and a bigger fool than he already was. Instead he raised his chin a little, and politely ignored the scrutiny of everyone in the room, and kept his eyes fixed on the King.

Randale smiled; it was an unexpected smile, and Stefen smiled hesitantly back. It was easy enough to be cocky among his own peers, but between Vanyel's attentions, and then the King's, Stef was getting very flustered.

He struggled to keep himself from dropping his eyes—the King's smile spread a little wider, then he turned away. He said something to Vanyel, something too quiet to overhear.

Then people were suddenly clearing out of the chamber—

Stefen blinked. *I guess the audience must be over.* In the bustle over getting the King out of his throne and on his feet, everyone seemed to have forgotten that Stef existed. He took a deep breath, and began to pack up his things. In one way he was relieved that he was no longer the center of attention, but in another, he was a little annoyed. After all, he'd just played his hands bloody for Randale's benefit—he'd be a week recovering, at least. If it hadn't been for him, there wouldn't have *been* a session of Court this afternoon.

Thank you, Stefen. You're very welcome, your Majesty. Think nothing of it. All in a day's—

Movement at the edge of his vision made him look up. Herald Vanyel was walking back toward him.

He looked back down at his gittern, and at the leather traveling case. His hands were shaking, which didn't make it any easier to get it into the tight leather case—and didn't make him look any more confident, either. He hastily fumbled the buckles into place, his heart pounding somewhere in the vicinity of his throat. *I'm jumping to conclusions,* he thought, stacking his music and putting it back into the carrier. *He's not coming toward me. He doesn't know me, he has more important people to worry about. He's really going to talk to somebody behind me before they leave. He's—*

"Here," said a soft, deep voice, as his music carrier vanished from his hand. "Let me help you with that."

Stefen looked up into the clouded silver of Vanyel's eyes, and forgot to breathe.

He couldn't break the eye contact; it was Vanyel who looked away, glancing down at Stefen's chording hand. The Herald's mouth tightened, and he made an odd little sound of something that sounded suspiciously like a reaction to pain.

Stefen reminded himself that blue was not his best color, and got his lungs to work again.

Then his lungs stopped working for a second time, as the Herald took his elbow as if he were a friend, and urged him onto his feet.

Vanyel looked back over his shoulder at the milling crowd, now clustered about the departing monarch, and his lips curled in a half smile. "No one is going to miss either of us," the Herald said. "Would you mind if I did something about those fingers?"

"Uh, no—" Stefen managed; at least he thought that was what he choked out. It must have sounded right, since Vanyel steered him deftly out of the room and toward the Heralds' Wing.

Stefen immediately stopped being able to think; he couldn't even manage a ghost of a coherent thought.

Vanyel took the young Bard's music carrier and gittern away from him, and gave the youngster a nudge toward the side door. He refused to let Stefen carry anything; the boy's fingers were a mess. He chided himself for not having noticed sooner.

For that matter, if I'd thought about how he'd been playing without a break, I'd have realized that no one, not even a Master Bard, can play all damned afternoon and not suffer damage. He tightened his jaw. *The boy must have been in some kind of a trance, otherwise he'd have been in agony.*

He guided the youngster through the door to his quarters, thanking whatever deities happened to be watching that no one seemed to have noticed their exit from the Audience Chamber together, and that there was no one in the halls that would have noticed the two of them on the way there. *The last thing I need is for this poor boy to end up with his reputation ruined,* he thought wryly, pushing Stefen down into the couch near the door, and putting his instrument and music case on the floor next to him.

The youngster blinked at him dazedly, confirming Vanyel's guess that he'd put himself in a trance-state. *It's just as well; once he starts to feel those fingers—*

Well, that was why Vanyel had brought the boy here; there was a cure for the injury. Two, actually, one of them residing in his traveling kit. Vanyel had become perforce something of an herbalist over the years—all too often he, or someone he was with, had been hurt with no Healer in reach. *He* had a touch of Healing Gift, but not reliable, and not enough to Heal anything serious. So he'd learned other ways of keeping himself and those around him alive. He kept a full medical kit with him at all times, even now, though here at the Palace he was unlikely to have to use it.

He found it, after a moment of rummaging, under the bed. He knew the shape of the jar he wanted, and fished it out without having to empty the entire kit out on his bed. A roll of soft bandage followed, and Vanyel returned to the boy's side with both in his hands.

A distinctive, sharp-spicy scent rose from the jar as soon as he opened it. "Cinnamon and marigold," he told the boy, and took the most maltreated hand in his to spread the salve on the ridged and swollen fingertips, feeling the heat of inflammation as he began his doctoring. "Numbs *and* heals, and it's good for the muscle cramps you'd be having if you hadn't played your fingers past *that* point. I'm surprised you have any skin left."

The boy smiled shyly but didn't say anything. Vanyel massaged the salve into the undamaged areas of the boy's hands and spread it gently on the blistered fingertips. With the care the raw skin merited, he wrapped each finger in a cushion of bandage, then closed his eyes and invoked the tiny spark of Healing talent *he* had along with his Empathy. He couldn't do much, but at least he could reduce the inflammation and numb some of the pain that the salve wouldn't touch.

But when he opened his eyes again, he was dismayed by the expression on the boy's face. Pure adoration. Unadulterated hero-worship. As plain as the condition of the boy's fingers, and just as disturbing.

It was bad enough when he saw it in the eyes of pages and Herald-trainees, or even younger Heralds. It made him uncomfortable to see it in the pages, and sick to see it from the Heralds.

He couldn't avoid it, so he'd learned to cope with it. He could distance himself from it when it was someone he didn't know, and wouldn't have to spend any amount of time with.

I can't leave it like this, he decided, feeling his guts knot a little. *I'll be working with him constantly, seeing him in Court—I can't allow him to go on thinking I'm some kind of godling.*

"So," he said lightly, as he put the boy's hand down. "According to my nephew, you're the best thing to come out of Bardic in an age." He raised an eyebrow and half-smiled. "Though if you don't show a little more sense, you'll play the ends of your fingers off next time, and *then* where will you be?"

"I suppose I could—uh—learn to play with my feet," the boy ventured. "Then I could *always* get a job at Fair-time, in the freak tent."

Van laughed, as much from surprise that the boy had managed a retort as at the joke. *There's more to this lad than I thought!* "Well, that's true enough—but I'd rather you just learned to pace yourself a bit better. I'll wager you haven't eaten yet, either."

Stefen looked guilty enough to convince him even before the boy shook his head.

Vanyel snorted. "Gods. Why is it that anyone under twenty seems convinced he can live on air and sunshine?"

"Maybe because anyone under fifteen is convinced he has to eat his weight twice a day," Stefen retorted, his eyes starting to sparkle. "So once you hit sixteen you realize you've stored up enough to live on your fat until you're thirty."

"Fat?" Vanyel widened his eyes in mock dismay. "You'd fade away to nothing overnight! Well, rank does have its privileges, and I'm going to invoke one of mine—" He reached for the bell-rope to summon a servant, then stopped with his hand around it. "—unless you'd rather go back to Bardic and get a meal there?"

"Me?" Stefen shook his head the awe-struck look back on his face. "Havens, no! But why would you want to—I mean, I'm just—"

"You're the first person I've had to talk music with in an age," Vanyel replied, stretching the truth just a trifle. "And for one thing, I'd like to know where you got that odd fingering for the D-minor diminished chord—"

He rang the bell as he spoke; a page answered so quickly Vanyel was startled. He sent the child off after provisions as Stefen attempted to demonstrate with his bandaged hand.

When the page returned a few moments later, laden with food and wine, they were deep in a discussion of whether or not the tradition was true that the "Tandere Cycle" had been created by the same Bard as "Blood Bound." Once into the heated argument (Vanyel arguing "for," based on some eccentricities in the lyrics, Stefen just as vehemently "against" because of the patterns of the melodies) the boy settled and began treating him as he would anyone else. Vanyel relaxed, and began to enjoy himself. Stefen was certainly good company—in some ways, very much older than his chronological age, and certainly able to hold his own in an argument. This was the first chance he'd had in weeks to simply sit back and *talk* with someone about something that had nothing whatsoever to do with politics, Randale, or a crisis.

The page had brought two bottles of wine with the meal; it was only when Vanyel was pouring the last of the second bottle into both their glasses that he realized how late it was—

And how strong that wine had been.

He blinked, and the candle flames blurred and wavered, and not from a draft.

I think maybe I've had a little too much—Vanyel forced his eyes to focus, and licked his lips. Stefen had curled up in the corner of the overstuffed couch with his legs tucked under him; his eyes had the soft, slightly dazed stare of someone who is drunk, knows it, and is trying *very* hard to keep everyone else from noticing.

Vanyel glanced up at the time-candle; well past midnight, and both of them probably too drunk to stand, much less walk.

Certainly Stefen couldn't. Even as Vanyel looked back at him, he set his goblet down with exaggerated care—on the thin air *beside* the table.

In no way is he going to be able to walk back to his room, Vanyel thought, nobly choking down the laugh that threatened to burst from his throat, and fumbling for a handful of napkins, as Stefen swore in language that was quite enough to take the varnish off the table, and snatched at the fallen goblet. *Even if he got as far as the Collegium building, he'd probably fall down the stairs and break his neck.*

He mopped at the wine before it could soak into the wood of the floor, Stefen on his knees beside him, alternately swearing and begging Van's pardon.

Seriously, if I send him back to his room, he'll get hurt on the way, I just know it. Maybe all he'd get would be a bruising, but he really could break his neck.

Stefen sat back on his heels, hands full of wet, stained napkins, and looked about helplessly for someplace to put them—some place where they wouldn't ruin anything else.

Vanyel solved his dilemma by taking the cloths away from him and pitching them into a hamper beside the wardrobe. He took no little pride in the fact that although *he* was just as drunk as Stefen, he managed to get the wadded cloths *into* the basket.

Aside from the fact that I like this youngster, there's the fact that he's proven himself valuable—after his performance this afternoon, I'd say that he's far too valuable to risk. Van sat back on his own heels and thought for a moment. He allowed his shields to soften a little, and did a quick "look" through the Palace. *None of the servants are awake. There's nobody I'd trust to see the lad safely over to his quarters except myself. And right now, I wouldn't trust me! I can still* think, *but I know damn well I can't walk without weaving.*

He became aware, painfully aware, that Stefen was looking at him with an intense and unmistakable hunger.

He flushed, and tried not to look in the boy's eyes. *Damn. Damn, damn, damn. If I let him stay—it is not* fair, *dammit! He's too young. He can't possibly know what he wants. He thinks he wants me, and maybe he does, right now. But in the morning? That's another thing altogether.*

He Felt Stefen's gaze, like hot sunshine against his skin, Felt the youngster willing him to look up.

And stubbornly resisted. The boy was too young; less than half *his* age. And the boy was infernally attractive. . . .

Damn it all, it's not fair. . . .

Stefen could hardly believe it. He was in Herald Vanyel's private quarters; the door was shut and they were quite alone together. He'd finally managed to redeem himself, at least in his own eyes, for looking like such an idiot. In fact, it looked like he'd impressed Vanyel once or twice in the discussion— at least, up until he'd spilled the wine.

And even then, he could tell that Vanyel was attracted; he sensed it in the way the Herald was carefully looking to one side or the other, but never directly at him, and in the way Vanyel was avoiding even an accidental touch.

Yet Vanyel wouldn't *do* anything!

What's the matter with him? Stefen asked himself, afroth with frustration. *Or is it me? No, it can't be me. Or is it? Maybe he's not sure of me. Maybe he's not sure of himself. . . .*

The wine was going to Stefen's head with a vengeance, making him bolder than he might otherwise have been. So when Vanyel reached blindly for his own goblet on the table beside them, Stefen reached for it, too, and their hands closed on the stem at the same time. Stefen's hand was atop Vanyel's—and as Vanyel's startled gaze met his own, he tightened his hand on the Herald's.

Vanyel's ears grew hot, and his hands cold. He couldn't look away from Stefen's eyes, startled and tempted by the bold invitation he read there.

No, dammit. No. Boy, *child,* you don't know what you're asking for.

In all his life, Vanyel had never been so tempted to throw over everything he'd pledged to himself and just do what he wanted, so very badly, to do.

Not that there hadn't been seduction attempts before this; his enemies frequently knew what his tastes were, and where his preferences lay. And all too often the vehicle of temptation had been someone like this—a young, seemingly innocent boy. Sometimes, in fact, it *was* an innocent. But in all cases, Vanyel had been able to detect the hidden trap and avoid the bait.

And there had been encounters that *looked* like seduction attempts. Young, impressionable children, overwhelmed by his reputation and perfectly willing to give him everything he wanted from them.

And that's what's going on here, he told himself fiercely, the back of his neck hot, his hand beneath Stefen's icy. *That's all that's going on. I swore by everything I consider holy that I was never going to take advantage of my rank and fame to seduce anyone, anyone at all, much less impressionable children who have no notion of what they're getting into. No. It hasn't happened before, and I'm not going to permit it to happen now.*

He rose to his feet, perforce bringing Stefen up with him. Once on his feet he took advantage of Stefen's momentary confusion to put the goblet down. The boy's hand slid from his reluctantly, and Vanyel endured a flash of dizziness that had nothing at all to do with the wine they'd been drinking.

"Come on, lad," he said cheerfully, casually. "You're in no shape to walk back to your bed, and I'm in no shape to see that you get there in one piece. So you'll have to make do with mine tonight."

He reached for the boy's shoulder before the young Bard could figure out what he was up to, and turned him about to face the bed. He gave the boy a gentle shove, and Stefen was so thoroughly intoxicated that he stumbled right to the enormous bedstead and only saved himself from falling by grabbing the footboard.

"Sorry," Vanyel replied sincerely. "I guess I'm a bit further gone than I thought; I can usually judge my shoves better than that!"

Stefen started to strip off his tunic, and turned to stare as Vanyel walked slowly and carefully to the storage chest and removed his bedroll.

"What are you doing?" the youngster asked, bewildered.

"You're my guest," Vanyel said quietly, busying himself with untying the cords holding the bedroll together. "I can do without my bed for one night."

The young Bard sat heavily down on the side of the bed, looking completely deflated. "But—where are you going to sleep?" he asked, as if he didn't quite believe what he was hearing.

"The floor, of course," Vanyel replied, unrolling the parcel, and looking up to grin at the boy's perplexed expression. "It won't be the first time. In fact, I've slept in places a lot less comfortable than this floor."

"But—"

"Good night, Stefen," Vanyel interrupted, using his Gift to douse all the lights except the night-candle in the headboard of the bed because he didn't trust his hands to snuff them without an accident. He stripped off his own tunic and his boots and socks, but decided against removing anything else. His virtuous resistance might not survive another onslaught of temptation, particularly if *he* wasn't clothed. "Don't bother to get up when I do—the hours I keep are positively unholy, and no one sane would put up with them."

"But—"

"Good *night*, Stefen," Vanyel said firmly, crawling in and turning his back on the room.

He kept his eyes tightly shut and all his shields up; after a while, he heard a long-suffering sigh, then the sound of boots hitting the floor, and cloth following. Then the faint sounds of someone settling into a strange bed, and the night-candle went out.

"Good night, Vanyel," came from the darkness. "I appreciate this."

You'll appreciate me more in the morning, Vanyel thought ironically. *And I hope you leave before there're too many people in the corridor, or you'll end up with people thinking* you *are shaych.*

But—"Good night, Stefen," he replied. "You're welcome to stay as long as you like." He smiled into the darkness. "In fact, you're welcome any time. Consider yourself my adoptive nephew if you like."

And chew on that for a while, lad, Vanyel thought as he turned over and stared at the embers of the dying fire. *I have the feeling that in the morning, you'll thank me for it.*

CHAPTER 4

HARD SURFACE BENEATH him. Too even to be dirt, too warm to be stone. Where?

Van woke, as he always did, all at once, with no transition from sleep to full awareness. And since he was not where he *expected* to be, he held himself very still, waiting for memory to catch up with the rest of him.

A slight headache between his eyebrows gave him the clue he needed to sort himself out. *Of course. I'm sleeping—virtuously—alone. On the floor. With a hangover. Because there's a Bard who's altogether too beautiful and too young in my bed. And I'll bet he doesn't wake up with a hangover.*

He heard Yfandes laughing in the back of his mind. *:Poor, suffering child. I shall certainly nominate you for sainthood.:*

Van opened his eyes, and the first morning light stabbed through them and straight into his brain. *:Shut up, horse.:* He groaned and closed his eyes tightly.

:No you don't,: Yfandes said sweetly. *:You have an appointment. With Lissandra, Kilchas, Tran, and your aunt. Remember?:*

He stifled another groan, and opened his eyes again. The sunlight was no dimmer. *:Now that you've reminded me, yes. I have done stupider things in my life than get drunk the night before a major spellcasting, I'm sure, but right now I can't recall any.:*

:I can,: Yfandes replied too promptly.

He knew better than to reply. In the state he was in now, she'd be a constant step ahead of him. *Some day,* he vowed to himself, *I'm going to find out how to make a Companion drunk, and when* she *wakes up, I'll be waiting.*

So there was nothing for it but to crawl out of his bedroll, aching in every limb from a night on the hard floor, to stare resentfully at the youngster who'd usurped his bed. Stefen lay sprawled across the entire width of the bed, a beatific half-smile on his face, deaf, dumb, and blind to the world. Dark red hair fanned across the pillow—*Van's* pillow—not the least tangled with restless tossing, as Van's was. No dark circles under Stefen's eyes—oh, no. The young Bard slept like an innocent child.

Vanyel snarled silently, snatched up his towels and a clean uniform, and headed for the bathing room.

The room was very quiet this early in the morning, and every sound he made echoed from the white-tiled walls. He might well have been the only person alive in the Palace; he couldn't hear anything at all but the noise *he* made. After plunging his head under cold water, then following that torture with a hot bath, he was much more inclined to face the world without biting something. In fact, he actually felt up to a breakfast, of sorts, perhaps a little bread and a great deal of herb tea.

Stefen was still blissfully asleep, no doubt, which made Van's room off limits. Well, it was probably too early for any of the servants to be awake.

He dressed quickly, shivering a little as the chill morning air hit his wet skin, and headed down the deserted hallways to the kitchen, where he found two cooks hard at work. They were pulling hot loaves from the ovens, anonymous in their floured brown tunics and trousers, their hair caught up under caps. They gave him startled looks—it probably wasn't too often that a Herald wandered into *their* purview—but they gave him a pot of tea and a bit of warm bread when he asked them for it, and he took both up to the library.

The Palace library was a good place to settle; the fire was still banked from last night, and a little bit of work had it crackling cheerfully under new logs, filling the empty silence. Vanyel chose a comfortable chair near it, his mug of tea on the hearthstone beside him, and nibbled at his bread while watching the flames and basking in the heat. The last of the headache faded under the gentle soothing warmth of the tea. Yfandes, having sensed, no doubt, that he had reached the limits of his patience, had remained wisely silent.

:Are you up to this?: she asked, when his ill-humor had turned to rueful contemplation of his own stupidity. *:It won't hurt to put it off another day, or even two.:*

He leaned back in his chair and tested all the channels of his mind and powers. *:Oh, I think so. No harm done, other than to my temper. Sorry I snapped.:*

She sent no real thoughts in reply to that, just affection. He closed everything down and thought about the planned session. They would be working magic of the highest order, something so complicated that no one had ever tried it before.

If he'd had any choice, Vanyel wouldn't be doing it now—but the ranks of the Herald-Mages had thinned so much that there was no one to replace any of the four Guardians should something happen to one of them. There were no spare Herald-Mages anymore. The Web, the watch-spell that kept the Heralds informed of danger, required four experienced and powerful mages to make it work; a Guardian of the Web was effectively tied to Haven—not physically, but psychically—as long as he or she was a Guardian. One fourth of the Guardians' energy and time were devoted to powering and monitoring the Web.

Van intended to change all that.

He had been gradually augmenting a mage-node underneath Haven for the past several years. He was no *Tayledras*, but he was Hawkbrother-trained; creating a new node probably would have been beyond him, but feeding new energy-flows into an existing node wasn't. He intended to power the new Web-spell with that node, and he intended to replace the Guardians with *all* the Heralds of Valdemar, Mage-Gifted or no.

And lastly, he intended to set the new Web-spell to do more than watch Valdemar; he intended to make it part of Valdemar's defenses, albeit a subtle part.

He was going to summon *vrondi*, the little air-elementals used in the Truth Spell, and summon them in greater numbers than anyone ever had before. Then he was going to "purpose" them; set them to watching for disturbances in the fabric of mage-energy that lay over Valdemar, disturbances that would signal the presence of a mage at work.

No one but a mage would feel their scrutiny. It would be as if there was something constantly tapping the mage's shoulder at irregular intervals, asking who he was.

And if the mage in question was not a Herald, it would report his presence to the nearest Herald-Mage.

This was just the initial plan; if this worked, Vanyel intended to elaborate his protections, using other elementals besides *vrondi*, to keep Valdemar as free as he could from hostile magics. He wasn't quite certain where to draw the line just yet, though. For now, it would probably be enough for every mage in Valdemar to sense he was being watched; it would likely drive a would-be enemy right out of his mind.

Well, sitting there thinking about it wasn't going to get anything accomplished.

Vanyel rose reluctantly from his chair, left his napkin stuffed into his mug on the hearth, and left the comforting warmth of the library for the chilly silence of the stone-floored corridors.

He headed straight for the Work Room; the old, shielded chamber in the heart of the Palace that had been used for apprentice Herald-Mages to practice their skills under the eyes of their teachers. But there were no apprentices here now, and every Herald-Mage stationed in Haven had his or her own private workrooms that would serve for training if any new youngsters with the Mage-Gift were Chosen.

Now the heavily shielded room could serve another purpose: to become the Heart of the new Web.

Tantras was already waiting for him when he arrived, arranging the furniture Vanyel had ordered. A new oil lamp hung from a chain in the center of the room. Directly beneath it was a circular table with a depression in the middle. Around it stood four high-backed, curved benches. Over in one corner, Tran was wrestling a heavy chair into place, putting it as far from the table as possible.

The older Herald looked up as Van closed the door behind him, raked graying hair out of his eyes with one hand, and smiled.

"Ready?" Vanyel asked, taking his seat, and putting his mage-focus, a large, irregular piece of polished tiger-eye, in the depression in the center. He hadn't been able to find a piece of unflawed amber big enough to use as a Web-focus, and fire-opals were too fragile to use in the Web. Fortunately when he'd replaced Jaysen as Guardian, he'd learned that he worked as well with Jaysen's tiger-eye as with opal and amber; flawless tiger-eye was *much* easier to find.

Vanyel looked back over his shoulder at his friend. "About as ready as I'm ever likely to be," Tantras replied, shrugging his shoulders. "This is the first time I've ever been involved with one of these high-level set-spells of yours. First time I've ever worked with *one* Adept, much less two."

"Nervous?" Vanyel raised an eyebrow at him. "I wouldn't blame you. We've never tried anything like this before."

"Me? Nervous? When you're playing with something that could fry my mind like a breakfast egg?" Tran laughed. "Of course I'm nervous. But I trust you. I think."

"Thanks for the vote of confidence—" Van began, when the door behind him opened and the other three Herald-Mages entered in a chattering knot.

The chattering subsided as they took their places around the table, Savil directly across from Van in the West, Kilchas in the South, Lissandra in the North.

Savil hadn't changed much in the last ten years; lean and spare as an aged greyhound, she moved stiffly, and seldom left Haven anymore. Her hair was pure silver, but it had been that color since she was in her early forties. Working with node-magic was the cause; the powerful energies bleached hair and eyes to silver and blue, and the more one worked with it, the sooner one went entirely silver. She placed her mage-focus, a perfect, unflawed natural crystal of rose-quartz, opposite the tiger-eye. She pursed her lips and contemplated the arrangement, then adjusted her stone until one side of the crystal was just touching the tiger-eye before she sat down. She smiled briefly at Vanyel, then her blue eyes darkened as she began opening up her own channels. Her face lost expression as she concentrated. What wrinkles she had were clustered around her eyes and mouth; there was nothing about her that told her true age, which was just shy of eighty.

On the other hand, Kilchas looked far older than Savil, although in reality he was twenty years younger. A wizened, shriveled old tree of a man, he had more wrinkles than a dried apple, hair like a tangle of gray wire, and a smile that could call an answering grin from just about anyone. At the moment, that smile was nowhere in evidence. He set his focus-stone touching Vanyel's and Savil's. A piece of translucent, apple-green jade, he'd had it carved into the shape of a pyramid. He fussed with it a moment until its position satisfied him. Then he took his seat and lowered his eyelids to concentrate, frowning a little, and his eyes were lost in his creased and weathered face.

Lissandra was the most senior of the Guardians, despite being younger than Vanyel. She had been a Guardian for much longer even than Savil. She had assumed the Northern quadrant along with her Whites, and although she was not quite Adept status, she wasn't far from it. Outside of her duties as a Herald-Mage, she specialized in alchemy, in poisons and their antidotes. Taller than many men, and brown of hair, eyes, and skin, her movements were deliberate, and yet oddly birdlike. She had always reminded Vanyel of a stalking marsh-heron.

Like a heron, she wasted no motion; she dropped her half-globe of obsidian in precisely the right place, and sat down in her chair, planting her elbows on the table and steepling her fingers in front of her face.

Tantras settled gingerly in his chair in the corner as Vanyel reached for the lamp, dimming it until everything outside the table was hardly more than a dim shadow. He reached into his belt pouch and felt for the final stone he'd selected for this spell; a single flawless quartz-crystal, perfectly formed, unkeyed, and as colorless as pure water.

And I must have gone through five hundred–weight of quartz to find it.

He closed his hand around it, a sharp-edged lump wrapped carefully in silk to insulate it, and brought it out into the light. The silk fell away from it as he placed it atop the other four, and it glowed with light refracted through all its facets.

Lissandra nodded her approval, Kilchas' eyes widened, and Savil smiled.

"I take it that we are ready?" Vanyel asked. He didn't need their nods; as he lowered all of his barriers and brought them into rapport with him, he Felt their assent.

Now he closed his eyes, the better to concentrate on bringing them all completely into rapport with himself and each other. He'd worked with Savil so many times that he and his aunt joined together with the firm clasp of longtime dancing partners.

:Or lovers,: she teased, catching the essence of the fleeting thought.

He smiled. *:You're not my type, dearest aunt. Besides, you'd wear me out.:*

He reached for Kilchas next, half expecting a certain reticence, given that Van was shaych—but there was nothing of the sort.

:I'm too old to be bothered by inconsequentials, boy,: came the acid reply, strong and clear. *:You don't spend most of your life in other peoples' heads without losing every prejudice you ever had.:*

Kilchas' mind meshed easily enough with theirs—not surprising, really, given that he was the best Mindspeaker in the Circle—but Vanyel found it very hard to match the vibrations of his magic. The old man was powerful, but his control was crude, which was why he had never gotten to Adept status; he was much like a sculptor used to working with an axe instead of a chisel. Every time Van thought he had their shields matched, the old man would Reach toward him impatiently, or his shields would react to the presence of alien power, and the protections would flare, which had the effect of knocking the meld of Van and his aunt away.

Vanyel opened his eyes, clenching his teeth in frustration, and saw Kilchas shaking his head. "Sorry about that, lad," he said gruffly. "I'm better at blasting things apart than putting them together. And I'm 'fraid some things have gotten instinctive."

"Would you object to having me or Savil match everything *for* you?" Vanyel asked, unclenching his fists and twisting his head to loosen his tensed shoulder muscles.

"You mean—you take over?" Kilchas frowned. "I thought Heralds didn't do that. Isn't that the protocol?"

"Well, yes and no," Savil replied, massaging her temples with her fingertips. "Yes, that's the protocol, but the protocol was never meant for Mindspeaking Adepts, especially not with the strong Gifts my nephew and I have. Van and I can get in there, show you what to do, then get out again without leaving anything of ourselves behind. Occasionally rules *were* made to be broken."

"You're sure?" Kilchas said doubtfully. "I don't want to find myself not knowing if an odd thought is a bit of one of you, left over from this spell-casting, or someone trying to squeak past my shielding."

"I'm positive," Van told him. "It's how the *Tayledras* trained me. One of them would take over, walk me through something, then get out and expect me to imitate them."

Kilchas sighed, and placed both his palms flat on the tabletop. "All right, then. Savil, by preference, Van. You're the one directing this little fireworks show—I'd rather you had your mind on that, and not distracted with one old man's wavering controls."

"Good enough." Vanyel nodded, relieved that it was nothing more personal than that; Kilchas' reasoning made excellent sense. "Let's try this again."

This time he waited, watching, for his aunt to take over Kilchas' mage-powers and bring them into harmony with her own, putting into place a much finer level of control than he had learned on his own. Not to fault Kilchas—for all that his hobby was the peaceable one of astronomy, he'd been primarily an offensive combat mage. He hadn't had much time to learn the kind of control Van and Savil had, nor had he any reason.

:*So we take a shortcut*,: Yfandes said softly. :*There's nothing wrong with a shortcut. I wish this were going faster, though.*:

:*So do I, love*,: Van replied, watching the edges of Kilchas' shields for the moment when the fluctuations ended, since that would signal Savil's success. :*I take it that the others are impatient?*:

:*Kilchas' Rohan is petrified*,: she said frankly. :*He's afraid Kilchas isn't up to this. Lissandra's Shonsea just wants it over; she's not happy about this, but she's confident that Lissandra can handle her part.*:

:*I don't blame her for being unhappy. I want it over, too. I'm not going to be worth much when we finish this job.*: Suddenly Kilchas' shields stopped pulsing, and the color smoothed to an even yellow-gold. :*Tell her it won't be long now.*:

He Reached out again to his aunt, and let her bring *him* into the meld, to avoid disturbing Kilchas' fragile control. Then, before the delicate balance could fall apart, he and Savil flung lines of power to Lissandra.

The fourth Guardian was used to working with Savil; she had been waiting for them, and with the smooth timing of a professional acrobat, caught them, and drew herself into the meld. Vanyel had, in the not-too-distant past, had more than one dislocated joint; the *snap* as Lissandra locked herself into place was a physical sensation very like having a bone put back in the socket. And once she was there, the meld stabilized; a ring instead of an arc. Vanyel breathed a sigh of relief, and Yfandes took that as the signal to bring the Companions into the meld.

They were to be the foundation, the anchoring point, so that none of them would be caught up in the currents of mage-power Vanyel would be using and find themselves lost. Kilchas and Lissandra would be contributing their powers and their presence, and Savil her expertise in handling *vrondi*, but most of this would be up to Vanyel.

Vanyel had worked this entire procedure out with the *Tayledras* Adepts of k'Treva, taking several years to research and test his ideas. The Hawk-brothers Moondance and Starwind, and their foster-son Brightstar were the ones that had helped him the most. No one knew node-magic like the *Tayledras* did; they were bred in and of it, and those that were Mage-Gifted handled it from the time their Gifts first began to manifest, which could be as young as eight or nine. And among the k'Treva clan, those three were the unrivaled masters of their calling.

In point of fact, it had been the spell that another master of an unidentified *Tayledras* clan had left behind in Lineas long ago, the one that bound Tashir's family to the protection of the heart-stone there, that had given Van the idea for this in the first place. In that case, the compulsions set by the spell had been relatively simple; guard the heart-stone, discourage the use of magic, keep the stone and the power it tapped out of the hands of unscrupulous mages. While *Tayledras* normally drained any area they abandoned of magic, they had left the heart-stone in what would become the capital of Lineas because the stone had been bound into another spell meant to Heal a mage-caused fault-line. That spell would take centuries to complete, and meanwhile, only magic was keeping the fault stable. If that magic were to be drained, the devastation caused by the resulting earthquake would be extensive, carrying even into Valdemar. Tashir's family had been selected precisely because they had *no* Mage-Gift and little talent with Mind-magic; although this would ensure that none of them would succumb to the temptation to use the magic, that meant that the creators of the spell had very little to work with.

Vanyel had all of the Heralds, and all their varied Gifts, to integrate into his spell. So what he planned to do was infinitely more complicated, though the results would be equally beneficial.

First things first, he told himself. *Get a good shield up around the four of us. If anything goes wrong, I don't* want *Tran caught in the backlash.*

The shield was the tightest he'd ever built, and when he was finished, the other three Guardians tested it for possible leaks and weak points. Ironically, of the five of them, it was Tantras, who sat *outside* that shield, who would be in the most danger if anything got loose. The Work Room itself was shielded, and so securely that even sounds from without came through the walls muffled, when they penetrated at all. Each of them had their own personal shields; that, in part, was what had been the cause of the difficulty Van had in melding with Kilchas—those shields *never* came down, and it was difficult to match shields one to another so that the power would flow between mages without interruption or interference. If the energy Van planned to call up got away from him, he and the others would be protected by their personal shields. The Work Room shields would protect those beyond the doors, but Tran would be caught in between the two. And since he wasn't a mage, he had none of his own. Van had spent many hours manufacturing protections for him, but they'd never been tested to destruction and he had no idea how much they would really take.

:*He knows that,*: Yfandes reminded him, :*And he agreed. Life is a risk;* our lives ten times the risk.:

Somehow that only made Vanyel feel guiltier.

But he had no choice; his decision to go ahead was based entirely on Valdemar's need. The problem was that the Mage-Gift had always been rare, and the troubles following Elspeth's passing had resulted in the deaths of more Herald-Mages than could be replaced. It had been appallingly clear to Vanyel after the death of Herald-Mage Jaysen that there weren't going to be enough Guardian-candidates to take over the vacant seat in the Web in the event of another death. Yet the Web was Valdemar's only means of anticipating danger before it crossed the Border. Heralds with no Mage-Gift, but with very powerful Gifts of Mindspeech or Farsight, had been tested in the seats; the Web-spell wouldn't work for them because it was powered by a Mage's own personal energies, and there was no way for a Herald without the Mage-Gift to supply that energy.

What Vanyel proposed was to modify that spell.

For the first time since his Gifts had been awakened, he dropped all but the last of his shields. Every mage ever born could establish a "line" to the mind of another with whom he had shared magic—but Vanyel had a line to every living Herald in Valdemar, by virtue of their being Heralds. When his shields were down, he found himself part of a vast network linking all the Heralds together. As delicate as a snowflake, as intricate as the finest lacework, the strands of power that bound them all were deep-laid, but strong. They pulsed with life, as if someone had joined every star in the night sky to every other star, linking them with faint strands of spun-crystal light. It was beautiful. He'd suspected this network existed from the glimpses he'd caught when following his lines to other Heralds, but this was the first time Vanyel had ever Seen the whole of it. Through his mind, the others Saw the same.

:*Amazing,:* Kilchas said at last. :*Why has no one ever spoken of this before?:*

:*Probably because unless your Gift is very strong, you can't detect it since the actual linkage is through the Companions,:* Vanyel replied. :*We share magic with the Heralds without the Mage-Gift through the Companions. That's the other reason I wanted them in the meld; I can See this without them, but with them, I can also manipulate it.:*

:*This must be what King Valdemar first saw when he created the Web.:* Savil's mind-voice was subdued.

:*Except that things were a lot less complicated in his day,:* Vanyel said dryly. :*Let's get to this before we lose the meld.:*

:*Or we get bored with your chatter and find something more interesting,:* Yfandes Mindspoke him alone.

:*One more comment like that, and I'll replace you with one of the* Tayledras *birds,:* Vanyel retorted. Before 'Fandes had a chance to respond, Savil had begun invoking the Web, and Van's attention was fully taken up with the task at hand.

As each Guardian responded, his or her focus-stone came alive with power. When Lissandra completed her response, the four stones were glowing softly, as brightly as the lamp flame above them, and the quartz crystal that topped them was refracting their light in little spots of rainbow all over the room.

Now Vanyel closed his eyes and Saw the Web overlaying the network lacing the entire Kingdom. There were secondary lines of power wisping out from the Web, as if the spell-structure was trying to make full contact with the entire body of Heralds, and yet lacked the power and direction to do so.

That was exactly what Moondance had surmised; the spell-structure was capable of linking all Heralds, but was incomplete and underpowered.

There was no way of knowing if King Valdemar had intended that, or not. Somehow the idea of legendary Valdemar being incapable of completing such a spell did not make Vanyel feel any easier.

If he couldn't, how in Havens can we?

Never mind; he was already committed, and it was too late to back out now. He Reached for the assemblage of focus-stones in the center of the table; Felt a sudden flare of heat/light/pressure as he melded with all five of them, then stabbed his power deep into the earth below Haven, to the ancient node there, a node he and Savil had reawakened. It was *very* deep, and hard to sense, but now that it was active it was one of the most powerful he'd ever used.

Finding it was like plunging into the heart of the sun; too overwhelming to be painful—it was beyond pain—and it threatened to burn him away from himself. It was easy to be lost in a node, and that was why the Companions were in this meld—after the first breathless, mind-numbing contact, he Felt them anchoring him, reminding him of where and what he was.

It took him a moment to lean on their strength and steady himself, to catch his breath. Then he took hold of the heart of the node, braced himself, and Pulled—

This was something no one outside of the *Tayledras* clans had ever attempted. Vanyel was going to create a heart-stone. A small one, but nevertheless, a true heart-stone.

He was fire, he was riven earth, he was molten rock. He was raging water and lightning. He was ancient and newborn. He was, with no memory, and no anchor. No identity. Then something prodded him. A name. Yfandes. He . . . remembered. . . .

With memory came sensation. He was agony.

He Pulled, though his nerves screamed and his heart raced, overburdened. He Pulled, though it felt as though he was pulling himself apart.

Slowly, reluctantly, the power swelled, then settled again at his command.

He Reached again, this time for the Web, and brought it into contact with the raw power of the node—

Contact wasn't enough.

He entered the Web itself; Reached from inside it with mental hands that were burned and raw, and with the melded will of the four Guardians and their Companions, forced it to match magics with the raw node-power and take it in—

And with the very last of his strength, keyed it.

The Web flared; from the heart of it, he Saw and Felt the power surging through it, opening up new connections, casting new lines, until the Web was no longer distinguishable from the fainter, but more extensive network he'd seen before.

He cast himself free from the new heart-stone, and sent delicate tendrils of thought along the new force-lines of the Web. And wanted to shout with joy at what he found, for the spell had taken full effect.

From this moment on, all Heralds were now one with Valdemar, and all were bound into the Web in whatever way their Gifts could best serve. When danger threatened, the Farseers would know "where," the Foreseers would know "when," and every Herald needed to handle the danger would find himself aware of the peril and its location.

At that moment, Vanyel Felt the Companions withdraw themselves from the meld.

For a moment, he panicked—until he Saw that the new Web was still in place, still intact.

Damn. I'd hoped—but they're still laws unto themselves, he thought ruefully. *They were apart from the Web before—and it looks like they've decided it's going to stay that way. Too bad; we could have used them to make up for Heralds with weak Gifts. And since every human magic I've seen has always left them unaffected, I was hoping they might have conferred that immunity on us. Companions have never done more than aid their Chosen, but it would have been nice if this time had been an exception.*

At least his original intentions were holding; the new Web was powered by the magic of the node, and only augmented by the Heralds instead of depending entirely on them. When the call came, those without more pressing emergencies would leave everything to meet greater threats to Valdemar.

Now for the addition to the Web protections. . . .

He dropped out of the meld, for this was something he had to handle alone. He stilled himself, isolated himself from every outside sensation, then brought Savil in closer. Together, they reached out to the *vrondi* and Called—

One came immediately, then a dozen, then a hundred. And still they Called, until the air elementals pressed around them on all sides, thousands of the creatures—

It was a good thing they didn't really exist on the same plane of reality where his body slumped in the Work Room, or he and everyone in it would have been smothered.

He Reached again, much more carefully this time, and created a new line to the Web and the power it fed upon. And showed it to the assembled *vrondi*, as Savil told them wordlessly that this power would be theirs for the taking—

—they surged forward, hungrily—

:—*if,*: said Savil, holding the line a bit out of their reach.

:*If?*: The word echoed from *vrondi* to *vrondi*, ripples of hunger/doubt/hunger. :*If? If?*:

They withdrew a little, and contemplated both of them. Finally they responded.

:*What?*:

Vanyel showed them, as Savil held the line. To earn the power, all they need do, would be to watch for mages. Always watch for mages. And let them know they were being watched.

They swirled about him, about Savil, thousands of blue eyes in little mist-clouds. :*All?*: they asked, in a chorus of mind-voices.

:*That's all,*: he replied, feeling the strength of his own power starting to fade. :*Watch. Let them know you watch.*:

The *vrondi* swirled around him, thinking it over. Then, just when he was beginning to worry—

:*YES!*: they cried, and seized on the line of power—and vanished.

And he let go of Savil, of the meld, and let himself fall.

"Gods," Kilchas moaned.

Vanyel raised his head from the table, where he'd slumped forward. "My sentiments exactly." Kilchas was half-lying on the table with his hands over his head, fingers tangled in his gray mane.

"I think," Lissandra said, pronouncing the words with care, "that I am going to sleep for a week. Did your thing with the *vrondi* work?"

"They took it," Vanyel replied, staring at the single globe of iridescent crystal in the center of the table where the grouping of five stones had been. "Every mage inside the borders of Valdemar is going to know he's being watched. That's going to make him uncomfortable if he doesn't belong here, or he's up to no good. The deeper inside Valdemar, the more *vrondi* he'll attract, and the worse he'll feel."

"And he'll have to shield pretty heavily to avoid detection," Savil added, leaning into the back of her chair and letting it support all her weight. "The *vrondi* are quite sensitive to mage-energy. And they're curious as all hell; I suspect wild ones will start joining our bound ones in watching out for mages just for the amusement factor."

"That's good—as far as it goes." Lissandra reached out and touched the globe in the center with an expression of bemusement. "But it doesn't let *us* know we have mages working on our territory, not unless you can get the *vrondi* to tell us."

"I do have some other plans," Vanyel admitted. "I'd like to get the *vrondi* to react to strange mages with alarm—and since they're now bound into the Web, that in itself would feed back to the Heralds. But I haven't got that part worked out yet. I don't want them to react that way to Herald-Mages, for one thing, and for another, I'm not sure the *vrondi* are capable of telling mages apart."

"Neither am I," Savil said dubiously. "Seems to me it's enough to let mages know they're being watched. If you're guilty, that alone is enough to make you jumpy."

Kilchas had managed to stand up while they were talking; he reached for the globe and tried to pick it up. His expression of surprise when he couldn't made Vanyel chuckle weakly.

"That's a heart-stone now," he said apologetically. "It's fused to the table, and the table is fused to the stone of the Palace and the bedrock beneath it."

"Oh," Kilchas replied, sitting down with a *thump*. Vanyel banished the shields, then turned to the only person in the room who hadn't yet spoken a single word.

Van leaned against the back of his chair, and faced Tantras. "Well?" he asked.

Tran nodded. "It's there, all right. There's something *there* that wasn't a part of me before—"

"What about the trouble-spots?" Vanyel asked.

The other Herald closed his eyes, and frowned with concentration. "I'm trying to think of a map," he said, finally. "I'm working my way around the Border. It's like Reading an object; I get a kind of sick feeling when I come up on some place where there're problems. I'll bet it would be even more accurate if I had a real map."

Vanyel sighed, and slumped his shoulders, allowing his exhaustion to catch up with him. "Then we did it."

"I never doubted it," Savil retorted.

:Nor I,: said the familiar voice in his head.

"Then it's time for me to go fall on my nose; I think I've earned it." Vanyel got to his feet, feeling every joint ache. "I think all of us have earned it."

"Aye to that." Lissandra copied him; Kilchas levered himself up with the aid of the table, and Savil needed Tantras' help to get her onto her feet. Vanyel headed for the door and pulled it open, leaving the others to take care of themselves. Right now all he could think about was his bed—and how badly he needed it.

He walked wearily down the corridor leading out of the Old Palace and toward his quarters, doing his best not to stagger. He was so tired that it would probably look as if he was drunk, and that wouldn't do the Heraldic reputation any good. . . .

:Oh, I don't know,: Yfandes chuckled. *:You might get more invitations to parties that way.:*

:I might. But would they be parties I'd want to attend?:

:Probably not,: she acknowledged.

It didn't occur to him until he was most of the way to the Herald's Wing that his bed might not be unoccupied. . . .

But it was; he pulled his door open to find his room empty, the bed made, and no sign of his visitor anywhere. Evidently the servants had already cleaned and tidied his quarters; there was nothing out of the ordinary about the room.

He clung to the doorframe, surprised by his own disappointment that the young Bard hadn't at least stayed long enough to make some arrangements to get together again.

This time with a little less wine. . . .

That disappointment made no sense; he'd only met the boy last night. And he couldn't *afford* close friends; he'd told himself that over and over.

Anybody you let close is liable to become a target or a hostage, he repeated to himself for the thousandth time. *You can't afford friends, fool. You should be grateful that the boy came to his senses. You can talk to him safely in Court. You know very well that after yesterday you're going to be seeing him there every day. That should certainly be enough. He had no idea what he was offering you last night; it was the wine and his hero-worship talking. You're too old, and he's too young.*

But his bed, when he threw himself into it, seemed very cold, and very empty.

CHAPTER 5

⟶ ◇ ⟵

A DOOR CLOSED, somewhere nearby. Stefen stretched, only half-awake, and when his right hand *didn't* hit the wall, he woke up entirely with a start of surprise. He found himself staring at a portion of wood paneling, rather than plaster-covered stone. It was an entirely unfamiliar wall.

Therefore, he wasn't in his own bed.

Well, that wasn't too terribly unusual. Over the course of the past couple of years, he'd woken up in any number of beds, with a wide variety of partners. What was unusual was that this morning he was quite alone, and every sign indicated he'd gone to sleep that way. He rubbed his eyes, and turned over, and blinked at the room beyond the bedcurtains. There on the floor, like a mute reproach, was a rumpled bedroll.

Looks like I did go to bed alone. Damn.

A pile of discarded clothing, unmistakably Heraldic Whites, lay beside the bedroll.

So it wasn't a dream. Stefen sat up, and ran his right hand through his tangled hair. *I really did end up in Herald Vanyel's room last night. And if he slept there and I slept here*—Stefen frowned. *He's shaych. I certainly made an advance toward him. He was attracted. What went wrong?*

Stef unwound the blankets from around himself, and slid out of Vanyel's bed. On the table beside the chairs on the opposite side of the room were the remains of last night's supper, and two empty bottles of wine. *I wasn't that drunk; I know what I did. It should have worked. Why didn't it? He was certainly drunk enough not to be shy. Should I have been more aggressive?*

He reached down to the floor, picked up his tunic and pulled it over his head. His boots seemed to have vanished, but he thought he remembered taking them off early in the evening. He found the footgear after a bit of searching, where they'd been pushed under one of the chairs, and sat down on the floor to pull them on, his bandaged left hand making him a little awkward.

No, I think being aggressive would have repelled him. I read him right, dammit!

Another thought occurred to him, then, and he stopped with his left foot halfway in the boot. *But what if he wasn't reading me right? What if he thinks I'm just some kind of bedazzled child? Ye gods, little does he know—*

Stef started to smile at that thought, when another thought sobered him. *But if he knew—or if he finds out, what would he think then?*

That was a disturbing notion indeed. *I haven't exactly been discreet. Or terribly discriminating.* He felt himself blushing with—shame? It certainly felt like it. *I was just enjoying myself. I never hurt anybody. I didn't think it mattered.*

But maybe to somebody like Vanyel, who had never had more than a handful of lovers in his life, it might matter. And before last night, Stef would have shrugged that kind of reaction off, and gone on to someone else.

Before last night, it wouldn't have mattered. But something had happened last night, something that made what Vanyel thought very important to Stefen.

Maybe that's it. Maybe it's that he's heard about me, heard about the way I've been living, and—

But that didn't make any sense either. Vanyel hadn't been repelled, or at least, he hadn't shown any sign of it. He'd just put Stefen to bed—alone, like a child, or like his nephew—and left him to sleep his drunk off. And had himself gone to some duty or other this morning, without a single word of reproach.

Stef stood up, collected his gittern and music case from where they were propped beside the door, and slipped out into the hallway, still completely at a loss for what to think.

All I know is, it's a good thing nobody knows I slept alone last night, or my reputation would be ruined.

There were no less than four messages waiting for him when he reached the room he shared with Medren. Fortunately, his friend wasn't in; he didn't want to face the older Journeyman until he could think of a reasonable excuse for what *hadn't* happened. There were times when Medren could be worse than the village matchmaker.

And he didn't even want to look at all those messages until after he was clean and fed.

The first was easily taken care of in the student's bathing room; the youngsters were all in class at this hour, and the bathing room deserted. The second was even easier; he'd learned when he was a student himself that his slight frame and a wistful expression could coax food out of the cooks no matter how busy they were. Thus fortified, he went back to his room to discover that the messages had spawned two more in his absence.

He sat down on his bed to read them. Four of the six messages were from Healers; one from the Dean of Healer's Collegium, two from Randale's personal physicians, and one—astonishingly—from Lady Shavri herself.

They all began much alike, with variations on the same theme. Effusive, but obviously genuine gratitude, assurance that he had done more for the King's comfort than he could guess. The Dean asked obliquely if he would be willing to allow the Healers to study him; the King's attending Healers hinted at requests to attach him directly to the Court. Shavri's note said, bluntly, "I intend to do everything I can to see that you are well rewarded for the services you performed for Randale. As King's Own, I will be consulting with the Dean of your Collegium and the head of the Bardic Circle. If you are willing to continue to serve Randale, Journeyman Stefen, I will do my best for you."

Stef held the last message in his bandaged hand, and contemplated it with amazement and elation.

Last night I thought they'd forgotten I existed. Vanyel was the only one who seemed to care that I'd played my hand raw for them. But this—

Then his keen sense of reality intruded. Shavri hadn't promised anything specific. The others had only been interested in finding out if he'd work with them, and while their gratitude was nice, it didn't put any silver in his pocket or grant him a permanent position. There were two more messages, and one was from the Dean of the Bardic Collegium. There was no telling what they held.

You spent too much time with Vanyel, Stef, he told himself. *All that altruism is catching.*

The fifth was from Medren, letting him know that his roommate was taking a week to travel up north of the city with a couple of full Bards for a Spring Fair. "I want to try out some new songs, pick up some others," the note concluded. "Sorry about running off like this, but I didn't get much notice. Hope things work out for you."

An oblique and discreet hint if ever I heard one, Stef thought cynically. *Obviously he noticed I didn't come back to the room last night, and I'll bet he's wondering if it was his uncle I was with. Unless somebody already told him.* Stefen sighed.

Horseturds, I hope not. If nobody knows, I'll have a chance to make something up to satisfy his curiosity between then and now.

That left the message from the Dean of the Collegium; Stefen weighed it in his hand and wished he could tell if it was good or bad news before he opened it. But he couldn't, and there was no point in putting it off further.

He broke the seal, hesitated a moment further, and unfolded the thick vellum.

Sealed, and written on brand new vellum, not a scrap of palimpsest. Very official—which means either very good, or very bad.

He skimmed through the formal greeting, then stopped cold as his eyes took in the next words, but his mind refused to grasp them.

". . . at the second noon bell, the Bardic Circle will meet to consider your status and disposition. Please hold yourself ready to receive our judgment."

What did I do? he thought wildly. *I only just made Journeyman—they can't be meaning to jump me to Master! But—why would they demote me? What could I have possibly done that was that bad? Unless they just found something out about my past. . . .*

That could be it; not something he'd *done*, but something he *was*. The lost heir to some title or other? No, not likely; that sort of thing only happened in apprentice-ballads. But there were other things that might cause the Circle to have to demote him, at least temporarily. If his family ran to inheritable insanity, for instance; they'd want to make sure *he* wasn't going to run mad with a cleaver before they restored his rank. Or if he'd been pledged to wed in infancy—

Now *there* was a horrid thought. In that case the only thing that would save him would be Apprentice-rank; apprentices were not permitted marriage. And galling as it would be to be demoted, it would be a lot worse to find himself shackled to some pudgy baker's daughter with a face like her father's unbaked loaves. But being demoted would give the Bardic Collegium all the time they needed to get him free of the pledge or simply outwait the would-be spouse, delaying and delaying until the parents gave up and fobbed her off on someone else.

Or until they found out about his sexual preferences. Even in Valdemar most fathers would sooner see their daughters married to a gaffer, a drunkard, or a *goat* than to someone who was shaych.

For one thing, they'd never get any grandchildren out of me, Stef thought grimly. *And as long as I'm an anonymous apprentice, there's no status or money to be gained by forcing a marriage through anyway.*

That seemed the likeliest—*far* likelier than that the Circle would convene to elevate an eighteen-year-old barely three months a Journeyman to Master rank.

Well, there was only one way to find out: get himself down to the Council Hall and wait there for the answer.

But first he'd better make himself presentable. He flung himself into the chest holding his clothing in a search for *one* set of Bardic Scarlets that wasn't much the worse for hard wearing.

Waiting was the hardest thing in the world for Stefen. And he found himself waiting for candlemarks outside the Council chamber.

He did not wait graciously. The single, hard wooden chair was a torture to sit in, so he opted for one of the benches (meant for hopeful tradesmen) instead. He managed to stay put rather than pacing the length and breadth of the anteroom, but he didn't sit quietly. He fidgeted, rubbing at the bandages on his fingers, tapping one foot—fortunately there was no one else in the room, or they might have been driven to desperate measures by his fretting.

Finally, with scarcely half a candlemark left until the bell signaling supper, the door opened, and Bard Breda beckoned him inside.

He jumped to his feet and obeyed, his stomach in knots, his right hand clenched tightly on his bandaged left.

The Council Chamber, the heart of Bardic Collegium, was not particularly large. In fact, there was just barely room for him to stand facing the members of the Bardic Council once the door was closed.

The Council consisted of seven members, including his escort, Breda. She took her place at the end of the square marble-topped table around which they were gathered. There was an untidy scattering of papers in front of the Chief Councillor, Bard Dellar.

The Councillor looked *nothing* like a Bard, which sometimes led to some awkward moments; set slightly askew in a face much like a lumpy potato was a nose that resembled a knot on that potato, separating a mouth so wide Dellar could eat an entire loaf of bread in one bite, and a pair of bright, black eyes that would have well suited a raven.

"Well," Dellar said, his mouth stretching even wider in a caricature of a grin. "You've certainly been the cause of much excitement this morning. And no end of trouble, I might add."

Stefen licked his lips, and decided not to say anything. Dellar looked friendly and quite affable, so the trouble couldn't have been that bad. . . .

"Cheer up, Stefen," Breda chuckled, cocking her head to one side. "You're not at fault. What caused all the problems was that we were trying to satisfy everyone without hurting anyone's feelings. Making you a Master and assigning you directly to Randale was bound to put someone out unless we did it carefully."

"Making me—*what?*" Stefen gulped. Dellar laughed at the look on his face.

"We're making you a full Bard, lad. Shavri was most insistent on that." The chief Councillor smiled again, and Stef managed to smile back. Dellar picked up the papers in front of him, and shuffled them into a ragged pile. "She doesn't want a valuable young man like you gallivanting about the countryside, getting yourself in scrapes—"

"Nonsense, Dell," Breda cut him off with an imperious wave of her hand, and pointed an emphatic finger at Stefen. "What Shavri did or didn't want wouldn't have mattered a pin if you weren't also one of the brightest and best apprentices we've had in Bardic in—I don't know—ages, at any rate. We don't make exceptions because someone with rank pressures us, Stefen. We *do* make them when someone is worthy of them. You are. You have no need to prove yourself out in the world, and your unique Gift makes you double valuable, to us, and to the Crown."

She gave Dellar a challenging look; he just shrugged and chuckled. "She's put it in a nutshell, lad. We need to keep you here for the King's sake, and the only way to do that is to assign you to King Randale permanently. The only way to give you the rank to rate *that* kind of assignment is for you to be a Master Bard. But there's a problem—"

"I can see that, sir," Stef replied, regaining his composure. "It's not the way things are supposed to be done. There's likely to be some bad feelings."

"That is an understatement," one of the others said dryly, examining her chording hand with care. "Bards are only human. There's more than a few that will want your privates for pulling this plum. About half of that lot will be sure you slept your way to it. And unless we can do something to head that jealousy off, gossip will dog your footsteps, and make both your job and your life infinitely harder. Need I remind you that we're dealing with Bards here, and experts with words? Before they're through, that risque reputation of yours will be the stuff of tavern-songs and stories from here to Hardorn."

Stefen felt his face getting hot.

"That's been the problem, lad," Dellar shrugged. "And this is where we had to make some compromises. So now I'll have to give you the bad news. You'll be assigned as the King's personal Bard, but it will be on the basic stipend. Bare expenses, just like now. No privileges, and your quarters will be your old room right here, rather than something plusher at the Palace. We'll have Medren move out so it's private, but that's the best we can do for you."

Stef nodded, and hid his disappointment. He was *still* going to be the youngest Master Bard in the history of the Collegium. He *still* had royal favor, and he would be in the Court, in everyone's eye, where he had the chance to earn rewards on the side. "I can understand that, sir," he said, trying to sound as if he was taking all this in stride. "If it looks like I'm not getting special treatment—if, in fact, it's pretty obvious that the only reason I've been made Master is so I can serve the King directly—well, nobody who's that ambitious is going to envy me a position with no special considerations attached."

"Exactly." Dellar nodded with satisfaction and folded his hands on top of his papers. "I'd hoped you would see it that way. You'll also be working with the Healers, of course. They're mad to know how it is you do what you do, and to see if it's possible for them to duplicate it."

Stefen sighed. That would mean more time taken out of his day, and less that he could spend getting some attention where it could do him some long-term good. He'd seen Randale now, and just how ill the King really was; he wouldn't last more than a few years, at best, and *then* where would Stefen be?

Out, probably. If nobody needs that pain-killing Gift of mine. And having nowhere else to go, unless I make myself into a desirable possession.

"Yes, sir," he replied with resignation he did his best to conceal.

Still, the Healers can't take up all my time. What I really need to find out is where the ladies of the Court congregate, since there isn't any Queen. The married ones, that is. The young ones won't have any influence—no, what I need is a gaggle of bored, middle-aged women, young enough to be flattered, old enough not to take it seriously. Ones I can be a diversion for. . . .

He realized suddenly that Bard Dellar was still talking, and he'd lost the last couple of sentences. And what had caught his attention was a name.

"—Herald Vanyel," Dellar concluded, and Stef cursed himself for his inattention. Now he had no idea at all what it was Vanyel had said or done or was supposed to do, nor what it could possibly have to do with himself. "Well, I think that about covers everything, lad. Think you're up to this?"

"I hope so, sir," Stefen said fervently.

"Very well, then; report to Court about midmorning, just as you did yesterday. Herald Vanyel will instruct you when you get there."

So, Vanyel's to be my keeper, hmm? Stefen bowed to the members of the Bardic Council, and smiled to himself as he left the room. *Well. Things are beginning to look promising.*

Despite the precautions, there was still jealousy. Stef found himself being ignored, and even snubbed, by several of the full Bards—mostly those who were passing through Haven on the way to somewhere else, but it still happened.

It wasn't the first time he'd been snubbed, though, and it probably wouldn't be the last. The Bards that stayed any length of time soon noticed that he wasn't getting better treatment than an ordinary Journeyman, and the ice thawed a little.

But only a little. They were still remote, and didn't encourage him to socialize. Stef was not at all happy about the way they were acting, and it didn't help that he had something of a guilty conscience over his rapid advancement. Making the jump from Journeyman to Master was much more than a matter of talent, no matter what the Council said; it was also a matter of experience.

Experience Stef didn't have. He wasn't that much different from Medren on that score. Nevertheless, here he was, jumped over the heads of his year-mates, and even those *older* than he was, getting shoved into the midst of the High Court—

The side of him that calculated everything rubbed its hands in glee, but the rest of him was having second and third thoughts, and serious misgivings. The way some of the other full Bards were treating him just seemed to be a confirmation of those misgivings.

And the Healers were beginning to get on his nerves. They wanted to monopolize every free moment of his time, studying him, and he had no chance during that first week to make any of the Court contacts he had intended to.

In fact, for the first time he was *using* that Gift of his every time he sang, and by the end of the day he was exhausted. If he wasn't singing for Randale's benefit, he was demonstrating for the Healers. If he'd had any time to think, he might well have told them, one and all, to chuck their Master Bardship and quit the place. But he was so tired at day's end that he just fell into bed and slept like a dead thing, and telling the Council to go take a long hike never occurred to him.

Maddeningly, he seldom saw much of Vanyel either, and every attempt to get the Herald's amatory attention fell absolutely flat.

Every time he pressed his attentions, the Herald seemed to become— nervous. He could *not* figure out what the problem was. Vanyel would *start* to respond, but then would pull back inside himself, and a mask would drop down over his face.

If he'd had the energy left, he'd have strangled something in frustration.

That was the way matters stood when Medren returned from his little expedition.

Stefen stared at himself in the mirror, then made a face at himself. "You," he said accusingly, pointing a finger at his thin, disheveled other self, "are an idiot."

"I'll second that," said Medren, popping up behind him startling Stef so much that he yelped and threw himself sideways into the wall.

While he gasped for breath and tried to get his heart to stop pounding, Medren thumped his back. "Good gods, Stef," his friend said apologetically, "what in the seventh hell's made you so jumpy?"

"No—nothing," Stef managed.

"Huh," Medren replied skeptically. "Probably the same 'nothing' that made you call yourself an idiot. So how's it feel to be a Master Bard?" When Stef didn't immediately answer, Medren held him at arm's length and scrutinized him carefully. "If it feels like you look, I think I'll stay a Journeyman. Don't you ever sleep?" A sly smile crept over Medren's face. "Or is somebody keeping you up all night?"

Stefen groaned and covered his eyes. "Kernos' codpiece, *don't* remind me. My bed is as you see it. Virtuously empty."

"Since when have you and virtue been nodding acquaintances?" Medren gibed.

"Since just before you left," Stef replied, deciding on impulse to tell his friend the exact truth.

"That's odd." Medren let go of his shoulders and moved back a step. "I would have thought that you and Uncle Van would have hit it off—"

Stef bit off a curse. "Since when—you've been—what do you—"

"I set you up," Medren said casually. "The opportunity was there, and I grabbed it—I knew Van would try anything to help the King, and I know you think he hung the moon. I figured neither one of you would be able to resist the other. Gods know I'd been *trying* to get you two in the same place at the same time for over a year. So—" Now he paused, and frowned. "So what went wrong?"

"*I* don't know," Stef groaned, and turned away, flinging himself down in a chair. "I can't think anymore. I've tried every ploy that's ever worked before, and I just can't imagine why they aren't succeeding now. The Healers are working me to death, and Herald Vanyel keeps sidestepping me like a skittish horse. I'd scream, if I could find the energy."

"Tell the Healers to go chase their shadows," Medren ordered gruffly. "Horseturds, Stef, you're exercising a *Gift*; that takes power, physical energy, and you're using yours up faster than you can replace it! No wonder you're tired!"

"I am?" This was news to Stefen. He'd always just assumed using his Gift was a lot like breathing. You just *did* it. And he said as much.

Medren snorted. "Good gods, doesn't *anybody* in this place think? I guess not, or the Healers wouldn't be stretching you to your limits. Or else nobody's ever figured the Bardic Gift was like any other. I promise you, it is; using your Gift *does* take energy and you've been burning yours up too fast. If the blasted Healers want to study you any more, tell them that. Then tell them that from now on they can just wedge themselves into a corner behind the throne and study you from there. Idiots. Honestly, Stef, Healers can be so damned focused; give them half a chance and they'll kill you trying to figure out how you're put together."

Stefen laughed, his sense of humor rapidly being restored. "That's why I was telling myself I was an idiot. I was letting them run me into the ground, but I couldn't think of a way to get them to stop. They can be damned persuasive, you know."

"Oh, I know." Medren took the other chair and sprawled in it gracelessly. "I know. Heralds are the same way; they don't seem to think ordinary folks need something besides work, work, and more work. I've watched Uncle Van drive himself into the ground a score of times. Once or twice, it's been *me* that had to go pound on him and make him rest. And speaking of Uncle Van, that brings me right back to the question I started with: what went wrong? You still haven't really told me anything. Take it from the beginning."

Stefen gave in, and related the whole tale, his frustration increasing with every word. Medren listened carefully, his eyes darkening with thought. "Hmm. I guess—"

His voice trailed off, and Stef snapped his fingers to get his attention. "You guess *what*?"

"I guess he's gotten really shy," Medren replied with a shrug. "It's the only thing I can think of to explain the way he's acting. That and this obsession he has about not letting anyone get close to him because they'll become a target."

Stefen felt a cold finger of fear run suddenly down his back. "He's not wrong," he told his friend solemnly, trying *not* to think of some of the things he'd seen as a street beggar. How during "wars" between street gangs or thief cadres, it was the lovers and the offspring who became the targets— and the victims—more often than not. And it was pretty evident from the Border news that a war between the nations and a war between gangs had that much in common. "It's a lot more effective to strike at an emotional target than a physical one."

Medren shook his head. "Oh, come on, Stef! You're in the heart of Valdemar! Who's going to be able to touch you here? That's even assuming Van *is* right, which I'm not willing to grant."

"I don't know," Stefen replied, still shivering from that odd touch of fear. "I just don't know."

"Then snap out of this mood of yours," Medren demanded. "Give over, and let's see if we can't think of a way to bring Uncle Van to bay."

Stefen had to laugh. "You talk about him as if he was some kind of wild animal."

Medren grinned. "Well, this is a hunt, isn't it? You're either going to have to coax him, or ambush him. Take your pick."

At that moment, one of the legion of Healers that had been plaguing Stefen appeared like a green bird of ill-omen in the doorway. "Excuse me, Bard Stefen," the bearded, swarthy man began, "but—"

"No," Stef interrupted.

The Healer blinked. "What?"

"I said, 'no.' I won't excuse you." Stefen stood, and faced the Healer with his hands spread. "Look at me—I look like a shadow. You people have been wearing me to death. I'm tired of it, and I'm not going to do anything more today."

The Healer looked incensed. "What do you mean by that?" he snapped, bristling. "What do you mean, we've been 'wearing you to death'? We haven't been—"

"I meant just what I said," Stef said coolly. "I've been using a *Gift*, Healer. That takes energy. And I don't have any left."

Now the Healer *did* look closely at him, focusing first on the dark rings under his eyes, then looking oddly *through* him, and the man's weathered face reflected alarm. "Great good gods," he said softly. "We never intended—"

"Probably not, but you've been wearing me to a thread." Stefen sat down again, feigning more weariness than he actually felt. The guilt on the Healer's face gave him no end of pleasure. "In fact," he continued, drooping a little, "if you *don't* let me alone, I fear I will have nothing for the King. . . ."

He sighed, and rested his head on the back of the chair as if it had grown too heavy to hold up. Through half-closed eyes he watched the Healer pale and grow agitated.

"We can't—I mean, King Randale's needs come first, of course," the man stammered. "I'll speak to—I'll see that you aren't disturbed any more today, Bard Stefen—"

"I don't know," Stefen said weakly. "I hope that will be enough, but I'm so tired—"

Out of the corner of his eye he saw Medren with his fist shoved into his mouth, strangling on his own laughter.

"Never mind, Bard," the Healer said, strangling on his own words. "We'll do something about all this—I—"

And with that, he turned and fled. Medren doubled up in silent laughter, and Stefen preened, feeling enormously pleased with himself.

"I really *am* tired, you know," he said with a grin, when Medren began to wheeze. "I honestly am."

"Lord and Lady!" the Journeyman gasped. "I know but—good gods, you should go on the stage!" He clasped the back of his hand to his forehead, and swooned theatrically across the back of his chair. "Oh la, good sir, I do believe I shall fai—"

The pillow caught Medren squarely in the face.

All right, Stefen thought, carefully putting his gittern back in its case. *I've left you alone except for simple politeness for three days, Herald Vanyel. Let's see if you respond to being ignored.* He began tightening the buckles holding the case closed. *I've never known anyone yet who could deal with* that.

He suppressed a smile as he caught Vanyel making his way through the crowd, obviously coming in Stef's direction. *Looks like you won't be the first to be the exception to the rule.*

"Bard Stefen?" Vanyel's voice was very low, with a note of hesitancy in it.

Stefen looked up, and smiled. He didn't have to feign the hint of shyness that crept into the smile; Vanyel *still* affected him that way. "I can't get used to that," he confessed, surprising himself with the words. "People calling me Bard Stefen, I mean. I keep looking around to see who you're talking to."

Vanyel smiled, and Stefen's throat tightened. "I know what you mean," he said. "If it hadn't been that I spent the winter with the Hawkbrothers and had gotten used to wearing white, I would have spent half every morning for the first couple of months trying to figure out whose Whites had gotten into my wardrobe."

Do I—no, I don't think so. Every time I've tried to touch him, he's started to respond, then pulled back. Let's keep things casual, and see if that works.

"I sometimes wish I'd never gotten Scarlets," Stef said, instead of trying to touch Vanyel's hand. "I never have any time for myself anymore. And I don't recognize myself anymore when I look in the mirror. I *used* to know how to have fun. . . ."

Vanyel relaxed just the tiniest bit, and Stefen felt a surge of satisfaction. *Finally, finally, I'm reading him right.*

The crowd was almost gone now; and Stefen wondered fleetingly what business had been transacted this time. He wouldn't know unless someone told him.

"You did a good day's work, Bard Stefen," Vanyel said, as if reading his mind. "Randi was able to judge three inter-family disputes that have been getting worse for the past year or more. I'll make you an offer, Stefen—*if* you promise not to get so intoxicated you can't navigate across the grounds." Vanyel smiled, teasingly. "We'll have dinner in my quarters, and you can show me those bar-chords you promised to demonstrate the night you played your fingers to bits."

I did? I don't remember promising that. For a moment Stefen was startled, because he thought he remembered everything about that evening. Then he suppressed a smile. *Clever, Herald Vanyel. A nice, innocent excuse. And you might even believe it. Well, I'll take it.*

"I don't make a habit of getting falling-down drunk, Herald," he replied, with a grin to take the sting out of the words. "And since the food is *much* better at the Palace, I'll accept that offer."

"You mean you're only interested in the food?" Vanyel laughed. "I suppose my conversation hasn't much impressed you."

He's a lot more relaxed. I think Medren's right, I'm either going to have to coax him or ambush him, and in either case I'm going to have to keep things very casual or I'll scare him off again. Damn. Stefen stood up and slung his gittern case over one shoulder before replying.

"Actually, I *am* much more interested in someone who'll talk to me," he said. "I'm not exactly the most popular Bard in the Collegium right now."

Vanyel grimaced. "Because of being advanced so quickly?"

Stefen nodded, and picked up his music carrier. "I had only just made Journeyman, and a lot of Bards resent my being jumped up like I was. A lot of the apprentices and Journeymen do, too. I can't say as I blame them too much, but I'm getting tired of being treated like a leper."

He fell into step beside Vanyel, and the two of them left through the side door.

"At least the Council's put it about that the whole promotion was at Herald Shavri's request," he continued. "That makes it a little more palatable, at least to some of the older ones. And the younger Bards can't claim I earned it in bed—that's one blessing, however small."

Vanyel raised one eyebrow at that last statement, but didn't comment. "I got something of the same treatment, though not for too long," the Herald told him. "Since it was Savil that gave me my Whites, there was an awful lot of suspicion of nepotism, or sympathy because of 'Lendel. . . .'"

The Herald's expression grew remote and saddened for a moment, then he shook his head. "Well, fortunately, Heralds being what they are, that didn't last too long. Especially not after Savil got herself hurt, and I cleaned out that nest of hedge-wizards up north. I pretty much proved then and there that I'd *earned* my Whites."

"I'm afraid I won't be able to do anything that spectacular," Stef replied, lightly. "It's not in the nature of the job for a Bard to do anything particularly constructive."

Instead of laughing, the Herald gave Stefen a peculiar, sideways look. "I think you underestimate both yourself and the potential power of your office, Stefen," he said.

Stefen laughed. "Oh, come now! You don't really expect me to agree with that old cliche that music can change the world, do you?"

"Things usually become cliched precisely because there's a grain of truth in them," was the surprising answer. "And—well, never mind. I expect you're right."

They had reached the Herald's Wing, that bright, wood-paneled extension of the Old Palace. Vanyel's room was one of the first beyond the double doors that separated the wing from the rest of the Palace. Vanyel held one of the doors open for Stef, then stepped gracefully around him and got the door to his own room open.

Stefen put his burdens down just inside the door, and arched his back in a stretch. "Brightest Havens—" he groaned. "—I feel as stiff as an old bellows. I bet I even creak."

"You're too young to creak," Vanyel chuckled, and pulled the bell-rope to summon a servant. "I don't suppose you play hinds and hounds, do you?"

Stefen widened his eyes, and assumed a patently false expression of naivete. "Why, no, Herald Vanyel—but I'd love to learn."

Vanyel laughed out loud. "Oh, no—you don't fool me with that old trick! You've probably been playing for years."

"Since I could talk," Stef admitted. "Can't blame me for trying."

"Since I might have done the same to you, I suppose I can't." Vanyel gestured at the board set up on the table. "Red or white?"

"Red," Stef replied happily. "And since *you're* the strategist, you can spot me a courser."

Stefen moved his gaze-hound into what he thought was a secure position, and watched with dismay as Vanyel captured it with a lowly courser. Then, to add insult to injury, the Herald maneuvered that same courser into the promotion square and exchanged it for a year-stag.

"Damn!" he exclaimed, seeing his pack in imminent danger of being driven off, and taking steps to retrench his forces. The "hind" side of hounds and hinds was supposed to be the weaker, which was why the better player took it. It was usually considered a good game if the play ended in stalemate.

Vanyel beat him about half the time.

It looked as though this game was going to end in defeat too. Three moves later, and Stef surveyed the board in amazement, unable to see any way out. Vanyel's herd had trapped his pack, and there was no way out.

"I yield," he conceded. "I don't know how you do it. You always take the hinds, and I can count the number of times I've won on one hand."

Vanyel replaced the carved pieces in their box with thoughtful care. "I have a distinct advantage," he said, after a long pause. "Until Randi got so sick that Shavri was spending all her time keeping him going, I helped guard the Karsite Border. I have a lot of experience in taking on situations with unfavorable odds."

"Ah," Stef replied, unable to think of anything else to say. He watched Vanyel's hands, admiring their strength and grace, and tried not to think about how much he wanted those hands to be touching something other than game pieces.

Ever since he'd stopped pursuing Van and started keeping things strictly on the level of "friendship," he'd found himself spending most evenings with the Herald. He was learning an enormous amount, and not just about hinds and hounds. Economics, politics, the things Vanyel had experienced over the years—it was fascinating, if frustrating. Being so near Vanyel, and yet not daring to court him, overtly or otherwise—Stef had never dreamed he possessed such patience.

This was an entirely new experience, wanting someone and being unable to gratify that desire.

It was a nerve-wracking experience, yet it was not completely unpleasant. He was coming to know Vanyel, the *real* Vanyel, far better than anyone else except Herald Savil. That was not a suspicion; he'd had the fact confirmed more than once, by letting some tidbit of information slip in conversations with Medren. And Medren would give him a startled look that told Stefen that once again, he'd been told something Vanyel had never confided to anyone else.

He knew Van better than he'd ever known any lover. And for all this knowledge, the Herald was still a mystery. He was no closer to grasping what music Vanyel moved to than he had been when this all began.

Which made him think of something else to say after all.

"Van?" he ventured. "You hated it out there—but you sound as if you wish you were back on the Border."

Vanyel turned those silver eyes on him and stared at him for a moment. "I suppose I did," he said, finally. "I suppose in a way I do. Partially because it would mean that Randi was in good enough health that Shavri could take her own duties up again—"

Stef shook his head. "There was more to it than that. It sounded like you *wanted* to be out there."

Vanyel looked away, and put the last of the pieces in their padded niches. "Well, it's rather hard to explain. It's miserable out there on the lines, you're constantly hungry, wet, cold, afraid, in danger—but I was doing some good."

"You're doing good here," Stefen pointed out.

Vanyel shook his head. "It's not the same. Any reasonably adept diplomat could do what I'm doing now. Any combination of Heralds could supply the same talents and Gifts. The only reason it's me is Randi's need and Randi's whims. I keep having the feeling that I could be doing a lot more good if I was elsewhere."

Stefen sprawled back in his chair, studying the Herald carefully. "I don't understand it," he said at last. "I don't understand you Heralds at all. You're constantly putting yourselves in danger, and for what? For the sake of people who don't even know you're doing it, much less that you're doing it for them, and who couldn't point you out in a crowd if their lives depended on it. Why, Van?"

That earned him another strange stare from the Herald, one that went on so long that Stef began to think he'd really said something wrong this time. "Van—what's the matter? Did I—"

Vanyel seemed to come out of a kind of trance, and blinked at him. "No, it's quite all right, Stef. It's just—this is like an echo from the past. I remember having exactly this same conversation with 'Lendel—except it was *me* asking 'Why?' and him trying to tell me the reasons." Vanyel looked off at some vague point over Stefen's head. "I didn't understand his reasons then, and you probably won't understand mine now, but I'll try to explain. It has to do with a duty to myself as much as anything else. I have these abilities. Most other people don't. I have a duty to *use* them, because I have a duty to myself to be the kind of person I would want to have as a—a friend. If I don't use my abilities, I'm not only failing people who depend on me, I'm failing myself. Am I making sense?"

"Not really," Stefen confessed.

Vanyel sighed. "Just say that it's a need to help—could you *not* sing and play? Well, I can't *not* help. Not anymore, anyway. And it doesn't matter if anyone knows what I'm doing or not; I know, and I know I'm doing my best. And because of what I'm doing, things are better for other people. Sometimes a great many other people."

"This is loyalty, right?" Stefen hazarded.

"Only in being loyal to people in general, and not any one land. I could no more have let those farmers in Hardorn be enslaved than I could have our own people." Vanyel leaned forward earnestly. "Don't you see, Stef? It's not that I'm serving Valdemar, it's that I'm helping to preserve the kind of people who leave the world better than they found it, and trying to stop the ones who take instead of giving."

"You sound like one of those *Tayledras*—"

"I am. Moondance himself has said so more than once. Their priority is for the land, and mine is for the people—but that's at least in part because the land is so damaged where they live." Vanyel smiled a little. "I wish you could see them, Stef. You'd want to write a thousand songs about them."

"If they're so wonderful, why are people afraid of them?" Stefen asked. "And why aren't you and Savil?"

Vanyel laughed at that. "Let me tell you about the first time I ever worked with Moondance—"

The story was almost enough to make Stefen forget his frustration.

CHAPTER 6

"**D**AMN!" MEDREN SWORE, pounding the arm of his chair. "This is *stupid*! I swear to you, my uncle is about to drive me mad!"

The windows to Stefen's room were open to the summer evening, and Medren was trying to keep his voice down to prevent everybody in the neighborhood from being privy to their plight. Stef evidently didn't *care* who overheard them. "About to drive *you* mad?" Stefen's voice cracked, and Medren winced in sympathy. Stef was pulling at his hair, totally unaware that he was doing so, and looked about ready to climb the walls. He shifted position so often that his chair was doing a little dance around the room, a thumblength at a time.

"I know, I know, it's a lot worse for you. I'm just frustrated. You're—" Medren paused, unable to think of a delicate way to put it.

"I'm *celibate*, that's what I am!" Stefen growled, lurching to his feet and beginning to pace restlessly. "I'm *worse* than celibate. I'm fixated. It's not just that Vanyel isn't cooperating, it's that I don't *want* anyone else anymore, and the better I know him, the worse it gets!" He stopped dead in his tracks, suddenly, and stared out the window for a moment. "I'm never happier than when I'm around him. I sometimes wonder how long I'm going to be able to stand this. There are times when I can't think of anything but him."

Medren stared at his friend, wondering if Stefen had really listened to himself just now. Because what he'd just described was the classic reaction of a lifebonded. . . .

Stef and Uncle Van? No. Not possible; not when Van has already been lifebonded once. . . . Or is it? Is there a rule somewhere that lifebondings can only happen once in a lifetime, even if you lose your bondmate?

A lifebonding would certainly explain a great deal of Stef's behavior. Medren had long ago given up on trying to second-guess his uncle. Vanyel was far too adept at hiding what he felt, even from himself.

"So, what have we tried so far?" Medren said aloud. Stef at least stopped pacing long enough to push his hair out of his eyes and count up all the schemes they'd concocted on his fingers.

"We tried getting him drunk again. He didn't cooperate. We tried that trip to the hot springs. That *almost* worked, except that we got company right when it looked like he was going to break down and do something. We tried every variation on my hurting myself and him having to help me, and all I got were bruises in some fascinating places." Stefen gritted his teeth. "We tried my asking him for a massage for my shoulder muscles. He referred me to a Healer. The only thing we haven't tried is catching him asleep and tying him up."

"Don't even *think* about that!" Medren said hastily. "Listen, first of all, you *won't* catch him asleep, and secondly, even if you did—you wouldn't want to be standing there if he mistook you for an enemy."

Like the last time he was home, when that idiot with the petition tried to tackle him in the bath. Medren shuddered. *I know Grandfather said he needed to replace the bathhouse—but that wasn't the best way to get it torn down.*

"He wouldn't hurt me," Stefen said with absolute certainty.

"Don't bet on that," Medren replied, grimly. "Especially if he doesn't know it's you. I've seen what he can do, and you wouldn't want to stand in the way of it. If he wants to level something or someone, he will, and anything in between him and what he wants to flatten is going to wind up just as flat as his target."

"No," Stef denied vehemently. "No—I swear to you, I know it. No matter what, he wouldn't hurt me."

Medren just shook his head and hoped Stef would never have to test that particular faith. "All right," he said after a moment's thought. "What about this—"

Vanyel closed his weary eyes for a moment, and thought longingly, selfishly, of rest, of peace, of a chance to enjoy the bright summer day.

But there was no peace for Valdemar, and hence, no rest for Herald Vanyel.

:Take a break tonight, Van,: Yfandes advised him. *:You haven't had young Stefen over for the past three evenings. And I think you can afford to let the Seneschal and the Lord Marshal hash this one out without you.:*

At least the news out of Karse was something other than a disaster, for a change.

"So there's no doubt of it?" he asked the messenger. "The Karsites have declared the use of magic anathema?"

The dust-covered messenger nodded. It was hard to tell much about her, other than the fact that she was not a Herald. Road grime had left her pretty much a uniform gray-brown from head to toe. "There's more to it than that, m'lord," she said. "They're outlawing everyone even suspected of having mage-craft. Just before I left, the first of the lucky ones came straggling across the Border. I didn't have time to collect much of their tales, but there's another messenger coming along behind me who'll have the whole of it."

"Lucky ones?" said the Seneschal, puzzled. "Lucky for us, perhaps, but since when has it been lucky for enemy mages to fall into our hands?"

"Aye, it wouldn't seem that way, but 'tis," she replied, wiping the back of her hand across her forehead, and leaving a paler smear through the dirt and sweat. "The ones we got are the lucky ones. They're the ones that 'scaped the hunters. They're burning and hanging over there, whoever they can catch. 'Tis a bit of a holy crusade, it seems. Like some kind of plague, all of a sudden half of Karse wants to murder the Gifted."

"Good gods." The Seneschal ran his hand over his closed eyes. "It sounds insane—"

"How did it start?" the Lord Marshall asked bluntly. "Or do you know?"

The messenger nodded. "Lord Vanyel's turning those demons back on Karse ten years ago was the start of it, but the real motivator seems to be from the priesthood."

"The *priesthood*?" Healer Liam exclaimed, sitting up straight. "Which priesthood?"

"Sunlord Vkanda," the messenger replied. "And there's not enough news yet to tell if it's only the one priest, or the whole lot of them."

At that moment, a servant appeared with wine. The messenger took it and gulped it down gratefully. Lord Marshall Reven leaned forward over the table when she'd finished, his lean face intent, his spare body betraying how tense he was.

"What else can you tell us?" he asked. "Any fragment of information will help."

The messenger leaned back in her chair. "Quite a bit, actually," she said. "I'm trained by one of your Heralds. The one that started this crusade's a nameless lad of maybe twenty or so; calls himself The Prophet. No one knows much else about him, 'cept that he started on that there was a curse on the land, on account of them using mages. That was a bit less than a month ago. Next thing you know, the countryside's afire, and Karse's got

more'n enough troubles to make 'em pull back every trooper they had on
the Border. That was how matters stood a week ago when I left; gods only
know what's going on in there now."

"Have we heard from any of our operatives in Karse itself?" the Seneschal asked Vanyel.

The Herald shook his head. "Not yet."

He was worried for those operatives—there were at least three of them,
one Mindspeaking Herald among them—but his chief reaction was relief. *I*
cannot believe that we pulled the last of the mages out less than a year ago. There is
no one in there now who should be suspected of magery. . . .

"You say this situation is causing some civil disorder?" Archpriest Everet
had a knack for understatement, but he was serious enough. His close-
cropped, winter-white hair was far too short to fidget with, so he fingered
his earlobe worriedly instead. Beneath his bland exterior, Vanyel sensed he
was deeply concerned.

Not surprising; while it might look as if this was unalloyed good news
for Valdemar, the fact that it was a religious crusade meant the possibility of
it spilling over the Border. There were several houses of the Sunlord within
the borders of Valdemar. If they joined their fellows in this holy war against
mages, not only would the Archpriest be responsible for their actions, he
would be obligated to see to it that they were stopped.

Which is about all he's thinking of. He doesn't see how much chaos this could
cause the entire country. If the followers of the Sunlord move against Heralds—

Some of us are mages; they might also count all Gifts as "magic."

And we have the backing of other religious orders. If the Heralds were attacked,
those orders might move before the Crown and Archpriest could. What would happen
if the acolytes of Kernos decided to take matters into their own hands and fight back
on the mages' behalf? After all, the order is primarily martial . . . fighting monks and
the like. And they favor the Heralds.

The situation, if it crossed the Border, could be as damaging to Valdemar
as to Karse.

"The Sunlord's the Karsite official state religion," the messenger reminded them. "If this Prophet has the backing of the priesthood, then he's
got the backing of the Crown. When I left, that was what things looked
like—but there's a fair number of people with a bit of magery in their blood,
and a-plenty of hedge-wizards and herb-witches that do the common folk
a fair amount of good. Not everybody can find a Healer when they need
one; when the big magics are flyin' about, the lords tend to forget about the

little ones that bring the rain and protect the crops. So not everybody is taking well to this holy crusade."

"I would suggest a series of personal visits to our own enclaves of the Sunlord, my lord Everet," Vanyel said mildly. "I suspect your presence will make cooler heads prevail, especially if you point out that this so-called 'Prophet' seems to be operating on nothing more than his charisma and his own word that he speaks for the Sunlord Vkanda."

Everet nodded, his mouth tight. "They owe their establishments to His Majesty's tolerance," he replied. "I shall be at pains to point that out."

"I'll assure him that you're already working on the potential problem," Vanyel told him, glancing at the empty throne. *Barring a miracle, Randi will never use that seat again. I wonder if we should have it taken out? It's certainly depressing to have it there.*

The Seneschal dismissed the messenger, who got stiffly to her feet, bowed, and limped out. "Well," Seneschal Arved said, once the door had closed behind her, "I think we have a Situation."

The Lord Marshal nodded. "If it stays within the Karse Border, this situation can only benefit us."

"If." Vanyel shook his head. "There's no guarantee of that."

:*And what about later?*: Yfandes prompted. :*After this crusade is over?*:

:*Good point.*: "We use magic openly in Valdemar, sanctioned and supported by the Crown," Van continued. "If this crusade doesn't burn itself out, if in fact *it* is sanctioned by the Karsite Crown, where does that leave us?"

"The deadliest of enemies " Everet answered grimly. "It will be worse than before; it will become a holy war."

Arved groaned, and closed his eyes for a moment. "You're right," he said, finally. "You're absolutely right. And if that situation occurs, there's nothing we can do to stop it."

"What we need now is information," Vanyel told them. "And that's my department. I'll get on it. *Whatever* happens, we'll have a respite from Karsite incursions for a couple of weeks while they get their own house in order. We should use that respite to our own advantage."

"Good," Arved said, shaking back his tawny hair. "Let's take this in manageable chunks. Herald Vanyel, you get us that information, and find out what the King wants us to do with refugees. We'll see what we can do to use this involuntary truce. Tomorrow we'll put together plans to cover all the contingencies we can think of. Everet—"

"I'll be making myself conspicuous in the Vkanda enclaves," the

Archpriest said, rising from his seat. "You'll have to go on without me. I think I'd better leave as soon as I can pack."

:He's going to be out of here within two candlemarks,: Yfandes said. *:He travels light.:*

"Lord Everet, I'll have a document from Randale for you before you leave, authorizing you to take whatever actions you think necessary with the followers of Vkanda," Vanyel said. "Please don't leave without it."

Everet paused in mid turn, and half-smiled. "Thank you, Herald. I would have gone charging off trusting in my office and so-called 'sanctity,' forgetting that neither apply to the Guard."

"Nor some highborn," the Lord Marshal reminded him. "And unless I miss my guess, there'll be one or two of those among the Sunlord's followers."

"Gentlemen, the Archpriest and I will get to our duties, and we'll leave you to work on this in our absence," Vanyel told them. He and Everet pushed their chairs aside and left the Council Chamber, going in opposite directions once they reached the door.

Randi first, then get in touch with Kera. . . . he thought, then Mindsent, *:'Fandes, can you boost me that far?:* knowing she'd been watching his surface thoughts.

:If not, we can at least reach someone stationed near the Border to relay.: She sounded quite confident, and Van relaxed a little. *:We'll have inside information shortly. And don't worry about Kera—thanks to that new Web we wove, if she was in trouble, we'd know. One of us would, anyway.:*

:Thanks, love.: He'd reached the door to Randale's quarters, and was such a familiar sight to the guards that one of them had already pushed the door open for him.

He thanked the man with a nod, and slipped inside.

Most of the time Randale was cold, so the room was as hot as a desert, with a fire in the fireplace despite the fact that it was full summer. The King lay on a day-bed beside the fire, bundled up in a blanket, Shavri on a stool beside him; he looked exhausted, but the pain lines about his mouth and eyes were mercifully few.

Those eyes were closed, but he wasn't sleeping. Vanyel saw his lids flutter a little the moment before he spoke. "So," he said quietly. "What's sent you flying out of the Council Chamber this time? Good news, or bad?"

"Wish I could tell you," Vanyel replied, dropping down beside the bed, and putting one hand on Shavri's shoulder. She brushed her cheek briefly against it, but didn't let go of Randale's hand. Van touched her dark, gypsy-tumble of curls for a moment, then turned his full attention back to the King. "We just got a messenger from the Border and the Karsites have just confirmed my belief that they're all completely mad."

He outlined the situation as quickly as he could, while Randale listened, with his eyes still closed. The King had long ago shaved off his beard, saying it no longer hid anything and made him look like the business end of a mop, he'd grown so thin. That was the day he'd finally acknowledged his illness, and the fact that he was never going to recover from it; the day Van had been reassigned permanently and indefinitely to the Palace.

All of Randale that could be seen, under the swathings of blankets, were his head and hands. Both were emaciated and colorless; even Randale's hair was an indeterminate shade of brown. Herald Joshe, who was something of an artist, had remarked sadly that the King was like an under-painting, all bones and shadows.

But there was nothing wrong with his mind, and he demonstrated that he'd inherited his grandmother's good sense.

"Rethwellan," he said, after listening to Vanyel. "They have mages in their bloodline; if Karse starts an anti-mage campaign, they'll be in as much danger as we. Get Arved to draft up some letters to Queen Lythiaren, feeling her out and offering alliance." He paused a moment. "Tell him to word those carefully; she doesn't entirely trust me right now after that mess with the Amarites."

"It wasn't your fault," Vanyel protested, as Shavri stroked her lifebonded's forehead. Randale opened his eyes and smiled slightly.

"I know that, but she can't admit it," he replied. "Have we got a 'limited powers' declaration around here somewhere? You'll need one for Everet."

"I think so," Vanyel answered, and got to his feet. After a moment of checking through the various drawers, he found what he was looking for—a pre-inscribed document assigning limited powers of the Crown, with blanks for the person and the circumstances. There was always pen, ink, and blotter waiting on the desk; in another moment Vanyel had filled in the appropriate blank spaces.

"Good, let me see it." Randale read it carefully, as he always did. "Your usual thorough and lawyerlike job, Van." He looked up at Vanyel, and smiled. "I hope you brought the pen with you."

"I did." Vanyel laid the bottom of the document over a book and held both so that Randale could initial the appropriate line. Blowing on the ink to dry it more quickly, he took the paper over to the desk and affixed the Seal of the Monarch. "What about the mages coming across the Border?" he asked over his shoulder.

"Unhindered passage via guarded trade-road into Rethwellan," Randale told him. "But I don't want to offer them sanctuary. This would be a good opportunity for Karse to get an agent into Valdemar. We can't know which are blameless, which are hirelings, and which are spies. Send them on, unless one of them happens to get Chosen."

"Not likely." Vanyel left the paper where it was, and returned to Randale's side. "How has today been?"

"Shavri's beginning to understand what it is that young Bard of yours actually does," Randale replied. "She's able to do a bit more for me. But yesterday was bad; I'd rather not give audiences today, because I don't think I can get past the door right now. No strength left."

Vanyel touched his shoulder; Randale sighed, and covered Vanyel's hand with his own. "Then don't try," Van said quietly. "Anything more I should do about Karse?"

"Get us inside information, then get our Herald operatives out of there," Randale replied. "Then send a few non-Gifted agents to deliver aid to the rest, then insinuate themselves into the trouble. And let's get moving on the Rethwellan situation."

By this time, the corners of his mouth were tight and pinched, and he was very pale. Vanyel felt a lump rising in his throat. Randale was proving a better King than anyone had ever expected; the weaker he became, the more he seemed to rise to the challenge. As his body set tighter physical limits on what he could do, his mind roved, keeping track of all of the tangles inside Valdemar and out.

Vanyel swallowed the lump that caught in his throat every time he looked at Randale. "Anything else?" he asked. "There's a lot of matters pending."

Randale closed his eyes and leaned back into the pillows. "Compromise in the Lendori situation by offering them the contract for the Guard mules if they'll cede the water rights to Balderston. Their animals are good enough, if priced a little high. The Evendim lot has their own militia; feel them out and see if they might be willing to spare us some men. Tell Lord Preatur that if he doesn't either take that little minx he calls his daughter and marry her off or send her back home, I'll find a husband for her; she's got half my Guard officers at dagger's point with each other. That's all."

"That's enough." Vanyel touched one finger to Randale's hot forehead, and exerted his own small Healing ability. Shavri had told him that every tiny bit helped some. "Rest, Randi."

"I'll do my best," the King whispered, and Vanyel took himself out before he started weeping.

Pages and acolytes were flying about Everet's rooms like leaves in a storm, while Everet stood in the middle of the chaos and directed it calmly. Vanyel dodged a running child and handed Everet the document.

Everet read it through as carefully as Randale had. "Excellent. Enough authority to cow just about anyone I might need to." He intercepted one of the acolytes and directed the young man to pack the document with the rest of his papers. "Thank you, Herald. Let's hope I don't need to use it."

"Fervently," Vanyel replied, and returned briefly to the Council Chamber to give the Seneschal the rest of King Randale's orders.

Sunlight on the water blinded him a moment. :*I feel like the Fair Maid of Bredesmere, waiting for her lover.*: 'Fandes Mindsent.

Vanyel squinted against the light, then waved to her; she was standing on the Field side of the bridge spanning the river separating the Palace grounds from Companion's Field. :*Well, you're all in white,*: he teased as he approached the bridge. :*And there's the River for you to get thrown into.*:

:*Just* try *it, my lad,*: she reared a little, and danced in place, the long grass muffling the sound of her hooves. :*We'll see who throws who in!*:

:*Thank you, I'd rather not.*: He ran the last few steps over the echoing bridge, and took her silken head in both his hands. "You're beautiful today, love," he said aloud.

:*Huh.*: She snorted, and shook his hands off. :*You say that every day.*: But he could tell by the way she arched her neck that she was pleased.

:*That's because you* are *beautiful every day,*: he replied.

:*Flatterer,*: she said, tossing her silver waterfall of a mane. Since they weren't in combat situations anymore, she'd told him to let it and her tail grow, and both were as long and full as a Companion's in an illuminated manuscript.

"It isn't flattery when it's true," he told her honestly. "I wish I had more time to spend with you."

Her blue eyes darkened with love. :*I do, too. A plague on reality! I just want to be* with *you, not have to work!*:

He laughed. "Now you're as lazy as I used to be! Come along, love, and let's get ourselves settled so we can make a stab at reaching Kera."

At one time there had been a grove of ancient pine trees near the bridge—the grove that had been destroyed when Herald-trainee Tylendel had lost control of his Gift in the shock following his twin brother's death. There was nothing there now except grass, a few seedlings and a couple of trees that had escaped the destruction. The dead trees had long since been cut up and used for firewood.

Since that night had been the start of the train of events that led to Tylendel's suicide, it would have been logical for Vanyel to shun the spot, but logic didn't seem to play a very large part in Vanyel's life. He still found the place peaceful, protective, and he and Yfandes often went there when they needed to work together.

There was a little hollow in the center of what had been the grove; Yfandes folded her legs under her and settled down there in the long grass. There wasn't so much as a breath of wind to stir the tips of the grass blades. Vanyel lowered himself down beside her, and braced his back against her side. The warm afternoon sun flowed over both of them.

"Ready?" he asked.

:When you are,: she replied.

He closed his eyes, and slid into full rapport with her; it was even easier with her than with Savil. He waited for a moment while they settled around each other, then Reached for Kera.

She couldn't know when someone was going to try to contact her, but Kera *had* to realize that they were going to do so eventually. Vanyel was counting on that, on the receptivity. He'd worked with Kera before this, so he knew her well enough to find her immediately *if* he could reach that far.

He strained to Hear her; to sort her out of the distant whispers on the Border of Karse. Most of those mind-voices were strident with anger; a few were full of panic. It was by the lack of both those traits that he identified Kera; that, and the carefully crafted shields about her. Savil's work, and beautiful, like a faceted crystal.

He stretched—it was like trying to touch something just barely within his grasp; the tips of his "fingers" brushed the edge of it. *:Kera.:* He offered his identification to her shields, which parted briefly and silently.

:Who?: came the thought; then incredulity. *:Vanyel?:*

She knew where he was and the kind of strain it was to reach her. Hard on that incredulity came the information he needed: exactly what was going on over in Karse, everything Kara knew about the Prophet, and that he was, indeed, backed by the full force of the Karsite Crown and the priesthood of the Sunlord.

:Get out of there,: Vanyel urged. *:Go over White Foal Pass if you have to, or get out through Rethwellan, but leave. Warn the others you're leaving if you can. With a Companion around you, however disguised, you're the most likely to be uncovered.:*

Fear, and complete agreement. Evidently she'd had some close calls already.

:Go,: she told him, courage layered over the fear. *:I've got my plans, I was just waiting for contact.:*

He released her, and dropped into clamoring darkness.

When he opened his eyes again, the last of a glorious scarlet sunset was fading from the clouds. Crickets sang in the grass near his knee, and he shivered with cold.

Not a physical cold, but the cold of depletion. Yfandes nudged him with her nose. *:I got it all, and I passed it on to Joshe's Kimbry, and Joshe passed it to the Seneschal.:*

"Good, 'Fandes," he coughed, leaning on her warm strength. "Thank you."

:I never suspected you had that kind of reach. You outdistanced me.:

"I did?" He rubbed his eyes with a knuckle. "Well, I don't know what to say."

:I do,: she replied, humor in her mind-voice, *:You're going to have a reaction-headache in a few more breaths. I suggest you stop by Randale's Healers on the way to your room.:*

"I'll do that." He got to his knees, then lurched to his feet. She scrambled up next to him, glowing in the blue dusk.

:Have you forgotten you'd invited young Stefen to your room tonight?:

"Oh, gods. I had." He was torn, truly torn. He was weary, but—dammit, he wanted the Bard's company.

:He wants yours just as badly,: Yfandes said, with no emotional coloring in her mind-voice at all.

"Oh, 'Fandes, he's just infatuated," Vanyel protested. "It'll wear off. If I told him to leave me alone—assuming I wanted to, which I don't—it would just make him that much more determined to throw himself in my way."

:I think it's more than infatuation,: she responded, and he thought he caught

overtones of approval when she thought about the Bard. *:I think he really cares a great deal about you.:*

"Well, I care about him—which is precisely why I'm going to keep this relationship within the bounds of friendship." Vanyel tested his legs, and found them capable of taking him back to the Palace, though the threatened reaction-headache was just beginning to throb in his temples. "He doesn't need to ruin his life by flinging himself at me." He stroked her neck. "Goodnight, sweetling. And thank you."

:My privilege and pleasure,: she said fondly.

He began the trek back to the Palace, dusk thickening around him, his head throbbing in time with his steps. *Friendship. Oh, certainly. Havens, Van,* he chided himself. *You know very well that you're just looking for excuses to see more of Stef.*

Now, finally, a breeze blew up; a stiff one, that made the branches bend a little. He had warmed up quite a bit just from the long walk, but although the cool air felt good against his forehead, it made him shiver. *Well, there's no harm in it, except to me. I'm certainly exercising all my self-control. . . .*

The depth of his attraction to the Bard bothered him, and not only because he felt the lad was still pursuing him out of hero-worship. As night fell around him and the lights of the Palace began to appear in the windows, he realized that over the past few weeks he had become more and more confused about his relationship with Stefen. Stars appeared long before he reached the doors to the Palace gardens, and he looked up at them, wishing he could find an answer in their patterns.

I don't understand this at all. I want to care for him so much—too much. It feels like I'm betraying 'Lendel's memory.

He turned away from the night sky and pulled open the door, blinking at the light from the lantern set just inside it.

He entered the hall, and closed the door behind him. *Great good gods, the boy should be glad I'm not 'Lendel,* he thought, with a hint of returning humor. *'Lendel would have cheerfully tumbled the lad into bed long before this. Gods, I need that headache tea—*

Evidently the gods thought otherwise, for at that moment, a page waiting in the hallway spotted him, and ran to meet him.

"Herald Vanyel," the child panted. "The King wants you! Jisa's done something horrible!"

*　　*　　*

The child couldn't tell him much; just that Jisa had come to Randale's suite with Treven and a stranger. There had been some shouting, and the page had been called in from the hall. Randale had collapsed onto his couch, Shavri and Jisa were pale as death, and Shavri had sent the page off in search of Vanyel.

An odd gathering waited for him in Randale's suite: the King and Shavri, Jisa and young Treven, the Seneschal, Joshe, and a stranger in the robes of a priest of Astera. And a veritable swarm of servants and Guards. By this time, Vanyel was ready to hear almost anything; a tale of theft, murder, drunkenness—but not what Jisa flatly told him, with a rebellious lift of her chin.

"Married?" he choked, looking from Jisa to Treven and back again." "You've gotten *married*? How? Who in the Havens' name would dare?"

"I did, Herald Vanyel." The stranger said, not cowed, as Vanyel would have expected, but defiantly. As he raised his head, the cowl of his robe fell back, taking his face out of the shadows. It was no one Vanyel knew, and not a young man. Middle-aged, or older; that was Van's guess. Old enough not to have been tricked into this.

"I wasn't tricked," the priest continued, as if he had read Vanyel's thought. "I knew who they were; they told me. No one specifically forbade them to marry, and it seemed to me that there was no reason to deny them that status."

"No reason—" Vanyel couldn't get anything else out.

"The vows are completely legal and binding," Joshe said apologetically. "The only way they could be broken would be if either of them wanted a divorcement."

Treven put his arm around Jisa, and the girl took his hand in hers. Both of them stared at Vanyel with rebellion in their eyes, rebellion, and a little fear.

Randale chose that moment to turn a shade lighter and gasp. Shavri was at his side in an instant, and in the next, had him taken out of the room into their private quarters.

"No reason," Vanyel repeated in disbelief. "What about Treven's duty to Valdemar? What are we going to do now, if the only way out of a problem is an alliance-marriage?"

He addressed the priest, but it was Treven who replied. "I thought about that, Herald Vanyel," he said. "I thought about it quite a long time. Then I did some careful checking—and unless you plan to have me turn shaych, there isn't anyone who could possibly suit as a marriage candidate, not even in Karse—unless there's some barbarian chieftain's daughter up north that nobody knows about. Of the unwedded, most are past childbearing, and the rest are infants. Of the wedded who might *possibly* lose their husbands in the next five years, most are bound with contracts that keep them tied to their spouse's land, and the rest are the designated regents for their minor children." Despite his relatively mild tone, Treven's expression boded no good for anyone who got in his way. "I didn't see any reason to deny ourselves happiness when we *know* that we're lifebonded."

"Happiness?" Shavri's voice sounded unusually shrill. "You talk about happiness, *here*?" She stood in the doorway, clutching a fold of her robe just below her throat. "You've put my daughter right back in the line of succession, you young fool! Do you have any idea how long and hard I fought to keep her *out* of that position? You've seen what the Crown has done to Randi, both of you—Treven, how can you possibly want that kind of pain for Jisa?"

:Shavri doesn't want the Crown, so she thinks her daughter shouldn't, either,: Yfandes observed. *:Your objection is rational, but hers is entirely emotional.:*

Jisa ignored her mother's impassioned speech, turning to Vanyel and the Seneschal. "If there's pain, I'm prepared to deal with it," she said calmly, addressing them and not her mother. "I don't blame Mother for not wanting the Crown—she doesn't want that kind of responsibility, she doesn't like being a leader, and she isn't any good at it. She says that the Crown means pain, and it does, for her—but—my lords, I'm *not* Mother! Why should she make my decisions *for* me?"

The priest nodded a little, and Shavri's face went white.

"Mother—" Now Jisa turned toward her, pleading. "Mother, I'm sorry, but we're two different people, you and I. I am a leader, I have been all my life, you've said so yourself. I'm not afraid of power, but I respect it, and the responsibility it brings. There's another factor here; Treven will be the King—I'll be his partner. We will be sharing the power, the responsibility, and yes, the pain. It will be different for us. Can't you see that?"

Shavri shook her head, unable to speak, then turned and fled back into the shelter of her room.

Arved was red-faced with anger. "Who gave you the authority to take it upon yourself to decide who and what was a suitable contract?" he snarled at Treven. The young man paled, but stood his ground.

"Two things, sir," he replied steadily. "The fact that Jisa and I are lifebonded, and the fact that a marriage with anyone except my lifebonded would be a marriage in name only, and a travesty of holy vows."

"In my opinion," put in the priest, "that would be blasphemy. A perversion of a rite meant to sanctify. Lifebonding is a rare and sacred thing, and should be treated with reverence. It is one thing to remain unwedded so as to give the appearance of being available, provided it is done for the safety of the realm. It seems to me, however, that to force a young person into an entirely unsuitable marriage when he is already lifebonded is—well, a grave sin."

Arved stared at the priest, then looked helplessly at Vanyel, and threw up his hands. "It's done," he said. "It can't be undone, and I'm not the one to beat a dead dog in hopes of him getting up and running to the hunt."

Joshe just shrugged.

Shavri had fled the room, Randale had collapsed—the Seneschal and his Herald had abrogated their responsibility. It was going to be left to Van to make the decision.

He ground his teeth in frustration, but there really was very little choice. As the Seneschal had pointed out, the thing was accomplished, and there would be no profit in trying to fight it further.

"Done is done," he said with resignation, ignoring Jisa's squeal of joy. "But I hope you realize you two have saddled me with the hard part."

"Hard part?" Treven asked.

"Yes," he replied. "Trying to convince the rest of the world that you haven't made a mistake, when *I'm* not sure of it myself."

CHAPTER 7

"I THOUGHT YOU'D be pleased," Jisa said sullenly. "You know how we feel about each other. I thought *you* would understand."

Vanyel counted to ten, and sighted on a point just above Jisa's head. They weren't alone; the priest was trying to talk Shavri around, Treven hovered right at Jisa's elbow, and there were at least half a dozen servants in the room. It wouldn't do to strangle her.

The only blessing was that Arved and Joshe were gone, which meant two less edgy tempers in a room full of tension.

"Whatever gave you the idea that I'd be pleased?" he asked. "And why should I understand?"

"Because you were willing to defy everything and everyone to have Tylendel," she replied, maddeningly. "You *know* what it's like to be life-bonded!" :Father,: she continued in Mindspeech, :*We've done everything else anyone ever asked of us. Why should we have to give up each other? And why can't you see our side of it?*:

He wanted to argue that *her* case was entirely different—that Tylendel was only an ordinary Herald-Mage trainee, that neither he nor 'Lendel was the Heir to the Throne—

But he couldn't. They were young and in love, and so it was useless to bring logic into the argument.

:*I can't understand why Treven's Companion didn't stop him,*: he replied, irritated by her relative calm.

:*Father, Eren not only didn't stop him, she helped us. She's the one that found Father Owain for us.*: She couldn't have kept the triumph out of her mind-voice, and she didn't even try.

"She *what*?" Vanyel exclaimed aloud. One of the servants picking up the clutter nearly jumped a foot, then glared out of the corner of his eye at them.

"Bloody 'Eralds," he muttered, just loud enough for Van to hear. "Standin' around *thinkin'* at each other . . . still can't get used to it."

"Eren helped us," Jisa persisted. "Ask Yfandes."

"I will," he told her grimly. *:'Fandes, what do you know about all this?:*
:Everything,: she replied.

:And you didn't stop them? You didn't even tell me?: He couldn't believe what he was hearing.

:Of course we didn't stop them,: she said sharply. *:We approve. You would, too, if you'd take a minute to think with your head and your heart. What else would you have? Jisa will make a fine Consort, better than anyone else your stuffy Council would have picked for Treven. The boy is entirely right; there are no female offspring of a suitable age among any of the neutrals, and why should he make an alliance-marriage with someone who's already an ally? If you'd have him hang about for years without wedding Jisa, I think you're a fool.:*

:But Randi—: he began.

:Randale's case is entirely different; for a start, there is—or was—a Karsite princess only a year older, and the Queen of Rethwellan is exactly his age. Before his illness became a problem, there was always the potential for an alliance-wedding.:

He was too taken aback to reply for a moment. and when he finally managed to recover, one of the pages appeared at his elbow, looking anxious.

"M'lord Herald?" the child said nervously. "M'lord, the King is doing poorly. The Healers said to tell you he was in pain and refusing to take anything and that you'd know what to do."

"Go fetch Bard Stefen," Vanyel told the boy instantly. "If he's not in his own rooms, check mine." He ignored the raised eyebrows as Shavri turned away from the priest and rounded on Jisa and Treven.

"*Now* see what you've done—" the distraught Herald-Healer began, her hair a wild tangle around her face, her eyes red-rimmed. "You've made him worse, your own father! I—"

Vanyel put a hand on her arm and restrained her, projecting calm at her. "Shavri, dearheart, in all honesty you can't say that. Randi goes in cycles, you know that—and you know he was about due for an attack. You can't say that's Jisa's fault—"

"But she brought it on!" Shavri exclaimed. "She made it worse!"

"You don't know that," Vanyel began, when the page reappeared with Stefen in tow.

The Bard strolled right up to the tense knot of people, ignoring the page's frantic tugs on his sleeve. He bowed slightly to Treven, and took Jisa's limp hand and kissed it. "Congratulations," he said, as Shavri went rigid and

Vanyel silently recited every curse he knew. "I think you did the right thing. I *know* you'll be happy."

He finally responded to the page's efforts, and turned toward the door to the private rooms. But before he could take more than a step, Shavri seized him by the elbow to stop him. "Wait!" she snapped. "Where did you hear this?"

He looked down at her hand, still clutching his elbow, then up at her face. "It's all over the Palace, milady Herald," he replied mildly, and looked down at her hand again.

She let go of him and pulled away, and clenched her hands in the folds of her robe. "Then there's no way we can hide this."

"I would say not, milady," Stefen replied. "By this time tomorrow it'll be all over the Kingdom."

He winked at Treven as Shavri turned back to the priest. To Van's amazement and anger, Treven winked back.

:You didn't——: he Mindsent to Jisa.

The anger in his eyes was met by matching anger in hers. *:Of course we did. The first thing we did was tell the servants and two of the biggest gossips in the Court, one of whom is Stef:*

:Why?: he asked, anger amplifying his mind-voice so that she flinched. *:Why? To make your mother a laughingstock?:*

:No!: she flared back, *:To keep you and her from finding some way to annul what we did! We thought that the more people that knew about it, the less you'd be able to cover it up.:*

:The Companions spread it about, too,: Yfandes said, complacently. *:I was told by Liam's Orser just as you found out.:*

"Dear gods," he groaned. "It's a conspiracy of fools!"

Jisa looked hurt; Yfandes gave a disgusted mental snort and blocked him out.

Stefen stepped back a pace and straightened his back, taking on a dignity far beyond his years. "You can call it what you like, Herald Vanyel," he said stiffly, "and you can think what you like. But a good many people think that these two did exactly the right thing, and I'm one of them."

And with that, he turned on his heel, and followed the frantic page to the doorway at the back of the room.

As the priest nodded in satisfaction and took Shavri's arm, Vanyel threw up his hands in a gesture of defeat, and left before his tattered temper and dignity could entirely go to shreds.

*   *   *

As the Seneschal had pointed out, it was done, and couldn't be undone. In the week following, Shavri forgave her daughter, Jisa reconciled with Vanyel—but the Council was unlikely to accept the situation any time soon. As Stefen remarked sagely, in one of the few moments he had to spare away from Randale's side, "They'd gotten used to having a pair of pretty little puppets that danced whenever they pulled the strings. But the puppets just came alive and cut the strings—and they don't have any control anymore. Younglings grow up, Van—and when they do, it generally annoys *somebody*. Do you want a potential King and Queen, or a couple of rag dolls? If you want the King and Queen, you'd better get used to those two thinking for themselves, because that's what they're going to have to do."

Vanyel hadn't expected that much sense out of Stefen—though why he should have been surprised by it after all their long talks made him wonder how well *he* was thinking. The young Bard was showing his mettle in the crisis, not only easing Randale's pain for candlemarks at a time, but soothing Shavri's distress and bringing about her reconciliation with Jisa and Treven. That left Van free to deal with Council, Court, and outKingdom: making decisions in Randale's name, or waiting for one of the King's coherent spells and getting the decrees from him. The two of them worked like two halves of a complicated, beautifully engineered machine, and Vanyel wondered daily how he had gotten along without Stefen's presence and talents before this. The Bard seemed always to be at the right place, at the right time, using his Gift in exactly the right way, but that wasn't all he did. He made himself indispensable in a hundred little ways, seeing that no one forgot important papers, that pages were on hand to fetch and carry, and that Shavri and Randale were *never* left alone except with each other. He had food and drink sent in to Council meetings; saw to it that ambassadors felt themselves treated as the most important envoys Valdemar had ever harbored.

If it hadn't been for Stefen, Vanyel would never have survived that week.

As it was, by the time the crisis was over, both of them looked like identical frayed threads.

And that was when the second shoe dropped.

Vanyel opened the door to his room, and stared in surprise at Stefen. The Bard was draped over "his" chair, head thrown back, obviously asleep. As Vanyel closed the door, the slight noise woke Stefen, who raised his head and rubbed his eyes with one hand.

"Van," he said, his voice thick with fatigue. "S—sorry about this. Shavri sent me out; they got two Healers that can pain-block now—they finally caught the trick of it this morning." He shifted around and grimaced as he tried to move his head. "I couldn't make it back to m'room. Too damned tired. Ordered some food for both of us and came here. Didn't think you'd mind. Do you?"

Vanyel threw himself down in the other chair and reached for a piece of cheese, suddenly ravenous. "Of course I don't mind," he said. "But why in Havens didn't you take the bed if you were so tired?"

Stefen frowned at him. "I put you out of your bed once. I'm not going to do it again. There's your mail." He pointed to a slim pile of letters weighed down with a useless dress-dagger. "Just came as I dozed off. Pass me some of that cheese, would you?"

Vanyel passed the plate to him absently and used the paperweight to slit the letters. He worked his way down through the pile, and then froze as he saw the seal on the last one.

"Oh, no," he moaned. "Oh, *no*. I do not need this."

"What?" Stef asked, alarmed. "What's the—"

Vanyel held up the letter, wordlessly.

"That's the Forst Reach seal," Stefen said, puzzled. Then comprehension dawned and his expression changed to a mixture of amusement and sympathy. "Oh. That. One of your father's famous missives. What is it now—sheep, your brother, or your choice of comrades?"

"Probably all three," Vanyel said sourly, and opened it. "Might as well get this over with."

He skimmed through the first paragraph, and found nothing out of the ordinary. "Well, Mekeal's doing all right with his warhorse project, which means that Father's grousing about it, but can't find anything to complain about. Looks like the Famous Stud has a few good traits—well hidden, I may add." The second paragraph was more of the same. "Good gods, Meke's first just got handfasted. What's he trying to do, start his own tribe? Did I—"

"Send something? What about that really awful silver and garnet loving-cup I've seen around?" Stefen had curled up in the chair with his head resting on the arm and his eyes closed. "Savil told me you kept things like that for presents, and the worse they are, the better your family likes them."

"Except for Savil, my sister, and Medren, the concept of 'good taste' seems to have eluded my family," Vanyel replied wearily. "Thank you.

Hmm. The last of the sheep has succumbed to black fly, and Father is gloating. Melenna and—good *gods!*"

"What?" Both of Stefen's eyes flew open, and he raised his head, staring blindly.

"Melenna and Jervis are *married!*" Van sat there with his mouth hanging open; the very idea of Jervis marrying *anyone*—

"Oh," Stef said indifferently. "There's a lot of that going around. Maybe it's catching." He put his head back down on the armrest, as Vanyel shook his head and proceeded to the third and final paragraph.

"Here's the usual invitation to visit home, which is invariably the prelude to something that kicks me in the—" Van stopped, and reread the final sentences. And read them a third time. They didn't make any more sense than they had before.

I suppose you know we've heard a lot about you from Medren. He's told us you have a very special friend, a Bard. 'Stefen' was the name he gave us. We'd really like to meet him, son. Why don't you bring him with you when you visit?

"Van?" Stefen waved a hand at him, and broke him out of his daze. "Van? What is it? You look like somebody hit you in the back of the head with a board."

"I feel like that," Van told him, putting the letter down and rubbing the back of his neck. "I feel just like that. There has to be a trick to it—"

"Trick to what?"

"Well—they want me to bring you with me. They want to meet you. And knowing my father, he's already assumed the worst about our friendship." Vanyel picked up the letter again, but the last paragraph hadn't changed.

Stefen yawned and closed his eyes. "Let him assume. He asked for it—let's give it to him."

"You mean you'd be willing to go with me?" Vanyel was astounded. "Stefen, you must be crazed! *Nobody* wants to visit my family, they're all insane!"

"So? You need somebody they can be horrified by so they'll leave you alone." Stefen was drifting off to sleep, and his words started to slur. "Soun's like—me—t'me. . . ."

I couldn't, Vanyel thought. *But—he's worn away to nothing. They* do *have two Healers to replace him, and those two can train more. Randi is as much recovered as he's going to get, and the Karse situation is stable. So—why not?*

＊　　＊　　＊

"Why not?" Savil said, and chuckled. "He's certainly asked for it."

Vanyel had finally prevailed on her to have her favorite chair re-covered in a warm gray; she looked like the Winter Queen, with her silver hair and her immaculate Whites. Taking her out of the Web had done her a world of good; there was a great deal more energy in her voice, though she still moved as stiffly as ever.

"But Savil," Vanyel protested weakly, "he thinks Stef is my lover! He *has* to!"

Savil leveled the kind of look at him that used to wither her apprentices. "So what if he does? *He* is the one who issued the invitation, entirely un-prompted. Call his bluff. Then confound him. Tell you what. I'll come with you."

"Kernos' Horns, Savil, what are you trying to do, get me killed?" Vanyel laughed. "Every time you come home with me, I wind up ears-deep in trouble! I might as well go parade up and down the Karsite Border in full panoply—it'd be safer."

"Nonsense," Savil scoffed. "It was only the once. Seriously, I daren't travel by myself anymore. And I could certainly use the break. They can't afford to let Herald-Mages retire anymore, there aren't enough of us."

"True," Van acknowledged. "You know, this really isn't a bad idea."

:Stef is a sack of bones and hair,: 'Fandes chimed in. *:The Healers are threatening mayhem if someone doesn't take him away for a rest. Savil needs one, too, and so do you, and neither of you will get one unless you're out of reach.:*

"'Fandes thinks it's a good idea," he mused. "And to tell you the truth, Mother and Father have been fairly civilized to me the last couple of visits. Maybe this *will* work."

"Give me two days," Savil said, looking eager.

"Don't take more than that," Vanyel told her, as he got up and headed for the door.

"Why?" she asked. "You don't take *that* long to pack!"

"Because if you take longer than that," he called back over his shoulder, "my courage will quite melt away, and you'll have to tie me to Yfandes' back to make me go through with this."

Two days later, they were on the road out of Haven, with Stefen riding between them on a sleek little chestnut palfrey, a filly out of Star's line. Vanyel's beloved Star had lived out her life at Haven, a pampered favorite whose good sense and sweet nature bred true in all the foals she'd thrown.

Star had, in fact, been Jisa's first mount. And although once he'd been Chosen Van had no more need of a riding horse, there had been trusted friends (and the occasional lover) who did—so Star, and Star's offspring, had definitely earned their keep. One of Star's daughters, this palfrey's dam, was now Jisa's mount.

Vanyel had made a present of this particular filly, Star's granddaughter Melody, to Stefen. Stef had reacted with dubious pleasure—pleasure, because it meant he'd be able to accompany Van on his daily exercise rides with 'Fandes. Dubious, because he didn't know how to ride.

Van had been surprised until he thought about it, then felt like a fool for *not* thinking. Stef had seldom had anything to do with a horse as a child; he was born into poverty, and in the city, so there was no reason for him ever to have learned how to ride. While Van, who had been tossed onto a pony's back as soon as he could walk, was a member of a privileged minority: the landed—which meant *mounted*—nobility.

He didn't often think of himself that way, but Stefen's lack of such a basic—to Van—skill made the Herald rethink a number of things in that light.

And then he'd seen to it that Stef learned to ride, among other things.

He was actually glad that Stefen was still such a tyro; it gave him a good excuse to stop fairly early each day. Savil wasn't up to long rides either, but she would never admit it. But with poor, saddle-sore Stefen along, she could be persuaded to make an early halt long before she ran into trouble herself.

By the third day of their easy trip, Stef was looking much more comfortable astride. In fact, he looked as though he was beginning to enjoy himself, taking pleasure in his mount and her paces. The chestnut filly was a good match for his dark red hair, and the two of them made a very showy pair.

:*I imagine they'd attract quite a bit of notice if we weren't around*,: Yfandes commented, echoing his thoughts.

:*Don't look now, beloved, but they attract quite a bit when we are around.*: With the late summer sun making a scarlet glory of the chestnut's coat and Stef's hair, and the two White-clad Heralds on their snowy Companions on either side of him, Stefen looked like a young hero flanked by savants.

:*It's a good thing he isn't the clothes-horse I was at his age,*: Van continued. :*Otherwise he'd outshine all of us.*:

:*He is rather striking, isn't he?*: There was a note of fondness in Yfandes' thoughts that pleased Vanyel. She didn't always like his friends; it was a relief when she did. One thing that helped was that Stef shared a habit with Jervis, the former armsmaster of Forst Reach. He talked directly to Yfandes, never talked *about* her in her presence, and included her in on conversations as if she could understand them—which, of course, she could.

Stef's filly snorted at a butterfly and pranced sideways, tossing her mane and tail playfully. Stefen laughed at her, and reined her in gently. A few weeks ago he would have clutched at the reins, probably frightening her and himself in the bargain. There was a patience and a confidence in the way he handled her that spoke to Vanyel of more than riding experience.

He's matured, Vanyel thought, with some surprise. *He's really grown up a lot in the last few weeks. He looks it, too, which is probably just as well. It's bad enough that my father is assuming he's my lover—if they knew how young he really is, my tail would truly be in the fire!*

He squinted ahead, trying to make out a distance post or a landmark through the bright sun. *Another week at most, even at this easy pace, and we'll be there. I wish I knew how much of a strain this was really going to be. It could be worse, I suppose. At least they're making an effort to be polite.*

The filly fidgeted, but Stef held her down to a fast walk, talking to her with amusement in his voice. Savil caught Vanyel's eye and grinned, nodding her head toward the young Bard.

:A month ago she'd have put him on his rump in the dust. Boy's doing all right, Van. I like him.: Her grin got a little wider. *:Beats the blazes out of some "friends" you've had.:*

He made a face at her. *:Now don't you start! I've told you; we're just friends and that's the way I intend to keep it.:*

She just gave him a look out of the corner of her eye that implied she knew better.

He ignored the look. By his reckoning, even if his parents were willing to admit that he was shaych that didn't imply they were minded to aid and abet him.

They're willing to meet my friends but they won't want to know *they're more than friends. I'll bet they keep half the hold between my room and Stef's,* he thought wryly. *Little do they know how much I'm going to appreciate that. It's been hard enough keeping things cool between us, and if they're going to help, that's just fine with me.*

Stefen slowed his filly and brought her alongside Yfandes. "If this is the way traveling always is, I'm sorry they jumped me out of Journeyman so quickly," he said, as Vanyel smiled. "I could get to like this awfully fast."

"You should have talked more with Medren," Van told him. "You're lucky. This is a good trip; the roads are fine, it hasn't rained once, and it's late summer. I'd say that on the whole, the bad days outnumber the good two to one. That's what it feels like when you're stuck out on the road, anyway."

Yfandes snorted and bobbed her head in agreement. Stef looked down at her.

"That bad, is it, milady?"

She whickered, and snorted again.

"I'll take your word for it. Both of you, that is. But this trip has been— entirely wonderful. I feel like a human being for the first time in weeks." He tilted his head sideways, and gave Vanyel a long, appraising look. "You look a lot better yourself, Van."

"I feel better," he admitted. "I just hope Joshel can hold things together for a few weeks."

"Huh," Savil said, entering the conversation. "If he can't, he's not worth his Whites."

"That's not fair, Savil," Vanyel objected. "Just because Joshe isn't a Herald-Mage—"

"That's not it," she replied. "At least, that's not all of it. You left him a clean slate, if he can't deal with it—"

"Then I'm sure we'll hear from someone," Stefen interrupted firmly. "I don't think it matters. They know where we are; if they really need you, they can contact you, Van. Why not relax?"

Stef was right, he thought reluctantly. He really should relax. This was another in a string of absolutely perfect summer days; the air was warm and still, without being sultry. They encountered a number of travelers, and all were completely friendly and ordinary, farmers, traders, children on errands—not a one had aroused his suspicions or Savil's. Birds chirped sleepily as they passed, and when the sun grew too oppressive, there always seemed to be a pleasant grove of trees or a tiny village inn to rest in for a little.

Maybe that's what's bothering me. It's too perfect. I mistrust perfection. I keep waiting for something to go wrong.

This afternoon was identical to the rest; at the moment they were passing through an area completely under cultivation. Open fields left fallow alternated with land under the plow. There were usually sheep or cattle grazing in the former, and farmfolk hard at work in the latter. The sheep would either ignore their presence or spook skittishly away from the road—the cattle gathered curiously at the hedgerows to watch them pass. Insects buzzed on all sides, in the fields and the hedges.

This is the way it should be, Van thought a little sadly, thinking of the burned-over fields, and ravaged villages of the South. *This is how Valdemar should be, from Border to Border. Will I ever see it that way in my lifetime? Somehow I doubt it. Dear gods, I would give anything if I could ensure that day would come. . . .*

Stefen gave the filly her head, and she danced away ahead of them, her hooves kicking up little puffs of dust.

Vanyel shook his head. *No use in brooding. I'll just do what I can, when I can. And keep Stef at arm's length until he comes to his senses.*

The Bard let his filly stretch into a canter, outdistancing both the Heralds. Van chuckled; the filly was headstrong, but hadn't learned her own limits yet. He and Savil would catch up to the two of them eventually, probably resting in the shade of a tree.

With any luck, this whole trip may end up with Stef doing just that—learning his limits. Especially after he meets Mother and Father. Chasing me is one thing, but trying to do so around them—and having to play little politeness games with them— He chuckled to himself, and Yfandes cocked an ear back at him. *Oh, Stef, I think you may have met your match. "Many's the marriage that's been canceled on account of relatives." This might be exactly what's needed to make him realize that he's been throwing himself at a legend, not a flesh-and-blood human. And when he sees that this human comes with a package of crazed relations, I won't seem anywhere near as attractive!*

They rode into Forst Reach in the late afternoon of the one day that hadn't been completely perfect. Clouds had begun gathering in late morning, and by mid-afternoon the sky was completely gray and thunder rolled faintly in the far south. Farmers were working with one eye on the sky, and Stefen's filly fidgeted skittishly, her ears flicking back and forth every time a peal of thunder made the air shudder.

Nevertheless, there was the usual child out watching the road for them, and by the time they came within sight of the buildings of Forst Reach the multitude had assembled. Withen Ashkevron had given in to fate, and begun adding to the building some ten years ago; now two new wings spread out from the gray granite hulk, sprawling untidily to the east and north. And scaffolding on the southern side told Van that yet another building spree was about to begin. The additions had totally altered the appearance of the place; when Vanyel was first a Herald it had looked foreboding, and martial, not much altered from the defensive keep it had originally been. Now it looked rather like an old warhorse retired to pasture; surrounded by cattle, clambered upon by children, and entirely puzzled by the change in its status.

And it appeared, as they drew nearer, that the entire population of the manor had assembled to meet them in the open space in front of the main building. Much to Van's amusement, Stefen looked seriously alarmed at the size of the gathering.

"Van, that can't be your family, can it?" he asked just before they got in earshot. "I mean, there's hundreds of them. . . ."

Vanyel laughed. "Not quite hundreds; counting all the cousins and fosterlings, probably eighty or ninety by now. More servants, of course. Farewells can take all day, if you aren't careful."

"Oh," Stefen replied weakly, and then the waiting throng broke ranks and poured toward them.

The filly shied away from the unfamiliar scents and sounds, but the people pressed closely around her were all well acquainted with the habits of horses. The children all scampered neatly out of the way of her dancing hooves, and before she could bolt, Vanyel's brother Mekeal took her reins just under the bit in a surprisingly gentle fist.

"This one of Star's get?" he asked, running a knowing hand over her flank. "She's lovely, Van. Would you consider lending me her to put to one of the palfrey studs one of these days? We're still keeping up the palfrey and hunter lines, y'know."

"Ask Bard Stefen; she's his," Vanyel replied, and dismounted, taking care to avoid stepping on any children. Not an easy task; they were as careless around adults as they were careful around horses. He moved quickly to help Savil down before she could admit to needing a hand, a service that earned him a quick smile of conspiratorial gratitude.

Stefen dismounted awkwardly in a crowd of chattering children and gawky and admiring adolescents, who immediately surrounded him demanding to know if he was a real Bard, if he knew their cousin Medren, if he knew any songs about their cousin Vanyel, and a thousand other questions. He looked a little overwhelmed. There weren't a great many children at Court, and those that were there were usually kept out of sight except when being employed as pages and the like. Vanyel debated rescuing him, but a moment later found himself otherwise occupied.

Withen bore down on him with Treesa in tow, plowing his way through the crowd as effortlessly as a draft horse through a herd of ponies. He stopped, just within arm's reach. "Van—" he said, awkwardly. "—son—"

And there he froze, unable to force himself to go any further, and unwilling to pull away. Vanyel took pity on him and broke the uncomfortable moment. "Hello, Father," he said, clasping Withen's arms for just long enough to make Withen relax without making him flinch. "Gods, it is good to see you. You're looking indecently well. I swear, some day I'm going to open a closet door somewhere, and finally find the little wizard you've been keeping to make your elixir of youth!"

Withen laughed, reddening a little under the flattery; in fact, he *was* looking well, less like Mekeal's father than his older brother. They both were square and sturdily built, much taller than Vanyel, brown-eyed, brown-haired, brown-completed. Withen's hair and beard were about half silvered, and he'd developed a bit of a paunch; those were his only concessions to increasing age.

Withen relaxed further, and finally returned the embrace. "And as usual, you look like hell, son. Randale's been overusing you again, no doubt of it. Your sister warned us. Kernos' Horns, can't we ever see you when you *haven't* been overworking?"

"It's not as bad this time, Father," Van protested with a smile. "My reserves are in fairly good shape; it's mostly sleep and peace I lack."

"But don't they ever feed you, boy?" Withen grumbled. "Ah, never mind. We'll get some meat back on those bones, won't we, Treesa?"

Vanyel held out his hands to his mother, who took both of them. Treesa had finally accepted the onset of age, though not without a struggle. She had permitted her hair to resume its natural coloring of silver-gilt, and had given up trying to hide her age-lines under a layer of cosmetics.

Yet it seemed to Van that there might have been a little less discontent in her face than there had been the last time he was here. He hoped so. It surely helped that Roshya, Mekeal's wife, was accepting her years gracefully, and with evident enjoyment. Whatever stupid things Mekeal had done in his time—and he'd done quite a few, including the purchase of a purported "*Shin'a'in* warsteed" that was no more *Shin'a'in* than Vanyel—he'd more than made up for them by wedding Roshya. At least, that was Van's opinion. Roshya stood right behind Treesa, a young child clinging to her skirt with grubby hands, giving Treesa an encouraging wink.

"Run along, dear," Roshya said to the child, with an affectionate push. The child giggled and released her.

Treesa smiled tentatively, then with more feeling. "Your father's right, dear," she said, holding him at arm's length and scrutinizing him. "You do look very tired. But you look a great deal better than the last time you were here."

"That's mostly because I am," he replied. "Mother, you look wonderful. Well, you can see that I brought Aunt Savil—and—" He hesitated a moment. "And the friend you wanted to meet. My friend, and Medren's. Stef—"

He turned and gestured to Stefen, who extracted himself from the crowd of admiring children and adolescents.

Van steeled himself, kept his face set in a carefully controlled and pleasant mask of neutrality, then cleared his throat self-consciously. "Father, Mother," he said, gesturing toward Stefen, "This is Bard Stefen. Stef, my father and mother; Lord Withen, Lady Treesa."

Stef bowed slightly to Withen, then took Treesa's hand and kissed it. "Mother? Surely I heard incorrectly. You are Herald Vanyel's younger sister, I am certain," he said, with a sweet smile, at which Treesa colored and took her hand away with great reluctance, shaking her head. "His mother? No, impossible!"

Withen looked a little strained and embarrassed, but Treesa responded to Stef's gentle, courtly flattery as a flower to the sun. "Are you really a full Bard?" she asked, breathless with excitement. "Truly a Master?"

"Unworthy though I am, my lady," Stef replied, "that is the rank the Bardic Circle has given me. I pray you will permit me to test your hospitality and task your ears by performing for you."

"Oh, *would* you?" Treesa said, enthralled. Evidently she had completely forgotten what else Stef was supposed to be besides Van's friend and a Bard. Withen still looked a little strained, but Van began to believe that the visit would be less of a disaster than he had feared.

Thunder rumbled near at hand, startling all of them. "Gods, it's about to pour. Meke, Radevel, you see to the horses," Withen ordered. "The rest of you, give it a rest. You'll all get your chances at Van and his f-friend later. Let's all get inside before the storm breaks for true."

Treesa had already taken possession of Stefen and was carrying him off, chattering brightly. Van turned protectively toward Yfandes, remembering that his father never *could* bring himself to believe she was anything other than a horse.

But to his immense relief, Meke was leading Stef's filly to the stables, but his cousin Radevel had looped the two Companions' reins up over their necks and was standing beside them.

"Don't worry, Van," Radevel said with a wink. "Jervis taught me, remember?" And then, to the two Companions, "If you'll follow me, ladies, one of the new additions to the stables are *proper* accommodations for Companions. Saw to 'em m'self."

Vanyel relaxed, and allowed his father to steer him toward the door to the main part of the manor, as lightning flashed directly overhead and the first fat drops of rain began to fall. *Good old Rad. Finally, after all these years, I get* one *of my family convinced that 'Fandes isn't a horse!*

CHAPTER 8

—◦—◇—◦—

" . . . SO, THAT'S THE SITUATION," Withen continued, staring out the bubbly, thick glass of the crudely-glazed window at the storm outside. "I don't think it's going to change any time soon. Tashir is turning out to be a fine young man, and a good ruler. His second eldest is fostered here, did I mention that?"

Thunder vibrated in the rock walls, and Vanyel shook his head. "No, Father, you didn't. What about farther north though, up beyond Baires?"

Withen sighed. "Don't know, son. That's still Pelagir country. Full of uncanny creatures, and odd folks, and without much leadership that I've been able to see. It's a problem, and likely to stay one. . . ."

Vanyel held his peace; the *Tayledras* weren't "leaders" as his father understood the term, anyway, although they ruled and protected their lands as effectively as any warlord or landed baron.

Rain lashed the outside of the keep and hissed down the chimney. He and his father were ensconced in Withen's "study," a room devoted to masculine comforts and entirely off-limits to the females of the household. Withen turned away from the window and eased himself down into a chair that was old and battered and banished to here where it wouldn't offend Treesa's sensibilities; but like Withen, it was still serviceable despite being past its prime. Van was already sitting, or rather, sprawling, across a scratched and battered padded bench, one with legs that had been used as teething aids for countless generations of Ashkevron hounds.

"So tell me the truth, son," Withen said after a long pause. "I'm an old man, and I can afford to be blunt. How much longer does Randale have?"

Vanyel sighed, and rubbed the back of his neck uneasily. "I don't know, Father. Not even the Healers seem to have any idea." He hesitated a moment, then continued. "The truth is, though, I don't think it's going to be more than five years or so. Not unless we find out what it is he's got and find a way to cure it, or at least keep it from getting worse. Right now—right now the Council's best hope is to be able to keep him going until Treven's trained and in Whites. We think he can hang on that long."

"Is it true the boy's wedded that young Jisa?" Withen looked as if he approved, so Vanyel nodded. "Good. The sooner the boy breeds potential heirs, the better off we'll be. Shows the lad has more sense than his elders." Withen snorted his disgust at those "elders." "It was shilly-shallying about Randale's marriages that got us in this pickle in the first place. Should have told the boy to marry Healer Shavri in the first damn place, and we'd have had half a dozen legitimate heirs instead of one girl out of the succession."

Withen went on in the same vein for some time, and Vanyel did not think it prudent to enlighten him to the realities of the situation.

"About the Pelagir lands, Father," he said instead. "The last few times I've visited home, I've heard stories—and seen the evidence—of things coming over and into Valdemar. Are they still doing that?"

When Withen hesitated, he began to suspect that something was seriously wrong. "Father, are these—visitations—getting worse? What is it that you aren't telling me?"

"Son," Withen began.

"No, Father, don't think of me as your son. I'm Herald Vanyel, and I need to know the whole truth." He sat up from his sprawled position, looked his father straight in the eyes. Withen was the first to look away.

"Well—yes. For a while they were getting worse." Withen looked at the fire, out the window—anywhere but at Van.

"And?"

"And we asked Haven for some help. For a Herald-Mage." Withen coughed.

"And?"

"And they said there weren't any to spare, and they sent us just a plain Herald." Withen's mouth worked as if he were tasting something bitter. "I won't say she was of no use, but—but we decided if Haven wasn't going to help us, we'd best learn how to help ourselves, and we sent her back. Let her think she'd taken care of the problem after a hunt or two. Had a talk with Tashir's people—after all, they've been doing without mages for one damned long time. Found out the ways to take out some of these things without magic. Worked out some more. Finally the things stopped coming across altogether. I guess they got some way of talking to each other, and let it be known that we don't like havin' things try and set up housekeeping over here."

"There's been no more sign of anything?" Van was amazed—not that there were no signs of further incursions, but that the people here had taken on the problem and dealt with it on their own.

"No, though we've been keepin' the patrols up. Tashir's people, too. But—"

"But what, Father?" Vanyel asked gently. "You can say what you like. I won't be offended by the truth."

"It's just—all our lives we've been told how we can depend on the Herald-Mages, how they'll help us when we need them—then when we need them, we get told there aren't any to spare, they're all down on the Karsite Border or off somewhere else—and here one of our *own* is a Herald-Mage—it just goes hard." Withen was obviously distressed, and Vanyel didn't blame him.

"But Father—you were sent help. You said so yourself. They sent you a Herald," he pointed out.

"A *Herald*?" Within scoffed. "What good's a plain Herald? We needed a Herald-Mage!"

"Did you give her a chance?" Vanyel asked, quietly. "Or did you just assume she couldn't be of any help and lead her around like a child until she was convinced there wasn't any real need for her?"

"But—she was just a Herald—"

"Father, nobody is 'just' a Herald," Vanyel said. "We're taught to make the best of every ability we have—Heralds and Herald-Mages. The only differences in us are the kinds of abilities we have. She would have done *exactly* as you did. She probably would have been able to help you, if you'd given her the chance. She wouldn't have been able to invoke a spell and destroy the creatures for you, but it's quite probable a Herald-Mage wouldn't have been able to either. I have no doubt she could have found the ones in hiding, perhaps, or uncovered their weaknesses. But you didn't give her a chance to find out what she could do."

"I suppose not," Withen said, after a moment. "I—don't suppose that was very fair to her, either."

Vanyel nodded. "It's true, Father. There aren't enough Herald-Mages. I'm afraid to tell you how few of us there are. I wish there were more of us, but there aren't, and I hope when you are sent help next time, you won't think of that help as 'just' a Herald."

"Because that's the best help Haven can give us," Withen concluded for him.

But he didn't look happy. And in a way, Van understood. But there was that stigma again—"just" a Herald—when there were Heralds who had twice the abilities of some of the Herald-Mages he'd known.

It was a disturbing trend—and unfortunately, one he had no idea how to reverse.

"Father, which would you rather have in a pinch—a Herald with a very strong Gift, a Gift that's exactly the kind of thing you need, or a Herald-Mage who may be able to do no more than *you* could on your own?" He paused for effect. "There have been no few Herald-Mages *killed* down on the Karsite Border precisely because they were mages, and because of that they tried to handle more than they were capable of. If I were spying on the enemy, I'd rather have a strongly Mindspeaking Herald doing it for me than a Herald-Mage who has to send up a flare of mage-fire when he needs to talk! If I were hunting up magical creatures, I'd rather have a Herald with powerful Farsight than a weak Herald-Mage who'd light up like a tasty beacon to those creatures every time he uses his magic."

"I never thought about it that way," Withen mumbled. "But still—"

"Please do think about it, Father," Van urged. "And please talk to others about it. Valdemar is short of friends and resources these days. We have to use everything we can, however we can. You have a powerful influence on the way people think in this area—"

"I wish your brother thought that," Withen mumbled, but he looked pleased.

"If you decide that I'm right, you can make an enormous difference in the way things are handled the next time. And that just may save you a great deal, including lives."

Withen sighed, and finally met his eyes. "Well, I'll think about it, son. That's all I'll promise."

Which is about as much of a concession as I'm ever likely to get out of him. "Thank you, Father," he said, hoping it would be enough. "That's all I can ask."

Dinner proved to be entertaining and amazingly relaxing. Only the immediate family and important household members assembled in the Great Hall anymore—there wasn't *room* for anyone else.

Vanyel was partnered with the priest who had replaced the late, unlamented Father Leren; a young and aggressive cleric with a thousand ideas whose fervor was fortunately tempered with wit and a wry good sense of humor. The young man was regrettably charismatic—before the meal was

over, Van found he'd been lulled into agreeing to broach a half dozen of
those ideas to his father.

Treesa had kidnapped Stef and ensconced him at her side, with herself
and Withen between the Bard and Vanyel. Since that was pretty much as
Van had *expected* things would go, he ignored Stef's mute pleas for help
throughout the meal. Given how much effort he'd been going to in order
to avoid the less platonic of Stef's continued attentions, he found it rather
amusing to see the Bard in the position of "pursued."

Immediately following dinner, Withen claimed his son for another conference. This time it included Withen, Radevel, Mekeal, and two cousins
Vanyel just barely knew. That conference left him with a profound admiration for how well the folk in this so-called "Border backwater" were keeping up with important news. They knew pretty well how much impact
Treven's marriage was going to have on situations outKingdom, had good
guesses about what concessions Randale was likely to have to make with
Rethwellan in order to gain their Queen's aid, and had a fair notion of the
amount of help Tashir was likely to be able to offer Valdemar.

What they wanted to know was the real state of the situation with Karse.
"We heard they'd outlawed magery," Radevel said, putting his feet up on
the low table they all shared, "and there was rumors about fightin' inside
Karse. All well an' good, if it's true, an' what's bad for Karse is likely to be
good for us 'twould look like, but what's that really gonna do to us? That
gonna end up spillin' across the Border, you reckon?"

Vanyel put his drink down on the table, and dipped his finger into a
puddle of spilled ale. "Here's the Karsite Border," he said, drawing it for
them. "Here's Rethwellan, and here's us. Now this is what we know so
far—"

In a few sentences he was able to sum up his own and Randale's analysis
of the situation, and the reasons why the alliance with Rethwellan was all
the more necessary.

"So we end up takin' hind teat if there's trouble out here, hmm?" one of
the cousins said cynically, around a mouthful of bread and cheese.

"To be brutally frank," Vanyel felt forced to say, "unless it's a major in-
cursion, yes. I wish I could tell you differently."

Radevel shrugged philosophically. "Somebody's gotta take second
place," he pointed out. "No way around that. Seems to me we've been doin'
pretty well for ourselves; we got some Guard, we got our own patrols, we
got Tashir an' his people. So long as nobody brings up an army, we should

be all right." Withen nodded, and refilled all their mugs, letting the foam run over the tops with casual disregard for the state of the furniture.

"I can do this much for you," Vanyel told them after a moment's thought. Five sets of eyes fastened on him. "You know I have limited Crown authority. I can authorize a general reduction in taxes for landholders who keep their own armed forces. And I can get you weapons—and I think some trainers. We've got some Guards that are minus legs or arms that would still make good trainers, even if they can't fight."

All of them brightened at that. Mekeal looked as if he was counting something up in his head.

:Probably would-be young heroes,: Yfandes said cynically. *:And he's reckoning how much he can get taken off the tax-roles by encouraging young hotheads to take their energy off to the Guard.:*

:Probably,: Van replied, thinking a little sadly of all the aspiring heroes who had found only early graves on the Karsite Border. And how many more he'd send there, if indirectly. . . .

But the fighters had to come from somewhere. Better that they came as volunteers, and well-trained. "I can probably even authorize tax credit if you send trained fighters for the Guard instead of cash or kind at tax time," he continued. "Randale's pretty loath to hire mercenaries, but he wants to avoid conscription, and right now the ranks down South are getting thinner than we'd like."

"I got another thought," Mekeal put in. "Give that credit across Valdemar, an' send the green 'uns to us for training an' seasoning. We'll get 'em blooded without the kind of loss you get in combat."

That made him feel less guilty. "Good gods," Vanyel replied, "I'm surrounded by geniuses! Why didn't *we* think of that?"

Meke shrugged, pleased. "Just tryin' to help all of us."

:It's an excellent solution to getting youngsters used to real combat at relatively low risk,: 'Fandes observed, with approval. *:I like the way your brother thinks.:*

:So do I, dearling.: He nodded at Meke. "That will help immensely, I truly think."

They discussed other matters for a while, but it was fairly evident that they'd touched on all the topics the others considered of the most import. Vanyel got to his feet and excused himself when the conversation devolved to small talk about hunting.

"I'll make an effort to get in touch with Herald Joshel and get confirmation on everything we covered," he told them, and grinned, seeing a chance to bring a point home. "That's the advantage of having a strong Mindspeaking Herald around when you need answers in a hurry. Joshe is actually a stronger Mindspeaker than I am, and he's taking my place with Randale while I'm gone. I know when he'll be free tomorrow, and I'll contact him then."

He was surprised at how late it was when he left them. The halls were quiet; the servants had long since gone to bed, leaving every other lamp out, and the ones still burning turned down low. His room would be the guest room he'd used every visit he'd made home, and he knew exactly where it was, despite the additions to the manor and the darkness of the halls.

He found himself yawning as he neared his door. *I didn't realize how tired I was*, he thought sleepily. *It's a good thing I didn't drink that second mug of ale Father poured. I wonder what room they put Stef in? I hope it wasn't the one overlooking the gardens; ye gods, he'll be up all night with mocker-birds screaming at his window. I'll take the old room any time, even if it isn't as cool in the summer. Havens, that bed is going to feel good. . . .*

He reached for the door handle and pulled it open just enough to slip inside. Some kind soul had left two candles burning, one above the hearth, one beside the bed. The gentle candlelight was actually quite bright compared to the darkened hallway; shadows danced as the candleflames flickered in the draft he had created by opening the door. As he stepped away from the door, he glanced automatically toward the right side of the hearth, beside the bed—the servants always left his luggage there, and he wanted to make sure his gittern was all right before he went to bed.

And he froze, for there were two sets of packs, and two gitterns. His—and Stefen's. And—he looked beyond the luggage to see if the furnishings had been changed; but they hadn't—only one bed.

Behind him, someone shot the bolt on the door.

He whirled; Stefen turned away from the door and faced him, the warm gold of candlelight softening his features so that he looked very young indeed. His loose shirt was unlaced to the navel, and his feet were bare beneath his leather riding breeches.

"Before you ask," he said, in a soft, low voice, "this wasn't my idea. This seems to have happened on your father's orders. But Van—I'm glad he did it—"

Vanyel backed up a step, his mind swimming in little circles. "Oh. Ah, Stefen, I'll just get my things and—"

Stef shook his head, and brushed his long hair back behind his ears with one hand. "No. Not until I get a chance to say what I have to. You've been avoiding this for weeks, and I'm not letting the one chance I've had to really talk to you get away from me."

Vanyel forced himself to relax, forced his mind to stop whirling as best he could, and walked over to one of the chairs next to the hearth. He stood beside it, with his hands resting on the back so that Stefen could not see them trembling. He glanced down at them; they seemed very cold and white, and he wondered if Stefen had noticed. "Ah . . . what is it you need to talk about that you couldn't have said on the road?" he asked, as casually as he could.

"Dammit, Van!" Stefen exploded. "You know very well what I want to talk about! You—and me."

"Stefen," Vanyel said, controlling his voice with an effort that hurt, "you are one of the best friends I've ever had. I mean that. And I appreciate that friendship."

Stef's eyes were full of pleading, and Vanyel forced himself to turn away from him and stare at a carved wooden horse on the mantelpiece. "Stef, you're very young; I'm nearly twice your age. I've seen all this before. You admire me a great deal, and you think—"

There were no footsteps to warn him; suddenly he found Stef's hands on his shoulders, wrenching him around, forcing him to look into the young Bard's face. Stef's hands felt like hot irons on his shoulders, and there was strength in them that was not apparent from the Bard's slight build. "Vanyel Ashkevron," Stef said, hoarsely, "I am shaych, just like you. I've known what I am for years now. I'm not an infatuated child. What's more—" Now the Bard flushed and looked away, off to Vanyel's right. "I've had more lovers in one year than you've had in the last ten. And—and I've never felt about *any* of them the way I feel about you. I—I think I love you, Van. I don't think I could ever love anyone but you."

He looked back up at Vanyel. The Herald could only gaze back into the darkened emerald of Stefen's eyes, eyes that seemed in the dim light to be mostly pupil. Vanyel was utterly stunned. This—this was considerably beyond infatuation. . . .

"Bards are supposed to be so cursed good with words," Stefen said unhappily, looking into Vanyel's eyes as if he was looking for answers. "Well, all my eloquence seems to have deserted *me*. All—all I can tell you is that I think I'd love you if you were a *hundred* years older than me, or a deformed monster, or—or even a woman."

The Bard's voice had lost any hint of training; it was tight and rough with tension and unhappiness. For his part, Vanyel couldn't seem to speak at all. His throat was paralyzed and his chest hurt when he tried to breathe. He felt alternately hot and cold, and his heart pounded in his ears. Stefen didn't notice his unresponsiveness, evidently, for he continued on without looking away from Van.

"Since you aren't any of those things," he said, his voice unsteady with emotion, "since you're w-wonderful, and w-wise, and beautiful enough to make my heart ache, and dammit, *not* old, I—I can't take this much longer." A single tear slid down one cheek, shining silver in the candlelight; Stefen either didn't notice it, or didn't care. "I—I'm only glib when it comes to making rhymes, Van. I love you, and I'm *not* a Herald. I can't *show* you how I feel—except physically. I want to be your lover. I don't want anyone else, not ever again."

When Vanyel didn't respond, a second tear joined the first, slipping silently from the corner of Stefen's eye; he swallowed, and broke eye contact to look down at his feet. He relaxed his hold on Vanyel's shoulders, but didn't release him.

"I suppose—I guess I must revolt you," he said, bitterly. "All my . . . other lovers . . . I don't blame you, I guess. I—"

That broke Vanyel's paralysis. That, and the ache his Gift of Empathy let him feel all too clearly, an ache that was matched by the one in his own heart. "No," he whispered. "No—Stef, I—just never knew you felt that strongly."

His hands hurt from clenching the back of the chair. He let go, and flexed them, then raised his right hand, slowly, and brushed the tear from Stefen's face with gentle, wondering fingers. "I never guessed," he repeated, no longer trying to hide the strength of his own feelings from himself.

Stefen let go of Vanyel's shoulders, caught Van's hand and looked back up into Vanyel's eyes, quickly. Whatever he read there made him smile, like the sun coming from behind a cloud; a smile so bright it left Vanyel dazzled. He kept Vanyel's right hand in his, and backed up a step. Then another. Vanyel resisted for a fraction of a second, then followed, drawn along like an obedient child. His knees were weak, and the room seemed too hot—no, too cold—

He's too young! part of him kept clamoring. *He can't possibly know what he's doing, what this means. He's hardly older than Jisa—*

His conscience nagged as Stefen blew out the candles, as the young Bard ran strong, callused hands under Vanyel's shirt, and drew him down onto the bed—

And then the voice was silenced as Stef gently proved beyond a shadow of a doubt that he was *just* as experienced as he had claimed. If there was someone being seduced, it wasn't Stefen. . . .

The last of Vanyel's misgivings dissolved as not-so-young Stefen showed him things he hadn't even imagined, and then proved that the sweet giving and receiving the Bard had just taught him was only the beginning. . . .

Overhead, sky a dead and lightless black. To either side, walls of ice—

He turned to the one standing at his side. 'Lendel—

But it was Stefen; wrapped in wool and fur, and so frightened his face was as icy-pale as the cliffs to either side of them.

"You have to go get help," he told the Herald—no, the Bard—

"I won't leave you," Stef said, stubbornly. "You have to come with me. I won't leave without you."

He shook his head, and threw back the sides of his cloak to free his arms. "Yfandes can't carry two," he said. "And I can hold them off for however long it takes you to bring help."

"You can't possibly—"

"I can," he interrupted. "Look, there's only enough room at this point for one person to pass. As long as I stand here, they'll never get by—"

Blink—

Suddenly he was alone, and exhausted; chilled to the bone. An army filled the pass before him, and at the forefront of that army, a single man who could have been Vanyel's twin, save only that his eyes and hair were deepest black—a dark mirror to Vanyel's silver eyes and silvered hair, and as if to carry the parody to its extreme, he wore clothing cut identically to Heraldic Whites, only of ebony black.

"I know you," he heard himself say.

The man smiled. "Indeed."

"You—you are—"

"Leareth." The word was Tayledras for "darkness." The man smiled. "A quaint conceit, don't you think?"

And Vanyel knew—

He woke, shaking like a leaf in a gale; his chest heaved as he gasped for breath, clutching the blanket.

He was cold, bone-cold, yet drenched with sweat. *It was the old dream, the ice-dream, the dream where I die—I haven't had that dream for years—*

Stefen lay beside him, sprawled over the edge of the bed, oblivious to Van's panting for air. Though the candles were out, Van could see him by moonlight streaming in the window. The storm had blown itself out, leaving the sky clear and clean; the moonlight was bright enough to read by, and Vanyel saw the bright points of stars glittering against the sky through the windowpane.

Vanyel controlled his breathing, and lay back, forcing his heart to slow. He blinked up into the dark canopy of the bed, still caught in the cold claws of the nightmare.

I haven't had that dream for years—except this time it was different. This time, it wasn't 'Lendel that was with me. Except—except it felt like 'Lendel. I thought it was 'Lendel until I turned around. and it was Stef. . . .

The young Bard sighed, and turned over, bringing his face into the moonlight. Lying beside Stef, for a moment—for a moment it had been, it had *felt* like being beside Tylendel, his love and life bonded.

Lifebonded.

Only then did he realize why Stefen "felt" like Tylendel. The tie was the same; Vanyel was not only in love with the Bard, he had lifebonded to him. There was no mistaking that tie, especially not for an Empath.

No—

But there was no denying it, either. Vanyel suppressed a groan; if being attracted to Stefen had been a betrayal of 'Lendel's memory, then what was this? He couldn't think; he felt his stomach knot and a lump in his throat. He had loved 'Lendel; he still did.

He thought that he would lie awake until dawn, but somehow exhaustion got the better of confused thoughts and tangled emotions, and sleep stole over him. . . .

:It's about time you got here,: Yfandes said, with a knowing look. *:Honestly, Van, you make things so complicated for yourself sometimes. Well, come on.:*

She turned adroitly, and flicked her tail at him, looking back at him over her shoulder. *:Well? Aren't you coming?:*

"Where am I?" he asked, looking about himself. There wasn't anything to be seen in any direction; wherever he looked, there was nothing but featureless gray fog. He and Yfandes were all alone in it, so far as he could see.

:Where are you?: she repeated, her mind-voice warm and amused. *:You're dreaming, of course. Or rather, in Dreamtime. There is a difference. Now are you coming, or not?:*

He followed her, having nothing better to do; the peculiar fog thickened until he could hardly see her. He tried to catch up with her, but she always managed to stay the same distance ahead of him. Finally, all he could make out of her was a vague, glowing-white shape in the swirling fog.

A tendril of fog wrapped around his head, blinding him completely. He faltered, tried to bat it away—

And stumbled into an exact duplicate of the grove in Companion's Field where he and 'Lendel had spent so many hours. The same grove that 'Lendel had destroyed. . . .

"Well, *ashke*," said a heartbreakingly familiar voice behind him. "You certainly took your time getting here."

He turned, slowly, afraid of what he might see, especially after what he and Stef had done.

"Don't be an idiot," Tylendel said, shaking back hair as gold as the summer sun filtering through the pine boughs above him. "Why should I mind?"

Tylendel lounged against the rough trunk of a tree with his arms crossed over his chest, looking little older than when he'd died, but dressed in the Whites he hadn't earned in life. He raised one golden eyebrow quizzically at Van, then grinned. "Why, Van—that's twice in one day you've been moonstruck. Is this getting to be a habit?" Then, softer, "What's wrong Vanyel-*ashke*?"

As Vanyel stood, rooted to the spot, Tylendel pushed himself away from the tree, crossed the few feet between them and took him in his strong, warm arms. Sharp scents rose from the crushed pine needles beneath their feet. Vanyel returned the embrace, hesitantly at first, then, with a sob that was half relief and half grief, held his beloved so tightly his arms hurt.

"Here, now," 'Lendel said, holding him gently. "What's the matter? Why should I be angry with you because you found someone to love who loves you?"

"Because—because I love you—" It seemed a foolish fear, now—

"Van-*ashke*, what's the point in suffering all your life for one mistake?" 'Lendel let go of him and stepped back a little, so that he could look down into Vanyel's eyes. "You don't give up a chance at happiness just because you've already been happy once in your life! Havens, that's like saying you'll never eat again because you've been a guest at one grand feast!"

'Lendel chuckled warmly; as his smile reached and warmed his brown eyes, Van found himself smiling back. "I guess that is kind of stupid," he replied with a touch of chagrin. "But I never did think too clearly when my emotions were involved."

'Lendel's smile faded a little. "Neither of us did," he said, soberly. "Me especially. Van—you know, I didn't love you enough, and I'm sorry."

Vanyel started to protest; 'Lendel put one finger on his lips to quiet him. "This is honesty; I didn't love you enough. If I had, I would have cared more about what was good for you than what *I* wanted. I'm sorry, *ashke*, and I think perhaps I've learned better. I hope so. Because—oh, Van—I want to make it up to you more than anything. If you can believe in anything, please, believe that. And believe that I love you."

He bent down and touched his lips to Vanyel's.

Vanyel woke with a start, wrapped in Stefen's arms. For a moment, he thought he could still smell the scent of crushed pine needles, and feel the breeze on his cheek.

"—love you," Stefen whispered in his ear, then subsided into deep breathing that told Van he was still really asleep.

'Lendel. That was 'Lendel. What in hell did all that mean? Van wondered, still slightly disoriented. *What in* hell *did all that mean?* He stared, wide-eyed, into the darkness. He would have liked to talk to Yfandes, but a gentle Mindtouch showed her to be deep in slumber.

The next time Stef turned over, releasing him, he eased out of bed, far too awake now to fall back asleep. The room was chilly; the storm had cooled things off in its passing. He slipped into a robe and began slowly pacing the floor, trying to unravel his dreams and nightmares, and making heavy work of it.

That second thing didn't feel like a dream, he thought, staring at the floor while he paced. *That felt real; as real as the Shadow-Lover, and I know He was real. It was 'Lendel, it couldn't have been anything I conjured up for myself out of guilt. Could it? I've never done anything like that before this. . . .*

And the old ice-dream has changed. I thought I'd gotten rid of it—thought I'd purged it away after I faced down Krebain. Why has it come back?

The square of moonlight crept across the floor and up the wall, then vanished as the moon set. And still Vanyel was wide awake, and too intent on his own thoughts to feel chilled. He kept pacing the floor, pausing now and again to look down on Stefen. The Bard slept on his lips curved in a slight smile, sprawled over the entire bed.

After a while, as the impact of the two dreams—if they were

dreams—began to wear off, that posture of Stef's began to amuse him. *I never would have believed that someone that slight could take up that much room all by himself,* he thought with a silent chuckle. *He's like a cat; takes up far more space than is even remotely possible under the laws of nature.*

It was nearly dawn; the pearly light of earliest morning filled the room, making everything soft-edged and shadowy. Vanyel continued to stare down at Stef, not thinking, really, just waiting for some of his thoughts to sort themselves out and present themselves to him in an orderly fashion.

Stefen stirred a little, and opened his eyes. He blinked confusedly at Van for a moment, then seemed to recollect where he was. "Van?" he asked, sleep blurring his voice. "Is something wrong, Vanyel-*ashke*?"

Vanyel froze. The words, the very tone, brought back the second dream with the impact of a blow above the heart.

*Tylendel leaning up against the shaggy tree trunk, a slight smile on his lips, his arms crossed over his chest. "What's wrong, Vanyel-*ashke?"

Ashke—it was the *Tayledras* word for "beloved," and Tylendel's special name for him, a play on Vanyel's family name of "Ashkevron."

But 'Lendel had been fluent in *Tayledras*; Savil had insisted that 'Lendel and Vanyel both learn the tongue, as she had always intended to take them to the Pelagir Hills territory claimed by her Hawkbrother friends as soon as Tylendel was ready for fieldwork. She didn't even offer the lessoning to Donni and Mardic, her other two pupils.

Stefen, on the other hand, knew only one word of pidgin-*Tayledras*; shaych, the shortened form of *shay'a'chern*, which had become common usage for those whose preferences lay with their own sex. He couldn't ever have heard the word he'd just used, must less know what it meant.

Wild thoughts of hauntings and possessions ran through Vanyel's mind. He'd seen so many stranger things as a Herald—"Stef," Vanyel said, slowly and carefully. "What did you just call me?"

"Vanyel-*ashke*," Stefen repeated, bewildered, and plainly disturbed by Van's careful mask of control. "Why? Did I say something wrong?"

"Is there a reason why you called me that just now?" Vanyel didn't move, though the hair was rising on the back of his neck. First the dreams, and now this . . . he extended a careful probe, ready at any moment to react if he found anything out of the ordinary.

"Sure," Stef replied, blinking at him, and rising up onto one elbow. "I've—" He blushed a little. "—I've been calling you that to myself for a while. Comes from your name, Ashkevron. It—it seems to suit you. You know how a Bard likes to play with words. It has a nice *sound*, you know?"

The probe met with nothing. No resistance, no aura of another presence. Vanyel relaxed, and smiled. It was nothing, after all. Just an incredible co-incidence. He wasn't being haunted by the spirit of a long-dead lover, nor was this love in any danger of being possessed or controlled by the last.

Not that 'Lendel would ever have done that, he reminded himself. *No, I'm just short on sleep and no longer thinking clearly, that's all. And so used to jumping at shadows that I'm overreacting to even a perfectly innocent pet-name.*

"Did I say something wrong?" Stefen asked again more urgently this time, starting to sit up as he pulled tangled hair out of his eyes with both hands. "If you don't like it—if it bothers you—"

"No, it's all right," Vanyel answered him. "I was just a little startled, that's all. *Ashke* is the *Tayledras* word for 'beloved,' and I wasn't expecting to hear that from you."

"If you'd rather I didn't—" Stef hastened to say, when Vanyel inter-rupted him.

"I do like it—just, I had some odd dreams, and coming on top of them, it startled me. That's all." Vanyel touched Stefen's shoulder, and the Bard flinched.

"Havens, you're *freezing*," Stef exclaimed. "How long have you been up? Never mind, it's probably too long. Get *in* here before you catch something horrible, and let me warm you up. After all," he added slyly, as Van shrugged off his robe and slid into bed beside him. "Whatever you catch, *I'll* probably get, and you wouldn't want to have the guilt of ruining a Bard's voice on your conscience, would you?"

"Anything but that," Van replied vaguely, then gasped as Stef curled his warm body around Van's chilled one.

"Oh?" the Bard said archly. *"Anything?"*

CHAPTER 9

A FTER STEFEN HAD warmed him and relaxed him—among other things—they both fell asleep for a second time as the first light of the sun sent strokes of pink and gold across the sky. This time Vanyel slept deeply and dreamlessly, and Stefen actually woke before him. Van awakened to find Stef lounging indolently next to him, watching him with a proprietary little smile on his face.

"Well, what are you looking at?" Van asked, amused by the Bard's expression. "And a copper for your thoughts."

Stefen laughed. "'Acres and acres, and it's *all mine*,'" he said, quoting a tag-line of a current joke. "If you had any idea of the number of times I've daydreamed of being right where I am now, you'd laugh."

"You think so?" Van smiled, and shook his head. "Oh, no, I promise, I wouldn't laugh."

"Well, maybe you wouldn't." Stefen searched his face for a moment, looking as if he wanted to say something, but couldn't make up his mind how to say it. Vanyel waited patiently for him to find the words. "Van," he said, finally, "I have to know. Are you sorry? I mean, I'm just a Bard, I haven't got Mindspeech; I can't, you know, mesh with you when we—" He flushed. "I mean, does that bother you? Do you miss it? I—"

"Stef," Vanyel interrupted him gently. "You're laboring under a misapprehension. I've never had a lover who shared his mind with me, so I wouldn't know what it was like."

"You haven't?" Stefen was flabbergasted. "But—but what about Tylendel?"

"My Gifts were all dormant while he was alive," Van replied, finding it amazingly easy—for the first time in years—to talk about his old love. "The only bond we had that I could share was the lifebond."

"Do you miss *that*, then?" Stef asked, shyly, as if he was afraid to hear the answer, but had to ask the question.

"No," Vanyel said, and smiled broadly. "And if you look inside yourself for a moment, you'll know why."

"If I—"

"Stef, you're a trained Bard; Bardic Gift is enough like Empathy for you to see what I mean." Van sent a brief pulse of wordless love along the bond, and watched Stef's face change. First surprise—then something akin to shock—then a delight that resonated back down through the bond they shared.

"I never dreamed—" Stef's voice was hushed. "I never—How? Why?"

"I don't know, *ke'chara*. and I don't care." Vanyel shook his head. "All I know is that it's happened, it's real. *And* I know that if we don't get out of bed and put in an appearance, we're never going to do so before noon—I'm afraid they might break the door down and find us in a very embarrassing position."

Stefen laughed. "You know, you're right. We should spare them that, at least. It's only fair."

Vanyel grinned wickedly. "Besides, if I know my mother, she's dying to carry you off to perform for her and her ladies. So come on, Bard. Your audience awaits."

Stefen struck a pose, and held it until Vanyel slid out of bed and flung his clothing at him.

"I warn you, you'd better hurry," the Herald advised him, "or I'll send her in to fetch you."

"I'm hurrying," Stefen replied, pulling on his breeches. "Trust me, I'm hurrying—" Then he stopped, with his shirt half on 'Van, about your mother—is she—ah, *serious?*'

Vanyel knew exactly what Stef was trying to ask, and laughed. "No, she's not really chasing you. She would probably be horrified if you took her seriously; in her way, she really loves Father, I think. She's just playing The Game."

Stefen heaved an enormous sigh of relief. "I couldn't tell; she's a little heavier-handed at it than the ladies at the Court."

"Not surprising," Van replied, checking his appearance in the mirror. "She's playing by rules that are thirty years out of date." He straightened his hair a little, then turned back to Stef, who was struggling into his tunic. "Under all the posing, she really has a good heart, you know. *She* was the one that saw that Medren had talent, even if she couldn't recognize the Gift, and saw to it that he got whatever training was available out here. Not much, but it was enough to give him a start." He crossed the room, to tug Stef's tunic down over his head. "She could have ignored him; he was nothing more than the bastard son of one of her maids, even if his father *is* my brother Meke. She *could* have dismissed Melenna; she didn't. Granted, she *was* holding Melenna as a last effort to 'cure' me, but still—she did her best for both of them, and that's a great deal more than many would have done."

Stef solved the problem of his tousled hair by shaking his head vigorously, then running his fingers through his mane a couple of times. "Then I'll get along fine with her. Anyone who's done anything for Medren gets my nod."

Vanyel chuckled. "Don't misunderstand me; Treesa's far from perfect. She can be selfish, inconsiderate, and completely featherheaded. She didn't dismiss Melenna, but that was at least partly because she'd have had to train a new maid *and* take care of all the things Melenna had until the new one was trained. And the gods know she's a shrewd one when it comes to her own comforts; she knew Melenna would be so grateful that she'd have devoted service out of the girl for years. But for all of that, she's good at heart, and I love her dearly."

Stef unlocked the door, with a sly smile over his shoulder for Van. "You know, this business of having a family takes an awful lot of getting used to. I have to confess it kind of baffles me."

Vanyel laughed, and followed Stefen out into the hall. "Stef, I hate to tell you this, but for all the privileges I grew up with, there have been any number of times I'd have traded places with any orphaned beggar-child on the street. My life would have been a great deal simpler."

Stefen grimaced. "I'll keep that in mind."

True to Vanyel's prediction, Treesa descended upon them once they reached the Great Hall, and appropriated Stefen to perform for her and her ladies as soon as they'd finished a sketchy breakfast.

That left Vanyel alone, which was exactly what he wanted right now. He strolled out the side door, heading ultimately toward the stables, taking care *not* to take a route that would put him along halls used by anyone except children and servants, or, once outside, under anyone's window. He wanted some time to think things through, and he'd had enough of family conferences for a while.

But there *was* someone who deserved his attention, first. *:'Fandes,:* he Mindsent, *:Good morning, love.:*

:Good morning, sleepy,: she Sent back, her mind-voice so full of pleased satisfaction that he chuckled. *:I trust you enjoyed yourself last night.:*

:You trust correctly,: he replied, just a tiny bit embarrassed.

:Good,: she said. *:It's about time. I want you to know that I heartily approve of this and I commend the lad's patience. The only question is, row what are you going to do?:*

He paused for a moment beside the mews, noting absently the chirrs and soft calls of the hooded raptors inside. *:That's something I need to work out, love. Would you be terribly hurt if I borrowed one of the hunters and rode off without you for a little bit? I want to be alone to think this through properly.:*

He caught a moment of surprise from her, and half-smiled. It wasn't often that he was able to catch her off-guard anymore. *:I suppose that makes sense,:* she said after a long pause. *:This really affects you a great deal more than me. No, I won't be hurt. Just don't make any stupid decisions like trying to get rid of the lad, will you? You need him, and he needs you, and you are very, very good for each other.:*

He laughed aloud, one of his worries taken care of—he was afraid that while she approved of Stef as a friend, she might not be as approving of the new relationship. *:I doubt I could remove him now with a pry-bar, love. And—thank you for understanding.:*

She Sent him a reply, not in words, but in emotion: love, trust, and shared happiness. Then she released the link.

He managed to reach the stables without being intercepted by anyone, though there were a couple of close calls avoided only because he saw Meke and his father before they saw him. Fortunately the stables weren't far; the double doors were standing wide open to catch every breeze and he walked inside.

Mekeal's famous Stud still had the best loose-box in the place, and the years had not improved the beast's looks or temper. It laid its ears back and snapped at him as he passed, then cow-kicked the side of its stall in frustration when it couldn't reach him. The only ones who had ever succeeded in riding the beast were Radevel and Jervis, and it was a fight every step of the way even for them.

"Watch it, horse," he muttered under his breath, "or I'll turn 'Fandes and Kellan loose on you again."

The horse snorted as if it could understand him, and backed off into a corner of its box.

Meke's warhorse mares were in this stable, along with the foals too young to sell. They watched him calmly as he passed them, some whickering as they caught his scent and recognized him for a stranger. That brought him the attention of one of the stablehands, a scruffy young man who came out of a loose-box at the sound of the first mare's call, grinning when he saw that it was Vanyel.

"Milord Herald," he said. "Can I serve ye?"

"I just want to borrow a hunter," he said. "'Fandes is tired and all I want to do is take a ride through Wyrfen Woods. Has Father got anything that needs exercise?"

"Oh, aye, a-plenty." The stablehand scratched his sandy head for a moment, thinking. "Habout Blackfoot yonder?" He pointed about three stalls down at a sturdy bay hunter-mare with a fine, intelligent eye. "Not too many can handle her, so she don't ever get all th' workin' she could use. She got a touchy mouth an' goes best neck-reined, an' she's a spooker. Needs some'un with light hands an' no nonsense. Reckon ye can still ride abaht anything, eh?"

"Pretty well," Vanyel replied. "I gentle all of the foals out of Star's line, if I have the time. I like your watchdogs, by the way—" He waved at the warhorse-mares, who were still keeping an eye on him. "—they're very effective."

"They are, that," the stablehand agreed, grinning, and showing that he, like Vanyel's old friend Tam, had lost a few teeth to the hooves of his charges. "Better at night. Anybody they dunno in here, an' they be raisin' a fuss. Leave one or two loose, and *they* be out o' their boxes—heyla!" He illustrated with his hands and the handle of his rake for a wall. "Got us one thief an' three o' them uncanny things that way. That old Stud breeds better'n he shows."

"I should *hope*!" Vanyel laughed, and went to fetch saddle and harness for his assigned mount.

Blackfoot was exactly as predicted: very touchy in the mouth, and working well under pressure of neck-rein and knee. Vanyel took her back to the stable long enough to switch her bridle for a bitless halter; as far as he was concerned, with a beast that touchy, it was better not to have a bit at all. If he *had* to rein her in, he was strong enough to wrestle her head down, and no horse out of Withen's hunter-line would ever run when she couldn't see.

He took one of the back ways into the Wood rather than the road through the village. Right now he didn't feel sociable, and the villagers would want him to be "Herald Vanyel Demonsbane," which was particularly trying. So he followed the bridle path out through the orchards, which were currently in fruit, but nowhere near ripe, so there was no one working in them. The apple trees were first, then nut trees, then the hedge that divided the orchards from the wild woods.

Riding a horse was entirely different from riding Yfandes; the mare required his skill *and* his attention. She tested him to see what she could get away with most of the way to the Wood, and subsided only when they had passed through a break in the hedge and the bridle path turned into a game trail. The silence of the Wood seemed to subdue her, and she settled down to a walk, leaving Vanyel free to turn most of his concentration inward.

Wyrfen Wood was still avoided by everyone except hunters and wood-cutters, and those who had to pass it traveled the road running right through the middle of it. The place had frightened Van half to death the first time he'd ridden through it; even dormant, he'd had enough Mage-Gift to sense the old magics that had once permeated the place. Those energies were mostly drained now, but there was still enough lingering to make anyone marginally sensitive uneasy. Animals felt it certainly, birds were few, and seldom sang, and Blackfoot's ears flickered back and forth constantly, betraying her nervousness.

Vanyel had made a fair number of exploratory trips into the Wood over the years, and he was used to it—or at least as used to residual magics as anyone ever got. He was aware of the dormant magic, but only as a kind of background to everything else, and a possible source of energy in an emergency. For all that Wyrfen Wood was an eerie place, it was relatively harmless.

Except that it attracted things from outside that were *not* harmless, and gave them an excellent place to hide. . . .

Which brought him right around to one of the very things he needed to think out.

The mare had slowed to a careful walk, picking her way along a game trail that was a bare thread running through the dense undergrowth. Vanyel let her have her head, settled back in the saddle, and spoke his thoughts aloud to the silent trees.

"There aren't enough Herald-Mages. There won't *be* enough Herald-Mages for years, even if Karse stops being a major threat tomorrow. That means the Heralds are going to have to start taking the place of Herald-Mages. Right?"

Blackfoot's ears flicked back, and she snorted.

"Exactly. Most people, including the Heralds themselves, don't think they can. But that's because they're looking at Heralds as if they

were—were—what? Replacements? No . . . substitutes. And when you substitute something, you're usually replacing something superior with something inferior, but—you substitute something *like* the original. And Heralds
aren't necessarily like Herald-Mages at all."

He thought about that, while Blackfoot picked her way across a dry
creek-bed.

"The point is that they *aren't* Herald-Mages. The point is to get Heralds
to use *their* Gifts the best they possibly can, rather than trying to do something they can't. I'm a tactician. Where's the tactical advantage in that?"

The game trail widened a little, and they broke into a clearing, a place
where lightning had set fire to a stand of pines last year to create a sizable
area of burnoff. Now the secondary growth had taken over; grass stood
belly-high to the mare, lush and tangled with morning-trumpet vines and
bright golden sun-faces. A pair of deer that had been grazing at the farther
end looked up at the noise they made, and bounded off into the deeper
woods.

"The tactical advantage," Vanyel told their fleeing backs, "is that most
mages *don't* have strong Gifts in anything other than sensing and manipulating magical energy. Which means—that they won't think of things like
that. They won't be protected against a Farseer spying on their work—or a
Thoughtsenser reading their minds. Or a Fetcher moving something they
need for a spell at a critical moment. That's it—that's it! I've got to do something to get the Heralds to stop thinking of themselves as second-rate mages
and start thinking of themselves as first-rate in the areas of their Gifts. And
we *have* to start matching the need *exactly* to the Gift, and not just throw the
first Herald who happens to be free at the need."

It wasn't the entire answer, but it was a start. It was more than they had
now.

Blackfoot had reacted to the lush meadow before her precisely as any
horse would have; she put her head down and began grazing greedily.
Vanyel was so used to Yfandes that the move took him completely by surprise. He started to pull her up, then thought better of the idea. The grass
would keep her occupied while he contacted Joshe, and the residual magics
made a good pool of energy to draw on so he wouldn't have to use his own
strength. Right now Joshe should be with Randale, going over what the
Herald would need to cover at the Council meeting. This would be an ideal
time to contact him.

He let her graze while he closed his eyes, getting used to the sounds around him so that he would be alerted by anything out of the ordinary. There weren't many; a light breeze in the branches high overhead, an air current that did not reach the ground, a few crickets and a locust singing, and the noise of Blackfoot tearing at the juicy grass and chewing it. Once everything was identified, he extended his Mage-Gift and made careful contact with the trickle of magic directly underneath him.

:??:

A curious touch, and one he did not expect. But not hostile; he identified that much immediately.

:??:

The touch came again; he caught it—and began laughing at himself. "Caught by my own trap!" he said aloud, and opened his eyes. Nothing to be seen—until he invoked Mage-Sight. There, right in front of him, hovered a little cloud, glowing a happy blue. A cloud with eyes: a *vrondi*.

"Hello," he said to it. It blinked, and touched him a second time. This time he sent back the proper reassurance.

:!!: it replied, and—well, *giggled* was the closest he could come to it. Then it vanished, leaving him free to tap the magic current again.

So far as Van knew, the Herald-Mages of Valdemar were the only ones to have ever discovered the *vrondi*. Their touch was not something that outKingdom mages would recognize, and even their appearance only showed that they were air elementals, and nothing more. Air elementals were the ones most commonly used as spies or scouts, which would only reinforce the impression he was trying to give. And even he, who had set the spell in the first place, had found that unexpected contact alarming. So a strange mage would feel something watching him as soon as he invoked any aspect of Mage-Gift or set any spell in motion. He wouldn't be able to identify it, he wouldn't know *why* it was watching him, and Vanyel heartily doubted he'd ever be able to catch it—*vrondi* were just too quick, and they were incredibly sensitive to hostility. Van decided he could almost feel sorry for that hypothetical future mage. The *vrondi* would drive him crazy. Yes, he could almost feel pity for someone faced with that situation.

Almost.

He settled back again; Blackfoot chewed on, happily oblivious to the magics going on around her, intent only on stuffing herself with the sweet grass. Oblivious—or ignoring them; with an ordinary horse, it was often hard to tell which. *First she gets spooky because she feels magic, then she totally ignores it going on above her ears. Stupid beast.* But 'Fandes would have been laughing at him by now for forgetting his own protection-spell, so Van wasn't entirely unhappy that she wasn't with him at the moment.

He Reached carefully for Joshe, drawing on the little stream of magic he'd tapped to boost him all the way to Haven.

:Vanyel?: came the reply. He caught at the proffered contact and pulled Joshe in, strengthening Joshe's faltering touch with his own augmented energies. The line between them firmed and stabilized.

Concern, overlaid with the beginnings of foreboding. *:Vanyel—is there anything wrong?:*

:No,: he said quickly. *:No, just some things came up out here and I need limited Crown authority to guarantee the things I promised. Is Randi up to that?:*

Relief, and assent. *:He's been better, but he's been worse. We've got Treven in full training, poor lad. I don't think he sees Jisa until bedtime, and he's up at dawn with the rest of us. A little more seasoning, and he'll be sitting in for Randale on the Council. What is it you need?:*

Vanyel explained as succinctly as he could. He sensed Joshe's excitement over the notion of taking more recruits in lieu of taxes, and then sending them to the Western Border for toughening instead of throwing them straight into combat after training.

:It's good, Van, all of it. Hold up a moment.: Van sensed Joshe's attention going elsewhere for a moment, then the contact strengthened as it came back. *:King Randale gives you full permission; the official documents will get drafted today or tomorrow, and go out by regular courier. He also said to tell you he thinks your family is slipping. They're not only degenerating into becoming normal, they're getting sensible. He says he's not sure how to take that—it sounds to him like the end of the world can't be far away.:*

So Randi was feeling good enough to make a joke. That *was* an improvement over the state he'd been in following Jisa's revolt. *:Tell him it isn't the end of the world, it's merely the result of my own patient application of a board to their heads for the last several years. Even they get the hint eventually.:*

Joshe's Sending was a simple laugh.

:I've also got some thoughts for you and the rest of the Heraldic Circle. I'd like you to call a meeting and put this before them, if you would. I really think it's important, especially now.:

He explained his own thoughts on the dichotomy, perceived and actual, between the Heralds and Herald-Mages, the problems he could see it causing, and his own tentative ideas for a solution to the problems. Joshe was silent all through his explanation, and for a short time afterward. Finally he answered.

:*I'm surprised you noticed,*: he replied slowly, with thoughts just under the surface that Vanyel couldn't quite read. :*Most of the other Herald-Mages either don't see it—or agree with the common perception that Heralds are some kind of lesser version of a Herald-Mage.*:

The bitter taste to his reply told Vanyel that this was something Joshe himself had encountered, and it hadn't gone down well. Joshe was immensely competent, and a match for Van in any number of spheres, and Vanyel didn't blame him for feeling resentment.

:*It's a problem, Joshe,*: he said, as carefully as he could. :*It's part of my peculiar mind-set to see problems. I think it needs to be dealt with now, before it causes serious damage. We can't do much about the perceptions of the general populace until we start to fix things in our own house.*:

Something followed that comment that was like a mental sigh of relief that follows after a far-too-heavy burden has been removed. Van nodded to himself, and pursued his advantage.

:*You'll never have a better time than now. The King is a Herald, the Heir is a Herald, the Herald-Mage in charge of the Karsite Border is much more Gifted in Fetching than magery and knows it, and you're sitting in for me. Savil will be sensible about this. You can keep this on the table as long as you need to in order to get the others to see that it is a problem, and you can call on the Heralds in the Circle to submit examples.*:

Now Joshe's resolution wavered. :*Do you think it's that important? It seems so trivial with everything else in front of us. The Karse situation, Randi's health.*:

:*It's important,*: he replied grimly. :*And it's only going to get more so. I think you can make the rest of the Circle see that. Point out the attrition among the Herald-Mages, and then quote what happened out here. People are supposed to trust us, and how can they if they think of some of us as being better than others?*:

:*Good point. Consider it on the boards.*: Vanyel knew that once Joshe made up his mind about doing something, he pursued it to its end. He felt a breath of relief of his own. The problem wasn't solved, but it would be. At least a start was being made.

:*Then I leave it in your capable and efficient hands. Wind to thy wings, brother.*:

:*And to yours.*: Vanyel felt Joshe break the contact, and dropped his end of it with a sigh.

Blackfoot was still stuffing herself, and showed no signs of stopping any time within the decade. He hauled her head up; she fought him every thumblength of the way, and returned to the game trail sullenly, and with ill grace.

I wish I had as clean an answer to what I should do about Stef, he thought, uncomfortably. *Gods, there's no denying what I feel about him—or the lifebond. But if I accept all that, and do so publicly, it flaunts the fact that I'm shay'a'chern in the faces of people I have to handle very carefully. Can I afford that? Can Valdemar? Or will knowing I have my weaknesses actually put me at an advantage? It might . . . I know that an awful lot of people come to me with the idea that I'm some kind of supernaturally wise and powerful savant, and that I can't possibly be interested in their problems. Knowing I have problems and weaknesses of my own might make me more accessible.*

But it also puts Stef right where I don't want him—in a position as an easy target for anyone who can't come directly at me. And he doesn't have any way to protect himself from that.

Maybe I ought to give him up. I don't know that I can afford a liability like that. Just make this a wonderful little idyll out here where it's safe to do so, then send him on his way when we get back to Haven. I'll make him understand, somehow. Maybe we could pretend to quarrel. . . .

No—I can't give him up. I can't. There has to be another way.

He was so intent on his own thoughts that he barely noticed when Blackfoot left the game trail for the road, and turned herself back toward Forst Reach.

Why is it I can solve the problems of the Kingdom, but can't keep my own life straight? Gods, I can't even control a stupid horse. He let her go for a moment, then reined her in to turn her back onto one of the game trails. He was still in no mood to face his fellows, and intended to return home the way he'd left.

He got her turned, though not without a fight. She had gotten her fill of picking her way through the brush, and let him know about it in no uncertain terms. She balked when they reached the break in the blackberry hedges that lined both sides of the road, and he finally had to dismount and lead her through.

That was when the spell of paralysis struck him, pinning him and Blackfoot where they stood.

One moment everything was fine; the next, with no warning at all, he was completely unable to move. Every muscle had locked, rigid as wood, and beside him Blackfoot shivered as the same thing happened to her. Magic tingled on the surface of his skin, and Mage-Sight showed him the cocoon of energy-lines that held him captive. It took him completely by surprise.

But only for half a breath; he hadn't spent all those years on the Karsite Border without learning to react quickly, even after being surprised.

His body was trapped, but his mind was still free—and he used it.

He tested the barrier even as he searched for the flare of mage-energy that would betray the location of his enemy as the other mage held the spell against him.

There—

And it was someone who was reacting exactly as he'd postulated ordinary mages would when faced with a Herald; armored to the teeth with shieldings to magic, but completely open to any of the Heraldic Gifts.

Van *could* use his own magic, and not the Mind-magic, of course. The stranger was nowhere near Vanyel's ability, and Van knew he could break the spell with a simple flexing of his own power, if he chose. But if he did that, the man might get away, and Van had no intention of letting him do that. Too many enemies had come back, better equipped, for second tries at him. Mages were particularly prone to doing just that, even one who was as outranked as this one.

Perhaps—*especially* this one. Because this was one whose power was stolen; siphoned from others with neither knowledge nor consent. Van saw *that* the instant before he struck. That may have been the other's motivation; to catch Vanyel off-guard and steal his power. There was no way of knowing until Van had him helpless and could question him at length.

Which—Vanyel thought angrily, as he readied his mental energies for a mind-to-mind blast—would be very shortly now. . . .

No mage of ill-intent should have been able to concentrate long enough to set a trap, he thought, looking down at the trussed-up body of his would-be captor, lying on his side in a bed of dead leaves. *Especially not in my home territory. The* vrondi *should have had him so confused and paranoid that he should have been firing off blasts at nothing. At the least he should have been leaking mage-energy sufficiently enough for me to detect him. I can't understand why he wasn't. Or why the* vrondi *didn't reveal him.*

The man stirred and moaned; he was going to have a dreadful headache for the next several days. The bolt Van leveled him with had been at full-power, just under killing strength. Van *could* kill with his mind—in fact, he *had*, once. It was something he never, ever wanted to do again. It had left him too sick to stand for a month, and feeling tainted for a year afterward. Even though the mage he'd destroyed had been a self-centered, power-hungry bastard, without a drop of compassion in his body, and with no interests outside his own aggrandizement, experiencing his death directly, mind-to-mind, had been one of the worst things Vanyel had ever endured. No, unless there was no other way, he didn't ever want to do *that* again.

Maybe he's unusually good at concentrating. Or maybe he's already so paranoid that having the vrondi *watching him didn't make things any worse for him.*

The mage at Van's feet was ordinary enough. He looked no different, in fact, from any number of petty nobles Van had encountered over the years; sandy hair and beard, medium build, a little soft and certainly not much accustomed to exercise or physical labor. His nondescript, blue-gray woolen clothing was that of "minor noble" quality, though cut a little differently from what was currently popular in Valdemar, and of heavier materials.

He must have come in over the Western Border; he certainly isn't from around here. Van waited impatiently for the mage to regain consciousness. He wanted to scan his mind, and wouldn't be able to do that effectively unless the mage was at least partially awake. The best information came when people reacted to questions, especially when they had something to hide.

The mage opened brown eyes that reflected his confusion when he felt he was tied up, and realized that he was lying in a pile of last year's leaves. Van moved closer, stirring the branches, and the mage focused on him immediately.

With no outward sign whatsoever of recognition.

But inside—the man's mind was screaming with fear.

Thoughts battered themselves to death against the inside of the mage's skull, none coherent, none lasting more than a breath. The only thing they had in common was fear. After a few moments of attempting to make sense of what was going on in there, Vanyel gave up and withdrew.

The mage was completely insane. There *was* no reason for his action, because he wasn't rational. He had trapped Vanyel because he had detected Van's use of magic the way the *vrondi* had, and thought that Van was after him. But then, he thought *everyone* was after him. His life for at least the past month had been spent in constant flight.

He didn't leak energy, because he *couldn't*; he had himself so wrapped up in mage-shields that nothing would leak past them. And the *vrondi*'s constant surveillance was only confirmation of what he already knew, that everybody was after him. And they were probably so confused by his insanity that they hadn't been able to make up their tiny minds about revealing him.

Vanyel sighed—then felt a twinge of guilt, and a sudden suspicion that sent him back to the mage's mind, probing the chaotic memories for confirmation he hoped he wouldn't find.

But he did. And this time he retreated from the chaos still troubled. The man had never been more than a hedge-wizard, but had convinced himself that "someone" was thwarting him from advancing beyond that status. To that end he began stealing power from others, specifically those whose Gift was even weaker than his. But since he really *wasn't* terribly adept or adroit, he failed to clean that power of little bits of personality that came with it. . . .

For at least the past four years, he'd been going progressively closer to the edge of insanity. He'd have gone over eventually; of that Vanyel had no doubt. But he had still been clinging to the last shreds of rational thought, when he crossed the Border into Valdemar and used his powers to search for another victim.

That had triggered Vanyel's Guardian spell, and the *vrondi* swarmed on him. It was at that point that he lost his grip on reality.

"In other words," he told the man, who stared at him blankly, "I might well be the one who sent you mad, in a roundabout fashion. Damn."

He crossed his arms, leaned back against the trunk of a tree, and thought over what he was going to have to do. Blackfoot snorted her disgust at being tied to a bush for so long with nothing she wanted to eat within reach. When Van didn't respond, she stamped her hooves impatiently. He continued to ignore her, and she heaved an enormous sigh and turned as much as her reins would allow to watch a moth fly past.

"I guess I'm going to have to take you back to Forst Reach," Vanyel said, reluctantly. "If I leave you with Father Tyler, he can find a Mindhealer to set you straight—and power-theft is really more in the provenance of the clergy than it is mine, since you didn't actually do any of that *inside* Valdemar. I really hate to have to take you there, but there's no place else."

With that, he hauled the mage to his feet, ignoring the man's struggles. He'd learned a thing or two on the Border, and one of those things was the best way to immobilize a prisoner. Blackfoot snorted with alarm when they approached her, but Van ignored her alarm as well as he ignored the man's attempts to struggle free.

At that point, Vanyel gave the man a taste of his own medicine; a touch of the paralysis spell he'd set on Van. With the man completely helpless,

Vanyel was able to haul him bodily to lie facedown over Blackfoot's saddle, like an enormous bag of grain. He felt the curious touch of the *vrondi*, attracted by his use of the spell, but ignored the creature; when he didn't invoke magic again, it got bored and vanished.

He was sweating and annoyed when he finally got the man in place; he considered using the spell to keep him quiescent during the walk back—but decided against it. It would be a waste of energy, since the ropes tying feet to hands under Blackfoot's belly would hold him perfectly well.

With a glance of annoyance at him, and a swat for Blackfoot, who decided to rebel against this unexpected burden, Vanyel took the reins and began leading the hunter along the game path, heading back to the manor.

And he couldn't help wondering if every half-mage in the Kingdom was going to take it into their heads to go mad.

The prospect was not an appetizing one.

CHAPTER 10

—➤— ◇ —❬—

"LAMENTABLE," SAID FATHER TYLER, regarding the trussed-up mage, who was propped against a corner of the low wall surrounding the father's stone cottage. From the look of things, the mage was neither happy nor comfortable, not that Van was inclined to wish him either of those states.

Father Tyler shook his head again, his tightly-curled blond hair scarcely moved. "Most regrettable."

"I wouldn't feel too sorry for him, Father," Vanyel said sourly, rubbing a pulled shoulder. The man had somehow gotten heavier when the time came to get him off Blackfoot's back, and Van had wrenched his back getting the mage to the ground. "He brought at least two thirds of this on himself. Maybe more; mages aren't supposed to cross into Valdemar without registering themselves, but I doubt you'll find a record of this one. Be that as it may, his problem stems from power-theft. He's certainly guilty of that, and he's managed to do as much harm to himself as he ever did to his victims."

"Just how serious is power-theft?" the priest asked, rubbing his chin, a look of intense concentration on his long face. "I admit the seminary never covered that."

"Somewhere between rape and larceny," Vanyel replied, absently, wondering if he could get Blackfoot back to the stables without running into his relatives. "Power becomes part of a mage; it has to, if he's going to be able to use it effectively. Because of that, having your power stolen is a little like rape; there's a loss of self that's very disturbing on a purely mental level. But that's why this fool ran into trouble. He wasn't good enough to cleanse the power he stole of all the personality overtones, and they became part of him. Pretty soon he never knew if what he was thinking stemmed from his own personality, or what was from outside, and he couldn't control what was going on in his dreams and random thought processes anymore. He put on tighter and tighter shields to stop the problem, which only made it worse.

The pressure in there must have been intolerable. Then the *vrondi* started spying on him, and he snapped completely. But if he hadn't stolen the power in the first place, this never would have happened."

"Well, it is your job to judge, Vanyel," the priest said, with a smile that made it clear he intended no insult. "But it is part of mine to forgive, and mend. I'll see what can be done for this poor fellow."

That only succeeded in making Van feel guiltier, but he smiled back and thanked the priest. He thought about warning him that the mage was strong and far from harmless—

But Father Tyler was younger than Vanyel himself, quite as strong as any of the stablehands; besides, he was the successor to Father Leren. He had been part of the united Temples' effort at cleansing their own ranks and was probably quite well acquainted with all the faces of treachery.

He'll be all right, Vanyel told himself as he made his farewell and took Blackfoot's reins. She was quite willing to go; in fact she tried her best to drag him to the stable. He would have been amused if he hadn't been so preoccupied.

He held Blackfoot to a walk by brute force, and turned again to his personal dilemma. The problem of Stef was no closer to a solution. Van still couldn't see how he would be able to reconcile all the warring factors in his life.

"What would *you* do?" he asked the mare, who only strained at the reins on her halter and tried to get him to quicken his pace. "Oh, I know what you'd do," he told her. "You'd eat."

She ignored him, and tugged impatiently as they crossed the threshold of the stable. Several of the stalls that had been occupied were empty when Blackfoot hauled him back to her loose-box. So luck was with him—it looked like the masculine contingent of Forst Reach had taken themselves off somewhere, en masse. And since Treesa had Stef as a semi-captive provider of entertainment, she wouldn't be looking for her son.

Vanyel unsaddled the mare and groomed her; evidently she was one of those animals that liked being groomed, as she leaned into his brushstrokes and sighed happily, behaving as charmingly as if she *hadn't* spent most of the ride fighting him. While he curried her, Van tried to think of somewhere about the keep he could go to think. What he needed was someplace where he could be found if someone really went looking for him, but a place no one would go unless they really *were* looking all over for him.

Then it occurred to him: the one side of the manor that hadn't yet been built on was the side with that relatively inaccessible porch. It was tree-shaded and quite pleasant, but since the only entry was through a pantry, hardly anyone ever used it. It was too open for trysting, and too awkward for anything else. Which meant it should be perfect for his purposes.

Blackfoot whickered entreatingly at him and rattled her grain bucket with her nose.

"You greedy pig—I'm surprised you aren't as fat as a pony!" he exclaimed, laughing. "Well, you don't fool me. I *know* the rules around here, girl, and you don't get fed until after evening milking."

She looked at him sourly, and turned her back on him.

"And you don't get to lounge around in your stall, either," he told her, as he swung the door to the paddock open. "It's a beautiful day, now get out there and move that plump little rear of yours."

He swatted her rump; she squealed in surprise and bolted out the open door. She dug all four feet in and stopped a few lengths into the paddock, snorting with indignation, but it was too late. He'd already shut the door.

He laughed at the glare she gave him before she lifted head and tail and flounced out into the paddock.

Then he turned tail himself, and headed back to the keep, and a great deal of thinking.

Once he'd fetched his instrument from their room, Stefen expected Treesa to lead him straight to the solar. That room was normally the ladies' sanctum—or at least it was for all the ladies *he* knew. But she didn't head in that direction; in fact, she led him outside and down a path through the gardens. The path was very well-used, and led through the last of the garden hedges and out into a stand of trees that continued for as far as he could see.

"Lady Treesa?" he said politely. "Where in Havens are we going?"

"Didn't Van tell you?" she asked, stopping for a moment to look back over her shoulder at him.

He shook his head and shrugged. "I am quite entirely in the dark, my lady. I expected you to take me to your solar."

"Oh—I'm sorry," she laughed, or rather, giggled. "During the summer we don't work in the solar unless there happens to be a lot of weaving to do—we come out here, to the pear orchard. No one is working in it at this time of year, and it's quite lovely, and cool even on the hottest summer days. The keep, I fear, is a bit musty and more than a bit damp—who would want to be indoors in fine weather like this?"

"No one, I suppose," Stef replied. At about that moment, the rest of the ladies came into view between the tree trunks. They had arranged themselves in a broken circle in the shade, and were already at work. Sure enough, they had their embroidery frames, their cushions, and their plain-sewing, just as if they were working in the heart of the keep. Spread out as they were on the grass beneath the trees, they made a very pretty picture.

They came up to the group to a chorus of greetings, and Lady Treesa took her seat—she was the only one with a chair, an ingenious folding apparatus—which, when Stef thought about it, really wasn't unreasonable given her age.

Now Stefen was the center of attention; Treesa let her ladies stew for a bit, though they surely must have known who he was *likely* to be. After an appropriate span of suspense, Treesa introduced him as "Bard Stefen, Vanyel's friend," and there were knowing looks and one or two pouts of disappointment.

Evidently Van's predilections were now an open secret, open enough that there were assumptions being made about what being Vanyel's "friend" entailed. Stefen ignored both the looks and the pouts, smiled with all the charm he could produce, took the cushion offered him at Treesa's feet, and began tuning his gittern, thankful that he'd put it in full tune last night and it only required adjusting now. The twelve-stringed gittern was a lovely instrument, but tuning it after travel was a true test of patience.

"Now, what is your pleasure, my lady?" he asked, when he was satisfied with the sound of his instrument. "For giving you pleasure is all my joy at this moment."

Treesa smiled and waved her hands gracefully at him. "Something fitting the day," she said. "Something of love, perhaps."

For one moment Stef was startled. *She can't possibly have meant that the way it sounded. She can't possibly be alluding to Van and me, can she?*

Then a second glance at her face told him that she was just "playing The Game" of courtly love. She'd meant nothing more than to give him the expected opening to flatter her.

Well, then—flatter her he would.

"Would 'My Lady's Eyes' suit you?" he asked, knowing from Vanyel that it was Treesa's favorite.

She glowed and tossed her head coyly, and he congratulated himself on reading her correctly. "It would do very nicely," she replied, settling back into the embrace of her chair, not even pretending an interest in her needlework.

Stefen smiled at her—only at her, as The Game demanded—and launched into the song.

By the third song he had grown to like Treesa quite a bit and not just because she was so breathlessly flattering to his ego, nor because she was Vanyel's mother. As Van himself had said, she had a very good heart. When he paused to rest his fingers, she asked him for news of Medren, and not just out of politeness' sake. Ignoring the sidelong glances of her ladies, she asked him several questions about her wood's-colt grandson after Stef's initial answer of "he's fine."

"Has he gotten advanced from his Journeyman status?" she asked, after several close inquiries to the state of Medren's health and progress—a question voiced wistfully, or so it seemed to Stef.

He paused for a moment to think, as the breeze ruffled his hair and sent a breath of cool down the back of his neck. "Not when we'd left, my lady," he replied, "But I honestly don't think it's going to be much longer. He's very good, my lady, and I'm not saying that just because he's my friend. The Council of the Bardic Circle is really waiting for the fuss to die down about my getting jumped to Master so quickly before they promote anyone else. And if you want to know the truth, I think they might have been waiting for me to leave so that no one could accuse me of using *my* influence to get him his full Scarlets."

"Bard Stefen," she said, and hesitated, looking at him oddly. This time he was certain that expression was of hope. "Do you think when he gets it, he would be willing to come *here* for a permanent post?" She smiled, and blushed a little. "I'm perfectly willing to trade shamelessly on his family ties if you think he'd be willing. Forst Reach would *never* rate a Master Bard, else."

Stefen pondered his answer for a moment before replying. Treesa was entirely right; Forst Reach *was* too small a place to demand the attentions of a Master Bard. Certainly there would be no chance for advancement here, under normal circumstances. But Forst Reach was also on the Border, and within reach of the newly-combined "kingdoms" of Baires and Lineas which were now ruled by Herald Tashir. Remarkable things had happened here—in fact, the solving of the mystery of who slaughtered Tashir's family was the subject of Medren's own planned Masterwork—and it was entirely possible that more remarkable things might occur. These were the sort of events that the Bardic Circle really preferred to have a full Bard on hand to record.

Furthermore, Medren had never shown the kind of ambition Stef harbored—he'd never talked about advancing in Court circles or gaining an important patron. It might well be that he'd be happy here.

"I think it might be worth asking him, my lady," Stefen replied with perfect truth. "And I know that if he wants it, the Circle would grant him leave to be here. Especially if you'd agree to share him with Tashir."

"I'd share him with *anyone* if it meant we'd have a Bard here," Treesa exclaimed. "And Tashir is such a dear boy, I'm certain he'd work out schedules with me so that we wouldn't both need Medren at the same time. It shouldn't be that hard even for seasonal celebrations—if I scheduled *ours* a bit early, and he scheduled *his* a bit late. . . ." Her voice trailed off, and she tapped her lips with one finger, obviously deep in thought. Stefen held his peace until she spoke again.

"Then I'll request it formally," she said aloud, and turned to Stef with both hands out in entreaty. "Would you—"

"I'll speak to him, my lady," Stefen assured her.

The dazzling smile she bestowed on him showed him something of the beauty she must have had in her prime. He bowed slightly to her, reinvoking The Game before she could get him to promise more than he could deliver. He had the distinct feeling that if she exerted herself, she could do just that.

He heard the sound of hooves on dry ground behind him at that moment, the steps slow and unhurried. He was about to turn to see who was riding out here, when Lady Treesa looked over his shoulder and smiled a second dazzling smile.

"And here is the *other* reason we meet out-of-doors in fine weather when Vanyel is at home," she said happily. "Especially if we can get Van to perform for us, or we have some other musician available. Welcome, Lady Yfandes! It would certainly present some difficulties attempting to get you up to the solar, would it not?"

Stefen turned; sure enough, it was Yfandes, who bowed—there was no doubt of it—to Lady Treesa, and whickered with what sounded like amusement. The Companion made her stately way to a spot that had evidently been left empty just for her, and folded herself down to it. That was the only way Stefen could think of the movement—it was a great deal more graceful than the way a horse would lie down, and was strongly reminiscent of a lady slowly taking a seat on the ground while minding all her voluminous skirts.

"Lady Yfandes is as fond of music as I am," Treesa told Stefen seriously.

"When Vanyel finally *told* me that, the thoughtless boy, I couldn't see any reason why she shouldn't be able to join us when she wished."

Stefen realized then, with a bit of shock, that Treesa was speaking of Yfandes as if she were a lady-guest, and doing so completely naturally. It seemed *she* had no problem with accepting Yfandes as a "person" and not a horse.

Which is a little better than I can manage at the moment, he thought ruefully. I have to keep reminding myself that she's not what she seems. And I'm a Bard, so I should know better!

"Well, in that case, my ladies all," he said, with a slight bow to Yfandes and another special smile for Treesa, "allow me to take up my gittern, and resume amusing you."

In fact, he was greatly enjoying himself. The entire little group seemed to be enthralled with having the talents of a full Bard at their disposal. Some of Treesa's ladies were quite pretty, and although Stef had no intention of following up on his flirtations, when they fluttered coyly at him, he preened right back. That was an accepted part of The Game, too. Best of all, none of this was work—he used only the barest touch of his Gift to enhance his performance, hardly enough for him to notice, unlike the deep-trance, draining effort he'd been putting out for the King.

It was a pity that Van had decided to vanish somewhere, but Stef was getting used to that. *Van broods,* he thought wryly. *And I must admit, he's had a lot to brood about lately. If I know him, no matter what we managed to build between us last night, he's going to have to agonize over it before he can accept it. Thank the gods he can't repudiate a lifebond, or I'd probably spend every night we're here reconvincing him he's not going to be rid of me. Of course, that could be quite enjoyable—but it could also be exhausting.*

He wondered what the Companion was making of all this. It would certainly help if Yfandes was on his side. He cast a brief glance at her; glowing white against the green of the orchard grass, and obviously watching him, her head nodding in time to his music. There was no doubt that there was a formidable intelligence behind those soft blue eyes.

Maybe the fact that she came out here is a sign that she likes me, he thought, when he couldn't detect any sign of hostility in her posture or her conduct. *I hope so. It would make my life so much easier. . . .*

Shortly after his second rest, Yfandes got up—doing so with a quiet that was positively unnerving; *nothing* that big had a right to move that silently!— and meandered off by herself. Stefen took that as a basically good sign. If

Van was having trouble thinking things through, 'Fandes was probably going to him. And no matter what was wrong, Stefen was certain that 'Fandes would help her Chosen get his head and emotions straightened out.

Just as he was about to begin again, Stefen spotted someone coming toward the little group on a wagon-road that bisected the grove of trees. He was moving slowly, and as he neared, Stef could see why; he was carrying two heavy baskets on a pole over his shoulders. A farmworker, then, not someone coming to look for himself or Treesa, and nothing to concern them.

He continued to exchange news of the Court with Treesa, while the other ladies leaned closer to listen, but there was something about the man that vaguely bothered him, though he couldn't put his finger on what it was. He watched the stranger draw closer out of the corner of his eye and could not figure out what it was about the man that gave him uneasy feelings.

Certainly none of the others seemed to think there was anything out of the ordinary about him. They ignored him as completely as if he didn't exist.

Then—*I thought Treesa said that no one works out here at this time of year. So what's* he *doing out here?*

He took a second, longer look at the stranger, and realized something else. Something *far* more alarming.

The man's clothing was of high quality—actually better than Stef's own Bard uniform.

What is that peasant *doing dressed like that?*

The feeling of *wrongness* suddenly peaked, and Stefen reacted instinctively, flinging himself at Treesa and her chair and knocking both to the ground.

Just in time, for something small, and with a deadly *feel* to it whizzed over both their heads, cutting the air precisely where Treesa had been sitting—

Vanyel leaned out over the edge of the balustrade. The granite was warm and rough under his hands, solid and oddly comforting. *I want solid things around me,* he thought slowly. *So much of my life is in flux—so much depends on luck and the things others do. I'd really like to have one point of stability; something I could always depend on.*

Or someone. . . .

The balustrade overlooked nothing; bushes were planted right up against it with trees beyond them, and had been allowed to grow until they blocked whatever view there might have been. With trees on all three open sides and the wall of the keep behind him, the porch wasn't good for much except the occasional lounger.

Sun beat down on Vanyel's head, warming him even though his Whites were reflecting most of the heat away. He stood so quietly that the little yellow-and-black birds that nested year-round in the branches of the bushes resumed the chatter he'd disturbed when he came out onto the porch, and actually began flitting to sit on the balustrade beside him.

:Brooding again, are we?:

He blinked, and came out of his nebulous thoughts. Yfandes was below him, barely visible through the thick branches of the bushes, a kind of white shape amid the green.

:I suppose you could call it brooding,: he admitted. *:It's abou—:*

:Stefen, of course,: she interrupted. *:I thought you'd probably had enough time to stew over it and make your insides knot up.:*

:Huh.: He raised an eyebrow. *:Dead in the black. Am I that predictable?:*

:On some topics, yes. And I expect by now you've laid to rest the fact that you're lifebonded, and that he really does love you on top of that. And that you love him. So what is it that's turning you inside out?:

He sighed, and looked up at the clouds crossing the cerulean sky. *:Danger, love. To him, and to me. To me, because he can be used as a hostage against me. To him, because he's going to be in harm's way as soon as it's obvious we're a pairing. I don't know that I can afford that kind of liability, and I don't know that it's right to put him at that kind of risk.:*

Yfandes withdrew for a moment. *:Well, as to the first—he's assigned to Haven, and a very valuable commodity, even with the Healers learning how to duplicate what he does. They still have to be in physical touch, and their subject responds best if both parties are in a trance. Try conducting negotiations that way, and see how far it gets you!:*

He chuckled at the mental image that called to mind.

:So far, Stef's the only answer to keeping Randi on his feet and functioning when he's in pain,: she continued. *:And as such, he'll have the best guards in Haven. And as for your second question—Stefen's a grown man. Why don't you ask him if he's willing to take the risks that come with being your lover? My bet is that he's already thought about them, and accepted them as the price he pays for having you.:*

He pushed away from the balustrade and folded his arms across his chest. *:Do you really think so?:* he asked, doubtfully.

He heard her snort in exasperation below him. *:Of course I think so, I wouldn't have said it otherwise! You know I can't lie mind-to-mind!:*

He felt comforted by her matter-of-fact attitude, and by her solid *presence*. No matter what happened, no matter what went wrong in his life, 'Fandes was always there for him. It made all of this a little easier—

In a single moment, the feeling of comfort vanished, to be replaced by one of immediate danger. All his internal alarms shrilled, and without a second thought, he leaped the balustrade and crashed through the intertwined bushes to land in a crouch at Yfandes' side.

She felt it, too—they were so closely linked she couldn't have ignored it. In the next second he had vaulted onto her back—

She evidently had signals of her own, for she plunged forward through the undergrowth, aimed toward the orchards, as soon as he was securely on her back. That gave him a direction: he clamped his legs around her barrel and twined his fingers in her mane, and invoked Farsight and Mage-Sight together.

Magic—

Strong, controlled, and near at hand.

Dear gods—his mind screamed. *The pear orchard!*

'Fandes leaped the hedge surrounding the gardens—they hurtled through, her hooves tearing great gouts of turf from the lawns—she leaped the second hedge on the other side and flew into the orchard.

Women were screaming at the tops of their lungs, and scattering in all directions—not with any great success, at least not the highborn. Their heavy skirts encumbered them, and they fell as much as they ran. The serving maids had already hiked their dresses above their knees and taken to the dubious shelter of tree trunks. Cushions were tumbled every which way, and the air was full of feathers where one or two of them had burst.

It was obvious whom they were fleeing, as a brown-clad stranger with his back to Vanyel and Yfandes raised his hands above his head.

A mage—and his target was equally obvious. Treesa and Stef lay sprawled helplessly just before him, and Van felt the gathering forces of energy as the mage prepared to strike them where they lay.

But—that's the man I caught—

Yfandes screamed a battle-challenge just before the man let loose a bolt of mage-fire. He half-turned in startlement at the noise, and the bolt seared the turf just beyond Bard Stefen and Vanyel's mother.

He was quicker than any mage Van had ever encountered in his life, at least in combat; before Vanyel could ready a blast of his own, he'd let fly with a second—just as Van realized that he and 'Fandes were completely unshielded.

Vanyel expanded the core of his own energies with a rush outward in a shield to cover the two of them, but just a fraction too late. Yfandes writhed sideways as she tried to evade the bolt, but was only partially successful. The edge of it hit them both.

He was protected; the shielding had covered that much—but Yfandes squealed as the bolt clipped her. She collapsed, going down in mid-leap, falling over onto her side. A sudden blank spot in Van's mind told him that she'd been knocked unconscious.

'Fandes!

He wanted, *needed* to help her. But there was no time—no time.

He managed to shove himself clear of her as she fell, hit the ground and rolled, and came up with mage-bolts of his own exploding from both hands. His hands felt as if he'd stuck both of them in a fire, but he ignored the pain.

The stranger dodged the one, and his shields absorbed the other. He struck back; a firebolt.

Vanyel sidestepped his return volley and let fly with a crackle of lightning at the stranger's feet. As he'd hoped, the mage's combat-shields did not extend that far down, and Vanyel's lightning found a target. The stranger shrieked and danced madly, but would not budge from his position, which was far too close to Stef and Van's mother for safety—

Vanyel sent a *sandaar*, a fire-elemental, raging straight for the enemy's face. He flinched, but stood his ground, and blew the elemental away with a shattering blast of power. That gave Van enough respite to take the offensive. Before the other mage had a chance to ready a counterblast, Van let fly three levinbolts in succession, and succeeded in driving him back, one step for each bolt.

When Van saw that the ploy was working, that the mage *was* being driven away from the Bard and Treesa, he Reached for energy in a frenzy, and sent bolt after bolt crashing against the enemy's shields. Though nothing penetrated, the force of impact was enough to continue to drive him backward, deeper into the orchard.

Van continued to fire off levinbolts as his own body shook with the strain of producing them out of raw magic, and his Mage-senses burned with the backlash of power. His whole world narrowed to the flow of energy, the target, and a vague awareness of where Treesa and Stefen lay.

Finally the enemy mage came exactly opposite the two lying on the ground. He didn't seem aware of them; certainly Van was keeping him occupied in defending himself. A few more steps, and Van would be able to include them in his own shielding—

Treesa chose that moment to struggle erect, though Stefen was trying to keep her down and protected with his own body. Her movement caught the mage's attention—

He looked directly into Vanyel's eyes, and smiled.

And reaching down into a pocket at the side of his boot, cast, not a weapon of magic or force, but one of material steel, following that with a levinbolt of his own. But not at Vanyel. At his mother.

"NO!" Vanyel screamed, and threw himself between Treesa and the oncoming blade—

And felt the impact in his shoulder as he crashed into his mother, sending them both to the ground—

And then a shock that twisted the world out of all recognition in a heart-beat, picked him up by the scruff of the neck, shook him like a dog shakes a rag, and flung him into the darkness.

Stef was trying to get Treesa down on the ground again, when another of those blinding flashes of light went off practically in the Bard's face. He cried out in pain as it burned his eyes; cried out again as two bodies crashed into his.

Can't see—can't breathe. Got to get out—

He struggled to get out from underneath them, his eyes streaming tears, with everything around him blurred.

He tried to make his eyes work. The only person still standing was the brown blot that was the mage that had attacked them. It raised two indis-tinct arms, and Stef struggled harder still to get free, knowing that there was nothing to stop him this time—that somehow he'd gotten rid of Van—

"Hey!"

A hoarse yell. The mage started, and turned just as Stef's eyes refocused. The mage's mouth opened in shock, and he tried to redirect the power he had been about to cast at his three victims.

Too late.

Radevel was already on him; he swung his weighted practice blade down on the mage's head as he tried to fend off the blow—or possibly hit Radevel with the mage-bolt meant for the others. It didn't matter. The blunt-edged metal sword snapped both his arms like dry sticks, and contin-ued with momentum unchecked. When the blade connected, it hit with a sound unlike anything Stef had ever heard before; the dull *thud* of impact, with a peculiar undertone of something wet breaking—like Rad had just smashed a piece of unfired pottery.

The mage collapsed, and Stef swallowed hard as his gorge rose and he fought down the urge to vomit. He'd seen any number of people dead before this—of cold, hunger, disease, or self-indulgence—but he'd never seen anyone *killed* before. It wasn't anything like that in songs.

He was having trouble thinking; vaguely he knew he should be looking for Vanyel, but he couldn't seem to get started. Finally he noticed that Van was one of the two people collapsed on top of him.

Van—he's not moving—

Yfandes struggled to her feet and shook her head violently, then looked around for Vanyel. She spotted him and the downed mage; pounded over and shouldered Radevel out of the way with a shriek of rage, and began trampling the body with all four hooves.

If he wasn't dead when he hit the ground, he is now.

Radevel stuck the blunt sword into his belt and turned. Half a dozen white-faced young men and boys walked slowly toward him from behind the trees—the sound of retching told Stef that there were probably more of them out there who weren't in any shape to walk yet.

"I hope you were paying attention," Radevel said matter-of-factly. "If you get the advantage of surprise on a mage about to spellcast, that's the best way to take him. Get his attention and interrupt his magic, then rush him before he has a chance to redirect it. Go for his arms *first*—most of 'em seem to have to wave their arms around to get a spell off. If you can, you want to keep 'em alive for questioning."

He glanced back over his shoulder at Yfandes, who was still squealing with rage and doing her best to pound what was left of the mage into the dirt.

"Of course," he continued, "when family or Heralds are involved, that usually isn't practical."

His expression didn't change, nor did the tone of his voice, but Stef noticed (with an odd corner of his mind that seemed to be taking notes on everything) that Radevel's eyes widened when he'd looked back at Yfandes, and he was retreating from her a slow, casual step at a time.

Servants had materialized as soon as the mage was down, and pulled Stef out from under the Herald and his mother. They ignored Stef, concentrating on trying to revive Lady Treesa and Vanyel. Radevel gathered his group of students and plowed his way through them to get to his aunt and cousin's side.

"What happened?" One of the ladies grabbed Radevel's arm as he passed. "Where did this man come from?"

"Van brought him in," Radevel said shortly, prying her hand off his arm. "Bastard jumped him, and Van thought he was crazy. Left 'im with Father Tyler. Must not've been as crazy as Van thought; first chance he got, once Tyler left him alone, he cut himself loose and stabbed the priest. Me, I was on the way to practice with this lot, and I found him—good thing, too, he'd've bled to death if I hadn't found him when I did. Anyway, just about then I saw Van pelting off this way, and I followed."

Radevel shook the lady off before she could ask him anything more, and knelt down beside Stef.

Stefen didn't know what to do; Van was as white as snow and about as cold, and Treesa wasn't much better off. He watched the servants trying to bring them around, and felt as helpless and useless as a day-old chick. Radevel looked at the haft of the tiny knife in Van's shoulder, but didn't touch it; laid his hand to the side of Treesa's face.

"Something's wrong here," he said to Stef. "This isn't natural. We need an expert. You—" He reached out and grabbed one of the older servant-women. "You keep anybody from muckin' with 'em. And don't nobody touch that knife. I'll get the Healer."

"I'll get Savil—" Stef offered, glad to find *something* he could do, getting unsteadily to his feet. He set off at a dead run before anyone could stop him, ignoring the way his eyes kept blurring and clearing, and the dizziness that made him stumble.

His breath burned in his throat, and his sides ached by the time he was halfway across the garden.

There seemed to be something wrong—he shouldn't have been that winded. It felt like something was draining him. . . .

Savil was already on the way—he was practically bowled over by Kellan in the entrance to the gardens. Her Companion stopped short of trampling him, and he scrambled out of the way, just barely avoiding her hooves.

"What happened?" Savil asked, reaching down to grab his arm, missing, and seizing his collar instead.

"A mage," Stef panted, holding his side. "He attacked me and Treesa— no, that's not right, he attacked Treesa, and I was just in the way. Van took him out, but he got Van—gods, Van is hurt and—and we can't get him or Treesa to wake up—"

"Enough, that's all I need to know for now." She turned away, dismissing him, and Kellan launched herself across the garden, leaving him to make his own way back.

He arrived winded and unable to speak; Savil was kneeling beside the Healer, and examining Vanyel's shoulder.

"I've been treating them for poison," the Healer said in a flat voice. "I thought Lady Treesa might have gotten nicked by one of those knives. But they aren't responding, and I don't know why."

"It's because you're not fighting poison, lad, you're fighting magic," Savil muttered, as Stef limped up and collapsed on the ground beside her with a sob. "It's a good thing you didn't try to pull that knife, you'd have killed him."

She looked up—in Stef's direction, but more *through* him than *at* him. "We can't do anything for them here," she said, after a moment. "Let's get them back to their beds. I hate to admit this to you, but I'm out of my depth. Van could probably handle this, but—well, that's rather out of the question at the moment."

Stef clutched his side and stifled a moan of panic, and she glanced sharply at him. "Don't give up yet, lad," she said quietly. "I'm out of my depth, but I'm not ready to call it finished."

Stef clenched his jaw and nodded, trying to look as if he believed her, while Van lay as pale as a corpse on the ground beside her.

Savil completed a more thorough examination than she was able to give in the orchard, and sat back in her chair, watching Van and thinking.

He wasn't prepared for a magic weapon, so he wasn't shielded against it. But something's got the thing slowed down considerably. Damned if I know what. Huh. A leech-blade. That's something I've only read about. I didn't know there was anyone that was enough of a mage-smith to make one anymore.

She glanced over at Stefen, who was recovering from magic-induced shock adequately on his own. Savil hadn't done anything to help him mostly because she reckoned that the lad could do with a little toughening. But he hadn't recovered as quickly, nor as completely as she'd expected, and Savil didn't know why that was happening either.

He sat on the other side of the bed, holding Vanyel's hand, in a pose that reminded her poignantly of the way Van had held 'Lendel's when her trainee was coming out of the trauma his twin's death had induced.

There was something else there that was poignantly like Van and her protege.

When it finally occurred to her, it was such an astonishing thought that she double-checked with her Companion to make sure she wasn't imagining things.

:Kell! Would you check with Yfandes and ask her if that boy's gone and life-bonded to Van?:

:If he's—: A moment of surprise. *:She says he has.:*

:Damn. Would that be why the leech-blade isn't draining Van as fast as I thought it would?:

:It's a good guess.: A pause. *:She says probably; something as deep as a lifebond is hard to monitor. She says Van is being fed from somewhere besides her, anyway.:*

:Sunsinger's Glory.: She invoked Mage-sight and stared at the evil thing. *It's working its way deeper, but slowly enough that I can take my time. He's got a couple of days before it'll do any lasting harm. Stef said it was thrown at Treesa; I wonder what it was supposed to do to her? Take her over, maybe; we'll never know now. So. I may be out of my depth, and Van may be out of reach, but I haven't exhausted the quiver yet. The only problem is that all the others that can handle this kind of weaponry are Tayledras. And I certainly can't take Van through a Gate in his condition; it would kill him.*

Well, that just means they're going to have to come to him, if I have to truss them up and drag them.

She heaved herself out of her chair, and saw Stef's eyes flick briefly to her before returning to Vanyel.

"Stefen," she said. "I want you to stay with him. Don't let anyone move him, and especially don't let anyone touch that blade. I'll be back shortly."

"Where are *you* going?" he asked, his head jerking up, his expression panicked.

"To get help," she replied. "Just remember what I told you, and do it."

And before he could get himself organized enough to stop her, she limped out of the room, and ducked down a side stair only an Ashkevron would know about.

I'll bring them, all right, she thought grimly, as she made her way down the twisting little staircase entirely by feel. *Whether they like it or not.*

CHAPTER 11

$\rightarrow\!\!\!\rightarrow \diamond \leftarrow\!\!\!\leftarrow$

SAVIL EMERGED FROM a linen closet on the ground floor, a legacy of her father's legendary building spree. At the far end of this hallway was the old family chapel, whose door Savil intended to use as a Gate-terminus. It had been used that way a number of times in the past, and the borderstones "remembered" those configurations. It was easier, and took far less energy, to build a Gate where one had been built before. And it was safer to anchor one end of a Gate on holy ground; there was less likelihood that something would come along and take control of it away from you.

We've shielded this chapel to a fare-thee-well, Savil thought, surveying the door for a moment. *It was well-shielded before, but it's a magical fortress now. That's good; less chance that the Gate-energy is going to get out and turn poor Van inside out. It's been twenty years, and his channels are still sensitive to Gate-energy. I'd rather not take a chance on making his condition any worse right now.*

A few months ago, she wouldn't have been able to do this, because she wouldn't have had the strength to spare. But when Van had changed the Web-Spell, he'd freed her and the other Guardians from the constant drain on their resources required by the Web. Now she had energy for just about any contingency, for the first time in years.

That freedom couldn't have come at a better time.

She braced herself, and invoked the four sides of the Gate: right side and left, threshold and lintel. When she had the "frame" built on the actual doorjambs, and the sides, bottom and top of the door were all glowing a luminous white, she invoked the second half of the spell. She fought a wave of weakness back for a moment, then sent the energy of the Gate out in little seeking threads, "looking" for the place she showed them, where they would build the second terminus.

It was easier this time than the last Gate she'd built to the Pelagirs, because she knew now where the k'Treva had relocated their Vale the last time they'd moved, and knew also where they built their own Gates inside the Vale.

Easier in terms of time; it was never "easy" to build a Gate, and the energy all had to be drawn from the mage himself; no outside sources could be used. As always, it felt as if bits of herself were spinning off and leaving her, as if she was trying to Fetch something that was just barely beyond her strength. It was hard to think, as if someone was actively preventing her mind from working. But there were no more than a few heartbeats between the moment she began the search and the moment she made contact with the other terminus.

There was a flare of light—and the chapel door no longer opened on a prosaic little family shrine, but on a riot of green leaves and twisted rock, with a hot spring bubbling off to the right.

K'Treva Vale.

She stumbled across the threshold, and into a circle of unblinking and hostile guards.

A half-dozen golden-skinned, blue-eyed warriors stared at her over the crystalline points of spear-or arrow-heads. Though not mages themselves, these guards knew the tiniest signs of the Gate being activated, and were prepared to handle anything or anyone coming through. This was the first time Savil had actually seen the Gate-guards at their posts, though she had met several of them during her visits to Moondance and Starwind— whenever one of the k'Treva mages needed to use the Gate, the guards generally cleared discreetly out of the way.

They stared at Savil for a very long moment, and she was altogether glad that she hadn't come with the intention of trying to cause trouble, because they looked more than capable of handling it.

Their no-nonsense attitude extended to their appearance. Most wore their hair shorter than was usual for *Tayledras*, barely past shoulder-length; and since it was summer, the normal silver-white had been dyed in mottled browns and dull yellow-greens. Their elaborate clothing was also dyed that way. In a tree or hiding in underbrush, they would be very hard to see.

Some few of them had the Mage-Gift, but none were primarily mages. These were members of the *Tayledras* Clan who, whether or not they had the Mage-Gift, preferred not to use what Gift they had. They served the Clan in other ways; as Healers and craftsmen, as scouts and border-guards, and as guards of the few places within the k'Treva shield that needed both tangible and intangible guards. After all, they didn't have to be sensitive to know when the Gate had been activated—the effect was fairly obvious.

Most of them were young; the life-expectancy of a *Tayledras* scout was about that of a Field-Herald, and for many of the same reasons.

"Savil!" exclaimed one of them, as Savil fought off her weakness and looked up. The circle of suspicious and hostile expressions changed in an instant. Someone knew her and recognized her. The weapons were lowered or set aside entirely, and two came to her aid as she swayed with fatigue and dropped to her knees on the bare stone in front of the Gate itself.

"Wingsister!" exclaimed the same one, a lean, sharp-faced young woman Savil knew as Firesong, whose spear clattered onto the smooth, bare stone as she tossed it aside. She helped Savil to her feet, and before the Herald-Mage could even voice her need, snapped out a series of commands.

"Windblade, get tea and honey. Hawkflight, find Brightstar; he should be with his weapons-teachers. Dreamseeker, find Starwind and Moondance. Suncloud, get me three more guards. Move on it!"

The four so designated handed their weapons to comrades, and sprinted off. Firesong helped Savil over to a seat on a magically smoothed boulder, supporting the Herald-Mage with one arm around her shoulders.

"How long can you hold the Gate?" Firesong asked as soon as Savil was settled.

"As long as I have to," Savil replied dryly. "Don't worry, the other terminus is secure. I wouldn't put k'Treva into any danger I could avoid."

"Good." Firesong looked as if she might have said more, but the youngster sent off for tea returned, as did the boy sent to fetch replacements. The guardswoman then had her attention fully claimed by the newcomers.

Like every set Gate-terminus Savil had ever seen constructed by *Tayledras*, this one was built around a cave-mouth. Unlike the last one, which she had helped shape, it was a very shallow cave this time; it went into the solid rock of the cliff-face scarcely more than two horse-lengths. The entrance had been cleared of dirt down to the bare rock, and ringed with boulders. It wasn't wise to allow anything to grow too near a place used often as a Gate-terminus; strange things happened to the plants. . . .

In spite of her claim to be able to hold the Gate, Savil was coming to the end of her strength. She huddled with her hands cupped around the hot cup of tea, and shivered. *They'd better come soon*, she thought, *or I'm going to lose this thing. We could call it up again, but that would take time, a good day before I'd be fit to try. We have time, but I don't think we have that much.*

But as if they heard her thoughts, Starwind and Moondance finally made their entrance, dramatically as always, bondbirds on their shoulders. Savil looked up from her tea, sensing them, more than hearing them—and there they were.

They *were* mages—Adepts, in fact—so their hair was its normal silver-white, elaborately braided and beaded, and flowing down past their waists. And being Adepts, they tended to a sense of the flamboyant that showed in their fantastically designed green tunics.

Savil smiled weakly at them; they wasted no time in formal greetings on seeing the depleted state she was in. They moved as one to augment her own failing energy.

She sighed as they each caught up one of her hands and she felt their energy flowing into her, strong and pure. With one sitting on either side of her, feeding her power to replace what she had lost, she felt able to talk to them.

It had been a while since she was last at k'Treva, but the years hadn't made much change in either of her friends. It was impossible to tell that Starwind was Savil's age, and Moondance only a little older than Vanyel. Adepts were long-lived, normally; node-magic tended to preserve them. *Tayledras* Adepts were even more long-lived, for they lived amid a constant flow of node-derived magic, magic that touched even the non-Gifted, whether born or raised among them, bleaching their hair and eyes to silver and blue in a matter of two years.

That bleaching effect was even more pronounced and took less time for the mages, a sign that working with node-magic changed them in deeper ways. The drawback was that when they *did* near the end of their allotted span—and not even an Adept could know when that would be—they would fail and die within a matter of weeks, as the magic burned them up from within.

Savil knew all that, but growled, "You two have little simulacrums locked away somewhere, don't you, that age for you."

"Now, Wingsister," Starwind chuckled. "You know that isn't true. You could enjoy the benefits we do, if you would accept our invitation to live here."

"Can't," she said shortly. "I have duties, and we've been through all that. Listen, I need your help—"

Briefly, she outlined everything that had happened, and waited for their response.

The initial reaction was pretty much as she'd expected.

"We do not leave k'Treva," Moondance began, uneasily, when she had finished. "You know that. Our place is here, as it has been for centuries—"

"That, *ash'ke'vriden*, is no excuse," said a light tenor voice from just beyond the trees planted at the edge of the "safe" boundary. A huge, white owl winged silently into the clearing to perch on a boulder, and following it was a younger version of the two *Tayledras* Adepts.

Except that instead of blue eyes, this striking young man had luminous silver, and there was something about the timbre of his strong, vibrant voice that would remind anyone who heard it of Vanyel.

Hardly surprising, since Vanyel was Brightstar's father—and apparently Brightstar was going to be Savil's unexpected ally.

"You yourselves have taught me that *Tayledras* have left their territories at need before," Brightstar said, taking a stand beside his owl, "and the world being what it is, likely will again." He lifted his chin in a way that reminded Savil irresistibly of Van in one of his aggressive moods. "If the need is great enough, what harm in answering it?"

Savil explained again, and Brightstar stiffened his back in outrage. "But you *must* go! I owe Wingbrother Vanyel my very existence. *I* would go, if I knew how to deal with these 'leech-blades'—" He spread his hands in a gesture of helplessness. "But I cannot."

"What, humility from the falcon who refused to admit there was any height he could not soar to?" Starwind raised a sardonic eyebrow.

They were taking this a little too lightly for her comfort, and evidently their adoptive son felt the same. Brightstar glowered. 'I do not think that we have time to waste while Vanyel lies in danger from this thing," he said. "And you are quite right that there are some things I am not suited for."

"So at last you recognize that yours is the Gift of changing the living and Healing the earth, and not things made by the hand of man." Moondance looked up, theatrically. "Has the sun turned green? Are fish learning to fly?"

"Is my honored father going to return to the point?" Brightstar retorted. "The question is—Vanyel is in need of us and cannot come to us. How do we answer that need? *I* say you must go to him before he comes to harm!"

Starwind nodded reluctantly. "Vanyel needs us, and indeed, we owe him much—but is our Clan served by our leaving the Vale? Or would this bring harm that outweighs any good we could do? My son, there are good reasons for keeping our presence as secret as we may."

A polite cough interrupted them. Savil turned slightly, and saw that Firesong was standing there, obviously waiting to be heard.

Starwind nodded at her, and she coughed again, self-consciously. "If you will excuse my intrusion," she said, standing at rigid attention with her hands clasped behind her. "It seems to me that the better question would be if the Vale and Clan are *harmed* by your leaving. And I cannot see that this would be the case. The debt of k'Treva to Wingbrother Vanyel is a high one, and our honor would be in doubt if we did not proffer help when it was asked of us. In my opinion, and speaking as the head of the scouts, I think that this overrides even our tradition of secrecy."

"So, I am twice rebuked," Moondance said with a slight smile. "And by the infants. I do believe that I hear a turtle singing."

"Lest the ground itself rise up to rebuke us a third time, *shay'kreth'ashke*," Starwind said, rising and holding out his hand to Savil, "or our son strike us down and drag us across the threshold, let us go."

"I'm very glad to hear you say that, *ke'chara*," Savil said, as they walked toward the Gate, and steeled themselves for the shock of crossing.

"Whyfor?" Starwind asked, pausing on the threshold of the Gate itself.

"Because," she said, "I'm getting too old to hit attractive men over the head and carry them off. And the sad part is, I'm so old that's the only way I can get them!"

And with that, she took his elbow and stepped across the threshold, taking him with her.

Though she was so exhausted that it felt like days since she'd left, it was hardly more than a candlemark. Either weariness had made it seem longer, or time did odd things when you passed through a Gate.

Or both, she thought, turning to face her creation. *No one really knows how the damn things work, anyway. Someday maybe an artificer will discover how to make us fly, and we can do without them altogether. If I had the choice between a nice journey in a comfortable seat, and one of these gut-wrenching Gates, I'd take the journey every time.*

She held up her hands and began unweaving her Gate, strand by careful strand, taking the energies back into herself. Tedious work, and dangerous; going too fast could send the power back into her at a rate she couldn't handle. And at her age, a shock like that could all too easily kill her.

Then again, that journey would probably mean entrusting myself to the competence of strangers. There's plenty of folk I wouldn't trust my baggage to, let alone my safety. Ah, well, it's a nice dream, anyway.

Building a Gate took most, if not all, of a mage's energies, but taking it down put a sizable amount of that energy back. Savil was feeling very much her cantankerous self when she turned back to Starwind.

"Well," she said, dusting her hands off on her tunic, "what kind of an entrance do you want to make?"

"Your pardon?" Starwind replied, puzzled by her turn of phrase.

"Do you want things to stay as quiet as possible?" she asked. "Would you prefer we kept your presence at Forst Reach a secret? It'd be hard, and frankly, we'd waste a lot of magic doing it, but we could, if that's what you want."

Starwind exchanged glances—and probably thoughts—with Moondance. He bit his lower lip, and looked at her measuringly before replying.

"I am of two minds," he said. "And the first thought is that it would be worth any effort to keep our presence unknown. Yet if we were to do that, we would be unable to accomplish many things that I would like. Moondance wishes to have speech of Vanyel's father, for one. If we are to do such a thing, we must be here openly."

Savil did her best to keep her surprise from showing. "I can't imagine why you'd want to talk to Withen, but—all right. So what's your choice?"

"Open," Moondance said promptly. "With as much drama as we may. If we are to break *Tayledras* silence, then I say we should leave your folk with a memory that will follow them all their days."

"You'll do more than that, my lad," Savil muttered, but nodded anyway. "However you want," she said a little louder. "I'd like you to look at Treesa first, if you would. Van can wait a little, and I'd rather get her on her feet before Withen comes home and has hysterics."

Starwind nodded. "Lead the way, Wingsister. We will follow your lead."

I doubt that, she thought, but didn't say it.

It was worth every odd look she'd ever collected from the members of her family to see their faces as she sailed into Treesa's sickroom, followed by the two *Tayledras*. They certainly knew how to time things for a particularly dramatic entrance, she gave them that. She shoved open the doors first, then made a half-turn to see if they were still coming—then, just before the doors swung completely shut, they flowed through, side by side, and paused to look around.

There were roughly half a dozen people in the room, all told. The only two Savil recognized were the Healer and Father Tyler, both of whom stared at the exotic Adepts with their mouths slowly falling open.

The rest drew back as far as they could get; years of being told as children to "be good, or the Hawkbrothers will get you" were bound to have an effect. And no one could doubt for a moment that these two were a pair of the fabled out-landers—for their birds were still perched calmly on their shoulders, as if they passed through Gates and were carried around strange keeps every day of the month.

Both birds were stark white now, though when Savil had last seen him, Starwind's bondbird, the younger of the pair, was still marked with gray where the darker colorations hadn't yet bleached out. She found herself marveling anew at the birds' calm; no falcon in the Ashkevron mews would sit unjessed and unhooded on a human's shoulder, nor tolerate being taken all over the keep. But then, these birds were to ordinary raptors what *Shin'a'in* warsteeds were to horses. Bred for centuries to be the partners of those they bonded with, their intelligence was a little unnerving. Just now Starwind's bird was watching Savil with a quiet, knowing look in its eyes, and Moondance's was watching the priest with what had to be an expression of wicked amusement.

Moondance himself strode toward the bed where Treesa had been placed. Those at her bedside melted out of his way without a single word. He held his hand briefly above her forehead, frowned for a moment, and then announced without turning around, "You were correct, Wingsister. It is simple mage-shock from being too near a blast. I can bring her out, if you'd like. It makes no difference to her recovery if she is awakened now or later."

"Do it now," Savil advised, "before Withen comes crashing in here like a bull with its tail on fire."

Moondance took both of Treesa's hands in his, and held them for a moment with his eyes closed. Treesa began to stir, muttering unintelligibly under her breath. Moondance waited for a moment, then opened his eyes and called her name, once.

"Treesa," he breathed. Only that, but somehow the name took on the flavoring of everything she was, and things Savil hadn't guessed she could be.

Treesa's eyes fluttered open, and the first thing she focused on was Moondance.

"Oh—" she said, weakly. "My." She gulped, and blinked at the *Tayledras* as if she could not look away from him, though he dazzled her. "Am—am I dead? Are—are you an angel?"

Starwind was too polite to burst out laughing, but Savil could tell by his too-calm expression and the creases around his twinkling eyes that he was doing his very best not to laugh at the notion of Moondance as an angel.

Moondance is never going to hear the last of this, Savil thought, holding back a smile that twitched the corners of her mouth despite the seriousness of the overall situation.

"No, my lady," Moondance said haltingly in the tongue of Valdemar. "I am only a friend of your son. We came here to help him, and you as well."

"To help—" All the color drained from Treesa's face. "Van—how badly is he hurt? Dear gods—"

She struggled to sit up, but the Healer prevented her from moving by holding her down with one hand on her shoulder. Moondance put his hand atop the Healer's, eliciting a gasp from both the Healer and Treesa.

"We go to him now, my lady," Moondance said, and smiled sweetly. "Be at ease; all will be well."

And with that, he turned and swept out of the room, Starwind joining him so that they left as they had entered, together. Savil smiled at Treesa, as reassuringly as she could, and followed them.

"Where is young Vanyel?" asked Starwind as soon as they were all in the stone-walled corridor.

"Up a flight and over a bit," Savil told him, taking the lead again, and moving as quickly as her aching hip would permit. "I should warn you about something. Seems he's lifebonded again, this time to a young Bard about half his age—"

Starwind exchanged a wry glance with Moondance. "Indeed? And where have I heard *that* tale before?"

"I would have no idea," Savil replied, her tone heavy with irony. "Just because you were near thirty and Moondance was all of sixteen. . . . At any rate, the boy's with him. Don't frighten him; he's had a bad few hours, and he's part of the reason why I haven't been frantic to get you here."

Moondance looked puzzled, but Starwind nodded knowingly. "Ah. The blade feeds on both of them. I had wondered why you were so calm about all this."

"So long as you didn't take a week to make up your minds, I reckoned we had time." She paused outside Vanyel's door. "Here. And remember what I told you."

This time Starwind held the door open for her, and followed her inside with no dramatics at all. Stefen, white-faced, was absorbed in Van—so completely that he didn't even notice they were there until Starwind laid a gentle hand on his shoulder.

Stefen jumped; he looked up at the *Tayledras* Adept, and his eyes grew very large, and very round. His mouth opened, but he couldn't seem to make a sound.

"We are here to help young Vanyel, little one," Starwind said kindly. "But for us to do so, you must move away from him."

Stefen lurched to his feet, knocking over the chair he'd been sitting on, and backed away, tripping over it in the process. Moondance caught him before he fell, and Savil wondered for a moment if the poor boy was going to faint on the spot. He recovered, and edged over to Savil, standing slightly behind her, his eyes never once leaving the *Tayledras*.

Starwind held one finger near to the leech-blade, but did not touch it. "A nasty piece of work, that," he said in his own tongue to Savil. "More than ordinary malice went into its making."

"But can you get rid of it?" Savil asked anxiously.

"Oh, aye. Not easily, but it is by no means the hardest task I have ever undertaken. *Ashke*—"

Moondance nodded, and moved to stand immediately behind him, with one hand resting lightly on his shoulder. Starwind ripped part of the ornamental silk from his sleeve; the cloth parted with a sound like the snarl of a hunting cat. He wrapped the bit of silk around his hand, and only then grasped the hilt of the leech-blade.

"Now we give it something else to seek after," he murmured, and held his other hand a few thumblengths away from the wicked little knife. Invoking Mage-Sight, Savil Saw that his hand glowed with life-force; far more than Vanyel possessed, even at the core of him. And she Saw how the blade loosened its hold on the Herald-Mage; how it turned in Starwind's hand, and lurched out of the wound like a hunger-maddened weasel.

"*Not* this time, I think," Starwind said aloud, pulling his unprotected hand away before the writhing blade could strike it. "Now, *ashke*—"

Moondance made an arc of pure power between his two hands, and Starwind brought the blade down into it.

The thing *shrieked*.

Stefen screamed, and clasped his hands over his ears. Savil very nearly did the same. The only reason she didn't try to block her ears was because she knew it wouldn't do any good. That hideous screaming was purely mental.

The scream of the blade continued for four or five breaths, then, as suddenly as it had begun, the thing fell silent. Moondance damped the power-arc, and when Savil's eyes and Mage-Sight recovered from the dazzle, she saw that Starwind held only a hilt. The blade itself was gone, and the air reeked of charred silk.

"And that," the *Tayledras* said with satisfaction, turning the blackened hilt over in his hand, and examining it carefully, "is that." He looked up at Savil. "And now, dearest Wingsister, we four can all join to bring our brother back to us."

She was placing her hands over Moondance's when she realized what he'd said.

Four? Huh. Well, why not?

"Come here, lad," she said over her shoulder to Stefen, who was hovering worriedly in the background. "They won't bite you."

"Much," Moondance said, in her tongue, with a sly grin for Stefen. Oddly enough, that seemed to relax him.

"What can I do?" he asked, taking his place at Savil's side.

"I have no idea," she admitted. "But *he* knows. So let's both find out."

Starwind smiled, and placed his hands atop theirs.

Savil took a long, deep breath and looked quickly down at Vanyel. He was breathing normally, deeply asleep, and his color was back. *He'll probably wake up in a candlemark or so. 'Fandes will be out about as long.*

"What happened?" Stef asked, dazedly. "What did we do?"

"Sit, Singer," Moondance said, pushing him down onto the bed. "We gave young Vanyel a path back to himself, and the strength to return upon it. But that strength came from us, you most particularly, and you should now rest." He nodded at the bed. "There is plenty of room there, and Vanyel would feel comforted by your presence."

"He would?" The youngster looked on his last legs, but was stubbornly refusing to admit his weariness. "Well—if you think so—"

"I think so." Moondance threw a light blanket over the Bard's shoulders. "Rest. You do not hasten his recovery by fretting."

"If you—" He stifled a yawn. "—say so."

Moondance shook his head at Starwind. "Children. Was *I* that stubborn-minded?" he asked in *Tayledras*.

"Oh, you were worse." Starwind grinned, and took Savil by the elbow. "Kindly show us where we will be staying, Wingsister. I think we will have to remain here some few days more, else Vanyel will foolishly exert himself and it will be all to do again."

:And just what do you have up your sleeve?: she asked him. *:You're right, of course, but there's more that you aren't telling the boy.:*

:Perceptive as always,: he replied. *:I wish you to hear this from Moondance, however.:*

She nodded at Moondance, who joined them at the door. "Sleep, Stefen," he ordered as he closed it. An indistinct mumble came from the general direction of the bed. It sounded like agreement.

"In the absence of anyone else I guess I'll make the decision of where to put you two," Savil said. "And because I don't know where else, I guess you might as well take the room next to Van's."

She opened the door to the next guest room, which looked about the same as Vanyel's in the dim light; with Forst Reach entertaining as many as a hundred visitors during the course of a year, no room ever sat long enough to take on an air of disuse. The only real sign that it was not occupied was the fact that the shutters were closed, and what light there was leaked in through the cracks.

"So, now, what was it you wanted to tell me about?" Savil asked Starwind, closing the door behind him. The older *Tayledras* went directly to the window and threw the shutters open.

"Not I," he said, "but Moondance." He sat on the window ledge and leaned out, looking with interest—though real or feigned, Savil couldn't tell which—at the grounds below.

"Well?" she asked impatiently of Moondance. The Healing-Adept looked very uncomfortable.

"I do not know how much you give credence to our beliefs," he said doubtfully.

"Depends on which one," she replied, sitting on the edge of the bed. "If it's the one about how people should live in trees, I still think you're out of your mind."

He ignored the sally. "We think—and have proved, insofar as such a thing is possible to prove—that souls are reborn, sometimes even crossing species' boundaries. Rebirth into something of like intelligence, a *hertasi* perhaps being reborn as a *kyree*, or a *kyree* as a human—"

"Must make things interesting at dinnertime," Savil jibed.

He glared at her. She gave him a sardonic stare right back.

"This is all very fascinating philosophy, but I don't see what it has to do with Van," she pointed out, tilting her head a little.

Moondance shook his head. "Not with Vanyel—with the Singer."

"Stef?" she exclaimed incredulously. "Why on earth Stefen? And why is it important?"

"Because my *shay'kreth'ashke* believes—as do I—that your Stefen is, or was, the young one called Tylendel," Starwind called from the window.

Savil's first reaction was surprise, then skepticism. "What, just because they lifebonded? Really, isn't that a little too neat, too pat? It makes a very nice tale, but—" She shrugged.

"No," Moondance said, walking to the window to stand beside Starwind. "No, it is not because of the lifebond, or not primarily. There are other things—memory traces of Vanyel many years ago, ties other than the lifebond." He paused, and looked up at the ceiling as if gathering his thoughts. "And there are reasons, pressing reasons, for this to have happened. The bond between Tylendel and Vanyel was strong, stronger even than most lifebonds I have seen. There is a debt owed to Vanyel because of what happened. There is unfinished business because Tylendel failed as a Herald." He looked at her expectantly for a moment, then shrugged. "I could go on at length, but that would only bore you."

"I doubt it," Savil replied, fascinated in spite of her skepticism. "But I can't see what relevance it has to the current situation, either."

Starwind left the window. "Only that the past has bearing on the present, and will color what happens in the present."

"So, should I tell them about this speculation of yours?" she asked curiously.

"Ah." Starwind clasped his hands behind his back, and gave his lifebonded a wry smile. "That is where we differ. I think perhaps yes, but I do not feel at all as strongly as Moondance, and am willing to be overruled."

"And I think that on no account should you tell them," Moondance said adamantly, leaning his back against the windowframe. "But our reasons for our feelings are much the same."

"We feel," Starwind took up the thread of conversation, "that this relationship should be permitted to develop without the baggage of the previous one. It is not the same set of circumstances at all, their meeting and bonding, nor are their relative status or ages the same. Therefore I think they should be told so that they may avoid misunderstandings that echoes of the past may bring."

"And I think that being told will only bring problems; that Vanyel will cease to react to Stefen as he has become, and that he will begin behaving in ways that will warp the relationship out of all recognition and health."

Moondance crossed his arms over his chest, and looked very stubbornly at Savil.

"I can think of one problem right off," she said slowly. "If Van thinks Stef's his old love, he's likely to do one of two things—pay *more* attention to Stef's opinions and advice, or *less*. Neither is healthy. Stef's got a good head on those shoulders, but he also has a lot of growing up to do yet. Right now Van's giving him about the same amount of slack he'd give any lad his age, and listening to him when he makes sense—"

"Which is the way it should remain," Moondance concluded.

She shook her head at Starwind. "Sorry, old friend, but my vote goes with Moondance."

He shrugged. "I had already told you I did not feel that strongly; I am content to be overruled."

"To change the topic, how long do you want to stay?" she asked. "I'll have to tell Withen something when he gets back."

"Three days, perhaps five. No more, certainly." Starwind shook his hair back. "Two days to keep Vanyel from overexerting, then however long it takes to unravel *who* did this thing, and *why*."

"If we can," Moondance said with resignation. "It is by no means certain. But with four Adepts at work, the odds are that what can be uncovered, will be."

"Which brings me to a request, dearest Wingsister," Starwind grinned. "Do you think this place is capable of producing garments of a suitable size for us? It seems that we forgot to pack. . . ."

"Oh, probably nothing good enough for you, you preening snow-birds," Savil grinned wryly, "but we may be able to rummage up *something*."

CHAPTER 12

Y ET ANOTHER OF Treesa's ladies had Savil and the elder *Tayledras* trapped in a conversation, this time just outside the keep as Starwind sent his falcon up for some exercise. There was no reason for this one-sided discourse; she'd done it purely for an excuse to gawk at the exotic. Savil closed her eyes for a moment, and wished that the chattering child-woman would come to the point. 'This," said Starwind under his breath, in his own language, "is not a family. it is a small army. And half of them are mad." He nodded to the young woman, smiled, and tried to interject a single word. "It—"

She ran right over the top of him without pausing for breath, and without taking her eyes from Starwind's face. "But my mother's cousin twice removed, you know, the Kyliera Grove Brendewhins not the Anderlin's Freehold lot, the ones who—"

:*Does she never cease speaking?*: Starwind asked. :*Even in sleep?*:

:*Not to my knowledge,*: Savil replied the same way.

:*Then I shall have to do something rude to free us from the chains of her words,*: he told her.

:*You're forgiven in advance,*: Savil assured him.

Suddenly, with no forewarning whatsoever, Starwind's white gyrfalcon swooped down out of the sky above them, and dove at the girl, missing her by a goodly distance, but frightening her into silence. The bird hovered just over Starwind's head, screaming at her, threatening to dive again.

"Your pardon," Starwind said, with a completely disarming smile, "but I think my bird must have taken a dislike to your apparel. I have never seen him act in this way before. He must believe that you are a threat to me."

The bird dove again, and this time the girl shrieked and fled. Starwind held up his arm, and the falcon settled on it immediately, then hopped to his shoulder and began preening itself with every sign of being completely calm.

Kellan wandered up. and put her nose up to the bird. It reached out with its wicked beak and gently nibbled at her upper lip before resuming its preening.

:*A bird with sense,*: Kellan told her Chosen, a wicked twinkle in her eye. :*I was considering charging you three just before Starwind asked Asheena to threat-dive.*:

:*The only problem with that is Lytherill would never have believed threat out of you,*: Savil said. :*She believes in the unquestionable goodness and purity of Companions.*:

Kellan hung her head and moaned. :*Does this mean I can expect her to garland me with roses, try to hug my neck, and speak to me in babytalk?*:

Savil laughed. :*No love, she's not quite that young, though a couple of years ago, before she discovered boys, you'd have been in danger.*:

:*How close are you to finding out what that mage was up to?*: Kellan asked, with the kind of abrupt change of subject Savil had come to expect from her over the years.

:*Close. We'll probably be able to run the spells tomorrow.*:

:*Indeed, Wingsister.*: A new mind-voice entered the conversation and both Savil and her Companion suppressed startlement. Adepts—or very powerful Mindspeakers—were so few that Savil seldom remembered that the *Tayledras* shared with Vanyel the ability to "overhear" any conversation that was not shielded against them. :*Pardon,*: he said apologetically. :*Yes, we should be prepared enough and Vanyel recovered enough to make the attempt tomorrow. Would the one who struck him were still in condition to be questioned.*:

Starwind sent his falcon up once more, this time in response to a pigeon taking wing from the keep eaves. Wild raptors, Savil knew, missed more often than they struck, but *Tayledras* bondbirds seldom stooped without a kill at the end. Starwind had his eyes closed, and his entire body stiffened with tension as his bird dove. A scream of triumph rang out as the bird pulled up for the kill and Starwind shivered a little, a tiny smile of satisfaction on his lips, as the falcon's talons struck home.

The gyrfalcon carried its prey to the roof to feed, and Starwind opened his eyes and smiled a little more broadly at Savil's knowing grin.

"Fantasizing someone other than a pigeon at the end of that stoop, hmm?" Savil asked.

"I?" Starwind was all innocence. And Savil didn't believe it for a moment.

"You. If I had that bastard in my reach right now—never mind. Come on, let's finish this walk." Savil headed out into the paddocks, and Starwind fell in beside her, Kellan following noiselessly behind.

"As for being waylaid by half-grown girls, half the problems you and Moondance are having you brought on yourselves," she told him frankly. "You two insisted on being spectacular, well, now you see what happens to a spectacle. I'm sorry, but I can't feel terribly sorry for you."

"I would not have insisted, had I known the sheer number of inhabitants in this place," he replied ruefully. "Gods of my fathers—*five* families, with no less than seven children in each, hundreds of men-at-arms, and then there are the servants, the fosterlings—" He shook his head in disbelief. "K'Treva is little larger, and it is an entire clan! It staggers the imagination."

"And every one of those people is dying for a close-up look at you," Savil sighed. "I tried to warn you."

"The warning came too late." He shrugged. "Though—I am glad to have met Withen's falconer, for all that he salivates every time he looks upon our winged brothers. And I am doubly glad to have met Vanyel's father and mother."

Savil strolled over to a fence surrounding the field that held the yearling fillies, and leaned on it, putting one foot on the lowest rung. "Withen's gotten better the last five years or so. I must say, I'm rather proud of him. Most men go more hidebound with age, but the old bastard seems to have relaxed some of his attitudes. Hellfires, he hardly ever bellows at me any-more."

"You think so?" Starwind replied, looking out over the field. "That is good. That is *very* good."

But why it was good, he refused to say.

Every night after dinner, Withen and Treesa had taken to inviting the *Tayle-dras*, Savil and Vanyel up to their private suite or (more often, since the weather was excellent) out to the secluded side porch Vanyel had favored before the orchard incident. In part, it was out of pity—to get them away from the Forst Reach herdes. And after the first evening, they included Stefen in on the invitation, although the Bard begged off, saying he had promised to entertain the younger set.

Tonight was no exception, but this time Vanyel, too, had gracefully asked pardon to decline. He didn't give a reason, but Savil told Withen as she joined the group out on the porch that he was missing an unusual experience.

"What is it?" Withen said curiously, handing Starwind a cup of wine. He'd had servants line the porch with festival-lanterns so that the place was well, but not brightly, lit.

"Someone managed to goad your son and his friend into challenging each other, musically speaking," she replied. "That's what they're up to right now, in front of most of the younglings of the keep—no, Treesa, trust me, it isn't anything you want to subject yourself to."

Treesa had begun to rise, but sank back down to her seat. "I do trust you, but why? I trust Van not to do anything that would upset the children's parents, so it can't be a bawdy-song contest, can it?"

"No, it's not," Savil said, grinning. "It's a *bad* song contest. They've challenged each other to come up with the worst songs they know. Trite, badly-rhymed, badly-scanned—you name it. Right now Van's going through some piece of drivel about being trapped in a magic circle for seventeen years, and it sounds like it may take seventeen years to sing it."

Treesa laughed. "It may, at that," she said, and filled a cup for the younger *Tayledras.*

Moondance took it, but his face was sober. "Lady Treesa, Lord Withen, I have a great wish to speak of something with you, and as it concerns your son, I think this moment of his absence gives me the opportunity. If you will permit." He paused, and looked first into Treesa's eyes, then into Withen's. "It is not comfortable."

Treesa dropped her gaze, but nodded. Withen cleared his throat. "Nothing about my son is particularly comfortable. I'm not sure he was ever created to inspire comfort. I think I would like to hear what you have to say. No, I would not *like* it, but I think I should hear it."

Moondance sighed, and sat down on the stone railing.

"Then, let me tell you something about a very young man, a boy, named Tallo."

Savil was considerably more than a little surprised; Moondance found the story of his own past so painful that he had rarely divulged it to anyone. She knew it, of course; she had found the boy . . . she had brought him to Starwind, nearly dead.

Moondance told his story in as few words as possible, his voice flat and without emotion.

"Some thirty years ago, in a village far from here, there lived a boy named Tallo. He was a recluse, a lone runner, an odd boy, given more to thought than deed. His parents hoped he would become a votary, and sent him to the priest to learn—but in the priest's books he found what he was truly Gifted with. Magic. His parents did not understand this, nor did they sympathize, for their lives had little to do with magic and mages. This made him further alone, more different, and his parents began to try to force him back to their own simple ways. It was too late for that—there were arguments. There were more when they attempted to bring him to wed, and he refused. He could not tell them what he felt, for what he yearned for were those of his own sex, and such a thing was forbidden."

Moondance's soft voice did not betray the pain the *Tayledras* Adept felt. Savil knew, no one better—but certainly Withen could never have guessed.

"One summer, after a winter of arguments and anger, there came a troupe of gleemen to the village—one among them was very handsome, and quite different from his fellows. Thus it was that Tallo learned he was not the only boy to feel yearnings of that kind. They became lovers—then they were discovered. Both were beaten and cast out of the village. In anger Tallo's lover repudiated him—and in pain and anger, Tallo called lightnings down upon him."

Moondance sighed, and shook his head. "He did not mean even to hurt, only to frighten—but he did not know enough to control what he called, and the young gleeman died in agony, crying out Tallo's name. And in remorse for what he had done, Tallo tried to take his own life. It was Herald Savil who found him, who brought him to her new friend, Starwind of the k'Treva. Who was also *shay'a'chern*, and Healed the young boy in body and spirit—but still, there was such grief, such remorse, that Tallo felt something must be given in sacrifice to the harm he had done. So did Tallo die, and in his place came Moondance."

Withen started. Moondance glanced sideways at him, and only now did the *Tayledras* show any emotion. "Tallo is no more," he said, his voice subdued. "And no one in Tallo's village would know Moondance. The *Tayledras* are stories to frighten children with, and they would not dare to recognize him. Those that were his family would only be afraid of what he has become. Never can the one who became Moondance reconcile with his family; he did not when he was Tallo, and now it is impossible to do so. And that, Lord Withen, Lady Treesa, is a desperate sadness."

He sipped his wine, as the insects sang in the darkness around them, and the lights in the lanterns flickered.

"It seems to me, Lord Withen," Starwind said, finally just before the long silence became too much to bear, "that a man's life must be judged by what he has done with it. Your son is a hero, not only to your people, but to ours, to the peoples of Baires and Lineas, even to some outside the Borders of your realm. Look at the good he has done—and yet always with him is a deep and abiding hurt, because he feels that *you* have seen nothing of the good he has done, that you feel he is something evil and unclean."

Withen swallowed his cup of wine in a single gulp. He stared up at the stars for a long time, then lowered his eyes to meet Starwind's for just a moment. He dropped them, then toyed with his cup, until the silence grew too much even for him to bear.

He cleared his throat, and furrowed his brow, looking very unhappy. "Thank you. You've given me a lot to think about," he said, awkwardly, and turned to lock gazes with Moondance. "Both of you have. And I promise you that I *will* think about it." He looked down at his cup, as if he was surprised to find it empty. "I think at the moment that I have had quite enough wine for one night." He smiled suddenly, stood up, and held out his hand to Treesa, who took it with a surprised expression. "By now that little contest should be over, and I do believe I'd like to find out who—and what—won."

And with that, he set his cup down, aided Treesa to her feet, and exited with a certain ponderous grace.

Savil blinked, and took a sip of her own wine. "What was that supposed to accomplish?" she asked. "And why on earth did you broach that subject now?"

Moondance put down his cup of wine untasted. "It was something that needed Healing," he replied. "I have done my poor best, and we may only see what time will bring."

Starwind nodded without speaking.

Savil looked up at the velvet of the night sky; no moon tonight, which made the stars seem all the brighter. "It felt right, if my opinion means anything to you," she said at last. "Right words, right time. If anything is going to happen—"

"It is in Withen's hands," Starwind sighed, then stretched. "Gods of my fathers—if there is anything more difficult than dealing with the heart, I do not know what it may be. I am to my rest."

"And I to mine," Savil said, putting her cup down. "Tomorrow is another day."

"Yes. And tomorrow we shall have finished the preliminaries over that

evil hilt. Tomorrow we shall look into its past, and that of its wielder."
Moondance shook his head. "This will not be pleasant."

"No," Savil agreed, moving toward the door with the other two. "And
I don't think the answers we're going to get will be pleasant either. So let's
enjoy our peace while we have it, hmm?"

"Indeed," Starwind said pausing to let her precede him. "For it is all too
fleeting and fragile a thing, peace."

Vanyel knew that Savil would have been happier in a fortified Work Room,
but the current situation wouldn't allow it. There really was no place suitable in all of the keep. The *Tayledras* felt more comfortable out-of-doors, and
the orchard was the place where the strange mage had died, so to the orchard they had all come. Savil had brought a cushion with her; the ground
was too much for her bones. The *Tayledras* sank down in their places with
no sign of discomfort at all. Vanyel wished belatedly that *he* had thought to
bring something to sit on, but it was too late now.

They sat in a circle, but with their backs to each other, rather than face-
to-face. All four of them would see this reenactment of the recent past; all
four of them would Hear the thoughts that had been strong enough to have
left an imprint there. They were looking outward, not inward, and hence,
the seating arrangement.

They were all in place now, as Vanyel eased himself down between Savil
and Starwind.

The little circle did not include Stefen, who was keeping Treesa and her
ladies occupied and out of the mages' way, but it was Starwind's opinion
that he was better employed in that capacity than in watching them work
magic he could not participate in.

Vanyel unwrapped the blackened hilt and laid it on the bare earth. He
looked up at Savil, whose expression made him think that her insides were
probably in knots. "You don't have to do this, you know," he reminded her.
"You don't have to help."

"I know that," she replied, "but I'd worry myself to bits until you three
finished this little exercise. I'd rather be in on it."

Vanyel nodded. "All right, then. Let's link."

He linked to Savil, while Starwind gathered Moondance in; familiar
bonds to familiar. Then the two halves joined, forming a meld that was as
close to seamless as anything Van had ever seen. It helped that the four of

them had wielded magics as a group before; it also helped that their friendship was as close as it was. But what made this work was that all four of them had actually trained together. They would take turns as leader and supporters in this, and there was no room for temperament or pride.

Savil took the lead for the first part, invoking from the hilt and from the blood-soaked ground the mage's last moments.

The peaceful orchard and his companions vanished from Vanyel's sight. Now he approached a ring of Treesa's ladies, listening to Stefen's music, as if he rode upon the mage's shoulder, and Vanyel knew that the others were Seeing what he Saw. All of the stranger's surface thoughts were open to them for that time period. Savil froze the scene at the moment the mage had attacked Treesa and Stefen, and they read then what was uppermost in his mind.

Vanyel was so startled he nearly fell out of the link. The man he had captured in the Wood and this mage might just as well have been two entirely different people! Not only was *this* mage not crazed, but his attitudes were drastically different, as well as what could be read of his past history and training.

The mage had not known that Vanyel was home; he had deduced who Vanyel was quickly enough, but had entrapped him by pure accident. He had been assuming that he would trap Withen's house-mage; most nobles outside Valdemar had one, to weave protections for themselves and their interests. Since he hadn't detected any of the arcane protections that would have shown him Withen's house-mage had a Work Room, he had supposed that his enemy must be some kind of woods' witch, or hedge-wizard, to do all of his spellcasting out-of-doors. The Wood, with all of its residual magics, would have been perfect for that. So the stranger had waited, snare at the ready, for the first sign of spellcasting. He had expected to catch another hedge-wizard.

He had gotten Vanyel. This was rather akin to setting a trap for a sparrow and catching a firebird. The mental blow that knocked him unconscious had caught him completely by surprise.

So when he came to, he had done so behind a screen prepared for just such an occasion. He had retreated behind a disguise that had been created for him by another mage—just in case he had discovered that the one he intended to neutralize had been more powerful than he. This was the false persona whose thoughts Vanyel had skimmed, the madman who interpreted everything as an attack or a threat to himself.

At this point the stranger had still not known that he'd caught Vanyel; he had only thought that Withen's house-mage was far more skilled than he had guessed. It wasn't until Vanyel actually came into his line-of-sight that he had realized who and what had caught him.

That had been the spark of recognition Vanyel had seen. After that, the man buried himself even deeper beneath the false persona, deciding to fall back on his secondary plan.

That involved getting inside Forst Reach itself—and Vanyel played right into his hands by taking him to Father Tyler.

He'd waited for Vanyel to probe him more carefully, and had been relieved when Van was too preoccupied to see if there was anything behind the persona-screen. That made his job all the easier.

He had disposed of Father Tyler, and had gone looking for Treesa or Withen. He'd found out where they were by the simple expedient of asking a servant. Then he'd gone hunting.

The final thought Vanyel read as the mage prepared to launch the leech-blade at Treesa was that his master would be very pleased.

That was, maddeningly, all.

Savil tried to Read further into the past than the moment of the attack, but once he was off Forst Reach lands, the mage had been screened and shielded, and there was nothing there to be Read. There was no image in the mage's mind connected with this "master"; he'd never seen the unknown mage in person. The "master" had only given him his orders, then given him the means to carry them out—*he* had set up the disguise-persona, had screened his servant against detection and back-Reading while off the Forst Reach lands, and had constructed the twin leech-blades for him.

The mage had only been a tool in the hands of someone bigger.

Vanyel shook off his disappointment, and began gently disengaging himself from the spell. Gradually the frozen scene faded from Mage-Sight and ordinary sight; then, with an abrupt, gut-wrenching shudder, it vanished completely, and Vanyel was back in the present, with a numb behind, and far too many unanswered questions.

He got up, breaking the circle, and stretched. He stood staring at the tree just in front of him for a while, trying to get everything he'd learned and everything he *hadn't* learned sorted out. When he turned around, Starwind was staring at him, a slight frown on his lips.

"You do realize what this attack means, do you not?" he said to Vanyel. "That you were vulnerable to the leech-blade was the purest accident; if you had been warded against magic the thing would have had no purchase upon you. Nevertheless, *you* were the target; the mage recognized you and knew that. He was to destroy you by indirect means, by destroying those you love. The one who sent him does not want to confront you—but does want you eliminated. This time the targets were to be Lady Treesa, Lord Withen, or both—hence the two blades."

"The protections I put on them won't hold against direct attacks," Savil admitted unhappily. "I can't stop an assassin. I don't think this is going to end with one attack, either, not with what I picked up. Van, I don't know what to say."

Vanyel sighed, and ran his fingers through his hair. "It's nothing I haven't anticipated, Savil. That's always been my worst fear, you know that. But if there is somebody, some powerful enemy of mine out there—where has he been all this time? What does he really want? And is he just *my* enemy, or is he Valdemar's enemy as well?"

Moondance stretched as Starwind clasped his shoulders and rubbed them absently. "This comes as quite a surprise to us as well, Wingbrother. We are reclusive, yes, but there are still signs of such a mage as this 'master' seems to be which we should have detected long before this."

Vanyel offered Savil his hands to pull her to her feet. "Except that you have a peculiar blind spot, my friends," Savil, said, accepting the aid. "You never look outside your own territory. Even the *Shin'a'in* Clans work together, but you don't; each of your Clans operates on its own. That's your strength, but that's also your weakness."

"Strength or weakness, it matters not," Starwind said shortly. "The question is, how is Vanyel to ensure the continued safety of his parents? As you have pointed out, Wingsister, this is not going stop at one attack."

"There's only one thing I can do," Vanyel said. "Since I can't be where they are—"

"Get them to move to where you are." Savil shook her head. "I don't know, Van. That may be harder than getting yourself transferred to Forst Reach."

"That may be," Vanyel said grimly, "but it has to be done."

Dinner was a cold lump in Vanyel's stomach, and his weariness made the lamplight seem harsher than it really was.

". . . . I have no choice but to insist on this, Father," Vanyel concluded, clasping his hands around his ale mug, and staring at the surface of the table.

"I know you never want to leave Forst Reach—and the gods know you never asked to have a Herald-Mage for a son. I'm asking this because I have to. I can't protect you, Savil can't protect you, Randale can't afford to keep a Herald here full-time to keep you safe; there aren't enough of them, and nothing less would do it. You could hire all the guards you wanted to; none of them would do any good against a mage. Hire a mage, and whoever this is will send a better one. This enemy of mine knows me very well, Father. If you or Mother died because of what I am—I—I'd never get over it." He looked up, at Withen's troubled face and at Treesa's frightened one. "There's no help for it, Father. You'll have to take up the Council seat for this district and move to Haven. Everyone would be glad to see you in it, and Lord Enderby never wanted it in the first place. You'd do a good job, and the Council could use your experience."

Treesa sighed happily and lost her fear instantly; *she* had wanted to move to Haven for years, ever since the last of her children wedded. "Oh, Withen," she said, her eyes sparkling, "You must! I've hoped for this for so long—"

Withen winced. "I think you mean you've hoped for a reason to make me go to the capital, and not that the reason would be that we're in danger otherwise!"

Treesa pouted. She'd recovered very quickly, showing a resilience that Moondance called "remarkable." "Of course that's what I meant! Withen, for all that you like to pretend that you're a plain and simple man, you've been running not only Forst Reach, but most of the county as well. And you very well know it. When something goes wrong, where's the first keep they go to? Here, of course. And it *isn't* to ask advice of Mekeal! I think Van is right; I think you'd make a fine Councillor."

Withen shook his head, and took a long drink of ale. "Ah, Treesa, I hate politics, you *know* that—and now you want me to go fling myself into them right up to the neck—"

Vanyel put his mug down. *I'm going to have to shock him into taking the seat, or he'll go, and pine away with boredom.* "Father, it's either that, or move to Haven *without* anything to do but sit around the Court all day and trade stories with the other spavined old war-horses," he said bluntly. "I was offering you an option that would give you something useful to do. You *are* going to Haven, whether or not you like it. I cannot afford to leave you here."

Withen bristled. "So I'm a spavined old war-horse, am I?"

Vanyel didn't rise to the bait. Withen expected him to try and back down, and he couldn't, not with so much riding on his persuading Withen that he was right. "In a sense, yes; you're too old to rejoin the Guard, even as a trainer. There's nothing else there for you. But that Council seat is crying for someone competent to fill it, and you *are* competent, you're qualified, and you won't play politics with Valdemar's safety at stake—and that puts you ahead of half the other Councillors, so far as I can see. And you, Father, are trying to change the subject."

Abruptly, Withen put his mug down and held up both hands in surrender. "All right, all right. I'll take the damned seat. But they'll get me as I am. No Court garb, no jewels and furbelows. Treesa can dress up all she likes, but I'm a plain man; I always have been, and I always will be."

Vanyel's shoulders sagged with relief. "Father, you can be anything you like; you'll be a refreshing change from some of the butterfly-brains we have on the Grand Council. Trust me, you won't be alone. There are two or three other old war-horses—no more 'spavined' than you, I might add—former Bordermen like you, who have pretty much the same attitudes. And I say, thank the gods for all of you."

Withen glowered. "I'm only going because you've got work for me," he said, grumbling. "Meke may think he runs Forst Reach, but Treesa's right: when there's trouble, it's me they all come to."

All the better for Meke, Vanyel thought. *Let him make his own mistakes and learn from them.*

But what he said was, "Then it's time to expand your stewardship, Father. More than time. I think you will serve Valdemar as well or better than you served Forst Reach."

He started to get up, when Withen's hand on his wrist stopped him. "Son," his father said, earnestly. "Did you really mean that about how you'd be hurt if something happened to your mother or me?"

"Father—" Vanyel closed his eyes, and sank back into his seat, swallowing an enormous lump in his throat. "Father, I would be devastated. I would be absolutely worthless. And somehow this mage knows that, which is why it's so important for you to be somewhere safe. Valdemar needs me, and needs me undamaged. And I need you. You're my parents, and I love you." He took a deep breath; what he was going to say was very hard, and it had cost him a lot of soul-searching. "I can't change the past, Father, but I can manage things better in the future. You've been very—good—about my relationship with Stef. If it would make you feel better, though, I'll see to it that he and I—don't see much of each other. That way you won't have—what I am—rubbed in your nose at Haven."

Withen flushed, and looked down at the table. "That's . . . that's very good of you, son. But I don't want you to do that."

Vanyel bit his lip with surprise. "You don't? But—"

"You're my son. I tried to see to it that you learned everything I thought was important. Honor. Honesty. That there are things more important than yourself. It seems to me you've been living up to those things." Withen traced the grain of the table with a thick forefinger. "There's only one way you ever disappointed me and—I don't know, Van, but—it just doesn't seem that important when you stack it up against everything else you've ever done. I don't see where I'd have been any happier if you'd been like Meke. I *might* have been worse off. Two blockheads in one family is enough. I'd say."

Withen looked up for a moment, then back down at his cup. "Anyway, what I'm trying to say is—is that I love you, son. I'm proud of you. That youngster Stefen is a good-hearted lad, and I'd like to think of him as one of the family. If he'll put up with us, that is. I can understand why you like him." Withen looked up again, met Vanyel's eyes, and managed a weak grin. "Of course, I'll admit that I'd have been a deal happier if he was a girl, but—he's not, and you're attached to him, and any fool can see he's the same about you. You've never been one to flaunt yourself—" Withen blushed, and looked away again. "I don't see you starting now. So—you and Stef stay the way you are. After all these years, I guess I'm finally getting used to the idea."

Vanyel's eyes stung; he wiped them with the back of his hand. "Father— I—I don't know what to say—"

"If you'll forgive me, son, for how I've hurt you, I'll forgive you," Withen replied. He shoved his seat away from the table and held out his arms. "I haven't hugged you since you were five. I'd like to catch up now."

"Father—"

Vanyel knocked over the bench, and stumbled blindly to Withen's side of the table. "Father—" he whispered, and met Withen's awkward embrace. "Oh, Father," he said into Withen's muscular shoulder. "If you only knew how much this means to me—I love you so much. I never wanted to hurt you."

Withen's arms tightened around him. "I love you, too, son," he said hesitantly. "You can't change what you are, any more than I can help what I am. But we don't have to let that get in the way any more, do we?"

"No, Father," Vanyel replied, something deep and raw inside him healing at last. "No, we don't."

CHAPTER 13

ORDINARILY STEF WOULD have been fascinated by the activities in the fields—he was city-born and bred, and the farmers at their harvest-work were as alien to him as the *Tayledras*, and as interesting. But Vanyel had been brooding, again, and finally Stef decided to ferret out the cause.

The road was relatively clear of travelers; with the harvest just begun, no one was bringing anything in to market. That, Savil had told Stef, would happen in about a week, when the roads would be thick with carts. This was really the ideal time to travel, if you didn't mind the late-summer dust and heat.

Stef didn't mind. But he *did* mind the way Van kept worrying at some secret trouble until he made both their heads ache.

And it seemed that the only way to end the deadlock would be if he said or did something to break it.

"Something's bothering you," Stefen said, when they were barely a candlemark from Haven. "It's *been* bothering you for the past two days."

He urged Melody up beside Yfandes, who obligingly lagged a little. Vanyel's lips tightened, and he looked away. "You won't like it," he said, finally.

Stef swatted at an obnoxious horsefly. "I don't like the way you've been getting all knotted up, either," he pointed out. "Whatever it is, I wish you'd just spit it out and get it over with. You're giving *me* a headache."

He eyed Savil, who was riding on Vanyel's right, hoping she'd get the hint. She raised one eyebrow at him, then held Kellan back, letting herself fall farther and farther behind until she was just out of earshot.

*Though how much that means when she can read minds—*Stef thought, then chided himself. *Oh, she wouldn't probe unless she had to. Heralds just don't do that to people, not even Van comes into my mind unless I ask him. I've got to get used to this, that they have powers but don't always use them. . . .*

"It's you," Van said quietly, once Savil had withdrawn her discreet twenty paces. "I'm afraid for you, Stef. The way I was afraid for my parents, and for the same reason." He shaded his eyes from the brilliant sun over-head, and looked out over fields full of people scything down hay, but Stef sensed he wasn't paying any attention to them. "I have an enemy who doesn't want a direct confrontation, so he'll strike at me through others. Once it's known that you and I are lovers, he won't hesitate to strike at you."

Gods. I was afraid I'd shocked or offended him. He's so—virginal. And Kernos knows I'm not. "Ah," Stefen said, relieved. "I was hoping it was just something like that, and not that—that I'd upset you or anything."

Vanyel turned to face him with an expression of complete surprise. "Stef, you've just *had* a taste of what it's like to be a target! How can you brush it off so lightly?"

"I'm not treating this lightly, but why are you bringing your parents to Haven if it isn't safe there?" Stefen pointed out with remorseless logic. "I thought that was the whole idea behind making them move there."

Vanyel looked away from him, up the road ahead of them.

It won't work, lover. You're never getting rid of me. Stefen had already made up his mind to counter any argument Van gave him, so he used Van's silence as an excuse to admire his profile, the way his long, fine-boned hands rested on his saddle-pommel, his perfect balance in the saddle . . .

"It's safer," Vanyel said, after a strained silence. "That doesn't mean it's safe. I don't want you hurt."

"I don't want to *be* hurt," Stefen said vehemently, then laughed. "You keep thinking I'm like a Herald, that I'll go throwing myself into danger the way you do. Look, Van, I am *not* a hero! I promise you, I have a very high regard for my skin! Bards are supposed to sing about heroes, not imitate them—there's no glory for a Bard in dying young, I promise you. I'll tell you what; at the first sign—the *very* first sign of trouble, I will most assuredly run for cover. I'll hide myself either behind the nearest Guard or the nearest Herald. Does *that* content you?"

"No," Vanyel said unhappily. "But I can't make you leave me, and that's the only thing that would keep you safe."

"Damned right you can't," Stefen snorted. "There's *nothing* that would make me leave you, no matter what happened."

"I only hope," Vanyel said soberly, peering up the road at the gate in the city walls, "that nothing makes you eat those words."

"I only hope nothing makes you eat those words." Was it only a few months ago I said that? I knew it could come to this, but will he understand?

"I'm sorry, Stef."

Vanyel spoke with his back to the Bard, looking out the window of his room as he leaned against the windowframe; he couldn't bear to look at Stefen's face. He didn't know how Stef felt, though he expected the worst; he was so tightly shielded against leaking emotions that he couldn't have told if Stef was angry, unhappy, or indifferent. But he didn't expect Stef to understand; the Bard couldn't possibly understand how a Herald's duty could come ahead of anything else.

Maybe nothing would make you leave me, ashke, *but nobody said anything about me leaving you. And I don't have a choice.*

"I can understand why you have to go—you're the only real authority who can speak for the King. But why can't I go with you?" Stefen spoke softly, with none of the anger in his voice that Van had expected—but Stef was a Bard, and used to controlling his inflections.

"Because I'm going to Rethwellan. They don't like shaych there. Actually, that's an understatement. If you came with me, they'd probably drive us both across the Border and declare war on Valdemar for the insult, if—when—they found out about the two of us." Vanyel gripped the side of the window tightly. The beautiful late-autumn day and the garden beyond the open window were nothing more than a blur to him. "We need that treaty, and we need it now—and the Rethwellan ambassador specifically requested me as Randi's proxy. I want you with me, but my duty to Valdemar comes first. I'm sorry, Stef."

Arms around his shoulders made him stiffen with surprise. "So am I," Stefen murmured in his ear. "But you said it yourself; Valdemar comes first. How long will you be gone?"

Vanyel shook his head, not quite believing what he'd just heard. "You mean you don't mind?"

"Of *course* I mind!" Stef replied, some of the anger Van had expected before this in his voice. "How can I not mind? But if there's one thing a Bard knows, it's how Heralds think. I've known all along that if you had to make a choice between me and your duty, I'd lose. It's just the way you are." His arms tightened around Vanyel's chest. "I don't *like* it," he continued quietly, "but I also don't like it that you can speak directly to my mind and I can't do the same to yours, and I'm learning to live with that, too. And you didn't answer me about how long you think you'll be gone."

"About three months. It'll be winter when I get back." The silence lasted a bit too long for Van's comfort. He tried to force himself to relax.

Stefen slid his hands up onto Van's shoulders, and began gently massaging the tense muscles of his neck.

"I'll miss you," the Bard said, eventually. "You know I will."

"Stef—promise me you'll stay safe—" Van hung his head and closed his eyes, beginning to relax in spite of himself.

"I'm the safest person in the Kingdom, next to Randale," Stefen chuckled. "Frankly, I'm much more concerned with knowing that you'll keep *yourself* safe. And one other thing concerns me very deeply—"

"What's that?"

"How I'm going to make sure tonight is so memorable you come *running* back here when you've got the treaty," Stefen breathed into his ear.

If 'Fandes wasn't so bone-deep tired, Van thought through a fog of weariness and cold, *I'd ask her to run. Ah well.*

Dull gray clouds were so low they made him claustrophobic; the few travelers on the road seemed as dispirited and exhausted as he was. Sleet drooled down as it had all day; the road was a slushy mire, and even the most waterproof of cloaks were soaked and near-useless after a day of it. Dirty gray snow piled up on either side of the road and made walking on the verge impossible. Van had stopped at an inn at nooning to dry off and warm up, and half a candlemark after they started out again he might as well not have bothered. Both he and Yfances were so filthy they were a disgrace to the Circle.

:No one would be able to stay clean in this,: 'Fandes grumbled. *:How far are we? I've lost all track of distance. Gods, I'm freezing.:*

:I think we're about two candlemarks out of Haven at this pace,: Vanyel told her.

She raised her head, a spark of rebellion in her eye. *:To the lowest hells with this pace,:* she said, shortly. *:I'm taking a new way home.:*

And with that, she pivoted on her hindquarters and leaped over the mounds of half-thawed snow that fenced the sides of the road. Vanyel tightened his legs around her barrel and his grip on the pommel with a yelp of surprise. He tried to Mindspeak her, but she wasn't listening. After three tries, he gave up; there was no reasoning with her in this mood.

She ranged out about twenty paces from the road, then threw her head up, her nostrils flaring. *:I thought so. This is where the road makes that long loop to the south. I can cut straight across and have us at the Palace gates in half a candlemark.:*

"But—" he began.

Too late. She stretched her weary legs into a canter, then a lope. She was too tired for an all-out run, but her lope was as good as most horses' full gallop.

"Look out!" Vanyel shouted. "—you're going through—"

She leaped a hedge, and cut through a flock of sheep, who were too startled by her sudden presence to scatter. Something dark and solid-looking loomed up ahead of them in the gusting sheets of thick sleet. She leaped again, clearing the hedge on the opposite side of the field, then lurched and slipped on a steep slope. Vanyel clung to her back as she scrambled down a cut, splashed through the ice-cold creek at the bottom, and clambered up the other bank.

Van gave up on trying to stop her, or even reason with her, and hung on for dear life.

The sleet thickened and became real snow; by now Vanyel was so cold he couldn't even feel his toes, and his fingers were entirely numb. Snow was everywhere, blown in all directions, including up, by the erratic gusts of wind. He couldn't see where Yfandes was going because of the snow being blown into his face; only the tensing of her muscles told him when she was going to make another of those bone-jarring jumps, into or out of someone's field, across a stream, or even through a barnyard.

Finally she made another leap that ended with her hooves chiming on something hard. Presumably pavement; she halted abruptly, ending in a short skid, and he was thrown against the pommel of his saddle before he could regain his balance. When he looked up, the walls of the city towered over them both, and here in the lee of the walls the wind was tamed to a faint breath. Already snow had started to lodge in the tiny crevices between the blocks of stone, creating thin white lines around each of them.

She moved up to the gate at a sedate walk, bridle bells chiming cheerfully as a kind of ironic counterpoint to her tired pacing.

The Guard at the gate started to wave them through, then took a second look and halted them just inside the tunnel beneath the walls, with a restraining hand on Yfandes' bridle. This tunnel, sheltered from the wind and snow, felt warm after the punishing weather outside.

Vanyel raised his head tiredly. "What—" he began.

"You're not goin' past me in *that* state, Herald," growled the Guard, a tough-looking woman who reminded Van of his own sister, Lissa. "Old man like you should know better than to—"

Old man? He shook his head so that his hood fell back, and she stopped in midsentence, her mouth falling open.

"If there were any flies to catch," he said, with tired good humor, "you'd be making a frog envious."

She shut her mouth with an audible snap.

"Beg your pardon, milord Vanyel," she said stiffly. "Just saw the white in your hair, and—"

"You did quite right to stop me, my lady," he replied gently. "I'm obviously not thinking, and it's from cold and exhaustion. We're far from infallible—*someone* had better watch out for us. Now what were you planning on doing with me—aside from telling me what a fool I was to be out in this muck?"

"I was goin' to give you a blanket to wrap up in," she said hesitantly. "Make you take off that soggy cloak. Gods, milord, it looks like you're carryin' half the road-muck 'twixt here and the Border on you."

"I think we are, but the Palace isn't far, and that's where we're heading," he said. "I think we can make it that far." He managed a real smile, and she smiled back uncertainly.

"If you say so, milord." She took her hand off Yfandes' rein, and stepped aside; he rode back out into the cold and snow.

But at least within the city walls they were sheltered from the wind. And it wasn't that far to the Palace. . . .

He must have blanked out for a while, a common enough habit of his, when he knew he was in relatively safe, but uncomfortable surroundings— riding on a patrolled road in the dead of winter, or waiting out an ambush in the pouring rain, for instance. The next thing he knew, he was in the dry and heated warming shed beside the stable; one of the grooms was at his stirrup, urging him to dismount.

:'Fandes?: he queried.

She turned her head slowly to stare at him, blinking. *Oh. We're home. I must have—:*

:You did the same thing I did; the minute we crossed inside the city we went numb. Get some rest, love. I'm going to do the same as soon as I make my report.:

"Get her closer to the heat," he told the groom, dismounting with care for his bruises. The warming shed was heated by a series of iron stoves, and on very cold nights, the door into the stable would be left open so that the heat would carry out into the attached building. "Get her dry, give her a thorough grooming, then a hot mash for her supper."

:Bless you.:

"Put two blankets on her, and take that tack away. It needs a complete overhaul." He took the saddlebags from the cantle and threw them over his shoulder, mud and all.

"Anything else, milord?" the groom asked, eyes wide with surprise at his state.

"No," Vanyel said, and dredged up another smile. "Thank you. I'm a little short on manners. I think they froze somewhere back about a candle-mark ago."

:Where are you going?: Yfandes asked, as she was being led away.

:To my room long enough to change, then to report,: he told her. *:Check with the others and tell me if Randi's holding Audience today, would you?:*

:He is,: she replied immediately. *:Stef's with him.:*

:Good. Thank you. Go get some rest, you deserve it.: He found a little more energy somewhere, and quickened his steps toward the door.

:So do you, but you won't take it,: she replied with resignation. Van sent her a tired but warm mental hug.

He strode out into the snow, which was coming down so thickly now that it completely hid the Palace from where he stood. *:I'll take it, love. Later. Randi's good hours are too rare to waste, and I have too much to report.:*

He was afraid; afraid of what he'd find when he saw Randale, afraid that Treven was not going to be able to cope with so many duties thrust on him so young, afraid that Shavri was going to fall apart at any moment—

Yes, and admit it. Afraid Stef's lost interest. That's what is really eating at you. He shivered, and forced himself to walk a little faster, as the snow coated him with a purer white than his uniform cloak was capable of showing just now.

The stable-side door opened just before he reached it, and someone pulled him inside, into warmth and golden light from the oil lamp mounted in the doorframe.

It took Vanyel a moment to recognize him; not because Tantras had changed, but because his numb memory couldn't put name and face together.

"Tran—" he croaked. *Ye gods, I doubt I'd recognize my own mother in this state.*

"Give me that cloak," Tantras said briskly, unfastening the throat-latch himself. "Delian has been watching for you two for days; as soon as he saw how mind-numb you were, he called me. There." The cloak fell from Van's shoulders, landing in a sodden heap on the floor. "Good. There isn't a lot of time to spare; Randi's Audiences rarely last more than a candlemark or two even with Stef to help. Come in here—"

He pulled Vanyel into a storage-chamber. There was a small lantern here on a shelf, and a set of Whites beside it. "Strip, and put these on," Tantras ordered. "What do you need out of your saddlebags?"

"Just the dispatch cases," Vanyel said, pulling at the lacings of his tunic, with hands that felt twice their normal size.

"I take it that you did all right?" Tantras pulled out the pair of sealed cases and laid them on the shelf where the uniform had been.

"It wasn't easy, but yes, I got the treaty Randi wanted." He had to peel his breeches off, they were so soaked. Tran handed him a towel, and he dried himself off, then wrapped it around his dripping hair before he began pulling on the new set of breeches. "Queen Lythiaren—gods, that's a mouthful!—has only heard rumors of what we are and what we can do. Heralds, I mean. She isn't familiar with Mind-magic; the very idea that someone could pick up their thoughts and feelings frightens most of the people of Rethwellan. I spent about as much time undoing rumor as I did at the bargaining table. But it's over, and I must say, it's a good thing Randi sent *me*, because I'll tell you the truth, I don't think anyone else has the peculiar combination of Gifts that would have let them pull it off."

"Your reputation doesn't hurt, either," Tran observed wryly.

Vanyel pulled the tunic over his head—one of Tran's and much too loose, but that wouldn't matter. He began toweling his hair, still talking. "That's true, though it almost did more harm than good. That's why I got out of there before the passes snowed up. I make them all very uneasy, and they were very happy to see my back."

"Here're your dispatches," Tran said, handing the cases to him as he ran his fingers through his hair to achieve a little order. "I'll take the rest of your stuff back to your room. And Randi looks like hell, so be prepared."

Vanyel took the twin blue-leather cases from his friend, and hesitated a moment. He wanted to say something, but wasn't certain what.

"Go," Tran said, holding open the door with one hand while he grabbed the lantern with the other. "You haven't got any time to waste."

Just how much worse can Randi have gotten in three months? he wondered, forcing tired legs into a brisk walk. The corridors were deserted; in fact, the entire Palace had an air of disuse about it. It was disquieting in the extreme, especially for someone who remembered these same corridors full of courtiers and servants, the way they had been in Elspeth's time. It was as if an evil spirit had made off with all the people, leaving the Palace empty, populated by memories.

The Throne Room was mostly empty; no sycophants, no curious idlers, only those who had business with Randale. Hardly more than twenty people, all told, and all of them so quiet that Van clearly heard Stef playing up at the front of the room. At first Van couldn't see Randale at all; then someone moved to one side, and Van got his first look at the King in three months.

With a supreme effort of will he prevented himself from crying out and running to Randale's side. Randale *had* changed drastically since summer.

It wasn't so much a physical change as something less tangible. Randale looked frail, as fragile as a spun-glass ornament. There was a quality of transparency about him; he could easily have been a *Tayledras* ice-sculpture, the kind they made for their winter-festivals, but one of a creature other than a man. One of the Ethereal Plane *Varrir*, perhaps.

That was, perhaps, the most frightening thing of all. Randale no longer looked quite human. Everything that was nonessential had been burned away or discarded in the past three months; he held to life by nothing less than sheer will. There was something magnificent about him; Vanyel would never have believed that poor, vacillating Randi, Randale who had never wanted to be King, could have metamorphosed into this creature of iron spirit and diamond determination.

He's holding on until Treven is ready, Van thought, watching as Randale listened carefully to the messenger from the Karsite Border. *He won't let go until Trev can handle the job. But that's all that's keeping him. I wonder if he realizes that?*

Shavri bent over him and touched his shoulder. He raised a colorless hand to cover hers, without taking his eyes or his attention away from the messenger. Vanyel Felt the strength flowing from her to him, and realized something else. Shavri was as doomed as Randi. She had, out of love, done the one thing no Healer ever did—she'd opened an unrestricted channel between them. She was giving him everything she had—they would burn out together, because she no longer had any way to stop that from happening.

She knew what she'd done; she *had* to. Which meant that was what she wanted.

Neither of them knows what the other is hiding. Randi doesn't know the channel Shavri opened is unrestricted; Shavri doesn't know how little Randi has left. I should tell them—but I can't. I can't. Let them keep their secrets. They have so little else except love.

Joshel beckoned to Van as the messenger bowed in response to something Randale said. Vanyel forced himself to walk briskly to the foot of the throne, as if he'd just come in from a pleasure ride. Randale was focused entirely on what came immediately before him; too focused to read past any outward seeming of well-being, if Van chose to enforce that kind of illusion. Which was precisely what Vanyel intended to do.

"Majesty," he said quietly, "your business with Rethwellan is successfully concluded." He handed the dispatch tubes to Joshel, who opened them and handed them to the Seneschal. "Here is your treaty, my King; exactly what you requested I negotiate for. Mutual defense pact against Karse, extradition of criminals, provision for aid in the event of an attack, it's all there."

Plus a few more things the Queen and I worked out. He watched as the Seneschal scanned each page and handed it on to Randale noted with tired satisfaction the surprised smiles as they came to the clauses he had gotten inserted into the document. It was a *good* treaty, fair to both sides. The rulers of Karse would have a rude awakening when they found out about this particular agreement.

He was proudest of the fact that he had negotiated the agreement despite having no formal training as a diplomat. Everything he knew, he'd picked up from Joshel or the Seneschal.

Randale knew that, and his smile showed that he realized the value of Van's accomplishment. "Well done, old friend," he said, in a breathless voice that told Van how much each word cost him in effort. "I couldn't have asked for more. I wouldn't have thought to ask for some of the things you got for us. I'm tempted to ask you to give up mage-craft in favor of politics."

"Oh, I think not, my liege," Vanyel said lightly. "I am far too honest. This is one situation where honesty was an asset, but that's usually not the case in politics."

Randale laughed, a pale little ghost of a chuckle, and leaned back into the padded embrace of his throne. "Thank you, Vanyel. I'm sure the Council will want to go over this with you in detail shortly, and I'd appreciate it if you'd brief Trev on how to handle the Queen."

This was clearly a dismissal, and Vanyel bowed himself out. He left the Throne Room entirely; he couldn't bear to see anything more of what Randale had become. Joshel followed him out into the corridor.

"I know you're exhausted, Van, but we need to convene the Privy Council on this and the Karse situation right away—" The haggard young

Herald paused, concern for Vanyel warring with the needs of the moment, and the conflict evident in his expression.

"It's all right, Joshe," Van told him. "The Council room is warm, and that's what I need most right now. I'm cold right down to my marrow."

"Can you go there now? I can get pages to bring everyone there in next to no time." Joshe's relief was so plain that Van wondered what else had gone wrong in his absence.

"Certainly," he replied. "Provided that no one minds that I look like a drowned cat."

"I doubt they'll mind," Joshel said, "We've got other things to worry about these days. They'd take you looking like a stablehand covered with muck; you're that important."

Frustration and anguish inside Vanyel exploded into words. "Important? Dammit, Joshe, what's the use of all this? I can level a building with the power I control, but I can't do anything for a friend who's dying in front of my eyes!"

Joshel sighed. "I know. I have to keep telling myself that it isn't Randi that we're working to preserve, it's Valdemar. Most of the time, it doesn't help."

"What good is having power if you can't use it the way it needs to be used?" Vanyel asked, his hand clenched into a fist in front of him. "I'm Vanyel Demonsbane, and I can't even keep my parents safe in their own home, much less keep Randi alive."

Joshe just shook his head; Vanyel could Feel the same anguish inside him, and unclenched his fist. "I'm sorry, Van. I wish I knew some answers for you. I should tell you one thing more before the Council meeting. The Heraldic Circle met today, and we're promoting Trev to full Whites."

Vanyel felt the news like a blow to the stomach. To promote Treven so young could only mean one thing—the King had to be a full Herald, and the Foreseers did not see Randale living through the next two years it would ordinarily take Treven to make his Whites.

Joshe nodded at Vanyel's expression. "You know what that means as well as I do," he said, and turned back to the door to the Throne Room.

Van walked the few steps down the corridor to the Council Chamber. Unlike the rest of the Palace, this room looked, and felt, as if it were in use. Heavy use, from the look of all the papers and maps stacked neatly about, and the remains of a meal on a tray beside the door. Here, then, was where the business of the Crown was being transacted, and not the Throne Room. Evidently Audiences were just for those things Randale had to handle personally, or for edicts that needed to come from the lips of the Sovereign in order to have the required impact.

This treaty, obviously, was one of those things, which was why Tran had hustled him into the Throne Room. Randale was probably signing it now, with what there was of the Court as witness, which made it binding from this moment on.

Van took his usual seat, then slouched down in it and put his feet up on the one beside it. *If Stef hasn't had a change of heart while I was gone, I could certainly use a massage,* he thought wistfully. The fire in the fireplace beside him burned steadily, and the generous supply of wood beside it argued that it had become normal practice to keep the Council Chamber ready for use at a moment's notice. That was in keeping with the rest of Van's observations, so it meant that the business of the Kingdom was being conducted at any and all hours.

After being told of Treven's promotion, he wasn't surprised when the door behind him creaked open, and Treven eased into the room, wearing a brand-new set of Whites.

The youngster sat down in the chair beside Vanyel with an air of uncertainty, as if he didn't know what his welcome would be. Van watched him through half-closed eyes for a moment, then smiled.

"Ease up, Trev. We're still friends. I've come to the conclusion that you and Jisa did the right thing."

The young man relaxed. "We've managed to convince Randale and Shavri, too," he said. "Though Jisa and her mother came awfully close to a real fight over it. I'm still not sure how I kept them from each other's throats. Early training for diplomatic maneuvering, I guess." He adjusted the fit of his white belt self-consciously.

"Feeling uncomfortable about that?" Van asked, gesturing at the white tunic.

Treven nodded. "I hadn't expected it quite so suddenly. I don't feel exactly like I've earned it. It feels like a cheat. And—and I don't like getting it because—because—"

The young Herald hung his head.

"I understand," Vanyel said. "I'd think less of you if you didn't have doubts, Trev. I'll give you my honest opinion, if you want it."

Treven grimaced. "Lady bless, that sounds like a bitter pill! Still—yes, I think so. At least I'd know what to measure myself against."

Vanyel took his feet off the chair, and straightened his aching back before facing Treven. The young man's honest blue eyes met his fearlessly, and Vanyel felt a moment of satisfaction. There weren't many people who could meet his gaze.

"I think you were rushed into this, Trev, and we both know why. No, I don't think you're ready—quite. I think you will be when you have to be, if you don't let that uniform fool you into thinking the Whites make the Herald."

Treven looked disappointed, and Vanyel knew he'd been hoping to be told—despite Van's warning that this would be an honest opinion—that he really was ready to be called a full Herald.

In some ways Treven was a boy still, and that had something to do with what Van had told him. He had a boy's optimism and a boy's belief in the essential fairness of the universe. This wouldn't have been a problem in an ordinary Herald—but neither belief had any place in the thinking of a Monarch. A King never assumed anything was fair; a ruler must always expect the worst and plan for it.

Treven would learn, as Randale had learned. As Jisa had learned.

As if his thought had summoned her, Vanyel felt Jisa's presence before she entered, the little mind-to-mind brush that was the Mindspeaker's equivalent of a knock.

:Hello, love,: he replied. :Holding on?:

:As well as I can,: she replied. :You saw.:

So, she hadn't missed what her mother had done, binding herself to her lifebonded's fate. And she wasn't blinded to Randale's condition by her love of him. There was resignation in her mind-voice, and a sadness as profound as if her parents were already gone.

:They've closed me out,: she said, in answer to the questions he couldn't bring himself to ask. :They've closed everyone out except each other. Most of the time I could be a thousand miles away, for all they notice I'm there.:

:Well, I notice you're here. Come on in.:

The door behind him creaked again, and Treven looked up and smiled. Vanyel started to get up, but Jisa pushed him back down into his chair with her hands on his shoulders.

"No you don't, Uncle Van. There's enough Healer in me to know how tired you are." She kissed him on the top of his head, and Sent, :Treven doesn't know, Father. I don't see any reason why he has to.:

:Thank you, dearheart.: "I won't deny you're right. Are you part of the Council now, too?"

She sat down beside Treven. "Both of us; I'm here as Mother's proxy. I have been ever since late fall."

"And doing very well at it, too." Jisa had left the door open, and the rest of the Council filed in, taking their usual seats. The Seneschal had said that last, and he stopped on the way to his seat at the head of the table, pausing with his hands on the back of Jisa's chair. His inflection told Vanyel he meant the compliment; there was nothing paternalistic or condescending in his voice. "I frankly don't know what we would have done without her earlier this fall; we had a situation with someone who claimed to be a high-ranking Karsite refugee. We suspected his motives, but he was shielded against casual Thought-sensing, and we didn't want to tip our hands by probing him. We badly needed someone whose Gift was Empathy—"

"But Mother was exhausted and in any case, wouldn't leave Father," Jisa said matter-of-factly. "So I went. He was a spy for the Prophet, sent to see if we were giving aid to their mages. It's hard to mistake fanatic devotion for anything else."

"That was when we put her on the Council," the Seneschal said, taking his seat. "And that brings us around to the Karsite situation."

The situation, so Seneschal Arved told them, was stalemate. The followers of the Prophet had won, and were consolidating their victory. As yet they had shown no signs of resuming the war the previous regime had begun—but they had also been probing to see if Valdemar had been aiding mages, or were offering aid to those who continued to evade the "witchfinders."

"They're just looking for an excuse to start things up again when they're ready," said the representative for the South, Lord Taving, with a sour grimace.

"I'm inclined to agree," Vanyel's father replied. "You know what they say: 'Nothing comes out of Karse but brigands and bad weather.' Whether they say their cause is for their god or for their greed, the Karsites always have been robbers and always will be."

Lord Taving looked gratified to find someone who shared his basic feelings toward Karse. "The only problem is, we're still in no shape to fight a war," he said, "or at least that's my understanding."

"You are correct, my lord," the Lord Marshal said. "Thanks to Vanyel's suggestions, we haven't had to resort to conscription, but our new Guards are still green as new leaves, and if faced with troops of seasoned fanatics, they wouldn't stand a chance."

"And why aren't they ready?" asked Guildmaster Jumay. "Zado knows we pay enough in taxes!"

"Largely because we've already lost more men to this war with Karse than in the whole of Elspeth's reign!" the Lord Marshal shot back heatedly.

"Which is why the treaty Vanyel brought back from Rethwellan is vital," the Seneschal said, pouncing on the opportunity to introduce the subject.

The rest of the Councillors—who had not been at the Audiences—reacted according to their natures. Lord Taving was not inclined to trust anything South of Valdemar's Border. Withen wanted to know where the catch was. The Lord Marshal heaved an audible sigh of relief, until he realized the thing included a mutual assistance pact.

Vanyel explained the details of the treaty at length until his head ached, pointing out the ones Randale had requested and the ones he had gotten inserted. They finally agreed that it was an excellent treaty as it stood—which was just as well, since Randale had already signed it.

When they finally let him go, it was clear that they were already preparing for Randale's death and a period in which Treven would be just one of the Council when it came to decision-making. Which was a good idea—but it brought home the fact that Randi's days were numbered, and probably less than a year.

He returned to his room very depressed, and paused outside the door for a moment to think where Stefen might be.

Then the door opened under his hand—

"I'm glad you're back," Stef said simply, and took his hand to pull him inside.

CHAPTER 14

S TEFEN HAD BEEN waiting for Van ever since the Audience session ended. He'd come straight to Vanyel's room once Randale had been put to bed. He'd had a page bring food and wine, and had gotten everything set up exactly like the supper he'd had with Vanyel the first night the Herald had brought him to this room. Except tonight he expected the end of the evening to be somewhat different.

He'd known Van was expected back at any time, but no one had been able to tell him exactly when the Herald would arrive, so he'd been as nervous and excited as a kid waiting for Festival for the past week.

When Van had made his presentation at the Audiences, even though he'd been in trance, Stef had known he was there. He had thought his heart was going to pound itself to pieces with joy. To stay in trance until Randale had no further need of him had been the hardest thing Stefen had ever done.

"I'm glad you're back," Stefen said simply, letting his voice tell Vanyel exactly how glad he really was. "I've missed you." He reached behind Vanyel and closed the door.

"I've missed you," Vanyel said, then unexpectedly pulled the Bard into his arms for an embrace with more of desperation in it than passion. Stef just held him, not entirely sure what had prompted the action, but ready to give Vanyel whatever he needed. Behind him, the fire crackled and popped, punctuating the silence.

Finally Van let him go. "I was afraid once I was gone you'd find someone who suited you better," he said hoarsely.

"We've lifebonded," Stef reminded him, pulling the Herald into the room and getting him to sit in the chair nearest the fireplace. "How could I find anybody who suited me better than that? That's not something that goes away just because there's some distance between us."

Vanyel laughed weakly. "I know, I was being stupid. It's just that in the middle of the night, when you're leagues and leagues away from me, it's hard to see why you'd choose to stay with me." Stefen reached for the food since Van was ignoring it, and poured some wine for him.

"You're still being stupid," Stef said, and put bread and cheese in one hand, and a mug of hot mulled wine in the other. "Eat. Relax. I love you. There, see? Everything's all right." He sat in the chair opposite Vanyel, and glared at him until he took a bite.

"I wish it could be that simple," Vanyel sighed, but he smiled a little when he said it. He ate what Stef gave him, then sipped at his wine, watching Stefen, his strange silver eyes gone dark and thoughtful.

"I have a surprise for you," Stef said, unable to bear the silence anymore. He got up, went to the desk, and took out the box he'd put there earlier. "I left it here in case you came back to your room before I got done. Here—"

He thrust it into Vanyel's hands and waited, hardly breathing, for the Herald to open it.

Vanyel turned the catch on the simple wooden box, saying as he did so, "You didn't have to do this—you don't have to give me things, Stef—" The lid came open, and he saw what nestled in the velvet and his mouth opened in a soundless "oh."

He took it out, his hands trembling a little. He'd told Stef once or twice that he was hampered in his mage-craft by not having a good focus-stone. The mineral he worked best with was amber, which wasn't particularly rare, but he had a problem similar to his aunt Savil's. For mage-work, the clearer and less flawed the stone, the better it focused power. And amber rarely appeared totally clear and without inclusions. When it did—it was expensive. Since the loss of his first focus-stone a few years ago, Van had never again found a piece even in the raw state that was flawless and large enough to be of use. Flaws in a stone could make it disintegrate or even explode when stressed by magic energies.

So, like Savil, Vanyel had to do most of the work that required a focus through his secondary stone, an egg-shaped piece of tiger-eye.

Stefen's present was a faceted half-globe of completely flawless, water-clear, dark gold-red amber, set in a thin silver band with a loop at the top so that it could be worn as a pendant. He'd begged a silver chain of Jisa just so that Van could wear it immediately. Jisa had given one to him without asking why, but when he'd told her, she'd been as pleased as if the gift had been for her.

"Stefen," Van said in a strange, strained voice. "You have to tell me. Where—and more importantly, *how*—did you get this?"

"I didn't steal it!" Stef exclaimed, stung.

"I didn't think you did, love—but there's no ordinary way *you* could afford something like this, and we both know it." Vanyel put the pendant back in the box and closed it. "I can't in good conscience wear this until I know."

He thinks I sold my bed-time for it, Stef thought suddenly. *Oh, gods—I have to put him right.*

"I met this gem-merchant," he said quickly. "He was giving some of the ladies I was playing for a private showing; amber, pearls, and coral, really unusual things, but he says he's been all over the world at one time or another. Anyway, he had this and I saw it, and he saw me looking at it. He told me it would be useless to me, that it was made to be a mage-focus . . . well, we got to talking, and I told him I wanted it for you, even though I knew I couldn't afford it."

He remembered what the merchant had told him, too: "What, a Bard like you? Gods, my friend, in my country you'd have been showered with baubles like this a thousand times over. A Gift such as yours is rarer than all my collection put together."

Then the merchant's face had grown thoughtful. "On the other hand, perhaps we could do each other a service. . . ."

"So anyway, he offered to give me the stone if I'd do him a favor. He had some more private showings planned, at the house he'd rented, for fellow gem-merchants. He said they were a lot harder to convince than pretty ladies and he wanted me to play for them—"

He faltered, for Vanyel was looking at him in a way that made him feel as if he *had* sold himself. "—he didn't ask me to do anything like make them buy things. Just to put them in a pleasant mood; make them feel good, and allow him to drop the fact that I was the King's Bard to impress them. That was all! I didn't do anything wrong!"

Vanyel was still looking at him doubtfully.

"Did I?" he asked, in a very small voice.

The Herald weighed the box in his hand. Stefen felt worse with every passing moment. He'd intended this to be a love-offering, and instead the thing had turned into a viper and bitten them both.

Finally Van opened the box, and took the amber out. Stef heaved a sigh of relief. Vanyel stared at the beautiful thing, and shook his head. "You didn't do anything wrong—but only by accident and the fact that I don't think your friend wanted you to get into trouble," he said, in a low voice.

"You came so close to misuse of your powers that I shudder to think about it. You must *never* use your Gift to manipulate people except at the orders of the Crown, Stef. You can be stripped of it, if you do. And it's wrong, Stef, it's just plain wrong. What if this man had been unscrupulous, and had been trying to sell trash—and what if he'd actually asked you to influence people to buy? What if he'd drastically overpriced his wares and asked you to make them think he was giving them a bargain? What if he'd brought in those who couldn't afford his merchandise and told you to make them want it enough to buy it no matter what?"

"Stop!" Stef cried, horribly ashamed of himself. Now he almost wished he *had* sold himself; it seemed more honest.

"Stef—" Vanyel caught his hand and drew him down beside his chair. "Stef, I didn't want to make you feel bad. You *didn't* do any of those things; you didn't misuse your powers. But it was a very near thing. You can thank that merchant for being an honest fellow, and *not* leading you into temptation."

Stefen vowed silently to *think* about what he was being asked to do before he did it. And he marveled a little at this change in himself. A year ago he would have done any of those things, and never considered them wrong.

"Van," he said quietly, "being with you . . . you've shown me that it's as wrong to play with peoples' minds and emotions as it is to steal—" He hesitated a moment, then added, "In a way, it *is* stealing from them. It's stealing their right to think and feel at their own will. I wouldn't have understood that before I met you, but I do now."

Vanyel relaxed completely, and closed his hand around the amber half-globe. "Then I can wear this, Stef, and I will, gladly, and I'll use it knowing it was a gift of love *and* honor." He bowed his head and chuckled. "I suppose that sounds rather pretentious and pompous, like something out of a ballad—but it's how I really feel, Stef."

"If you thought any differently, you wouldn't be Vanyel," Stef replied, flushing happily as Van pulled the chain over his head and laid his right hand on Stef's shoulder.

"You give me too much credit, lover," Vanyel said quietly. "I'm as prone to being a fool as anyone else. And just now, I'm a very sore fool. Could I possibly get you to use those talented hands of yours to unknot my shoulders?"

"And give me a chance to have my hands on you?" Stef grinned. "Of course you could, and I will. Gladly."

Vanyel finished off his wine in a single gulp, peeled off his tunic, kicked off his boots, and sagged back into his chair. Stefen got up and moved around behind him, and began kneading his shoulders with steady, firm pressure.

"What's wrong, Van?" he asked. "You just got back with everything the King asked you for and more."

"Sometimes I feel like everything I've done is useless," Vanyel said dispiritedly. "Randi is going to be dead before the year's out, every enemy Valdemar has will take that as a signal to strike while Treven is so young, and a good half the treaties we made will fall apart, because they were made with Randale and not Trev. Karse is likely to declare holy war on us any day. The West is full of half-mad mage-born, any one of whom might be another Krebain, but with wider plans. I have a personal enemy out there somewhere; I don't know who or why, only that he, she, or it is a mage."

Stefen dug his thumbs into Vanyel's shoulders a little harder and tried to think of things to say that would make a difference. "Randale is the mind behind the Crown, but about half of the work is being done by Trev and the Council," he offered. "Trev's bright, especially on short-term planning, and Randale's doing long-range planning that ought to hold good for the next five years. Trev's a little too idealistic, maybe, but he'll get that knocked out of him soon enough—and Jisa is practical enough for two. They'll be all right."

"How do *you* know so much about this?" Vanyel asked suddenly, after a long silence.

"I'm right there whenever Randale is working, and I'm beginning to be able to listen to what's going on while I'm in trance." Stefen was rather proud of that. It wasn't much compared with the kinds of things Vanyel could do, but it was more than he'd been able to manage before Van's trip.

"That's pretty impressive," Vanyel told him, without even a trace of patronization. "Bards usually don't have a Gift that requires being in trance, and I'm surprised you learned how to manage that on your own. What about Jisa and Trev?"

"I spent a lot of time with them after you'd gone," Stef replied, working on Van's neck, flexing and stroking as though he were playing an instrument. The muscles were very stiff, so tight they were like rope under tension, and Stef had no doubt they were giving Van a headache of monumental proportions. "With Jisa especially. The Seneschal is the only one who doesn't underestimate her, and he likes it that way."

"A very wise lady," Vanyel said, his voice a little muffled. "Did you know she's my daughter, and not Randi's?"

It should have been a shock. Somehow it wasn't. "No. But it makes sense. She's very like you, you know." He thought about the situation for a moment. "Obviously Randale must know; I mean, a Healer like Shavri can prevent any pregnancy she cares to, so it wasn't an accident, which means she *wanted* Jisa. . . ."

"Shavri was desperate for a child, and the two of them asked me to help. I've never told anyone but you, not even my parents," Van replied. "I have three other children, but the only one I ever see is Brightstar, the boy Starwind and Moondance are raising. The others are a Mage-Gifted girl one of the other *Tayledras* has, named Featherfire, and a girl two of Lissa's retired shaych Guards are raising, who has no Gifts at all so far as I can tell."

Stefen wasn't sure how he should be feeling about these revelations. "Why?" he asked finally. "I mean, why did you do it? I can see why Shavri would have asked *you*, rather than somebody else, but why the others?"

Vanyel sighed, and flexed his shoulders. "For pretty much the same reasons as Shavri had. People I knew and cared for wanted a child, but for one reason or another couldn't produce one without outside help. Featherfire's mother isn't shaych, but there wasn't a single *Tayledras* male she felt the right way about to have a child with. She had twins; Brightstar is Feather's brother."

Stef recalled all the fantasies he'd had about his parentage, how he'd never known who even his mother was. "Do you ever wish you'd—I don't know, had more of a hand in their raising?" He worked his thumbs into the nape of Vanyel's neck, with the silky hair covering both hands. "I know they've got parents who really want them, but—"

"That's just it; they have parents who really *want* them," Van replied. "Ah, that's it, that's the worst of the aches, right there. I see what 'Fandes means about musicians having talented hands. Really, love, the only reason Brightstar and Jisa know I'm their father is that it's necessary for them to know. Brightstar evidently has all my Gifts; Jisa could get backwash from a magical attack on me, because she has Mage-Gift in potential. They have to be prepared. Featherfire is so like her mother they could be twins, and Arven doesn't even carry potential as far as I was able to check. They all know who their *real* parents are—the ones who love them."

He chuckled then. "What's funny?" Stef asked.

"Oh, just that whatever it is that makes someone shaych, it probably isn't learned *or* inherited. Brightstar has a half dozen young ladies of the *Tayledras*

with whom he trades feathers on a regular basis, and he'd probably have
more if he had the stamina."

"Trades feathers?" Stef said with puzzlement.

"*Tayledras* custom. When you want to make love to someone you offer
them a feather. If you want a more permanent relationship, it's a feather from
your bondbird."

"Oh." That gave his fertile imagination something to work on. And
feathers were easier come by in the dead of winter than, say, flowers. . . .

Van was finally relaxing under his hands. In fact, from the way his head
kept nodding, the Herald was barely awake. Which meant Stef could probably coax him into bed without too much trouble.

Of course, he may not get much sleep. Stefen sighed contentedly, and slowly
ran his fingers through Vanyel's hair, grateful just for his lover's presence.

Van relaxed for the first time in three months, and gave himself over completely to the gentle strength of Stef's callused hands. Stef felt the cold more
than most—he was so thin it went straight to his bones—so he'd built the
fire up to the point where *he* was comfortable. That meant that even without his tunic, Van basked in drowsy warmth.

The mage-focus glowed just above his heart, touching him with a different sort of warmth. That piece of amber was truly extraordinary. It might
have been made for him, fitting into his cupped hand perfectly, meshing
with his power-patterns and channeling them with next to no effort on his
part. Given how things had worked out, perhaps it had been, in the same
way that the rose-quartz crystal he'd given Savil years ago had seemingly
been made for her, though it had been given to him.

He'd told Stef the truth, though; if the Bard had bought the thing with
dishonorable coin, he couldn't have worn it. If Stef had failed to realize *why*
that kind of perversion of his Gift was wrong, Vanyel would have had misgivings every time he put it on.

Stef had changed, though Van had never tried to change him. He'd
become a partner, someone Van could rely on, despite his youth. *And because
he's my partner, he had to know about Jisa and the others. Partners shouldn't have
secrets from one another. That information could be important some day. It's good to
be able to tell someone—especially him. . . .*

It was so easy to relax, letting all his responsibilities slide away for a
moment. He felt himself drifting off into a half-doze, and didn't even try to
stop himself.

PAIN!

He didn't realize that he'd jumped to his feet until he found himself staring at Stef from halfway across the room. He blinked, and in that instant between one breath and the next, knew—

Kilchas! That pain was Herald-Mage Kilchas, and he was dying. Or being killed. Suddenly. Violently.

An unexpected side effect of the new Web. Unless someone was magically cut out of the Web, every Herald would know when another Herald died, as the Companions already knew.

And as Vanyel knew that something was wrong.

The Death Bell began tolling, and he grabbed his tunic from the back of the chair beside the one he'd been sitting in, pulling it on hastily over his head. Something was wrong, something to do with Kilchas, and he was the only one who might be able to see what it was. But he had to get there.

Stef fell back a step, startled. "Van, what did I—"

The Death Bell tolled, drowning out the rest of his words.

Stef had been at Haven long enough to know what *that* meant. But he'd never seen a Herald react to it the way Vanyel had—and he'd never heard of a Herald who had reacted *before* the tolling of the Bell.

"Van?" he said, and the Herald stared at him as if he'd never seen him before.

"Van?" he said again, which seemed to break Vanyel out of whatever trance he'd gotten stuck in. Vanyel grabbed his uniform tunic and began pulling it on over his head.

"Van," Stef protested. "It's the Death Bell. There's nothing you can *do*, and even if there were, you just got back! You're tired, and you've earned a rest! Let somebody else take care of it."

Van shook his head stubbornly, and bent down to reach for his boots. "I have to go—I don't know why, but I have to."

Stefen sighed, and got both their cloaks; his, that had been draped on a hook behind the door, and Vanyel's spare from the wardrobe. As soon as the Herald straightened up from pulling his boots on, Stef handed him the white cloak and swung his own scarlet over his shoulders. Vanyel paused, hands on the throat-latch of his garment.

"Where are *you* going?" he asked, in a startled voice.

Stefen shrugged. "With you. If you're going to run off the first night you're home, at least I can be with you."

"But Stef—" Vanyel protested. "You don't have to—"

"I know," he interrupted. "That's one reason why I'm doing it anyway, lover." He held the door open for the Herald, and waved him through it. "Come on. Let's get going."

Someone had already beaten Vanyel to the scene; there were lights and moving shadows at the base of one of the two flat-topped towers at the end of Herald's Wing. The storm had blown off some time after Vanyel got in; the sky was perfectly clear, and the night windless and much colder than when he'd arrived. The slush had hardened into icy ridges that he and Stef slipped and stumbled over to get to the death-scene.

Kilchas lay facedown on the hardened snow, one arm twisted beneath him, head at an unnatural angle. He was dressed in a shabby old tunic and soft breeches, with felt house-shoes. Treven, cloak wrapped tightly around him, knelt beside the body. A very young, blond Guardsman stood next to him, holding a lantern that shook as the hand that held it trembled. "—there was this kind of cry," he was saying, as Van stumbled within hearing distance. "I looked up at the tower, and he was falling, limplike; like somebody'd thrown a rag doll over. I ran to—to catch him, to try to help, but he was—" The young man shuddered and gulped. "So I came to get help, my lord."

"Which was when you bowled me over in the corridor," Treven said coolly, touching the body's shoulder with care. "You can go get me a Healer, but I think he'll just confirm that the poor old man died of a broken neck and smashed skull." Though the young Heir spoke with every sign of complete composure, Van Felt him shaking inside. This was Trev's first close-up look at the violent death of a fellow human, and all his calm was pretense.

Not that it ever got easier emotionally with time and repetition; it was just easier to be calm about taking care of it.

"Trev." Vanyel touched the young man's shoulder at the same time as he spoke; Trev and the Guardsman both jumped. The lantern swung wildly in the Guardsman's hand, making the shadows jerk and dance, and making the body appear to move for an instant.

"Trev, I'll take it from here if you want, but I think you've got things well in hand." His first impulse had been to take over; this, after all, was not the first time he'd seen death near at hand—it was not even the first time he'd seen the death of someone he knew and cared for. No, that had happened so often he'd given up counting the times . . . but taking over from

Trev would have meant shoving the young Heir into the position of hanger-on, when what he *needed* to do was start assuming his authority. The sooner he started doing so, the more readily others would accept that authority when Randi died.

So even if the young Heir didn't have any experience in handling situations like this, Trev should be the one in charge.

Treven took a deep breath, and looked very much as if he wanted to hand that authority right back to Van. But instead, he said only, "This really isn't my area of expertise, Herald Vanyel. Would you mind having a look here?"

Van nodded. Beside him, Stef shivered, and pulled his cloak a little tighter. Vanyel knelt down beside the white-faced Heir, and examined the body without visible sign of emotion, though he wanted to weep for the poor old man. "The neck is broken, and the front of the skull as well," he said quietly. He looked up, though all he could see of the top of the tower was the dark shape of it against the sky. "Kilchas has an observatory up on the top of this tower," he told Treven. "Did he say anything about going up there tonight?"

Another pair of Heralds had joined them; Tantras and Lissandra; Lissandra huddled in on herself, as though she was too cold for her cloak to warm her. "Oh, gods," the woman said brokenly. "Yes, he told me that he was going up there if it cleared at all tonight. Phryny was conjuncting Aberdene's Eye, or some such thing. Only happens once in a hundred years, and he wanted to see it. He was so excited when it cleared up at sunset—" She sobbed, and turned away, hiding her face on Tran's shoulder. He folded his cloak around her, and looked down at the three kneeling in the snow.

"Poor old man," Tantras said hoarsely. "He must have gotten so wrapped up in what he was doing that he forgot to watch his step."

"There're probably ice patches all over the top of that tower," Trev replied, "and the parapet is only knee-high. It's only enough to warn you that you're at the edge, not save you from falling." He stood up, folding dignity around himself like a new cloak that was over-large, stiff, and a trifle awkward. "Guard, would you please see that Kilchas' body is taken to the Chapel? I'll inform Joshel, and have him see to what's needed from there." The Guardsman stood up, saluted, and trudged toward the Guard quarters, leaving the lantern behind. Before too long his dark blue uniform had been absorbed into the night.

Treven turned to Vanyel. "Thank you, Herald Vanyel. If Tantras and

Lissandra don't mind, I'll have them stay with me to get things taken care of. You've just come in from a long journey, and you should get some rest." He coughed uncomfortably, as if he wasn't sure what to say or do next.

Vanyel started to object, but realized that he didn't have any grounds for objection. It *looked* like an accident. Everyone else accepted it as an accident.

But Van didn't—couldn't—believe that it was.

Nevertheless, all he had to go on were vague and ill-defined feelings. Nothing even concrete enough for a Herald to accept.

So he thanked Treven—to Stefen's quite open relief—and returned across the crusted snow to the warmth and light of the Herald's Wing.

He was at the door, when Yfandes Mindtouched him. *:Van,:* she said, sounding troubled. *:We've found Kilchas' Companion, Rohan. He's dead. He was off in the far Western corner of the Field.:*

:And?: he prompted her.

:And I don't like it. There's no sign of anything wrong, but I don't like it. We just don't—fall over like that. Unless we die in battle or by accident, we're Called, and we generally have time to say good-bye to our friends before we go.:

: Could the shock of his Chosen dying like that have killed Rohan?: Van asked.

: May be,: she replied reluctantly. *:Most of the others think that's what did it.:*

:But you're not convinced.: It was kind of comforting that she shared his doubts.

:I'm not convinced. It doesn't feel right. I can't pinpoint why, but it doesn't.:

"Van, are you going to stand there all night?" Stef asked, holding the door open and shivering visibly.

"Sorry, *ashke*," Vanyel said giving himself a little mental kick. "I was talking to 'Fandes. The others found Kilchas' Companion. Dead. She says it doesn't feel right to her."

The heat of the corridor hit him and made him want to lie down right then and there. He fought the urge and the attendant weakness. Stefen looked at him with puzzlement. "I thought that Companions never outlived their Chosen," he said. "And vice versa. So what's wrong?"

"'Fandes just doesn't like the way it seems to have happened—Rohan was off by himself in the farthest corner of the Field, and none of the others knew he was gone until they found him."

Stefen looked disturbed. "That's not the way things are supposed to happen," he replied slowly. "At least not the way I understand them. I think you're both right. There's at least something odd about this."

Van reached the door of his room first, and held it open for the Bard. "It may just be the new Web-spell," he said as he closed the door behind them, took off his cloak, and flung it into a chair. "It's supposed to bind us all together; some of that may be spilling over in unexpected ways, like onto our Companions."

Stefen draped his own cloak on top of Vanyel's. "Here," he offered. "Let me help you out of that tunic and go lie down; we can talk about this while I give you a better massage than the one that was interrupted. I'll play opposition, and try to find logical explanations for everything you find wrong."

"Stef, I'm absolutely exhausted," Vanyel warned, unlacing his tunic and allowing Stef to pull it off. "If you really get me relaxed, I'll probably fall asleep in the middle of it. And once I do, you wouldn't be able to wake me with an earthquake."

"If that's what you need, then that's what you should do," the Bard replied, pushing him a little so that he sat down—or rather, collapsed—onto the bed. "Meanwhile, let me get the knots out of you while we talk about this. Why don't you pull 'Fandes into this, too? If she's worried, you probably should, anyway, and she may find holes in *my* arguments."

:'Fandes?: Van called.

:Here—:

:Want to listen in on this? We're going to try and see if I'm just overreacting to Kilchas' death because of exhaustion.:

:Neatly put, and that could be my problem, too. Go ahead. I'll be listening.: She sounded relieved.

Vanyel yielded to Stef's wishes, and sprawled facedown on the bed. Stefen straddled him and reached into the top drawer of the little bedside table.

"What—" Vanyel began, turning his head to look; then when Stefen pulled out a little bottle of what was obviously scented oil, asked in surprise, "How did that get in there?"

"I put it there," Stef said shortly. "Get your head back down and relax." In a few moments, his warm hands were slowly working their way upward along Van's spine, starting from the small of his back. Vanyel sighed, and gave himself up to it.

"Now, what doesn't fit in the way Kilchas died?" Stef asked. "And don't you start tensing up on me. You can think *and* stay relaxed."

"Kilchas has a little enclosure up there," Van said, thinking things through, slowly. "The roof is glass. If he doesn't want to, he doesn't *have* to go out in the cold. I can't see why he would have been outside, and he certainly wasn't dressed for the cold."

"What if the glass was covered with snow or ice?" Stef countered. "It probably was, you know."

:I agree,: Yfandes said reluctantly. :Everything else was.:

"Good point. But why was he wearing slippers, rather than boots?"

Stefen rolled his knuckles along either side of Vanyel's spine while he thought. "Because he didn't know the glass was going to be iced over until he'd already climbed the stairs to the roof, and it was too far for him to climb down and back up again just for his boots. He was an old man, after all, and his quarters are down here on the ground floor."

Van gasped as Stef hit a particularly sore spot. "All right, I can accept that, too. But he's had that observatory for years. He always knows—knew—exactly where he is up there. Why should he suddenly misstep now?"

"Because he didn't," Stef answered immediately. "He was doing something he'd never had to do before. He was cleaning the glass on the roof of his little shelter, trying to chip the ice off. He lost his balance, or he slipped."

:That sounds just like Kilchas. Stubborn old goat.:

Vanyel tried not to tense as Stef hit another bad knot and began working it out. "Why not get a servant to do it?" he asked.

"No time?" Stef hazarded, as the fire in the fireplace cracked and popped. "This thing he was going to be watching—it would have been about to happen, and he figured if he had to find a servant, then wait for him to do the job, he'd miss part of what he wanted to see. Either that, or he was sure a servant wouldn't do it right. Or both."

:That sounds like Kilchas, too,:

The air filled with the gentle scent of sendlewood. Vanyel felt sleep trying to overcome him and fought it off. "If he just fell—" he said, slowly, "Why, when I felt him die, did I only feel pain? Why didn't I feel him fall?"

"I don't know," Stef said, pausing with his hand just over Van's shoulderblades. "I don't know how these Gifts of yours are supposed to work. But Kilchas was an old man, Van. What if he was already dead when he fell? What if his heart gave out on him? That's pretty painful, I guess. And if his heart suddenly gave out, couldn't that cause his Companion's to do the same? Maybe that's why he was found the way he was."

Vanyel closed his eyes, suddenly too tired to try to find something wrong with what appeared to be a perfectly ordinary situation.

"You're probably right," he said, :'Fandes, do you agree?:

:Quite reasonable,: she said, wearily. *:That's very typical of heart-failure; the shock goes straight to us, too. And Kilchas' Rohan was as old as he was. That's a much more logical explanation than foul play—it's just that so few of you live long enough these days for your hearts to fail that I forgot that. I think we may be overreacting because we're tired and we're so used to treachery and ambush that we ignore other answers, love.:*

"'Fandes agrees with you—" he began; then Stef started something that had nothing to do with a therapeutic massage, and he murmured a little exclamation of surprise.

"Have we disposed of the topic, *ashke*?" Stef asked, breathing the words into his ear, his chest pressed against Vanyel's back.

:I think,: Yfandes said tactfully, *:that it's time for me to get some sleep. Good night, dearheart,:*

:Good night, love,: he replied—then his attention was taken elsewhere.

And it was quite a while before either he or Stefen actually slept.

CHAPTER 15

VANYEL FORGOT ALL about his misgivings in the weeks that followed. His time was devoured by Council meetings, Audience sessions
where he and Treven stood as proxies for Randale, and long-distance spell-
casting. Desperation at being unable to be two places at once had led him
to discover that he could work magic *through* a Herald without the Mage-
Gift, provided that the Herald in question was both a Thoughtsenser and
carried Mage-Gift in potential. He immersed himself in the nodes so often
he began to feel very much akin to the *Tayledras*.

He often returned to his room at night long past the hour when sane folk
retired. When he did so, he found Stef invariably curled up sleepily next to
the fire, light from the flames making a red glow in his hair, for he refused
to take his own rest until Van returned. The Bard's patient care was the one
constant in his life besides Yfandes, and as fall deepened into winter, he
came to rely more and more on both of them, just to keep a hold on sanity
and optimism in a world increasingly devoid of both.

Karse *had* declared holy war on the "evil mages of Valdemar," though as
yet they had done nothing about it. The agents both the Lord Marshal and
the Seneschal had in place reported that the Prophet-King (as he styled
himself) had his hands full with rooting out "heresy" in his own land. But
no one was under any delusions; the consensus was that as soon as the followers of the Sun Lord needed an outside enemy to unify what was left of
the populace, there would be an army of fanatics hammering the Southern
Border.

That would only add to the bandits who had taken over the buffer zone
between the two countries, motley bands of brigands who had escaped or
been turned loose during the revolution, those who had been accused of
magery and fled their homes but had declined to cross the Border, and op-
portunists who preyed on both sides.

"At least there won't be any mages in the Prophet's pay," the Seneschal said, as they all leaned over the maps and tried to find weak points in their defenses.

"Maybe," the Archpriest replied dubiously. His tour of the south had garnered mixed results. On the whole he was happy with the outcome, for his presence had kept any overt activities to a minimum. The net result, however, was that there were no enclaves of the Sun Lord in Valdemar anymore. Roughly half of the devotees had been so revolted by the Father-House's actions that they had converted to some other way. The rest had decamped across the Border to Karse, to join their fellows. The holdings themselves had gone to those who had remained behind, thus staying in the hands of those who had remained loyal to Valdemar.

Supposedly loyal, at any rate. Both the Seneschal and the Archpriest were keeping a wary eye on them in case some of these "conversions" were intended as a ruse, to cover later subversion. That there were spies planted in the midst of these enclaves was a given.

"What do you mean, 'maybe'?" asked the Seneschal, hand poised above a marker representing a Guard detachment.

"What's the difference between a miracle and a magic spell?" the Archpriest asked, looking from Arved to Van and back again.

"A miracle comes from the gods; magic comes from a mage," the Seneschal replied impatiently.

"That's purely subjective," the Archpriest pointed out. "To the layman, there is no discernible difference. The Prophet can easily have mages *within* his own ranks, claim their powers are from the Sun Lord, and be completely within strict doctrinal boundaries."

"Damn. You're right," the Lord Marshal said softly. "I wonder how many he *does* have?"

"There's no way of knowing," Vanyel replied, as they all turned to look at him. "I *don't* think he has anyone a Herald couldn't counter, though. My operatives aren't reporting any 'miracles' other than Healing and the odd illusion, not even when the Prophet's Children are trying to capture mages. The powerful mages in the pay and employ of the Karsite Crown were all known as such, and have either been killed or fled the country. That's not to say that the Mage-Gifted won't end up in the Sun Lord's priesthood in the future; I'd virtually guarantee that. But they won't get effective training, because there won't be anyone experienced enough to train them thoroughly, and they probably won't be permitted to use their Gift combatively."

"Why not?" the Archpriest asked.

Van smiled thinly, and fingered a marker representing an agent. "Because if they learn what they can do, what's to stop them from declaring *themselves* the chosen of the God and doing exactly what the Prophet did?"

"Only with more success, because they have 'miracles' to prove their power," the Archpriest mused, his eyes half-closed. "Interesting speculation. It's fortunate that you are on our side, Vanyel."

Van bowed with intended irony. "A Herald tends to be altogether too well acquainted with the ways of treachery for anyone's comfort. including his own, my lord," he said. "One could say that it is part of the job."

"To know, and not use?" The Archpriest's smile was genuine and his eyes warmed with it. "I am aware of that, my son. I think that most of you would have been comfortable within the ranks of the clergy had there been no Companions to Choose you."

"Most?" Vanyel chuckled, knowing the Archpriest was blissfully unaware of his relationship with Stefen. "Some, maybe, but I assure you, my lord, not all. By no means all. We are far too worldly for most orders to ever accept us!"

He would have said more, but suddenly—

His eyes burned. A giant hand closed itself around his chest, as his lungs caught fire. He tried to breathe, and only increased the pain. His heart spasmed, once, twice—then exploded.

He found himself sprawled facedown over the table, the rest of the Councillors, his father among them, frantically trying to revive him. He stared at the lines of the map just under his nose, unable to remember what they were.

"Vanyel!"

He was very cold, and his chest hurt.

"Turn him over you fools, he can't breathe!"

He blinked as the shadows danced around him, trying to recall exactly where—and who—he was.

:Van?: Yfandes said weakly, making a confusion of voices inside his head and out. *:Are you all right?:*

"What's wrong? What happened? Has he ever had a spell like this before?"

He stirred, dazed, the map-paper under him crackling.

The Council meeting. I was in the Council meeting.

:Van?: A little more urgent.

:'Fandes. Give me a moment. . . .:

"What—" he gasped. He tried to push himself away from the table, but his arms were too weak and trembling, and he was too dazed to even think of what to do. Someone—two someones—grabbed his arms, one on either side, and pulled him up. Trev and Joshel; they lowered him into a chair—

Just as the Death Bell began tolling.

Lissandra—He knew it, even as the other two looked at each other over his head and spoke the name simultaneously.

"You go," Treven told Joshel. "Find out what happened." He shook Vanyel's shoulder gently. "Is that what you Felt? Is that what happened to you just now?"

Vanyel nodded, and schooled himself to reply. "I—yes. Something very painful, very sudden. Like what happened with Kilchas, only worse." He shuddered. "I don't understand—why am I Feeling them die? Why is this happening to me, and no one else?"

"Maybe because you set the spell," Treven hazarded. "The rest of us know what happens after the fact, but you feel it at the time. Or maybe it's happening just because the two of them were in the original Web with you. Or because they're close by physically. We haven't had any Herald deaths at Haven but Kilchas and Lissandra."

"I suppose. . . ." He put his head down on his knees, still dizzy. "A lot of good I'm going to be if I black out every time a Herald dies." He was still in too much quasi-physical pain and too much in shock to feel the emotional impact of the other Herald-Mage's death.

:'Fandes? What about her Companion?:

:We're looking,: Yfandes said shortly. *:Shonsea dropped out of our minds just as you Felt Lissandra die. Are you going to be all right?:*

:I think so—I—:

:We found her,: Yfandes interrupted. *:The northern end of the Field. It looks as though she was running, and fell and broke her neck.:*

Vanyel sighed and closed his eyes. *:If she felt what I did, I'm not surprised it came as enough of a shock to make her fall. Something horrendous happened, whatever it was.:*

His head throbbed with aftershock, and it was increasingly hard to think. He raised his head with an effort when Joshel came back into the Council Chamber, coughing.

"It looks like she had an accident with her alchemical apparatus," Joshe said. "When we got to her chamber, it was full of fumes of some kind. We had to open a window to clear them out. Look—"

He held up a glass jar; it was frosted on the outside.

"That's what those fumes did closest to the spill; ate into things. We found a container of some kind over a small firepot had broken. That was where the fumes were coming from. All we can guess is that it cracked and spilled the stuff into the fire, and Lissandra breathed in a fatal dose before she could get the window open."

"It Felt like my lungs were on fire," Vanyel said. "I couldn't breathe, and my eyes were burning."

"She might not even have been able to see to get the window open," Joshe continued. "As corrosive as those fumes were, she must have been nearly blind. We found her halfway between her workbench and the door."

Lissandra should have known better than to work with something that dangerous in her chamber, Vanyel thought vaguely. *What on earth possessed her to do such a thing? The still-room at Healer's Collegium has adequate ventilation against accidents, and she hasn't got any secrets from the Healers. . . .*

But his head was pounding, and he couldn't seem to get any further than that.

"I need to get something for my head," he said thickly, getting to his feet. Treven looked at him in concern.

"This hit you awfully hard," he said. "I know you've been overworking. Do you want to take this session up later?"

He shook his head. "No," he replied. "We haven't the time to spare. You have Audiences right after this, then Randi has a private Audience session with the Rethwellan ambassador. I'll be all right."

Treven smiled weakly. "You always are," he said with gratitude. "I don't know what we'd do without you."

"Someday you'll *have* to do without me," Van reminded him grimly. "I'm not immortal. Well, let's get on with this. My operatives say the next move will be for Karse to declare holy war on Rethwellan, too, trusting that the mountains will keep the Queen from coming at them."

"The more fools, they," the Lord Marshal replied. "Here's what she's pledged us if they make a move like that. . . ."

The fire in Savil's room hissed and popped at them, and the late-afternoon sun shone weakly down on the gardens outside the window. Van sat back in his chair and tried not to look as if he were tired of hearing his aunt's plaints.

"I don't like it," Savil said fretfully. "First Kilchas, then Lissandra. Both of them Herald-Mages. It's no accident."

"What else could it be?" Vanyel asked reasonably, rubbing one of his shoulders. He was still stiff and sore from his fit this afternoon. "We've been all over that. No one found anything out of the ordinary. No signs of tampering, magical or otherwise. Just the result of miscalculation."

A coal fell down to the grate, and a shower of sparks followed it.

"I still don't like it," she replied, stubbornly shaking her head. "What if the tampering wasn't with their equipment, but with *them*—their minds or their bodies? A Healer could easily have stopped Kilchas' heart. A Mindhealer could have made Lissandra think she was putting something harmless on the fire. You'd never detect that kind of tampering."

She's getting old, he thought sadly. *She's getting old, and frightened of everything.* In her oversized, overstuffed chair she looked thinner, and terribly frail. There were lines in her face that had never been there until this winter. It seemed that, like the *Tayledras*, she was failing all at once. *She's aged more in the last six months than in the last six years.* "Savil, love, why would a Healer do something like that?" he asked. "It just isn't logical."

"You don't have to be a Healer to have Healing Gifts," she countered. "You have them; so do I. Moondance *is* a Healing Adept. It could be a rogue mage with the Gift. A kind of anti-Healer."

Great good gods. Now she's inventing enemies. Whoever heard of anything like that? "All right, then," he replied patiently. "*Who?* We've no indication that anyone is using mages against Valdemar right now."

She frowned. "What about the one that nearly killed you?"

"There's no sign of that kind of magical attack in either Kilchas' death or Lissandra's," he reminded her. "And the attempt on me was not directed at Valdemar. I think that must have been a purely personal vendetta and nothing more. I've made a lot of enemies in the last few years, and it's all too likely to have been one of them."

"Van," she said unhappily, "I'm worried. I think it's stretching coincidence—first the incident with you, then Kilchas is killed, then Lissandra. Please listen to me—"

Vanyel sighed. "I'll tell you what, Aunt Savil. If it'll make you feel more confident, I'll strengthen your wards. But I don't think they need it. You're an eminently capable mage, as you very well know—you're *my* superior at ritual magics. Kilchas was very old and inclined to try and do things he shouldn't because he was stubborn. Lissandra worked with very dangerous substances all the time. The odds just caught up with both of them."

Savil scowled at him, and the fire hissed as if it felt her anger. "Vanyel Ashkevron, you're being more than usually dense. If I were ten years younger—"

Abruptly she deflated, and shrank back down into her chair. "But I'm not," she said sadly. "I'm older than Kilchas, and just as vulnerable. I'm holding you to your promise, Van. Strengthen my wards. I'll take any help I can get, because I believe I will be the next target and I can't get anyone else to agree with me, not even you."

Vanyel stood up, feeling guilty. "Savil, I don't blame you for overreacting. You knew both of the others better than I did. I'll be happy to strengthen your wards as soon as I get a moment free, and I'm absolutely certain that in a few more weeks we'll be laughing about this."

"I hope so," Savil said unhappily as he moved toward the door. "I truly hope so."

He stifled a surge of annoyance, and bade her good night as affectionately as he could manage. It wouldn't cost him more than a candlemark and a little energy to strengthen her wards, and if it made her less paranoid, it was worth it.

He closed the door behind himself, and literally ran into Stefen in the hall outside.

"I hope you're through for the day," the Bard said in a weary voice as he caught Vanyel's arm. "Because I certainly am. It's my turn to need a backrub. The Rethwellan ambassador wouldn't talk unless I was out of the room and Randale couldn't sit up unless I was *in* the room, so they compromised by sticking me in a closet."

Vanyel chuckled tiredly, and put his arm around Stefen's shoulders. "Nobody has me scheduled for anything more, and I'm not inclined to let them know I'm free. Let's go; I'll give you that backrub."

"More than a backrub, I hope," Stef said, shyly.

"I think I might be able to manage that," Vanyel said into the Bard's ear.

"Good," Stef said. "I'll hold you to that. . . ."

Later, much later, as Vanyel drifted off to sleep, he remembered what he had promised Savil.

Oh, well, he thought drowsily. *I can take care of it tomorrow. It's not that urgent. And I didn't promise exactly when I'd do it, just that I would when I got some free time.*

The fire had burned down to coals, with a few flames flickering now and again above them, and Stef was already asleep, his head resting on Vanyel's shoulder. It was the first moment of peace together they'd had since returning from Forst Reach—the first entire evening they'd been able to spend together without either of them being utterly exhausted or worried about something.

And it was the first evening Van hadn't had to spend in the nodes, drawing energy for later use, or channeling it elsewhere.

He stroked Stef's silky, fine hair, and the Bard murmured a little in his sleep. *I'm not going to spoil it now. It can wait until morning.*

He watched the fire through half-closed eyes, listening to Stef breathe, and waited for sleep to take him.

Then the peace of the evening shattered.

:VANYEL!:

He was out of bed and grabbing his clothes before Stef woke.

:VAN—:

Savil's cry was cut off, abruptly, and Vanyel doubled up and fell to the floor—

Pain—

—knives of fire slicing him from neck to crotch—

—lungs aching for air—

—teeth fastening in his throat—

Then, nothing—

He found himself gasping for breath, curled in a fetal position on the floor, Stefen staring at him from the bed with his eyes wide with fear. It had felt like an eternity, yet it had taken only a few heartbeats from the moment Savil called him until now.

Savil!

He grabbed his robe from the floor beside him where he had dropped it and struggled to his feet, pulling it on. He burst out the door and ran down the corridor—joined by every other Herald in the wing just as the Death Bell tolled. *This* time he hadn't been the only one to feel the death-struggle.

And this time there was no doubt. This was no accident.

Savil's door was locked; Vanyel kicked it open. His aunt lay in the center of a circle of destruction; furniture overturned, lamps knocked over, papers scattered. Blood everywhere. Some of the others, Herald-trainees who had probably never seen violent death before, gasped and turned green—or blanched and fled.

Claw and teethmarks on Savil's throat and torso showed that she'd put up a fight. A trail of greenish ichor and a broken-bladed knife told that her enemy had not escaped unscathed.

But there was no sign of it, and the trail ended at the locked door.

Not that it mattered to him. The damage was already done, and this time Vanyel's hard-won detachment failed entirely. While the others checked the locks, and looked for clues or any sign of what had attacked her, he sank down to his knees beside the body, and took one limp hand in his—and wept.

Oh, gods—Savil, you were right, and I didn't listen to you. Now you're gone, and it's all my fault. . . .

Some of the others stopped what they were doing, and looked at him with pity and concern. Very few of them had ever seen Vanyel emerge from behind the cool mask of the first-ranked Herald-Mage of Valdemar. Fewer still had seen him break down like this, especially in public. He had heard that he had a reputation for such coolness and self-isolation that even fellow Heralds seemed to think nothing could crack his icy calm.

They were finding out differently now. "She—thought someone was—targeting the Herald-Mages," he said brokenly, to no one in particular. "She was afraid she was going to be next; she asked me to help her, and I just thought she was being hysterical. I promised to strengthen her wards, and I didn't; I forgot. This is all my fault—"

She's never going to sit there in her chair and expound at me again. I can't ever ask her for advice. She'll never take on Father for me—she was my mother in every-thing but flesh, and I failed her, I failed her, when I'd promised to help her.

He hung his head, and closed his eyes, choking down the sob that rose and cut off his breathing.

Savil, Savil, I'm so sorry—and sorry isn't enough. Sorry won't bring you back.

Tears escaped from under his closed eyelids, and etched their way down his cheeks. He couldn't swallow; he could hardly breathe.

A hand touched his shoulder. He looked up, slowly, through eyes that burned and vision that wavered with tears.

"Van?" Tantras said quietly. "I know you're in no shape to do anything, but you're the only Herald-Mage left, and we can't check all the magical locks she had to see if they were violated."

He blinked, then reckoned up in his head all the deaths over the last couple of years.

Oh, gods—I'm not just the only Herald-Mage they have left here, *I'm the very* last *Herald-Mage. There aren't any more but me.*

He wiped the back of his hand across his eyes and rose slowly to his feet. "Clear everyone out," he said in a low, and deadly calm voice, as a coldness settled in his heart and icy anger steadied his thoughts. "I'll need some room to work."

The wards weren't violated. Van stood in the middle of the room and scanned every inch of it with Mage-Sight. The wards were fading now that Savil was dead, but they were still strong enough to read. She had warded all four directions, above and below, weaving protection atop protection, and all glowed with the bright blue that meant no strand and no connection had been broken, and the only hole was the one he himself had made when he broke down the door.

The wards weren't violated. The locks and locking-spells are all intact. Whatever it was came in before *she set the wards.*

What was the damned thing, anyway?

There was still a trace of the greenish ichor left, more than enough to identify the creature if it was something Vanyel had encountered before this. But it wasn't; it wasn't even close to anything he knew, and the magical signature it had left behind when it broke the spell that gave it its disguise was entirely new.

It's intelligent, he decided. *It has to be. And it's not Abyssal, or I'd at least recognize that much of its signature, which only leaves one possibility. It's created, or it's from the Pelagirs. Or both—*

His only option now was to try alone what he and Savil and the two *Tayledras* had done together; try to See into the immediate past. He wouldn't have tried it if he hadn't seen it done by an expert, and if the time he wanted to See hadn't been so recent, he wouldn't have been able to do it alone.

The longer he waited, the fainter the traces would be. His best chance at discovering anything would be to cast the spell now, this instant.

You son of a bitch, whoever, whatever you are, you're not getting away! I'm going to hunt you down if it takes me the rest of my life—

He sat down on the cold, bare floor, next to where Savil had been found, and tapped recklessly into the node far below Haven. His need, anger, and sorrow drove him deeper into it than he had ever been or dared to go before; he grasped the raw power with unflinching "hands," manipulating it like soft, half-molten iron. He forged it into the spell on the anvil of his will and tuned it to himself through the medium of his mage-focus. Then he cast it loose.

When he opened his eyes, the room was as he had left it when he'd last seen Savil alive. He was sitting just beside Savil's big chair; it was early evening by the thin light coming in the windows, and she didn't seem to be in the room. *This must be just after I met Stef,* he thought, and guilt ate at him, acid in his wounds of loss. The wards were *not* up. And there was nothing in the room that did not belong there.

Vanyel froze the moment and searched everywhere, even behind and underneath the furniture. Nothing. Everything was entirely as it should be.

He gritted his teeth and let time proceed again, waiting as the twilight deepened and became true night; as one of the servants came in, lighting the lamps and leaving fresh candles in the sconces. Another brought in a heavy load of wood, and fueled the fire. Nothing at *all* out of the ordinary—

Wait a moment!

He froze the time-stream again, and examined the candles, minutely, with Mage-Sight.

Nothing at all odd about the candles—but when he turned his Sight on the wood, the entire pile glowed an evil green, and when he dug deeper at it, the wood gave him the same signature as the ichor.

But it wasn't enough; not quite. He needed to see how the thing had looked when it dropped its disguise, and where it had gone afterward.

He forced himself to let the time-stream start up again; his heart lurched when he saw Savil enter the room. *No, not now,* he told himself, forcing himself to be cold and unemotional. *It's not the time for that—not while I'm tapping a node. I can't afford to give up concentration for emotion.*

He regained control over himself, just as his aunt turned away from him and put up her wards.

Even though he was watching the woodpile, he didn't see it actually change; the creature was that fast. He froze time again; catching it in mid-leap and Savil in mid-turn.

Well, at least I'm not slipping, he thought, still locked in that icy detachment. *That creature isn't anything I've ever encountered before.* It was mostly like a raven, but with toothed beak, evil red eyes, and powerful legs that ended in feet bearing knife-sharp, hand-sized talons.

Not even the *Tayledras* knew all of the creatures that roamed the Pelagirs, but somehow this bird-thing didn't have the feeling of anything natural—if that word could ever be applied to a beast from that magic-haunted area. Still, the bird looked wrong; the teeth were too long for it to be able to actually eat with them, and those claws were no good for anything except rending. Certainly it couldn't perch on anything like a tree limb with those talons. And how would it feed young?

Vanyel could not leave his own position, but he could let the beast continue its leap, little by little, until he could see all of it. He did so, steadfastly ignoring the look of fear on his aunt's face, the panic as she realized she could not ready a blast of mage-energy before it reached her. It was thumb-lengths away from her when he stopped the thing again, and close examination of the rear proved what he had suspected. It had no genital slit; in fact, it had nothing at all, not even a vent. It was as featureless behind as a feather-covered egg.

It was a construct, a one-of-a-kind, probably created specifically for this task out of a real raven. The only way it could obtain nourishment would be magically; it was utterly dependent on the mage that created it, and there would be no young that might escape the mage's control. That meant that the mage who had targeted Savil was at the least more ruthless than Vanyel, and very likely more powerful as well.

Power doesn't count for everything, Vanyel thought, clenching his jaw on a rising tide of anger. *There's skill, and there's how much you're willing to pay for what you want. I want this bastard, and I don't intend to lose him.*

He sped up the time-stream, skipping ahead to the moment when Savil was already dead and he had started to kick in the doorway. He watched dispassionately as the bird-thing, wounded and bleeding, again assumed its guise of a pile of wood, this time beside the door. He watched as he allowed himself to be overcome with grief, and the creature took that moment of distraction to slip out the door.

He tracked it as it fled from the Palace by the first exit. It paused just long enough to attack one lone Companion, down and in shock with the loss of her Chosen—the others came to Kellan's aid, but too late. The thing rose up in triumph and fled, its talons and beak red with the mingled blood of Herald and Companion, while the rest of the herd shrieked their impotent anger after it.

And still he tracked it. North. North for several days' ride, on wings sped by more magic, until it dropped back down to earth, exhausted and weakened by its injury. He sensed from its primitive thoughts that it was going to stay there for at least a week, healing. It knew it was safe enough. No one knew it was there . . . and no one could follow it that quickly.

That was all he could bear to see. He let loose his control of the spell, and it dissolved away, leaving him sitting alone in the middle of the empty, ruined room, with dawn just beginning to color the sky outside the windows, and Stefen huddled in a cloak just inside the door.

"They t-told me not to disturb you," the Bard stuttered, looking pale and wan in the thin, gray light. "But nobody said I couldn't wait here until you w-were done. Van, I'm sorry, I w-wish I could do something—"

"You can," Vanyel replied shortly. "You can guard the door and keep everyone else out." There was hurt in Stef's eyes at his coldness, but he ignored it.

:'Fandes?: he called.

The rage in her mind-voice colored everything a bloody red. :Gods damn them to the lowest hells! That thing got Kellan on its way out, Van—:

:I know that,: he interrupted. :And I'm about to extract a little revenge right now. Will you link and cover my back while I go hunting?:

:Hunt away,: she snarled. :I'm right behind you.:

That was all the assurance he needed. Once again he dove into the node, pulled in all the raw power he could hold through the buffering effect of his amber focus, and launched himself out again with all his channels scorched and tender but still perfectly functional.

He knew the general area where the thing had gone to earth, and he still had that trace of ichor to use to find its exact location. While he had that bit of the beast's life-fluid, it could never escape him, no matter how many disguises it assumed, or how much magic it called up to cloak its presence.

With Yfandes guarding his back. he knew he needn't waste half his energy watching for ambush; he tracked the thing into its hiding place with infinite patience. He still had his tap into the node; he could afford whatever expense of power it took to find the construct.

When he found it, he also found something else; it had shielding far more powerful than he had expected. The creature's master wanted it back, evidently, which made it all the more valuable to Vanyel. His resources were already stretched thin by distance; he couldn't smash through those shields at this range.

But he didn't need to. . . .

It was protected against "real" magic, not Mind-magic. And one of his Gifts was Fetching—with all of the power of the node to back him. Because

he had both real and Mind-magic, he could fuel his mind-powers with
mage-energies as no other Herald could. Which was where his enemy had
made a fundamental misjudgment.

He seized the thing, shields and all; belatedly it tried to escape, but it hadn't
a chance at that point and its master hadn't given it the ability to call for help. It
had been too late for the creature to escape the moment he knew its physical
location. As it struggled, he could Feel its rising panic, and he smiled—

And *Pulled.*

:Yes—: Yfandes hissed eagerly in his mind—by no means enough to
distract him; he was used to her commentaries and encouragements in the
back of his thoughts after all these years. *:Yes! Bring it* here *and we'll show them
we're not to be slaughtered at anyone's whim—:*

The thing grabbed on to where it was and resisted his pull; he simply
tapped deeper into the node, ignored the pain, the rivers of fire that ran
along his channels, and pulled harder. He ripped it loose as it shrieked in
desperation; Yfandes supported him as he hauled it in. She cushioned him
from the effects of a reaction-headache, something she'd never done before,
enabling him to fling the creature down right on the spot where it had
killed Savil, and pin it to the floor with raw node-power.

Stefen gave a strangled croak when it appeared, but wisely remained
where he was. Wise—or perhaps frozen with fear; Van Felt the panic coming from him in waves, but had no time to worry about the Bard just now.
While the beast squirmed and screamed both mentally and vocally, he
stripped the protections from its crude thoughts and ripped away every
detail he could concerning its master.

North, the direction it had fled in the first place; the direction no one
expected for an enemy. North, and an impression of the vast wilderness that
could only be the Forest of Wendwinter and the Ice Wall mountains beyond. But of the master himself, nothing; only darkness. After ruthless
probing that left the bird's mind a broken, bleeding rag, Vanyel decided that
this was all the construct had ever seen of its master.

He contemplated the writhing creature at his feet with his mouth set in
a grim line. He had left it a ruin, with nothing remaining to tell it how to
get home, or even how to defend itself. It could no longer work the borrowed magics it had been given, and it might not even remember how to
fly. If he let it go, it would slowly starve itself to death, and its master would
never know what had become of it, or even whether or not it had been
successful in its task.

Even Yfandes' lust for revenge seemed satisfied now; at any rate, she was silent, and her anger no longer seethed at the back of his mind.

But *his* need for vengeance was not filled.

He gathered all the node-power he could handle, poured in channels that burned as hotly as his own need for revenge. He made certain that there was still a line open between the bird and its creator. It was too bad that the line was such a thin one—one that he could not follow to its source. He was going to have to find the perpetrator the hard way.

But the line was enough to punish the master through. . . .

And he smashed the thing with one hammer-blow of pure, wild power.

The construct screamed its agony, and as it died in the cold flames of magic, the energy backlashed up the line Van had left open to its creator.

The scream ended; the thing glowed with the power Van poured into it—then incandesced until it was too bright to look at. And still he fed the fire, until the last of it was eaten away, and there was nothing left but a few wisps of white, feathery ash.

He turned toward Stefen, knowing that at any moment he would feel the effects of what he had just done. Yfandes couldn't protect him from the reaction-headache of overexertion of Mind-magic much longer; it was incredible enough that she'd done it in the first place. And his channels were pure agony that would take several hours of self-Healing to repair.

The Bard stared at him, his eyes wide and frightened, his face pale as skimmed milk. "W-what did y-you do th-that for?" he whispered, looking at Vanyel as if he expected the Herald to lash out at him next.

"I sent a message," Vanyel said quietly. "One that can't be mistaken for anything but what it is. A challenge, and a warning. Whoever did this, whoever murdered Savil, is going to pay for it with his own life. Because this wasn't a personal vendetta; this bastard is the same one that's responsible for Kilchas' death, and Lissandra's and probably made the attempt on me as well. So it's a threat to Valdemar, and as such, I am going to eliminate the source of the threat."

The reaction-headache hit then; he brought one hand slowly to his head and swayed a little. Stef was instantly at his side, supporting him.

He recalled the hurt in Stefen's eyes when he'd cut him off earlier, and grimaced. "Stef," he said, awkwardly. "I'm sorry. I loved Savil, she was— she was—" He couldn't continue; tears interrupted him.

"She was the most remarkable and sweetest old bitch the gods ever created," Stef replied angrily, with tears in his own eyes. "There's never going to be anyone to match her. Whoever did this to her—I want his hide, too. Not as much as you do, but I want it too, and I'll do anything I can to help you get it." He held Vanyel, half supporting him, half embracing him. "It's all right, I understand."

Vanyel shook his aching head. "I just hope you can keep understanding, Stef," he said through the pain, "because this isn't finished yet. It isn't even close."

CHAPTER 16

V ANYEL HAD CONVENED the entire Council as soon as he was able to speak coherently. The *entire* Council, including Randale, which meant that they met in his bedroom with Shavri in attendance.

Four stone walls surrounded them; like the Work Room, the Royal Bedchamber was an interior room, entirely windowless. Hard on Randi, who seldom got to see the sun anymore—but mandated by security. Assassins can't climb in the window if there aren't any windows.

The room was warm, but not stifling. For the sake of appearances, Randi had been moved from his bed to a couch, one as soft and comfortable as his bed, but with a padded back so that he could sit up with full support. The rest of the Councillors brought in chairs from the outer rooms of the suite, and arranged them around the couch with no regard for rank.

Most of them took in Vanyel's pronouncement—framed as a request—with a stunned silence.

All but the King.

"Absolutely not," Randale said, actually sitting up in alarm. His voice sounded stronger than it had in months. Shavri paled a little and clutched the side of the couch. "We can't possibly spare you."

"You can't afford not to let me go, Randale," Vanyel replied tightly, keeping a rein on his temper. "Whoever this is, whatever his motive, he's been targeting Heralds, and that makes him an enemy of Valdemar. And if he can pick Herald-Mages off from *outside* the Border, he can pick off anyone, including you, any time he chooses."

He'd hoped that personal threat would give the King pause, but Randale didn't hesitate a second. "That's not a factor. What is a factor is that you are the *last* Herald-Mage. Who's going to train the youngsters with the Mage-Gift? Who would even know what the Mage-Gift *looks* like? And who is going to counter attacks by mage-craft on the Border if you aren't here?"

"To answer the last question first," Van replied, "Heralds. 'Ordinary'

Heralds. They're not only capable of it; I've managed to convince them that they *can*, which was no mean feat."

"He has trained several Heralds in just that already," Joshel said reluctantly. "And we've learned from our operatives that there aren't any mages on the Karsite side anymore; at least, none with any power. After declaring magic anathema, *they* won't have anyone to train mages either—"

"As for the youngsters—" Van continued, grimly, "In case you hadn't noticed, no one has had any trainees with Mage-Gift for the past two years. It was never that common to begin with, and it seems to be appearing entirely in potential now."

"Only in potential?" Shavri said, looking shocked, her glance going from Vanyel to Joshel and back again. "But—why? What's happened?"

Van shrugged, and rubbed his thumb nervously along the arm of his chair. "I don't know—but consider this—so far as I can tell, this enemy has picked Herald-*Mages* as his targets. What if he's been making his job easier by killing the children with the Mage-Gift before they can be Chosen? It wouldn't be that hard. All you'd have to do is wait for the Gift to manifest and send something to cause an 'accident.' No one would ever guess that the deaths were connected in any way."

"That makes it all the more imperative that you stay—" Shavri began, her face settling into a stubborn scowl.

"That makes it all the more imperative that I *go*," Vanyel countered, pounding the arm of his chair with his fist. "What am I supposed to do, tap into the nodes and sit around scanning the entire countryside, waiting for some spell or creature to target an unknown child somewhere? I don't even know if that's what's happening—and if it is, how do I stop it?" His throat tightened with grief and guilt, but he forced himself to continue. "The thing that got Savil spirited itself *into* the Palace, in *Haven*, and killed an experienced Herald-Mage under our very noses! Dear gods, she called to me for help, and I'm just down the hall from her and I was *still* too late to save her! How in the seven hells am I supposed to catch this enemy again when I not only don't know where and when he'll strike, but who? I *have* to carry the fight to him; it's the only way to neutralize him. And if we don't—he has to have a larger plan, he can't be doing this for the fun of it. Do we wait for him to be ready to make his move, or do we take him *before* he's ready? Which is better tactics?"

"I can't argue tactics with you, Vanyel," Shavri said resentfully, as Randale collapsed back against his cushions, "but I can't see what good it's going to do you, us, *or* Valdemar to go haring off into the unknown after some nebulous enemy who may just be—"

Vanyel was about to interrupt her, when Yfandes stopped him. *:Hold your temper, Van,:* she said firmly. *:We're behind you. And we're going to take care of this.:*

We? he thought in surprise. But before he could ask her what she meant, the face of every Herald in the room went blank, and Shavri stopped in midsentence.

There was a long moment of silence, broken only by the sounds of non-Heralds stirring restlessly in their seats. The candles placed in sconces all around the room flickered only when someone moved, creating a momentary current in the air. Someone coughed uncomfortably.

:'Fandes?: Vanyel Sent. *:What's going on?:*

:You have to go, Van,: she replied firmly. *:This mage is too much of a threat. We—the Companions, I mean—have been talking it over since you decided to go after him, and we think you're right. So we're backing you. And if the others won't listen to their own Companions, they'll hear from all of us.:* The overtones to her mind-voice sounded both smug and a little ominous. *:We'll just see how long any of them can hold out against that.:*

Joshel shook his head at that point. "All right," he said aloud, breaking the silence so suddenly that the non-Heralds started. He gave Vanyel a long-suffering look. "I don't know how you managed this," he told the dumbfounded Herald-Mage, mixed admiration and annoyance in his expression, "I've never heard of all the Companions uniting to back a Herald against King and Council before. I hope you're right, Vanyel Ashkevron—and I hope this isn't going to be too much for even you to handle."

One by one the others gave in, Shavri the last, possibly because Shavri's bond with her Companion was the weakest.

But finally even she acquiesced, though not happily. "I hope you're satisfied, Herald Vanyel," she said, on the verge of tears. "I thought you were our friend—"

The others of the Council looked uneasy, embarrassed, or both, at this display of "womanly vapors." Vanyel, who knew it was more than that, dared not waver from his resolve. He knew why she was trying emotional blackmail; she was afraid for Randale and Jisa, but there was too much riding on this for him to allow her to manipulate his feelings for her, Randi, and their daughter.

"I am, Shavri. But Valdemar comes first; you know that as well as I do," he replied coolly, bringing home to her the same lesson he'd given Randale years ago.

"Then how *dare* you ride off and leave Valdemar unprotected?" she cried passionately, making her hands into fists.

"Because I *am* protecting Valdemar," he said, just as passionately. "This mage, whoever he is, doesn't dare leave me alive, not after the way I destroyed his creature. While he concentrates on me, he'll be ignoring Valdemar and anyone in Valdemar. You should all be perfectly safe while he brings all his resources to bear on me."

"And what if he k-k-kills you?" Shavri said miserably. "What will protect us then?"

"Shavri," he said, leaning toward her and catching and holding her gaze, "If I die, I'll either take him with me, or leave him so crippled he'll be no threat. So help me, I will protect Valdemar with my last breath, and if there is a way to protect her after my death, I'll find it!"

He stared into her eyes for a long moment, during which no one seemed to breathe. Then he sat back, breaking the spell himself. "But I don't intend to die," he said, with a grim smile. "I intend to find this bastard, and make him pay for what he did to Savil and the others. And if I have your permission to do so—?"

Randale nodded wearily. "There doesn't seem to be much choice in the matter," the King said. "For what it's worth, you have the permission of Crown and Council."

Vanyel stood, and bowed with deliberate grace to all of them. "I'm sorry if you feel that your decision has been forced," he said, "but I can't feel sorry that you came to it. Valdemar is more important than any one man, however powerful he seems to be. Thank you; I'll be leaving in the morning. Treven is ready to take full responsibilities as Randale's proxy and the Heir, Joshel knows how to contact my operatives in Karse, and Tantras can take over everything else I've been doing, just as he's done in the past." He looked around at the various faces of the Councillors, his father included. "I'm not indispensable, you know," he finished quietly. "No one is. You're all the most capable people I know, and if there's safety for anyone in this realm, it's in your hands, not mine, ultimately. *Zhai'helleva*, my friends."

And with that, he turned and left the room before anyone else could break down—including himself.

Stefen slipped inside Vanyel's door and shut it behind him, quietly. Van was beside the bed, neatly folding clothing and stowing it away in his travel-packs. While he did not look up from his packing, Stefen knew that Vanyel was well aware he'd come in.

Stef bit his lip, unable to think of how to start, what to say. Vanyel continued to ignore his presence, perhaps hoping that Stef would become discouraged and leave. The silence lengthened, as Stefen's palms grew sweaty and his throat tighter and tighter. Finally he blurted out the first words that came into his head.

"*You're not leaving without me.*" He tried to make it sound defiant, but it came out plaintive. He pressed his back against the wood of the door as if he could physically bar Vanyel's way and waited for Van's response.

"Stef," Van said without turning around, "I can't take you with me, you know that." He sounded as distant and cold as if he were on the moon.

"Why not?" Stefen asked, around the lump in his throat. He was well aware that his words were very similar to what might be coming out of a petulant adolescent, and too anxious to care. "You're not going into Rethwellan this time. There's no one to care if we're lovers! What's the difference if I'm with you or not?"

Finally Vanyel turned around; his face was set in a stony mask, and his eyes were inward-focused, as if he was trying not to see Stef, only his shadow. "The difference is that you're not a Herald, you're not combat-trained, you can't even defend yourself from one man with a sword. You're a liability, Stef. I told you when we first—"

"How am I any safer here?" he interrupted, desperately, playing shamelessly on the guilt he knew Vanyel felt over Savil's death. "Savil wasn't safe! If someone wants to use me against you, all they have to do is wait until you're gone, and *take* me. Anybody who can do what's been done so far could make one of those Gate-things, grab me while everybody's asleep, and be gone before I could yell for help! You said yourself I couldn't protect myself from one man with a sword—how am I going to protect myself against something like *that?*"

He balled his hands into fists, to keep from gouging the wood of the door with his nails. The room was much too hot, and it was very hard to breathe. Vanyel seemed to waver for a moment, the mask cracking—then his lips tightened. The fire flared up, making his face look even harsher and more masklike.

"I don't have time for this, Stef. I have a job to do, and you're only going to get in the way." The words were deliberately hurtful, and if Stef hadn't felt a trace of contrary emotions through the bond that tied them together, he might have fled at that moment.

He's so driven—but I can crack that shell. I have to. Just enough so that he'll let me come with him . . . but it's a mistake to bring up Savil again. That's what's driving him.

"I'm coming with you," he said stubbornly, moving away from the door and toward Vanyel. "If you won't take me with you, I'll follow you. If you set somebody to watch me, I'll get away somehow. If you won't let me stay with you, I'll ride an hour behind you." He stopped for a moment, then made the last two steps in a rush, taking Vanyel in his arms before the Herald could evade the embrace. Vanyel held himself away, as stiffly as the night they'd first met, but Stef hid his face in Vanyel's jerkin anyway. "I don't care what you do," he said into Vanyel's shoulder, his cheek pressed tightly against the smooth leather. "I love you, and I'm following you. I don't care what happens to me, as long as I can be with you."

"What about Randale?" Vanyel asked in a strange, hollow voice.

"I'm not in love with Randale," Stef replied, a little defensively. "I'm not a Herald, you said that yourself, and I don't see that I owe him anything. There're a dozen Healers that can pain-block now; three of them can do it while Randale's awake and talking. I'm just a convenience; he doesn't *need* me anymore, and with Treven taking over full Heir's duties, he won't even have to do anything he doesn't feel up to."

"Shavri would probably dispute that," Vanyel said dryly, but his rigid posture was softening.

"She did," Stefen told him, encouraged by that tiny sign. "And I told her she could force me to stay, but she couldn't force me to play. She looked like she wanted to throw something at me, but she didn't. She just told me what she thought of me. It started with 'traitor' and went downhill from there."

"I imagine it did," Vanyel replied with a little cough.

"She told me she'd have me demoted, that she'd have me banned from the Bardic Circle," Stef continued, feeling that Vanyel was relaxing further. "I told her I didn't care. And I don't." He released Vanyel a little, and looked up into the Herald's face, lifting his chin defiantly. "It doesn't matter to me. If I wanted a high position and all the rest of that, I could have gone with that gem-merchant. I *used* to want that kind of thing, but I don't anymore."

"What do you want, Stef?" Vanyel asked softly, his strange silver eyes full of pain, and haunted by thoughts Stef could only guess at.

"Besides you? I don't know," Stefen said truthfully. He'd *intended* to say "just you," but something about the way Van had asked the question compelled him to the exact truth. "I only know that without you, no rank or fame would be worth having."

"And what would you have done if Randale had still needed you?" Vanyel continued, holding Stef's eyes with his.

Stefen swallowed. His throat tightened again, and a cold lump formed in the pit of his stomach. "I d-d-don't know," he replied miserably. "It's too hard a choice, and I didn't have to make it, so does it matter? He *doesn't* need me, and he told Shavri so."

"He did?" For the first time since Savil's death, Vanyel smiled—a very faint smile, but a genuine one. "You didn't tell me that part."

"You didn't let me get to it," Stef reminded him, with an uncertain grin. "Randale told Shavri that *he* didn't need me, and that I'd only pine myself away to nothing if I had to stay. He said I should follow my heart, and that I shouldn't let you stop me. And that we needed each other."

Vanyel's arms came up and slowly closed around Stefen. "I guess we do, at that," he said in a whisper, and held Stef so tightly the Bard could hardly breathe.

"Will you let me come with you now?" he asked, when he was certain Van wasn't going to let go of him any time soon.

"Don't you ever give up?" Vanyel asked, amusement warring with exasperation, and amusement winning.

"No," the Bard replied, sure now that he'd won. "I already told you that." He felt Van's hand stroking his hair, and sighed, relaxing himself, the cold lump in his stomach vanishing.

"All right—but only because I think you're right." Vanyel pushed him away enough so that the Herald could look into his eyes. "You're probably a lot safer with me than here. I can put better protections on you than I've ever put on anyone else, including myself; you'll be invisible to Mage-Sight because I'll make them all passive defenses that don't manifest unless you're attacked, and it's harder to find a moving target. But Stef—please, *please* promise me that if it comes to a physical battle, you'll run. You *don't* know anything but street-fighting, and I don't have the time to teach you enough of anything to do you any good. I've lost Savil—if I lost you—"

The look in Vanyel's eyes was not altogether sane, and reminded Stef uneasily of the expression he'd seen once in the eyes of a broken-winged bird. Stefen shuddered, and pulled the Herald back into an embrace. "I promise," he said. "I told you, I value my skin. I won't risk it doing something stupid."

"Good," Vanyel sighed. "Well—I guess I should let you go pack. . . ."

He let go of Stef, reluctantly. Stefen backed a step away, and grinned up at the Herald. He returned to the door, opened it, and pulled his packs in from the hallway.

"I already have," he said simply.

Vanyel was awake at dawn, and Stef somehow managed to shake himself into a facsimile of alertness, even though his body protested being up at such an unholy hour, and his mind refused to admit that he was actually moving about.

Van had gone completely over his packs the night before; fortunately Medren had helped Stef put his kit together, and there was nothing Vanyel insisted upon that he did not already have, and very little he insisted Stef discard. Stef had already been in bed and asleep by the time Van finished his own packing, but he could be a very light sleeper if he chose, so the night had not been entirely wasted.

Although as he yawned his way through a sketchy breakfast, he wondered if the night might not have been better spent in sleeping, after all.

It was so dark that the stablehands were working by lantern light. Vanyel saddled Yfandes with his own hands, but suggested absently to Stefen that he stand back and let the experienced grooms deal with his little filly.

They placed a different sort of saddle on her than Stef was used to; one identical to Vanyel's, with the rear and front a little higher than his riding saddle, and rings and snaffles all over the skirting. He couldn't imagine what all those fastenings could be for, especially when there weren't any straps in evidence to be attached to them.

But then he didn't know much about horses, anyway. If that was the kind of thing Vanyel wanted him to use, he and Melody would cooperate. At least, he hoped Melody would cooperate; she looked rather affronted by the rump-band.

Then the grooms brought out two of the oddest animals Stefen had ever seen. Horse-tall, spotted brown and white, as hairy as the shaggiest of dogs, they had long necks and rabbit-like faces with big, round, deep-brown eyes. One of them craned its long neck in Stefen's direction, its nostrils widening and its split upper lip lifting.

Stef tried to back out of its reach, but Melody was in the way and he was hemmed in by stalls on either side. The grooms were so busy loading the beasts with packs that they didn't notice what the one nearest Stef was trying to do.

He braced himself, waiting for the thing to try and bite him, hoping he could dodge out of the way before it connected.

But the creature only snuffled at him, stirring his hair with its warm, sweet breath. Melody twitched the skin of her neck and turned her head to see what was disturbing her.

Stefan fully expected her to have a fit when confronted by the odd beast, but she didn't even widen her eyes. She just snorted in equine greeting, and the beast stretched its neck still further to touch noses with her before going back to snuffling Stefen's hair as if in fascination.

Finally the groom looked up from strapping the last pack down, and saw what the creature was doing. "Here now," he said, slapping its shoulder lightly. The beast pulled its head back, and turned a gaze full of disappointment on its handler.

"Don't you go a-lookin' at me like that, missy," he said. "Them's not roses you was a-smellin', 'twas the young lad's hair."

She sighed, as deep and heartfelt as any crestfallen maiden, and closed her eyes. The groom pulled the final strap tight, and turned toward Stef. "Chirras," he said, shaking his head. "Curious as cats, they are. You watch this 'un; she likes flowers, an' anything that's bright-colored she'll go sniffin' at just in case it might be some posy she ain't never seen afore." He grinned. "Some fool Herald name of Vanyel gave 'er a snow-rose once, an' ever since she's been lookin' fer flowers where there can't be none."

"She'd just carried my packs through a blizzard, Berd," Vanyel replied without turning around. "I thought she deserved a reward, and I didn't have any sweets with me. Listen, we plan to leave these two at the Border, at the last Guard post. Is that all right?"

"What're you gonna do for supplies?" the groom asked skeptically.

"What I generally do; live off the land." Now Vanyel turned to face them. "I wouldn't have asked you for them now except that Stef isn't used to this kind of trip, and I don't want to make it too hard on him at the beginning."

"Whatever you say," the groom replied. "The Guard post is fine. Next replacement to come back down can bring 'em with."

"That's pretty much what I thought." Vanyel took the lead-rope of the other chirra from a young boy and fastened it to the cantle of his saddle, while Berd did the same with the flower-loving chirra and Melody's saddle. Van mounted once his chirra was secure, and Stef followed his example.

"You take care, m'lord Van—" Berd called after them, as they rode out into the dark and cold. Vanyel half-turned in his saddle to wave, but he neither replied nor smiled.

Outside the walls of the city, there was nothing to be seen except snow-covered hills and a farmhouse or two. By the time they were a candlemark from Haven, the sky was as light as it was likely to get for the rest of the day. The clouds hung low, heavy, and leaden; the air felt a little damp, and the only place Stef wasn't cold was where his legs were warmed by contact with his horse.

Vanyel lifted his head and sniffed the light breeze, a few strands of silvered hair escaping from the hood of his cloak. "Smells like snow," he said, the first words he'd spoken since leaving the Palace grounds. Stef sampled the air himself, but it didn't smell any differently to him. "How can you tell?" he asked, his voice sounding loud over the snow-muffled footfalls of the beasts on the road.

"It just does," Van replied. "Like rain, only fainter and colder." He looked back at Stef, and got Yfandes to slow so that they were riding side by side. "I won't stop for you, and I won't hold my pace back for you, Stef," he said warningly. "I don't dare. I'm holding back enough as it is, taking chirras for the first leg. The *only* reason I'm catering to your inexperience on this first stage is because my enemy is going to assume I'm coming straight for him at a Companion's pace, and I hope this will throw him off."

"I understand," Stef hastened to say. "I won't hold you back. I'll keep up."

"You might, but your filly isn't a Companion," Van began. Then he got that "listening" expression that meant his Companion was talking to him. "'Fandes says she'll help," he replied, looking a little surprised. "I don't know what she plans to do; maybe do something so that Melody can keep up with her. I hope so; a Companion is good for a lot more in the way of speed and endurance than an ordinary horse. I bred both those qualities into Star's line, but there's still only so much a horse can do."

"I'll keep up," Stef repeated, vowing to himself that he'd die before he complained of soreness or fatigue.

He's so strange, he thought, *so cold. It's like there's nothing in the world that's important except getting this enemy of his. I've never seen him like this before. Is he always like this when he's working, I wonder?*

"I have to stop this mage," Vanyel said quietly, as if he'd heard Stefen's thoughts. "I have to, Stef, it's the most important thing I've ever had to do. Can you understand that? I'm sorry if it seems as though I'm being cold to you—"

Stefen shook his head. "No, it's all right," he said hastily, even though it *didn't* feel all right. "I told you I wouldn't fall behind, and I won't. You'll have no reason to feel that bringing me along was a bad idea."

"I hope you're right," Van replied bleakly. "Although I must admit that it looks as though the weather is going to be a bigger factor in our progress than you are."

Even as he spoke, the first big, fluffy flakes began falling from the lowering clouds. Stef looked up in puzzlement. "It doesn't look that bad," he protested, shifting in his saddle to relieve strained muscles inside his thighs.

Vanyel's eyes were closed, and his brows knitted with concentration. "It's not bad now," he said slowly. "But it could get that way very quickly, very easily. This storm system goes all the way up to the Border, and the balances in it are quite delicate. Right now it looks as though it's going to snow steadily, but things can change that balance all too easily."

"Oh," Stef replied. "I didn't know you could predict weather like that."

Vanyel opened his eyes and raised an eyebrow at him. "I can't," he said. "I can only read weather, I can't predict what it's going to do. It's one of the first things I was taught after I got control of my Mage-powers. The kind of magic I can do often disrupts weather patterns, and I need to know if I'm going to kick up a storm if I build a Gate or something of that nature."

"Oh, like when 'Lendel died—" Stef replied absently, lost in his own worries.

But Vanyel stiffened, and turned completely in his saddle to face the Bard. "How did you know that?"

Stefen brushed snow away from his face, and felt an odd little chill down his spine at the tone of Vanyel's voice and the odd expression he wore. Van actually looked frightened. Mostly startled, but a little frightened.

"Savil must have told me, or maybe Jisa," he said, trying to make sense of his own muddled memories and Vanyel's reaction. "I remember *somebody* must have told me there was a big storm caused mostly by the Gate being made. It was probably Savil, since there was a lot of stuff about how magic works involved in the explanation. I know Savil talked to me about it after I asked her—"

"Why?" Van asked. "Why did you ask her?"

"Because it's a part of you that's important," Stefen replied in a quietly defensive tone. "I never asked you about it because it seemed like you avoided the subject—I didn't want to hurt you or anything. So I asked Savil if *she'd* mind talking about it, and she said no, it had been long enough ago that she didn't mind anymore. That was while you were getting back to yourself after that mage attacked us."

Vanyel relaxed, and lost his haunted look.

"I talked to your parents a lot, too," Stef said. "I hope you don't mind." He tried to muster up a hint of mischief. "Treesa and I have a lot in common; she says I'm more fun to have as company than any of her ladies. I helped her get herself settled in when they got here, you know."

"I didn't know," Vanyel replied with a kind of absent-minded chagrin. "I just saw Father taking to the job of Councillor like a hound to the chase, and I guess I just assumed Mother would be all right."

She wasn't all right; she got here and found out that she was in the same position Savil said you were in when you first came here—a provincial noble from the backwater, twenty years behind the fashions, with no knowledge of current gossip or protocol, Stef thought. *She saw less of you than before. She was terribly lonely, and if there had been a way to get home, she'd have taken it.*

"I thought she was fine. It just seemed like after the first couple of weeks, she was as happy as Father," Van continued, peering through the curtain of snow at the road ahead. "Every time I'd see her she was the center of attention, surrounded by others." He paused for a moment, then said, "Was that your doing?"

"Some of it," Stef admitted. "I coached her, and I introduced her to Countess Bryerly and Lady Gellwin. You probably hadn't noticed, but there isn't much 'court' at Court with Randi so sick and Shavri's time taken up with it. The real Court, the social part, has pretty much moved out of the Crown section of the Palace and into the nobles' suites. And those are the two that really run it. Countess Bryerly is distantly related to the Brendewhins, so that made everything fine. Lady Gellwin took Treesa under her wing as a kind of protege, put her in charge of a lot of the younger girls once she found out that your mother did a lot of fostering."

A month ago, Vanyel would have been deeply upset that he hadn't thought to make sure his mother was well settled in. Now he only said, "Thank you, Stef. I appreciate your helping her," and continued to peer up the road.

That's not like him, Stef thought, worriedly. *I've never seen him so obsessed before. If he thought we could make any better time by getting off 'Fandes and pushing her, he'd do it. I don't understand what's gotten into him.*

The snow was getting thicker; there was no doubt about that. It still wasn't enough to stop them, or to slow them by too much, but Vanyel was obviously concerned. He spoke in an absent tone of voice whenever Stef asked him a direct question, but otherwise he was absolutely silent and inward-centered. The morning lengthened into afternoon, and Stef was afraid to ask him to stop for something to eat and a chance to warm up, even though they passed through three villages with inns that Stef eyed longingly. He was hungry, but worse than the hunger was the cold. Snow kept getting in under his hood and melting, sending runnels of icy water down the back of his neck. He could hardly feel his hands or his nose. There wasn't any wind, but they were creating their own breeze just by moving, and it kept finding its way in through the arm-slits of his cloak. And Melody was suffering, too; she walked steadily in Yfandes' wake with her head down and her eyes half-closed; she was tired, and probably missed her warm stable as much as Stefen missed his room and fireplace.

Finally Yfandes planted all four hooves in the middle of the road and refused to go any farther. Melody actually ran right into her rump before the filly realized the Companion had stopped.

Van seemed to come out of a trance. "All right," he said crossly. "If that's the way you want it, I guess I don't have a choice."

"What?" Stef said, startled.

"Not you, *ashke*, Yfandes. She says she's cold and hungry and she's stopping whether I like it or not." He dismounted and led her and the chirra over to the side of the road, kicking his way through the soft snow. Stef had to make two tries at dismounting before he could get off; he'd never been so stiff and sore in his life, and he had the sinking feeling it was only going to get worse.

But when he got under the tree, he felt a little resistance in the air—and when he passed it, a breath of warmth melted the snow stuck to his hair. It was more than just a breath of warmth; the entire area beneath the branches was warm, about as warm as a summer day; what snow Van hadn't cleared away was melting, and Yfandes was looking very pleased with herself.

"Van—" Stef said hesitatingly. "Is this a good idea? I mean, I guess you used magic to do this, won't somebody spot it?"

Vanyel shook his head. "I used a *Tayledras* trick; it's how they shield their valleys. From the outside, even to Mage-Sight, this place looks absolutely the same as it did before we got here; snow-covered trees, and no humans. It'll stay that way until well after we've gone on." He brushed snow from his cloak and grimaced. "There will still be a trace of magic-use here, though, and if my enemy knows I trained with the *Tayledras* he'll be able to track us by that, about two days behind our real trail. I'd rather not have done this, but 'Fandes said her joints were getting stiff and she had to get warm, so I didn't have much choice."

Stef had a sneaking suspicion that 'Fandes had insisted as much for *his* sake as her own, and he gave her a look of gratitude he hoped she could read. To his astonishment, she turned to look right at him and gave him a slow, deliberate wink when Vanyel's back was turned, rummaging in the chirras' packs.

"Could we sort of change direction every once in a while to throw him off?" Stef said, hoping this meant Van was going to warm up their resting place every time they stopped.

"It won't do much good; he knows we're coming north after him, and there's only a limited number of ways we can travel." Vanyel sighed, and looked over Stef's shoulder as if he wished they could get back on the road immediately.

Stefen ate his meal in silence. Yfandes sidled up to him and he leaned on her, grateful for the support and for her warmth. *It looks like the best I can hope for is that he'll wait until I'm warm clear through before getting back on the road.*

"At any rate, this is how we'll camp at night," Vanyel continued, handing him cold meat, bread, cheese, and two apples. "I don't want to stop at inns; there could be spies there, and I don't want this mage to know exactly where we are."

Stef split his second apple and fed half to Yfandes and half to Melody. "Whatever you say, Van," he replied, hoping he'd be able to get back *on* his horse when Vanyel wanted to leave. "As long as I can be with you."

CHAPTER 17

S NOW FELL, AS it had fallen for the past three weeks, as it seemed it would continue to fall for the next three weeks. Not a blizzard; the wind, when there was one, was gentle, and the temperature relatively warm. But the snow was wet and heavy; good snow for playing in, as dozens of children making snow-beasts in their yards could attest—but it increased their travel time fourfold. Ironically, considering how much stress Vanyel had put on the fact that he would leave Stef behind if he had to, the chirras were forcing a path through the snow for the two riding, and their progress was set by the chirras' pace.

"How many days can a snowstorm last?" Stef asked, cuddled on Melody's back, shivering despite woolen under-drawers, a sweater and a shirt under his tunic, and two sweaters and his cloak over that.

"It's not the same storm, *ashke*," Vanyel replied, as he consulted a map, then looked for landmarks. They were supposed to reach the last Guard outpost today, at least according to Vanyel's calculations. That outpost marked the end of the lands Valdemar claimed, and the beginning of territory held by no one except wolves—two and four-legged. And other things—the Pelagirs reached into that territory, and where they ended was anyone's guess. Probably only the *Tayledras* knew. It also marked the point at which Vanyel and Stefen's "easy" travel ended. They'd be leaving the chirras behind, and what little was left of the supplies, and going on with what Yfandes and Melody could carry—and what Vanyel could conjure up.

By now, Stef was no longer so sore in the morning that he would far rather have died than get up and remount his horse—but the cold never varied, and once out of their little shelter of mage-born warmth in the morning, he was chilled and miserable within a candlemark.

"What do you mean, it isn't one storm?" Stef asked. "It hasn't stopped snowing since we left Haven."

"It's a series of storms, all coming out of the north," Van replied, folding the map and storing it carefully in a special pocket on his saddle. "They generally blow out during the night, and a new one moves in just before dawn. The post isn't more than a couple of furlongs away; we should make it there by dusk." He looked back critically at Stefen. "If they have it to spare, we should get you some warmer clothing. And a better cloak. If I had known you'd feel the cold this badly, I'd have gotten it for you before we left."

Stefen held his peace.

"You're going to need it," Vanyel continued, urging the chirra forward, with Yfandes following at its tail. "After this, when we leave the gear and the extra supplies, this trip is going to be much harder on you."

And not on you? What are you made of, Van? Stone and steel? "I don't see how it can," Stef replied, since for once, Van seemed to be waiting for an answer. "I'm already frozen most of the time."

"Because we may be frozen *and hungry* most of the time," Vanyel told him, looking back over his shoulder. "We'll eat what I can hunt. I refuse to use magic to bring helpless creatures to me unless I'm literally starving to death."

"I'm probably a lot more used to being hungry than you are, Lord Vanyel Ashkevron," Stefen snapped. "I spent most of my life being hungry! I may not be woods-wise, but I'm not as helpless as you keep trying to make me out to be!"

Vanyel recoiled a little; his mouth tightened, and he turned away. "I hope for your sake that's true, Stefen," was all he said as he presented his back to the Bard.

Stef bit his lip and tasted the salt-sweet of blood. *Bright move, Stef. Very bright move. What do you use for a mind, dried peas?* He brushed snow and hair out of his eyes with a movement that had become habit, and stared at the snow-blanketed woods to his right and left. *But dammit, I wish he'd give me credit for being something more than a useless piece of baggage. All right, I'm not a Herald, I don't know how to survive on my own in the woods—but I can help and I've been helping—when m'lord bothers to give me instructions.*

Unhappiness, colder and more bitter than the cold, welled up in his throat. *Maybe he was right. Maybe I shouldn't have come. Maybe this whole trip is just showing him how little he needs or wants me. Maybe I should stay behind at this Guard post—*

Suddenly Yfandes stopped; Melody kept moving past the Companion until Vanyel reached over and caught her reins out of Stefen's hands.

Then he caught Stefen's hands, themselves. "I'm sorry, Stef," he said, that same wounded-bird look back in his eyes. "I don't give you enough credit. 'Fandes just gave me an earful for some of the things I've been saying and doing to you."

Stefen tried to smile. "It's all right, really it is—"

"No it's not, but I can't help myself, Stef," the Herald said through clenched teeth. "I'll probably go right on doing this to you, making you hurt, making you feel like you wish you'd stayed behind. I just hope you can forgive me, because it isn't going to stop. Everything has to take second place to what I'm doing about this enemy of mine, can you understand that?"

"No," Stefen said truthfully. "But I'll try."

Vanyel dropped his eyes. "I'm glad you're with me, Stef," he said, in a whisper. "I'm glad you're sticking this out with me. It would be a lot harder without you. You remind me I'm still human just by being here. You remind me there's something else besides the task I've been set. Something worth more than revenge . . . but I say things I shouldn't because sometimes I don't want to be reminded of that."

Stefen couldn't think of anything profound to say, but the lump in his throat and stomach were gone, and he felt a great deal warmer than he had in weeks. He freed one hand from Vanyel's and touched his glove to Van's cheek. "I love you," he said simply, as Vanyel's silver eyes met his again. "That's all that matters, isn't it?"

Vanyel smiled, a flicker of his old self, and patted Stef's hand. "Let's go," he said, and let go of the Bard's other hand. "The sooner we get into shelter, the happier you'll be."

The listening look crossed his face again, and he coughed. "'Fandes says, 'to the nine hells with you humans, you have cloaks. The sooner we get to the shelter, the happier *I'll* be.'"

Stefen smiled—and when Vanyel had turned his attention back to the trail ahead, exchanged winks with the Companion.

Lady, he thought at her, *we may not be able to Mindspeak at each other, but I have the feeling you and I are communicating very well, lately.*

The Guard post meant a real fire, a real bed, and hot food. And, almost as important, human voices, voices that weren't his and Vanyel's.

There was warmer clothing available, wool underclothes from the Guards' winter stores, sweaters one of the Guardswomen knitted from mixed sheep and chirra wool, the new, fur-lined cloak that had belonged

(Stef tried not to think of the ill omen) to a Guardsman that had died of snow-fever before he could ever wear it.

And there was news of the North, news that was at odds with their own mission.

They sat by the fire, hot cider brewing in a kettle. Vanyel and the Post Commander slouched across a tiny table in the corner, while Stef warmed his bones right on the hearth.

"Lady bless, not a thing but the occasional bandit and a bout of snow-fever," said the Commander, a handsome woman with iron-gray hair and a firm jaw. "Since last summer we haven't even seen the odd Pelagir critter coming over."

"Not even rumors?" Vanyel asked, as Stef warmed his feet at the fire and played someone's old lute that had been found in the storeroom. The tone wasn't exactly pure, but the Guardsfolk were certainly enjoying it, so he tried not to wince at the occasional dull note. "No hint of activity up there at all?"

"Not a thing," the Commander replied positively. "The only odd thing's this snow. Never seen it snow so much as it has in the past few weeks. Well, you can see for yourself; we shouldn't have more than one or two thumb-lengths on the ground right now, and we've got it up to our waists with no end in sight."

"You mean this *isn't* normal winter weather?" Vanyel asked, sitting up straight. "I thought—my nephew was up here and carried on like the snow was above the rooftops by midwinter!"

"Hellfires, no, this isn't normal," the woman laughed. "If your nephew was that young Journeyman Bard we had through here—poor lad, one snowfall and he thought the end of the world was coming in ice! But that was *after* some of my people scared him half to death with their tales. Normal winter gives us snow every couple of weeks, not day after day. Can't say as I mind it, though. Weather like this is harder on the bandits than it is on us. We got clearing crews; they don't, and it's damn difficult to move through woods this deep in soft snow."

Stef knew that look, the one Vanyel was wearing now. He finished the song he was on, just about the same time as Van made a polite end to his conversation and headed back to their room.

He gave the lute back to its finder, claiming weariness, and ignoring the knowing looks as he hurried after the Herald.

The guest room did not have a fireplace, and it was in the area of the barracks farthest from the chimneys. Given his choice, this was not where Stef would have gone. The corridor was lit by a couple of dim, smoking lanterns, and Stef would have been willing to swear he saw the smoke freeze as it rose into the air. Vanyel was a dim white shape a little ahead of him; he managed to catch up with the Herald before he reached their door.

"What was it?" he asked, seizing Van's elbow. "What did she say?"

He was half afraid that Van would pull away from him, but the Herald only shook his head and swore under his breath.

"I can't believe how stupid I was," he said quietly, as he opened the door to their room and motioned Stef to go inside. The candle beside the door and the one next to the bed sprang into life as they entered—the kind of casual use of magic that impressed Stef more than the nightly creation of their shelter, because the use of magic to light a candle implied that Van considered it no more remarkable than using a coal from the fire for the same purpose. *That* was frightening—that Van could afford to "waste" power that way. . . .

"How were you stupid?" Stef persisted. "What did she tell you other than the fact that they're having odd weather this winter?"

"Odd weather?" Vanyel grimaced. "That's rather like saying Randi's a little ill. You heard her, they've had *weeks* of snow, not the couple of days' worth they should have had."

He took his cloak down from the hook next to the door and bundled himself up in it. "Do you still want to be useful?" he asked, sitting down on the edge of the bed and looking up at Stef with the candle flames reflecting in his eyes.

"Of course I want to be useful—" Stef said uncertainly.

"Good. Stand by the door and make sure nobody comes in." Vanyel put his back against the wall, and pulled the cloak in tightly around himself. He cocked an eyebrow at Stef as the Bard shuffled his feet, hesitantly. "That's *not* a light request. I'm going into trance. I made the basic mistake of assuming that since I didn't sense any magic in the weather *around* us that it wasn't wizard weather. Obviously I was wrong."

"Obviously," Stef murmured, seeing nothing at all obvious about it.

"So, I'm going to be doing some very difficult weather-working, but I'm going to have to do it at some distance, where these snowstorms are being generated. When I do that, I'll be vulnerable." He waited for Stefen to respond.

After a moment, light did dawn. "Oh—so if there're any agents here—"

"Right. This would be the time for them to act. And since my magical protections are pretty formidable, the easiest thing would be to come after me physically." Vanyel settled back and closed his eyes.

"Van, what do you want me to do if somebody forces their way in here?" Stef asked, feeling for the hilt of his knife.

Vanyel opened his eyes again. "I want you to stop them however you have to," he said, his eyes focusing elsewhere. "This is one place where your street-fighting skill is going to do us some good. Take them alive if you can, but don't let them touch me. One of those leech-blades just has to touch the skin to be effective."

"All right," Stefen replied, feeling both a little frightened, and better than he had since this trip started. At least *now* he was doing something. And Van had admitted to needing him to do it. "You can count on me."

"If I didn't think I could," Van told him, closing his eyes again, "I wouldn't have asked you, lover."

Stef started at another noise; the candle had long since burned down to nothing, but he hadn't dared light another. Several times he'd thought he'd heard something outside the locked shutters on the room's single window, but nothing had ever happened.

The sound came again, but this time he realized it was coming from the bed. He groped his way over and sat down; the shapeless bundle of Van moved, and the cloak parted, letting out a faint mist of golden light. Stef gaped in surprise; his present, the amber mage-focus around Van's neck, was glowing ever so slightly. The light it gave off was just enough to see by.

"Anything happen?" Van asked, shaking long, silver-streaked hair out of his eyes. He looked like the old Vanyel; his face had lost some of that hard remoteness. And he *sounded* like the old Van, as well, his voice held concern for Stef as well as need to know if anything had gone wrong.

"I thought I heard something a couple of times, but other than that, nothing," Stef told him, still staring at the pendant. "Does it always do that?"

"Does—oh, yes, at least it has for a while. That's the best gift anyone's ever given me, especially now," Van said, his eyes and voice both warming. He stretched, throwing his cloak back a little and reaching high over his head, ending with one hand lying lightly on Stef's knee. "Having the focus to feed raw power through has made a lot of this much easier on me. I don't always have *time* to use it, but when I do, it extends my reach and my strength. I'm glad you cared enough about me to find it for me, *ashke*." He smiled, and Stef warmed all through. "The snow should stop in about a candlemark, and it won't start again the way it has been."

The abrupt change of subject didn't confuse Stef as much as it might have this time. "So it *was* wizard weather, then. Did you find out where it was coming from?"

"Vaguely. On the other side of this forest; possibly up in the mountains." Van massaged his right hand with his left. "That's the strange part, Stef. I've never heard of a powerful mage coming out of that area before. A few tribal shamans, certainly, but never an Adept-class mage."

"Who says he has to have come from there?" Stef replied, taking Van's hand and massaging it for him. *He's treating me like a partner now, and not like a liability.* "He could have come from somewhere else, the Pelagirs or Iftel, maybe, and moved in there *because* there's no one there. That's what *I* would do if I were a mage and wanted to build myself up before I took on the world. I'd go up where there aren't any mages. No rivals, no competition."

"That's reasonable, I suppose," Van admitted. "Listen, lover, how upset would you be at not staying the couple of days we planned here—at leaving at first light?"

"I told you I wasn't going to hold you back," Stefen said, with a purely internal sigh of regret. "I'm not going to start now by breaking that promise. If you want to leave, we'll leave."

"I was hoping you'd say that," Van replied, kicking off his boots. Stef took his cloak from him, and started peeling off his own clothing, expecting that, as usual, the use of magery would have left Vanyel too tired to do anything but sleep.

Until he felt Van's hands sliding under his shirt.

"Here," the Herald breathed in his ear. "Let me help you with that. This may be our last real bed for a while. . . ."

In the morning, that brief glimpse of the old Vanyel was gone. Van was back to his new patterns; remote, silent, face unreadable, eyes wary. Stef sighed, but he hadn't really expected anything different. *At least I know that down under the obsession, he's still the same person*, he thought, dressing quickly in a room so cold that his breath frosted. *So when this is over, I'll have him back again the way he was. It was beginning to look like I'd lost the Van I love. . . .*

They saddled up and rode out without more than a cursory farewell. Stef had learned how to take care of Melody entirely on his own while they'd been on the road; now he didn't even think twice about getting her brushed down and saddled, he just did it without waiting for the groom's help.

Most of what they were carrying was food for Yfandes and Melody. There was a certain amount of provender out here, even in the depth of winter, and Vanyel could, if he chose, force-grow more overnight in their shelters. He could even Fetch a limited amount every night from the stores here at the Guard post, which was probably what he was going to do. But the fact was it was harder to feed the horse and the Companion out here in the winter woods than it was to feed the humans, so their needs took priority over Van and Stef's.

Stef was very glad for his new clothing, motley though it was, the moment they got out of the shelter of the palisade around the Guard post. Though the sky was as clear as Van had promised—in fact, for the first time in weeks, Stef saw the Morning Stars, Lythan and Leander, on the eastern horizon—it was colder than it had been while it was snowing.

A lot colder. Already Stef's nose was numb, and he was very glad of the wool scarf wrapped around his ears under the hood of his cloak.

Vanyel looked to the east, where the sky was just beginning to turn pink, and frowned a little. But he said nothing, only urged Yfandes on, into the marginally clearer place between the trees that marked what passed for a road up here.

The sun rose—and at the moment it got above the tree-tops, Stef knew what had caused Van to frown. Though weak by summer standards, the clear sunlight poured through the barren branches and reflected off of every surface, doubling, even tripling its effect on the eyes. The ground was a blinding, undulating expanse of white, bushes and undergrowth were mounds of eye-watering whiteness—in fact, Stef pulled his head completely inside the hood of his cloak and rode with his eyes squinted partly shut after a few moments. The only relief was when they passed through sections of conifers that overshadowed the road and blocked the sunlight. Once out of their shade, the reflected sunlight seemed twice as painful as before.

Still Vanyel pressed on, even though Melody and even Yfandes tripped and stumbled because they couldn't see where they were going, and couldn't guess at obstacles under the cover of snow. The farther they got from the Border, the thinner the snow-cover became, but the snow and the light reflected from it were still *there*, still a problem, even past midday—and they did not take their usual break to eat and rest. Finally Stef pulled Melody to a halt. She hung her head, breath steaming, sweating, obviously grateful for a chance to stop. Yfandes went on for a few more lengths, then paused. It took Vanyel several moments to notice that Stef was no longer behind him.

He turned and peered back through the snow-glare; hooded, White-clad Herald on his white Companion, he was hard to make out against the snow, and he looked like an ice-statue.

His voice was as cold as the chill air. "Why did you stop?"

"Because Melody and Yfandes need the rest you didn't take," Stef told him bluntly. "Look at Yfandes, look at how heavily she's breathing, how she's sweating! They don't have the chirras in front of them to break a path, Van, they need their rest at noon more than ever—"

"We don't have the time," Vanyel snapped, interrupting him.

"We don't have a *choice*," Stef countered. "Yfandes will carry you until she drops, but what good are you going to be able to do if you kill her?" He nudged Melody with his heels, and she covered the few steps between them stiffly and reluctantly. He gestured at Yfandes, who had taken the same posture as Melody; head down, eyes closed, sides heaving. "Van, look at her, look at what you're doing to her. Hellfires, look at what you're doing to yourself! You can't see, you haven't eaten or had anything to drink since before dawn, and for what? This enemy of yours isn't *going* anywhere—he's going to be right where he's been all along!"

"But he knows we're coming—" Vanyel began.

"So what difference does that make?" Stefen sniffed, fighting back that traitorous lump that kept getting in the way of what he wanted to say, and rubbed his nose with the back of his glove. "He hasn't done much except throw a little snow at us so far, and that snow might not even have been thrown at *us*. Van, you're forgetting everything that makes you someone special, that makes you a Herald, every time you start focusing in on this enemy of yours. I mean, that's really it, he isn't an enemy of Valdemar any-more, he's a personal enemy, someone *you* want to take on by yourself—and you're running over everything and everybody in your path to get at him! Me, Randale, even Yfandes; none of us matter, as long as you can personally *destroy* this mage! Don't you see that? Don't you see what you're becoming?"

"You—" Vanyel's expression hardened still more, and he drew himself up, stiffly. "You have no idea of what you're talking about. You aren't a Herald, Stefen—you wouldn't even stand by Randale. How can you pre-sume to judge—"

That was as far as he got. Yfandes jerked her head up, and trumpeted an alarm, but it was too late.

Men—hundreds, it seemed—burst through the snow-covered bushes on either side of the road. Melody started awake at Yfandes' scream, then shied violently at the shouting creatures running toward her. Stef clung to her saddle, bewildered—

Ambush? he thought, trying to hold onto Melody as she bucked and shied again, while Vanyel did something with his hands and balls of fire appeared from nowhere to burst in their attackers faces. *But—*

The exploding fire was the last straw so far as Melody was concerned. She screamed and fled, stumbling, down their backtrail, and bucked Stef off before they had gone more than two lengths.

Stefen went flying headfirst into a snowdrift, and came up, scraping snow out of his eyes, just in time to see Vanyel cut an axe-wielding attacker in half with his sword, while Yfandes mashed in a second man's face with her hindfeet.

At that moment Stef forget everything he ever was, and everything he ever knew. He was no longer thinking, only feeling—and the only thing he felt was fear.

And the only thing of any importance in the entire world was getting *away* from there.

He turned and ran. Ran as hard as he'd ever run in his life, with fear driving him and nipping at his heels. Ran along the backtrail and then off into the bushes, with branches lashing at him and buried protrusions tripping him.

Ran until he simply *couldn't* run anymore, until the sounds of fighting were lost in the distance, until he ran out of breath and strength and collapsed into the snow, lungs on fire, mouth parched, sides an agony, legs too weak to hold him.

He lay where he fell, waiting for one of the ambushers to come after him and kill him, fear making him whimper and tremble, but too spent even to crawl.

But nothing happened.

He pulled in great shuddering breaths of air, sobbing with fright, while his body finally stopped shaking with exhaustion and began shivering with cold. And still nothing happened.

He levered himself up out of the snow, and there was nothing in sight; no enemies, not even a bird. Only the snow-covered bushes he had fallen into, blue sky, bare tree-branches making a pattern of interlace across it, and the churned-up mess of snow and dead leaves of his backtrail through the undergrowth.

He listened, while fear ebbed and sense returned, slowly. He heard nothing, nothing whatsoever.

And finally thought returned as well. *Van! Dear gods—I left him alone back there—*

He struggled to his feet, and fought his way back through the bushes, staring wildly about. Still there was neither sight nor sound of anything.

Dearest gods, how could I do that—

Once again he ran, this time driven by guilt, along the swath his flight had cut through the snow and the forest undergrowth. He burst through a cluster of bushes onto the road, and literally stumbled onto the site of the ambush.

There was blood everywhere; blood, and churned-up snow and dirt, and bits of things that made Stef sick when he saw them—bits of things that looked like they had belonged to people.

Then his eyes focused on the center of the mess, on something he had first taken for a heap of snow.

Yfandes. Down, lying in a crumpled heap, like a broken toy left by a careless child, blood oozing from the stump where her tail had been chopped off.

No sign of Vanyel.

No—

Stef stumbled to Yfandes' side, afraid of what he would find. But there was nothing, no body, nothing. Yfandes had been stripped of her harness and saddle, and a trail of footprints and bloody snow led away from where she lay.

No—

His legs wouldn't hold him. His mind could not comprehend what had happened. In all the endless things he had imagined, there had been nothing like this. Vanyel had never been defeated—he never *could* be defeated.

No, no, no—

His heart tried to deny what his eyes were telling him; his mind was caught between the two in complete paralysis. He touched Yfandes' flank with a trembling hand, but she did not move, and Vanyel did not reappear to tell him that it was all a ruse.

His heart cracked in a thousand pieces.

NO!

He flung back his head, and howled.

*   *   *

"Damen!"

The boy started, fear so much a part of him that he no longer noticed it, and looked up from the pot he was tending on the hearth across the smoke-filled hall to the doorway.

The Lord. He cringed into the ashes on the hearthstones, expecting Lord Rendan to stalk over and deliver a blow or a kick. The men had gone out every day for the past two weeks on the orders of Master Dark, and had always come back empty-handed. Tempers were short, and Damen was usually the one who bore the brunt of those tempers.

But nothing happened, and his fear ebbed a little; he coughed and took a second look, raking his hair out of his eyes with a greasy hand and peering through a thicker puff of smoke and soot that an errant breeze sent down the half-choked chimney. Lord Rendan stood blocking the open doorway, arms laden with something bulky, a scowl on his face. But it wasn't the scowl Damen had come to dread these past two weeks, the one that told of failure on Rendan's part and punishment to come for Damen—

The boy scrambled to his bare feet, slipping a little on a splash of old tallow, and scuttled through the rotting straw and garbage that littered the floor to the lord's side. "Here," Rendan growled, thrusting the bundle at him. Damen took it in both arms, the weight making him stagger, as Rendan grabbed his shoulder and turned him toward the hearth. "Put it over there, on the bench," the lord snapped, as his fingers dug into Damen's shoulder, leaving one more set of bruises among the rest. The boy stumbled obediently toward the bench and dropped his burden, only then seeing that it was a saddle and harness, blood-spattered, but of fine leather and silver-chased steel.

A saddle? But we don't have any horses—

The lord threw something else atop the pile; white and shining, a cascade of silver hair—

A horse's tail; a white horse's tail, the raw end still bloody.

Before Damen could stir his wits enough to wonder what that meant, the rest of the men crowded in through the keep door, cursing and shouting, bringing the cold and snow in with them. Damen rubbed his nose on his sleeve, then scuttled out of the way. He stood as close to the fire as he could, for in his fourth-hand breeches and tattered shirt he was always cold. He counted them coming in, as he always did, for the number varied as men were recruited or deserted and may the gods help him if he didn't see that all of them had food and drink.

One hand's-worth, two hands, three and four hands—and five limp
bodies, carried by the rest. One cut nearly in half; Gerth the Axe—

An' no loss there, Damen thought, with a smirk he concealed behind a
cough. *One less bastard t' beat me bloody when 'e's drunk, an' try an' get into me
breeches when 'e's sober.*

The others dropped Gerth's hacked-up body beside the door. Two more
bodies joined his, bodies blackened and burned; Heverd and Jess. Damen
dismissed them with a shrug; they were no better and no worse than any of
the others, quite forgettable by his standards.

A fourth with the face smashed in was laid beside the rest, and Damen
had to take account of the other faces before he decided it must be Resley
the Liar. A pity, that—the Liar could be counted on to share a bit of food
when the pickings were thin and there wasn't enough to go around, provided a lad had something squirreled away to trade.

But there was a fifth body, white-clad and blood-smeared; certainly no
one *Damen* recognized. And that one was thrown down beside the pile of
harness, not next to the door. An old man, he thought, seeing the long,
silver-threaded hair; but that was before they dumped him unceremoniously
beside the bench. Then the face came into the flickering firelight, and
Damen blinked in confusion, for the face was that of a young man, not an
old one, and a very handsome young man at that, quite as pretty as a girl.
He was apparently unconscious, and tied hand and foot, and it occurred to
Damen that *this* might be what Master Dark had set them all a-hunting these
past two weeks.

He didn't have any time to wonder about the prisoner, for a few of the
men set to stripping the bodies of their fellows and quarreling over the
spoils, while the rest shouted for food and drink.

Damen gathered up the various bowls and battered cups that served as
drinking vessels, and balanced them in precarious stacks in his arms. He
passed among the men while they grabbed whatever was uppermost on the
pile in his arms and filled their choice from the barrel atop the slab table in
the center of the hall. Drink always came first in Lord Rendan's hall; sour
and musty as the beer always was, it was still beer and the men drank as
much of it as they could hold. Damen returned to the hearth, wrapped the
too-long sleeves of his cast-off shirt around his hands and grabbed the end
of the spit nearest him, heaving the half-raw haunch of venison off the fire.
It fell *in* the fire, but the men would never notice a little more ash on the
burned crust of the meat. He staggered back to the table under his burden

of flesh, and heaved it with a splatter of juices up onto the surface beside the barrel, on top of the remains of last night's meal. Those that weren't too preoccupied with gulping down their second or third bowl of beer staggered over to the table to hack chunks off with their knives.

Now the last trip; the boy picked up whatever remained of the containers that hadn't been claimed as drinking vessels, and filled them one at a time from the pot of pease-pottage he'd been tending. He brought them, dripping, to the table, and slopped them down beside the venison, saving only one for himself. *He* was not permitted meat until the last of the men had eaten their fill, and he was not permitted beer at all.

He sat on his heels next to the hearth, and watched the others warily, gobbling his food as fast as he could, cleaning the bowl with his fingers and then licking it and them bare of the last morsel. Too many times in the past, one or more of the men had thought it good sport to kick his single allotted bowl of porridge out of his hands before he'd eaten more than half of it. Now he tried always to finish before any of the rest of them did.

But tonight the men had other prey to occupy them. As Damen tossed his bowl to the side and wrapped his arms around his skinny legs, Lord Rendan got up, still chewing, and strolled over to the side of the prisoner. The man was showing some signs of life now, moaning a little, and twitching. The Lord kicked him solidly in the side, and Damen winced a little, grateful that he wasn't on the receiving end of the blow.

Then Rendan reached down and untied the man, who didn't seem to understand that he'd been freed. The man acted a great deal like Rendan's older brother had, after his skull had been broken. Lord Gelmar hadn't died, not right away, but he couldn't walk or speak, and he'd acted as if he was falling-down drunk for more than a week before Rendan got tired of it and had him "taken outside."

"Careful, Rendan, he's like t' do ye—" one of the men called out.

"Not with that spell on 'im," the Lord laughed. "That powder Master Dark sent down with his orders was magicked. This 'un can hear and see us, but he can't *do* nothing." He kicked the man again, and the prisoner cried out, scrabbling feebly in the dirt of the floor.

"Just what *is* this beggar, anyway?" Kef Hairlip asked. "What's so bleedin' important 'bout him that the Master wants 'im alive an' talkin'? 'Ow come 'e 'ad us an' ever' other bunch 'twixt 'ere an' the mountains lookin' fer 'im?"

Tan Twoknives answered before the Lord could, standing up with a leaky mug in one hand and one of his knives in the other. "Kernos' balls, boy, haven't you never seen a Herald before?" He hawked and spat a gobbet of phlegm that fell just short of the prisoner's leg. "Bloody bastards give us more trouble'n fifty Kingsmen 'cross the Border, an' stick their friggin' noses inta ever'body's business like they got nothin' else t'do."

He shoved his knife back into his belt and swigged the last of his beer, then slammed the mug down on the table and strode forward to prod the prisoner himself.

Some of the others muttered; they all looked avid, greedy. More than half the band had long-standing grudges against Heralds; Damen knew that from the stories they told—though few of them had ever actually seen one. Mostly they'd been on the receiving end of Herald-planned ambushes or counter-raids, or been kicked in the teeth by Herald magic, without ever seeing their foe face-to-face. Heralds, Damen had reckoned (at least until now) were like the Hawkmen of the deep woods. You heard plenty of stories about them, and maybe even saw some of what they did to others that crossed their path, but if you were lucky, you never encountered one yourself.

Well, now they *had* one, and he didn't seem quite so formidable. . . .

"So, what's the Master's orders about this bastard, Rendan?" Tan asked, prodding the prisoner with his toe again. "He's gotta be alive and talkin', but what else?"

Rendan crossed his arms, and looked down at the man, who had gone very silent and stopped moving. "He hasta be alive," Rendan said after a moment. "But the Master didn't say no more than that. The reward's th' same whether or not he's feelin' chipper."

Tan smiled crookedly, his yellowed and broken teeth flashing as he tucked his thumbs into his belt. "Well, if *that's* all he said—what'dye say t' gettin' some of our own back, eh?"

Damen nodded to himself, and tucked himself back farther next to the fireplace in the damp corner that he called his own. He knew that smile, knew that tone of voice. He blanked what had followed the *last* time he heard it out of his mind. He did *not* want to remember.

"I think that's a very good idea, Tan," Lord Rendan replied with a matching smile. He hauled the prisoner up by the front of his tunic, and threw him to Tan, who held him up until he stood erect—

Then punched him in the stomach with all his considerable strength.

The man doubled over and staggered backward toward Rendan, who leaned back against the table and kicked him toward one of the other men.

This amused them for a while, but after everyone had a turn or two, the novelty of having a victim who couldn't fight back and couldn't really react properly to the pain he was in began to bore them—as Damen had known it would, eventually. The only thing that actually did fight back was the thing the man had around his neck—it had burned whoever tried to take it, and eventually they left it on him.

Tan was the last to give up; he kneed the man in the groin and let him drop to the ground, limbs twitching. He stared at the Herald for a long time, before another slow smile replaced the scowl he'd been wearing.

He picked up a piece of the fancy horse-harness, a blue-leather strap embellished with silver brightwork, and turned it around and around in his hands. The prisoner moaned, and tried to crawl away, but succeeded only in turning over onto his back. He opened blind-looking silver eyes and stared right at Damen, though there was no sign that he actually saw the boy. There was a bruise purpling one cheekbone, and his right eye was just beginning to swell—but those injuries were nothing at all. Most of the blows had been to the vulnerable parts of the body, and Damen knew of men who'd died from less than the Herald had taken.

The Herald closed his eyes again, and made a whimpering sound in the back of his throat. That seemed to make up Tan's mind for him.

He reached for the man's hair with one hand, still holding the harness-strap in the other.

"Ah . . . y'sweet little horsey! Hah!" Tan rose from his knees, breathing heavily, refastening his breeches. "Who's next?" he asked, laughing. "Which o' ye stallion's gon' mount our little white mare? Little pup's 's good's a woman!"

Damen couldn't watch. *He'd* been in that position before, when they'd first lured him out here, and away from another band, with promises of gold and feasting. Exactly the same position, except that he'd been forced over the bench, not a saddle, and he'd been whipped and brutally tied with rope-ends instead of harness. That was what he had tried hard not to remember—

He curled up in his corner, and buried his head in his arms, trying to block it all out. He could hide his eyes, but there was nowhere to hide from the sounds; the weak cries of pain, the rhythmic grunts, the soft wet sounds and throaty howls of pleasure, the creak of leather and jingle of harness.

It ain't me this time, he said to himself, over and over. *It don't matter. It ain't me.* He rubbed his wrists and stared in frightened paralysis at the floor, remembering how the ropes had torn into *his* skin, and how the men had laughed at *his* cries of agony.

And finally, he managed to convince himself, though he waited with shivering apprehension for the ones who hadn't yet had a turn to remember that *he* was in the hearth-corner, and that the bench was still unoccupied.

Not everyone had a taste for Tan's sport, though—either they weren't drunk enough, or the man wasn't young enough to tempt them, or any other of a dozen possible reasons, including that they still secretly feared the Herald despite his present helplessness.

Or they weren't convinced that Master Dark would be pleased with the results of this little diversion.

They all forgot Damen was even there—those that joined Tan in the helpless man's rape and those that simply watched and laughed, then wandered off to drink themselves stuporous and fall into one of the piles of old clothing, straw, and rags that most of them used for beds. Finally even Tan had enough; the noises stopped, except for a dull sound that could have been the Herald's moaning, or the wind.

Damen dozed off then, only to feel the toe of a boot prodding the sore spot on his rib cage from the last kick he'd gotten. He leapt to his feet, cowering back against the wall, blinking and shivering.

It was Lord Rendan again. "Go clean that mess up, boy," he said, jerking his chin at the huddled, half-clothed shape just at the edge of the firelight. "Clean him up, then lock him in the storeroom."

Damen edged past the Lord, then fumbled his way across the drunk and snoring bodies to where the prisoner still lay.

He'd been trussed and gagged with the harness, knees strapped to either end of the saddle, and as a kind of cruel joke, the silvery-white horse-tail had been fastened onto *his* rump. He was very thin, even fragile-looking, and his pale skin was so mottled with purple bruises he looked like the victim of some kind of strange plague.

Damen struggled with the strange straps and buckles and finally got him free of the saddle, but even after the boy had gotten him completely loose, the prisoner wouldn't—or maybe couldn't—do anything but thrash feebly and moan deep in his chest. Damen tugged his clothing more-or-less back into place, but the Herald didn't even notice he was there.

Get 'im inta the storeroom, 'e says. 'Ow 'm I s'pposed t' do that? Damen spat in disgust, squatted on his heels to study the situation, and finally seized the man by the collar and hauled him across the floor and through the store-room door.

The Lord lit a torch at the fire and brought it over, examining the prisoner by its light. The Herald had curled upon his side in a fetal position, and even Damen could tell he was barely breathing.

They did 'im, fer sure, he thought. *'It 'im too hard one way or 'tother. 'E don' look like 'e's gonna last th' night.*

Evidently Lord Rendan came to the same conclusion. He cursed under his breath, then threw the torch to the ground, where it sputtered and went out. Damen waited for the accustomed kick or slap, but the Lord had more important matters to worry about.

When Lord Rendan wanted to make the effort, he could have even hardened animals like Tan jumping to his orders. Before Damen could blink, he had a half dozen men on their feet, shaking in their patched and out-at-heel boots. Before the boy had any idea what the Lord had in mind, those men were out the door and into the cold and dark of the night.

The Lord returned to the storeroom with another torch, and stuck it into the dirt of the floor. And to Damen's utter surprise, Lord Rendan wrapped the prisoner in his own cloak, and forced a drink of precious brandywine down his throat.

"Stay with him, boy," the Lord ordered, laying the man back down again. "Keep him breathing. Because if he don't last till the Healer gets here—Master Dark is goin' t' be real unhappy."

Damen began shivering, and squatted down beside the man, piling everything that could pass for a covering atop him. He remembered what had happened to Lord Rendan's younger brother, the last time Master Dark had been unhappy with the band.

Sometimes you could hear him screaming when the wind was right. Master Dark had decided to recreate a legend, about a demigod whose eyes were torn out, and whose flesh was food for the birds by day and regrew every night. . . .

Not even Tan ate crewlie-pie after that, though the carrion-birds grew sleek and fat and prospered as never before.

No, Damen did not want Master Dark to be unhappy. Not *ever*.

*   *   *

Old Man Brodie bent over and ran his hands along the roan colt's off foreleg. He let his Healing senses extend—carefully—into the area of the break, just below the knee.

And let the energy flow.

A few moments later, he checked his progress. *Bone callus; good. And under it . . . hmm . . . knitting nicely. No more running about creekbeds for you, my lad; I'll bet you learned your lesson this time.*

He withdrew—as carefully as his meager skills would allow him to. The horse shuddered and champed at the unexplainable twinge in its leg, sidled away from the old man, then calmed. *Ach . . . too rough on leaving.* He regretted his lack of polish every day of his life since he'd failed as a Healer, the way he'd barely get a job done, never completely or with anything approaching style.

And never without causing as much pain to his patient as he was trying to cure—pain which he shared, and pain which he could, after several years of it, bear no longer.

His teachers had told him that he was his own worst enemy, that his own fear of the pain was what made it worse and made him clumsy. He was willing to grant that, but knowing intellectually what the problem was and doing something about it proved to be two different matters.

And *that* hurt, too.

Finally he just gave up; turned in his Greens and walked north until the road ran out. Here, where no one knew of his failure and his shame, he set himself up as an animal Healer, making a great show of the use of poultices and drenches, purges and doses, to cover the fact that he was using his Gift. His greatest fear had been that someday, someone would discover his deception, and uncover what he had been.

He stood up, cursing his aching back, and the colt, with the ready forgiveness of animals, sidled up to him and nibbled his sleeve. Brodie's breath steamed, illuminated by the wan light from the cracked lantern suspended from the beam over his head. He was glad the farmer had brought the colt into the barn; it would have been hellish working on a break kneeling in the snow. "That'll do him, Geof," Brodie said, slinging the bag that held his payment—a fat, smoke-cured ham—over his shoulder. The farmer nodded brusquely, doing his best to mask his relief at not having to put down a valuable animal. "He won't be any good for races, and I'd keep him in the barn over winter if I was you, but he'll be pulling the plow like his dam come spring, and a bad foreleg isn't going to give him trouble at stud."

The colt sniffed at the straw at his feet.

"Thankee, Brodie," Geof Larimar said, abandoning his pretense at calm. "When I found 'im, allus I could think of was that 'is dam's over twenty, an' what was I gonna do come spring if she failed on me? I 'preciate your comin' out in th' middle of th' night an' all."

"I appreciate the ham—" Brodie replied, scratching the colt's ears, "and I'd rather you called me when the injuries are fresh; it's easier to treat 'em that way."

"I coulda swore that leg was broke, though," Geof went on inexorably, and Brodie went cold all over. "He couldn't put a hair worth o' weight on it—"

"Bad light and being hailed out of bed are enough to fool any man," Brodie interrupted. "Here—feel the swelling?" He guided the farmer's hand to the area he'd just treated, still swollen and hot to the touch from the increased blood flow he'd forced there. "Dislocation, and a hell of a lot easier to put back in when it's just happened than if he'd had it stiffen overnight."

"Ah," the farmer said, nodding sagely. "That'd be why 'e couldn't put weight on it."

"Exactly." Brodie relaxed; once again he'd managed to keep someone off the track. He yawned hugely. "Well, I'd best be on my way. Could stand a bit more sleep."

Geof showed him out and walked with him as far as the gate. From there Brodie took the lonely little path through the creek-bottom to his isolated hut.

Not isolated enough, he brooded. *That Dark bastard managed to find me. . . .*

For he hadn't been able to keep his secret from everyone. Three years ago, a handsome young man had come strolling up to his very door and proceeded to tell him, with an amused expression, everything he *didn't* want anyone to know. Then informed him that he would make all this public— unless Brodie agreed to "do him a favor now and again."

The "favors" turned out to be Healing an endless stream of ruffians and bandits who came to his door by night, each bearing "Master Dark's" token. Their injuries were always the kind gotten in combat—Brodie asked no questions, and they never said anything. But after the first two, when it became evident that these patients were never better than thieves and often worse, Brodie began taking a twisted sort of satisfaction in his *lack* of skill where they were concerned. It only seemed right that in order to be Healed these cutthroats suffered twice the pain they would have if they'd recovered naturally.

Brodie was altogether glad that it was the dead of winter. He seldom saw more than two or three of them during the coldest months. . . .

He squinted up at the sky; first quarter moon, and the sky as clear as crystal. It would be much colder, come dawn.

He heaved himself up the steep, slippery side of the cut, and onto the path that led to his hut.

And froze at the sound of a voice.

"About time, ye ol' bastid," growled a shadow that separated itself from a tree trunk and strode ruthlessly toward him. "Time t' pay yer rent agin. Th' Master needs ye."

CHAPTER 18

"WHAT IN KERNOS' name did you *do* to him?" Brodie sputtered, white and incoherent with rage. Having to patch up one of these bastards was bad enough—but being called on to save one of their half-dead victims, presumably so that they could deliver similar treatment to him again—it was more than Brodie was willing to take silently.

The man was catatonic and just barely alive. Raped, beaten to unconsciousness, a cursory examination told Brodie he was bleeding internally in a dozen places, and only a wiry toughness that gave the lie to his fragile appearance had saved him from death before Brodie ever got there.

The so-called "Lord" Rendan shrugged. "It's none of your concern, Healer," he growled. "Master Dark wants this man, and he wants him alive and able to talk. You Heal him; that's all you need to know. You'd better do a good job, too, or else. . . ."

Rendan smirked, showing a set of teeth as rotten as his soul, and his less-than-subtle threat chilled Brodie's heart. This was more than simple risk of exposure, then; this was his life that was in danger now.

But if he showed his fear . . . working with beasts had taught him that displaying fear only makes the aggressor more inclined to attack.

"Get out of here, and let me work in peace," he growled, hoping the flickering of the single candle Rendan had brought into the storeroom hid the shaking of his hands. "Animals, the lot of you. Worse than animals, not even a rabid pig would do something like this! Go on, get out, and I'll see if anything can be done. And leave the damned candle! You think I'm an owl? And send in the boy—I may need him. He's practically useless, but the rest of you are worse."

Rendan lost his smirk, confronted by defiance where he didn't expect it, demands where he expected acquiescence, and reluctantly sidled out, leaving Brodie alone with his desperate work.

Gods of light—Brodie didn't have to touch the man to know that it was a good thing he was unconscious. Every nerve was afire with pain. Brodie removed the heap of rags covering him carefully, all too aware of how the least little movement would make what was agony into torture for both of them.

The man was already a strange one; hair streaked with silver as any old gaffer, yet plainly much younger, and under the bruises was a face that would set maidens swooning. When Brodie got down to his clothing he frowned, trying to remember where he'd heard of white garments like this man wore.

Something out of Valdemar, wasn't it? Kingsmen of some kind. Not Harpers— Heralds? What's a Kingsman of Valdemar doing outside his borders?

Well, it didn't much matter; the man's labored breathing told Brodie that if he didn't do something quickly, this particular Kingsman would be serving from under the sod.

All right, you poor lad, Brodie thought, nerving himself for the plunge. *Let's see how bad you really are. . . .*

Stef's throat was raw, and his eyes swollen when he finally got control of himself again. He scrubbed at his eyes with the back of his hand, and carefully slowed his breathing.

Oh, gods, control yourself. Look at the facts, Stef; Van's gone. This isn't doing anybody any good. He's not dead, or there'd be a body. Besides, I'd know if he was dead. That means they took him away somewhere. They left a trail even I can follow, which means wherever they took him, I can find him. And if I can find him, maybe I can get him loose.

He took steady, deep breaths of air so cold it made his lungs ache, and looked up at the dark, star-strewn sky. Night had fallen while he'd cried himself senseless; there was a clear quarter-moon, so he should have no trouble reading the trail the ambushers had left. The moon was amazingly bright for the first quarter; so bright he had no trouble making out little details, like the drops of blood slowly oozing from the stump where poor Yfandes' tail had been chopped off—

Suddenly his breath caught in his throat. *She's bleeding!* Dead *things don't* bleed!

But if she isn't dead, why does she look dead?

Magic—has to be. And magic's the only way they'd have taken Van down . . . like the magic that got Savil and the others. And since I didn't see anything that acted like a mage before I—

Well, that means it was probably a magic weapon, something any fool could use. Probably something still here.

Galvanized by the thought, he began searching Yfandes' body meticulously, thumblength by thumblength, searching for something—anything that might qualify as a weapon. He wasn't certain what it would be, except that he had a vague notion it might be something very like that leech-dagger—the ploy had worked once, and people tended to repeat themselves . . . another dagger, maybe, or an arrow.

Almost a candlemark later, he found what he thought might be what he was looking for; a tiny dart, hardly longer than the first joint of his index finger, buried in Yfandes' shoulder, hidden by her mane. It tingled when he touched it, in the way he'd come to associate with magic. Maybe it wasn't what he thought it was—

But he gripped it as carefully as he could, and pulled, praying he wasn't leaving anything behind.

Yfandes drew a great, shuddering breath. Then another.

And suddenly Stefen was bowled over backward into a heap of blood-stained snow as she surged to her feet, and pivoted on her hindquarters, teeth bared, eyes rolling, looking for a target.

Her eyes met his.

Brodie ignored the aches of his body, the noisy breathing of the child beside him. He found himself doing things he never thought he could, driven by a rage that increased with every new injury he uncovered.

The young man had some slight Gift of Healing, and a boundless store of energy, which was certainly what had kept him alive all this time.

The Feel of blue-green Healing power was unmistakable, and Brodie approached the man's injuries cautiously after he first passed the man's low-level shields and encountered it. It was well that he did so. . . .

Dear gods—Everywhere he looked there was Healing magic; low-level, but comprehensive. There was a fine net of Healing holding each critical hurt stable, sealing off the worst of the bleeding, keeping the swelling down. Brodie had to insinuate himself delicately into that net, replacing its energies with his own. But once he did that, he found that he now had an awesome amount of power available to him—such a tremendous amount that it was frightening.

He isn't a Healer—and I can't See that he's a mage, much less an Adept-class—but where in the gods' names did he get this reservoir of power from? What is he? And why is it Dark wants him?

But there was something subtly interfering with Brodie's own powers, and keeping the man from doing anything effective about his hurts. Then Brodie identified what it was—when he finally had a breath to spare and could take a more leisurely look at the major repair work he had ahead of him.

For when he probed into the man's abilities, beneath a shell of *external* blockage was something that Brodie suspected had to be Mage-Gift, though the blockage had it so sealed off that until then the Healer had not seriously considered that the man might be a mage. But Mage-Gift tied in and integrated with all the others in quite a remarkable way, so that interference with it rendered the rest of the man's abilities ineffective or impaired.

Brodie smiled, withdrew a little, and contemplated the external matrix of the spellblock. From within it was perfectly smooth, perfectly created to leave no crack and no opening that a mage so entrapped could use to break it open.

But from the outside—that was a different story entirely. The outside of the thing was rutted, creviced and full of weak spots. Brodie had no doubt that even a simple Healer like himself could find some way to break it open. After all, if a Healer could get through another person's shields to treat him, he ought to be able to break into a blocking-spell providing he could find something *his* power could work on. Half the battle was being able to See what was wrong; or so his teachers had always told him. "If you can See it, you can act on it" was the rule.

Brodie had never heard of a Healer breaking a spell, but after all the things he'd done so far, things he'd have sworn that *he*, at least, couldn't do, he was willing to try this one.

The spell probably accounted for the man's catatonia—and no one had ordered Brodie *not* to interfere with it. Rendan had, in fact, told him to do "whatever it takes." He actually had permission, if oblique, to do exactly what he wanted to do.

He smiled again, seeing the perfect revenge for everything Rendan and Master Dark had done to him within reach, for when this man came back to himself again and found he was no longer blocked. . . .

"I just can't Heal him without cracking this thing," he said aloud to the boy, just on the chance that the child might be a spy for his master. He savored the words as he spoke them. "My goodness, I can't imagine what it could be for, but it's certainly keeping me from doing *my* job."

The boy scratched his head, then caught and killed a flea crawling across his forehead. He looked at the wall beyond the Healer incuriously. Brodie smiled again. *The child's no more than he seems. No one is going to interfere.*

And with that, he set himself to examining the spell-net, energy-pulse by energy-pulse. And found, much sooner than he expected, the point of vulnerability.

The spell was also tied into the man's physical condition, rendering his sense of balance useless and confusing his other senses, so that sight and sound were commingled and impossible to sort out. The man would be *seeing* speech as well as hearing it, for instance, and hearing color as well as seeing it.

But where the spell touched on the physical, the Healer had a point where *his* power could affect it. And since the spell was an integrated unit, once a weakness was exploited, the rest could be disintegrated and destroyed from within.

Brodie laughed out loud, formed his power into a bright green stiletto-point, and set to work, chiseling his way into the spell.

Stef froze. Yfandes' eyes were glowing, a deep, angry red that cast a faint red light on the white skin around them. He'd never seen or heard of anything like it; it was a reflection of rage he guessed, and he wasn't sure she even recognized him. He'd seen what those hooves could do—

:*Where is he?*: growled a female voice, seeming to come from everywhere and nowhere.

He couldn't help himself; he gasped and looked wildly around, wondering how anyone had come up on him without him noticing.

:*It's me, Bard.*: Yfandes stalked stiffly up to him, and shoved his shoulder with her nose, knocking him over sideways. :*What happened to Van? Where is he? All I remember is being darted.*:

He stared at Yfandes, stunned. *She must be Mindspeaking me, but how? I don't have the Gift*—"I don't know," he said aloud. "I—I ran away—"

:*I know that, boy,*: she snorted, mentally and physically. :*Which was exactly what Van told you to do, if you'll exercise your damned memory and stop having a crisis of conscience. And I can Bespeak anyone I choose to; it's one of the abilities Companions try not to use if there's any way around it. Now how much time have you been wasting? Were the bastards still around, or were they gone when you came back here?*:

"I—uh—they were gone," he stammered, clambering to his feet. "But they didn't exactly try to hide their trail—"

He pointed at the trampled snow just beyond her. She swung her head around then turned back to him. :*How long?*: she demanded again.

"It isn't much past sunset now—" He gulped, and continued bravely. "It was late afternoon when I found you. I thought you were dead. I just sort of—"

:Tyreena's blessed ass, you went into shock, Bard, you've never seen combat, you've never lost a beloved, and you went into thrice-damned shock. You pulled yourself together, which is more than I would have given you credit for being able to do. Now, are you ready to come with me and save him?:

He nodded, unable to speak.

:Then tie off my tail-stump so I don't leave a track for the wolves to follow, and let's get on with it, shall we?: She raised her head, and her eyes continued to glow with that strange crimson light. *:I can't Sense him, which probably means they had more than just the dart and he's spellblocked from me. But he's not dead. They couldn't kill him without my knowing.:*

Stefen searched what little had been left behind, and found a thong tied to the handle of a broken axe. He approached her flank with trepidation, the thong held out stiffly in front of him.

She swung her head in his direction and snorted again. *:Felias' tits, Bard, I'm not a horse, I'm not going to kick you! Get on with it':*

He stumbled over the lumps of frozen snow in his haste, but managed not to fall too heavily against her. He could feel her muscles stiffening, bracing herself to keep him erect until he regained his balance. He tied the bleeding stump of her tail off as hard as he could, felt her wincing a little, but didn't quit binding it until the bleeding stopped.

She craned her neck and rump around to survey his handiwork, and nodded with approval. *:Good. Gods, that hurts, though. Now, have you ever ridden bareback?:*

"No—" he replied.

:Well, you're about to learn.:

Vanyel prowled the dark, sheltered corner of his mind that was the only place free of pain, the only place that was still *his* and his rage seethed with all the red-hot, pent fury of a volcano about to erupt. Periodically he tested his bonds, but they never yielded, and he was forced to retreat again. He wanted revenge; he wanted to feel *those others* die beneath the lash of his anger as the construct had died. He wanted to hear them shriek in pain and fear; he wanted to destroy them so utterly that there would not even be a puff of ash to blow away on the breeze when he was finished.

And there was nothing he could do. The spell confusing his senses was too strong to break out of; even when they'd freed his hands and feet, he'd been unable to act on that freedom. Whoever had sent that spell powder had known what Van was capable of, and had integrated magic-blocking with Mind-magic-blocking, until there was nothing he could use to lever himself out of his encapsulation.

Whoever? No—this could only be the work of his enemy. No one else knew him so well, knew his weaknesses as well as his strengths. And Vanyel had tipped his hand by using Fetching to retrieve the construct, telling his enemy, in effect, exactly what he was dealing with.

He cursed himself for having the stupidity to play right into his enemy's hands.

And his anger built until that was all there was—white rage and the hunger to kill.

Then, suddenly, one of the walls he had been flinging himself against vanished, giving him the opening he needed.

He burst his mage-born bonds and roared up out of himself, wild as a rabid beast, every deadly weapon in his arsenal sharp and ready, and looking only for a target.

Any target.

Stef found that riding bareback—at least on Yfandes—was not as hard as he'd thought it would be. Moon or no, in broad daylight Melody had stumbled and missed paces, and he had no idea how Yfandes was finding her way in the near-darkness. She flowed along the rough ground like a scent-hound, nose to the ground, relying on him to keep watch for enemies. What he was supposed to *do* about those enemies, he had no idea—

Snow had blown over the tracks they were following once they got up out of the sheltered hollow where they'd been ambushed. That didn't seem to bother Yfandes, much. Only once did she cast about herself for the trail, when they came up on a large meadow, silver and seamless under the moonlight, with a stiff breeze still scudding snow across it in sinuously snaking lines.

She looked out over the white expanse, and circled around the edge under the trees until she came to a place where she could pick the trail up again.

Stef felt entirely useless, just a piece of baggage on Yfandes' back.

:You won't be useless when we find them,: came the dry, unsolicited voice in

his head. *:You may be more involved than you'd prefer. Now will you kindly think of snow, please?:*

"What?" he replied, startled.

:You're broadcasting distress to anyone able to pick up thoughts, and that distress is very much centered on Van. I don't think they have a real mage or Mind-Gifted with them, but we daren't take the chance. So will you please think about snow? Or concentrate on how cold you are. Those are ordinary enough thoughts that they shouldn't give us away.:

He huddled down a little further into his cloak, and did as he was told, looking up at the thin clouds drifting over the moon, shivering every time the breeze found its way down the back of his neck or in the arm-slit of his cloak. He tried very hard to concentrate on how miserable he was feeling, on how he wished he was sitting beside a roaring fire, with wine mulling on the hearth, and Vanyel—

Dammit.

With wine mulling on the hearth and nowhere to go. Or sinking into a warm featherbed—

He stopped that one before it started.

Or standing before a feasting-hall crowded with adoring listeners, his stomach full of a fine dinner and better wine, and his ears full of praise—

He managed to dwell on that image for quite some time, until a particularly sharp gust of wind cut right through his cloak and gave him more thoughts of cold and misery to dwell on.

He managed to feel quite sorry for himself before very long, and dwelling on his own unhappiness made it a lot easier to "forget" Van, and what their attackers might be doing to him.

It seemed as if they'd been traveling for an awfully long time, though.

:It's nearly dawn,: 'Fandes said. *:But that's not too surprising. I hardly expected them to ambush us too near their own stronghold. The trail is getting very fresh, though, and—:*

She stopped, suddenly, and flung her head up to catch the breeze, hitting *him* in the face with the back of her skull, and nearly knocking his front teeth out.

:Sorry. They're near. I smell woodsmoke, heated stone, burned venison, and them. Get down, and we'll take this quietly. There's bound to be a sentry, but whether it'll be on the walls or outside them—:

Let's hope it's outside, Stef thought, flexing his stiff hands, then sliding off her back to land knee-deep in snow. *We won't be able to get past him if there's a sentry on the wall, and I don't know the first thing about taking one out.*

He let Yfandes lead the way, picking his feet up carefully to keep from falling over anything. Finally she stopped, right on the edge of a screening of bushes.

:Careless, lazy, or stupid,: she said, and for a moment he wondered if she meant *him*—

:They've let all this undergrowth spring up on the edge of their clearing,: she continued, her mind-voice thick with contempt. *:We can come right up to the walls without anyone ever seeing us. Ah, there he is. Stef, look up there, just above the door. See him?:*

Stef picked his way up to the bushes and looked—sure enough, there was *something* there, pacing back and forth a little. A shadow among shadows, on the top of a wall that even in the dim moonlight showed severe neglect. The square-built keep would not have lasted a candlemark in a siege.

:That's the sentry and that's the only one they have.: She paused a moment. *:Now what that means is that this is probably the only way into the building, which is not very good for us.:*

"I could just walk up there," he offered. "I'm a Bard, I could just pretend I'm a traveling minstrel—"

:In the dead of winter, the middle of nowhere? Minstrels don't travel in winter if they can help it. How the blazes did you get out here, and why did you come? They may be stupid, but they're probably suspicious bastards.:

"Uh—I could say I was turned out of my post—"

She snorted. *:Have you seen any Great Houses since three days before the Border?:*

"My inn, then—the innkeeper's wife and I——"

:Why here? This isn't a very promising place. It's all but falling to pieces.:

"I'm cold and hungry, and I wouldn't care if it was the first place I saw with people and food and fire—"

:Wait.: She raised her head to look over his. *:Something's happening.:*

With no more warning than that, the center of the building went up with an ear-numbing roar in a sheet of red and green flames.

Stef squeaked, and hid his eyes with his forearm, then peeked under the crook of his elbow. The entire front of the building had burst outward in the time he'd hidden his eyes; the door was splinters, and the right side of the keep had already collapsed outward. There were screams, but no sign of fire, and Stef realized then that what he'd just seen was an explosion of mage-power.

:*Get on!*: Yfandes ordered, and he scrambled onto her back. She didn't even wait this time until he'd settled himself; she just leapt through the bushes with the Bard clinging to her mane and trying desperately to get a grip on her with his legs.

She raced across the small expanse of clear ground between the bushes and the keep, and crashed through what was left of the door, coming to an abrupt halt just inside. He blinked, his eyes burning from the foul smoke blowing into them, and tried to make out what was going on. Here, inside the building, there were fires, small ones. Furniture burning. Piles of rags, smoldering—

Men.

With horror and nausea, Stefen realized that fully half of what he had thought were burning piles of flotsam were actually burning bodies, aflame with the same blood-red fires Van had used to destroy the raven-thing. And some of the piles were thrashing and screaming.

He tumbled from Yfandes' back as she pivoted, lashing out with hooves and teeth at a man running by. He tried to make some sense of the confusion, looking, without consciously realizing he was doing so, for Van.

And then the fires rose higher, reflecting off a single figure, the red glare concealing until this moment the fact that the man wore shredded Whites. Scarlet mage-fires turned his white-streaked hair into a cascade of ripping shadow threaded with blood. Just beyond, a group of terrified men crouched against the far wall, cowering away from him; some pleading, some simply trying to melt into the stone of the wall in numb fear.

"Vanyel!" Stef shouted. The Herald turned around for a moment, but a movement by one of the men he had cornered made him turn back to face them. It *was* Vanyel, but not a Van that Stefen recognized. Like Yfandes, his eyes and the mage-focus around his neck glowed an identical, angry red, and beneath the glow the eyes were not sane. His clothing was tattered and bloodstained, and his face disfigured with bruises, but it was not that mistreatment that made him impossible to identify. It was those furious, mad eyes, eyes which held nothing in common with humanity at all.

Vanyel gestured, and one of the men shivering against the wall jerked upright, and stumbled toward him. As he did so, the last of the screaming stopped, though the fires continued to burn in eerie silence. In that silence, the man's whimpering pleas for mercy were sickeningly clear.

Vanyel laughed. "What mercy did you grant *me*, scum?" he replied in a soft, conversational voice. "It seems to me that I remember you. It seems to me that you were the first and the last to sate yourself. 'Little white mare,' I believe you called me." He gestured again, and the bandit stooped, like a clumsily-controlled marionette, and picked something up from the floor.

It was the splintered end of a spear-shaft, ragged, but as sharp as anything of metal. The bandit's arms jerked again, and the jagged end of it was placed against his stomach.

The bandit's eyes widened; his mouth opened, but nothing emerged. There was a popping sound, and as the point of the wood penetrated the bandit's clothing, Stefen realized with horror that Vanyel was forcing the brigand to disembowel himself, controlling his body with Mind-magic.

"No!" he screamed. *"Van, no!"*

He flung himself between the two, and faced that frightening mask of insanity, his hands held out in pleading. "Van, you're a *Herald*, no matter what they did to you, you *can't* do that to him!"

The red glow died from Van's eyes for a moment; then his jaw hardened, and something like an invisible hand pushed Stefen out of the way. The Bard stumbled and fell to the filthy floor, but was up again in a breath, and right back between the Herald and his victim. The brigand fell onto his back, writhing, then stiffened as Vanyel stepped forward.

"Van—Van, don't! If you do this, *you'll be just as bad as he is.* Don't let *him* do that to you! Don't let *them* make you into something like they are!"

Vanyel froze, with his hand still outstretched.

Then the angry red glow faded, first from his eyes, then from the pendant at his breast. He blinked, and sanity returned to his face.

He looked around at the carnage he caused, and his face spasmed; his mouth twisted as if he was going to be sick, but his eyes went to two bodies beside a storeroom door, and stayed there. One of those bodies was that of an old man, with the kind of pouch an herb-Healer often carried spilled out on the floor beside him. The other body was too small to be an adult; it had to be a child.

Van's posture betrayed him—tense, and legs slightly bent.

He's going to bolt—Stef realized, wondering if he could tackle the Herald before he broke and ran.

:*No, he's not,*: Yfandes said firmly, and interposed herself between Vanyel and the door.

Something—broke open. And suddenly Stef felt what Vanyel was feeling. Absolute revulsion at the deaths, the massacre *he* had caused. Despair at the knowledge that he had killed at least one innocent; two if the boy could be counted in that category. Contemptible. Worse than contemptible . . . *hateful. Insane.* . . .

Under the self-loathing, the fear that Yfandes and Stef would both repudiate him, would hate him for what he'd done, and cast him out of their lives and hearts.

"No—Van—" Stef walked carefully toward him, slowly, with Yfandes maneuvering to keep Van's escape blocked. "Listen to me, it's not your fault. You were in pain, your mind was confused, you weren't able to think of anything except hurting them back. That's part of you—*everybody* has that as a part of them. You're not a god, above mistakes! It's just a part of you that you lost control of for a little. If it had been *me,* I'd probably have done a lot worse things than you did—"

'Fandes herded the Herald in close enough that Stef could get Vanyel in his arms. He did so, before Van could evade his embrace. The Herald shuddered all over his body, like a terrified animal.

:We've a problem, Bard: Yfandes said grimly. *:There's a lot worse damage than we thought.:* And through her powers, she permitted him a glimpse of a little of what had been done to Van, a glimpse that suddenly made Van's speech about being "sated" and "little white mares" understandable. Stefen choked—and then had to make a conscious effort to start breathing again.

The bandits seemed to realize that Vanyel was no longer a threat, and began slipping past the three of them to vanish into the thin, gray light of dawn beyond the walls. Stef ignored them; they didn't matter. What mattered was Van.

He held Vanyel, but not in a way that would confine him—lightly—and tried to send back love along the link between them. The last of the brigands, the man who'd nearly impaled himself at Vanyel's command, crawled toward the shattered door, leaving a blood-smeared trail. He scrambled to his feet when he reached it, and tumbled out of sight beyond a pile of toppled stone blocks. *I don't think he'll live long out there,* Stefen thought. *I can't really admit to caring much if he does.*

Gray light filled the hollow of the wrecked hall, and the mage-fires died and went out, leaving smears of black ash where the burning bodies had been. Vanyel stood shivering and tense in Stefen's arms, while the sun rose over the walls of the keep. Finally, as the sun touched his blood-soaked, tangled hair, he collapsed into Stef's embrace.

Yes, Stefen thought. *We've won the first round—*

:*It won't be the last,*: Yfandes said, smoldering anger beneath her words. :*They've broken him.*:

Then it's up to us to put him back together.

"Come on, Vanyel-*ashke*," he said softly. "Let's go. Let's get you somewhere warm and safe."

Stef found the tack, and the configurations it had been twisted into made him tight with anger. He managed to get it all untangled, got Yfandes saddled and bridled; then she knelt and Van practically fell into her saddle.

:*I'd ask you to put the supports on him,*: she said after she stood up again, :—*but*—:

"I have a pretty good idea," Stef answered her, wishing that the bandit Van had nearly impaled hadn't gotten away. "I'm nowhere near as innocent as Van still thinks I am. He'd just get thrown back to last night if he felt restraints."

Vanyel had fallen into a half-stupor; shock, Stef guessed. And at this point, the last thing he wanted to do was rouse him.

"I can walk beside, and steady him in the saddle, if you don't go too fast," he told the Companion.

:*Good. Thank you.*: She moved off a few steps. :*How's that?*:

"That will do." He kept one hand in the small of Vanyel's back, holding his sword-belt, and one clutching the front of Van's saddle. Now, if Stefen tripped, he wouldn't fall and take Van with him. "Where are we going?" he asked, as she led him through the wreckage of the doorway and into the sunlight. Several trails of footprints led away from the place, and she looked around for a moment.

:*Anywhere except where those lead,*: she replied, finally. :*Other than that, I really don't know. . . .*:

:*Perhaps, white sister,*: said a strange, very dry voice, :*you should determine a direction before setting out.*:

The bushes directly ahead of them rustled, and something large—*very* large—stepped out from among them.

:*Perhaps I can help,*: the voice continued.

Stef groped after a knife, his eyes fixed on the creature, his heart right in his throat. This beast—whatever it was—looked something like a wolf, but was much bigger than any wolf Stef had ever heard of or seen. Its shoulder was as tall as his waist; it had a thin, rangy body with long legs, and a head with a very broad, rounded forehead, forward-facing eyes, and jaws—

Dear gods, that thing could bite my arm in half and never notice—

:I could, singer, but I won't.: The thing lolled out its tongue in a canine grin. *:I see you recognize my Folk, white sister. Tell him:*

:That's a kyree, *Stef. A neuter, I think.:* Yfandes bowed her head to the creature, and Stef relaxed marginally. *:One with a very powerful Gift of Mind-speech, or you wouldn't be able to hear him . . . er, it.:*

:Indeed, right on all counts.: The *kyree* padded elegantly across the snow toward them. *:I am the FarRanger for the Hot Springs Clan. I felt the magic, and I came. We are like in power, white sister, and you know my kind. Can I give you a direction?:*

:Do you know the Tayledras?: she asked. The *kyree* nodded. *:We have a treaty with them, all Clans of the Folk.:*

:This one is Wingbrother to k'Treva.: She tossed her head at her rider.

He raised his head and peered keenly at Vanyel. *:Then we are honor-bound to give you more than direction; we must give you aid and shelter. Though of my own will,:* he added over his shoulder as he turned, *:I would have done so anyway.:* His lip lifted as he sniffed audibly. *:The things here were a foul, uncleanly folk, and the world is well rid of them. In time, they might have been a danger to my Clan.:*

Yfandes followed the *kyree* beneath the trees, where it turned northward. *:I am Yfandes, this is Stefen, and my Chosen is Vanyel,:* she said formally.

The *kyree* looked back over its shoulder for a moment. *:I am Aroon,:* he replied, just as formally. *:There is deep mind-hurt with the one you call your Chosen.:*

Stef felt Yfandes' shoulder muscles relax a little. *:Yes. Have you a Mind-healer among your Clan?:*

:I fear not,: Aroon replied, regretfully. *:Yet the talents of the singer and yourself, and the safety of our caves may suffice. Do not count the prey escaped until it wings into the sky.:*

"I think you should know, sir," Stef said hesitantly, "That the men that were here served someone who is our enemy. He's killed a lot of people, and he's a very powerful mage."

:Adept-class, easily: Yfandes interjected.

"I doubt very much that he'll be pleased with the way things have turned out. And he won't hesitate to kill *you* if you give us shelter and protection." Stef took a deep breath, afraid this would mean the creature would change its mind, yet feeling better that he'd *told* the *kyree* about the dangers involved.

The dry voice warmed a great deal. :*We have often been called insular, and isolationist,*: Aroon replied. :*And there is some truth to that. But if the one you speak of would indeed kill those of whom he knows nothing to achieve his vengeance on you, then he is our enemy as well, and you are well deserving of our protection. And as the* Tayledras *and the white sister will tell you, that is not inconsiderable, particularly for a Clan with a Winged One.*:

Yfandes heaved a great sigh. :*You have a shaman, then?*:

:*Indeed,*: the *kyree* chuckled. :*Comparable to your Adept-class. And I doubt me that this enemy of yours has ever encountered the magic of the Folk. If he can even find* you *on this continent, I would be greatly surprised. So—tell me all that you know of him. Warned ahead is armed ahead.*:

Yfandes touched Van's leg with her nose before answering. :They *called him Master Dark—*:

Sunset saw them entering the mouth of the cave-complex that the *kyree* called home, in the foothills of the very mountains Vanyel had been aiming for. To Stefen's considerable amazement, the caves were not dark; they were lit by glowing balls of light of many colors—each one, so Aroon told them, representing the last life-energy of a *kyree* shaman, created before he, she, or it passed out of the world.

:*The blue are those that were mages,*: he told them, as he led them through a gathering crowd of curious *kyree* that had gotten word of their arrival. The *kyree* didn't press about them, or hinder them in any way, but Stef felt their eyes on him, alight with a lively curiosity. :*The green,*: Aroon continued, :*those that were Healers. The yellow, those that were god-touched, and the red, those that had mostly Mind-magic:* The globes of softly glowing light showed Stef wonders he'd have been glad to stop and examine more closely, if he hadn't been so worried about Van. Stone icicles grew toward stone tree trunks; stone pillars flowed toward the ceiling on either hand. Stone curtains, as rippling and fluid as real fabric, cloaked off farther chambers—light from globes behind them showed that, and the light passing through them made Stef catch his breath in wonder at their beauty.

And it was warm down here, and getting warmer.

"What's making it so warm?" Stef asked, throwing his cloak back and taking off his scarf.

:*The springs,*: Aroon told him. :*We have both hot and cold springs here. I shall ask you while you stay here that you light no fires—the smoke will be trapped, you see, and cause us difficulties. But do not fear the winter's cold, or that you must eat your food raw. There is one spring fully hot enough that you may cook meat in it. And as for the white sister, I think we can provide—:*

:I'd worried about that,: she admitted.

:Tubers, grain that we shall Fetch from those humans greedy enough to deserve being robbed, and mushrooms that we grow ourselves.: He laughed silently. *:We are not wholly carnivores.:*

:I'm relieved to hear it,: Yfandes began, when they passed beneath a smooth, nearly circular arch and into an enormous cavern centered with a stone formation so incredible Stef could hardly take it in. The *kyree* apparently appreciated it as well, for it was surrounded by glowing lights, placed to display it best. The thing looked like some kind of incredible temple, but one that had grown rather than been built. . . .

At the foot of this enormous structure lay a snow-white *kyree*, one with eyes as blue as Yfandes', Stef saw when they approached her closely.

:Forgive me for not rising,: the *kyree* whispered into their thoughts, *:But I am fatigued from cloaking your arrival.:* She chuckled. *Something I am sure you appreciate. I am Hyrryl, the shaman of the Hot Springs Clan. Be welcome.:*

Yfandes bowed as deeply as she could without dislodging Van.

"Our thanks, gracious Lady," Stef said for them both.

:My thanks for your honesty with Aroon. I think that first, to warm you from your journey and to cleanse you, the springs would be the best place for all of you.: She looked up at the semi-conscious Herald appraisingly. *:You have one deeply hurt; the Healing will not be easy.:*

Stef finally blurted out what he'd been thinking since they met Aroon. "Lady—I don't think I can! I'm just a Bard, I don't know anything about— about Healing something like *this!* I—"

:You are one who loves, and is beloved,: she replied gravely. *:That is not the answer to everything, but it will give you a beginning. You are a Bard, and you are practiced with words. Use that. Words can Heal—words and love together can more often achieve what magic cannot.:*

Aroon bowed and moved away then; Yfandes followed, and Stef had no choice but to go along. As they left that cavern for another, Stef noticed it was getting hotter—and there was a great deal of moisture in the air. Shortly after that, he knew why, as they emerged into a cave filled with multileveled hot springs.

Yfandes stopped beside one that steamed invitingly, lit from above by a globe as yellow as sunshine. *:Get him down, Stef. Strip him, and get him into the water. And get into there yourself. Then—do what seems best.:*

"Why?" he asked, doing as he was told.

:I'm going with Aroon. Hyrryl is a Healer, and I need that Gift right now. Don't worry, I'll be back—and if Van starts having problems, I'll be there in a blink.:

He stripped Vanyel of his boots, shirt, and tunic—hesitated over the underbreeches, and decided to leave them on. Yfandes turned and headed wearily back toward the cavern entrance, and Stef saw how she limped—the cuts he hadn't noticed before in his anxiety for Van—how worn and exhausted she looked, and decided not to ask her to stay, even though he felt badly in need of her support.

"All right, *ashke*," he said quietly, as he slipped Van down into the hot water, and the Herald started to revive from the stupor he'd been in. "Let's see if words and love really *are* enough."

Life in the *kyree* caverns had a curious, dreamlike quality to it. Stef ate when he was hungry, slept when he was weary, and forced himself to put all thoughts of time and urgency out of his mind. Any weakness in Vanyel would be fatal once he left the caverns—Master Dark would surely be eager to have them in his hands, and sooner or later, they *had* to leave the protection and hospitality the *kyree* Clan was providing them. Yfandes helped, helped a great deal, in fact—but it became very obvious that since most of Van's mental and emotional trauma stemmed from the brutal serial rape he'd suffered, it was his lover that would have to be the prime mover in helping him become whole again.

Stef discovered a patience in himself that he had never once suspected. He took things so slowly that it was frequently Yfandes who fretted at the pace he was setting. Sometimes Van needed to be alone more than he needed either of them—when that happened, Stef took himself off to some other cavern, and made Yfandes come with him. There he usually found himself surrounded by *kyree*, all as hungry for music as any group of humans he'd ever encountered. He didn't have an instrument, but they considered his voice instrument enough. They'd accompany him with surprisingly complex rhythms tapped out on skin drums made for the use of paws and tails, and a low crooning drone they sang deep in their chests. Their sound was so unique, it filled him with a compulsion he would never have expected: it made him want to *compose* something for them, something to use their distinct sound.

He soaked with Vanyel in the hot springs, Yfandes lying in the heat nearby. It was days before Van could bear to have Stef touch him. . . .

And far longer for anything more.

And sometimes Stef was so tied up inside with frustration, longing, and emotions so confused he couldn't sort them out himself that he'd go off to some dark corner and cry himself hoarse. Hyrryl would find him there, and when he was ready he would talk to her, for hours, as Van talked to him, never minding that his was the only voice, and she ran on four feet instead of two. She spoke to him in strong, affectionate terms, and gently encouraged him to continue his "song-carving" with the *kyree*. He was flattered, and admitted that it actually seemed to be helping him more than it was entertaining the Clan. Hyrryl closed her eyes and chuckled silently, assuring him wordlessly not to be too sure about that. Stefen found himself telling her everything about his life over the "days," many things he had never told Vanyel, and some things he'd never before thought of as significant. He often wondered if Van ever confided in her as well, but if he did, Stef never learned of it.

Then, one "night," Van sought his solitary bed. Not for loving—but for comfort, which was by far the harder for him to need again—the comfort of arms around him, and the trust to sleep in the same bed as someone else.

And from that moment, there was no turning back.

CHAPTER 19

$\diamond$

VANYEL HAD CALLED a private meeting of the three of them as soon as he felt he was ready to face the world again. Aroon had directed them to a small side-chamber lit only by a single green globe.

"All right," Vanyel said quietly, sitting cross-legged against a stone pillar, sipping at a tin cup (rescued from his saddlebags) full of cold water. "Here's what we're up against."

He looked from Stef's troubled eyes to Yfandes' calm ones. *At least I had enough sense to clean out Rendan's mind before I killed him—even if I didn't do it in the approved manner.*

"I got all this from ransacking the bandit lord's thoughts. This mage, this 'Master Dark,' has been operating for a long, long time." Vanyel sat back, and grasped his crossed ankles, nervously. "Rendan's *father* served him, in fact. This past year he actually began recruiting bandit groups seriously, but before that, he had at least four or five along the Border at any one time."

"Why?" Stef asked, puzzled. "What's the point, if he's up past the mountains and we're down here?"

:Because he didn't plan to stay there,: Yfandes replied.

Van nodded, and ran his hand through his hair. "Exactly. As I said, he's been operating a *long* time. Long enough that he began all this before Elspeth was born. The northlands are harsh, cold, and populated mostly by nomadic hunters and caribou herders. He wanted power over somewhere more civilized."

:Valdemar.: Yfandes cocked her head sideways. *:Why us?:*

"Because—this is a guess, mind—the Pelagirs are protected by the *Tayledras*, and Iftel was too tough a nut to crack." He smiled, crookedly. "Iftel is very quiet unless you rouse them, and that deity of theirs—*whatever* it is—takes a very proprietary and active interest in the well-being of its people. Not even a circle of Adept-class mages wants to tackle a god."

I could wish we could get it to act beyond its Borders. . . .

"So, he decided he wanted Valdemar." Stef sat in the far corner and mended Van's tunic with careful, tiny stitches. Some of the gear had been retrieved with Yfandes' saddlebags, but most was lost, and Vanyel hadn't wanted to go back for it. "What's he been doing about it?"

"He's been killing Heralds," Van said bluntly. "But doing it so carefully that no one ever suspected. Rendan knew a fair amount, more than he ever told his men—Rendan's father was in a real position to know a great deal, since he had enough Mage-Gift to be useful to Master Dark."

Vanyel knew a great deal more than that; since he hadn't been exactly concerned with ethics at the time, he'd raped Rendan's mind away from him in a heartbeat. *He couldn't subvert us, he couldn't take us on openly, so he destroyed us singly. The Herald-Mages were the easiest for him to identify at a distance—and the ones he considered most threatening. And I was right; he's been killing children and trainees, making it look like accidents, for a very long time now. Getting the children the moment their Mage-Gift manifested, if he could. Like Tylendel. . . .*

Like me.

"He's been doing this for *years* without detection," Vanyel continued, "and the only reason he tipped his hand with me is because I was a different and more powerful mage than he expected. And because I'm the last; he didn't have to worry about detection by the others, and he really *wanted* me out of the way. And—"

"And?" Stef prompted.

Vanyel closed his eyes a moment. "And because he's ready. He's bringing his forces down here to invade. Rendan didn't know when, but probably this spring."

He was lying, and he knew it. So did Yfandes, but she didn't call him on it. *All those dreams—the ones of dying in the pass. They weren't allegories for something else; they were accurate. But I still don't know when he's coming through—if I go get help now, it could be too late to stop him. One mage can hold him and however many troops and minor mages he has with him if it's done in the pass. But an army couldn't stop him if he makes it to the other side, and the Forest.*

"So what are we going to do, get help?" Stef asked, looking relieved.

Vanyel shook his head. "No, not until I've got accurate information. We're going up through Crookback Pass, so I can see what he's got." *That's why I've been fighting myself, love. I knew just as well as you did that any weakness would give him an opening to destroy me. And that includes wanting vengeance.*

Van felt strangely calm—whatever came, he hoped he was ready. He had tried to deal with all his fears alone, and what he had left was resignation and purpose. He hoped it would be enough to carry him through what was to come.

Master Dark *had* to be stopped. If it would take a sacrifice of one to stop him, Vanyel would willingly be that sacrifice.

Yfandes understood; she, too, had fought for Valdemar and the people of Valdemar all her life. But Van didn't think Stef would. So Stef wouldn't learn the truth until it was too late.

This was something quite different from the need for revenge that had driven him up here. He didn't hate Master Dark with the all-consuming passion that had eaten him as well—he hated coldly; what the mage had done, and what he wanted to do. Valdemar was in peril—but more than that, if this mage was permitted to take Valdemar, he would move on to other realms. Yfandes and Hyrryl agreed—

I'll cherish the time I have left—and I'll stop him however it takes. And if my death is what it takes—I'll call Final Strike on him. Not even an Adept can survive that.

"All right," Stef agreed reluctantly. "If that's what you want, that's what we'll do."

Van smiled, a little sadly. "Thank you, *ashke*. I was hoping you'd say that."

Stef trudged alongside Yfandes, with Vanyel walking on the other side, both of them holding to her saddle-girth so that she could help them over the worst obstacles. The path was knee-deep in snow, and wound through stony foothills covered in virgin forest. Fallen limbs and loose rocks provided plenty of things to stumble over.

Crookback Pass was so near the *kyree* caverns that Hyrryl and Aroon were visibly agitated to learn of Master Dark's plans. The Pass was the southernmost terminus of the only certain way through the mountains that anyone knew—at least in Valdemar.

Stef looked over 'Fandes' back at the Herald, toiling along with his head down and the sun making a halo of the silver strands in his hair. Van caught him at it, and gave him one of those peculiar, sad smiles he'd been displaying whenever he looked at Stef lately. Van had been very strange since he'd recovered. Loving—dear gods, yes. But preoccupied, inward-focused, and a little melancholy—but quite adamantly determined on this expedition.

So far it had been fairly easy, except for the heavy snow and the odd boulder. The *kyree* kept this area of the forest free of snow-cats and wolves—and it was really quite beautiful, if you had leisure to *look* at it. Which they didn't; both Van and Yfandes seemed determined to get up to the Pass as quickly as possible. With only one riding beast (Melody had vanished completely, and Stef only hoped she'd found her way to some farm and not down a wolf's throat), the only way to make any time was to do what they were doing, both of them walking, but using 'Fandes' strength to get them over the worst parts.

The hills they'd been traversing got progressively steeper and rockier, and by midafternoon they were in the mountains just below the Pass itself.

That was when Vanyel called a halt. Stef was afraid that Van was going to insist on a cold camp—but he didn't. They searched until they found a little half-cave, then spent the rest of the time until dark searching out dead wood. With the provisions the *kyree* had given them—more dead rabbits than Stef had ever seen at one time in his life—and the fire Van started, they had a camp that was almost as comfortable as the *kyree* caves.

Stef would have preferred a real bed over the pine boughs and their own cloaks, but that was all they'd have.

Van smiled at him from across the fire, the damage to his clothing and person a bit less noticeable in the dim firelight. "Sorry about the primitive conditions, *ashke*, but I'd rather not let him know we were coming. Any display of magic will do that. If he's still trying to guess where we are, I'll be a lot happier."

Stef tore another mouthful of meat off his rabbit-leg, wiped the grease from the corners of his mouth, and nodded. "That's all right, I don't mind, I'm just glad you're not *after* him the way you were. And *I'd* rather he didn't know where we were, either! I'm just glad we're finally going to get this over with. Then we can go home and just be ourselves for a while."

Vanyel blinked, rapidly, then pulled off his glove and rubbed his eyes. "Smoke's bad on this side—" He coughed, then said softly, "Stef, you've been more to me than I can tell you. You've made me so happy—happier than I ever thought I'd be. I—never did as much for you as I'd have liked to. And if it hadn't been for you, back there, I—"

Stef scooted around to Van's side of their tiny fire. "Tell you what—" he said cheerfully. "I'll let you make it up to me. How's that for a bargain?"

Vanyel smiled, and blinked. "I might just do that. . . ."

By midafternoon of the third day, they were into real mountains; though sunlight still illuminated the tops of the white-covered peaks around them, down on the trail they were in chill gloom. Stef shivered, and hoped they'd be stopping soon—then they rounded a curve in the trail and Crookback Pass stretched out before them.

A long, narrow valley, it was as clean a cut between two ranks of mountains as if a giant had cut it with a knife.

Too clean. . . .

Stef took a closer look at the sides of the pass. The rock faces looked natural enough until about ten man-heights above the floor of the pass. From there down they were as sheer as if they *had* been sliced, and as regular.

"Magic," Van whispered. "He must have carved every difficult pass from here back north this way. Dear gods—think of the power—think of what it took to *mask* the power!"

He looked up, above the area that had been carved. "If we walk along the floor of the pass, we'll be walking right into the path of—of anything coming along—"

Stef looked where *he* was looking and saw what looked like a thin thread of path. "Is that the original pass up there, do you think?"

Van nodded. "Look—see where it joins the route we're on? This is the original trail right up until this point. Then the old trail climbs, and the new one stays level."

Stef studied the old trail, what he could see of it. "You couldn't bring an army along that—at least not quickly."

"But you can on this." Van studied the situation a moment longer. "Let's take the old way as far as we can. We might have to turn back, but I'd rather try the old route first. I'd feel too exposed, otherwise."

Stef sighed, seeing his hopes for an early halt vanish. "All right, but if I spend the night camped on a ledge, I won't be responsible for my temper in the morning."

Van turned suddenly and embraced him so fiercely that Stef thought he heard ribs crack. "It's not your temper I'm worried about, *ashke*," he whispered. "It's you. I don't want anything to happen to you. I need that, to know you're safe. If I know that, I can do anything I have to."

Then, just as suddenly as he had turned, he released the Bard. "Let's get going while there's still light," he said, and began picking his way over the rocks to the old trail. Yfandes nudged Stef with her nose, and he took his place behind Van, with the Companion bringing up the rear.

From then on, he was too busy watching where he put his feet to worry about anything else. The trail was uneven, icy, and treacherous; strewn with spills of boulders that marked previous rockslides. After they came across one pile that had what was clearly a skeletal hand protruding from beneath it, Stef started looking up nervously at every suspicious noise.

And to add to the pleasure of the climb, the right side of the trail very frequently dropped straight down to the new cut.

It was not an experience Stef ever wanted to repeat—although for the first time in days—or the daylight, at least—he wasn't cold; the opposite, in fact. There was *something* to be said for the exertion of the climb, after all.

Night fell, but the full moon was already high in the sky, and Vanyel elected to push on by its light. They were about halfway across the Pass, and according to the *kyree*, there was a wide, flat meadow on the other side, and a good-sized stand of trees. That meant firewood, and a place to camp safe from avalanche.

Stef was very much looking forward to anything wide and flat. His back and legs ached like they'd never hurt before, and once the sun was down, the temperature dropped. His labor was no longer enough to keep him warm, and his hands were getting numb.

:Just one more rise, Bard,: Yfandes whispered into his mind. *:Then it's downhill—:*

Suddenly, Vanyel dropped flat, and Stef did the same without asking why. He crawled up beside the Herald, who had taken shelter behind a thin screening of scrawny bushes.

Vanyel turned a little and saw him coming; put his finger to his lips, and pointed down. Stef wriggled up a little farther so he could see, expecting a scouting party or some such thing below them.

Instead, he saw an army.

They covered the meadow. The snow was black with them, and they were *not* camped for the night; there were no bivouacs, no campfires, just rank after rank of men, lined up like a child's toy soldiers. Stef wondered what they were waiting for, then saw that there was movement at the farther edge of the meadow, where the next stretch of the trail began. More men were pouring into the meadow with every candlemark, and they were probably waiting for the last of them to join the rest before making the last push through the mountains. By night, so that no prying eyes would see them.

Master Dark was bringing his army into Valdemar, and there was nothing on the Northern Border that could even delay them once they came across the pass.

Vanyel wriggled back; Stef followed him.

"What are we—" Stef whispered in a panic. Van placed his finger gently on Stef's lips, silencing him.

"You're going to alert the Guard post; Yfandes will take you, and with only you on her back, she'll be able to do anything but fly. I'll hold them right here until the Guard comes up."

"But—" Stef protested.

"It's not as stupid an idea as it sounds," Van said, looking back over his shoulder. "Back there where the old trail meets the new, one mage can hold off any size army. And if the Guard can come up quickly enough, one detachment can *keep* that army bottled up on the trail below the Pass for as long as it takes for the rest of the army to get here. But none of that is going to work if I don't stop them now, *here*."

Stef wanted to object—but he couldn't. Vanyel was right; even a Bard could see that—this was a classic opportunity and a classic piece of strategy, and Master Dark couldn't possibly have anticipated it. "You'd better— just—" Stef began, fiercely, and couldn't continue for the tears that suddenly welled up. "Dammit, Van! I—"

Vanyel took Stef's face in both hands and kissed him, with such fierce passion that it shook the Bard to his marrow. "I love you, too. You're absolutely the best friend, the dearest love I've ever had. I'll love you as long as there's anything left of me. Now go—quickly. I won't have my whole attention on what I'm doing if you're not safe."

Stef backed away, then flung himself on Yfandes' back before he could change his mind.

:Hang on,: she ordered, and he had barely enough time to get a firm grip on the saddle with hands and legs when she was off.

Vanyel watched them vanish with the speed only a Companion could manage—just short of flying. Stef weighed far less than he did, which should improve Yfandes' progress. . . .

Then he climbed down the sheer slope to the floor of the new trail. He had to make the best possible time to get to the end and the bottleneck, and the only way he was going to be able to *do* that would be to take the easiest way. Getting down was the hard part—when he got there, he found that the ground was planed so evenly that he could run.

First, he began a weather-magic that would bring in the clouds he sensed just out of sight. Then, run he did. He was out of breath by the time he reached his chosen spot, but he had plenty of leisure time to recover when he got there. In fact, the worst part was the waiting; he had placed himself right where the old trail made that sharp turn into the new, and they wouldn't be able to see him until they were right on top of him. And *he* couldn't see them, which made things worse.

He tried not to look around too much; this was the exact setting of his dreams, and he didn't want to be reminded of how they had all ended.

Foresight is just seeing the possible *future*, he reminded himself, probing beneath the skin of the land for nodes, and setting up his tap-lines *now*, filtering them through his mage-focus so that the power would be attuned to him and he wouldn't have to use it raw. *Moondance told me that ages ago, and if anyone would know, the* Tayledras *would. The first dream was almost twenty years ago! Things have to have altered since then. And if I remember what happened in them, I may be able to alter the outcome. Some of those dreams even had 'Lendel in them with me, instead of—*

Stef. Twenty years. 'Lendel had died at seventeen. Van had met Stef when the Bard was seventeen. There was time enough, between 'Lendel's death and now—Stef was exactly the right age to have been born about that time.

More things sprang to mind. The Dreamtime encounter with 'Lendel—the things he had said—the way the *Tayledras* treated Stef and the way Savil had taken the Bard under her wing after that—it was all beginning to make a pattern.

The way he called me ashke *without ever knowing the word. No. Yes. What other answer is there? He came back to me, 'Lendel came back as Stef, somehow—and Savil and the Hawkbrothers knew—*

But there was no opportunity to think about this revelation, for the first of Master Dark's forces had just begun to round the bend in the trail, and it was time to put his plans into motion.

As little bloodshed as I can manage, particularly with the fighters. They could be spell-bound, ignorant—whatever.

The clouds he had been calling loomed above the mountains, hiding the peaks, and full of lightning-crackles just waiting to be released. Vanyel was happy to oblige them; he called lightnings down out of them to lash the ground just ahead of the first rank, as he simultaneously illuminated himself with a blinding blue glare of mage-light.

The lightning exploded the trail in front of him, the ice-covered rocks screaming as the powerful force lashed them, heating them enough to turn the ice into steam in an eye-blink. Vanyel kept his eyes sheltered by his forearm, so that he alone was not blinded. The first ranks of the forces were, however; black-armored men stumbled blindly forward, pushed by the ranks behind them, shouting in fear and anger.

All right, that's one point of difference from the dreams, already. I fought them magic-against-weaponry, I didn't intimidate them right off.

The chaos calmed, as Vanyel stood, ready, energies making his mage-focus glow the same blue as the light behind him, his hands tingling with power. The ranks of armed men and strange beasts stirred restively, the fighters watching him through the slits in their helms. In this much, too, the dreams had been right. Under the armor, they were a motley lot, and only half of them looked human, but they were armed and armored with weapons and protection made of some dull black stuff, and carried identical round, unornamented black shields. And the stumbling chaos he had caused had been righted in short order; that argued for a great deal of training together. This *was* the army he had taken it for.

The ranks in front parted, as in the dreams, and a wizard stepped through. There was no doubt of *what* he was; he was unarmed and unarmored, and the Power sat heavily in him, making him glow sullenly to Mage-Sight. But it was the power of blood-magic—

As was the power of the second, the third, and the fourth.

Four-to-one, then Master Dark to follow. Vanyel flexed his fingers, and hoped Yfandes had gotten Stef to safety by now. *Let's see if these lads know how to work together, or if I can divide them—*

Stefen hung on and closed his eyes, fighting his own panic. He'd never been on—or even near!—anything going this fast before. The ground rushing by his feet and the violent lurching as Yfandes leapt obstacles were making him sick and frightened, with the kind of fear that no rational thought was going to overcome.

They had already covered the same amount of ground that had taken the three of them a day, and now Stef was quite lost.

:I'm doing a kind of Fetching, Bard, only I'm doing it with us. That's why we seem to be jumping a great deal, and why you're sick. Besides, you two got rather sidetracked. You had to come at the Pass obliquely. I'm going straight back.:

Stef gulped. *She's doing Fetching, only with us. No wonder my stomach thinks it got left behind—it may have. . . .*

Lights showed up ahead, against the dark of the trees. Torches along the top of a wall—the lights of the Guard post. Stef couldn't believe it. It hadn't been *nearly* long enough—

But it was. Yfandes thundered into the lighted area in front of the gate, as sentries came piling down off the walk—

She stopped with all four hooves set, in a shower of snow—and bucked. Violently.

Stefen wasn't expecting that. He flew over her head and landed in a snowbank—

He thought he was going to land all right, but his breath was knocked out of him and his head cracked against a buried log and he saw nothing but stars—

—and heard hoofbeats vanishing into the distance, followed by a babble of voices.

Hands hauled him out of the snow; he shook his head to clear his eyes and immediately regretted doing so. His head felt like it was going to explode, and colored lights danced in front of him. But his vision cleared enough for him to see as he looked up that one of the people striding out of the gate was the Commander.

She recognized him immediately. "Great good gods!" she exclaimed. "What in the nine hells are you doing here? Where's the Herald?"

His head was swimming, and his vision blacking out, but he managed to get all of his message out—

The Commander turned white, and barked a series of orders. The alarm bell began ringing. So did Stef's ears. The Commander's aide shoved Stef over to one side, and men and women began pouring out of the barracks, hastily arming and armoring themselves as they ran into their ranks. Stef wasn't sure if he was going to be able to stand much longer; his knees were going weak. The post Healer emerged, took one look at him, and started toward him, arms forward.

And that was all Stef knew, before the ground quietly but violently introduced itself and darkness came over him.

Vanyel trembled with exhaustion—but the nodes were still pouring their power into him, and two of the wizards lay charred and dead on the icy ground in front of him. Of the other two, one had tried to flee and been cut down by his own men, and the other was a mindless, drooling thing that crawled over to the side of the trail and lay there curled on its side.

There's another difference. I didn't defeat the wizards, in the dream. I fought them to a standstill. He assessed the damage to himself, and came up relatively satisfied. There was a slight wound to his right leg; blood was running down his leg and into his boot to freeze there. He was a bit scorched, but really, the damage so far was light.

Although a young boy who'd never been in combat—as I was then—would have been convinced that every hurt was fatal. That may be the reason for that "difference"; it may not be a difference at all. Well. Now it's time for Master Dark to appear.

The front ranks parted again, and a single, elegantly black-clad figure paced leisurely through, lit by red mage-light as Vanyel was lit by blue.

Right on cue.

The young man was wearing black armor and clothing that had to be a conscious parody of Heraldic Whites. He was absolutely beautiful, with a perfectly sculptured face and body. Somehow that face looked oddly familiar—

It could just be that the face was so perfect, it looked like the statue of a god.

Of course, if I didn't care how I wasted power, I could look like anything I wanted, too.

He was a reverse image of Vanyel in every way, from sable hair to ebony eyes to night-black boots.

"Why do you bother with this nonsense?" he asked, sweetly, his lips curving in a sensual smile. "You are quite alone, Herald-Mage Vanyel." His voice was a smooth, silky tenor; he had learned the same kind of perfect control over it that he had over his body.

The familiarity of his features bothered Vanyel. At first he thought it was because he very closely resembled the Herald himself, but there was more to it than that. A kind of racial similarity to someone—

"You are," the young man repeated, with finely-honed emphasis, "quite alone."

Tayledras. *He looks* Tayledras, *only reversed. Did he always look that way, or did he tailor himself? Either way, he's making a statement about himself, the Hawk-brothers, and the Heralds—*

"You tell me nothing I didn't already know. As I know *you,*" he heard himself saying. "The *Tayledras* have a name for you. You are *Leareth*. The name means—"

"Darkness," Leareth laughed. "Oh yes, I quite consciously chose that *Tayledras* name. Hence, 'Master Dark' as well. A quaint conceit, don't you think? As are"—he waved at the men behind him, in their sinister panoply—"my servants."

"Very clever," Vanyel replied. *This has already deviated from the dreams—in the dreams, the mages stand behind him, and this time there were four instead of three. The fighters stayed out of reach, letting the mages handle me. Maybe if I can stall the final confrontation long enough, Stef can get to the Guard and they can get here in time.*

"You need not remain alone, Vanyel," Leareth continued, licking his lips sensuously. "You need only give over this madness—stretch out your hand to me, join me, take my Darkness to you. You will never be alone again. Think how much we could accomplish together! We are so very similar, we two, in our powers—and in our pleasures."

He paced forward; one swaying step that rippled his ebony cloak and his raven hair. "Or if you prefer—I could even bring your long-lost love to you. Think about it, Vanyel—think of Tylendel, once more alive and at your side. He could share our life and our power, Vanyel, and nothing, *nothing* would be able to stand against us."

Vanyel stepped back, and pretended to consider the offer.

Dear gods, doesn't he understand us at all? Nothing is worth having if it comes at the kind of cost he demands. Can't he understand how much I would be betraying Stef—'Lendel—if I betrayed Valdemar?

The cold seemed to gather about him, chilling him and stiffening his wounded leg.

He can't know that I know he's lying—either about his abilities or about the reward if I turn traitor. Or both—

I wonder if I can hold against him. Or even—take him?

Hope rose in him, and he probed a little around Leareth's shields.

And hid a shock of dismay. *He's better than I am. Much better. He's able to tap node-magic through other mages so that it doesn't burn him out. He's got a half dozen of those mages feeding him power from the other side of the mountain, from tapped nodes! He's going to kill me—and then he's going to march right through here and take Valdemar: And I don't have enough left even in the nodes to call the Final Strike that will take him—*

"Well?" Leareth shifted his weight impatiently.

How can I stall for more time?

Oh, gods—I'm going to die—alone—

And for nothing—

Then—like a gift from the gods, the hoofbeats of a single creature, behind him.

Yfandes thundered to a halt beside him, and screamed her defiance at the

Dark Mage. He stepped back an involuntary pace or two, his eyes wide with surprise. Yfandes raised her stump of a tail high and bared her teeth at him as Vanyel placed one hand on her warm flank.

:*I told you I would never leave you when I Chose you,*: she said calmly. :*I knew what our bond would come to then, when I first Chose you—and I don't regret my choice. I love you, and I am proud to stand beside you. There is not a single moment together that I would take back.*:

:*Not one?*: he asked, moved to tears.

:*Not one. I will not let you face him alone, beloved. And I can give my strength to you, for whatever you need.*:

Her strength added to his would be enough—just enough—to overcome Leareth's protections on a Final Strike.

Vanyel raised his eyes to meet Leareth's, and with one smooth motion, mounted and settled into Yfandes' saddle, and answered the mage's offer with a calm smile and a single word.

"No."

"*Vanyel!*"

Terrible pain—then, nothing. A void where warmth should be.

Stefen leapt from the cot, screaming Van's name—the Healer tried to hold him down, but he fought clear of the man, throwing the blankets aside in a frenzy of fear and grief.

I felt him die—oh, gods. No, no I can't have, it's just something else, some magic—he's still alive, he has to be—

He ran, out of the barracks, out into the snow, shoving people out of the way. He stumbled blindly to the stables and grabbed the first horse he saw that didn't shy away, saddling it with tack that seemed oddly familiar—

The filly snorted in his hair as he reached up to bridle her—and he recognized her. It was Melody—

But that didn't matter, all that mattered was the ache in his heart, in his soul, the empty place that said *Vanyel*—

He flung himself on Melody's back and spurred her cruelly as soon as he was in the saddle; she squealed in surprise and launched herself out of the stable door, as the Healers and sentries shouted after him, too late to stop him.

Days later, he came upon the battlefield, riding an exhausted horse, himself too spent to speak. The battle was long over, and still the carnage was incredible.

At the edge of camp, one of the Guardsmen stopped Melody with one hand on her bridle, and Stef didn't have the strength to urge her past him. He simply stared dully at the man, until someone else came—a Healer, and then someone in high-rank blue. He ignored the Healer, but the other got him to dismount.

The Commander, her face gray with fatigue, her eyes full of pain.

"I'm sorry, lad," the Commander said, one arm around his shoulders. "I'm sorry. We were all too late to save him. He was—gone—before we ever got here. But . . . I'd guess you know that. I'm sorry."

The dam holding his emotions in check broke inside him, and he turned his face into her shoulder; she held him, as she must often have held others, and let him cry himself out, until he had no more tears, until he could scarcely stand. Then she helped him into her own tent, put him to bed on her own cot, and covered him with her own hands.

"Sleep, laddy," she whispered hoarsely. "'Tain't a cure, but you need it. He'd tell you the same if—"

She turned away. He slept, though he didn't think he could; the mournful howls of *kyree* filled his thoughts . . . and Vanyel's face, Vanyel's touch. . . .

Candlemarks later, he woke. Another Guardsman sat on a stool next to the cot, keeping watch beside him.

He blinked, confused by his surroundings—then remembered.

"I want to see him," he said, sitting up.

"Sir—" the Guardsman said hesitantly, "There ain't nothin' to see. We couldn't find a thing. Just—them. Lots of them."

"Then I want to see where he was," Stef insisted. "I have to— please—"

The Guardsman looked uncomfortable, but helped him up, led him out and supported him as he climbed back up the pass. Bodies were being collected and piled up to be burned; the stench and black smoke were making Stef sick, and there was blood everywhere. And at the narrowest point of the pass, where the mortuary crews hadn't even reached, it was even worse.

Stefen's escort tightened his grip suddenly and yelped, as a white-furred shape appeared beside them. Hyrryl's blue eyes spoke her sympathy wordlessly to Stefen, and he heard himself saying, "It's all right . . . they're friends," as another fell in on his left—Aroon. The Guardsman swallowed, and they resumed their walk.

Blackened, burned, and mangled bodies were piled as many as three and four deep, and all of them wore ebony armor or robes. The carnage centered around one spot, a place clean of snow and dirt, scoured right down to the rock, with the stone itself polished black and shining. Hyrryl and Aroon took up positions on either side of the pass, and sat on their haunches, almost at attention, watching over the Bard. The Guardsman bowed and retreated wordlessly, and no one else came near.

Stef stumbled tear-blinded through the heaped bodies, looking for one—one White-clad amid all the black—.

There was nothing, just as the Guardsman had told him. Stef shook his head, frantically, then began looking for anything, a scrap of white, any-thing at all.

Finally, after candlemarks of searching, a glint of silver caught his eye. He bent—and found a thin wisp of blood-soaked, white horsehair. And beside it, the mage-focus he had given Vanyel; the chain gone, the silver setting half-melted and tarnished, the stone blackened, burned, cracked in two.

He clutched his finds to his chest; his knees gave way, and he fell to the stone, his grief so all-encompassing that he could not even weep—only whisper Vanyel's name, as if it were an incantation that would bring him back.

The trees were a scarlet glory behind the dull brown of the Guard post. "You're the Bard, ain't you? Stefen? The one that was with—" Awe made the boy's eyes widen, his voice drop to a whisper. "—Herald Vanyel."

Stef tried unsuccessfully to smile at the young Guardsman. "Yes. I'd heard about what's happening up here and I came to see for myself."

That got a reaction; the boy started, and his eyes widened with fear. Then the youngster straightened and tried to look less frightened than he was. "'Tis true, Bard Stefen. Anybody comes into that Forest as has bad intentions, they don't come out again. Fact is, it looks like it started the night Herald Vanyel died. We found lots of them fellahs in the black armor as had run off inta the Forest, and ev' one of 'em was cold meat."

"I'd heard that," Stefen said, dismounting carefully. "But I'd also heard some tales that were pretty wild." The autumn wind tossed his hair and Melody's mane as he handed her reins to the Guardsman.

"They ain't wild, m'lord Bard. The men as we found—stuck right through with branches, or even icicles, up t' their waists in frozen ground—they was spooky enough. But Lor' an' Lady! There was some tore t'little *bits* by somethin', and more just—dead. No mark on 'em, just dead—and the awfullest looks on their faces—" The boy shivered. "Been like that ever since. Once in a while we go in there, have a look around, sure enough, we'll find some bandit or other th' same way."

"They say the Forest is cursed," Stef said absently, shading his eyes with his hand, and peering into the shadows beneath the trees beyond the Guard barracks. "It sounds more like a blessing to me."

"Blessed or cursed, 'tis a good thing for Valdemar, an' we reckon Herald Vanyel done it."

Stefen slung his gittern-bag over one shoulder, his near-empty pack over the other, and headed, not for the Guard post, but the Forest.

"Hey!" the boy protested. Stef ignored him, ignored the shouts behind him, and began his solitary trek into the Forest they now called "Sorrows."

Near sunset he finally stopped. *Near enough,* he thought, looking around. *I don't need to be in the Pass to do this. And this is where we were last happy together. This, or a place very like this.*

He was at the foot of a very tall hill—or small mountain; the sun was setting to his left, the moon rising to his right, and there was no sign of any living person. Just the hill, with a shallow cave under it, the trees, and the birds.

He gathered enough wood for a small fire, started it, and took out his gittern. He played until the sun just touched the horizon; all of Van's favorites, all the music he'd composed since—even the melody of the song for the *kyree,* and the song he'd left a copy of back at Bardic Collegium, the one he'd never performed in public—the one he had written for Vanyel, that he called "Magic's Price."

And then he put the gittern down, carefully. He'd thought about breaking it, but it was a sweet little instrument, and didn't deserve destruction for the sake of an unwitnessed dramatic scene. He settled on wrapping it carefully and stowing it in the back of the cave. Perhaps someone would find it.

The ache in his soul had not eased in all these months. People kept telling him that time would heal the loss, but it hadn't. They'd kept a close watch on him for months after he returned from the Pass, but lately they hadn't been quite as careful.

But then, lately there had been other things to think about than one young Bard with a broken heart.

He'd taken the opportunity offered by the confusion of King Randale's death and King Treven's coronation to escape them and make his way up here.

It hadn't been easy to get that vial of argonel, and finally he'd had to buy it from a thief. He took it out of the bottom of his pack, and weighed the heavy porcelain vial in his hand.

A lethal dose for ten or so he said. Should be enough for one skinny Bard.

He set it down in front of him, staring at it in the fading, crimson light. *You drift into sleep. Not so bad. Easier death than he had. Easier than Randi's. A lot easier than Shavri's—*

Finally he reached for it—

A shower of stone fragments shook themselves loose from the roof of the cave, and one struck the bottle of poison. It tipped over and rolled out of his reach, then the cork popped out and it capriciously poured its contents into the dust. He scrambled after it with a cry of dismay, glancing worriedly at the ceiling of the cave—

:*Go through with it, you idiot,:* said a cheerful voice in his mind, :*and I'll never forgive you.:*

That voice—Stef froze, then turned his head, very slowly.

Something stood there, between him and the forest.

Van.

A much younger-looking Vanyel. And a very transparent Vanyel. Stef could see the bushes behind him quite clearly—

Before he had a chance to feel even a hint of fear, Van smiled—the all-too-rare, sweet smile Stef had come to cherish in their time together—a smile of pure love, and real, unshadowed happiness.

"Van?" he said, hesitantly. *It can't be—I'm going mad—oh, dear gods, please let it be—*

Tears began to well up, and he shook them out of his eyes as he reached out with a trembling hand. "Van? Is that really—"

Van reached out at the same time; his hand—and just his hand—grew solid momentarily. Solid enough that Stef was able to touch it before it faded to transparency again.

It was real; real, and solid and warm.

It is. Oh, gods, it is—

"How?" Stef asked, through the tears. "What happened?"

Vanyel shrugged—a completely Van-like shrug. *Something happened, after I took Leareth out with the Final Strike. I had a choice. Most Heralds have a couple of choices; they can go on to the Havens, or come back, like the Tayledras say people come back—I was given another option.:*

"Another option? *This?*"

:I know it doesn't look like much—: Vanyel smiled again, then sobered. :The problem is that I was the last Herald-Mage. Valdemar needs a guardian on this Border, a magical one—Master Dark wasn't alone, and he left apprentices. So—that was my choice, to stay and guard. Yfandes, too. 'Fandes and I are part of the Forest now—:

He hesitated a moment. :Stef—I asked for something before I agreed, and you get the same choice. You can join me—but—:

"But?" Stefen cried, leaping to his feet, stirring the dust from the now-forgotten pebble attack. "But what? Anything, ashke—whatever I have to do to be with you—"

Vanyel moved closer, and made as if to touch his cheek. :You can join me, but there are conditions. You can only come when it's time. There are things I can't tell you about, but you have to earn your place. There's something that needs to be done, and you are uniquely suited to do it. I won't lie to you, beloved—it's going to take years.:

"What is it?" Stef demanded, his heart pounding, his throat tight. "Tell me—"

:You remember how worried I was, about people thinking that Heralds were somehow less than Herald-Mages?:

Stef nodded. "It's gotten worse since you—I mean, you were the last. There's no one to replace you, no one to train new ones, no way to find new ones. I mean, now you're a legend, Van, and the people tend to think of legends as being flawless. . . ."

:That's where you come in. You have to use your Gift to convince the people of Valdemar that the Gifts of Heralds are enough to keep them safe. You, and every Bard in the Circle. Which means that first you have to convince the other Bards, then the Circle has to convince the rest of the realm.: Vanyel held out both hands in a gesture of pleading. :The Bards are the only ones that have a hope of pulling this off, Stef. And you are the only one that has a hope of convincing the Bards.:

"But that could take a lifetime!" Stefen cried involuntarily, dismayed by the magnitude of the task. Then, as Vanyel nodded, he realized what that meant in terms of "earning his place."

:Exactly,: Van said, his eyes mournful. :Exactly. Do you still love me enough to spend a lifetime doing the work I've left to you? A lifetime alone? I wouldn't blame you if—:

"Van—" Stef whispered, looking deeply into those beloved silver eyes. "Van—I love you enough to die for you—I still do. I always will. I guess—"

He hesitated a moment more, then swallowed down his tears. "I guess," he finished, managing to dredge up a shaky, tear-edged smile, "if I love you enough to die for you, it kind of follows that I love you enough to *live* for you. And there are worse ways to die for somebody than by old age—"

:*Tell me about it:*. For one moment, all the starlight, the moonlight, seemed to collect in one place, then feed into Vanyel. The figure of the Herald glowed as bright as the full moon for a heartbeat, and he solidified long enough to take Stefen into his arms—

:*Oh*, ashke—: he murmured, and smiled lovingly.

Then he was gone. Completely. And without the evidence of the spilled bottle and the dust in his hair, Stef would never have known Vanyel was there except in his mind.

The Bard looked around frantically, but there was no sign of him. "Van, wait!" he shouted into the still air, "Wait! How will I know when I've earned my place?"

:*You'll know,:* came the whisper in his mind. :*We'll call you.:*

EPILOGUE

✦

HERALD ANDROS LEANED back in his saddle, and stretched, enjoying the warm spring sunshine on his back. He looked behind him to make sure his fellow traveler was keeping up all right.

The old Bard was nodding off again; it was a good thing that Ashkevron palfrey had easy paces, or the poor old man would have fallen off a half dozen times.

:Why on earth do you suppose he wants to visit Sorrows?: he asked Toril.

His Companion shook her head. *:Damned if I know,:* she replied, amusement in her mind-voice. *:The very old get pretty peculiar. He should be glad there's been peace long enough that someone could be spared to ferry him up here.:*

:It still wouldn't have happened if I wasn't on my way to the Temple in the first place,: he said. *:Poor old man. Not that anyone is going to miss him—all of his old cronies are gone, and hardly anyone even knows he's at Court anymore.:*

Toril tested the breeze for a moment. *:Maybe he's making a kind of memorial trip. Did you know he's the Stefen? Vanyel's lifebonded?:*

:No!: He turned in his saddle to stare back at the frail, slight old man, dozing behind him. *:I thought Stefen was dead a long time ago! Well, I guess he deserves a little humoring. He's certainly earned it.:*

She shook her head in silent agreement, and slowed until they were even with the Bard. "Bard Stefen?" he said, softly. The Bard's hearing was perfectly good—and he didn't want to startle the old man.

The Bard opened his eyes, slowly. "Dozed off again, did I?" he asked, with a hint of a smile. "Good thing this old man has you to watch out for him, son."

"Do you have any idea of where you're going?" Andros asked. "We've been inside the border of Sorrows for the last couple of candlemarks."

The Bard looked around himself with increased interest. "Have we now? Well—could be why I felt comfortable enough to go on sleeping. I wish you'd told me; I could have saved you a little riding."

He pulled his old mare to a halt, and slowly dismounted, then pointed at a little grove of goldenoak at the foot of a rocky hillside. "That'll do, lad. All I want is to be left alone for a bit, eh? I know that sounds a bit touched, but the old get pretty peculiar sometimes."

Andros blushed at this echoing of his own thoughts, and obediently turned Toril away.

:Well, my lady,: he said, :Where would you like to go?:

:I'd like a good long drink of spring water,: she replied firmly, :And I can smell running water just over that ridge.:

The water not only tasted good—it felt good. Andros became very much aware of how dusty and sweaty the trip had made him, and Toril allowed that she wouldn't object to a bath, either. By the time the two of them were dry, it was late afternoon, and Andros figured the old man would be ready to continue his journey.

When he returned to the grove, the old man was gone.

The gittern was there, though, and the mare—so Andros just sighed, and assumed he'd gone off for a walk. He began a search for the Bard, growing more and more frantic when not even a footprint turned up—

Toril imposed herself in front of him, waiting for him to mount. He blinked at her, wondering what on earth he was doing, wandering around in the woods like this.

:I must have had sun-stroke,: he told her, shaking his head in confusion. :What am—what was I doing?:

:I wondered,: she replied with concern, :You wanted to see the battle site, and I tried to tell you it wasn't here, but you insisted it was. Don't you remember?:

:No,: he replied ruefully. :Next time knock me into a stream or something, would you?:

He caught a twinkle in her eye, but she replied demurely enough, :If it's necessary. It's just that now we're late, and they really need a Herald out here for relay work. Every moment we're not there is trouble for the Healers. It's just a good thing there's a full moon tonight.:

"Oh, horseturds," Andros groaned aloud. "You don't expect me to ride all night, do you?"

:Why not? I'm the one doing all the work. Now get the packmare and let's get going.:

"Why is there a saddle on this mare?" he asked, frowning, as he approached the palfrey. "And why isn't she fastened to your saddle already?"

:The second—because you unfastened her. You'd better have the Healers look at you when you get there.: Her mind-voice was dense with concern. :I think you *really must have had a serious sunstroke. She's got a saddle because she's a present from Joserlyn Ashkevron to his sister, and saddles don't grow on trees, not even this close to the Pelagirs.:*

"You're right," Andros said, rubbing his head, then mounting. "I'd better talk to them. Well, let's get going."

They rode off, leaving a gittern behind them, propped up against a tree. When they were quite out of sight—and hearing-distance—the strings quivered for a moment.

A knowledgeable listener might have recognized a ballad popular sixty or seventy years earlier—a love-song called "My Lady's Eyes."

And a very keen-eared listener might have heard laughter among the trees; young male laughter, tenor and baritone, making a joyful music of their own.

To this day, that gittern is grown into the tree it leaned against then, the goldenoak's roots entwined around its strings in a gentle embrace, and there are bright days, when the winds whispers through the trees, that the Forest of Sorrows seems the most inappropriate name possible.

APPENDIX

Songs of Vanyel's Time

Nightblades

They come creeping out of darkness, and to darkness they return.
In their wake they leave destruction; where they go, no one can learn.
For they leave no trace in passing, as if all who watched were blind.
Like a dream of evil sending,
Nightblades passing, nightblades rending,
Into darkness once more blending
Leaving only dead behind.

First a threat—and then a death comes in the darkness of the night
And a dozen would-be allies have begun to show their fright.
When the nightblades strike unhindered, and can take a life at will,
There's no safety in alliance
And much peril in defiance,
It is best to show compliance
And the Karsite ranks to fill.

The chief envoy summons Vanyel, for one ally still seems brave
And the treaty may be salvaged if Vanyel this life can save.
Herald Vanyel feigns refusal, senses one would play him fool;
Thinks of treachery in hiding,
Lets his instincts be his guiding.
His own counsel he is biding,
He'll be no unwitting tool.

Garbed in black slips Herald Vanyel to their last lone ally's keep;
Over wall and into window, past all gates and guards to creep.
Past all gates and guards—no magic has them wrapped in deadly spell—
They are drugged, and they are dreaming.
Some foe strikes in friendly seeming—
See—a metal dart there gleaming!
Vanyel knows the symptoms well.

Now he hears another's footstep soft before him in the dark
And he hastes to lay an ambush while the nightblade seeks his mark.
Now he waits beside the doorway of the ally's very room
And the nightblade, all unknowing,
With a single lamp-beam showing,
To a confrontation going,
Not to fill another tomb.

Out of shadow Vanyel rises and he bars the nightblade's way.
He has only that slim warning—Vanyel has him soon at bay.
When the guards have all awakened, then he bares the nightblade's face—
And all minds but his are reeling
When he tears off the concealing—
And the envoy's face revealing—
Brings the traitor to disgrace.

My Lady's Eyes

(This is drivel. It's *supposed* to be. It's Vanyel's mother's favorite song.
Van puts up with it because he can show off his fingering.)

My Lady's eyes are like the skies
A soft and sunlit blue,
No other fair could half compare
In sweet midsummer hue.
My Lady's eyes cannot disguise
Her tender, gentle heart,
She cannot feign, she feels my pain
Whenever we must part.

    (Instrumental)
Now while I live I needs must give
Her all my love and more,
That she may know I worship so
This one that I adore.
And while away, I long and pray
The days may speed, and then,
I heartward hie, I flee, I fly,
To see her eyes again.

    (Instrumental)
My Lady's eyes, each glance I prize,
As gentle as a dove,
And would that I could tell her why
I dare not speak my love.

Too high, as far as any star
Her station is to mine,
Too wide that space to e'er embrace,
Beneath her I repine.

    (Instrumental)

Shadowstalker

It was just a week till Sovven, and the nights were turning chill
And the battle turned to stalemate, double-bluff, and feint and drill,
When a shadow drifted northward, just a shadow, nothing more.
No one noticed that the shadows all grew darker than before.
No one noticed, while the shadows seemed to creep into the heart,
But from then the fight for freedom seemed a fool's quest from the start.
All the hopes that they had cherished seemed unreasoned and naive
Nothing worth the strength to pray for, or to strive for, or believe.

And the shadows stole the sunlight from the brightest autumn day,
As they sang a song of bleakness that touched every heart that heard
As they whispered words of hopelessness, all courage fled away,
And they wove a smothering blanket over all that lived and stirred.

Herald Vanyel came upon them, and he sensed a subtle wrong,
And there was some magic working; deeply hidden, yes, but strong.
And it moved and worked in secret, like a poison in the vein
Like a poison meant to weaken, this was magic meant to drain.
Herald Vanyel saw the Shadows, and they turned their wiles on him
For one moment even he began to feel his spirit dim—
But he saw their secret evil, and he swore e'er he was done
He would stalk and slay these Shadows, and destroy them, one by one.

Herald Vanyel, Shadow Stalker, hunted Shadows to their doom
They turned all their powers upon him, turned away from other men
And although they strove to take him, he unwove their web of gloom.
So the Shadows fled his anger, their creator sought again.

Herald Vanyel faced the Singer who had sung them into life
And she sang to him of grief and loss that cut him like a knife
And she sang to him of self-hate, and she wove a net of pain
With her songs of woe and hopelessness bent to be Vanyel's bane.
"So now what is there to strive for?" was the song she sang to him.
And the shadow came upon his heart, the world grew gray and dim.
But the Singer of the Shadow did not know the foe she fought,
Nor how dear he held his duty, nor by what pain power was bought.

Herald Vanyel looked upon her, and he saw through her disguise
And she strove then to seduce him into death or madness sweet.
Herald Vanyel looked within him, and he saw her songs were lies,
And he gathered up his magic then, her powers to defeat.

Herald Vanyel raised his golden voice and sang of life and light,
Of the first cry of a baby, of the silver stars of night.
Herald Vanyel sang of wisdom, sang of courage, sang of love,
Of the earth's sweet soil beneath him, of the vaulting sky above,
Sang of healing, sang of growing, sang of joy and hope and dreams,
And the Singer of the Shadows felt the death of all her schemes.
It was then she tried to flee him, but his song and magic spell
Struck her down and held her pinioned and she faltered, and she fell.

Then the Singer of the Shadows saw her Shadows shatter there,
Saw her lies unmade before her, saw her darkness turned to day
And how empty and how petty was the spirit then laid bare—
Like her Shadows then she shattered, and in silence passed away.

Windrider Unchained

Windrider, fettered, imprisoned, and pinioned,
Wing-clipped by magic, his power full drained,
Valdemar's Heir is defeated and captive,
With his Companion by Darklord enchained.

Darklord of shadows his fetters is weaving,
Binds him in darkness as deep as despair,
Mocks at his anger and laughs at his weeping,
"Where is your strength now, oh Valdemar's Heir?"

Darklord has left them by shadows encumbered,
Darshay and Windrider trapped in his gloom,
Deep in his prisons, past hope, past believing,
Heir and Companion, will this be your tomb?

Out of the shadows another draws nearer,
Out of the twilight steals one furtive light.
Shadows dance pain, while the Light sings despairing,
Drawn here by Darshay and Windrider's plight.

Power new-won have the Singer and Dancer,
Power to shatter their curses at last—
Power that also could free the sad captives;
Power to break the bonds holding them fast.

Heart speaks to heart in the depths of the darkness
Grief calls to grief, and they falter, afraid—
Why should they sacrifice all for these *strangers*?
Then new-won compassion sends them on to aid.

Dancer in Shadows, she weeps as she dances,
Dancing, unmaking the shadow-born bands.
Sunsinger now through tears gives up his power—
Sings back the magic to Windrider's hands.

Spent now, the twain unseen fall into shadow,
Gifted to strangers all that they had gained.
Darklord returns, and by fear is confounded—
Flees the avenger, Windrider unchained!

Demonsbane

Along a road in Hardorn, the place called Stony Tor
A fearful band of farmers flees Karsite Border war.
A frightened band of farmers, their children, and their wives,
Seeks refuge from a tyrant, who wants more than their lives.

Now up rides Herald Vanyel. "Why then such haste?" says he.
"Now who is it pursuing, whose anger do you flee?
For you are all of Hardorn, why seek you Valdemar?
Is Festil no protection? Bide all his men too far?"

"Oh, Vanyel, Herald Vanyel, we flee now for our lives,
Lord Nedran would enslave us, our children and our wives—
He'd give our souls to demons, our bodies to his men.
King Festil has not heeded, or our peril does not ken."

Now up speaks Herald Vanyel. "The Border is not far—
But you are all of Hardorn, and not of Valdemar.
You are not Randale's people—can call not on his throne—
But *damned* if I will see you left helpless on your own!"

So forth goes Herald Vanyel, and onward does he ride.
On Stony Tor he waits then, Yfandes at his side.
With Nedran's men approaching, he calls out from on high,
"You shall not pass. Lord Nedran! I shall not let you by!"

Now Herald Vanyel only stands blocking Nedran's way
"Now who are you, fool nothing, that you dare to tell me nay?"

Now up speaks Herald Vanyel in a voice like brittle glass;
"The Herald-Mage called Vanyel—and I say you shall not pass!"

Now there stands great Lord Nedran, and behind him forty men,
Beside him is his wizard—but he pales, and speaks again—
"So you are Herald Vanyel—but this place is not your land.
So heed me, Herald Vanyel; turn aside and hold your hand."

"Let be; I'll give you silver, and I shall give you gold,
And I shall give you jewels fair that sparkle bright and bold,
And I shall give you pearls, all the treasures of the sea,
If you will step aside here, and leave these fools to me."

"What need have I of silver more than sweet Yfandes here?
And all the gold I cherish is sunlight bright and clear.
The only jewel I treasure's a bright and shining star,
And I will protect the helpless even outside Valdemar."

"Now I shall give you beauty, slaves of women and of men,
And I shall give you power as you'll never see again,
And I shall give you mansions and I shall give you land,
If you will turn aside here, turn aside and hold your hand."

"Now beauty held in bondage is beauty that is lost.
And land and mansions blood-bought come at too high a cost.
And power I have already—all power is a jade—
So turn you back, Lord Nedran, if of me you are afraid!"

Lord Nedran backs his stallion; the wizard he comes nigh.
"Prepare yourself, bold Vanyel, for you shall surely die!"
The wizard calls his demons, the demons he commands,
And Vanyel, Herald Vanyel, only raises empty hands.

The wizard calls his demons, the sky above turns black.
The demons strike at Vanyel, he stands and holds them back.
The demons strike at Vanyel, they strike and hurt him sore,
But Vanyel stands defiant, to raise his hands once more.

The sky itself descending upon bare Stony Tor
Now hides the awful battle. The watchers see no more.
The wizard shouts in triumph—too soon he vents his mirth.
For Vanyel calls the lightning, and smites him to the earth!

The clouds of black have lifted; upon the barren ground
Stands Vanyel hurt, but victor, the demons tied and bound.
He looks down on Lord Nedran; his eyes grow cold and bleak—
"Now shall I give you, Nedran, the power that you seek—"

Now Vanyel frees the demons, and Nedran screams with fear,
He sets them on the Karsites, who had first brought them here.
He sets them on the Karsites, and on the Karsite land.
They look down on Lord Nedran. They do not stay their hand.

Now Vanyel calls the farmers. "Go tell you near and far,
How thus are served the tyrants who would take Valdemar.
I am the bane of demons, who flees them I defend.
Thus Heralds serve a foeman—thus Heralds save a friend!"

The Shadow-Lover

Shadow-Lover, never seen by day,
Only deep in dreams do you appear.
Wisdom tells me I should turn away,
Love of mist and shadows, all unclear—
Nothing can I hold of you but thought
Shadow-Lover, mist and twilight wrought.

Shadow-Lover, comfort me in pain.
Love, although I never see your face,
All who'd have me fear you speak in vain—
Never would I shrink from your embrace
Shadow-Lover, gentle is your hand
Never could another understand.

Shadow-Lover, soothe me when I mourn
Mourn for all who left me here alone,
When my grief is too much to be borne,
When my burdens crushing-great have grown,
Shadow-Lover, I cannot forget—
Help me bear the burdens I have yet.

Shadow-Lover, you alone can know
How I long to reach a point of peace
How I fade with weariness and woe
How I long for you to bring release.
Shadow-Lover, court me in my dreams
Bring the peace that suffering redeems.

Shadow-Lover, from the Shadows made,
Lead me into Shadows once again.
Where you lead I cannot be afraid,
For with you I shall come home again—

In your arms I shall not fear the night.
Shadow-Lover, lead me into light.

Magic's Price

Every year Companions Choose, as they have done before,
The Chosen come with shining hopes to learn the Herald's lore.
And every year the Heralds sigh, and give the same advice—
"All those who would hold Magic's Power must then pay Magic's Price."

Oh there was danger in the North—that's all that Vanyel knew.
An enemy of power dark sought Heralds out—then slew.
But only those with Magic's Gift were slain by silent rage—
Till Vanyel of them all was left the only Herald-Mage.

Yes, from the North the danger came, beyond the Border far—
The Forest did not stay Dark Death, nor did the mountains bar.
And Vanyel cried—"We die, my liege, and know not why nor where!
So send me North, my King, that I may find the answers there!"

Then North went Vanyel—not alone, though 'twas of little aid
A Bard was like to be to him; and Stefen was afraid—
He feared that he would fail the quest, a burden prove to be—
Dared not let Vanyel go alone to face dark sorcery.

So out beyond the Border there, beyond the forest tall,
Into the mountains deep they went that stood an icy wall—
To find the wall had cracked and found there was a passage new,
A path clean cut that winding ran a level course and true.

This path was wrought by magecraft; Vanyel knew that when he saw
The mountains hewn by power alone, a power he felt with awe—
But to what purpose? Something moved beyond them on the trail;
They watched and hid—and what they found there turned them cold and pale.

An army moved in single file, by magic cloaked and hid—
An army moved on Valdemar that marched as they were bid—
A darker force than weaponry controlled the men and place,
For Vanyel looked—and Vanyel knew an ancient evil's face.

Then Vanyel turned to Stefen, and he told the Bard to ride
To warn the folk of Valdemar—"They call me 'Magic's Pride.'
It's time I earned the name—now go! I'll hold this army back
Until the arms of Valdemar can counter their attack."

So Stefen rode, and so it is no living tongue can tell
How Vanyel fought, nor what he wrought, nor how the Herald fell.
The Army came—but not in time to save the Herald-Mage,
Although the pass was scorched and cracked by magic power's rage.

They fought the Dark Ones back although they came on wave by wave.
No trace they found of Vanyel, nor of his Companion brave—
They only found the focus-stone, the gift of Stefen's hand—
Now blackened, burned, and shattered by the power that saved their land.

They only found the foemen who into the woods had fled
And each one by unseen, uncanny powers now lay dead.
As if the Forest had somehow bestirred itself that day—
Had Vanyel with his dying breath commanded trees to slay?

And still the forest of the North guards Valdemar from harm—
For Vanyel's dying curse is stronger far than mortal arm.
And every year the Chosen come, despite the old advice—
"All those who would be Magic's Pride must then pay Magic's Price."